Maeve Binchy

Maeve Binchy

Circle of Friends
Silver Wedding

CRESSET EDITIONS

This edition published by Cresset Editions
in 1993
an imprint of the Random House Group
20 Vauxhall Bridge Road
London SW1V 2SA

Circle of Friends was first published by Century
in 1990
Silver Wedding was first published by Century
in 1988

ISBN 0 7529 0426 4

Jacket illustration by David Holmes

Typeset in Baskerville 11/12.5 by
Pure Tech Corporation, Pondicherry, India
Printed and bound by
Griffin Paperbacks, Australia

CONTENTS

Circle of Friends

1

Silver Wedding

485

Circle of Friends

For my dear love Gordon Snell

CHAPTER ONE

1949

The kitchen was full of the smells of baking. Benny put down her school bag and went on a tour of inspection.

'The cake hasn't been iced yet,' Patsy explained. 'The mistress will do that herself.'

'What are you going to put on it?' Benny was eager.

'I suppose Happy Birthday Benny.' Patsy was surprised.

'Maybe she'll put Benny Hogan, Ten.'

'I never saw that on a cake.'

'I think it is, when it's a big birthday like being ten.'

'Maybe.' Patsy was doubtful.

'And are the jellies made?'

'They're in the pantry. Don't go in poking at them, you'll leave the mark of your finger and we'll all be killed.'

'I can't believe I'm going to be ten,' Benny said, delighted with herself.

'Ah, it's a big day all right.' Patsy spoke absently as she greased the trays for the queen cakes with a scrap of butter paper.

'What did you do when you were ten?'

'Don't you know with me every day was the same,' Patsy said cheerfully. 'There was no day different in the orphanage until I came out of it and came here.'

Benny loved to hear stories of the orphanage. She thought it was better than anything she read in books. There was the room with the twelve iron beds in it, the nice girls, the terrible girls, the time they all got nits in their hair and had their heads shaved.

'They must have had birthdays,' Benny insisted.

'I don't remember them,' Patsy sighed. 'There was a nice nun who said to me that I was Wednesday's child, full of woe.'

'That wasn't nice.'

'Well, at least she knew I was born on a Wednesday. . . . Here's your mother, now let me get on with the work.'

Annabel Hogan came in carrying three big bags. She was

1

surprised to see her daughter sitting swinging her legs in the kitchen.

'Aren't you home nice and early? Let me put these things upstairs.'

Benny ran over to Patsy when her mother's heavy tread was heard on the stairs.

'Do you think she got it?'

'Don't ask me, Benny, I know nothing.'

'You're saying that because you *do* know.'

'I *don't*. Really.'

'Was she in Dublin? Did she go up on the bus?'

'No, not at all.'

'But she must have.' Benny seemed very disappointed.

'No, she's not long gone at all. . . . She was only up the town.'

Benny licked the spoon thoughtfully. 'It's nicer raw,' she said.

'You always thought that.' Patsy looked at her fondly.

'When I'm eighteen and can do what I like, I'll eat all my cakes uncooked,' Benny pronounced.

'No you won't, when you're eighteen you'll be so busy getting thin you won't eat cakes at all.'

'I'll always want cakes.'

'You say that now. Wait till you want some fellow to fancy you.'

'Do you want a fellow to fancy you?'

'Of course I do, what else is there?'

'What fellow? I don't want you to go anyway.'

'I won't get a fellow, I'm from nowhere, a decent fellow wouldn't be able to talk about me and where I came from. I have no background, no life before, you see.'

'But you had a *great* life,' Benny cried. 'You'd make them all interested in you.'

There was no time to discuss it further. Benny's mother was back in the kitchen, her coat off and down to business with the icing sugar.

'Were you in Dublin at all today, Mother?'

'No, child, I had enough to do getting things ready for the party.'

'It's just I was wondering . . .'

'Parties don't run themselves, you know.' The words sounded

2

sharp but the tone was kindly. Benny knew her mother was looking forward to it all too.

'And will Father be home for the cake bit?'

'Yes, he will. We've asked the people for half past three, they'll all be here by four, so we needn't sit down to the tea until half past five, and we wouldn't have got to the cake until your father has the business closed, and is back here.'

Benny's father ran Hogan's Outfitters, the big menswear shop in the middle of Knockglen. The shop was often at its busiest on a Saturday, when the farmers came in, or the men who had a half day themselves were marched in by wives to have themselves fitted out by Mr Hogan, or Mike the old assistant, the tailor who had been there since time immemorial. Since the days when young Mr Hogan had bought the business.

Benny was glad that her father would be there for the cake, because that was when she might be given her present. Father had said it was going to be a wonderful surprise. Benny *knew* that they must have got her the velvet dress with the lacy collar and the pumps to go with it. She had wanted it since last Christmas when they went to the pantomime in Dublin and she had seen the girls on the stage dancing in pink velvet dresses like this.

They had heard that they sold them in Clery's, and that was only a few minutes from where the bus stopped when it went to Dublin.

Benny was large and square, but she wouldn't look like that in the pink velvet dress. She would be just like the fairy dancers they had seen on the stage, and her feet wouldn't look big and flat in those shoes because they had lovely pointy toes, and little pom poms on them.

The invitations to the party had been sent out ten days ago. There would be seven girls from school, farmers' daughters mainly from outside Knockglen. And Maire Carroll, whose mother and father owned the grocery. The Kennedys from the chemist were all boys so they wouldn't be there, and Dr Johnson's children were all too young so they couldn't come either. Peggy Pine who ran the smart clothes shop said that she might have her young niece staying with her. Benny said she didn't want anyone they didn't know, and it was with some relief that they heard the niece Clodagh didn't want to go amongst strangers either.

Her mother had insisted she invite Eve Malone and that was

bad enough. Eve was the girl who lived in the convent and knew all the nuns' secrets. Some people at school said look how Mother Francis never gives out to Eve, she's the real pet; others said the nuns had to keep her for charity and didn't like her as much as they liked the other girls whose families all contributed something to the upkeep of St Mary's.

Eve was small and dark. She looked like a pixie sometimes, her eyes darting here and there, forever watchful. Benny neither liked Eve nor disliked her. She envied her being so fleet and lithe and able to climb walls. She knew that Eve had her own room in the convent, behind the curtain where no other girl was allowed to step. The girls said it was the room with the round window that faced down the town and that Eve could sit at the window and watch everyone and where they went and who they were with. She never went on holidays anywhere, she stayed with the nuns all the time. Sometimes Mother Frances and Miss Pine from the dress shop would take her on an outing to Dublin, but she had never stayed away a night.

Once, when they had gone on a nature walk, Eve had pointed to a small cottage and said that it was her house. It stood in a group of small houses, each separate and surrounded by a little stone wall. They looked down into the big disused quarry. When she was older she would live in it all on her own and there would be no milk allowed in the door, and no clothes hangers. She would put all her things on the floor because it was hers to do what she liked with.

Some of them were half afraid of Eve, so nobody denied the story, but nobody really believed it either. Eve was so strange, she could make up tales and then, when everyone had got interested, she would say, 'Fooled you'.

Benny didn't really want her to come to the party, but for once Mother had been insistent.

'That child has no home. She must come to this one when there's a celebration.'

'She *has* a home, Mother, she's got the run of the whole convent.'

'That's not the same. She's to come here, Benny, that's my last word.'

Eve had written a very neat correct letter saying that she accepted the invitation with pleasure.

'They taught her to write nicely,' Benny's father had said approvingly.

'They're determined to make a lady out of her,' Mother had said. No one would explain why it seemed so important.

'When it's her birthday she only gets holy pictures and holy water fonts,' Benny reported. 'That's all the nuns have, you see.'

'God, that would turn a few of them over in their graves up there under the yew trees,' Benny's father had said, but again there was no explanation of why.

'Poor Eve, what a start for her,' Benny's mother sighed.

'I wonder was she born on a Wednesday like Patsy?' Benny was struck by something.

'Why would that matter?'

'She'd be miserable. Wednesday's child is full of woe,' Benny parroted.

'Nonsense.' Her father was dismissive.

'What day was I born on?'

'A Monday, Monday September 18th, 1939,' her mother said. 'At six o'clock in the evening.'

Her parents exchanged glances, looks that seemed to remember a long wait for a first and, as it turned out, an only child.

'Monday's child is fair of face,' Benny said, grimacing.

'Well, that's true certainly!' her mother said.

'You couldn't have a fairer face than Mary Bernadette Hogan, spinster of this parish, almost ten years of age,' said her father.

'It's not really fair, I mean I don't have fair hair.' Benny struggled to fit in with the saying accurately.

'You have the most beautiful hair I have ever seen.' Her mother stroked Benny's long chestnut locks.

'Do I really look nice?' she asked.

They reassured her that she looked beautiful, and she knew they had bought the dress for her. She had been worried for a bit but now she was certain.

At school next day, even the girls who hadn't been asked to the party wished her a happy birthday.

'What are you getting?'

'I don't know, it's a surprise.'

'Is it a dress?'

'Yes, I think so.'

'Ah, go on, tell us.'

'I don't know yet, really. I won't have it till the party.'

'Was it got in Dublin?'

'I think so.'

Eve spoke suddenly. 'It might have been got here, there's lots of things in Mrs Pine's.'

'I don't think so.' Benny tossed her head.

Eve shrugged. 'Okay.'

The others had gone away.

Benny turned on Eve. 'Why did you say it was got in Mrs Pine's? You don't know, you don't know anything.'

'I said okay.'

'Have *you* got a frock?'

'Yes, Mother Francis got one at Mrs Pine's. I don't think it's new. I think someone gave it back because there was something wrong with it.'

Eve wasn't apologetic. Her eyes flashed, she was ready with the explanation before anyone else could make the accusation.

'You don't know that.'

'No, but I think it. Mother Francis wouldn't have the money to buy me a new frock.'

Benny looked at her with admiration. She softened in her own attack.

'Well, I don't know either. I think they got me this lovely velvet one. But they mightn't.'

'They got you something new anyway.'

'Yes, but I'd really look great in this,' Benny said. 'It would make anyone look great.'

'Don't think about it too much,' Eve warned.

'Maybe you're right.'

'It's nice of you to ask me. I didn't think you liked me,' Eve said.

'Oh, I do.' Poor Benny was flustered.

'Good. Just as long as you weren't told to, or anything.'

'No! Heavens no!' Benny was far too vehement.

Eve looked at her with a measured glance. 'Right,' she said. 'See you this afternoon.'

They went to school on Saturday mornings, and at 12.30 when the bell went they all poured out of the school gates. All except Eve, who went to the convent kitchen.

'We'll have to feed you up with a good meal before you go,' said Sister Margaret.

'We wouldn't want them to think that a girl from St Mary's would eat all before her when she went out to tea,' said Sister Jerome. They didn't want to spell it out too much for Eve, but it was a big event, the child they had brought up being invited out to a party. The whole community was delighted for her.

As Benny had walked down the town, Mr Kennedy called her into the chemist.

'A little bird told me it was your birthday,' he said.

'I'm ten,' Benny said.

'I know. I remember when you were born. It was in the Emergency. Your Mam and Dad were so pleased. They didn't mind at all that you weren't a boy.'

'Did they want a boy do you think?'

'Everyone with a business wants a boy. But I don't know, I've three of them, and I don't think one of them will ever run this place for me.' He sighed heavily.

'Well, I suppose I'd better be . . .'

'No, no. I brought you in to give you a present. Here's a pack of barley sugar all for you.'

'Oh, Mr Kennedy . . .' Benny was overwhelmed.

'Not at all. You're a grand girl. I always say to myself, there's that little barrel Benny Hogan coming along.'

A bit of the sunlight went out of the barley sugar. Moodily Benny tore the corner off the packet and began to eat a sweet.

Dessie Burns, whose hardware shop was next door to Kennedy's, gave her a shout of approval.

'That's it, Benny, like myself, always head in the nosebag. How are you in yourself these days?'

'I'm ten today, Mr Burns.'

'Jaysus isn't that great, if you were six years older I'd take you into Shea's and put you up on my knee and buy you a gin and it.'

'Thank you, Mr Burns.' She looked at him fearfully.

'What's your father doing over there?' Don't tell me he's after hiring new staff. Half the country taking the emigrant ship and Eddie Hogan decides to expand.'

Dessie Burns had small piggy eyes. He looked across the street towards Hogan's Gentleman's Outfitters with huge unconcealed interest. Her father was shaking hands with a man – or a boy, it was hard to see. He looked about seventeen, Benny thought, thin and pale. He had a suitcase in his hand. He was looking up at the sign over the door.

'I don't know anything about it, Mr Burns,' she said.

'Good girl, keep your mind out of business, let me tell you it's a heart scald. If I were a woman I wouldn't have the slightest interest in it either. I'd just get myself a fine eejit of a man to keep me in barley sugar all day.'

Benny went on down the street, past the empty shop which people said that a real Italian from Italy was going to open up. She passed the cobbler's shop where Paccy Moore and his sister Bee waved out to her. Paccy had a twisted leg. He didn't go to Mass, but it was said that the priests came down to him once a month and heard his confession and gave him Holy Communion. Benny had heard that they had sent to Dublin and maybe even Rome for him to have a dispensation, and it wasn't a question of his being a sinner or outside the Church or anything. And then she was home to Lisbeg. The new dog which was half collie, half sheepdog, sat sleepily on the step loving the September sunshine.

Through the window she could see the table set for the party. Patsy had cleaned the brasses specially, and Mother had tidied up the front garden. Benny swallowed the barley sugar rather than be accused of eating sweets in the public view, and let herself in the back.

'Not a word out of that dog to let you know I was coming,' her mother said crossly.

'He shouldn't bark at you, you're family,' Benny defended him.

'The day Shep barks for anything except his own amusement there'll be white blackbirds. Tell me did you have a nice day at school, did they make a fuss of you?'

'They did, Mother.'

'That's good. Well they won't know you when they see you this afternoon.'

Benny's heart soared. 'Will I be getting dressed, like in anything new, before the party?'

'I think so. I think we'll have you looking like the bee's knees before they come in.'

'Will I put it on now?'

'Why not.' Benny's mother seemed excited about seeing the new outfit herself. 'I'll just lay it out for you above. Come up and give yourself a bit of a wash and we'll put it on.'

Benny stood patiently in the big bathroom while the back of her neck was washed. It wouldn't be long now.

Then she was led into her bedroom.

'Close your eyes,' said Mother.

When Benny opened them she saw on the bed a thick navy skirt, a Fair Isle jumper in navy and red. A big sturdy pair of navy shoes lay in their box and chunky white socks folded nice and neatly beside them. Peeping out of tissue paper was a small red shoulder bag.

'It's an entire outfit,' cried Mother. 'Dressed from head to foot by Peggy Pine . . .'

Mother stood back to see the effect of the gift.

Benny was wordless. No velvet dress, no lovely soft crushed velvet that you could stroke, with its beautiful lacy trim. Only horrible harsh rough things like horse hair. Nothing in a misty pink, but instead good plain sensible colours. And the shoes! Where were the pumps with the pointed toes?

Benny bit her lip and willed the tears back into her eyes.

'Well, what do you think?' Her mother was beaming proudly. 'Your father said you must have the handbag and the shoes as well, it would make it a real outfit. He said that going into double figures must be marked.'

'It's lovely,' Benny muttered.

'Isn't the jumper perfect? I'd been asking Peggy to get something like that for ages. I said I didn't want anything shoddy . . . something strong that would stand up to a bit of rough and tumble.'

'It's gorgeous,' Benny said.

'Feel it,' her mother urged.

She didn't want to. Not while she still had the velvet feel in her mind.

'I'll put it on myself, Mother, then I'll come and show you,' she said.

She was holding on by a thread.

Fortunately, Annabel Hogan needed to go and supervise the shaking of hundreds and thousands on the trifle. She was just heading off downstairs when the telephone rang. 'That'll be your father.' She sounded pleased and her step was quicker on the stair.

Through her sobs which she choked into the pillow, Benny heard snatches of the conversation.

'She loved it, Eddie, you know I think it was almost too much for her, she couldn't seem to take it all in, *so* many things, a bag and shoes, and socks, on top of everything. A child of that age isn't used to getting all that much at once. No, not yet, she's putting it on. It'll look fine on her . . .'

Slowly Benny got off her bed and went over to the mirror on the wardrobe to see if her face looked as red and tearstained as she feared. She saw the chunky figure of a child in vest and knickers, neck red from scrubbing, eyes red from weeping. She was not a person that anyone would ever dream of putting in a pink velvet dress and little pumps with pointed toes. For no reason at all she remembered Eve Malone. She remembered her small earnest face warning her not to think about the dress from Dublin too much.

Perhaps Eve knew all the time, maybe she had been in the shop when Mother was buying all this . . . all this horrible stuff. How awful that Eve knew before she did. And yet Eve had never had anything new, she knew that whatever dress *she* got for today would be a reject. She remembered the way Eve had said 'They got you something new anyway'. She would never let them guess how disappointed she was. Never.

The rest of the day wasn't very clear to Benny because of the heavy cloud of disappointment that seemed to hang over the whole proceedings. For her anyway. She remembered making the right sounds and moving like a puppet as the party began. Maire Carroll arrived wearing a proper party dress. It had an underskirt that rustled. It had come from America in a parcel.

There were games with a prize for everyone. Benny's mother had bought cones of sweets in Birdie Mac's shop, each one wrapped in different-coloured paper. They were all getting noisy but the cake had to be delayed until Mr Hogan returned from the shop.

They heard the angelus ringing. The deep sound of the bells rolled through Knockglen twice a day, at noon and at six in the evening, great timekeepers as much as reminders to pray. But there was no sign of Benny's father.

'I hope he wasn't delayed rameishing on with some customer today of all days,' Benny heard her mother say to Patsy.

'Not at all, Mam. He must be on his way. Shep got up and gave himself a good stretch. It's always a sign that the Master is heading home to us.'

And indeed he was. Half a minute later Benny's father came in full of anxiety.

'I haven't missed it, we're not too late?'

He was patted down and given a cup of tea and a sausage roll to bolster him up while the children were gathered and the room darkened in anticipation.

Benny tried not to feel the rough wool of the jumper at her neck. She tried to smile a real smile at her father, who had run down the town to be here for the big moment.

'Do you like your outfit . . . your first entire outfit?' he called over to her.

'It's lovely, Father, lovely. Do you see I'm wearing it all.'

The other children in Knockglen used to giggle at Benny for saying 'Father'. They used to call their fathers Daddy or Da. But by now they were used to it. It was part of the way things were. Benny was the only one they knew without brothers and sisters, most of them had to share a Mam and a Dad with five or six others. An only child was a rare occurrence. In fact they didn't know any, except for Benny. And Eve Malone of course. But that was different. She had no family at all.

Eve was standing near Benny as the cake came in.

'Imagine that's all for you,' she whispered in awe.

Eve wore a dress that was several sizes too big for her. Sister Imelda, the only nun in the convent who was good with the needle, had been in her sick bed so a very poor job had been done on taking up the hem. The rest of it hung around her like a curtain.

The only thing in its favour was that it was red and obviously new. There was no way that it could be admired or praised, but Eve Malone seemed to have risen above this. Something about the way she stood in the large unwieldy garment gave Benny courage. At least her horrible outfit fitted her, and though it was far from being a party dress, let alone the dress of her dreams, it was reasonable, unlike Eve's. She put her shoulders back and smiled suddenly at the smaller girl.

'I'll give you some of the cake to take back if there's any left over,' she said.

'Thanks. Mother Francis loves a slice of cake,' Eve said.

Then it was there, the blurry light of the candles and the singing Happy Birthday and the big whoosh . . . and the clapping, and when the curtains were open again Benny saw the thin young man that her father had been shaking hands with. He was far too old for the party. They must have brought him back to tea with the grown-ups who would come later. He was very thin and pale, and he had a cold hard stare in his eyes.

'Who was he?' Eve asked Benny on Monday.

'He's the new assistant come to work with my father in the shop.'

'He's awful, isn't he?'

They were friends now, sitting on a schoolyard wall together at break.

'Yes, he is. There's something wrong with his eyes, I think.'

'What's his name?' Eve asked.

'Sean. Sean Walsh. He's going to live in the shop.'

'Ugh!' said Eve. 'Will he go to your house for meals?'

'No, that's the great thing. He won't. Mother asked him to come to Sunday lunch and he made some awful speech about not assuming, or something.'

'Presuming.'

'Yes, well whatever it is he's not going to do it and it seems to mean coming to meals. He'll fend for himself he said.'

'Good.' Eve approved of that.

Benny spoke hesitantly. 'Mother said . . .'

'Yes?'

'If you'd like to come any time . . . that would be . . . it would be all right.'

Benny spoke gruffly as if fearing the invitation would be spurned.

'Oh, I'd like that,' Eve said.

'Like to tea on an ordinary day, or maybe midday dinner on a Saturday or Sunday.'

'I'd love Sunday. It's a bit quiet here on Sundays, a lot of praying, you see.'

'Right, I'll tell her.' Benny's brow had cleared.

'Oh, there is one thing though . . .'

'What is it?' Benny didn't like the intense look on Eve's face.

'I won't be able to ask you back. Where they eat and I eat, it's beyond the curtain, you see.'

'That doesn't matter at all.' Benny was relieved that this was the only obstacle.

'Of course, when I'm grown up and have my own place, you know, my cottage, I could ask you there,' Eve said earnestly.

'Is it really your cottage?'

'I told everyone.' Eve was belligerent.

'I thought it might only be a pretend cottage,' Benny said apologetically.

'How could it be pretend? It's mine. I was born there. It belonged to my mother and my father. They're both dead, it's mine.'

'Why can't you go there now?'

'I don't know. They think I'm too young to live on my own.'

'Well, of course you're too young to live on your own,' Benny said. 'But to visit?'

'Mother Francis said it was sort of serious, my own place, my inheritance she calls it. She says I shouldn't be treating it as a dolls' house, a playing place when I'm young.'

They thought about it for a while.

'Maybe she's right,' Benny said grudgingly.

'She could be.'

'Have you looked in the windows?'

'Yes.'

'Nobody's gone and messed it all up on you?'

'No, nobody goes there at all.'

'Why's that? It's got a lovely view down over the quarry.'

'They're afraid to go there. People died there.'

'People die everywhere.' Benny shrugged.

This pleased Eve. 'That's true. I hadn't thought of that.'

'So who died in the cottage?'

'My mother. And then a bit later my father.'

'Oh.'

Benny didn't know what to say. This was the first time Eve had ever talked about her life. Usually she flashed back with a Mind Your Own Business, if anyone asked her a question.

'But they're not in the cottage, they're in Heaven now,' Benny said eventually.

'Yes, of course.'

There seemed to be another impasse.

'I'd love to go and look through the window with you some time,' Benny offered.

Eve was about to reply when Maire Carroll came by.

'That was a nice party, Benny,' she said.

'Thanks.'

'I didn't know it was meant to be fancy dress though.'

'What do you mean?' Benny asked.

'Well, Eve was in fancy dress, weren't you, Eve? I mean that big red thing, that wasn't meant to be ordinary clothes, was it?'

Eve's face tightened into that hard look that she used to have before. Benny hated to see the expression come back.

'I thought it was quite funny myself,' Maire said with a little laugh. 'We all did when we were coming home.'

Benny looked around the schoolyard. Mother Francis was looking the other way.

With all her strength Benny Hogan launched herself off the wall down on Maire Carroll. The girl fell over, winded.

'Are you all right, Maire?' Benny asked in a falsely sympathetic tone.

Mother Francis came running, her habit streaming behind her.

'What happened, child?' She was struggling to get Maire's breath back, and raise her to her feet.

'Benny pushed me . . .' Maire gasped.

'Mother, I'm sorry, I'm so clumsy, I was just getting off the wall.'

'All right, all right, no bones broken. Get her a stool.' Mother Francis dealt with the panting Maire.

'She did it purposely.'

'Shush, shush, Maire. Here's a little stool for you, sit down now.'

Maire was crying. 'Mother, she just jumped down from the wall on me like a ton of bricks . . . I was only saying . . .'

'Maire was telling me how much she liked the party, Mother. I'm so sorry,' Benny said.

'Yes, well Benny, try to be more careful. Don't throw yourself around so much. Now, Maire, enough of this whining. It's not a bit nice. Benny has said she was sorry. You know it was an accident. Come along now and be a big girl.'

'I'd never want to be as big a girl as Benny Hogan. No one would.'

Mother Francis was cross now. 'That's quite enough, Maire Carroll. Quite enough. Take that stool and go inside to the cloakroom and sit there until you're called by me to come away from it.'

Mother Francis swept away. And as they all knew she would, she rang the bell for the end of break.

Eve looked at Benny. For a moment she said nothing, she just swallowed as if there were a lump in her throat.

Benny was equally at a loss, she just shrugged and spread out her hands helplessly.

Suddenly Eve grasped her hand. 'Some day, when I'm big and strong, I'll knock someone down for you,' she said. 'I mean it, I really will.'

'Tell me about Eve's mother and father,' Benny asked that night.

'Ah, that's all long ago now,' her father said.

'But I don't know it. I wasn't there.'

'No point in raking over all that.'

'She's my friend. I want to know about her.'

'She used not to be your friend. I had to plead with you to let her come to the party,' Mother said.

'No, that's not the way it was.' Benny couldn't believe now that this was so.

'I'm glad the child's coming here to her dinner on Sunday,' Eddie Hogan said. 'I wish we could persuade that young skinny-malinks above in the shop to come too, but he's determined not to trespass, as he calls it.'

Benny was pleased to hear that.

'Is he working out well, Eddie?'

'The best you ever saw, love. We'll be blessed with him, I tell you. He's so eager to learn he almost quivers like Shep there, he repeats everything over and over again, as if he's learning it off by heart.'

'Does Mike like him?' Benny's mother wanted to know.

'Ah, you know Mike, he likes nobody.'

'What does he object to?'

'The way Sean keeps the books. God, it's simple to understand, a child could do it, but old Mike has to put up a resistance to everything. Mike says he knows everyone's measurements, and what they paid and what they owed. He thinks it's like a kind of insult to his powers to write things down.'

'Couldn't you keep the books, Mother?' Benny suggested suddenly.

'No, no, I'd not be able to.'

'But if it's as simple as Father says . . .'

'She'd well be able to but your mother has to be here, this is our home, she runs it for you and me, Benny.'

'Patsy could run it. Then you wouldn't have to pay Sean.'

'Nonsense, Benny,' her father said.

But she wasn't to be stopped. 'Why not? Mike would like Mother being in there. Mike loves Mother, and it would be something for Mother to do all day.'

They both laughed.

'Isn't it great to be a child?' said her father.

'To think that the day isn't full already,' agreed her mother.

Benny knew very well that her mother's day was far from full. She thought that it might be nice for Mother to be involved in the shop, but obviously they weren't going to listen to her.

'How did Eve's parents die?' she asked.

'It's not a thing to be talking about.'

'Why? Were they murdered?'

'Of course not.' Her mother sounded impatient.

'Why then . . . ?'

'Lord, why, why, why,' her father sighed.

'At school they're always telling us to ask why. Mother Francis says that if you have a questioning mind you get to know all the answers.' Benny was triumphant.

'Her mother died giving birth, when Eve was being born. And then a bit later, her poor father, may the Lord have mercy on him, went out one evening with his wits scattered and fell over the cliff into the quarry.'

'Wasn't that desperate!' Benny's eyes were round with horror.

'So, it's a sad story, all over long ago, nearly ten years ago. We don't start bringing it all up over and over.'

'But there's more to it, isn't there . . . there's a kind of secret.'

'Not really.' Her father's eyes were honest. 'Her mother was a very wealthy woman, and her father was a kind of handyman who helped out in the convent, and did a bit of work up at Westlands. That caused a bit of talk at the time.'

'But it's not a secret or a scandal or anything.' Annabel Hogan's face was set in warning lines. 'They were married and everything in the Catholic Church.'

Benny could see the shutters coming down. She knew when to leave things.

Later she asked Patsy.

'Don't ask me things behind your parents' back.'

'I'm not. I asked them, and this is what they told me. I just wanted to know did you know any more. That's all.'

'It was before I came here, but I heard a bit from Bee Moore . . . Paccy's sister, she works above in Westlands you see.'

'What did you hear?'

'That Eve's father did a terrible act at the funeral, cursing and shouting . . .'

'Up in the church, cursing and shouting . . . !'

'Not *our* church, not the real church, in the Protestant church, but that was bad enough. You see Eve's mother was from Westlands – from the big house beyond. She was one of the family and poor Jack, that was the father, he thought they'd all treated her badly . . .'

'Go on.'

'That's all I know,' Patsy said. 'And don't be asking that poor child and upsetting her. People with no parents don't like endless questions.'

Benny took this as good advice not only about Eve, but about Patsy herself.

Mother Francis was delighted to see the new friendship developing, but far too old a hand in dealing with children to say so.

'Going down to the Hogans again are you?' she said, sounding slightly put out.

'Do you mind?' Eve asked.

'No, I don't mind. I can't say that I mind.' The nun tried hard to conceal her enthusiasm.

'It's not that I want to be away from here,' Eve said earnestly.

Mother Francis felt an urge to take the child in her arms as

17

she used to do when Eve was a baby given into their care by the accident of her birth.

'No, no, of course, child. Strange though this place is, it is your home.'

'It's always been a lovely home.'

The nun's eyes filled with tears. 'Every convent should have a child. I don't know how we're going to arrange it,' she said lightly.

'I wasn't a nuisance when I arrived?'

'You were a blessing, you know that. It's been the best ten years St Mary's ever had . . . you being here.'

Mother Francis stood at a window and watched little Eve go down the long avenue of the convent out to Sunday lunch on her own with the Hogans. She prayed that they would be kind to her, and that Benny wouldn't change and find a new friend.

She remembered the fights she had to keep Eve in the first place, when so many other solutions were being offered. There was a cousin of the Westwards in England who would take the child, someone who would arrange Roman Catholic instruction once a week. The Healys who had come to start the hotel were reported to be having difficulty in starting a family. They would be happy to have Eve in their home, even after their own children came along, if they did. But Mother Francis had fought like a tiger for that small bundle that she had rescued from the cottage, on the day she was born. The child they had reared until some solution could be found. Nobody had seen that Jack Malone's solution would involve throwing himself over the quarry one dark night. After that there had been no one with better claim to Eve than the nuns who had reared her.

It was the first of many Sunday dinners in Lisbeg for Eve. She loved coming to the house. Every week she brought something which she arranged in a vase. Mother Francis had shown her how to go up the long windy path behind the convent and pick leaves and wild flowers. At the start she would rehearse arranging them with the nun so that she would do it well when she got to the Hogans, but as the weeks went by she grew in confidence. She could bring armfuls of autumn colours and make a beautiful display on the hall table. It became a ritual.

Patsy would have the vases ready to see what Eve would bring today.

'Don't you have a lovely house!' she would say wistfully and Annabel Hogan would smile, pleased, and congratulate herself on having brought these two together.

'How did you meet Mrs Hogan?' she would ask Benny's father. And 'Did you always want to run a business?' The kind of questions Benny never thought to ask but was always interested in the answers.

She had never known that her parents met at a tennis party in a county far away. She had never heard that Father had been apprenticed to another business in the town of Ballylee. Or that Mother had gone to Belgium for a year after she left school to teach English in a convent.

'You make my parents say very interesting things,' she said to Eve one afternoon as they sat in Benny's bedroom, and Eve marvelled over being allowed to use an electric fire all for themselves.

'Well, they've got great stories like olden times.'

'Yes . . .' Benny was doubtful.

'You see, the nuns don't have.'

'They must have. Surely. They can't have forgotten,' Benny said.

'But they're not meant to think about the past, you know, and life before Entering, they really start from when they became Brides of Christ. They don't have stories of olden days like your mother and father do.'

'Would they like you to be a nun too?' Benny asked.

'No, Mother Francis said that they wouldn't take me, even if I did want to be a nun, until I was over twenty-one.'

'Why's that?'

'She says it's the only life I know, and I might want to join just because of that. She says when I leave school I have to go out and get a job for at least three years before I even think of Entering.'

'Wasn't it lucky you met up with them?' Benny said.

'Yes. Yes, it was.'

'I don't mean lucky that your mother and father died, but if they had to wasn't it great you didn't go somewhere awful?'

'Like in stories with wicked stepmothers,' Eve agreed.

'I wonder why they got you. Nuns usually don't get children unless it's an orphanage.'

'My father worked for them. They sent him up to Westlands to earn some money because they couldn't pay him much. That's where he met my mother. They feel responsible, I think.'

Benny was dying to know more. But she remembered Patsy's advice.

'Well, it all turned out fine, they're mad about you up there.'

'Your parents are mad about you too.'

'It's a bit hard sometimes, like if you want to wander off.'

'It is for me too,' Eve said. 'Not much wandering off above in the convent.'

'It'll be different when we're older.'

'It mightn't be,' Eve said sagely.

'What do you mean?'

'I mean, we have to show them we're terribly trustworthy or something, show them that if we *are* allowed to wander off, we'll wander back in good time.'

'How could we show them?' Benny was eager.

'I don't know. Something simple at the start. Could you ask me to stay the night here, for one thing?'

'Of course I could.'

'Then I could show Mother Francis that I'd be back up in the convent in time for Mass in the chapel, and she'd get to know I was to be relied on.'

'Mass on a weekday?'

'Every day. At seven.'

'No!'

'It's quite nice. The nuns sing beautifully, it's nice and peaceful. Really I don't mind it. Father Ross comes in specially and he gets a lovely breakfast in the parlour. He says the other priests envy him.'

'I didn't know that . . . every day.'

'You won't tell anyone will you?'

'No. Is it a secret?'

'Not a bit, it's just that I *don't* tell anything, you see, and the Community likes that, they feel I'm part of them. I didn't have a friend before. There wasn't anyone to tell.'

Benny smiled from ear to ear. 'What night will you come? Wednesday night?'

'I don't know, Eve. You don't have any smart pyjamas or anything to be going to stay with people. You don't have a good sponge bag, things that people who go visiting need.'

'My pyjamas are fine, Mother.'

'You could iron them, certainly, and you have a dressing gown.' She seemed to be faltering. 'A sponge bag though?'

'Could Sister Imelda make one for me? I'll do extra clearing up for her.'

'And what time will you come back?'

'I'll be at my prie-dieu in time for Mass, Mother.'

'You won't want to get up that early if you're visiting people.' Mother Francis's face was soft.

'That's what I'd want, Mother.'

It was a great evening. They played rummy with Patsy in the kitchen for a long time because Mother and Father went across the road to Dr and Mrs Johnson's house. It was a supper to celebrate the christening of their new baby.

Eve asked Patsy all about the orphanage, and Patsy told more details than she had ever told Benny. She explained how they used to steal food, and how hard it was when she came to Hogans', her first job, to realize she didn't have to take any stray biscuit or a fistful of sugar and put it into her apron.

In bed that night Benny said in wonder, 'I don't know why Patsy told us all that. Only the other day she was saying to me that people with no parents didn't like being asked questions.'

'Ah, it's different with me,' Eve said. 'I'm in the same boat.'

'No you're not!' Benny was indignant. 'Patsy had nothing. She had to work in that awful place and get nits and steal and be beaten for wetting the bed. She had to leave there at fifteen and come here. It's not a bit like you.'

'No. We are the same, she has no family, I don't. She didn't have a home like you do.'

'Is that why you told her more than you told me?' Benny had been even more astounded at the questions Patsy felt free to ask. Did Eve hate the Westwards who were so rich for not taking her into the big house? Eve didn't, they couldn't, they were Protestants, she explained. Lots more, things Benny wouldn't have dared to ask.

'You don't ask things like that,' Eve said simply.

21

'I'd be afraid of upsetting you,' Benny said.

'You couldn't upset a friend,' Eve said.

Benny and Eve, who had lived all their lives in the same village, were each amazed at the things the other didn't know about Knockglen.

Benny didn't know that the three priests who lived in the presbytery had been given the game of Scrabble, which they played every night, and sometimes rang the convent to ask Mother Francis questions like how you spelt 'quixotic' because Father O'Brien was going to get a triple word score.

Eve hadn't known that Mr Burns in the hardware shop was inclined to take to the drink or that Dr Johnson had a very bad temper and was heard shouting about God never putting a mouth into the world that he didn't feed. Dr Johnson was of the view that there were a lot of mouths, especially in the families with thirteen children, that God had forgotten to feed.

Benny didn't know that Peggy Pine was an old friend of Mother Francis, that they had been girls years ago and that when she came to the convent she called Mother Francis Bunty.

Eve hadn't known that Birdie Mac who ran the sweet shop had a man from Ballylee who had been calling for fifteen years, but she wouldn't leave her old mother and the man from Ballylee wouldn't come to Knockglen.

It made the town far more interesting to both of them to have such insights. Particularly because they knew these were dark secrets not to be shared with anyone. They pooled their knowledge on how children were born, and hadn't any new enlightenments to offer. They both knew that they came out like kittens, they didn't know how they got in.

'It's got something to do with lying down one beside the other, when you're married,' Eve said.

'It couldn't happen if you weren't married. Suppose you fell down beside someone like Dessie Burns.' Benny was worried.

'No, you have to be married.' Eve knew that for certain.

'And how would it get in?' It was a mystery.

'It could be your Little Mary,' Benny said thoughtfully.

'What's your Little Mary.'

'The bit in the middle of your tummy.'

'Oh your tummy button is what Mother Francis calls it.'

'That must be it,' Benny cried triumphantly. 'If they all have different names for it, that must be the secret.'

They practised hard at being reliable. If either said she would be home at six o'clock then five minutes before the hour struck and the Angelus rang she would be back in place. As Eve had anticipated, it did win them much more freedom. They were thought to be a good influence on each other. They didn't allow their hysterical laughing fits to be seen in public.

They pressed their noses against the window of Healy's Hotel. They didn't like Mrs Healy. She was very superior. She walked as if she were a queen. She always seemed to look down on children.

Benny heard from Patsy that the Healys had been up to Dublin to look for a child to adopt but they hadn't got one because Mr Healy had a weak chest.

'Just as well,' Eve had said unsympathetically. 'They'd be terrible for anyone as a mother and father.' She spoke in innocence of the fact that Knockglen had once thought that she herself might be the ideal child for them.

Mr Healy was much older than his wife. It was whispered, Patsy said, that he couldn't cut the mustard. Eve and Benny spent long hours trying to work out what this could mean. Mustard came in a small tin and you mixed it with water. How did you cut it? Why should you cut it?

Mrs Healy looked a hundred but apparently she was twenty-seven. She had married at seventeen and was busy throwing all her efforts into the hotel since there were no children.

Together they explored places where they had never gone alone. To Flood's, the butchers, hoping they might see the animals being killed.

'We don't really want to see them being killed do we?' Benny asked fearfully.

'No, but we'd like to be there at the beginning so that we could if we want to, then run away,' Eve explained. Mr Flood wouldn't let them near his yard so the matter didn't arise.

They stood and watched the Italian from Italy come and start up his fish and chip shop.

'Weel you leetle girls come here every day and buy my feesh?' he asked hopefully to the two earnest children, one big, one small, who stood watching his every move.

'No, I don't think we'll be allowed,' Eve said sadly.

'Why is that?'

'It would be called throwing away good money,' Benny said.

'And talking to foreign men,' Eve explained to clinch matters.

'My seester is married to a Dublin man,' Mario explained.

'We'll let people know,' Eve said solemnly.

Sometimes they went to the harness maker. A very handsome man on a horse came one day to enquire about a bridle that should have been ready, but wasn't.

Dekko Moore was a cousin of Paccy Moore's in the shoe shop. He was very apologetic, and looked as if he might be taken away and hanged for the delay.

The man turned his horse swiftly. 'All right. Will you bring it up to the house tomorrow, instead?' he shouted.

'Indeed I will sir, thank you sir. I'm very sorry sir. Indeed sir.' Dekko Moore sounded like a villain who had been unmasked in a pantomime.

'Lord, who was that, I wonder?' Benny was amazed. Dekko was almost dead with relief at how lightly he had escaped.

'That was Mr Simon Westward,' Dekko said, mopping his brow.

'I thought it must be,' Eve said grimly.

Sometimes they went into Hogan's Gentleman's Outfitters. Father always made a huge fuss of them. So did old Mike, and anyone else who happened to be in the shop.

'Will you work here when you're old?' Eve had whispered.

'I don't think so. It'll have to be a boy, won't it?'

'I don't see why,' Eve had said.

'Well, measuring men, putting tape measures round their waists, and all.'

They giggled.

'But you're the boss's daughter, you wouldn't be doing that. You'd just be coming in shouting at people, like Mrs Healy does over in the hotel.'

'Um.' Benny was doubtful. 'Wouldn't I need to know what to shout about?'

'You could learn. Otherwise Droopy Drawers will take over.'

That's what they called Sean Walsh, who seemed to have become paler, thinner and harder of the eye since his arrival.

'No, he won't, surely?'

'You could marry him.'

'Ugh. Ugh. Ugh.'

'And have lots of children by putting your belly button beside his.'

'Oh, Eve, I'd hate that. I think I'll be a nun.'

'I think I will too. It would be much easier. You can go any day you like, lucky old thing. I have to wait until I'm twenty-one.' Eve was disconsolate.

'Maybe she'd let you enter with me, if she knew it was a true vocation.' Benny was hopeful.

Her father had run out of the shop and now he was back with two lollipops. He handed them one each proudly.

'We're honoured to have you ladies in our humble premises,' he said, so that everyone could hear him.

Soon everyone in Knockglen thought of them as a pair. The big stocky figure of Benny Hogan in her strong shoes and tightly buttoned sensible coat, the waif-like Eve in the clothes that were always too long and streelish on her. Together they watched the setting up of the town's first fish and chip shop, they saw the decline of Mr Healy in the hotel and stood side by side on the day that he was taken to the sanatorium. Together they were unconquerable. There was never an ill-considered remark made about either of them.

When Birdie Mac in the sweet shop was unwise enough to say to Benny that those slabs of toffee were doing her no good at all, Eve's small face flashed in a fury.

'If you worry so much about things, Miss Mac, then why do you sell them at all?' she asked in tones that knew there could be no answer.

When Maire Carroll's mother said thoughtfully to Eve, 'Do you know I always ask myself why a sensible woman like Mother Francis would let you out on the street looking like Little Orphan Annie,' Benny's brow darkened.

'I'll tell Mother Francis you wanted to know,' Benny had said quickly. 'Mother Francis says we should have enquiring minds, that everyone should ask.'

Before Mrs Carroll could stop her Benny had galloped out of the shop and up the road towards the convent.

'Oh, Mam, you've done it now,' Maire Carroll moaned. 'Mother Francis will be down on us like a ton of bricks.'

And she was. The full fiery rage of the nun was something that Mrs Carroll had not expected and never wanted to know again.

None of these things upset either Eve or Benny in the slightest. It was easy to cope with Knockglen when you had a friend.

CHAPTER TWO

1957

There hadn't been many teddy boys in Knockglen, in fact no one could ever remember having seen one except on visits to Dublin when there were groups of them hanging round corners. Benny and Eve were in the window of Healy's Hotel practising having cups of coffee so that they would look well accustomed to it when they got to the Dublin coffee houses.

They saw him pass by, jaunty and confident in his drainpipe trousers, his long jacket with velvet cuffs and collar. His legs looked like spider legs and his shoes seemed enormous. He seemed oblivious of the stares of the whole town. Only when he saw the two girls actually standing up to peer at him past the curtains of Healy's window did he show any reaction. He gave them a huge grin and blew them a kiss.

Confused and annoyed they sat down hastily. It was one thing to look, another to call attention to themselves. Making a show of yourself was high on the list of sins in Knockglen. Benny knew this very well. Anyone could have been looking out the window seeing them being cheap with the teddy boy. Her father maybe, with the tape around his neck, awful sleeveen Sean Walsh, who never said a word without thinking carefully of the possible effect it might have. He could have been looking. Or old Mike, who had called her father Mr Eddie for years, and saw no reason to change.

And indeed everyone in Knockglen knew Eve as well. It had long been the nuns' ambition that Eve Malone be thought of as a lady. She had even joined in the game herself. Eve didn't want it to get back to the convent that she was trick acting in Healy's Hotel and ogling teddy boys out of the window. While other girls with real mothers resisted all the attempts to gentrify themselves, Eve and Mother Francis studied books on etiquette and looked at magazines to see how nice people dressed, and to pick up any hints on behaviour.

'I don't want you to put on an artificial accent,' Mother

Francis had warned, 'nor do I want you sticking out your little finger when you're drinking tea.'

'Who are we trying to impress?' Eve had asked once.

'No, look at it the other way. It's who you're trying not to let down. We were told we were mad and we couldn't rear you. It's a bit of human, nonsaintly desire to be able to say "I told you so" to the begrudgers.'

Eve had understood that immediately. And there was always hope that the Westward family would see her one day as an elegant lady and be sorry they hadn't kept in touch with the child who was after all their own flesh and blood.

Mrs Healy approached them. A widow now, formidable as she had always been, she managed to exude disapproval at fifty yards. She could not find any reason why Benny Hogan from the shop across the road and Eve Malone from the convent up the town should not sit and drink coffee in her bay window, but somehow she would have preferred to keep the space for wealthier and more important matrons of Knockglen.

She sailed towards the window. 'I'll adjust the curtains – they seem to have got all rucked up,' she said.

Eve and Benny exchanged glances. There was nothing wrong with the heavy net curtains of Healy's Hotel. They were as they always were: thick enough to conceal those within while giving a perfect view out.

'Well, isn't that a terrible poor ibex!' exclaimed Mrs Healy, having identified easily what the girls had been looking at.

'I suppose it's only his clothes really,' Eve said in a sanctimonious tone. 'Mother Francis always says it's a pity to judge people by the garments they wear.'

'Very admirable of her,' snapped Mrs Healy, 'but of course she makes sure that the garments of all you pupils are in order. Mother Francis is always the first to judge you girls by the uniforms you wear.'

'Not any more, Mrs Healy,' Benny said happily. 'I dyed my grey school skirt dark red.'

'And I dyed mine black, and my grey jumper purple,' Eve said.

'Very colourful.' Mrs Healy moved away like a ship under full sail.

'She can't bear us being grown up,' Eve hissed. 'She wants

to tell us to sit up straight and not to put our fingers on the nice furniture.'

'She knows we don't feel grown up,' Benny said gloomily. 'And if awful Mrs Healy knows then everyone in Dublin will know.'

It was a problem. Mr Flood the butcher had looked at them very strangely as they walked up the street. His eyes seemed to burn through them in disapproval. If people like that could see their awkwardness, they were indeed in a bad way.

'We should have a rehearsal – you know, go up for a couple of days ahead of everyone else so we won't look like eejits.' Eve was hopeful.

'It's hard enough to get up there when we have to. There's no point in asking to go up there in order to waltz around a bit. Can you see them agreeing to that for me at home?'

'We wouldn't call it waltzing around,' Eve said. 'We'd call it something else.'

'Like what?'

Eve thought hard. 'In your case, getting books listed and timetables – there's endless things you could say.' Her voice sounded suddenly small and sad.

For the first time Benny realized properly that they were going to live separate lives though in the same city. Best friends from the age of ten, now they would go down different roads.

Benny was going to be able to go to University College, Dublin, to study for a BA degree because her parents had saved to pay for her. There was no money in St Mary's convent to send Eve Malone to university. Mother Francis had strained the convent's finances already to provide secondary education for the daughter of Jack Malone and Sarah Westward. Now she would be sent to a convent of the same order in Dublin where she would do a secretarial course. Her tuition fees would be waived in exchange for some light housework.

'I wish to God you were coming to college, too,' Benny said suddenly.

'I know. Don't say it like that, don't let your voice get drippy or I'll get upset.' Eve spoke sharply, but without harshness.

'Everyone keeps saying that it's great, we have each other, but I'd see more of you if you were still in Knockglen,' Benny complained. 'Your place is miles across the city, and I have to come home on the bus every night, so there'll be no meeting in the evenings.'

'I don't think there's much of the night life planned for me either,' Eve said doubtfully. 'A few miles of convent floor to polish, a few million sheets to hem. A couple of tons of potatoes to peel.'

'They won't make you do that!' Benny was horrified.

'Who knows what light housework means? One nun's light could be another nun's penal servitude.'

'You'll need to know in advance, won't you?' Benny was distressed for her friend.

'I'm not in much of a position to negotiate,' Eve said.

'But they never asked you to do anything like that here.' Benny nodded her head up in the direction of the convent at the end of the town.

'But that's different. This is my home,' Eve said simply. 'I mean, this is where I live, where I'll always live.'

'You'll be able to get a flat and all when you get a job.' Benny sounded wistful. She didn't think she would ever see freedom.

'Oh yes, I'm sure I'll get a flat, but I'll come back to St Mary's, like other people come home from flats on holidays,' Eve said.

Eve was always so definite, Benny thought with admiration. So small and determined with her short dark hair and white elfin face. No one had ever dared to say that there was anything different or even unusual about Eve living in the convent, sharing her life with the Community. She was never asked about what life was like beyond the curtain where the nuns went, and she never told. The girls also knew that no tales would be told of their own doings. Eve Malone was nobody's spy.

Benny didn't know how she was going to manage without her. Eve had been there for as long as she remembered to help her fight her battles. To deal with the jibes of those who called her Big Ben. Eve had made short work of anyone who took advantage of Benny's gentle ways. They had been a team for years: the tiny wiry Eve with her restless eyes never settling long on anything or anyone; the big handsome Benny, with her green eyes and chestnut-brown hair, tied back with a bow always, a big soft good-quality bow a bit like Benny herself.

If there had only been some way they could have gone in the doors of University College together and come home on the bus each night, or better still got a flat together, life would have been perfect. But Benny had not grown up expecting life to be totally perfect. Surely it was enough to have got as much as she had.

Annabel Hogan was wondering whether to change the main meal of the day to the evening. There were a lot of arguments for this and a lot against.

Eddie was used to his dinner in the middle of the day. He walked back from the shop and the plate of meat and potatoes was put in front of him with a regularity that would have pleased an army officer. As soon as Shep started his languid stroll out to meet the master at the turn of the road, Patsy began to heat the plates. Mr Hogan would wash his hands in the downstairs cloakroom and always profess pleasure at the lamb chops, the bacon and cabbage, or the plate of cod and parsley sauce on a Friday. Wouldn't it be a poor thing to have the man close his shop and walk back for a kind of half-hearted snack. Maybe it might even affect his work and he wouldn't be able to concentrate in the afternoon.

But then think of Benny coming back from Dublin after a day in the university: wouldn't it be better if they saved the main meal for her return?

Neither husband nor daughter had been any help. They both said it didn't matter. As usual the burden of the whole house fell on herself and Patsy.

The meat tea was probably the answer. A big slice of ham, or grilled bacon, or a few sausages, and they could put a few extra on Benny's plate in case she felt the need of it. Annabel could hardly believe that she had a daughter about to go to university. Not that she wasn't old enough – she was well old enough to have seen a family through university. She had married late, at a time she had almost given up hope of finding a husband. She had given birth at a time when she thought miscarriages would be all she ever knew.

Annabel Hogan walked around her house: there was always some little thing to be done. Patsy was in the big, warm kitchen, the table covered with flour and crockery, but it would all be swept away and scrubbed by meal time.

Lisbeg was not a big house, but there was plenty to do in it. There were three bedrooms and a bathroom upstairs. The master bedroom looked out over one side of the front door and Benny's bedroom was on the other. At the back of the house, the dark spare room and the big, old-fashioned bathroom with its noisy pipes and its huge wood-surrounded bath.

Downstairs if you came in the front door (which people rarely did) you would find a large room on each side. They were hardly ever used. The Hogans lived in the back of the house, in the big shabby breakfast room that opened off the kitchen. There was hardly ever a need to light a fire in the breakfast room because the great heat of the range came through. There was a big double door kept permanently open between the two rooms, and it was as comfortable a place as you could imagine.

They rarely had visitors, and if ever anyone was expected the front drawing room in its pale greens and pinks with damp spots over the wall could be aired and dusted. But in the main, the breakfast room was their home.

It had three big red plush armchairs, and the table against the wall had three dining chairs with plush seats as well. A huge radio stood on the big sideboard, and shelves of ornaments, and good china and old books were fixed precariously to the wall.

Now that young Eve had become such a regular guest in the household, a fourth chair had been found, a cane chair rescued from one of the sheds. Patsy had tied a nice red cushion to it.

Patsy herself slept in a small room beyond the kitchen. It was dark and had a tiny window. Patsy had always told Mrs Hogan that it was like being dead and going to Heaven to have a room of your own. She had always had to share with at least two other people until the day she came to Lisbeg.

When Patsy had walked up the short avenue and looked at the square house with its creeper and its shabby garden it seemed to her like a house on the front of a calendar. Her small room looked out on the back yard, and she had a window box. Things didn't grow very well in it because it was in shadow and Patsy wasn't much of a gardener, but it was her own, and nobody ever touched it, any more than ever went into her room.

Patsy was as excited as any of them about Benny going to university. Every year on her annual holidays, Patsy paid a dutiful visit of one half day to the orphanage which had reared her, and then she went to stay with a friend who had married in Dublin. She had asked her friend to take her to see where Benny would be a student. She had stood outside the huge pillars of University College, Dublin and looked at it all with satisfaction. Now she would know where Benny went and studied; she would know the look of the place.

And indeed it was a big step for Benny, Annabel Hogan realized. No more safe trotting to and fro from the convent. It was life in the big city with several thousand other students from all kinds of places, with different ways and no one to force you to study like Mother Francis. It was not surprising that Benny had been as excited as a hen walking on hot coals all summer long, never able to keep still, always jumping up with some further excitement.

It was a relief to know that she was with Eve Malone for the morning, those two could talk until the cows came home. Annabel wished that there had been some way young Eve could have been sent to university too. It would have made things more fair somehow. But things rarely turned out nice and neatly in this life. Annabel had said as much to Father Ross the last time he had come to tea, and Father Ross had looked at her sternly over his glasses, saying that if we all understood the way the Universe was run what would there be left for God to tell us on the Last Day.

To herself Annabel thought that it wouldn't interfere with the running of the Universe if enough money could be found some-where for the university fees and accommodation for Eve Malone, the child who had no home except the big bleak convent with the heavy iron gates.

Mother Francis had asked God very often for a way to send Eve Malone to university but so far God had not seen fit to show her one. Mother Francis knew it must be part of his divine plan, but at times she wondered had she prayed hard enough, had she examined every possibility. She had certainly been up every road as far as the Order was concerned. She had written to the Mother General, she had put Eve's case as persuasively as she could. The girl's father, Jack Malone, had worked all his life for the convent as handyman and gardener.

Jack had married the daughter of the Westward family, as unlikely a match as was ever known in the country, but necessary since a child was on the way. There had been no problem in having Eve brought up as a Catholic, since the Westwards had never wanted to know about her at all, and didn't care what faith she was raised in just as long as they never had to hear her name.

Mother General's view was that enough had been done for the child already. To provide a university education for her might mark her out as a favoured pupil. Would not others from needy backgrounds expect the same?

It had not stopped there. Mother Francis had taken the bus to their convent in Dublin and spoken to the very difficult Mother Clare who held sway there. With so many young nuns starting university education in the autumn and lodging in the Dublin convent was there not a chance that Eve might join them? The girl would be happy to do housework to earn her place among the students.

Mother Clare wouldn't even consider it. What an extraordinary suggestion, to put forward a girl – a charity child who was not a Sister, a novice, a postulant, nor anyone with the remotest intention of becoming a nun – and raise her up above the many Sisters in the community who were all hoping and praying for a chance of higher education . . . what would they feel if a girl who had already been pampered, it seemed, by the convent in Knockglen, were put in to study, over their heads? It would be an outrage.

And perhaps it was outrageous of her, Mother Francis thought sometimes. It was just that she loved Eve as much as any mother could love a daughter. Mother Francis the celibate nun who had never thought she could know the joy of seeing a child grow up in her care had loved Eve in a way that might well have made her blind to the feelings and sensitivities of other people. Mother General and Mother Clare were indeed right, it would have been preferential treatment to have financed Eve's university education from the convent funds.

But when all was said and done, Mother Francis wished she could be sure that they would treat Eve well up in Mother Clare's convent. St Mary's had always been a home for Eve; the fear was that she might find the sister house in Dublin more like an institution, and worse still she might find her own role there not that of an honoured daughter, but more that of a maid.

When Benny and Eve came out of Healy's Hotel, they saw Sean Walsh watching them from the doorway of Hogan's across the street.

'If you keep talking to me he might think we haven't seen him,' Benny hissed out of the corner of her mouth.

'Not a chance. Look at him standing there with his thumbs in behind his braces, copying the way your father stands.'

Eve knew only too well Sean Walsh's expectations: he had a longterm career plan, to marry the daughter of the house, the heir to Hogan's Gentleman's Outfitters, and inherit the lot.

They had never been able to like Sean Walsh, not since the very first day he had turned up at Benny's tenth birthday party. He had never smiled. Not once in all those years had they seen a real smile on his face. There were a lot of grimaces, and a little dry bark sometimes, but never a laugh.

He didn't throw his head back like Peggy Pine did when she laughed, or giggle into his fist like Paccy Moore; he didn't make big gestures like Mario in the fish and chip shop, or even get wheezing and coughing fits like Dessie Burns often did. Sean Walsh seemed watchful the whole time. Only when he saw others smiling and laughing did he give the little barks.

They could never get him to tell anything about the life he had lived before he came to Knockglen. He didn't tell long stories like Patsy did, or wistful tales like Dekko Moore about the time he made harnesses for the Lords of the Soil somewhere down in Meath. Sean Walsh would not be drawn.

'Oh, dear, you don't want to hear my stories,' he would say when Benny and Eve plagued him for some information.

The years had not improved him: he was still secretive and insincerely anxious to please. Even his appearance annoyed Benny, although she knew this was unreasonable. He wore a suit that had seen a lot of pressing, and was obviously carefully looked after. Benny and Eve used to tell each other in fits of laughter that he spent hours in his little room above the shop pressing all his ambitions into the suit with a damp cloth.

Benny didn't really believe Eve about Sean having ambitions to marry into the shop, but there was something deeply unsettling all right about the way he looked at her. She had so much wanted to be fancied, it seemed a cruel blow to think that if it ever happened it might only be by someone as awful as Sean Walsh.

'Good morning, ladies.' He made an exaggerated bow. There was an insult in his voice, a sneer that he hadn't intended them to notice. Other people had called them 'ladies', even that very morning, and had done so without any offence. It was a way of acknowledging that they had left school and would shortly start a more grown-up life. When they had been in the chemist's buying shampoo, Mr Kennedy had asked what he could do for the two young ladies and they had been pleased. Paccy Moore had said they were two fine ladies when they had gone to have heels put on Benny's good shoes. But with Sean Walsh it was different.

'Hallo, Sean.' Benny's voice was lacklustre.

'Surveying the metropolis, I see,' he said loftily. He always spoke slightly disparagingly of Knockglen, even though the place he came from himself was smaller and even less like a metropolis. Benny felt a violent surge of annoyance.

'Well, you're a free agent,' she said suddenly. 'If you don't like Knockglen you could always go somewhere else.'

'Did I say I didn't like it?' His eyes were narrower than ever, almost slits. He had gauged this wrong, he must not allow her to report his having slighted the place. 'I was only making a pleasant remark comparing this place to the big city. Meaning that you'll have no time for us here at all soon.'

That had been the wrong thing too.

'I'll have little chance of forgetting all about Knockglen considering I'll be coming home every night,' said Benny glumly.

'And we wouldn't want to anyway,' Eve said with her chin stuck out. Sean Walsh would never know how often she and Eve bemoaned their fate living in such a small town which had the worst characteristic any town could have: it was actually within striking distance of Dublin.

Sean hardly ever let his glance fall on Eve, for she held no interest for him. All his remarks were directed to Benny. 'Your father is so proud of you, there's hardly a customer that he hasn't told about your great success.'

Benny hated his smile and his knowing ways. He must know how much she hated being told this, reminded about how she was the apple of their eye, and the centre of simple boastful conversation. And if he knew why did he tell her and annoy her still further? If he did have designs on her, and a plan to marry Mr Eddie Hogan's daughter and thereby marry into the business, then why was he saying all the things that would irritate and upset her?

Perhaps he thought that her own wishes would hardly be considered in the matter. That the biddable daughter of the house would give in on this as she had on everything else.

Benny realized she must fight Sean Walsh. 'Does he tell everyone I'm going to college?' she asked, with a smile of pleasure on her face.

'Only subject of conversation.' Sean was smug to be the source of information but somehow disconcerted that Benny didn't get embarrassed as he had thought she would.

Benny turned to Eve. 'Aren't I lucky?'

Eve understood. 'Oh, spoiled rotten,' she agreed.

They didn't laugh until they were out of sight. They had to walk down the long straight street past Shea's pub with its sour smell of drink coming out on to the street from behind its dark windows, past Birdie Mac's sweet shop where they had spent so much time choosing from jars all their school life. Across the road to the butcher's where they looked in the window to see back at the reflection of Hogan's Outfitters and realize that Sean Walsh had gone back inside to the empire that would one day be his.

Only then could they let themselves go and laugh properly.

Mr Flood, of Flood's Quality Meat Killed On The Premises, didn't appreciate their laughter.

'What's so funny about a row of gigot chops?' he asked the two laughing girls outside his window. It only made them laugh more.

'Get on with you then, do your laughing somewhere else,' he growled at them. 'Stop making a mock and a jeer out of other people's business.'

His face was severely troubled and he went out into the street to look up at the tree which overhung his house.

Mr Flood had been seen staring into that tree a lot lately, and worse still having conversations with someone he saw in its branches. The general thinking was that Mr Flood had seen some kind of vision, but was not ready yet to reveal it to the town. His words to the tree seemed to be respectful and thoughtful, and he addressed whatever he saw as Sister.

Benny and Eve watched fascinated, as he shook his head sorrowfully and seemed to agree with something that had been said to him.

'It's the same the whole world over, Sister,' he said, 'but it's sad it should come to Ireland as well.'

He listened respectfully to what he was hearing from the tree, and took his leave. Vision or no vision, there was work to be done in the shop.

The girls only stopped laughing by the time they had reached the convent gates. Benny turned to go back home as usual. She never presumed on their friendship with Eve by expecting to be let in to the inner sanctum. The convent in holidays was off limits.

'No, come on in, come in just to see my room,' Eve begged.

'Mother Francis? Wouldn't they think . . . ?'

'It's my home, they've always told me that. Anyway, you're not a pupil any more.'

They went through a side door; there was a smell of baking, a warm kitchen smell through the corridors, then a smell of polish on the big stairway, and the wide dark hall hung with pictures of Mother Foundress and Our Lady, and lit only by the Sacred Heart lamp.

'Isn't it desperately quiet in the holidays?'

'You should be here at night. Sometimes when I've come home from the pictures and I let myself in, it's so quiet I'd nearly talk to the statues for company.'

They went up to the small room where Eve had lived for as long as she could remember. Benny looked around with interest.

'Look at your wireless, right beside your bed!' The brown bakelite electric radio, where, like every other girl in the country, Eve listened at night to Radio Luxembourg, was on her night table. In Benny's house, where she was considered a very pampered only child, she had to borrow the kitchen radio and then perch it on a chair because there wasn't any socket near enough to her bed to plug it in.

There was a neat candlewick bedspread and a funny nightdress case shaped like a rabbit.

'Mother Francis gave me that when I was ten. Isn't it awful?'

'Better than holy pictures,' Benny said.

Eve opened a drawer in which there were piles of holy pictures each one bound up with a rubber band.

Benny looked at them, fascinated. 'You never threw them away!'

'Not here. I couldn't.'

The small round window looked down over Knockglen, along the tree-lined drive of the convent through the big gates and down the broad main street of the town.

They could see Mr Flood fussing round the window of his shop as if he were still worried about what they could have found so amusing in its contents. They saw small children with noses pressed against the window of Birdie Mac's, and men with caps pulled well down over their faces coming out of Shea's pub.

They saw a black Ford Prefect pull up in front of Hogan's and knew it was Dr Johnson. They saw two men walking into Healy's Hotel, rubbing their hands. These would be commercial travellers, wanting to write up their order books in peace. They could see a man with a ladder up against the cinema putting up the new poster, and the small round figure of Peggy Pine coming out of her dress shop to stand and look admiringly at her window display. Peggy's idea of art was to put as much in the window as could possibly fit without falling over.

'You can see everything!' Benny was amazed. 'It's like being God.'

'Not really, God can see round corners. I can't see your house, I can't see who's having chips in Mario's; I can't see over the hill to Westlands. Not that I'd want to, but I can't.'

Her voice was tight when she spoke of her mother's people in the big house. Benny knew from old that it was a thorny subject.

'I suppose they wouldn't . . .'

'They wouldn't.' Eve was firm.

They both knew what Benny was going to say: that there was no chance of the wealthy Westwards paying for a university education for Eve.

'Do you think Mother Francis might have approached them?'

'I'm sure she did, lots of times over the years, and she always got the door slammed in her face.'

'You can't be certain,' Benny said soothingly.

Eve looked out of the window down the town, standing as she must often have done over the years.

'She did every single thing to help me that anyone could. She *must* have asked them, and they must have said no. She didn't tell me because she didn't want me to feel worse about them. As if I could.'

'In a fairy story one of them would ride up to the avenue

39

here on a white horse and say they'd been wanting you as part of their lives for years,' Benny said.

'And in a fairy story I'd tell him to get lost,' Eve said, laughing.

'No, I wouldn't let you, you'd say thank you very much, the fees are this price, and I'd like a nice flat of my own with carpets going right up to the wall and no counting how much electric fire we use.' Benny was gleeful.

'Oh yes, and a dress allowance of course, so much a month put into Switzer's and Brown Thomas for me.'

'And a holiday abroad each year to make up for not seeing you much over the past while!'

'And a huge contribution to the convent building fund for the new chapel to thank the nuns for doing the needful.'

Benny sighed. 'I suppose things like that *could* happen.'

'As you said, in a fairy story,' Eve said. 'And what would be the best happening for you?'

'Two men to get out of a van down there in a minute's time and tell my father that Sean Walsh is a criminal wanted for six murders in Dublin and that he has to be handcuffed and out of there this instant.'

'It still leaves the business of you having to come home from Dublin on the bus every night,' Eve said.

'Listen, don't go on at me. For all that you've been in and out of our house a thousand times you don't know the way they are.'

'I do,' Eve said. 'They idolize you.'

'Which means I get the six ten bus back every night to Knockglen. That's what being idolized does for you.'

'There'll be the odd night surely in Dublin. They can't expect you home every single night.'

'Where will I stay? Let's be practical – there'll be no nights in Dublin. I'll be like bloody Cinderella.'

'You'll make friends, you'll have friends with houses, families, you know, normal kinds of things.'

'When did you and I have anything approaching a normal life, Eve Malone?' Benny was laughing to cheer them up and raise the mood again.

'It'll soon be time for us to take control, seriously.' Eve refused to laugh at all.

Benny could be equally serious.

'Sure it will. But what does it mean? You're not going to hurt Mother Francis by refusing to go to this place she's sending you. I'm not going to bring the whole world down on us by telling my mother and father that I feel like a big spancelled goat going to college and having to come back here every night as if I were some kind of simpleton. Anyway, you'll be out of there and you'll get a great job and be able to do what you like.'

Eve smiled at her friend. 'And we'll come back to this room some day and laugh at the days when we all thought it would be so dreadful.

'We will, we will, and Sean Walsh will be doing penal servitude . . .'

'And the Westwards will have lost all their money and their land.'

'And Mrs Healy will have thrown away her corsets and be wearing a short skirt.'

'And Paccy Moore will own a fleet of shoe shops throughout the country.'

'And Dr Johnson will have learned to smile.'

'And Mother Francis will be the Reverend Mother General of the whole Order and can do what she likes, and go to see the Pope, and everything.'

They laughed, delighted at the thought of such wonders.

CHAPTER THREE

Emily Mahon stood in front of the gas cooker and grilled the ten rashers that she served every morning except Friday. Her white blouse hung neatly in the corner of the room. She wore a nylon jacket to make the breakfast lest her clothes get spattered before she went out to work.

She knew that Brian was in a mood this morning. He hadn't a word to throw to a dog. Emily sighed as she stood in the shabby kitchen. Theirs must be the least improved house in Maple Gardens. It was always the same, they say that the shoemaker's children are never shod. So it was logical that the builder's wife would be the only one in the road without a decent kitchen to work in. She had seen the jobs that were done on other people's houses. Kitchens that were tiled so that they only needed a wipe down the walls and a quick mop of the floor. There were units that all fitted together like a continuous counter rather than the cupboards and tables of different sizes that Emily had lived with for twenty-five years. It was useless trying to change him. 'Who sees it but us?' was the reply.

Very few visitors came into 23 Maple Gardens. Brian's builder's yard was the centre of his social activities, such as they were. The boys, Paul and Nasey, had never brought their friends home, and now they too worked with their father in the yard. That's where fellows called to pick them up, or to take them over to a pub for a pint.

And Nan, the baby of the family, eighteen years old and about to start at university today, Nan had not been one for inviting friends home either.

Emily knew that her beautiful daughter had a dozen friends at school, she had seen her walking down the street when classes were over, surrounded by other girls. She went to the houses of friends, she was invited everywhere, but not one of her school-mates had crossed the door of Maple Gardens.

Nan was not just beautiful in Emily's eyes. This was the opinion of everyone. When she was a small child people had stopped in the street asking why this little girl with the blonde, almost white, curls had never been chosen for the Pears soap advertisement . . . the one where it said, 'Growing up to be a beautiful lady'. In truth Emily did have dreams that one day in a park or on the street a talent scout would stop and see the perfect features and flawless skin of this child and come to the house begging on bended knees to transform her life.

Because if there was anything that Emily Mahon wanted for her little princess, it was a transformed life.

Emily wanted Nan to have everything that she had never had. She didn't want the girl to marry a bullying drunk like her mother had done. She didn't want a life of isolation stuck out here in a housing estate, only allowed to go out to work as a favour. Emily had read a lot of magazines, she knew that it was perfectly possible for a girl with Nan's looks to rise to be the highest in the land. You saw the very beautiful wives of rich businessmen, and the really good-looking women photographed at the races on the arms of well-known people from important families. It was obvious that not all these people could have come from the upper classes. *Their* women were often plain and horsey. Nan was in the running for that kind of life, and Emily would do everything in her power to get it for her.

It had not been hard to persuade Brian to come up with the fees for university. In his sober moods he was inordinately proud of his beautiful daughter. Nothing was too good for her. But that was when he was sober.

And then, during this last summer, Nan had said, 'You know, one day he'll break your jaw and then it'll be too late.'

'I don't know what you mean.'

'He hit you last night, while I was out, when the boys weren't here. I know he did.'

'Now you know nothing of the sort.'

'Your face, Em. What will you tell them today?'

'The truth. That I got up in the night and walked into an open press.'

'Is it going to be like that always? Will he get away with it for the rest of his life?'

'You know how sorry he is, Nan. You must know how he'd give any of us the moon after he's been – not himself.'

'It's too high a price to pay for the moon,' Nan had said.

And now today she was going to start out as a student, this

lovely girl that Emily still looked on with awe. Brian had been handsome before alcohol had thickened his face, and she herself had good features, high cheekbones and deep-set eyes. Their daughter seemed to have taken the best features and left the bad ones. Nan had no trace of the coarseness that was in her father's face. Nor did she have any of the pale and slightly apologetic stance of her mother.

As Emily Mahon stood in the kitchen she hoped that Nan would be warm and pleasant to her father this morning. Brian had been drunk last night, certainly, but there had been no dog's abuse out of him.

Emily turned the rashers expertly. There were three for Paul, three for Nasey and four for Brian. Neither she nor Nan ate a cooked breakfast. Just a cup of tea and a slice of toast each. Emily filled the washing-up bowl with hot soapy water. She would collect their plates to steep when they had finished. Usually everyone left the house around the same time; she liked to have the table cleared before she closed the door behind her, so the place looked respectable when they came in again in the evenings. That way nobody would raise too many objections about Emily going out to work. It had been a battle hard fought.

Nan had been so supportive during the long war waged with Brian. She had listened wordlessly to her father saying, 'No wife of mine is going to work. I want a meal on the table. I want a clean shirt . . .' She had heard her mother say that she could provide these things, but that the days were long and lonely on her own and she would like to meet people and to earn her own money, no matter how small.

The boys, Paul and Nasey, had not been interested, but played the game to win and stuck with their father in the need to have a nice warm house and meals.

Nan had been twelve then, and it was she who had tipped the balance.

'I don't know what you're all talking about,' she had said suddenly. 'None of you are ever in before six, winter or summer, and so there *will* be a meal. And if Em wants more money and will do all your washing and clearing as well, then I can't see what the fuss is about.'

Nobody else could either.

So Emily had worked in a hotel shop since then; her own

little world surrounded by nice things: glass and linen and high-class souvenirs for tourists. At first the hotel had been unwilling to employ someone with a young daughter. She would constantly need time off, they told her. Emily had been able to look them straight in the eye even then and say that Nan would cause no trouble. And she had been right. It was only Brian who had ever interrupted the even style of her working life by phoning or calling, to ask idiotic questions about things that had already been agreed or arranged, but forgotten through drink.

She called them, as she did every morning. 'Breakfast going on the table.'

Down they came, her two big sons, dark like their father, square and looking as if they had been manufactured by a toy firm to look like younger versions of a father in a game. Then came Brian, who had cut himself shaving, and was dabbing the blood on his chin. He looked at his wife without pleasure.

'Do you have to wear that bloody garment in the house? Isn't it bad enough going out to work as a skivvy in someone's shop without dressing as a skivvy at home.'

'It's to keep my blouse clean,' Emily said mildly.

'And you have your clothes draped around so that the place looks like a hand-me-down shop,' he grumbled.

Nan came in at that moment. Her blonde curls looked as if she had just come from a hairdresser rather than from the hand basin in her own bedroom which was where she had washed her hair this morning. Brian Mahon might have skimped on comfort for the rest of the house, but his daughter's bedroom had the best of everything. A wash basin neatly boxed in, a big fitted wardrobe with even a rail for her shoes in it. Nothing had been spared on Nan's room. Each item was an apology for a drunken bout. She wore a smart blue skirt, and her new navy three-quarter-length coat over her shoulders; a white lacy blouse with a navy-blue trimming. She looked like the cover of a magazine.

'That's right, attack Em for leaving her blouse there, but if it's seven of your shirts and seven each of the boys', that's twenty-one shirts ironed for you and there's no word of it being a hand-me-down shop then, is there?'

Her father looked at her in open admiration. 'They're going to look twice when you walk in the door of University College,' he said.

Nan showed no pleasure at the compliment – in fact Emily seemed to think it irritated her.

'Yes, that's all very well, but we never discussed the matter of pocket money.'

Emily wondered why Nan brought it up now. If she were to ask her father on her own he would give her anything.

'There's never been any shortage of pocket money in his house.' His face was red and angry already.

'Well, there hasn't been any question of it up till now. Paul and Nasey went in to work for you, so they got a wage from the start.'

'A *sort* of wage,' Paul said.

'More than any other human would give a lout like you,' his father retorted.

Nan continued, 'I wanted it to be clear from the start rather than having to ask every week.'

'What's wrong with asking every week?' he wanted to know.

'It's undignified,' she said shortly.

That was exactly what Emily had felt each week asking for her housekeeping; now she could work out a budget to suit herself.

'What do you want?' He was annoyed.

'I don't know. I'm not really entitled to anything. I'm going to be dependent on you for three or four years. What do *you* suggest?'

He was at a loss. 'We'll see.'

'I'd prefer if we could decide today. It would get things off to a good start. I'd know what I could buy, how long it would take me to save for something . . . a new dress or whatever.'

'I bought you that coat there! It cost an arm and a leg – it's an ordinary navy coat to me, and it cost as much as a fur.'

'It's very well cut, that's why. It will last for years.'

'I should hope so,' he muttered.

'So you see in order not to have discussions like this all the time, don't you think . . .'

Emily held her breath.

'A pound a week for . . .'

'Fares and lunches, yes, that's fair . . .' She stood looking at him expectantly.

'And what else is there . . . ?'

'Well, I suppose there's cinema, newspapers, books, coffee, going to a dance.'

'Another two pounds a week for that?' He looked anxiously at her.

'Oh, that's very generous, thank you. That would be marvellous.'

'And what about clothes then . . . ?' He nodded over at the coat that had cost him an arm and a leg.

'I could manage stockings out of what you've given me.'

'I want you as well dressed as the next man's daughter.'

Nan said nothing.

'What would it cost?' He was like a child now.

Nan looked at him thoughtfully, as if she knew he was in her power now.

'Some people's fathers give them an allowance by the month for clothes. A sum like . . . I don't know . . . twenty . . . but I don't know . . .'

'You'll have thirty pounds a month, nothing is short-changed in this house.' He almost roared it.

Emily Mahon watched Nan start to smile.

'Thank you very much, Daddy, that's more than generous,' she said.

'Well,' he was gruff, 'I won't have you saying I'm not generous.'

'I never said that, never once,' she answered him.

'Well, all this business putting me on the carpet . . . implying that I might leave you short.'

'In your right mind, Daddy, you'd never leave me short, but I don't want to rely on your always being in your right mind.'

Emily caught her breath.

'What do you mean?' He was like a turkeycock now.

'You know exactly what I mean. You're two people, Daddy.'

'You're in no position to be giving me lectures.'

'I'm not. I'm explaining why I wanted it on a regular arrangement so that I wouldn't have to be annoying you when you're . . . well, when you've had a drink I suppose.'

There was a moment's silence. Even the boys wondered what would happen now. The usual way of coping with their father had been to make no reference to anything untoward that might have happened, for fear of bringing it all upon them again. But Nan had chosen her time and place well.

The silence was broken by Emily.

'Well, that's a very good allowance, there can't be many girls setting off today who'd get that.'

'No indeed.' Nan was undisturbed by the tension around her. 'I mean it, Daddy. And I honestly think that if you are going to give me that much, it's probably easier for you to do it once a month.'

'Yes, that's agreed,' he said.

'So will I ask you for forty-two pounds today and then not come near you for a month?'

Paul and Nasey looked at each other with widened eyes.

'Forty-two pounds?' Her father seemed astounded.

'You said three pounds a week, and thirty pounds for clothes.' She seemed apologetic. 'It is a lot, I know.'

'I'm not going back on my word.' He reached into his back pockets and took out a wad of old notes. He peeled them off.

Emily willed her daughter to show the right amount of gratitude, she prayed that the girl wouldn't take it for granted.

But as usual Nan seemed to know better than everyone what to do.

'I'm not going to go down on my knees and thank you, Daddy, because that would just be words. I'll try to make you proud of me. Make you feel glad you've spent so much to put a daughter through college.'

Brian Mahon's eyes misted slightly. He swallowed but could say nothing. 'That's it. Now could a man have a cup of tea in this place does anyone think?'

In a big terraced house in Dunlaoghaire, another household was getting ready for the opening of the university term. Almost a town in itself, Dunlaoghaire was some miles from the centre of Dublin, a big harbour where the mail came in and left every day for Holyhead bringing the holiday visitors. Full also on the out-going journeys with emigrants about to seek their fortune in London.

Ever since the days it had been called Kingstown, it had been a lovely place to live; tropical palm trees along the coast line made it seem like somewhere much more exotic than it really was. The sturdy Victorian houses spoke of a time when this was a place of substance and quality. It was healthy too; the two great arms of piers reached out into the sea and were a regular walking spot for anyone in need of a breath of air or some exercise.

It was a curious mixture of staid respectability with overtones of holiday fun. Every year there was a big noisy carnival with its ghost trains and chairoplanes, and yet matrons with shallow baskets did sociable shopping excursions usually ending with coffee in Marine Road and tutt-tutting over the state of the borough.

Kit Hegarty moved swiftly around her large house in a quiet road that led down to the sea. She had a lot to do. The first day was always important, it set the tone for the whole year. She would cook them all a good breakfast and make it clear that she expected them to be at the table on time.

She had kept students for seven years now, and was known as one of the university's favoured landladies. Normally they didn't like to sanction a digs so far away from the city and the university buildings, but Mrs Hegarty had been quick to explain how near her house was to the railway station, how short was the train journey into town, how good the bracing sea air.

She didn't need to plead for long; soon the authorities realized that this determined woman could look after students better than anyone. She had turned her big dining room into a study; there each boy had his own place at the big felt-covered table, books could be left undisturbed. It was expected in Kit's house that there would be some period of study after supper, most nights at any rate. And her only son Frank studied with them too. It made him feel grown up sitting at the same table as real university students, engineers and agricultural science students, law or med-icine, they had all sat and studied around the Hegarty dining table while young Frank was working for his Intermediate and his Leaving Certificate.

Today he would join them as a fully fledged student himself.

Kit hugged herself with pleasure at the thought that she had raised a son who would be an engineer. And raised him all on her own. Joseph Hegarty had been long gone now, his life in England was no concern of hers any more. He had sent money for a little while, and dates when he was going to be back; and then excuses, and little money. And then nothing.

She had tried not to bring up Frank with any bitterness against his father. She had even left a photograph of Joseph

Hegarty in the boy's room lest he should think that his father was being banished from his memory on top of everything else. It had been a heady day when she noticed the photograph no longer in a place of honour, on the chest of drawers, but moved to a shelf where it could hardly be seen, and then face down, and then in the bottom of a drawer.

Tall, gangly Frank Hegarty didn't need any mythical father's picture any more.

Kit wondered whether Joseph, if he had stayed around, would have had any views on Frank's motorbike. It was a black 250cc BSA – his pride and joy.

Probably not. He had never been a man to face up to anything unpleasant. And Frank's bike was unpleasant. And dangerous, and it was the only black cloud in her life on this morning when her son started university.

In vain she had pleaded and begged him to use the train. They were only minutes from the railway station, the service was frequent. She would pay for his weekly ticket. He could make as many journeys as he liked. It was the only thing he had ever stood out for.

He had gone to Peterborough and worked long hours in a canning factory only so that he could own this bike. Why did she want to take away the one possession that was truly valuable to him? Just because she didn't know how to ride a motorbike or even want to, it was unfair that she should try to stop him.

He was eighteen years and six months. Kit looked at the statue of the Infant of Prague that she kept in the house to impress the mothers of the students who boarded with her. She wished she had a stronger conviction that the Infant of Prague might be any earthly use in keeping her son safe on this terrible machine. It would be nice to have been able to offload your worries on to someone or something like that.

Patsy asked Mrs Hogan if she'd like her to wet another pot of tea.

'Ah, go on, Mam, you'd need tea on a bad day like this,' Patsy said encouragingly.

'That would be nice, Patsy.' She sank back into her chair, relieved.

It hadn't been so wet earlier, when Benny had left for her

first day at college. Benny in her navy jumper and white blouse with the navy and grey check skirt.

'You'll be the belle of the ball,' Eddie had said to her, bursting with pride.

'Oh, Father, I won't. I'm so big and drab-looking,' Benny had said suddenly. 'I'm like some kind of hearse. I caught sight of myself in the mirror.'

Eddie's eyes had filled with tears. 'Child, you're beautiful,' he had said. 'Don't talk about yourself like that. *Please*. Don't upset your mother and me.'

Annabel had wanted to hug her and tell her that she looked lovely. Big, certainly, but with that lovely glowing skin and all that chestnut hair tied back in a navy and white ribbon, she looked what she was: a girl from a nice family, from a house in the country, whose father ran an established business.

But it wasn't a morning for hugging. Instead she had reached out her hand.

'You are a handsome, lovely girl, and they'll all see that,' she said softly.

'Thank you, Mother,' Benny said dutifully.

'And what's more, you'll be very, very happy there. You won't be going back to dreary little bedsitters like a lot of girls have to do, or being half starved in some digs . . .' Annabel sighed with pleasure. '*You'll* be coming home to your own good home every night.'

Benny had smiled at her but again it had seemed a little as if it were expected.

The girl was nervous, as any girl would be starting out in a new place, with strangers.

'It'll be a quiet house from now on, Mam.' Patsy arrived with the teapot and put it on the stand. She placed the quilted cosy on it and patted it approvingly.

'I expect she'll make friends.' Annabel was doubtful. There had always been Eve and only Eve; it was going to be a big wrench.

'And will she be bringing them down here to stay do you think?' Patsy's eyes shone at the excitement. She loved speculating.

'I hadn't thought of that. But I'm sure she will. After all she can't possibly stay up in Dublin with people we don't know or have never heard of. She knows that.'

Mother Francis was thinking about Eve as she watched the rain fall steadily on the convent grounds. She would miss her. Obviously she had to go to Dublin and stay in the convent there; this was the only way she could train for a career. Mother Francis hoped that the Community in Dublin would understand the need to make Eve feel important and part of the place as they had always done here in Knockglen. Eve had never felt remotely like a charity child, nor had there been any pressure on her to join the Order.

Her father had worked long hours for the convent in his time, he had paid many times over in advance for his child to be housed and educated, had he but known it. Mother Francis sighed and prayed silently that the Lord would look after the soul of Jack Malone.

At times there had been other options. Mother Francis and her old school friend of years ago Peggy Pine discussed it long and often.

'I could let her serve her time to me, and make her fit for a job in any shop in Ireland, but we want more than that for her, don't we?'

'Not that it isn't a very worthwhile career, Peggy,' Mother Francis had said diplomatically.

'You'd love the few letters after her name though, wouldn't you now, Bunty?' Few people on earth called Mother Francis that and got away with it.

And what Peggy said was true. Mother Francis *did* want everything that might help to push Eve up some kind of ladder. She had been such an innocent victim from the start it seemed only fair to help her all they could now.

There had never been enough money to dress the child properly and even if there had been they didn't have the style or the know-how. Peggy had advised from the wings, but Eve didn't want outside charity. Anything that came from the convent she regarded as her right. St Mary's was her home.

It was certainly the only place she thought of as home. The three-room cottage where she had been born had lost its interest for Eve as her dislike of the Westwards had grown. When she was a youngster she was forever going up the long path through the convent kitchen gardens, past the briars and brambles and peering in its windows.

When she was about ten she had even started to plant flowers outside it. Mother Francis had nurtured them behind the scenes, just as she had taken cuttings from the various bushes and plants in the convent garden and made a garden around the stony waste ground, the ugly edge of the cliff where Jack Malone had ended his life.

It was hard to know when this hatred of her mother's family had begun. But Mother Francis supposed it was only natural. A girl brought up in a convent with the whole town knowing her circumstances could not be expected to feel any warmth towards the people who lived in splendour over in Westlands. The man who used to ride around Knockglen as if it were all part of his estate; that was Eve's grandfather, Major Charles Westward. A man who had shown no wish to know his daughter's child. He had not been seen much in recent years, and Peggy Pine – who was Mother Francis's line of communication with the outer world – said that he was now in a wheelchair as a result of a stroke. And that small, dark young man Simon Westward, who was seen from time to time around Knockglen, he was Eve's first cousin. He looked very like her, Mother Francis thought, or maybe she was being fanciful. There was another child, too, a girl, but at some fancy Protestant school up in Dublin, hardly ever seen around the place here.

As Eve's resentment of the family had grown, so had her interest in the cottage dwindled. It stood empty. Mother Francis had never given up hope that Eve would live there one day, with a family maybe, and bring back some happiness to the little house that had known only confusion and tragedy.

And it was such a comforting little place. Mother Francis often sat there herself when she came up to tidy the place. It had always been the custom in St Mary's for the nuns to go anywhere in the grounds to read their daily Office. You were as close to God in the gardens, under the big beech tree, or in the walled garden with its smell of rosemary and lemon balm, as you were in the chapel.

Nobody thought it odd that Mother Francis often went up the path past the blackberries to read her Office up by the cottage. She kept a watchful eye on any leaks that might have sprung. If there was anything she couldn't cope with herself she would ask Mossy Rooney, a man of such silence and discretion that he found it hard to reveal his own name in case it might incriminate someone.

If anyone were to ask whether the cottage was for sale or rent, Mother Francis was always ready with a helpless shrug of the shoulders and say that things hadn't been fully sorted out yet, but that it was in Eve's name and nothing could be done until she was twenty-one. Nobody ever brought the matter up with Eve; and as for Mossy Rooney, who had replaced some of the window frames and the guttering, it would have been pointless asking him for information. The whole town knew he was silent as the tomb, a man of deep thoughts, none of them revealed; or possibly a man of no thoughts at all.

Mother Francis would have loved that old cottage to be Eve's home; she could see in her mind's eye a kind of life where Eve would bring her student friends home from university to stay there for weekends, and they would call to the convent and have tea in the parlour.

It was such a waste of a little stone house with a wooden porch and a view across the county as well as down the craggy rocks of the stone quarry. The cottage had no name. And the way things were it might never have a name or a life of its own.

Perhaps she should have approached the Westwards directly. But the reply to her letter had been so cold. Mother Francis had deliberately written on plain paper, not on the heavily embossed convent paper with Our Lady's name all over it. She had spent a sleepless night composing the right words, words that would sound neither sleeveen nor grasping. Evidently she hadn't found them. The letter from Simon Westward had been courteous, but firm and dismissive. His aunt's family had raised no objections to her daughter being brought up in a Roman Catholic convent, and that was where their interest in the matter ended.

Mother Francis had not told Eve about the letter. The girl had hardened her heart so much; there was no point in giving her further cause.

The nun sighed heavily as she looked back at her sixth-year class, heads bent over their composition books all intent on their essay 'The Evils of Emigration'. She wished she could believe that Mother Clare in Dublin would welcome Eve and tell her that the Dublin convent would be her new home for the next year.

It wasn't Mother Clare's style, but God was good, and perhaps she had, for once, been open-hearted and generous.

She might have been generous; but on the other hand she probably hadn't been. There had been no word from Eve for a week, which was not a good sign.

Eve's room in the Dublin convent had no bedside table with a small radio on it. There was no candlewick bedspread. A small neat iron bed with a shabby well-washed coverlet had one lumpy pillow and sheets which were hard to the touch. There was a narrow, poky cupboard and a jug and basin from early times but possibly necessary still today since the bathroom was a long way away.

It wasn't like a prison cell, it was like a maid's room, Eve told herself firmly. And in a sense that was how they must view her, a difficult prickly maid up from the country. Worst of all, a maid with airs and graces.

Eve sat on her bed and looked around the room. She could hear the regretful, gentle voice of Mother Francis telling her that life was never meant to be easy and that her best course was to work very hard now and get out of this place in record time. Study her grammalogues in the shorthand, take sharp interest in the book-keeping, flex her fingers for the typing, practising over and over. Listen and take notes on office procedure. In a year's time or less she would land herself a good job, and a place to live.

Never again would anyone offer her an iron bed in a dark poky little room.

The Wise Woman would grit her teeth and get on with it, Eve told herself. That was a phrase she and Benny used all the time. What would the Wise Woman do about Sean Walsh? The Wise Woman would pretend that he did not exist. The Wise Woman wouldn't buy another half pound of toffees in Birdie Mac's because she'd get spots. The Wise Woman would do her homework because Mother Francis was on the warpath.

After a week Eve realized that the Wise Woman would also need to be a canonized saint to adapt to the new surroundings.

Mother Clare had suggested a regime of light housework, 'to cover all your obligations, my dear'.

And Eve would admit that she did have obligations. She was

getting a free residential course for which others paid handsomely. There was no history of association with this convent as there was with St Mary's in Knockglen. She would have been eager to help from a sense of justice and also to do Mother Francis credit. But this was different.

Mother Clare's idea of covering obligations centred around the kitchen. She thought perhaps that Eve might like to serve the breakfast in the refectory and clear away, and that she should also leave classes ten minutes before lunch and be back in the refectory to serve soup to the other students when they came in.

In all her years in St Mary's Eve Malone had never been seen by the other girls to perform one menial task. She had been asked to help behind the scenes as would any girl in her own home. But in front of the other pupils Mother Francis had made an iron-hard rule that Eve must never be seen to do anything which would give her a different status.

Mother Clare had no such qualms. 'But my dear girl, you don't know these other pupils,' she had said when Eve had politely requested that she should not be put in a public position of a non-fee-paying student.

'And I hardly *will* get to know them if they think I'm there on some different basis to themselves,' she had said.

Mother Clare's eyes had narrowed. She sensed trouble in this girl, who seemed to have taken in the entire community below in Knockglen.

'But isn't that the case, Eve? You are here on a different basis,' she had said, smiling very sweetly all the while.

Eve knew the battle had to be fought and won there and then before the other students arrived.

'I am happy to cover my obligations in whatever way you suggest, Mother, but not in view of my fellow students. Can I ask you to rethink your plans for me.'

Two spots of red appeared on Mother Clare's cheeks. This was pure insolence. But Mother Clare had fought many battles since she had taken her vows and she always realized when she was on poor ground. Like now. The Community in Knockglen would defend Eve vociferously. Even some of the Sisters here in Dublin might see that the girl had a point.

'I'll tell you tomorrow,' she had said and turned to swish her long black skirts and veil down the polished corridor.

Eve had spent the day wandering around Dublin with a heavy heart. She knew she had visited heavy housework upon herself because of her attitude.

She looked in shop windows and willed herself to think of the days when she would be able to afford clothes like she saw there.

Imagine if you could go in and buy maybe four of the pencil-slim skirts in different colours. They were only twelve shillings and eleven pence each. It didn't matter that they were not great quality, you could have all these colours. And there was cotton gingham at two shillings a yard, you'd have a smashing blouse out of that at six shillings, maybe four of them to go with each of the skirts.

Eve dismissed the swagger coats. She was too short, they were too sweeping, they'd envelop her, but she'd love six pairs of the fully fashioned very sheer nylons just under five shillings each. And tapered slacks in wine or navy; she saw those everywhere. They varied in price, but usually around a pound a pair.

If she had a wallet of money she'd go and buy them now. This minute.

But it wasn't money for clothes that she wanted. Eve knew that only too well. She wanted a different kind of life entirely. She wanted to study, to spend three, even five, years at university. She was prepared to make sacrifices for it, but there seemed to be no way she could even begin.

There were stories of people putting themselves through college by working during the day and studying at night. But that would still mean the year with the terrible Mother Clare to qualify herself for any kind of work. Eve noticed that almost without realizing it her journey had taken her up through St Stephen's Green towards the big grey buildings of University College. It was still empty and she wandered at will around the main hall, seeing only those involved in administration moving about.

The term would start next week. Lucky Benny would arrive as would hundreds of first-year students from all over Ireland.

Eve realized that there were thousands like herself who would never get there. But their expectations hadn't been raised. They hadn't been encouraged and treated well and led to believe that they had brains and insights like she had. That's what made it so hard.

Eve knew that through these doors next week would come

girls who only intended to use university as part of their social life. There would be unwilling students, who didn't want to be here at all, who had other plans and other dreams, but came to satisfy the wishes of parents. There would be those who drifted in and would use the time to make up their minds. She felt a boiling rage about the Westwards, the family who cut off their own flesh and blood, who let her be raised by the charity of the nuns and never bothered themselves to think that she was now of university age.

There was no fairness on earth if someone who would appreciate it and work hard was kept out just because of a greedy, uncaring family who would prefer to forget the child of an unsuitable union rather than make a generous gesture and ensure that some right was done at the end of the day.

She looked in the glass-fronted noticeboards and read of the societies that would be re-forming when term started, and the new committees and the sports arrangements and the practice times, and the appeals for people to join this group and that club.

And she saw the big staircases leading up to the libraries and the lecture halls. She saw the red plush benches which would be filled with students next week, and she ached to be amongst them. To spend her days reading and writing and finding out more and talking to people, and to spend no time at all trying to outwit awful people like Mother Clare.

The Wise Woman would get on with her life and stop dreaming. Then she thought how tiring it was going to be for the rest of her life trying to be the Wise Woman all the time. It would be great to be the very Unwise Woman on occasions.

Benny took the bus to Dublin on the first day of term with more trepidation than she would ever have expected. At home they had behaved as if she were a toddler going to a first party in a party frock rather than a huge ungainly student eighteen years of age going to university dressed from head to toe in dark clothes.

She could still see the tableau this morning; her father with tears of pride in his eyes – she knew he would go to the business and bore everyone to death with tales about how this wonderful daughter was going to university. Benny could see her mother sitting there stretching her hand out full of what she had been full of for months now: the huge advantages of being able to come home every night by bus. Patsy, looking like the faithful old black mammy slave in a film except that she was white and she was only twenty-five. It had made Benny want to scream and scream.

And she had other worries too, as she sat on the bus and started her university career. Mother Francis had told her that the bold Eve hadn't written or telephoned, and that all the Sisters were dying to hear from her. Yet Eve had phoned Benny twice in the last week to say that life in the Dublin convent was intolerable and she would have to meet her in Dublin because otherwise she would go mad.

'But how can we meet? Don't you have to stay in that place for lunch?' Benny had asked.

'I've told them I have to go to hospital for tests.'

As long as she had known her, Eve had hardly ever told a lie. Benny had to tell a lot of little lies in order to be allowed out late or indeed at all. But Eve had been resolute about never lying to the nuns. Things must be bad in Dublin if she had gone this far.

And then there was Sean Walsh. Naturally she had not wanted to go out with him, but both her mother and father stressed how nice it was of him to take such an interest in the fact that she was going off to university and wanted to take her to the pictures as a treat. She had decided to take what might be the easiest way out and accept. After all, if it were to be something to mark the beginning of a new stage in her life, then she could make it clear that this new life wouldn't involve any further outings with him.

Last night they had gone to the film *Genevieve*. Almost everyone else in the world must have loved it, Benny thought grimly, all over the place people left cinemas humming the tune and wishing they looked like either Kay Kendall or Kenneth More. But not Benny. She had left in a black fury.

All through the film Sean Walsh had put his thin bony arm around her shoulder or on her knee and even on one particularly unpleasant occasion managed to get his hand sort of around her back under her arm and around her breast. All of these she had wriggled out of, and as they were leaving the cinema he had the nerve to say, 'You know, I really respect you for saying no, Benny. It makes you even more special, if you know what I mean.'

Respected her! For saying no to *him*? That was the easiest thing she had ever done, but Sean was the type who thought that she enjoyed it.

'I'll go home now, Sean,' she had said.

'No, I told your father we'd have a cup of coffee in Mario's. They won't be expecting you.'

She was trapped again. If she *did* go home they would ask why the coffee hadn't materialized.

Next to the cinema, Peggy Pine's shop had some new autumn stock. Benny had looked at the cream-coloured blouses and soft pink angora sweaters. In order to talk about something that did not have to do with fondling and stroking she spoke of the garments.

'They're pretty, aren't they, Sean?' she had said, her mind barely on them. She was thinking instead that once she got to university she would never need to see him again.

'Well, they are, but not on *you*. You're much wiser not to draw attention to yourself. Wear dark colours. Nothing flashy.'

There had been tears in her eyes as she crossed the road with him to Mario's and he brought two cups of coffee and two club milk chocolate biscuits to the plastic-topped table where she waited for him.

'It's an ill wind,' he had said.

'What do you mean exactly?'

'Well, that brought Eve off to Dublin and out of your life.'

'Not out of my life. I'm going to be in Dublin.'

'But not in her world. Anyway, you're grown up now, it's not for you to be as thick as thieves with the likes of *her*.'

'I like being as thick as thieves with her. She's my friend.' Why do I have to explain this to him, Benny had thought.

'Yes, but it's not seemly. Not any more.'

'I don't like talking about Eve behind her back.'

'No, I'm just saying, it's an ill wind. Now that she's gone you won't always be saying that you're off to the pictures with her. I can take you.'

'I won't have much time for the pictures any more. Not with study.'

'You won't be studying every night.' He had smiled at her complacently. 'And don't forget, there's always weekends.'

She had felt a terrible weariness.

'There's always weekends,' she repeated. It seemed easier somehow.

But Sean had felt like making a statement. 'Don't think that it's going to come between us, you having a university education,' he had said.

'Not come between us?'

'Exactly. Why should it? There are some men that might let it but I'm not one. I tell you something, Benny, I've always modelled myself a lot on your father. I don't know whether you know this or not.'

'I know you work with him, so I'm sure you must learn from him.'

'Much more than that. I could learn from any outfitters in the country. I could learn tailoring by sitting at a bench. No, I watch the way Mr Hogan has faced the world, and I try to learn from that.'

'What have you learned in particular?'

'Well, not to be proud, for one thing. Your father married an older woman, a woman with money. He wasn't ashamed to put that money into his business, it's what she wanted and he wanted. It would have been a foolish, bull-necked man who would have looked a gift horse in the mouth . . . so I like to see myself in a small way as following in his footsteps.'

Benny had stared at him as if she had never seen him before.

'What exactly are you trying to say, Sean?' she had asked.

'I'm trying to say that none of it means anything to me. I'm above all that sort of thing,' he had said loftily.

There was a silence.

'Just to make my point clear,' he had ended.

That had been last night.

Mother and Father had seemed pleased that she had spent time having coffee with Sean.

If that's what they want for me, Benny asked herself, why on God's earth are they allowing me to go to university? If they want to take it all away in the end and match me up with that slimy halfwit, why then take me up to the mountain and show me the world? It was too hard to answer, as was Eve's problem. Eve had said not only was she going to be free for lunch, she would meet Benny off the bus and walk her up to University College. Hanged for a sheep was what Eve had said on the phone.

Jack Foley woke with a start. He had been dreaming that he and his friend Aidan Lynch were on Death Row in some American prison and they were about to die in the electric chair. Their crime seemed to be that they had sung the song 'Hernando's Hideaway' too loudly.

It was a huge relief to find himself in the big bedroom with its heavy mahogany furniture. Jack said you could hide a small army in the various wardrobes around the house. His mother had said that it was all very well to mock but she had stood many long hours at auctions all over the city finding the right pieces.

The Foleys lived in a large Victorian house with a garden in Donnybrook, a couple of miles from the centre of Dublin. It was a leafy place, professional people, merchants, senior civil servants had lived around here for a long time.

The houses on the road didn't have numbers; they all had names, and the postman knew where everyone lived. People didn't move much once they got to a road like this one. Jack was the eldest of the family and he had been born in a smaller house, but he didn't remember it. By the time he was a toddler his parents had arrived here.

He noticed that in the photographs of his childhood the rooms looked a lot less furnished.

'We were building up our home,' his mother had told him. 'No point in rushing and getting the wrong type of thing entirely.'

Not that Jack or any of his brothers really noticed the house much. It was there for them as it had always been. Like Doreen had always been putting the food on the table, like the old dog Oswald had been there for as long as they could recall.

Jack shook off his dream about Death Row and remembered that all over Dublin today there would be people waking to the first day of term.

The first day of term in the Foley household meant that Jack would put on a college scarf and head into UCD for the first time. In the dining room of the big Donnybrook house there was a sense of excitement. Dr John Foley sat at the head of the table, and looked at his five sons. He had assumed they would all enter medicine as he had, so it had been a shock when Jack had chosen law. Perhaps the same thing would happen with the others. Dr

Foley looked at Kevin and Gerry. He had always seen them somewhere in the medical field as well as on a rugby pitch. His eye fell on Ronan. Already he seemed to have the reassuring kind of manner one associated with being a doctor. That boy Ronan could convince even his own mother that the wounds he got in a playground were superficial, that the dirt on his clothes would easily wash out. That was the personality you needed in a good family doctor. Then there was Aengus, the youngest: his owlish glasses made him look studious and he was the only Foley boy not to be chosen for some kind of team in the school. Dr Foley had always seen his son Aengus as going into medical research when the time came. A bit too frail and woolly for the rough and tumble of ordinary practice.

But then he had been wrong about his eldest son. Jack said he had no wish to study physics and chemistry. The term he had spent at school trying to understand the first thing about physics had been wasted. Nor did he want botany and zoology, he'd be no good at them.

In vain Dr Foley had pleaded that the pre-med year was a necessary term of purgatory before you started the real business of medicine.

Jack had been adamant. He would prefer law.

Not the Bar either, but being apprenticed as a solicitor. What he would really and truly like was to do this new degree course for Bachelor of Civil Law. It was like doing a BA but all in law subjects. He had discussed it with his father seriously and with all the information to hand. He could be apprenticed to his mother's brother, surely. Uncle Kevin was in a big solicitors' practice: they'd find a place for him. He timed his request well. Jack knew that his father's head was buried as deeply in the world of rugby as the world of medicine. Jack was a shining schoolboy player. He was on the pitch for his school in the Senior Cup final. He scored two tries and converted one of them. His father was in no position to fight him. Anyway it would have been foolish to force someone into a life so demanding. Dr Foley shrugged. There were plenty of other boys to follow him down the good physician's route to Fitzwilliam Square.

Jack's mother Lilly sat at the far end of the table opposite her husband. Jack could never remember a breakfast when she had not presided over the cups of tea, the bowls of cornflakes, the slices of grilled bacon and half tomato which was the start to the day every morning except Fridays and in Lent.

His mother always looked as if she had dressed up for the occasion, which indeed she had. She wore a smart Gor-Ray skirt, always with either a twinset or a wool blouse. Her hair was always perfectly done, and there was a dusting of powder on her face as well as a slight touch of lipstick. When Jack had spent the night in friends' houses after a match he realized that their mothers were not like his. Often women in dressing gowns with cigarettes put food on kitchen tables for them. The formal breakfast at eight o'clock in a high-ceilinged dining room with heavy mahogany sideboards and floor-to-ceiling windows wasn't everyone else's way of life.

But the Foley boys weren't pampered either; their mother had seen to that. Each of them had a job to do in the mornings before they left for school. Jack had to fill the coal scuttles, Kevin to bring in the logs, Aengus had to roll yesterday's papers into sausage-like shapes which would be used for lighting the fires later, Gerry, who was meant to be the animal lover, had to take Oswald for a run in the park, and see that there was something on the bird table in the garden, and Ronan had to open the big heavy curtains in the front rooms, take the milk in from the steps and place it in the big fridge and brush whatever had to be brushed from the big granite steps leading up to the house. It could be cherry blossom petals or autumn leaves or slush and snow.

When breakfast was finished the Foley boys placed their plates and cutlery neatly on the hatch into the kitchen before going to the big room where all their coats, boots, shoes, school bags and often rugby gear had to be left.

People marvelled at the way Lilly Foley ran such an elegant home when she had five rugby-playing lads to deal with, and marvelled even more that she had kept the handsome John Foley at her side. A man not thought to be easy to handle. Dr Foley had a wandering eye as a young man. Lilly had not been more beautiful than the other women who sought him, just more clever. She realized that he would want an easy uncomplicated life where everything ran smoothly and he was not troubled with domestic difficulties.

She had found Doreen at an early stage, and paid her over

the odds to keep the house running smoothly. Lilly Foley never missed her weekly hair-do and manicure.

She seemed to regard her life with the handsome doctor as a game with rules. She kept an elegant attractive home. She put on not an ounce of fat, and always appeared well groomed at golf club or restaurant, as well as at home. This way he didn't wander.

Today when the four younger boys left for school, Jack helped himself to another cup of tea.

'I'll know what you two talk about when you're alone now,' he grinned. He looked very handsome when he smiled, his mother thought fondly. Despite reddish-brown hair which wouldn't stay flat, those freckles on his nose, he really was classically good looking, and when Jack Foley smiled he would break any heart. Lilly Foley wondered would he fall in love easily, or did the rugby take so much time that he would just be satisfied with the distant adulation of the girls who watched and cheered the games.

She wondered would he be as hard to catch as his father had been. What would some wily girl see in him that he would respond to? She had captured his father by promising an elegant uncluttered lifestyle very different from the neglected unhappy home he had come from. But this would not be the way to lure away her Jack. He was happy and well looked after in this home. He wouldn't want to flee the nest for a long time yet.

'Are you sure you won't take a lift?' Dr John Foley would have been proud to drive his eldest son up to Earlsfort Terrace and wave him into his first day at university.

'No, Dad, I told a few of the lads . . .'

His mother seemed to understand. 'It's not like school, it's sort of more gradual, isn't it? There's no bell saying you all have to be there at such a time.'

'I know, I know. I've been there, remember.' Dr Foley was testy.

'It's just that I said . . .'

'No, your mother is right, you want to be with your own friends on a day like this, and the best of luck to you, son, may it turn out for you just as well as you ever hoped. Even if you're not doing medicine.'

'Ah, go on, you're relieved. Think of all the malpractice suits.'

'You can get those in law just as well as medicine. Anyway,

there's no reason why they shouldn't pick a law student for the first fifteen.'

'Give me a bit of time, Dad.'

'After the way you played in the Schools Cup? They're not blind in there. You'll be playing in the Colours match in December.'

'They never have Freshers for that.'

'They'll have you, Jack.'

Jack stood up. 'I'll be on it next year. Will that do you?'

'All right, if you play for UCD in 1958 that'll do me. I'm a very reasonable, undemanding man,' said Dr Foley.

When Benny got off the bus on the Quays, she saw Eve waiting, with her raincoat collar turned up against the rain. She looked cold and pale.

'God, you really will end up in hospital this way,' Benny said. She was alarmed by the look in Eve's eyes and the uncertainty of the future.

'Oh, shut up will you? Do you have an umbrella?'

'Do I have an umbrella? We're lucky that I don't have a plastic bubble encasing me, the weather was tested all night, I think. I have a folding mac that makes me look like a haystack in the rain, I have an umbrella that would fit most of Dublin under it.'

'Well, put it up then,' Eve said, shivering. They crossed O'Connell Bridge together.

'What are you going to do?' Benny asked.

'Anything. I can't stay there. I tried.'

'You didn't try very hard, less than a week.'

'If you saw it, if you *saw* Mother Clare!'

'You're the one who's always telling me that things will pass, and to make the best of them. You're the one who says we can stick anything if we know where we're going.'

'That was before I met Mother Clare, and anyway I don't know where I am going.'

'This is Trinity. We just keep following the railings, and up one of the streets to the Green . . .' Benny explained.

'No, I don't mean here. I mean, where I'm going really.'

'You're going to get a job and get shot of them as quick as possible. Wasn't that the plan?'

Eve made no reply. Benny had never seen her friend so low.

'Isn't there anyone nice there? I'd have thought you'd have made lots of friends.'

'There's a nice lay Sister in the kitchen. Sister Joan, she's got chapped hands and a streaming cold, but she's very kind. She makes me cocoa in a jug while I'm washing up. It has to be in a jug in case Mother Clare comes in and thinks I'm being treated like someone normal. I just drink it straight from the jug, you see, no cup.'

'I meant among the others, the other girls.'

'No, no friends.'

'You're not trying, Eve.'

'You're damn right I'm not trying. I'm not staying either, that's for good and certain.'

'But what will you *do*? Eve, you can't do this to Mother Francis and everyone.'

'In a few days I'll have some plan. I won't live in that place. I won't do it.' Her voice had a slightly hysterical ring about it.

'All right, all right.' Benny was different now. 'Will you come home on the bus tonight, back to Knockglen, back to the convent?'

'I can't do that. It would be letting them down.'

'Well, what would it be standing shivering around the streets here, telling lies about being in hospital? What'll they say when they hear that? Will we walk through the Green? It's nice, even though it's wet.' Benny's face looked glum.

Eve felt guilty. 'I'm sorry, I'm really making a mess of your first day of term. This is not what you need.'

They had reached the corner of St Stephen's Green. The traffic lights were green and they started to cross the road.

'Look at the style,' Benny said wistfully. Already they could see students in duffle coats, laughing and talking. They could see girls with pony tails and college scarves walking in easy friendship with boys along the damp slippery footpaths up towards Earlsfort Terrace. Some did walk on their own, but they had great confidence. Just beside them Benny noticed a blonde girl in a smart navy coat; despite the rain, she still looked elegant.

They were all crossing together when they saw the skid, the boy on the motorbike, out of control and ploughing towards the sedate black Morris Minor. It all seemed like slow motion, the way the boy fell and the bike swerved and skidded. How the car tried to avoid it and how both motorbike and car came sideways into the group of pedestrians crossing the wet street.

Eve heard Benny cry out, and then she saw the faces frozen as the car came towards her. She didn't hear the screams because there was a roaring in her ears and she lost consciousness, pinned by the car to the lamp post. Beside her lay the body of the boy Francis Joseph Hegarty, who was already dead.

CHAPTER FOUR

Everyone said afterwards it was a miracle that more people hadn't been killed or injured. It was another miracle that it was so near the hospital, and that the driver of the car, who had been able to step out of it without any aid, had in fact been a Fitzwilliam Square doctor himself, who had known exactly what to do. Clutching a handkerchief to his own face, he felt blood over his eye but he assured them it was superficial, he gave instructions which were followed to the letter. Someone was to hold up the traffic, another to get the guards, but first someone was sent down the side lane towards St Vincent's Hospital to alert casualty and summon help. Dr Foley knelt beside the body of the boy whose motorbike had lost control. He closed his own eyes to give a silent prayer of relief that his own son had never wanted to ride a machine like this.

Then he closed the eyes of the boy with the broken neck, and placed a coat over him to keep him from the eyes of the students he would never get to know. The small girl with the wound in her temple had a slightly slow pulse and could well be concussed. But he did not think her condition critical. Two other girls had been grazed and bruised, and were obviously suffering from shock. He himself had bitten his tongue from what he could feel in his mouth, probably loosened a couple of teeth and had a flesh wound over his eye. His task now was to get things into the hands of the professionals before he asked anyone to take his blood pressure for him.

One of the injured girls, a big, soft-faced girl with chestnut-coloured hair and dark, sensible clothes, seemed very agitated about the one lying unconscious on the ground.

'She's not dead is she?' The eyes were round in horror.

'No, no, I've felt her pulse. She's going to be fine,' he soothed her.

'It's just that she didn't have any life.' The girl's eyes were full of tears.

'None of you have yet, child.' He averted his glance from the dead boy.

69

'No. Eve in particular. It would be terrible if she weren't all right.' She bit her lip.

'I've told you. You must believe me, and here they are...' The stretchers had been brought the couple of hundred yards from the hospital. There wasn't even a need for an ambulance.

Then the guards were there, and the people directing the traffic properly, and the little procession moved towards the hospital. Benny was limping slightly and she paused to lean on the girl with the blonde curly hair who she had noticed seconds before the accident.

'Sorry,' said Benny, 'I didn't know if I could walk or not.'

'That's all right. Did you hurt your leg?'

She tested it, leaning on it. 'No, it's not much. What about you?'

'I don't know. I feel all right, really. Maybe too all right. Perhaps we'll keel over in a moment.'

Ahead of them on the stretcher was Eve, her face white. Benny had picked up Eve's handbag, a small cheap plastic one which Mother Francis had bought for her in Peggy Pine's shop as a going-to-Dublin present a few weeks ago.

'She's going to be fine, I think,' Benny explained in a shaky voice. 'The man with all the blood on him, the man driving the car, he says she's breathing and her pulse is all right.'

Benny looked so worried that anyone would have wanted to take her in their arms and stroke her, even though she was bigger than most people around.

The girl with the beautiful face, now grazed and muddy, the girl in the well-cut navy coat, now streaked with blood and wet mud, looked at Benny kindly.

'That man's a doctor. He *knows* these things. My name is Nan Mahon, what's yours?'

It was the longest day they had ever known.

The hospital machinery moved into action, but slowly. The guards took charge of the dead boy as regards telling his family. They had been through his things. His address was on a lot of his belongings. They had deputed two young guards to go out to Dunlaoghaire.

'Can you tell her it was instantaneous?' John Foley said.

'I don't know,' said the young officer. 'Can we tell her that?'

'It's true, and it might be some comfort to her,' John Foley said mildly.

The older Garda sergeant had a different view.

'You never know, Doctor, many a mother might like to think their son had time to whisper an Act of Contrition.'

John Foley turned his head away lest his annoyance be seen.

'And it wasn't his fault, be sure to tell her that,' he tried.

'I'm afraid my men can't . . .' the sergeant began.

'I know, I know.' The doctor sounded weary.

The nurse said of course they could use the phone, but they should have themselves looked at first. Then they'd be in a position to tell their parents what had happened. It made a lot of sense.

The news was good: minor cuts, nothing deep, anti-tetanus injections just in case, mild sedative for shock.

Eve was a different matter. Cracked ribs and mild concussion. Several stitches at the edge of her eye, and a broken wrist. She would be in hospital for some days, possibly a week. They wanted to know who to inform.

'Give me a minute,' Benny said.

'Well, you must know who it is, you're her friend.' The almoner was puzzled.

'Yes, but it's not that easy.'

'Well, what about her wallet?'

'There's nothing in it, no next of kin or anything. Please let me think, I just want to work out what's best.'

Benny was also putting off telling her own parents about the accident, but she had to decide which of the two nuns to talk to on Eve's behalf. Would Eve be furious if Mother Francis heard the whole earning of the lies, the unhappiness and the circumstances that had brought her to the other side of the city and now into a hospital bed?

Would Mother Clare be as bad as Eve had said?

The woman was a nun after all, she must have some redeeming qualities if she were to keep her vows all her life.

Benny's head ached as she tried to work it all out.

'Would it be any help to tell me?' Nan Mahon asked. They had cups of sweet milky tea and they sat at a table.

'It's like a Grimms' fairy tale,' Benny said.

'Tell it,' Nan said.

So Benny told it, feeling slightly disloyal.

Nan listened and asked questions.

'Ring Mother Francis,' she said at the end. 'Tell her that Eve was about to ring her today.'

'But she wasn't.'

'It'll make the nun feel better, and what does it matter what day she was going to ring?'

It made sense. It made a lot of sense.

'But what about Mother Clare?'

'The baddy?'

'Yes, she sounds really awful and she'll crow over Mother Francis, the good one. It's awful to let her in for all this.'

'It's much better than ringing the bad one and bringing all the torments of Hell down on yourself for nothing.'

'I think you're right.'

'Good. Will you go and tell that Sister there, she's beginning to think you have delayed concussion or something. And by the way, put someone medical on to tell her about Eve's injuries. You'll only frighten her to death.'

'Why do you not want to tell your parents?'

'Because my mother works in a hotel shop where they don't really go a bundle on employing married women in the first place, so I don't want to get her all into a fluster for nothing. And my father . . .' Nan paused.

Benny waited.

'My father, that's different.'

'You mean he wouldn't care?'

'No, I mean the very opposite, he'd care too much. He'd come in here ranting and raving and making an exhibition of himself, saying that his poor little girl was injured, scarred for life and who was to blame.'

Benny smiled.

'I mean it. He's always been like that. It's good and bad. Good mainly because it means I can get what I want.'

'And bad?'

'Oh, I don't know. Bad too,' Nan shrugged. The confidences were over.

'Go on and ring the Good Sister before we have the starched apron in on us again.'

Kit Hegarty was in the big front bedroom, the one she had left to the two brothers from Galway. Nice sensible boys, she thought, well brought up by their mother, hung their clothes up neatly, which made a nice change. They wouldn't be much trouble during the year, one doing agriculture, one studying for a B.Comm. No matter what they said, it was the farmers who had the money. There were a good many farmers' sons going in the doors of University College today for the first time.

She thought of her own son amongst the crowd today. He would walk up those steps with a confidence he didn't feel, she knew that. She had seen so many of the students set out from her door, awkward and anxious, and after a few weeks it was as if they had been studying there all their lives.

It would be easier for Frank because he knew Dublin already. He didn't have to get to know a new city like the boys from the country did.

She heard the front gate squeak open, and as she saw the two young Garda officers look up at the windows and come slowly up her path, Kit Hegarty suddenly knew without any doubt what they were coming to tell her.

Jack Foley had met several fellows from school. Not necessarily close friends, but it was amazing how welcome they were in that sea of faces. And they too seemed glad to see him.

There was an introductory lecture at twelve, but until then there wasn't much to do except get their bearings.

'It's like school without the teachers,' said Aidan Lynch, who had paid very little attention to any teacher during his days at school with Jack Foley.

'This is what's meant to be forming our character, remember?' Jack said. 'It's like being on your honour to work all the time.'

'Which means we don't have to work at all,' Aidan said cheerfully. 'Will we go round the corner to Lesson Street? I saw armies of beautiful women all heading in that direction.'

Aidan was a better authority on women than any of the rest of them so they followed him willingly.

At the corner they saw that there had been an accident. People still stood around talking about it. It was a student, they said, very badly hurt, possibly dead. The blanket was over his face when they carried him away.

He had been on that motorbike, which was in bits over beside the wall. Someone said he was going to be doing engineering.

Aidan looked at the twisted wreck of steel and metal.

'Jesus, I hope it wasn't that fellow who was canning peas in Peterborough with me during the summer. That's the bike he was getting. Frank Hegarty. He was going to do engineering.'

'There could have been hundreds of people . . .' Jack Foley began, but then he saw the car that had been pulled away from the corner where it had crashed. There was blood and glass all over the road. The car had been moved in order to let the traffic get through.

It was his father's car.

'Was anyone else hurt?'

'A girl. A young girl. She looked very bad,' said the man. The kind of man you always find at an accident, full of information and pessimism.

'And the man, the man driving the car?'

'Oh, he was all right. Big fancy coat on him, with a bit of fur on the collar. You know the type. Walked out of the car, giving orders left, right and centre, just like a general.'

'He's a doctor, he's meant to do that,' Jack said defensively.

'How do you know that?' Aidan Lynch was astonished.

'It's our car. You go on and have coffee. I'm going into the hospital to see if he is all right.'

He ran across the wet road and over to the hospital entrance before any of them could answer him.

'Come on,' Aidan said. 'The main thing with women is to be the first person they meet. They love that. It gives you a huge advantage.'

It was much easier to tell Mother Francis than Benny had feared. She had been calm and not at all put out about Eve having abandoned all the plans that had been so carefully thought out for her. She had also been very practical.

'Tell me as simply and quickly as you can, Bernadette, where does Mother Clare think that Eve is today?'

'Well, Mother . . .' Benny felt as if she were eight years of age again, instead of almost eighteen. 'It's a bit awkward . . .' It was partly to do with Mother Francis calling her 'Bernadette'. It put her straight back in the classroom, in her gym slip again.

'Yes, I'm sure, but the best thing is if I know everything, then I can judge how much has to be said to Mother Clare.' The nun's voice was smooth. Surely she couldn't be planning to go along with the lies.

Benny risked it. 'I think she thinks that Eve is sort of in hospital already. I think that's what Eve would have been telling you had she been able to give you a ring . . .'

'Yes, of course, she would. Please stop fretting, Bernadette. I am much more concerned that Eve gets well and is aware that we have all made things easier. Can you give me more details . . . ?'

Biting the corner of her lip Benny haltingly told a tale of mythical blood tests. It was noted crisply.

'Thank you, Bernadette. Now can you put me on to someone qualified to tell me about Eve's injuries.'

'Yes, Mother.'

'Bernadette?'

'Yes, Mother?'

'Ring your father at work first. Say you couldn't get through to your mother. It's easier to talk to men. They fuss a lot less.'

'But look at you, Mother, you don't fuss at all.'

'Ah, child, I'm different altogether. I'm a nun,' she said.

Benny gave the phone to the Sister, and sat down with her head in her hands.

'Was it awful?' Nan was sympathetic.

'No, like you said, it was easy.'

'It always is, if you do it right.'

'Now, I have to ring my parents. How do I do that right?'

'Well, what are you hiding from *them*?' Nan seemed amused.

'Nothing. It's just that they'll make such a fuss. They think of me as in nappies.'

'It all depends on how you begin. Don't say "Something terrible happened".'

'What do I start with, then?'

Nan was impatient. 'Maybe you *should* be in nappies,' she snapped. Benny felt her heart sink. It was probably true. She was a big baby, soft in the head.

'Hello, Father,' she said into the phone. 'It's Benny. I'm absolutely fine, Father, I was trying to ring Mother but there was something wrong with the number. Wouldn't it be great to have the automatic exchange?' She looked across at Nan, who was giving the thumbs-up sign.

'No, I'm not actually *in* the college, but I'm just beside it. These people here are very over careful you know, they just like to cover every eventuality so they asked us all to ring our families even though there isn't a thing wrong . . .'

Sean Walsh ran through Knockglen to tell the news to Annabel Hogan. Mrs Healy saw him running as she looked from her bow window and knew that something must be amiss. That young man always moved very correctly. He didn't pause as Dessie Burns called out to him from the hardware shop, he didn't notice Mr Kennedy looking over his glasses at all the bottles and apothecary jars in the window display of the chemist's shop. He ran past the chip shop where he had had coffee with Benny only last night, past the newsagents', the sweetshop, the pub and Paccy Moore's cobbler's shop. Up the short avenue to the Hogans' house; the ground was wet and covered with leaves. If *he* owned his house, he thought to himself, he would give it a good coat of paint, put a smart gate on it. Something more imposing than the way the Hogans had it.

Patsy answered the door. 'Sean,' she said, without much enthusiasm.

Sean felt his cheeks redden slightly. If he were master of the house, no maid would address a senior employee of the master's by his Christian name. It would be Mr Walsh, thank you very much, or sir. And she would wear something to show that she was a maid, a uniform, or a white collar and apron anyway.

'Is Mrs Hogan at home?' he asked haughtily.

'Come in, she's on the phone,' Patsy said casually.

'The phone? It's working again?'

'It never wasn't.' Patsy shrugged.

She led him into the sitting room. He could hear Mrs Hogan in the distance talking to someone. They had the phone in the breakfast room off the kitchen. He wouldn't have had it that way. A telephone should be on a half moon table in the hall. A highly polished table under a mirror, perhaps a bowl of flowers beside it reflecting in the table. Sean had always looked around him when he went into people's houses. He wanted to know how things should be done. For when the time came.

The sitting room had shabby chintz furniture, and faded curtains in the long window alcove. It could have been a very smart room, Sean thought, mentally ticking off the changes he would make. He hardly noticed Patsy, who had come back in.

'She says you're to come out to her.'

'Mrs Hogan isn't coming in here?' He didn't want to be telling the news in the territory where the maid could be involved, but followed obediently to the shabby breakfast room.

'Ah, Sean.' Annabel Hogan was polite to him even if her maid wasn't.

'I'm very sorry to be the bearer of bad news, but there's been an accident,' he said in the sepulchral tones of an undertaker.

'I know, poor Eve, Mother Francis was on to me about it.'

'But Mrs Hogan . . . Benny was involved in it . . .'

'Yes, but she's not hurt at all, she was talking to Mother Francis and to her father. There was some fault on the phone here or else I was on the phone myself talking to Father Rooney about the Station.'

'She got scratches and a sprained ankle.' Sean couldn't believe this calm acceptance. He had expected to be the deliverer of the news and then the great consoler, but Mrs Hogan was making light of it. It was incomprehensible.

'Yes, but she's perfectly all right. She's going to sit there in the hospital, and they'll keep an eye on her and someone will put her on the evening bus, just as she planned. It's only the shock, Mother Francis says. Better to let her sit calmly there with people who know all about it.'

Sean felt all this thunder being stolen from him.

'I had thought I would drive to Dublin and collect her,' he said.

'Ah, Sean, we couldn't ask you to do that.'

'She might not like hanging around hospital, you know, sick people, smells of disinfectant . . . it's early closing and I was going to ask Mr Hogan for a loan of the car.'

Annabel Hogan looked at Sean Walsh's concerned face and at a stroke all the careful, calming work of Mother Francis was destroyed.

'You're very kind, Sean, but maybe if it's as bad as that my husband would want to go himself . . .'

'But Mrs Hogan, if I might presume, it's very hard to find a place to park the car in the centre of Dublin. Mr Hogan hasn't been used to driving in the city traffic of recent years, and I had planned to go to Dublin to collect the samples of material. You could ask them till kingdom come to put them on the bus, but they never do . . .'

'Will I come with you, do you think?'

Sean Walsh's mind did a slow careful calculation, then he came to a decision.

'I'll go on my own, Mrs Hogan, if that's all right. Then you can make all the preparations here.'

It had been the right thing to say. Annabel saw herself in the role of getting ready to welcome the invalid home.

Sean smiled as he left the house. This time he didn't run up the main street of Knockglen. He walked on the other side of the road. He nodded to Dr Johnson, who was coming out of his surgery. He glanced in the window of Peggy Pine's women's outfitters and saw with distaste the pastel colours that Benny had admired last night. Benny was such a big girl, she could hardly have wanted them for herself. Still, it was good that she sought his advice.

He saw that *Monsieur Hulot's Holiday* was coming to the cinema this weekend. That was good. Benny wouldn't be well enough, and Sean didn't like foreign-language films. They put him at a disadvantage.

He held his shoulders back. There was no reason for him to feel at a disadvantage. Things were working out fine.

All he had to do now was to let Mr Hogan know how distressed Mrs Hogan was and how he had saved the day.

Dr Foley said he'd just go in and see how that child was in casualty before he left.

'They've cancelled my appointments for this morning . . . Maybe you'd walk me down to the Shelbourne for a taxi?' he asked Jack.

'I could get one here, and come home with you.'

'No, no, you know I don't want that. Stay here in the waiting room, will you, Jack?'

Jack moved into the over-bright room with the yellow walls. Two girls sat at a table. One of them was a spectacularly pretty blonde; the other, a big girl with long chestnut hair tied back in a bow, had a bandage on her foot. He realized they must have been in the accident.

'Was it terrible?' he asked, looking questioningly at the empty chair, as if asking their permission to sit down. They pulled the chair forward and told him about it. They told him they had heard that the doctor had managed to avoid them all by driving into the lamp post. Only Eve, who had been hit by the moving car, was seriously hurt and even Eve would be out of hospital in a week.

They talked easily. Benny stumbled from time to time, and became tongue-tied when she looked at the handsome boy sitting beside them. Never before had she held a conversation with anyone like this, and she would begin a sentence and not know how to finish it.

Jack Foley's eyes rarely left Nan's face, but she seemed to be unaware of this and talked as if all three of them were equal partners in the conversation. Jack explained that it had been his father driving the car. Nan said that both she and Benny were busy trying to play down their bruises and scratches because it would cause such almighty upheavals in both their homes.

'I don't feel like going in to college now. Do you?' she looked from one to the other. It was as if she knew a solution would be proposed.

'Why don't I take the pair of you for a plate of chips?' Jack asked.

Benny clapped her hands like a child. 'I didn't know that's what my soul cried out for, well possibly not my soul, but there was a cry there definitely,' she said. They both smiled at her.

'I'll just see my father to a taxi and come back for you.' He was looking straight into Nan's eyes.

'Where would we go? It's the best offer we've had all day,' Nan said.

'He's very nice,' Benny said, when Jack had gone.

'He's the college hero before he even gets there,' said Nan.

'How do you know?'

'I saw him play in the Schools Cup.'

'Play what?'

'He was on the wing.' Nan saw Benny's mystification and explained. 'Rugby. He really is very good.'

'How did you go to a rugby match?'

'Everyone does. It's a kind of social event.'

Benny realized that there were going to be a great many areas where she would be at a loss. Rugby matches would only be a very small part of them, and none of these gaps in her knowledge would be helped by continuing to live in Knockglen all her life.

She wished suddenly that she were someone totally different, that she were much smaller and had a small face and tiny feet like Nan had. That she could look up at men rather than over or down at them. She wished her parents lived in the Aran Islands and that there could be no question of her having to go home every night. She felt a sudden desire to dye her hair blonde and keep dyeing it every day so that the roots would never show. There was nothing she could do about her size. Even if she were thinner she would still have huge shoulders and great big feet. No operation had been invented to give you small feet.

She looked at them with distaste in their sensible shoes and thick bandage. Her mother had normal feet, her father had, why did Benny's have to be the way they were? At school they had once heard of some animal which had become extinct because of its huge flat feet. Benny hadn't known whether to envy it or be sorry for it.

'Is it hurting much?' Nan had seen Benny studying her foot and thought it must be paining her.

Jack came back at that moment.

'Well,' he said to Nan.

She stood up. 'I think Benny's foot is hurting her.'

'Oh, I'm sorry.' He looked at her briefly with a sympathetic smile.

'No, it's fine,' she said.

'If you're sure?' He was polite. Perhaps he wanted to go off with Nan on his own. She didn't know. But it would always be like this anyway so there was no point in getting upset about it.

'You were looking at it and frowning,' Nan said.

'No, I was only thinking about all those prayers we say for the conversion of China. Do you put three Hail Marys on to the Rosary for it?'

'I think it was the conversion of Russia in ours,' Jack said. 'But I'm not sure. Just shows you how well I'm able to escape it.'

'Well, I can't think why we should be praying for them,'

Benny said with mock indignation. 'They have lovely habits out there. They bind everyone's feet.'

'What?'

'Oh yes, as soon as they're born, so there's no problem about people falling over them. Everyone has tiny feet and nice squashed-up bones. So elegant-looking.'

Jack seemed to realize she was there for the first time.

'And now chips,' he said, looking straight at her. 'Four plates, one plate each and one to pick off. And lashings of tomato ketchup.'

Then she heard the nurse tell someone that Miss Hogan was out in the waiting room, and there was Sean Walsh coming towards them. Her face fell.

'I've come to drive you home, Benny,' he said.

'I told Father I was coming home on the bus,' she said coldly.

'But he gave me the car...'

Jack looked politely from the thin-faced boy to the big girl with the red-brown hair.

No introductions were made.

Benny spoke with an authority she didn't know that anyone could have, let alone herself.

'Well, I hope you had some other work to do in Dublin, Sean. That you didn't come up specially, because I have to leave now. And I will be home on the bus as arranged.'

'What do you have to do? You're to come home. Now. With me.' Sean sounded petulant.

'She has to go for some more treatment,' Jack Foley said. 'I'm just taking her there. You wouldn't want her to miss that.'

CHAPTER FIVE

Benny knew they would come to meet her off the bus. But she hadn't expected all three of them, not Patsy as well, and not the car. Sean must have driven home with dire tales to have brought such a gathering to the bus stop. Before Mikey had swung the bus around and brought it to a stop she had seen their pale faces in the wet night, the two umbrellas. She felt the familiar surge of irritation mixed with guilt. No one on earth had such a loving family, no one on earth felt so cooped up and smothered.

She walked with a heavy heart to the front of the bus.

'Goodnight, Mikey.'

'Good girl, Benny. Something wrong with your foot?'

'I hurt it,' she said, realizing his wife would probably have the tale already.

'It's all this drunken life as a student. That's what it is,' he said, roaring with laughter at his wit.

'That's what it is,' she repeated it in a dull, polite way.

'There she is!' cried her father, as if there had ever been any doubt about her arrival.

'Oh, Benny, are you all right?' Her mother's eyes were wide with anxiety.

'Mother, I *told* Father on the phone. I'm fine. Fine.'

'Then why did you have to go back for treatment?' Annabel Hogan had the face of someone who thought that very bad news was being kept from her. 'We were very alarmed when Sean told us that they needed to look at you again, and you didn't ring a second time . . . so we were afraid . . .'

Her father's face had lines of worry.

'Sean had no business coming up there for me, interfering and giving orders and upsetting everyone here and there.' Benny's voice was calm, but a little louder than normal.

She saw Mrs Kennedy from the chemist turn and look at her. That would be a subject for discussion in *their* house tonight, a scene, no less, at the bus stop with the Hogan family of all people. Well, well, well. Hadn't it been a' mistake to let that Benny go to Dublin on her own after all?

'He went to set our minds at ease,' Benny's father said. 'We were very worried.'

'No, Father, you weren't. You were quite happy for me to come home on the bus. I talked to you and you were grand, and you said Mother would be grand and then suddenly Sean manages to spoil everything.'

'The boy drove the whole way to Dublin on his half day to bring you home and then drove straight back and said you had to see another doctor. Do you blame us for being worried?' Eddie Hogan's face was working with distress: beside him Annabel raked her face for more information. Even Patsy didn't seem convinced that all was well.

'I didn't *want* him to come for me. You never said he was coming. There was nothing wrong with *me*, for God's sake. You *must* see that. I was perfectly all right, but a boy was killed. He was killed in front of my eyes. He was alive one minute and then he was dead with his neck broken. And Eve's in a hospital ward with broken ribs and concussion and all kinds of things. And all Sean Walsh can do is stand like a stuffed dummy in that hospital and talk about me!'

To her horror Benny realized that there were tears pouring down her face, and that a small circle of people were watching her in concern. Two schoolgirls from the convent who had been in Dublin to buy books with one of the young nuns turned to see what was happening. It would be all around the convent before bed time.

Benny's father decided to act. 'I'll get her into the car,' he said. 'Patsy, will you run down to Dr Johnson's like a good girl and ask him to come over as soon as he can. Now, Benny, it's all right. It's all right. It's natural, just shock.'

Benny wondered was there a condition which might be known as Rage. Because that was definitely what she felt her condition to be. Helpless rage.

Everyone in Knockglen heard about it in record time, but what they heard bore little relation to the facts. Mrs Healy said that she heard the girls were running and laughing like they had done in Knockglen and they were hit by a car. As a precaution they had both been admitted to hospital, but Sean Walsh had driven up and got Benny discharged. It was a lesson on how to conduct yourself in huge menacing Dublin traffic if you came from a small place like Knockglen.

Mr Flood was silent and blessed himself a great deal when he heard the news. He said that it was obviously meant as some kind of warning. What kind of a warning he couldn't say, but his family noticed with alarm that he had gone out to consult the tree again. They had hoped that this little habit had died down.

Mrs Carroll said it was a waste of good money sending girls to university. Not if the grocery was three times the size of Findlater's in Dublin would they send Maire and her sisters there. You might as well take money and shovel it down the drain. What did they do on the very first day except walk under the first vehicle they saw? Maire Carroll, serving in the shop and hating it, felt a firm and vicious sense of satisfaction over the fate of Eve and Benny, but of course she pretended great care and concern.

Bee Moore, who worked in Westlands and was a sister of Paccy Moore the shoemaker, had heard that Eve was dead from horrible injuries and that Benny was in such shock she couldn't be told. The nuns would all be going up to Dublin to collect her body shortly.

Birdie Mac in the sweet shop told people that it took a great amount of faith these days to realize that God was fair-minded. Wasn't it hard enough on that poor child to know no parents, to be totally disowned by her relations up in Westlands, to be brought up an orphan in the convent in second-hand clothes, and sent to a secretarial course when she had her heart set on going to university without being mown down by a car on her first week. Birdie sometimes questioned the fairness of life, having spent overlong looking after an ailing mother and missing her chances with a very suitable man from Ballylee who married another, who wasn't bound to an ailing parent.

Dessie Burns said that there was a lot of truth in the theory that if you fell down drunk, you never hurt yourself, a theory he had tested only too often. It was a girl like Eve Malone, a little

pikasheen who wouldn't have had a drink on her at all, that would
end up in hospital.

Father Ross said that Mother Francis would take it badly. She
felt as much for that girl as if she had been her own flesh and
blood. No mother could ever have done more for the girl. He
hoped Mother Francis wouldn't get too great a shock.

Mother Francis had acted swiftly when she heard about Eve. She
had gone straight to Peggy Pine and waited demurely until the
shop was free of customers.

'Do me a great favour, Peg.'

'Whatever you want.'

'Could you close the shop and drive me to Dublin?'

'When?'

'As soon as you can, really, Peg.'

Peggy pulled down the orange sheets of plastic intended to
keep the glare off her goods in the window, both in summer when
there might have been sunshine and in winter when it was
unnecessary.

'Off we go,' she said.

'But the business?'

'One thing about you, Bunty, you have the good sense to ask
a favour at the right time. You decide to leap over the convent
wall and hightail it to England to a new life, and you have the
wit to do it on early closing day.' She picked up her handbag,
rooted for her keys and then put on her tweed coat and closed
the door behind her. There were advantages about the single state.
You didn't need to tell anyone what you were doing. Or why.

You didn't even need to ask why.

'Mother Francis!' Eve's voice was weak.

'You're going to be fine.'

'What happened to me? Please, Mother. The other people
just say "Hush" and "Rest".'

'Not much point in saying either of those words to you.' The
nun was holding Eve's thin hand. 'Broken ribs, but they'll knit
together. A wrist that's going to be painful for a while, but it will
heal. A few stitches. Truly I never lied to you in my life. You're
going to be fine.'

'Oh, Mother, I'm so sorry.'

'Child, you couldn't have stopped it.'

'No. About you. Having to find out about me this way.'

'I know you were *going* to ring me. Benny told me that. She said you were about to phone.'

'I never lied to you, either, Mother. I wasn't going to phone.'

'Not immediately, perhaps, but you would have some time.'

'Do you still think any question must be answered?'

'Of course.'

'What'll I do, Mother, what on earth will I do when I get out of here?'

'You'll come home to get well and then we'll think of something else for you.'

'And Mother Clare?'

'Leave her to me.'

Jack came in the side door and found Aengus sitting in the cloakroom studying his glasses.

'Oh, Jesus, not *again*.'

'It's not my fault, Jack, I don't do anything, I swear I don't. I just went past these fellows and one of them shouted, "Hey, speccy four-eyes," and I ignored them like you told me and then they came and took them off and stamped on them.'

'So, it's my fault.' Jack looked at the glasses; they were beyond repair. Sometimes he had been able to fit the frames back and push in the lenses; not this time.

'Listen, Aengus, don't make a big thing out of it. They've had enough here today.'

'Well, what will I say?' Aengus looked naked and defenceless without his spectacles. 'I mean I can't say I stamped on them myself.'

'No, I know. Listen, I'll go in tomorrow and kick the shit out of the fellows who did it.'

'No, no, Jack, please. That would make it worse.'

'Not if I beat them to a pulp it won't. They won't try anything again. They'd be afraid they'd have to deal with me again.'

'But they'll know you won't be there all the time.'

'I can be there at odd times. You know, just happen to be passing when they're going out of school.'

'Wouldn't they think I was a telltale?'

'Nope.' Jack was casual. 'You're smaller. You have to wear glasses to see, if they don't respect that then you have to bring in reinforcements . . . that's the system.'

There was no need for a gong in their household, Lilly Foley said that Holy Mother Church looked after all that for them. As soon as they heard the angelus ring they gathered from all over the big house to the supper table. Jack's father had asked him not to mention the accident in front of the younger children. He didn't want to go into the fact that someone had died. His father looked pale, Jack thought, his eye slightly swollen but maybe he wouldn't have noticed it if he hadn't been involved. Certainly none of his brothers saw anything amiss. Ronan was entertaining them; he was a good mimic and this time he was doing a fussy Brother in the school trying to get everyone to sit still in the big hall for a lecture. Then he went on to a merciless performance as an inarticulate Guarda, who had called to the school to deliver the annual lecture on road safety.

Ronan had picked the wrong day for this story.

Another time his father might have laughed or mildly remonstrated about the cruelty of the imitation. But today Dr Foley's face was grey and set.

'And whatever his accent or his defects, I don't suppose one of those blockheads making a jeer of him listened to a word he was saying.' The voice was harsh.

'But, Daddy . . .' Ronan was bewildered.

'Oh, you can "But, Daddy" at me all you like – it's not going to bring you, or any of those amadans mocking the poor guard, back to life when they walk out under a ten-ton truck.'

There was a silence. Jack watched his brothers look at each other in alarm, and saw his mother frown slightly down the table at his father.

For no reason Jack remembered something that girl Benny had said earlier in the day. It was something about wishing she had the power to control conversations. If you could do that you could rule the world, she had laughed.

'You mean like Hitler?' he had teased her.

'I mean the reverse of Hitler. I mean sort of patting things down, not stirring them up.'

That was the moment when the fabulous Nan Mahon had flashed her eyes. Anyone could pat things down, she had said with a toss of all that blonde curly hair. The point was to liven things up. She had looked straight at Jack when she said it.

Nan Mahon turned the key in Number 23 Maple Gardens. She had no idea whether there would be anyone home yet. It was six fifteen. Whoever came in first turned on the electric heater in the hall to take the chill off the house, and then lit the gas fire in the kitchen. They had all their meals at a big kitchen table; there was never any company, so it didn't matter.

The hall was already slightly warm so somebody was home. 'Hallo,' Nan shouted.

Her father came out of the kitchen.

'That was a fine message you left. That was a great day's work, frightening the bloody lives out of us.'

'What is it?'

'What is it? What is it? Meek as milk! God Almighty, Nan, I've been here for the past two hours without knowing hair nor hide of you.'

'I left a message. I said there had been an accident. I wouldn't have, but the hospital said we had to. I left a message at the yard. I told Paul to tell you I was all right. Isn't that what he said?'

'Who'd believe the daylight out of that fool, reading magazines with one hand, stuffing his face with another . . .'

'Well, you were out.' Nan had taken her coat off and was examining the mud stains. She hung it up carefully on a big wooden coat hanger and began to brush hard at the dried mud.

'Someone was killed, Nan. A boy died.'

'I know,' she spoke slowly. 'We saw it.'

'And why didn't you come straight home?'

'To an empty house?'

'It wouldn't have *been* empty. I'd have come back. We'd have got your mother back out of that place.'

'I didn't want to get her back, disturbing her when there was nothing she could do.'

'She's worried sick too. You'd better ring her. She said she'd stay put in case you came by the hotel.'

'No, *you'd* better ring her. I didn't get her worried.'

'I can't understand why you're being so callous . . .' He looked at her bewildered.

Nan's eyes were blazing. 'You haven't even begun to *try* to understand . . . you haven't a notion what it was like, all the cars and the blood and the glass and the boy with the blanket over him, and a girl breaking her ribs, and all the hanging about and waiting . . . it was . . . it was . . . just awful.' He came towards her, arms outstretched, but she avoided him.

'Oh, Nan, my poor baby,' he was saying.

'That is precisely why I didn't want you to come to the hospital. I'm not anyone's poor baby. I only had scratches. I didn't want you making an exhibition of yourself. And of me.'

He flinched.

Nan continued. '*And* I didn't ring Em because it's hard enough to get a job in any place as a married woman without having hysterical daughters ringing up crying for Mamma. Em's been working in that kip for six years, since I was twelve. And there *have* been days I'd have liked her at home when I had a headache or one of the nuns had roared at me at school. But I thought of her. You, you never give anyone a thought but yourself. You'd ring her if you couldn't find your socks where you thought they should be.'

Brian Mahon's hand was in a fist. He moved closer to where his daughter was starting again to brush the mud from the coat that hung on the side of the kitchen dresser.

'By God, you won't speak to me like that. You may well be upset, but you're not going to get away with treating me like dirt. Your own father out slaving day and night so that you'd have a college education. By God, you're going to take that back or you're going to get out of this house.'

Not a muscle of Nan's face moved, her stroke never faltered as she brushed and watched the flakes fall down on the newspaper she had spread beneath. She said nothing.

'Then you'll not stay under my roof.'

'Oh, but I will,' said Nan. 'For the moment anyway.'

Mother Francis had been putting off her visit to Mother Clare as long as possible. There had been a deliberately vague telephone call. But it became clear that she would soon have to go out in the rain and get a bus to their sister convent. She had sent Peggy home. It was not a visit she relished making.

Still, she thought, bracing her shoulders, if she had been a real mother she would have had to endure many such problems with a teenage daughter. As a schoolteacher she knew only too well the dance they led their parents. Natural mothers had to put up with a great deal. This was the very thought in her head as she turned the corner of the corridor and back into the waiting room and saw the weeping figure of a woman hunched over and hugging herself with grief.

Beside her stood a pleasant-looking, round, grey-haired woman, unsure of what to do, hesitating about whether to hush the weeping figure or let her cry.

'Frank,' the woman sobbed. 'Frank, tell me it's not true. Tell me it's someone else, tell me it was just someone that looked like you.'

'They're going to get the nurse again,' said her companion. 'She was fine a minute ago. We have a taxi ordered. I was taking her home with me...'

'Was it her son...?' Mother Francis asked.

'Her only child.' The woman's eyes were eager but anxious. 'I'm her neighbour. She's going to spend the night with me. I've sent my sister in to look after the other lads.'

'Lads?'

'She keeps students, you see. This was her boy's first day at college.'

The nun's face was sad. Beside them, the anguished figure of Kit Hegarty rocked to and fro.

'You see Sister, Mother, I'm the worst one for her. I have everything. A husband, and a family, and Kit has nothing now. She doesn't want to be with the likes of us. She doesn't want anything nice and normal and safe. It's only reminding her of what she hasn't got.'

Mother Francis looked at the women with appreciative eyes. 'You're obviously a very good friend Mrs...?'

'Hayes, Ann Hayes.'

Mother Francis was kneeling down beside Frank Hegarty's mother. She reached out and held the woman's hand.

Kit looked up, startled.

'In a few days, when the funeral's over, I want you to come and stay with me,' she said softly.

The ravaged face looked at her. 'What do you mean? Who are you?'

'I'm someone like you. I've lost my child, in a sense. I could tell you about it, maybe you could advise me. You see, I'm not a real mother. You are.'

'I was.' Kit smiled a terrible twisted grimace.

'No, you are, you still are, you'll always be his mother, nobody can take that away from you. And all you gave him, all you did for him.'

'I didn't give him much. I didn't do much for him. I let him have that bike.' She clawed at Mother Francis's hand as she spoke.

'But you had to. You had to give him freedom. That was the greatest gift, that was what he would have wanted most. You gave him the best he could want.'

Nobody had said anything like this to Kit all day. Somehow she managed to take a proper breath, not the little shallow gasps she had been giving up to now.

Mother Francis spoke again. 'I live in the convent in Knockglen. It's simple and peaceful. And you could spend a few days there. It's different, you see, that's the main thing. It wouldn't have memories.'

'I couldn't go. I can't leave the house.'

'Not immediately, of course, but whenever you're ready. Ann will look after things for a few days. Ann Hayes and her sister.'

Somehow her voice had a hypnotic effect. The woman had become less agitated.

'Why are you offering me this?'

'Because my heart goes out to you. And because my girl was hurt in the same crash . . . she's going to be all right, but it's a shock seeing her so pale in a hospital bed . . .'

'She's going to be all right.' Kit's voice was flat.

'Yes, I know. I know you would accept your son to have any injury if you thought he was going to come out.'

'Your girl, what do you mean . . . ?'

'She was brought up in our convent. I love her every bit as much as if she were my natural daughter. But I'm no use as a mother. I'm not out in the world.'

Through her tears Kit managed something like a real smile.

'I will come, Mother. The convent in Knockglen. But how will I know you? Who will I ask for?'

'I'm afraid you won't have any difficulty in remembering the name. Like your son, I was called after St Francis.'

Mario looked at Fonsie's yellow tie with disapproval.

'You're going to frighten them away.'

'Don't be an eejit, Mario. This is the way people dress nowadays.'

'You no call me eejit. I know what eejit means.'

'It's about the only word of English you *do* know.'

'You no speak to your uncle that way.'

'Listen, Mario, pass me those biscuit tins. If we put the player on top of something tinny it'll sound a bit more like real music.'

'Eet soun horrible, Fonsie. Who will come to hear things so very, very loud?' Mario put his hands on his ears.

'The kids will.'

'The kids have no money.'

'The old ones wouldn't come in here in a fit anyway.'

The door opened and Sean Walsh walked in.

'Now do you see!' Fonsie cried.

At the very same moment Mario said, 'Now, what did I tell you!'

Sean looked from one to the other with distaste. It was a place he rarely went, and now he had been twice in twenty-four hours; last night with Benny, and tonight because he was so late and fussed getting back from his useless journey to Dublin. He had not been able to buy himself provisions, both grocery shops were closed. Normally Sean Walsh divided his custom. One day he might patronize Hickey's, beside Mr Flood; other days he would go to Carroll's, immediately next door to Hogan's. It was as if he were preparing for the day he would be a big man himself in this town and wanted everyone on his side, wanted them all to think of him as a customer. If he had been a drinking man he would have had a half pint in every establishment. It was the way to get on. But tonight there had been no time to get the cheese or sardines or cold ham that made his evening meal; Sean never liked to cook in his bed-sit above the premises of Hogan's lest the smell of food linger and be deemed offensive. He had thought that he might slip in for a quick snack that would keep body and soul together before he went back to his room to brood about the situation that he had handled so badly.

Now it appeared that Mario and his halfwit nephew were making fun of him.

'He's old and he's come in here two times,' Mario was saying.

'He's not old, and the word is twice, you gobdaw,' the unappealing Fonsie said.

Sean wished that he had gone down to Birdie Mac's and knocked on the door for a bar of Kit-Kat, anything rather than face these two.

'Are you serving me food, or am I interrupting some kind of talent contest?'

'How old are you, Sean?' Fonsie said. Sean looked at him in disbelief: the huge spongy soles making him four or five inches taller than he really was, the hair slicked into waves with some filthy oil, his narrow tie and huge, mauve-coloured jacket.

'Are you mad?'

'You tell how old you are.' Mario looked unexpectedly ferocious.

Sean felt the whole world had tilted. First Benny had turned her back on him in public and told him to go home without her after he had driven up especially to collect her. Now both men in the chipper. It was one of the rare occasions in his life when Sean Walsh spoke without calculation.

'I'm twenty-five,' he said. 'Since September.'

'There!' Fonsie was triumphant.

'No!' Mario was equally sure he was right.

'What *is* this?' Sean looked angrily from one to the other.

'Mario thinks the place is for old people. I say it's for young fellows like yourself and myself,' Fonsie said.

'Sean is not a fellow, he is a businessman.'

'Oh, Jaysus, does it matter? He's not on two sticks like most people in the town. What do you want, Sean? Rock salmon or cod?'

Patsy had gone for a walk with Mossy Rooney.

He had waited wordlessly in the kitchen until the daughter of the house had been soothed and put to bed. Mossy, a little like Sean Walsh, would have wished that the kitchen and living quarters of the Hogan household were more separate. Then he would have been able to sit down at the table, loosen his shirt collar, his shoelaces, and read the evening paper until Patsy was ready. But the Hogans lived on top of you when you went to that house. There was the master, a man of importance in the town that you'd think would want a house properly run for himself.

And the mistress, much older by all appearances than her husband, who fussed too much over that great big daughter.

There had been a great deal of fussing tonight. The doctor had come and given her two tablets to take, he had said there wasn't a thing wrong with her that wouldn't be wrong with any red-blooded girl who had seen a fatal accident. She was shocked and upset and what she needed most was to be allowed to rest, alone.

Mossy Rooney, a man who though he spoke little, noticed a lot, saw the look of relief pass over Benny Hogan's face, as she was sent to bed with a hot-water bottle and a cup of hot milk. He saw also the way the Hogans looked after her as she left the kitchen. He had seen that look on the faces of mother ducks when they took their little flocks down to the river for the first time.

If he had been walking out with any other girl in service in the town they could have stayed in on a wet night and talked by the kitchen range, but with the Hogans hovering around he had to bring Patsy out into the rain.

'Would you not like to take your ease indoors on a bad night like this?' Mrs Hogan had said kindly.

'Not at all, Mam, a nice fresh walk would be grand,' Patsy said with little enthusiasm.

For a long time Annabel and Eddie Hogan sat in silence.

'Maurice said that we're not to worry about a thing,' Eddie said eventually.

Maurice Johnson obviously realized who were the real patients in the house. He had uttered more words of advice to them than to the girl he was meant to be treating.

'It's easy for Maurice to say that. We don't worry about his children,' Annabel said.

'True, but to be fair he and Grainne don't worry much about them either.'

Kit Hegarty lay in her own narrow bed and heard the fog horn and the town hall clock, heard the occasional sound of a car going past. The sleeping tablets hadn't worked. Her eyes were wide open.

Everyone had been so kind. Nobody had counted the time or the trouble. The boys in the house, ashen-faced at the shock, had offered to leave. Their parents had telephoned from the country. And that little Mrs Hayes next door, who she hardly knew, had been a tower of strength, sending her sister in to cook and keep the place going. And the priests in Dunlaoghaire had been great, in and out all evening, three or maybe four of them saying nice things and talking to other people, making it seem somehow more normal, drinking cups of tea. But she had so wanted to be left alone for a while.

The only thing that stuck out in a day that seemed to have been a hundred hours of confusion was that nun. The aunt, possibly, of a girl who had been injured in the accident. *She* had understood that Frank had to have the bike. Nobody else appreciated that. Fancy a nun being able to realize it. And she had been insistent in her invitation. Kit thought that she would go and see her in that convent. Later, when she was able to think.

Judging from all the chatter, everyone in UCD must have got to know each other pretty quickly, Benny thought as she went up the steps the following morning. The main hall was thronged with people standing in groups, there were shouts of laughter and people greeting each other.

Everyone had a friend of some sort.

On another day it might have worried Benny, but not today.

She walked down a stone staircase to a basement where you could hang your coat. It smelled faintly carbolic, like school. Then up to the ground floor again and into the Ladies' Reading Room. This was not at all like school. For one thing nobody seemed to think that a reading room was a place you were meant to read. There were girls fixing their make-up at a mirror over the mantelpiece, or scanning notices on the board – items for sale, extra tuition offered, rooms to share, sodalities to join.

A very confident group laughed and reminisced about their summers abroad. They had been in Spain, or Italy, or France . . . the only thing in common was how little of the language they had learned, how monstrous the children they had had to mind had been, and how late everyone ate their meals in the evening.

They were happy to be back.

Benny soaked it all up for Eve. She would visit her again at lunch time. This morning she had been pale, still, but cheerful as anything. Mother Francis was going to sort it out. There would be no recriminations.

'I'm going to try to get to college, Benny,' she had said, her face blazing with the intensity of it. 'I'll only be a few weeks late. I'll get a job, really I will. So you just watch out for everything for me, and take notice, so that I'll catch up.'

'Are you going to ask the Westwards?'

'I'm not going to rule it out.'

There were always a great many students who took English as a subject in First Arts. The lectures were held in a big hall, confusingly called the Physics Theatre. Benny streamed in with the others. It was so different to the classrooms at school. More like an amphitheatre, with rows of seats in semicircles high up at the back. There were some young student nuns already in place, they were in the front rows, eager and anxious to miss nothing. Benny walked slowly up towards the high seats at the back where she thought she might be more inconspicuous.

From her vantage point she watched them come in: serious-looking lads in duffle coats, earnest women in glasses and hand-knitted cardigans, the clerical students from the religious seminaries in their black suits all looking remarkably cleaner and neater than the other males not bound for religious life. And the girls, the confident, laughing girls. Could they really just be First Years, these troupers in brightly coloured skirts, flouncing their hair, aware of the impression they were creating? Perhaps they had spent a year abroad after they left school, Benny thought wistfully. Or even had a holiday job during the summer. Whatever it was, it didn't bear the hallmark of life in Knockglen.

Suddenly she saw Nan Mahon. Nan wore the smart navy coat she had worn yesterday, but this time over a pale yellow wool dress. Tied loosely around the strap of her shoulder bag was a navy and yellow scarf. Her curly hair was back from her face more than yesterday, and she had yellow earrings. As she walked in, flanked by a boy on each side, each competing for her attention, Nan was the object of all eyes. Her eyes roamed the banks of seats, deciding where to sit. Suddenly she saw Benny.

'Hallo, *there* you are!' she cried.

People turned round to see who she was waving at. Benny reddened at the stares, but Nan had left the two admirers and was bounding up to the back row. Benny was taken aback. She felt sure that Nan would know everyone in UCD in days. It was surprising to be singled out. And so warmly.

'Well, how did it go?' she asked companionably.

'What?'

'You know, you sent the young man packing and he more or less said you'd rue the day. I haven't seen anything so dramatic for years.'

Benny was dismissive. 'You couldn't get a message through to him. Mercifully he didn't turn up at home. I thought he'd be there, with big cows' eyes.'

'He's probably more madly in love with you than ever, now.' Nan was cheerful, as if this was good news.

'I don't think he has a notion of what love is. He's like a fish. A fish with an eye to the main chance. A gold-digging goldfish.'

They giggled at the thought.

'Eve's fine,' Benny said. 'I'm going to see her at lunch time.'

'Can I come too?'

Benny paused. Eve was often so prickly even when she was in the whole of her health. Would she like seeing this golden college belle at her bedside?

'I don't know,' she said at last.

'Well, we were all in it together. And I know all about her, and the business of Mother Clare and Mother Francis.'

For a moment Benny wished she hadn't told the story in such detail. Eve certainly wouldn't like her business being discussed as she lay unconscious.

'That got sorted out,' Benny said.

'I knew it would.'

'Do you think you could come tomorrow instead?'

CHAPTER SIX

The body of Frank Hegarty was brought to the church in Dunlaoghaire.

Dr Foley attended the prayers and the Removal service with his eldest son.

Also in the church was Mother Francis, who had found it necessary to spend a little longer in Dublin than she had hoped, sorting things out with Mother Clare. Peggy had offered to collect her later. She knew there was some kind of trouble, but didn't ask what it was. She had given her own kind of encouragement to Mother Francis.

'Whatever that one says to you, Bunty, remember that her people were tinkers.'

'They weren't.'

'Well, dealers, anyway. That should give you the upper hand dealing with her.'

It hadn't, of course, any more than it should have. Mother Francis had a grim face as she waited in the big church for the funeral party to arrive. She didn't know why she was there; it was as if she wanted to represent Eve.

Nan Mahon went out on the bus to Dunlaoghaire and stood among the group at the back of the church. She was instantly spotted by Jack Foley who went to join her.

'That's nice of you, to come all the way out,' he said.

'You did too.'

'I came with my father. But do you see that group there, those are fellows who worked with him in the summer. That's Aidan Lynch – he was at school with me, and a whole lot more. They were all canning peas together.'

'How did they know?'

'His picture was in the paper, and there was some kind of announcement at the engineering lectures today,' he said. 'Where's Benny? Did you see her today?'

'Yes, but she couldn't come tonight. She had to go home, you see, every evening on this one bus.'

'That's hard on her,' Jack said.

'It's very foolish of her,' Nan said.

'What can she do about it?'

'She should make a stand at the outset.'

Jack looked at the attractive girl beside him. She would have made a stand, he knew that. He remembered the big soft-featured Benny.

'She stood up to that awful fellow with the white face who tried to take her off with him yesterday.'

'If you couldn't stand up to *him* you shouldn't be allowed out,' Nan said.

'This is Eve Malone,' Benny said, as Nan sat on the end of the hospital bed.

She wanted Eve to like Nan, to recognize that Nan could have been anywhere but had chosen to come and see Benny's friend. Benny had heard this fellow Aidan Lynch almost begging Nan to come and have lunch with him.

Nan had not brought flowers or grapes or a magazine; instead she had brought the one thing that Eve truly wanted, a college handbook. All the details of registration, late registration, degree courses, diplomas. She didn't even greet the girl in the bed. Instead she spoke about the matter which was uppermost in Eve's mind.

'I gather you're trying to get into college. This might be of some use to you,' she said.

Eve seized it and let her thumb riffle through the pages. 'This is just what I need, thank you very much indeed,' she said.

Then her brow darkened slightly.

'How did you think of bringing me this?' she asked suspiciously.

Nan shrugged. 'It's all in there,' she said.

'No, what made you think I'd need it?'

Benny wished Eve wouldn't be so prickly. What did it matter that Nan Mahon knew her hopes? There was no need to be secretive.

'I asked, that's all. I asked what you were doing and Benny said you hadn't enrolled yet.'

Eve nodded. The tension was over. She fingered the book again with gratitude and Benny felt a pang of regret that *she* hadn't thought of something so practical.

Little by little Eve was losing her look of wariness. And as Benny watched the girls talk easily she realized they were kindred spirits.

'Will you have it sorted out fairly soon do you think?' Nan was asking.

'I have to go and ask a man for money. It's not easy but it won't get any easier by delaying,' Eve said.

Benny was astounded. Eve never talked of her business to anyone and the matter of approaching the Westwards for money was one she had only barely acknowledged to Benny herself. Nan was unaware of this.

'Will you play up the being injured bit?' she enquired.

Eve was on the same wavelength. 'I might. I've been considering it, but he's the kind of fellow who might regard that as weakness and snivelling. I'll have to work out how to play it.'

'What's it all about?' Nan asked with interest.

And as Eve began to tell her the story of the Westwards, the story never spoken aloud to anyone, Benny realized with a shock that Nan was in fact pretending to Eve that she hadn't heard any of this already. She had asked Nan to be discreet, and she certainly had followed the instructions to the letter. And judging by the way Eve was confiding, the instructions had been unnecessary.

It had been harder to deal with Mother Clare than Mother Francis would ever have believed possible. Sometimes Mother Francis talked directly to Our Lady about it and asked for immediate and positive advice.

'I've *said* I was sorry, I've *said* that we will look after Eve from now on, but she goes on and on and says it's her duty to know what plans are being made for the girl. Why can't she just stay out of it? Why, Holy Mother, tell me?'

As it happened, Mother Francis got an answer which she presumed had come from the Mother of God, even though it was spoken by Peggy Pine.

'What that auld rip wants is to be able to prance around like the cock of the walk saying "I told you so, I told you so". She wants you to humble yourself, then she'll give up on it and start torturing someone else.'

Mother Francis agreed to use the tactics of humbling herself. 'You were right all along, Mother Clare,' she wrote in the most hypocritical letter she had ever penned. 'We were wrong to ask you to take on someone like Eve who had been given a wholly exaggerated set of expectations by our small Community here. I can only say that I bow to your wisdom on this as in so many other matters and hope that the Sisters were not unduly inconvenienced by the experiment which you knew was destined to be full of pitfalls.'

It had been the right approach. The regular bewildered and hurt interrogations from Mother Clare ceased.

And just in time too. Eve was pronounced fit to leave hospital a week to the day after she had been admitted.

'I'll come on the bus, with Benny,' Eve had said on the telephone.

'No, you won't, there's half a dozen people who'll go and collect you. I don't like to ask Peggy again but Mrs Healy will be going up.'

'*Please*, Mother.'

'All right, Sean Walsh? No, don't even tell me . . . !'

'I've caused you enough trouble. I'll go with anyone you say, though I *would* rather go on the bus.'

'Mario?'

'Marvellous. I love Mario.'

'All right, we'll see you tomorrow. I'm so glad you're coming home, Eve. I missed you.'

'And I missed you, Mother. We'll have to talk.'

'Of course we will. Wrap up warmly, won't you.'

When Eve hung up Mother Francis sat for a moment. It was true they would have to talk. Talk seriously.

As she sat there the telephone rang again.

'Mother Francis please?'

'Speaking.'

There was a pause.

'Mother, in a fit of generosity you said to me . . . I mean you wondered if I'd like . . . and isn't it odd, in the middle of everything I kept remembering it. I wonder would you think it strange if I *did* come to see you . . . ?'

The woman's voice stopped again hesitantly.

A great smile lit up Mother Francis's face.

'Mrs Hegarty, I'm delighted to hear from you. This weekend would be lovely. You tell me which bus and I'll walk over and meet you. It's only a couple of minutes from the convent gate. I'm very pleased you're going to come and see us.'

She wondered where she would put the woman to sleep. She had thought of her as staying in Eve's room. But there was the extra parlour that they had always been meaning to do up as a guest room. All it needed was curtains. She'd get some material from Peggy and ask Sister Imelda to ask the senior girls to run them up at domestic science class. She'd get a bedside light from Dessie Burns and a nice cake of soap in Kennedy's chemist.

'Eve's going home today,' Benny reported when she met Nan for coffee in the Annexe as she did every morning.

'I know. She told me last night.'

'What?'

'Well, it's at night she really wants people to go in and see her, and you've long gone so I took a couple of fellows in to cheer her up.'

Benny felt a jolt. She knew that Nan and Eve got on well . . . but taking fellows in to a hospital bed!

'What fellows?' she asked lamely.

'Oh, you know, Aidan Lynch and some of that gang. Bill Dunne – do you know him?'

'No.'

'He's very nice, does Commerce. I bet you know him to see, he's always outside the History Library with a group.'

'Did Eve like them coming in?'

'Yeah, she loved it. Did you think she wouldn't?'

'It's just that she's a bit edgy sometimes . . . you know, on the defensive a bit.'

'I never noticed that.'

It was true. Eve had seemed much lessy chippy whenever Nan came in. Nan had a gift of making things simple, everyone went along with her way. Just then four boys approached the table. They were all looking at Nan.

'Would you girls like to come down Grafton Street and get some real coffee? Decent coffee for a change,' said the spokesman, a thin boy in an Aran Island sweater.

Nan smiled up at them warmly.

'Thanks a lot, but no, we have a lecture at twelve. Thanks anyway.'

'Come on, that's only a big lecture, no one'll miss you.' He was encouraged by her smile to think it was only a matter of saying it often enough.

'No, honestly.' Nan stopped suddenly as if she had been thoughtless. 'I mean I'm only speaking for myself. Benny, do you want to go?'

Benny reddened. She knew the boys didn't want her. It was Nan who had attracted them. But they had nice faces and seemed a little bit lost, like everyone else.

'Why don't you sit down with us?' she suggested with a big smile.

That was exactly what they wanted to do. Chairs and benches were pulled up, names exchanged. School names given. Did they know this person or that? What were they studying? Where were they staying? It was much easier than Benny had thought to be in the middle of a group like this. She had completely forgotten that she was big and that they were boys. She asked eagerly about the societies, and which ones were good, and where were the best dances.

Nan didn't make as much effort, but she was very pleased to hear all the information. Her smile was so bright that Benny could see the boys almost loosening their collars as she turned it towards them.

The boys said that the Debating Society on a Saturday night was great. And then when it was over you could go to the Solicitor's Apprentice or down at the Four Courts. They looked from one girl to the other.

Benny said that unfortunately she had to stay in the country at weekends. As she said it she realized what a death knell it sounded, so she cheered up at once and said that this was only for this term. Maybe things would change then. She looked around brightly and the boys seemed pleased with her. She knew they were all mad keen for Nan to go with them this Saturday, and Nan wasn't a bit flirtatious.

If she could, she would. She hadn't wanted to go because she didn't know anyone, she said.

'You know us,' said the thin boy in the grubby white sweater.

'I do, of course,' Nan's smile nearly broke his heart.

Benny knew that it would be a great night. She could see it. Of course, she would be in Knockglen. But her smile was bright.

After all, one of the things she had been afraid of was that she wouldn't know how to talk to fellows when she got to college. She didn't have much practice at home. But it seemed to be easy enough, like talking to ordinary people. That was what she must think about. The good side. Not always dwelling on the bad side like having to go home before the fun began.

When Mario collected Eve in his ice-cream van it was Fonsie who ran lightly up the steps of the hospital to escort the patient to her transport.

'You're to take it easy, you'll remember that.' The Sister looked doubtfully at Fonsie as a companion.

'Nothing faster than slow jive.' Fonsie leaned back and clicked his fingers slowly. Sister was not amused.

'And you *are* staying in a convent?'

'Don't be prejudiced now,' Fonsie warned. 'Just because I don't look like your idea of a nun doesn't mean . . .'

'Oh shut up, Fonsie, Mario's nearly having a fit down there in the van.'

It was the first time she had seen the outside world for over a week. Eve shuddered when she saw the corner where the crash had taken place. They tucked her up in the van and drove back to Knockglen arguing all the while.

Some arguments she was able to take part in – like having brighter lights and music in the chip shop, like calling the chip shop a café, like having 'Island in the Sun' so that you could hear it from the street and it would make you want to come in.

'Make you want to call the guards, more likely,' Mario said.

There were other arguments she couldn't contribute to – like whether Mario's brother had been mad to marry an Irish girl, Fonsie's mother, or whether Fonsie's mother had been mad to marry an Italian, Mario's brother. She drifted off to sleep during that particular saga which she felt would never be solved anyway.

Eve sat up in bed and drank her beef tea.

'Sister Imelda made it. Have a taste?'

Benny sipped some from the cup.

'Patsy told me she heard her in Flood's talking about shin beef, and pointing to her ankle in case she wasn't making herself clear. Mr Flood was saying, "I know where the shin is, Sister, God forgive me I may not know much but I know where the shin is." '

'Is Patsy still going out with that dumbo, Mossy?'

'Yes, mother's terrified she'll marry him.'

'Is he that bad?'

'No, we just don't want Patsy to marry anyone, because she'll leave.'

'A bit hard on Patsy,' Eve said. 'I feel like the prodigal son. I never had any time for him in the gospel, but still it's a nice feeling. The accident saved me, everyone's so sorry for me they forget I told all those lies and was so rude to awful Mother Clare. Listen, I meant to tell you, the most extraordinary thing. The boy that got killed, Frank Hegarty . . . Mother Francis met his mother that day. I don't remember it clearly, but anyway they got talking and she's coming here to stay for a few days. Here to Knockglen.'

'Will she stay in Healy's?'

'No, here in the convent would you believe? They've done up one of the parlours as a bedroom.'

'Go on!'

'She's coming on the bus today. It's going to be very hard to know what to say to her.'

'I know,' Benny agreed. 'I mean anything could be the wrong thing. She mightn't want to talk about it at all, but then it could be considered callous to start up chats about other things.'

'Nan would know what to say,' Eve said suddenly.

Benny felt a cold lurch in her heart. It was an unworthy thought, considering how kind Nan was to her and how she included her in everything. But Benny did feel that Nan got *too* much credit for things. Was it right that she would know what to do in every circumstance?

A little wave of pure jealousy came over her. She said nothing. She was afraid it might show in her voice.

Eve hadn't noticed. She was still musing what Nan would do or say.

'I think it's because she doesn't dither, like we do. She always sounds as if she knows what she's doing, whether she does or not. That's the secret.'

'I suppose it is,' Benny said, hoping the glum, mean note didn't sound in her voice.

'Nan could make anyone do anything,' Eve said. 'She got them to let us smoke in the ward!'

'But you don't smoke!' Benny was startled.

Eve giggled. 'Oh, I did for the fun of it, the others all did. It was the principle of the thing.'

'What will she do all day? Mrs Hegarty?' Benny asked.

'I don't know. Walk around. She's going to feel lonely and odd here.'

'She would at home too, I suppose,' Benny said.

'Have you talked to Sean since?'

'Not really. He was on his high horse last weekend, you know, head turned the other way when he saw me at Mass, a fit of the sulks. Unfortunately, that didn't last and he came round last night to discuss the pictures. I'm afraid I used you shamelessly. I said I couldn't make any plans until I knew what you'd be doing.'

'*That* didn't please him.'

'Well, he said that from what he heard you'd most likely be in Mario's, clicking your fingers with Fonsie. . . . He was full of disapproval.'

Eve pealed with laughter.

'I wonder what Fonsie said. He's very funny, really he is. He thinks he's going to be Mr Big of Knockglen.'

'Lord, that wouldn't be hard.'

'I know, I told him. But he said I'd missed the point. He said that by becoming a Mr Big he would make Knockglen big too, he would drag it up with him.'

'It can't happen soon enough,' Benny said gloomily.

'God, you sound like a cross between Father Rooney and Mrs Healy with your dire voice,' Eve warned her.

'Maybe that's who I am. Maybe my parents were given the wrong baby.'

'Boy, would *that* be the wrong baby,' Eve said and that started them off all over again.

Kit Hegarty said she never saw such a lovely room. It was exactly what she wanted. It was small and low-ceilinged and there were no shadows or corners in it to keep her awake at night. She knew she would sleep here as she had not slept since it happened. She would love to do something to help, she said. She hadn't many skills, but she was used to running a house.

Mother Francis was soothing. Not now, later maybe, now she must rest. She showed her the chapel. It was quiet and dark. Two nuns knelt in front of the altar where Mother Francis explained that the Blessed Sacrament was exposed. There would be Compline later, if she liked to come and listen to the nuns singing their office.

'I'm not sure . . .'

'Neither am I,' Mother Francis said firmly. 'It might make you too sad, on the other hand it might be just what you need, to sit in a church with people you don't know and weep for your son. And there are the glasshouses. I'll show you those. They're not in very good condition. We don't have the money or the people to look after them. Ah, if only you'd known them when Eve's father was alive . . .'

She told the woman the story that was rarely told, the workman and the restless daughter of the big house, the unsuitable relationship, the pregnancy, the marriage and the birth of Eve and the two deaths.

There were tears in Kit Hegarty's eyes.

'Why are you telling me this?' she said.

'I suppose it's a clumsy attempt to let you know other awful things happen in the world,' said Mother Francis.

'Are you not going out tonight?' Annabel Hogan asked as Benny pulled up a chair with them in the breakfast room after supper. 'Out' meant out with Sean Walsh. Benny pretended not to realize this.

'No, Eve has to take it easy. She's up and everything and coming down for supper tonight with the nuns and Mrs Hegarty.' Her face was bland.

'I meant, nothing on at the pictures?' her mother asked equally innocently.

'Ah, of course there's something on, Mother. It's meant to be very exciting – about the sound barrier.'

'And wouldn't you like to be at that?' her father asked.

'I don't really like going by myself, Father. If we were *all* going now . . .' The Hogans hardly ever went to the cinema.

She knew that they liked to see her stepping out with Sean from time to time. Somewhere in their confused minds they must think it was company for her, entertainment, a date even. And from Sean's point of view, they knew he considered it an honour to take the daughter of the house out for all to see. Somehow it made things nice and orderly. Safe.

Sean wouldn't leave them, go to a better shop in a bigger town if he was happy, and this must be their view, however short term and foolish.

'You know we don't go to the pictures,' her mother said. 'We wondered were you going to go with Sean?'

'Sean! Sean Walsh?' asked Benny as if the town were full of Seans, all of them craving to take her to the cinema.

'You know I mean Sean Walsh.' Annabel's voice was sharp.

'Oh no, I don't think it's a good idea to go with him all the time.'

'You don't go all the time.'

'No, but with Eve not being here, there'd be a danger I could slip into the way of it.'

'And what would be the harm of that?'

'Not a bit of harm, Mother, but you know.'

'Did he not ask you? He told *me* he was going to ask you.' Eddie Hogan looked puzzled. He didn't like things that weren't clear.

'I said no to Sean because I didn't want Sean to think and me to think, and the whole of Knockglen to think, we were a twosome.'

It was the first time such a notion had ever been mentioned in their household.

Benny's parents looked at one another at a loss.

'I wouldn't say going to the pictures occasionally is making you into a twosome,' Annabel Hogan said.

Benny's face lit up. 'That's exactly my point too. I think it's fine to go to the pictures with Sean *occasionally*, but not every week. Occasionally was the very word I said, I think.'

Actually the words she had said were 'Sometimes, perhaps, but not in the immediate future', and he had looked at her with his cold small eyes, and she had shivered. But there would be little point in trying to explain this to her parents. It was quite enough to have told them as much as she had already told them.

Jack Foley and Aidan Lynch decided to go to the debate on Saturday night. It was held in the big Physics Theatre, and was fairly rowdy, despite the dinner jackets worn by the Committee and the Visiting Speakers.

As they stood at the doorway watching from the sidelines Aidan saw the blonde head of Nan Mahon in the centre of a sea of male duffle coats. She was laughing, her head thrown back and her eyes sparkling. She wore a white frilly blouse with a rose pinned to the top button, and a black skirt. She was the most attractive girl in the room.

'Look at the lovely Nan,' Aidan said, whistling a low envious sound through his teeth. 'I asked her to come with me to this and she said she'd rather be free.'

'So, she'd rather be free,' Jack said, looking at her closely.

'I thought she liked me.' Aidan sounded mock desolate.

'No, you didn't. You thought she liked Bill Dunne. In fact *I* thought she liked *me*,' said Jack.

'There's enough of them liking you,' Aidan grumbled. 'No, I thought I was special with Nan. She took me to see her friend in hospital.'

'You're a natural hospital visitor,' Jack laughed. 'Look at Nan over there. She likes everyone.'

He looked with a pang of regret at the girl in the centre of the crowd.

'What was the friend like in hospital?' he asked Aidan in order to take their minds off lost opportunities with Nan.

'Okay,' Aidan said unenthusiastically. 'A bit skinny and ready to bite your head off about everything, but all right, I suppose.' Even as he said it, Aidan realized that it might not sound all that gallant. 'Not that I'm exactly an Adonis myself,' he added.

'But you are, you are!' Jack Foley said. 'Listen, I've had enough of this caper looking at our girl in the middle of that crowd. Will we go for a pint?'

'You're on,' Aidan said.

Jack looked long and hard at Nan as they went out of the hall, but if she saw them come in and go out her eyes gave not a flicker of recognition. Jack could have sworn she was looking straight at them, but then perhaps there were so many in the crowd at the door she just didn't see them.

Eve was disappointed in the way that Mother Francis had invited Frank Hegarty's mother to stay. It would mean that their talk had to be put off for one thing, and she was restless and eager to know the nun's view on how she should approach the Westwards. She intended only to ask for her university fees. She would find a place to live where she could mind children. It must be possible. Not every single student who went in the doors of University College could have parents with money to pay for everything. There had to be some of them working their way through a degree. Eve had refused to consider a daytime job and night studying. She had heard of course of those who had done it, but the atmosphere was different. The students were old and greyer. They scurried in for lectures and scurried out again. It wasn't just the letters after her name that Eve Malone wanted. It was the life of a student. The life she could have had if things had been different.

She hoped that the Hegarty woman wouldn't stay long in Knockglen, because Eve needed to act soon. She must not malinger in the convent and prove Mother Clare's point about how she was a liability. Also if she were going to aim to be enrolled in UCD this year then she must do so within the next few days. And if there were to be an unpleasant interview with Simon Westward, the sooner it was over the better. She wished she had Mother Francis's attention to herself.

After supper Eve sat in the warm kitchen. Sister Imelda had clucked around for a while getting her some warm milk with a little pepper shaken on top, which was known to cure any condition. The tea towels had been washed and laid out on the Aga. The smell was familiar, it was home; but Eve didn't feel the sense of comfort that the place usually brought her.

Moving quietly as she always did, Mother Francis came in and sat down opposite her. 'Don't drink that if it's horrible. We'll pour it away and rinse the mug.'

Eve smiled. It had always been the two of them against the world.

'It's all right . . . not something you'd choose, though, if you had a choice.'

'You *do* have a choice, Eve, a series of them.'

'It means going up to Westlands, doesn't it?'

'If your heart is set on it . . . then yes.'

'And what will I say?'

'We can't write a script, Eve.'

'I know, but we could try to work out what would be the best way to approach them.' There was a silence. 'I expect you *have* approached them for me already?' It was the first time Eve had ever mentioned this.

'Not for a long time, not since you were twelve, and I felt that we should ask them in case they might want to send you to a posher boarding school in Dublin.'

'And no response?'

'That was different. That was six years ago and there was I, a nun wearing black, covered in beads and crucifixes . . . that's the way they might see it.'

'And was that the last time? You didn't ask them about university fees did you?'

Mother Francis looked down. 'Not in person, no.'

'But you wrote?'

The nun passed over the letter from Simon Westward. Eve read it, her face set in hard lines.

'That's fairly final, isn't it?'

'You could say that, or you could look at it differently. You could say that then was then and now is now. It's you, you can ask them for yourself.'

'They might say I never went near them except to ask for money.'

'They'd be right.'

Eve looked up startled.

'That's not fair. Mother. You knew how I felt all these years. I wouldn't lower myself to go to them cap in hand when you had all done so much for me and they had done nothing. It would have been letting the convent down.' She bristled at the injustice of the nun's remark.

Mother Francis was mild. '*I* know that. Obviously I do. I'm trying to look at it from their point of view. There's no point otherwise.'

'I'm *not* going to say I'm sorry. I'm *not* going to pretend . . .'

'True, but is there any point in going at all if you go with that attitude?'

'What other attitude is there?'

'There are many, Eve, but none of them will work unless . . .'

'Unless . . . ?'

'Unless you mean it. You don't have to cringe and pretend

111

a love you don't feel, you don't have to go up there with a heart filled with hate either.'

'What would your heart be full of, going up there?'

'I told you. It's *your* visit.'

'Help me, Mother.'

'I haven't been much help to you so far. Do this one on your own.'

'Have you lost interest in me? And what happens to me?' Eve's chin jutted up as it always did when she was warding off a hurt.

'If you believe that . . .' Mother Francis began.

'I don't. It's just that it's like a series of dead ends. Even if I *do* get the fees I'll have to find somewhere to live, some work.'

'One step at a time,' Mother Francis said.

Eve looked at her. The nun's face had that look she used to have years ago when there was some surprise in store.

'Do you have any ideas?' Eve asked eagerly.

'My last idea wasn't very successful, now was it? Go to bed, Eve. You'll need all your strength to deal with the Westwards. Go up there in the late morning. They'll be going to Church at eleven.'

The avenue was full of pot holes, and there were clumps of weeds rising in the middle of what must once have been a well-kept drive. Eve wondered if her father had worked on this very road. Mother Francis had always been vague about Jack Malone when pressed. He had been a good man, a kind man and very loving of his little daughter. That was really the sum total of it. And it was what you *would* tell a child, Eve realized.

And about her mother there was even less information. She had looked very beautiful when she was young. She had always been very gracious, Mother Francis had said. But what else could she say about a gardener and the disturbed daughter of the Big House? Eve was determined that she would not lose her clear-sighted way of looking at her background. She had long realized that there was no mileage in romanticizing her history. She squared her shoulders and approached the house. It was shabbier close up than it looked from the road. The paint on the conservatory was all peeling. The place looked untidy and uncared for. Croquet mallets and hoops were all thrown in a heap as if someone had played a game many months ago, but no one had ever bothered to tidy the set away or to have another game since. There were wellington boots in the hall, old golf clubs splintering, with their bindings coming undone. Tennis racquets slightly warped stood in a big bronze container.

Through the glass doors Eve could see a hall table weighed down with catalogues and brochures and brown envelopes. It was all so different from the highly polished convent where she lived. A stray piece of paper would never find its way on to the hall table under the picture of Our Lady Queen of Peace. If it did it would soon be rescued and brought to the appropriate place. How extraordinary to live in a house where you could hardly *see* the hall table for all that was covering it.

She rang the bell, knowing that it would be answered by one of three people. Bee, the sister of Paccy Moore, the shoemaker. Bee was the housemaid in Westlands. Or possibly the cook might come to the door if it was Bee's Sunday off. Mrs Walsh had been in the family for as long as anyone could remember. She hadn't come from Knockglen in the first place and didn't fraternize with the people of the town, even though she was a Catholic and seen at early Mass. She was a large woman who looked rather ominous on her bicycle. Or perhaps Simon Westward himself would come to the door. His father was in a wheelchair and reported to be increasingly frail, so he would not appear.

Ever since she could remember Eve had played a game. It was like not stepping on the cracks in a footpath. It was what Mother Francis would have called superstition, probably. But she had always done it. 'If the next bird to hop up on the window sill is a thrush then I'll get my exam. If it is a blackbird, I'll fail. If I have to wait until I count twenty-five at the door of the convent in Dublin, I'm going to hate it.' For some reason she always felt like doing it at doors.

As she stood outside the unfamiliar door of the place that was once her mother's home, Eve Malone told herself firmly that if Bee Moore came to the door it would be a good omen, she would get the money. If Simon Westward himself came it would be bad. If it was Mrs Walsh the thing could go either way. Her eyes were bright as she waited and heard the sound of running feet.

She saw the figure of a schoolgirl, about ten or eleven years old, running towards the door. She reached up to open it and stood looking at Eve with interest. She was wearing the very short tunic that girls in Protestant schools always wore. In the convent everything had to be a bit more droopy and modest. She had her hair tied in two bunches, one sticking out over each ear almost like handles, as if someone were going to pick her up and carry her by them. She wasn't fat, but she was square and stocky. She had freckles on her nose and her eyes were the same dark blue as her school uniform.

'Hallo,' she said to Eve. 'Who are you?'

'Who are *you*?' Eve asked. She wasn't afraid of anyone in the Big House if they were this size.

'I'm Heather,' the child replied.

'And I'm Eve.'

There was a pause while Heather tried to work something out.

'Who did you come to see?' she said, after some consideration.

Eve looked at her with admiration. The child was trying to work out whether Eve was for the master or for the staff. She had phrased the question perfectly.

'I came to see Simon Westward,' she said.

'Oh, sure, well come in.'

Eve walked behind the little figure through the hall, full of dark pictures, hunting prints maybe. It was impossible to see. Heather? Heather? She didn't know of any Heather in the household, but then she didn't really keep up with who was who in this family. If people in Knockglen spoke of them she didn't join in the conversation. Sometimes the nuns mentioned them, but Eve would toss her head and turn away. Once she came upon an article about them in the *Social and Personal* magazine and she had turned the pages on angrily in case she would find out any more about them and their goings on. Benny had always said that if the Westwards had been *her* family she would have wanted to know everything about them and would probably have made a scrapbook as well. But that was Benny all over. She'd probably have been doing their errand for them by now, and thanking them for everything instead of guarding the cold indifference that Eve had nurtured for so long.

'Are you one of Simon's girlfriends?' the child asked conversationally.

'No, indeed,' Eve said with no emotion.

They had reached the drawing room. The Sunday papers were spread out on a low coffee table, a sherry decanter and glasses stood on a silver tray. Over by the window in his wheelchair sat Major Charles Westward, his shoulders sloped down, and it was obvious even from a distance that he was not really aware of his surroundings. A rug over his knees had partly slipped to the floor.

This man was Eve's grandfather. Most people hugged their grandfather, they called them Grandad, and sat on their knee. Grandfathers gave you two-shilling pieces and took pictures of you on First Communion and Confirmation days. They were proud of you and introduced you to people. This man had never wanted to see Eve, and if he was in the whole of his sense he might have ordered her out of his house, as he had done her mother.

Once upon a time she had thought he might see her from his horse or his car and ask who was that lovely child. She had a look of the family about her. But that was long ago. She felt no sense of loss looking at him, no wish that things had been different. She was not embarrassed by his infirmity nor upset by looking at him closely after the years of rejection.

Heather looked at her curiously. 'I'll go and find Simon for you now. You'll be all right here?' she said.

The child's face was open. Eve found it hard to be stiff with her.

'Thanks. Thanks a lot,' she said gruffly.

Heather smiled at her. 'You don't look like his girlfriends usually look.'

'No?'

'No, you look more normal.'

'Oh good.' Despite herself Eve smiled.

The child was still curious. 'Is it about the mare?'

'It's not about the mare. I wouldn't know a mare from a five-bar gate.'

Heather laughed good-naturedly and headed for the door. Eve surprised herself by giving the information the child had been looking for.

'I'm not one of his girlfriends,' she called. 'I'm one of his cousins.'

Heather seemed pleased. 'Oh, then you're a cousin of mine too. I'm Simon's sister.'

Eve said nothing because of a slight lump in her throat. Whatever she had thought would happen when she went to Westlands it was not this. She would never have believed that any Westward would have been pleased to see her.

Mother Francis told Kit Hegarty that there was no need for her to hurry back to Dublin. She could stay as long as she liked, a week maybe.

'Don't go back too soon. The peace of this place could wear off you if you went back to the city too quickly.'

'Ah, that's country people for you. You think Dublin is all like O'Connell Street. We're out in *County* Dublin you see, by the seaside. It's a grand place full of fresh air.'

Mother Francis knew that the peace of Knockglen had nothing to do with it being in the country or the city. The advantage was, the place was far from the home where Frank Hegarty would return no more.

'Still, stay here a while and take our air.'

'I'm in the way.' Kit had sensed Eve's eagerness to have Mother Francis to herself.

'On the contrary. You are very helpful in that Eve needs time to talk to other people before she commits herself to *any* plan. There's no point in she and I going round in circles. Much as I hate it, I realize that she *has* to make up her own mind.'

'You would have made a marvellous mother,' Kit said.

'I don't know. It's easier one step removed.'

'You're not removed. You just manage not to do what all the rest of us wish we didn't do. You don't nag.'

'I don't think you were a nagger either,' Mother Francis smiled.

'Did you not want to marry and have children?' Kit asked.

'I wanted a wild unsuitable farmer's son that I couldn't have.'

'Why couldn't you have him?'

'Because we hadn't a farm or land to go with me. Or so I thought. If he had really wanted me he'd have taken me, farm or no farm.'

'What happened to him?'

'He married a girl who had legs much better than Bunty

Brown, and who *did* have a farm to go with her. They had four children in five years, then he found another, as they say.'

'And what did the wife do?'

'She made a fool of herself the length and breadth of the county. That's not what Bunty Brown would have done. *She* would have thrown him out, started a guest house, and held her head high.'

Kit Hegarty laughed. 'Are you telling me *you* are Bunty Brown?'

'Not any longer. Not for a long time.'

'He was a fool not to take you.'

'Ah, that's what I said too. I said it for three years. They didn't want to take me in the convent at first. They thought I was just running away, trying to hide from the world.'

'And do you regret it, not waiting for a different farmer's son?'

'No, not a bit.'

Her eyes were far away.

'And you've had everything, in a way,' Kit said. 'You've had all the joy of children in a school.'

'It's true,' Mother Francis said. 'Every year, new children, every year new young faces coming in.' She still looked sad.

'It will work out for Eve.'

'Of course it will. She's probably talking to him now.'

'Who is she talking to?'

'Her cousin, Simon Westward. Asking him for fees. I hope she doesn't lose her temper. I hope she won't throw it all away!'

Heather had left the room as soon as her brother came in. Simon went over first to the figure in the wheelchair, picked up the rug, and knelt to tuck it in around the old man. He stood up and came back to the fireplace. He was small and dark, with a thin handsome face, dark-eyed, and his brown hair fell into his eyes. He had had to shake it away so often it was now a mannerism. He wore riding breeches and a tweed jacket with leather cuffs and elbows.

'What can I do for you?' His voice was cold and polite.

'Do you know who I am?' Eve's voice was equally cold.

He hesitated. 'Not really,' he said.

Her eyes blazed. 'Either you do or you don't,' she said.

117

'I *think* I do. I asked Mrs Walsh. She said you were the daughter of my aunt Sarah. Is that right?'

'But you know of me, surely?'

'Yes, of course. I didn't recognize you coming up the drive, so I asked.'

'What else did Mrs Walsh say?'

'I don't think that's relevant. Now can I ask you what it's about?'

He was so much in command of the situation that Eve wanted to cry. If only he could have looked ill at ease, guilty about his family's treatment of her, confused and wondering what lay ahead. But Simon Westward would always know how to handle things like this.

She was silent as she looked at him. Unconsciously imitating his stance, hands behind her back, eyes unflinching, mouth set in a hard thin line. She had dressed carefully, deciding not to wear her best outfit in case he would think she had put it on specially, or had come from Mass. Instead she had worn a tartan skirt and grey cardigan. She had a blue scarf tied around her throat in what she had thought was a jaunty look.

Her glance didn't fall from his stare.

'Would you like a glass of sherry?' he asked, and she knew she had won the first round.

'Thank you.'

'Sweet or dry?'

'I don't know the difference. I've never had either.' She spoke proudly. There was going to be no aping the manners of her betters from Eve Malone. She thought she saw him raise his eyebrows in surprise that bordered on admiration.

'Then try the sweet. I'll have that too.'

He poured two glasses. 'Will you sit down?'

'I'd rather stand. It won't take long.'

'Fine.' He said nothing more, he just waited.

'I would like to go to university this term,' she began.

'In Dublin?'

'Yes. And there are a few things standing in the way.'

'Oh yes?'

'Like that I cannot afford it.'

'How much does it cost in Trinity now?'

'It's not Trinity and you know that well. It's UCD.'

'Sorry, I didn't know, actually.'

'For years Trinity wouldn't let Catholics in, and now when it does, the Archbishop has said it's a sin to go there, so you know it's UCD.'

He put his hands out as if warding her off. 'Peace, peace,' he said.

Eve continued. 'And since you ask, the fees are sixty-five pounds a year for three years for a BA, and after that I would like to do a Diploma in Librarianship so that would be another sixty-five pounds. There would be books to buy. I am talking about one hundred pounds a year.'

'And?'

'And I was hoping you would give it to me,' she said.

'Give? Not lend?'

'No, give. Because I wouldn't be able to pay it back. It would be a lie to ask for a loan.'

'And how will you live there? You'll have to pay for rooms and everything.'

'I told you. It's not Trinity. There are no rooms. I'll get a job in a family, earn my keep. I'd be able to do that. It's just the fees I don't have.'

'And you think we should pay them?'

'I'd be very glad if you did.' Not grateful, Eve told herself firmly, she had sworn she would not use that word. No matter how much Mother Francis had warned her. Glad was the nearest she could get.

Simon was thinking. 'A hundred pounds a year,' he repeated.

'It would be for four years,' Eve said. 'I couldn't really start unless I knew I wouldn't have to come and beg for it every year.'

'You're not begging for it now,' said Simon.

'That's right, I'm not,' Eve said. She felt a great pounding in her head. She hadn't known it was going to be remotely like this.

He smiled at her, a genuine smile. 'I never beg either, it must be a family trait.'

Eve felt a hot flush of anger. Not only was he going to refuse her, he was going to make fun of her as well.

She had known that she might be refused, she thought it would be with apologies cold and distant, closing the door firmly, and this time for ever. She had steeled herself against it. There

119

would be no tears. No pleading. Neither would there be recriminations. She had heard enough in the gossip of the town to know that her father had sworn and cursed this family long years ago. She wasn't going to let history repeat itself.

She had rehearsed staying calm. 'So what do we do now?' she asked in a level voice. There was nothing arrogant or pleading about it.

'That seems perfectly reasonable,' Simon said.

'What?'

'What you ask for. I don't see any reason why not.' His smile was very charming.

She felt that to smile back would put her in some kind of danger.

'Why now?' she asked. 'Why not before?'

'You never asked me before,' he said simply.

'Not personally,' she agreed.

'Yes. It's quite different to be asked indirectly, by a religious order who never made any other approach to me.'

'What approach might they have made?'

'Oh, I don't know. Hard to say. I can't say I'd have liked them to ask me to tea or to pretend a friendship I didn't feel. But it was rather bald just to ask for money on your behalf as if you hadn't a mind or a voice of your own.'

She considered it. It was true. Of course it was also true that she should never have had to ask him or any of the Westwards for what was rightfully hers. And Mother Francis had been sent away twice with a flea in her ear.

But these were not the subjects at issue. And the need was for calm, not for raking up the past.

'I see,' she said.

Simon had almost lost interest in it. He was prepared to talk about other things.

'When does term start, or has it started?'

'Last week. But there's late registration.'

'Why didn't you register in time?'

'I tried another kind of life. I couldn't bear it.'

He must have been used to short answers. It seemed to satisfy him.

'Well, I'm sure you won't have missed very much in a few days. All I ever see in Dublin when I go there is students from both universities drinking coffee and talking about changing the world.'

'They might, one day.'

'Of course.' He was courteous.

She was silent. She couldn't ask him to get the money now, she didn't want to launch into any thanks. The word grateful might slip out. She sipped her sherry thoughtfully.

Their eyes met. 'I'll get a cheque book,' he said, and went out to the hall. Eve heard him rooting around amongst the papers and documents stacked on the table.

By the window the old man sat silently staring with unseeing eyes at the unkempt garden. Out on the lawn the sister who must have been nearly twenty years younger than her elder brother played with a couple of large dogs, throwing them sticks. It was like a foreign land to Eve.

She stood there like the visitor she was, until Simon came back in.

'You'll have to forgive me, I am not saying this in any way to be offensive, but I don't know if your name is Maloney or O'Malone, or what?'

'Eve Malone.' She spoke without expression.

'Thank you. I didn't want to go out and check with Mrs Walsh. It was one or the other, ask you or ask her.' He smiled.

Eve did not return the smile. She nodded her head slightly. He wrote the cheque slowly and deliberately, then folded it in half and handed it to her.

Common politeness must make her thank him. The words stuck in her throat. What had she said before, what had been the word which had pleased her? Glad.

She used it again. 'I'm glad you were able to do this,' she said.

'I'm glad too,' he said.

They did not use each other's names, and they knew there was no more to say. Eve put the cheque in the pocket of her cardigan and stretched out her hand.

'Goodbye,' she said.

Simon Westward said exactly the same thing at the same time.

She waved cheerfully at the child who seemed disappointed to see her go, and walked down the avenue of the house that had been her mother's home with her back straight, because she knew that she was being watched from the house. From the kitchens, from the garden where the dogs were playing, from the drawing room and from a wheelchair.

She didn't let the skip come into her step until she was outside.

In the convent Mother Francis and Kit Hegarty were having lunch in the window of the Community dining room, and a place had been set for Eve.

'We didn't wait for you,' Mother Francis said, her eyes anxiously raking Eve's face for the answer.

Eve nodded twice. The nun's face lit up.

'I'll go now. I have a lot of things to do. Eve, your meal's in the kitchen. Bring it out and sit here with Mrs Hegarty like a good girl.'

'Perhaps...' Kit looked uncertain. 'Can't I go and let you two talk?'

'No, no, no you've not finished yet, I have. And this is Eve's home and mine. We have years to talk. You'll be going away soon.'

Eve brought out her heaped plate of bacon and floury potatoes with a white sauce. She placed it on the table and saw the sad tired face of the older woman watching her.

'Sister Imelda's always trying to fatten me up, but it's no use. When you've got my kind of way of going on it just burns up food.'

Mrs Hegarty nodded.

'I expect you're the same,' Eve said. She felt almost light-headed with relief. She was only making small talk until the lunch was over, until she could run up the road to tell Benny the news, until she could talk to Mother Francis alone when this sad woman went away.

'Yes, I am the same,' Kit Hegarty said. 'I never rest, I hardly ever sleep. I think about everything too much.'

'You've had a lot to think about,' Eve said sympathetically.

'Not always. Frank used to say to me that I couldn't sit down, that my eyes were never still.'

'People say that to me, too,' Eve said, surprised.

They looked at each other with a new interest, the two who had been competing for Mother Francis' time and attention. They didn't think it odd that she hadn't come back to them. They didn't notice that Sister Imelda never came in to take away their plates. As the grey clouds that raced along behind the big banks of convent trees turned black, as the short winter afternoon turned into evening, they talked on.

Their stories fell into place, like pieces of a jigsaw. Eve Malone needed somewhere to live, a place where she could earn her keep. Kit Hegarty needed someone to help her with her guest house. She had no heart to stay in it all day now that Frank, the reason for all the work, had gone. They both could see the solution and yet were afraid to voice it.

It was Eve who spoke first. In the convent which had been her home, Eve softened her voice to ask. Eve, who could never ask for a favour, who hadn't been able to form words of thanks for the £400 in her cardigan pocket was able to ask Kit Hegarty could she come and live with her.

And Kit Hegarty leaned across the table and took Eve's hands in hers.

'We'll make some kind of a life out of it,' she promised.

'We'll make a great life out of it,' Eve assured her.

Then they went to tell Mother Francis, who seemed very surprised and thought it must be the direct intervention of God.

CHAPTER SEVEN

Brian Mahon had been drinking now for several days. Not a real batter, nothing that had involved any violence or a brawl as it sometimes did, but steady drinking. Emily knew that things were shaping up for a fight. And this time it was going to be about Nan's bedroom.

Nan had decided that from now on she would study there in the evenings. She had said it was not possible to study downstairs with the radio on and the family coming and going all the time. Nasey had fixed her up a simple desk and Paul had put a plug on an electric fire. This is where she would work from now on. Emily sighed. She knew that Brian would object as soon as it was brought to his notice. Why had he not been consulted? Who was going to pay for the electricity? Who did Nan think she was?

The answer to the last part was that Nan thought she was a lot too good for Brian Mahon and Maple Gardens. Her mother had ensured that over the years. As she brushed her daughter's golden hair, Emily had always made the girl believe that there would be a better and a different life. Nan had never doubted it. She felt no need to conform to the lifestyle of a house ruled by an often drunken father.

Nan Mahon was not afraid of her father because she knew with a certainty which her mother had helped to create that her future didn't lie in her father's kind of world. She knew without arrogance that her beauty would be her means of escape.

Emily wished that there was some way that she could take Brian aside and talk to him in a way that he would listen. Really listen and understand. She could say to him that life was short and there was no point in crossing Nan. Let her work up in the bedroom if that's what she wanted. Be nice – be pleasant about it, then she'd come down and sit with them afterwards.

But Brian didn't listen to Emily these days. If he had ever listened to her. She sighed to herself as she opened up the new delivery of Belleek china, and put the packing neatly into a big container under the counter. She arranged the little jugs and plates on a shelf so that they would best catch the eye and began to write out price tags in her meticulous handwriting. Emily Mahon sighed again. It was so easy to run a hotel shop, and so hard to run a family. People didn't realize how often she'd like to make her bed in the corner of this little world, amongst those nice car rugs and cushions with celtic designs on them. It would be simpler by far than going back to Maple Gardens.

She had been quite right of course. The row had well begun when Emily Mahon let herself into the family home.

'Do you know anything about all this?' Brian roared.

Emily had decided to try and play it lightly.

'Well, I must say that's a great greeting to one of the workers of the world,' she said, looking from her husband's hot, red face to Nan's cool and unruffled expression.

'Aw, shut up with that workers of the world crap, will you? We all know there isn't a reason in the world for you to be going out to work. Only because you took some figario. If you'd stayed at home and minded your business we wouldn't have all this trouble now.'

'What trouble?' Emily was weary.

'Well might you ask what trouble. Sure you don't know what's going on in your own house.'

'Why are you picking on Em?' Nan asked. 'She's only in the door, she hasn't her coat off, or her shopping put down.'

Her father's face was working. 'Don't call your mother by her Christian name, you young pup.'

'I'm not.' Nan was bored with this argument. 'I'm calling her M, short for Mother, Mama, Mater.'

'You're dismantling that contraption you have upstairs, and coming back down here to where we have the house heated. You'll study your books in this room like a normal human being.'

'Excuse me,' Nan asked. 'Excuse my mentioning it, but what kind of study could anyone get in a room like this with people bellowing and shouting.'

'Listen to me, you impertinent young rossie . . . you'll feel the weight of my hand on you if there's any more of this.'

'Ah, Dad, don't hit her . . .' Nasey had stood up.

'Get out of my way . . .'

Nan didn't move. Not an inch did she stir from where she stood, proud, young, confident in her fresh green and white blouse and her dark green skirt. She had her books under her arm, and she could have been a model picture for student fashion.

'Am I breaking my back for you to speak to me like that in front of the family? Am I working to make you into a bad-mannered tinker?'

'I haven't said anything bad-mannered at all, Dad, only that I'm going up to work, to get a bit of peace. So that I'll get my degree eventually, so that you'll be prouder of me than ever.'

The words were inoffensive, but Brian Mahon found the tone of his daughter almost more than he could bear.

'Get up there out of my sight then, we don't want to see hair or hide of you this evening.'

Nan smiled. 'If you want me to give you a hand, Em, just call me,' she said, and they heard her light step going up the stairs.

The three students in Mrs Hegarty's digs were delighted to hear of Eve's arrival. They had felt awkward and unsure of themselves in a place where the son of the house had been killed so tragically. Now at least an attempt was being made to return to normality.

They liked Eve too, when she appeared. Small, attractive in a wiry kind of way and prepared to put up with no nonsense from the very start.

'I'll be getting your breakfast from now on. Mrs Hegarty is feeding you like fighting cocks so you get bacon and egg and sausage every day and scrambled eggs on a Friday. But I have a nine o'clock lecture three days a week so I was wondering if you could help me clear and wash those days, and the other days I'll run round after you like a slave . . . pouring you more cups of tea and buttering you more toast.'

They went along with her good-naturedly, and they did more than she asked. Big lads who wouldn't have known where the hoover was kept in their own homes were able to lift it out for Eve on a Tuesday before they went to catch the train to college. They wiped their feet carefully on the hall mat. They said they never again wanted to risk anything like the reception that they got when they had accidentally walked some mud in on top of a carpet that Eve had cleaned. They kept the bathroom far cleaner than they had ever done before Eve had come on the scene. Kit

Hegarty told her privately that if she had known how much the presence of a girl would smarten the lads up, she might have had a female student years ago.

'Why didn't you? They'd have been easier.'

'Don't you believe it, always washing their hair, wanting the lavatory seat put down, drying their stockings over chairs, falling in love with no-hopers . . .' Kit had laughed.

'Aren't you afraid of any of those things happening with me?' Eve asked. They got on so well now they could talk easily on any subject.

'Not a chance of it. You'll never fall for a no-hoper. Hard-hearted little hannah that you are.'

'I thought you said I was like you?' Eve was making bread as she spoke. Sister Imelda had taught her to make soda bread when she was six. She had no idea of the recipe, she just did it automatically.

'Ah, you *are* like me, and I didn't fall for a no-hoper, there was lots of hope in Joseph Hegarty. It's just that as time went on it didn't seem to include me.' She sounded bitter and sad.

'Did you make any attempt to find him, you know, to tell him about Frank?'

'He didn't want to know about Frank when there was something to tell like when he learned to swim, or when he lost his first tooth, or when he passed his Inter. Why tell him anything now?'

Eve could see a lot of reasons, but she didn't think it was the time or the place.

'Suppose he came back,' Eve asked. 'If Joe walked in the door one day . . .'

'Funny I never called him Joe, always Joseph. I'm sure that tells us something about him or me. Suppose he came back? It would be like the man coming to read the meter. I gave up looking at that gate years ago.'

'And yet you loved him? Or else thought you did?'

'Oh, I did love him. There's no use denying it just because it wasn't returned and didn't last.'

'You're very calm about it.'

'You didn't know me years ago. Let me see. Around the time you were one or two, if you'd known me then you wouldn't have said I was calm!'

'I've never loved anybody,' Eve said suddenly.

'That's because you were afraid to.'

'No, the nuns were much more liberal than people think. They didn't fill me with terror of men.'

'No, I meant afraid to let yourself go . . .'

'I think that's right. I feel things very strongly, like resentment. I resent those bloody Westwards. I hate asking them for money. I can't tell you how much it took to make me walk up there that Sunday. And I feel very protective too, if anyone said a word against Mother Francis or Sister Imelda I'd kill them.'

'You look very fierce with that knife. Put it down, for God's sake.'

'Oh.' Eve laughed, realizing she was brandishing the carving knife, which she had used to put a cross on the top of the soda bread. 'I didn't notice. Anyway it wouldn't harm anyone. It's as blunt as anything. It wouldn't cut butter. Let's get one of those budding Engineers inside there to take it into the lab and sharpen it up for us.'

'You *will* love somebody one day,' Kit Hegarty said.

'I can't imagine who.' Eve was thoughtful. 'For one thing he'd have to be a saint to put up with my moods, for another I don't see many good examples, where love seems to have worked out well.'

'Have you anything planned on Sunday?' Dr Foley asked his eldest son.

'What am I letting myself in for if I haven't?' Jack laughed.

'Just a simple answer. If you're busy I'll not bother you.'

'But then I might miss something great.'

'Ah, that's what life is all about, taking risks.'

'What is it, Dad?'

'You *are* free then.'

'Come on, tell me.'

'You know Joe Kennedy, he's a chemist in the country. He wants to see me. He's not well, I think. We go back a long way. He wondered if I'd come and call on him.'

'Where does he live?'

'Knockglen.'

'That's miles away. Don't they have doctors there?'

'They do, but he wants a friend more than a doctor.'

'And you want me to come, is it?'

'I want you to drive me, Jack. I've lost my nerve a bit.'

'You can't have.'

'Not altogether, but just for a long wet drive, slippy roads. I'd be very grateful.'

'All right,' Jack said. 'What'll I do while you're talking to him?'

'That's the problem. I wouldn't say there's all that much *to* do there, but maybe you could go on a drive or sit in the car to read the Sunday papers.'

Jack's face brightened. 'I know. There's a girl that lives there. I'll give her a ring.'

'That's my boy. Only a couple of months at university and already there's a girl in every town.'

'She's not a girl in that sense. She's just a nice girl,' Jack explained. 'Have you the phone book? There can't be that many Hogans in Knockglen.'

Nan was very excited when Benny said that Jack Foley had rung her.

'Half the girls in college would give anything to have *him* coming to call on them, let me tell you. What'll you wear?'

'I don't think he's coming to call, not in that sense. I mean it's not something to get dressed up for. I won't wear anything,' Benny said, flustered.

'That should be a nice surprise for him when you open the door,' Nan said.

'You know what I mean.'

'I still think you should get dressed up, wear that nice pink blouse, and the black skirt. It *is* a party when a fellow like Jack Foley comes to call. If he was coming out to Maple Gardens I'd dress up. I'll get you a length of pink ribbon and a black one and you can tie them both round your hair to hold it back. It'll look great. You've got gorgeous hair.'

'Nan, it won't look great on a rainy Sunday in Knockglen. Nothing looks great there. It'll just look pathetic.'

Nan looked at her thoughtfully. 'You know those big thick brown bags, the ones they sell sugar in. Why don't you put one of those over your head and cut two slits for eyes. That might look right.'

Annabel Hogan and Patsy planned to make scones, and queen cakes and an apple tart. There would be bridge rolls first with chopped egg on one plate and sardines on the other.

'Maybe we shouldn't overdo it,' Benny suggested.

'There's nothing overdone about a perfectly straightforward afternoon tea for your friend.' Benny's mother was affronted at the notion that this might not have been their normal Sunday afternoon fare.

They were going to light a fire each day in the drawing room to heat it up for the occasion and after tea had been cleared away Benny's parents would withdraw to the breakfast room, leaving the young people the run of the good room on their own.

'There's not any question of having the run of the place,' Benny had begged, but to no avail. 'He's only coming here because he has to kill the time,' she pleaded. They wouldn't hear of it, a nice young man telephoning courteously several days in advance to know if he could call. It wasn't a matter of killing time. There was a rake of things he could do in Knockglen.

Personally Benny could think of very few. Window shopping didn't bear thinking about. The cinema wasn't open in the afternoon. Healy's Hotel would pall after half an hour, and Jack Foley wasn't likely to put away an afternoon in Mario's, however entertaining Fonsie might be. The Hogans were the only game in town. Still, it was nice that he remembered her. Benny rehearsed the pink and black ribbon. It looked well. She started wearing it on Friday evening so that the household wouldn't think it was part of the dressing up.

When Sean asked her to the pictures she said no, that since she was having a friend from Dublin she had to stay at home on Saturday and get things ready.

'A friend from Dublin!' Sean sniffed. 'And might we know her name?'

'It's a him, not a her,' Benny said mulishly.

'Pardon me,' Sean said.

'So that's why I can't go, you see,' she added lamely.

'Naturally.' Sean was lofty and knowing.

For some reason that she couldn't explain Benny heard herself saying, 'It's just a friend, not anything else.'

Sean's smile was slow and cold. 'I'm sure that's true, Benny.

I wouldn't have expected anything less of you. But it's good of you to say it straight out.'

He nodded like a self-satisfied bird. As if he were being generous and allowing her to have her own friends until the time came. And a pat on the head for defining that there was nothing but friendship involved.

'I hope it's a very pleasant visit. For all of you,' Sean Walsh said, and bowed in what he must have thought was an elegant or a gracious manner. Something he had seen Errol Flynn or Montgomery Clift do, and stored up for a suitable occasion.

Jack Foley was the easiest guest they had ever known in Hogans'. He ate some of everything put in front of him. He praised it all. He had three cups of tea. He admired the teapot and asked was it Birmingham 1930s silver. It was. Wasn't that amazing? they said; no, Jack said, that's what his parents' silver was. He just wondered was it the same. He punched Benny playfully like a brother when they talked about university. He said how marvellous it was to have boys and girls in the same classes. He had felt so gauche when he had come there from a single-sex school. Benny saw her mother and father nodding sagely, agreeing with him. He spoke of his parents and his brothers, and the boy Aengus with the glasses, which were always getting broken at school.

He said that the debates were great on a Saturday night, you learned a lot from them as well as having fun. Had Benny been? No, Benny hadn't. You see there was this problem about getting back to Knockglen, she said in a flat voice. Oh, that was a pity he thought, they really were part of college life. Perhaps Benny could stay with her friend Nan, he sometimes saw her there. They all nodded. Perhaps. Some Saturday.

He was discreet about why his father wanted to meet Mr Kennedy. It could be anything, he said, rugby club business, or new drugs on the market, or old school reunions. You never knew with his father, he had so many irons in the fire.

Benny looked at him with admiration. Jack Foley didn't even look as if he were putting on an act.

The only other person she knew who could do that was Nan. In many ways they would be ideally suited.

'It's nice and fine. Do you think you could show me the town?' he asked Benny.

131

'We were just going to leave the two of you to ... er, chat,' Benny's mother began.

'I've eaten so much ... I think I do need a walk.'

'I'll get proper shoes.' Benny had been wearing flat pumps, like party shoes.

'Get boots, Benny,' he called after her. 'We're really going to walk off this fabulous tea.'

They walked companionably together. Benny in her winter coat, with the pink collar of her smart blouse showing over it. She had put on wellingtons, and she felt that the cold wind was making her cheeks red, but it didn't matter. Jack wore his purple and green Law Society scarf wound round his neck.

Several people were out walking in the wintry sunshine which would soon turn into a sunset.

'Where will we go?' he asked at the Hogan's gate.

'Through the town, out the other side, and up to Westlands. That'll undo the harm of all the apple tart.'

'Poor Mr Kennedy's dying. He wanted to talk to my father about it. He doesn't get much joy out of the local man, apparently.'

'That's very sad. He's not old,' Benny said. 'That's where the local man, as you call him, lives.' She waved across the road to Dr Johnson's house, where the children were throwing sticks for a dog.

'I didn't mention that to your parents ...' Jack began.

'Nor will I, don't worry,' Benny said.

They knew the story would travel the length of the one-street town.

Benny pointed out places, and gave a little commentary. Bee Moore called out from the doorway of Paccy Moore's cobbler's shop that there were lovely new skirts arrived into Peggy Pine's.

'They're just right for you, Benny,' Bee said, and added, with no sense of offence, 'they'd fit an elephant, and there's a great stretch in them.'

'Beautiful!' Jack commented, with a grin.

'Ah, she doesn't mean any harm,' Benny said.

In Mario's, both Fonsie and his uncle blew extravagant kisses out to Benny. And in Dessie Burns' hardware shop they wondered who could have written 'Useful Gift' over a saw. They passed

Kennedy's chemist swiftly without saying anything about the man inside talking to Jack's father. Benny took him across to point out some of the finer points of Hogan's Gentleman's Outfitters.

Jack admired the shop courteously, and said it was very discreet. You'd never know from the outside what it was like on the inside. Benny wondered was that a good thing, but decided it probably was. Country people were different. They didn't like anyone knowing their business.

She asked Jack to keep staring in the window and to notice the reflection of Mrs Healy across the road watching them beadily from her hotel. Jack heard about Mrs Healy's corsets, and what amazing structural feats they were. There was a rumour that Mrs Healy was quite a plump, soft person, but nobody except the late Mr Healy would have had any proof of this. New and ever more taxing underpinnings were bought every time she went to Dublin, and there was a rumour that she had once gone to London on a corset-buying spree, but this might only be a rumour.

When she had gone back into her hotel Benny felt it safe to move on. She showed Jack the clean white slabs of Mr Flood's the butcher's. She said that Teddy Flood, his son, didn't really want to work there, but what else could he do? It was hard to be born into the business if you were a boy. Mr Flood was becoming very odd these days.

Jack said he could see that without being told. It was surely highly questionable to have so many cows and pigs and lambs around the wall in a highly coloured gambolling state. It must make people feel sensitive about buying them in their very dead condition, and eating them. Benny said that this was nothing. Mr Flood had always had piteous-looking animals peeping at you from the walls. The real thing was that he now had a fairly permanent vision of something up a tree. A saint possibly, but definitely a nun. It was a source of worry to the family and a cause of great fits of giggling among the customers when he would suddenly pause in sawing or chopping and go out of doors for a brief consultation upwards.

They passed the church and paused to study the details of the Men's Mission, which would be coming to the church shortly. Benny said that during the two weeks of the missions little wooden stalls selling prayer books and beads, and holy objects and Catholic Truth Society pamphlets did huge business outside the church. Was it the same in Dublin? Jack was apologetic. He didn't really know. He had gone to the mission of course, but like everyone he and Aidan had always wanted to try and find out which had the lecture on sex. That was the one that was usually packed out, but the missioners were becoming more and more cunning. They sort of hinted each night that the big sex sermon would be tomorrow and they had crowds coming in every night, in case they missed it.

Benny said that men were much more honest than women, really. Girls felt exactly the same but didn't admit it.

She showed him the square where the bus came in. Mikey was just drawing up.

'How's Benny?' he called out.

'Great altogether,' Benny said, with her big smile.

They paused in front of the gates of St Mary's and she pointed out the landmarks to him. The big long lawns, the camogie field, the glasshouse, the windy path through the kitchen gardens that went uphill to the quarry path, where Eve had her cottage.

She knew everything and everyone, he told her, and there was a story attached to whatever they saw.

This pleased her. At least he wasn't being bored.

Neither of them saw Sean Walsh looking at them from inside Birdie Mac's sweet shop. Birdie often made tea and toast of a Sunday afternoon and Sean Walsh had taken to dropping in. His eyes were cold as he watched Benny Hogan and the arrogant young pup that she had gone off with that very first day, trick acting and showing off right outside the convent gates in full view of the town. It didn't please him one little bit.

They stood on the five-bar gate that had a good view down over the Westwards' land. Benny pointed out places to him. The graveyard where all the Westwards lay. The small war memorial in it that had wreaths of poppies in November, because so many of them had died in wars.

'Wasn't it odd to think of them all fighting in those wars when they lived here?' she said.

'But that would be their whole culture and tradition and everything,' Jack said.

'I know, but when the others would be talking about home-land and fatherland and king or queen and country . . . they'd only be talking about Knockglen.'

'Don't knock Knockglen,' he said, laughing.

'Don't let Fonsie in the chipper bar hear you say that, he'll be trying to turn it into a hit single. Move over Bill Hayley ... that's Fonsie ...'

'Where did he get the name?'

'Alphonsus.'

'God.'

'I know. Didn't you escape lightly, Jack Foley, with your nice normal name?'

'And what about you ... Benedicta was it?'

'No, nothing as exotic. Mary Bernadette, I'm afraid.'

'Benny's nice. It suits you.'

It was dark as they walked back. The lights were on up in the convent. Benny told Jack of Eve's life there, and the lovely bedroom where you could sit and look down the town.

'Now I have you home safely in good time,' she said, delivering him to the door of Kennedy's chemist.

'Will you come in?'

'No, he might be upset.'

'Thanks, Benny. It was a lovely visit.'

'I enjoyed your being here. Wasn't it lovely for me too?'

'Will you come out one night in Dublin?' He spoke suddenly, almost surprising himself.

'Not at night. I'm Cinderella, remember. But I'll see you round.'

'Maybe a lunch?'

'Wouldn't that be grand?' she said, and walked off down the dark street.

'Poor Joe,' his father said after a long silence in the car.

'Has he got cancer?'

'Riddled with it. He's only a couple of months, I'd say, from the sound of things.'

'What did you tell him?'

'He wanted me to listen.'

'Has he no one here who'll do that?'

'No. According to him there's an arrogant, bad-tempered GP, a wife who thinks it's all safe and in the hands of the Little Flower or the Infant of Prague, or some such helpful authority and won't brook any discussion on the matter ... However, enough's enough.

How was your friend? Joe said she was a nice girl, big horse of a girl he called her.'

'Isn't it a pity he couldn't have found a better way to describe people.'

'Let me get this straight again,' Nan said, her eyes wide with disbelief. 'He asked you out. I mean he said the words "I would like you to come out with me one night", and you said no?'

'No, I didn't say no, and he didn't ask me out like that.'

Nan looked to Eve for guidance. They were all three together waiting for the lecturer to arrive. They sat away from the main body of the students in order to get this matter sorted.

'Well, did he or didn't he?' Eve asked.

'It was like you'd ask a friend. Casual. It wasn't like a date.'

'It certainly wasn't if you said no,' Eve said dryly.

'Don't go on like that.' Benny looked from one to the other. 'I swear, if he *does* ask me out I'll go. Now are you satisfied?'

'And where will you stay the night in Dublin?' Eve asked.

'I could stay with you, couldn't I, Nan?'

'Oh yes, sure.' The reply was half a second late.

Benny looked to Eve. 'Or if there was any problem with that I could stay with you, Eve, out in Dunlaoghaire.'

'Easily.' That was said quickly, but of course Mother and Father would never let her stay in a guest house full of boys with a woman they didn't know, even if Eve did live there in a semi-work capacity. Benny was philosophical. It wouldn't happen anyway. What were all the plans for?

In the Ladies' Reading Room stuck into the criss-cross tapes on the notice board was a folded piece of paper. 'Benny Hogan, First Arts.' She opened it casually. It must be from that pale-faced clerical student who had missed the history lecture and she had promised to give him the notes. Benny had remembered to take carbon paper with her. He could keep the copy for himself. She didn't know his name. He was a worried young man, definitely not strong, his white face made even whiter by the black clothes. She got an odd feeling when she saw that the letter was from Jack Foley. It was like the sudden jolt you get if you touch something too hot or too cold.

Dear Benny,

I remember you said evenings were difficult at the moment, so what do you say to lunch in the Dolphin? I've never been there but I'm always hearing about it. Would a Thursday be good? I remember you saying you didn't have a tutorial or anything on Thursdays. I'll probably see you before then, but if you can't make it or don't want to, can you leave a note in the porter's office? I hope I won't hear from you because that means I'll see you in the Dolphin at one fifteen on Thursday week.

And thank you for the lovely afternoon in Knockglen.

Love, Jack

Love, Jack. Love, Jack. She said it to herself over and over. She closed her eyes and said it again. It was possible, wasn't it? Just possible that he did like her. He didn't *need* to ask her out, or to remember that she had a free afternoon on Thursdays, or be so kind as to think of lunch. He could have sent a postcard if he wanted to be mannery, as her father would call it. Jack Foley didn't need to ask her to lunch in a big posh hotel where the high of the land went. He must have done it because he liked being with her, and that he liked her.

She didn't dare to believe it.

Benny heard Nan's infectious laugh in the corridor outside. Hastily she pushed the note deep into her shoulder bag. It seemed a bit shabby considering how enthusiastic Nan and Eve always were on her behalf, but she couldn't bear them giving her advice on what to wear and what to say. And worst of all she couldn't bear them to think that Jack Foley might in fact fancy her, when she so desperately hoped it was true.

CHAPTER EIGHT

Benny decided she would be thin on Thursday week. She would have hollows in her cheeks and a long narrow neck. It would, of course, involve eating nothing. Not easy to do at home where Patsy would put a bowl of porridge, a jug of cream and the silver sugar basin in front of her to start the day. Then there was the brown bread and marmalade. And on either side of her, a parent determined she should have a good start to the day.

Benny realized that you'd need great ingenuity if you were to lose an ounce of weight as a resident of Lisbeg in Knockglen. So she first pretended that she had gone off porridge. In fact she loved it, swimming in cream and dusted with brown sugar. Then she would leave her departure until as late as possible and cry 'Is that the time? I'll take my bread and butter with me.' When no one was looking she would tip it into Dr Johnson's hen run or drop it into the bin outside Carroll's or Shea's.

Then there was lunch time. She found it beyond human endurance to go into the cafés where the smell of sausage and chips in one kind of place or almond buns in another would drive her taste buds wild.

She told Nan and Eve that she had to work and stayed resolutely in the library all the time.

The stuffiness of the library and no food made her feel headachy and weak all afternoon. It was another test of will to pass the sweet shops when she knew a packet of Rollos would give her the energy to struggle down to the quays and get the bus. Then back in Knockglen she had to cope with the meat tea as well.

'I had a huge feed-up in town today,' she'd say apologetically.

'What did you do that for when there's good food waiting for you here?' her mother would reply, puzzled.

Or else she'd try the angle that she didn't feel like it because she was tired. They didn't like that either. Should they have a word with Dr Johnson about her? What could be making a normal healthy girl tired? Benny knew that it would be useless to tell them the truth, that she wanted to lose some weight. They would tell her she was fine. They would worry and discuss it endlessly. Meals would become a battleground. It was quite hard enough already to resist slices of Patsy's treacle tart, and to toy with one piece of potato cake when she craved half a dozen. Benny knew that the road to beauty was not meant to be an easy one, but she wondered grimly whether it was such hard going for everyone else.

She wondered should she wear a corset like Mrs Healy, or better still not like Mrs Healy's very obvious whalebone. There was the one she had seen advertised. 'Nu Back corset . . . expands as you bend, stoop or twist . . . returns to position easily and cannot ride up when sitting.' It cost 19/11d, almost a pound, and it did seem to promise everything you could dream of. Except of course it didn't hold out any hope for the cheeks and the neck.

Benny sighed a lot. Wouldn't it have been great going to lunch in a smart Dublin place if she were small and neat like Eve was? Or better still if she looked like Nan. If she looked so gorgeous that everyone would look and Jack Foley would be so proud and pleased that he had asked her.

Because Benny was never available for lunch any more, Nan and Eve often found themselves walking together to one of the cafés near the university. Eve watched with a wry amusement as the boys came to join them wherever they went.

Nan put on an amazing performance, Eve thought to herself. She had a practised charm, but no gush whatsoever. Eve had never known anyone play such a role. But then she asked herself, *was* it a performance? She seemed totally natural and was invariably warm and pleasant to those who approached. Almost regal, Eve thought. It was as if she knew that there would be admiration everywhere and was quite accustomed to coping with it.

Eve was always included in the conversations and, as she told Kit Hegarty in their easy companionship out in Dunlaoghaire, it was the best introduction you could have to every single male in UCD.

'Of course they do see me as a pale shadow,' Eve said sagely. 'Like the moon not having any light of its own, it reflects the light of the sun.'

'Nonsense,' Kit said loyally. 'That's not a bit like you to be so humble.'

'I'm being practical,' Eve said. 'I don't mind it at all. There's only one Nan in every generation.'

'Is she the sort of College Belle?'

'I suppose so, though she doesn't act it. Not like that Rosemary, who thinks she's at a party all day every day. Rosemary has a foot of make-up on, and she has eyelashes about ten inches long, you wouldn't believe it. She keeps looking up and down so that no one will miss them. I wonder that doesn't make herself dizzy or blind herself.' Eve sounded very ferocious.

'But Nan's not like that?' Kit Hegarty had yet to meet this paragon.

'No, and she's just as nice to awful fellows as she is to real hunks. She spends ages talking to ones that are covered in pimples and can hardly string two words together. Which drives the hunks out of their minds.'

'And does she not have her eye on anyone for herself?' Kit asked. She thought that Eve was seeing far too much of the dazzling Nan and not nearly enough of her old friend Benny Hogan.

'Apparently not.' Eve was surprised too. 'Because she could have anyone she liked, even Jack Foley, but she doesn't seem to want them. It's as if there's something else out there that we don't know about.'

'Martians?' Kit suggested.

'Nothing would surprise me.'

'How's Benny, by the way?' Kit's voice was deliberately casual.

'Funny you should ask. I haven't seen her all week, except at lectures, and then only to wave across to.'

Kit Hegarty knew better than to probe or criticize, but her heart went out to that big untidy girl with the bright smile, the girl who had been Eve's friend through thick and thin and now seemed to be left out in the cold. It was tough on ordinary moths and insects when a gorgeous butterfly like Nan came on to the scene.

'Eve, are you going to the Annexe?' Aidan Lynch seemed to be everywhere. He had a fawn duffle coat which had seen much better days, long curly hair which fell into his eyes, and dark horn-rimmed spectacles that he always said were plain glass but made him look highly intellectual.

'I wasn't thinking of it, no.'

'Could the thought of my company there and back and the distinct possibility that I would buy you a coffee and a fly cemetery make you change your mind?'

'I'd love a fly cemetery,' Eve said, referring to the pastries with the black, squashy filling. 'I cook breakfast for huge greedy men and I forgot to have any myself today.'

'Huge, greedy men?' Aidan was interested. 'Do you live in a male harem?'

'No, a digs. I help with the housework to earn my keep.' She spoke without self-pity or bravado. For once the joky Aidan was without words. But not for long.

'Then it's my duty, not just my pleasure, to feed you up,' he said.

'Nan won't be there. She has a tutorial.'

A flicker of annoyance passed over his face. 'I didn't want Nan to be there. I wanted you.'

'Well recovered, Mr Lynch.' She smiled at him.

'Is there anything more harsh in this life than to be misjudged, and have one's motives entirely misunderstood?' he asked.

'I don't know. Is there?' Eve liked the lanky law student. She had always thought of him as part of Jack Foley's gang. Full of nonsense of course and all that lofty talk. But basically all right.

They walked companionably down the corridor towards the stone stairs that led to the Annexe, the college coffee shop. They passed the Ladies' Reading Room on the way. Through the door Eve caught a glimpse of Benny sitting in a chair on her own.

'Aidan, just a minute. I'll ask Benny to come with us.'

'No! I asked *you*,' he said petulantly.

'Well, God Almighty, the Annexe is open to everyone in the whole place. It's not as if you'd asked me to a candlelit dinner for two,' Eve blazed at him.

'I would have, but I don't know where they serve them at this time of the morning,' he said.

'Don't be a clown. Wait here a second.'

Benny's mind seemed far away. Eve touched her shoulder.

'Oh, hallo,' she said, looking up.

'Good, you admit you know me. Let me introduce myself. My name is Eve Malone. We met some years ago in . . . where was it . . . Knockglen . . . yes that's where it was!'

'Don't, Eve.'

'What is it? Why don't you play with me any more?'

'I can't tell you.'

'You can tell me anything,' Eve said, kneeling down beside the chair.

Out in the corridor Aidan Lynch cleared his throat.

'No, go on, there's a fellow waiting for you.'

'Tell me.'

'I'm on a diet,' Benny whispered.

Eve threw back her head and pealed with laughter. Everyone in the room looked over at them. Benny's face got red.

'Now look what you've done,' she hissed furiously.

Eve looked into her friend's eyes. 'I'm only laughing with relief, you great fool. Is that all? Well, I don't think there's any point in it. You're grand as you are, but if you want to, be on one, but don't run away from everybody. I thought I'd done something awful to you.'

'Of course not.'

'Well, come on, come and have a coffee with Aidan and myself.'

'No, I can't bear the smell of food', Benny said piteously. 'My only hope is to keep away from where it is.'

'Will we have a walk in the green at lunch then? There's no food there,' Eve suggested.

'We might see someone feeding the ducks and I could snatch the bread and run off stuffing it down my throat,' Benny said with a hint of a smile.

'That's better. I'll pick you up in the main hall at one.'

'Don't tell anyone.'

'Oh, Benny, honestly!'

'What was all that about?' Aidan said, pleased to see that Eve had returned alone.

'I was letting Benny know where I was going and explaining that if I wasn't back by a stated time she was to ring the guards,' Eve said to him.

'Aren't you very droll.'

'Well, you're not a great one at taking life too seriously yourself,' she said with spirit.

'I knew we were suited, I knew from the very first minute I saw you. In bed.'

Eve just raised her eyes, not to encourage him. But Aidan was warming to the theme.

'It will be a nice thing to tell our grandchildren in years to come.'

'What?'

Aidan spoke in a child's voice. ' "Tell me, Grandad, how did you and Grandma meet?" and then I'll say, "Ho, ho, ho, little boy, we met when she was in bed. I was introduced to her in bed. It was like that way back in the fifties. It was a racy time, ho, ho, ho." '

'You are an idiot,' Eve laughed at him.

'I know. I said we were well suited,' he said, tucking her arm into his as they joined the crowds on the stairs down to coffee.

Benny took out a small mirror from her handbag. She put it inside a copy of *Tudor England* and examined her face carefully. Five days with no food to speak of and her face was still round, her jaw was still solid and there was no sign of a long swan-like neck. It would almost make you give up believing in God.

'Are there women after you in college?' Aengus asked Jack Foley.

'I never looked.' Jack wasn't concentrating.

'You'd know. They'd be breathing heavily,' Aengus explained.

Jack looked up from his notes. 'They would?'

'So I hear.'

'Where do you hear this?'

'Well, mainly from Ronan. He was doing a very funny imitation of people in a car, huffing and puffing. He says that girls get like that when they're passionate.'

'And where did he see all this that he could be imitating it?' Jack asked, a trifle anxiously.

Aengus was innocent. 'I don't know. You know Ronan.'

Jack did know his brother Ronan, and had an uneasy feeling that there had been someone in the vicinity when he was saying goodbye to Shirley the other night. Shirley was quite unlike most of the other girls in UCD. She had been in America for a year, which made her very experienced. She had offered Jack a lift home from the Solicitors' Apprentice Dance last Saturday night at the Four Courts. She had her own car and her own code. She had parked right outside his house under a street light.

When he had murmured that they might have more shade, Shirley had said, 'I like to see what I'm kissing.'

Now it looked as if his brother had also seen whatever kissing had been going on.

Jack Foley made a note to leave Shirley alone. Next time it would be Rosemary or even the ice-cool Nan Mahon. No more crazy ladies, thank you very much.

Benny ate an apple walking around St Stephen's Green at lunch time and felt a little bit better. Eve never spoke of the diet again. Benny knew she didn't even need to warn her not to tell Nan. It wasn't that Nan wouldn't be helpful, she'd be very helpful. It was just that Nan didn't ever need to try. She just was perfect already, and it put her in a different world.

Instead they talked about Aidan Lynch and how he was going to come out to Dunlaoghaire tonight and take Eve to the pictures. He understood that she had to wash up after supper. He'd come out on the train.

'I've missed you a lot, Eve,' Benny said suddenly.

'Me too. Why can't you stay in town some evening?'

'You know.'

Eve did know. The arguments about the evenings drawing in, the dark nights, it would be such hard work they decided they should wait until Benny had a real date, a real reason to stay in town. It almost seemed like frittering it away to use a night off just for the two of them to be together like the old days.

'I'd love it if you'd come home to Knockglen,' Benny said. 'And not that I'm twisting your arm, but I know Mother Francis would too.'

'I will,' Eve promised. 'It's just that I've got obligations too. It's then that I'm the most help to Kit. I get the Saturday tea over so quickly it would make your head swim. I keep telling the lads they have to be on the six thirty train into town to see the action. They don't know what I mean but it gets a bit of urgency into them. Otherwise they'd be dawdling there all night.'

Benny giggled. 'You're a terrible tyrant.'

'Nonsense. I was raised by an army general in St Mary's, that's all. Mother Francis would get her way over anything. Then on Sundays we have this rule. They get a big Sunday lunch, and there's a plate of salad left under a tea towel for each of them in the evening, no serving or anything.'

'I'm sure she's delighted with you,' Benny said.

'I'm a bit of company. That's all.'

'Does she ever talk about her son?'

'Not much. But she cries over him at night. I know that.'

'Isn't it extraordinary that people can love their children so much that they kind of live for them?'

'Your parents do. That's part of the problem. Still, it's nice to know they do,' Eve said.

'Yours would have, if they'd stayed around long enough.'

'And if they'd been sane,' Eve said dryly.

Benny sat beside Rosemary at the history lecture. She had never really spoken to her before. She wanted to look at Rosemary's make-up and wondered was there anything she could learn.

As they waited for the lecturer to arrive they talked idly.

'Knockglen?' Rosemary said. 'That's the second time I heard of that today. Where is it?'

Benny told her, and added glumly that it was too far to be accessible and too near to let you live in Dublin.

'Who was talking about it?' Rosemary puckered up her face, trying to think. She often applied a little Vaseline to her eyelashes in the privacy of the lecture hall. It was meant to make them grow. She did so openly in front of Benny, who was no rival that must be kept out of beauty secrets.

Benny watched with interest. Then Rosemary remembered.

'I know. It was Jack. Jack Foley. He was saying that a friend of his fancies someone from Knockglen. It's not you by any chance?'

'No, I don't think so.' Benny's heart was like lead. Rosemary was on such close terms with Jack, and Jack was making a joke out of Knockglen.

'His friend Aidan. You know, goofy Aidan Lynch. He's quite witty actually, it sort of makes up for everything else.'

Benny felt her cheeks burning. Is this the way people talked? People like Jack and Rosemary and maybe even Nan, for all she knew. Did handsome people have different rules?

'And did Jack approve of whoever Aidan fancied?' She wanted to keep Jack's name in the conversation, however painful it was.

'Oh yes. He said it was a great place. He's been there.'

'Really.' Benny remembered every moment of the day that Jack Foley had been in her town in her house in her company. She could probably give a transcript like they did in court cases of every word that had been said.

'He's really out of this world,' Rosemary confided. 'You know, not only is he a rugby star, but he's bright. He got six honours in his Leaving, and he's nice.'

So Rosemary had prised out of Jack how well he had done in his exams leaving school, just like she had.

'Are you going out with him?' Benny asked.

'Not yet, but I *will* be, that's my project,' Rosemary said.

All during the lecture on Ireland under the Tudors Benny sneaked little looks at her neighbour. It was so monstrously unfair that a girl like Rosemary should have a bar of KitKat in her bag and have no spots and no double chin.

And when had she had all these conversations with Jack Foley? In the evenings probably. Or even the early evenings, when poor Benny Hogan was sitting like a big piece of freight on the bus back to Knockglen.

Benny wished she hadn't eaten the apple. Perhaps what her system had wanted was a complete shock. No food at all after eighteen years of too much food. Maybe the apple had delayed the process.

She looked at Rosemary and wondered was there any hope that she would fail in her project.

'How's work, Nan?' Bill Dunne prided himself on getting on well with women. He thought that Aidan Lynch's reputation was quite unjustified. That was fine at school when everyone was joky. But in university, women were there because they were studious. Or because they wanted people to think they were studious. You couldn't go on trick acting and making schoolboy jokes to university women. You pretended to take their studies seriously.

Nan Mahon smiled one of her glorious smiles. 'I suppose it's like it is for everyone else,' she said. 'When you like the lectures, when you enjoy the subject, it's fine. When you don't, it's hell, and there's going to be hell to pay at the end.'

The words themselves were meaningless, but Bill liked the tone. It was warm and almost affectionate.

'I wonder could I take you to dinner one night?' he asked.

He had thought this out carefully. A girl like Nan must get asked to hops, and to pubs and to parties and to cinemas all the time. He wanted to move it one grade up the ladder.

'Thank you, Bill.' The smile was still warm. 'I don't go out very much. I'm a real dull stick. I study a bit during the week, you see. In order to keep up.'

He was surprised and disappointed. He had thought dinner would work.

'Perhaps we could dine at a weekend, then. When you're not so tied up.'

'Saturdays, I usually go to the debate, and then down to the Four Courts. It's become a bit of a ritual.' She smiled apologetically.

Bill Dunne wasn't going to beg. He knew that would get him nowhere.

'I'll catch you at one of those rendezvous then,' he said loftily, refusing to let his pique be seen.

Nan's room became her living quarters. She had an electric kettle there and two mugs. She took her tea with lemon, so there was no need for milk and sugar.

Sometimes her mother came in and sat with her.

'It's peaceful in here,' Emily said.

'That's why I wanted it this way.'

'He's still annoyed.' Nan's mother sounded as if she were about to plead.

'He has no reason to be, Em, I am perfectly polite always. He's the one who uses the language and loses control of himself.'

'Ah, if only you understood.'

'I do. I understand that he can be two different people. I don't have to be dependent on his moods. So I won't be. I won't sit down there wondering when he'll come home and what condition he'll be in.'

There was a silence.

'Neither should you, Em,' Nan said at last.

'It's easy for you. You're young and beautiful. You've the world ahead of you.'

'Em, you're only forty-two. You've a lot of the world ahead of you.'

'Not as a runaway wife, I wouldn't.'

'And anyway you don't want to run away,' Nan said.

'I want *you* to be away from it.'

'I will be, Em.'

'You don't go out with any young men. You never go out on dates.'

'I'm waiting.'

'What for?'

'For the Prince, the white knight, the Lord, or whatever it was you said would come.'

Emily looked at her daughter, alarmed.

'You know what I meant. Something much better than here. Something far above Maple Gardens. You meet people amongst your friends, these law students, these young engineers . . . these boys with fathers who have big positions.'

'That's only the same as Maple Gardens except a bit more garden and a downstairs cloakroom.'

'What do you mean?'

'I haven't held on to this dream just to end up in another Maple Gardens, Em, with another nice fellow who'd turn out to be a drinker like Dad.'

'Hush, don't say that.'

'You asked me. I told you.'

'Yes, I know. But what do you hope to get?'

'What you told me I'd get, anything I wanted.'

She looked so proud and confident there at her desk, her mug of tea in her hand, her blonde hair back from her brow, her face unruffled by the kind of conversation they were having.

'You could too.' Emily felt the belief she had always held in her heart soar back again.

'So there's no point in going out with the people I don't want to live amongst. It's only a waste of time.'

Emily shivered. 'There could be some very, very nice people in all that number.'

'There could, but not what you and I want.'

Emily's glance fell on the desk and amongst Nan's books and files were magazines, *The Social and Personal, The Tatler, Harpers and Queen*. There were even books of etiquette borrowed from the library. Nan Mahon was studying a great deal more than First Arts.

Mrs Healy looked through the thick net curtains and saw Simon Westward getting out of his car. He had his small stocky sister with him. Perhaps he was going to take her into the hotel for a lemonade. Mrs Healy had long admired the young Squire, as she called him. Indeed she had half harboured some little notions about him. He was a man of around thirty, within a few years of her own age.

She was a fine substantial widow in the town, a person of impeccable reputation. Not exactly his social class of course, and not the right religion. But Mrs Healy was a practical woman. She knew that when people were as broke as the Westwards would appear to be a lot of the old standards might not be as firm as they used to be.

She knew that Simon Westward owed Shea's since last Christmas for the drink he had bought to cover the Hunt and what they called the Boxing Day party. Many a traveller came and had a drink in Healy's Hotel and spoke indiscreetly because he would have thought that the lofty and distant landlady had not the remotest interest in the tittle-tattle of the neighbourhood.

In most cases they would have been correct, but in terms of the Westwards, Mrs Healy had always been interested. She had grown up in England where the Big House had always been much more a part of the town. It had never ceased to amaze her, back home again in her native land, that nobody seemed to know or care about the doings up at Westlands. .

To her disappointment the Westwards went into Hogan's Gentleman's Outfitters cross the road.

What could they want there? Surely they would deal in Callaghan's up in Dublin, or Elvery's. But perhaps credit had run out in those places. Maybe they were going to try locally where a man as nice as Eddie Hogan would never ask to see the colour of their money before lifting the bale of material down from the shelf and starting to write the measurements into his book.

From the inside of his dark shop, peering through his dark window with its bales of materials and its shutters that never fully opened, Eddie Hogan saw with delight that Simon Westward and his small sister were coming into the premises. He wished he had time to smarten the place up.

'You'll never guess . . . ' he began to whisper at Sean.

'I know,' Sean Walsh hissed back.

'It's very dark,' Heather complained, screwing up her eyes to get used to the change from the bright winter sunshine outside.

'Shush.' Her brother didn't want her to seem rude.

'This is an honour,' Eddie Hogan said.

'Ah good morning, Mr . . . Hogan, isn't it?'

'Of course it is,' Heather said. 'It's written outside.'

Simon looked annoyed; Heather immediately became repentant.

'Sorry,' she muttered, looking at the ground.

'It is indeed Edward Hogan at your service and this is my assistant, Sean Walsh.'

'How do you do, Mr Walsh.'

'Mr Westward,' Sean bowed slightly.

'I'm afraid after all that, it's only something rather small. Heather wants to buy a present for my grandfather. It's his birthday. Just a token.'

'Ah yes. Might I suggest some linen handkerchiefs.' Eddie Hogan began to produce boxes of them, and open a drawer where they were stocked singly.

'He's got more hankies then he knows what to do with,' Heather explained. 'And he's not great at blowing his nose anyway.'

'A scarf, maybe?' Eddie Hogan was desperate to please.

'He doesn't go out, you see. He's very, very old.'

'It's a puzzler all right.' Eddie scratched his head.

'I thought you might have some sort of gewgaws,' Simon said, smiling from one man to the other. 'It doesn't really matter what. Grandfather isn't really in a position to appreciate anything . . . but . . . you know.' With a flick of his head he indicated Heather, who was prowling earnestly around the shop.

Eddie Hogan had now ventured into the whole problem. 'Might I suggest, Miss Westward, if it's something just to give your grandfather a feeling of pleasure that you remembered him and marked his birthday, you might think in terms of sweets, rather than clothing.'

'Yes.' Heather was doubtful.

'I know I may appear to be turning business away, but we want to think of what's best for everyone. A little box of jellies possibly. Birdie Mac would wrap it up nicely and you could get a card.'

Simon looked at him with interest. 'Yes, that's probably much more sensible. Silly of us not to see it. Thanks.'

He must have seen the look of naked disappointment on Eddie Hogan's face. 'Sorry to have bothered you, Mr Hogan, wasting your time and everything.'

Eddie eagerly looked back at the small dark confident young man.

'It was an honour, as I said, Mr Westward,' he said foolishly. 'And maybe now that you've been in our place you'll come back again.'

'Oh, undoubtedly.' Simon held the door open for his sister and escaped.

'That was very clever of you, Mr Hogan,' Sean Walsh said approvingly. 'Putting him under a compliment to us.'

'I was only trying to think of a present for the little girl to give her grandfather,' Eddie Hogan said.

Thursday arrived. Benny looked at herself in the bathroom mirror. She stared long and hard. There was a possibility that she had lost some weight around her shoulders. Only a possibility, and even if it were true what a useless place to lose it.

She had washed her hair the night before and it looked nice and shiny. The skirt that Peggy Pine had said might crush, did indeed crush. It looked awful. But it was a lovely blue colour, not like all the sensible navy and brown that she had worn like a school uniform. The kind of colours that wouldn't draw attention to you. The blouse looked a bit raggy too, not like the heavy ones she normally wore. But it was much more feminine. If she were sitting across a table from a gorgeous man like Jack Foley he would have nothing to look at except her top. She *had* to have something fancy, not look as if she were a governess or a school prefect.

Her heart soared and plummeted a dozen times as she dressed. He had been so easy and natural that day he was here in Knockglen. But in college it was different. You always heard people talking about him as if he were some kind of Greek god. Even real Holy Marys in her class spoke of him. These were girls with straight hair and glasses and shabby cardigans, who worked harder than the nuns and seemed to have no time for fellows or a social life, even those kind of girls knew of Jack Foley.

And he was asking her out today. She'd love to tell Rosemary. She would really adore to see her face. And lots of them, she'd love to go up to Carroll's shop now and kick on the door and tell horrible Maire Carroll who used to call her names at school how well things were turning out. Maire who didn't get called to the Training College like she had thought, and was sulking in her parents' grocery shop, while Benny would be having lunch in the Dolphin with Jack Foley.

Benny folded the flimsy blouse up and put it in her big shoulder bag. She also put in a small tube of toothpaste and a toothbrush, her mother's Blue Grass talcum powder, which she would say she had borrowed by mistake if it were noticed. It was seven thirty-five. In six hours' time she would be sitting opposite him. Please God may she not talk too much and say stupid things that she'd regret. And if she did say stupid things let her remember not to give a great laugh after them.

She felt a flicker of guilt that she hadn't told Eve about the outing. It was the first time she had kept anything from her friend. But there hadn't been time, and she was afraid that Eve would tell Nan – there was no reason not to after all. And Nan would have been great and lent her a nice handbag or a pair of earrings to match her skirt. But she didn't want it all planned and set up. She wanted to do it on her own, and be herself. Or sort of herself. Benny smiled wryly at her reflection. It wasn't exactly her own ordinary self that would walk into the Dolphin in six hours' time. It was a starved over-polished shiny Benny who hadn't given one minute's thought to her books for the last ten days.

'I wish you'd tell me what's wrong with the porridge, Benny.' Patsy was on her own in the kitchen when Benny came down.

'Nothing, Patsy, I swear.'

'It's just that if ever I married I'd want to be able to put a decent pot of porridge for a man and his mother on the stove.'

'His mother?'

'Well, I'd have to marry in somewhere, wouldn't I? I've nowhere for anyone to marry into.'

'Do you fancy anyone, Patsy?'

'Divil a point in yourself or myself fancying anyone. I haven't a penny to bless myself with, and you'd have to be sure he'd be a grand big ox of a fellow the size of yourself,' said Patsy cheerfully.

Somehow the morning passed. Benny skipped her twelve o'clock lecture. She didn't want to have to run through the Green, down Grafton Street and round by the Bank of Ireland in order to be in the Dolphin at one fifteen. She would be able to do it, but she didn't want to arrive flushed and panting. She would walk down slowly and take her ease. Then at the last moment she would change somewhere nearby in the ladies' cloakroom of a pub or a coffee shop and put on more talcum powder and brush her teeth. She would look so relaxed and unfussed.

She pitied the people she saw as she walked slowly through the Dublin streets. They looked grey and harassed. They had their heads down against the wind that blew instead of holding themselves high and facing it as Benny did. They were all going to have dull ordinary things at lunch. Either they would go home on a bus to a house where the radio would be on and children were crying, or they would queue up for a meal in a city restaurant where it would be crowded and the smell of other people's dinners would be unattractive.

She checked herself finally, and decided she was as good as she could be. She should of course have started the diet much earlier. Like maybe three years ago. But there was no point in crying over that.

She had been big and fat when he had met her in Knockglen only a couple of weeks ago. It hadn't stopped him asking her out in a place like this. She looked up at the Dolphin unbelievingly. He hadn't said which part. She knew his letter off by heart. But he must mean the hall.

There were three men in the entrance. None of them was Jack. They were much older. They were wealthy looking, possibly people who went racing.

She saw with the shock that comes with recognition that one of them was Simon Westward.

'Oh, hallo,' said Benny, forgetting she didn't actually know him, just all about him from Eve.

'Hallo,' he was polite but mystified.

'Oh, Benny Hogan, from the shop in Knockglen.'

She spoke naturally, with no resentment at not being recognized. Simon's smile was warm now.

'I was in your father's shop yesterday.'

'He told me. With your little sister.'

'Yes, he's a very courteous man, your father. And his assistant . . . ?'

'Oh, yes.' Benny wasn't enthusiastic.

'Not the same type of person?'

'Not at all, but you couldn't tell my father that. He thinks he's fine.'

'No boys in the family to help him run it?'

'No, only me.'

'And do you live in Dublin?'

'Oh, I wish I did. No, I go up and down every day.'

'It must be exhausting. Do you drive?'

Simon lived in a different world, Benny decided.

'Only on the bus,' she said.

'Still it makes it a bit better if you can have nice lunches in a place like this . . .' He looked around him approvingly.

'This is the first time I've been here. I said I'd meet someone. Do you think I should wait in the hall?'

'The bar, I think,' he said, pointing.

Benny thanked him and went in. It was crowded but she saw him immediately over in a corner . . . He was waving.

'There she is!' Jack cried. 'Now we're all complete.'

He was standing up smiling at her, from the middle of a group of seven people. It wasn't a date. It was a party. There were to be eight people. And one of them was Rosemary Ryan.

Benny didn't really remember much about the party before they went into the dining room. She felt dizzy, partly with the shock and partly with the lack of food over the past few days. She looked wildly to see what the others were drinking. Some of them had glasses of club orange, but it could have been gin and orange. The boys had glasses of beer.

'I'd like one of those.' She pointed weakly to a beer glass.

'Good old Benny, one of the lads,' said Bill Dunne, a boy she had always liked before. Now she would have liked to pick up the heavy glass ashtray and beat him over the head with it until she was perfectly sure he was dead.

They were all chatting easily and happily. Benny's eyes raked the other girls. Rosemary was as usual looking as if she had come out from under the hair dryer and hours of ministration in the poshest place in Dublin. Her make-up was perfect. She smiled at everyone admiringly. Carmel was small and pretty. She had been going out with her boyfriend Sean since they were sixteen or maybe even fifteen. They were known as the college's Perfect Romance. Sean looked at Carmel with adoration and he listened to every word she said as if it were a pronouncement. Carmel was no threat. She would have eyes for nobody, not even Jack Foley.

Aidan Lynch, the long lanky fellow who had taken Eve to the pictures, was there too. Benny breathed a prayer of relief that she had told nobody about what she had thought was her date. How foolish she would have felt had the story got around. But of course Aidan would tell Eve that Benny was there, and Eve might very reasonably wonder why nothing had been mentioned. Benny felt cross and hurt and confused.

The other girl was called Sheila. She was a law student. A pale sort of girl, Benny thought, looking at her savagely; pale and rather dull-featured. But she was small. God, she was small. She had to look up at Jack Foley, not over at him like Benny did. She remembered Patsy talking about her needing a big ox of a man. She willed the tears back into her eyes.

None of them had ever been there before. It was all Jack's great plan, they said . . . a scheme that would make them well-known, highly respected personages here by the time they qualified. Lots of lawyers and a lot of racing people met there. The thing to do was to establish yourself as a regular.

The words of the menu swam in front of Benny. She was going to eat real food for the first time in ten days. She knew it would choke her.

She was sitting between Aidan Lynch and the wordless Sean when the final seating arrangements had been made. Jack Foley was between Rosemary and Sheila across the table from her. He looked boyish and pleased, delighted with his notion of getting the four boys to pay for a smart lunch like this.

The others were pleased with him too.

'I must say you went out and plucked the best of the bunch for us to be seen with,' Aidan Lynch said extravagantly.

155

Faithless pig, Benny thought to herself, remembering that he had sworn such undying devotion to Eve Malone earlier in the week.

'Only the best is good enough.' Jack's smile was warm and included everyone.

Benny's hand was reaching for the butter, but she pulled back. To her fury, Bill Dunne saw her.

'Ah, go on, Benny, hanged for a sheep as a lamb,' he said, pushing the butter dish towards her.

'You should see the marvellous teas that go on the table in Benny's house,' Jack said, trying to praise her. 'I was down there not long ago and you never saw the style. Scones and savouries and tarts and cakes, and that was just an ordinary day.'

'That's the country for you. They like to feed them up down there. Not like us poor starved Town Mice,' Aidan said.

Benny looked around them. The thin blouse with the frills had been no good, nor had the blue skirt. The waft of Blue Grass that she could feel coming from under her arms and down the front of her bra. She wasn't the kind of girl that people would admire and want to protect like they felt about Rosemary Ryan and the little loving Carmel and the pale but interesting Sheila from the Law Faculty. Benny had been brought along only as a joky person. Someone that they'd all talk to about big feeds and being hanged for a sheep as well as a lamb.

She smiled a brave smile.

'That's it, Aidan. You come down to Knockglen and we'll fatten you all right. You'd be like one of those geese that they stuff so that they'll have nice livers.'

'Benny, please.' Rosemary fluttered her lashes and looked as if she were going to come over all faint.

But Bill Dunne was now interested. 'Yeah, we could be seeing Lynch's Liver on menus.'

Jack was entering into it, too. 'A Knockglen speciality. Fattened fifty miles from Dublin,' he said.

'I'd have to go into hiding. They'd want me dead, not alive. God, Benny, what have you got planned out for me?'

'But think of what a delicacy you'd be,' said Benny. Her cheeks were glowing. Fattened fifty miles from Dublin. Had Jack really said that? Had he meant it as a joke about her? The most important thing was not to seem hurt.

'It's a high price to pay.' Aidan was looking thoughtful as if he were considering it as a serious possibility.

'I think it's all rather awful to joke about raising poor defenceless animals to eat them,' Rosemary said, looking fragile.

Benny wished she could remember what Rosemary had ordered. But she didn't need to. Jack did.

'Come on, that's hypocritical,' he said. 'You've ordered veal chops . . . the calves didn't exactly enjoy getting ready to become that, now did they?'

He smiled at her across the table. The knight who had come to her rescue.

Rosemary sulked and pouted a little, but when nobody took any notice she recovered.

Rosemary and Sheila competed all during the meal for Jack's attention. Carmel only cared what her Sean thought of this or that item on the menu; they ate little pieces from each other's plates. Benny entertained Bill Dunne and Aidan Lynch as if she had been a hired cabaret. She worked at it until she could feel beads of sweat on her forehead. She was rewarded with their attention and their laughter. She could see Jack straining to join in at times, but he seemed pinioned by the warring women on each side.

The less she tried to seek his attention, the more he tried to engage her in chat. It was obvious that he liked her company, but only as someone who was a load of fun. With a smile that nearly cracked her face Benny knew inside that Jack Foley liked to be where there was laughter, and good times. He wouldn't in a million years have thought of asking someone like Benny out alone.

Simon Westward passed the table.

'See you back in Knockglen sometime,' he said to Benny.

'Who's he? He's rather splendid?' Rosemary asked. She seemed to be losing slightly on points to Sheila who had the advantage of being able to compare notes about lecturers with Jack. Rosemary must have decided on the making-him-jealous route.

'He's one of the ones we didn't manage to fatten up properly in Knockglen,' she said.

The others all laughed at this, but Jack didn't.

'Don't knock Knockglen,' he said softly.

He had said that before to her. This time he seemed to be saying something else.

Mossy Rooney worked on the roof of the cottage over the quarry. There had been a high wind and eleven slates had been lifted right off. They probably lay in smithereens now at the foot of the quarry.

He had been asked by Mother Francis to come urgently and repair the damage.

The nun came up and watched anxiously as he worked out what needed to be done.

'It won't be very dear, will it, Mossy?'

'Not to you, Mother Francis.' His face was expressionless as always.

'But you must be paid for your work.' She looked worried.

'It won't bankrupt you and the Order,' he said.

Never once did he hint that it was odd of the convent to maintain a small house up here that nobody used. By nothing in his tone was there any trace of surprise that a place which had seen two deaths nearly two decades ago was still kept as a kind of shrine for a young rossie who was above in Dublin getting a university education, if you don't mind, and never came next or near the place.

Mossy wasn't a person to speculate about things like that. And even if he were, his mind was too busy. He had another thought in it.

He might ask Patsy to meet his mother. He was collecting information about her first. He didn't want to get into anything he might have to extricate himself from later . . .

'Simon, will you come and see me at school?'

'What?' He was studying a ledger.

'You heard. You only say "what" to give yourself time to think,' Heather said.

'I can't, Heather. I have far too much to do here.'

'You haven't,' she grumbled. 'You're always going to Dublin. Even to England. Why can't you stop for a day and come and see me? It's awful. You've no idea. It's like a prison.'

'No it's not, it's perfectly all right. All school is boring. It gets better when you get older.'

'Did yours?'

'What?' He laughed. 'Yes, it did. Look, the holidays come quickly. You're having a lovely half-term now, and then you'll be back for Christmas before you know it.' His smile was very broad.

'Haven't we any other relations? They only let relations come.'

'Not here, you know that.'

They had cousins in England and in Northern Ireland. But Simon, Heather and their old grandfather were the only surviving members of the Westward family to live on the big estate in Westlands.

Nobody ever said it, but the crazed crying out of Jack Malone praying that none of the family should die in their beds seemed to have been heeded. There were very few Westwards about.

'I saw your friend Benny yesterday, I expect she told you,' Aidan Lynch said to Eve as he sat patiently in Kit Hegarty's kitchen waiting for the washing-up to be finished so that they could go out.

'Take a tea towel, Einstein, and we'll be finished quicker,' Eve said.

'She didn't tell you, then?'

'Amazingly no. You may find this hard to believe but a day passed by in the forest without a record of your movements being sent by the tomtoms.'

'I thought she might have dropped it, after all it isn't every day one goes to the Dolphin.'

'Benny was in the Dolphin?'

'And I was, I was there, don't forget about me.'

'It's not easy,' Eve admitted.

'Perhaps she was covering up for me.'

Eve had lost interest in Aidan's ramblings, she was much more curious as to what Benny had been doing in the Dolphin. ·

'Was she eating anything?' she enquired.

'Like a horse. She ate everything before her,' he said.

'I didn't know you knew Jack Foley,' Rosemary said next day to Benny.

'Not very well.'

'Well enough for him to go to tea with you in Knockglen.'

'Oh, he was just passing through. His father had to see someone.'

Rosemary wasn't satisfied. 'Are they family friends then?'

'No. It was a nice lunch, wasn't it?'

'Yes, it was. Aidan Lynch is an awful eejit, isn't he?'

'I think he's rather nice. He takes a friend of mine to the pictures now and then. She says he's great fun.'

Rosemary Ryan did not look convinced.

'Sean and Carmel would make you sick, wouldn't they, all that gooey stuff.'

'They seem very well settled certainly.' Benny's eyes were dancing with mischief.

She knew the next attack would be on Sheila.

'Did you know that one, Sheila, from the BCL course before?'

'No.' Benny's face was innocent. 'She seemed to be very well up in all her studies. I thought they all seemed very fond of her.'

Rosemary returned to her notes in disgust. Benny noticed that she had a bar of Fruit and Nut and nibbled at it from time to time. Comfort eating is what that was. Benny knew it well.

Bryan Mahon was very drunk on Friday night. Nan heard only some of it. She locked her door and turned on her radio so that she couldn't hear what was being said. She knew her mother wasn't a whore, and so did Paul and so did Nasey. So did her father when he was sober. But when he was drunk he seemed to want to say at the top of his voice that not only was she a whore but a frigid one and that the sooner people realized this the better. Nan also knew that her mother would never leave the home where such humiliations were forced on her with ever greater frequency.

'It's for you, Eve.' One of Kit's students answered the phone on Saturday morning.

'Oh, good.' Eve hoped it was Benny. Maybe she would go down to Knockglen on the lunch-time bus. Kit had said that she was free to go whenever she wanted.

But it wasn't Benny. It was Nan.

'Can I tempt you out for a walk today?'

'Yes, that would be nice. Will I come in your way and learn a bit of that side of town? I could pick you up.'

'No.' Nan spoke sharply. Then her voice softened. 'Anyway

it's much nicer out your side. We could go down the pier. I'll pick *you* up.'

'Sure.'

Eve felt a vague sense of disappointment. She would have preferred it to be Benny saying she'd meet her off the bus.

Five minutes later Benny rang. But it was too late now.

'Can't you ring Nan and tell her you're coming home?'

'I can't. I don't have her number. Do you?'

'No.' Benny too had hoped that Eve would come back.

'You never told me you were at the Dolphin,' Eve challenged.

'I was going to tell you all about it.'

'Not only that, but threatening to pickle Aidan's liver.'

'I had to say something.'

'Why?'

'They expected me to.'

'They sure as hell didn't expect you to say that,' Eve said. 'But they seemed to enjoy it. And are you back on your food again?'

'Oh yes. Patsy's making currant bread here. You should smell it.'

Nan wore a white pleated skirt and a dark green jacket. The boys who were in the digs looked up with great interest when she came in.

Kit Hegarty too looked at her with interest. She was indeed a striking young woman. Most of all because she seemed so much in control of herself. She spoke in a low clear voice as if she expected that others would listen without her having to make any effort.

She went to Eve's bedroom with her and Kit could hear her exclaiming with admiration.

'A sea view as well. Lord, you are lucky, Eve.'

With the familiar feeling of loss she always felt, Kit heard Eve explain, 'It used to be Frank Hegarty's room. I wanted to keep some of his things around it, but Kit said no.'

'What are you going to wear?' Nan asked.

'Why? It's only a walk on the pier!' Eve protested.

'Everywhere's only a walk somewhere. So that you look nice. That's why.'

Kit Hegarty heard Eve sigh, and the door close as she

changed into the red blazer and red tartan skirt which really did look nice on her, and went well with her dark colouring.

But Kit in her heart agreed with Eve. It was only a walk on the pier. Nan was making it seem like a public appearance. Maybe that's what she did everywhere.

They walked companionably along with the crowds from Dublin, among people who had come out from Dublin City to walk off the effects of lunch or who were trying to keep children and mothers-in-law entertained.

'Look at those kids,' Nan said suddenly, pointing out a crocodile of small schoolgirls walking purposefully with two well-wrapped-up women teachers.

'What about them?' Eve asked.

'Look, one of them's waving at you.'

Eve looked over. It was true, one of the small blue-clad figures was making great signs.

'Eve, hallo Eve,' she called behind her hand so as not to alert the teachers.

'Who is she?' Nan asked.

'No idea.' Eve looked bewildered. The child was wearing a school beret and had a round face, snub nose and freckles. Then Eve saw the two bunches of hair, one on each side of the head like two jug handles.

It was Heather Westward. Simon's little sister.

'Oh hallo,' Eve said lamely, and without much enthusiasm.

'Do you live near here?' the girl hissed at her.

'Why?' Eve was wary.

'I was wondering would you come and take me out some time. Just for a bit?'

Eve looked at her dumbstruck. 'Take you out? Where? What for?'

'Anywhere. I'd be no trouble.'

'Why me?'

'We can only go out with relations. You're my cousin. Please?'

'I can't. It's not possible.'

'Yes, it is. If you phoned the school and said you're my cousin.'

'But your brother?'

'He never comes up. He's too busy at home. Trying to organize things.'

'Your other relations?'

'I don't have any.'

The crocodile which had been pausing to look at the big mail boat moored at the jetty was now moving on. The teachers were shepherding them for the off.

'Please,' called Heather Westward.

Eve stood there wordlessly looking after them.

'Well?' Nan asked her.

'I suppose I'll have to,' Eve said.

'Of course you will.'

'She's only a child. You can't disappoint a child,' Eve said crossly.

'And it would be foolish. Look at all the housepoints you'd get.'

'Housepoints?'

'Well, they'll have to ask you to the Big House if you're a friend of Heather's. And they'll owe you. Don't forget that. You won't be going cap in hand any more.'

'I won't go there, anyway, cap or no cap.'

'Yes you will,' said Nan Mahon firmly. 'And what's more you'll take me with you.'

CHAPTER NINE

Peggy Pine regarded the arrival of her niece Clodagh as something of a mixed blessing. The girl wore very, very short skirts; she was loud and flamboyant. She had worked for two years in shops in Dublin and spent a summer in London. According to her aunt she felt herself a world authority on dress and the buying habits of the female population.

There was much about her aunt's shop she was going to change.

'She *might* be a nice friend for you,' Annabel Hogan told Benny, weighing it up. 'But we should wait and see. She might be altogether too flighty for Knockglen, from what Peggy says, and indeed from first impressions.'

'Oh, Sean up in the shop is full of disapproval of her,' Eddie Hogan observed.

'Then I like her already,' Benny chimed in.

'You need a friend now that you don't see Eve any more,' Annabel said.

Benny's eyes flashed. 'What do you mean, Mother? Don't I see Eve three or four times a week in college?'

'But it's not the same,' her mother said. 'She never comes home here any more, and she has her own friends out in Dunlaoghaire in that house she works in. And there's this Nan. You never say Eve any more, it's always Eve and Nan.'

Benny was silent.

'It was only to be expected,' her mother consoled. 'And you'll make lots of new contacts, where you need them. Round here.'

'Who have you asked to the dance?' Bill Dunne asked Jack as they walked out of their lecture together. One of the big college dress dances was coming up in a few weeks' time.

'I knew your mind wasn't on constitutional law,' Jack said.

'We have a written Constitution here. No need to upset ourselves about it,' Bill said.

'All the more reason, it would appear. I haven't done anything yet. What about you?'

'I was waiting to see who you were going to ask so that I could pick up the crumbs from the rich man's table.'

'You're a pain. You're beginning to talk as obscurely as Aidan.'

'I think he's all right. He's going to ask Eve Malone, I think, when he gets up enough courage. She's inclined to bite off his head. I'm more interested in knowing what *you're* going to do.'

'I wish I knew.'

'Well ask somebody,' Bill begged, 'and leave the field clear for the rest of us.'

That was the problem. Who should he ask? Jack had been vague any time Shirley phoned. He had been busy disentangling himself there, and Sheila who sat beside him at lectures had dropped fairly heavy hints. But the gorgeous Rosemary Ryan had rung him only last week saying she had two free tickets to a show which meant of course that she had gone out and bought two tickets for a show, but didn't want him to know that.

And Nan Mahon had smiled a lot at him across the Annexe and the main hall and places where she had been and he had been. He would like to ask her in many ways. She was so lovely and yet so unattainable.

Suddenly he had an inspiration.

'I know what we'll do,' he said to Bill Dunne, banging him on the arm enthusiastically. 'We'll ask them all. All the girls we fancy. Tell them to pay for themselves, and then we'll have our pick.'

'We couldn't do that!' Bill gasped at the audaciousness of the plan. 'It would be very mean. They wouldn't say yes. They'd go with fellows who'd pay for them.'

'We could have a little party first.' Jack was thinking on his feet.

'Where? You're not going to get girls in evening dress to go into Dwyer's or Hartigan's.'

'No, in a house.'

'Whose house?'

'Mine, I suppose,' Jack said.

'Why can't you just take a girl to a dance like every normal boy?' Jack's father grumbled.

'I don't know who to take,' Jack said simply and truthfully.

'It's not committing you for life, there won't be a breach of promise action if you take the wrong girl to a dance in your first term.'

'I thought that you both might like to use the opportunity . . . ?' Jack looked hopefully from his mother to his father.

'Use it for what, might one ask?' Lilly Foley asked.

'Well, you know, the way you're always saying that you mean to have people in for drinks . . .'

'Yes . . . ?'

'And you know the way you're always grousing that you never meet any of my friends . . .'

'Yes . . . ?'

'I thought you could have a sherry party on the night of the dance, and sort of kill two birds . . . ?'

Jack's smile was very powerful. In minutes it was all agreed.

Rosemary Ryan offered Benny a peppermint. She must be about to divulge some information or do some detective work. Benny wondered which it was. It turned out to be both.

'Jack Foley's asked me to the big dance,' she said.

'Oh, that's nice.' Benny's heart was like lead.

'Yes, well I did tell you earlier in the term I was sort of making him my project.'

'You did indeed.'

'I think it's a large party.'

'Well, they usually are, I hear,' Benny said. She had heard little else in conversations in the Ladies' Reading Room and overheard in the cloakrooms and the cafés. People went to the dress dances in parties of ten or twelve. The boys decided on the groupings and the girls were their guests. The tickets were about twenty-one shillings, and there was dinner, and everyone danced with everyone else apparently, but with their own special date most of all and at the end.

She had a vain hope that Aidan Lynch might get up a party for it and include her. But then he couldn't really unless she had been asked by some other fellow. Those were the rules.

Rosemary was chewing her pencil as well as the peppermint.

'It's a bit odd, though. It's like a big group, and we're all meeting at Jack's house first. I was wondering were you going?'

'Not as far as I know.' Benny was cheery.

'You weren't asked?'

'No, not as yet. When were *you* asked?'

'About an hour ago,' Rosemary admitted grumpily.

'Oh well, then, there's every hope.' Benny wondered did your face break by putting these false smiles on.

After the lecture she met Jack Foley in the main hall by chance.

'Just the girl I was looking for. Will you join our group? It's a sort of Dutch party for the big dance.'

'Lovely,' Benny said. 'Will we dress in clogs?'

'No, I meant like we all sort of get our own tickets.' Jack looked embarrassed.

'That makes much more sense, then we can all be free as birds,' she said.

He looked at her, surprised. 'Birds?'

'Different kinds of birds. Sparrows, emus, but free,' she said, wondering was she actually going mad to be having this stupid conversation.

'You'll come then?'

'I'd love to.'

'And we'll have drinks in my house. I'll write down the address. My parents are having friends of their own age in. Would your parents like to come, do you think?'

'No.' Her voice was like a machine gun. 'No, what I mean is thank you, but they hardly ever come up to Dublin.'

'This might be the excuse they need.' He was politely courteous. He had no idea how much she would hate them there.

'It's very kind of you, but I think not. However, I certainly would love it.'

'That's great,' he said, pleased. 'We need someone to cheer us up in these dim and dismal days.'

'Ah, I'm the one for that,' Benny said. 'Never short of a word, that's me.'

The wind lifted his hair, and his shirt collar stood high around his neck over his navy sweater, coming out over his navy jacket. He looked so handsome she wanted to reach out and stroke him.

His smile seemed as if he had never smiled for anyone else in the world.

'I'm really glad you're going to be there,' he said.

'Stop looking as if you're going to your execution,' Kit said to Eve. 'She's only a child.'

'In a big posh Protestant school,' Eve grumbled.

'Not at all. It's shabbier than our own, I can tell you.'

'Still, full of airs and graces.'

'She can't have that many airs and graces. She wouldn't have begged an old misery boot like you to come and see her.'

Eve grinned. 'That's true. It's just we won't have anything to say to each other.'

'Why don't you bring a friend? It might be easier.'

'Oh God, Kit, who could I bring on an outing like this?'

'Aidan Lynch?'

'No, he'd frighten the wits out of her.'

'Nan?'

'Not Nan,' Eve said.

Kit looked up sharply.

There was something about Eve's tone that meant the matter was closed. Mother Francis had warned Kit about this. She said that Eve had areas where nobody followed her.

Eve was now miles away from the conversation. She was thinking about what Nan had said, using the child to get accepted into the life at Westlands.

It wasn't a joke either. She had meant it. She had said that she would go down to Knockglen and stay with Benny if there was a chance of meeting the Westward family socially.

'But they're a senile old man, a kid and Simon, an uppity fellow with an accent you could cut, who wears riding breeches,' Eve had exclaimed.

'They're a start,' Nan had said perfectly seriously.

It had made Eve shiver to think that someone could be so determined and so cool.

Also so graceful in defeat. When Eve had said that Nan would *never* visit Westlands through her introduction, Nan shrugged.

'Someone else, somewhere else then,' she had said, with her easy smile.

Heather had her coat and beret on when Eve arrived at the school. She was received by the headmistress, a woman with hair cut so short it might have been shaved at the back of her head. How could she have thought this looked attractive,

Eve wondered. It was such an old style, so like pictures in school stories of the way schoolmistresses looked in the twenties and thirties.

'Miss Malone. How good of you to arrive so promptly. Heather has been ready since she got up, I do believe.'

'Good. Well, we said two o'clock.' Eve looked around the parlour. It was so strange to be in a school without pictures of saints everywhere on the walls. No statues, no little Sacred Heart lamps. It didn't feel like a school at all.

'And Heather must return for supper at six, so we like the girls to be back at five forty-five.'

'Of course.' Eve's heart sank. How could she entertain this child for nearly four hours?

'As you suggested, we telephoned Mr Simon Westward, but he wasn't at home. We spoke to Mrs Walsh, the housekeeper, who confirmed that you are indeed a cousin.'

'I just wanted to make sure that they agreed. I haven't been in close contact with the family for a long time.'

'I see,' said the headmistress, who saw only too well. A slightly shabby girl with the surname Malone, that was *indeed* likely to be a relation not in close contact. Still, the housekeeper had said it was all in order.

'Enjoy yourself, Heather, and don't be too much trouble for Miss Malone.'

'Yes, Miss Martin. No, Miss Martin,' Heather said.

Together they walked down the avenue.

There were no words and yet the silence didn't seem uncompanionable.

Eve said, 'I don't know what you'd like to do. What do you normally do when you go out?'

'I've never been out,' Heather said simply.

'So what do you think you'd like to do?'

'I don't mind. Honestly. Anything. Just to be out, to be away from it all is smashing.'

She looked back at the school as an escaped prisoner might.

'Is it awful?'

'It's lonely.'

'Where would you rather be?'

'At home. At home in Knockglen.'

'Isn't that lonely too?'

169

'No, it's lovely. There's my pony Malcolm, and Clara the dog, and Mrs Walsh and Bee and of course Grandfather.'

She sounded enthusiastic when she talked about them all. That big empty house was home. The school full of chattering children her own age and class was prison.

'Would you like an ice cream in a glass?' Eve said suddenly.

'I'd love it. At the end of the afternoon if that would be all right. We have it to look forward to . . . as the crown of the day.'

Eve smiled a big wide smile. 'Right, the crown of the day it will be. In the meantime we'll have a good walk down to the sea to get up an appetite.'

'Can we go near it and feel the spray?'

'Yes, that's the best bit.'

Their legs were tired when they reached the Roman Café.

'They always stop us from going near the spray when we're out on school walks,' Heather said.

'I'll have to tidy you up a bit so that they'll not discover.'

'Are you going to have a Knickerbocker Glory?' Heather asked, studying the menu.

'No, I think I'll just have a coffee.'

'Is Knickerbocker Glory too dear?' Heather asked.

Eve took the menu. 'It's on the dear side, but it is the crown of the day so that's all right.'

'You're not just having coffee because of the cost?' Heather was anxious.

'No, truly. I want a cigarette. It goes better with coffee than ice cream.'

They sat contentedly. Heather chatted about the games at school, lacrosse and hockey.

'Which did you play?' she asked Eve.

'Neither. We played camogie.'

'What's that?'

'Well might you ask! It's a sort of gaelicized version of hockey in a way, or a feminine version of hurley.'

Heather digested this with some interest.

'Why didn't we know you before, Simon and I?' she asked.

'I'm sure you must have asked Simon that, the day I came to your house.'

'I did,' Heather said, truthfully. 'But he said it was a long story.'

'He's right.'

'But it's not a mystery or a crime or anything is it?'

'No,' Eve said thoughtfully. 'No. It's not either of those things. My mother was called Sarah Westward, and I think she may have been wild or a bit odd or something, but whatever caused it she fell in love with a man called Jack Malone. He was the gardener in the convent, and they were mad about each other.'

'Why was that odd?'

'Because she was a Westward and he was a gardener. And anyway they got married, and I was born. And when I was being born my mother died. My father carried me down from the cottage to the convent. The nuns went rushing up to the cottage, but it was too late. They sent for Doctor Johnson and there was a terrible commotion.'

'And what happened then?'

'Well, apparently there was some kind of row and a lot of shouting at my mother's funeral.'

'Who shouted?'

'My father, I believe.'

'What did he shout?'

'Oh, a lot of old rameis . . . rubbishy stuff about some of the Westwards dying in their beds . . . because they hadn't behaved better to Sarah.'

'And where was the funeral?'

'In the Protestant church. Your church. She's buried in your family grave. Under the name Westward, not Malone.'

'And what happened to the cottage?'

'It's still there. It's mine, I suppose. I never use it though.'

'Oh, I know I wouldn't either.

'And was Sarah my aunt?' Heather asked.

'Yes . . . your father was her older brother . . . there were five in the family, I believe.'

'And they're all dead now,' Heather said factually. 'Whatever your father was shouting at that funeral seems to have worked.'

'What happened to your parents?'

'They were killed in India, in a car accident. I don't remember them. Simon does of course, because he's so old.'

'How old is he?'

'He's nearly thirty. I wonder. Did he know all about the

shouting and everything at your mother's funeral? I suppose he was there.'

'He might have been. He'd have been about eleven.'

'I'm sure he was.' Heather was scraping the bottom of her glass.

'I wouldn't necessarily . . .' Eve began.

Heather looked up and their eyes met. 'Oh, I wouldn't tell him all about our conversation,' she said. And changing to something that interested her much more, she leaned across the table eagerly. 'Tell me, is it true that nuns put on shrouds and sleep in their coffins at night like vampires?'

Eddie and Annabel Hogan were pleased that their daughter had been asked to the dance.

'It's nice that it will be just a group of friends going to it, isn't it?' Annabel sought reassurance. 'It's not as if she had a special boy yet that she was keen on or anything.'

'In my day the men took the women to dances, paid for them and went to their houses to pick them up,' Eddie complained.

'Yes, yes, yes, but who's going to come the whole way down to Knockglen to the door and pick Benny up and then deliver her back again? Don't go saying that now, and making trouble where there isn't any.'

'And you're happy enough to let her stay in this boarding house in Dunlaoghaire?' Eddie looked at his wife anxiously.

'It's not a boarding house. There you go again, getting it all wrong. You remember the woman who was down staying with Mother Francis in St Mary's, whose son was killed. That's where Benny will stay. They'll put another bed in Eve's room.'

'Well, as long as you're happy.' He patted her on the hand.

Shep sat between them at the fire, and looked up from one to the other as if pleased to see this touching.

Benny was out at the pictures with Sean Walsh.

'I'm happy enough about her going to the dance and staying with Eve, of course I am. I want her to have a great night, something she'll always remember.'

'What are you not happy about then?'

'I don't know what's going to happen to her. Afterwards.'

'You said she'd go back to this house that isn't a real boarding house.' Eddie was bewildered.

'Not after the dance. After . . . after everything.'

'None of us know what will happen in the future.'

'Maybe we're wrong sending her up there. Maybe she should have done a book-keeping course and gone into the shop with you. Forget all these notions of getting a degree.'

Annabel was chewing her lip now.

'Haven't we been talking about this since she was born?'

'I know.'

They sat in silence for a while. The wind whistled around Lisbeg, and even Shep moved closer to the grate. They told each other they were glad to be indoors on a night like this, in and settled, not out in Knockglen where people were still sorting out their lives. Sean and Benny would be leaving the cinema shortly and going for a cup of coffee at Mario's. Patsy was up with Mrs Rooney being inspected as a suitable candidate for Mossy. Peggy Pine's niece Clodagh was going through the order books with her aunt. People said that it was a fallacy nowadays that the young didn't work. In fact, some young people couldn't stop working. Look at Clodagh, and Fonsie and Sean Walsh. Between them they would change the face of Knockglen in the next ten years.

'I hope they'll change it into a place we'll like to live in,' Eddie said doubtfully.

'Yes, but we won't have all that much longer to live in it. It's Benny we should be thinking about.'

They nodded. It was nearly always Benny that they were thinking about anyway, and what the future had in store. They had lived their whole adult lives in a thirty-mile radius of this place. A huge city like Dublin on their doorstep had never affected them.

They simply couldn't envisage a life for their daughter that didn't revolve around Knockglen, and the main street business of Hogan's Gentleman's Outfitters. And, though they hardly dared speak of the matter to each other, they thought too that it might best revolve around Sean Walsh.

Benny looked across the table in Mario's at Sean Walsh. In the very bright light his face looked thin and pale as always, but she could see the dark circles under his eyes.

'Is it hard work in the shop?' she asked him.

'Not hard, exactly, not in terms of physical work . . . or hours . . . just trying to know what's best, really.'

'How do you mean?'

For the first time ever, Benny was finding it easy to talk to Sean. And it was all thanks to Nan Mahon. Nan, who knew what to do in every situation.

Nan said that Benny should always be perfectly pleasant to Sean. There was nothing to be gained by scoring points off him. She should let him know in a variety of ways that there was no question of ever sharing any kind of life or plans with him, but that he was highly thought of as her father's employee. That way he couldn't fault her, and it would also keep her parents happy.

'I'm sure I'll do it wrong,' Benny had said. 'You know me. I'll think I'm being pleasant and distant, and I'll end up walking up to Father Ross arranging for the banns to be read out.'

But Nan had said it was easy. 'Ask him all about himself, sound interested but don't get involved. Tell him things about yourself that you'd like him to know and never answer any question directly, that's the secret.'

So far it seemed to be working quite well. Sean sat there in Mario's and, raising his voice to compete with Guy Mitchell on the new record player, he told a tale of how the clothing industry was changing and how men were going to Dublin and buying ready-made suits off the peg, and how the bus from Knockglen stopped so near McBirney's on the quays in Dublin it was as bad as if McBirney's had opened a branch next to Mr Flood's.

Sean said that it was sometimes hard to convince Mr Hogan of the need for change. And perhaps not his place to do so.

Benny listened sympathetically with her face and about a quarter of her mind. The rest of her thoughts were on the dance and what she should wear. She was back on her diet again, drinking bitter black coffee instead of the frothy, sugary cups that everyone else in the café was having. She moved the chocolate biscuits on the plate around, making patterns of them with the yellow ones underneath and the green ones on top. She willed her hands not to rip one open and stuff it into her mouth.

There were no dresses big enough for her, in any of the shops in Dublin. Well, there *were*, but not the kind of shops she'd go to. Only places that catered for rich, older women. Dresses with black jet beading on them, or dove grey with cross-over fronts. Suitable for someone in their sixties at a state banquet. Not for Benny's first dance.

Still, there was plenty of time, and there were dressmakers, and there were friends to help. Nan could probably come up with a solution for this as well as everything else. Benny had asked Nan if she could stay the night in her house after the dance.

Nan hadn't said yes or no. She asked why Benny didn't stay with Eve.

'I don't know. It *is* the place she's working, after all.'

'Nonsense. It's her home. You two are old friends, you'd enjoy staying there.'

Perhaps this is what Nan meant by not answering any question directly. Certainly Benny hadn't felt even slightly offended. It would be wonderful to know how to deal with people like Nan did.

Sean was still droning on about the need to have a sale. And the dangers of having a sale. Mr Hogan felt that if a place like Hogan's had a sale it might look to customers as if they were getting rid of shoddy goods. Also what would people who had paid the full price for similar items a few weeks previously think if they saw them reduced now?

Sean saw the reason in this, but he also wondered how you could attract local people to buy their socks and shoes in Hogan's instead of going up to O'Connell Street in Dublin on a daytrip and coming home sliding past the door trying to hide the name Clery's on the package?

Benny looked at him and wondered who would marry him and listen for the rest of her life. She hoped that this new policy of being polite but uninvolved would work.

'What about next week?' Sean said, as he walked her down the town and round the bend of the road to Lisbeg.

'What about it, Sean?' she asked courteously.

'*Jamaica Inn*,' he said triumphantly, having read the posters.

The old Benny would have made a joke and said that Jamaica was a bit far to go on an outing. The new Benny smiled at him.

'Oh, Charles Laughton, isn't it, and Maureen O'Hara?'

'Yes,' Sean said, a trifle impatiently. 'You haven't seen it, I don't remember it being here before.'

175

Never answer a question directly. 'I loved the book. But I think I preferred *Rebecca*. Did you read *Rebecca*?'

'No, I don't do much reading. The light's not very good up there.'

'You should have a lamp,' Benny said eagerly. 'I'm sure there's one in the spare room we never use. I'll mention it to Father.'

She beamed such enthusiasm for this helpful idea, and put out her hand so firmly to shake his, that he couldn't press her for a yes or a no about the pictures next week. Nor could he press his cold, thin lips on hers with any dignity at all.

Mother Francis moved around the small cottage. She had been very heartened by Kit Hegarty's report on the meeting between Eve and Heather. Perhaps the way to a reconciliation was opening up after all. The agreement to pay the fees had done nothing to soften Eve's heart to the cold distant family who had treated her mother, her father and herself so shabbily.

In some ways it had almost strengthened her resolve not to give in to them in any way.

If only Mother Francis could get her to stay a night in this cottage, to sleep here, to feel the place was her own. If Eve Malone were to wake in this place and look out over the quarry she might feel she belonged somewhere rather than perching here and there, which was what she felt now. Mother Francis had high hopes that she might be able to install Eve by Christmas. But it was work of high sensitivity.

It would be no use pretending that she needed Eve's room in the convent. That would be the worst thing to do. The girl would feel she had been evicted from the only home she knew. Perhaps Mother Francis could say that the older members of the Community would like a little outing and that since they couldn't leave the convent grounds perhaps Eve might arrange a tea party for them in her cottage. But Eve would see through that at once.

When Mother Francis and Peggy Pine were young together, Peggy used to say, 'It will all come clear in the end.'

Mainly it had. This cottage was an area where it had taken a long time for things to come clear.

She was always careful to lock the door with the big key, and put it under the third stone in the little wall near the iron gate. There was a big padlock that Mossy had suggested she put on the gate as well, but it looked ugly and forbidding. Mother Francis decided to risk doing without it.

Not many came up this way unless they had business here. Either you came through the briar and bramble-covered paths of the convent or else if anyone wanted a view of the big stone escarpments they chose a much better and broader way which went up at a gradual incline from the square where the bus turned every day.

To her shock, when she turned around she saw a figure standing only a few feet away.

It was Simon Westward. He had his back to her and was looking out over the dark, misty view. She rattled the gate so that he would hear her and not be startled.

'Oh . . . um, good afternoon,' he said.

'Good afternoon, Mr Westward.'

In religious life a part of the day was known as the Great Silence. It meant the nuns did not feel uneasy when there was no conversation. Mother Francis waited easily for the small dark man to speak again.

'Rotten weather,' he said.

'Never very good, November.' She could have been at a garden party instead of on top of a quarry in the mist and rain with a man she had crossed swords with several times.

'Mrs Walsh said you come up here a lot,' he said. 'I told her I didn't feel I'd be quite in place in the convent. I wondered where I might run into you casually, as it were.'

'You'd be very welcome in the convent, Mr Westward, you always would have been.'

'I know. Yes, I know.'

'But anyway you've found me now.'

It would have been more sensible for them to go back into the cottage but there was no way that she would take him over Eve's doorstep. It would have been the final betrayal. He looked at the house expectantly. She said nothing.

'It's about Eve,' he said eventually.

'Oh yes.'

'It's just that she very kindly went and took my sister out from school. I'm afraid Heather very probably asked her to do so, in fact I know she did. But anyway Eve took her on a nice day out and is going to again . . .'

'Yes.' Mother Francis had cold eyes and a heavy heart. Was he going to ask Eve to stay clear of the family? If so, she would have a heart as hard as Eve's.

'I was wondering if you could tell her . . .'

The nun's glance didn't waver.

'If you could tell her how grateful I am. I mean truly.'

'Why don't you tell her yourself?' Mother Francis felt the words come out of her mouth in a quick breath of relief.

'Well, I would, of course. But I don't know where she lives.'

'Let me write it down for you.' She began to seek deep in the pockets of her long black skirt.

'Let me. Farmers always have backs of envelopes to scribble things on.'

She smiled at him. 'No, let *me*. Nuns always have little notebooks and silver-topped pencils.'

She produced both from the depths of her pockets and wrote with a shaking hand what she thought might be the outline plans for an olive branch.

Clodagh Pine came into Hogan's shop.

'How are you, Mr Hogan? Do you have a loan of a couple of hat stands?'

'Of course, of course.' Eddie Hogan went fussing off to the back of the shop to look for them.

'Opening a millinery section are we?' Sean Walsh said to her in a lofty tone.

'Watch your tone with me, Sean. You don't know what you're dealing with here,' she said, with a loud laugh.

Sean looked at her without pleasure. She was pretty, certainly, in a flashy sort of way. But she had her long legs exposed for all to view, in a ridiculously short skirt. She wore a lime-green dress with a black jacket over it, a pink scarf, and her earrings, which were long and dangly, were precisely the same green as her dress, and her very obviously tinted blonde hair was held up with two black combs.

'No, I probably don't.'

'Well, you will,' she said.

There were just the two of them standing in the shop. Old Mikey was at his tailoring and Mr Hogan was out of earshot.

'I'll hardly miss you, that's for sure.'

'You'd be wise not to.' She deliberately misunderstood him. 'We can be rivals or friends. It's probably more sensible to be friends.'

'I'd say everyone's your friend, Clodagh.' He laughed a scornful little laugh.

'You'd be wrong there. A lot of people aren't my friends at all. However, my aunt is. I'm doing a major reorganization of her window. Every notice saying "A Fashion Ship" has already been burned. Wait till you see the new display.'

'On Monday, is it?' He was still superior.

'No, genius. This afternoon, early closing day, the only day anyone really looks in your window. And tomorrow we'll let it rip.'

'I should congratulate you.'

'Yes, you should. It's harder for me coming in than it is for you. I haven't any plans to marry my aunt.'

Sean looked nervously at the back storeroom where Eddie Hogan had found some hat stands and was returning with them triumphantly.

'I'm sure your new windows will be a great success,' he said hastily.

'Yes, they'll be fabulous,' she said. She gave the surprised Eddie Hogan a kiss on the forehead, and was gone in a flash of colour, like a bird of paradise.

'I'm not spending hard-earned money on a dress,' Eve said with a ferocious scowl when Nan started talking about what they would wear.

She expected Nan to tell her that you are how you look, and that you must expect people to take you or leave you on the way you present yourself. It was one of Nan's theories.

'You're right,' Nan said unexpectedly. 'Whatever you buy it shouldn't be an evening dress.'

'So?' Eve was wrong-footed now. She had expected an argument.

'So what will you do?' Nan asked.

'Kit said I can look through her things, just in case. She's taller than I am, but then so's everyone. I could take the hem up, if I found something.'

'Or you could have my red wool skirt,' Nan said.

'I don't think so . . .' Eve began, the prickles beginning to show.

'Well, nobody's seen it in college. Red looks great on you. You could get a fancy blouse or maybe Kit Hegarty has one. Why not?'

'I know it sounds ungrateful, but I suppose it's because I don't want to wear your cast-offs,' Eve said straight out.

'But you wouldn't mind wearing Kit Hegarty's, is that it?' Nan was quick as a flash.

'She offers them because . . . because she knows I wouldn't mind taking them.'

'And what about me? Haven't I got the same motive?'

'I don't know, to be honest.' Eve fiddled with her coffee spoon.

Nan didn't plead with her, and she didn't shrug. Very simply she said, 'It's there, it's nice, it would look well on you.'

'Why are you lending it to me, I mean what's in your mind?' Eve knew she sounded like a five-year-old but she wanted to know.

'Because we're a group of friends going to this dance. I want us to look knock-out. I want us to wipe the eyes of people like that stupid Rosemary and that dull Sheila. That's why!'

'I'd love it,' Eve said, with a grin.

'Mother, would it be awful if I was to ask you for a loan of money, like to get some material for a dress?'

'We'll buy you a dress, Benny. Your first big dance. Every girl should have a new dress from a shop.'

'There isn't one to fit me in the shops.'

'Don't be full of misery like that. I'm sure there is. You haven't looked.'

'I'm not even remotely full of miseries. People don't come in my size until they're old. I don't mind now that I *know*. I used to think people were born with big bones and large frames, but apparently these grow when you're about sixty-eight. You'd better watch it, Mother, it could happen to you.'

'And where did you develop this nonsensical theory, may I ask?'

'After slogging round every shop in Dublin. Lunch times, Mother, I didn't miss my lectures!'

She looked not remotely put out about it, Annabel was relieved to see. Or perhaps she was, inside. With Benny it was hard to tell.

There was nothing to be gained by probing. Benny's mother decided to be practical.

'What material had you in mind?'

'I don't know. Something rich ... I don't know if this is ridiculous, but I saw something in a magazine. She was a biggish woman and it was like tapestry ...'

Benny's smile was broad, but not totally sure.

'Tapestry?' Her mother sounded doubtful.

'Maybe not. It might make me look like a couch or an armchair.'

Annabel wanted to take her daughter in her arms, but she knew she must do nothing of the sort.

'Do you mean brocade?' she asked.

'The very thing.'

'I have a lovely brocade skirt.'

'It wouldn't fit me, Mother.'

'We could get a bit of black velvet let into it, maybe, as panels, and then a top of black velvet and some of the brocade to trim it. What do you think?'

'We couldn't cut up your good skirt.'

'When will I ever wear it again? I'd love you to be the belle of the ball.'

'Are you sure?'

'Of *course* I am. And it's better than anything you'd buy in the shops.'

It was. Benny knew that. Her heart sank though at the thought of what her mother might envisage as a design.

A sudden picture of her tenth birthday flashed before Benny. The day she thought she was going to get a party dress and had been given that sensible navy-blue outfit. The pain of it was as real now as then. But there seemed few alternatives.

'Who'd make it, do you think?'

'Peggy's niece is a great hand with the needle, we hear.'

Benny brightened. Clodagh Pine looked anything but frumpish. The project might not be doomed after all.

Dear Eve,

Just a very brief note to thank you most sincerely for your visit to my sister at her boarding school. Heather has written glowingly of your kindness. I wanted to express my appreciation, but to tell you not to feel in any way obligated to this in consideration of any assistance with fees that this family may have given you. I need hardly add that you are very welcome to call at Westlands during the Christmas vacation should you wish to do so.

Yours in gratitude,
Simon Westward

Dear Simon,

I visit Heather because I want to and she wants me to. It has nothing to do with considerations, as you call them. During the Christmas vacation I shall be in residence at St Mary's Convent, Knockglen. You are very welcome to call there, should you wish to do so.

Yours in explanation,
Eve Malone

Dear Mr and Mrs Hogan,

As Benny may have told you, a group of us are going to the end of term dress dance next Friday week. My parents are having a small sherry party in our house in Donnybrook, where we will all gather before setting off for the dance. They asked me to suggest to some of the parents that they might like to drop in for the drinks party should they be in the area. I realize it is rather far away, but just in case there was a chance, I thought I would mention it.

Thank you again for that wonderful afternoon at your home weeks ago during my visit to Knockglen.

Kind regards,
Jack Foley

Dear Fonsie,

I'm going to have to ask you very firmly to cease writing these notes to me. My aunt thinks there is only one Miss Pine in the world and that she is it. She has read aloud to me your letters about being groovy, and inviting me to where the action is. She has begun to ask me what 'turning someone on' is about, and why do people say 'It's been real'.

I have a healthy respect for my aunt. I have come here to help her modernize her shop and improve her business. I do

not intend to spend every morning listening to her reading
See you later Alligator at me.

I am perfectly happy to meet you and talk to you, but the
correspondence must now cease.

Cordially,
Clodagh

Dear Mother Francis,
I intend to spend Christmas at St Mary's in Knockglen for a
variety of reasons. I hope this will not unduly disturb the
Community. I shall be in touch later with full details.

Your Sister in Christ,
Mother Clare

Lilly Foley was pleased about the party. John would enjoy it. He
would like seeing their big house filled with lights and flowers and
the rustle of evening dresses, beautiful girls.

Her husband would enjoy playing host to a roomful of
handsome young people. It would make him feel their age.

She was determined it would be just right, and that she herself
would look her very best. There was no way he could be allowed
to look across at her and think she was drab and grey compared
to all the glitter around them.

She would think of her own outfit later. In the meantime
she must plan it properly. She could not let Jack know how
welcome the excuse was. She would let him and his father know
what a wonderful wife and mother she was to cope with his
demands.

'Will they want sausages and savouries, do you think?' Lilly
asked.

'They'll want whatever we give them.' Jack had no interest
in details.

'Who'll serve it? Doreen will need help.'

Jack looked round the table. 'Aengus,' he said.

'Can I wear a napkin on my arm?' Aengus asked.

'You'd probably better wear one on your bottom as well,'
Ronan said.

His mother frowned.

'It's for *your* friends, Jack. I wish you'd pay some attention.'

'And for yours and Dad's. Look, aren't the pair of you

delighted? You've got those new curtains you've been talking about and you had the gate painted.'

'It'd be like you to tell everyone that.'

'Of course I won't. I keep telling you that I think it's great all your friends are coming round.'

'And all yours!'

'Mine will only be here for an hour or two. Yours will stay all night and disgrace themselves. I'm as well off not to be a witness to it.'

'And what about the oldies, as you call them? The parents of your friends.'

'I asked Aidan Lynch's parents. You know them already.'

'I do.' Mrs Foley raised her eyes to heaven.

'And Benny Hogan's parents, the people from Knockglen. But they can't come. They wrote to you, remember? It's only going to be people like Uncle Kevin and the neighbours, and all your own crowd. You'll hardly notice my few.'

'I wish I knew why you've inflicted this on us,' his mother said.

'Because I couldn't decide which girl to ask, so I asked them all.' Jack beamed at her in total honesty.

The weekend before the dance, Eve came home to Knockglen.

'I've left it far too long,' she confessed to Benny on the bus on the Friday evening. 'But it really was that I didn't want to run out on Kit. Do you think Mother Francis knows that?'

'Tell her,' Benny said.

'I will. She said she had a favour to ask of me. What do you think it could be?'

'Let's guess. Help her set up a poteen still in the kitchen garden?'

'I'd be good at that. Or maybe, based on my huge experience beating off the advances of Aidan Lynch, she wants me to give Sixth Year a course of lessons in sex education.'

'Or take the older nuns to Belfast on a day excursion to see a banned film.'

'Or bring Sean Walsh in to the art room and drape a duster over his vital parts and have him for a life class.'

They laughed so much that Mikey the driver said they put him off concentrating.

'The pair of you remind me of those cartoons of Mutt and Jeff, do you know the ones I mean?' Mikey shouted at them.

They did. Mutt was the big one, Jeff was the tiny one. Mikey was always pretty subtle.

'I can't turn her away,' Mother Francis pleaded with Eve in the kitchen.

'Yes you can, Mother, yes you bloody can.'

'Eve! Please!'

'No, honestly, you can do anything. You've always been able to do anything you wanted. Always.'

'I don't know where you got this idea.'

'From living with you, from watching you. You can tell Mother Clare that it damn well won't suit the Community to have her here just because her own lot above in Dublin want to be shot of her for Christmas.'

'It's hardly a charitable thing to say, or do.'

'Since when has that had anything to do with it?'

'Well, we must have raised you under some misapprehension here. Charity is meant to have quite a lot to do with the religious life, actually.'

They both laughed at that.

'Mother, I couldn't be in the same house as her.'

'You don't *have* to Eve. The rest of us do.'

'What do you mean?'

'You have your own house, if you want to use it.'

'Another of your ploys!'

'On my word of honour. If you think that I went to all the trouble to arrange that Mother Clare came here just so that I could manoeuvre you into that cottage, then you really don't understand anything at all.'

'It would be going a bit far, certainly,' Eve agreed.

'Well, then.'

'No.'

'Why? Just one good reason.'

'I won't take their charity. I won't live in their bloody grace and favour home like some old groom who broke his back looking after horses for the squires and gets some kind of bothan and tugs his remaining bit of hair out in gratitude for the rest of his life.'

'It's not like that.'

'It *is*, Mother, it is. She was thrown out, not good enough to walk through their doors, never let back in again. But they didn't want her to die on the side of the road so they gave her that cottage that no one wanted because it was miles from anywhere and in addition, horror of horrors, beside the Roman Catholic convent.'

'They liked it, Eve. It was where they wanted to live.'

'It's not where I want to live.'

'Not even look at it? I go to so much trouble minding it for you, always hoping, I thought you'd be delighted.'

Mother Francis looked tired, weary almost.

'I'm sorry.'

'I was so sure you'd be so relieved to have a place to escape . . . but I suppose I got it wrong.'

'I wouldn't mind having a look, Mother. To please you. Nothing to do with them.'

'Tomorrow morning, then. We'll go up, the pair of us.'

'And my room here . . .'

'Will be your room here until the day you die.'

'What do you think?' Benny looked anxiously at Clodagh.

'It's a gorgeous bit of stuff. A pity to cut it up.'

'You've seen people going to these places. Will it look all right?'

'When I'm through with it and you, it will be a sensation.'

Benny looked doubtfully at Clodagh's own outfit, which was a white smock over a mauve polo-necked jumper and what looked like mauve tights. It was very far ahead for anywhere, let alone Knockglen.

'We'll cut the bodice well . . . well down like this.'

Benny stood in her slip. Eve sat companionably on a radiator smoking and giving her comments.

Clodagh made a gesture with the black velvet top which implied a startlingly low neckline.

'Cut it where?' Benny screamed. Clodagh gestured again.

'That's what I thought you said. I'd fall into my dinner, for God's sake.'

'Presumably you'll be wearing some kind of undergarment to prevent this.'

'I'll be wearing a bra made of surgical steel . . .'

'Yes, and we must push your bosom right up and in like this.'
Clodagh made a grab at her and Benny gave a yell.

'I haven't had as much fun in years,' Eve said.

'Tell her, Eve. Tell her my mother's paying for this. She won't
let me out like the whore of Babylon.'

'It's a dance, isn't it?' asked Clodagh. 'It's not a function to
put forward the cause of your canonization or anything, is it?'

'Clodagh, you're off your head. I can't. Even if I had the
courage.'

'Right. We'll give you a modesty vest.'

'A what?'

'We'll cut the thing the way it should be cut and mould you
into it. Then I'll make a bit of pleated linen or something and a
couple of fasteners and we can tell your mother that this is what
you'll be wearing. You can take it out as soon as you are outside
the city limits of Knockglen.'

Clodagh fiddled and draped and pinned.

'Put your shoulders back, Benny,' she ordered. 'Stick your
chest out.'

'Jesus, Mary and Joseph, I look like the prow of a ship,' said
Benny in alarm.

'I know. Isn't it great?'

'Fellows love the prows of ships,' Eve said. 'They're always
saying it.'

'Shut up, Eve Malone. I'll stick the scissors in you.'

'You will not. Those are my expensive pinking shears. Now
isn't that something?' Clodagh looked pleased.

Even in its rough and ready state they could see what she
had in mind for Benny. And it looked very good indeed.

'The Wise Woman wouldn't let her mother near the fittings
for this dress,' Eve said sagely.

'They'll be climbing all over you in this,' Clodagh said happily
as she began to unpin it.

'Wouldn't that be fantastic,' Benny said, smiling delightedly
at her reflection in the mirror.

CHAPTER TEN

'It's great that you'll be working late tonight,' Nan said to her mother. They poured another cup of coffee at the kitchen table. The dance was in the same hotel as Emily's shop. Nan planned to bring her friends in to introduce them and parade their finery.

'You don't have to, you know, I can always peep out and see you going into the ballroom.'

'But you know that I'd love to, Em. I want you to meet them and them to meet you.'

Between them, unspoken, lay the certainty that Nan would never bring them home to Maple Gardens.

'Only if it seems right at the time. There might be people there that you don't want to bring into a shop . . . you know.'

Nan laid her hand on her mother's.

'No, I don't know, as it happens. What do you mean?'

'Well, we've had such hopes for you . . . you and I, that you'll get out of all this.' Emily looked round the small, awkward house. 'You mightn't want to be bringing grand people in on top of me in a shop.' She smiled apologetically.

'It's a gorgeous shop. And you run it like a dream. I'd be proud to have them see you there,' Nan said.

She didn't say that she was not relying on the Aidan Lynches, the Bill Dunnes or the Jack Foleys to take her out of Maple Gardens. She had set her sights much higher than that.

'I wish you'd come in tonight for the drinks bit,' Eve said to Kit.

'No, I'd be no good at a thing like that, all falling over my words. I was never any good at social occasions.'

'Aidan Lynch's parents are going to be there. You could talk about him!'

'God, Eve, leave me alone. I'd a million times prefer to be here. Ann Hayes and I are going to the pictures. That's much more our style than having cocktails with doctors in Ailesbury Road.'

'It's not Ailesbury Road,' Eve said defensively.

'It's not far off it.' Her face softened. 'To be asked is enough. Have you the bed made up for Benny?'

'I have. We won't make a noise and wake you.'

'It's easy to wake me. I sleep very lightly. Maybe you'll tell me about it. That outfit is gorgeous on you. I never saw anything like it.'

They had a dress rehearsal the night before, with evening bag borrowed from Mrs Hayes next door, and the good white lacy blouse from Kit's wardrobe starched and pressed until it was like new. Now Kit's surprise gift was produced. Scarlet earrings exactly the same colour as the skirt.

'No, no. You can't be buying me things,' Eve stammered.

Something in Kit's face reminded Eve that Frank Hegarty might have been dressing up in a dinner jacket this night to go to the dance if things had been different.

'Thank you very, very much,' she said.

'You really are very beautiful. Very striking.'

'I think I look a bit like a bird,' Eve said seriously. 'A sort of crazed blackbird with its head on the side before it goes picking for things.'

Kit pealed with laughter. 'I mean it. I really do,' she said. 'You *are* very attractive, mad as a brush of course, but with any luck people might not notice that.'

Benny's outfit had been packed in a box in tissue paper. It had been much admired at home. There had been a dangerous moment when Patsy had giggled and said she hoped nobody would snatch Benny's modesty vest away. The Hogans looked at each other, alarmed.

'Why would a thing like that happen?'

Benny had glared at Patsy, who went back to the range in confusion.

'I'd love to see you all dressed up setting out tonight,' Benny's mother said. 'You and Eve and all your friends.'

'Yes, well you could have come up of course to Dr Foley's. You *were* invited.'

Benny felt hypocritical. She would have hated them to have been there.

'Yes, it was very civil of them certainly,' Eddie Hogan said. 'Repaying the hospitality we gave to that boy.'

Benny felt herself wince with embarrassment. How provincial and old-fashioned they were compared to people in Dublin. Then a wave of guilt came over her and she felt protective about them. Why *should* they have the same style and way of going on as people who went to cocktail parties?

'And you'll be home on the morning bus?' Her mother said hopefully.

'Maybe the later one. It would be nice to get value out of the visit, and meet the girls for coffee . . . or lunch.'

'But you'll ring?' her father asked.

'Of course I will.' She was dying to be gone. 'Tomorrow morning.'

'You'll be fine, up in Dublin,' her father said, sounding as doubtful as if she were going to the far side of the moon.

'Don't I go there every day, Father?'

'But not every night.'

'Still I'm safe with Mrs Hegarty, you know that.' Oh, please let them let her go.

'And enjoy every minute of it,' her mother said.

'I'd better go for the bus, Mother. I don't want to be rushing, not carrying this parcel.'

They stood at the door of Lisbeg – Mother, Father, Patsy and Shep. If Shep had known he would have raised his paw to wave. He would have.

'Enjoy the dance, Benny,' Dr Johnson called to her.

Clodagh, already rearranging her now much talked-of windows in Pine's shop made marvellous gestures, miming Benny ripping off a modesty vest and exposing enormous amounts of bosom.

Fonsie watched this from across the street with interest.

'Fabulous bird, isn't she?' he said.

'There's great talent here in Knockglen,' Benny agreed.

'Keep on rocking,' Fonsie encouraged her.

Outside Hogan's, Sean Walsh was polishing the brasses.

'Tonight's the big night,' he said with a slow smile.

Remember Nan's advice: It doesn't hurt to be nice. It often helps.

Benny smiled back. 'That's it, Sean,' she said.

'I was trying to persuade your father to let me drive them up to that reception he was invited to.'

'It wasn't a reception. It was more a few drinks in Dr Foley's house.'

190

'The very thing. He showed me the letter inviting them. I said it would be a matter of nothing for me to drive them.'

'But they refused.' She knew her voice was high-pitched now.

'Ah, sure what would that be except to lift the phone and say they were able to come after all? I told them they owed it to themselves to go out once in a while.'

'Did you?'

'Yes. And I said, when better than on the night of Benny's big dance?'

'What a pity they weren't able to take you up on it.'

'The day's young yet,' Sean Walsh said, and went back into the shop.

He was only saying it to annoy her. He must have known how much she would hate her parents to be at something like this. She felt slightly faint and leaned against the wall of Birdie Mac's.

Birdie knocked on the window, mouthing at her.

God, Benny thought, this is all I need. She's going to give me some broken chocolate or something now to build me up.

'Hallo, Miss Mac,' she tried to make her voice steady. She must try to be sane. Her parents had just said goodbye to her. They had no intention of coming to Dublin. There would have been preparations for a week.

Birdie was at the door. 'Benny, I just had a phone call from your mother. She wants me to give her a home perm this morning. I forgot to ask her, does she have a hair dryer at home?'

Birdie Mac looked at Benny anxiously.

'Are you all right, child? You're very pale.'

'A home perm you say.'

'Yes. It's easy for me, I can run down now and wind it on, and then come back later and do the neutralizing. It's the dryer I was wondering about . . .'

'There is a dryer.' Benny spoke like a robot.

She moved up to the square without realizing it. She was startled by the hooting of the bus.

'Well, Benny, are you going to get on? Do you need a special invitation?'

'Sorry, Mikey. Are you leaving? I didn't notice.'

'No, not at all. We've all day, and all night. Leisure is the keynote in our bus service, never hurry a passenger, that's our motto.'

She sat down and looked unseeingly out.

They couldn't have decided to come up to Dublin. Not to the Foleys'. Not tonight.

Rosemary wasn't at her history lecture.

'She's gone to the hairdresser,' said Deirdre, a busy, fussy girl who knew everything. 'Apparently she's going to the big dance tonight in a party. They're all going to drinks in Jack Foley's house first. Imagine. In his house.'

'I know,' Benny said absently. 'I'm going too.'

'You're what?'

'Yes.' Benny looked up at the girl's highly unflattering surprise.

'Well, well, well,' Deirdre said.

'Nobody's taking anyone. We're all paying for ourselves.' She was determined to bring Rosemary down, in some respects anyway.

'Yes, but to be included. Heavens.' Deirdre looked Benny up and down.

'I'm looking forward to it.' Benny knew she had a grim, despairing look on her face.

In addition to all her anxieties she now feared that her parents would be there, fumbling and apologizing and mainly horrified by the amount of bosom she would be revealing. It was not beyond the possible that they might actually order her out of the room to cover herself. The thought made Benny go hot and cold.

'I suppose it's being friendly with that Nan Mahon that does it,' Deirdre said eventually.

'Does what?'

'Gets you invited to lots of places. It's a great thing to have a friend like that.'

Deirdre had shrewd, piggy eyes.

Benny looked at her for a moment or two with dislike.

'Yes. I usually choose my friends for that reason,' she said.

Too late she remembered how Mother Francis had warned them to beware of sarcasm.

'It's a way to go, certainly,' Deirdre said, nodding her head sagely.

The day seemed very long. She met Eve and they went out to Dunlaoghaire on the five o'clock train. There were a lot of office workers going home. And at some of the stations schoolchildren in uniform got on. Eve and Benny nudged each other in pleasure to be part of a different world. A world of going to a big dress dance, as part of a big, glittering circle.

Kit had sandwiches for them.

'I'm too excited,' Eve protested.

'I've been on a diet. I'd better not fall at the last fence,' Benny explained.

Kit was adamant. She wasn't going to have them fainting at the dance, and anyway the food had to be digested and turned into fat, and there wouldn't be time for that to happen. There was no fear that Benny would burst through her outfit. Kit had declared the bathroom a no-go area for her lodgers, though she said that was not strictly necessary. Most of them didn't see the need to spend hours in it.

The coffee and sandwiches were on a tray in their room. Kit seemed to understand their need to giggle and reassure each other.

The meal that night was her responsibility, she said. Eve wasn't to think of either preparing it or serving it.

They zipped and hooked each other. They held the light at a better angle for the application of eyeliner and eyeshadow. They advised on the amount of lipstick blotting, and they dusted a lot of powder over Benny's bosom, which was whiter than her neck and arms.

'Probably everyone's is. It's just we don't get a chance to see them.'

Benny's hand flew to her cleavage.

'Don't *do* that. Remember Clodagh says it looks as if you're drawing attention to it.'

'It's easy to say that. Specially wearing a smock like she does.'

'Come on, how. Didn't she make you look marvellous?'

'Did she, Eve? Or did she and I make me look a fool?' Benny looked so troubled and upset, Eve was startled.

'Come on. We're all a bit nervous. I think I look like a horrible bird of prey, but when I try to be objective I think that's probably not so.'

'Of course it's not so. You look terrific. You must *know* that.

Look at yourself in the mirror, for heaven's sake. You're so petite, and colourful.' Benny's words were stumbling over each other in their eagerness to convince her small worried friend.

'And so must *you* know you look great. What's wrong? What don't you like?'

'My chest.'

'Not again!'

'I'm afraid of what people will think.'

'They'll think it's terrific . . .'

'No, not fellows. Ordinary people.'

'What kind of ordinary people?'

'Whoever's there first. You know, at the drinks bit. They might think I'm fast.'

'Don't be stupid.'

Kit called up the stairs. 'Can I come and see you? Mr Hayes will be here to drive you in in about ten minutes.'

'Come on up and talk sense into my friend.'

Kit came in and sat on the bed. She was full of praise.

'Benny's worried about her cleavage,' Eve explained.

'She shouldn't be. Let the other girls worry about it, and envy it.' Kit said it as one who knew there was no argument.

'But . . .'

'It's not Knockglen. Your parents aren't going to be here.' Eve stopped suddenly. 'What's wrong?'

'Nothing.' Benny's eyes were too bright.

Eve and Kit exchanged glances.

'Mrs Hegarty, could I use your phone do you think?'

'Certainly,' Kit said. 'It's a coin-operated one, I'm afraid.'

Benny snatched up her handbag and ran downstairs.

They looked at each other in bewilderment.

'What's that about?'

'I've no idea,' Eve said. 'Something to do with Knockglen. She's ringing home. You can bet on it.'

'Hallo, Patsy. It's Benny.'

'Oh, are you at the dance yet?'

'Just setting out. Is Mother there, or Father?'

'No, Benny. They're out.'

'They're what?'

'They're out. They went out about six o'clock.'

'Where did they go?'

'They didn't tell me,' Patsy said.

'Patsy, they must have. They always say where they're going.'

'Well, they didn't. What did you want them for?'

'Listen, were they dressed up?'

'What do you mean?'

'What were they wearing, Patsy? *Please.*'

'God, Benny, I never notice what people are wearing. They had their outdoor clothes on.' Patsy was doing her best.

'Are they in Dublin do you think?'

'Surely not. Surely they'd have said?'

'Did Sean Walsh collect them?'

'I don't know. I was out in the scullery.'

'You must have noticed something.' Benny's voice was very impatient. Patsy got into a huff.

'I'd have noticed plenty had I been told there was going to be a Garda inquiry on the phone,' she said, offended.

'I'm sorry.'

'It's all right,' said Patsy, but it wasn't.

'I'll see you tomorrow and tell you all about it.'

'Oh, very nice.'

'And if they do come back . . .'

'Well, Mother of God, Benny, I hope they will come back.'

'If they do come back, just say I rang to thank them for everything, and the lovely dress and all.'

'Sure, Benny. I'll say you rang all sweetness and light.'

Benny stood in the hall for a few moments to catch her breath. She would not burden Eve with the whole thing. She would put her shoulders back and her chest forward. She would go to this party. If her parents turned up she would tell them she had lost the modesty vest. That it had blown away when she took it out of the parcel. She would be fun and make jokes and be jolly.

Even if her parents said mortifying things to people like Rosemary, if they made crass remarks about hospitality being repaid, she would hold her head up high.

Nobody would know that in these hoops of steel which were meant to be called an uplift brassière there was a heart of lead surrounded by a lot of wavy, nervous, fluttery feelings.

The doorbell rang and she answered it. A man in a hat and overcoat stood there.

'I'm Johnny Hayes, to drive two ladies into Donnybrook,' he said and, looking at the expanse of bosom approvingly, he added, 'though it wouldn't take much to make me drag a grand armful like yourself into the car and head off for the Dublin mountains.'

Now that it had started Lilly Foley was beginning to enjoy herself. Jack had been right. It was indeed well time they gave a party, and this was an ideal occasion. Their neighbours could admire the young people heading off to the dance. The house could be filled with young men in dinner jackets and girls in long, sweeping dresses without it looking pretentious. That was the style these big houses were meant for, Lilly Foley told herself. But she didn't tell her husband or sons. They had a habit of sending her up over what they called her notions. If Lilly Foley liked to see cars draw up in their tree-lined road and hear the sound of long dresses swishing up the steps to the hall door then she kept that little pleasure to herself.

An early arrival was Sheila, one of Jack's fellow students. To Lilly Foley she had been a fairly constant voice on the telephone, wanting to go over some notes with Jack. Now here in the house she was an attractive girl, in a yellow and black dress, over-eager to impress Lilly thought, busy explaining that she had an uncle a Judge and a cousin a Senior Counsel so that she was practically born to be a barrister. Soon, a young couple, Sean and Carmel, arrived, who talked animatedly to each other and no one else. Lilly was pleased to see Bill Dunne . . . a personable and easygoing young man. He made a nice antidote to that Aidan Lynch, whose antics she had never understood and whose parents both had voices like fog horns.

She looked proudly at Jack who was extraordinarily handsome in his rented dinner jacket, welcoming people in and laughing his easy laugh. He had an arm around first this girl and then another. You'd need to be a better detective than Lilly Foley considered herself to know which of them he liked most. The very pretty but rather over made-up girl, Rosemary, had allowed her glance to fall only briefly on Lilly before turning the full-voltage charm on Dr Foley.

Aengus was extremely solemn in his duty as waiter. He stood at the foot of the stairs with his glasses steaming, his new spotted bow tie resplendent. He felt the centre of attention, the figure that everyone would be aware of as they came in and left their coats in the dining room.

So far it had all been strangers. He was relieved to recognize Aidan Lynch, Jack's friend from school.

'Good evening,' Aidan said to him formally. 'Are you from a catering agency? I don't remember seeing you much on the social scene around Dublin.'

'I'm Aengus,' Aengus said, overjoyed not to have been recognized.

'You're very kind to let me use your first name. I'm Aidan Lynch. My parents have gone ahead into the drawing room and I think are having their drink requirements met by Dr Foley. Do I give you my order . . . er, Aengus, is it?'

'Aidan, I'm Aengus, Jack's brother.' The smile of triumph was wide on his face.

'*Aengus*. So you are. I didn't realize!' Aidan said, smiting his forehead.

'You can have dry sherry, or sweet sherry or a beer or a club orange,' Aengus said.

'My goodness,' Aidan was lost in indecision.

'But only one at a time.'

'Ah, that's disappointing. I was just about to ask for them all together in a glass with a dollop of whipped cream on top,' he looked saddened.

'Seeing that you're a friend of Jack's I'll ask if you can . . .' Aengus was about to set out for the kitchen where the drink was.

'Come back, you fool. Listen, did a beautiful, small dark girl come in?'

'Yes, she's in there. She's with some fellow. She keeps licking his ear and drinking out of his glass.'

Aidan pushed past him into the drawing room. How could Eve be behaving like this? Maybe she too had mixed all her drinks. But she was nowhere to be seen. His eyes went round the big room with its warm lights, its huge Christmas tree in the window. He saw a lot of familiar faces, but no Eve.

He came back to Aengus.

'Where is she? Quick.'

'Who?' Aengus was alarmed.

'The beautiful dark girl.'

'The one licking the fellow's ear?'

'Yes, yes.' Aidan was testy.

Aengus had come to the door. 'There!' He pointed at Carmel and Sean, who were, as usual, standing very close to each other.

Relief flooded over Aidan.

Carmel and Sean saw him and waved.

'What was all the pointing about?' Carmel asked.

'You look utterly beautiful, Carmel,' Aidan said. 'Leave this man instantly. I'll give you a better life. You have disturbed my dreams so much . . . Come and disturb my waking hours as well!'

Carmel smiled a wise, mature woman-of-the-world smile and patted Aidan's hand.

At the same moment, Aidan heard Eve's voice behind him.

'Well, hallo Aidan. Here you are tongue-tied and wordless as ever.'

He turned and looked at her. She looked so good that he got a lump in his throat and for a few seconds he was literally unable to find words.

'You're gorgeous,' he said. Very honestly and unaffectedly.

Nan had warned Eve not to say that the red skirt was on loan. If it was praised then thank for the praise, Nan had said. Why throw people's compliments back in their faces?

Eve had never spoken to Aidan in anything other than joky terms. But his admiration had been unqualified.

'Thank you,' she said simply.

Then it was as if the mist had cleared and they went back to their old way of going on.

'I'm glad you arrived just when you did, because Carmel was propositioning me here. It's been deeply embarrassing in front of Sean, but what can I do?' Aidan looked at her helplessly.

'It's something you're going to have to cope with all your life. I'd say it's a physical thing, you know the way animals give off scents. It couldn't be intellectual or anything.'

Eve laughed happily and spun around to the admiring glance of Bill Dunne.

'You look *terrific*,' Bill Dunne said to her. 'Why don't you dress like that all the time?'

'I was just going to ask you exactly the same question,' she laughed up at him.

Bill fixed his tie and smiled foolishly. Aidan looked put out. He spoke hastily to Jack, who was at his elbow.

'I don't know whether this was such a good idea.'

'What?' Jack looked at the glass of beer in Aidan's hand. 'Is it flat?'

'No. I mean asking all the girls. We thought we'd have them under our control. Maybe we'll lose them all.'

'Jack?' Aengus had arrived, looking anxious.

'Aha, Mr Fixit is here,' Aidan said, looking malevolently at the small boy he would never forgive for confusing him so at the outset of the evening.

'Jack, will I bring out the sausages yet? Mummy wants to know is everyone here.'

'Nan's not here yet. Wait another few minutes.'

'Everyone else is here, are they?' Aidan looked round the room. He didn't like the way Bill Dunne was making Eve laugh. He didn't like the way everyone in the older set seemed to be making his parents laugh too loudly.

'I think so. Look, here's Nan now.'

Standing at the door utterly naturally, as if she had entered a crowded room like this every evening of her life, was Nan Mahon. She had a beautiful lemon dress, the skirt in flowing silk, the top a strapless bodice of thousands of tiny seed pearls on a lemon taffeta base. Her shoulders were graceful, rising from the dress; her hair, a mass of golden curls, was scooped up into a clasp, also decorated with tiny pearl ornaments. Her skin looked as if she had never known a spot or a blemish.

Jack went over to greet her, and take her to meet his parents.

'Is that Jack's lover, do you think?' Aengus asked Aidan Lynch hopefully. Aidan was the kind of person who sometimes told you unexpected things.

He was disappointed this time.

'You are a remarkably foolish and unwise young man to talk about lovers to boys who have been through a Catholic education and know that such things must be confined to the Holy Sacrament of Matrimony.'

'I meant like in the pictures . . .' Aengus pleaded.

'You don't know what you mean, your mind is a snake pit of confusion. Go and get the sausages while you still have a few brain cells left alive,' Aidan ordered him.

'They're not all there,' Aengus was mutinous.

'Yes, they are.'

'No, there's someone in the cloakroom. She's been there since she came in.'

'She probably got out the window and left,' said Aidan. 'Get the sausages or I'll tear the face off you.'

Aengus knew it had all been going too well. The bow tie, the attention and people thanking him. Now Aidan Lynch was speaking to him just like he had at school.

He went gloomily out towards the kitchen in search of the party food.

In the hall a big girl was looking at herself in the mirror without very much pleasure.

'Hallo,' he said.

'Hallo,' she replied. 'Am I the last?'

'I think so. Are you Nan?'

'No. She just went in, I heard her.'

'They said I couldn't serve the sausages until Nan arrived. She was the only one missing.'

'Well, I expect they forgot me,' she said.

'They must have,' he said comfortingly.

'Are you Jack's brother?'

'Yes, I'm Aengus Foley.'

'How do you do. I'm Benny Hogan.'

'Do you like sausages?'

'Yes, why?'

'I'm getting some now. I thought you could have a few before you went on, to stock up like.'

'Thanks, but I'd better not. I'm afraid of bursting out of my dress.'

'You've burst out of most of it already,' said Aengus indicating her bosom.

'Oh God,' said Benny.

'So you might as well have the sausages anyway,' he said cheerfully.

'I'd better go in,' she said.

She straightened her shoulders and trying not to look at the small boy who had thought her dress was ripped open, she held back her shoulders as she had promised Clodagh Pine she would and moved into the drawing room feeling like an ocean liner.

Bill Dunne and John O'Brien saw her first.

'God, is that Big Benn? Doesn't she look fantastic?' Bill said, behind his hand.

'Now, that's what I call a pair of Killarneys,' John O'Brien said.

'Why Killarneys?' Bill was always interested in explanations of things.

'It's an expression.' John O'Brien was still looking at Benny. 'She's not bad-looking at all, is she?'

Benny saw none of them. Her eyes were roaming the room to see if in the middle of this happy and confident throng her parents were standing, awkward and ill at ease. Worse, would she find them holding forth on subjects of interest only in Knockglen? Worst of all, would they make a scene when they saw her dress?

But as far as she could see there was no sign of them. She peered and twisted, looking at the backs of people's heads, trying to see if they were hidden in that group of older people, where a man with a very loud laugh stood holding court.

No, they definitely weren't there.

She had seen a Morris Cowley pull away from the footpath just as they arrived. It was driven by one person. It was dark and hard to see either the face or the registration number. It *could* have been their car. That was what had unhinged her. She had fled straight into the cloakroom hissing at Eve to go in without her.

'I'll wait for you,' Eve had said, thinking that she was just going to the lavatory.

'If you do, I'll kill you, here and now in front of everyone. There'll be so much blood your blouse will be the same colour as your skirt.'

'You've made your point. I'll go in without you,' Eve had said.

For fifteen minutes Benny had sat in the Foleys' downstairs cloakroom.

Several times she felt the door handle rattle when a girl wanted to go in and check her appearance. But there was a mirror in the dining room and they made do with that.

Finally, she realized that there were no more sounds of people arriving and she emerged.

She felt foolish now, and a dull flush of anger with Sean

201

Walsh for having tricked her into thinking that her night would be spoiled spread over her face. She felt a sense of rage with the unfortunate Patsy that she hadn't found out where the master and mistress had gone on a rare evening out. But most of all she felt an overpowering sense of annoyance with herself.

Now that she was sure they were not in the room she could ask herself what would have been so very terrible if they had turned up.

Slowly normality came back and she realized she was the centre of a lot of very interested attention.

'That's a very classy-looking outfit.' Rosemary didn't even bother to disguise her surprise.

'Thanks, Rosemary.'

'So, where did you get it?'

'Knockglen.' Benny's answer was brief. She wanted to catch Eve's eye and tell her that she was all right again. But Eve had her back turned.

Before she could get to her there were several more compliments. As far as she could see they were genuine. And mainly unflattering in their astonishment.

Still, it was heady stuff.

She touched Eve on the shoulder.

'I'm back,' she said, grinning.

Eve turned away from the group. 'Am I allowed to talk to you or do you still have some kind of plan to carve me up?'

'That's over.'

Eve lowered her voice. 'Well then.'

'What is it?'

'Every single person in the room is looking at the pair of us. We're a Cinderella story come true.'

Benny didn't dare to look.

'I mean it,' Eve said. 'The glamour pusses like Rosemary and Sheila and even Nan are expected to look great at a dance. You and I are the surprise element. We're going to be danced off our feet. Mark my words.'

'Eve, what would the Wise Woman do now?'

'In your case the Wise Woman would get a drink, and hold it in one hand and your evening bag in the other. That way you physically can't start covering up your bosom.'

'Don't call it bosom,' Benny begged.

'Sister Imelda used to call it the craw. You know, like in a bird. "Make sure you cover your craw, Eve," she'd say. As if I had one to cover.'

'As if any of us took any notice of her.'

Nan came up and put her arm into each of theirs. It was no treat for Nan to be admired, and she seemed to see nothing staggering about her two friends having emerged from the chrysalis. She behaved as if she had expected them to look magnificent.

She spoke almost as a cat would purr.

'Now, haven't we knocked those awful Rosemarys and Sheilas into a cocked hat?'

They all laughed happily, but Benny would have been happier if there had been any sign that Jack Foley, the handsome young host who was handing round plates with his little brother, had even by a flicker of his eye acknowledged that she was in the room, with most of her bosom bare, and if you were to judge by everyone else's glances, looking very well indeed.

The last car door banged as the young people left. John and Lilly Foley stood on the top step and waved goodbye. Inside there was still a lively drinks party with their own friends, and Aidan Lynch's parents. Lilly knew she looked well. It had taken a lot of time, but she had found exactly the right cocktail dress, glittery without being overdone, dressy without it looking as if she should be going to the dance with the youngsters. It was a heavy lilac silk and she had earrings to match it. Her feet hurt in her new shoes, but no one would know that, certainly not the tall handsome man beside her.

'That was lovely, wasn't it? You were a great host.' She smiled at her husband, full of congratulation as if it were he rather than she who had organized everything.

'You're wonderful, Lilly,' he said, giving her a kiss on the forehead, and he put his arm around her as they closed the door and rejoined the guests.

All the work had been worth it, just for that.

The ladies' cloakroom was full of excited girls combing and lacquering their hair and flattening their lips out into grotesque shapes in order to apply lipstick. Two women behind a counter took their coats and gave them pink cloakroom tickets which the girls tucked into their bags.

There was a smell of perfume and face powder and a little nervous sweat.

Nan was ready before anyone else, unaware of the slightly jealous glances from others in the room. Suddenly their own strapless dresses looked a bit like something from the metal industry. They became aware of how the firm supports cut into their flesh. How could Nan's hair look so perfect without having to be licked into shape with cans of hair spray? Why didn't she need to dab at her chin and hide spots with tubes of covering paste?

'I'm just going to have a wander round until you're ready,' she said to Benny and Eve. 'Then I'll take you into the shop to meet my mother.'

She left gracefully in a sea of other girls who were bouncing or bobbing or running up and down the carpeted stairs. She looked serene.

Nan walked in one side of the hotel bar smiling politely around her as if she were waiting to meet someone.

It was a place with dark oak panelling and red plush seats. By the bar a lot of men stood talking. Drinks here were very much more expensive than in an ordinary Dublin pub. This was a bar where the wealthy met.

You would find county people, up in Dublin for the bloodstock sales, or some kind of land business. There might be stockbrokers, bankers, visitors from England, people with titles. It was not the kind of bar where you could ever come in on your own.

But on the night of a dance in the hotel ballroom, a lone girl looking for her partner would be quite acceptable. Nan stood where the light fell on her and looked around her. It wasn't long before everyone in the place saw her. She was aware without having to look at individual groups that everyone had seen her, and that they were admiring the cool young woman in the exquisite dress with the golden hair who stood confidently at the door.

Just when they had all had sufficient time to look at her, she turned around and with a wave of delight moved off to the foyer, where Eve and Benny were waiting.

'What were you up to?' Eve asked.

'Surveying the talent in the bar,' Nan replied.

'Won't there be enough of it at the dance? My God, you're insatiable, Nan Mahon.'

'Yes, well less of that to my mother.'

Nan led them into the hotel shop where an attractive, rather tired-looking woman sat by the till. She had fair hair too, like her daughter, but it was faded. She had a nice smile, but i⁺ was wary. Nan must have got her really striking good looks from her father, Eve decided. Her father who was hardly ever mentioned at all in Nan's conversation.

Nan did the introductions and they paraded their dresses for her. Emily Mahon said all the right things. She told Eve that the scarlet skirt looked much better on a dark person. It had drained the colour from Nan's face. She told Benny that anyone could see at ten miles that this was beautiful expensive brocade, and that the girl who had remodelled it for her must be a genius. She had never mentioned the huge cleavage which cheered Benny greatly. If anyone else mentioned it she was going to dig out that modesty vest and reinstate it.

'And do any of you have any particular boyfriends tonight?' Emily asked eagerly.

'There's a fellow called Aidan Lynch who fancies Eve a lot,' Benny said proudly, and then in order to define things properly for Mrs Mahon she added, 'And everyone fancies Nan.'

'I think you're going to have a deal with Johnny O'Brien yourself,' Nan said to Benny. 'He's been following you around as if you had a magnet somewhere about your person.'

Benny knew only too well what part of her person John O'Brien was following around.

Emily was pleased that her daughter had such nice friends. She had rarely met anyone that Nan knew. They had never been invited to the school plays or concerts like other parents. Nan had never wanted her father to know anything about school activities. It had always been her dread as a child that he would turn up the worse for wear at her convent school. To meet Eve and Benny was a big occasion for Emily Mahon.

'I'd offer you a spray of perfume from the tester, but you all smell so lovely already,' she said.

They said they didn't smell nearly nice enough. They'd love a splash of something.

They leaned over to Emily, who doused them liberally with Joy.

'The only problem is that you'll all smell the same,' she laughed. 'The men won't know one of you from the other.'

'That's good then,' Nan said approvingly. 'As a group we'll have made an impact on them. They'll never forget us.'

They were aware that a customer had come into the shop and might want to be served.

'We'd better move on, Em, we don't want you sacked,' Nan said.

'It's a treat to see you. Have a wonderful evening.' Her eyes hated to see them go.

'Don't hurry on my account,' the man said. 'I'm just browsing.'

His voice made Eve turn sharply.

It was Simon Westward. He hadn't seen her. He had eyes only for Nan.

As usual Nan seemed unaware that anyone was looking at her. She had probably grown up with those looks of admiration, Eve thought, like she herself had grown up with the sound of the convent bell. It became part of the scenery. You didn't notice it any more.

Simon did indeed start to browse among the shelves of ornaments and souvenirs, picking some up and examining them, looking at the prices on the box.

Emily smiled at him. 'Tell me if you want any help. I'm just having a chat here . . .'

She saw Nan frown at her slightly.

'No, honestly . . .' He looked straight at Nan.

'Hallo,' he said warmly. 'Did I see you in the bar a moment ago?'

'Yes, I was looking for my friends.' Her smile was radiant. 'And now I found them.' She spread her hands out to indicate Eve and Benny.

Out of politeness he moved his eyes from Nan to acknowledge them.

'Hallo,' Benny grinned. Simon looked at her startled. He knew her from somewhere certainly, but where? A big, striking girl, very familiar.

He looked at the smaller dark girl. It was his cousin Eve.

'Well, good evening, Simon,' she said slightly mocking. It was as if she had the advantage of him. She had already recognized him and had been watching while he ogled her friend.

'Eve!' There was warmth in his smile. Swift warmth.

Now he remembered who Benny was also. She was the Hogan girl.

'Small world, all right,' Eve said.

'Are you all going to a dance?'

'No, heavens no. This is just our casual Friday night out. We dress up a lot in UCD, you know. Not scruffy Trinity students shuffling round in duffle coats.' Her eyes danced, taking the sharpness out of her response.

'I was just going to compliment you and say you all looked splendid, but if it's like this every Friday, then I *have* been missing out on the social scene.'

'Of course it's a dance, Simon,' Benny said.

'Thank you, Miss Hogan.' He couldn't remember her name. He waited expectantly to be introduced to Nan, but it didn't happen.

'Will you be going to see Heather this weekend?' Eve asked.

'Alas no. I'm going to England, actually. You really have been frightfully good to her.'

'I enjoy meeting her. She has a lot of spirit,' Eve said. 'And she'd need it in that mausoleum.'

'It's meant to be the best . . .'

'Oh, it's about the only place for you lot to send her, certainly,' Eve reassured him. But she did imply that if Simon and his lot were less blinkered there would have been many more places to send the child.

Simon let another tiny pause develop, enough for him to be presented to the blonde girl if he was going to be. But no move was made.

She didn't stretch out her hand and introduce herself, and he wasn't going to ask.

'I must get on with my purchases and leave you all to enjoy the dance,' he said.

'Was it anything in particular?' Emily was professional now in her manner.

'I wanted a gift, a small gift for a lady in Hampshire,' his eyes were resting on Nan as he spoke.

'Something particularly Irish?' Emily asked.

'Yes, not too shamrocky though.'

Nan had been fiddling with a small paperweight made of Connemara marble. She left it back rather pointedly on the shelf.

Simon picked it up.

'I think you're right.' He looked straight into her eyes. 'I think this is a very good idea. Thank you so much.' He ended the sentence on a rising note, where if anyone was going to give a name it would be given now.

'It's very attractive,' Emily said. 'And if you like I could put it in a little box for you.' His eyes were still on Nan.

'That would be lovely,' he said.

Aidan Lynch appeared at the door.

'I know I'm always the spectre at the feast, but was there any question of you ladies joining us? It's not important or anything. It's just that the people at the door want to know where the rest of our party is and it's a question that's becoming increasingly hard to answer.'

He looked from one to the other.

Nan made the decision.

'We got sidetracked,' she explained. 'Come on, Aidan, lead us to the ball.'

She gathered the other two with her like a hen clucking at chickens.

Benny and Eve said their goodbyes, and Nan smiled from the door.

'Goodbye, Em, I'll be seeing you.'

She didn't say she'd be seeing her tonight, or at home. Simon watched them as they walked with Aidan Lynch towards the ballroom.

'What a very beautiful girl that is,' Simon said.

Emily looked after the three girls and boy walking through the crowded hotel.

'Isn't she?' said Emily Mahon.

They had a table for sixteen on the balcony. Dancing was well under way when they trooped in. Girls at other tables looked up when they saw Jack Foley, and people craned to see who he was with.

They had no luck in guessing. He went in talking to Sean and Carmel.

Boys at the other tables saw with envy that Jack Foley's table had Rosemary *and* Nan Mahon. That seemed too much for one party. College beauties should be spread about a bit. Some of them wondered how that goofy Aidan Lynch always seemed to be in the thick of everything, and one or two asked each other who was the very tall girl with the wonderful cleavage.

At their table the plan of campaign was under way. Everyone was drinking a glass of water from the large jug on the table. Then as soon as it was empty the eight boys would each pour the quarter bottle of gin which they had in their pockets into the jug. For the rest of the evening, only minerals would be ordered. They would ask for more and more club oranges, and the gin could be added from the jug.

Nobody could afford hotel prices for spirits. This was the clever solution. But the trick was not to let them remove the jug of so-called water, or worse still, fill it up, thus watering the gin. The table was never to be left empty and at the mercy of waiters.

The bandleader called out that they were to take the floor for a selection of calypsos.

Bill Dunne was first on his feet with his hand out to Rosemary. She had positioned herself near Jack, but that had been the wrong place. She should have sat opposite him, she realized too late. That way he could have caught her eye. With a hard, forced smile she stood up and went down to join the dancers.

Johnny O'Brien asked Benny. She stood up eagerly. Dancing was something she was good at. Mother Francis had employed a dancing teacher who came once a week and they learned the waltz and the quickstep first, but she had also taught them Latin American dancing. Benny smiled at the thought that girls from Knockglen would probably beat any Dublin girls when it came to doing the samba the mambo or the cha cha cha.

They were playing 'This is my Island in the Sun'. Johnny looked with open admiration at Benny.

'I never knew you had such a nice . . .' He stopped.

'Nice what?' Benny asked him directly.

Johnny O'Brien chickened out. 'Nice perfume,' he said.

It *was* nice, too, the perfume. It was heady, like a cloud around her. Of course he hadn't meant perfume at all, but he was right. That was nice also.

Aidan was dancing with Eve.

'This is the first time I've been able to hold you in my arms without your beating at me with your bony little fists,' he said.

'Make the most of it,' Eve said. 'The bony little fists will be out again if you start trying to dance with me in your father's car.'

'Were you talking to my father?' Aidan asked.

'You know I was. You introduced me to him three times.'

'He's all right really. So's my mother – a bit loud but basically all right.'

'They're no louder than you are,' Eve said.

'Oh they are. They boom. I just talk forcefully.'

'They talk more directly, normally. Sentences and everything,' Eve said, thinking about them.

'You're very beautiful.'

'Thank you, Aidan. And you look great in a dinner jacket.'

'When are you going to stop fighting this hopeless physical passion you have for me and succumb? Allow yourself to have your way with me.'

'Wouldn't you drop dead if I said I would?'

'I'd recover pretty quickly, I tell you.'

'Well, it mightn't happen for a while. The succumbing bit, I mean. A good while.'

'That's the trouble about being brought up by nuns. I might have to wait for ever.'

'They weren't nearly as bad as everyone says.'

'When are you going to take me to meet them?'

'Don't be ridiculous.'

'Why not? I took you to meet *my* family.'

'You didn't. They just happened to be there.'

'You didn't arrange for your nuns to rent motorbikes and roar up to the party. I think that was socially rather inept of you,' Aidan said.

'They couldn't make it,' Eve explained. 'Friday's their poker night and they just won't change for anyone.'

Sean and Carmel danced entwined. The music played 'Brown Skin Girl Stay Home and Mind Bay-bee'.

'Imagine, that won't be long now,' Carmel said.

'Another four years,' Sean said happily.

'And we've been together four years already if you count the year before Intermediate Cert.'

'Oh, I do count that. I couldn't get you out of my mind that year.'

'Aren't we lucky?' Carmel said, holding him tighter.

'Very lucky. Everyone in the room envies us,' said Sean.

'Wouldn't Sean and Carmel sicken you?' Eve said to Benny as they all went back up the stairs.

'Not much value out of asking them anywhere, certainly,' Benny agreed.

'They remind me of those animals in the zoo that keep picking at each other, looking for fleas,' Eve said.

'Don't, Eve,' Benny laughed. 'Someone will hear.'

'No, you know, monkeys obsessed with each other. Social grooming I think it's called.'

Back at the table Jack Foley and Sheila were sitting. Jack had elected to mind the jug of gin for the first watch. Sheila was pleased to have been chosen to sit with him, but she would have preferred to have been on the dance floor.

Nan came back to the table with Patrick Shea, an Architectural student, a friend of Jack's and Aidan's from school. Patrick Shea was hot and sweating. Nan looked as if she had been dancing on an ice rink in a cool breeze. There wasn't a sign of exertion on her face.

Benny looked across the table at her admiringly. She was so much in command of every situation and yet her mother was quite shy, and not a confident person at all. Perhaps Nan got it all from her father. Whom she never mentioned.

Benny wondered why Eve hadn't introduced her to Simon. It was rather gauche not to. If it had been anyone else Benny would have made the introduction herself, but Eve was always so chippy about those Westwards.

Still Nan had said nothing, and knowing Nan, if she had wanted an introduction she would have asked for one.

Johnny O'Brien was offering her a glass of orange. Benny took a great gulp of it thankfully and it was only when she had swallowed it she remembered it was full of gin.

She choked it back and saw Johnny O'Brien looking at her admiringly.

'You're certainly a woman who can hold her drink,' he said.

It wasn't the characteristic she would most like to be praised for, but at least it was better than having gagged or got sick.

Rosemary had been looking at her.

'I envy you being able to do that,' she said. 'I get dizzy after even a little drink.'

She looked around her, knowing that there would be silent praise and admiration for this feminine trait.

'I'm sure,' Benny said gloomily.

'It must be coming from the country,' Rosemary said, still with the look of mock admiration. 'I expect they drink a lot there, don't they?'

'Oh, they do,' Benny said. 'But differently. I mean when I drink gin in the country it's usually by the neck out of a bottle. It's a rare treat to get it in a glass and mixed with club orange.'

They laughed as she had known they would.

It was never hard to make them laugh. It was very hard to make them look at you with different eyes, though.

Benny looked at Jack, relaxed and happy, leaning back in his chair surveying the scene both around him and down on the tables near the dance floor. He would be the perfect host. He would ask every girl at the table to dance.

She felt an extraordinary urge to reach across and stroke his face, just touch his cheek gently. She wondered was she going mad? She had never known an urge like that before.

He would ask her to dance soon. Maybe now, perhaps the very next dance, he would lean across the table and smile. He would put out his hand towards her and smile with a slight questioning look. She could see it happening so clearly she almost believed it had happened already.

'Benny?' he might say, just like that, and she'd get up and walk down the stairs with him, hands touching lightly. And then they would just move towards each other.

The bandleader had said that their vocalist would knock strips off Tab Hunter in any singing context and he would now sing 'Young Love' to prove it.

Benny willed Jack to catch her eye and dance three soft slow numbers with her, beginning with 'Young Love'.

But Rosemary caught his eye first. Benny didn't know how

she did it, it might have been something to do with some awful beating of her eyelashes, but she managed to drag his glance over to her.

'Rosemary?' he said in that voice which he should have used to say 'Benny?'

Her heart was like a lump of lead.

'Will you risk it, Benny?' Aidan Lynch was at her elbow.

'Lovely, Aidan, thank you.'

She stood up and went downstairs to the floor where Jack Foley and Rosemary were dancing and Rosemary had put both her arms around Jack's neck and was leaning back a bit away from him as if to study him better.

The dance was a success every year. This year the organizers seemed to think it was better than ever. They measured these things by enthusiasm. The spot prizes went very well.

'First gentleman up with a hole in his sock.'

Aidan Lynch won that easily. He pointed out that the part you put your foot in was a hole. They had to give it to him. He got a huge cheer.

'How did you know that?' Benny was impressed.

'A friend of mine was a waiter here once. He told me all the spots.'

'What are the other questions?' Benny asked.

'There's one which says "The first lady up with a picture of a rabbit". That's easy too.'

'It is? Who'd have a picture of a rabbit?'

'Anyone with a threepence. There's a rabbit on the thruppenny piece.'

'So there is. Aren't you a genius, Aidan?'

'I am Benny, I am, but not everyone apart from yourself and myself recognizes this.'

They were welcomed as heroes back to the table and the wine they had won was opened.

'More drink. Aren't you marvellous, Benny?' Rosemary said. She had somehow managed to nestle her body into Jack's by leaning against him. Benny wanted to get up and smack her face hard. But fortunately Jack had moved away and the need that she felt to separate them passed.

Some waltzes were announced. Benny didn't want to dance

this set with Jack. Waltzes were too twirly, too active. No time to lean against him, to touch his face even accidentally.

The others were starting to go downstairs as the music soared up at them. 'Che Sera, Sera, whatever will be, will be.'

A tall, handsome boy came over to the table and asked courteously, 'May I ask Nan for just one dance please, you have her all evening . . . is that all right? Nan, will you?'

Nan looked up, everyone else seemed to be occupied.

'Of course,' she said, and went smiling to the dance floor.

Benny remembered at school when you were picked for teams the awful bit about being the last one to be chosen. Or worse when there was an uneven number and Mother Francis would say 'All right, Benny, you go with that team' at the very end. She remembered the musical chairs and being the first one out. She had an uneasy feeling that it was all going to happen again.

Jack was with Rosemary again! She saw Bill Dunne and another boy, Nick Hayes, talking at the end of the table, miles from where she was. If they had noticed her and come to sit with her or asked them to join her that would have been all right.

Benny sat with a fixed smile on her face, fiddling with the menu which said they would have melon soup, chicken and trifle. She wondered absently had they forgotten it was a Friday. She poured out a fizzy orange drink into her glass and drank it. From the corner of her eye she saw a waiter approaching with a large metal jug about to refill the water jugs on the table.

Benny stood up, 'No,' she said. 'No, they don't want any.'

The waiter looked an old man. He looked tired. He had seen too many of these student dances, and danced at none of them.

'Excuse me, Miss, let me fill it.'

'No.' Benny was adamant.

'Even if you don't want any, the ones that did get to dance might want it when they come back,' he said.

There was something in the mixed pity and scorn of his speech that brought a sharp sting of tears to her eyes. 'They said they didn't *like* any more water. Before they went off to dance. Truly.'

She must not make him suspicious either. Suppose he reported something odd about their table.

A great weariness came over her. 'Listen,' she said to him. 'I don't give a damn. They told me they didn't want any more but I don't care. Fill it up if you're set on it. What the hell.'

He looked at her uneasily. He obviously thought she was slightly mad, and that it was kind of somebody to have given her an outing.

'I'll go on to the next table,' he said hastily.

'Great,' Benny said.

She felt awkward sitting on her own. She would go to the ladies'. There was no one to excuse herself to. Nick and Brian were having an animated discussion at the far end of the table; they didn't see her go.

In the lavatory she sat and planned. The next dance would probably be rock and roll. That wasn't what she wanted for her dance with Jack either. She wouldn't catch his eye for this one. She'd wait until it was something lovely and slow again. Maybe they'd have 'Unchained Melody'. She loved that. Or 'Stranger in Paradise'. That was nice too. 'Softly, Softly' was a bit too sentimental. But it would do.

To her surprise she heard Rosemary's voice at the hand basins outside.

The waltzes couldn't be over yet, surely. They normally had three of them.

'He is utterly gorgeous, isn't he?' Rosemary was saying to someone. 'And he's nice too, not full of himself like a lot of those sporty fellows are if they're any way good-looking.'

Benny didn't recognize the other girl's voice. Whoever she was, she thought that Jack and Rosemary were together.

'Have you been going with him long?' she asked wistfully.

'No, I'm not going out with him at all. *Yet*, that is,' she added menacingly.

'He looked pretty keen out there.'

Benny's heart lurched.

'He's a good dancer as well as everything else. The waltz isn't my strong point. I pretended I had turned my ankle. I just wanted to come in here for a rest.'

'That was clever.'

'Well, you have to use every trick in the book. I said to him that I'd grab him for another dance later because we didn't finish this one.'

'You've got no competition.'

'I don't like the look of Nan Mahon. Did you see her dress?'

'It's out of this world. But you look just as good.'

'Thanks.' Rosemary was pleased.

'Where is he now?'

'He said he'd finish off the waltzes with Benny.'

Benny's faced burned. He had *known* she was a wallflower. He had bloody known. He hadn't deigned to ask her for a full dance, but when ravishing Rosemary walked out on him, he'd get good old Benny for the rest of it.

'Who's Benny?'

'She's that huge girl – from way down the country. He knows her through her family or something. She's always turning up at these things.'

'No competition there then?'

Rosemary laughed. 'No, I don't think so. Whoever she is, her people must have money. They know the Foleys somehow and she's wearing a very expensive dress. I don't know where she got it, but it's fabulous, brocade and beautifully cut. It takes stones off her. She says she got it in Knockflash or wherever she lives.'

'Knockflash?'

'Somewhere, real hick town. She no more got it there than she got it in the Bog of Allen.'

Their voices faded. They had freshened themselves up, re-sprayed their hair, put on more perfume. They were ready to go out again, full of confidence, and face it all.

Benny sat on the lavatory. Ice cold. She was huge. She was no competition for anyone. She was the kind of person someone would come and finish off a dance with but not choose in the first place.

She looked at the small wristwatch her mother and father had given her for her seventeenth birthday. It was five to ten.

More than anywhere in the world she wanted to be sitting by the fire in Lisbeg. Her mother in one chair, her father in another and Shep looking at pictures in the flames and wondering what it was all about.

She would like to be hearing the kitchen door latch go and Patsy come in from her walk with Mossy and make them all a cup of drinking chocolate. She didn't want to be in a place where people said she was huge and no competition and must have lots of money and be a family friend of the Foleys to be invited anywhere. She didn't want to be fighting to save jugs of gin on tables for people who wouldn't dance with her.

But wishing wouldn't get her home out of this humiliating place. Benny decided that she would take the good out of what she had overheard. It was good that her dress looked expensive and well cut. It was good though sad that it was necessary to hear that it took stones off her. It was good that Rosemary wasn't any way sure of Jack. And it was good that he hadn't found her sitting at the table, lonely and abandoned, and now he couldn't feel he had fulfilled his obligation to dance with her. There were lots of good things, Benny Hogan told herself as she took the little piece of cotton wool that Nan's mother had soaked in Joy perfume for them and rubbed it behind her ears.

She would go back and Rosemary would never know that her cruel dismissive remarks had only served to make Benny feel more positive and confident than ever.

They were making an announcement from the stage that the meal would be served shortly, and thanks to a special dispensation from the Archbishop's House the Friday abstinence need not be observed. There was a huge cheer.

'How did they get that?' Eve asked.

'The Archbishop knows we've all been so good he wants to reward us,' Jack suggested.

'No, it's just that chicken's the easiest to serve. You know everyone gets a wing. They breed special chickens for functions, with ten wings,' Aidan said.

'But why would the Archbishop want us to have chicken, seriously?' Benny asked.

'It's a deal,' Aidan explained. 'The dance organizers promise not to have dances on Saturday night that might run into the Sabbath day and the Church lets them eat chicken on Fridays.'

'You ran away on me.' Jack leaned over to Benny just as the soup was being served.

'I what?'

'You ran off. I was looking for you to waltz with me.'

'No, I didn't,' Benny said smiling. 'That was Rosemary that ran off on you. She hurt her ankle. I expect you mix us all up, we all look the same to you.'

The people around laughed, Rosemary didn't. She looked at Benny suspiciously. How did she know about the ankle?

Jack used the chance to make a flowery compliment. 'You don't all look the same. But you all look marvellous. I mean it.' And he was looking straight at Benny when he said it. She smiled back and managed not to make a joke or a smart remark.

There was a raffle during the meal, and the organizers came around to invite Rosemary and Nan to go and sell tickets.

'Why us?' Rosemary said. She didn't want to leave her post. The committee didn't want to explain that it was easier to force people to buy tickets if beautiful women were doing the asking. Nan had stood up already.

'It's for charity,' she said. 'I certainly don't mind.'

Rosemary Ryan looked very annoyed. Nothing had been going her way this evening. Nan had won all the honours in this little incident and that big Benny across the table seemed to be smiling at her in some awful smug knowing way.

'Of course I'll come too,' she said, jumping to her feet.

'Mind your ankle,' Jack said, and she looked at him sharply. He was probably just being concerned, but there was something about Benny's eyes she didn't like.

The man who thought he was streets ahead of Tab Hunter but just hadn't got the breaks also thought he was a pretty good Tennessee Ernie Ford and went down to great depths in his version of 'Sixteen Tons', a song Benny had detested since it had been popular when they were studying for the Leaving Certificate and Maire Carroll had always managed to be singing it when she was near Benny.

Benny was dancing with Nick Hayes.

'You're very light to dance with. It's like holding a feather,' he said in some surprise.

'It's easy to dance if someone leads well.' She was polite.

He was all right, Nick Hayes, but only all right.

Jack was dancing with Nan.

Somehow it was more disturbing than watching him dance with Rosemary.

Nan didn't make those very obvious little efforts. She really made no play for him at all and that must be maddening to someone like Jack Foley who was used to everyone adoring him. In fact they were very much alike, those two. She hadn't really noticed it before.

Both so sure of themselves because they didn't need to fight for anyone's attention like everyone else seemed to have to do. But just because they were so sure, they could afford to be nice and easygoing. Those kind of good looks freed you to be whatever kind of person you wanted to be.

'I never see you round anywhere in the evenings,' Nick was saying.

'Nobody does much,' Benny said. 'What kind of places do you go?'

She didn't care where he went. She just wanted to get him talking so that she could take her mind off the awful tune they were dancing to, and think more of Jack.

'I have a car,' he was saying right across her happy thoughts of the next dance when surely Jack must choose her.

'I could come and see you in Knockglen some time. Jack said he had a very nice day when he went to your house.'

'He did? Good, I'm glad he enjoyed it.' This was hopeful. This was very good indeed. 'Maybe you'll come back together one time and I'll try and entertain you both.'

'Oh no, that's not the idea. The idea would be to keep you to myself,' Nick said with a leer. 'One doesn't want Jack Foley getting in on all one's discoveries, does one?'

He was putting on an accent deliberately trying to pretend he was being posh. Somehow it was flat and silly and didn't work. He couldn't make people laugh like Aidan Lynch could, like she herself could.

She tried to dull the pain she felt watching Nan and Jack dance together.

Nick Hayes was looking at her, waiting for a response.

'I always hate this song,' she said to him suddenly.

'Why? It's quite nice I think.'

'The words.'

'I owe my soul to the company store,' he sang along with the vocalist. 'What on earth's wrong with those words?' he asked, mystified.

She looked at him. He genuinely didn't remember the first line – you load sixteen tons and what do you get?

He had made no connection.

It was there only in her mind. Nobody else in the room heard the song title and swivelled their eyes to Benny Hogan. She must remember this. And she must remember that both Johnny O'Brien and Nick Hayes were asking her for a date.

These were the things she would remember from the night. As well as the dance with Jack when he asked her.

He asked her at twenty-five to twelve. When they had dimmed the lights and the vocalist had told them that since Frankie Laine hadn't been able to show he would sing Frankie's song, 'Your Eyes are the Eyes of a Woman in Love', Jack Foley leaned across the table and said, 'Benny?'

They danced together easily, as if they had been partners for a long time.

She forced herself not to prattle and chatter and make fifteen jokes.

He seemed to be happy to dance without conversation.

Sometimes, looking over his shoulder she saw people looking at them. She was as tall as he was, so she couldn't have looked up at him to speak anyway, even if she had wanted to.

He drew her a little closer which was great except that she feared the place he had his hand on her back was just the part where the heavy-duty bra ended and there was a small roll of flesh.

God, suppose he held that bit of her – it would be like a lifebelt. How could she get him to move his hand up her back. How? These were the things you needed to know in life, rather than what was set out in a syllabus for you.

Mercifully the number ended. They stood beside each other companionably waiting for the next one to start. He leaned over and touched a lock of her hair.

'Is it all falling down?' Benny asked, alarmed.

'No, it's lovely. I just pretended it was out of place so that I could touch your face.'

How extraordinary that he had wanted to feel her face as she had yearned to touch his all night.

'I'm afraid . . .' she began.

She was going to say 'I'm afraid it's a very sweaty face, your finger might get stuck to it.'

But she stopped herself.

'What are you afraid of?' he asked.

'I'm afraid other Fridays are going to seem very dull after tonight.'

'Don't knock Knockglen.' He always said that. It was like a special phrase between them.

'You're right. We have no idea what plans Mario and Fonsie have for the place.'

The singer was sorry that Dino couldn't make it so he was going to give his own rendition of the Dean Martin number 'Memories are Made of This'.

Benny and Jack drew towards each other, and this time his hand was higher on her back. The devil roll of flesh like a lifebelt was not in evidence.

'You're a marvellous person to have in a party anywhere,' he said.

'Why do you say that?' Her face showed nothing of what she felt. None of the despair that he only thought of her as some kind of cabaret.

'Because you are,' he said. 'I'm only an ignorant old rugby player. What do I know of words?'

'You're not an ignorant old rugby player. You're a great host. We're all having a great night because you got us all together and invited us to your home.' She smiled and he gave her a little hug. And when he had held her tight he didn't release her again.

Into her ear he whispered, 'You smell absolutely lovely.'

She said nothing. She didn't close her eyes. It looked too confident. She didn't look around and see the envious glances as she was held by the most sought-after man in the room. She just looked down. She could see the back of his dinner jacket, and the way his hair curled at the back of his neck. Pressed close to her she could feel his heart beating, or maybe it was her heart. She hoped it was his, because if it was hers it seemed a bit over-strong.

Even when the third song, 'The Man from Laramie', was over Jack didn't suggest going back to the table. He wanted the next dance.

Benny blessed that dancing teacher who used to drive around in a battered old car teaching the tunic-clad girls of Ireland to dance. She blessed her with all her heart as she and Jack did stirring versions of 'Mambo Italiano' and 'Hernando's Hideaway'. Laughing and flushed they came back to the table. Sheila wasn't even pretending to listen to Johnny O'Brien and Rosemary looked distinctly put out. Nan caught Benny's eye and gave her a discreet thumbs-up sign. Eve sitting across the table with Aidan Lynch's arm loosely round her shoulder gave her a huge grin of solidarity. They were on her side.

'We thought we'd lost you for the night,' Nick Hayes said waspishly.

Neither Benny nor Jack took any notice. Aidan Lynch had won yet another spot prize – this time a huge box of chocolates which were opened. Carmel was busy feeding Sean with the soft-centred coffee ones he liked.

Rosemary foolishly grabbed the box to offer it to Jack.

'You must have one before they're all gone,' she said. But her movement was too swift and she spilled them all.

Benny looked on. It was the kind of thing she would normally have done. How perfect that it should be Rosemary who did it tonight.

'You owe me another dance for the one we didn't finish,' Rosemary said, as people tried to retrieve the chocolates.

'I do indeed. I wasn't going to let you forget it,' Jack said gallantly.

His fingers were still touching Benny's slightly. She was sure he had been going to dance with her again.

Then suddenly and unbelievably the last dance was announced. They wanted to see everyone on the floor for 'California Here I come'.

Benny could have cried.

Somehow, yet again, she had lost the high ground to Rosemary Ryan. She was going to have the last dance with Jack. Nick had his hand out to her, and so had Johnny O'Brien. She thought she saw a look of regret on Jack's face. But she must have imagined it, because when she and Johnny O'Brien took to the floor Jack and Rosemary were whirling around both laughing. Though she couldn't be sure, she thought she saw him push some of the hair out of Rosemary's eyes as he had done to her.

She kept a happy smile on her face for Johnny O'Brien as she clicked through her brain the possibilities that Jack Foley was just a fellow who liked everyone, and said nice things to every single woman he met. Not out of devious cunning, but because he genuinely did feel that every woman had some attraction for him.

This *must* be the case, Benny thought, because the way he

had held her when they were dancing together was suspiciously like the way he held Rosemary when everyone was dancing to 'Goodnight Sweetheart, See You in the Morning.'

There was a lot of excitement at the door where the photographers gathered to take snaps. They gave out little pink cards with the address of the places where the small prints could be inspected next day.

Benny was leaving just as Jack called.

'Here,' he called. 'Benny, come here and let's pose for posterity.'

Hardly able to believe that he had called her, she leaped to his side.

Just then Nan came down the steps.

'Nan too,' he said.

'No, no,' she moved away.

'Come on,' he said, 'the more the merrier.'

The three of them smiled at the flash. And then with a lot of calling goodnight, and see you, and wasn't it great, they were all in the cars that Jack had organized. Nick Hayes was to drive Benny, Eve and Sheila home because they all lived on the south side. The others were within a couple of miles of the city centre.

Nan was going with Sean and Carmel.

Rosemary, to her great rage, had a lift with Johnny O'Brien, who lived in the same road.

Kit had left sandwiches for them and a note saying that she had been out late playing cards so not to wake her until morning.

They crept up to bed.

'He's really nice, Aidan Lynch,' Benny said as they got undressed. 'I mean really nice. Not just all jokes and playing the fool.'

'Yes, but he talks like the Goons, nine tenths of the time. It's like having to learn a new language understanding him,' Eve complained.

'He seems very fond of you.'

'I ask myself what can be wrong with him then. Hereditary insanity maybe. His parents are like town criers. Did you hear them?'

Benny giggled.

'And what about you and Jack? You were doing great.'

'I thought I was.' Her voice was heavy and sad. 'But I wasn't really. He's just a dreamboat who's nice to everyone. He likes to be surrounded by the whole world, and have the whole world in a good humour.'

'It's not a bad way to be,' Eve said. She lay in her bed with her arms folded behind her neck. She looked so much more cheerful and happy than she had a few short months ago.

'No, it's not a bad way to be. But it's not a good thing to hitch your star to. I must keep remembering that,' Benny said.

Next morning they were woken by Kit.

'There's a call for you, Benny.'

'Oh God, my parents.' She leapt out of bed in her nightie.

'No, not at all. A young man,' Kit said, raising her eyebrows in approval.

'Hallo, Benny. It's Jack. You said you were staying with Eve. I asked Aidan for the phone number.'

Her heart was beating so strangely now, she thought she might fall down.

'Hallo, Jack,' she said.

'I was wondering if you'd like to have lunch,' he said.

She knew what lunch was now. Thank God. Lunch was a lot of people gathered together in a crowd around a table, with Benny entertaining them.

He certainly was someone who liked all his friends around him all the time. Benny was glad that she had identified that last night to Eve. That she hadn't allowed herself to build up any hopes.

She paused for a couple of seconds before she accepted. Only because she was thinking it all out.

'I meant on our own,' he said. 'This time just the two of us.'

CHAPTER ELEVEN

Eddie and Annabel Hogan had raised their eyebrows at each other in surprise as Patsy banged around the kitchen getting breakfast and muttering to herself. They had no idea what it was about.

They could decipher parts of her muttering . . . in all the years she had been in this house she had never been spoken to like that, shouted at, given dog's abuse. Mutter, mutter, crash, crash.

'Probably had words with Mossy,' Annabel whispered as Patsy went out to give some scraps to the four hens in their little wire-covered run.

'If so, she must be the first who ever had. I never knew such a silent man,' Eddie whispered back.

They had managed to get the information that Benny had telephoned from Dublin shortly before she went to the dance while they had gone for a walk.

Dr Johnson had said that Annabel should take more exercise and form the routine of a regular walk. Last night they had taken Shep on a long and invigorating journey half a mile out along the Dublin road. So they had missed the call.

'It was only to say thank you for the dress again, is that all, Patsy?' Annabel asked, yet again.

'That's what she said it was,' Patsy said darkly.

Benny's parents were mystified.

'She was probably overexcited,' Eddie said, after a lot of thought.

'She was that all right,' Patsy agreed.

Clodagh Pine told her aunt they should stay open at lunch time.

'Child, you'll have us all in the County Hospital if we work any more.'

Peggy Pine couldn't believe that she had thought this niece of hers was going to be a lazy lump. Already she had increased the turnover of the shop significantly, and despite her own appearance, which was to say the least of it eccentric, she had managed not to alienate any of the old customers either.

'But look at it, Aunt Peg. When else would people like Birdie Mac be able to come down and look at cardigans? When would Mrs Kennedy come over and see the new blouses? Mrs Carroll closes the grocery for lunch. She doesn't spend the whole lunch hour eating, by the look of her, thin string of misery that she is. Wouldn't she walk down and see what the new skirts are like?'

'It might seem a bit unfair somehow. Unfair on the others.' Peggy knew her thinking was confused.

'Tell me, Aunt Peg, have I missed something in my walks up and down Knockglen? Are there several women's draperies, open and competing with us? Is there a whole circle of women running shops like ours thinking that we're a bit sharp opening at lunch time?'

'Don't be impertinent,' Peggy said.

'Seriously. Who would object?'

'They might think we were anxious to make money. That's all.' Peggy was defensive.

'Oh, gosh wouldn't that be dreadful. And there you were all those years not trying to make a penny. Trying to lose it. How could I have been so stupid?' Clodagh put on a clowning face.

'We'll be dropping off our feet.'

'Not when we get another girl in we won't.'

'There'd never be the call for it.'

'Go over the books with me today and you'll see.'

Mrs Kennedy looked without pleasure on the picture of Fonsie who stood in her shop.

'How's the drugs business, Mrs K?' he asked. He always winked slightly at her as if she were engaged in something shady.

'What can I do for you?' she asked in a clipped voice.

'I'm looking for a nice fancy cake of soap.'

'Yes ... Well.' She managed to suggest that it was not a moment before time.

'For girls, like,' Fonsie said.

'A gift?' She seemed surprised.

'No, for the new ladies' room,' Fonsie said proudly.

He had spent a long time persuading Mario that they should do up the two outhouses as toilets. And make the female one look attractive. Girls liked to spend time painting themselves and doing their hair. Fonsie had driven out to an auction and bought a huge mirror. They put a shelf underneath it. All they needed now was a couple of nice towels on a roller and a bit of smart soap to start off with.

'Would Apple Blossom be a bit too good for what you had in mind?' Mrs Kennedy brought out what was called a gift pack of soap.

Fonsie made a mental note to tell Clodagh to stock soaps and talcs. Sneak them in before Peggy could protest that they were taking business from the chemist. Mrs Kennedy was an old bat, and a bad old bat at that. She didn't deserve to have the monopoly on the town's soap.

She wouldn't have, not for much longer.

But in the meantime . . .

'That's precisely what we need, Mrs Kennedy, thank you so much,' he said with a great beam and handed the money across the counter without even wincing at the cost.

Sean Walsh saw from the shop window that Mrs Healy across the road was polishing the brass sign for the hotel. She was looking at it critically. He wondered had it been defaced, she was frowning so much. There was nobody in Hogan's so he strolled across the road to see what was happening.

'It's hard to get in and out of the letters,' Mrs Healy said. 'Bits remain in there clogging them up.'

'You shouldn't be doing this, Mrs Healy, it's not fitting,' he said. 'A member of your staff should do the brasses.'

'You do the ones across the road. I've seen you,' she countered.

'Ah, that's different. It's not my place, across there.'

'Not yet,' said Mrs Healy.

Sean ignored this. 'You must have somebody, Mrs Healy, one of the kitchen maids.'

'They're so unreliable. Just standing chatting to people instead of getting on with it.' Mrs Healy seemed quite unaware that this is what she was doing herself.

'If you like, I'll do yours when I'm doing ours,' Sean offered. 'But early in the morning, before anyone would see.'

'That's extraordinarily kind of you.' Mrs Healy looked at him, surprised, as if wondering why he would do this. She prided herself in being able to understand human nature. Running a hotel you met all sorts and you had to make judgements about people. Sean Walsh was a difficult person to categorize. It was obvious that he had his eye on the daughter of the house. A big strong-willed girl with a mind of her own. Mrs Healy thought that Sean Walsh would be wise to make some contingency plans. Just because she was a large girl who might not get many offers, Benny Hogan, once she had her degree from Dublin, might well hightail it off somewhere else. Leaving Sean Walsh's plans in tatters.

Mother Francis was pleased that it was a nice bright Saturday morning and not drizzling with rain like it had been most mornings in the week.

She would go up to the cottage for an hour when school finished and see what else needed to be done. Sometimes she told herself that she was like a child with a dolls' house. Perhaps all the aching that a woman out in the world might have for her own home was coming to the surface. She hoped that this wasn't going to threaten the whole basis of her vocation to the religious life. You were meant to put your own home and family behind you and think only of your calling. But there was nothing in any rules that said you couldn't help to build up a home for an orphan who had been sent by the intervention of God into your care.

Mother Francis wondered how her orphan had got on at the dance last night. Kit Hegarty had phoned to say that Eve looked splendid. Mother Francis wished it hadn't been in a borrowed skirt, no matter how elegant and how rich a red.

She wished that class would be over and she could release the girls who were dying to escape anyway and go to Mario's café and look in the very much changed windows of Peggy's shop. Wouldn't it be wonderful if she could just ring the bell now, at eleven thirty in the morning and shout 'You're free'.

The children would remember it all their lives. But undoubtedly it would get to the ears of Mother Clare. Her heart sank as it always did at the thought of her sister in religion. If Mother Clare hadn't been coming they might have invited Kit Hegarty for Christmas. They couldn't now. Mother Clare would say they were turning a religious house into some kind of boarding house.

In two and a half hours she would be taking the key from its place in the wall and going into the cottage, polishing the piano and covering the damp stain on the wall with a lovely gold-coloured wall hanging.

One of the missionary Sisters had brought it from Africa. They had all admired it, but it wasn't a holy picture. It didn't really seem suitable to put it up in the convent. Mother Francis had kept it carefully. She knew just where it would be useful. And maybe she might get some gold-coloured material somewhere and Sister Imelda could run up a couple of cushion covers too.

Eve was almost bouncing up and down on her bed when she heard about the invitation to lunch.

'I *told* you, I *told* you,' she kept saying.

'No, you didn't. You said he *looked* as if he was enjoying dancing with me. That's all.'

'Well, you thought he looked as if it was Purgatory on earth and that he was making eyes at people over your shoulder to rescue him.'

'I didn't quite think that,' Benny said. But she had almost thought it.

When she had played the whole thing over in her mind again and again, those six lovely dances they had together, she was torn between believing that they were as enjoyable for him as they were for her, and that they were a simple courteous duty. Now it looked as if he really had liked her. The only problem was what to wear to the lunch.

Only the old cast-off clothes of yesterday were available. You couldn't wear a ball gown and expose your bosom on a November Saturday. So much the pity!

'I have seventeen pounds. I could lend you some if you wanted to buy something,' Eve offered.

But buying was no use. Not for Benny. They simply didn't have the clothes in her size.

If it had been Eve they could have run up Marine Road in Dunlaoghaire to Lee's or McCullogh's and got something in two minutes. If it were Nan all she would have to do was open a cupboard and choose. But Benny's clothes, such as they were, were fifty miles away in Knockglen.

Knockglen.

She had better ring her parents. And find out where they had been. And tell them it would be the evening bus, and say something to Patsy.

She got the coins and went back down to the phone.

They were delighted to hear from her and pleased that the dance had gone well, and wanted to know what had been served for supper. They were very startled to hear about the dispensation to eat meat. They had been out for a walk when she had telephoned last night. It was very good of her. And had the party in the Foleys' house been nice? And had she explained again how grateful they were to be asked?

Benny felt her eyes misting.

'Tell Patsy I have a pair of stockings for her as a present,' she said suddenly.

'You couldn't have chosen a better time to give her something,' Benny's mother said in a low, conspiratorial voice. 'She's been like a weasel all day. A weasel with a head cold if you ask me.'

Eve said that Kit would find a solution to the clothes problem. Kit had an answer for everything.

'Not about huge clothes.' Benny was gloomy.

But she was wrong. Kit said that one of the students who stayed in the house had a gorgeous emerald-green jumper. She'd borrow it off him. Say it needed a stitch or something. Boys never noticed that kind of thing. If he wanted to wear it today he bloody couldn't. That was all, Then Kit would sew a nice lacy collar of her own on it and lend Benny her green handbag. She'd be dressed to kill.

Fonsie wanted Clodagh to be the first to see the new ladies' cloakroom.

'God, it's lovely.' She was full of admiration. 'Pink towels, pink soap, and purple curtains. It's fabulous.'

He was anxious about the lighting. Was it too bright?

Clodagh thought not. If they were old people, who didn't want to see wrinkles, then yes, have it subdued. But they'd be young. Let them see the worst in their faces.

Clodagh wished she could get her aunt to install two fitting rooms. Peggy said that it wasn't needed in somewhere like Knockglen. People could take things on approval. If they didn't like them they could bring them back.

This was uneconomic and with the increased volume of stock they carried, hard to organize. There was a storeroom that Clodagh had her eye on. All it needed was light mirrors, carpet and bright curtains. They sighed, Clodagh and Fonsie, at the uphill battles with their relations.

'Will we go and have a drink in Healy's?' Fonsie said suddenly.

'I don't know. I said I'd unpack a whole lot of stuff that came in this morning.'

'To celebrate my new bathrooms and to plan your new fitting rooms,' he pleaded.

They walked companionably up the street, Clodagh in her short white wool dress worn over a pair of baggy mauve trousers and mauve polo-necked jumper. Great white plastic hoops of earrings dangled under a man's tweed hat with a ribbon of mauve and white on it.

Fonsie's spongy shoes made no sound on the footpath. His red crushed velvet jacket was bound in a yellow braid, his shirt neck was open and a red thin string like a tie hung down on each side of the collar. His dark red trousers were so tight that it appeared that every step would cause him pain in most of his body.

On Saturdays at lunch time the bar in Healy's Hotel was like a little club. Eddie Hogan would call in for a drink and meet Dr Johnson coming back from his rounds. Sometimes Father Ross would appear, and if Dessie Burns was off the drink he would sip a club orange loudly and know he was welcome in their midst.

Mr Flood hadn't been in much recently. The visions he had been seeing were preoccupying him. He had been seen standing in front of his shop looking thoughtfully up at the tree. Mr Kennedy when he was alive had been a regular. His wife would not have dreamed of coming in his stead. Sometimes Peggy had gone in for a swift gin and vermouth with Birdie Mac.

Clodagh and Fonsie paused at the entrance to the bar; they didn't want to join the group of old people and yet it would have been rude to ignore them.

As it happened they didn't have to make the decision.

Suddenly between them and the room stood the well-corseted figure of Mrs Healy.

'Can I do anything for you?' She looked from one to the other without hiding her distaste.

'Very probably, but I think we'll confine it to just having a drink at the moment,' Fonsie laughed, and ran his hand through his mop of dark and well-greased hair.

Clodagh giggled and looked down.

'Yes, well, perhaps Shea's or somewhere might be nice for a drink,' Mrs Healy said.

They looked at her in disbelief. She could not be refusing them entrance to her hotel?

Their silence unsettled her. Mrs Healy had been expecting a protest.

'So maybe we could see you, here, when you are ... um ... more appropriately dressed,' she said, with an insincere smile on her lips, but nowhere near her eyes.

'Are you refusing to serve us a drink, Mrs Healy?' Fonsie said in a very loud voice, intended to make every head in the place look up.

'I'm suggesting that perhaps you might present yourself for a drink in garb that is more in tune with the standards of a town like this and a hotel of this calibre,' she said.

'Are you refusing us because we are the worse for drink?' Clodagh asked. She looked over to the corner where two farmers were celebrating a small field bought and sold and were distinctly the worse for wear.

'I think out of respect for your aunt, who is one of our most valued customers, you might mind your tongue,' Mrs Healy said.

'She's joking, Clodagh. Don't mind her,' Fonsie said, trying to push past.

Two spots of red on Mrs Healy's face warned everyone that she most certainly was not joking.

Fonsie said that there were four men in the bar without ties, and he was perfectly willing to close his tie if it meant he could get a half pint of Guinness.

Clodagh said that if any of her garments offended Mrs Healy she would be very happy to remove them one by one until she was in something acceptable like a vest and knickers.

Eventually they tired of the game. With exaggerated shrugs and bewildered expressions, they left the bar. They both turned at the door with the sad, bloodhound faces of condemned criminals, but their laughter could be heard all the way down the corridor and out into the street.

The group in the corner looked at each other in some alarm. The main problem was Peggy, one of the town's most respected citizens. How would she take to her niece being refused entrance to the hotel? The little group of people that Mrs Healy cherished in her hotel looked down furtively.

Mrs Healy spoke in a steady voice. 'One has to draw the line somewhere,' she said.

Lilly Foley said that Aidan Lynch's terrible parents never knew where to draw the line.

Jack asked why they hadn't stopped serving drink, then the Lynches would have gone home. That apparently had been done early on. The bottles had been physically taken away from Aengus, but they had still stayed on and boomed.

'It irritated your father,' Lilly told Jack.

'Why didn't he do something about it then, like saying "Good God, is that the time?"' Jack saw no problems in the tardy Lynch parents.

'It's a woman's place to organize these things. It was left to me. As things always are,' Lilly Foley seemed put out.

'But apart from that it was a great party. Thanks a lot.' Jack grinned at her.

It mollified her a bit. She noted that her son had been on the phone already asking some girl out to lunch. She couldn't hear which one, but she assumed it was the glamorous Rosemary, who kept boasting of her relations in the Law, or the very beautiful girl, Nan, in the dress with all the little pearls on it. The girl who had said hardly anything, but was still the centre of attention.

Lilly looked affectionately at her eldest son. His hair was tousled, he smelled of Knight's Castille soap, he had eaten a huge breakfast and read the sporting pages of two newspapers. He had given Aengus half a crown for all his help at the party.

Lilly knew that like his father before him Jack Foley was a heartbreaker, and would be one until the day he died.

He had said the name of the restaurant as if everyone knew it. Carlo's. Benny had heard of it. It was down near the quays, her old stamping ground getting on and off the bus from Knockglen. It was small and Italian, and she had once heard Nan say she had been there in the evening and they had candles in wine bottles like you saw in the pictures.

Much too early as usual, she went into a big store and examined the cosmetics. She found a green eyeshadow and smeared some on each lid.

It was exactly the same colour as the veterinary student's enormous jumper that she was wearing. The shop assistant urged her to buy it, insisting that it was often hard to find exactly the right shade when you were looking for it and you should seize the hour.

Benny expained that it wasn't her sweater. It was borrowed from a fellow. She wondered why she needed to tell so much to strangers.

'Maybe he'll lend it to you again,' said the girl in the short pink nylon coat whose job was to sell cosmetics.

'I doubt it. I don't even know who he is. His landlady pinched it for me.'

Benny knew she was sounding very peculiar but conversation of any kind made her feel less anxious. It filled that great empty echo chamber of anxiety she felt about the lunch that lay ahead.

It had been so easy when she smelled of Joy and when she was able to be in his arms. It would be quite different now, in a green sweater across a table. How would she smile and attract him, and hold him. There must have been something about her that appealed to him last night. It couldn't have been all naked bosom, could it?

'Do you think I could have a spray of Joy perfume without buying any?' she begged the girl.

'We're not meant to.'

'Please.'

She got a small splash. Enough to remind him of last night.

Carlo's had a small door. That was a poor start. Benny hoped it wouldn't have those awful benches, the kind of church pew seats that were popular now. They were desparately hard to squeeze into. Even though it was bright out on the street, with a cold, wintry sun picking everything out sharply, it was dark and warm inside.

She gave her coat to the waiter.

'I'm to meet someone here,' she said.

'He is here already.'

That meant that Jack must be well known in this place, she thought with a wave of disappointment. Maybe he came every Saturday with a different girl.

'How do you know it's the right person?' she asked the waiter anxiously. It would be humiliating to be led to the wrong table in front of everyone and for Jack to have to rescue her.

'There is only one person here,' the waiter said.

He stood up to greet her.

'Don't you look lovely and well-rested considering the night that was in it?' he said admiringly.

'That's the good bracing air of Dunlaoghaire,' she said.

Why had she said that? There were words like bracing you didn't say. They reminded people of big, jolly girls on hikes. Like the word strapping.

But he hadn't made any unfortunate word associations. He still seemed quite admiring.

'Whatever it is, it works. Our house is full of the-day-after feeling, glasses and ashtrays piled up in the kitchen.'

'It was a lovely party, thank you very much.'

'It was fine. Aengus sends you his regards. He was very taken with you.'

'I think he thought I was mad.'

'No. Why should he think that?'

It had been the wrong thing to say. Why had she said it? Bringing herself down, why couldn't she have asked about Aengus?

The waiter came and fussed over them. He was a kindly man, like a thinner version of Mario. Benny wondered was he any relation. There couldn't be that many Italians working in Ireland.

Benny decided to ask him.

'Do you have a relative working in Knockglen?'

He pronounced the name of her home town over and over, rolling it around, but his eyes narrowing suspiciously.

'Why do you think I have relations in Knocka Glenna?'

'There's an Italian there, called Mario.'

Benny wished the purple and red sunburst carpet would open up at her feet and suck her into it, then close over her head.

Jack rescued her. 'It's probably a bit like, do you know my uncle Mo in Chicago?' he said. 'I'm always doing that.'

She couldn't imagine him ever doing it. Was there any way at all of trying to get back some of the magic of last night?

They hadn't even begun the lunch and already he must have regretted asking her. She had talked about the bracing air of Dunlaoghaire, reminding him of fat ladies on postcards. She had assumed that his younger brother must think she was mad. She had engaged the waiter in an endless and confused dialogue about whether he knew another Italian living miles away. What a great fun person she was. And there wasn't even anybody in the restaurant to distract him, to make him feel that the outing had any excitement at all. Benny wished she were back in the Dolphin hotel with half of Dublin there and all the Rosemarys and Sheilas and even Carmel and Sean picking at each other and feeding each other bread rolls.

Anything was better than this catastrophic setting.

'Isn't it super to have it to ourselves,' Jack said at that moment. 'I feel like a sultan, or some millionaire. They do – you know – ring up restaurants and say they want to book all the tables so that they won't be disturbed.'

'They do?' Benny asked eagerly.

At least it was conversation and he seemed to be making the best of the place being empty.

'Well, I did it today, of course! Carlo, we need the whole place to ourselves . . . a pianist possibly. No? Well, all right. Just a few violinists at the table later. Just don't let any hoi polloi in, no awful Dubliners having their lunch or anything sordid like that.'

They laughed and laughed just like last night.

'And what did Carlo say?'

'He said, "For you Messter Foley anything you like, but only eef the Signorina ees lovely."'

The words were bitten back. She was about to say, 'Well, we fell down on that one, didn't we?'

She was going to put herself down for fear of thinking that she might actually believe herself to be acceptable. But something warned her it wasn't the right thing to do. She put her head on one side and smiled at him.

'And then you arrived and he saw you were very beautiful, so he has now put a House Full sign on the door,' Jack said.

'Is that Carlo who's serving us, do you think?' Benny asked.

'No idea,' Jack said. 'He looks much more like a man who has a secret cousin in Knockglen, but doesn't want anyone to know.'

'I must remember every detail of this place to tell Mario about it,' Benny said, looking happily around.

'You're lovely, Benny,' Jack said, and laid his hand on hers.

Clodagh told her aunt that she had been barred from Healy's. It didn't matter all that much because it wasn't a place she planned on visiting much anyway, but she felt that Peggy should know from her before anyone else told her.

'What were you doing, the pair of you?' Peggy asked.

'I'd tell you if we *were* doing anything, you know that. But as it happened we just walked in. She decided she didn't like the look of us.'

'She can't do that under the Innkeeper's Act.'

'I think she can. Management reserves the right and all that. We thought you ought to know, you and Mario, but honestly Fonsie and I don't care. That's the truth.'

The truth also was that Peggy and Mario did care. Very much. Neither of them liked the way that the young people dressed, in fact it was a source of great common grumbling between them. But to be refused service in the town's only hotel. That was something else. That was war.

It wasn't long before Mrs Healy discovered how the lines were being drawn. Mr Flood, who was having one of his clear spells where he neither saw nor mentioned the nun in the tree who had been visiting him with messages, said that it was time that someone had taken a stand. Those two were an abomination. He had read in the papers that there was an international movement to take over the civilized world, and that its members knew each other by these kind of garish clothes. It was no accident that Fonsie and Clodagh had gravitated to each other, he said, nodding his head sagely. Mrs Carroll was with Mrs Healy too. The sooner this very undesirable influence in the town was stamped on, the better. Neither of these two young people had parents to deal with them, relying only on a maiden aunt and a bachelor uncle. No wonder they had run wild. Her own daughter Maire, who was working in the shop and doing book-keeping by correspondence course, had often been drawn to the bright lights in the café, and to the garish clothes in what had once been a respectable window. Mrs Healy had been quite right to make her point.

237

Mrs Kennedy on the other hand took a different view. She was heard to say that Mrs Healy had a cheek. She hadn't even been born in Knockglen. Who did she think she was, making rules and regulations for the people of the town? Mrs Kennedy said that there were many unsavoury people seen in the corner of Healy's bar on a Fair Day and when commercial travellers had too much to drink and knew they could always get a drink in the hotel. Mrs Kennedy, who had never liked the young widow and thought that her own husband used to spend too many evenings there, was outraged that she should think of refusing a drink to a niece of Peggy Pine, no matter how unwisely the poor girl garbed herself.

Birdie Mac wasn't sure. She was a timid woman who had lived all her life looking after an aged mother. She had neither wanted to do this or not wanted to. It was just that Birdie was unable to make a decision. She had never made her own mind up about anything. Even though she was a friend of Peggy's she also listened to what Mrs Carroll said. Even though Mario was a good customer and bought biscuits from her every day, she still agreed with poor Mr Flood that Mario's nephew was going too far altogether and how could it be stopped unless somebody shouted stop?

She didn't like Mrs Healy personally, but she admired her courage in running a business so well in a man's world, instead of retreating humbly behind the counter of a sweet shop, which was all that Birdie had been able to do in terms of independent living.

Dr Johnson said that Mrs Healy was free to serve or refuse whosoever she wanted. Father Ross wouldn't be drawn at all. Paccy Moore told his cousin Dekko that Mrs Healy had two bunions, one on each foot. That was his only comment. It was taken to be support for Clodagh and Fonsie.

Eddie and Annabel Hogan discussed it for a long time over their Saturday lunch. There were ways of course that Clodagh and Fonsie had misunderstood Knockglen and gone too far. They both looked as if they were in fancy dress almost all of the time. But they were hard workers, it couldn't be denied, and that was their great saving grace. If they had been standing smoking on the corner there would have been no sympathy for them.

But nobody could accuse either of them of being idle. And

in Knockglen that would cover a multitude of sins, like dressing so mutinously.

'If someone came into your shop, you'd serve them no matter how they were dressed, wouldn't you, Eddie?'

'Yes, but if they had manure on their boots I'd ask them not to walk it in,' he said.

'But they weren't walking anything in,' Annabel Hogan said. She had always thought that Mrs Healy had a special smile for the men and nothing nearly so warm for their wives. And also Clodagh had made such a lovely dress for Benny it would be hard not to be on her side. All that brocade had looked so well, there were little bits of chestnut colour in it, just like Benny's hair, and that beautiful dash of white at the front, that pleated insert over the bosom. It had given the whole thing such a classy touch. So elegant and ladylike, and not at all the kind of thing you'd ever have thought Clodagh would have dreamed up.

Mother Francis heard about the scene in the hotel as well. Peggy drove up to the convent that afternoon for tea and advice.

'Rise above it, Peggy. Rise right above it.'

'That's not easy to do if you're out in the world, Bunty.'

'It's not easy to do if you're inside a convent either. I have that Mother Clare descending on me for Christmas. Imagine trying to rise above that.'

'I'll never go in there for a drink again.'

'Think carefully, Peggy, think. If you do want a drink where will you go? The spit and sawdust in Shea's maybe? The poky little snugs of the other places? Don't do anything rash.'

'God, Bunty, for a nun you've a great knowledge of all the bars in town,' said Peggy Pine admiringly.

They talked about the dance, and how wonderful Aidan had been. No other table had won so many spot prizes. And there had been an incident Jack told her where a girl fainted at another table and when they had loosened her clothes and tried to revive her, two bread rolls had fallen out of her bra. Jack laughed good-naturedly at this. Benny thought of how the girl must be feeling today, and how she would never be able to remember the dance with anything but shame.

'Oh, go on, it *is* funny,' he said. She knew she must see the lighthearted side. 'Yes, and full of crumbs, very scratchy I'd say.'

She felt like Judas to this girl she didn't even know, but she was rewarded with the smile.

'Not anything you'd ever need, Benny,' he said, smiling at her across the table.

'Everyone's different.' She looked down very, very embarrassed.

'You're different in a good way,' he said.

At least the veterinary student, whoever she was, had a nice floppy jumper. You couldn't see the outline of her breasts. She looked at her front, relieved. What could she say now to change the subject?

The door opened and another couple came in. Jack shrugged.

'I said only people from Napoli could come, and then only if they stayed quiet.' He looked at them warningly.

They were a pair of middle-aged Dubliners. Cold and shivery.

'Probably civil servants having an affair,' Benny whispered.

'No, two school inspectors planning to make everyone fail the Leaving Certificate next year,' he countered.

Most of the time it was easy to talk to him. He was so normal and relaxed, and there really was nothing in his manner that made her feel anxious. It was just herself. Benny realized that she had spent years sending herself up and playing the fool. When it came to the time to play the romantic lead, she didn't have a clue. And worse, she wasn't at all sure that was the part she was actually being cast to play. She wished she could read his signals, and understand what he was saying.

If only she could know then she could respond.

The ice cream was offered. The waiter explained cassata, a beautiful Neapolitan ice cream, he said, lovely bits of fruit and nuts chopped up in it, some candied peel, some macaroons. *Bellissima*.

Something told Benny that the right thing was to have it, not to talk of diets or calories or waistlines.

She saw Jack's face light up. He'd have some too.

The waiter saw them smile at each other.

'It's a very dark afternoon. I light a little candle to give you light to see each other when you talk,' he said.

Jack's open shirt over his navy sweater was a pale pink. It looked beautiful in the candlelight. She felt again that urge to stroke him. Not to kiss his lips or press against him, just to reach out and rub her hand softly from his cheek to his chin.

She had drunk only one glass of wine. It couldn't be some drink-crazed feeling.

Benny watched as if it was happening to someone else as she leaned across and stroked his face softly three times.

The third time he caught her hand and held it to his lips.

He kissed it with his head bent over it so that she couldn't see his eyes.

Then he gave it back to her.

There was no way he was making fun of her, or making a silly extravagant gesture like Aidan might.

Nobody would hold your hand like that and kiss it for such a long time unless they wanted to.

Would they? Would they?

Dessie Burns said that Mrs Healy could be a bit uppity in herself, and there had indeed been times when she had spoken to him more sharply than was called for. But to be fair, there had been a question of drink involved and perhaps there were those who would say that the woman had been within her rights. There was nothing more scrupulously and boringly fair than Dessie Burns when he was on the dry.

And when all was said and done that young Fonsie was a pup, and a pup needed a good spanking now and then if he was to grow into a good dog, so that's all that had happened. Fonsie had been told he couldn't walk around this town as if he owned it. Who was he? The nephew of an Eyetie, with no sign of the Eyetie mother and the Dub father since the day he'd set foot in the place. That was a young lad without a background, without a history, in Knockglen. Let him take things more slowly. And as for Peggy's niece, she was a sore trial with the get-up of her. Maybe this would make her settle down.

Mario said that he would go up and stand on the step of Healy's Hotel and spit in the door and then spit out the door, and then he'd come home and spit at Fonsie.

Fonsie said that none of this would advance them, they should instead go to Liverpool and buy a beautiful second-hand Wurlitzer juke box that he had seen advertised there.

Mario developed a most unexpected loyalty to Fonsie. Having denounced him to everyone in the town individually and generally he now said that his sister's child was the salt of the earth, the mainstay of Mario's old age and the shining hope for Knockglen.

He also said with a lot of pounding on whatever surface he was near that he would never drink in Healy's again. Which, considering he had never drunk there anyway, was a threat more powerful in the utterance then the deed.

Simon Westward came into Healy's that afternoon to enquire if they did dinners.

'Every day, Mr Westward.' Mrs Healy was delighted to see him in the place at last. 'Might I offer you a little something on the house to celebrate your first visit to us?'

'Very kind of you ... er ... Mrs ... er ...'

'Healy.' She looked rather pointedly at the hotel sign.

'Ah yes, how stupid of me. No, I won't stay for a drink now. You do do dinners. That's wonderful. I wasn't sure.'

'Every day from noon until two-thirty.'

'Oh.'

'Do those hours not suit you?'

'No, I mean they're perfectly fine hours. I was thinking of dinner in the evening.'

Mrs Healy always prided herself on being ready when Opportunity came to call.

'Up to now Mr Westward we have merely served high teas, but coming up to the Christmas season and thereafter we will indeed be serving dinner,' she said.

'Starting?'

'Starting next weekend, Mr Westward,' she said, looking him straight in the eye.

The waiter thought they must have a sambucca. It was a little Italian liqueur. This was with the compliments of the house. He would put a coffee bean in it and set it alight. It was a wonderful drink to have at the end of a lunch on a winter's day.

They sat there and wondered would the disgruntled couple get one too, or was it only for people who looked happy.

'Will we see you next weekend?' the waiter asked eagerly. Benny could have killed him. She was doing so well. Why must the waiter bring up the subject of another date?

'Certainly another time, I hope,' Jack said.

They walked along the Quays, which had often looked cold and wet to Benny, but this afternoon there was a glorious sunset, and everything had a rosy light.

The second-hand booksellers had wooden stands of books on display outside.

'It's like Paris,' Benny said happily.

'Were you ever there?'

'No, of course I wasn't,' she laughed good-naturedly. 'That's me, just showing off. I've seen the pictures and I've been to the films.'

'And you're studying French of course, you'd be able to take it in your stride.'

'I doubt that. Great chats about Racine and Corneille in English would be more my line.'

'Nonsense. I'll be depending on you to be my guide when I'm playing in the Parc des Princes,' he said.

'I bet you will,' she said.

'No, that's me showing off. I'll never play for anyone if I keep eating like I did last night and today. I'm meant to be in training. You'd never know it.'

'You're lucky you didn't have practice today. You often do on Saturdays, don't you?'

'We did. I skipped it,' he said.

She looked at him suddenly. The old Benny would have made a joke. The new Benny didn't.

'I'm glad you did. It was a lovely lunch.'

She had her overnight bag in a shop near the bus stop. The woman handed it over the counter to her and together they walked towards the bus.

'What will you do tonight?' he asked her.

'Go to Mario's café and tell people about the dance. What about you?'

'No idea. Hope there are some invitations when I get home.' He laughed lazily, the kind of man who didn't have to plan his own life.

He passed her zippered bag on to the bus. Benny willed Mikey not to make any smart-aleck remarks.

'There you are, Benny. I knew we didn't have you yesterday. The weight in the bus was lighter altogether,' he said.

Jack hadn't heard, or if he had heard he hadn't understood

243

Mikey's mumblings. That's what she told herself as she sat and looked out at the darkening city and the beginnings of the countryside.

She had danced close to Jack Foley, who had then invited her out to lunch. She had said nothing too stupid. He had said he'd see her in the Annexe on Monday. He had kissed her hand. He had said she was lovely.

She was absolutely exhausted. She felt as if she had been carrying a heavy weight for miles and miles in some kind of contest. But whatever contest it was, and whatever the rules, it looked as if she had won.

CHAPTER TWELVE

Heather wanted to know all about the dance and mainly what they had for pudding. She was stunned that Eve couldn't remember. She found it beyond comprehension that there could be too much else happening to remember pudding.

She broke the news that Simon said he was going to join them on their outing.

'I didn't know anything about this,' Eve said, annoyed.

'I didn't tell you in case you wouldn't come.' Heather was so honest that it was hard to attack her.

'Well, if you have him . . .'

'I want you,' Heather said simply.

Simon arrived in the car.

'Think of me as the chauffeur,' he said. 'You ladies are in charge.'

Almost immediately he gave them his own plan for the afternoon. A drive through County Wicklow and afternoon tea in a rather nice hotel he knew.

Eve and Heather had been planning to take the train to Bray, go on the bumpers and have ice creams with hot butterscotch sauce. Eve was pleased that Simon's outing sounded so dull and tame compared to her own. She knew which Heather would have preferred.

But Heather was a dutiful sister, and she saw far too little of Simon already. She gave a mild show of enthusiasm. Eve after a deliberate pause did the same.

Simon looked from one to the other. He knew that this was second best. He was very cheery and answered all Heather's questions about her pony, about Clara's puppies, about Woffles the rabbit.

He explained that Mrs Walsh was still as silent and as majestic on her bicycle as ever. That Bee Moore was upset over some young man she had wanted and he had turned his attentions to Another. Eve had to put her hand over her face when Heather's questioning revealed the man to be Mossy Rooney and Another to be Patsy.

'How's Grandfather?' Heather asked.

'The same. Come on, we're boring Eve.'

'But he's Eve's grandfather too.'

'Absolutely.'

The subject was closed. Eve knew he wanted something. She had no idea what it was.

At tea time he brought it up.

'That was a remarkably beautiful girl, your friend.'

'Which friend?'

'In the shop, at the dance. The blonde girl.'

'Oh yes?'

'I was wondering who she is?'

'Were you?'

'Yes, I was.' He was short now.

For ages afterwards Eve hugged herself with delight and congratulations that she had managed not to answer such a direct question with any kind of response that would please him. And yet she had remained perfectly polite. For the girl who used to speak so unguardedly, whose temper was a legend in St Mary's, it was a triumph.

'Who is she? Oh, she's a student at UCD, doing First Arts, like about six hundred of us.'

Her smile had told Simon Westward that this was all he was going to get.

The veterinary student was a nice boy called Kevin Hickey. He was very polite and he thanked Mrs Hegarty for having taken his new green sweater to sew a tape on the back of it in case he wanted to hang it up with a loop. He had thought you should fold them, or put them on a clothes hanger, but still, it was very nice of her. He might wear it tonight. It was a great colour. When he picked it up he thought there was a faint smell of perfume, but he must have imagined it. Or else it was Mrs Hegarty's perfume. Kevin Hickey's mother was dead. It was nice to live in a house where there was a kind woman looking after him. He had asked his father to send her a turkey for Christmas. It would come by train, wrapped in straw and tied well with string.

He smelled his green jumper again. There was definitely some cosmetic. Maybe if he hung it up in the fresh air by the window it would go away.

He heard the gate opening and drew back. He wouldn't like Mrs Hegarty to see him airing the jumper. But it wasn't Mrs Hegarty back from her shopping. It was a dark-haired man he hadn't seen before.

The doorbell rang and rang, so Kevin ran down to answer it. Mrs Hegarty was out, he said. The man wanted to wait. He looked respectable. Kevin was at a loss.

'It really is all right.' The man smiled at him. 'I'm an old friend.'

'And what's your name?'

'It's Hegarty also, as it happens.'

As Kevin went back upstairs he turned and saw the man who was sitting in the hall pick up the picture of Mrs Hegarty's son who had died. Possibly he was a relation.

Sheila noticed that Jack ran off immediately after his law lectures these days. No hanging around and chatting. No little jokes, just off like an arrow. Once or twice she asked him why he needed to run so fast.

'Training.' He had smiled at her with that boyish kind of laugh which meant he knew he would be forgiven anything.

Sheila decided that he must be seeing that Rosemary Ryan in First Arts.

She enquired from Carmel if that was true. It was easy to talk to Carmel because she wasn't really playing in the same game, she was so preoccupied with Sean that other people were only a vague background to her.

'Rosemary and Jack? I don't think so,' Carmel said after a lot of thought. 'No, I haven't seen them together at all. I've seen Jack in the Annexe a couple of mornings, but only talking to Benny Hogan.'

'Ah, well, that's all right, so,' said Sheila with some relief.

Benny and Patsy were friends again. It had taken the promised stockings plus a tin of French Moss talcum powder and an explanation that her nerves were overwrought because she was frightened of going to the dance. Once Patsy had come round she was as usual a strong champion of the daughter of the house.

'What did you have to be frightened of? Aren't you a fine big girl who shows all the signs of being well fed and well looked after all her life?'

That was one of the things that Benny feared was only too obvious. But it was hard to explain to small, stooped Patsy who had been brought up without enough to eat in an orphanage.

'How's your romance?' she asked instead.

'He's not much with the words,' Patsy complained.

'But the words he does say? Are they nice?'

'It's very hard to know with men what they mean,' Patsy said sagely. 'You'd need someone standing at your shoulder saying this means this, and this means the other.'

Benny agreed fervently. When Jack Foley said he had missed her at a party did he mean that he had looked around and thought it would be lovely if only Benny had been there? Had he thought it all evening, or only once? And if he missed her that much why had he gone to it? At the party in Jack's house Aengus had asked Benny if she was one of the ones who was always phoning looking for Jack. She had decided that she would never be one of those. It had worked so well the way things were. Or had it? Patsy was right. With men it was impossible to know what they meant. Nan used to say they never meant anything, but that was too depressing to contemplate.

Mrs Healy had been disappointed not to see Sean Walsh arriving full of support for her predicament. She knew his distaste for Fonsie and Clodagh and the kind of lifestyle they represented. But then Sean was not a customer in Healy's Hotel. It had something to do with not presuming, she imagined. Not putting himself forward, styling himself as Mr Hogan's equal when he was in fact a hired hand.

It was nice to see that kind of respect but sometimes Sean carried it too far. Like polishing the brasses, like living in a cramped room over the shop. He seemed to be biding his time and maybe he might bide it too long.

'You should invite young Sean Walsh in for a drink with you sometime,' she suggested to Eddie Hogan.

Eddie's honest face told her what she already knew. 'I've asked him a dozen times, but he won't come in with me. I don't think he's a drinking man. Weren't we blessed the day he arrived in Knockglen?'

Emily Mahon marvelled at the way her daughter kept her clothes and her room. Every garment was sponged and hung up when it was taken off. Her coats and jackets always looked as if they had come straight from the dry cleaners.

The shoes had newspapers stuffed in the toes and stood on a small rack by the window. She polished her belts and handbags until they gleamed. On the wash-hand basin in her room were samples of soaps that Emily had been able to get her through the hotel. There was a book on how to apply make-up. Nan Mahon didn't rely on weekly magazines or Sunday newspapers to teach her style. She did the thing thoroughly.

Emily smiled affectionately as she saw the books on etiquette that Nan studied as well as her university texts. Nan had once told her mother that anyone could talk to anyone if they knew the rules. It was a matter of learning them.

The book was open at a section telling you how introductions are made.

'Marquesses, Earls, Viscounts, Barons and their wives are introduced as Lord or Lady X, Honourables as plain Mr.' Imagine if Nan was in a world where such things would be of use to her. But then it wasn't all that far beyond the possible. Look at the way she had looked at that dance. People who weren't even part of the student crowd were admiring her. She might very well end up in twinset and pearls on the steps of a big house, with dogs beside her and servants to do her work.

It had always been Emily Mahon's dream for her daughter. The only problem was what part would she play in it. And it didn't bear thinking about how little a part Nan's father might be expected to take in any such lifestyle.

If Nan were to get there it was easy to see that she would no longer be any part of Maple Gardens.

Rosemary Ryan wore far too much make-up for the daytime. Benny could see that quite clearly now. There was a ridge at the side of her jaw where it stopped.

She was also brighter than people gave her credit for. When she was with a crowd she always simpered and played the dumb blonde, but in tutorials she was sharp as a razor.

'What are you going to do when this is over?' she asked Benny.

'Go to the Annexe.' Benny was meeting Jack. She hoped Rosemary wouldn't come too. 'I have to meet a whole lot of different people,' she said hastily, to discourage her.

'No, I meant this. All of this.' Rosemary waved a vague hand around the university.

'Do a postgrad diploma and be a librarian, I think,' Benny said. 'What about you?'

'I think I'll be an air hostess,' Rosemary said.

'You don't need a degree for that.'

'No, but it helps.' Rosemary had it worked out. 'It's a great way to get a husband.'

Benny didn't know whether she meant doing a degree was a good way or being an air hostess. She didn't like to ask. It was such a strange coincidence that Rosemary should say that, because only the day before Carmel had asked Nan would she think of joining Aer Lingus. She had the looks and the style. And she'd meet lots of men.

'Only businessmen,' Nan had said, as if that settled it.

Carmel's eyes had narrowed. Her Sean was doing a B.Comm. and was aiming hard to be a businessman.

'Carmel says Nan doesn't think it's a good job.' Rosemary was probing. 'Do you think Nan's going out with Jack Foley?'

'What makes you think that?'

'I don't know. He hasn't been sighted much. I wondered was he holed up with someone mysterious.'

'*I* see him from time to time,' Benny said.

'Oh, that's all right then.' Rosemary was pleased. 'He's around. He hasn't been snatched away from under our noses. What a relief!'

Kit Hegarty let herself in and found her husband Joseph sitting in the kitchen.

She put her shopping on the floor and steadied herself with a hand on the kitchen chair.

'Who let you in?' she asked.

'A boy with freckles and a Kerry accent. Don't say anything to him. He interrogated me and asked me to sit in the hall.'

'Which you didn't.'

'I was cold.'

'Did you tell him who you were?'

'Just that my name happened to be Hegarty. Sit down, Kit. I'll make you a cup of tea.'

'You'll make me nothing in my kitchen,' she said.

But she did sit down and looked at him across the table. He was fifteen years older than he was the day he had taken the mail boat out of their lives.

How long had she cried herself to sleep at night wanting him to return? How often had she played the scene where he would come back and she would forgive him? But always in that version Francis would be young and would run towards them both, arms outstretched, crying out that he had a daddy and a real home again.

He was still handsome. His hair had only little bits of grey, but he looked shabbier than she remembered, as if he were down on his luck. His shoes weren't well polished. They needed to be taken to a cobbler's. His cuffs were not frayed exactly, but thin.

'Did you hear about Francis?' she said.

'Yes.'

The silence hung long between them.

'I came to tell you how sorry I was,' he said.

'Not sorry enough to see him ever, to care to be involved in his life when he had a life.'

She looked at him without hate, the man who had abandoned them. She had been told that he had gone to live with a barmaid. At the time somehow that had made it worse, more humiliating that the woman was a barmaid. It was such an obvious kind of thing to do. Now she wondered why the woman's job had been remotely important.

She thought of all the questions she had parried and eventually answered while her son grew up asking about his father, and wondering why he didn't have what everyone else at the Christian Brothers school had in their homes.

She thought of the day Francis had got his Leaving Certificate and run home with the results, and how she had an urge to find her long-lost husband that day – only a few months ago – and tell him that the child they had produced together would go to university.

In those long nights when she had not been able to find any sleep and thoughts had run scampering around in her head, she remembered with relief that she hadn't raised the hopes of this philandering husband and led him to believe that he had fathered a university student.

She thought of all this as she looked at him sitting in her kitchen.

'I'll make you tea,' she said.

'Whatever you think.'

'Did she throw you out?' Kit asked. She asked because he hadn't the look of a man who was cared for by a woman, not even a woman who had been brassy and taken him, even though she must have known he had a wife and child in Ireland.

'Oh, that all ended a long time ago. Years and years ago.'

It had ended. But he had not come back. Once gone he was truly gone. Somehow that was sadder than the other. For years she had seen him in some kind of domesticity with this woman. But in fact he might have been living alone, or in digs or bedsitters.

That was worse than leaving her for a grand passion, however ill advised. She looked at him with a look of great sadness.

'I was wondering . . .' he said.

She looked at him, kettle in one hand and teapot in the other.

He was going to ask, could he come back.

Nan wanted to know if Eve had taken Heather out at the weekend. She often enquired about Heather, Eve noticed, rarely about the digs and Kit or the convent and Mother Francis.

She said they went to Wicklow and it had been wet and misty, and they went to a hotel where tea and sandwiches cost twice what real food like ice cream and butterscotch sauce would cost.

'You must have gone in a car to a place like that,' Nan said.

'Yes.' Eve looked at her.

'Did Aidan drive you?'

'Lord, I couldn't let Aidan near her. He's quite frightening enough for our age. He'd give a child nightmares.'

Nan left the subject of Aidan Lynch.

'So who did?'

Eve knew it was ridiculous not to tell her. She'd get to know some day. It was like being an eight-year-old, having secrets at school. Anyway it was making too much of it all.

'Her brother Simon drove us,' she said.

'The one we saw in my mother's shop at the dance, and you didn't introduce me.'

'The very one.'

Nan pealed with laughter. 'You're marvellous, Eve,' she said. 'I'm so glad I'm your friend. I'd really hate to be your enemy.'

Most of the cottages on the road up by the quarry behind the convent were fairly dilapidated. It was never a place that anyone would really seek out to live. It had been different when the quarry was operating, in those days there had been plenty of people wanting to live there. Now there were very few lights in windows. Mossy Rooney lived in a small house there with his mother. There had been rumours that Mossy had been seen with building materials and a consequent speculation that he might intend building an extra room at the back. Could this mean that he had plans to marry?

Mossy was not a man to do things in a hurry. People said that Patsy shouldn't count her chickens too soon.

Sean Walsh sometimes went for a walk up that way on a Sunday. Mother Francis would nod to him gravely and he always returned the greeting very formally.

If he ever wondered what the nun was doing pushing her way past the dark green leaves of the wild fuchsia and rolling up her sleeves to polish and clean he never gave any sign of his curiosity. Neither did she pause to think why he walked there. He was a lonely young man, not very attractive to speak to. She knew that Eve had always disliked him. But that might just have been a childish thing, a loyalty to Benny Hogan, who had some kind of antipathy towards her father's assistant.

She was surprised when he addressed her. With a long preamble of apology he asked if she knew who owned the cottages and whether they might perhaps belong to the convent. Mother Francis explained that they had once belonged to the Westlands estate, and had devolved somehow to various quarry workers and others. Politely with her head on one side in her enquiring manner she wondered why he wanted to know.

Equally courteously Sean told her that it had been an idle enquiry but the nature of small towns being what it was, perhaps an enquiry that might remain confidential between the two of them.

Mother Francis sighed. She supposed the poor fellow who had scant hope of making much of a living in Hogan's might be looking to the day when he could buy a house for himself and start a family, and that he was realistic enough to start looking up on this wild craggy road where nobody would really live by choice.

Benny hated going into the Coffee Inn. The tables were always so small. She was afraid that her skirt or her shoulder bag would swoop someone's frothy coffee off on to the floor.

Jack's face lit up when he saw her. He had been holding a seat with some difficulty.

'These awful country thicks wanted to take your stool,' he hissed at her.

'Less running down the country people,' Benny said. She glanced up and saw with a shock that the three students who had lost the battle for the seat were Kit Hegarty's students, the boys who lived where Eve worked. And one of them, a big fellow with freckles, was wearing his lovely emerald-green sweater.

Aidan Lynch asked Eve to come home and meet his parents.

'I've met them,' Eve said ungraciously, handing him another dinner plate to dry.

'Well, you could meet them again.'

Eve didn't want to meet them again; it was rushing things. It was saying things that weren't ready to be said like that Eve was Aidan's girlfriend, which she wasn't.

'How is this relationship going to progress any further?' Aidan asked the ceiling. 'She won't get to know my family. She won't let me near her body. She won't go on a date with me unless I come out to Dunlaoghaire and do the washing-up after all the culchies first.' He sounded very sorry for himself.

Eve's mind was on other things. Aidan could amuse himself for hours when he was in one of his rhetorical moods. She smiled at him absently.

Kit was out. For the very first time since Eve had been in the house; what was more, there was no message.

Kevin, the nice freckled vet student whose jumper had been purloined for Benny's date, had said that Mrs Hegarty had gone out with a man.

'Everyone goes out with men,' Aidan had interrupted. 'It's the law of nature. Female canaries go out with male canaries. Sheep go out with rams. Women tortoises go out with men tortoises. Only Eve seems to have reservations.'

Eve took no notice. She was also thinking about Benny. Almost every day for a week now Benny had met Jack Foley, either in the Annexe or the Coffee Inn or a bar. She said he was very easy to talk to. She hadn't put a foot wrong yet. Benny's face had looked as if someone had turned on a light inside when she talked about Jack Foley.

'And of course this Eve that I have the misfortune to be besotted with . . . she won't even stay in Dublin for the Christmas parties. She's leaving me on my own for other women to have their way with, and do sinful things with my body.'

'I have to go to Knockglen, you idiot,' he said.

'Where there will be no parties, where people will go out and watch the grass grow and see the rain fall and moo-cows will walk down the main street swishing their foul tails.'

'You've got it wrong,' Eve cried. 'We'll be having a *great* time in Knockglen, down in Mario's every evening, and of course there'll be parties there.'

'Name me one,' Aidan countered.

'Well, I'll be having one for a start,' Eve said, stung.

Then she stood motionless with a dinner plate in her hands. Oh God, she thought. Now I have to.

Nan rang the *Irish Times*, and asked for the sports department. When she was put through she asked them to tell her what race meetings would be held before Christmas.

Not many, she was told. Things slackened off coming up to the festival season. There'd be a meeting every Saturday, of course, Navan, Punchestown, run-of-the-mill things. But on St Stephen's Day it would all get going again. The day after Christmas there'd be Leopardstown and Limerick. She could take her pick of those. Nan asked them what did people who usually went racing do when the season slackened off. In a newspaper people are accustomed to being asked odd questions on the phone. They gave it some consideration. It depended on what kind of people. Some might be saving their pennies, some might be out hunting. It depended.

Nan thanked them in the pleasant unaffected voice that had never tried to imitate the tones of another class she wanted to join. An elocution teacher at school had once told them that there was nothing more pathetic than people with perfectly good Irish accents trying to say 'Fratefully naice'. Nothing would mark you out as a social climber as much as adopting that kind of accent.

They sat in a café in Dunlaoghaire, Mr and Mrs Hegarty. Around them other people were doing ordinary things, like having a coffee before going to an evening class in typing, or waiting for the pictures to start.

Ordinary people with ordinary lives and nothing bigger to discuss than whether the electric fire would eat up electricity or if they could have two chickens instead of a turkey for Christmas day.

Joseph Hegarty fiddled with his spoon. She noticed that he didn't take sugar in his coffee now. Perhaps the woman had put him off that. Perhaps his travels had taken him to places where there were no sugar bowls on the table. He had left one insurance company and gone to another. He had moved from that to working with a broker, to having a book himself, to working with another agent. Insurance wasn't the same, he told her.

She looked at him with eyes that were not hard, or cold. She saw him objectively. He was kindly and soft spoken, as he had always been. In those first agonized months after he had left that was what she had missed above all.

'You wouldn't know anyone here any more,' she said haltingly.

'I'd get to know them again.'

'It'd be harder to find insurance work here than there. Things are very tight in Ireland.'

'I wouldn't go back on that. I thought maybe I could help you . . . build up the business.'

She thought about it, sitting very still and with her eyes down so that she wouldn't meet the hope in his. She thought of the way he would preside over the table, make the place seem like it was run by a family. She could almost see him giving second helpings, making boys like Kevin Hickey laugh, being interested in their studies and their social lives.

But why had he not done that for his own son? For Francis

Hegarty who might still be alive this day if he had had a firm father who would brook no nonsense about a motorbike.

'No, Joseph,' she said, without looking up. 'It wouldn't work.'

He sat there very silent. He thought about his son, the son who had written to him all these years. The son who had come to see him during the summer, on a weekend from canning peas. Frank, the boy who had drunk three pints with his father and told him all about the home in Dunlaoghaire and how maybe his mother's heart was softening. But he had never told his mother about the visit or the letters. Joseph Hegarty would keep faith with the dead boy. Frank must have had reasons, his father would not betray him now or change his mother's memory of him.

'Very well, Kit,' he said. 'It's your decision. I just thought I'd ask.'

The Westwards were in the telephone book. The phone was answered by an elderly woman.

'It's a personal call for Mr Simon Westward from Sir Victor Cavendish.' Nan spoke in the impersonal voice of a secretary. She had taken the name from *Social and Personal*.

'I'm sorry, Mr Westward isn't here.'

'Where can Sir Victor find him, please?'

Mrs Walsh responded immediately to the confident tone that expected an answer.

'He's going to have lunch in the Hibernian, I believe,' she said. 'Perhaps Sir Victor could telephone him there.'

'Thank you so much,' Nan said, and hung up.

'I want to give you your Christmas present today,' Nan said to Benny in the main hall.

'Lord, Nan, I didn't bring anything in for you.' Benny looked stricken.

'No, mine is a treat. I'm taking you to lunch.'

She would listen to no refusals. Everyone deserved to have lunch in the Hibernian at least once in their life. Nan and Benny were no exceptions. Benny wondered why Eve wasn't being included.

They met Bill Dunne and Johnny O'Brien as they were crossing St Stephen's Green.

The boys suggested a Christmas drink. When that was turned down, they came up with chicken croquette and chips in Bewley's with sticky almond buns to follow. Laughing, Benny said they were going to the Hibernian.

'You must have a pair of sugar daddies then,' Bill Dunne said crossly to hide his disappointment.

Benny wanted to tell them that it was Nan's treat, but she didn't like to. Perhaps Nan mightn't want to admit that it was just the two of them. She looked hopefully at her friend for some signal. But Nan's face gave no hints of anything. She looked so beautiful Benny thought, again with a pang. It must be amazing to wake up in the morning and know your features were going to look like that all day, and that everyone who saw your face would like it.

Benny wished that Bill Dunne didn't look so put out. On an ordinary day it would have been lovely to have gone to Bewley's with him. Jack was up at the rugby club all afternoon. She would love to have been with Bill and Johnny in many ways. They were Jack's people. They were part of his life. She felt disloyal to Nan and her generous present. And wasn't it marvellous to go inside the Hibernian for something better than walking through its coffee lounge to the ladies' cloakroom at the back which was all she had ever done before.

Eve had no lectures in the afternoon. She couldn't find either Benny or Nan. Aidan Lynch had invited her to join his parents, who liked to combine an hour of Christmas shopping and four hours of lunch several times in the weeks leading up to the festive season. She had declined, saying it sounded like a minefield.

'When we're married we'll have to see them, you know, invite them over for roast lamb and mint sauce,' he had said.

'We'll face that when we come to it in about twenty years' time,' Eve had said to him grimly.

You couldn't put Aidan Lynch off. He was much too cheerful, and totally confident that she loved him. Which of course she didn't. Eve didn't love anybody, as she had tried to explain. Just very strong affections for Mother Francis and Benny and Kit. Nobody had ever shown her why love was such a great thing, she told him. Look what it had done for her mother and father. Look how boring it made Sean and Carmel. Look at the way it had wrecked Kit Hegarty's life.

Thinking about Kit made her think that that was where she would go, home to Dunlaoghaire. Kit had looked very strange in the last couple of days. Eve hoped that she wasn't sick, or that the man who had come back hadn't been who Eve feared it had.

She took the train out to Dunlaoghaire and let herself in. Kit was sitting in the kitchen with her head in her hands. Nothing had been touched since Eve had left that morning. Eve hung up her coat.

'Sister Imelda had a great saying. She used to believe that there was no problem on the face of the earth that couldn't be tackled better with a plate of potato cakes. And I must say I agree with her.'

As she spoke she took the cold mashed potato from the bowl, opened a bag of flour and dropped a lump of butter in the frying pan.

Eve still didn't look up.

'Not that it solved everything, mind you. Like I remember when nobody would tell me why my mother and father were buried in different churchyards. We had potato cakes then, Mother Francis and I. It didn't really explain it, or make me feel better about it. But it made us feel great eating them.'

Kit raised her head. The casual voice and the ritual actions of cooking had soothed her. Eve never paused in her movements as Kit Hegarty told her the story of the husband who had left and come back and been sent away again.

Nan had spotted Simon Westward the moment that she and Benny were led into the dining room. The waiter had been intending to put two such young-looking female students away in a corner, but Nan asked could they have a more central table. She spoke like someone who had been there regularly. There wasn't any reason why she shouldn't get a better table.

They studied the menu and Nan asked about the dishes they couldn't understand.

'Let's have something we never had before,' she suggested.

Benny had been heading for lamb because it looked nice and safe. But it was Nan's treat.

'Like what?' she asked fearfully.

'Brains,' Nan said. 'I never had those.'

'Wouldn't it be a bit of a waste? Suppose they were awful?'

'They wouldn't be awful in a place like this. Why don't you have sweetbreads or guinea fowl or snipe?'

'Snipe? What's that?'

'It's with game. It must be a bird.'

'It can't be. I never heard of it. It's a belt, taking a snipe at someone.'

Nan laughed. 'That's taking a swipe, you idiot.'

Simon Westward looked up just then. Nan could see him from the corner of her eye. She had been aware that he was at a table with a couple, a very tweedy, older man and a younger, horsey-looking woman.

Nan knew that she had been seen. She settled back into her seat. All she had to do now was wait.

Benny struggled with the things they didn't know on the menu.

'I could have scampi, I don't know that.'

'You know what it is. It's a big prawn in batter.'

'Yes, but I've never tested it, so it would be new to me.'

At least she had got out of brains and sweetbreads and other strange-sounding things.

'Miss Hogan. Don't you dine in the best places?' Simon Westward was standing beside her.

'I hardly ever go anywhere posh, but any time I do you're there.' She smiled at him warmly.

He didn't even have to look enquiringly across the table before Benny introduced him. Very simply, very correctly.

In Nan's books of etiquette she would have broken no rule, not that she had ever read them.

'Nan, this is Simon Westward. Simon, this is my friend Nan Mahon.'

'Hallo, Nan,' said Simon, reaching for her hand.

'Hallo, Simon,' said Nan, with a smile.

'You were out with a sugar daddy. I heard,' Jack accused her laughingly next day.

'No, indeed I wasn't. Nan took me to the Hibernian for lunch, as a treat. A Christmas present.'

'Why did she do that?'

'I told you. A Christmas present.'

Jack shook his head. It didn't add up.

Benny bit her lip. She wished now that she hadn't gone. In fact she wished at the time that she hadn't gone. She had ordered potatoes with the scampi and hadn't known that you were meant to have rice until she saw surprise on the waiter's face. She had asked for a little of everything from the cheeseboard instead of just picking two cheeses, which is what other people did. She had asked for nice frothy cappuccino coffee and was told gravely that it wasn't served in the dining room.

And there was something about Simon and Nan that made her uneasy too. It was as if they were playing some game, a game that only they understood. Everyone else was outside.

And now here was Jack implying that Nan must have had some kind of ulterior motive to take her to lunch.

'What's wrong? He saw her looking distressed.

'Nothing.' She put on her bright smile.

There was something very vulnerable about it. Jack could see Benny as what she must have been like when she was about four or five pretending that everything was all right even when it wasn't.

He put his arm around her shoulder as they walked across at the traffic lights between Stephen's Green and Grafton Street.

All the shops were done up with Christmas decorations. There were lights strung across the street. A group of carol singers shivering in the cold were starting 'Away in a Manger'. The collection boxes were rattling. Her face looked very innocent. He felt a need to protect her from all sorts of things. From Bill Dunne who said that a big girl like that with an enormous chest would turn out to be a great court. From drunks walking round with bottles in their hand wild-eyed and with wild hair. He wanted to keep her on the footpath so that the busy Christmas traffic wouldn't touch her, and from the small children with dirty faces who would wheedle the last pennies of her pocket money from someone gentle like Benny Hogan. He didn't want her to go back to Knockglen on the bus this afternoon, and to be there for nearly three weeks of the holidays.

'Benny?' he said.

She turned her face to him to know what he wanted. He held her face in both his hands and kissed her very softly on the lips. Then he drew away and looked to see the surprise in her eyes.

He put his arms around her then, standing right at the top of the busiest street in Dublin, and held her to him with his arms. He felt her arms go round him and they clung to each other as if it were the most natural thing in the world.

CHAPTER THIRTEEN

Fonsie had a new black velvet jacket for Christmas. Clodagh had made him a set of lilac-coloured button covers, and a huge flouncy handkerchief to put in his breast pocket.

He startled most of Knockglen by moving very deliberately up the church to receive Communion in his outfit.

'He has added blasphemy to the list of his other crimes,' Mrs Healy hissed at the Hogans, who were sitting near her.

'He must be in a State of Grace, otherwise he wouldn't go,' Annabel said. She thought Mrs Healy was making too much of this vendetta. She envied Peggy and Mario for having such lively young blood in their businesses. If only Benny and Sean had made a go of it, then perhaps the dead look of failure might not hang around the door of Hogan's, while the other two establishments went from strength to strength. She looked at Eddie beside her. She wondered what he was praying about. He always seemed genuinely devout, as if he were talking to God when they were in the church, unlike herself. Annabel found that being at Mass seemed to concentrate her anxieties about daily life rather than raise her nearer to God. Benny wasn't praying. That was for sure. Nobody who was praying had such a strange faraway look on their face.

Annabel Hogan was fairly sure that her daughter was in love.

Clodagh Pine looked at her friend Fonsie with pleasure. He really did look smart. And he *was* a smart fellow. She had never thought she would meet anyone remotely like Fonsie when she was banished to Knockglen in a foolish effort to quieten her by sending her to a backwater. And her aunt had been very good to her also, much better than Clodagh had dared to hope. She had been generous with her praise for the developments, while at the same time resisting each new one that came along. Once she had accepted an idea, Peggy Pine would get the bit between her teeth and run with it. Like the smart home knits which were now attracting people to come to Dublin.

Like the idea of designer labels with the word Pine on them.

All had added greatly to the shop's turnover. And the place looked smart and lively. It had been a success for both of them.

Clodagh decided that she would not outrage the sensitivities of Knockglen, so for Christmas day Mass she wore a short herringbone tweed coat with a black leather belt. She wore high black boots and a black leather beret pulled down the side of her head. It would have looked really good with big chunky flashy earrings. But for Christmas Mass Clodagh showed restraint. She was unaware that her aunt knelt with her head in her hands and asked the Mother of God why a girl so good and helpful as Clodagh should dress like a prostitute.

Sean Walsh knelt stiffly. He had the look of someone who was poised waiting for a blow. He looked rigidly in front of him, lest he be caught gazing around.

Sean had been invited to Christmas lunch at the Hogans' this year. Other Christmases he had gone home to his own people, a world of which he spoke not at all, in a town which no one could remember because Sean Walsh had never referred to it. But this year he had persuaded Mr Hogan to stay open late on Christmas Eve and not close at lunchtime, as they had done in other years.

Most people had a few presents still to buy on Christmas Eve, Sean reasoned. And if Hogan's wasn't open they could always buy men's handkerchiefs in Peggy Pine's, or boxes of cheroots in Birdie Mac's, or masculine-smelling soaps in Kennedy's. All those places would now be open to catch the trade. Knockglen was changing fast.

'But you can't do that,' Mr Hogan had pleaded. 'You'll miss your bus home.'

'There's not going to be much of Christmas there anyway, Mr Hogan,' Sean had said apologetically, knowing that now an invitation would have to be forthcoming.

Sean was looking forward to sitting at Christmas lunch with the Hogans as if he were a person of status. He had bought a dried flower arrangement for Mrs Hogan, something that could stand on her table all year, he would say. And a talcum powder called Talc de Coty for Benny. It was 4/11d, a medium range talcum powder that would please her, he thought, without embarrassing her by its grandness.

She had been pleasant this morning, smiled at him very

affably and said she was glad he was coming to lunch and that they'd see him about one o'clock in Lisbeg.

He had been pleased to be told what time they expected him. He was wondering if he should have gone back with them after Mass. It was as well to have it pointed out to him.

Benny had realized that since Sean was inevitable, she might as well be polite about it. Patsy told her that her mother and father had been worried in case she'd make a fuss.

'It's only lunch. It's not a lifetime,' Benny had said philosophically.

'They'd be well pleased if it was a lifetime.'

'No, Patsy, you can't be serious. Not any more. Surely not any more. Once they may have thought about it.'

'I don't know. You can't lay down laws for what people think and hope.'

But Patsy was wrong. Benny knew that her parents couldn't have any hopes that she should consider Sean Walsh. Business was poor. Money was tight. She knew this. And she knew that they couldn't have embarked on the whole costly business of letting her have a university education unless they had hopes of better things for her. If they believed she would marry Sean Walsh and that he would run Hogan's, they would have tried to force her into doing a secretarial course and book-keeping. They would have put her into the shop. They would never have let her near a world that had all it had in it. The world that had given her Jack Foley.

The Mass in the convent was always a delight. Father Ross loved the pure clear voices of the younger nuns in the choir. There was never coughing or spluttering or fidgeting when he said Mass in the Chapel of St Mary's. The nuns chanted responses and rang the bells perfectly. He didn't have to deal with sleepy or recalcitrant altar servers. And there was nothing like the amazing and highly disrespectful fashion show to which the parish church in Knockglen had been treated this morning. Here everybody was in the religious life except of course young Eve Malone, who had grown up here.

His eyes rested on the small dark girl as he turned to give the final blessing 'Ite Missa Est'.

He saw her bow her head as reverently as any of the sisters when she said 'Deo Gratias'.

He had been worried to hear that she was going to live in that house where her mother had died, out of her senses in childbirth, and where her poor father too had lost his life. She was too young a child to have a place on her own, with all the dangers that this might involve. But Mother Francis, who was an admirably sensible woman, was in favour of it.

'It's only up the garden, Father,' she had reassured him. 'In a way it's part of the convent. It's as if she never left us at all.'

He looked forward now to his breakfast in the parlour. Sister Imelda's crisply fried rashers, with triangles of potato cakes which would make a man forget everything in the world and follow its smell and its taste wherever it led.

Mrs Walsh cycled back to Westlands from Knockglen. Mr Simon and Miss Heather would go out to church at eleven thirty. The old gentleman hadn't gone to any service for a long time. It was sad to see him so feeble in his chair and yet at times he would remember very clearly. Usually things best forgotten. Sad incidents, accidents, disasters. Never happy times, no weddings, christenings or festivities.

Mrs Walsh never spoke of her life in the Big House. She could have had a wide audience for tales of the child sitting talking to Clara about her puppies, to Mr Woffles about his Christmas lettuce and to the pony about how she was going to become a harness maker and invent something softer than the bit for his poor tender mouth.

Mrs Walsh had warned Bee Moore that she didn't want to hear any stories coming from her reporting either. People were always quick to criticize a family which was different to the village. And the Westwards were a different religion, a different class and also a different nationality. The Anglo-Irish might consider themselves Irish, Mrs Walsh said very often, to make her point more firmly to Bee Moore. But of course they were nothing of the sort. They were as English as the people who lived across the sea. Their only problem was that they didn't realize it.

Mr Simon, now, he had his eye on a lady from England, from Hampshire. He was going to invite her to stay. But not in Westlands. He was going to put her up at Healy's Hotel, which was his way of saying that he hadn't made his mind up about her enough to have her at the house.

Mrs Walsh cycled back to cook the breakfast and thought that Mr Simon was ill advised. Healy's Hotel was no place to put a rich woman from Hampshire. It was a place with shabby fittings and cramped rooms. The lady would not look favourably on Mr Simon and on Westlands, and on the whole place. She would go back to Hampshire with her thousands and thousands of pounds.

And the object of the invitation surely had been for her to stay and marry into the family, bringing more English blood and, even more important, bringing the finances the place needed so desperately.

Mother Clare looked at Eve with a dislike she barely attempted to conceal.

'I'm pleased to see that you have recovered from all your various illnesses, such as they may have been,' she said.

Eve smiled at her. 'Thank you, Mother Clare. You were always very kind to me. I am so sorry that I didn't repay it properly at the time.'

'Or at all,' sniffed Mother Clare.

'I suppose I repaid it in some form by getting myself out of your way.' Eve was bland and innocent. 'You didn't have to think about me any more and try to fit me in to your world, just out of kindness to Mother Francis.'

The nun looked at her suspiciously, but could find no mockery or double meaning in the words.

'*You* seem to have got everything you wanted,' she said.

'Not everything, Mother.' Eve wondered whether to quote St Augustine and say that our hearts were restless until they rested in the Lord. She decided against it. That was going over the top.

'Not every single thing, but a lot certainly,' she said. 'Would you like me to show you my cottage? It's a bit of a walk through the briars and everything, but it's not too slippy.'

'Later, child. Another day, perhaps.'

'Yes. It's just I didn't know how long you were staying . . .' Again her face was innocent.

Last night, as on so many Christmas Eves, she had sat and

talked with Mother Francis. This time even telling the nun a little about Aidan Lynch and the funny quirky relationship they had.

Mother Francis had said the worst thing about Mother Clare's visit was that it seemed to be open-ended. She couldn't ask the other nun when she was going to leave. Eve had promised to do it in her stead.

Mother Clare did not like to be asked her plans so publicly. 'Oh . . . I mean . . . well,' she stammered.

'What day *are* you going, Mother Clare, because I want to be sure I can show it to you. You brought me into your home, the least I can do is bring you into mine.'

She forced Mother Clare to give a date. Then by an amazing surprise it turned out that Peggy Pine was driving to Dublin that day. The departure was fixed.

Mother Francis flashed a glance of gratitude to Eve.

A glance of gratitude and love.

Patsy had had a watch from Mossy for Christmas. That meant only one thing. The next present would be a ring.

'Eve says she thinks he's building on to the back of the house,' Benny said.

'Ah, it's hard to know with Mossy,' Patsy said.

They set the table with crackers, and criss-cross paper decorations as they had done every year as long as Benny could remember.

Around the house they had paper lanterns. The Christmas tree in the window had the same ornaments on it for years. This year Benny had brought some new ones in Henry Street and Moore Street in Dublin.

She felt a lump in her throat when her father and mother examined them with pleasure as if they were anything except the most vulgar red and silver tatty objects you could come across.

They were so touched at anything she did for them, and yet she was the one who should be thanking them. You didn't need to be Einstein to see that the business was not doing well. That it was a struggle for them to keep going and to give her what they did. And yet there was no way to tell them that she would one million times prefer to do what Eve was doing, to work her own way through college, staying in a house helping with the work, or minding children.

Anything at all, including being down on her hands and knees cleaning public lavatories. If it meant that she didn't have to come back to Knockglen every single night, if it meant that she would live in the same town as Jack Foley.

'Poor Sean. He won't be any trouble?' Benny's mother spoke in a question.

'And I couldn't let him work all day yesterday and not ask him for a bite to eat today, seeing that he missed his bus home?' Benny's father's remark was a question too.

'Will he ever get a place to live himself, you know, a house here?' Benny asked.

'Funny you should say that. There's talk that he's above on the road over the quarry looking at this place and that. Maybe that's what's on his mind.'

'He'll have his job cut out for him saving enough for a house with what he's paid above in the shop.' Eddie Hogan was regretful.

He didn't need to say, because they all knew it, that there wasn't a question of Sean being underpaid. It was just that the takings were so poor there wasn't much to pay anyone at all out of it.

Everything happened at the same time. Sean Walsh knocked on the front door which nobody ever used, but he thought that on Christmas day things would be different. Dessie Burns arrived at the back door as drunk as a lord saying that he only wanted a stable to sleep in, just a stable. If it was good enough for Our Saviour, it would be good enough for Dessie Burns, and perhaps a plate of dinner brought out to him wouldn't go amiss. Dr Johnson came roaring out of his avenue to borrow Eddie Hogan's car. 'Of all the bloody times that thoughtless bastard up in Westlands has to go and have a turn it has to be bloody Christmas day just as I was putting my fork in the bloody turkey,' he roared and drove off in the Hogans' Morris Cowley.

Birdie Mac arrived agitated saying that Mr Flood, who had normally seen one nun in the tree above his house, now saw three and was out with a stick trying to attract their attention and get them to come in for a cup of tea. Birdie had been down to Peggy Pine to ask her advice and Peggy had been something akin to intoxicated and told her to tell Mr Flood to get up in the tree with them.

And Jack Foley rang from Dublin, braving the post office which hated connecting calls on Christmas day unless they were emergencies.

'It *is* an emergency,' he had explained.

And when Benny came on the line he said that it was the greatest emergency in his whole life. He wanted her to know how much he missed her.

Patsy went for a walk with Mossy, when everything had been cleared away. This year for the first time, Benny suggested that they should all take part in the washing-up. They opened front and back doors to let out the smells of food. Benny said it was hardly tactful to the hens to let them smell the turkey dinner, but perhaps hens had closed-off sections of their minds on this subject. Sean didn't know how to react to this kind of chat. He debated several attitudes and decided to look stern.

The big grandfather clock in the corner ticked loudly as first Eddie Hogan and then Annabel fell asleep in the warm firelight. Shep slept too, his big eyes closing slowly and unwillingly as if anxious not to leave Benny and Sean to talk on their own.

Benny knew that she could sleep too, or pretend to. Sean would regard this not as the rudeness it was, but as some kind of sign that he was a welcome intimate in their home. Anyway she was too excited to sleep.

Jack had phoned from his own house where he had said they were all playing games and had sneaked away to tell her that he loved her.

Benny was as wide awake as she ever had been. She longed for better company than Sean Walsh, and yet she felt sorry for him. Tonight he would go back to that small room two floors above the shop. Nobody had telephoned to say they missed him. She could afford to be generous.

'Have another chocolate, Sean.' She offered the box.

'Thank you.' He even managed to look awkward eating a simple thing like a sweet. It went slowly down his neck. There was a lot of swallowing and clearing his throat.

'You look very . . . um . . . nice today, Benny,' he said, after some thought. Too much thought for the remark that resulted.

'Thank you, Sean. I suppose everyone feels well on Christmas day.'

'I haven't particularly, not up to now,' he confessed.

'Well, today's lunch was nice, wasn't it?'

He leaned across from his chair. 'Not just the lunch. *You* were nice, Benny. That gives me a lot of hope.'

She looked at him with a great wave of sympathy. It was something she never thought would happen. Within an hour two men were declaring themselves to her. In films the women were able to cope with this, and even play one off against the other.

But this was no film. This was poor, sad Sean Walsh seriously thinking that he might marry into the business. She must make sure that he realized this was not going to happen. There had to be words somewhere that would leave him with a little dignity and make him realize that things would not be improved by his asking again. Sean was of the old school that thought women said 'No' when they meant 'Yes', and all you had to do was ignore the refusals until they became an acceptance.

She tried to think how she would like to hear it herself. Suppose Jack were to tell her that he loved someone else, what would be the best way for her to find out? She would like him to be honest, and tell her directly, no apologies, or regrets. Just the facts. And then she would like him to go away and let her digest it all on her own.

Would it be the same for Sean Walsh?

She looked into the changing pictures and leaping flames of the fire as she spoke. There was a background of her parents' heavy breathing. The clock ticked, and shep whimpered a little.

She told Sean Walsh her plans and her hopes. That she would live in Dublin, and she had great hopes that it would all work out.

Sean listened to the news impassively. The part about the person she loved caused him to smile. A crooked little smile.

'Would you not agree that this might be just what they call a crush?' he asked loftily.

Benny shook her head.

'But it's not based on anything, any shared hopes or plans, like a real relationship is.'

She looked at him astounded. Sean Walsh talking about a real relationship as if he would have the remotest idea what it was.

She was still humouring him. 'Well, of course you're right. It might not work out, but it's my hope it will.'

The smile was even more bitter. 'And does he, this lucky man, know anything about your infatuation. Is he aware of all this . . . hope?'

'Of course he is. He hopes too,' she said, surprised. Sean obviously thought that she just fancied someone from afar like a film star.

'Ah well, we'll see,' he said, and he sat looking into the fire with his sad pale eyes.

Patsy had been up in Mossy's house for the evening wearing her new watch and going through a further inspection by Mossy's mother. Mossy's married sister and her husband had come in to give the encounter even further significance.

'I think they thought I was all right,' she told Benny, with some relief.

'Did you think *they* were all right?'

'It isn't up to me to be having opinions, you know that, Benny.'

Not for the first time Benny wanted to find the orphanage where Patsy had grown up with no hope and no confidence and strangle everyone in it. Patsy wanted to know what time Sean Walsh had left, because she saw him walking around up on the quarry path at all hours. He had looked distraught, she reported, as if he had something in his mind.

Benny wanted to know no more of this. She changed the topic. Were there lights on in Eve's cottage? she wanted to know.

'Yes, it looked lovely and cosy. She had a little Christmas crib in the window with a light in it. And there was a tree too, a small tree with lots of things hanging on it.'

Eve had told Benny about the crib, a gift from the convent, and every single nun had made a decoration for the tree as well. Angels with pipe cleaners and coloured wool. Stars made out of foil wrapping paper, little pom pom balls, little figures cut out of Christmas cards and given a stiff cardboard backing. Hours of work had gone into those presents.

The Community was alternately proud and sad that Eve had moved to her own house. But they had grown used to her being in Dublin. In those first weeks they had missed her running through the convent, and sitting up in the kitchen talking to them.

And as Mother Francis said it was only at the other end of the garden.

Mother Francis never said that to Eve herself. She always stressed that the girl must come and go, using the ordinary path when she wished. It was her house and she must entertain whom she liked.

When Eve asked about having a party, Mother Francis said she could have half the county if she pleased. Eve admitted ruefully that she seemed to be having half of Dublin. Because of her boasting they all thought Knockglen was the place to be.

Mother Francis said that this was only the truth and wondered how Eve was going to cope. She wondered what Eve was going to do about food for half of Dublin.

'I've brought a lot of stuff. Clodagh and Benny are going to come in on St Stephen's day and help.

'That's great. Don't forget Sister Imelda would always love to be asked to make pastry.'

'I don't think I could . . .'

'You know, I believe they eat sausage rolls all over the world, including Dublin. Sister Imelda would be honoured.'

Clodagh and Benny were up at the cottage early.

'A soup, that's what you want,' Clodagh said firmly.

'I don't have a big pot.'

'I bet the convent does.'

'Why did I take this on, Clodagh?'

'As a housewarming. To warm your house.' Clodagh was busy counting plates, making lists and deciding where they would put coats. Benny and Eve watched her with admiration.

'That one could rule the world if she was given a chance,' Eve said.

'I'd certainly make a better stab at it than the eejits who are meant to be in charge,' said Clodagh cheerfully.

The Hogans were surprised to see Sean Walsh come in through the gate of Lisbeg on St Stephen's day.

'We didn't ask him again, today?' Annabel asked, alarmed.

'I didn't, certainly. Benny may have.' Eddie sounded doubtful.

But nobody had invited Sean Walsh. He had come to have a discussion with Mr Hogan about business. He had taken a long walk last night up around the quarry and he had sorted everything out in his head. Sean Walsh had a proposition to put to Mr Hogan, that he should be taken on as a partner in the firm.

He realized that there wasn't sufficient cash flow to make him a more attractive salary offer. The only solution would be to invite him to be a full partner in the business.

Mario looked on as Fonsie backed the station wagon up to the door and loaded the record player into the back.

'We go back to the peace and the quiet?' he asked hopefully.

Fonsie didn't even bother to answer. He knew that nowadays anything Mario said was more in the nature of a ritual protest than a genuine complaint.

The café was unrecognizable from the run-down place it was when Fonsie had arrived in town. Brightly painted, cheerful, it was attracting all kinds of clientele that would never have crossed its doorstep in the old days. Fonsie had seen that there was an opportunity for morning coffee for an older set, and he had gone all out to get it. This was the time of day when the younger set, the real customers, were tied up at school or working, so the place was almost empty.

Fonsie played old-style music and watched with satisfaction while Dr Johnson's wife, and Mrs Hogan, Mrs Kennedy from the chemist and Birdie Mac all took to call in for a coffee that was cheaper than Healy's Hotel in an atmosphere that was distinctly less formal.

And as for the youngsters, he had plans for a magnificent juke box which would pay for itself in six months. But there would be time enough to explain that to his uncle later. In the meantime he just said that he was lending the player they had to Eve Malone for her party.

'That's a better place to play it than here,' Mario grumbled. 'Up on the quarry is good. It will only deafen the wild birds that fly around in the air.'

'You won't stay too late at this party now, will you?' Benny's father was looking at her over his glasses.

It made him look old and fussy. She hated him peering like

that. Either look through them or take them off, she wanted to shout with a surge of impatience.

She forced a reassuring smile on to her face.

'It's the only party there's ever been in Knockglen, Father, you know that. I can't come to any harm, just up at the back of the convent garden.

'That's a slippy old path through the convent.'

'I'll come back by the road then, down through the square.'

'It'll be pitch dark,' her mother added. 'You might be better coming through the convent.'

'I'll have plenty of people to come back with me. Clodagh or Fonsie, Maire Carroll even.'

'Maybe I could walk up that way myself about the time it would be ending. Shep, you'd like a nice late-night walk wouldn't you?'

The dog's ears pricked up at the thought of any kind of walk.

Please let her find the right words. The words that would stop her father walking out in the dark out of kindness and peering through the window at Eve's party, wrecking it for everyone, not only Benny.

Please could she say the right thing that would stop him in this foolish well-meant wish to escort her safely home.

Nan would know how to cope with this. What would Nan do? Nan always said stick as close to the truth as possible.

'Father, I'd rather if you didn't come up for me. It would make me look a bit babyish, you know, in front of all the people from Dublin. And it's the only party that's ever been given in Knockglen and maybe the only one that ever will be. Do you see how I don't want to be taken there and collected as if I were a child?'

He looked a bit hurt, as if a kind offer had been refused.

'All right, love,' he said eventually. 'I was only trying to be helpful.'

'I know, Father, I know,' she said.

This Christmas Nan's father had been worse than usual. The festive season seemed to bring him no cheer. The boys were almost immune to him. Paul and Nasey spent very little time in Maple Gardens.

Emily tried to excuse him. She spoke of him apologetically to Nan.

'He doesn't mean it. If you knew how full of remorse he is after.'

'I do,' Nan said. 'I have to listen to it.'

'He'll be so sorry he upset us. He'll be like a lamb today,' Em pleaded for understanding.

'Let him be like anything he likes, Em. I'm not going to be here to look at it. I'm going to the races.'

She had rehearsed this outfit over and over. It seemed to be just right. The cream camel-hair suit with the brown trimmings, the hat that fitted so perfectly into the blonde curly hair. A small, good, handbag and shoes that would not sink in the mud. She went to the races on the bus, along with other Dubliners going on a day out.

But while they talked form and record and likely outsiders, Nan Mahon just sat and looked out of the window.

She had very little interest in horses.

It didn't take her long to find him, and position herself in a place where she could be seen. She stood warming her hands at one of the many coal braziers placed around the enclosure. She appeared to concentrate very much on the heat as she saw him from the corner of her eye.

'How lovely to meet you again, Nan Mahon,' he said. 'Where are your supporting group of ladies?'

'What do you mean?' Her smile was warm and friendly.

'It's only I never see you without a great regiment of women in tow.'

'Not today. I came with my brothers. They've gone to the Tote.'

'Good. Can I bear you off to have a drink?'

'Yes. I'd love that, but just one. I must meet them after the third race.'

They went into the crowded bar, his hand under her elbow guiding her slightly.

There were smiles here and there and people calling to him. She felt confident that she was their equal. There were no pitying looks. Not one of those people would ever know the kind of house she had left this morning to get here on the bus. A house where drink had been spilled, where a lamp had been broken, where half the Christmas pudding had been thrown against the wall in a drunken rage. These people accepted Nan as an equal.

Eve looked around her little house with pleasure.

The oil lamps were lit and they gave a warm glow. The fire burned in the grate.

Mother Francis had left what she called a few old bits and pieces around the place. They were exactly the kind of thing that Eve wanted. A big blue vase in which she could put the wild catkins she had gathered. A handful of books to fill a corner shelf. Two slightly cracked china candlesticks for the mantelpiece, an old coal scuttle polished and burnished.

In the kitchen on the old range there were saucepans which must have come from the convent. Nothing much useful had been left from her parents' time.

Only the piano. Sarah Westward's piano. Eve ran her fingers over it and wished yet again that she had paid attention and tried to learn when Mother Bernard had been giving her lessons. Mother Francis had wanted so much for Eve to share what must have been a great love of music. Her mother had a piano stool stuffed with sheet music, and books and scores in a cupboard. They had been neatly tidied and kept free of damp by Mother Francis over the years.

When the piano tuner came to the school he was always asked to do a further chore and had been led through the kitchen gardens up the path to the piano which he always told Mother Francis was twenty times better than anything they had in the music room of St Mary's.

'It's not ours,' Mother Francis used to say.

'Then why am I tuning it?' he used to ask every year.

Eve sat down at the fire and hugged herself.

As in so many things, Mother Francis had been right. It was very nice to have a place of your own.

The Hogans had decided not to talk to Benny yet about Sean Walsh's proposition. Or ultimatum.

It had been very courteously couched, but there was no question about it. If he were not invited to be a partner in the business he would leave, and it would be known why he left. Nobody in Knockglen would think that he had been fairly treated. Everyone knew what his input had been, and how great his loyalty.

Sean did not need to spell out what would be the future for

the business if he were allowed to leave. As it was, he was the one holding it together. Mr Hogan had no real business sense in terms of what today's customers wanted. And old Mike in the shop wasn't going to be any help to him in that regard.

They would talk to Benny about it, but not now. Not since she had put herself out to be polite and courteous to him during the Christmas meal. She might flare up again and they didn't want to risk that.

'Has Sean been asked to the party above in Eve's cottage?' Eddie asked, although he knew that there was no question of the boy having been invited.

'No, Father.'

To Benny's relief the telephone rang. But it was startling to have someone call at nine o'clock in the evening. She hoped that it wasn't Jack to say he wasn't coming.

Benny answered it. Nan Mahon was on the line, pleading, begging that she could come to stay tomorrow night for the party. Nan had said that she didn't think she would be able to come to Knockglen when the party was first mentioned. What had changed her mind? A lot of things, apparently. She would explain everything when she arrived. No, she wouldn't need to be met on the bus. She'd be getting a lift. She'd explain all that later too. No, no idea what time. Could she say she'd see Benny at the party?'

Next morning, on the day of the party, Benny went up early to Eve's cottage to tell her the news.

Eve was furious.

'What does she think she's doing, announcing her arrival like some bloody old king from the olden days?'

'You did ask her to the party,' Benny said mildly.

'Yes, and she said no.'

'I don't know what *you're* bellyaching about. It's just one more for the party. I'm the one who was dragging beds all night with Patsy and checking that there's no dust on the legs of the furniture in case Nan does a household inspection.'

Eve didn't know why she was annoyed. It was, on the face of it, unreasonable. Nan was her friend. Nan had lent her that beautiful red skirt for the dance. Nan had advised Eve on everything from how to put on eyeliner to putting shoe trees in every shoe every night. The others would be delighted to see her. It would make the party go with an even bigger swing. It was strange that she felt so resentful.

They sat having coffee in the kitchen of Eve's home, the two of them puzzling out who was giving Nan a lift. Benny said it couldn't be Jack because he was coming in a car with Aidan and Carmel and Sean. They knew it wasn't with Rosemary Ryan and Sheila, still deadly rivals and driving discontentedly with Bill Dunne and Johnny O'Brien.

Benny was thinking about Jack and how after tonight surely Rosemary and Sheila would have to give up their hopes of him, once they had seen how he and Benny felt about each other. To say straight out that he had missed her. To say it on the phone on Christmas day. It was the most wonderful thing that could have happened.

Eve's brow was furrowed. She wished she could think that Nan was just coming for the party. She felt sure that it was in order to wangle an invitation to Westlands. Which she would not get from Eve, and that was for sure and for certain.

Heather came to call wearing her hacking jacket and little hard hat.

'You look as if you've just got off a horse,' Eve said.

'I have,' and Heather proudly showed her pony tied to the gate.

It was eating some of the bushes within its reach. Eve leaped up in panic. Those were her only decoration, she said, and now this terrible horse was hoovering it all up. Heather laughed, and said nonsense, her beautiful pony was only nuzzling. He wouldn't dream of eating anything between meals. Benny and Eve went out and stroked the grey pony, Malcolm, the light of young Heather's life. They kept away from the mouth with the big yellow teeth and marvelled at how fearless Heather seemed to be. Heather had come to help. She thought she would be useful in setting up the games and was very perplexed when there seemed to be no games to set up. No ducking for apples like at Hallowe'en. Heather was at a party where they had advertisements all cut out of papers, just the words. The thing that was being advertised was cut out. Everyone had a pencil and paper and the one who got most of them right won.

In desperation they suggested she blow up balloons. That pleased her. She had plenty of breath, she said proudly. As she sat in an ever-increasing heap of green, red and yellow balloons Heather asked casually if Simon had been invited to the party.

'No, it's not really his kind of party,' Eve said. 'And besides, he'd be very old for it.'

She wondered why she was making excuses for not inviting this man for whom she had felt nothing but dislike all her life. But then who could ever have foreseen the way things would turn out. That she would be very fond of his younger sister, and that she would have been settled in this house where she had vowed never to live. The day might well come when her cousin Simon Westward could cross this door, but not for a long time yet.

Jack Foley was recognized as the expert on Knockglen. He had been there before, after all. He knew Benny's house. He had been given clear instructions on how to get to the quarry road. You came in like the bus to the square and took a hilly path that had no signpost on it, but looked as if it were leading to a farmhouse.

There was another way through the convent, but you couldn't take the car and Eve had been adamant that there was to be no horseplay anywhere near her nuns.

Aidan wanted them to go and have a look at the convent first. He stared out of the passenger seat at the high walls and the big wrought-iron gate.

'Imagine being brought up in a place like that. Isn't it a miracle that she's normal?' he said.

'But *is* she normal?' Jack wanted to know. 'She does appear to fancy you, which doesn't augur well for her state of mind.'

They wound their way up the perilous track. The curtains were pulled back in the cottage and they could see firelight, and oil lamps, a Christmas tree and balloons.

'Isn't it gorgeous?' breathed Carmel, whose plans for the future when Sean was an established businessman now widened to include a small country cottage for weekends.

Jack liked it too.

'It's away from everywhere. You could be here and nobody know a thing about it.'

'Unless of course the sounds of "Good Golly, Miss Molly"

were coming out of every window,' Aidan Lynch said happily, leaping from the car and running in to find Eve.

Clodagh had brought a clothes rail and hangers up from the shop. It meant that Eve's bed wouldn't be swamped with people's garments and there would be room for the girls to sit at the little dressing table to titivate themselves.

Benny was in there doing a final examination of her face when she heard Jack's voice. She must not run out and fling herself into his arms as she wanted to. It was more important than ever now that she let him make the first move. A man like Jack used to having girls throw themselves at him would not want that.

She would wait, even if it killed her.

The door of Eve's bedroom opened. It was probably Carmel, coming in to dab her face and say something cosy about Sean.

She looked in the mirror and over her shoulder she saw Jack. He closed the door behind him and came over to her, leaning his hands on her shoulders and looking at her reflection in the mirror.

'Happy Christmas,' he said in a soft voice.

She smiled a broad smile. But she was looking at his eyes, not her own, so she didn't know how it looked. Not too broad and toothy, she hoped.

Clodagh had covered a strapless bra in royal blue velvet to look like one of those smart boned tops, and then put a binding of the same material down a white cardigan.

Naturally Benny had worn a blouse under it when she left Lisbeg, but the blouse had been removed and was folded neatly to await the home journey.

He sat on the edge of Eve's bed, and held both her hands.

'Oh, I really missed you,' he said.

'What did you miss?' She didn't sound flirtatious. She just wanted to know.

'I missed telling you things, listening to you telling things. I missed your face, and kissing you.' He drew her towards him, and kissed her for a long time.

The door opened and Clodagh came in. She was dressed from head to foot in black lace with a mantilla and a high comb in her hair. She looked like a Spanish dancer. Her face was powdered dead white and her lips were scarlet.

'I was actually coming to see if you wanted any assistance with your dress, Benny, but it appears you don't,' Clodagh said, without seeming the slightest confused by the scene she had walked in on.

'This is Clodagh,' mumbled Benny.

Jack's face lit up as it did when he was introduced to any woman. It wasn't that he was eyeing them up and down. He didn't even try to flirt with them. He liked women. Benny remembered suddenly that his father was like that too. At the big party in their house Dr Foley had been pleased to greet each new girl who was presented to him. There was nothing but warmth and delight in his reaction. So it was with Jack. And tonight when all the others arrived he would be the same.

It must be a wonderful thing to be so popular, she thought, to be able to please people just by being there.

Clodagh was explaining to Jack how she had got the lace in an old trunk upstairs in the Kennedys' house. Mrs Kennedy had told her she could go and rummage there and she had found marvellous things altogether. In return she had made Mrs Kennedy four straight skirts with a pleat in the back. It was amazing with all the plumage available that some people still wanted to dress like dowdy sparrows.

Jack put his arm around Benny's shoulders.

'I've hardly seen any sparrows in Knockglen. You're all pretty exotic birds to me.'

Together with his arm around her shoulder and followed by Clodagh in her startling black and white they came out of Eve's room and in full view of Sheila and Rosemary, of Fonsie and Maire Carroll, of Bill Dunne and Johnny O'Brien, they joined the party.

Without Benny Hogan having to manoeuvre it one little bit, they joined the party as a couple.

There never had been a party like it. Everyone agreed on that. From Fonsie's wonderful solo demonstrations to the whole place on its feet, from Guy Mitchell and 'I Never Felt More Like Singing the Blues'. The soup had been a magnificent idea. Bowl after bowl of it disappeared, sandwiches, sausage rolls and more soup. Eve served it from the big convent cauldron, her face flushed and excited. This was her house. These were her friends. It couldn't be better.

Only during the supper did she remember that Nan hadn't arrived.

'Perhaps she didn't get a lift after all.' Benny was on a cloud of her own.

'Did we tell her how to find the house?'

'Anyone in Knockglen would tell her where you live.' Benny squeezed Eve's arm. 'It's going wonderfully isn't it?'

'Yes. He can't take his eyes off you.'

'I don't mean that. I mean the party.'

Benny did mean that of course as well. Jack had been at her side all night. He had had a few dances with the others as a matter of form, but for the most of the night he was with her, touching, laughing, dancing, holding, swaying, including her in every conversation.

Rosemary Ryan watched them with some bewilderment for the first few dances.

'I didn't know anything about you and Jack,' she said, as she and Benny were having a glass of punch.

'Well, I did tell you I met him from time to time in the Annexe.'

'That's right. You did.'

Rosemary was quite fair-minded. Benny had said she was meeting Jack. If Rosemary read nothing into it then it was her own fault.

'You do look very well,' she said grudgingly, but again struggled to be just. 'Have you lost a lot of weight or put on more make-up or what?'

Benny didn't even react. She knew that whatever it was, Jack seemed to like it. And he didn't care who else knew. Benny had thought that somehow it would have had to be a secret about them.

Aidan asked Eve for a pound of sugar.

'What do you want that for?'

'I read that if you put it in the carburettor of a car, then the car won't start.'

'How about trying to find some discovery that would make it start?' That seems to me to be the better invention,' Eve said.

'You're wrong. I want Jack's father's car never to start again. Then we can stay here in this magical place and never go away.'

'Yeah, terrific. And I'll have to put up Sean and Carmel for the night as well,' Eve said.

'If I stayed, would you take me to meet the nuns tomorrow?' Aidan asked.

Eve told him that there was no question of his staying, at any time, but least of all now when Mother Clare was below watching every move. Or indeed maybe outside in the fuchsia bushes with a torch, for all they knew. But she was glad that he liked the place. And when the weather got finer, he might come and spend a whole day. Aidan said they would probably be spending much of their adult life here. During the long vacations when he was called to the Bar. They would want to escape here with the children, away from the loud booming voices of his parents.

'And what about my job?' Eve asked, entertained in spite of herself by the fantasy.

'Your job will of course be to look after me, and our eight fine children, using your university education to give them a cultured home background.'

'You'll be lucky, Aidan Lynch.' She pealed with laughter.

'I have been lucky. I met you, Eve Malone,' he said, without a trace of his usual joky manner.

Bill Dunne was the first to see Nan when she came in the door. Her eyes were sparkling and she took in the scene around her with delight.

'Isn't it wonderful?' she said. 'Eve never said it was anything like this.'

She wore a white polo-necked jumper and a red tartan skirt, under a black coat. She carried a small leather case with her, and asked to be shown to Eve's bedroom.

Benny called to the kitchen to let Eve know that Nan was here.

'Bloody hell, we've finished the soup,' Eve said to Aidan.

'She won't expect it, not at this hour,' he soothed her.

It was a late hour to arrive. Eve had thought she heard a car pull away down the track a few moments ago, but she had told herself she was imagining it.

Still someone must have left Nan at the door. It was raining outside and Nan looked immaculate. She could not have climbed up that path in this weather.

Eve put some sausage rolls and sandwiches on a plate, and took them through the sitting room, skirting Fonsie and Clodagh, who were doing such a spirited rendering of the Spanish Gypsy Dance that everyone had formed a circle to clap and cheer. She knocked on the door of her own bedroom in case Nan was changing, but she was sitting down at the dressing table exactly as she was; Rosemary Ryan was sitting on the bed, telling the mystery-of-the-year story. Jack Foley and Benny Hogan, of all people, were inseparable.

'Did you know?' Rosemary was asking insistingly.

'Yes, sort of.' Nan didn't sound as if it mattered very much. Her mind seemed to be elsewhere.

Then she saw Eve. 'Eve, it's fabulous. It's a jewel. You never told us it was like this.'

'It's not always like this.' Despite herself, Eve was pleased. Praise from Nan was high praise.

'I brought you something to eat . . . in case you were changing,' she said.

'No, I'm all right like this.' Nan hadn't thought of changing. She was of course all right in whatever she wore. It wasn't very dressy. All the others had put on the style. Parties weren't so run of the mill that you went in a jumper and skirt. But on Nan it looked beautiful.

They all went into the room. Nan loved it. She was busy stroking everything, the polished oil lamps, the wonderful wood in those shelves, the piano. Imagine having a piano of your own. Could she see the little kitchen?

Eve took her through and down the stone step. The place was covered with pots and pans and debris. There were boxes and bottles and glasses. But Nan saw only things she could praise. The dresser, it was wonderful. Where did it come from? Eve had never asked. And that lovely old bowl. It was the real thing, not like horrible modern ones.

'I'm sure a lot of those things came from your mother's home,' she said. 'They have a look of quality about them.'

'Yes, or maybe they bought them together.' Somehow Eve felt defensive about her father, and the thought that there could be no look of quality attached to him.

Nan said she was too excited to eat. It was marvellous to be here. Her eyes were dancing. She looked feverish and restless.

Everyone in the room was attracted to her, but she was aware of none of them. She refused any offer to dance, saying she had to take it all in. And she wandered around touching and admiring, and sighing over it all.

She paused by the piano and opened it to look at the keys.

'Weren't we all very unlucky that we never learned to play?' she said to Benny. It was the first time Benny had ever noticed Nan Mahon sounding bitter.

'Are you ever going to dance, or is this tour of inspection going to go on all night?' Jack Foley asked her.

Suddenly Nan seemed to snap out of it. 'I'm being appallingly rude, of course,' she said, looking straight at him.

'Now, Johnny,' Jack said to Johnny O'Brien. 'I knew that all you had to do was wake her out of the trance, and it would work. Johnny says he's been asking you to dance for ten minutes and you can't even hear him.'

If Nan was disappointed that Jack had not been inviting her to dance there was no way that anyone would have known. She smiled such a smile at Johnny that it almost melted him into a little puddle on the floor.

'Johnny, how lovely,' she said, and put her arms straight around his neck.

They were playing 'Unchained Melody', a lovely slow smoochy number. Benny was so pleased that Jack hadn't left her for Nan just as Fonsie had put that one on. It was one of her favourite songs. She had never dreamed that she would dance to it, here in Knockglen with the man she loved, who had his arms wrapped around her, and seemed to love her too. In front of all her friends.

They put more turf and logs on the fire, and when one of the oil lights flickered down, nobody bothered to replace it.

They sat around in groups or in twosomes, the evening drawing to a close.

'Can anybody play that beautiful piano?' Nan asked.

Amazingly Clodagh said that she could. Fonsie looked at her in open admiration. There was nothing that woman couldn't do, he told people proudly.

Clodagh settled herself at the keys. She had a repertoire that staggered them. Frank Sinatra numbers that they all joined in, ragtime solos, and she even got people to sing solos.

Bill Dunne startled them all by singing 'She Moved Through the Fair' very tunefully.

'That was a well-kept secret,' Jack said to him as they clapped him to the echo.

'It's only when I'm out of Dublin and can't be sent up by all you lot that I'd have the courage,' Bill said, red with pleasure from all the admiration.

Everyone said that Knockglen had not been properly praised up to this, and now that they knew where it was they'd be regular visitors. Fonsie told them to come earlier next time, when it was opening time in Mario's, soon to be Ireland's premier stylish café. Trends had to start somewhere and why not Knockglen?

Eve was sitting on the floor next to one of her two rather battered armchairs; on Clodagh's advice they had draped bedspreads over the shabby furniture. It looked exotic in the flickering light.

She thought she should get up and make more coffee for the departing guests, but she didn't want it to end, and the way Aidan had his arm around her and was stroking her, he didn't want to make any move to go either.

Nan sat on a tiny three-legged stool, hugging her knees.

'I met your grandfather today,' she said suddenly to Eve.

Eve felt a cold shock run through her. 'You did?'

'Yes. He really is a charming old man, isn't he?'

Benny felt she wanted to move away from Jack's arm and go over and support Eve physically. In some way she wanted to be a barrier between her and what Nan was saying.

Please may Eve not say anything brittle or hurtful. Let her just mumble for the moment. Let there not be a scene now to end the party on a sour note.

Eve might have read her mind.

'Yes. How did you meet him?' Although she knew. She knew only too well.'

'Oh, I met Simon at the races yesterday and we got talking. He offered me a lift if I was going to this part of the world. So we got here a bit early . . . and, well, he took me to Westlands.'

If they had got here so bloody early, Eve thought, then Nan might have been on time rather than turning up when the supper was finished.

She didn't trust herself to say any more. But Nan had in no way finished with the subject.

'You could really see what he must have been like before. You know, very upright and stern. It must be terrible for him to be like that in his chair. He was having his tea. They serve it beautifully for him. Even though he's sometimes not able to manage it.'

She had been there since tea time. Since five o'clock and she hadn't bothered to come next or near them until after nine in the evening. Eve felt the bile rise in her throat.

Nan must have sensed it. 'I did keep asking Simon to drive me up here, but he insisted on showing me everything. Well, I suppose you've been over it dozens of times.'

'You know I haven't.' Eve's voice was dangerously calm.

Only Benny and Aidan who knew her so well would have got the vibrations.

Aidan exchanged a glance with Benny. But there was nothing he could do.

'Well, you must, Eve. You must let him take you all through the place. He's so proud of it. And he describes it so well, not boasting or anything.'

'Where's this?' Sheila always liked to hear of places that were splendid and people that were important.

'Eve's relations, up at the big house. About a mile over ... that way ... is it?' Nan pointed with her arm.

Eve said nothing. Benny said that it was more or less that way. Benny also wondered did anyone want coffee, but they didn't. They wanted to sit dreamily with low music on the player and to chat. And they wanted Nan to have the floor. There was something about the way her face was lit up by the fire and by the place she was talking about ... they wanted her to go on.

'He showed me all the family portraits. Your mother was very beautiful, wasn't she, Eve?' Nan spoke in open admiration. There was nothing triumphalist about her having been there, about her having been taken on a tour and shown the picture that had not been shown to Eve on her one visit.

Nan had always said that Eve should bury her differences. Nan would have thought that Eve knew what her mother looked like.

'You must have had quite a tour.' The words nearly choked her.

'Oh yes. The trouble was getting away.'

'Still, you managed it,' Aidan Lynch said. 'Fonsie, if we're not going to be given cells in the convent for the night, which I was distinctly promised, I think we should have something to loosen up our limbs for the journey home. What would you suggest, man?'

Fonsie had long realized that Aidan was a fellow spirit. He leaped to his feet and flipped through a few record covers.

'I think it comes down to a straight contest between Lonnie Donegan "Putting on the Style" and Elvis being "All Shook Up" Man,' he said after some thought.

'Man, let's not insult either of those heroes. Let's have them both,' Aidan said, and he went around the room clapping his hands at people to get them going.

Benny had followed Eve to the kitchen.

'She doesn't understand,' Benny said.

Eve clutched hard with both her hands at the sink.

'Of course she does. How often have we talked about it?'

'Not to her. Seriously not to her. With Nan we usually pretend things are fine. Otherwise she gets you to change them. Remember?'

'I'll never forgive her.'

'Yes, of course you will. You'll forgive her this minute, otherwise it will change everything about the party. It was the most wonderful party in the world. Truly.'

'It was.' Eve softened. Inside she saw Aidan beckoning to her.

Everyone was on the floor. Benny went back. Jack and Nan were dancing, laughing happily, neither of them knowing that anything was amiss.

CHAPTER FOURTEEN

Dear Mr and Mrs Hogan,
Thank you very much for my lovely visit to Knockglen. You were both so hospitable to me I felt very welcome. As I said to you, I think your house is beautiful. You have no idea how lovely it is to come and stay in a real Georgian house. Benny is very lucky indeed.

You very kindly asked me if I would come back again some time. Nothing would give me more pleasure. My regards to Patsy, also, and thank her for the lovely breakfasts.

Yours sincerely,
Nan Mahon

Eddie Hogan said to his wife that there were some people in life for whom it was a real pleasure to do the smallest thing, and that Benny's friend Nan was one of them.

Annabel agreed completely. They had never met a more charming girl. And such perfect manners too. She had given Patsy half a crown when she was leaving. She was a perfect lady.

Dear Kit,
The more I think of it, the more I realize that it was ridiculous of me to assume that I could just walk in years later and take up as if nothing had happened. Considering the way I treated you and how little I gave you and Frank over the years you would have had every reason to throw me out on my ear.

But you were very calm and reasonable, and I'll always be grateful for that.

I just wanted you to know that I have always had an insurance policy for you, in case anything happened to me, so that you and our son might have had something good to remember me by. I wish you all the luck and happiness that I didn't bring to you myself.

Love, Joe

Kit Hegarty folded the letter from the man that everyone else had called Joe. She had never called him anything but Joseph. Meeting him had been so different to the way she thought it would have been. She had intended to hurl everything at him if she ever saw him again. But in fact he was just like a distant friend who was down on his luck. He gave an address. She couldn't even acknowledge the letter.

Dear Mother Francis,
My sincerest thanks for being invited to spend the Holy Feast of Christmas with you and the Community in St Mary's. Thank you also for arranging the lift back to Dublin with your friend Miss Pine. An outspoken person, but no doubt a good Christian with a heavy cross to bear in that niece that she has.

I was very pleased to see that Eve Malone had settled down and begun to repay some of the work our Order has put into her education. It was gratifying to see that she studies so hard.
Your sister in Christ,
Mother Mary Clare

Mother Francis smiled grimly as she read the letter, particularly the part about how they had 'invited' Mother Clare. But it was wonderful that she had been able to forewarn Eve of the surprise visit that Mother Clare had intended to pay. Mossy Rooney had come along quietly with his cart and removed all the bottles and boxes. The cottage was flung open to the winter air to clear the fumes of smoke and drink from the previous night.

Mother Clare, to her great rage, had discovered Eve sitting blamelessly studying instead of what she had hoped to find as the aftermath of a party, and would have found had it not been for Mother Francis.

Dear Sean,
As you asked me to do I am confirming in writing that I intend to invite you to become a partner in Hogan's Gentleman's Outfitters. I shall arrange with Mr Gerald Green of Green and Mahers, Solicitors to come to Knockglen and we will formalize the details early in the New Year.

I look forward to a successful partnership in 1958.
Yours sincerely,
Edward James Hogan

Mrs Healy read the letter carefully, word by word, and then nodded approvingly at Sean Walsh. It was never any harm getting these things in writing, she told him, with the best will in the world people could always go back on what they said. And not a word against Eddie Hogan. He was the nicest man you'd meet in a day's walk, but it was time someone realized Sean Walsh's worth, and acknowledged it.

Eddie Hogan died on a Saturday at lunch time. After he had finished his cup of tea and queen cake, he stood up to go back to the shop.

'If Sean has his way, there'll be no closing for lunch . . .' he began, but he never finished the sentence.

He sat down on the sofa with his hand to his chest. His face was pale and when he closed his eyes his breathing was strange. Patsy didn't need to be asked to run across the road for Dr Johnson.

Dr Johnson came in his shirt sleeves. He asked for a small glass of brandy.

'He never takes spirits, Maurice, you know that!' Annabel's hand was at her throat in fear. 'What is it? Is it a kind of fit?'

Dr Johnson sat Annabel Hogan down on the chair. He handed her the brandy.

'Sip it slowly, Annabel, that's the girl.'

He saw Patsy with her coat on as if to go for Father Ross.

'Just a little drop at a time. It was totally painless. He never knew a thing.'

The doctor beckoned Patsy over.

'Before you get the priest, Patsy, where's Benny?'

'She's in Dublin for the day, sir. She went up to meet Eve Malone. They were going to a special lecture, I think she said.'

'Get Eve Malone to bring her back,' said Dr Johnson. He had managed to take a rug and cover the figure of Eddie Hogan, who lay on the sofa looking for all the world as if he were taking a quick nap before he went back to the shop.

Annabel sat rocking to and fro, moaning in disbelief.

Dr Johnson went to the door after Patsy.

'No need to tell that bag of bones in the shop yet.'

'No sir.'

Dr Johnson had always disliked Sean Walsh. He could almost

see him picking one of the best black ties from the stock and combing his thin lank hair. He could visualize him putting on the correct expression of grief before he came to offer his condolences to the widow, and her daughter.

Whenever they found her.

Benny and Jack walked hand in hand over Killiney Hill. It had been one of those cold, crisp winter afternoons, which was going to end soon. Already they could see the lights of Dunlaoghaire twinkling far below them, and then the great sweep of Dublin Bay.

They would meet Aidan and Eve later in Kit Hegarty's house. Kit had promised them all sausages and chips before they went into the town on the train to the L and H. Tonight the motion was going to be about Sport, and Jack half threatened to speak. He said he didn't know whether he needed huge encouragement and masses of support, or if it would be easier to speak one night on his own when there were no friends to hear him make a fool of himself.

Not since the great dance before Christmas had Benny been able to spend a night in Dublin. Jack had been increasingly impatient.

'What am I going to do with my girl always miles away? It's like having a penfriend,' he had complained.

'We see each other in the day.' But her throat had narrowed in fear. He sounded cross.

'What's the use? It's at night I need you to go to things.'

She had wheedled this Saturday by pretending there was a lecture, and asking if she could tack the night on as well.

And she had another worry. He was very insistent that she go for a weekend to Wales with him.

His team were going to play a friendly match. There would be lots of people going. He really wanted her to go.

'It's not normal,' he had fumed. 'Anyone else could go. Rosemary, Sheila, Nan, they all have families who'd realize that if they're old enough to have a university education they're old enough to be let out on a simple boat trip for two days.'

She hated him saying her family weren't normal. She hated them for not being normal enough to let her go.

Soon it was more dark than it was day. They came down the springy turf together and walked along the Vico Road looking down at Killiney Bay, which people said was meant to be as beautiful as the Bay of Naples.

'I'd love to go to Naples,' Benny said.

'Maybe they'll let you when you're about ninety,' Jack grumbled.

She laughed, though she didn't feel like it.

'Race you down to the corner,' she said, and laughing they ran down to the railway station where they caught a train to Dunlaoghaire.

As soon as Kevin Hickey opened the door to them Benny knew something was wrong.

'They're in the kitchen,' he said, refusing to meet her eye. Behind him she saw the tableau of Kit and Eve and Aidan waiting to give them some very bad news.

It was as if everything had stopped. The sound of the traffic outside, the clocks ticking, the seagulls over the harbour.

Benny walked forward slowly to hear what they were going to tell her.

Shep seemed to be in everyone's way, all the time. He was looking for Eddie, and there seemed to be no sign of him. Almost everyone else in Knockglen seemed to be in and out of Lisbeg, but no sign of the master.

Eventually he went out and lay down beside the hen house; only the hens were behaving normally.

Peggy Pine arranged two big trays of sandwiches. She also asked Fonsie to collect drink from Shea's.

'I think your man is going to get some at Healy's.'

'Well, your man will be too late then,' Peggy said, taking ten pound notes from her till. 'We'll have paid cash. There's nothing he can do about that.'

They smiled at each other. The one bright spot in a dark day being the thought of besting both Sean Walsh and Mrs Healy at the same time.

By tea time everyone in the town knew. And everyone was shocked. By no standards was Eddie an old man, they speculated happily. Fifty-two at most, at the very most. Maybe not even fifty. The wife was older. They tried to work it out. And not a man for the drink, and not a day sick. Hadn't he and his wife taken to going on healthy walks recently? Didn't that show you that your hour was marked out for you and it didn't really matter what you did, you couldn't put it off once it came.

And such a gentleman. Never a harsh word out of him. Not a one to make a quick shilling here and there, he'd not hurry a farmer who hadn't paid a bill for a while. Not one to move with the times, the windows of Hogan's hadn't changed much in all the time he was there. But such a gentleman. So interested in everyone who came in and their family and their news. All the time in the world for them. And he kept poor Mike on there too, long after he might have needed him.

The prayers that were added on to the family rosary that evening for the repose of Eddie Hogan's soul, were prayers that were warm and genuine. And prayers that people said were hardly needed. A man like Eddie Hogan would have been in Heaven by two o'clock.

Eve had managed to ward off Sean Walsh's attempts to come to Dublin to collect Benny.

She had also managed to say that Benny was at a lecture where it was impossible to disturb her, because it was a kind of field trip. Nobody knew where they had gone. They would have to wait until she came home at six o'clock.

'They're never bringing her father to the church tonight?' Eve had said.

It was unthinkable that Benny would not be there when her father's body was brought to lie overnight in Knockglen parish church.

'They might have done, if they had known where to find Benny.' Sean sounded aggrieved.

Jack said he'd get his father's car.

'They might need it.' Benny's face was wan and empty. 'They might need it for something important.'

'There's nothing more important than this,' said Jack.

'Will we go with them?' Aidan Lynch asked Eve.

'No,' Eve said. 'We'll go down by bus tomorrow.'

She could hardly bear to look at Benny's fce as she sat looking unseeingly in front of her.

From time to time she said 'Dead' in a low voice, and shook her head.

She had spoken to her mother on the phone, her mother had sounded sleepy, she said. That too seemed hard to accept.

They gave her a sedative, to calm her down. It makes her feel sleepy,' Kit explained.

But none of it made any sense to Benny, no matter what tablet you took. It couldn't make you feel sleepy. Not when Father had died. Died. No matter how many times she said it, it wouldn't sink in.

Mr Hayes next door drove them in to the Foleys' house.

Jack's mother was at the door. Benny noticed that she wore a lovely woollen suit with a cream blouse underneath. She had earrings on, and she smelled of perfume.

She gave Benny a hug of sympathy.

'Doreen has packed you a flask of coffee and some sandwiches for the car journey,' she said.

She made it sound as if Knockglen were at the other side of Europe.

'We're both very, very sorry,' she said. 'If there's anything at all we can do . . .'

'I think I'd better get her on the road,' Jack cut short the sympathies.

'Were they going out somewhere tonight?' Benny asked.

'No. Why?'

He was negotiating the early Saturday evening traffic in Dublin, and trying to get out towards the Knockglen road.

'She looked all dressed up.'

'No, she didn't.'

'Is she like that all the time?'

'I think so.' He was surprised, glancing over at her.

She sat in silence for a while, staring ahead. She felt very cold and unreal.

She wished over and over the most futile wish. That it could be this morning. If only it were eight o'clock this morning.

Her father had said that it was going to be a nice bright day.

'Isn't it a pity you have this lecture now. You could have had a great day here in Knockglen, and maybe yourself and Shep would have come up and got me out of the shop early for a bit of a walk!'

If only she had the time again. There'd have been no lies

about lectures that didn't exist. There'd have been no shame at accepting his praise for her eagerness to study.

She'd have cancelled everything, just to have been there, to have been with him when he began to leave his life.

She didn't believe it was so instant that he didn't know. She would like to have been in the room.

And for her mother too. Mother, who never had to make a decision of her own . . . being alone to handle everything.

Benny's eyes were dry but her heart was full of shame that she hadn't been there.

Jack couldn't find any good words. Several times he almost had the right thing. But always he stopped.

He couldn't bear it any longer. He pulled into the side of the road. Two lorries hooted at him angrily, but he was parked now up on a grass verge.

'Benny, darling,' he said, and put his arms around her. 'Benny, please cry. Please cry. It's awful to see you like this. I'm here. Benny cry, cry for your father.'

And she clung to him and wept and wept until he thought that her body would never stop shaking with the sobs and the grief.

They were all like characters in a play, Benny thought. People moving off stage and on stage all evening. One moment she would look and there was Dekko Moore talking earnestly in the corner, the small tea cup and saucer looking ridiculous in his large hands. Then she would glance again and in that corner Father Ross was standing mopping his brow as he listened to the visions of poor Mr Flood and wondered how best to cope with them.

In the scullery Mossy Rooney stood not wanting to form part of the main gathering that spread through the whole house, but ready when Patsy called him to help. On the stairs sat Maire Carroll whom Benny had so disliked at school. Tonight, however, she was sympathetic and full of praise for Benny's father. 'A very nice man with a word for everyone.'

Benny wondered wildly what kind of a word her father would have been able to dredge up for the charmless Maire Carroll.

Her mother sat in the middle, accepting the sympathy, and she was the most unreal figure of all. She wore a black blouse that Benny had never seen before. She worked out that Peggy must have produced it from the shop. Mother's eyes were red, but she was calmer than Benny would have thought possible, considering.

The undertakers had told her that Father was lying upstairs. Jack went up with her to the spare room, where candles burned and everything seemed to have been miraculously tidied and covered. It didn't look like the spare bedroom at all. It looked like a church.

Father didn't look like Father either. One of the nuns from St Mary's was sitting there. It was something they did, go around to people's houses when someone died and sit there by the body. Somehow it made people more calm and less frightened to see the figure of a nun keeping guard.

Jack held her hand tightly as they knelt and said three Hail Marys by the bed. Then they left the room.

'I don't know where you're going to sleep,' Benny said.

'What?'

'Tonight. I thought you could stay in the spare room. I forgot.'

'Darling, I have to go back. You know that. I have to take the car back for one thing . . .'

'Of course, I forgot.'

She had thought that he would be there with her, standing beside her for everything.

He had been such a comfort in the car, when she had wept on his shoulder. She had begun to assume that he would always be there.

'I'll come back for the funeral. Obviously.'

'The funeral. Yes.'

'I should go soon.'

She had no idea what time it was. Or how long they had been home. Something inside her told her that she must pull herself together now. This minute, and thank him properly for his kindness. She must not allow herself to be a drag.

She walked him out to the car. It was a blowy night now, the dark clouds were scudding across the moon.

Knockglen looked very small and quiet compared to the bright lights of Dublin they had left . . . some time ago. She didn't know how long ago.

He held her close to him, more a brotherly hug than any kind of kiss. Perhaps he thought it was more suitable.

'I'll see you on Monday,' he said softly.

Monday.

It seemed so far away. Imagine her having thought he was going to stay for the weekend.

Eve and Aidan came on Sunday.

They walked from the bus down the main street.

'That's Healy's Hotel. Where I wanted you to stay.'

'Until I reminded you I am an impoverished student, who has never spent a night in a hotel in my life,' Aidan said.

'Yes, well . . .'

She showed him the Hogans' shop with the black-rimmed notice in the window. She told him about how nice Birdie Mac in the sweet shop was, and how horrible Maire Carroll in the grocery was. From time to time Aidan turned and looked back up at the convent. He had wanted to be invited there first, but Eve had refused. They hadn't come on a social call, she said, they had come to help Benny. There would be time later to meet Mother Francis and Sister Imelda and everyone.

They passed Mario's café, which even when closed on a Sunday radiated cheer, and life and excitement.

They turned the corner at the end of the street and went to Benny's house.

'It's awful only going to people's houses when they're dead,' Aidan said suddenly. 'I'd like to have come here when he was alive. Was he nice?'

'Very,' Eve said. She paused with her hand on the gate.

'He never saw any bad in anyone, and he never saw anyone grow up either. He always called me Little Eve. He always thought Benny was nine, and he saw no harm in that Sean Walsh, who'll be lording it inside.'

'Will I deal with Sean Walsh, make verbal mincemeat of him?' Aidan asked eagerly.'

'No, Aidan, thank you, but that wouldn't be what's required.'

It was an endless day, even with Eve and Aidan there. Benny had a headache that she thought would never leave her. There had been so many wearying encounters. Mrs Healy for example, wanting to know if there was any way she had offended the family.

No? Well, she was certainly glad to hear that, because she

had been so ready and eager to supply the drink that would be needed and then was told that her participation would not be necessary. And then Benny had to cope with old Mike from the shop. There had been words said, words that Mr Eddie had not meant the way that Mr Walsh thought he had meant them.

Mr Walsh? Yes, Mike had been told that it wasn't fitting for a partner to be called Sean any more, even though Mike had been head tailor when Sean Walsh had come in as a schoolboy.

Benny had been coping with Dessie Burns who was in that perilous state of being off the jar but threatening to go back on to it at any moment because if there was one thing a man should not be it was doctrinaire, and with Mario who said that in Italy people would cry, cry and cry again over the death of a good man like Eddie Hogan, not just stand in his house talking and drinking.

And then the church bells began to toll. So often in Lisbeg they heard the bells and it just meant the angelus, or time for Mass, or someone else was being brought to the church. Benny put on her black lace mantilla and walked with her mother behind the coffin up the street, where people had come to their doors and to stand outside their businesses on the cold Sunday afternoon.

And as she walked past their shop her heart grew heavier. It would be Sean's shop from now on. Or Mr Walsh as he would want people to call him.

She wished she could talk to her father about old Mike and ask him what was going to happen. The procession paused momentarily outside Hogan's. And then moved on. She could never talk to her father again about his shop or about anything. And he was powerless now to do anything about the shop he had loved so much.

Unless of course she were to do something herself to try and sort it out.

Aidan Lynch was introduced to Mother Francis.

'I have appointed myself guardian of Eve's morals while she is at university,' he said solemnly.

'Thank you very much.' Mother Francis was formally grateful.

'I hear nothing but good of the way you brought her up. I wish I'd been left to a convent.' His smile was infectious.

'There might have been more problems with you,' the nun laughed.

Mother Francis had thought it was very sensible for Aidan Lynch to spend the night in Eve's cottage, while Eve slept at the convent. Everyone liked the thought of Eve being back under their roof again, and her bedroom was going to be there for ever. This had been a promise.

Eve showed Aidan how to rake the range.

'I think when we're married we might have something more modern,' he grumbled.

'No, surely with the eight children we can have them stoking it, going up the chimney even.'

'You don't take me seriously,' he said.

'I do. I just believe in child labour, that's all.'

Back in the convent, having cocoa with Mother Francis in the kitchen, it was impossible to believe that she had ever left these walls.

'A very nice young man,' Mother Francis said.

'But basically a beast of course, like you told us all men were, ravening beasts.'

'I *never* told you that.'

'You hinted at it.'

They were more like sisters these days than mother and daughter. They sat companionably in the warm kitchen and talked of life and death and the town and Mr Flood's visions and how hard everything was on poor Father Ross. Because if the vision was as true as Fatima and everybody believed it, why could they not make the leap of imagination and believe it might all be true in Knockglen?

Possibly because Mr Flood the butcher was such an unlikely person to be visited by a holy nun in a tree. Or even on the ground according to Mother Francis.

The funeral Mass was at ten o'clock. Benny and her mother and Patsy went in the church mourners' car provided by the undertaker.

As she linked her mother up the aisle to sit in the front row, Benny was aware of the people who had come to pay their respects. Farmers had come yesterday, in their Sunday suits, they would be out in their fields on a weekday morning. Today she saw men in suits, commercial travellers, suppliers, people from two parishes away. She saw her father's cousins, and her mother's brothers. She saw standing in a comforting crowd her own circle of friends.

There was Jack, so tall that everyone in the church must have seen him. He wore a black tie and he turned round to see them coming. It was almost like being at a wedding, where people turn around to see the bride . . . the thought came and went.

Bill Dunne had come too, which was very nice of him, and Rosemary Ryan. They stood beside Eve and Aidan, their faces full of sympathy.

And Nan was there, in a black blazer and a pale grey skirt. She wore gloves and carried a small black bag. Her mantilla looked as if it had been made by a dress designer to sit in her blonde hair. Everyone else wore a mantilla that looked like a rag, or a headscarf. Clodagh wore a hat, though. A big black straw hat. It was her only concession to mourning colours. The rest of her outfit was a red and white striped coat dress, considerably shorter than Knockglen would have liked.

But then it was hard to please Knockglen since there was also disapproval for Fonsie's coat – a long one like de Valera would wear except it had a huge velvet collar and small finishings of fake leopard fur at the pockets, collars and cuffs.

Mother looked very old and sad. Benny glanced at her from time to time. Sometimes a tear fell on Mother's missal, and once or twice Benny leaned over and wiped it away. It was as if Mother hadn't noticed.

Mercifully, Sean Walsh had not presumed upon them too much. Startled by the rebuff over obtaining supplies from Healy's Hotel, he had been more cautious in his overtures than Benny had dared to hope. He had not sat anywhere near them now in the church, in the role of a chief mourner. She must keep her head and not let him take over. His style was so different to her father's, his humanity so little in comparison.

Benny wished she had someone who could talk it through with her, someone who really understood. Her glance fell on Jack Foley, whose face was stony in its sympathy. But she knew she wouldn't burden him with it.

The tedious in-fighting over a small shabby country shop. Nobody would bother Jack Foley with all that.

Not even if she loved him, and he loved her.

Outside the church, the people of Knockglen talked to each other in low voices. They commented on the group of young people down from Dublin. Must be friends of Benny, they deduced.

'Very handsome-looking couple that tall boy and the blonde girl. They're like film stars,' Birdie Mac said.

Eve was nearby.

'They're not a couple,' she heard herself saying. 'The tall boy is Jack Foley . . . he's Benny's boyfriend. He and Benny are a couple.'

She didn't know why she said it, or why Birdie Mac looked at her so oddly. Perhaps she had just spoken very loudly.

Or it didn't seem suitable to talk of Benny having a boyfriend at a time like this.

But in fact she thought Birdie didn't believe her.

As they walked to the open grave past the headstones Eve stopped and pointed out a small stone to Aidan.

'In loving memory of John Malone,' it said.

'It was nicely kept, weeded and with a little rose tree.

'Do you do this?' he asked.

'A bit, mainly Mother Francis, wouldn't you know it.'

'And your mother?'

'Across the hill. Over in the Protestant graveyard. The posh one.'

'We'll go and see hers too,' he promised.

She squeezed his hand; for one of the few times in her life she was without words.

They were very good to her, all Benny's friends. They gave her great support. They were courteous to the people of Knockglen and helpful back at the house after the funeral.

Sean Walsh thanked Jack for coming, as if Jack were there somehow as an act of respect to Hogan's Outfitters. Benny gritted her teeth in rage.

'Mr Hogan would have been very honoured by your presence,' Sean said.

'I liked him very much when I did meet him. I came to tea

here with Benny months and months ago.' He smiled at her warmly, remembering the day.

'I see.' Sean Walsh, to Benny's disappointment, now did see. 'You didn't stay overnight, did you?' Sean asked loftily.

'No, I didn't. I came down this morning. Why?'

'I heard that one of Benny's friends did stay, up in the cottage on the quarry.'

'Oh, that was Aidan.' Jack was easy. If he tired of Sean and this pointless conversation he didn't show it, but he managed to manoeuvre Benny away.

'That's the creep, isn't it?' he whispered.

'That's how it is.'

'And he had notions of you.'

'Only notions of the business, which he more or less got without having to have me as well.'

'Then he lost the best bit,' Jack said.

She smiled dutifully. Jack was going to be off soon, she knew. She had heard him tell Bill Dunne that they had to be out of Knockglen by two at the latest. He had asked Bill to make the move.

She made it easy for him. She said that he had been a tower of strength, and everyone had been wonderful to come all that distance. She begged him to get on the road while there was still plenty of daylight.

They were all going to squeeze into Bill Dunne's car. There had been four coming down, but they were going to try and fit Eve and Aidan in as well.

Benny said that was terrific, rather than have them just hanging on waiting for a bus.

She smiled and thanked them without a quiver in her voice.

It was the right way to be, she could see Jack looking at her approvingly.

'I'll ring you tonight,' he promised. 'About eight. Before I go out.'

'Great,' she said, eyes bright and clear.

He was going out. Out somewhere on the night of her father's funeral.

Where could he be going on a Monday night in Dublin?

She waved at the car as it went around the corner. It didn't matter, she told herself. She wouldn't have been there anyway.

Last Monday night when Father was alive and well, Benny Hogan would have been safely back in Knockglen by eight o'clock.

That's the way things had always been, and would always be. She excused herself from the group of people downstairs, saying she was going to lie down for twenty minutes.

In the darkened room she lay on her bed and sobbed into her pillows.

Selfish tears too, tears over a handsome boy who had gone back to Dublin smiling and waving with a group of friends. She cried for him as much as for her father, who lay under heaps of flowers up in the graveyard.

She didn't hear Clodagh come in and pull up a chair. Clodagh still wearing her ludicrous hat, who patted Benny's shoulders and soothed her with exactly the words she wanted to hear.

'It's all right, it's all right. Everything will sort itself out. He's mad about you. Anyone can tell. It's in the way he looks at you. It's better he went back. Hush now. He loves you, of course he does.'

There was an enormous amount to do.

Mother was very little help. She slept a lot of the time, and dozed off, even in a chair. Benny knew that this was because Dr Johnson had prescribed tranquillizers. He had said she was a woman who had focused her whole life around her husband. Now that the centre had gone she would take a while to readjust. Better let her get used to things gradually, he advised, not make any sudden changes or press her for decisions.

And there were so many things to decide, from tiny things like thank-you letters, and taking Shep for a walk, and Patsy's wages, to huge things like had Sean Walsh been made a partner yet, and could the business survive, and what were they going to do for the rest of their lives without Father?

Mr Green, the solicitor, had come to the funeral, but said that there would be ample opportunity for them to discuss everything in the days that followed. Benny hadn't asked him whether he meant Sean Walsh to be in on the discussions or not.

It was something she wished she had said at the time. Then it would have been a perfectly acceptable question as someone distressed and not sure of what was going on. Afterwards it looked more deliberate, and as if there was bad feeling. Which there wasn't – except on a personal level.

It was extraordinary how many of Nan's sayings seemed to be precisely appropriate for so many situations. Nan always said tht you should do the hardest thing first, whatever it was. Like the essay you didn't want to write, or the tutor you didn't want to confront with an unfinished project. Nan was always right about everything.

Benny put on her raincoat on the morning after the funeral and went to see Sean Walsh in the shop.

The first thing she had to do was to avoid old Mike, who started to shuffle up to her with every intention of finishing the conversation he had begun in her house. Briskly and loudly so that Sean could hear she said that she and her mother would be very happy to talk to Mike later, but for the moment he would have to excuse her, she had a few things she wanted to get settled with Sean.

'Well, this is nice and businesslike.' He rubbed his hands together in that infuriating way, as if he had something between his palms that he was trying to grind to a powder.

'Thank you for everything, over the weekend.' Her voice was insincere. She tried to put some warmth into it. He *had* stood long hours greeting and thanking. It wasn't relevant that she hadn't wanted him there.

'It was the very least I could do,' he said.

'Anyway, I wanted you to know that Mother and I appreciated it.'

'How *is* Mrs Hogan?' There was something off-key about his solicitude, like an actor not saying his lines right.

'Fairly sedated at the moment. But in a few days she will be herself again and able to participate in business matters.'

Benny wondered, did Sean have this effect on other people? Normally, she never used words like 'participate'.

'That's good, good.' He nodded sagely.

She drew a deep breath. It was something else Nan had read. That if you inhaled all the air down to your toes and let it out again it gave you confidence.

She told him that they would arrange a meeting with the solicitor at the end of the week. And until then perhaps he would be kind enough to keep the shop ticking over exactly as he had been doing so well over the years. And out of respect to her father she knew that there would be no changes made, no changes *at all*; her head inclined towards the back room where old Mike had gone fearfully.

Sean looked at her astounded.

'I don't think you quite realize . . .' he began. But he didn't get very far.

'You're quite right. I *don't* realize.' She beamed at him as if in agreement. 'There are whole areas of the way this business has been run, and the changes in it that are planned and under-way, that I know nothing about . . . that's what I was saying to Mr Green.'

'What was Mr Green saying?'

'Well, nothing, obviously, on the day of a funeral,' she said reprovingly. 'But after we have talked to him then we should all talk.'

She congratulated herself on her choice of words. However often he played the conversation over to himself again he wouldn't be able to work out whether he was included in the conversation with the lawyer or not.

And he would not discover the huge gap in Benny's own information.

She didn't know whether in fact he was a partner in the business yet, or whether the deed of partnership might not have been signed.

She had a distinct feeling that her father had died before matters were completed, but another even stronger feeling, that there was a moral obligation to carry out what had been her father's wishes.

But Benny knew that if she were to survive in the strange clouded waters that she was now entering, she must not let Sean Walsh know how honourably she would behave to him. Even though she disliked and almost despised him, she knew that Sean had earned the right to be her father's successor in the firm.

Bill Dunne said to Johnny O'Brien that he half thought of asking Nan Mahon to the pictures.

'What's stopping you?' Johnny asked.

What was really stopping him, of course, was the thought that she would say no. Why invite rejection? But she wasn't going out with anyone else. They knew that. It was odd, considering how gorgeous she was. You'd think half the men in college would want to take her out. But perhaps that was it. They *wanted* to, and yet did nothing about it.

Bill decided to invite her.

Nan said no, she didn't really like the cinema. She was regretful, and Bill didn't think she had closed the door.

'Is there anything you would like to go to? he asked, hoping he wasn't making himself too humble, too pathetic.

'Well, there is . . . but I don't know.' Nan sounded doubtful.
'Yes? What?'

'There's a rather posh cocktail party at the Russell. It's a sort of pre-wedding do. I'd like to go to that.'

'But we weren't invited.' Bill was shocked.

'I know.' Nan's eyes danced with excitement.

'Bill Dunne and Nan are going to crash a party,' Aidan said to Eve.

'Why?'

'Search me.'

They thought about it for a while. Why go to a place where you might be unwelcome? There were so many places where Nan Mahon could just walk in and everyone would be delighted. She looked like Grace Kelly, people said, confident and beautiful without being flashy. It was a great art.

'Maybe it's the excitement,' Aidan suggested.

It could be the fear of being caught, the danger element like gambling.

Why else would you want to go to a wedding party with a whole lot of horsey people from the country, neighing and whinnying? Aidan asked.

Once Eve knew it was that kind of party she knew immediately why Nan Mahon wanted to go. And why she needed someone very respectable and solid like Bill Dunne to go with her.

Jack Foley thought it was a marvellous idea.

'That's only because you don't have to do it,' Bill grumbled.

'Oh, go on. It's easy. Just keep smiling at everyone.'

'That would be all right if we all had your matinée-idol looks. Advertising toothpaste all over the place.'

Jack just laughed at him.

'I wish she'd asked me to escort her. I think it's a great gas.'

Bill was doubtful. He should have known there would be trouble involved once he had dared to ask out someone with looks like Nan Mahon. Nothing came easy in life.

And it was all so mysterious. Who on earth would want to go to a thing like that, where they'd know nobody and everyone else knew everyone?

Nan wouldn't explain. She just said that she had a new outfit and thought it would be a bit of fun.

Bill offered to pick her up at home, but she said no, they'd meet in the foyer of the hotel.

The new outfit was stunning. A pale pink sheath dress with pink lace sleeves. Nan carried a small silver handbag with a silk rose attached to it.

She came in without a coat.

'Better in case we have to make a quick getaway,' she giggled.

She looked high and excited, like she had looked when she came into Eve's party in Knockglen. As if she knew something nobody else did.

Bill Dunne was highly uneasy going up the stairs, loosening his collar with a nervous finger. His father would be furious if there was any trouble.

There was no trouble. The bride's people thought they were friends of the groom, the groom's thought they were on the bride's side. They gave their real names. They smiled and waved and because Nan was undoubtedly the most glamorous girl in the room it wasn't long before she was surrounded by a group of men.

She didn't talk very much, Bill noticed. She laughed and smiled and agreed, and looked interested. Even when asked a direct question she managed to put it back to the questioner. Bill Dunne talked awkwardly to a dull girl in a tweed dress who looked over at Nan sadly.

'I didn't know it was meant to be dressy-uppy,' she said,

'Ah. Yes, well.' Bill was trying to imitate Nan's method of saying almost nothing.

'We were told it was a bit low key,' the tweed girl complained. 'Because of everything, you know.'

'Ah yes, everything,' Bill mumbled desperately.

'Well, it's obvious isn't it? Why else wouldn't they wait until spring?'

'Spring. Indeed.'

He looked over her head. A small dark-haired man was talking to Nan. They looked very animated, and they hardly seemed to notice that anyone else in the room existed.

Lilly Foley looked at herself in the mirror. It was hard to believe that lines would not go away. Not ever.

She had been used to little lines when she was tired or strained. But they always smoothed out after rest. In the old days.

In the old days, too, she didn't have to worry about the tops of her arms, whether they looked a little crepey and even a small bit flabby.

Lilly Foley had been careful about what she ate since the day her glance had first fallen on John Foley. She had been thoughtful, too, about what she wore, and even, if she were honest, about what she said.

You didn't win the prize and keep it unless you lived up to the role.

That's why it was heartbreaking to think that big overgrown puppy dog of a girl Benny Hogan should think that she had a chance with Jack. Jack was so nice to her, he had his father's manners and charm. But obviously he couldn't have serious notions about a girl like that.

He had driven her to Knockglen and gone to the funeral out of natural courtesy and concern. It would be sad if the child got ideas.

Lilly had been startled to hear Aidan Lynch talking of Benny and Jack as if they were a couple.

At least Benny had the sense not to keep telephoning him like other girls did.

She *must* realize that there could be nothing in it.

Benny sat at the kitchen table and willed the phone to ring. She was surrounded by papers and books.

She intended to understand all about the business before

talking to Sean and Mr Green at the end of the week. She could ask no help and advice from old Mike in the shop and her mother was not likely to be any help either. Benny had bought a box of black-bordered writing paper. She had listed the people who sent flowers, hoping that her mother would write a short personal note to each of them. She even addressed the envelopes.

But Annabel's hand seemed to feel heavy and her heart listless. She never managed more than two letters a day. Benny did them herself eventually. She ordered the mortuary cards, with little pictures of her father, and prayers on them which people would keep in their missals to remind them to pray for his soul. It was Benny, too, who had ordered the black-rimmed cards printed with a message of gratitude for the sympathies offered.

Benny paid the undertakers, and the gravediggers, and the priest, and the bill in Shea's. She paid everyone in cash as she had drawn a large sum from the bank in Ballylee. Fonsie had driven her there in his van.

'Wait till we get Knockglen on the map,' Fonsie had said. 'Then we'll have a bank of our own, not having to wait till the bank comes on Thursdays as if we were some one-horse wild west outpost.'

The man in the bank in Ballylee had been most sympathetic, but also slightly uneasy about advancing the sum.

'I'm meeting Mr Green the solicitor on Friday,' Benny reassured him. 'Everything will be put on a proper footing then.'

She hadn't imagined the look of relief on the banker's face.

She realized that she hadn't the first idea about how her father had run his business all these years, and she had only had a few days to find out.

As far as she could see it was a matter of two big books and a till full of pink slips.

There was the takings book. Every item was entered in that as it was received. Some of them were pitiably small. The sale of collar studs, sock braces, shoehorns, shoe polishing brushes.

And then there was the lodgement book, a big brown leather volume with a kind of window in the front of it. It was ruled in three columns: cheques, cash and other. Other could mean postal orders or in one case dollars from a passing American.

Each Thursday her father had queued up with others when the bank came to town. The bank signature at the end of each week's lodgement was the receipt and acknowledgement that the money had been put in the account.

In the till there were always pink raffle tickets, books that had been sent on spec by Foreign Missions, ideal for tearing off to write out what had been taken out. Each time there was a sum listed and a reason. 'Ten shillings: petrol.'

It was Wednesday, early-closing day. She had lifted both books from the shop and put them into a large carrier bag.

Sean had remonstrated with her, saying that the books never left the premises.

Benny had said nonsense. Her father had often pored over the ledgers at home, and her mother wanted to see them. It seemed a small comfort at a time like this.

Sean had been unable to refuse.

Benny didn't even know what she was looking for. She just wanted to work out why the business was doing so badly. She knew that there would be seasonal highs and lows. After the harvest when the farmers got paid for the corn they all came and bought new suits.

She wasn't looking for discrepancies, or falsification.

Which was why she was so surprised when she realized that the takings book and the lodgement book didn't match up. If they took so much a week, then that much should have been lodged, apart from the small pink tickets called drawings from the till, which were very insignificant.

But as far as she could see by reading it and adding everything laboriously, there was a difference between what was taken and what was lodged, every single week. Sometimes a difference of as much as ten pounds.

She sat looking at it with a feeling of shock and despair. Much as she disliked him and wished him a million miles away from Knockglen, she did not even want to think for a moment that Sean Walsh had been taking money from her father's business. It was so unlikely, for one thing. He was such an over-respectable person. And for another, if he was to be made a partner why steal from his own business? And most important of all, if this had been going on for months and months, and maybe years, why was Sean Walsh living in threadbare suits in a cramped room two floors above the shop? She sat numbed by the discovery, and hardly heard the telephone ring.

Patsy answered it and said that a young man was looking for Benny.

'How are you?' Jack was concerned. 'How's everything?'

'Fine. We're fine.' Her voice sounded far away.

'Good. You didn't ring.'

'I didn't want to be bothering you.' It was still unreal. Her eyes were on the books.

'I'd like to come down.' He sounded regretful, as if he were going to say he couldn't. She didn't want him here anyway. This was too huge.

'No, heavens no. Please.' She was insistent, and he knew it. He seemed cheered.

'And when will you come back up to me?'

She told him she should have things sorted out in some way by next week. Maybe they could meet for coffee in the Annexe on Monday.

Her lack of pursuit was rewarded. He really *did* seem sorry not to see her.

'That's a long time away. I miss you, you see,' he explained.

'And I miss you. You were wonderful, all of you, to come to the funeral.'

When he was gone from the phone he went from her mind too.

There was nobody she could ask about the books.

She knew that Peggy, Clodagh, Fonsie and Mario would understand. As would Mrs Kennedy, and many other business people in the town.

But she owed it to the memory of her father not to reveal him as an incompetent bungler, and she owed it to Sean Walsh not to mention a word of her suspicion until she knew it was true.

'Why won't you let me take you home?' Simon asked Nan after dinner.

It was the second time they had met that week after the extraordinary coincidence of their meeting at the cocktail party.

Nan looked at him and spoke truthfully.

'I don't invite anyone home with me. I never did.'

She sounded neither apologetic nor defiant. She was saying it as a fact.

'Might one ask why?'

She smiled at him mockingly. 'One might, if one was rather pushing and curious.'

'One is.' He leaned across the table and patted her hand.

'What you see is the way I am, the way I see myself. And how I feel and the way I am always going to be. Were you, or anyone to come home with me, it would be different.'

For Nan it was a long speech about herself. He looked at her with surprise and some admiration.

He realized that she was from somewhere in North Dublin. He knew her father was in building. He had thought that perhaps they lived in a big nouveau-riche house somewhere. They must have money. Her clothes were impeccable. She was always at the best places. He felt quite protective about her wish to keep her home life to herself, and her honesty in saying that this was what she was doing.

He told her gently that she was a silly. He didn't feel ashamed of *his* home, a falling down, crumbling mansion in Knockglen, a place that had seen better days, where he lived with underpaid retainers, a senile grandfather and a pony-mad little sister. It was a pretty weird background to introduce anyone into. Yet he had invited her there after Christmas. He held his head on the side quizzically.

Nan was not to be moved. It was not a pleasure for her to bring her friends home. If Simon felt uneasy about this, then perhaps they had better not see each other again.

As she had known he would, he agreed to dismiss the matter from their conversation and their minds.

In a way he was actually relieved. It was better by far than being paraded at a Sunday lunch and having expectations raised.

Heather was very bad at needlework at school. But after a conversation with Dekko Moore, the harness maker in Knockglen, she had decided that she should try to be good at it. He said that she might have a future for herself making hunting attire for ladies, and that they could be sold through Pine's or Hogan's.

It was Heather's project for the new term to learn to sew properly.

'It's awful, things like cross stitch, not real things like clothes,' she grumbled to Eve. It was Heather's twelfth birthday and the school allowed her to spend the evening out with a relation just as long as she was back by eight.

They had a birthday cake in Kit's house and everyone clapped when she blew out the candles. The students liked Heather, and her overwhelming interest in food.

They discussed the teaching of sewing in schools and how unfair it was that boys never had to learn cross stitch.

'At least you don't have to make big green knickers with gussets in them like we did at school,' Eve said cheerfully.

'Why did you have to make those?' Heather was fascinated by the tales of the convent.

Eve couldn't remember. She thought it might have had something to do with wearing them over their ordinary knickers and under their tunics when they were doing handstands. Or maybe she was only making that up. She really didn't know. She was annoyed with Simon for not taking his sister out on her birthday and only sending her a feeble card with a picture of a crinoline lady on it. There were hundreds of nice horsey birthday cards around that he could have got.

But more than that, she was worried about Benny. There was some problem, some worry about the business. Benny had said she couldn't talk about it on the phone, but she'd tell all next week.

It was something she had said at the end that wouldn't go out of Eve's mind.

'If you ever say any prayers, Eve, prepare to say them now.'

'What am I to pray for?'

'Oh, that things will turn out all right.'

'But we've been praying for that for years,' Eve said indignantly. She wasn't to start praying for unspecified things, she told Benny.

'The Wise Woman would leave them unspecified for a bit,' Benny had said.

Benny didn't sound very wise or very happy.

'Simon's got a new girlfriend,' Heather said chattily. She knew Eve was always interested in such tales.

'Really? What happened to the lady from Hampshire?'

'I think she's too far away. Anyway this one's in Dublin, so Bee Moore told me.'

Ah Eve thought, that's going to be one in the eye for our friend Nan Mahon and her notions.

Then the thought came to her suddenly. Unless of course it *is* Nan Mahon.

CHAPTER FIFTEEN

Benny returned the account books to the shop very early on the following morning. She took Shep with her for the outing. The dog looked around hopefully in case Eddie might come out of the back room beaming and clapping his hands, delighted to see his dear old dog arriving for a visit.

She heard a footstep on the stair and realized that she had not been early enough. Sean Walsh was up and dressed.

'Ah, Benny,' he said.

'I should hope so too. We wouldn't want anyone else letting themselves in. Where'll I leave these for you, Sean?'

Was she imagining it or did he eye her very closely? He took both books and laid them in their places. It was a good three quarters of an hour before the shop opened.

The place smelled musty and heavy. There was nothing about it that would encourage you to spend. Nothing that would make a man feel puckish and buy a bright tie or a coloured shirt when he had always worn white. She looked at the dark interior and wondered why she had never taken the time to notice these things when her father was alive, less than a week ago, and talk to him about them.

But she knew why. Almost immediately she answered her own question. Her father would have been so pleased to see her taking an interest, it would have raised his hopes again. The whole subject of a union with Sean Walsh would have been aired once more.

Sean watched her looking around.

'Was there anything in particular . . . ?'

'Just looking, Sean.'

'There'll have to be great changes.'

'I know.' She spoke solemnly and weightily. That was the only language he understood, heavy pontificating phrases. But she thought a look of alarm came into his eyes as if her words had been menacing.

'Did you find what you were looking for in the books?' His glance never left hers.

'I wasn't looking for anything, as I told you I just want to familiarize myself with the day-to-day workings before I met Mr Green.'

'I thought your mother wanted to see them.' His lip curled a little.

'She did. She undersands much more than any of us realized.'

Benny didn't know why she had said this. Annabel Hogan knew nothing of the business that her dowry had helped to buy. She had deliberately stayed away from it, thinking it to be a man's world where the presence of a woman would be an intrusion. Men didn't buy suits and get measured in a place with a woman around it.

Suddenly Benny realized that this had been the tragedy of her parents' life. If only her mother *had* been able to get involved in the shop, how different things would have been. They would have shared so much more, their interest in Benny would not have been so obsessive. And her mother, in many ways a sharper, more practical person than Eddie Hogan, might have spotted this discrepancy, if such it was, and headed it off long ago. Long before it looked as serious as it looked now.

Emily Mahon knocked on the door of Nan's bedroom and came in carrying a cup of tea.

'Are you sure you don't want any milk in it?'

Nan had taken to having a slice of lemon instead. It was puzzling for the rest of the family, who poured great quantities of milk in their tea which they drank noisily from large mugs.

'It is nice, Em. Try it,' Nan urged.

'It's too late for me to change my ways, and no point in it either – not like you.'

Emily knew that her daughter had found a special person at last.

She knew from the amount of preparation that went on in the bedroom, from the new clothes, the wheedling money from her father and mainly from the sparkle in Nan's eyes.

On the bed lay a small petal hat. It matched exactly the wild silk-dress and bolero in lilac trimmed with a darker purple. Nan was going to the races today. An ordinary working day for most people, a studying day for students, but a day at the races for Nan.

Emily was on late shift; they had the house to themselves.

'You'll be careful, love, won't you?'

'How do you mean?'

'You know what I mean. I don't ask you about him because I know you think it's bad luck, and we wouldn't want to be meeting him anyway, lowering your chances. But you will be careful?'

'I haven't slept with him, Em. I haven't a notion of it.'

'I didn't mean only that.' Emily had meant only that, but it seemed a bit bald to hear it all out in the open. 'I meant, careful about not neglecting your college studies, and not going in fast cars.'

'You meant sleeping, Em,' Nan laughed affectionately at her mother. 'And I haven't, and I won't, so relax.'

'Are you and I going to keep teasing each other for ever, or will we give in to ourselves and go to bed together soon?' Simon asked Nan as they drove to the race meeting.

'Are we teasing each other? I didn't notice.'

He looked at her admiringly. Nothing threw her. She was never at a disadvantage.

And she looked really beautiful today. Her photograph would probably be in the papers. Photographers always looked for somebody classy as well as the ladies with silly hats. His companion was exactly the girl they would seek out.

They got stuck with a lot of people as soon as they went into the Enclosure. At the parade ring Molly Black, a very bossy woman with a shooting stick, looked Nan up and down with some care. Her own daughter had once been a candidate for Simon Westward's interest. This was a very different type of girl for him to parade. Handsome certainly. A student by all accounts, living in Dublin, and, giving nothing away whatsoever about herself or her background.

Mrs Black moaned about the decree from Buckingham Palace abolishing the Debutantes' presentation at Court.

'I mean, how will anyone know who anyone is once that goes?' Molly Black said, staring at Nan with gimlet eyes.

Nan looked around for Simon, hurt he wasn't at hand. She resorted to her usual system, answering a question with another.

'Why are they abolishing it, really, do you think?'

'It's obvious. You have to be presented by someone who was herself presented. Some of these are on rather hard times, and they take a fee from really dreadful businessmen to present their ghastly daughters. That's what caused it all.'

'And did you have someone to be presented?' Nan's voice was cool and her manner courteous.

She had hit home.

'Not my immediate family, no, obviously,' said Mrs Black, annoyed. 'But all one's friends, one's friend's children. It was so nice for them, such a good system. They met like-minded people until all this crept in.'

'But I suppose that it's easy to tell like-minded people, to recognize them, do you think?'

'Yes it is, quite easy.' Molly Black was gruff.

Simon was at her elbow again.

'Having a most interesting conversation about doing the Season with your little friend here,' Mrs Black said to him.

'Oh good.' Simon moved them away.

'What a battle-axe,' he said.

'Why do you bother with her then?'

'Have to.' He shrugged. 'She and Teddy are everywhere. Guarding their daughters from fortune hunters like myself.'

'Are you a fortune hunter?' Her smile was light and encouraging.

'Of course I am. You've seen the house,' he said. 'Come and let's have a very large drink and put a lot of money we can't afford on a horse. That's what living is all about.'

He took her by the arm and led her across the grass through the crowds into the bar.

The meeting with Mr Green was very low key. It was held in Lisbeg. Benny had woken her mother up enough to attend by strong coffee and a stern talking to.

Her mother must not ask that things be put off, or postponed until later. There was no later, Benny insisted. Hard as it was on all of them, they owed it to Father to make sure that things didn't end in a giant muddle.

Benny had begged her mother to recall any conversations about Sean's partnership. The letter existed, the letter saying that the intention was there. Had there been anything at all that made her think it had been formalized?

Wearily, Annabel said that Father had kept saying there was no need to rush things, that they'd wait and see, that everything got done in time.

But had he said that about things in general, or about Sean's partnership?

She really couldn't remember. It was very difficult for her to remember, she complained. It seemed such a short time ago Eddie Hogan had been alive and well and running his own business. Today he was buried and they were meeting a solicitor to discuss business dealings that she knew nothing of. Could Benny not be more patient and understanding?

Patsy served coffee in the drawing room, aired and used now because of the stream of sympathizers who had filled the house. There were just the three of them. Benny said they would telephone Sean Walsh and ask him to join them after a suitable period.

Mr Green told them what they already knew, which was that the late Mr Hogan, despite numerous reminders, suggestions and cautions, had made no will. He also told them what they didn't know, which was that the Deed of Partnership had been drawn up and prepared ready for signature, but it had not been signed.

Mr Green had been in Knockglen as was his wont on four Friday mornings in January, but on none of these occasions had Mr Hogan approached him with a view to signing the document.

On the one occasion that Mr Green had reminded him of it, the late Mr Hogan had said that he still had something to think about.

'Do you think he had discovered anything that made him change his mind? After all he did write that letter to Sean before Christmas?' Benny was persistent.

'I know. I have a copy of the letter. It was sent to me in the post.'

'By my father?'

'I rather think by Mr Walsh.'

'And there were no hints or feelings . . . Did you get any mood that the thing was wrong, somehow?'

'Miss Hogan, you'll have to forgive me for sounding so formal, but I don't deal in the currency of feelings or moods. As a lawyer I have to deal in what is written down.'

'And what is written down is an intent to make Sean Walsh a partner, isn't that right?'

'That is correct.'

Benny had no proof, only an instinct. Possibly in the weeks before his death her father too had noticed that they seemed to be lodging less than they took. But there had been no confrontation. Had there been a face-to-face accusation he would have told his wife about it, and Mike in the workroom would have heard every word.

Perhaps her father had been waiting to find proof, so this is what she too must do.

Like her father she would ask to delay the partnership agreement, by saying that it was hard to know who should be the parties to it.

Mr Green, who was a cautious man, said that it was always wise to postpone any radical change until well after a bereavement. They agreed that now would be the time to have Sean Walsh to the house.

Fresh coffee was brought in when Sean arrived.

He explained that he had closed the shop. It was impossible to allow Mike to remain in control. He was a man who had given untold service in the past, no doubt, but as Mr Hogan used to say, poor Mike wasn't able for a lot in today's world.

Her father used to say that, Benny remembered, but he had said it with affection and concern. He had not said it with the knell of dismissal echoing around it.

The arrangement was that for the moment everything would carry on as it was. Did Sean think they needed to employ somebody on a temporary basis? He said that all depended.

Depended on what, they wondered? On whether Miss Hogan was thinking of abandoning her university studies and coming to work in the shop with him. If that were to happen there would be no need to employ a casual.

Benny explained that nothing was further from her father's dreams. Her parents were both anxious that she should be a university graduate, but she would nonetheless take a huge and continuing interest in the shop. She almost kicked her mother into wakefulness and a few alert statements that she would do the same thing.

Very casually and with no hint of anything being amiss, Benny asked if the very simple book-keeping system could be explained to them. Laboriously Sean went through it.

'So what's in the takings books should be more or less as what's in the lodging book each week.' Her eyes were round and innocent.

'Yes. Give or take the drawings,' he said.

'Drawings?'

'Whatever your father took out of the till.'

'Yes. And the little pink slips; they say what those were, is that right?'

'When he remembered.' Sean's voice was sepulchral and he sounded as if he were trying not to speak ill of the dead. 'Your father was a wonderful man, as you know, but forgetful in the extreme.'

'What might he have taken money out for?' Benny's heart was cold. There would never be any proof, not if this was believed.

'Well, let me see.' Sean looked at Benny. She was wearing her best outfit, the new skirt and bolero top that she had been given as a Christmas present.

'Well, maybe for something like your clothes, Benny. He might have taken money out to pay for an outfit without remembering to sign a drawing slip.'

She knew now that she was defeated.

Kevin Hickey said that his father was coming up from Kerry and wondered could Mrs Hegarty recommend a good hotel in Dunlaoghaire?

'God, Kevin, you pass a dozen of them yourself every day,' Kit said.

'I think he wanted your choice rather than mine.'

Kit suggested the Marine, and she booked it for him.

She supposed that Kevin's father would like to see the house where his son lived all through the academic year, and urged the boy to bring him round for a cup of tea during his visit.

Paddy Hickey was a big, pleasant man. He explained that he was in machinery in the country. He had a small bit of land, but there wasn't the streak of a farmer in any of them. His brothers had all gone to America, his sons had all done degrees in something, but none of them in agriculture.

Like all Kerrymen he said he put a great emphasis on education.

Kit and Eve liked him. He talked easily about the boy of the house who had died, and asked to see a picture of him.

'May he rest in peace, poor young lad who never got a chance to know what it was like down here,' he said.

It was awkward but affecting. Neither Kit nor Eve felt able to say anything in reply.

He thanked them for giving his son such a good home, and encouraging him to study.

'No hope he's getting anywhere with a fine-looking young girl like yourself?' he asked Eve.

'Ah no, he wouldn't look at me,' Eve said, laughing.

'Besides, she has a young law student besotted about her,' Kit added.

'That must leave you lonely here sometimes, Mrs Hegarty,' he said. 'When all the young folk go out of an evening.'

'I manage,' Kit said.

Eve realized that the man was revving up to ask Kit Hegarty out. She knew that Kit herself was quite unaware of this.

'You do manage,' Eve said. 'Of course you do. And people want you everywhere, but I'd love you to go out and be silly, just once.'

'Well, talking of being silly,' said big Paddy Hickey, 'I don't suppose there's a chance you'd accompany a poor lonely old Kerry widower out for a night on the town.'

'Well, isn't that *great*,' cried Eve, 'because we're all going out tonight, every single one of us.'

Kit looked startled.

'Come back for her about seven o'clock, Mr Hickey. I'll have her ready for you,' Eve said.

When he was gone Kit turned on Eve in a fury.

'Why are you behaving like that? Cheap and pushy. It isn't at all like you.'

'It's not like me for *me*, but by God I'd need it for you.'

'I can't go out with him. I'm a married woman.'

'Oh yes?'

'Yes, I am. No matter what Joseph did in England I'm married anyway.'

'Oh, belt up Kit.'

'*Eve!*'

'I mean it. I really do. Nobody's asking you to commit adultery with Kevin's father, you great fool, just go out with him, tell him about your living encumbrance across the channel if you want to. I wouldn't personally, but you will. But don't throw a decent man's invitation back in his face.'

She looked so cross that Kit burst out laughing.

'What'll I wear?'

'That's more like it.' Eve gave her a big squeeze as they went upstairs to examine both their wardrobes.

'I was wondering would you consider Wales a sort of break . . .' Jack asked Benny hopefully.

'No, it's too soon.'

'I just thought it could be a change. They always say that's a good thing.'

Benny knew what he meant. She longed to go to Wales with him. She longed to be his girl, on a boat sailing out from Dunlaoghaire to Holyhead. She longed to be sitting beside him on a train, and meeting the others and being Benny Hogan, Jack Foley's girl, with everything that that implied.

And she knew that a change could clear her head of the thoughts and the suspicions that buzzed around in it.

She had tried to get her mother to make a visit. To go to her brothers and their wives. They had been very solicitous at the funeral. But Annabel Hogan told Benny sadly that they had never approved of her marrying Eddie all those years ago, a man younger than she was with no stake in any business. They had thought she should have done better for herself. She didn't want to go to stay in their homes, large country places, and tell them tales of a marriage which had worked for her but which they had never thought anything of.

No, she would stay in her home and try to get used to the way things were going to be from now on.

But Benny didn't want to explain all this to Jack. Jack wasn't a person to weigh down with problems. The great thing was that he seemed so glad to see her. He took no notice of the admiring glances coming at him from every corner of the Annexe. He sat on his hard wooden chair and drank cup after cup of coffee. He had two fly cemeteries, but Benny said she had gone off them.

In fact her whole being cried out for one, but she was eating no cakes, bread puddings, chips or biscuits. If she had not had Jack Foley to light up everything for her, it would have been a very dull life indeed.

Nan was delighted to see Benny back at lectures.

'I had no one to talk to. It's great to see you again,' she said.

Despite herself, Benny was pleased.

'You had Eve. Lord, I envy the two of you being here all the time.'

'I don't think Eve is too pleased with me,' Nan confided. 'I've been going out with Simon, you see, and she doesn't approve.'

Benny knew that was true: Eve did not approve, but then it would have been the same with anyone who went out with Simon. She felt that he should have made some effort to make provisions for his cousin once he was old enough to understand the situation.

And she felt that Nan had been sneaky. Eve always claimed that Benny had been dragged to the Hibernian with the express purpose of making the introduction. Benny thought that was impossible, but there were some subjects on which Eve was adamant.

'And where does he take you?' Benny loved to hear Nan's cool comments on the high life that Simon Westward was opening up.

She described the back bar in Jammet's, the Red Bank, the Baily and Davey Byrne's.

'He's so much older, you see,' Nan explained. 'So most of his friends meet in bars and hotels.'

Benny thought that was sad. Imagine not going to where there was great fun, like the Coffee Inn, or the Inca or the Zanzibar. All the places she and Jack went to.

'And do you like him?'

'Yes, a lot.'

'So why do you look so worried? He obviously likes you if he keeps asking you to all these places.'

'Yes, but he wants to sleep with me.'

Benny's eyes were round. 'You won't, will you?'

'I will, but how? That's what I'm trying to work out. Where and how.'

Simon as it turned out had decided where and how. He had decided that it was going to be in the back of a car parked up the Dublin mountains. He said it was awfully silly to pretend they both didn't want it.

Nan was ice cool. She said she had no intention of doing anything of the sort in a car.

'But you do want me?' Simon said.

'Yes, of course I do.'

'So?'

'You have a perfectly good house where we can be comfortable.'

'Not at Westlands,' Simon said.

'And most definitely not in a car,' said Nan.

Next day Simon was waiting at the corner of Earlsfort Terrace and Leeson Street as the students poured out at lunch time, wheeling bicycles or carrying books. They moved off to digs, flats and restaurants around the city.

Nan had said no, when Eve and Benny asked her to come to the Singing Kettle. Chips for Eve and black coffee for strong-willed Benny.

They didn't see her eyes dart around as if she knew someone would be waiting for her.

They didn't notice as Simon stepped out and took her hand.

'How amazingly crass I was last night,' he said.

'Oh, that's perfectly all right.'

'I mean it. It was unpardonable. I wondered if you might come down to a pretty little hotel I know for dinner and we might stay overnight. If you'd like to.'

'I'd like to, certainly,' Nan said. 'But sadly I'm not free until next Tuesday.'

'You're making me wait.'

'No, I assure you.'

But she was indeed making him wait. Nan had worked out the safe period, and next Tuesday was the earliest she dared go to bed with Simon Westward.

Clodagh was sitting in her back room sewing. She had a glass door and could see if there was a customer who needed personal attention. Otherwise her aunt and Rita, the new young girl they had taken on, could manage fine without her.

Benny came in and sat beside her.

'How's Rita getting on?'

'Fine. You've got to choose them – quick enough to be of some use. Not so quick that they'll take all your ideas and set up on their own. It's the whole nature of business.'

Benny laughed dryly. 'I wish someone had told that to my father ten years ago,' she said ruefully.

Clodagh went on sewing. Benny had never brought up the subject of Sean Walsh before. Even though it had been a matter of a lot of speculation in the last weeks. Just after Christmas there had been talk of him becoming a partner. Those who drank in Healy's Hotel said Mrs Healy spoke of it very authoritatively. Clodagh, since the day she had been barred from Healy's, made it her business to find out everything that went on there, and all subjects discussed at its bar.

She waited to hear what Benny had to say.

'Clodagh, what would happen if Rita was taking money from the till?'

'Well, for a start I'd know it at the end of the day, or else the end of the week.'

'You would?'

'Yes, and then I'd suggest cutting off her hands at the wrists, and Aunt Peggy would say we should just sack her.'

'And suppose you couldn't prove it?'

'Then I'd be very careful, Benny, so careful you wouldn't believe it.'

'If she had put it in a bank someone would know?'

'Oh yes. She wouldn't have put it in a bank, not around these parts. It would have to be in cash somewhere.'

'Like where?'

'Lord, I'd have no idea, and I'd be careful I didn't get caught looking.'

'So you might have to let it go if you couldn't prove it.'

'Crucifying as it would be, I might.'

Benny heard the warning in her voice. They both knew they were not talking about the blameless Rita out in the shop. They each realized that it would be dangerous to say any more.

Jack Foley said he'd ring Benny when he got to Wales. They were staying in a guest house. He was going to share a room with Bill Dunne, who was going for the laugh and a beer.

'You won't need me at all,' Benny had said, laughing away her disappointment that she couldn't be there.

'Fine though Bill Dunne is and everything, I don't think there's much comparison. I wish you were coming with me.'

'Well, ring me from the height of the fun,' Benny said.

He didn't ring. On night one, or night two, or night three. Benny sat at home. She didn't take her mother up to Healy's Hotel to try out one of their new evening dinners, at Mrs Healy's invitation.

Instead she stayed at home and listened to the clock ticking and to Shep snoring and to Patsy whispering with Mossy while her mother looked at the pictures in the fire and Jack Foley made no phone call from the height of the fun.

Nan packed her overnight bag carefully. A lacy nightie, a change of clothes for the next day, a very smart sponge bag from Brown Thomas, with talcum powder and a new toothbrush and toothpaste. She kissed her mother goodbye.

'I'll be staying with Eve in Dunlaoghaire,' she said.

'That's fine,' said Emily Mahon, who knew that wherever Nan was going to stay it was not with Eve in Dunlaoghaire.

Bill Dunne ran into Benny in the main hall.

'I'm meant to bump into you casually and see how the land lies,' he said.

'What on earth do you mean?'

'Is our friend in the doghouse or isn't he?'

'Bill, you're getting worse than Aidan. Talk English.'

'In plain English, your erring boyfriend, Mr Foley, wants to know if he dares approach you, he having not managed to telephone you.'

'Oh, don't be so silly,' Benny said, exasperated. 'Jack knows I'm not that kind of girl, going into sulks and moods. He knows I don't mind something like that. If he couldn't phone he couldn't.'

'Now I see why he likes you so much. And why he was so afraid that he'd upset you,' Bill Dunne said admiringly. 'You're a girl in a million, Benny.'

Heather Westward didn't really like the thought of Aidan coming on their outings, but that was before she got to know him. Soon

Eve complained that she liked Aidan more than she liked Eve. His fantasy world was vastly more entertaining than her own.

He told Heather that he and Eve were going to have eight children, with ten months between each child. They would marry in 1963 and keep having children until late 1970.

'Is that because you're Catholics?'

'No, it's because I want something to occupy Eve during my first hard years at the Bar. I shall be in the Law Library all day and night in order to make money for all the Knickerbocker Glories that these children will demand. I shall have to work at night in a newspaper as a sub-editor. I have it all worked out.'

Heather giggled into her huge ice cream. She wasn't absolutely sure if he was being serious. She looked to Eve for confirmation.

'....... what he thinks now, but actually what's going to happen is that he's going to meet some brainless little blonde who'll flutter long lashes at him and giggle, and he'll forget all about me and the long-term plan.'

'Will you mind?' Heather spoke as if Aidan weren't there.

'No, I'll be quite relieved really. Eight children would be exhausting. Remember how Clara felt with all those puppies?'

'But you wouldn't have to have them all at the same time?' Heather took the matter seriously.

'Though it would have its advantages,' Aidan was reflective. 'We'd get free baby things, and you could come and help with the babysitting, Heather. You'd change four while Eve changed the other four.'

Heather laughed happily.

'I wouldn't want a brainless little blonde, honestly,' Aidan said to Eve. 'I'm no Jack Foley.'

Eve looked at him, astonished. 'Jack?'

'You know, the Wales outing. It's all right. It's all right, Benny's forgiven him. Bill Dunne says.'

'She's forgiven him for not phoning her. She doesn't know anything about a brainless blonde that should be forgiven.'

'Oh . . . I don't think it was anything really . . .' Aidan backtracked.

Eve's eyes glinted.

'Well, only a ship that passed in the night, or the evening, a blonde, silly Welsh ship. I don't know, for God's sake. I wasn't there. I was only told.'

'Oh, I'm sure you were told, and all the gory details.'

'No, really. And Eve, I wouldn't go and say anything to Benny.'

'I'm her friend.'

'Does that mean you will or you won't?'

'It means that you'll never know.'

Nan settled herself into Simon's car.

'You smell beautiful,' he said 'Always the most expensive of perfumes.'

'Most men don't recognize good perfume,' she complimented him. 'You're very discerning.'

They drove out of Dublin south through Dunlaoghaire, past Kit Hegarty's and past Heather's school.

'That's where my sister is.'

Nan knew this. She knew that Eve went there on Sundays when Simon did not. She knew Heather was unhappy there and would much prefer a day school within reach of her beloved pony and dog and the country life she loved so much, pottering around Westlands. But she didn't let Simon know that she knew any of this.

With Simon she was determined to play it cool and distant. To ask little and seem to know little of his family and home life, so that he would not feel justified in prying into hers. Later, when she had really captivated him, then it would be time for him to get answers to his questions.

And by then he would know her well enough to realize that a drunken father and a messy family would form no part of the life that she led.

She believed that she had flirted with him for long enough and that she was timing it right to go to this hotel with him tonight.

She had looked the hotel up in a guide book, and knew all about it. Nan Mahon would not arrive anywhere, even at a hotel to lose her virginity, unprepared and uninformed about the social background of the place.

He smiled at her, a crooked lopsided smile. He really was most attractive, Nan thought, even though he was smaller than she would have chosen. She didn't wear her really good high-heeled shoes when she was out with him. He was very confident of her, as if he had known that this day would come sooner rather than later.

In fact that thought must have been on his mind.

'I was very glad when you agreed to come to dinner and let us spend a whole evening together instead of rushing away at a taxi rank,' he said.

'Yes, it's a lovely place, I believe. It has marvellous portraits and old hunting prints.'

'Yes. How do you know that?'

'I can't remember. Someone told me.'

'You haven't been here with any of your previous boyfriends?'

'I've never been to a hotel with *anyone*.'

'Come on now.'

'True.'

He looked slightly alarmed. As if the thought of what lay ahead was now more arduous and complicated than he had supposed. But a girl like Nan would not go ahead with something like this unless she intended it.

And when she said she had never been to a hotel with a chap, she might be speaking the literal truth. But a girl like this must have had some kind of experience, whether it was in a hotel bedroom or a sand dune. He would not face that problem until he had to.

There were candles on the table, and they sat in a dark dining room with heavy oil paintings of the hotelier's stern ancestors.

The waiter spoke respectfully like an old retainer, and they seemed to recognize Simon, and treat him with respect.

At the next table sat a couple. The waiter addressed the man as 'Sir Michael'. Nan closed her eyes for an instant. In many ways being here was better than being in Westlands. He had been right.

It was like a stately home, and they were being treated like the aristocracy. Not bad for the daughter of Brian Mahon, builders' provider and drunk.

Nan had not been telling him any lies, Simon realized with surprise and some mild guilt. He was indeed the first man she had gone to a hotel with in any sense of the word. She lay there with the moonlight coming through the curtains and catching her perfect sleeping face. She really was a very beautiful girl, and she seemed to like him a lot. He drew her towards him again.

Benny knew that Sean Walsh's partnership could not be postponed for ever. If only she could get her mother to take an interest in the matter. Annabel woke heavy and leaden from a sleep that had gained through tablets. It took her several hours to shake off the feeling of torpor.

And when she did the loneliness of her position came back to her. Her husband dead before his time, her daughter gone all day in Dublin and her maid about to announce an engagement to Mossy Rooney, and only holding up the actual date out of deference to the bereavement in the family.

Dr Johnson told Benny that these things took time. Sometimes a lot of time, but eventually, like Mrs Kennedy in the chemist's, if the wife could be persuaded to take an interest in the business they would recover.

Dr Johnson looked as if he were about to say something and thought better of it.

He had always hated Sean Walsh. Benny wondered could it have been about him?

'The problem is Sean, you see,' she began tentatively.

'When was it not?' Dr Johnson asked.

'If only Mother was in the shop and properly there, taking notice . . .'

'Yes, I know.'

'Do you think she'll ever be able to do that? Or am I just running after a pipe dream?'

He looked affectionately at the girl with the chestnut hair, the girl he had watched grow from the chubby toddler into the big awkward schoolgirl and now fined down a bit he thought, but still by anyone's standards a big woman. Benny Hogan may have had more comforts than some of the other children in Knockglen whose tonsilitis and chicken pox and measles he had cured, but she never had as much freedom.

Now it looked as if the chains that bound her to home were growing even stronger.

'You have your own life to live,' he said gruffly.

'That's not much help, Dr Johnson.'

To his own surprise he heard himself agreeing with her.

'You're right. It isn't much help. And it wasn't much help saying to your mother, "Stop grieving and try living". She won't listen to me. And it was no help at all, all those years ago, telling Birdie Mac to put her mother into a home, or telling Dessie Burns to go to the monk in Mount Mellary who gets people off the jar. But you have to keep saying these things. Just to stay sane.'

As long as she had known him Benny had never known Dr Johnson make such a speech. She stared at him open-mouthed.

He pulled himself together. 'If I thought it would get that long drink of water, Sean Walsh, out of your business and miles from here, I'd give Annabel some kind of stimulant to keep her working in there twelve hours a day.'

'My father had an undertaking to make Sean a partner. We'll have to honour it.'

'I suppose so.' Dr Johnson knew that this was so.

'Unless there was any reason my father didn't sign the deed.' She looked at him beseechingly. It was the smallest hope in the world that Eddie Hogan might have confided his suspicions to his old friend Maurice Johnson. But no. With a heavy heart she heard Dr Johnson say gloomily that he didn't know any reason.

'It's not as if he was the kind of fellow who'd ever be caught with his hands in the till. He hasn't spent tuppence on himself since the day he arrived.'

Sean Walsh was having his morning coffee in Healy's. From the window he could see if anyone entered Hogan's.

Mike could cope with an easy sale, or measuring a regular customer. Anything more difficult would have to be monitored.

Mrs Healy sat beside him. 'Any word of the partnership?'

'They're going to honour it. They said so in front of the solicitor.'

'So they might. It should be done already. Your name should be above the shop, for all to see.'

'You're very good to have such a high opinion of me . . . um . . . Dorothy.' He still thought of her as Mrs Healy.

'Nothing of the sort, Sean. You deserve to make more of yourself. And be seen to be what you are.'

'I will. One day people will see. I move slowly. That's my way.'

'Just as long as you're moving, not standing still.'

'I'm not standing still,' Sean Walsh assured her.

'When can I see you again?' Simon said as he dropped Nan off outside University College.

'What do you suggest?'

'Well, I'd suggest tonight, but where could we go?'

'We could go for a drink anywhere.'

'But afterwards?'

'I'm sure you know some other lovely hotels.' She smiled at him.

He did, but he couldn't afford them. And he couldn't take her to Buffy and Frank's place where he stayed when he was in Dublin. And she wasn't going to take him to her home. A car seemed out of the question, and Westlands was off limits as far as he was concerned.

'We'll think of something,' he promised.

'Goodbye,' Nan said.

He looked after her with admiration. He hadn't met a girl like this in a long time.

'Benny, you look awful. You haven't even combed your hair,' Nan said.

'Thanks a bundle, that's all I need.'

'It's *is* what you need, actually,' Nan said. 'You've got the most handsome man in college panting after you. You can't turn up looking like a mess.'

'I'll comb my hair then,' Benny said ungraciously.

The most handsome man in college was not panting after her. He was looking like a guilty sheep, every time he met her he apologized for the whole Wales thing. Benny had said he must forget it, these things happened. And she wasn't making an issue of it, so why should he?

She had even arranged to stay in town this Friday, and suggested they have an evening together. She had asked Eve if they could stay in Dunlaoghaire. She had told Patsy that she would be gone and she had explained to her mother that she needed one night a week in Dublin. That everyone got over a loss in their own way, and her way had to be spending time with her friends.

Her mother's eyes, dull and listless, had clouded as if this was one further blow.

Worst of all Jack said that Friday wasn't a good night for him. They had a meeting in the rugby club, and then they'd all go for a drink afterwards.

'Make it another night,' he said casually. Benny had wanted to smack him very hard. He was as thoughtless as any child.

Why did he not realize how hard it was for her to arrange anything at all? Now she had to go and unpick everything she had arranged. Eve, Kit, Patsy, her mother. Bloody hell, she wouldn't. She'd stay in Dublin anyway that night and maybe go to the pictures with Eve and Aidan. They had asked her often enough, and to have a curry afterwards.

They were still whistling the theme tune of *Bridge on the River Kwai* when they arrived at the Golden Orient in Leeson Street. They met Bill Dunne coming out of Hartigan's, and he joined them for the meal.

Aidan took them through the menu as an expert.

Everyone was to order something different, then they could taste four dishes and become curry bores.

'But we all like kofta,' Eve complained.

'Too bad. The mother of my children is not going to be a one-dish lady,' Aidan said.

'Where's Jack?' Bill Dunne enquired.

'At a rugby club meeting.' Benny spoke casually.

She thought she saw the boys exchange glances, but decided that she was imagining it. All that watching of Sean Walsh made her see glances and looks where none existed.

Jack Foley rang, very cross, on Saturday.

'I believe there was a great outing last night. The only night of the week I couldn't get away,' he said.

'You never told me. You always said Fridays were marvellous nights in Dublin.' Benny was stung by the injustice of it all.

'And so they were for some, Bill Dunne was telling me.'

'What night *are* you free next week, Jack? I'll arrange to stay in town.'

'You're sulking,' he said. 'You're sulking over the Wales thing.'

'I told you, I understand that you didn't have time to ring me. I am *not* sulking over a phone call.'

'Not the phone call,' he said. 'The other thing.'

'What other thing?' asked Benny.

Nan and Simon met three times without being able to do what they both wanted to do, which was to make love.

'What a pity you don't have a little flat in town,' he said to her.

'What a pity you don't,' she countered.

What they really needed was a small place where nobody would see them, somewhere they could steal in and out of.

It needn't be in Dublin. It could be miles away. Petrol was no problem. Apparently Simon put it all down for the farm. It was complicated, but it was free.

He just needed to be back in Knockglen to fill up.

Nan remembered Eve's cottage by the quarry.

She had seen where Eve put the key under a stone in the wall. Nobody went there. Except sometimes a nun to keep an eye on the place. But the nun wouldn't be keeping an eye on the place at night.

There were only lights in one cottage. Nan remembered that this was the one where a silent man called Mossy lived. She had heard Benny and Eve talking about him once.

'That's the man our Bee Moore wanted for herself, but some other took him away,' Simon said, smiling loftily at his local knowledge.

Nan had brought a pair of sheets, pillowcases and two towels. Plus her sponge bag, this time with soap as well. They must leave no trace of their visit.

Simon couldn't understand why they didn't just ask Eve. Nan said this was not even remotely possible. Eve would say no.

'Why? You're her friend. I'm her cousin.'

'That's why,' Nan said.

Simon had shrugged. They were here, so what did it matter? They dared not light the fire or the range. They brought the bottle of champagne to bed immediately.

Next morning it was very chilly.

'I'll have to bring my primus stove if I can find it,' Simon said shivering.

Nan folded the sheets and towels carefully and put them into the bag.

'Can't we leave them here?' he asked.

'Don't be ridiculous.'

Washed briskly in cold water, but as yet unshaven, Simon examined the cottage for the first time.

'She has some nice things here,' he commented. 'That came from Westlands, definitely.' He nodded at the piano. 'Does Eve play?'

'No, I don't think so.'

He touched other things. This was definitely from the house, and that might have been. He seemed to know even though he was only a child when his aunt had begun the ill-advised marriage, and started to live in this cottage instead of a Big House similar to the one she grew up in.

He laughed at a statue in place of honour on the mantelpiece.

'Who's he, when he's at home?' he said looking at a china figure of a man with a crown and a globe and a cross.

'The Infant of Prague,' Nan replied.

'Well, what's he doing on display like this?'

'Probably one of the nuns gave it to her. They do come and clean the house. Why not leave it there to please them when you don't have to look at it yourself?' Nan asked.

He looked at her admiringly. 'You're a businesswoman as well as everything else, Nan Mahon.'

'Let's go,' she said. 'It would be terrible to be caught first time.'

'You think there'll be others?' he teased.

'Only if you get your primus stove going,' she laughed.

On the first floor of Hogan's the rooms were big and high-ceilinged. That was where the family that owned the shop formerly used to live. It was where Eddie Hogan and his bride lived for the first year of their marriage. They had bought Lisbeg just before Benny was born.

The rooms on that first floor were still filled with lumber. To the furniture which was already stacked there came extra lumber, old rails not used in the shop, bales empty now of material, boxes. It was not a pretty sight.

The rooms where Sean Walsh had his home for going on ten and half years were on the floor above that.

A bedroom, another room which could be a sitting room, and a very old-fashioned bathroom with a geyser that looked like a dangerous missile.

Benny had not been up there since she was about eight or nine.

She remembered her father saying that he had asked Sean would he like a key to his own area. But Sean had been insistent that he did not.

If he had taken the money he would not have hidden it in his own rooms. Since that was the first place that would be searched if it ever were found out. It would be pointless for her to search. Pointless and dangerous. She had not forgotten Clodagh's heavy warning.

Things would be quite bad enough if Sean Walsh were not made a partner. There would be an outrage in Knockglen if he were wrongfully accused of stealing from her father. Benny did not relish the thought of hunting in his private rooms for some evidence. But she felt so sure that there must be something, perhaps in the form of a post office book from some faraway branch.

In the beginning as she had ploughed through her father's simplistic and even then not very thorough book-keeping methods, she had only *suspected* that Sean must be taking away a sum of money each week. But now she knew it. She knew it because of one simple lie he had told.

When she had tried to ask him to explain the system of drawing slips in front of Mr Green, she had asked for an example. Sean Hogan had pointed to the outfit she wore and suggested that Benny's own clothes might be something that her father drew money from the till to pay for. The thought had raised a lump in her throat.

Until she had looked at the cheques that were returned with the bank statement. Her father had paid for every single garment he had bought for her. Clothes she had liked, clothes she had hated, each one paid for in Pine's by cheque with his slanting writing.

She wished it were all over. That Sean had been unmasked, and that he had left town. That her mother had recovered her spirit and gone in to run the business. And most of all that someone would tell her exactly what had happened in Wales.

Simon brought his primus stove. Nan brought two pretty china candlesticks, and two pink candles.

Simon brought a bottle of champagne. Nan brought two eggs, and herbs, and bread and butter. She brought some instant coffee powder too. She made them a glorious omelette in the morning.

Simon said it made him feel so excited they should go straight back to bed.

'We've just remade it with all her things, silly,' Nan said. Nan never referred to Eve by name.

After a time Simon stopped calling her Eve as well.

'Where does that daughter of yours spend the nights?' Brian Mahon asked.

'You were very drunk a couple of times, Brian. I think she was frightened. She goes out to her girlfriend, Eve, in Dunlaoghaire. They all get on together, that Eve and Benny down in Knockglen. They're her friends. We should be glad she has them.'

'What's the point of rearing children and having them stay out at night?' he grumbled.

'Paul and Nasey often don't come home. You never worry about them.'

'Nothing could happen to them,' he said.

'Nor Nan either,' Emily Mahon said, with a small silent prayer.

Nan was out three nights a week at least nowadays.

She did hope most fervently that nothing would happen to her beautiful golden daughter.

Mossy Rooney saw lights there one evening. He walked straight by.

Eve Malone must have come home quietly for a night, he thought to himself.

None of his business.

The very next day Mother Francis asked him if he would do

a job on the guttering at the cottage. She came up to show him where it was falling away.

'Eve hasn't been back for weeks, the bold child,' Mother Francis scolded. 'If it wasn't for yourself and myself, Mossy, the place would fall down around her ears.'

Mossy kept his peace.

Eve Malone might have wanted to come back to her house without letting the nuns know.

Sean Walsh walked the quarry road at night. It was a place you didn't meet many people. It left him free to think of his plans, his hopes, his future. It was a space where he could consider Dorothy Healy and the interest she showed in him. She was several years older than him. There was no denying that. He had always thought in terms of marrying a much younger woman. A girl in fact.

But there were advantages in a union with an older woman. Eddie Hogan had done so after all. It had never hurt his prospects. He had been perfectly happy in his life, limited though it was. He had fathered a child.

Sean's thoughts were in a turmoil as he passed the cottage. He wasn't really aware of his surroundings.

He thought he heard music coming from inside. But he must have been imagining it.

After all, Eve wasn't at home and who else would be in there at midnight playing the piano?

He shook his head and tried to work out what length of time Mr Green the solicitor had in mind when he spoke about the regrettably snail-like process of the law.

Dr Johnson pulled his prescription pad across the desk. Mrs Carroll had always been a difficult person. He felt that she needed the services of Father Ross more than himself, but was it fair to dump all the neurotic moaners on to the local priest and call the whole thing a religious crisis?

'I know I'm not going to be popular for saying so, Dr Johnson, but I have to say what's true. That cottage up in the quarry is haunted. That woman died roaring and her poor halfwitted husband, God be good to him, may have taken his own life, God bless the mark afterwards. No wonder a house like that is haunted.'

341

'Haunted?' Dr Johnson was weary.

'No soul died at peace there. No wonder one of them comes back to play the piano at night,' she said.

Heather rang Westlands. She was coming home next weekend. Bee Moore said that was grand, she'd tell Mr Simon.

'I'll be going to tea with Eve in her cottage,' Heather said proudly.

'I wouldn't fancy that myself. People say it's haunted,' said Bee Moore, who had heard that for a fact.

Heather and Eve sat making toast by the fire in the cottage. They had long toasting forks that Benny had found for them.

She said there were amazing things on the first floor of Hogan's shop, but she didn't like to denude the place entirely in case bloody Sean *was* going to be a partner. So she had just brought something he could hardly sue for through every court in the land.

'Is it definite about the partnership?' Eve wanted to know.

'Some time, when you have about thirty-five hours...'

'I have.'

'Not now.'

'Do you want me to go away? I could go out to the pony,' Heather said.

'No, Heather, it's a long, long story, and it would depress me telling it and depress Eve listening to it. Stay where you are.'

'Right.' Heather put another of Sister Imelda's wonderful tea cakes on the toasting fork.

'Anything new though?' Eve thought Benny looked troubled.

But Benny shook her head. There was a resigned sort of look on her face that Eve didn't like. As if Benny wanted to get into a big fight over something and lacked the energy.

'I could help. Like the old days. The Wise Woman would let two people tackle it.'

'The Wiser Woman might give in to the inevitable.'

'What does your mother say?'

'Very little.'

'Benny, will you have a toasted cake?' Heather's solution for nearly every crisis.

'No. I'm fooling myself that if I don't eat, this fellow will like me more and stop going off with Welsh floozies.'

Eve sighed heavily. So someone had told her.

They cycled along cheerfully, Eve saluting almost everyone they passed. Heather knew no one. But she knew fields that would have donkeys at the gate, and a gap in the hedge where you could see a mare and two foals. She told Eve about the trees and their leaves and how her nature scrapbook was the only thing she was any good at. She wouldn't mind school work if it was all to do with pressing flowers and leaves and drawing the various stages of a beech tree.

Eve thought how odd it was about two first cousins, with only seven years between them, living only a mile and a half apart, never having met, and one knowing every person who walked the road and the other every animal in every farm.

It was strange to ride up the ill-kept ridge-filled drive of Westlands with the young woman of the house.

Even though she was no outsider, coming to ask for a handout, Eve still felt odd and out of place.

'We'll go in through the kitchen.' Heather had thrown her bicycle up against the wall.

'I don't know . . .' Eve began. Her voice was an almost exact copy of Heather's when lunch at the convent was suggested.

'Come on,' Heather said.

Mrs Walsh and Bee Moore were surprised to see her, and not altogether pleased.

'You should have come in at the front when you had a guest,' Mrs Walsh said reprovingly.

'It's only Eve. We had lunch in the kitchen of the convent.'

'Really?' Mrs Walsh's face expressed very clearly that Eve had been unwise to receive the daughter of the Big House so poorly. The very least that might have been arranged was lunch in the parlour.

'I told her you made great shortbread,' Heather said hopefully.

'We must make up a nice little box of it some time,' Mrs Walsh was polite, but cold. She definitely didn't want Eve Malone on her patch. From inside the house, Eve heard someone playing a piano. 'Oh, good,' Heather said, pleased. 'Simon's home.'

Simon Westward was charming. He came forward with both his hands out to Eve.

'Lovely to see you here again.'

'I didn't really intend . . .' She wanted terribly to tell him that she had no intention of being a casual visitor to his house. She must make him understand that she was doing it to please a child, a lonely child who wanted to share the place with her. But those words were hard to find.

Simon probably had no idea of what she was trying to say.

'It's great you're here now, it's been far too long!' he said.

She looked around her. This was not the drawing room she had been in on her first visit. It was another, south-facing room, with faded chintz and old furniture. A small desk stuffed with papers stood in the corner, a large piano near the window. Imagine one family having so many rooms and enough furniture to fill them.

Enough pictures for their walls.

Her eyes roamed around the portraits, hoping to find the one of her mother. The one she had not known existed.

Simon had been watching her. 'It's on the stairs,' he said.

'I beg your pardon?'

'I know Nan told you. Come, and I'll show it to you.'

Eve felt her face burn. 'It isn't important.'

'Oh, but it is. A painting of your mother. I didn't show it to you that first day because it was all a bit strained. I was hoping you'd come again. But you didn't, and Nan did, so I showed it to her. I hope you're not upset.'

'Why should I be?' Her fists were clenched.

'I don't know, but Nan seemed to think you were.'

How dare they talk about her. How *dare* they, and whether or not she was upset.

With tears stinging at the back of her eyes, Eve walked like a robot to the foot of the stairs where hung a picture of a small dark woman, with eyes and mouth so like her own she felt she was looking in a mirror.

She must have so little of her father about her, if there was so much of Sarah Westward there already.

Sarah had her hand on the back of a chair, but she didn't look relaxed and at peace. She looked as if she were dying for it all to be over so that she could get away. Somewhere, anywhere.

She had small hands and big eyes. Her dark hair was cut

short, as the thirties fashion would have dictated. But looking at her you got the feeling that she might have preferred it shoulder length and pushed behind her ears. Like Eve's.

Was she beautiful? It was impossible to know. Nan had only said that she was in order to let Eve know that she had seen the picture.

Nan. Nan had walked around this house, as a guest.

'Has Nan been back here since then?' she asked.

'Why do you say that?'

'I just wondered.'

'No. That was the only day she was at Westlands,' he said.

There was something slightly hesitant about the way he said it, but yet she knew it was the truth.

Out in the kitchen they were getting a grudging afternoon tea ready. Eve thought that the food they were eating this day would never end, but Heather was loving it and it would be a pity to spoil it for her now.

Eve admired the pony and the way Heather had cleaned its tack. She admired Clara's puppies and refused the offer of one as guard dog.

'It would be good to look after your property,' Heather tried to persuade her.

'I'm not there often enough.'

'That's all the more reason. Tell her, Simon.'

'It's up to Eve.'

'I'm hardly ever there. Only the odd weekend. A dog would die of loneliness.'

'But whoever *is* there could walk him.'

Heather held an adorable little male puppy up for inspection. It was seven-eighths labrador, she explained, all the best, but with a little of the silliness taken out.

'No one but me, and Mother Francis from time to time.'

'Does she sleep there?' Heather asked.

'Heavens no. So you see, no need for a guard dog.'

She didn't think to ask why Heather supposed the nun might sleep in her little cottage. She just assumed it was part of Heather's continuing ignorance of convent life. And she didn't notice any change of expression in Simon's face.

Mrs Walsh came to tell them that tea was served in the drawing room.

Eve walked in to meet her grandfather for the second time in her life.

The grandfather that Nan Malone had told everyone was so charming and such a wonderful old man. She felt herself pushing her shoulders back, and taking those deep breaths that Nan said were so helpful if you had to do something that was a bit stressful. As if Nan would know!

He looked about the same. Possibly a bit more alert than on the previous occasion. She had heard that he had been taken ill on Christmas Day, and that Dr Johnson had been summoned, but that it had all passed.

It was touching to see Heather, the child who had grown up with him and who loved him as part of the only life she knew, sit beside him, nestling in to him and helping him with his cup.

'No need to cut up the sandwiches for you today, Grandfather. They're absolutely tiny. It must be to impress Eve.'

The old man looked across at where Eve sat awkwardly in a hardbacked and uncomfortable chair. He looked at her long and hard.

'You remember Eve, don't you?' Heather tried.

There was no reply.

'You do, of course, Grandfather. I was telling you how good she's been to Heather, taking her out of school . . .'

'Yes, yes indeed.' He was cuttingly distant. It was as if someone told him that a beggar on the street had once been a fine hard worker.

She could have just smiled and let it pass. But there was something about the way he spoke which went straight to Eve's heart. The temper that Mother Francis had always said would be her undoing bubbled to the surface.

'Do you know who I am, Grandfather?' she said in a loud, clear voice. There was a note of challenge in her voice that made them all look at her startled, Heather, Simon and the old man. Nobody helped him out.

He would have to answer now or mumble.

'Yes. You are the daughter of Sarah and some man.'

'The daughter of Sarah and her husband Jack Malone.'

'Yes, possibly.'

Eve's eyes blazed. 'Not possibly. Definitely. That was his

name. You may not have received him here, but he was Jack Malone. They were married in the parish church.'

He raised his eyes. They were the same dark almond-shaped eyes that they all had, except that Major Westward's were smaller and narrower.

He looked hard at Eve. 'I never doubted that she married the handyman Jack Malone. I was saying that it is possible he was your father. Possible, but not at all as definite as you believe . . .'

She was numb with shock, the words filled with hate seemed to make no sense. His face, slightly lopsided, was working with the effort of speaking clearly and making himself understood.

'You see, Sarah was a whore,' he said.

Eve could hear the clock ticking.

'She was a whore with an itch, an itch that many handymen around the place found it easy to satisfy. We lost so many good grooms, I remember.'

Simon was on his feet in horror. Heather sat where she had been, on the little footstool, the one with beaded trimming at her grandfather's feet. Her face was white.

He had not finished speaking.

'But let us not think back over unpleasant times. You may indeed be the child of the handyman Jack Malone. If you wish to believe that, then . . . that is what you must believe . . .'

He reached for his tea. The effort of speaking had exhausted him. His cup shook and rattled against the saucer.

Eve's voice was low, and because of that all the more menacing.

'In all my life there has only been one thing I was ashamed of. I was ashamed that my father used a religious occasion, the funeral of my mother, to call down a curse on you. I wished he hadn't chosen a graveyard by a church. I wished he had more respect for the people who had come down to mourn. I even thought that God might have been angry with him for it. But now I know he didn't curse you hard enough, and his wish wasn't answered. You have lived on full of hate and bile. I will never look on your face again. And I will never forgive you for the things you said today.'

She didn't pause to see how the others took her departure. She walked straight out of the door, and through the big hall into the kitchen. Without speaking to Mrs Walsh or to Bee Moore she let herself out of the back door. She got on her bicycle and without a backward glance cycled down the rutted avenue that led from her grandfather's house.

At the window of the drawing room Heather stood, tears pouring down her face.

When Simon came to comfort her she pummelled him with her fists.

'You let her go. You let her go. You didn't stop him. Now she'll never be my friend again.'

Dearest Benny, dearest, dearest Benny,
Do you remember those shaking tempers I used to get at school? I thought they had passed over like spots do, but no. I was so desperately and hurtfully insulted by that devil in a wheelchair out in Westlands that I am not normal to speak to, and I'm going back to Dublin. I haven't told Mother Francis about the row, and I won't tell Kit, or Aidan. But I will tell you when I'm able. Please forgive me for running off, and not meeting you tonight. I've asked Mossy to take this note in to you, but honestly it's the best thing.
See you on Monday.
Love from a very distraught Eve

When Mossy handed her the note Benny first thought it was from Sean Walsh, that it was some kind of threat or instruction to back off her investigations.

She was deeply upset to hear of a row bad enough to send Eve away in one of her very black moods. Sorry, too, because that nice child would be caught in the middle of it.

And selfishly she was sorry, because she had hoped to spend the evening telling Eve all about her ever-growing belief that Sean Walsh had been salting away money and to ask her advice about where they should look for it.

When Eve let herself in to the house, Kevin Hickey was in the kitchen.

'Not out, wowing the girls on a Saturday night, Kevin?' she said.

She had promised herself that she would be a professional.

This was her job, this house her place of work. She would not allow her personal anger to rub off on the guests.

Kevin said, 'I did have a sort of a plan, but I thought I'd hang around.' He nodded with his head, indicating upstairs towards Kit's room.

'She's had some bad news, apparently. Her old man died in England. I know she hated him, but it's a shock all the same.'

Eve came into the dark room with two cups of tea and sat beside the bed. She knew Kit would not be asleep.

Kit lay, head propped up by pillows and cushions, smoking. Through the window the lights of Dunlaoghaire harbour were glinting and shining.

'How did you know I needed you?'

'I'm psychic. What happened?'

'I'm not sure. An operation. It didn't work.'

'I'm very sorry,' Eve said.

'She said it was very unexpected, the operation, that he had no idea that there was anything wrong with him. That if ever he were to die she was to ring me and say he had no idea there was anything wrong.'

'Who said all this?'

'Some landlady. He had given her fifty pounds in an envelope and said it was for her.'

Eve was silent. It was all curious and complicated and messy, like everything Joseph Hegarty seemed to have touched in his life.

'What's worrying you, Kit?'

'He must have known he was dying. That's why he came back. He must have wanted to spend the last few weeks here. And I didn't let him.'

'No, didn't he make a big point about that? He didn't know.'

'He *said* that because of the insurance.'

'The what?'

'Insurance policy. He's done what he never did in his life, he's made sure I'm provided for.'

Eve felt a big lump in her throat.

'They're going to bury him in England next weekend. They're extraordinary over there. Funerals aren't the next day. It's at a weekend so people could get there. Will you come with me, Eve? We could go on the boat.'

349

'Of course I will.'

Dear Heather,
I have to go to a funeral in England. Kit's ex-husband died.
She needs me to go with her. That's why I won't be there
on Sunday. Nothing to do with other things. See you the
weekend after. Maybe Aidan will come as well.
Just so that you know it's urgent, otherwise I'd come.

Love, Eve

Heather read the letter silently at breakfast. Miss Thompson, who
was the only nice teacher in Heather's opinion, looked at her.
'Everything all right?'
'Yes.'
Miss Thompson shrugged and left her alone. You couldn't
push adolescent girls for confidences they didn't want to give.
She's never coming again, Heather said to herself over and
over. She said it during morning prayers, during mathematics and
during geography. Soon it became like the refrain of a song you
can't get out of your mind. 'She's never coming again.'
Miss Thompson didn't remember about the letter, but she did
say that she had noticed Heather was extremely quiet and withdrawn during the week. And she went back over it all, as they
all had to on Friday night when Heather Westward didn't turn
up for supper, and couldn't be found anywhere on the school
premises. And she had not turned up at home. It had to be
admitted by all those who didn't want to believe it, that Heather
had run away from school.

CHAPTER SIXTEEN

As soon as Simon heard that Eve Malone had gone to England he said that was where they would find Heather.

Eve had not acknowledged his note of apology and explanation that his grandfather's hardening of the arteries made him unstable and unreliable and therefore someone whose opinions and views were best ignored.

Simon wondered had the note been too formal? He had told Nan about it, and to his surprise she had been critical of him. Normally she had been so cool, unruffled and giving so little of herself and her views.

'Why was it such an awful letter?' he asked anxiously.

'Because it sounds icy, like your grandfather.'

'It wasn't meant to be. It was meant to be low key, to try and bring down the temperature.'

'It did that all right,' Nan agreed.

On Friday when the school had been in touch he rang Nan.

'You know what you were saying about the letter . . . do you think that's why she took Heather?'

'Of course she didn't take Heather.' Nan was dismissive.

'So where is Heather then?'

'She ran away because you were all so awful.'

'Why don't you run away then?' He sounded petulant.

'I like awful people. Didn't you know?'

The schoolgirls were frightened. Nothing like this had ever happened before. They were all being asked extraordinary questions. Had they seen anyone come in to the school, had they seen Heather leave with anyone else?

Her school coat was gone, her hated school beret left on the bed. Her pyjamas and sponge bag, her book of pressed flowers, her snaps of the pony and Clara and her puppies had disappeared. They were normally on display beside her bed where other girls had pictures of their families.

Heather's classmates were asked had she been upset? They hadn't noticed.

'She's very quiet really,' said one of them.

'She doesn't like it here,' said another.

'She's not much fun. We don't take much notice of her,' said the class bully.

Miss Thompson's heart was heavy.

There had been no sign of Heather on the bus. Mikey said he knew her well. A big thick lump of a child as square as a half door. Of course he'd have noticed her.

She would have had eleven shillings at the most, and possibly a lot less. Heather was known to spend a few pennies on sweets.

By the time Simon arrived at the school they had called the guards.

'Is it really necessary to have the police?' he said.

The headmistress was surprised. 'Since she hasn't gone home and you could throw no light on anywhere she might be . . .'

Miss Thompson looked at Simon with some dislike.

'And we have assumed that there was nothing for her to run home to apart from her pony and her dog, and she didn't go there anyway, so we thought you would have wanted us to call in the guards. It would be the normal thing for anyone to do, the normal thing to do.'

Simon looked at her miserably. Until now he hadn't realized how far from normal poor Heather's life had been.

He would make it up to her, when they got her back from England, which was undoubtedly where Eve had taken her.

At the guest house in Dunlaoghaire, the guards and Simon found three students holding the fort. Mrs Hegarty had gone to England to a funeral. Eve Malone had gone with her. Yes, of course they had left an emergency number where they could be contacted.

Mrs Hegarty had said she would ring anyway next morning to see if they had managed their breakfasts.

It was now eleven o'clock on a Friday night. The mail boat would not yet have arrived at Holyhead. Mrs Hegarty would not be in London until seven in the morning. She and Eve would take the mail train to Euston.

There was a discussion about telephoning the police in Wales to look for Heather.

There was some doubt on the part of the two guards who were busy taking down details.

'You're absolutely sure this is where your sister is, sir?' they asked again.

'There's nowhere else she could be.' He was sure of that.

'Did anyone see Mrs Hegarty and Miss Malone off at the boat?' one guard asked.

'I did.' The boy who said he was Kevin Hickey, veterinary student, was spokesman.

'And were they accompanied by a twelve-year-old girl?'

'You mean Heather?'

Simon and the guards had not explained the purpose of their enquiries.

'Was she with them?' Simon asked.

'Of course not. That's the problem. Eve was worried because she was going to this funeral. She was afraid Heather wouldn't understand that she simply *had* to go away.'

Eve had left a box of chocolates which she had instructed Kevin to deliver to the school on Sunday, with a note from Eve.

'Could you give them to her, if you're connected?' he asked Simon.

They asked to see the note.

It was simple and to the point: 'Just to show I haven't forgotten you. Next week, *you* choose where we go. Love, Eve.'

Simon read it and for the first time since his sister's disappearance had been discovered tears came to his eyes.

On Saturday morning there could hardly have been anyone in Knockglen who didn't know about it. Bee Moore had done her fair share of telling, and Mr Flood, who had been one of the early recipients of the news, had been out consulting with the nuns in the tree, but finding to his disappointment that there was no heavenly message about Heather.

'I had hoped she might have been in Heaven. Well, her kind of Heaven,' he said, remembering that he mustn't lose sight of the fact that the Westwards were Protestants.

Dessie Burns said there'd be a fine reward for anyone who found her, and mark his words she was kidnapped, and what's more kidnapped by someone in the know.

Paccy Moore said that the chances of being kidnapped by anyone in the know were slim. If you knew anything about the Westwards you'd know they could hardly pay their bills. If the poor child had been kidnapped it was by some gombeen Dubliner who thought that she was wealthy because she had a posh accent and came from a big house.

Mrs Healy said to Sean Walsh that they'd be singing a different song up at Westlands now. They had always been so distant and different, and things that happened to ordinary people never happened to them.

Sean wondered why she had turned against them. And Mrs Healy said it wasn't a matter of that so much as being slightly peeved. Mr Simon Westward had implied that he would be having the most important of people to stay at the hotel in the near future, if they had evening dinners. Mrs Healy had put on those dinners, but Mr Westward had never partaken.

'But other people have,' Sean Walsh said. 'You've made your profit on them, that's all that matters.'

Mrs Healy agreed, but you didn't like to be hopping and jumping like people in a gate cottage just for the whims of the aristocracy.

She said as much to Mrs Kennedy from the chemist who looked at her thoughtfully, and said that it was a sad thing to have a hard heart when there was a child's life at stake, and Mrs Healy changed her tune drastically.

Clodagh told the news to Peggy Pine. Clodagh thought that a man in a raincoat had offered poor Heather a whole box of chocolates in Dunlaoghaire harbour.

Mario said that all the men of Knockglen should go out and beat the hedges with sticks looking for her.

'You see too many bad films,' Fonsie complained.

'Well, where do you think she is, Mister Smartie Pants?' Mario enquired.

'I see too many bad films too. I think she went for that bloody horse of hers, and rode off into the sunset.'

But it was one of the many theories that didn't hold up because the pony was still up in Westlands.

Peggy Pine went up to the convent to talk to Mother Francis.

'Eve was on the phone from London,' Mother Francis said. 'I could hear her grinding her teeth from there. Apparently they thought she had taken Heather with her. I dread to think what she'll do when she gets back.'

'But Eve would never had done that.'

'I know, but there was some kind of row up in Westlands last week. Needless to say Miss Malone didn't tell *me* anything about it . . . Lord, Peggy, where would that child be?'

'When you think about running away you think about running to somewhere you were happy.' Peggy Pine was thoughtful. It didn't get them much further.

Heather had never seemed to be all that happy anywhere.

Sister Imelda had started the thirty days prayer. She said it had never been known to fail.

'The poor child. I never met a girl who was as appreciative. You should have heard her telling me how much she enjoyed toasting my tea cakes up in Eve's cottage.'

Suddenly Mother Francis knew where Heather was.

She reached into the gap in the wall and as she suspected the key wasn't there.

Mother Francis moved softly to the front door of Eve's cottage. It was closed. She peeped in the window and saw a large box on the table. There was something moving inside it, a cat she thought first, a black cat. Then she saw it was a bird.

A wing of black feathers came at an awkward angle out of the box.

Heather had found a wounded bird and had decided to cure it. Not very successfully, by all appearances. There were feathers and bits of torn-up newspaper everywhere.

Heather, flushed and frightened-looking, was trying to get a fire going. She seemed to be using only sticks and bits of cardboard. It would flare for a moment, and then die down.

Mother Francis knocked on the window.

'I'm not letting you in.'

'All right,' Mother Francis said unexpectedly.

'So there's no point in staying. Seriously.'

'I brought your lunch.'

'No, you didn't. It's a plot. You're going to rush me as soon as I open the door. You have people out behind the wall.'

'What kind of people? Nuns?'

'The Guards. Well, maybe nuns as well, my brother. People from school.'

Mother Francis sighed. 'No, they all think you're in London. That's where they're looking for you as it happens.'

Heather stood on a stool and looked out of the window.

There did not seem to be anyone else.

'You could leave the lunch on the step.'

'I could. But it would get cold, and I'll need the dish for Sister Imelda, and it means I don't get any.'

'I'm not coming home or anything.'

Mother Francis came in. She left a covered dish and the big buttered slices of bread on the sideboard.

She looked first at the bird.

'Poor fellow. Where did you find him?'

'On the path.'

Gently Mother Francis lifted the bird. She kept up a steady stream of conversation. It was only a young crow. The young often fell from the high trees. Some of them were quite clumsy. It was a myth to believe that all birds were graceful and could soar up in the air at will.

The wing wasn't broken, she told Heather. That was why the poor thing had been trying so hard to escape. It had just been stunned by the fall.

Together they felt the bird and smiled at the beating of the little heart and the anxious bird eyes not knowing what fate was in store for it.

Mother Francis gave it some bread crumbs, and then together they took it to the door.

After a few unsteady hops it took off in a low lopsided flight, just clearing the stone wall.

'Right, that's the wildlife dealt with. You get rid of all those feathers and newspapers and put back this box in the scullery. I'll see to lunch.'

'I'm still not going back, even if you did help me with the bird.'

'Did I say a thing about going back?'

'No, but you will.'

'I won't. I might ask you to let them know you're safe, but that's all.'

Mother Francis got the fire going. She explained to Heather about the dry turf, that stood leaning against the wall. She showed her how to make a little nest of twigs and get that going with a nice crackling light before putting on the turf. Together they ate Sister Imelda's lamb stew, and big floury potatoes, and dipped their bread and butter into the rich sauce.

There was an apple each and a piece of cheese for afterwards. Mother Francis explained that she couldn't carry much more, because the path was quite slippy and anyway she didn't want to arouse suspicion about where she was going.

'Why did you come for me?' Heather asked.

'I'm a teacher, you see. I imagine I know all about children. It's a little weakness we have.'

'There's nothing you can do.'

'Ah now, we never know that till we've examined all the possibilities.'

Eve rang Benny from England. She said she had spent more time making cross-channel phone calls than she had spent being any help to Kit. The whole thing was so infuriating she was going to tear off Simon Westward's affected little cravat and tie it round his thin useless neck and pull it hard until he was blue in the face and only when she saw his tongue and eyeballs protruding would she stop pulling.

'You're wasting time,' Benny said.

'I am. I suppose there's no news, is there?'

'Not that we've heard.'

'I've just had an idea where she might be. It's only an idea,' said Eve.

'Right. Who will I tell. Simon?'

'No, go on your own. Just go up as if you happened to be passing, and if the key isn't there you'll know she's inside. And Benny, you know how comforting you can be. She'll need that. Tell her I'll sort it out when I get back.'

On her way up the town Benny thought that she might buy some sweets. It would break the ice if Heather was there and needed to be talked out of the place. She had no money, but she knew that her credit would be good in Birdie Mac's.

As she passed the door of Hogan's she suddenly thought of the drawing slips. She could sign a pink piece of paper and write '£1 miscellaneous goods' on it. Why should she, from one business premises in the town, ask credit from Birdie in another.

Sean watched carefully.

'There, I think that's in order, isn't it?' she smiled brightly.

'You've taken a great interest in the mechanics of the business,' he said.

She knew he had something to hide. She *knew* it. But she must be careful. She continued in her same cheery tone.

'Oh well, one way or another I'll have to be much more involved from now on,' she said.

He repeated the phrase with an air of wonder.

'One way or another?'

She shouldn't have said that. It implied that there might be doubt over his partnership. She had told herself so often to be careful. Best now to play the role of someone who was not the full shilling.

'Oh, you know what I mean, Sean.'

'Do I?'

'Of course you do.'

She almost ran from the shop. In and out of Birdie's and up to the square. She had better not go through the convent, even though it was quicker. The nuns would see her and ask her what she was up to.

Eve wanted this done on the quiet.

They had been over a lot of ground, Mother Francis and Heather Westward. The school in Dublin and the games and the other girls having lots of family coming to see them and houses to go to at weekends.

And how much Heather loved Westlands and how horrible Grandfather had been to Eve, and the fear that Eve might not come again.

And how nice it would be if there was a school that she could cycle to every day.

'There is,' Mother Francis said.

There were some areas that had to be argued through. Mother Francis said that there wouldn't be any effort made to convert Heather to Catholicism because the main problem these days was keeping those that were already in the flock up to the mark.

And there would be no idols of the Virgin Mary to bow down to and worship. There would however be statues of the same Virgin Mary around the school to remind anyone who wished to be so reminded of the Mother of God.

And there would be no need for Heather to attend religious doctrine classes, and she need have no fear that history would be taught with an emphasis on the Pope being always right and everyone else being wrong.

'What was it all about, the split?' Heather asked.

'The Reformation do you mean?'

'Yes. Was it about your side worshipping idols?'

'I think it was more about the Real Presence at Mass. You know, whether Communion is truly the Body and Blood of Jesus, or just a symbol.'

'Is that all it was about?' Heather asked, amazed.

'It started that way. But it developed, you know the way things do.'

'I don't think there should be all that much fuss then.'

Heather seemed greatly relieved that the doctrinal differences of three hundred years appeared to be so slight. They were just shaking hands on it when there was a knock on the door.

'You said you didn't tell anyone.' Heather leapt up in dismay.

'Nor did I.' Mother Francis went to the door.

Benny stood there with her speech ready. Her jaw dropped when she saw the nun and the angry little figure inside.

'Eve rang. She wondered whether Heather might have been here. She asked me to come and . . . and well . . .'

'Did you tell anyone?' Heather snapped out the question.

'No, Eve particularly said not to.'

The face relaxed.

Mother Francis said she had to be going now before the Community assumed that she too was a missing person and started broadcasting appeals for her on the wireless.

'Are they doing that for me?'

'Not yet. But a lot of people are very worried and afraid that something bad might have happened to you.'

'I'd better tell them . . . I suppose.'

'I could if you like.'

'What would you say?'

'I could say that you'll be back later this afternoon, that you'll be calling in to the convent to borrow a bicycle.'

She was gone.

Benny looked at Heather. She pushed the box of sweets over to her.

'Come on, let's finish it. We'll tear through it, both layers.'

'What about the man who fancies Welsh women, the one you're getting thin for?'

'I think it's too late.'

Happily they ate the chocolates. Heather asked about the school and who were the hard teachers and who were the easy ones.

Benny asked about her grandfather and whether he knew all the awful things he had said.

'Did she tell everyone?' Heather looked ashamed.

'Only me. I'm her great friend.'

'I don't have any great friends.'

'Yes, you do. You have Eve.'

'Not any more.'

'Of course you do. You don't understand Eve if you'd think a thing like that mattered. She didn't want to like you in the first place because she had all the bad memories about that old business years ago. But she did, and she always will.'

Heather looked doubtful.

'Yes, and you can have me, too, if you want me, and Eve's Aidan as a sort of circle of friends. I know we're way too old for you, but until you make your own.'

'And what about the man who goes off with thin Welsh people? Is he in the circle?'

'On the edges,' Benny said.

In a way that was more true than she meant it to be. She had met Jack twice during the week, and he had been rushing. There was a lot of training, and hardly any time to speak alone.

He had been very contrite about some still unspecified incident during the friendly match played in Wales. Some girls had come to the club, and it had all been a bit of fun, a laugh, nothing to it. Tales had been greatly exaggerated. In vain Benny tried to tell him that she had heard no tales so nothing could be made better or worse because there had been no stories to exaggerate.

Jack had said that everyone was entitled to a bit of fun, and he never minded her jiving away in Mario's when he wasn't around. It had been highly unsatisfactory.

There was an uneven number of sweets, so they halved the last one, a coffee cream.

They tidied up Eve's house and damped the embers of the fire. Together they left and replaced the key in the wall.

Mossy nodded to them gravely as he passed by.

'Who was that?' Heather whispered.

'Mossy Rooney.'

'He's broken Bee Moore's heart,' Heather said disapprovingly.

'Not permanently. She's going to be Patsy's bridesmaid when the time comes.'

'I suppose people get over these things,' Heather said.

Mother Francis handed Heather Eve's bicycle.

'Off you go. Your brother will be waiting for you. I said he should let you go home on your own pedals.'

The nun produced Heather's small bag of possessions, her nature book, her pyjamas, the photographs of the horse and dog and the small sponge bag. She had wrapped them neatly in brown paper and twine and clipped them on to the back of the bicycle.

Benny and Mother Francis watched her cycle off.

'You guessed! Eve always said you had second sight.'

'If I have then I'd say you have some big worry on your mind.'

Benny was silent.

'I'm not prying.'

'No, of course not.' Benny's murmur was automatic politeness.

'It's just being what people laughingly call out of the real world . . . I hear a great deal about what goes on amongst those who are in it.'

Benny's glance was enquiring.

'And Peggy Pine and I were school friends years ago, like you and Eve . . .'

Benny waited. Mother Francis said that if it was of any use to Benny she should know that Sean Walsh had enough money, from whatever source, to think himself able to buy one of the small cottages up in the quarry road. Cash deposit.

Benny's mother said that Jack Foley had rung. No, he hadn't left a message. Benny thought harsh things about Heather Westward for having taken her out of the house when the call came. And she wished that she had not run so readily to do Eve's bidding.

But then Eve would have done the same for her. And if he loved her and wanted to talk to her, he would ring again.

If he loved her.

Nan's mother came to say that there was a Simon Westward on the phone.

Nan's tone was cold.

'Did I give you my phone number?' she asked.

'No, but that's irrelevant. Heather's home.'

'Oh, I am glad. Where was she?' Nan was still wondering how he knew where to telephone. She had been adamant about not telling anyone how to contact her.

'She was in Eve's cottage, as it happens.'

It had been a distinct possibility that Nan and Simon might have been there also. The thought silenced them both for a moment.

'Is she all right?'

'She's fine, but I can't leave. I have to sort her out.'

Nan had been ironing her dress for the last hour. It had complicated pleats in the linen. Her hair was freshly washed and she had painted her toenails a pearly pink.

'Yes, of course you must stay,' she said.

'Oh good. I thought you'd be annoyed.'

'The main thing is that she's safe.'

There was no hint of the rage that Nan was feeling. His tone was so casual.

Simon said that apparently Heather had been very unhappy at the school in Dublin. Nan sighed. Eve had been saying this for months. Heather had probably been saying it for years, but Simon had not listened. There were just a few schools that were suitable for his sister and she would jolly well have to learn to like the one she was in. That had been his attitude.

'So maybe tomorrow?' He was confident and sure.

'Sorry?'

'Tomorrow, Sunday night. Things will have sorted themselves out here . . .'

'And?'

'And I was hoping you might come down . . . for the night?'

'Well, I'd love to.' Nan smiled. At last he had invited her. It had taken some time, but he was inviting her to Westlands. She would be given a guest room. She was going there as Mr Simon's young lady.

'That's marvellous.' He sounded relieved. 'You get the last bus. I'll go to the cottage and set things up for us.'

362

'The cottage?' she said.

'Well, we know Eve's in England.'

There was a silence.

'What's wrong?' he asked.

'Suppose Heather decides to call again?'

'No, by heavens, she'll get a strict talking to about respecting other people's property.'

He saw no irony in this at all.

'I think not,' she said.

'Nan?'

She had hung up on him.

Joseph Hegarty had made a few, but not many, friends during his years in England. They had gathered to speak well of him after his funeral.

In the back room of a bar they sat, an ill-assorted group. A landlady who had been fond of him; whenever he didn't have the rent, he always did so many repairs around the house, it was twenty times better than having a lodger, she confided. Eve could see the pain in Kit's face. That Joseph Hegarty should be without the rent was bad enough, but that he should do plumbing and carpentry for a strange woman in England rather than in his own house in Dunlaoghaire was even worse.

If the barmaid was amongst the group she did not declare herself. The whole thing had such an unreal atmosphere about it, Eve felt that they were taking part in some play. Any moment the curtain would fall and they would all start talking normally again.

The only clue to why Joseph Hegarty might have stayed so long in this twilight world where he touched so little on people around him came from Fergus, a Mayo man, who said he was a friend.

Fergus had left a long time ago. There had been no row, no one thing that drove him out of his smallholding in the West of Ireland. He just felt one day that he wanted to be free and he had taken a train to Dublin, and then the boat.

His wife was now dead, his family grown. None of them wanted anything to do with him, and in many ways it was for the best. If he had gone back, he would have had to explain.

'At least Joe saw his son last summer. That was the great thing,' he said.

Kit looked up, startled.

'No, he didn't. Francis never saw him since he was a child.'

'But didn't he write to him and all?'

'No.' Kit's voice was clipped.

Eve went to stand beside Fergus the Mayoman at the bar later.

'So he did keep in touch with his son then?'

'Yes, I think I was out of order. The wife is very bitter. I shouldn't have said . . . I didn't know.'

'In time she'll be glad. In time I'll tell her properly. And maybe she'll want to talk to you.' She took out a diary and a pen. 'Where would you be . . . if we wanted to get in touch?'

'Ah, now, that's hard to say.' The look in the eyes of Fergus became wary. He wasn't a man who liked to plan too far ahead.

There was a discussion with the man from the insurance, and some documents to sign. Eve and Kit went to Euston and took the train to Holyhead.

For a long time Kit Hegarty looked out of the window at the land where her husband had lived for so long.

'What are you thinking about?' Eve asked.

'About you. You were very good to come with me. Several people thought you were my daughter.'

'I seem to have been on the phone most of the time.' Eve was apologetic.

'Thank God it turned out all right.'

'We don't know that yet. They're a weird bunch. They could send her back there. I hate being beholden to them, I really do.'

'You don't have to be,' said Kit. 'The first thing I'm going to do when I get the insurance money is to give you a sum. You can walk back up that avenue, and throw it back. Throw it on the floor.'

Patsy said that with all their talk about teaching them to work in a house, the orphanage had been very bad at teaching them to sew.

Mossy had said that his mother was expecting Patsy to have made a lot of things for her hope chest, like pillowcases, and hemmed them herself.

She was struggling away in the kitchen. The trouble was that often she pricked her fingers and the nice piece of linen got stained with blood.

'He's mad. Can't you buy grand pillowcases for half nothing up in McBirney's in Dublin?' Benny said indignantly.

But this wasn't the point. Apparently Mrs Rooney expected a suitable bride for Mossy to be able to turn a hem properly and sew dainty stitches. Patsy had to try harder and put up with all this nonsense because she had nothing else to bring to the marriage. No family, no bit of land, not even her father's name.

'Does it have to be hand done? Couldn't it be on a machine?' Benny was worse than useless, her own stitching was in big loops, irregular and impatient.

'What's the difference? We haven't a machine that works.'

'We'll ask Paccy to mend it. Let's look on it as a challenge,' Benny said.

Paccy Moore said that a horse with heavy hooves must have been using the sewing machine, and that if you had a fleet of highly paid engineers they wouldn't be able to put it back in working order. Tell the lady of the house to throw it out, was his advice. And surely they must have had an old one years ago, one of those nice firm ones that people like Benny and Patsy couldn't break.

They went sadly back to Lisbeg. There wasn't much point in telling the lady of the house anything. The listless manner hadn't changed. They *did* have an old sewing machine somewhere with a treadle underneath. Benny remembered seeing it once, even playing at it. But it was useless to talk to Mother. She would try to remember and then say that her headache was coming back.

But Benny hated to see Patsy, who had started life with so little, continue in this struggle to please.

'You see, I can't have bought ones, Benny. The old rip gives me the material herself, just to make sure.'

'I'll ask Clodagh to do them for you. She loves a challenge too,' said Benny.

Clodagh said they should both be shot for not knowing how to do a simple seam. She showed them on the machine.

'Go on, do it yourselves,' she urged.

'There isn't time for that. You do it and we'll do something in return for you. Tell us what you want us to do.'

'Ask my aunt to lunch and keep her there all afternoon. I want to rearrange everything in the shop: if I knew someone was looking after Peg I could get a gang in to help me. When she comes back it'll be too late to change it.'

'When?'

'Thursday, early closing day.'

'And you'll do all these pillowcases and some sheets and two bolster cases?'

'It's a deal.'

Jack Foley said he was going to skip lectures on Thursday and they'd go to the pictures.

'Not Thursday. Any other day.'

'Bloody hell. Isn't that the day you don't have lectures?'

'Yes, but I have to go back to Knockglen. There's this great scheme . . .'

'Oh, there's *always* some great scheme in Knockglen,' he said.

'Friday. I can stay the night in Dublin.'

'All right.'

Benny knew she would have to do something to try and smooth down Jack's ruffled feelings. She was very much afraid it might involve doing something more adventurous in the car than they had done already.

As Patsy said, at least three times a day, men were the divil.

Nan had taken a risk in hanging up on Simon. She had also left the phone slightly off the hook in case he called again. She went angrily up to her room and lay on her bed. The freshly ironed dress hung on its hanger, her pink nails twinkled at her, she really should go out somewhere and get value from all this primping and preening.

But Nan Mahon didn't want to arrange a meeting with Bill Dunne, or Johnny O'Brien, or anyone. Not even the handsome Jack Foley, who had been prowling discontentedly since Benny was never around.

Benny. Simon must have got her telephone number from Benny. He had probably pleaded with her and said it was urgent. Benny was very foolish, Nan thought. A handsome man like Jack Foley should not be left on his own in Dublin. All very well to say that the Rosemary Ryans and Sheilas knew he was spoken for. But when it came to it people often forgot loyalties. In Dublin things were more immediate than that.

'You're very cross,' Heather said.

'Of course I am. Why couldn't you have told us how awful it was?'

Heather had, many times, but nobody had listened. Her grandfather had looked away dreamily, and Simon had said everyone hated school. You just had to grin and bear it. Mrs Walsh had said that in her position Heather had to have a suitable education, meeting the people she would be meeting socially later on, not the daughters of every poor fellow down on his luck which is what you'd meet in a village school.

She hadn't expected Simon to be so annoyed. He had been on the phone to someone and had come back in a great temper.

'She hung up on me,' he had said, several times.

At first Heather had been pleased to see him distracted, but she realized that it wasn't making their conversation about her future any easier.

'Mother Francis will talk to you about the school,' she began.

'That's all that bloody woman wants. First they got Eve, and now they want you.'

'That's not true. They took Eve because nobody else wanted her.'

'Oh, they have *you* well indoctrinated, I can see that.'

'But who did want her, Simon? Tell me.'

'That's not the point. The point is that we have planned an expensive education for you.'

'It'll be much cheaper here, much. I asked. It's hardly anything.'

'No. You don't understand. It's not possible.'

'*You* don't understand,' Heather said, twelve years of age and confronting him with her fists clenched. As she told him that she would run away every single time she was sent back to that school, her eyes flashed and she reminded him suddenly of the way Eve had looked that day she came to Westlands.

Jack seemed to have got over his bad temper. On Thursday morning he took Benny to coffee in the Annexe. She ate a corner of one of his fly cemeteries in order to prevent him from over-dosing on them, and being pronounced unfit to play in the next match.

He put his hand over hers.

'I am a bad-tempered boorish bear, or bearish boor, which ever you like,' he apologized.

'It won't be long now. I'll have everything sorted out, I swear,' Benny said.

'Days, weeks, months, decades?' he asked, but he was smiling at her. He was the old Jack.

'Weeks. A very few weeks.'

'And then you'll be able to romp shamelessly around Dublin with me, giving in to my every base wish and physical lust.'

'Something like that,' she laughed.

'I'll believe it when I see it,' he said, looking straight at her. 'You do know how much I want you, don't you?'

She swallowed, not able to find the right words. As it happened, she didn't need to. Nan had approached.

'Is this a Sean-Carmel impersonation, or can I join you for coffee?'

Benny was relieved. Jack went back to the counter to collect it.

'I'm not interrupting anything am I, seriously?' Nan was marvellous. You could actually ask her to take her coffee off and join another group. Nan wouldn't mind. She was a great apostle of the solidarity between girls. But in fact it was much better not to walk any further down the path of discussing sex.

'I wanted Benny to come to *Swamp Women* but she's stood me up,' Jack said, in a mock mournful voice.

'Why d'ya not go to *Swamp Women* with the nice gentl'man, honey?' Nan asked. 'I sho would in yore place.'

'Then come with me,' Jack suggested.

Nan looked at Benny, who nodded eagerly.

'Oh, please do, Nan. He's been talking about *Swamp Women* for days.'

'I'll go and keep him from harm,' Nan promised.

On their way to the cinema they met Simon Westward.

'Have you been avoiding me?' he asked curtly.

Nan smiled. She introduced the two men. Anyone passing by would have thought they made an extraordinarily handsome tableau standing there, two of them in college scarves, the third small, and very county.

'We're going to *Swamp Women*. It's about escaped women prisoners and alligators.'

'Would you like to join us?' Jack suggested.

Simon looked up at Jack, a long glance.

'No, thanks all the same.'

'Why did you ask him to come with us? Because you knew he wouldn't?' Nan asked.

'Nope. Because I could see how much he fancied you.'

'Only mildly, I think.'

'No, seriously, I think,' Jack said.

Because Nan knew that Simon would have turned to look after them, she took Jack's arm companionably.

Benny went back to Knockglen on the bus in high good humour. Jack was cheerful again. He did say he wanted her, he couldn't have been more explicit. And now she didn't even have to worry about him being left high and dry. Nan had gone to the silly film with him.

All Benny had to do now was keep Peggy Pine entertained while unmentionable things went on in her shop. She knew that Fonsie, Dekko Moore, Teddy Flood and Rita were all poised. Peggy must be kept off the scene until at least five o'clock.

When she got into Lisbeg Benny was pleased to see that Patsy had made a good soup, and there were plain scones to be served with it. Mr Flood had sent down a small leg of lamb, there was the smell of mint sauce made in a nice china sauce boat.

Mother wore a pale grey twinset with her black skirt, and even a small brooch at the neck. She looked more cheerful. Probably she needed company, Benny realized. She certainly seemed a lot less listless than on other days.

Peggy drank three thimblefuls of sherry enthusiastically, and so did Mother. Benny had never known Clodagh's aunt in better form. She told Mother that business was the best way to live your life, and that if she had her time, and her chances, all over again she would still think so.

She confided to them, something that they already knew, which was that she had been Disappointed earlier in life. But that she bore the gentleman in question no ill will. He had done her a service in fact. The lady he had chosen did not have the look of a contented person. Peggy Pine had seen her from time to time over the years. While she in her little shop was as happy as anything.

Mother listened interested, and Benny began to have the stirrings of hope that Peggy might be able to achieve for Mother what she had not been able to do. Peggy might make Annabel Hogan rediscover some kind of reason for living.

'The young people are the hope, you know,' Peggy said.

Benny prayed that the transformation taking place in the shop at this moment would not be of such massive proportions as to make Peggy withdraw this view.

'Ah, yes, we've been blessed with Sean Walsh,' Annabel said.

'Well, yes, as long as you'll be in there to keep the upper hand,' Peggy warned.

'I couldn't be going in interfering. He did fine in poor Eddie's time.'

'Eddie was there to be a balance to him.'

'Not much of a balance I'd be,' Annabel Hogan said. 'I don't know the first thing about it.'

'You'll learn.'

Benny saw the dangerous trembling of her mother's lip. She hastened to come in and explain to Peggy, that things were a little bit up in the air at the moment. There had been a question of Sean being made a partner and that should be cleared up before Mother went into the shop.

'Much wiser to go in before the deed is signed,' Peggy said.

To her surprise Benny saw her mother nodding in agreement. Yes, it did make sense to go in and be shown the ropes. It wouldn't look as if she were only going in afterwards to make sure they got an equal share.

And after all they might need more hands around the shop, so Sean if he was going to be a partner would prefer an unpaid one than someone who would need a wage. She told an astonished Benny and Patsy that she might go in on Monday for a few hours to see how the daily routine worked.

Peggy looked pleased, but not very surprised.

Benny guessed that she might have planned the whole thing. She was a very clever woman.

Nan and Jack came out of the cinema.

'It was terrible,' Nan said.

'But great terrible,' Jack pleaded.

'Lucky Benny. She's back in Knockglen.'

'I wish she didn't spend so much time there.'

They had a cup of coffee in the cinema café and he told her how hard it was to have a girlfriend miles away.

What would Nan do if she had a chap down in Knockglen, at the far end of civilization?

'Well, I do,' Nan said.

'*Of course*, the guy in the cavalry twill and the plummy accent.'

But Jack had lost interest. He wanted to talk about Benny and how on earth they could persuade her mother to let her live in Dublin.

He wondered was there any hope that she could have a room in Nan's house? Nan said there was none at all.

They said goodbye at the bus stop outside the cinema. Jack ran for a bus going south.

Simon stepped out of a doorway.

'I wondered if you were free for dinner?' he said to Nan.

'Did you wait for me?' She was pleased.

'I knew you wouldn't see *Swamp Women* round a second time. What about that nice little hotel we went to in Wicklow? We might stay the night.'

'How lovely,' Nan said, in a voice that was like a cat purring.

It was a marvellous night in Knockglen.

Peggy Pine absolutely loved the changes in the shop. The new lighting, the fitting rooms, and the low music in the background.

Annabel Hogan had called on Sean Walsh and said that she hoped to come and join him in the shop on Monday and that he would be patient with her and explain things simply. She mistook his protestations as expressions of courtesy and insisted that she turn up at nine a.m. on the first day of the week.

Mossy Rooney said that his mother thought that Patsy was a fine person and would be very happy for them to go to Father Ross and fix a day.

And best of all Nan Mahon telephoned Benny and said that *Swamp Women* was the worst film she had ever seen, but that Jack Foley obviously adored Benny and wanted nothing but to talk about her.

Tears of gratitude sprang to Benny's eyes.

'You're so good, Nan. Thank you, thank you from the bottom of my heart.'

'What else are friends for?' asked Nan as she packed her little overnight bag and prepared to meet Simon for their visit to Wicklow.

Sean Walsh was in Healy's Hotel.

'What am I going to do?'

'Let her come in. She'll tire of it in a week.'

'And if she doesn't?'

'You'll have someone to help you do the errands. It makes it harder for her to refuse you the partnership. She can't be avoiding your eye and the issue if she's working beside you.'

'You're very intelligent . . . um . . . Dorothy,' he said.

Rosemary Ryan knew what was going on everywhere. Eve said she was like those people during the war who had a map of where their troops were and their submarines and they kept moving them about like pieces on a board.

Rosemary knew Jack had been to the pictures with Nan. She was checking that Benny knew.

'Aren't you the silly-billy to go off and leave your young man wandering around unescorted,' Rosemary said.

'He wasn't unescorted for long. I sent him to the pictures with Nan.'

'Oh, you did. That's all right.' Rosemary seemed genuinely relieved.

'Yes, I had to go back to Knockglen and he had declared an afternoon off for himself.'

'You spend too long down there.' Rosemary was trying to warn her about something.

'Yes, well, I'm staying in town tonight. We're all going to Palmerston. Are you coming?'

'I might. I have ferocious designs on a medical student. I'll send out a few enquiries to know whether he'll be there or not.'

What could Rosemary be warning her about? Not Nan, that was clear. Everyone knew that Nan was besotted with Simon Westward. Sheila had given up on him. There was nobody else. Perhaps it was just that he was getting used to being on his own at social occasions. Perhaps by staying so long in Knockglen

Benny was letting Jack think that he was free to ramble, and there might have been a bit of rambling, possibly the Welsh type of rambling . . . that she didn't know about. Benny dragged her mind back to Tudor Policy in Ireland. The lecturer said that it was often complicated and hard to pin down since it seemed to change according to the mood of the time. What else is new, Benny wondered? Jack, who had been so loving about her when talking to Nan, was annoyed again now.

He had thought she was going to stay in town for the weekend apparently and had made plans for Saturday and Sunday too. But Benny had to go back to prepare her mother for work on Monday. If he couldn't understand that what kind of friend was he? Eve would say he wasn't meant to be a friend. He was meant to be a big handsome hunk who happened to fancy Benny. But there had to be more to it than that.

Eve and Kit discussed plans.

They would put a hand basin in each bedroom, and build an extra lavatory and shower. That would stop the congestion on the landings in the morning.

They would have a woman to come in and wash on Mondays. They would have the house rewired, some of those electrical installations didn't bear thinking about.

They would be able to charge a little more if the facilities were that much better. But the real benefit would be they needn't keep students they didn't like. The boy who never opened his bedroom window, who had Guinness bottles under the bed and who had left three cigarette burns on the furniture would be given notice to mend his ways or leave. Nice fellows like Kevin Hickey could stay for ever.

For the first time in her life Kit Hegarty would have some freedom.

'Where does that leave me?' Eve asked lightly. 'You won't need me now.'

But she knew Kit did need her. So she spoke from a position of safety.

They had decided after reflection that the money would not be cast back on the drawing room floor of Westlands. It would be put for Eve in a post office account. Ready to be taken out and thrown, the moment Eve wanted to.

They danced at the rugby club and Benny realized there were people who came here every Friday night and that all of them knew Jack.

'I love you,' he said suddenly as they sat sipping club oranges from bottles with straws. He pushed a damp piece of hair out of her eyes.

'Why?' she asked.

'Lord, I don't know. It would be much easier to love someone who didn't keep disappearing.'

'I love you too,' she said. 'You delight me.'

'That's a lovely thing to say.'

'It's true. I love everything about you. I often think about you and I get a great warm feeling all over me.'

'Talking about great feelings all over us, I have my father's car.'

Her heart sank. Once in the car it was going to be very, very hard to say no. Everything they had been told at school, and at the mission, and in all those sermons on purity, made it seem like a simple choice. Between sin and virtue. You were told that virtue was rewarded, that sin was punished, not only hereafter, but in this life. That boys had no respect for the girls who gave in to their demands.

But nobody had ever told anybody about how nice it felt, and how easy it would be to go on, and how cheap you felt stopping.

And about how you feared greatly that if you didn't go ahead with what you both wanted to do then there would be plenty more who would.

People of the temperament and lack of scruples up to now only discovered in Wales.

'I hope we didn't drag you away from each other too early.' Eve spoke dryly as they settled down to sleep in Kit Hegarty's.

'No, just in time, I think,' Benny said.

It had been the opportune demands of Aidan and Eve to let hem into the car before they froze to death out of discretion.

'Why can't you stay the weekend?' Eve too seemed to be warning her about something. It was like a message that she was getting from everyone. She should stay around.

But there was no way that she could stay, no matter how great the danger. Things were at a crossroads in Knockglen.

'Have you a cigarette?' she asked Eve.

'But you don't smoke.'

'No, but you do. And I want you to listen while I tell you about Sean Walsh.'

They turned on the light again, and Eve sat horrified as the tale of the money and the suspicions and the partnership was unfolded.

The hopes that Benny's mother might find a life of her own in the shop, the support that would be needed. Eve listened and understood. She said that it didn't matter how much temptation was thrown into Jack Foley's path, some things were more important than others, and Benny had to nail Sean Walsh, no matter what.

Eve said she'd come down herself and help to search for the money.

'But we can't go into his rooms. And if we were to get the guards he'd hide it.'

'And he's such a fox,' Eve added. 'You'll have to be very, very careful.'

There was now a Saturday lunch-time trade at Mario's, toasted cheese slices and a fudge cake with cream. The place was almost full as Benny walked past.

She went in to admire Clodagh's drastic changes. There were half a dozen people examining the rails and maybe four more in the fitting rooms.

Between them Clodagh and Fonsie had brought all the business in the town to their doorstep. There were even people who might well have gone to Dublin on a shopping trip browsing happily.

'Your mother's in great form altogether. She's talking of shortening her skirts, and smartening herself up.'

'Mother of God, who'll shorten her skirts for her? You're too busy.'

'You *must* be able to take up a simple hem. Didn't you say you had a sewing machine somewhere?'

'Yes, but I don't know where it is in the lumber and rubble up in the shop.'

'Up in the Honourable Sean Walsh's territory?'

'No, he's right upstairs. The first floor.'

'Ah, get it out, Benny. Get someone to drag it down to your house. I'll come round for ten minutes and start you off.'

'It mightn't be working,' Benny said hopefully.

'Then your mother'll have to look streelish, won't she?'

Benny decided she'd go back to the shop and see if the machine really was there and looked in workable condition before she asked Teddy Flood or Dekko Moore or someone with a handcart to help her home with it.

Sean wasn't in sight in the shop. Only old Mike saw her go upstairs.

She saw the sewing machine behind an old sofa with the springs falling out. It couldn't have been used for nearly twenty years.

It looked like a little table. The machine part was down in it. Benny pulled, and up it came, shiny and new looking as well it might be, considering how little use it had had. It was quite well made, she thought, with those little drawers on each side, probably for spools of thread and buttons and all the things that sewing people filled their lives with.

She opened one of the little drawers. It was stuffed with small brown envelopes, pushed up one against the other. It seemed an extraordinary way to keep buttons and thread. She opened one idly and saw the green pound notes, and the pink ten-shilling notes squeezed together. There were dozens and dozens of envelopes, old ones addressed to the shop, originally with invoices, each with its post mark. With a feeling of ice water going right through her body, Benny realized that she had found the money Sean Walsh had been stealing from her father for years.

She didn't remember walking home. She must have passed Carroll's and Dessie Burn's and the cinema as well as Pine's and Paccy's and Mario's. Maybe she even saluted people. She didn't know.

In the kitchen Patsy was grumbling.

'Your mother thought you must have missed the bus,' she said. Benny saw her preparing to put the meal on the table.

'Could you wait a few minutes, Patsy? I want to talk to Mother about something.'

'Can't you talk and eat?'

'No.'

Patsy shrugged. 'She's above in the bedroom trying on clothes that stink of mothballs. She'll run them out of the shop with the smell of camphor.'

Benny grabbed the sherry bottle and two glasses and went upstairs.

Patsy looked up in alarm.

In all her years in this house she had never been excluded from a conversation with the mistress and Benny. And never would she have believed that there was any subject that needed a drink being brought to the bedroom.

She said three quick Hail Marys that Benny wasn't pregnant. It was just the kind of thing that would happen to a nice big soft girl like Benny. Fall for a baby from a fellow who wouldn't marry her.

Annabel listened white-faced.

'It would have killed your father.'

Benny sat on the side of the bed. She chewed her lip as she did when she was worried. Nan had said she must try to get out of the habit. It would make her mouth crooked eventually. She thought about Nan for a quick few seconds.

Nan wouldn't pause to care about her father's business. Not if it was being robbed blind by everyone in it. It was both terrible and wonderful to be so free.

'I wonder if Father knew,' Benny said.

It was quite possible that he had his suspicions, but that being Eddie Hogan he had put them away. He wouldn't have opened his mouth unless he had positive proof. But it was odd that he had delayed the partnership deal. Mr Green had said he was surprised that it had not been signed. Could Father have had second thoughts about going into partnership with a man who had his hand in the till over the years?

'Your father would not have been able to bear the disgrace of it all. The guards coming in, a prosecution, the talk.'

'I know,' Benny agreed. 'He'd never have stood for that.'

They talked as equals sitting in the bedroom that was strewn with the clothes Annabel had been trying on to wear on her first day in the shop. Benny didn't urge her to make decisions and Annabel didn't hang back.

Because they were equals they gave each other strength.

'We could tell him we know,' Annabel said.

'He'd deny it.'

They couldn't call the guards, they knew that. There was no way that they could ask Mr Green to come in, climb the stairs to the first floor and inspect the contents of the sewing machine. Mr Green wasn't the kind of lawyer you saw in movies who did this sort of thing. He was the most quiet and respectable of country solicitors.

'We could ask someone else to witness it. To come and see it.'

'What good would that do?' Annabel asked.

'I don't know,' Benny admitted. 'But it would prove it was there in case Sean were to shift it and hide it somewhere else. You know, when we speak to him.'

'*When* we speak to him? We have to, Mother. When you go in there on Monday morning, he has to be gone.'

Annabel looked at her for a long time. She said nothing. But Benny felt there was some courage there, a new spirit. She believed that her mother would face what lay ahead. Benny must find the right words to encourage her.

'If Father can see us, it's what he'd want. He'd want no scandal, no prosecution. But he wouldn't want you to stand beside Sean Walsh as a partner knowing what we know now.'

'We'll ask Dr Johnson to witness the find,' Annabel Hogan said with a voice steadier than Benny would ever have believed.

Patsy said to Bee Moore that evening that you'd want to have the patience of a saint to work in Lisbeg these days. There was that much coming and going, and doors closed, and secrets, and bottles of sherry and no food being eaten and then food being called for at cracked times.

If this is what it was going to be like when the Mistress went up into the shop then maybe it was just as well she was going to marry Mossy Rooney and his battle-axe of a mother and be out of it.

Patsy remembered Bee's former interest in Mossy and altered her remarks slightly. She said she knew she was very lucky to have been chosen by Mossy and was honoured to be a part of his family. Bee Moore sniffed, wondering again how she had lost him to Patsy. She said that things were equally confusing in her house. Everyone in Westlands seemed to have gone mad. Heather had started in St Mary's and was bringing what Mrs Walsh called every ragtag and bobtail of Knockglen back up to the house to ride her pony. The old man had taken to his bed, and Mr Simon was not to be seen, though it was reliably reported that he had been in Knockglen at least two nights without coming home. Where on earth could he have stayed in Knockglen if he hadn't come home to his own bed in Westlands? It was a mystery.

Maurice Johnson said that he was a man whom nothing would surprise. But the visit of Annabel Hogan and her daughter, and its reason, caught him on the hop.

He listened to their request.

'Why me?' he asked.

'It's you or Father Ross. We don't want to bring the Church into it. It's involving sin and punishment. All we need is someone reliable.'

'Let's not delay,' he said. 'Let's go this minute.'

There were two customers in the shop when they went in. Sean looked up from the boxes of V-necked jumpers that he had opened on the counter.

There was something about the deputation that alarmed him. His eyes followed them as they went to the back of the shop towards the stairs.

'Is there anything . . . ?' he began.

Benny paused on the stairs and looked at him. She had disliked him ever since she had first met him, and yet at this moment she felt a surge of pity for him. She took in his thin greasy hair and his long white narrow face.

He had not enjoyed his life or enriched it with the money he had taken.

But she must not falter now.

'We're just going to the first floor,' she said. 'Mother and I want Dr Johnson to see something.'

She saw the fear in his eyes.

'To witness something,' she added, so that he would know.

Dr Johnson went down the stairs quietly. He walked through the shop, his eyes firmly on the floor. He didn't return Mike's greeting. Nor did he acknowledge the figure of Sean standing there immobile with a box in his hands. He had said to the Hogans that he would confirm that in his presence they had removed upwards of two hundred envelopes each containing sums of money varying from five to ten pounds.

There had been no gloating in the downfall of a man he had never liked. He looked at the little hoard in tightly screwed-up envelopes. The man was buying himself some kind of life, he supposed. Had he thought of wine, or women, or song when he had stashed Eddie Hogan's money away? It was impossible to know. He didn't envy the two women and their confrontation, but he admired them for agreeing to do it at once.

They sat in the room and waited. They knew he would come upstairs. And both of them were weak with the shock of their discovery and the shame that they would have to face when Sean came up to meet them.

Neither of them feared that he would bluster or attempt to deny that it was he who had put the money there. There was no way now for him to say they had made it up. Dr Johnson's word would be believed.

They heard his step on the stair.

'Did you close the shop?' Annabel Hogan asked.

'Mike will manage.'

'He'll have to a lot of the time from now on,' she said.

'Have you something to say? Is there some kind of accusation?' he began.

'Let's make it easy,' Annabel began.

'I can explain,' Sean said.

They could hear the Saturday afternoon noises of Knockglen, people tooting their car horns, children laughing and running by, free from school since lunch time. There was a dog barking excitedly, and somewhere a horse drawing a cart had been frightened. They sat, the three of them, and heard him whinnying until someone calmed him down.

Then Sean began to explain. It was a method of saving, and Mr Hogan had understood, not exactly agreed, but acknowledged. The wages had not been great. It was known that Sean did the lion's share of the work. It had always been expected that he should build a little nest egg for himself.

Annabel sat in the high-backed chair, a wooden one they had never thought of bringing to Lisbeg. Benny sat on the broken sofa, the one she had pulled out to find the sewing machine. They hadn't rehearsed it, but they acted as a team, neither of them said a word. There were no interruptions or denials. No nods of agreement or shaking of the head in disbelief. They sat there and let him form the noose around his neck. Eventually his voice grew slower, his hand movements less exaggerated. His arms fell to his sides, and soon his head began to hang as if it were a great weight.

Then he stopped altogether.

Benny waited for her mother to speak.

'You can go tonight, Sean.'

It was more decisive even than Benny would have been. She looked at her mother in admiration. There was no hate, no revenge, in her tone. Just a simple statement of the position. It startled Sean Walsh just as much.

'There's no question of that, Mrs Hogan,' he said.

His face was white, but he was not now going to ask for mercy, or understanding, or a second chance.

They waited, to hear what he had to say.

'It's not what your husband would have wanted. He said in writing that he wanted me to become a partner. You have agreed that with Mr Green.'

Annabel's glance fell on the table full of envelopes.

'And there is no one to confirm or deny that this was an agreement.'

Benny spoke then. 'Father would not have liked the police, Sean. I know you would agree with that. So mother and I are going along with what we are sure would be his wishes. We have discussed this for a long time. We think he would have liked you to leave this evening. And that he would like us to speak to no person of what has happened here today. Dr Johnson, as you need hardly say, is silent as the grave. We only asked him here to give substance to our request that you leave, without any fuss.'

'And what'll happen to your fine business when I leave?' His face had become crooked now. 'What's to become of Hogan's, laughing stock of the outfitting business? Will it have its big closing down sale in June or in October? That's the only question.'

Agitated and with his features in the form of a smile he walked around rubbing his hands.

'You have no idea how hopeless this place is. How its days are numbered. What do you think you'll do without me? Have old Mike, who hasn't two brains to rub together, talking to the customers and God blessing them, and God saving them, like Barry Fitzgerald in a film? Have you, Mrs Hogan, who don't know one end of a bale of material from another? Have some greenhorn of an eejit serving his time from some other one-horse town? Is this what you want for your great family business? Is it? Tell me, is it?'

His tone was becoming hysterical.

'What did we ever do to you that makes you turn on us like this?' Annabel Hogan asked, her voice calm.

'You think you were good to me. Is that what you think?'

'Yes. In a word.'

Sean's face was working. Benny realized she had never remotely suspected that he could feel so much.

He told a tale of being banished upstairs to servant's quarters, being patronized and invited to break bread from time to time with the air of being summoned to a palace. He said that he had run the business single-handed for a pittance of a wage and a regular pat on the head. The cry that they would be lost without Sean Walsh, said often enough to render it meaningless. He said that his genuine and respectful admiration for Benny, the daughter of the house, was a matter of mockery, and had been thrown back in his face. He had been honourable and would have been proud to escort her to places even when she was not a physically beautiful specimen.

Neither Annabel nor Benny allowed a muscle to move in the face of the insults.

He had not intruded, imposed or in any way traded on his position. He had been discreet and loyal. And this was the thanks he was getting for it.

Benny felt a great sadness sweep over her. There was some sincerity in the way Sean spoke. If this was his version of his life, then this was his life.

'Will you stay in Knockglen?' she asked unexpectedly.

'What?'

'After you leave here?'

Something clicked then. Sean knew they meant it. He looked at them, as if he had never seen either of them before.

'I might,' he said. 'It's the only place I've really known, you see.'

They saw.

They knew there would be talk. A lot of talk. But on Monday the shop would open with Annabel in charge. They had only thirty-six hours to learn the business.

Mrs Healy agreed to see Sean in her office. Even given his usual pallor, she thought he looked badly as if he had just had a shock.

'May I arrange to have a room here for a week?'

'Of course. But might I ask why?'

He told her that he would be leaving Hogan's. As of now. That he would therefore be leaving his accommodation there. He was vague in the extreme. He parried questions about the partnership, denied that there had been any fight or unpleasantness. He said that he would like to transfer his belongings across the road at a time when half the town wouldn't be watching, like when they were gone home to their tea.

Fonsie saw him of course, saw him carrying one by one the four cardboard boxes that made up his possessions.

'Good evening, Sean,' Fonsie said gravely.

Sean ignored him.

Fonsie went straight back to tell Clodagh.

'I think I see a love nest starting. Sean Walsh was bringing twigs and leaves and starting to build it across in Healy's.'

'Was he moving across, really?' Clodagh didn't seem as surprised as she should be.

'In stealth and with lust written all over him for Dorothy,' Fonsie said.

'Well done, Benny,' said Clodagh, closing her eyes and smiling.

Maire Carroll had come up to the convent to ask for a reference. She was going to apply for a job in a shop in Dublin. As Mother Francis struggled to think of something to say about Maire Carroll that was both truthful and flattering, Maire revealed that Sean Walsh had been seen taking all his belongings and going to live in the hotel.

'Thank God, Benny,' Mother Francis breathed to herself.

Sunday was the longest day that any of them had worked. It had an air of unreality because the shutters were closed so that nobody should know they were there.

They would have looked a very strange crew to anyone who saw them. Patsy in her overalls scrubbing out the small room which had been filled with the results of a thousand cups of ill-made tea. Old Mike said that they took it in turns to make the tea and open the biscuits. The place had all the signs of it. The Baby Belling had been brought down from Sean's quarters upstairs. From now on there would be proper tea, and even soup or toast made.

Hogan's was going to change.

And to help it change, Peggy Pine and Clodagh were there, as was Teddy Flood.

To none of them had any explanation been given apart from the fact that Sean Walsh had left, and they were in need of some advice. Clodagh said one business was the same as another. If you could run one you could run the lot, and she always hoped she might be seconded to get a steel works or a car plant on its feet.

Mike, who had never been the centre of such attention, was asked respectful questions. It was the general opinion that Mike must be addressed slowly, and his answers weighed with the same deliberation that he gave them.

To fuss Mike would be counter-productive. Let him think there was all the time in the world.

Let him wander down no lanes of regret about Mr Eddie and no tight-lipped mutterings about that Sean Walsh who wanted to be called Mister.

Slowly they pieced it together, the way the business was run. The people who had credit, and those who didn't. The way the bills had been sent out, the reminders. The salesmen who came with their books for orders. The mills, the factories.

Haltingly Mike told it all. They listened and worked out the system, such as it was.

A thousand times Annabel Hogan cursed herself for not taking an interest and forming a part of the company when her husband was alive. Perhaps he would have liked it? It was only her own hidebound feelings that had kept her at home.

Benny wished that she had come to help her father. If only

she could have had the time over again, then she would have spent Saturday afternoons here with him, learning about his life at work.

Would he have been proud of her and pleased that she was taking such an interest? Or would he have thought that she was a distraction in the all-male world of gentleman's outfitters? It was impossible to know. And anyway she had avoided the shop a lot because of Sean Walsh.

As they toiled on, working out which bales of material were which, Benny let her mind wander. Could her parents seriously have expected her to marry Sean just because he had been helpful in the business? And even worse, suppose she had gone along with their views? Promised herself to him, allowed his disgusting advances and been engaged to him now? Think then how impossible it would have been once they discovered his theft. The mean, grubbing, regular stealing from a kind employer who had wished him nothing but well.

Patsy had heated up the soup and served the sandwiches. They sat companionably and ate them.

'Is it wrong of us, do you think, to work on a Sunday?' Mike was fearful about the whole thing.

'*Laborare est orare*,' Peggy Pine said suddenly.

'Could you translate for those of us without the classical education, Aunt?' Clodagh asked.

'It means that the Lord thinks working is a form of prayer,' Peggy said, wiping away the crumbs and settling down to writing out proper sales tickets which Annabel could understand.

They had opened up the back door of the shop late on Saturday night so they could come and go by the lane at the rear of the premises.

The sun shone on the disused back yard with its rubbish and clutter.

'You could make a lovely conservatory here,' Clodagh said admiringly.

'What for?' Benny asked.

'To sit in, you clown.'

'Customers wouldn't want to sit down, would they?'

'Your mother and you.'

Benny looked blank.

'Well, you are going to live here, aren't you?'

'Lord no. We'll be living in Lisbeg. We couldn't live over the shop.'

'Some of us do, and manage fine,' Clodagh said huffily.

Benny could have bitten off her tongue. But there was no point in trying to take it back now.

Clodagh didn't seem a bit upset.

'Good for you if you can,' she said. 'I thought the object of all this was to try and turn this place round. You won't do that if you don't put some money into it. I assumed you were going to sell your house.'

Benny wiped her forehead. Was there ever going to be any end to all this? When could she get back to living an ordinary life again?

Jack Foley telephoned Benny from nine in the morning until noon.

'She can't be at Mass *all* bloody morning,' he grumbled.

Benny telephoned Jack at home.

She got his mother.

'Is that you, Sheila?' she asked.

'No, Mrs Foley. It's Benny Hogan.'

She heard that Jack was out and not expected back until late. He had left quite early.

'I thought he was down in your neck of the woods, actually,' Mrs Foley said.

She made it sound like a swamp with alligators in it. Like the film Benny hadn't seen.

She forced her voice to be light and casual. No message. Just to say that she had rung for a chat.

Mrs Foley said that she'd write it down straight away. She managed to make it sound as if the name of Benny Hogan would be added to a long list of those who had already telephoned.

It was over, and she longed to celebrate. Everything she had wanted for the shop since the day Father had died had been achieved. They had had huge support from their friends in Knockglen. Sean had been rendered unimportant.

It was a night of triumph she wanted to tell Jack all about. The awful bits and the funny bits, the look on Sean's face, Patsy making more and more tea, and sandwiches. Old Mike getting surges of energy like Frankenstein's monster. Peggy Pine showing her mother how to ring up a sale. She wanted to tell him that from now on she wouldn't be needed so desperately at home. She would be free to spend several nights a week in Dublin.

She had a terrible foreboding that she had left it all too late. That she had been away too long.

CHAPTER SEVENTEEN

Brian Mahon said that it was great to be spending all that money paying fees for a university student when she didn't get up for her bloody lectures.

Emily said he should hush. That was unfair. Nan worked very hard, and it was rare the girl had a lie-in.

'When she *is* in the house it would be nice to see her, just now and again,' he said.

Nan told them that she stayed with Eve out in Dunlaoghaire, on the occasions when she didn't come home. Her father said it was a pity that woman in the guest house didn't pay her fees and buy her clothes for her.

But he had to meet a man who had come in on the boat to the North Wall. He'd been down in a docker's pub. There was a deal about a consignment.

Emily sighed. There might be a deal about a consignment, but there would also be a day's drinking. When he had gone she went upstairs.

Nan was lying on her bed with her arms folded behind her head.

'Aren't you well?'

'I'm fine, Em. Honestly.'

Emily sat down on the stool opposite the dressing table.

There was something troubled in Nan's face, some look she had never seen before. It was surprise mixed with indecision.

Nan had never known either, not since she was a little girl.

'Is it . . . Simon?'

Normally Emily never mentioned his name. It was almost like tempting fate.

Nan shook her head. She told her mother that Simon was most devoted and attentive. He was down in Knockglen. She'd be seeing him for dinner tomorrow night. Emily was not convinced. She shook her head as she went downstairs, tidied away the breakfast things, put on her smart blouse and set out for work.

As she stood at the bus stop she wondered what was wrong with her daughter.

Back in her bedroom Nan lay and looked ahead of her. She knew there was no need to have sent the specimen to Holles Street Maternity Hospital. Her period was seventeen days late. She was pregnant.

Eve and Kit were up early. They had builders arriving and they wanted to show them from the beginning that this was a house with rules, a house like they had never known before.

They had left bags of cement and sand in the back yard the night before. The name on the sacks was Mahon.

'You must tell Nan that we're putting a few shillings into her father's pocket,' Kit said.

'No, Nan wouldn't like to hear that. She doesn't want to be reminded of her father and his trade.'

Kit was surprised.

Nan always seemed remarkably unpretentious for such an attractive girl. You never caught her stealing a look at herself in the mirror, or blowing about the people she had been out with.

Eve had liked her so much at the beginning, but had been very resentful of Nan taking up with the Westwards.

'You're not still bearing a grudge against her because she went out with Simon Westward are you?'

'A grudge? Me?' said Eve, laughing. She knew that most of her life had been spent bearing grudges against the family that had disowned her.

And anyway Kit had used the wrong tense. Nan was still going out with Simon. Very much so.

Heather had been on the phone, squeaking with excitement about her life in the convent and how funny and mad and superstitious everyone was.

'I hope you don't *say* any of that,' Eve said sternly.

'No, only to you. And I have another secret. I think Simon's doing a line with Nan. She rings sometimes, and I know he goes off to meet her, because he packs a bag. And he doesn't come home at night.'

Eve was sure that Nan and Simon were Going All The Way. Simon wouldn't be remotely interested in a girl unless she would. It wasn't a sin for him anyway, and he wouldn't take Nan out, no matter how gorgeous she looked, unless he was getting value for it.

Because Eve knew very well that Nan was not someone her cousin Simon was going to bring home to Westlands.

When she telephoned it was as she had known it would be. The pregnancy test was positive.

Nan dressed carefully and left the empty house in Maple Gardens. She took the bus to Knockglen.

She walked past the gates of St Mary's Convent and looked up the long avenue. She could hear the sounds of children at play. How strange of Simon to let his sister stay there, amongst all the children of people who worked on the estate.

But from her own point of view it was good. It meant that he was tied more to Knockglen. She could come more frequently to the cottage. And there would be fewer crises about Heather being unhappy and running away from the school where she should be.

She couldn't remember clearly how far it was from the village to Westlands, but decided that it was too far to walk. Knockglen didn't have the air of a place that would have a taxi. She had heard so much bad about Healy's Hotel from Benny, Eve and Simon that she dared not risk asking them to arrange her a lift.

Nan would wait until a suitable car passed by.

A middle-aged man in a green car came into view. She hailed him and as Nan had known he would, he stopped.

Dr Johnson asked her where she was heading.

'Westlands,' she said simply.

'Where else?' the man said.

They talked about the car. He explained it was a Morris Cowley, the cheapest end of the Ford range. He'd love a Zodiac or even a Zephyr, but you had to know when to draw the line.

'I don't think you do,' said the beautiful blonde girl, whom Dr Johnson remembered seeing somewhere before.

She had a slightly high, excited look about her. He asked no questions about her visit.

She said that a lot of people were too timid, they didn't reach for things. He should reach for a Zephyr or a Zodiac, not assume that they were beyond his grasp.

Maurice Johnson smiled and said he would discuss the notion of reaching with his wife and with his bank manager. He could see neither of them agreeing with this view, but he would certainly present it.

He turned in the gates of Westlands.

'Were you going here anyway?' Nan asked, alarmed. She didn't want to clash with another visitor.

'Not at all. But a gentleman, even in a Morris Cowley, always sees a lady right to the door.'

She gave him a smile of such brightness, he thought to himself that men like Simon Westward who were knee high to a grasshopper had all the luck when it came to getting gorgeous women, just because they had the accent and the big house.

Nan looked up at the house. It wasn't going to be easy. But then nothing that was important had ever been easy. She took three deep breaths, and rang at the door.

Mrs Walsh knew well who Nan Mahon was. She had heard the name on the telephone many times, and even though she discouraged Bee from gossiping, she knew that this girl, who had been in the house a couple of days after Christmas, was a friend of Eve Malone and Benny Hogan.

But just to keep things as they should be, she asked her name.

'Mahon,' Nan said, in a clear, confident voice.

Simon was coming out of the morning room anyway. He had heard the car pull up and draw away.

'Was that Dr Johnson, Mrs Walsh? He seems to have driven off without seeing Grandfather . . .'

He saw Nan.

His voice changed.

'Well, hallo,' he said.

'Hallo, Simon.'

She stood, very beautiful in a cream-coloured suit with a red artificial flower pinned to the lapel. Her handbag and shoes were the same red. She looked as if she were dressed to go out.

'Come in and sit down,' he said.

'Coffee, Mr Simon?' Mrs Walsh asked, but she knew she would not be needed.

'No thanks, Mrs Walsh.' His voice was light and easy. 'No, I think we'll be all right for the moment.'

He closed the door firmly behind them.

Aidan Lynch came up to Jack in the pub and said that Benny had taught him the Charleston.

It was really quite simple, once you learned to work the two legs separately.

'Yes,' Jack Foley said.

And it looked very snazzy, Aidan said, and possibly Benny should give up her notion of becoming a librarian, and be a teacher. After all anyone could check books in and out of a library, but not everyone could teach. Impart knowledge.

'True,' Jack Foley agreed.

And so Aidan wondered, how much more was he going to have to go on making inane chat until they could get down to the point, the point being that he and Eve, who were so to speak Love's Young Dream of the university at the moment, leaving Sean and Carmel in the halfpenny place, wanted to know had there been a falling out between Benny and Jack.

'Ask her,' Jack said.

'Eve has. And she says no, it's just that she can never find you.'

'That's because she's always looking for me in Knockglen,' Jack said.

'Have you been able to ... you know,' Aidan was the old confiding mate now.

'Mind your own business,' Jack said.

'That means you haven't. Neither have I. Jesus, what do they teach them in these convents?'

'About people like us, I suppose.'

They forgot about women and talked about the match and the way that some people couldn't kick a ball out of their way if it was laid down in front of them.

Aidan hadn't any more information for Eve about Benny. But at least he could report that no new person had come on the scene.

'This is a surprise,' Simon said. The small narrow frown that was just a half line between his eyes showed it wasn't entirely a welcome surprise.

Nan had rehearsed it. No point in small talk, and fencing.

'I waited until I was certain. I'm afraid I'm pregnant,' she said simply.

Simon's face was full of concern.

'Oh no,' he said, moving towards her. 'Oh no, Nan no, you poor darling. You poor, poor darling.' He embraced her and held her close.

She said nothing. She felt his heart beat against hers. Then he drew her away, examining her face, looking to see how upset she was.

'How awful for you,' he said tenderly. 'It's not fair is it?'

'What isn't?'

'Everything.' He waved his hands expansively.

Then he went over to the window and ran his hands through his hair. 'This is awful,' he said. He seemed very upset.

They stood apart, Nan with her hand on the piano, Simon by the window, both of them looking out the long window at the paddock where Heather's pony stood and across at the fields where the grazing had been let and cattle moved slowly round.

Everything seemed like slow motion, Nan thought. Even the way Simon spoke.

'Will you know what to do?' he asked her. 'Will you know where to go?'

'How do you mean?'

'Over all this.' He waved a slow wave of his hand vaguely in the direction of her body.

'I came to you,' she said.

'Yes, I know, and you were right. Utterly right.' He was anxious she should know this.

'I never thought it could happen,' Nan said.

'Nobody ever does.' Simon was rueful, as if it happened all over the place, to everyone he knew.

Nan wanted to speak. She wanted desperately to say 'What do we do now?'

But she must give him no chance to say anything hurtful or careless that she would have to respond to angrily. She *must* leave silences. The expression was Pregnant Pauses, she thought with a little giggle that she fought back. Simon was about to speak.

'Nan, sweetheart,' he said, 'this is about as terrible as it can be. But it will all be all right. I promise you.'

'I know,' she looked at him trustingly.

And then her ears began to sing a little as he told her of a friend who knew someone and it had all been amazingly simple, and the girl had said that it was much easier than going to a dentist.

And there had been no ill effects. Well, actually Nan had met the girl, but it wouldn't be fair to name names. But she was someone terribly bubbly and well-adjusted.

'But you don't mean . . . ?' She looked at him shocked.

'Of course I'm not going to abandon you.' He came towards her again and took her in his arms.

Relief flooded through her. But why had he talked about this silly bubbly woman who had been to have an abortion? Had he changed when he saw her stricken face?

Simon Westward stroked her hair.

'You didn't think I'd let you look after it all on your own, did you?' he said.

Nan said nothing.

'Come on now, we both enjoyed ourselves. Of course I'll look after it.'

He pulled away from her and took a cheque book out of a drawer.

'I don't know what this chap said, he did tell me a figure, but this should cover it. And I'll get the name and address of the place and everything. It's in England of course, but that's all for the best, isn't it?'

She looked at him unbelieving. 'It's your child. You know that?'

'Nan, my angel, it's not a child at all. Not a speck yet.'

'You do know that you were the first and there has been nobody else?'

'We're not going to upset ourselves over this, Nan. It can't be between us. You know that, I know it, we've known it since we went into our little fling.'

'Why can't it be? You want to get married. You want an heir for this place. We get on well together. I fit in with your world.' Her voice was deliberately light.

But she was playing for everything in this plea. She never thought she would have had to beg like this. He had said he loved her. Every time they made love he called out how much he loved her. It was unthinkable that he was reaching for a cheque book to dismiss her.

He was gentle with her. He even took her hand.

'You know that you and I are not going to marry Nan. You, of all people, so cool, so reasonable, so sensible. You know this. As do I.'

'I know you said you loved me,' she said.

'And so I do, I love every little bit of you. I don't deny it.'

'And this is love then? A cheque and an abortion?'

His face looked troubled. He seemed surprised that she took this view.

'And it wouldn't have mattered, I suppose, if my father was a rich builder instead of a shabby builder.'

'It has nothing to do with that.'

'Well, it certainly has nothing to do with religion. It's 1958 and neither of us believes in God.'

He opened her hand and pressed the folded cheque into it.

She looked at him in disbelief.

'I'm sorry,' he said.

She was still silent. Finally she said, 'I'm going back now.'

'How will you get home?' he asked.

'I was stupid enough to think I was coming home.' She looked around her, at the portraits on the wall, the piano, the view from the window.

Something about her face touched him. She was always so very, very beautiful.

'I wish . . .' he began, but couldn't finish the sentence.

'Do you know someone who would drive me back to Dublin?'

'I will, of course.'

'No, It would be too artificial. Someone else.'

'I don't really know anyone else . . . anyone that I could ask . . .'

'No. You do keep yourself to yourself. But I know what we'll do. I'll take your car just down to the square,' she said. 'There'll be a bus soon. You can collect it later in the day.'

'Let me at least . . .'

He moved towards her.

'No, please stay away from me. Don't touch me.'

He handed her the car keys.

'It needs a lot of choke,' he said.

'I know. I've been in it a great many times.'

Nan walked down the steps of Westlands. He watched from the window while she got into his car and drove away.

He knew that from the kitchen window Bee Moore and Mrs Walsh were watching and speculating.

He looked at her with admiration as she started his car and drove down the long avenue without looking back.

She left the keys in the car. Nobody would dare to steal the car of Mr Simon Westward in this feudal backwater. They'd all be afraid of crossing anyone at the Big House.

Mike was turning the bus. He'd be going back to Dublin in five minutes, he told her. She paid her fare.

'You could have got a return, it would have been cheaper.' Mike was always anxious to give people a bargain.

'I didn't know I'd be going back,' Nan said.

'Life's full of surprises,' said Mike, looking at this blonde girl in the cream and red outfit, who looked much too smart for this part of the world anyway.

Bill Dunne saw Benny come into the Annexe. She was looking around, hunting for Jack, but there was no sign of him. She stood in the line with the other students. If Jack had been there he would have kept a table, and she could have gone straight to join him.

Bill waved and said he had an extra coffee. In fact he hadn't begun his own, but it seemed a way of calling her over. She looked very well today, in a chestnut-coloured sweater, the exact colour of her hair, and a pale yellow blouse underneath.

Bill and Benny talked easily. If she was glancing around for Jack she never mentioned it. And he never showed that he noticed Benny was so easy to talk to. They discussed banning the bomb and if it would ever work. Benny said she was afraid it was like asking boxers to tie one hand behind their backs, or like saying we should go back to bows and arrows once they had invented gunpowder. They wondered would Elvis really join the US Army or was it just a publicity stunt? They talked of Jack Kerouac. Would every single person that he met On the Road have been interesting? Surely some of them must have been deadly bores.

The time flew, and they had to go back to lectures. If Benny was disappointed that Jack Foley hadn't turned up she showed no sign of it. But then women were known to be very good at hiding their feelings. Most people didn't know what they were up to half the time.

Rosemary saw everything and noted it all. She watched Bill and Benny chatting animatedly. They seemed like great friends. Perhaps he was consoling her about Jack. Rosemary had often thought that the feeling was unworthy, but she felt that Jack was too handsome for Benny. She thought it was like a mixed marriage. A Black and a White, a Catholic and a non-Catholic. You heard of those that did work. But the usual rule was that they didn't. It wasn't a view that anyone would agree with so she didn't express it. Anyway people might think she was after Jack Foley for herself. Which oddly enough was not true. She had met a very nice medical student called Tom. He wouldn't be qualified for years, which would give Rosemary time to be an air hostess or something with a bit of glamour in the meantime.

Sean Walsh stood on the Quays waiting for the bus back to Knockglen. He had stayed in a men's hostel in Dublin for five days to think things out. During the daytime he had walked through the menswear shops in Dublin trying to see himself working in any of them.

The prospect began to look less and less likely. He would not come armed with a reference. He would be unlikely to be taken on anywhere.

Little by little he began to realize how his horizons had narrowed. The idea of buying his own place, renovating a cottage up over the quarry, was now only a fantasy. The notion of standing at the door of his own business and watching the town walk by was not one he could hold any more in his dreams. His name would be over no premises in Knockglen, the town where he had lived for ten years, and which, when all was said and done, he thought of as home.

He was going to go back now with a proposition.

He saw a very good-looking girl get off the bus, a blonde girl in a cream suit with red trimmings. He recognized her as the friend of Eve and Benny. The girl who had been at Mr Hogan's funeral, and had been up at Westlands around Christmas time. She didn't acknowledge him. She looked as if her mind were set on something else entirely.

Sean got on to the bus and looked without pleasure at Mikey, a man who was over-familiar and with an unfortunate habit of referring to people's physical appearance.

'There you are Sean, with a face as long as a wet week. Is it the return of the Prodigal we see?'

'I wish I understood what you meant, Mikey.'

'It's a reference to a story Our Lord told in the New Testament, Sean. A man like yourself nearly eating the altar in the church should know that.'

'I am well aware of the parable of the Prodigal Son, but since he was a man who spent his life in wrong-doing, I'm afraid I can't see the similarity.'

Mikey looked at Sean shrewdly. His wife had given him some highly coloured speculation about what might or might not have happened in Hogan's Outfitters. But obviously Sean Walsh had not run away.

'I was only wondering where the fatted calf was going to be killed, Sean,' Mikey said. 'Maybe they're basting it already down in Healy's Hotel.'

Nan let herself into the house that she had left that morning. She took off her cream suit and hung it carefully on a padded hanger. She sponged it lightly with lemon juice and water. She put shoe trees in her red shoes, and she rubbed her red leather bag with some furniture cream, before wrapping it carefully in tissue paper and placing it beside her other four handbags in a drawer. She put on her best college clothes, combed her hair and went out to stand for a second time at the bus stop across the road.

Mrs Healy had tidied up her office. She placed a big jug of daffodils on the window and two small hyacinths in plastic bowls on the filing cabinet.

She had been to Ballylee to have her hair done.

The new corset was very well fitting. It managed to distribute the flesh very well. So well, in fact, that a tight skirt looked remarkably fine. She wore her high-necked blouse and cameo brooch. The ones reserved for special occasions.

And after all it would be a special occasion this afternoon. She knew that Sean Walsh was coming back today. And that he was going to make a proposal of marriage.

It was lunch time in the convent, and Mother Francis had her turn on dinner duty. That meant she walked up and down keeping order as the girls had their sandwiches. Then she supervised the tidying up of the hall, the careful cleaning and refolding of the greaseproof paper for tomorrow's packed lunch, the airing of the room and the quick exercise in the yard.

She saw a group of the girls explaining to Heather Westward the nature of rosary beads.

'Why do you call them a pair, there's only one?' Heather looked at the necklace of beads.

'They're always called a pair.' Fiona Carroll, the youngest of the badly behaved Carroll children from the grocery, was scornful.

'What does it mean "Irish Horn"?' Heather was interested.

'That's just what they're made from,' Siobhan Flood, the butcher's granddaughter, dismissed it.

'So what does it *do*?' Heather demanded, looking fearfully at the rosary beads.

She was not at all convinced that it did nothing, that you did things with it, you used it to pray with, that was all. That the spacings on the beads meant that you said ten Hail Marys and then stopped and said a Glory Be and then an Our Father.

'Like the Lord's Prayer?' Heather asked.

'Yes, but the proper way,' Fiona Carroll said, in case there should be any doubt about it.

They explained that the whole point was not to say one Hail Mary more than was needed. That was why they were made.

Mother Francis had an art of listening to one set of conversations while being thought to be in the middle of others. Her heart was heavy when she heard the explanations being given to the unfortunate Heather.

After all her teaching, this is what they thought. They thought the point of this beautiful prayer to Our Lady was never to let yourself say one more Hail Mary than was necessary.

Wouldn't a teacher be very foolish to think that anything ever got into their heads? Perhaps the Mother of God would be touched and pleased by the innocence of children. Mother Francis would, at this particular lunch time, have liked to take them out individually and murder them one by one.

Kit answered the phone at lunch time. It was Eve wanting to know if Benny could stay the night. She knew the answer would be yes, but between them there had always been courtesies like this.

Kit was pleased. She wanted to know was there a dance or an occasion?

'No, there's not.' Eve sounded worried. 'She said she wants her mother to get used to her being away from home.'

'And what about Jack Foley?'

'That's the question I wanted to ask and didn't,' Eve said.

Hogan's had closed for lunch. Annabel, Patsy and Mike adjourned to the back room and ate shepherd's pie and tinned beans. Mike said he hadn't felt as well in years. These midday dinners in the shop would build you up for the afternoon. Patsy said it was a grand, handy place to cook. They should move up here altogether.

Nan tried three pubs before she found them. It was nearly closing time. Almost the Holy Hour when the Dublin city pubs closed between half past two and half past three.

'Well, look who's here.' Bill Dunne was pleased.

'Caught you, Nan. You're on a pub crawl,' said Aidan.

Jack as always said the right thing. He said it was great to see her and what would she like.

Nan said she was sick and tired of studying and she had come out to find a few handsome men to take her mind off her books. They were all flattered to think she had set out to look for them. They sat around her in an admiring circle.

She looked fresh in her pale green jumper with a dark green skirt and jacket. Her eyes sparkled as she laughed and joked with them.

'How goes the romance with Milord?' Aidan asked.

'Who?'

'Come on. Simon.'

'I haven't seen him for ages,' she said.

Aidan was surprised. Only last night Eve had been fulminating about it all.

'Did it end in tears?' Aidan knew that Eve would demand the whole story from him, not just half said, half understood bits of conversation.

'Not a bit. Nothing could come of it. We knew that. He's one world, I'm another,' Nan said.

'That's establishment baloney. Just because he's part of the crumbling classes,' Bill Dunne said.

'Exactly. And much as I know we should be nice to the crumbling classes, they're a bit hard to take,' said Nan.

Bill, Jack and Aidan realized immediately that this Simon was besotted with Nan, but that she had thrown him over because she couldn't go along with all that would be involved if she was to play the game as they wanted to play it at the Big House.

Aidan knew that Eve would be very pleased with this news. Jack knew that Nan was just saying what he knew already. Only a few weeks ago he had seen Simon approach Nan and beg to be taken back into her warmth, while she had been polite and distant. Bill Dunne was pleased that he could report to everyone else that Nan Mahon was in circulation again.

The barman mentioned that drinking up time had long been exceeded. He looked stern, young law students weren't going to be much help to him if he got an endorsement on his licence.

Bill and Aidan drifted back to the university.

Jack dallied and spoke to Nan.

'I don't suppose you'd think of being really bad and coming to the pictures with me?'

'Lord no, more *Swamp Women*!'

'We could look at a paper.'

They bought an *Evening Herald*.

Nan said, 'What about Benny?'

'What about her?'

'I mean where is she?'

'Search me,' said Jack. There was nothing they could agree on. They walked slowly through the Green debating this one and that, heads close together inside the pages of the newspaper.

It took them a long time to get to Grafton Street. They still hadn't made up their minds. The pubs were open again now. the Holy Hour was well over.

'Let's have a drink and discuss it,' Jack suggested.

He had a Guinness. Nan had a pineapple juice.

Jack told her a long, sad saga about Benny never being there. He said he knew things were difficult in Knockglen and that

Benny was trying to get her mother started in the shop. But he wondered was she taking it all on her shoulders too much?

'She shouldn't stay holding her hand,' Nan agreed with him. She explained that she had never felt responsible for her mother, who went out to work every day and didn't need anyone to mind her.

Jack brightened. He had been afraid that he was being selfish. No, Nan told him, it was a sign of how much he liked Benny around that he missed her.

He warmed to this view. Take tonight for example. There was a club dance. Everyone brought a partner. And here would he be, Jack Foley, yet again with no partner.

He looked across at her suddenly.

'Unless, of course . . . ?'

'I wouldn't like to. Benny might . . . ?'

'Oh, come on. Benny won't mind. Didn't she ask us to go to the pictures together?'

Nan looked doubtful.

'You're not worried about your old pal Cavalry Twill, are you?'

'I told you, that's long forgotten. He's no part of my life.'

'Well then.' Jack was easy and somewhat cheered. 'Will we meet at the club?'

Carmel was on the Ladies' Committee. It involved helping to prepare the supper for the functions. Sean liked her to be involved. He was Treasurer of course, and very important. She was buying bread for the sandwiches when she met Benny, who was trying to turn her back on the sweet counter and make do with an apple.

'It's the Tiffin Bar that's almost reaching out its arms at me from the shelf,' Benny said. 'Thank God you came in. I was nearly going to buy it.'

'It'd be a shame to go back on the Tiffin now,' Carmel said.

Benny didn't like the feeling that seemed to hang unspoken that there had been years of wedging chocolate bars down her throat. She bought the apple unenthusiastically.

'It's a pity you're not going to be here tonight,' Carmel said. 'The party's going to be great. They've given us much more money than usual. We're going to have sponge flans filled with whipped cream and decorated with chocolate flake. Oh, sorry, Benny, but you're not here, so you won't be tempted anyway.'

'I am here as it happens. I'm staying with Eve,' Benny said.

'Great,' said Carmel warmly. 'See you tonight.'

'Ring him,' Eve said. 'Ring him and tell him you're in town.'

'He knows. He must know. I told him.'

'They never listen. Ring him.'

Benny said she'd have to talk to that woman, Jack's mother, who always made people sound as if they were looking for autographs instead of trying to speak to her son. Eve said that was nonsense. Benny had only phoned the house once. She must ring now. Jack would be delighted.

From the house in Dunlaoghaire Benny eventually did phone.

'I'm sorry, but he's gone out to the Rugby Club. They're having some kind of party tonight. He said he'd be late back.'

'He can't have known you were in town,' Eve said.

'No.'

They sat at the kitchen table. Neither of them suggested that Benny should just dress up and go in to the club anyway.

Neither of them said it had all been the forgetfulness of men, and that Jack would be delighted to see her.

They concentrated instead on Kit Hegarty who was going out with Kevin Hickey's father.

'Don't cheapen yourself now, remember,' Eve warned.

'He won't respect you,' said Benny.

Kit said that it was wonderful to see the high moral tone of the younger generation. She was relieved to know that this was their attitude.

'It's not our attitude for ourselves. We have no restraint at all,' Eve assured her. 'It's only for you.'

'I wish we had no restraint,' Benny said gloomily. 'We might be better off.'

Annabel Hogan had brightened up the shop considerably by taking away some of the wooden panels and surrounds in the window. It did not look nearly so sepulchral and solemn. She had V-necked jumpers in several colours displayed on stands. For the first time a man coming into Hogan's might be able to browse and choose rather than knowing what he wanted before he came in the door.

It also meant that she could see out much more clearly, without having to peer.

She saw Sean Walsh walk into Healy's Hotel without a backward glance at the business where he had worked for so long.

She knew that he had left his belongings there while he went away to make his plans. Perhaps he had got a job somewhere and he had returned to collect his belongings. Peggy Pine had said that Sean had hopes of Mrs Healy. Annabel doubted it. Dorothy Healy was no fool. She would know quicker than most that Sean would not have left Hogan's as he did unless there had been an incident. He was no longer an aspiring merchant in the town.

'I'm no longer a person of substance in this town,' Sean Walsh said to Mrs Healy.

She inclined her head graciously. There had been a time when he thought he would have more to offer, something to bring to the request he was going to make. But circumstances had changed.

Her head was angled like a bird considering its options. Sean spoke of his admiration for her. The respect in which she was held. The potential in Healy's Hotel, a potential as yet not fully realized.

He said there was a need for an overseer, someone to look after the daily business, the nuts and bolts, while Mrs Healy's own flair was used where it was of most use in greeting the customers, and being a presence.

Dorothy Healy waited.

He spoke of his admiration, his gratitude for her interest in him and his career, the affection that he hoped he was correct in thinking had grown between them. He was sorrier than he could ever say that things had not worked out as he would have liked. He had always envisaged himself making this speech, when he was a partner in a business and the owner of a small property on the Quarry Road.

He spoke a lot of the time with his head hanging, and addressed many of his remarks to Mrs Healy's knees. She gazed at his dead-looking hair, which would be perfectly all right if he used a good shampoo and went to a proper barber. When he looked up at her anxiously, his pale face working with the anxiety of his proposal, she smiled at him encouragingly.

'Yes, Sean?'

'Will you accept my proposal of matrimony?' he said.

'I shall be happy to accept,' said Dorothy Healy.

She saw some colour flood into his face and join the look of disbelief.

He reached out and touched her hand.

He didn't realize that he was a far likelier prospect now than he had been before.

Mrs Healy wanted no refurbished cottage up on a path by the quarry.

She wanted no connections with a dying clothing business across the road. She needed a man who could manage the heavy and duller side of the hotel for her. And she knew, since Sean Walsh must have been thrown out because he was found with his hand in the till across the road, that he would have to be careful in his new employ.

She had him where she wanted him now.

'I don't know what to say,' he said.

But as the afternoon became evening they found a lot to say. Plans were made, big plans and little plans. A jeweller in Ballylee would be visited for a ring. Father Ross would be consulted about a date. Sean would visit Dublin and buy three suits off the peg, since he was a stock size. Sean would be declared the Manager as of Monday. He would live in the new building which had been erected at the back. Sean hadn't been aware of its purpose. He had thought it some kind of store house. Together they looked at it. It had all the makings of a fine family house.

As if Mrs Healy had known that this would happen one day.

Paddy Hickey was a fine dancer. And he said Kit was light as a feather.

'It was the hand of God that directed my son to your house,' he said.

'That and the notice I have up in the university,' Kit replied.

'Will you come down to Kerry with me?' he asked.

She looked at his big square handsome face. He was an honourable man, who wouldn't run away from her.

'I might, one day, go down and see the place you're from,' she said.

He had told her that his family was reared. That Kevin was the youngest lad. That his place was grand and modern, the kitchen had the best Formica in it, and you could eat your dinner off the tiled floor.

He said he had nice neighbours and relatives who knew all about Mrs Hegarty the widow in Dublin who had given such a home to Kevin.

'I'm only a recent widow,' Kit said.

'Well, I didn't know that, until you told me, and they need never know it, and I suppose Joe Hegarty would be pleased to know that someone was looking after you.'

'I never called him Joe, in all the years. I never called him that,' she said almost wonderingly.

'Maybe that was part of it all,' said Kevin Hickey's father, who had every intention of making this woman his wife.

The mournful sound of the fog horn boomed around Dunlaoghaire Harbour. Eve was so used to it now that she hardly heard it any more.

But she stirred and looked at her clock with the luminous hands. It was half past three.

She listened. Benny didn't seem to be breathing the way a sleeping person does. She must be lying there awake.

'Benny?'

'It's all right. Go back to sleep.'

Eve turned on the light. Benny was propped up against her pillows in the small camp bed. Her face was tearstained.

Eve swung her legs out of the bed and reached for her cigarettes.

'It's just that I love him so much,' wept Benny.

'I know, I know.'

'And he must have gone off me. Just like that.'

'It's a misunderstanding. For God's sake, if he was going with anyone else we'd know.'

'Would we?'

'Of course we would. You should have rung earlier. You'd have saved yourself all this. You'd be out somewhere in a steamy car trying to keep your clothes on you.'

'Maybe I kept them on me too much.'

'Stop blaming yourself. You always think it's your fault.'

'Would you tell me if you knew? Really and truly would you tell me? You'd not keep it from me to be kind?'

'I swear I'd tell you,' Eve said. 'I swear I'd not let you be made a fool of.'

The party was great. Carmel was in the kitchen most of the time and so didn't see the way Jack Foley and Nan Mahon danced together. And how they found everything funny, and hardly talked to anyone else.

Carmel was busy washing plates when Jack Foley got Nan's coat and took her home.

'I'm honoured to be allowed to take you home. Bill Dunne and the boys say you never tell them where you live.'

'Maybe I don't want *them* to know,' Nan said.

They sat outside the door of Maple Gardens and talked. The light of the street lamp on Nan's face made her look very beautiful. Jack leaned across and kissed her.

She didn't move away when he bent over to kiss her. Instead she clung to him eagerly.

It was very easy to kiss and hold Nan Mahon. She didn't move away and pull back just as you were feeling aroused. He stroked her breast through the lilac silky dress she wore under her coat.

His voice was husky. There was no other sensation outside this car.

When she did pull away she spoke to him, cool and unruffled and different to the woman he had held in his arms, pliant, eager and wrapping herself close to him.

'Jack, don't you think we should talk about Benny?'

'Nope.'

'Why not?'

'She's not here.' He realized that it sounded too harsh, too dismissive. 'What I mean is that anything between Benny and me has nothing to do with this.' He reached for her again.

She leaned over and kissed him on the nose.

'Goodnight, Jack,' she said, and vanished. He saw her let herself into the house and the door close behind her.

It was the same ritual of hanging up the clothes, sponging them and brushing them.

Cleaning her face with cream and doing her stretching exercises. Though she might have to change those exercises. Nan lay in her bed and thought about the events of the day. She laid her two hands on her stomach where a lab report had proved what she knew already. That a child was beginning to grow. She did not think about Simon Westward. She would never think about him again, no matter what happened.

She lay in the bedroom that she and her mother had decorated over the years, the years when they had told each other Nan was like a princess, and that she would leave Maple Gardens and find a prince.

Her first attempt had not been very successful.

Nan stared ahead of her unseeingly and thought out the options.

She did not want to go to this person and have something that was less important than tooth extraction. She did not want the sordidness of it, the shabby end of something that had been important. She didn't think it was a speck, as Simon had said. But she didn't believe it was a baby either.

If it were done, then it would all be over, the slate would be clean, she could continue with her studies.

She looked over at her desk. She didn't enjoy them. They took up too much time. They ate into the hours she should have been grooming herself, and preparing for the places to go. She found no great joy sitting in those large musty chalk-smelling halls, or the cramped tutorial rooms. She wasn't academic. Her tutor had told her more than once that she would not make the Honours group. What was the point of struggling on doing a pass degree while the kudos was on the Honours students?

She could go to England and have the child. She could have it adopted. Take less than a year out of her life. But why have a child to give it away? Go through all that just to make some anonymous couple's dream come true?

If she lived in a remote country village in the West of Ireland, the community might have excused a beautiful girl falling for the Squire and bringing up his child, ashamed but still accepted.

In parts of working-class Dublin, an unexpected child would

have been welcomed in the family. The child would grow up believing its granny was its mother.

But not in Maple Gardens. It was the beginnings of respectability for the Mahons and their neighbours. And for Nan and Em it would be the end of the dream.

It looked as if a lot of the options weren't really options after all.

It was too early for morning sickness. But she didn't take any breakfast.

Em looked at her anxiously.

'You'll be seeing Simon this evening, is that right?' she asked, hoping to see Nan's face light up.

But she was disappointed.

'I haven't seen Simon for weeks and weeks, Em.'

'But I thought you said . . .'

'I'm saying now, and I want you to remember it, I haven't been going out with Simon Westward since just after Christmas.'

Emily Mahon looked at her daughter astonished.

But there was something about the set of Nan's jaw that made it seem very important.

Emily nodded, as if she had taken the instruction to heart. It didn't make it any easier to understand. Either Nan had been lying when she told her of the outings to smart places with Simon, or else she was lying now.

Jack came into the Annexe. Benny waved eagerly from a table. She had been holding a chair against all comers, by draping her scarf and her books all over it.

She looked so glad to see him and a lurch of guilt shook him.

Nobody had reported his long hours dancing with Nan to her anyway; he was slightly afraid that Carmel might have seen it as her duty to make sure that Benny was informed.

But Benny's eyes were shining with pleasure to see him.

'How was the party?'

'Oh, you know, these things are always the same. Everyone was fine, very cheerful.' There had been two wins to celebrate, some fine playing and thanks to Sean they were in funds. He told her all those details and little about the night itself.

'It was a pity you couldn't have been in Dublin.'

'But I was. Remember I said it would be early-closing day and Mother was going to have a rest and an early night.'

'I'd forgotten,' Jack admitted.

There was a pause.

'And of course you didn't know about the party.'

'Well, I did, because I ran into Carmel when she was shopping for it. And she told me.'

She looked unsure. He felt a heel, not just for holding Nan so close last night, but because Benny had thought he mightn't have asked her.

'I'd have loved you to have been there. I just forgot. Honestly, I'm so used to your not being there. What did you do?'

'I went to the pictures with Eve.'

'You should have rung me.'

'I did, but it was too late.'

Jack hadn't even looked at the message pad this morning. His mother would have written the names of anyone who called.

'Ah, Benny, I'm very sorry. I'm stupid.' He banged his head as if it were wood.

He seemed very sorry.

'Well, no harm done,' she said.

'I ran into Nan. And since she wasn't doing anything I asked her to come instead. I think she quite enjoyed it.'

Benny's smile was broad. Everything was all right. He had genuinely forgotten. He wasn't trying to tell her anything. He wasn't wriggling out. He would have loved her to have been with him last night.

Thank God he had met Nan and invited her.

Now she had nothing to worry about.

CHAPTER EIGHTEEN

Jack woke suddenly with his heart pounding. He was in the middle of a very violent dream. It was so real it was hard to shake it off. Benny's father, Mr Hogan, was standing at the top of the quarry pushing the black Morris Minor belonging to Dr Foley over the edge.

Mr Hogan had red burning coals where his eyes should be, laughing while the car bounced to the bottom of the quarry with a crash.

It was the crash that had jerked Jack awake.

He lay there, panting.

Beside him lay Nan, sleeping innocently, her hands folded under her face, a little smile on her lips.

They lay in Eve's cottage, the place he had come for a party just after Christmas.

They had needed somewhere to go, Nan said. This was a perfectly safe place. Nobody ever passed by. The key was in the stone wall.

Nan had been wonderful. So cool and practical, saying they must bring a spirit lamp and perhaps their own sheets and towels.

Jack would never have thought of that. She said they should keep the curtains very tightly drawn and leave the car hidden in the square lest anyone see it. There was a place behind the bus shelter where nobody would think to look.

She was naturally observant.

She had said that she never thought it was possible that she could desire someone so much.

He had been worried about everything of course, but she said that it would be all right. The alternative was just to go on being a tease. She wanted to love him completely and honestly. It had been so wonderful, compared to that girl in Wales, which had all been just rushed and quick and awkward. Nan's beautiful body was magical in his arms. She seemed to love everything as much as he did.

It must have been awful for her the first time, but she had made no complaint. What excited him most was her calm exterior when they met in college. The cool Nan Mahon looking fresh and immaculate was the same girl who wrapped herself around him and gave him an ecstasy that he had not known could exist.

This was their third visit to the cottage.

He had still not spoken to Benny.

It was just that he didn't know what to say.

There was going to be an Easter Pageant at the School. Heather wanted to take part.

'We told your brother that you wouldn't be involved in religious instruction,' Mother Francis explained.

'But this isn't religion. It's drama. It's only a play,' Heather pleaded.

It had been an exercise in spirituality intended to give the children some feeling of the message of Easter by re-enacting the Passion of Our Lord. Mother Francis sighed.

'Well, who'll explain it to your brother? Will you, or will I?'

'I don't think we'll bother him about it. He's like a weasel. Could I be Hitler, please, Mother, please!'

'Could you be *who*?'

'Um . . . Pontius Pilate. I got confused . . .'

'We'll have to see. But first I will have to discuss it with Mr Westward.'

'It's too late,' said Heather triumphantly. 'He's gone to England today. To Hampshire. To look for a wife.'

Mossy Rooney cleared out the back of Hogan's shop, and made the derelict yard look as if it had always intended to be a garden. Benny and her mother decided they must put flowers and even shrubs in it.

Mossy said that they could even have a bit of a garden seat. The place was nice and sheltered.

Patsy had told him that if the mistress had an ounce of sense she'd sell Lisbeg and move into the shop good and proper. There was plenty of room in it, and why did she want to be rattling around like a tin can in a big empty house?

If they were in the shop it would be easier for Patsy to come and do a bit of daily work. It wouldn't be as heavy and constant as looking after a big house where nobody lived. Annabel Hogan had not admitted it to herself yet, but as she stood beside Benny watering in the fuchsias that they had taken at Eve's request from the cottage, she began to think that it might be the wisest course.

In a way it would be nice just to walk upstairs and be home. Or be able to stretch out your feet on the sofa.

But time enough to think of that later. There was more than enough to sort out already.

Benny had been careful not to make the first floor, the lumber room where they had found the money in the sewing machine, a place they didn't visit. Bit by bit she managed to get rid of what had to go. Very gradually she started to ferry things up from Lisbeg. Little by little she and Patsy were transforming that big room into a place where it would be quite possible to sit and spend an evening. They took a wireless, some chairs that did not have the springs protruding. They polished a shabby old table and put place mats on it. Soon they were having their meals up here. Shep spent more time nosing around the lane, prowling the small garden which he regarded as his own exercise yard, and sitting proprietorially in the shop, than he did lording it over an empty Lisbeg.

Soon the shop was beginning to feel like home.

Soon Benny would be able to feel more free.

Dekko Moore asked Dr Johnson was there a chance that Mrs Hogan might part with Lisbeg.

Very often customers came in to him, people from big places, loaded down with money, and they often enquired were there any houses of a certain style going to come up on the market.

'Give them a few months, yet,' Dr Johnson said. 'I imagine they'll be moved up above by the end of the summer, but you wouldn't want to rush them.'

Dekko said it was extraordinary the way things had gone already. He had gone into the shop to buy a pair of socks the other day, and he had spent a fortune.

Nan and Jack ran down the track from the quarry walk to the square. The Morris Minor was hidden behind the bus shelter. For the third time they were lucky nobody was about. It was only six thirty in the morning. The car started and they were on the road to Dublin.

'One morning it won't start. And then we're for it,' Jack said, squeezing her hand.

'We're very careful. We won't be caught,' she said. She looked out of the window, as they sped past the fields and farms on their way to Dublin.

He sighed, thinking of the nights and early mornings they had spent in Eve Malone's small bed.

But a part of him felt almost sick at the risk they were taking. Eve would kill them if she knew they were using her house like this. Knockglen was a village. Someone must see them sooner or later. Knockglen was much more than a village. It was Benny's home town.

Benny.

He tried to put her out of his mind. He had managed to see her only with other people for the last two weeks. Since this amazing explosive thing with Nan had begun. He didn't think that Benny noticed. He made sure that Bill or Aidan or Johnny was there, or else he called over people to join them.

They never went to the pictures alone; on the hard-fought nights that Benny was able to stay in Dublin he made sure they went out in a group. He tried not to include Nan with them, though sometimes Benny brought her along.

Nan told him that she accepted exactly what he said, that whatever happened between them had nothing to do with Jack and Benny. They were two different worlds.

Yes, he had said that in the heat of the moment, but when he saw Benny's trusting face, and laughed at her funny remarks . . . when she turned out on a cold afternoon to watch him at a practice match, when she offered to help Carmel with the sandwiches, when he realized that he actually wanted to be with her alone and to touch her the way he touched Nan, then he felt confused.

It was easy to say that your world was compartmentalized. But in real life it wasn't easy.

Nan must be much more mature than all of them if she could accept that what Jack felt for her was a huge and almost overpowering passion. It had everything to do with desire and very little to do with sharing a life. They didn't talk much in the car, while with Benny they would both find the words stumbling over each other.

Jack felt a great sense of anxiety as the traffic began to build up a little on the road and they approached Dublin. Nan told him nothing of her home and family.

'How do they let you stay out all night?' he had asked.

'How do yours let you stay out all night?' she had replied.

The answer was simple. That he was a boy. Nothing terrible could happen to him, like getting pregnant.

But he didn't say it. He didn't dare to say it out of politeness, and out of superstition.

Nan watched fields turn into first factory premises and then housing estates. They would soon be home. She would ask him to leave her at the corner of Maple Gardens. As soon as his car had disappeared, Nan would go to the bus stop.

She would come into college early and get herself ready for lectures.

Not that her heart was in them. But she couldn't go home. Her father thought she was staying with Eve Malone in Dunlaoghaire, instead of sneaking into Eve's cottage in Knockglen.

It would confuse and worry her mother. Let Jack go home to his house with hot water and clean shirts, and a mildly perplexed mother and maid putting bacon and egg on the table. He had nothing to worry about, a lover and a patient loving girlfriend. From what you read in books it was what all men wanted.

Nan bit her lip as they drove along in silence. She would have to tell him very soon. She could see no other way out.

That night when she lay on her bed she examined the options. This was the only one that looked as if it might possibly work.

She was not going to think about Benny. Jack had said that was his business. It had nothing to do with what was between them. Nan didn't really believe that. But he had said that it was up to him to cope with. She had enough to worry about.

She could not confide in one single person because there was nobody alive who would condone what she was about to do. For the second time in a month she was going to have to tell a man that she was pregnant. And with the unfairness of life, the second one who had no duty or responsibility would probably be the one to do the right thing.

Mossy's mother said that May was nice for a wedding. Paccy Moore said they could have the reception in the room behind his shop. After all, his sister Bee was being the bridesmaid, and Patsy didn't have a home of her own.

It wasn't what Patsy had hoped. The guests coming through the cobbler's shop. But it was either that or let it be known she was coming in with nothing to her mother-in-law's house and have the gathering there.

What she would really have liked was to be able to use Lisbeg, and have the reception in the Hogans' house, but it didn't look likely. The master would only be four months gone. The mistress and Benny spent that much time above in the shop they would have little time and energy to spare for Patsy. She was getting a dress at Pine's. She had been paying for it slowly since Christmas.

Clodagh told Benny about Patsy's hopes. 'It may be impossible, I'm not suggesting you do it, it's just that you'd hate to hear afterwards and not have realized.'

Benny was very grateful to be told. It was bad of them not to have thought of it in the first place. They had assumed that all the running would be made by Mossy's side and didn't even think of suggesting a venue.

Patsy's joy knew no bounds. It was one in the eye for Mossy's mother. She began to get the wedding invitations printed.

'And how's your own romance?' Clodagh enquired. 'I believe he was down here the other night.'

'God, I wish he had been. I *think* it's going all right. He's always coming looking for me and suggesting this and that, but there's a cast of thousands as well.'

'Ah well, that's all to the good. He wants to show you to his friends. And he has friends. That lunatic across the road there has no friends except people who sell pinball machines and juke boxes. I could have sworn I saw him at Dessie Burns' getting petrol.'

'Who? Fonsie?'

'No, your fellow. Oh well, I suppose there's dozens of handsome blokes in college scarves getting petrol in Morris Minors.'

'It's not only Mr Flood who's seeing visions,' Benny said to Jack next day. 'Clodagh thought she saw you getting petrol in Knockglen the other night.'

'Would I have come to Knockglen and not gone to see you?' he asked.

It was a ridiculous question. It didn't even need an answer. She had only brought it up to show him that he was a person there, that he had an identity.

He breathed slowly through his teeth and remembered the shock that he and Nan had got when he realized the petrol gauge was showing empty. They had to fill up there and then. There would be nowhere open when they made their dawn escape.

Another very near miss. He wouldn't tell Nan about it. He hoped Benny wouldn't.

Sean Walsh was taking his early morning walk. These days he was accompanied by the two unattractive Jack Russell terriers with whom he would be sharing his home. They were less yappy and unpleasant if they were wearied by this harsh morning exercise.

He had ceased to look at the houses with the resentment and longing that he had once felt.

Things had turned out very much better than he would have dared to hope.

Dorothy was a woman in a million.

From Eve Malone's cottage he saw two figures emerge. The early sunlight was in his eyes and he couldn't see who they were.

They ran hand in hand, almost scampered down the way that led to the square. He squinted after them. They both looked vaguely familiar. Or perhaps he was imagining it. They must be Dublin people who had rented or borrowed the cottage.

But where were they going?

It was much too early for a bus. There had been no cars in the square.

It was a mystery, and that was something Sean Walsh didn't like at all.

Lilly Foley spoke to her husband about Jack.

'Three nights last week, and three again this week, John. You'll have to say something.'

'He's a grown man.'

'He's twenty. That's not a grown man.'

'Well, it's not a child. Leave him be. When he's passed over for a team, or fails an exam, *that*'s the time to talk to him.'

'But who could he be with? Is it the same girl, or a different one each time?'

'It's a fair distance on the old milometer, I notice, whoever it is.' Jack's father laughed roguishly.

He had found a receipt for petrol from Knockglen. It must be that big girl Benny Hogan. Which was a turn-up for the books, and where on earth did they go? Her father had died, but her mother was strict. Surely she wouldn't have been able to entertain Jack in her house?

Heather rang Eve. 'When are you coming home? I miss you.'

Eve felt absurdly flattered.

She said she'd come soon, next weekend or the weekend after.

'It doesn't have to be the weekend.'

Eve realized that was true. It didn't.

She was free to leave any afternoon. She could travel on the bus with Benny. She'd have tea with Mother Francis and the nuns and then take Heather up to the cottage. She'd hear at first hand how the plans for the Easter Pageant were going. She could go to see Benny's mother and admire the changes in Hogan's. She could call to Mario's to end the evening. Knockglen was full of excitement these days. She might go tomorrow, but she had better check it wasn't a night that Benny was coming to town. It would be silly to miss her.

Benny said they'd skip a lecture and meet on the three o'clock bus. That way they'd have a bit of time. They had sandwiches in the place that the boys liked. The pub with the relaxed view about the Holy Hour.

Aidan, Jack and Bill were there. Rosemary had called in to borrow ten shillings. She needed to have a hair-do in a very good place. Tom the medical student had been harder to pin down than she had hoped. It was time for heavy remedies now, like new hairstyles.

Nobody felt like work, but Eve and Benny refused the offer of being taken to play some slot machines in an amusement arcade.

'I'm getting the bus,' said Benny.

'Goodbye, Cinderella,' Jack blew her a kiss. His eyes were very warm. She must have been mad to worry about him.

Benny and Eve left the pub.

Aidan said that he felt sure those two would be up all night and maybe bopping till dawn in Mario's.

'What?' Jack spilled some of his drink.

He hadn't realized that Eve was going back to her cottage. He had arranged to meet Nan on the Quays at six o'clock. They had been planning to go to the very same place.

Nan Mahon walked briskly down towards the river. Her overnight bag contained the usual sheets, pillowcases, candlesticks, breakfast and supper materials. Jack just brought a primus stove and something to drink.

But this time Nan had packed a bottle of wine as well. They might need it. Tonight was the night she was going to tell him.

Heather was overjoyed to see Eve. As she went through the school hall she called her over excitedly. There was a rehearsal in progress, and she was wearing a sheet. Heather Westward was playing Simon of Cyrene, the man who helped Jesus to carry his cross.

It was something that Knockglen would not have believed possible a few short weeks ago.

'Are you coming to cheer me on when we do it for real?' Heather wanted to know.

'I don't think cheering you on is what Mother Francis had in mind . . .'

'But I'm one of the good people. I help him. I step forward and lighten his burden,' Heather said.

'Yes. I'll certainly come and support you.'

'You see, I won't have any relations here like everyone else has.'

Eve promised that she would be there when the pageant was performed. She might even bring Aidan so that Heather would have two people. Eve Malone knew very well what it was like to be the only girl in the school who had nobody to turn up with a cake for the sale of work or with applause for the pageants and the plays. That had been her lot all during her years in St Mary's.

She let Heather get back to rehearsal and said she'd see her later in the cottage. It was time to talk to Mother Francis.

Eve said she had to go down to Healy's Hotel to have a cup of coffee so that she could get a close-up look at Love's Young Dream, Dorothy and Sean, Great Lovers of our Time. Mother Francis said she wasn't to be making a jeer out of them. Everyone was being very restrained, and Eve must be the same.

Hadn't it turned out better than anyone dared to hope, Mother Francis said sternly, and Eve realized that she must have known or suspected something of the secret Benny had told her, the missing money and the terror of the confrontation.

But if she did, it would never be discussed.

Up in her own cottage, waiting for Heather to come pounding up the convent path, Eve looked around.

There was something different. Not just the way things were placed. Mother Francis came here often. She polished and she dusted. Sometimes she rearranged things. But this was different.

Eve couldn't think what it was. It was just a feeling that someone else had been there. Staying there, cooking even. Sleeping in her bed. She ran her hand across the range. Nobody had used it. Her bed made with the neat corners she had learned at school.

Eve shivered. She was becoming fanciful. All those stories about the place being haunted must have got to her. But on a bright April evening this was ridiculous.

She shook herself firmly and started getting the fire going. Heather would need toast within minutes of her arrival.

Later, down in Healy's Hotel, Eve saw Sean. In his dark manager's suit.

'Might I be the first to congratulate you?' she said.

'That's uncommonly gracious of you, Eve.'

Eve enquired politely about when they intended to marry. Was courteously interested in the expansionist plans for the hotel, the honeymoon that would include the Holy City and the Italian lakes, and enquired whether Mrs Healy was around so that she could express her congratulations and pleasure personally.

'Dorothy is having a rest. She does that in the early evenings,' Sean said, as if he were describing the habits of some long extinct animal in a museum.

Eve stuffed her hand into her mouth to stop any sound coming out.

'I see you've decided to capitalize on your property,' Sean said.

Eve looked at him blankly.

'Let your cottage out to people.'

'No, I haven't,' she said.

'Oh, I'm sorry.'

She thought he was manoeuvring the conversation around to a point where he would ask her to rent it to him or to let it to someone he knew.

A feeling of revulsion rose in her throat. She decided that this must be nipped in the bud. Sean Walsh must be left under no illusion that her home could be let to anyone, not to anyone for money.

'No, I'm sorry for speaking so sharply Sean. It's just that I never intend to. I'm keeping it for myself and my friends.'

'Your friends. Yes,' he said.

Suddenly he realized who he had seen coming out of Eve's cottage. It was that blonde girl he had seen several times before, most recently getting off the Knockglen bus, on the Quays in Dublin.

And the man. Of course he remembered who he was. He was Benny's boyfriend. The doctor's son.

So *that* little romance hadn't lasted long. And there had been precious little said about its being over.

He smiled a slow smile. There was something about it that made Eve feel very uneasy. That was twice this afternoon she had got goose-bumps. She must be getting very jumpy. Aidan was right. Eve Malone was a deeply neurotic woman. She felt an overwhelming urge to be away from Sean Walsh and out of his presence.

She jumped up and started to hasten out of the hotel.

'You'll pass on my good wishes to Mrs Healy,' she tried to say Dorothy, but somehow the word wouldn't form in her mouth.

The traffic was bad on the Quays. Jack saw Nan but he couldn't attract her attention. She was leaning against the wall, and looking down into the Liffey. She seemed many miles away.

Eventually by hooting and shouting he managed to make her

hear him. She walked threading her way confidently between the parked cars in the traffic jam. He thought again how beautiful she was, and how hard it was to resist these nights with her. However, he would have to resist it tonight. His heart nearly stopped when he realized how near they had been to discovery. In future they would have to check and double check that Eve was not going home mid-week.

It was terrifying enough that time they had seen the man with the dogs, the tall thin fellow that Benny hated so much, the one there had been all the fuss over about getting him to leave.

Nan slipped into the car easily and laid her overnight bag on the back seat.

'Change of plan,' he said. 'Let's have a drink and discuss it.'

It was always something that made Benny smile, that phrase. Nan didn't know it.

'Why?'

'Because we can't go down there. Eve's going home.'

'Damn!' She seemed very annoyed.

'Isn't it lucky we discovered?' He wanted to be congratulated on the amazing accident that made Aidan reveal this to him.

'Isn't it unlucky that she chose tonight of all nights to go down there?'

Jack noticed that Nan never referred to Eve by name.

'Well, it *is* her house,' he said with a little laugh.

Nan didn't seem amused.

'I really wanted to be there tonight,' she said. Even frowning she looked beautiful.

Then her face cleared. She suggested this lovely hotel in Wicklow. It was absolutely marvellous. Very quiet and people didn't disturb you. It was exactly where they could go.

Jack knew the name. It was a place where his parents had dinner sometimes. It was much too expensive. He wouldn't be able to afford it and he told her so.

'Do you have a cheque book?'

'Yes, but not enough money in the bank.'

'We'll get the money tomorrow. Or I will. Let's go there.'

'And stay the night. Nan, we're not married. We can't.' He looked alarmed.

'They don't ask for your wedding certificate.'

He looked at her. She changed her voice slightly.

'I've heard of people who've been there, and stayed the night. There was no problem.'

As they drove out south past Dunlaoghaire they saw the house where Eve lived with Kit Hegarty.

'Why on earth can't she be there tonight?' Nan said.

Jack thought it would certainly be a lot cheaper for everyone if she were.

He dreaded the thought of writing a cheque that bounced in this hotel, and having to face his mother and father when it all came out.

He wished that Nan could just have faced the fact that this was one night they would have to put off. Benny would have been most agreeable and understanding.

He wished he didn't keep thinking of Benny at times like this. It was as hypocritical as hell.

Benny and Eve met in the square next morning. They sat in the shelter and waited for Mikey to arrive with the bus.

'Why do we call this a square?' Eve asked. 'It's only a bit of waste ground really.'

'That's until the young tigers get their hands on it. It might be a skating rink next week,' Benny laughed.

It was true that Clodagh and Fonsie were tireless in their efforts to change Knockglen. They had even frightened other people into improving their business.

Fonsie had gone to Flood's and said that if ever he owned a fine frontage like that he'd have the lettering repainted in gold. Mr Flood, terrified that somehow it would be taken from him unless he lived up to this young man's expectations, had the signwriters in next day. Clodagh had stood in Mrs Carroll's untidy grocery and chatted about the food inspectors who were closing shops down all over the place. It was amazing what a coat of paint and a spring clean did to fool them. All the time she pretended she was talking in the abstract. But she could have told Mossy Rooney that he would be called in next day, as indeed he was.

Clodagh told Mossy to put up a fitting for an awning without being asked. Dessie Burns was now stocking various colours of big canvas blinds. Clodagh and Fonsie were going to have their town looking like a rainbow before they finished.

'I suppose they'll get married,' Eve said.

'Clodagh says never. There's too many nuptials coming up, she says we'll be sick of weddings. Mrs Healy and Mr Walsh, Patsy and Mossy, and Maire Carroll home from Dublin with a fiancé already, I gather, unlike the two of us who were very slow off the mark.'

They were giggling as usual when they got on the bus. Nothing had changed since they were schoolgirls.

Rosemary was full of smiles. The hair-do had been highly successful, she said. Benny had lent her three shillings. It was counted meticulously back to her. Tom had been very impressed.

'It looks a bit flattened,' Benny said, examining the hair-do.

'Yes, I know,' Rosemary said delightedly. 'I owe Jack a shilling. Will you give it to him for me?'

Benny said she would. She'd be seeing him in the Annexe anyway.

Sean and Carmel had a table. Benny joined them with Jack's shilling clutched in her hand so that she wouldn't forget to give it to him.

'Jack was looking for you everywhere this morning,' Sean said. Benny was pleased.

'He went and stood outside a Latin lecture, he thought it was yours, but it was Baby Latin.'

'Oh, I'm not Baby Latin,' Benny said proudly. She was just one step above it. Everyone in First Arts had to do some kind of Latin in their first year. Mother Francis would have killed her if she had gone into the easy option.

Bill Dunne joined them.

'Jack said if I saw you, to say that he'll meet you at one o'clock in the main hall,' Bill said. 'Though if you want my personal opinion you wouldn't touch him with a bargepole. He hasn't shaved. He's like a bear with a sore head. He's not worthy of you.'

Benny laughed. It made her feel as high as a kite when Bill Dunne said things like this in front of everyone. It confirmed somehow that she was Jack's girl.

'He's not coming here now, then.' She had been looking at the door.

'Him come anywhere? I asked him about cars and all for the outing to Knockglen after Easter. He said not to talk to him about cars, outings or Knockglen or he'd knock my head off.'

Benny knew that Bill was dramatizing it all, so that he could cast himself in the role of the beautifully mannered nice person and Jack the villain.

Since this was different to the way things were, everyone knew it was a joke. She smiled at Bill affectionately. She knew Jack was longing for the great weekend in Knockglen. It would be even better than Christmas.

Everyone had been planning it for ages. Sean had been collecting money from people, a shilling now and a shilling then. The fund was building up.

There would be a gathering in Eve's, in Clodagh's, and very possibly something upstairs in Hogan's. The rooms were so big and with high ceilings they positively called out to have a party. Benny had been sounding her mother out. And the signs looked good.

She was pleased that Jack was looking for her.

For the past few weeks he had never wanted to see her on her own.

Benny hoped that he might want them to go off to lunch together, like that time ages ago when they had gone to Carlo's.

Maybe she should take *him* there for a treat. But she'd wait and see his mood. She didn't want to be too pushy.

Bill was right. Jack *did* look very badly. Pale and tired as if he hadn't slept all night. He still looked just as handsome, maybe even more so. There was less of the conventional College Hero and more of the lead player in some film or theatre piece.

Yes, Jack Foley looked as if he were in a play.

And he spoke as if he were in one too.

'Benny, I have to talk to you. Where can we go that's away from all these people?'

She laughed at him good-naturedly.

'Hey, you were the one who said the main hall at one o'clock. I didn't choose it. Did you think it would be deserted and just the two of us?'

The crowds swarmed past them in and out, and just standing around in groups talking, duffle coats over arms now, scarves loosely hanging. The weather was getting too warm for them, but they were the badge of being a student. People didn't want to discard them entirely.

'Please,' he said.

'Well would you like to go to Carlo's, you know that lovely place we went . . .'

'*No.*' He almost shouted it.

Everywhere else would be full of people they knew. Even if they were to sit in Stephen's Green, half the university would pass by on its way to stroll down Grafton Street at lunch time.

Benny was at a loss, and yet she knew she had to make the decision.

Jack looked all in.

'We could sit by the canal?' she suggested. 'We could get apples for us and some stale bread in case we see the swans.'

She looked eager and anxious to please him.

It seemed to distress him still further.

'Oh, Jesus, Benny,' he said, and pulled her towards him. A flicker of fear came and went. She felt something was wrong, but then she was always feeling that and it never was.

There was a place near one of the locks where they often sat. There was a bit of raised ground.

Benny took off her coat and laid it down for them to sit on.

'No, no, we'll ruin it.'

'It's only clay. It'll brush off. You're as bad as Nan,' she teased him.

'It's Nan,' he said.

'What is?'

'She's pregnant. She found out yesterday.'

Benny felt a jolt of shock for her friend. At the same time she felt the sense of surprise that Nan of all people had been going all the way with Simon Westward. Nan. So cool and distant. How had she made love properly? Benny would have thought that she would have been the last person on earth to have found herself in this position.

'Poor Nan,' she said. 'Is she very upset?'

'She's out of her mind with worry,' he said.

They sat in silence.

Benny went over the whole awfulness of it in her mind. A university career in ruins, a baby by the age of twenty. And possibly from the look of sympathy on Jack's face a problem about Simon Westward.

Eve would have been right about him.

He would never marry Nan Mahon from the North Side of Dublin, a builder's daughter. And beautiful though she was, the fact that she had given in to him would make him less respectful of her than ever.

'What's she going to do? I suppose she's not going to get married?'

She looked at Jack.

His face was working with emotion. He seemed to be struggling for words.

'She *is* getting married.'

Benny looked at him alarmed. This wasn't normal speech.

He took her hand, and held it to his face. There were tears on his face. Jack Foley was crying.

'She's getting married . . . to me,' he said.

She looked at him in disbelief.

She said absolutely nothing. She knew her mouth was open and her face red with fright.

He was still holding her hand to his face.

His body was shaking with sobs.

'We have to get married, Benny,' he said. 'It's my baby.'

CHAPTER NINETEEN

Eve was in the Singing Kettle when she saw Benny at the door. At first she thought that Benny was going to join them and was about to pull up another chair.

Then she saw her face.

'See you later,' she said hastily to the group.

'You haven't finished your chips.' Aidan was amazed. Nothing could be that pressing.

But Eve was out in Leeson Street.

She drew Benny away from the doorway where they were in the main path of almost everyone they knew.

Then, leaning against the iron railings of a house, Benny began to tell her the tale. Sometimes it was hard to hear the words, and sometimes she said the same words over, and over and over again.

Like that he said he loved her, he loved Benny. He really did and he wouldn't have had this happen for the world. But there was nothing else that could be done. The announcement would be in the *Irish Times* on Saturday.

Eve looked across the road and saw a taxi letting someone off at St Vincent's Private Nursing Home. She dragged Benny through the traffic and pushed her into the back of it.

'Dunlaoghaire,' she said briskly.

'Are you girls all right?' The taxi driver watched them in the mirror. The big girl look particularly poorly, as if she might get sick all over his car.

'We have the fare,' Eve said.

'I didn't mean that,' he began.

'You did a bit.' They both grinned.

Eve said to Benny that she should rest. There'd be plenty of time to talk when they got home.

Kit was out. She was shopping for a new outfit for Easter when she was going to Kerry as a guest of Kevin Hickey and his father.

They had the kitchen to themselves. Benny sat at the table

and through a blur saw Eve prepare a meal for them. She noticed her small thin hands cut deftly through the cold cooked potatoes and trim the rinds from rashers of bacon. She saw thin fingers of bread dipped in a beaten egg.

'I don't want any of this,' Benny said.

'No, but I do. I left my whole lunch in the Kettle, remember?' Eve took a bottle of sherry from inside a cornflake packet.

'It's to hide it from the drinky students,' she explained.

'I'm not having any.'

'Medicinal,' Eve said, and poured out two huge tumblers for them as she placed the big white plates of comfort food in front of them.

'Now start at the very beginning and tell me slowly. Start from when you sat down on the coat by the canal, and don't tell me that he loves you or I'll get up and throw every single thing that's on this table on the floor and you'll have to clear it up.'

'Eve, please. I know you mean to help.'

'Oh, I mean to help all right,' said Eve. Benny had never seen her face looking so grim. Not in all that long war she had waged with the Westwards, not in the fight with Mother Clare or in her hospital bed had she seen Eve Malone's face so hard and unforgiving.

They talked until the shadows got longer. Benny heard Kit let herself in. She looked around at the untidy kitchen and the half finished sherry bottle.

'It's all right,' Eve said gently, 'she'll understand. I'll do a quick clear-up.'

'I should be going for my bus.'

'You're staying here. Ring your mother. And Benny . . . she'll ask are you seeing Jack. Tell her you don't see Jack any more. Prepare her for it being over.'

'It needn't be over. He doesn't want it to be over. He says that we have to talk.'

Kit came to the door and looked around her in surprise. Before she could make any protest Eve spoke.

'Benny's had a bit of a shock. We're coping with it the best we can, by eating most of tomorrow's breakfast. I'll go up to the huckster's shop and replace it later.'

Kit knew a crisis when she saw one.

'I have to hang up my finery. See you in half an hour to prepare supper. That's if there's any of that left.'

She nodded encouragingly and disappeared.

Annabel Hogan said that was fine. She had a lot of work to do in the shop. It would save them making a supper. She and Patsy would just get something from Mario's. Benny thought bitterly of all the nights she had left Jack Foley to his own devices in Dublin while she had trundled wearily home to keep her mother company. Now she was less in the way staying in Dublin.

'Are you going out with Jack?' Mother asked.

Despite Eve's warning, Benny couldn't do it. She couldn't tell her mother that it was over. Even to say it meant it might be true.

'Not tonight,' she said brightly. 'No, tonight I'm just going out with Eve.'

Benny lay on Eve's bed and bathed her eyes with cold water while Eve served the supper downstairs. The curtains were drawn and she could hear the clatter of plates and cutlery below. Kit had looked in briefly with a cup of tea. She had made no attempt to cheer her or sympathize. Benny could see why she must be such a restful person to live with.

She dreaded the bucketfuls of sympathy that Mother would pour on her, the endless wondering and speculating and ludicrous little suggestions. Maybe if you wore paler colours or darker colours, perhaps if you went round to his house to talk to his mother. Men like girls who get on well with their mothers.

She wouldn't tell Mother that Nan was pregnant. It demeaned them all somehow.

It put everything on a different level.

They walked, Benny and Eve, for what seemed and felt like hours and miles.

Sometimes they argued, sometimes Benny stopped to cry again. To say that Eve wouldn't be so harsh if only she could have seen Jack's face, and Eve would tighten her lips and say nothing. As they walked up the Burma road and into Killiney Park, Benny said that it was all her fault. She hadn't understood how a man needs to make love. It's a biological thing. And when they sat by the obelisk and looked down on the bay she said that Jack Foley was the most dishonest cheating man in the whole world, and why in God's name did he keep saying he loved her if he didn't?

'Because he did love you. Or thought he did,' Eve said. 'That's the whole bloody problem.'

It cheered Benny that Eve could find some ray of hope and sincerity in the whole thing. She thought that Eve had set her heart against him.

'I'm not against him,' Eve said softly. 'I'm only against the idea of your thinking that somehow you'll get him back.'

'But if he still loves me . . .'

'He loves the idea of you, and hates hurting you. That's totally different.'

Eve put her small hand over Benny's. She wished she had better words, softer ones. But she knew that Benny mustn't sleep a night in false hopes. She pointed out that there was very little hope in a situation where one party was explaining things to an unbelieving family in Donnybrook and another in Maple Gardens.

'Why didn't I sleep with him? Then we'd be explaining things tonight in Knockglen.'

When it was dark and they got back to Dunlaoghaire, Eve said Benny should have a bath.

'I don't feel like going to bed.'

'Who said anything about that? We're going out, on the town.'

Benny looked at her friend as if she were mad. After these hours of listening and appearing to understand she must have had no realization of how Benny felt, if she suggested going out.

'I don't want to meet anyone now. I don't want to be taken out of myself.'

Eve said that wasn't the object of the outing. They were going to go everywhere and meet everyone. They were going to talk about Jack and Nan before it became gossip, and long before it appeared as an engagement announcement in the papers. Eve said that it was the only thing that could be done now. Benny must be seen to hold her head high. She didn't want to live with the sympathy vote for the rest of her life. She didn't want to be written off as someone who was let down. Let nobody be the one to tell Benny the news. Let Benny be the one to tell it everywhere.

'What you are asking is ridiculous,' Benny asked. 'Even if I could do it, everyone would still see through me. They'd know I was upset.'

'But they would never think you had been made a fool of,' Eve said, eyes burning. 'The one good thing about Jack that came out of all this is that he told you first. He told you before he told his mates and asked them for advice. He gave you the story before he gave it to his parents, to the chaplain. You must use that advantage.'

'I don't like to . . . and I suppose I keep hoping that his parents won't let him.'

'They will. When they hear the sound of shotguns coming from Nan's family and moral responsibility from the clergy. And he's a man of twenty. In a few months he won't even have to ask them.'

It was a shadowy night. She only remembered patches of it. Bill Dunne asking was it an April Fool? He couldn't believe that Jack was going to *marry* Nan Mahon. If he was going to marry anyone it should have been Benny. He said that three times in front of Benny.

Three times she answered brightly that she was far too busy becoming a tycoon in Knockglen and trying to get an Honours BA to get married.

Carmel held her hand too tightly and too sympathetically. Benny wanted to snatch it away, but she knew Carmel meant well.

'It could be all for the best, and we'll still be seeing lots of you, won't we?'

Sean said that he could be knocked over with a feather. And how was Jack going to manage as a married man, with all those years ahead of him? Perhaps he was going to give up his degree and go straight into his uncle's firm as an apprentice. And where were they going to live? The whole thing was startling in the extreme. Had Jack given any indication of what he was going to live on? And presumably a family was planned. Fairly imminently. Hence the haste. Had Jack given Benny any idea of what he was going to live on? Through clenched teeth Benny said that he hadn't.

Johnny O'Brien said he wondered where they'd done it. It gave the lie to the fact that you couldn't get pregnant in a Morris Minor.

When they lay exhausted in their beds in Dunlaoghaire, Benny said sarcastically that she hoped that Eve had found the evening worthwhile, and that it had served her purposes.

'Most certainly it has,' Eve said cheerfully. 'Firstly, you're so tired that you'd sleep standing up, and secondly you've nothing to dread going in tomorrow. They know you've survived the news. They've seen you surviving.'

Aengus Foley had a toothache. He had been given whiskey on a piece of cottonwool. But not much sympathy and no attention. His mother's voice had been sharp as she asked him to go to bed, close the door and realize that pain had to be borne in this life. It wasn't permanent, it would go, probably at the precise moment they took him to Uncle Dermot the dentist.

They seemed to want to talk to Jack interminably in the sitting room. Twice he had come down to hear what it was all about, but the voices were low and urgent, and even the phrases that he could hear he couldn't understand.

John and Lilly Foley were both white with fury as they stood in their drawing room listening to their eldest son describe how he had ruined his life.

'How could you have been so stupid?' his father said over and over again.

'You can't possibly be a father, Jack, you're only a child yourself,' said his mother with tears coming down her face. They begged, they pleaded, they cajoled. They would visit Nan's parents, they would explain about his career. How it couldn't be ruined before it had begun.

'What about her career? That has been ruined no matter what happens.' Jack's voice was flat.

'Do you want to marry her?' His father asked, exasperated.

'I don't want to marry her now, in three weeks' time, obviously I don't. But she's a wonderful girl. We made love. I was the one who wanted to, and now we have no other option.'

The pleas began again. She might like to go to England, and give the child for adoption. A lot of people did that.

'It is my child. I'm not going to give it to strangers.'

'Forgive me, Jack, but do we know that it is your child? I have to ask you this.'

'No, you don't have to ask me, but I'll answer you. Yes, I'm absolutely certain that it's my child. She was a virgin the first night I slept with her.'

Jack's mother looked away in disgust.

'And are we also absolutely sure that she *is* pregnant? It's not just a false alarm? A frightened young girl. These things can happen, believe me.'

'I'm sure they can, but not this time. She showed me the report from Holles Street. The lab test was positive.'

'I don't think you should marry her. Truly I don't. She's not even someone you've been going out with for a long time. Someone you've known, that we've all known, for years.'

'I met her on the first day in college. She's been in this house.'

'I'm not saying that she's not a very lovely girl ...' Jack's father shook his head. 'You're shocked now and frightened. Leave it. Leave it for a few weeks.'

'No, it's not fair on her. If we say we'll wait she'll think I've been persuaded to change my mind. I'm not going to let her think that.'

'And what do her parents think of all this mess ... ?'

'She's telling them tonight.'

Brian Mahon was sober. He sat at his kitchen table wordless as Nan in an even tone explained to her father, mother and two brothers that she would be getting married to Jack Foley, a law student, in three weeks' time.

She saw her mother twist her hands and bite her lip. Em's dream lay broken into a thousand pieces.

'You'll do nothing of the sort,' Brian Mahon roared.

'I think it would be better for everyone if I did.'

'If you think ... I'm going to let you ...' he began, but stopped. It was all bluster anyway. The damage had been done.

Nan sat looking at him cool and unflustered, as if she were telling him that she was going to the cinema.

'I suppose you knew all about this.' He looked at his wife.

'I deliberately didn't tell Em, so that you couldn't accuse her of covering things up,' Nan said.

'And by God there's plenty to cover. He's put you up the pole, I suppose.'

'Brian!' Emily cried.

'Well, if he has, he'll pay good and proper, for whatever we decide to do.' He looked foolish as he sat there angry and red-faced, trying to be the big man in a situation over which he had no control.

'You'll decide nothing,' Nan said to him coldly. 'I decide. And our engagement will be in the *Irish Times* on Saturday morning.'

'Janey Mac, the *Irish Times*,' Nasey said. It was the poshest of the three papers, not often seen in the Mahon household.

'While you're living in my house . . . I tell you that I make decisions.'

'Well, that's just it. I won't be living here much longer.'

'Nan, are you sure that this is what you want to do?'

Nan looked at her mother, faded and frightened. Always living her life in the shadow of someone else, a loud drunken husband, a mean-spirited employer at the hotel, a beautiful daughter whose fantasies she had built up.

Emily would never change.

'It is, Em. And it's what I'm going to do.'

'But university . . . your degree.'

'I never wanted one. You know that. We both know that. I was only going there to meet people.'

They talked, mother and daughter, as if the men didn't exist. They spoke to each other across the kitchen, across the broken dream, without any of the accusations or excuses that would be the conversation of most girls in this situation.

'But it wasn't a student you were going to meet. Not this way.'

'The other didn't work, Em. The gap was too wide.'

'And what do you expect us to do, coming home with this kind of news . . .' Brian wanted to put a stop to the conversation that he didn't even understand.

'I want to ask you a question. Are you prepared to put on a good suit and behave well for four hours at a wedding, without a drink in your hand, or are you not?'

'And if I'm not?'

'If I even *think* you're not, we'll go to Rome and get married there. I will tell everyone that my father wouldn't have a wedding for us.'

'Go on, do that then,' he taunted her.

'I will if I have to. But I know you, you'd like to blow and blow and boast to your pals and the people you sell supplies to that your daughter's having a big society wedding. You'd like to hire the clothes, because you're still a handsome man and you know it.'

Emily Mahon looked at her daughter in amazement. Unerringly she had gone for the right targets. She knew exactly how to make her father give her a wedding.

Brian would think of nothing else. No expense would be spared.

'Go home with her for the weekend,' Kit urged Eve.

'No, she has to do it on her own.'

Knockglen was quick to judge, and it was important who began to spread the story. If Benny was there saying to people that her romance with Jack Foley was a thing of the past, then no serious whispers would begin. Benny was going to have to live with enough this summer without having to live with the pity of Knockglen as well. Eve was an expert on avoiding the pity of Knockglen.

Mother was still in the shop. It was after seven, and Benny had only looked in automatically and seen her there. Benny let herself in with the key she carried on her key ring.

'Glory be to God, you put the heart across me.'

Annabel Hogan was standing on a chair trying to reach something that had slid away on the top of a cupboard. Annabel was hoping that it was some nice rolls of paper with the name Hogan's on it. Eddie had bought it years ago, but it had proved impractical to cut. It hadn't been thrown out. It might be up here covered with dust.

Benny looked up at her animated face. Perhaps when people were older they did recover from things. It was impossible to believe that this was the same listless woman who had sat by the fire with the book falling from her hand. Now she was lively and occupied, her eyes were bright and her tone had light and shade.

Benny said she was bigger, she'd reach. And true there it was, rolls of it. They threw it down on the floor. Tomorrow they would dust it, see if it was usable.

'You look tired. Was it a busy day?' Mother asked. It had been a day of heartache to walk the corridors and sit in lectures while the rumour about Jack and Nan spread like a forest fire.

Sheila actually came and offered her sympathy as one would for a bereavement. Several groups had stopped speaking as Benny approached.

But Eve had been right. Better let the other story spread too, the news that Benny was not wearing mourning. That she had been able to talk about it cheerfully. There had been no sign of either Nan or Jack in college. Benny kept thinking that Jack was going to appear by magic, all smiles, tucking his arm into hers, and that the whole thing would have been a bad dream.

Mother knew none of this, of course. But she did realize that Benny looked worn out.

She thought she knew just what would cheer her up.

'Come up and look at what Patsy and I were doing today. We've pulled around a lot of the furniture on the first floor. We thought it would be grand for your party before we get the place painted. Then you could make as much mess as you liked without having to worry about it . . . you could even have some of the boys stay here and the girls stay at Lisbeg . . .'

Benny's face was stony. She had forgotten the party. The great gathering planned for the weekend after Easter. She and Jack had talked of little else as they sat with their groups of friends over the last weeks. And all the time, every night possibly, he was saying goodbye to her and making love with Nan.

She gave a little shudder at how she had been deceived, and how he had said with his eyes full of tears that he couldn't help himself, and he was sorrier than he could ever say. She walked wordlessly up the stairs behind her mother and listened to the animated conversation about the party that would never be.

Gradually her mother, noticing no response, let her voice die away.

'They are still coming, aren't they?' she said.

'I'm not sure. A lot of things will have changed by then.' Benny swallowed. 'Jack and Nan are going to get married,' she said.

Her mother looked at her open-mouthed.

'What did you say?'

'Jack. He's going to marry Nan, you see. So things might change about the party.'

'Jack Foley . . . your Jack?'

'He's not my Jack any more. Hasn't been for some time.'

'But when did this happen? You never said a word. They can't get married.'

'They are, Mother. The engagement will be in tomorrow's *Irish Times*.'

The look on her mother's face was almost too much to bear. The naked sympathy, the total incomprehension, the struggling for words.

Benny realized that Eve was probably right in this harsh face-saving exercise. Bad as it was now, it would be worse if she had said nothing and her mother had found out through someone else. Like today in college, it was over now, the shock and the pity and the whispering. They couldn't continue indefinitely if Benny seemed to be in the whole of her senses. What was very hard was this pretence that she and Jack had been just one more casual romance, with no hearts broken at the end of it.

'Benny, I'm so sorry. I can't tell you how sorry I am.'

'That's all right, Mother. You were always the one to say that college romances come and go . . .' The words were fine, but the tone was shaky.

'I suppose she's . . .'

'She's very excited, certainly, and . . . and . . . everything.'

If her mother said the wrong thing now she would lose the little control she still held on to. Please let Mother not embrace her or say something about the fickleness of men.

Being in business for a few weeks must have taught Annabel a great deal about life.

There were just a few headshakes at the modern generation, and then a suggestion that they go home for tea before Patsy sent a search party out to look for them.

After supper she called on Clodagh. She moved restlessly around, picking things up and putting them down again as they talked. Clodagh sat and stitched, watching her carefully.

'Are you pregnant?' Clodagh asked eventually.

'I'm not the one who is, unfortunately,' Benny said. She told the tale. Clodagh never put down her needle. She nodded, and agreed, and disagreed and asked questions. At no time did she say that Jack Foley was a bastard, and that Nan Mahon was worse to betray her friend. She accepted it as one of the things that happen in life.

Benny grew stronger as she spoke. The prickling of her nose and eyes, the urge to weep, had faded a little.

'I still believe that it's me he loves,' she said timidly at the end of the saga.

'It might well be,' Clodagh was matter of fact. 'But that's not important now. It's what people do is important, not what they say or feel.'

She sounded so like Eve, so determined, so sure. In the most matter-of-fact way she said that Jack and Nan would probably make no better or no worse a fist of getting married and having a child than most people did. But that's what they would be. A couple with a child. And then another and another.

Whether Jack still loved Benny Hogan was irrelevant. He had made his choice. He had done what was called the decent thing.

'It was the right thing,' Benny said, against her will.

Clodagh shrugged. It might have been, or it might not, but whatever it was it was the thing he had done.

'You'll survive, Benny,' she said comfortingly. 'And to give him his due, which I don't want to do at this moment, he wants you to survive. He wants the best for you. He thinks that's love.'

Late that night at the kitchen table Patsy said that all men were pigs and that handsome men were out and out pigs. She said he had been well received and made welcome in this house, and that he was such a prize pig he didn't know a lady when he saw one. That Nan wasn't a lady for all her fine talk. He'd discover that when it was too late.

'I don't think it was a lady he wanted,' Benny explained. 'I think it was more a lover. And I wasn't any use to him there.'

'Nor should you have been,' Patsy said. 'Isn't it bad enough that we're going to have to do it over and over when we're married, and have a roof over our heads. What's the point in letting them have it for nothing before?'

It seemed to shed a gloomy light on the future that lay ahead for Patsy and Mossy. It was almost impossible to imagine other people having sex, but depressing to think that Patsy was dreading it so much.

Patsy poured them more drinking chocolate and said that she wished Nan not a day of luck for the rest of her life. She hoped that her baby would be born with a deformed back and a cast in its eye.

The engagement is announced between Ann Elizabeth (Nan), only daughter of Mr and Mrs Brian Mahon, Maple Gardens, Dublin and John Anthony (Jack), eldest son of Dr and Mrs John Foley, Donnybrook, Dublin.

'I saw the *Irish Times* this morning.' Sean Walsh had made it his business to exercise the two Jack Russells up and down the street until he met Benny.

'Oh yes?'

'That's a bit of a surprise, isn't it?'

'About Princess Soraya?' she asked innocently. The Shah of Persia was about to divorce his wife. There had been a lot about it in the press. Sean was disappointed. He had hoped for a better reaction, a hanging of the head. An embarrassment even.

'I meant your friend getting married?'

'Nan Mahon? That's right. You saw it in the paper. We didn't know when they'd be making it official.'

'But the man . . . she's marrying your friend.' Sean was totally confused now.

'Jack? Of course.' Benny was bland and innocent.

'I thought you and he . . .' Sean was lost for words.

Benny helped him. They had indeed been friends, even walking out . . . as people might put it. But college life was renowned for all the first-year friendships, people moved around like musical chairs. Sean looked at her long and hard. He would not be cheated of his moment of victory.

'Well, well, well. I'm glad to see that you take it so well, Benny. I must say that when I saw them here, around Knockglen, I thought it was a . . . well, a little insensitive, you know. But I didn't say anything to you. I didn't want to upset anybody.'

'I'm sure you didn't, Sean. But they weren't here. Not here around Knockglen. So you were mistaken.'

'I don't think so,' said Sean Walsh.

She thought about the way he said it. She thought about Clodagh having seen Jack at Dessie Burns' petrol pump. She thought about Johnny O'Brien wondering where they did it. But it was beyond belief. *Where* could they have gone? And if Jack loved her, how could he have come back to her home town to make love to someone else?

Somehow the weekend passed. It was hard to remember that when the phone rang it wouldn't be Jack. It was hard when Fonsie talked about the party to realize that nobody would come to it. It was hard to believe that he wouldn't be waiting in the Annexe with eyes dancing, waving her over, delighted to see her.

The hardest thing was to forget that he had said on the banks of the canal that he still loved her.

It was easy for Eve and Clodagh to dismiss that. But Benny knew Jack wouldn't have said it unless he meant it. And if he did still love her none of the other business made sense.

She didn't even allow herself to think about meeting Nan. The day would come, probably next week, when she would have to see her.

There had been conflicting stories. Nan was going to continue and finish her degree, while her mother did the babysitting. Or that Nan was going to leave immediately. That she was out already flat hunting. Benny had kept the cutting from the newspaper. She read it over and over to make it have some meaning.

John Anthony. She had known that. And even more, like that the name he took at Confirmation was Michael, so his initials were JAM Foley. She hadn't known that Nan would have been baptized Ann Elizabeth. Probably Nan had been a pet name when she was a beautiful little baby. A baby who could get what she wanted. All the time.

Perhaps she hadn't been able to get Simon Westward, and so she had taken Jack instead. How unfair of Simon not to want Nan. That's what must have happened. Benny raged at him, and his snobbery. Nan was exactly the kind of person who would have livened up Westlands. If only that romance had continued then none of this would have happened.

Benny stood behind the counter in the shop, in order to free her mother and Mike for earnest discussions on new cloth. Heather Westward came in in her St Mary's uniform.

She had come in to buy a handkerchief for her grandfather. It was a treat because he was so ill, and it would cheer him up. Was there one for under one and six? Benny found one, and wondered should it be wrapped up for him? Heather thought not. He wouldn't be able to open the wrapping paper, maybe just a bag.

'He mightn't even know what it is, but he's not well, you have to do something?' She looked at Benny for approval.

Benny thought she was right. She handed over the hand-kerchief for the old man who had shouted at Eve and called Eve's mother a whore.

He might have done the same if Simon had married Nan.

Suddenly with a jolt Benny wondered if Nan had slept with Simon.

Suppose she had. Just suppose that she had, then this baby might be his, and not Jack's after all.

Why hadn't she thought of it before?

The whole thing that looked as if it could never be solved, might in fact have a solution after all.

She looked wild-eyed at the thought of it. She saw Heather watching her in alarm.

She *must* say it to Jack. She had to. He couldn't be forced to marry someone he didn't love, when it might not be his child. No matter that he had slept with Nan. Benny would forgive him. Like she had forgiven him over that business in Wales. It wouldn't matter, just as long as he loved her.

But the feeling of excitement, the ray of hope, died down. Benny realized that she was clutching at straws. That Jack and Nan must have had this discussion. She wished she could remember how long ago it was that Nan had been talking enthusiastically about Simon, but if it was over for ages . . . then there was no hope.

And anyway Jack wouldn't be foolish enough . . .

He'd know, wouldn't he? Men always did. That's why you had to keep your virginity until you married, so that they'd know it was the first time.

No, it was just a mad, wild hope.

But suppose she believed it to be true. It would only lead to a huge confrontation, and almighty indignation if she were to suggest it to Jack. Imply that Nan was passing off someone else's child on him.

The thought had better go back to where it came from.

Heather was still in the shop. She seemed to be hovering as if about to ask a favour.

'Is there anything else, Heather?'

'You know the Easter Pageant. Eve and Aidan are going to come. It's on Holy Thursday. I was wondering would you like to come too? As part of my group.'

'Yes, yes I will, thank you.' Her mind was still far away.

'I'd have forced Simon to come, but he's in England. He mightn't even be back for Easter.'

'What's he doing there?'

'Oh, they think he's going to ask this woman to marry him. She's got pots and pots of money.'

'That would be nice.'

'We could get the drainage and the fencing done.'

'Would you mind, someone else coming in there?'

'No, I'd hardly notice.' Heather was practical.

'And this romance with the lady in England . . .' Benny enquired. 'Has it been going on for a while or is it new?'

'For ages,' Heather said. 'It's about time they made some move.'

So that was that. The wild little hope that Simon could be drawn into the whole business seemed to have faded.

Benny looked distant and abstracted. Heather had been about to tell her that there had been some great row with Nan. That Nan had come to Westlands about four weeks ago all dressed up and there had been words in the Morning Room and she had driven Simon's car to the bus and wouldn't let him come with her.

Heather remembered the date, because it was when they were casting for the Easter Pageant and she had been very nervous. If she had told Benny then, Benny would have realized that it was the very same day as the party in the rugby club. The one she hadn't gone to, but Nan had. The very night it had all begun.

Nan went to Sunday lunch at the Foleys' to meet the family. She was immaculately dressed, and Lilly thought that they would have no apologies or explanations to make for her on grounds of appearance. Her stomach was flat, and her manner was entirely unapologetic.

She came up the steps of the large Donnybrook house as of right, not as the working-class girl who had been taken advantage of by the son of the house. She spoke easily and without guile. She made no effort to ingratiate herself.

She paid more attention to Dr Foley than to his wife, which would have been the appropriate attitude of any intelligent girl coming to the house.

She was pleasant, but not effusive to Kevin, Gerry, Ronan and Aengus. She didn't forget their names or mix them up, but neither did she seek their approval.

Lilly Foley watched her with dislike, this cunning, shrewd girl with no morals who had ensnared her eldest son. There were few ways she could fault the public performance. The girl's table manners were perfect.

At coffee afterwards in the drawing room, just the four of them, Nan spoke to them with such a clear and unaffected stance that both of Jack's parents were taken aback.

'I realize what a disappointment all this must be to you, and how well you are covering this. I want to thank you very much.'

They murmured, startled words denying any sense of disappointment.

'And I am sure that Jack has told you my family are all much simpler people than you are, less educated, and in many ways their hopes for me have been realized rather than crushed. If I am to marry into such a family as yours.'

She went on to explain to them the kind of ceremony that she would like to provide and for which her father would pay. A lunch for perhaps twenty or thirty people in one of the better hotels. Very possibly the one where her mother worked in the hotel shop.

There would be minimum speech-making because her father was not a natural orator, and she thought that she would wear an oyster satin coat and dress instead of a long, white dress. She would hope that some of Jack's and her friends would attend. On her side she would provide two parents, two brothers, two business associates of her father and one aunt.

When Jack took her away on their journey for afternoon tea in Maple Gardens, John and Lilley Foley exchanged glances.

'Well?' she said.

'Well?' he answered.

He filled the silence by pouring them a small brandy each. It was never their custom to have a drink like this in the afternoon, but the circumstances seemed to call for it.

'She's very presentable,' said Jack's mother grudgingly.

'And very practical. She had the Holles Street report in her handbag, left open for us to see in case we were going to question it.'

'And very truthful about her own background.'

'But she never said one word about loving Jack,' Dr Foley said with a worried frown.

In Maple Gardens the table was set for tea. A plate of biscuits with sardines on them, another with an egg mayonnaise. There was a bought swiss roll and a plate of Jacob's USA assortment. Nasey and Paul were in navy suits and shirts. Brian Mahon wore his new brown suit. It hadn't cost as much as it should have because he had been able to give the man in the shop a few cans of paint for his own house. Cans of paint that hadn't cost anything in the first place.

'There's no need to tell all that to Jack Foley when he arrives,' Emily had warned.

'Jesus Christ, will you stop nagging at me? I've agreed to stay away from the jar until after they've been and gone, which is a fine imposition to put on a man who's going to lash out for a fancy society wedding. But still, give you lot an inch and you take a bloody mile . . .'

Jack Foley was a handsome young fellow. He sat beside Nan during afternoon tea. He tried a little of everything. He thanked Mr Mahon for the generous plans for the wedding. He thanked Mrs Mahon for all her support. He hoped Paul and Nasey would be ushers in the church.

'You'd hardly need ushers for that size of a crowd,' said Nasey, who thought twenty people was the meanest he ever heard of.

'Who's going to be your best man?' Paul asked.

Jack was vague. He hadn't thought. One of his brothers, possibly.

He felt awkward asking Aidan, what with the whole Eve and Nan friendship. And Bill Dunne or Johnny . . . it was all a bit awkward, to be honest.

He turned to Nan. 'Who'll be the bridesmaid?' he asked.

'Secret,' Nan said.

They talked about places to live, and flats. Brian Mahon said that he'd be able to give them the name of builders who did good conversion jobs if they found an old place and wanted to do it up.

Jack said that he would be working in his uncle's office, first as a clerk, and then as an apprentice. He was going to take lessons in book-keeping almost at once, in order to be of some use in there.

Several times he felt Nan's mother's eyes on him, with a look of regret.

Obviously she was upset about her daughter being pregnant, but he felt it was something more than that.

As Nan talked on cheerfully of basements in South Circular Road, or top-storey landings in Rathmines, Emily Mahon's eyes filled with tears. She tried to brush them away unseen, but Jack felt that there was some terrible sorrow there, as if she had wanted something very different for her beautiful daughter.

When they had gone Brian Mahon loosened his collar.

'You can't say too much against him.'

'I never said anything against him,' Emily said.

'He had his fun and he's paying for it. At least that's to his credit.' Brian was grudging.

Emily Mahon took off her good blouse and put on her old one automatically. She tied an apron around her waist and began to clear the table. She could puzzle for a thousand years and never understand why Nan was settling for this.

Nan and she had never wanted cheap bed-sitters, student flats, cobwebby conversion jobs. For years they had turned the pages of the magazines and looked at the places where Nan might live. There was never a moment when they planned a shotgun marriage to a student.

And Nan was adamant about saying that her relationship with Simon Westward was long over. And had never been serious. She was almost too adamant when she was telling her mother how long it had been over.

Brian changed into his normal clothes for going to the pub.

'Come on, lads, we'll get a pint and talk normally for a while.'

Emily filled the sink with hot water and did the washing-up. She was very worried indeed.

Jack and Nan sat in his father's car.

'That's the worst over,' she said.

'It'll be fine,' he assured her.

She didn't believe the worst was over, and he didn't believe everything would be fine.

But they couldn't admit it.

After all, it was there in black and white in the paper. And the chaplain would be able to give them a date very shortly.

Aidan Lynch said that Sundays weren't the same without Heather.

Eve said that he had been invited to watch Heather in a sheet helping Our Lord to carry his burden. Next week, on Holy Thursday, could he bear to come? Aidan said he'd love it, it would count as his Easter Duty. Would they bring a First Night present for Heather?

Eve said that he was worse than Heather. The thing was meant to be some kind of religious outpouring, not a song and dance act. Still it was great that he'd come down, and he could even stay the night in the cottage.

'It'll make up for us not having the party,' Eve said.

'Why won't we have the party?' Aidan asked.

Rosemary was sitting in the Annexe with Bill and Johnny. She was telling them that Tom, her medical boyfriend, had very healing hands. She refused to listen to ribald jokes on the subject. She said that she had an unmerciful headache and he had massaged it right away.

'I'm very sorry that there'll be no party now, down in Knockglen,' she said. 'I was looking forward to Tom coming and meeting you all properly.'

'Why won't there be a party?' asked Bill Dunne.

'I never heard anything about it being off,' said Johnny O'Brien.

Jack was not at his lectures now. He hadn't officially given up, but he was in his uncle's office all day. Learning the ropes. Aidan was going to meet him at six o'clock.

'He has time to go out and drink pints, has he?' Eve said disapprovingly.

'Listen, he hasn't been sent to Coventry. He's not in disgrace. He's just getting married. That's not the end of the earth,' Aidan said.

Eve shrugged.

'And what's more, I'm going to be his best man, if he asks me.'

'You're not!' She was aghast.

'He's my friend. He can rely on me. Anyone can rely on a friend.'

Nan made an appearance in college. She went to a ten o'clock lecture and then joined the crowds streaming down the stairs to the Annexe.

There was a rustle as they saw her coming to join the queue.

'Well, I'm off now,' Rosemary said under her breath to Carmel. 'If there's one thing I can't bear, it's the sight of bloodshed.'

'Benny won't say anything,' Carmel whispered back.

'Yes, but have you seen Eve's face?'

Benny was trying to calm Eve down. It was ridiculous to say that Nan didn't have a right to show her face in college. Benny begged Eve not to make a scene. What had been the point of urging her to get over everything publicly if Eve was going to ruin it all now?

'That's quite right,' Eve said suddenly. 'It was just a surge of bad temper.'

'Well, why don't you go now, in case it surges again?'

'I can't, Benny. I'd be afraid you'd be so bloody nice and ask her all about the wedding dress and offer to knit bootees.'

Benny squeezed her friend's hand. 'Go on, Eve, please. I'm better on my own. I won't do any of that. And anyway she won't join us.'

Nan went to another table. She drank her coffee with a group she knew from another class.

She looked across at Benny, who looked back.

Neither of them made a gesture or mouthed a word. Nan looked away first.

Nan lay on her bed. Jack was going out with Aidan, which

surprised her. She thought that there would be a heavy boycott from Eve's side of things.

But men were easier, more generous at forgiving. Men were more generous at everything. She lay with her feet raised on two cushions.

If Em had been a different kind of mother, she would have pursued the question she had been skirting around. Emily Mahon knew that her daughter was carrying Simon Westward's child. What she didn't know was why she, the princess, was going to let this one mistake spoil a lifetime of planning. Emily would suggest going to England, having the child adopted, and starting all over again.

The pursuit, the quest, the path to a better life. But Em didn't know that Nan was tired. Tired and weary of pretending. And that for once she had met someone, a good and honest person, who didn't have a life plan . . . a system of passing black as white. That's what she had been doing. Like Simon had been passing as rich.

Jack Foley was just himself.

When told that a child was his he accepted that it was. And when it was born, it would be theirs. She could leave university. She had made a good impression on the Foley parents. She could see that. There was a small mews at the end of their garden. In time it would be done up, in more time they would live in a house similar to his parents'. They would entertain, they would have dinner parties, she would keep in touch with her mother.

It would all be a great sense of peace compared to the never-ending contest. The game where the goalposts kept moving, and the rules changing.

Nan Mahon was going to marry Jack Foley, not just because she was pregnant, but because at the age of almost twenty she was tired.

Kit Hegarty had a lemon-coloured suit and a white blouse for her trip to Kerry.

'You need some colour to go with it. I keep forgetting we can't ask Nan.'

'Have you spoken to her at all?' Kit asked.

'Nope.'

'God, you're a tough girl. I'd hate to make you my enemy.'

The Hayes next door had come in to wish Kit well. Ann Hayes said what she needed was a big copper-coloured brooch and she had the very thing at home.

Mr Hayes looked at Kit admiringly.

'Lord bless us, Kit, but you're like a bride,' he said.

'Stop putting so much hope in this. It's only an outing.'

'Your Joseph would have been glad for you to meet another fellow. He often said.'

Kit looked at him startled. Joseph Hegarty would have said little to the Hayes, he hardly knew them.

She thanked him, but said as much.

'You're wrong, Kit. He did know us. He sent us letters for his son.'

Eve's heart chilled. Why did this man have to tell Kit now?

'He wanted to keep in touch with his boy. He wrote every month, giving his address as he moved on from place to place.'

'And Francis read these?'

'Frank read them all. He went to see him last summer when he was canning peas in England.'

'Why did he never say, why did neither of them ever say?'

'They didn't want to hurt you. The time wasn't right to tell you.'

'And why is the time right now?'

'Because Joe Hegarty wrote to me before he died. He wrote to say that if you met a good man I was to explain that you must never worry about having deprived your son of his father. Because you didn't.'

'Did he know he was going to die?'

'Sure, we're all going to die,' said Mr Hayes, as his wife came back in and pinned the brooch on Kit Hegarty's lapel.

Kit smiled, unable to speak. It was something she had been worrying a lot about lately. When she saw how close Paddy Hickey was to his sons, she wondered had she done wrong letting Francis grow up without knowing a father?

She was glad that it had been explained in front of Eve. It showed how much Eve was part of the family.

The Hayes were going to keep an eye on the house for two weeks. The outing was going to be much longer than Kit had first thought when it had been described as a weekend. And Eve would be down in Knockglen. Kit was delighted they had decided to go ahead with their party. It would be a further betrayal to admit that there could be no party now. That the stars had gone.

When Carmel's Sean had been organizing the finances, he had given some money to Jack as an advance. Jack was the one with most access to a car. Jack could get them a reduction through a wine merchant. He had been the one who was going to bring the drink. But obviously everything had changed now. And no one liked to remind Jack that he was already in possession of eleven pounds of the communal money.

Carmel's Sean suggested they should forget it. The other boys agreed. Jack had quite enough on his plate without reminding him that he owed the kitty eleven pounds.

Heather was wonderful in the pageant.

Aidan, Eve and Benny were enormously proud of her. She was a stockier, more solid, Simon of Cyrene than was normally shown by artists, but then surely they would have pulled from the crowd someone strong to help in the journey up the hill of Calvary.

Mother Francis had always urged the children to make up their own words.

Heather had been adept at this.

'Let me help you with that cross, Jesus, dear,' she said to Fiona Carroll, who was playing Our Lord with a sanctimonious face.

'It's a difficult thing to carry going uphill,' Heather added. 'It would be much easier on the flat, but then they wouldn't see the Crucifixion so well, you see.'

There was tea and biscuits in the school hall afterwards and Heather was greatly congratulated.

'It's the best Easter ever,' she said, with her eyes shining. 'And Eve says I can be a waitress at her party, next week, so long as I go home before the necking starts.'

Eve looked at Mother Francis sadly. A grown-up look of collusion, of admitting how children would hang you. Heather was unaware of anything amiss.

'Will your friend be here again?' she asked Benny.

'Which one?'

'The man that took to fancying Welsh girls for a bit, but came back.'

'He went off again,' Benny said.

'Better leave him to go then,' Heather advised. 'He sounds a bit unreliable.'

Standing there in her sheet, in the middle of the party, Heather had no idea why Eve, Aidan and Benny got such a fit of hysterical laughter, and had to wipe the tears out of their eyes. She wished she knew what she had said that was so funny, but she was glad anyway that it had pleased them all so much.

Everyone was delighted to be going to Knockglen. Not for just a party, but for a series of outings.

They would arrive on the Friday after six o'clock, when there would be drinks in Hogan's, and then they would all adjourn to Mario's for the evening. There were bunk beds and sofas and sleeping bags for the boys in Hogan's shop; the girls were going to stay in Eve's and Benny's houses. Then there would be a great trek to Ballylee for lunch and a walk in the woods on Saturday and back for the main event, the proper party in Eve's cottage.

They all said that the one at Christmas would take some beating. Eve said it would be better than ever now. An April moon, and the blossom out on the hedges and grass instead of mud around. There would be wild flowers all over the disused quarry, it would look less like a bomb site than it had done in winter. No one would slip on the mucky paths this time. They wouldn't need to huddle by the fire.

Sister Imelda was as usual aching to be asked to help with the cooking.

'It's no fun for you, Sister, if you can't see them enjoying it,' Eve pleaded.

'It's probably just as well I don't see all that goes on up there. It's enough for me to be told they like it.'

'If Simon and the woman from Hampshire come home that weekend, are you going to ask them?' Heather asked.

'No,' said Eve.

'I thought you only hated Grandfather. I thought you and Simon got on well enough.'

'We do.' Eve was dry.

'If he had married Nan, would you have come to the wedding?'

'You ask an awful lot of questions.'

'Mother Francis says we should have enquiring minds,' Heather said primly.

Eve laughed heartily. That was true. Mother Francis *had* always said it.

'I might have, if I'd been asked. But I don't think your brother would ever have married Nan.'

Heather said it would all depend whether Nan had money or not. Simon couldn't marry anyone poor because of the drainage and the fencing.

He had thought that Nan's father was a wealthy builder in the beginning. She heard a lot of this from Bee Moore, but Bee always had to stop when Mrs Walsh came in because Mrs Walsh didn't like gossip.

Heather was helping to tidy up the cottage garden. They had a big sack, which they were filling with weeds. Mossy would take it away later.

They worked easily, the unlikely friends and cousins, side by side.

Eve said that maybe they shouldn't talk too much about Nan over the weekend. She was going to marry Jack Foley shortly. Neither of them would be here. There was nothing hush hush, just better not to bring the subject up.

'Why?' Heather asked.

Eve was a respecter of the enquiring mind. As they dug the dandelions and slashed back the nettles, she told an edited version of the story. Heather listened gravely.

'I think you're taking it worse than Benny,' she said eventually.

'I think I am,' Eve agreed. 'Benny fought all my battles for me at school. And now there's nothing I can do for her. If I had my way, I'd kill Nan Mahon. I'd kill her with my bare hands.'

The night before they were all due to arrive, Benny lay in bed and couldn't sleep.

She would close her eyes and think that a lot of time had passed, but when she saw the luminous hands of the little pink clock she realized that it had only been ten minutes.

She got up and sat by her window. Out in the moonlight she saw the shape of Dr Johnson's house opposite, and the edge of Dekko Moore's, where young Heather said she was going to work as a harness maker.

What had Benny wanted when she was Heather's age, twelve? She had grown out of the wish for pink velvet dresses and pointed shoes with pom poms. What had she wanted? Maybe a crowd of friends, people that she and Eve could play with without having to be home at a special time. It wasn't very much.

And they had got it, hadn't they? A whole crowd coming down from Dublin to herself and Eve. How little you knew when you were twelve. Heather Westward wouldn't want to be a harness maker when she was twenty. She'd forget that this is what she had wanted now.

She couldn't get Jack out of her mind tonight. The weeks in between had passed by without touching her. His face was just as dear as it always was, and never more dear than when he had cried on the canal bank and told her he still loved her and that he wouldn't have had this happen for all the world.

She wondered what he and Nan talked about. Did Nan ever tell him how she had helped Benny to put on make-up, and to use good perfume? How Nan had advised Benny to hold in her tummy and push out her chest?

But it was madness to suppose that they ever talked about her at all.

Or to suppose that either of them even remembered that they had been intending to spend this weekend in Knockglen.

'What are you going to wear?' Clodagh asked her next morning.

'I don't know. I've forgotten. I can't get interested. Please, Clodagh, don't nag me.'

'Wouldn't dream of it. See you at Mario's tonight then.'

'What about up above the shop first, that's where we're starting.'

'If you can't be bothered to get dressed for it, why should I be bothered to go?'

'Damn you to Hell, Clodagh. What'll I wear?'

'Come into the shop and we'll see,' said Clodagh, smiling from ear to ear.

By six o'clock they were coming up the stairs, exclaiming

and praising. The huge rooms, the high ceilings, the lovely old windows, the davenport, the marvellous frames on the old pictures.

It was like Aladdin's Cave.

'I'd live here if I were you,' Bill Dunne said to Benny's mother. 'Not that your own house isn't terrific . . .'

'I'm half thinking about it,' Annabel Hogan said to him.

Benny felt her heart soar. The groundwork was beginning to pay off. She was afraid to smile too much. Clodagh had sewed her into a very tight country and western type bodice. She looked as if she were going to take out a guitar and give them a song. Johnny O'Brien said that she looked utterly fantastic. Fabulous figure, out-in-out, he said, showing her with his hands. Jack must be mad, he said helpfully.

They were all in high form to cross the street to rock the night away in Mario's.

Eve nudged Benny as Sean Walsh, Mrs Healy and the two Jack Russells went for an evening constitutional around the town.

Mario was delighted to see them, rather over-welcoming, Fonsie thought, until he heard that Mr Flood had been in with a message from the nun in the tree saying that his café was a den of vice and must not only be closed down, but should be exorcized as well.

Any company other than Mr Flood looked good to Mario at the moment.

Fonsie's new juke box, which Mario secretly thought looked like the product of a diseased mind, spat out the music. The tables were pushed back and those who couldn't fit in the café watched and cheered from outside.

With a mixture of regret and amazement Mario looked back on the days before his sister's son had come to work with him. The peaceful poverty-stricken days when his till hardly ever rang and most people couldn't have told you there was a chip shop and a café in Knockglen.

On Saturday Benny and Patsy fried a breakfast for Sheila, Rosemary and Carmel. Then they went up to the shop and did the same for Aidan, Bill, Johnny and the man who was always called Carmel's Sean.

'I do have an identity of my own,' he grumbled when Benny called out to know if Carmel's Sean would like one egg or two.

'In this town if your name is Sean, you'd be wise to give yourself some other handle,' Benny said. Patsy got a fit of the giggles. It was magical to be able to mock Sean Walsh in these very premises.

Slowly the day took shape. The journey to Ballylee began. Never had the countryside looked lovelier. Benny turned round in the car twice to point things out to Jack. She wondered would it take her long to remember he wasn't there. And wouldn't ever be there again.

Bill Dunne and Eve got separated from the others as they walked up to see an old folly. A summer house facing the wrong way that a family even more unused to the land than the Westwards were had built.

'Benny's fine over all this Jack business, isn't she?' Bill asked, looking for confirmation.

'Hasn't she plenty of fellows looking for her attention? Of course she's fine,' Eve was burningly loyal.

'Has she?' Bill seemed disappointed.

He told Eve that nothing had ever surprised him as much. Jack was inclined to talk, the way fellows do, the way girls did too amongst each other, he supposed. He never mentioned a word about Nan. Oh, he used to complain that Benny was a convent girl through and through which presumably meant she wouldn't go to bed with him, despite all his blandishments, and that she wasn't in Dublin enough. But not till the night of the rugby club party did Jack even go out with Nan, he knew that for a fact.

'That was only a few weeks ago,' Eve said, surprised.

'Yes, didn't the other business happen very quick?' Bill shivered in case talking about it might make him the putative father of someone's child.

'Well, it only takes once, that's what they always say.' Eve's voice was light.

'That must have been all it was.' Bill was sympathetic.

Eve changed the subject. Bill's line of thinking was dangerously near to her own. That the pregnancy had happened too suddenly.

She had not been able to pinpoint Jack and Nan's first encounter until now, and that night was only a few weeks ago. It was the night she and Benny had gone to the pictures in Dunlaoghaire. Even with Benny's poor mathematics, that was surely too soon for anything to have happened and be confirmed. Surely they would know this. Surely Jack's father, a doctor, would know?

And that meant something almost impossible to believe. It meant that Nan Mahon was pregnant with someone else's child, and had taken Benny's Jack to be its father.

Her mind was racing, but the race came to an abrupt end. The engagement was announced. The marriage date was fixed. This is what Nan and Jack were going to do. It wasn't a melodrama of blood tests and confrontations. It would go ahead, no matter what.

To cast any suspicions would only raise Benny's hope again and break her heart further.

And then there was the possibility that she could be wrong. Eve had never been sure where Simon and Nan could have made love, and had been forced to dismiss the possibility that they ever had. Westlands was out, Maple Gardens was out, so was a car. Simon had no money for hotels. Nan had no friends. None at all except Benny and Eve. She was having great difficulty in finding anyone to be her bridesmaid.

Eve had been forced reluctantly to believe that they might not have been lovers at all. Which was disappointing, as it meant there was no chance of being able to blame the pregnancy on Simon.

But then if there had been any possibility of doing that, surely Nan would have done it. She wouldn't have let a chance like that pass by.

But there had been no tales of any rows with Simon. According to all accounts, or to Nan's account, the friendship had ended amicably a long time ago.

'You're muttering to yourself,' Bill Dunne criticized her.

'It's my only unpleasant habit. Aidan says it's a tiny flaw in an otherwise perfect character. Come on, I'll race you up to the folly.'

She wanted no more of these buzzings in her mind.

The house looked beautiful. It had been well worth it to have Mossy give the door a coat of paint. And the garden was a tribute to Heather's and Eve's hard work. Heather was inside in a white chef's hat made for her by Clodagh, and a butcher's apron. It seemed excessive for passing plates of savouries, but she felt important in it. The dusk was turning to darkness. The stars were coming out in the clear sky.

Figures came up the path to the party. Teddy Flood, Clodagh Pine, Maire Carroll and her new fiancé, Tom, the medical student that Rosemary had such ferocious designs on. A few more from college who were just coming for the night rather than making a whole weekend out of it.

Aidan was explaining that tomorrow was called Low Sunday and that this was probably prophetic. With the amount they had eaten, drunk and danced, low would be exactly how they would feel.

'Keep the drink moving, will you?' Eve said. 'I have to carve this beast.'

They had a huge joint of pork boned and rolled by Teddy Flood for them. He said you'd be able to cut it like butter. Honestly, it would be like carving a swiss roll. But Eve didn't want to make a mess of it. She closed the door behind her so that she could be on her own in the kitchen.

And as she prepared the place for herself, the huge carving dish, something that Benny had found in the shop, the plates that were heating in the bottom of the range, she was concentrating so hard that she didn't hear the door open and two extra guests arrive.

Carrying bottles of wine and cans of beer, in came Jack and Nan.

Rosemary was the nearest to the door and therefore the first to see them. She let her arm drop from Tom's shoulder where it had rested all evening to mark clearly lines of possession.

'My God,' she said.

Jack smiled his easy smile. 'Not exactly. Just his deputy,' he said.

Carmel was nuzzling Sean on a bench close by. 'You didn't say they were coming,' she accused Sean in a whisper.

'I didn't bloody know,' Sean hissed back.

Johnny O'Brien was doing a complicated tango step with Sheila.

'Hey, it's the black sheep,' he called happily.

Sheila whirled around to see if she could see Benny. She was just in time to see Benny look up from where she and Bill Dunne were sorting out records. And to see the colour go out of Benny's face as she dropped three of the EPs straight from her hands.

'Thank God for the passing of the seventy-eights,' said Fonsie, whose record collection would have been the loser.

'There's a surprise,' Bill said.

Even though the music of 'Hernando's Hideaway' was thumping and thudding itself all round them, Nan and Jack must have felt the silence and the chill.

Jack's legendary smile came to his rescue.

'Now, come on, did you think I'd forgotten I said I'd get the drink?' he laughed. He had put it down on the floor, his hands were wide apart, being held out helplessly in the little gesture Benny knew and loved.

It *must* have been a dream. All of it, and now that he was back it was over.

She felt herself smiling at him.

And he saw the smile. All the way across the room.

'Hallo, Benny,' he said.

Now everyone could feel the silence. Everyone except the Johnson Brothers, who were singing 'Hernando's Hideaway'. Clodagh had dressed Benny in black and white for the party. A big black corduroy skirt, a white blouse with a black velvet trim. She looked flushed and happy at the moment that Jack saw her.

He was walking over to her.

'How's your mother and the shop?'

'Fine, going great. We had a party there last night.' She spoke too quickly. She looked over his shoulder. Aidan Lynch had taken the bottles of wine from Nan and laid them on the table. Clodagh was trying to explain to Fonsie out of the corner of her mouth.

Johnny O'Brien, who could always be relied on to say something, if not the right thing, came over and punched Jack warmly on the arm.

'It's great to see you. I thought you were barred,' he said.

Aidan poured Jack a drink. 'Jack the lad!' he said. 'Like old times.'

459

'I thought it would be silly to act as if there was a feud or something.' Jack looked only mildly anxious that he had done the right thing.

'What feud would there be?' Aidan asked, looking nervously over at where Nan stood beside the door, hardly having moved since she came in.

'Well, that's what I thought. Anyway I couldn't make off with all the money for the jar.'

They both knew it had nothing to do with the drink.

'How are things?' Aidan asked him.

'Fine. A bit unreal.'

'I know,' said Aidan, who didn't know and couldn't possibly imagine it. He thought it safer to move to different waters.

'And your uncle's office?'

'Crazy. They're all so petty, you wouldn't believe ...' Jack had his arm upon a tall chest of drawers and was talking easily. Benny had moved slightly away. She felt very hot and then very cold. She hoped she wasn't going to faint. Perhaps she could get some air.

Then she realized that Eve didn't know they were here. She must go into the kitchen and tell her.

Aidan had realized this at the same time. He had moved Fonsie in to talk to Jack and headed Benny off at the kitchen door.

'I'll do it,' he said. 'Come in to rescue me if I'm not out in an hour and there's no sign of supper.'

She gave a watery smile.

'Are you all right?' he asked, concerned.

'I'm okay.' For Benny that was like saying she was terrible. Aidan looked around him and caught Clodagh's eye. She moved over to join them.

As Aidan went into the kitchen, Clodagh said, 'She can stand there at the bloody door all night. She's got some nerve coming here, I tell you. She got short shrift from me.'

'What?'

'She said, "Hallo, Clodagh", nice as pie. I looked through her. She said it again. "Do I know you?" is what I said.' Clodagh was pleased with her repartee.

'People will have to speak to her.'

'Let them. I'm not going to.'

And indeed Nan did seem curiously isolated, while Jack was the centre of his mates.

Benny looked across the room. Nan's face, serene and beautiful as ever, looked around her in that interested, slightly questioning way. She gave no sign that she might feel unwelcome, ungreeted. She looked perfectly at ease standing just where she had come in, when Aidan had removed the wine bottles from her arms.

Benny looked at Nan as she had done so often, admiringly. Nan knew what to say, how to behave, what to wear. Tonight she was in yet another new outfit, a very flowery print, all mauve and white. It looked so fresh, you'd think it had come straight off a shop rail five minutes ago, not from a long car drive.

Benny swallowed. For the rest of her life, Nan would drive in a car with Jack, sit beside him sharing all the things that *she* had once shared. Tears of disappointment came into her eyes. Why had she not done as he asked, taken off her clothes and lain down beside him, loved him generously and warmly, responded to him, instead of buttoning herself up and moving away and saying they should be going home?

If it were Benny who was pregnant, surely he would have been pleased and proud.

He would have explained to his parents, and to her mother as he had done for Nan. Big tears welled up in her eyes at her own foolishness.

Nan saw and came towards her.

'I haven't been avoiding you,' Nan said.

'No.'

'I was going to write to you, but then we never wrote each other letters, so that would be artificial.'

'Yes.'

'And it's hard to know what to say.'

'You always know what to say.' Benny looked at her. 'And you always know what to do.'

'It was never intended to be like this. I assure you.'

There was something in Nan's voice that sounded phony. Benny realized with a shock that Nan was lying. Perhaps it was intended to be like this. That this was exactly the way Nan had planned it.

In the kitchen Eve was white-faced.

'I don't believe you,' she said to Aidan.

'Put those things down.' He looked at the carving knife and fork in her hand.

'Well, they're getting out. They're getting straight out of my house, let me tell you.'

'No, they're not, Eve.' Aidan was unexpectedly firm. 'Jack is my friend, and he is not going to be ordered out. It was always planned that he'd come here . . . he brought the drink.'

'Oh, don't be a fool,' Eve blazed. 'Nobody wanted the bloody drink. If he was that worried about it couldn't he have sent it . . . they're not welcome here.'

'They're our friends, Eve.'

'Not any more. Not now.'

'You can't keep up these things for ever. We've got to get back to normal. I think they were absolutely right to come.'

'And what are they doing inside? Lording it over everyone?'

'Eve, please. These people are your guests, our guests in a way since you and I are a couple. Please don't make a scene. It would ruin the party for everyone. They're all behaving fine in there.'

Eve went over and put her arms around Aidan.

'You're very generous, much nicer than I am. I don't think we'll work as a couple.'

'No, you're probably right. But could we sort that one at another time, not just when they're going to have their supper?'

Bill Dunne came through the kitchen to go to the bathroom.

'Sorry,' he said, as he saw Aidan and Eve in each other's arms. 'You wouldn't know where to put yourself these days.'

'All right,' Eve conceded, 'just so long as I don't have to talk to her.'

Benny was dancing with Teddy Flood when Eve went into the room. Jack was talking to Johnny and Sean. He was as handsome and assured as ever. He looked delighted to see her.

'Eve!'

'Hallo, Jack.' Unenthusiastic, but not rude. She had made a promise to Aidan. Hospitality must never be abused.

'We brought you a vase, a sort of glass jug. It would be nice for all the daffodils and everything,' he said.

It was a nice jug. How did someone like Jack Foley do the right thing so often? How did he know she had daffodils, he hadn't been here since Christmas, when there was nothing but holly in bloom.

'Thanks. That's lovely,' she said. She moved around the room, emptying ashtrays, making spaces where the plates could be put down.

Nan stood on her own on the edge of a group.

Eve couldn't bring herself to say any words of greeting. She opened her mouth, but she couldn't find anything to say. She went back to the kitchen and stood at the table leaning on both hands. The rage she felt was a real thing, you could almost take it out of her and see it, like a red mist.

She remembered how Mother Francis, and Kit Hegarty, and many a time Benny, had warned her that this temper wasn't natural. It would only hurt her in the end.

The door opened, and Nan came in. She stood there in her fresh flowery print, the breeze from the window slightly lifting her blonde hair.

'Listen, Eve . . .'

'I won't, if you don't mind. I have a meal to prepare.'

'I don't want you to hate me.'

'You flatter yourself. Nobody hates you. We despise you. That's different altogether.'

Nan's eyes flashed now. She hadn't expected this.

'That's a bit petty of you, isn't it? A bit provincial? Life goes on. Aidan and Jack are friends . . .'

She looked proud and confident. She knew she held all the winning cards. She had broken all the rules and yet she had won. Not only was she able to take away her only friend's boyfriend, find somewhere, the Lord knew where, to sleep with him, and then get him to agree to marry her, she was also expecting everything to remain the same as it had been in their social life.

Eve said nothing. She looked at her dumbfounded.

'Well, say something, Eve,' Nan was impatient. 'You must be thinking something. Say it.'

'I was thinking that Benny was probably your only friend. That of every one of us she was the only one who just liked you for being you, not just for being glamorous.'

Eve knew that this was pointless. Nan would shrug. If she physically didn't shrug her shoulders, she would mentally. She would say that these things happened.

Nan would take, she would take everything she saw. She was like a child crawling towards a shining object. She took just by instinct.

'Benny's better off. She'd have had a lifetime of watching him, of wondering.'

'And you won't?'

'I'll cope.'

'I'm sure you will, you've coped with everything.'

Eve realized she was shaking. Her hands were trembling as she filled the jug with water and started to arrange a bunch of flowers that someone else had brought.

'I chose that for you,' Nan said.

'What?'

'The vase. You don't have one.'

Suddenly Eve knew where Jack and Nan had spent their nights together. Here in this house, in her bed.

They had driven to Knockglen, come up the track, taken her key and let themselves in. They had made love in her bed.

She looked at Nan aghast. That was why she had had the feeling that someone had been in the house. The strange undefined sense of someone else's presence.

'It was here, wasn't it?'

Nan shrugged. That awful dismissive shrug. 'Yes, sometimes. What does it matter, now . . .'

'It matters to me.'

'We left the place perfect. No one would ever know.'

'You came to my house, to my bed, to take Benny's Jack in my bed. In Benny's town. Jesus Christ, Nan . . .'

Now Nan lost her temper, utterly.

'By God, I'm sick of this. I am sick of it. This Holy Joe attitude, all of you desperate to do it, playing around the edges, not having the guts or the courage, confessing it, titillating everyone still further . . .'

Her face was red and angry.

'And don't talk to me about this cottage . . . don't talk as if it was the Palace of Versailles. It's a damp, falling down shack . . . that's what it is. It hasn't electricity. It has a Stanley Range that we couldn't light for fear you'd find the traces. It has leaks and draughts, and it's no wonder they say the place is haunted. It feels haunted. It smells haunted.'

'Nobody says my house is haunted.' There were tears of rage in Eve's eyes.

Then she stopped. People had said that they heard someone playing the piano here at night.

But that was ages ago. Jack didn't play the piano. It must have been before Jack.

'You brought Simon here too, didn't you?' she said.

The memory of Simon playing the piano at Westlands came back to her. That day she had gone up there with Heather, the day the old man had cursed at her and called her mother a whore. Nan said nothing.

'You brought Simon Westward to my bed, in my house. You knew I'd never have let him over the doorstep. And you brought him in here. And then, when he wouldn't marry you, you tricked Jack Foley . . .'

Nan was suddenly pale. She looked around her at the door to the room where the others were dancing.

The music of Tab Hunter was on the record player.

'Young love, first love . . .'

'Take it easy . . . ' Nan began.

Eve had picked up the carving knife. She started to move towards her, the words came tumbling out. She couldn't control them if she tried.

'I will *not* take it easy. What you have done, by Christ, I won't take it easy.'

Nan wasn't near enough to reach the handle of the door to the sitting room. She backed away, but Eve was still moving towards her, eyes flashing and the knife in her hand.

'Eve, stop!' she cried, moving as fast as she could out of range. She lurched against the bathroom door so hard that the glass broke.

Nan fell, sliding down on the ground, and the broken glass ripped her arm. Blood spurted everywhere, even on to her face.

The dress with mauve and white print became crimson in a second. Eve dropped the knife on the floor. Her own screams were as loud as Nan's as she stood there in her kitchen amid the broken glass, the blood and the meal ready to be served, and the sound of everyone joining in the song in the room next door.

'Young love, first love, is filled with deep emotion.'

Eventually someone heard them and the door opened.

Aidan and Fonsie were in first.

'Whose car is nearest?' Fonsie asked.

'Jack's. It's outside the door.'

'I'll drive it. I know the road better.'

'Should we move her?' Aidan asked.

'If we don't she'll bleed to death in front of our eyes.'

Bill Dunne was great at keeping everyone back out of the kitchen. Only Jack, Fonsie and of course Tom, the medical student, in case he knew something the rest of them didn't, were allowed in. Everyone else should stay where they were, the place was too crowded already.

They had opened the back door. The car was only a few yards away. Clodagh had brought a rug and clean towels from Eve's bedroom. They wrapped the towel around the arm with the huge, gaping wound.

'Are we pushing the glass further in?' Fonsie asked.

'At least we're keeping the blood in,' Aidan said.

They looked at each other in admiration. Jokers yes, but when it came to the crunch, they were the ones in charge.

Benny sat motionless in the sitting room, her arm around Heather.

'It's going to be all right,' she kept saying, over and over. 'Everything's going to be all right.'

Before he got into the car Aidan came over to Eve.

'Don't let anyone go,' he warned. 'I'll be back very soon.'

'What do you mean?'

'Don't let them crawl away because they think it's expected. Give them something to eat.'

'I can't . . .'

'Then get someone else. They need food anyway.'

'Aidan!'

'I mean it. Everyone's had too much to drink. For God's sake feed them. We've no idea who'll be in on top of us now.'

'What do you mean?'

'Well, if she dies, we'll have the guards.'

'Die! She can't die.'

'Feed them, Eve.'

'I didn't . . . she fell.'

'I know, you fool.'

Then the car, with Jack, Fonsie, Aidan and a still hysterical Nan, left.

Eve straightened herself up.

'I think it's ludicrous myself, but Aidan Lynch says we should all have something to eat, so could you clear a little space and I'll bring it in,' she said.

Stricken, they obeyed her. Even though they would never have suggested it, it was exactly the right thing to do.

Dr Johnson looked at the arm and phoned the hospital.

'We're bringing someone in, severed arteries,' he said crisply. The three white faces of the boys looked at him as he hung up.

'I'll drive her,' he said. 'Just one of you. Which one?'

Fonsie and Aidan stood back, and Jack stepped forward. Maurice Johnson looked at him. His face was familiar. A junior rugby player, he had been in Knockglen before. In fact Dr Johnson had a feeling that he was meant to be Benny Hogan's boyfriend. There had been talk that she was walking out with a spectacularly handsome young man.

He wasted no time speculating. He nodded to Fonsie and Aidan and drove out of his gate.

It was an endless Sunday. The whole of Knockglen had heard that there had been a terrible accident and an unfortunate girl from Dublin had slipped and fallen, cutting herself on a glass door.

Dr Johnson had been quick to say that there wasn't any horseplay and everyone seemed to him to be stone cold sober. In fact he had no idea whether this was true or not, but he couldn't bear the tongues to wag, and Eve Malone to get further criticism for things that were beyond her control.

Dr Johnson also told everyone in sight that the girl would recover.

And recover she did. Nan Mahon was out of danger on the Sunday night. She had received several blood transfusions and there had been a time when her heartbeat had slowed down, causing alarm. But she was young and healthy. It was wonderful, the recuperative powers of the young.

Some time on the Monday night, she miscarried. But the hospital was very discreet. After all, she wasn't a married woman.

CHAPTER TWENTY

It was summer before Jack Foley and Nan Mahon had the conversation they knew that they would have to have. After her stay in the hospital in Ballylee she had gone back to Dublin.

That was at her insistence. She had seemed so agitated that Dr Johnson agreed.

Jack still worked in his uncle's office, but he studied for his first-year examination as well. There was, unspoken, the thought that he might return and do his degree in Civil Law. Aidan kept the notes from lectures.

Aidan and Jack met a lot, but they never talked about what was uppermost in their minds. Somehow it was easier to chat and be friends if they didn't mention that.

Brian Mahon wanted to sue. He said that by God people were always suing his customers for harmless jackass incidents. Why shouldn't they get a few quid out of it? That girl had to have some kind of insurance, surely?

Nan was very weak but her wound was healing, the livid red scar would fade in time.

Since she had never said aloud to her family that she was pregnant she did not have to report that this was no longer the case. She lay long hours in the bed where she had lain full of dreams.

She would not let Jack Foley come to see her.

'Later,' she had told him. 'Later, when we are able to talk.'

He had been relieved. She could see that in his eyes. She could also see he wished it to be finished, over, so that he could get on with his life.

But she wasn't ready yet. And she had had terrible injuries. He owed her all the time she needed to think about things.

'There's no sign of your fiancé,' Nasey said to her.

'It's all right.'

'Da says that if he leaves you now because of your injuries, we can sue him for breach of promise,' Nasey said.

She closed her eyes wearily.

Heather told over and over the story about the fall and the blood. She knew she would never have such an audience again. They hung on her every word. Heather aged twelve had been at a grown-ups' party wearing a chef's hat, and had seen all the blood. Nobody had taken her home or said she wasn't to look. She didn't tell them that she had felt dizzy and had cried into Benny's chest most of the time. She didn't tell them that Eve had sat white-faced, saying nothing for hours.

Eve took a long time to get over the night. She told only three people about having had the carving knife in her hand.

She told Benny, and Kit and Aidan. They had all said the same thing. They told her she hadn't touched Nan, she was only gripping it. They told her that she wouldn't have, that she would have stopped before she got near her.

Benny said that you couldn't be someone's best friend for ten years and not know that about them.

Kit said she wouldn't have anyone living in the house unless she knew what they were like. Eve would shout and rage. She wouldn't knife someone.

Aidan said the whole thing was nonsense. She had been gripping that knife all evening. Hadn't he asked her to put it down himself? He said the future mother of his eight children had many irritating qualities, but she was not a potential murderess.

Gradually she began to believe it.

Little by little she could go into her kitchen and not see in her mind's eye all that blood and broken glass.

Soon the strained look began to leave her face.

Annabel Hogan said to Peggy Pine that they would never know the full story of the night above in the cottage, no matter how much they asked. Peggy said that it was probably better not to ask any more. To think on more positive things like Patsy's wedding, like whether she should sell Lisbeg and move in over the shop. Once people heard that it might be for sale there were some very positive enquiries, and figures that would make poor Eddie Hogan turn in his grave.

'He'd turn with pleasure,' Peggy Pine said. 'He always wanted the best for the pair of you.'

It was the right thing to say. Annabel Hogan began to look at the offers seriously.

Benny found the summer term at University College was like six weeks in another city. It was so different to everything that had gone before. The days were long and warm. They used to take their books to the gardens at the back of Newman House in St Stephen's Green and study.

She always meant to ask about these gardens and who looked after them. They belonged to the university, obviously. It was peaceful there and unfamiliar. Not like almost every other square inch of Dublin, which she associated with Jack.

Some nights she stayed with Eve in Dunlaoghaire, other nights they both went home on the bus together. There was a divan couch in Eve's cottage; sometimes she spent the night up there. Mother, absorbed with plans and redecoration, seemed pleased that Benny had Eve to talk to. They called it studying, but in fact it was talking; as fuchsias started to bud, as the old roses began to bloom, the friends sat and talked. They spoke very little about Nan and Jack and what had happened. It was too soon, too raw.

'I wonder where they went,' Benny said once, out of the blue. 'A couple of people said they saw them here in Knockglen, but where could they have stayed?'

'They stayed here,' Eve said simply.

She didn't have to tell Benny that it was without her permission, and that it had broken her heart. She saw tears in Benny's eyes.

There was a long silence.

'She must have lost the baby,' Benny said.

'I expect so,' Eve said.

She found herself thinking unexpectedly of the curse her father had laid on the Westwards.

And how so many of them had indeed had such bad luck.

Could this have been more of it? A Westward not even to survive till birth?

Mr Flood was referred to a new young psychiatrist, who was apparently a very kind young man. He listened to Mr Flood endlessly, and then prescribed his medication. There were no more nuns in trees. In fact, Mr Flood was embarrassed that he

should ever have thought there were. It was decided that it should
be referred to as a trick of the light. Something that could happen
to anyone.

Dessie Burns said that what was wrong with the country was this
obsession with drink. Everyone you met was either on the jar or
off the jar. What was needed was an attitude of moderation. He
himself was going to be a moderate drinker from now on, not all
this going on tears or going off it totally. The management in
Shea's said that it all depended on your interpretation of the word
moderation, but at least Mr Burns had cut out the lunch-time
drinking and that could only be to everyone's advantage.

Knockglen was cheated of the wedding of Mrs Dorothy Healy
and Mr Sean Walsh. It was decided, they told people, that since
the nuptials would be second time around for Mrs Healy and
since Sean Walsh had no close family to speak of, they would
marry in Rome. It would be so special, and although they would
not be married by the Holy Father they would share in a blessing
for several hundred other newly married couples.

    'They couldn't rustle up ten people between them who'd come
to the wedding,' Patsy told Mrs Hogan.

    Patsy was thrilled by the decision. It would mean that her
own wedding would now have no competition.

Eve was surprised to get an invitation to Patsy's wedding. She
had expected just to go to the church to cheer her on. She realized
that of course she and Patsy would be neighbours, up on the
quarry path. She assumed that Mossy's mother had heard dire
reports of the goings-on at the party, and would look on her as
a shameless hussy who gave drunken parties. Eve didn't realize
that Mossy told his mother as little as he told anyone else. She
was getting increasingly deaf, and since she only knew about the
world what he told her, she knew remarkably little.

    She knew that Patsy was a good cook, and didn't have a
family of her own to make demands, so Patsy would be free to
look after Mossy's mother in her old age.

Mother Francis saw Dr Johnson passing the school in his car. She
was looking out of the window as she often did when the girls

were doing a test and thinking about the town. How she would hate to leave Knockglen, and go to another convent within the Order. Every year in summer the changes were announced. It was always a relief to know that she had another year where she was. Holy Obedience meant that you went without question where Mother General decided.

She hoped unworthily each year that Mother Clare would not be sent to join them. She didn't exactly pray that Mother Clare would be kept in Dublin, but God knew her views on that. Any day now they would know. It was always an unsettling couple of weeks waiting for the news.

She wondered where Dr Johnson was going, what a strange demanding life, always out to see someone being born or die or go through complicated bits in between.

Major Westward was dead when the doctor arrived. He closed the eyes, pulled a sheet over the head and sat down with Mrs Walsh. He would phone the undertakers and the Vicar, just to alert them, but first someone had better find Simon.

'I telephoned him this morning. He's on his way from England.'

'Right then. Not much more that I can do.' He stood up and reached for his coat.

'Not much loss,' he said.

'I *beg* your pardon, Dr Johnson?'

He had looked at her levelly. She was a strange woman. She liked the feeling of being in the Big House, even though it was Big rather than Grand. She would probably stay if Simon brought home a bride, grow old here, feel that her own state had been ennobled by her contact with these people.

It wasn't fair of him to be snide about the dead man. He had never liked old Westward, he had thought the man arrogant and ungiving to the village that was on his doorstep. He had found the disinheriting of Eve Malone beyond his comprehension.

But he must not tread on the sensibilities of other people. His wife had told him that a thousand times.

He decided to change his epitaph.

'Sorry, Mrs Walsh, what I said was, "What a loss, such a loss." You'll pass on my condolences to Simon, won't you?'

'I'm sure Mr Simon will telephone you, Doctor, when he gets back.'

Mrs Walsh was tight-lipped. She had heard very well what he had said the first time.

Jack Foley's parents said that he was behaving most unreasonably. What were they to think, or indeed to say? Was the wedding on or was it off? Obviously since the urgency had gone out of it and the three-week run-up time had been and gone, they could assume that she was no longer pregnant. Jack had snapped and said he couldn't possibly be expected to discuss all this with them at this early stage while Nan was still convalescing.

'I think we can be expected to know whether you now have reason to call off this rushed marriage.' His father spoke sharply.

'She had a miscarriage,' he said. 'But nothing else is clear.'

He looked so wretched they left him alone. After all their main question had been answered, the way they hoped it would be.

Paddy Hickey proposed to Kit Hegarty at a window table in a big Dunlaoghaire hotel. His hands were trembling as he asked her to marry him. He used formal words, as if a proposal was some kind of magic ritual and wouldn't work unless he asked her to do him the honour of becoming his wife.

He said that all his children knew he was going to ask her, they would be waiting, hoping for a yes, like himself. He spoke so long and in such flowery tones that Kit could hardly find a gap in the speech to say yes.

'What did you say?' he asked at length.

'I said I'd love to and I think we'll make each other very happy.'

He got up from his side of the table and came round to her, in front of everyone in the restaurant dining room he took her in his arms and kissed her.

Somehow, even in the middle of the embrace he felt that people had laid down their cutlery and their glasses to look at them.

'We're going to get married,' he called out, his face pink with pleasure.

'Thank God I'm going off to the wilds of Kerry, I'd never be able to come in here again,' said Kit, acknowledging the smiles and handshakes and even cheers of the other diners at the tables around them.

Simon Westward wondered could his grandfather possibly have known how inconvenient was the day he took to die. The arrangements with Olivia were at a crucial stage. He did not need to be summoned to a sick bed. But on the other hand, he would be in a better position to talk to her once he was master of Westlands in name as well. He tried to feel some sympathy for the lonely old man. But he feared that he had brought a lot of his misery on himself.

So, it mightn't have been easy to welcome Sarah's ill-matched husband, a handyman, to the house, but he should have made some overtures of friendship to their child.

Eve would have been a good companion for all those years. Petted and fêted in the Big House, she would not have developed that prickling resentment which was her hallmark as a result of being banished.

He didn't like thinking about Eve. It reminded him uncomfortably of that terrible day in Westlands when the old man had lashed out all around him.

And it reminded him of Nan.

Somebody had sent him a cutting from the *Irish Times*, with the notice of her engagement. The envelope had been typed. At first he thought it might have been from Nan herself, and later he decided that it was not her style to do that. She had left without a backward glance. And as far as he could see from his statement, had not cashed that cheque. He didn't know who had sent the newspaper cutting. He thought it might have been Eve.

Heather asked Mother Francis, would Eve be coming to their grandfather's funeral?

Mother Francis said that somehow she thought not.

'He used to be very nice once, he got different when he got old,' she said.

'I know,' Mother Francis said. Her own heart was heavy. Mother Clare was going to be sent to Knockglen. It was all very well for Peggy Pine to urge Mother Francis to take the whip hand, and to show her who was master, and a lot of other highly unsuitable instructions for religious life. It was going to disrupt the Community greatly. If only there was some kind of interest, some area she could find for Mother Clare to be hived off.

'Are you in a bad humour, Mother?' Heather asked.

'Oh, Lord, child, you really are Eve's cousin. You have exactly the same way she had of knowing when anything was wrong. The rest of the school could tramp past and never know anything.'

Heather looked at her thoughtfully.

'I think you should put more faith in the Thirty Days Prayer. Sister Imelda says it's never been known to fail. She did it for me when I was lost, and look at how well it turned out.'

Mother Francis sometimes worried about how Heather had latched on to some of the more complicated aspects of the Catholic faith.

Nan asked Jack to meet her.

'Where would you like?' he asked.

'You know Herbert Park. It's quite near you.'

'Is that not too far from you?' They were curiously formal.

If anyone saw this handsome couple walking there they would have assumed that this was another summer romance, and smiled at them.

There was no ring to give back. There were very few arrangements to unpick.

She told him that she was going to London. She hoped to do a course in dress designing. She wanted to be away for a while. She didn't really know exactly what she did want, but she knew what she didn't want.

She talked flatly, with no light and shade in her voice. Jack fought down the guilty, overwhelming surge of relief, that he was not going to have to marry this beautiful dead girl and spend the rest of his life with her.

When they left the small park with its bright rows of flowers and the pit-pat of people playing tennis they knew that they would probably never see each other again.

The day dawned bright and sunny for Patsy's wedding. Eve and Benny were there to help her dress. Clodagh would be down to see that those two clowns didn't get anything wrong.

Paccy Moore was going to give her away. He had said that if she wanted someone with a proper leg he wouldn't be a bit insulted, and he might make a bit of clatter with the iron going up the church, but Patsy would have no one else.

His cousin Dekko was going to be the best man, and his sister Bee the bridesmaid. It gave the appearance of a family.

The best silver was out despite Patsy saying that a couple of Mossy's cousins might be light fingered. There was chicken and ham, and potato salad, and a dozen different types of cake, and trifle and cream.

It would be a feast.

Clodagh had plucked Patsy's eyebrows and insisted on doing a make-up.

'I wonder would there be a chance that my mother might see me up in Heaven?' Patsy said.

For an instant, none of the three girls could find an answer. They found it too moving to think that Patsy would need the support of a mother she had never known, and her easy confidence that this woman was in Heaven.

Benny blew her nose loudly.

'I'm sure she can see you, and she's probably saying you look lovely.'

'God, Benny, don't blow your nose like that in the church. You'd lift half the congregation out of their seats,' Patsy warned.

Dr Johnson was driving the party up to the church.

'Good girl, Patsy,' he said, as he settled Paccy and the bride into the back of his Morris Cowley. 'You'll tear the sight out of the eyes of that old rip above.'

It was exactly the right remark, the partisan response to show Patsy that she was on the winning team, that Mossy's mother wouldn't even be a starter in the race.

Dessie Burns had abandoned moderation that morning. He tried to wave a cheery greeting at them from his front door, but it wasn't easy with a bottle in one hand and a glass in the other. He somehow went into a spin and fell down. Dr Johnson looked at him grimly. That would be his next call, stitching up that eejit's head.

It was a great wedding. Patsy had to be restrained several times from clearing up or going to the kitchen to bring out the next course.

They were waved away at four o'clock.

Dekko was going to drive them to the bus, but Fonsie said he had to drive to Dublin anyway, so he'd take them to Bray.

'Fonsie should be canonized,' Benny said to Clodagh.

'Yes, I can see his statue in all the churches. Maybe they'd even make this a special place of pilgrimage for him. We'd outsell Lourdes.'

'I mean it,' Benny said.

'Don't you think I don't know?' A rare look of softness came into Clodagh's face.

That night Mother asked Benny if she'd mind if they sold Lisbeg.

She knew she mustn't appear too eager. But she said thoughtfully that it was a good idea, there'd be money to build up the shop. It was what Father would have liked.

'We always wanted you to be married from here. That's the only thing.'

The signs of Patsy's wedding were still everywhere, the silver ornaments from the cake, the paper napkins, the confetti, the glasses around the house.

'I don't want to get married for a long, long time, Mother. I mean that.' And oddly she did.

All that pain she had felt over Jack seemed much less now.

She remembered how she had ached all over at the very thought of him and how she had wanted to be the one leaving to walk up the church to a smiling Jack Foley.

That ache was a lot less painful now.

Rosemary said that they should have a party in Dublin just to show that it wasn't only the socialites in Knockglen who could organize things. A barbecue maybe, the night their exams were over, down by White Rock, on the beach, between Killiney and Dalkey.

They'd have a huge fire, and there'd be sausages and lamb chops and great amounts of beer.

Sean and Carmel would not be in charge this time. Rosemary would do the food, and her friend Tom would collect the money. The boys started contributing.

'Will we ask Jack?' Bill Dunne said.

'Maybe not this time,' said Rosemary.

Eve and Benny were going to share a flat next year. The digs in Dunlaoghaire would be closed. They were very excited and kept looking at places now before the vacation so that they'd be ahead of the posse in September.

They were full of plans. Benny's mother would come and stay, maybe even Mother Francis might come and visit. There had been wonderful news from the convent. Mother Clare had broken her hip. Not that Mother Francis *called* it wonderful news, but it did mean that Mother Clare would need to be near a hospital and physiotherapy, and all the stairs and the walking in St Mary's wouldn't be advisable. Mother Francis was in the middle of the Thirty Days Prayer when this happened. She told Eve that it was her biggest crisis of faith yet. Could the prayer be *too* powerful?

As they left one flat they had been examining, they ran into Jack.

He looked at Benny.

'Hallo, Jack.'

Eve said she had to go, seriously, and she'd see Benny later out in Dunlaoghaire. She was gone before they could say anything.

'Would you come out with me tonight?' he asked her.

Benny looked at him. Her eyes went all around the face that she had loved so much, every line, every fold of the skin so dear to her.

'No, Jack, thank you.' Her voice was gentle and polite. She was playing no games. 'I'm going out already.'

'But that's just with Eve. She won't mind.'

'No, it's impossible. Thanks all the same.'

'Tomorrow then, or the weekend?' His head was on one side.

Benny remembered suddenly the way that his mother and father had stood on the steps of their house that night. His mother watchful and wondering.

Little things that she had learned during the past month about the Foleys made her think that this was always the way things were.

Benny didn't want to wonder and watch over Jack for the rest of her life. If she went out with him now, it would be so easy. They would be back to where they had been before. In time Nan would be forgotten like the incident in Wales had been sort of forgotten.

But she would always worry about the next one.

The next time she just wasn't around, ever smiling, always ready. It was too much to ask.

'No.' Her smile was warm.

His face was surprised and sad. More sad than surprised.

He began to say something.

'I only did what . . .' Then he stopped.

'I never meant it to . . .' He stopped again.

'It's all right, Jack,' Benny said. 'Honestly, it's all right.'

She thought she saw tears in his eyes and looked away quickly. She didn't want to be reminded of that day on the canal bank.

The firelight danced and they threw more and more logs on. Aidan had said he wondered were he and Eve leaving the conception of their eight children too late; and she assured him that they weren't, it would be wrong to rush these things. He sighed resignedly; he had known she would say this.

Rosemary was flushed and pretty, and Tom paid her the most extravagant compliments; Johnny O'Brien was in disgrace because he had whirled a blazing log and it had set fire to a great bowl of punch. The blaze had been spectacular, but the drink severely diminished.

Fonsie and Clodagh had come up from Knockglen. It would be a long time before anyone forgot their dazzling jive display on the big flat rock.

Sean and Carmel nuzzled up to each other as they had done from the beginning of time, Sheila from the law faculty had a new hair-do and a happier smile. Benny wondered why she hadn't liked her so much in the old days.

It was all over Jack, probably. Like everything had been.

The clouds that had been in front of the moon scudded past and it was almost as bright as daylight.

They laughed at each other, delighted. It was as if someone had shone a huge searchlight over them, then more clouds came and made it discreet again.

They were tired now from singing and from dancing to the little record player that Rosemary had provided. They only wanted to sing something gentle.

Not anything that would make Fonsie start to dance again. Someone started the song about 'Sailing Along on Moonlight

Bay'. Everyone groaned because it was so awful and old-fashioned, but everyone sang it because they knew the words.

Benny was leaning half against a rock and half against Bill Dunne, who was sitting beside her. Bill was so enjoying the night, and was looking after her, getting her nice bits of burned sausage on a stick and some tomato ketchup to dip it in. Bill was a great friend. You wouldn't have to spend your life watching him and wondering about him. You wouldn't have to spend the night worrying if he was having a good time or too good a time.

She was thinking how comfortable he was when she saw Jack coming down the steps.

It was very dark and to the others it might just have looked like a figure in the distance. But she knew it was Jack coming to join the summer party. Asking to belong again.

She didn't make any move. She watched him for a long time; sometimes he stopped in the shadows, as if doubtful of his welcome.

But Jack Foley would never be doubtful for long. He would know that these were his friends. The long winding steps were quite a distance from the rocks where they sat around their fire. Probably not very far, but it seemed a long time for him to cross the sand.

Long enough for her to realize how often she had seen his face everywhere. She used to see his face smiling and frowning. She used to see it like Mr Flood saw visions, up in trees and in the clouds. She used to see it in the patterns of leaves on the ground. When she woke and when she slept there was no other image in the foreground, and not because she summoned it there. It just wouldn't go away.

That was the way it had been for a very long time, when things were good and when things were bleak.

But tonight she would have difficulty in seeing his face. She would have to wait until he came in to the firelight to remember what he looked like. It was oddly restful.

They were still in full voice when someone saw Jack. The song didn't stop. They were all exaggerating the words anyway, and laughing. A few people waved to him.

He stood on the edge.

Jack Foley on the edge of things. Nobody waved him into the

centre of the group. He smiled around him, glad to be back. His nightmares brushed away, his sins, he hoped, forgiven. He seemed happy to be part of the court again. Not even his worst enemy would ever have accused him of having wanted to be king. That's just the way it had turned out.

Across the fire his eyes sought Benny. It was hard to know what he was asking her. Permission to be there? Pardon for everything that had gone before? Or the right to come and hold her in his arms?

Benny smiled the big, warm smile that had made him fall in love with her. Her welcome was real. She looked lovely in the light of the flames, and she did what no one else had done. She pointed him to where the drink was, where the long sticks lay for cooking the food. He opened a beer and moved slightly towards her. That had been an encouragement, hadn't it?

There wasn't much room on the rug where she sat leaning against Bill Dunne and the craggy bit of rock.

Nobody moved over to make space. They assumed he would sit down where he was.

After a few moments Jack Foley did that. Perched on a rock. On the edge.

Bill Dunne, who had his arm lightly around Benny's shoulder, didn't take it away because she hadn't moved as he had thought she might.

The song was over and someone had started 'Now is the Hour'. They sang in exaggerated poses and mimes, in funny accents and pretence of huge passion. Benny looked into the fire.

It was peaceful here. There would be other nights like this. More like floating along than racing along. And as she saw the sticks move and huge showers of sparks fly up to the sky over the dark hills, she couldn't see Jack's face.

All she could see were the flames and the sparks, and the long shadows out over the sand, and the edge of the sea with tiny bits of white coming in over the stones and the beach.

And the friends, all the friends sitting in a great circle, looking as if they were going to sing for ever.

Since they were into sentimentality, Fonsie said, they shouldn't overlook 'For Ever, and Ever, my Heart will be True'.

The voices soared up to the sky with the smoke and the sparks and nowhere in the sky did Benny Hogan see the face of Jack Foley.

And Benny sang with the others, knowing that Jack Foley's face was somewhere with all the faces around the fire, not taking over the whole night sky.

Silver Wedding

For Gordon Snell my dear love and my best friend.

1

Anna

Anna knew that he was doing his best to be interested. She could read his face so well. This was the same look she saw on his face when older actors would come up and join them in the club and tell old tales about people long gone. Joe tried to be interested then too, it was a welcoming, courteous, earnest look. Hoping that it passed as genuine interest, hoping that the conversation wouldn't last too long.

'I'm sorry, I'm going on a bit,' she apologized. She pulled a funny face at him as she sat at the other end of the bed dressed only in one of his shirts, the Sunday papers and a breakfast tray between them.

Joe smiled back, a real smile this time.

'No, it's nice that you're so het up about it, it's good to care about families.'

He meant it, she knew, in his heart he thought it was a Good Thing to care about families, like rescuing kittens from trees and beautiful sunsets and big collie dogs. In principle Joe was in favour of caring about families. But he didn't care at all about his own. He wouldn't have known how many years his parents were married. He probably didn't know how long he had been married himself. Something like a silver anniversary would not trouble Joe Ashe.

Anna looked at him with the familiar feeling of tenderness and fear. Tender and protective – he looked so lovely lying there against the big pillows, his fair hair falling over his face, his thin brown shoulders so relaxed and easy. Fearful in case she would lose him, in case he would move on gently, effortlessly, out of her life, as he had moved into it.

Joe Ashe never fought with people, he told Anna with his big boyish smile, life was much too short for fights. And it was true.

When he was passed over for a part, when he got a bad

review, there was the shrug – Well, so it could have been different but let's not make a production out of it.

Like his marriage to Janet – It was over, so why go on pretending? He just packed a small bag and left.

Anna feared that one day in this very room he would pack a small bag and leave again. She would rail and plead as Janet had done and it would be no use. Janet had even come around and offered Anna money to go away. She wept about how happy she had been with Joe. She showed pictures of the two small sons. It would all be fine again if only Anna would go away.

'But he didn't leave you to come to me, he had been in a flat by himself for a year before he even met me,' Anna had explained.

'Yes, and all that time I thought he would come back.'

Anna hated to remember Janet's tear-stained face, and how she had made tea for her, and hated even more to think that her own face would be stained with tears like this one day, and as unexpectedly as it had all happened to Janet. She gave a little shiver as she looked at the handsome easy boy in her bed. Because even if he was twenty-eight years of age he was still a boy. A gentle cruel boy.

'What are you thinking?' he asked.

She didn't tell him. She never told him how much she thought about him and dreaded the day he would leave.

'I was thinking it's about time they did another film version of *Romeo and Juliet*, you're so handsome it would be unfair on the world not to get a chance to look at you,' she said laughingly.

He reached out and put the breakfast tray on the floor. The Sunday papers slid after it.

'Come here to me,' said Joe. 'My mind was running on the same lines entirely, entirely at all, at all as you Irish say.'

'What a superb imitation,' Anna said drily, but snuggling up to him all the same. 'It's no wonder that you're the best actor in the whole wide world and renowned all over the globe for your great command of accents.'

She lay in his arms and didn't tell him about how worried she was about this silver wedding. She had seen from his face that she had already been going on about it far too long.

In a million years Joe would not understand what it meant in their family. Mother's and Father's twenty-fifth anniversary.

They celebrated everything in the Doyle household. There were albums of memories, boxes chronicling past celebrations. On the wall of the sitting room at home there was a gallery of Major Celebrations. The wedding day itself, the three Christenings. There was Grannie O'Hagan's sixtieth birthday, there was Grandpa Doyle's visit to London with all of them standing beside a sentry outside Buckingham Palace, a solemn young sentry in a busby who seemed to realize the importance of Grandpa Doyle's visit.

There were the three First Communions, and the three Confirmations; there was a small sporting section, Brendan's school team the year he had been on the Seniors. There was an even smaller academic section, one graduation portrait of Anna herself, very studied and posed, holding her certificate as if it were a ton weight.

Mother and Father always joked about the wall and said it was the most valuable collection in the world. What did they want with Old Masters and famous paintings, hadn't they got something much more valuable, a living wall telling the world what their life was all about?

Anna had winced whenever they said that to people who came in. She winced now lying in Joe's arms.

'Are you shuddering at me or is that passion?' he asked.

'Unbridled passion,' she said, wondering was it normal to lie beside the most attractive man in London and think not of him but of the sitting room wall back in the family home.

The family home would have to be decorated for the silver wedding. There would be a lot of cardboard bells and silver ribbon. There would be flowers sprayed with a silver paint. They would have a tape of the 'Anniversary Waltz' on the player. There would be window sills full of cards, there might indeed be so many that it would call for an arrangement of streamers with the cards attached as they had for Christmas. The cake would have traditional decorations, the invitations would have silver edges. Inviting people to what? That was what was buzzing around Anna's head. As a family this was something they should organize for their parents. Anna and her sister Helen and her brother Brendan.

But it really meant Anna.

She would have to do it all.

Anna turned towards Joe and kissed him. She would not think about the anniversary any more now. She would think about it tomorrow when she was being paid to stand in a bookshop.

She wouldn't think of it at this moment when there were far better things to think about.

'That's more like it, I thought you'd gone to sleep on me,' Joe Ashe said, and held her very close to him.

Anna Doyle worked in Books for People, a small bookshop much patronized by authors and publishers and all kinds of media. They never tired of saying that this was a bookshop with character, not like the big chains which were utterly without soul. Secretly Anna did not altogether agree.

Too many times during her working day she had to refuse people who came in with perfectly normal requests for the latest bestseller, for a train timetable, for a book on freezer cookery. Always she had to direct them to a different shop. Anna felt that a bookshop worthy of the name should in fact stock such things instead of relying for its custom on a heavy psychology section, a detailed travel list, and poetry, sociology and contemporary satire.

It wasn't as if they were even proper specialists. She had intended to leave a year ago, but that was just when she met Joe. And when Joe had come to stay it happened to coincide with Joe not having any work.

Joe did a little here and there, and he was never broke. There was always enough to buy Anna a lovely Indian scarf, or a beautiful paper flower or find the most glorious wild mushrooms in a Soho delicatessen.

There was never any money for paying the rent or for the television, or the phone or the electricity. It would have been foolish of Anna to have left a steady job without having a better one lined up for herself. She stayed in Books for People, even though she hated the name, believing that most of the buyers of books *were* people anyway. The others who worked there were all perfectly pleasant, she never saw any of them outside work but there were occasional book signings, poetry evenings and even a cheese and wine evening in aid of a small nearby theatre. That was when she had met Joe Ashe.

Anna was at work early on Monday morning. If she wanted

time to think or to write letters then to be in before the others was the only hope. There were only four of them who worked there: they each had a key. She switched off the burglar alarm, picked up the carton of milk, and the mail from the mat. It was all circulars and handbills. The postman had not arrived yet. As Anna put on the electric kettle to make coffee, she caught sight of herself in the small mirror that was stuck to the wall. Her eyes looked large and anxious, she thought. Anna stroked her face thoughtfully. She looked pale and there were definitely shadows under the big brown eyes. Her hair was tied up with a bright pink ribbon matching exactly her pink tee-shirt. She must put on a little make-up, she thought, or she would frighten the others.

She wished she had gone ahead and got her hair cut that time. It had been so strange, she had made an appointment in a posh place where some of the Royal Family went to have their hair done. One of the girls who worked there as a stylist came in to the bookshop and they had got talking. The girl said she would give Anna a discount. But the night she met Joe at the benefit evening for the theatre he had told her that her thick dark hair was beautiful the way it was.

He had asked her, as he so often did still, 'What are you thinking?' And in those very early times she told him the truth. That she was thinking about having her hair cut the following day.

'Don't even consider it,' Joe had said, and then suggested that they go to have a Greek meal and discuss this thing properly.

They had sat together in the warm spring night and he had told her about his acting and she had told him about her family. How she lived in a flat because she had thought she was becoming too dependent on her family, too drawn into everything they did. She went home of course on Sundays, and one other evening in the week. Joe had looked at her enthralled. He had never known a life where adults kept going back to the nest.

In days she was visiting his flat, days later he was visiting hers because it was more comfortable. He told Anna briefly and matter-of-factly about Janet and the two little boys. Anna told Joe about the college lecturer she had loved rather unwisely during her final years, resulting in a third-class degree and in a great sense of loss.

Joe was surprised that she had told him about the college lecturer. There was no hassle about shared property, shared children. He had only told her about Janet because he was still married to her. Anna had wanted to tell everything, Joe hadn't really wanted to hear.

It was only logical that he should come to live with her. He didn't suggest it, and for a while she wondered what she would say if she were invited to take up residence in his flat. It would be so hard to tell Mother and Father. But after one long lovely weekend, she decided to ask Joe would he not move in properly to her small ground-floor flat in Shepherd's Bush?

'Well I will, if that's what you'd like,' Joe had said, pleased but not surprised, willing but not over-grateful. He had gone back to his own place, done a deal about the rent and with two grip bags and a leather jacket over his arm he had come to live with Anna Doyle.

Anna Doyle, who had to keep his arrival very secret indeed from her mother and father who lived in Pinner and in a world where daughters did not let married men come to spend an evening let alone a lifetime.

He had been with her since that April Monday a year ago. And now it was May 1985 and by a series of complicated manoeuvres Anna had managed to keep the worlds of Pinner and Shepherd's Bush satisfactorily apart while flitting from one to another with an ever-increasing sense of guilt.

Joe's mother was fifty-six but looked years younger. She worked at the food counter of a bar where lots of actors gathered, and they saw her maybe two or three times a week. She was vague and friendly, giving them a wave as if they were just good customers. She hadn't known for about six months that they lived together. Joe simply hadn't bothered to tell her. When she heard she said, 'That's nice, dear,' to Anna in exactly the same tone as she would have spoken to a total stranger who had asked for a slice of the veal and ham pie.

Anna had wanted her to come around to the flat.

'What for?' Joe had asked in honest surprise.

Next time she was in the pub Anna went to the counter and asked Joe's mother herself.

'Would you like to come round and see us in the flat?'

'What for?' she had asked with interest.

Anna was determined. 'I don't know, a drink maybe.'

'Lord, dear, I never drink, seen enough of it in this place to turn you right against it, I tell you.'

'Well, just to see your son,' Anna went on.

'I see him in here, don't I? He's a grown-up now, love, he doesn't want to be looking at his old mum, day in day out.'

Anna had watched them since with a fascination that was half horror and half envy. They were just two people who lived in the same city, and who made easy casual conversation when they met.

They never talked of other members of the family. Nothing about Joe's sister who had been in a rehabilitation centre on account of drugs, nor the eldest brother who was a mercenary soldier of some sort in Africa, nor the youngest brother who worked in television as a cameraman.

She never asked about her grandchildren. Joe had told Anna that Janet did take them to see her sometimes, and occasionally he had taken the boys to a park nearby where his mother lived and she had come along for a little while. He never took them to her home.

'I think she has a bloke there, a young fellow, she doesn't want a lot of grandchildren trailing in to her.' To Joe it was simple and clear.

To Anna it was like something from another planet.

In Pinner if there were grandchildren they would have been the central pivot of the home, as the children had been for nearly a quarter of a century. Anna sighed again as she thought of the celebrations that lay ahead and how she would have to face up to them, as she had to face up to so many things on her own.

It was no use sitting in an empty bookshop with a coffee and a grievance that Joe wasn't as other men, supportive and willing to share these kinds of things with her. She had known there would be nothing like that from the first evening together.

What she had to do now was work out how the silver wedding could be organized in October in a way that wouldn't drive everyone mad.

Helen would be no use, that was for certain. She would send an illuminated card signed by all the sisters, she would invite Mother and Father to a special folk Mass with the Community, she would get the day off and come out to Pinner in her drab grey jumper and skirt, her hair dull and lifeless and the big cross on a chain around her neck constantly in her hand. Helen didn't even look like a nun, she looked like someone a bit dopey and badly dressed retreating behind the big crucifix. And in many ways that's what she was. Helen would turn up all right if everything was organized, and in her canvas bag she would take back any uneaten food because one nun loved gingerbread and another had a weakness for anything with salmon in it.

With a sense of despair Anna could see into the future months ahead with her younger sister Helen, a member of a religious community in South London, picking her way through the food like a scavenger and filling a biscuit tin with foil-wrapped tit-bits.

But at least Helen would be there. Would Brendan come at all? That was the real worry, and the one she had been trying to avoid thinking about. If Brendan Doyle did not get the train and boat and then the train again and make it to Pinner for his parents' twenty-fifth wedding anniversary they might as well call the whole thing off now. The disgrace would never be disguised, the emptiness would never be forgotten.

An incomplete family picture on the wall.

They would probably lie and say that he was in Ireland and couldn't be spared from the farm, the harvest or the shearing or whatever people did on farms in October.

But Anna knew with sickening clarity that it would be a paper-thin excuse. The Best Man and the Bridesmaid would know there had been a coldness, and the neighbours would know, and the priests would know.

And the shine would be taken off the silver.

How to get him back, that was the problem. Or was it? What to get him back for? Perhaps that was a bigger problem.

Brendan had always been so quiet when he was a schoolboy. Who would have known that he felt this strange longing to go away from the family to such a remote place? Anna had been so shocked the day he told them. Utterly straightforward and with no care about what it would do to the rest of the family.

'I'm not going back to school in September, it's no use trying to persuade me. I'll never get any exams, and I don't need them. I'm going to Vincent. In Ireland. I'll go as soon as I can leave.'

They had railed and beseeched. With no success. This is what he was going to do.

'But why are you doing this to us?' Mother had cried.

'I'm not doing anything to you.' Brendan had been mild. 'I'm doing it for me, it's not going to cost you any money. It's the farm where Father grew up, I thought you'd be pleased.'

'Don't think he'll make the farm over to you automatically,' Father had spluttered. 'That old recluse could just as well leave it to the missions. You could easily find you've put in all that graft for nothing.'

'Father, I'm not thinking of inheritances and wills and people dying, I'm thinking of how I'd like to spend my days. I was happy there and Vincent could do with another pair of hands.'

'Well if he does isn't it a wonder that he never married and provided himself with a few pairs of hands of his own around the place without asking strangers in to him?'

'Hardly a stranger, Father,' Brendan had said, 'I am his own flesh and blood, his brother's child.'

It had been a nightmare.

And the communication since had been minimal, cards at Christmas and on birthdays. Perhaps anniversaries. Anna couldn't remember. Anniversaries. How was she going to assemble the cast for this one?

The Bridesmaid, as they always called her, was Maureen Barry. She was Mother's best friend. They had been at school together back in Ireland. Maureen had never married, she was the same age as Mother, forty-six, though she looked younger. She had two dress shops in Dublin – she refused to call them boutiques. Perhaps Anna could talk to Maureen and see what would be best. But a warning bell went off loudly in her head. Mother was a great one for not letting things go outside the family.

There had always been secrets from Maureen.

Like the time that Father had lost his job. It couldn't be told.

Like the time that Helen ran away when she was fourteen. That was never breathed to Maureen. Mother had said that nothing mattered in the end, everything could be sorted out just so long as family matters weren't aired abroad, and neighbours and friends weren't told all of the Doyle business. It seemed to be a very effective and soothing cure when things went wrong, so the family had always stuck to it.

You would think that Anna should ring Maureen Barry now and ask her as Mother's oldest friend what was best to do about Brendan and about the anniversary in general.

But Mother would curl up and die if she thought there was the remotest possibility of any member of the family revealing a secret outside it. And the coldness with Brendan was a big secret.

There were no family members who could be asked to act as intermediaries.

So what kind of party? The day was a Saturday, it could be a lunch. There were a lot of hotels around Pinner, Harrow, Northwood, and restaurants and places used to doing functions like this. Perhaps a hotel would be best.

It would be formal for one thing, the banqueting manager would advise about toasts and cakes and photographs.

There wouldn't have to be weeks of intensive cleaning of the family home and manicuring the front garden.

But a lifetime as the eldest of the Doyles had taught Anna that a hotel would not be right. There were all those dismissive remarks about hotels in the past, destructive and critical remarks about this family who couldn't be bothered to have the thing in their own home, or the other family who would be quite glad to invite you to a common hotel, an impersonal place, but wouldn't let you over their own doorstep, thank you very much.

It would have to be home, the invitation would have to say in silver lettering that the guest was being invited to Salthill, 26 Rosemary Drive, Pinner. Salthill had been a seaside resort over in the West of Ireland where Mother and Maureen Barry used to go when they were young, it had been lovely, they said. Father had never been there, he said there was little time for long family holidays when he was a boy making his way in Ireland.

Wearily Anna made the list; it would be this size if there wasn't an Irish contingent, and that size if there were. It could be this size if there was to be a sit-down meal, that size if it were a buffet. This size if it were just drinks and snacks, that size if it were a proper meal.

And who would pay for it?

Very often the children did, she knew that.

But Helen had taken a vow of poverty and had nothing.

Brendan, even if he did come which wasn't likely, was working for an agricultural worker's wages. Anna had very little money to spend on such a party.

She had very little money indeed. By dint of hard saving, no lunches and a few wise buys at Oxfam she had saved £132. It was in the building society hoping to become £200 and then when Joe had £200 they were going to Greece together. Joe had £11 at the moment so he had a longer way to go as regards saving. But he was sure to get a part soon. His agent had said there were a lot of things coming up. He'd be working any day now.

Anna hoped that he would, she really and truly did.

If he got something good, something where they recognized him properly, something steady, then everything else could fall into place. Not just the Greek holiday but everything. He could arrange a settlement for his sons, give Janet something that would make her feel independent, he could begin the divorce proceedings. Then Anna could risk leaving Books for People and go to a bigger shop, she would easily get promotion in a large bookshop, a graduate, experienced in the trade already. They would love her.

The time had gone by in thought, and soon the keys were turning in the door and the others arriving. Soon the door was open to the public. Planning was over, yet again.

At lunch time Anna made up her mind, she would go out to Pinner that evening and ask her parents straight out how they would like to celebrate the day. It seemed less celebratory than telling them that it was all in hand. But to try and do that was nonsense really, and she could still get it wrong. She would ask them straight out.

She rang them to say she would be coming over. Her mother was pleased.

'That's good, Anna, we haven't seen you for ages and ages, I was just saying to Daddy I hope Anna's all right, and there's nothing wrong.'

Anna gritted her teeth.

'Why would there be anything wrong?'

'Well it's just been so long, and we don't know what you do.'

'Mother, it's been eight days. I was with you last weekend.'

'Yes, but we don't know how you are getting on . . .'

'I ring you almost every day, you *know* how I'm getting on and what I do, get up in Shepherd's Bush and get the tube in here, and then I go home again. That is what I do, Mother, like a great many million people in London do.' Her voice rose in rage at her mother's attitude.

The reply was surprisingly mild. 'Why are you shouting at me, Anna my dear child? I only said I was delighted you were coming over this evening, your father will be overjoyed. Will we have a little steak and mushrooms? That's what we'll have as a celebration to welcome you back. Yes, I'll run down to the butcher's this afternoon, and get it ... That's simply great you're going to come back. I can't wait to tell your father, I'll give him a ring at work now and tell him.'

'Don't ... Mother, just ... well I mean ...'

'Of course I'll tell him, give him pleasure, something to look forward to.'

When she hung up, Anna stood motionless, hand on the receiver, and thought about the one time she had brought Joe to lunch at Salthill, 26 Rosemary Drive. She had invited him as 'a friend' and had spent the entire journey making him promise not to reveal that he was (a) living with her, and (b) married to someone else.

'Which is the more dangerous one to let slip?' Joe had asked, grinning.

'They're both equally dangerous,' she had said with such seriousness that he had leaned over and kissed her on the nose in the train in front of everyone.

It had been all right as a visit, Anna had thought, Mother and Father had inquired politely about Joe's acting career and whether he knew famous actors and actresses.

In the kitchen Mother had asked was he by way of being a boyfriend?

Just a friend, Anna had insisted.

On the way home she asked Joe what he had made of them. 'Very nice but very tense people,' he had said.

Tense? Mother and Father. She had never thought of them as tense. But in a way it was true.

And Joe didn't know what they were like when there was no outsider there, Mother, wondering why Helen hadn't been there on two occasions during the week when they had telephoned her convent. Father striding around the garden snapping the heads off flowers and saying that boy was so restless and idle that he could only end up with the job of village idiot sucking straws on a small farm, it was hard to know why he had to go back to the one village in Ireland where they were known, and live with the one man in Ireland who could be guaranteed to give the worst impression of the Doyles and all their activities, his own brother, Brendan's Uncle Vincent. Just to inherit that miserable farm.

Joe had seen none of this side of things and yet he still thought her parents tense.

She had pursued it. Why? How did it show itself?

But Joe didn't want to be drawn.

'It's like this,' he had said to her, smiling to take any hurt out of his words. 'Some people just live that kind of life where this can be said and that can't be said, and people think what can be told and what can't. It's a way of going on where everything is a pretence, an act ... Now that doesn't bother me if people want to live like that. It's not my way, but people make up a lot of rules and live by them ...'

'We're not like that!' She was stung.

'I'm not criticizing you, my love. I'm just telling you what I see ... I see Hare Krishnas shaving their heads and dancing and waving bells. I see you and your family acting things out just like they do. I don't let the Hare Krishnas get up my nose, I won't let your old man and old lady either. Right?' He had grinned at her winningly.

She had grinned back with a hollow empty feeling inside her and resolved not to go on about home any more.

The day came to an end. One of the nicer publishing reps was there as the shop closed. He asked her to come and have a drink.

'I'm going to darkest Pinner,' Anna said. 'I'd better set out now.'

'I'm driving that way, why don't we have a drink en route?' he said.

'Nobody's driving to Pinner,' she laughed.

'Oh, how do you know I don't have a mistress out that way, or am hoping to acquire one?' he teased.

'We wouldn't discuss such things in Rosemary Drive,' Anna said, mock primly.

'Come on, get in, the car's on a double yellow line,' he laughed.

He was Ken Green, she had talked to him a lot at the bookshop. They had both started work the same day, it had been a common bond.

He was going to leave his company and join a bigger one, so was she; neither of them had done it.

'Do you think we're just cowards?' she asked him as he negotiated the rush-hour traffic.

'No, there are always reasons. What's holding you back, these moral folk in Rosemary Drive?'

'How do you know they're moral folk?' she said, surprised.

'You just told me there'd be no talk of mistresses in your house,' Ken said.

'Too true, they'd be very disappointed to know that I was one myself,' Anna said.

'So would I.' Ken seemed serious.

'Oh, come on out of that,' she laughed at him. 'It's always easy to pay compliments to someone you know is tied up, much safer. If I told you I was free and on the rampage you'd run a hundred miles from me instead of offering me a drink.'

'Absolutely wrong. I left your bookshop to the last specially, I was thinking all day how nice it would be to see you. Don't you accuse me of being faint-hearted, hey?'

She patted his knee companionably. 'No. I misjudged you.' She sighed deeply. It was easy to talk to Ken, she didn't have to watch what she said. Like she would when she got to Salthill in Rosemary Drive. Like she would when she got back to Joe later on.

'Was that a sigh of pleasure?' he asked.

With Joe or with Mother or Father she would have said yes.

'Weariness: I get tired of all the lies,' she said. 'Very tired.'

'But you're a big girl now, surely you don't have to tell lies about your life and the way you live it.'

Anna nodded her head glumly. 'I do, truly I do.'

'Maybe you only think you do.'

'No, I do. Like the telephone. I've told them at home that my phone has been taken out, so that they won't ring me. That's because there's a message on the answerphone saying "This is

Joe Ashe's number". He has to have it, you see, because he's an actor and they can't be out of touch.'

'Of course,' Ken said.

'So naturally I don't want my mother ringing and hearing a man's voice. And I don't want my father asking what's this young man doing in *my* flat.'

'True, he might well ask that, and why he hadn't a machine of his own and number of his own,' Ken said sternly.

'So I have to be careful about not mentioning things like paying the phone bill, I have to remember I'm not meant to *be* on the phone. That's just one of the nine million lies.'

'Well, is it all right at the other end of the line, I mean you don't have to lie to this actor chap?' Ken seemed anxious to know.

'Lie? No, not at all, what would I have to lie about?'

'I don't know, you said all the lies you had to tell everywhere. I thought maybe he was a jealous macho fellow, you couldn't tell him you went for a drink with me. That's if we ever get anywhere near a drink.' Ken looked ruefully at the tailbacks.

'Oh no, you don't understand, Joe would be glad to think I went for a drink with a friend. It's just . . .' Her voice trailed away. What was it just? It was just that there was an endless utterly endless need to pretend. Pretend she was having a good time in the odd club place where they went. Pretend she understood this casual relationship with his mother, his wife, his children. Pretend she liked these fringe theatres where he played small parts. Pretend she enjoyed lovemaking every time. Pretend she didn't care about this heavy family business ahead of her.

'I don't lie to Joe,' she said as if she were speaking to herself. 'I just act a bit.'

There was a silence in the car.

'Well, he *is* an actor, I suppose,' Ken said, trying to revive the conversation a little.

That wasn't it. The actor didn't act at all, he never pretended to please anyone else. It was the actor's girlfriend who did all the acting. How odd that she had never thought of it that way before.

They sat and talked easily when they eventually found a pub.

'Do you want to ring your people to say you've been delayed?' Ken suggested.

She looked at him, surprised that he should be so thoughtful.
'Well, if they've bought steak and everything . . .' he said.

Mother was touched. 'That was nice of you dear, Father was beginning to look out for you. He said he'd walk down to the station.'

'No, I'm getting a lift.'

'Is it that Joe? Joe Ashe the actor?'

'No, no, Mother, Ken Green, a friend from work.'

'I don't think I got enough steak . . .'

'He's not coming to supper, he's just driving me there.'

'Well, ask him in, won't you? We love to meet your friends. Your father and I often wish you brought friends back here more often. That all of you did over the years.' Her voice sounded wistful, as if she were looking at her wall of pictures and not getting a proper charge from them.

'I'll ask him in for a moment then,' Anna said.

'Could you bear it?' she asked Ken.

'I'd like it. I can be a beard.'

'What on earth is that?'

'Don't you read your gossip magazines? It's someone who distracts attention from your real love. If they get to meet upright fellows like me they won't get the wind of evil sensual actor lovers who have their answering machines tied to your phone.'

'Oh shut up,' she laughed. It was easy laughter, not forced.

They had another drink. She told Ken Green about the anniversary. She told him briefly that her sister was a nun, her brother had dropped out and gone to work on the farm of her father's eldest brother Vincent, a small rundown place on Ireland's west coast. Feeling a little lighter and easier already, she told him that this was why she was having supper with her parents. For the first time in a long while she was going to come right out in the open, ask them what they wanted, tell them the limitations. Explain the problems.

'Don't go too heavily on the limitations and problems, if they're like you say, dwell more on the celebratory side,' he advised.

'Did your parents have a silver wedding?'

'Two years ago,' Ken said.

'Was it great?' she asked.

'Not really.'

'Oh.'

'When I know you better I'll tell you all about it,' he said.

'I thought we knew each other well now?' Anna was disappointed.

'No. I need more than one drink to tell the details of my whole life.'

Anna felt unreasonably annoyed that she had told him all about Joe Ashe and about how he had to be kept a secret at home.

'I think I talk too much,' she said contritely.

'No, you're just a nicer person. I'm rather buttoned up,' Ken said. 'Come on, drink that back and we'll head for the Saltmines.'

'The what?'

'Isn't that what you said your house was called?'

Anna laughed and hit him with her handbag. He made her feel normal again. The way she had felt a long time ago when it was great to be part of the Doyle family, instead of walking through a minefield which is what it was like these days.

Mother was waiting on the step.

'I came out in case you had any difficulty parking,' she explained.

'Thanks, but it seemed to be quite clear . . . we were lucky.' Ken spoke easily.

'We haven't heard much about you, so this is a nice surprise.' Her mother's eyes were bright, too bright.

'Yes, it's a surprise for me too. I don't know Anna very well, we just talk when I go to the bookshop. I invited her for a drink this evening and as it was one of her evenings for coming to Pinner it seemed like a good chance of a drive and a chat.'

Ken Green was a salesman, Anna remembered. He earned his living selling books, getting bigger orders than booksellers wanted to give, forcing them to do window displays, encouraging them to take large cardboard presentation packs. Naturally he would be able to sell himself as well.

Her father liked him too.

Ken managed to ask the right questions, not the wrong ones. He asked easily what line of business Mr Doyle was in. Her father's usual mulish defensive look came on his face. His voice took on the familiar pitch he had when he spoke of work, and rationalization.

Most people shuffled and sort of sympathized, mixed with jollying Desmond Doyle along when he began the tale of woe, the company that had been going along very nicely thank you until in the cause of rationalization a lot of jobs, perfectly sound secure jobs, went. Desmond Doyle's job had got changed, he told Ken Green. Changed utterly. It wasn't the same breed of men in business these days.

Anna felt weary. It was always the same, Father's version of the story. The truth was that Father had been sacked over what Mother called a personality conflict. But it was a secret. A great secret nobody was to know. At school it was never to be mentioned. Anna's first great habits of secrecy must have begun then, she realized. Perhaps that was when the secrecy all began. Because a year later Father was employed again by the same firm. And that was never explained either.

Ken Green didn't mutter agreement about the world in general and the ways of businessmen in particular.

'How did you manage to survive the rationalization? Were you in some essential post?'

Anna's hand flew to her mouth. No one had been as direct as this before in this household. Anna's mother looked with alarmed glances from one face to another. There was a short pause.

'I didn't survive it; as it happens,' Desmond Doyle said. 'I was out for a year. But they brought me back, when there was a change of personnel along the line, when some personality differences had been ironed out.'

Anna's hand remained at her mouth. This was the first time that Father had *ever* acknowledged that he had been a year unemployed. She was almost afraid to see how her mother had taken it.

Ken was nodding in agreement. 'That often happens, it's something like putting all the pieces into a paper bag and shaking a few of them back on to the board. Though the pieces aren't always put back in the right holes?' He smiled encouragingly.

Anna looked at Ken Green as if she had never seen him before. What was he doing, sitting in this room interrogating her father about forbidden subjects? Was there the remotest possibility that Mother and Father would think she had discussed private business with him?

Mercifully, Father hadn't taken it at all badly; he was busy explaining to Ken that people had indeed been relocated into the wrong positions. He himself who should have Operations Manager was in fact Special Projects. Special Projects meant as little or as much as anyone wanted it to mean. It was a non-job.

'Still, that leaves it up to you to make what you will of it, that's the thing with non-jobs. I have one, Anna has one, and we try in our different ways to make something of them.'

'I have *not* a non-job!' Anna cried.

'It could be called that, couldn't it? There's no real ceiling, no proper ranking or way of getting recognition, you make it a good job because you're interested in publishing, you read the catalogues, you understand why books appear and who buys them. You could stand filing your nails like that colleague of yours with the purple hair.'

Anna's mother giggled nervously.

'Of course you're right when you're young, Ken, people have chances to make something of their job, but not when they're old ...'

'So you were all right, then.' Ken was bland.

'Come now, don't be flattering me ...'

'I wasn't.' Ken's face showed that nothing was further from his intentions. 'But you can't be more than forty-six, can you, forty-six or forty-seven?'

Anna fumed at her own stupidity, inviting this lout home.

'That's right, forty-seven next birthday,' Father was saying.

'Well, that's never old, is it? Not *old* like fifty-eight or sixty-two.'

'Deirdre, can we make that steak stretch to four pieces? This young fellow's doing me good, he has to stay for supper.'

Anna's face burned. If he said yes she would never forgive him.

'No, thank you, Mr Doyle, no, I mean it Mrs Doyle. I'm sure it would be lovely but not tonight. Thanks again. I'll just finish my drink and let you get on with your evening.'

'But it would be no trouble and we'd like to ...'

'Not tonight, Anna wants to talk to you, I know.'

'Well, I'm sure if it's anything...' Anna's mother looked wildly from her daughter to this personable young man with the dark hair and dark brown eyes. Surely Anna couldn't have come home with some announcement about him. Was the message written in her face...?

Ken put her out of her misery. 'No, it's got nothing to do with me. It's a family thing, she wants to talk about your silver wedding anniversary and how you're going to celebrate it.'

Desmond Doyle was disappointed that Ken was definitely leaving. 'Oh, that's not for months,' he said.

'Anyway, whenever it is, the main thing is that you discuss it and do what you both want, and I know that's what Anna came home to talk to you about, so I'll leave you to it.'

He was gone, there had been handshakes all round and a quick grip of Anna's arm with his other hand.

They watched him pull out into the road and he tooted his horn very gently, just an acknowledgement.

The three Doyles stood almost wordless on the doorstep of Salthill, number 26 Rosemary Drive.

Anna faced them. 'I just told him casually that we were going to make plans, I don't know why he made such a big thing out of it.'

She got the feeling that neither of her parents was listening to her.

'That wasn't the only reason I came back. I came anyway to see you both.'

Still a silence.

'And I know you won't believe it but I just said that to him because ... well, because I had to say something.'

'He's a very pleasant young man,' Desmond Doyle said.

'Good-looking too. Smartly turned out,' Deirdre Doyle added.

A wave of resentment washed over Anna. They were already comparing him favourably to Joe Ashe, Joe whom she loved with her body and soul.

'Yes,' she said in a dull voice.

'You haven't talked much about him before,' her mother said.

'I know, Mother, so you told him two seconds after you met him.'

'Don't be insolent to your mother,' Desmond Doyle said automatically.

'I'm twenty-three years of age, for Christ's sake, I'm not insolent like a child,' Anna stormed.

'I can't think what you're so upset about,' her mother said. 'We have a lovely supper for you, we ask a civil question, pass a remark about how nice your friend is, and get our heads bitten off.'

'I'm sorry.' This was the old Anna.

'Well, that's all right, you're tired after a long day. Maybe the little drinks on top of all that driving didn't agree with you.'

Anna clenched her fists silently.

They had walked back into the house and stood, an uneasy threesome, in the sitting room. They were beside the wall of family pictures.

'So what do you think we should do, eat now?' Mother looked from one to the other helplessly.

'Your mother went down to the shops especially when she heard you were coming tonight,' Father said.

For a mad moment she wished that Ken Green hadn't left after all, that he was here to drive a wedge through this woolly mass of conversation, this circular kind of talk that went nowhere. It just rose and fell, causing guilt, creating tension, and then was finally patted down.

If Ken were still here he might have said: 'Let's leave the meal for half an hour and talk about what you would really like to do for your anniversary.' Yes, those had been his very words. He hadn't said anything about what should be done or what might be expected, or what was the right way to go about it. He had said as he was leaving that Anna would want to talk to her parents about what they would both like for this day.

Like. That was a breakthrough in this family.

On an impulse she used exactly the words she thought Ken Green would say.

Startled, they sat down and looked at her expectantly.

'It's your day, it's not ours. What would *you* like best?'

'Well, really . . .' her mother began, at a loss. 'Well, it's not up to us.'

'If you all want to mark it, that would be very gratifying of course . . .' her father said.

Anna looked at them in disbelief. Did they really think that it wasn't up to them? Could they possibly live in a wonderland where they thought that life was a matter of all their children deciding to mark the occasion together? Did they not realize that in this family everything was acting . . . and that one by one the actors were slipping off the stage – Helen to her convent, Brendan to his remote rocky farm in the West of Ireland. Only Anna who lived two rail journeys away was even remotely around.

A great wave of despair came over her. She knew she must not lose her temper, that the whole visit would have been useless if it ended in a row. She could hear Joe asking her mildly why on earth she took such long wearying journeys on herself if it only ended up making them all tense and unhappy.

Joe had life worked out all right.

She felt an ache, a physical ache to be with him, and to sit on the floor by his chair while he stroked her hair.

She hadn't known it was possible to love somebody so intensely, and as she looked at the troubled man and woman sitting obediently on the sofa in front of her she wondered, had they ever known any fraction of this kind of love? You never could think of your parents expressing love, it was gross beyond imagining to think of them coupling and loving like real people did . . . like she and Joe did. But Anna knew that everyone felt that about their parents.

'Listen,' she said, 'I have to make a phone call. I want you to stop worrying about dinner for a moment, and just talk to each other about what you'd really like, then I'll start organizing it. Right?' Her eyes felt suspiciously bright, maybe the little drinks hadn't agreed with her.

She went to the phone. She would find an excuse to talk to Joe, nothing heavy, just to hear his voice would make her feel fine again. She would tell him that she'd be home a little earlier than she thought, would she get a Chinese takeaway, or a pizza or just a tub of ice cream? She wouldn't tell him now or later how bleakly depressing her old home was, how sad and low her parents made her feel, how frustrated and furious. Joe Ashe wanted to hear none of this.

She dialled her own number.

The phone was answered immediately, he must have been in the bedroom. It was a girl's voice.

Anna held the phone away from her ear like people often do in movies to show disbelief and confusion. She was aware she was doing this.

'Hallo?' the girl said again.

'What number is that?' Anna asked.

'Hang on, the phone's on the floor, I can't read it. Wait a sec.' The girl sounded good-natured. And young.

Anna stood there paralysed. In the flat in Shepherds Bush, the phone was indeed on the floor. To answer it you had to lean out of bed.

She didn't want the girl to struggle any more, she knew the number.

'Is Joe there?' she asked. 'Joe Ashe?'

'No, sorry, he went out for cigarettes, he'll be back in a few minutes.'

Why hadn't he put the answering machine on, Anna asked herself, *why* had he not automatically turned the switch, like he did always when leaving the flat? In case his agent rang. In case the call that would mean recognition came. Now the call that meant discovery had come instead.

She leaned against the wall of the house where she had grown up. She needed something to give her support.

The girl didn't like silences. 'Are you still there? Do you want to ring him back or is he to ring you or what?'

'Um . . . I'm not sure.' Anna fought for time.

If she got off the phone now, he would never know that she had found out. Things would be the same as they were, nothing would have changed. Suppose she said wrong number, or it doesn't matter, or I'll call again, the girl would shrug, hang up and maybe might not even mention to Joe that someone had called and rung off. Anna would never ask, she wouldn't disturb what they had.

But what had they? They had a man who would bring a girl to her bed, to *her* bed as soon as she was out of the house. Why try to preserve that? Because she loved him and if she didn't preserve it there would be a big screaming emptiness and she would miss him so much she would die.

Suppose she said she'd hold on, and then confront him? Would he be contrite? Would he explain that it was a fellow actress and they were just learning their lines?

Or would he say it was over? And then the emptiness and ache would begin.

The girl was anxious not to lose the call in case it might be a job for Joe.

'Hang on, I'll write down your name if you like, won't be a jiff, just let me get up, should be up anyway . . . Let's see, there's some kind of a desk over here by the window, no it's a dressing table . . . but there's an eyebrow pencil or something. Right, what's the name?'

Anna felt the bile bitter in her throat. In her bed, lying under the beautiful expensive bedspread she had bought last Christmas was a naked girl who was now going to carry the phone across to the simple table where Anna's makeup stood.

'Does the phone stretch all right?' Anna heard herself asking. The girl laughed. 'Yes it does, actually.'

'Good. Well, put it down for a moment on the chair, the pink chair, and reach up on to the mantelpiece, good, and you'll find a spiral-backed pad with a pencil attached by a string.'

'Hey?' The girl was surprised but not uneasy.

Anna continued, 'Good, put back the eye pencil, it's kohl anyway, it wouldn't write well. Now just put down for Joe: "Anna rang. Anna Doyle. No message." '

'Sure he can't ring you back?' A hint of anxiety had crept into the voice of yet another woman who was going to spend weeks, months, even years of her life trying to please Joe Ashe, say the right thing, not risk losing him.

'No, no, I'm with my parents at the moment. In fact I'll be staying here the night. Could you tell him that?'

'Does he know where to find you?'

'Yes, but there's no need to ring me, I'll catch up on him another time.'

When she had hung up she stood holding on to the table for support. She remembered telling them that the hall was the very worst place to have a telephone. It was cold, it was too public, it was uncomfortable. Now she blessed them for having taken no notice of her.

She stood for a few moments but her thoughts would not be gathered, they ran and scurried like mice around her head. Finally when she thought she had at least recovered the power of speech she went back into the room where her mother and father sat.

They who had never known the kind of love she knew nor the kind of hurt. She said that if it wouldn't put them out she'd like to stay the night, then they'd have all the time in the world to discuss the plans.

'You don't have to ask can you stay the night in your own home,' her mother said, pleased and fussing. 'I'll put a hot-water bottle in the bed just in case, the rooms are all there for you, not that any of you ever come and stay in them.'

'Well, I'd love to tonight.' Anna's smile was nailed firmly on her face.

They had got to the actual numbers that should be invited when Joe rang. She went to the phone calmly.

'She's gone,' he said.

'Has she?' Her voice was detached.

'Yes. It wasn't important.'

'No. No.'

'No need for you to stay over and make a big scene and meaning of life confrontation.'

'Oh no, none of that.'

He was nonplussed.

'So what are you going to do?' he asked.

'Stay here, as I told your friend.'

'But not for ever?'

'Of course not, just tonight.'

'Then tomorrow night after work . . . you'll be home?'

'Yes indeed, and you'll be packed.'

'Anna, don't be so dramatic.'

'Absolutely not, calmness itself. Stay there tonight of course, no, for heaven's sake there's no need to go immediately. Just tomorrow evening. Right?'

'Stop this, Anna, I love you, you love me, I'm not lying to you.'

'And neither am I to you, Joe, about tomorrow night. Truly.' She hung up.

When he called back ten minutes later, she answered the phone herself.

'Please don't be tiresome, Joe. That's a great word of yours . . . tiresome. You hate when people press you on things and ask you about things that concern them, tiresome you call it. Maybe I'm learning from you.'

'We have to talk . . .'

'Tomorrow after work. After *my* work that is, you don't have any work, do you? We can talk then for a bit like about where I'm to send your mail, and there won't be any answering machine messages so you'd better set something else up.'

'But . . .'

'I won't come to the phone again, you'll have to talk to my father, and you always said he was a nice bloke with nothing to say . . .'

She went back to the discussion. She saw that her mother and father were wondering about the phone calls.

'Sorry for the interruptions, I've been having a row with Joe Ashe, my boyfriend. It's very antisocial to bring it into this house, if he rings again I won't talk to him.'

'Is it serious, the row?' her mother asked hopefully.

'Yes, Mother, you'll be glad to know it's fairly serious as rows go. Possibly final. Now let's see what people should have to eat.'

And as she told them about a very nice woman called Philippa who ran a catering business, Anna Doyle's mind was far away. Her mind was back in the days when things had been new and exciting and when her life was filled to every corner by the presence of Joe.

It would be hard to fill up all those parts again.

She said that they could ask for sample menus and decide what they wanted. They would write to everyone in very good time, individual letters, personal letters with the invitation, that would mean it was special.

'It is special, isn't it? Twenty-five years married?' She looked from one to the other hoping for reassurance. The cosy claustrophobic sense of family that the Doyles had managed to create around them. To her surprise and regret it didn't seem to be there tonight. Mother and Father looked uncertain about whether a quarter of a century of marriage had been a good thing. This was the one time in her life that Anna needed some sense that things were permanent, that even if her own world was shifting the rest of civilization was on fairly solid ground.

But maybe she was only reading her own situation into it all, like those poets who believed in the pathetic fallacy, who thought that nature changed to suit their moods, and that skies were grey when *they* were grey.

'We'll make it a marvellous occasion,' she told her father and mother. 'It's going to be even better than your wedding day, because we're all here to help celebrate it.'

She was rewarded with two smiles and she realized it would at least be a project for the great yawning frighteningly empty summer that lay ahead of her.

2

Brendan

Brendan Doyle went to the calendar to look up the date that Christy Moore was coming to sing in the town twenty miles away. It was some time next week, and he thought he'd go in to hear him.

He had written it down on the big kitchen calendar the day he had heard it billed on the radio. To his surprise, he realized that today was his birthday. It came as a shock to think it was already eleven o'clock in the morning and he hadn't realized that it was his birthday. In the olden days he would have known it was his birthday weeks in advance.

'Only three weeks to Brendan's birthday,' his mother would chirrup to anyone who might listen.

He had hated it when he was very young, all the fuss about birthdays. The celebrations. The girls had loved it of course, wearing smart frocks. There were never any outsiders there; Brendan couldn't remember having a real party, one with other children and crackers and games, just the family all dressed up and crackers and jelly with whipped cream and hundreds and thousands on it. There would be presents from all the others, wrapped properly, with little tags, and birthday cards as well which would all be arranged on the mantelpiece. Then there would be a photograph of The Birthday Boy all on his own, maybe wearing a paper hat. And then one with the rest of the family. These would be kept in the album, and brought out triumphantly when any guests arrived. The first of the birthdays, Brendan, wasn't he getting so big? And then this was Helen's birthday, and then Anna's. Look. And people looked and praised Mother. She was marvellous they said, marvellous to do all that for them, go to so much trouble.

His mother never knew how he hated it. How he had hated the singing, and seeing her clapping her hands and running for the camera during the 'For He's a Jolly Good Fellow'.

He wished they could just sit down and get on with it instead of all these antics and actions. As if they were all on stage.

And all the secrecy too. Don't tell Auntie Maureen about the new sofa. Why? We don't want her to think that it's new. Why don't we want her to think that? We just don't want them saying we put a lot of store by it, that's all. But it's gorgeous, isn't it? Yes, but we don't want them to say that we think it's something special, when Auntie Maureen asks about it just say "Oh the sofa, it's all right", as if you weren't impressed. *You* know.'

Brendan didn't know, he had never known. They always seemed to be hiding something from somebody. From the neighbours, from people at school, from people in the parish, from Maureen Barry, Mother's great friend, from Frank Quigley who worked with Father, who was meant to be the greatest friend of the family. And specially from everyone back in Ireland. Don't tell this to Grannie O'Hagan, and never let a word of that be said in front of Grandpa Doyle.

It was quite simple to live by Mother's and Father's rules if you understood that nothing was to be said outside the family.

Brendan thought that there was very little of importance said within the family either.

He remembered his birthday the year that Father had lost his job. There had been *huge* secrecy at that stage of their lives. Father used to leave the house in the mornings at the usual time and come back again as if things were normal. What was it all for, Brendan had wondered then and wondered still.

And here in Vincent's farm, the smallholding on the side of a hill where his father had grown up, he felt even more remote from the man than he had done when he lived in Rosemary Drive pretending that he was bright at school, pretending that he was going to get A levels and go to university. When all the time he knew he was going to come back here to this stony place where nothing was expected and nothing claimed to be what it was not.

He had never been *Uncle* Vincent, even though he was the oldest of Father's brothers, he was Vincent from the start. A tall stooped man, much lined and weatherbeaten. He never spoke until he had something to speak about. There was no small talk in the small house on the side of the hill, the house where Father had grown up one of six children. They must have been very poor then. Father didn't speak of it or those times. Vincent didn't speak of any times. Although a television aerial waved from almost every small farm in the countryside hereabouts, Vincent Doyle saw no need of one. And the radio he had was small and crackly. He listened to the half-past six news every evening, and the farm report that went before it. He sometimes came across some kind of documentary on the Irish in Australia, or some account of the armies of Napoleon coming to the West of Ireland. Brendan never knew how he tracked these features down. He didn't buy a daily newspaper nor any guide to look up what was on. And he wasn't a regular enough listener to know what was being broadcast when.

He wasn't a hermit, a recluse or an eccentric. Vincent always wore suits. He had never come to terms with a world of jackets and trousers. He bought a new suit every three years, and the current one was moved down a grade, so that one day it would have been the good suit for going to Mass and the day after a new purchase it would have been relegated to a different league. It could be worn when he went to tend the sheep, and even when lifting them in and out of his trailer.

Brendan Doyle had loved this place that strange summer when they had come for the visit. Everyone had been very tense all the way over on the boat and train, and there were so many things to remember. Remember not to talk about sitting up all night on the way to Holyhead. Remember not to talk about the crowds sitting on their luggage or people would know they had gone steerage. Remember not to say that they had waited for ages on a cold platform. There were to be no complaints, it was all to have been fun. That was the message that Mother kept repeating over and over during the endless journey. Father had said almost the opposite, he had told them not to go blowing and boasting to their Uncle Vincent about all the comforts they had in London. Brendan remembered asking a direct question; he had felt slightly sick before he asked it, as if he knew it wasn't the thing to say.

'Well – which are we? Are we rich like we're pretending to Grannie O'Hagan, or are we poor like we're pretending to Uncle Vincent and Grandpa Doyle?'

There had been a great pause.

Horrified, his parents had looked at each other.

'Pretend!' they had cried almost with one voice. There was

no pretending, they protested. They had been advising the children not to gabble off things that would irritate their elders or bore them. That was all.

And Brendan remembered the first time he saw the farm. They had spent three days with Grannie O'Hagan in Dublin and then a long tiring train journey. Mother and Father seemed upset by the way things had gone in Dublin. At least the children had behaved properly, there had been no unnecessary blabbering. Brendan remembered looking out the window at the small fields of Ireland. Helen had been in disgrace for some horseplay at the station, the main evil of it was that it had been done in the presence of Grannie O'Hagan. Anna was very quiet and stuck in a book. Mother and Father talked in low voices over and over.

Nothing had prepared him for the sight of the small stone house, and the yard with the bits of broken machinery in it. At the door stood his grandfather, old and stooped, and wearing shabby old clothes, a torn jacket and no collar on his shirt. Beside him was Uncle Vincent, a taller and younger version but wearing a suit that looked as if it were respectable.

'You're welcome to your own place,' Grandpa Doyle had said. 'This is the land you children came from, it's a grand thing to have you back from all those red buses and crowds of people to walk your own soil again.'

Grandpa Doyle had been to London once on a visit. Brendan knew that because of the pictures, the one on the wall taken outside Buckingham Palace, and the many in the albums. He couldn't really remember the visit. Now as he looked at these two men standing in front of the house he felt an odd sense of having come home. Like those children's stories he used to read when an adventure was coming to an end and they were coming out of the forest. He was afraid to speak in case it would ruin it.

They had stayed a week there that time. Grandpa Doyle had been frail, and hadn't walked very much further than his front door. But Vincent had taken them all over the place. Sometimes in the old car with its bockety trailer; the trailer had not changed since that first visit. Sometimes Vincent couldn't be bothered to untackle it from the car even though there might be no need to transport a sheep, and it rattled along comfortingly behind them.

Vincent used to go off to see his sheep twice a day. Sheep had a bad habit of falling over on their backs and lying there, legs heaving in the air; you have to right them, put them the right way up.

Anna had asked was it only Uncle Vincent's sheep that did this or was it all sheep? She didn't want to speak about it when she got back to London in case it was just a habit of the Doyles' sheep. Vincent had given her a funny look but had said quite agreeably that no harm could come from admitting that sheep fell over, it was a fairly common occurrence in the breed, even in England.

Then Vincent would stop and mend walls; sheep were forever crashing through the little stone walls and dislodging bits of them, he explained. Yes, he confirmed to Anna before she had to ask, this too was a general failing in them as a species.

In the town he brought them into a bar with high stools and bought them lemonade. None of them had ever been in a public house before. Helen asked for a pint of stout but didn't get it. Vincent hadn't minded. It was the barman who had said she was too young.

Even way back then, Brendan had noticed that Vincent had never bothered to explain to people who they were; he didn't fuss and introduce them as his brother's children, explain that they were over here for a week's visit, that in real life they lived in a lovely leafy suburb of North London called Pinner, and that they played tennis at weekends in the summer. Mother and Father would have managed to tell all that to almost anyone. Vincent just went on the way he always did, talking little, replying slowly and effortlessly when he was asked a question.

Brendan got the feeling that he'd prefer *not* to be asked too many questions. Sometimes, even on that holiday, he and Vincent had walked miles together with hardly a word exchanged. It was extraordinarily restful.

He hated it when the week was over.

'Maybe we'll come back again,' he had said to Vincent as they left.

'Maybe.' Vincent hadn't sounded sure.

'Why do you think we might not?' They were leaning on a gate to the small vegetable area. There were a few drills of potatoes there and easy things like cabbage and carrots and parsnips. Things that wouldn't kill you looking after them, Vincent had explained.

'Ah, there was a lot of talk about you all coming back here, but I think it came to nothing. Not after they saw the place.'

Brendan's heart skipped.

'Coming back . . . for more than a holiday do you mean?'

'Wasn't that what it was all about?'

'Was it?'

He had seen his uncle's eyes looking at him kindly.

'Yerra, don't worry yourself, Brendan boy, just live your life the best you can, and then one day you can go off and be where people won't be getting at you.'

'When would that day be?'

'You'll know when it arrives,' Vincent had said without taking his eyes away from the few rows of potatoes.

And indeed Brendan *had* known when the day arrived.

Things changed when they went back home to London after that visit. For one thing Father got his job back, and they didn't have to pretend any more that he had a job when he hadn't. And there had been all kinds of terrible rows with Helen. She kept saying that she didn't want to be left in the house alone. She would interrogate them all each day about what time they were going out and coming back, and even if there seemed to be five minutes of unaccounted-for time, she would arrange to go and meet Brendan when school finished.

He had tried to ask her what it was all about, but she had shrugged and said she just hated being by herself.

Not that there was ever much fear of that in Rosemary Drive. Brendan would have loved some time on his own instead of all the chit-chat at mealtimes, and getting the table ready and discussing what they ate and what they would eat at the next meal. He couldn't understand why Helen didn't welcome any chance of peace with open arms.

Perhaps that was why she had gone to be a nun in the end. For peace. Or was it because she still felt the need to be with people, and she thought the numbers were dropping at Rosemary Drive, with Anna moving out to her flat and Brendan a permanent resident in Ireland?

It was strange to have lived for so long with this family, and lived so closely during weeks, months, years of endless conversation and still to know them so little.

Brendan had decided to go back to that stone cottage on the

day that his school ran a careers exhibition. There were stands and stalls giving information about careers in computing, in retailing, in the telephone service, in London Transport, in banking, in the armed forces. He wandered disconsolately from one to another.

Grandpa Doyle had died since that family visit when he welcomed them to the soil they came from. They had not gone home for the funeral. It wasn't really *home*, Mother had said, and Grandpa would have been the first to have agreed. Uncle Vincent wouldn't expect it, and there were no neighbours who would think it peculiar and talk poorly of them for not going. There had been a special Mass said for the repose of his soul in their parish church and everyone they knew from the parish sympathized.

The headmaster said that a decision about how to spend the years of one's life was a very major decision; it wasn't like choosing what cinema to go to or what football team to support. And suddenly like a vision Brendan realized that he had to get away from this, he had to escape the constant discussions and whether this was the right decision or the wrong one, and how he must tell people he was a management trainee rather than a shopworker or whatever new set of pretences would appear. He knew with the greatest clarity that he had ever possessed that he would go back to Vincent's place and work there.

Salthill, 26 Rosemary Drive, was not a house that you walked out of without explanations. But Brendan realized that these would be the very last explanations he would ever have to give. He would regard it as an ordeal by fire and water, he would grit his teeth and go through it.

It had been worse than he could ever have imagined. Anna and Helen had wept, and pleaded and begged him not to go away. His mother had wept too and asked what she had done to deserve this; his father had wanted to know whether Vincent had put him up to this.

'Vincent doesn't even know,' Brendan had said.

Nothing would dissuade him. Brendan hadn't known that he possessed such strength. For four days the battle went on.

His mother would come and sit on his bed with cups of drinking chocolate. 'All boys go through a period like this, a time of wanting to be on their own, to be away from the family apron strings. I've suggested to your father that you go on a little holiday over to Vincent, maybe that will get it all out of your system.'

Brendan had refused. It would have been dishonest. Because once he went he would not come back.

His father made overtures too. 'Listen, boy, perhaps I was a bit harsh the other night saying you were only going to try and inherit that heap of old stones, I didn't mean that to sound so blunt. But you know the way it will look. You can see how people will look at it.'

Brendan couldn't, not then, not now.

But he would never forget the look on Vincent's face when he arrived up the road.

He had walked all the way from the town. Vincent was standing with the old dog, Shep, at the kitchen door. He shaded his eyes from the evening light as Brendan got nearer, and he could make out the shape in the sunset.

'Well now,' he said.

Brendan had said nothing. He had carried a small grip bag with him, all his possessions for a new life.

'It's yourself,' Vincent had said. 'Come on in.'

At no time that evening did he ask why Brendan had come or how long he was staying. He never inquired whether they knew his whereabouts back in London, or if the visit had official approval.

Vincent's view was that all this would emerge as time went by, and slowly over the weeks and months it did.

Days came and went. There was never a harsh word between the two Doyles, uncle and nephew. In fact there were very few words at all. When Brendan thought he might go to a dance nearby, Vincent said he thought that would be a great thing altogether. He had never been great shakes at the dancing himself but he heard that it was great exercise. He went to the tin on the dresser where the money was and handed Brendan forty pounds to kit himself out.

From time to time Brendan helped himself from the tin. He had asked in the beginning, but Vincent had put a stop to that, saying the money was there for the both of them, and to take what he needed.

Things had been getting expensive, and from time to time Brendan went and did an evening's work in a bar for an extra few pounds to add to the till. If Vincent knew about it he never acknowledged it, either to protest or to praise.

Brendan grinned to himself, thinking how differently things would have been run back in Rosemary Drive.

He didn't miss them; he wondered could he ever have loved them, even a little bit? And if he hadn't loved them did that make him unnatural? Everything he read had love in it, and all the films were about love, and anything you heard of in the papers seemed to be done for love or because someone loved and that love wasn't returned. Maybe he was an odd man out, not loving.

Vincent must have been like that too, that's why he never wrote letters or talked to people intensely. That's why he liked this life here in the hills and among the stony roads and peaceful skies.

It was a bit unnatural, Brendan told himself, to become twenty-two all by yourself, without acknowledging it to another soul. If he told Vincent, his uncle would look at him thoughtfully and say 'Is that a fact?' He would offer no congratulations nor suggest a celebratory pint.

Vincent was out walking the land. He would be back in by lunch. They would have that bacon cold, and plenty of tomatoes. They would eat hot potatoes with it because a dinner in the middle of the day without a few big floury potatoes would be no use to anyone. They never ate mutton or lamb. It wasn't out of a sense of delicacy to the sheep that were their living, it was that they had no big freezer like some of their neighbours who would kill a sheep each season. And they couldn't bear to pay the prices in the butcher's shop for animals that they had sold for a greatly smaller sum than would warrant such a cost by the time they got to the butcher's cold store.

Johnny Riordan the postman drove up in his little van.

'There's a rake of letters for you, Brendan, it must be your birthday,' he said cheerfully.

'Yes it is.' Brendan had grown as taciturn as his uncle.

'Good man, will you buy us a pint later?'

'I might do that.'

The card from his father was one with a funny cat on it. Quite unsuitable from an estranged father. The word 'Father' was written neatly. No love, no best wishes. Well, that was all right.

He sent an automatic card to Father with just 'Brendan' on it each year too.

Mother's was more flowery, and said she could hardly believe she had such a grown-up son, and wondered whether he had any girlfriends and would they ever see him married.

Helen's card was full of peace and blessings. She wrote a note about the Sisters and the hostel they were going to open and the funds that were needed and how two of the Sisters were going to play the guitar busking at Piccadilly station and how the community was very divided about this and whether it was the right way to go. Helen always wrote with a cast of thousands assuming he knew all these people and remembered their names and cared about their doings. At the end she wrote, 'Please take Anna's letter seriously.'

He had opened them in the right order. He opened Anna's slowly. Perhaps it was going to tell him some bad news, Father had cancer, or Mother was going to have an operation? His face curled into a look of scorn when he saw all the business about the anniversary. Nothing had changed, simply nothing, they had got trapped in a time warp, stuck in a world of tinsel-covered cards, meaningless rituals. He felt even more annoyed about the whole thing because of Sister Helen's pious instruction to take Anna's letter seriously. Talk about passing the buck.

He felt edgy and restless as he always did when drawn into family affairs. He got up and went outside. He would walk up the hills a bit. There was a wall he wanted to look at. It might need a bit more work than just rearranging the stones like they did so often.

He came across Vincent with a sheep that had got stuck in the gate. The animal was frightened and kicking and pulling so that it was almost impossible to release her.

'You came at a good time,' Vincent said, and together they eased the anxious sheep out. She bleated frantically and looked at them with her silly face.

'What's wrong with her at all, is she hurt?' Brendan asked.

'No. Not a scratch on her.'

'Then what's all that caterwauling out of her?'

Vincent looked long at the distressed sheep. 'That's the one that lay on its lamb. Crushed the little thing to death,' he said.

'Stupid thicko sheep,' Brendan said. 'Sits on her own perfectly

good lamb, then gets stuck in a gate, that's what gives sheep a bad name.'

The ewe looked at him trustingly and gave a great baaa into the air.

'She doesn't know I'm insulting her,' Brendan said.

'Divil a bit she'd care. She's looking for the lamb.'

'Doesn't she know she suffocated it?'

'Not at all. How would she know that?' Vincent said.

Companionably the two men walked back towards the house to make their lunch.

Vincent's eyes fell on the envelopes and cards.

'Well now, it's your birthday,' he said. 'Imagine that.'

'Yes.' Brendan sounded grumpy.

His uncle looked at him for a while.

'It's good of them to remember you, it would be scant remembering you'd get if you had to rely on me.'

'I don't worry about remembering . . . not that sort.' He was still bad-tempered as he washed the potatoes at the sink and put them into the big saucepan of water.

'Will I put them up on the mantelpiece for you?'

Vincent had never said anything like that.

'No, no. I wouldn't like that.'

'All right so.' His uncle collected them neatly and left them in a little pile. He saw Anna's long typed letter but made no comment. During the meal he waited for the boy to speak.

'Anna has this notion I should go over to England and play games for some silver wedding celebrations. *Silver*,' he scoffed at the word.

'That's how many?' Vincent asked.

'Twenty-five glorious years.'

'Are they that long married? Lord, Lord.'

'You weren't at the wedding yourself?'

'God Brendan, what would take me to a wedding, I ask you?'

'They want me to go over. I'm not going next or near it.'

'Well, we all do what we want to do.'

Brendan thought about that for a long time.

'I suppose we do in the end,' he said.

They lit their cigarettes to smoke while they drank their big mugs of tea.

'And they don't want me there, I'd only be an embarrassment.

Mother would have to be explaining me to people, and why I didn't do this or look like that, and Father would be quizzing me, asking me questions.'

'Well, you said you weren't going so what's the worry about it?'

'It's not till October,' Brendan said.

'October, is that a fact?' Vincent looked puzzled.

'I know, isn't it just like them to be setting it all up now?'

They left it for a while but his face was troubled, and his uncle knew he would speak of it again.

'In a way, of course, once in a few years isn't much to go over. In a way of looking at it, it mightn't be much to give them.'

'It's your own decision, lad.'

'You wouldn't point me one way or the other, I suppose?'

'Indeed I would not.'

'It might be too expensive for us to afford the fare.' Brendan looked up at the biscuit tin, maybe this was an out.

'There's always the money for the fare, you know that.'

He did know it. He had just been hoping that they could use it as an excuse. Even to themselves.

'And I would only be one of a crowd, if I were to go it would be better to go on my own some time.'

'Whatever you say yourself.'

Outside they heard a bleating. The sheep with the foolish face, the one that had suffocated her lamb was still looking for it. She had come towards the house hoping that it might have strayed in there. Vincent and Brendan looked out the kitchen window. The sheep still called out.

'She'd have been a hopeless mother to it even if it had lived,' Brendan said.

'She doesn't know that, she's just living by some kind of instinct. She'd like to see it for a bit. To know that it's all right, sort of.'

It was one of the longest speeches his uncle had ever made. He looked at his uncle and reached out to touch him. He put his arm gently around the older man's shoulder, feeling moved to the heart by the kindness and generosity of spirit.

'I'll go off into the town now, Vincent,' he said, taking his arm away. 'I'll write a couple of letters maybe and maybe work pulling a few pints tonight.'

'There's enough in the biscuit tin,' Vincent said gently.

'There is, I know. I know.'

He went out into the yard and passed the lonely ewe still calling for her lost lamb and started up the old car to drive to the town. He would go back for their silver anniversary. It was only a little time out of this life. The life he wanted. He could give a little time to show them he was all right and that he was part of the family.

3

Helen

The old man looked at Helen hopefully. He saw a girl in her twenties with a grey jumper and skirt. Her hair was tied back in a black ribbon but it looked as if any moment it might all escape and fall wild and curly around her shoulders. She had dark blue restless eyes and freckles on her nose. She carried a black plastic shopping bag which she was swinging backwards and forwards.

'Miss,' said the old drunk, 'can you do me a favour?'

Helen stopped at once, as he had known she would. There were passers-by who went on passing by and those who stopped. Years of observation had taught him to tell one sort from the other.

'Of course, what can I do?' she asked him.

He almost stepped back. Her smile was too ready, too willing. Usually people muttered that they didn't have change or that they were in a hurry. Even if they did seem about to help a wino they didn't show such eagerness.

'I don't want any money,' he said.

'Of course not,' Helen said as if it was the last thing that a man with a coat tied with string and an empty ginger-wine bottle in his hand would want.

'I just want you to go in there and get me another bottle. The bastards say they won't serve me. They say I'm not to come into the shop. Now if I were to give you two pounds into your hand, then you could go in and get it for me.'

From his grizzled face with its wild hair above and its stubble below his small sharp eyes shone with the brilliance of the plan.

Helen bit her lower lip and looked at him hard.

He was from Ireland of course, they all were, or else Scotland. The Welsh drunks seemed to stay in their valleys, and the English didn't get drunk in such numbers or so publicly. It was a mystery.

'I think you've had enough.'

'How would you know whether I've had enough or not? That's not what we were debating. That, as it happens, was not the point at issue.'

Helen was moved, he spoke so well, he had such phrases ... the point at issue. How could a man who spoke like that have let himself go so far and turn into an outcast?'

Immediately she felt guilty about the thought. That was the way Grandmother O'Hagan would talk. And Helen would immediately disagree with her. Here she was at twenty-one thinking almost the same thing.

'It's not good for you,' she said, and added spiritedly, 'I said I'd do you a favour, it's not a favour giving you more alcohol, it's a downright disservice.'

The drunk liked such niceties and definitions, he was ready to parry with her.

'But there is no question of your *giving* me alcohol, my dear lady,' he said triumphantly. 'That was never part of our agreement. You are to act as my agent in purchasing the alcohol.' He beamed at his victory.

'No, it's only going to kill you.'

'I can easily get it elsewhere. I have two pounds and I will get it elsewhere. What we are now discussing is your word given and then broken. You said you would do me a favour, now you say you will not.'

Helen stormed into the small grocery-cum-off-licence.

'A bottle of cider,' she asked, eyes flashing.

'What kind?'

'I don't know. Any kind. That one.' She pointed to a fancy bottle. Outside, the drunk knocked on the window and shook his head of shaggy hair, trying to point to a different brand.

'You're not buying it for that wino?' asked the young man.

'No, it's for myself,' Helen said guiltily and obviously falsely. The drunk man was pointing feverishly at some brand.

'Listen, don't give it to him, lady ... I beg you.'

'Are you going to sell me this bottle of cider or are you not?' Helen could be authoritative in short bursts.

'Two pounds eighty,' the man said. Helen slapped the money, *her* money, down on the counter, and in an equally bad temper the bottle was shoved into a plastic bag for her.

'Now,' Helen said. 'Did I or did I not do what you asked me?'

'You did not, that's only rat's piss, that stuff, fancy bottles for the carriage trade. I'm not drinking that.'

'Well don't then.' There were tears starting in her eyes.

'And what's more I'm not spending my good money on it.'

'Have it as a present.' She was weary.

'Oh high and mighty, Lady Muck,' he said. He had a good quarter of it drunk from the neck by this stage. He was holding it still by its plastic carrier bag.

Helen didn't like the look of his face, the man was working himself up into some kind of temper, or even fit. She looked at him alarmed, and saw a huge amount of the despised cider vanishing down his throat.

'The urine of rodents,' he shouted. 'Bottled by these creeps of shopkeepers and dignified with the name of alcohol.'

He banged on the window again loudly. 'Come out, you cheat and rogue, come out here and justify this garbage.'

There were vegetable boxes piled neatly with apples and oranges, with potatoes loose and mushrooms in baskets. The man with the near-empty cider bottle began to turn them over on to the street systematically.

The staff ran from the shop; two of them held him, another went for the law.

'Thank you very much,' said the boy who had served Helen. 'That was a very nice day's work.'

'You wouldn't bloody listen to me,' shouted the man, who had foam flecks at the side of his mouth by now.

'Her sort don't listen to anyone, mate,' said the irate shopkeeper who was trying to immobilize him.

Helen moved from the scene awkwardly. She walked away almost sideways as if she were trying not to turn her back on the chaos and distress she had created. But then this happened so often.

It was always happening, Helen found, everywhere she went.

Back in the convent she wouldn't say anything to Sister Brigid about it. It would be so easily misunderstood. The sisters wouldn't grasp that it would all have happened anyway. The man might have got even more violent and upset if nobody had bought him the drink. He might have broken the window or hurt someone.

But Helen wouldn't tell the upsetting tale. Brigid would be bound to look at her sadly and wonder why trouble seemed to follow Helen Doyle wherever she went.

It might even put further away the day when they would allow Helen to take her vows and become a member of the Community rather than just a hanger-on. How much did she have to prove? Why did Sister Brigid keep putting off the time when Helen should be considered seriously as one of their Community? She worked as hard as any of them, she had been with them for three years and still there was this feeling that it was somehow a passing whim.

Even the most minor and accidental events made them see Helen as unstable in some way. It was terribly unfair and she wouldn't add to the long list by telling them about the confusion she was walking away from. Somehow it would be seen as her fault.

Instead she would think about the silver wedding celebrations and what she could do best to help.

Well obviously she hadn't any money or anything so there could be nothing expected from her on that score. And as well as the vow of poverty that she had taken – or to be more honest was trying to take – she was a bit unworldly these days, she had left the mainstream of everyday life. And even if she did go out to work each day, as all the Sisters did, she didn't see the side of life that Mother and Anna would be concentrating on, the more material end of things. And she wouldn't be any good rounding up neighbours and friends. Perhaps she could see whether they might have a special Mass or Liturgy . . . But Helen was doubtful whether the old priest in the parish church where the Doyles went was going to be well up on the modern liturgy of renewal.

Better leave it to Anna who had plenty of time for all that sort of thing. Anna got so tetchy often when Helen did things to help, it was often better to do nothing, to say in a calm voice, Yes Anna, No Anna, Three Bags Full Anna. This is what Brigid would suggest. Brigid was very big on the calm voice. Or on Helen's developing it. It often sounded like blandness, and even hypocrisy to Helen, but Brigid said that it was what the world in general seemed to want. And there were times when Helen thought gloomily that she might be right.

Certainly Mother always wanted things underplayed and understated, and in most cases not mentioned at all. Mother would like not so much calm as silence. Perhaps Mother might be pleased if Helen had been born deaf and dumb.

By this stage she had arrived at St Martin's, the house where the Sisters lived. Brigid never called it the Convent, even though that is what it was. Brigid called it just St Martin's, or home. She didn't criticize Helen Doyle for using a more formal and official word to describe the redbrick house where eleven women lived and went about their daily business as social workers in various London agencies.

Nessa was working with young mothers, most of them under sixteen, and trying to teach them some kind of mothering skills. Nessa had a child herself a long time ago, she had brought the baby up on her own but the child had died when it was three. Helen couldn't remember whether it was a boy or a girl. The other Sisters didn't talk about it much. But it did give Nessa the edge when it came to looking after children. Brigid usually worked in the day centre for vagrants. Serving them lunches, trying to organize baths and delousing. Sister Maureen worked with the group that were rehabilitating ex-prisoners. The days were gone when these kinds of nuns just polished the big tables in the parlour in the hopes of a visit from a bishop. They went out to do God's work and found plenty of opportunity to do it in the streets of London.

Helen had moved from one area to another since she had come to join St Martin's. She would like to have worked with Sister Brigid running the day centre. What she would really have liked is if Brigid would let her run it on her own, and just call in from time to time to see how things were getting along. This way Helen felt she would be really useful and special, and that once seen in a position of calm control over the wellbeing of so many people, she would have no difficulty in proving her readiness to be a full member of the Community.

She realized that Obedience was very much part of it, and like Poverty and Chastity this was no problem to her, Helen believed. She didn't want to be laying down the law and making rules, she would obey any rule. She didn't want money for jewels or yachts, she laughed at the very notion of such things. And Chastity. Yes she was very sure she wanted that in a highly positive way. Her one experience of the reverse side of that coin was quite enough to reassure her on this particular score.

She had worked in the kitchen, done her turn as a skivvy. She was never sure why Brigid hadn't liked her using that term. Skivvy. She had not been able to understand that people used that word quite respectably nowadays, as a sort of a joke. Debs said they were skivvying for a while before going skiing, it meant minding someone's house. Australians over here for a year often got jobs in bars, in restaurants, or as skivvies. It wasn't an insulting term.

Helen sighed, thinking of all the gulfs in understanding there were everywhere. She let herself in the door of St Martin's. It was Sister Joan's month for running the house, as Brigid liked it called. Joan called out from the kitchen as she heard her come in.

'Just in time, Helen, I'll take the stuff from you now. You couldn't have timed it better, as it happened.'

With a lurch Helen remembered the reason she had taken the large black plastic carrier bag that had been swinging emptily beside her on her journey home. She had meant to come by the market and buy cheaply what the sellers hadn't got rid of during the day. She had forgotten it once, and that was why she had been heading towards the grocery and off-licence where she had assisted her compatriot to destroy his liver even faster than he was already doing. She had been given three pounds to buy the vegetables. She had spent it on cider for an alcoholic.

'Sit down, Helen. It's not the end of the world,' said Joan, who didn't know the details of the story but recognized the substance and knew there would be no vegetables for the casserole.

'Sit down, Helen, stop crying. I'll put on a cup of tea for you just as soon as I've scrubbed some of those potatoes. We'll have jacket potatoes with a little bit of cheese. It will be just as nice.'

Nessa was tired; it had been a particularly bad day.

An eighteen-year-old mother had sat whimpering in a corner while her fate was being discussed by social workers and a woman police officer. Her baby would live, thanks to Nessa, but what kind of life?

The mother had not turned up at the centre for two days running and Nessa became worried. The door to the block of flats always swung open and as Nessa went in she almost fell over Simon crawling along the filthy corridor. Beer cans and bottles were strewn everywhere, the place smelled of urine, there were dangers every few feet, broken bicycles, crates with sharp corners. Simon was crawling earnestly towards the open door. In a minute he would have been on the street where no car or motor bicycle would have expected a child to crawl. He would have been dead.

As it was he was alive, the sores from his stinking nappies being treated. Anti-tetanus injections were being given against the germs he must have encountered, and his bruised eye was pronounced mercifully intact.

His mother hadn't beaten him, of this Nessa was sure, but she was too feeble-minded to look after him. He would be in care when he came out of hospital. A lifetime of care lay ahead of him. But care with a capital C.

Nessa was not in the mood for Helen's tears and explanations. She cut her very short.

'So you forgot the vegetables again. So what, Helen? Let's have a little peace. That's what would be really nice.'

Helen broke off mid-sentence. 'I was only taking it all on myself, I didn't want you to blame Sister Joan.'

'Oh for God's sake, Helen, who in their right mind would blame Sister Joan or any Sister? Cut it out, will you?'

It was the sharpest remark that had ever been made in St Martin's House, a place of peace and consideration.

Sister Joan and Sister Maureen looked shocked at Nessa with her white tired face going up the stairs.

Helen looked at all three of them and burst into tears again.

Sister Brigid never seemed to be aware of any little atmosphere. It was one of her characteristics. Sometimes Helen thought it was a weakness, a rare insensitivity in an otherwise remarkable character. Other times she wondered whether it might in fact be a blessing and something that Sister Brigid cultivated purposely.

There was no mention made of Helen's red eyes and blotchy face as they sat, heads bent, waiting for Sister Brigid to say the simple blessing over their food. Nobody acknowledged that Nessa looked white and drawn, though they were solicitous about passing her things and smiling at her a little more often than they smiled at the rest of the table. Eleven women including Brigid, the quiet Mother Superior who never used that title. She had been very stern with Helen for calling her Reverend Mother.

'But isn't that what you are?' Helen had been startled.

'We are sisters here, it's a community, this is our home, it's not an institution with ranks and rules and pecking orders.'

It had been hard to grasp at first, but after three years Helen felt that she had surely earned her place. Biting her lip she looked at the ten women chattering around the simple meal. Made more simple still by the fact of her forgetting the vegetables.

They talked easily about the work they had done during the day, the practicalities, the funny things, the optimisms, the chance of more help here, of fighting the cuts there. Brigid had said that they must not bring their problems to the supper table or even home to the house, otherwise St Martin's would be weighed down by the collective grief and anxiety of these workers in the sad end of society. They would become so depressed if they were to dwell every night on the amount of misery and pain they had seen in their different worlds that it would be counter productive. People needed escape, time out, retreat. They didn't have the luxury of going *on* retreat like the nuns of a previous generation, but neither did they have the demands and responsibilities that many trained social workers who were married women or men had. There were no children needing time, love and attention, there were no social demands nor the intensity of one-to-one relationships. Brigid told them often that small communities of nuns like theirs were ideally situated to serve the many and apparently increasing needs around them in London. The only thing they had to fear was too great an introspection or a depth of worry which might render their help less effective because it was becoming self-important.

Helen looked around at their faces: apart from Nessa who was still looking frail the others were like women who had few cares. You would not know from listening to them that some of them had spent the day in magistrates' courts, in police stations, in welfare centres or in squats and rundown council estates, or like herself in a clothing centre.

She was pleased that they laughed when she told them about the bag lady who had come in to get a coat that morning. Helen's job was to arrange the sorting, the dry-cleaning and mending of clothes that came in to the bureau. A generous dry-cleaning firm let them use the big machine free at off-peak hours if they ensured that paying customers didn't realize they were sharing with hand-me-downs for tramps.

The woman had been very insistent. 'Nothing in green, I've always found green an unlucky colour, Sister. No, red's a bit flashy, in my day only a certain kind of woman wore red. A nice mauve, a lilac shade. No? Well, safer to settle for a brown then. Not what you'd call cheerful for spring. But still.' A heavy sigh. Helen Doyle was a good mimic, she caught the woman perfectly, all the others could see her as clearly as if they had been there.

'You should be on the stage, Helen,' said Joan admiringly.

'Maybe she will one day,' said Maureen innocently.

Helen's face clouded. 'But how can I? I'll be here. Why don't any of you believe I'm going to stay? I've joined as much as you'll let me.' The lip was trembling. Dangerously.

Sister Brigid intervened. 'What did she look like in the brown coat, Helen?' she asked firmly. The warning was plain.

With an effort Helen pulled herself back to the story. The woman had asked for a scarf too, something toning she said, as if she had been in the accessories department of a fashion store.

'I found her a hat in the end, a yellow hat with a brown feather in it, and I gave her a yellow brooch I was wearing myself. I said it sort of brought the whole colour scheme together. She nodded like the Queen Mother and was very gracious about it, then she picked up her four bags of rubbish and went back to the Embankment.'

'Good, Helen.' Sister Brigid was approving. 'If you can make it seem like a fashion store with a bit of choice then you're doing it exactly right, that woman would never have taken what she thought was charity. Well done.'

The others all smiled too, and Nessa's smile was particularly broad.

'There's no one like Helen for these old misfits,' Nessa said, as if to make up for her earlier outburst. 'You always get on to the wave length so well.'

'It's probably that I'm there already,' Helen said. 'You know, about taking one to know one and all that.'

'You'd never be a bag lady, Helen,' Brigid said affectionately. 'You'd lose the bags.' The laughter around the supper table in St Martin's was warm and good-natured.

Helen felt very much at peace and very much at home.

She thought she heard Nessa get up in the middle of the night and go downstairs. It was an old house full of creaks and sounds. They could each recognize the others' steps and coughs. Like a family.

Helen was about to get up and follow her down to the kitchen for cocoa and a chat. But she hesitated. Brigid had often said that when people were upset the last thing they needed was someone to arrive in on top of them offering tea and sympathy. Helen had listened without agreeing. It was what she always wanted. There hadn't been any of it at home. Daddy too tired, Mother too anxious, Anna too busy, Brendan too withdrawn. It was why she had found this other family. They always had time to sympathize. It was what their work was all about. Listening.

Surely she should go down now and listen to Nessa, and maybe tell her all about the drunk today and how upsetting it had been. But maybe not. As Helen was deciding she heard Sister Brigid's light step go down the stairs.

She crept to the landing to hear what they were talking about.

Strangely it was all about the garden, and what they should plant. Shrubs would be nice to sit and look out on, Brigid said.

'When do you ever sit down?' Nessa spoke in a tone that was both scolding and admiring.

'I do sit down, lots of times. It's like that thing we got to charge the batteries for the radio, it puts new energy into me, into all of us.'

'You never seem tired, Brigid.'

'I feel it, I tell you. I'm getting old anyway, I'll be forty soon.'

Nessa laughed aloud. 'Don't be ridiculous, you're only thirty-four.'

'Well, forty is the next milestone; I don't mind, it's just that I don't have as much energy as I used to. Who'll do the garden, Nessa? I'm too full of aches and pains. You can't be spared from the children.'

'After today I think I could be spared only too easily. I don't have any judgement...'

'Shush, shush... Who will we ask to do it? It's hard work, you know, trying to make that little patch look like something restful and peaceful.'

'Helen maybe?' Nessa sounded doubtful.

Helen on the landing felt a dull red come up her neck and to her face.

'Oh, she'd do it certainly, and she'd be full of imagination ...' Sister Brigid sounded doubtful too. 'The only thing is ...'

Nessa came in immediately. 'The only thing is she'd lose interest halfway through after we'd bought all the plants, and they'd die. Is that what you mean?'

Helen felt a wave of fury come over her.

'No, it's just that I don't like her to think that we're shunting her to do something that isn't really... our work, you know.'

'But it's *all* our work, isn't it?' Nessa sounded surprised.

'Yes, you know that, I know that, Helen doesn't. Anyway we'll see. Come on, Nessa, if us old ones are to be any use to this Community we'd better get a few hours of sleep a night.' She was laughing, Sister Brigid had a lovely warm laugh that included you and wrapped you up.

'Thank you, Brigid.'

'I did nothing, said nothing.'

'It's the way you do it, say it.' Nessa was obviously feeling better now.

Helen slipped back into her room and stood for a long time with her back to the door.

So they thought she wouldn't finish things? She'd show them, by heavens would she show them.

She'd dig that garden single-handed, she'd build a magic garden where they could all sit and think and be at peace and they would realize that Sister Helen more than any of them knew that anything done for the Community was as important as any other thing. Then they would have to let her take her vows. And she would be completely part of their world. And safe. Safe from everything else.

Like everything Helen had touched, the building of the garden had its highs and lows. Helen found three boys who said they were anxious to help the Sisters in their great work building a refuge and they'd be happy to join in with a bit of the heavy work. They brought spades and shovels and Sister Joan said it was beyond the mind's understanding how much tea they wanted, how they couldn't have this butter on their bread, or marge, it had to be a particular spread. And they wondered was there a little something going at lunch time. Sister Joan said nervously that the nuns all had their meal in the evening, but fearing that the volunteer workforce would abandon everything, she ran out and bought provisions.

After three days Sister Brigid thanked them and said that there could be no further imposition on their kindness.

The lads had begun to enjoy the good food and over-powering gratitude of the nuns and didn't really want to leave at all.

They left the place in a possibly greater mess; earth had been turned over certainly, but no pattern or plan had emerged.

But Helen soldiered on, she dug until she had blisters, she spent her scant off-time in bookshops reading the sections of gardening books that concentrated on 'Starting Out'.

She learned the differences between one kind of soil and another.

She told the Sisters amazing things each evening about the sexuality of growing things.

'They never told us a word about this at school,' she said indignantly. 'It's the kind of thing you should know, about everything being male and female even in the garden, for heaven's sake, and going mad to propagate.'

'Let's hope it all does propagate after your hard work,' Brigid said. 'You really are great, Helen, I don't know where you find the energy.'

Helen flushed with pleasure. And she was able to remember those words of praise too a little later when the problem of the bedding plants came up. The nice woman who said she really admired the Sisters even though she wasn't a Roman Catholic herself and disagreed with the Pope about everything, brought them some lovely plants as a gift. Red-faced with exertion from planting them, Helen assured the others that evening they were very very lucky. It would have cost a fortune if they had to buy all these, nobody knew how expensive things were in garden centres.

She had barely finished talking when the news came that the plants had all been dug up from a park and a nearby hotel. The repercussions were endless. The explanations from every side seemed unsatisfactory. Helen said she had to protect her sources and wouldn't give them the name of the benefactor. But in mid conversation she mentioned to the young policewoman that Mrs Harris couldn't possibly have taken them deliberately, she wasn't that kind of person, and that was enough for the two constables to identify exactly who she was talking about. Mrs Harris had been in trouble before. A latter-day Robin Hood was how she was known down at the station, taking clothes from one washing-line, ironing them and presenting them as gifts to another home.

Only Helen could have got herself involved with Mrs Harris, the other nuns sighed. Only Helen could have got them all involved, was Brigid's view, but she didn't say anything at the time.

Helen realized that the garden couldn't be considered her full-time work. And even when she had reassured the Community that she was taking on no further assistance from gargantuan eaters of meals or compulsive plant thieves she felt she should take on more than just a horticultural role. She was determined to play her part as fully as possible. She said she would do half the skivvy work, leaving Sister Joan or Sister Maureen free for a half day to do something else.

It worked. Or it sort of worked.

They all got used to the fact that Helen might not have scrubbed the table or taken in their washing when it started to rain. They knew that she would never know when they were running out of soap or cornflakes. That she wouldn't really rinse out and hang the dishcloths up to dry. But she was there, eager and willing to help.

And she did answer the phone and more or less coped when people came to call.

Which is why she was there when Renata Quigley came to see the Sister in charge.

Renata. Tall and dark, somewhere in her mid-thirties. Married for fifteen years to Frank Quigley.

What on earth could she want, and how had she tracked Helen down to St Martin's? Helen felt her heart race and she could almost hear it thumping in her ears. At the same time there was a sense of ice-cold water in the base of her stomach.

She hadn't seen Renata since the wedding, but she had seen pictures of her of course, in magazines and in the trade papers Daddy had brought home. Mrs Frank Quigley, the former Miss Renata Palazzo, exchanging a joke or enjoying herself at the races or presenting a prize to the apprentice of the year or walking among the high and mighty at some charity function.

She was very much more beautiful than Helen had thought, she had skin that Mother would have called sallow but looked olive-like and beautiful with her huge dark eyes and her dark shiny hair with its expensive cut. She wore her scarf very artistically caught in a brooch and draped as if it were part of her green and gold dress. She carried a small leather handbag in green and gold squares.

Her face was troubled and her long thin hands with their dark red nails were twisting round the little patchwork bag.

'Can I please speak to the Sister in charge?' she asked Helen.

Helen looked at her, open-mouthed. Renata Quigley didn't recognize her. Suddenly the memory of an old movie came back to her, and some beautiful actress looking straight at the camera and saying, 'Nobody looks at the face of a nun.' It was the kind of thing that would drive Sister Brigid mad. Helen had never forgotten it. Until this moment she had never realized how true it was. There was Renata Quigley on her doorstep looking straight into her eyes and she didn't recognize Helen, the daughter of Deirdre and Desmond Doyle, her husband's friends.

Helen who had caused so much trouble that time.

But perhaps she had never known. With another shock Helen realized that Renata might have been told nothing at the time.

While all this was going through her mind, Helen stood at the door, a girl in a grey jumper and skirt, with a cross around her neck, her hair tied back with a black ribbon, her face perhaps covered in grime from the garden where she had been when she heard the doorbell.

Perhaps she didn't even look like a nun.

It was obvious that Renata didn't connect her with the child she had known in Rosemary Drive, Pinner, when she had come to call.

'I'm sorry, there's nobody here but me,' Helen said, recovering slightly.

'Are you one of the Community?' Renata looked doubtful.

'Yes, well yes. I'm here in St Martin's, part of the house, one of the Sisters.' It was straining the truth but Helen was not going to let Renata Quigley go until she knew why she had come here in the first place.

'It's a little complicated, Sister,' Renata said nervously.

Helen's smile nearly split her face in half.

'Well, come on in and sit down and tell me, that's what we're here for,' she said.

And she stood back and held the door open while Frank Quigley's wife walked into St Martin's. Into Helen's home.

That face, that dark lean face with the high cheekbones. Helen Doyle knew it so well. She remembered well her mother saying with some satisfaction that it would run to fat all the same in the end, mark her words, all the middle-aged Italian women you saw with several chins, they too had been lean girls with long, perfectly formed faces. It was in their diets, in their lifestyles, in the amount of olive oil they managed to put away.

When she was a child Helen had been irritated with her mother for all this kind of niggling. What did it matter? Why was Mother so anxious to criticize, to find fault?

But later, later Helen was to look at pictures of the face and wish that her own were like it, that she had hollows and soft golden skin instead of round cheeks and freckles. She would have killed to get that dark heavy hair she saw in the photographs, and wear those loop earrings, which made Helen look like a tinker running away from an encampment, but made Renata Palazzo Quigley look glamorous as an exotic princess from a far land.

'I came here because I heard that there is a Sister Brigid . . . I thought perhaps . . .' She faltered.

'I suppose you could say I'm Sister Brigid's deputy,' Helen said. In ways it could be true. She *was* in charge of the house when they were all out, that could be considered being a deputy. 'I'll be glad to do what I can.'

Helen fought back the other thoughts in her mind. She simply closed a door on Renata's picture in a silver frame on a small table with a long white cloth reaching to the floor. She closed another door on Frank Quigley, her father's friend, with tears in his eyes. She tried to think only of this moment. A woman had come to St Martin's for help in some way, and Sister Brigid was out. Helen was in charge.

'It's just that you're very young . . .' Renata was doubtful.

Helen was reassuring. She had her hand on the kettle and paused to look at Renata.

'No, no, I'm much more experienced than you think.'

She felt a little light-headed. Could she really be saying these words to Frank Quigley's wife?

It had been impossible in Rosemary Drive that time when Father had lost his job. Helen thought back on it and it flashed in front of her as if she were watching a video on that machine that she had got for St Martin's once because the company had *assured* her it was free for a month and there would be no obligation. It had all been very difficult, the business about the video, like everything.

But nothing was as frightening as the time her father had left Palazzo. There was a council of war every night and Mother had warned them that they must tell nobody.

'But why?' Helen had begged. She couldn't bear her sister and brother to accept that this was the way things should be from now on. 'Why does it have to be a secret? It's not Daddy's fault that they changed the place. He can get another job. Daddy can get *any* job.'

She remembered still how Mother had snapped at her.

'Your father doesn't want *any* job, he wants his job at Palazzo back. And he will have it back soon, so in the meantime nothing is to be said. Do you hear me, Helen? Outside this house not one word is to be said. Everyone is to think that your father is going to work as usual in Palazzo.'

'But how will he earn money?' Helen had asked.

It was a reasonable question. To this day she didn't regret it, like she sometimes regretted the things she had said, the offers she had made, the questions she had asked.

Anna had said nothing, for an easy life she had explained.

Brendan had said nothing because nothing was what Brendan always said.

But Helen couldn't say nothing.

She was sixteen years old, grown up, in her last year at school. She would not stay on and do A levels like Anna. Even though she felt she was twice as bright as Anna in many ways. No, Helen was going to see the world, try her hand at this and that, get on-the-job experience.

She was so full of life, at sixteen some people thought she was years younger, a big schoolgirl. Other people thought she was years older, a lively student going on twenty.

Frank Quigley had no idea how old she was the afternoon she went to see him in his office.

The dragon woman Miss Clarke had protected him as she always had. Helen wondered could she possibly be there still? It was years ago. Surely she had given up hoping that Mr Quigley was going to look into her eyes and say that she was beautiful without her glasses?

Helen had left her school blazer downstairs with the doorman, and had opened the top buttons of her school shirt in order to look more grown up. The dragon woman had eventually let her in. There were very few who could withstand Helen when she was in full flow. Explanation came hard upon explanation, and all the time she was moving towards his office. Before the dragon realized it, Helen was in.

She was flushed and excited.

Frank Quigley had looked up, surprised.

'Well, well, Helen Doyle. You're not meant to be here, I'm sure.'

'I know.' She laughed easily.

'You should be at school, not bursting into people's offices.'

'I do a lot of things I shouldn't do.'

She had sat on the corner of his desk swinging her legs, shoulders hunched up. He looked at her with interest. Helen knew she had been right to come here, the silence of Rosemary Drive was no way to handle things. There had to be confrontation.

'What can I do for you?' He had a mock gallantry. He was quite handsome in a way, dark with curly hair. Old of course, as old as her father, even. But different.

'I suppose you could take me to lunch,' she said. It was the kind of thing people said in films and in plays on telly. It worked for them, perhaps it would for her too. She gave him a smile much braver and more confident than she felt inside.

'Lunch?' He laughed in a short bark. 'Lord, Helen, I don't know what kind of lifestyles you think we live down here . . .' He broke off, looking at her disappointed face.

'Aw hell, I've not had lunch out for years.'

'I never had,' Helen said simply.

That did it.

They went to an Italian restaurant which was almost dark like night and there were candles on the table.

Every time Helen tried to bring up the subject of her father he skirted around it. She knew that in those television series about big business they always came to the point at the coffee stage.

There was no coffee. There was a Zambucca. A liquorice-tasting liqueur. With a little coffee bean in it and the waiter set it alight. Helen had never seen anything so marvellous.

'It's like a grown-up's birthday cake,' she said delightedly.

'You're fairly grown up for seventeen,' Frank said. 'Or is it older?'

This was to her advantage, if he thought she was older than sixteen he would listen better. Take her more seriously.

'Almost eighteen,' she lied.

'You've been around, despite the schoolgirl get-up,' he said.

'I've been around,' Helen said.

The more travelled he thought she was, the more he would listen when the time came to talk.

The time didn't come to talk.

He had been affectionate and admiring and had patted her cheek and even held her face up to the candlelight to see if there was any telltale ring of red wine around her mouth before she went back to school.

'I'm not going back to school,' Helen said very definitely. She looked Frank Quigley straight in the eye. 'You know that, and I know that.'

'I certainly hoped it,' he said, and his voice sounded a bit throaty. Something about the way he stroked her cheek and lifted her hair made it difficult to talk about her father's job, Helen had felt it would somehow be wrong to bring the subject up when he was being so attentive. She was relieved when he suggested they go back to his place so that they could talk properly.

of what she wanted to say, heedless of timing or other people's feelings.

She saw a look of pain cross Frank Quigley's face.

'Your father will get a job. He told me that he didn't need one, that he was looking about, that he had plenty of offers.' Frank's voice was cold. 'He will be reinstated in Palazzo. Not overnight, I have to talk to Carlo, these things have to be done tactfully. They can take a little time.'

Helen nodded vigorously.

'And you, Helen. Will you be all right, will you forgive me?'

'Of course. It was a misunderstanding.' Her voice sounded eager, as if she too wanted to be let off a hook.

'That's what it was, Helen, and Helen listen to me, please. The only thing I can tell you is that it won't always be like this ... it will be lovely and happy ...' He was straining to try to tell her that this gross happening would not be the pattern for the rest of the lovemaking in her life.

He might as well have been talking to the wall.

'Are you sure I couldn't do anything about the sheets, like a launderette or anything?'

'No.'

'But what will you say?'

'Please, Helen, please.' His face was pained.

'Will I go now, Frank?'

He looked unable to cope.

'I'll drive you ...' His voice trailed away. His face showed that he didn't know where he was to drive her.

'No, it's all right, I can get the bus. I know where I am, I'll just get the bus home and say ... say I don't feel well.' Helen gave a little giggle. 'It's true in a way. But listen, Frank, I don't have the bus fare, could I ask you ...'

She couldn't understand why Frank Quigley had tears pouring down his face when he handed her the coins and closed her hand over them.

'Will you be all right?' He was begging to be reassured. He was not ready for what she told him.

'Frank.' Helen gave a little laugh. 'I'm not a child, for heaven's sake, I was sixteen last week. I'm a grown-up. I'll find my way home on the bus.'

She left then because she couldn't bear the look on his face.

'Do you mean the office?' She was doubtful. The dragon would keep interrupting.

'I don't mean the office,' he said very steadily, looking at her. 'You know that and I know that.'

'I certainly hoped it,' she said, echoing his words.

The apartment block was very luxurious. Mother had always said she could not understand why Frank Quigley hadn't bought himself a proper house now that he was a married man. But then he probably had expectations of the big white house with the wrought-iron gates and the large well-kept gardens. The house of the Palazzos.

But Mother couldn't have known how splendid the flat was. Flat wasn't the word for it, really. It was on two floors, there was a lovely staircase leading up to a floor which had a big balcony with chairs and a table outside, the balcony ran along the whole length of the place, past the sitting room and the bedroom.

They went out the sitting room door to look at the view from the balcony. And Helen's heart lurched with a sudden realization as they left the balcony to return indoors through the bedroom.

Her hand went to her throat in an automatic gesture of fright. 'Your wife ... ?' she said.

Long long afterwards when she played it back in her mind, she thought of all the things she could have said, should have said, might have said. How had it been that the only thing which *did* come to her to say was something that could obviously be taken to mean that she was willing and enthusiastic, but just afraid of discovery?

'Renata isn't here, Helen,' Frank Quigley said softly. 'You know that and I know that, just as we both knew you weren't going back to school.'

She had heard that it wasn't healthy to try to blot something out of your memory, to try to pretend that it had never happened. Helen didn't care whether it was healthy or not, for a long time she tried to forget that afternoon.

The moment of no return, the look of bewilderment and anger when she had shied away from him first.

The urgency, and the pain, the sheer hurt and stabbing and fear that he was so out of control that he might do literally anything and kill her. The way he rolled away and groaned, not like that first groan but with shame and then with fury.

'You told me, you said you'd been around,' he said with his head in his hands as he sat on one side of the bed, white, naked and ridiculous-looking.

She lay on the other beside the silver-framed photograph of the lean olive-faced Renata. Silent and disapproving-looking beside her marriage bed. As if she had always known what might happen there one day.

Helen had lain there and looked at the picture of Our Lady, it was the one you saw everywhere called Madonna of the Wayside. At least Our Lady hadn't had to go through all this to get our Lord. It had been done miraculously. Helen looked at the picture because that meant she didn't have to look at her father's friend Frank Quigley who was crying into his hands. And it meant she didn't have to look at the white sheets which were stained with blood and she didn't have to think about how badly he had injured her and if she would have to go to a doctor. Or if she might be pregnant.

She didn't know how long it was before she made a move to the bathroom and cleaned herself up. She didn't seem to have been very badly injured, the bleeding had stopped.

She dressed herself carefully and dusted herself with Renata's talcum powder which wasn't in a tin like ordinary powder, it was in a big glass bowl with a pink swansdown puff.

When she came out, Frank was dressed. And white-faced.

'The bed . . . ?' she began.

'Forget the bloody bed . . .'

'I could . . .'

'You've done enough,' he snapped.

Helen's eyes filled with tears. 'I've done enough? What did I do, I came to talk to you about my father and why he'd been sacked, it was you, you who did all this . . .' With her hand she waved in the direction of the bed.

His face was contrite. 'Your father. You did this to try and get Desmond back his piffling little job. Jesus Christ, you'd whore around to get your father a penny-farthing nothing place in a supermarket.'

'It is not a nothing job.' Helen's face burned with anger. 'He was a very important person there, and now, now he's been

sacked and Mother says we are not to tell anyone, neighbours, relatives, anyone, and he goes off each morning pretending he's going to work . . .'

Frank looked at her in disbelief.

'Yes he does, and I just wanted to have lunch with you and tell you straight out how bad it was and you'd understand because you were Dad's friend way back at school in the Brothers when you used to climb over stone walls . . . he told me . . . and you're doing so well there and married to the boss's daughter and everything . . . And *that's* all I wanted, I didn't whore around, I've never slept with anyone in my life and I didn't mean to sleep with you, I wasn't to know you'd fall in love with me and all this would happen, and now you say it's all my fault.' She burst into tears.

He put his arms around her and held her close to him.

'Christ, you're only a child, what have I done? Christ Almighty what did I do?'

She sobbed against his jacket for a bit.

He held her away from him and his eyes were full of tears.

'I'll never be able to make amends. Literally there's nothing I can do to tell you how sorry I am. I'd never . . . never if I hadn't thought . . . I was so sure that . . . but that doesn't matter now. What matters is you.'

Helen wondered had he always loved her or was it only now People could fall in love so easily.

'We'll have to forget this,' she said. She knew that a wom[an] had to take the lead in such matters. Men would dither and [give] in to temptation. Anyway there was no temptation for Hele[n], this was what it was like then the rest of the world could h[ave] as far as she was concerned.

'It happened, it can't be forgotten. I'll do anything t[o make] it up to you.'

'Yes, but we can't keep on seeing each other, it wo[uldn't be] fair.' She looked over at the picture of Renata.

She thought he looked puzzled. 'No, of course,' [he said.]

'And we won't tell anyone, either of us.' She [was somehow] eager about this.

'Lord no, nobody at all,' he said, looking high[ly relieved.]

'And my father?' She spoke without guile [as]
Helen always spoke, eager to get over the mea[ning and]

Of course he had to stay away from the house in case he wasn't able to control himself when he saw her. That's what she told herself.

She never remembered him coming to Rosemary Drive again after that. There had always been some excuse, he was on a conference, he was abroad, he and Renata were going to see some of her relations in Italy. He was terribly sorry, it was such bad timing. Mother said he was getting above himself, still wasn't it great that they never had to go to him cap in hand to ask him to reinstate his old friend in Palazzo's? At least that idea had come straight from Mr Palazzo himself, who had realized that this was no way to treat valued managerial staff.

Helen never knew whether her father realized that it was Frank. It was hard to talk to her father, he had built a little shell around himself almost for fear of being hurt, like Mother's shell for fear of letting themselves down somehow.

She had found those last school terms endless, the world had changed since that strange afternoon. She was always frightened of being misunderstood. She had started to scream one day when the singing master at school asked her to come into the storeroom and help him carry down the sheet music to the school hall. The man hadn't touched her but she had this sudden claustrophobic fear that he would think she was encouraging him somehow, and that he would begin this hurtful business and then blame her. As things turned out he *did* blame her very much indeed and had said that she was a neurotic hysterical fool, a troublemaker, and if she were the last female on earth he wouldn't touch her with a barge-pole.

The Principal of the school seemed to agree with him and asked Helen sharply why she had begun to scream if she agreed that there had been no question of an attack or even an advance.

Helen had said glumly that she didn't know. She had felt that she was in some kind of situation she couldn't handle and that unless she *did* scream something else would happen and it would all be too late and too complicated.

'Has anything of this sort happened to you before?' The Principal was not entirely sympathetic. Helen Doyle had always been a difficult pupil, gushy, anxious to please, always creating waves of trouble around her.

Helen had said no, unconvincingly.

The Principal had sighed. 'Well, you can be certain that it will keep happening to you, Helen. It's your personality. This sort of thing will turn up in your life over and over again, situations that you can't handle. That is unless you pull yourself together and take control of your own actions.'

She sounded so final it was as if she were passing a life sentence.

Helen had been dazed at the unfairness of it all.

It was then that she decided to be a nun.

And now, years later, she was almost a nun. Well, she would be a nun if Sister Brigid had not been so adamant about telling her that she was only using the convent as a crutch, that she was using it as a place to hide and that those days were over in religious life.

Helen felt safe in St Martin's. And even as she made a mug of coffee and sat down to join the beautiful Renata Palazzo Quigley whose face had looked at her from a silver frame on that frightening day . . . she felt safe. Safe from the memories and the fear of that time.

'Tell me what you want and I'll see if there's anything we can do,' she said with the big smile that made everyone love Helen. When they met her first.

'It's very simple,' Renata said. 'We want a baby.'

It was very simple. And very sad. Helen hugged her mug of coffee to her and listened. Frank was too old at forty-six. Too old. How ridiculous, but adoption societies wouldn't consider him. Also he had a poor medical history, some heart trouble, nothing very serious, due to stress at work, and all businessmen had this in today's world. Natural mothers and fathers were allowed to bring a child into the world into any kind of appalling conditions, tenements, places of vice, nobody stopped them and said that they couldn't have any children. But for adoption everything had to be over-perfect.

Renata had heard that sometimes, if she were only to meet the right person, there must be occasions where a child could be given to a good loving home, to a father and mother who would love the little boy or girl as their own. There surely were cases when this happened.

There was a look of longing in her eyes.

Helen patted the hand of the woman who had once looked at her from the silver frame.

She had told Renata that they would meet again in a week when she would have made some inquiries. She thought it wiser not to consult Sister Brigid for the moment. Sister Brigid being an authority figure had to keep so well within the limits of the law ... Better just let Helen inquire a little. All right? All right.

She told nobody. They said she looked feverish and excited, and Helen entertained the Community with tales of how she made her garden grow.

'Anyone call?' Brigid asked.

'No. Not anyone really, you know, usual callers.' Helen avoided her eye. It was the first time she had told a direct lie in St Martin's. It didn't feel good but it was for the best in the end.

If she could do this one thing, if she could do what she hoped she might be able to do, then even at the age of twenty-one her whole life would have been worth living.

It was Nessa's turn to do the kitchen for half a day. Nessa was the one woman at St Martin's who found Helen almost impossible to get on with. Normally when they worked together Helen stayed out of Nessa's way. But this time she positively hung around her neck.

'What happens when the children are born to really hopeless mothers, Nessa? Don't you wish you could give them to proper homes from the start?'

'What I wish isn't important, I don't rule the world.' Nessa was short, she was scrubbing the kitchen floor and Helen kept standing in her way.

'But wouldn't a child be much better off?'

'Mind, Helen, please. I've just washed there.'

'And you always have to register the births, no matter what kind of mother?'

'What do you mean?'

'I mean do you have to go to the town hall or the registry office or whatever and sort of say who the child is?'

'No, I don't always.'

'Oh, why not?'

'Because I'm usually not the one who does it, it depends. It depends. Helen, do you think that if you're not going to do any work you could move out of the kitchen so that I could clean it?'

'And no babies end up without being registered?'

'How could they?'

'I don't know.' Helen was disappointed. She had thought there might be long twilight times when nobody knew who or what the baby was. She hadn't understood how the Welfare State at least checked its citizens in and out of the world.

'And foundlings, babies in phone boxes, in churches, where do they end up?'

Nessa looked up in alarm. 'God, Helen, don't tell me you found one?'

'No, worse luck,' Helen said. 'But if I did would I have to register it?'

'No, Helen, of course not, if *you* found a baby you could keep the baby and dress him or her up when you remembered, and feed the child when it occurred to you, or when there was nothing else marginally more interesting to do.'

'Why are you so horrible to me, Nessa?' Helen asked.

'Because I am basically pretty horrible.'

'You can't be, you're a nun. And you're not horrible to the others.'

'Ah, that's true. The real thing about being horrible is that it's selective.'

'And why did you select me?' Helen didn't seem put out or hurt, she was interested. Actually interested.

Nessa was full of guilt.

'Oh, for heaven's sake, I'm just short-tempered, I hate doing this bloody floor, and you're so young and carefree and get everything you want. I'm sorry, Helen, forgive me, I'm always asking you to forgive me. Really I am.'

'I know.' Helen was thoughtful. 'People often are, I seem to bring out the worst in them somehow.'

Sister Nessa looked after her uneasily as Helen wandered back into the garden. There was something more than usual on her scattered brain and it was weighing very heavily.

Helen rang Renata Quigley. Same address, same apartment, same bed presumably. She said that she was still inquiring but that it wasn't as easy as people thought.

'I never thought it was easy,' sighed Renata. 'But somehow it does make all the going out to functions and to this celebration and that celebration a little easier if I think that somebody as kind as you, Sister, is looking out for me.'

With a thrill of shock that went right through her body Helen Doyle realized that she would meet Frank and Renata Quigley at her parents' silver wedding party.

Frank Quigley had been the best man back in those days when he and Father were about equal.

Before everything had changed.

The garden was finished and more or less ran itself. Sister Joan loved being in the clothing centre, and she was quick with a needle, so that she could do an alteration on the spot, move the buttons on a jacket for an old man, praise him, admire him, say that the fit made all the difference in the world. Let him think it was custom tailored.

There was no real work for Helen, no real place.

Once more she asked Brigid about taking her vows.

'It's very harsh to keep me on the outside, seriously I have been here for so long, you *can't* say it's a passing fancy any more now, can you?' She begged and implored.

'You're running, Helen,' Brigid said. 'I told you that from the word go. This is not like a convent in the films, a place in a forest where people went to find peace, it's a working house. You have to have found peace already to bring it here.'

'But I've found it now,' Helen implored.

'No, you're afraid of engaging with real people, that's why you're with us.'

'You're all more real than anyone else. Honestly I've never met any group I like so much.'

'That's not the whole story. We shelter you from something. We can't go on doing that, it's not our role. If it's men, if it's sex, if it's the cut and thrust of the business world . . . we all have had to face it and cope with it. You're still hiding from something.'

'I suppose it is sex a bit.'

'Well, you don't have to keep indulging in it,' Brigid laughed. 'Go back out into the world, Helen, I beg you, for a couple of years. Stay in touch with us and then if you still feel this is your home, come back and we'll look at it all again. I really do think you should go. For your own good.'

'Are you asking me to leave. Truly?'

'I'm suggesting it, but do you see what I mean about this not being like the real world? If this was a real place, I'd be telling you to go or promoting you. It's too protective here for you, I feel it in my bones.'

'Let me stay for a little while. Please.'

'Stay until after your parents' twenty-fifth wedding anniversary,' Brigid said unexpectedly. 'That seems to be preying on your mind for some reason. And then after that we'll see.'

Helen went away from Sister Brigid's little workroom, more wretched than she had been for a long time.

She looked so sad that Sister Nessa asked did she want to come and help with the young mothers. This was the first time the invitation had ever been made.

Helen went along, for once silent and without prattle.

'Don't be disapproving or anything, will you Helen?' Nessa asked nervously. 'We're not meant to be passing judgement, just helping them cope.'

'Sure,' Helen said.

She sat listless as any of the girls who were on low-dosage anti-depressants or who lived in fear of a pimp who had wanted them to have an abortion. Nessa looked at her from time to time with concern. But Helen was quiet and obedient. She did everything she was asked to do. She was useful too in a way. She went out to the flats of those who had not turned up. Nessa had always been nervous since the incident of the little Simon who had crawled out of his flat almost into the mainstream of rush-hour traffic.

In the late afternoon Nessa asked Helen to go and find Yvonne, who was eight months pregnant with her second child. Her eldest, a beautiful girl with Jamaican eyes like her father long gone, and a Scottish accent like her mother who gave birth to her at sixteen, was waiting at the door.

'Mummy's gaen do wee wee,' she said helpfully.

'That's great,' Helen said, and brought the toddler back into the house.

From the bathroom came the groans and the cries of Yvonne. Suddenly Helen found courage.

'You're better in your bedroom,' she said suddenly to the chubby child and moved a chest of drawers to make sure the child couldn't get out.

Then she went to cope with what she thought was a miscarriage in the lavatory.

But in the middle of the blood, the screams and the definite smell of rum all around the place, Helen heard a small cry.

The baby was alive.

Yvonne remembered nothing of it all. She had been so drunk that the day passed in a terrible blur.

They told her she had lost the child, that she had flushed it down the lavatory.

The ambulance men had been tender and gentle as they lifted her on to the stretcher, they had looked around the place and even down the lavatory bowl in confusion.

'They told us she was near to her time, she couldn't have got rid of a full-term foetus, surely.'

But Helen, the cool-eyed girl who said she was a voluntary welfare worker at the mother and child centre, and that she lived with the Sisters in St Martin's, assured them that she had not been able to get in to the flat and had heard continuous flushing of the chain and then found the place covered in blood.

The small round three-year-old seemed to back her up, saying that her mother had been long time wee wee and that Helen had been long time at the door.

Nessa, ashen-faced and trying not to let herself believe that this would never have happened if she had sent anyone else but Helen, agreed that Helen had been gone ages and ages and could get no reply. Helen had made a call to Nessa saying that there were problems but that she knew she would get in if she could persuade the child to open the door. She had called from a nearby shop where she had stopped to buy a bottle of milk for herself because she felt faint thinking of what might be inside.

That night, with Yvonne in her hospital bed, with Yvonne's three-year-old lodged temporarily in a local orphanage until the care order could be signed, Helen told Brigid she felt restless and she would like to go out for a walk.

'You *are* restless tonight,' Brigid said absently. 'You've been out to the garden a half a dozen times.'

'I wanted to make sure it was all right,' Helen said.

Carefully she picked up the little bundle, the boy who would inherit the Palazzo millions, and took him in her arms. She had him wrapped carefully in a towel and in one of her own nighties. She had a soft blue rug, which used to lie folded on the back of her chair, wrapped well around him.

She slipped out the back gate of St Martin's and walked until her legs were tired. Then in a shop where nobody would recognize her and mention to one of the sisters that they had seen one of the Community carrying a baby, she found a phone and telephoned Renata.

'I have it,' she said triumphantly down the phone.

'Who is this, you have what?'

'Renata, it's Sister Helen from St Martin's, I have your baby.'

'No, no, it's not possible.'

'Yes, but I must give him to you now, tonight, now this minute.'

'It's a little boy, you got us a little boy?'

'Yes. He's very very young, he's only one day old.'

Renata's voice was a screech. 'But no, one day, he will die, I cannot know what to do for a child of one day . . .'

'I don't know either, but I bought him a bottle of milk, he seems to be taking it off my finger,' Helen said simply.

'Where are you?'

'I'm in London of course, about two miles from the convent. Renata, have you any money?'

'What kind of money?' She sounded worried.

'Enough to pay for a taxi.'

'Yes, yes.'

'So will I come to your flat. And give him to you. No one must know.'

'Yes, I don't know, perhaps I should wait till . . . I don't know what to do.'

'I went to great trouble to get him for you.' Helen sounded tired.

'Oh I know, Sister, I'm so foolish, it's just that it's so quick and he is so very little.'

'I'm sure you'll learn, you can always ring someone and ask them. Will I get a taxi now, it might cost pounds?'

'Yes, come now.'

'And Frank's not there is he?'

'Frank, how did you know my husband is Frank?'

'You told me,' Helen said, biting her lip.

'I suppose I must have. I don't know what to say.'

The taxi man said that this wasn't where he wanted to go. He was on his way home. South London is what he wanted. Not miles out to Wembley.

He saw the tears beginning to form.

'Get in before I change my mind,' he said. 'Anyway, at least you've had it, let's look on the bright side, I could have ended up delivering it.'

'That's true,' Helen said, and the taxi driver looked at her anxiously, wondering would he get his fare when he got to Wembley.

She recited the address of the apartment block as if by rote and asked the driver to wait. The lady of the house would be down in a moment and would pay him.

He told the other cab drivers afterwards that he had spotted her as trouble the very moment he saw her. The moment that her eyes had filled with tears when he said perfectly normally of an evening that he wanted to go south of the river rather than up to this neck of the woods in Wembley. Anyway, he said, it all seemed to have happened at once, the lady came down and was carrying a purse with money. Classy she was and foreign, she took one look at the baby and she started to scream.

'He's got blood on him, he's not properly formed, no, no, I didn't want this! This is a baby that still is not ready to be a baby. No, no.'

She backed away from the girl in the grey skirt and jumper with her hand up to her mouth and at that moment a fellow in a Rover came along and leaped out, he took one look at what was happening and he shook the foreign woman till her head near as anything fell off, then he took the child and seemed to recognize the girl in the grey. He kept saying 'Oh my God' too, as if she were something from outer space.

Then there was a bundle of notes stuffed in the taxi man's

window, four times the fare out to bloody Wembley. So he had to go and he never knew what it was all about and how it ended.

It ended badly. As everything Helen Doyle had ever touched seemed to end.

She had refused to go into the flat, crying too now, louder than Renata, but neither of the women cried as much as the bewildered hungry baby that had been born in a lavatory that morning.

Sister Brigid was summoned eventually to make some sense out of the whole scene. She came with Nessa, white-faced but calm.

Nessa saw to the baby and Brigid listened to the hysterical explanations.

The Italian woman was saying that she had intended only to inquire if any mother wanted to give her baby privately for adoption, she hadn't asked anyone to take one for her.

The tall Irish businessman was pleading for Helen, saying that she had done it for the best as she had always done everything for the best, but the world was never able to perceive it that way. He sounded tender towards her and yet terrified of her as well.

He knew her parents, he explained. Desmond Doyle had been one of his oldest friends.

'She is the daughter of those Doyles?' Shock was being piled on shock for Renata.

'Yes, she can't have known it was us.'

There was something in the way the man spoke. There was something that sounded a warning. Brigid looked from one stricken face to another to try and read the signals.

Helen was opening her mouth. 'But I *did* know, I *did* know, it's only because it *was* Frank that I'd do this, I'd never have taken a baby, and told all those lies. If it hadn't been Frank I'd not have risked the baby's life. I felt I owed it to him, after all, after everything . . .'

Brigid had worked with people for all her adult life. Mainly people who were in some kind of distress. She didn't know what was going to be said now but she felt it was crucial that whatever it was, Helen should not say it. Helen was in mid-flight, through the tears and the gulps the story was coming out.

'I never meant it to be like this, but they could have given it such a good life, so much money, and Frank's too old to adopt a child, and she said he had been having heart attacks . . .'

'You told her that?' Frank snapped at his wife.

'I thought she was a nun miles away, how did I know she was bloody Doyle's daughter?'

Helen was oblivious. 'I wanted to make amends, to make up for everything. To try and put things right. After all, my life worked out all right and I got everything I wanted, but Frank didn't, he had no children and he had heart attacks, he was punished . . . I wanted to try and even it out.'

Renata was looking from one to another now in confusion. Out in the other room Sister Nessa had quietened the baby and Helen was gathering breath again.

'You work with Mr Doyle still?' Brigid asked quickly.

'Yes, and he helped my father when he was sacked, he asked Mr Palazzo to give him back his job . . .'

Brigid saw an avenue of escape. She stood up as she spoke.

'So Helen with her usual impetuous nature decided to thank you for this by getting you a child when it was not going to be easy through the proper channels. Isn't that right?'

Frank Quigley looked into the grey eyes of Sister Brigid, competent, unemotional, strong. Irish perhaps a generation ago, but now with a London accent. She reminded him of bright men he met in business.

'That's it. Exactly, Sister.'

Helen hadn't stopped crying. Brigid felt she might not have stopped speaking either. With what seemed like a deliberate effort she put her arm around the girl's shoulder.

'Let's take you home, Helen, back to St Martin's. That's the best thing now.'

'Will I drive you?' Frank asked.

'No, but if you could get us a mini-cab or a taxi, Mr Quigley.'

At this moment Nessa came in; the baby was asleep. They would take him to the hospital, the one they knew, and where they were known. He would be looked after.

'It seems a pity in a way, Sister.' Frank looked at Sister Brigid, and she looked back. The glance was a long one.

It was a pity in many ways. They could give the boy

everything, including more love than he would ever know from Yvonne.

'Yes, but if we do this, everything breaks down. Every single thing.'

He felt she was tempted.

'Not everything, just one little bit of form-filling. The mother thinks he is dead.'

'Please,' Renata said. 'Please, Sister.'

'I'm not God, I'm not even Solomon,' said Brigid.

They knew it was hard for her, and they drew together, the handsome couple. Helen watched them with a look of pain in her face.

The porter had been asked to hail a taxi, and the unlikely foursome walked to the lift, Helen tearful and supported by Sister Brigid, red-haired Sister Nessa carrying the tiny baby wrapped in its blue rug.

Renata stretched out her hand to touch Helen's arm.

'Thank you, Sister Helen, I know you meant kindly for me,' she said.

'Sister Helen has a great big heart,' Brigid said.

'Thank you,' Frank said at the door. He did not look at Helen, he looked instead admiringly into the grey eyes of Brigid.

'There are countries where it is all legal. If you like, some day you can ask me and I will tell you what I know,' she said.

'Goodbye, Frank,' Helen said.

'Thank you, Helen. Sister Brigid is right, you have a great big heart.' He touched her cheek.

In the taxi they were silent, until Helen said, 'You called me Sister Helen, does this mean I can stay?'

'It means we won't ask you to go yet. But maybe now that you have faced some things you haven't faced before, it mightn't be as necessary to hide as it once was. Perhaps you will be able to make your life somewhere else. Travel the world, even.'

This time Helen didn't think that Sister Brigid was asking her to leave. She felt better than she had felt for a long time.

She looked at Sister Nessa holding the tiny boy close to her breast.

'Isn't it sad that you can't keep the baby, Nessa,' Helen said with a rush of generous spirit. 'To make up for the one you had

that died. It could be a kind of substitute, couldn't it? A consolation.'

She didn't even notice the two women glance at each other
and then look out the windows on each side of the taxi.

4

Desmond

Of course the corner shop was more expensive than the super-market but then it *was* on the corner, that's what you were paying for. And the fact that it stayed open so late at night.

Desmond liked calling in there. There was a mad magical feel about the place and the way Suresh Patel was able to pack in so many goods on his shelves . . . and in such a way that they didn't all come tumbling down. Desmond often said that Mr Patel must have a secret. Over in the big supermarket chain Palazzo Foods where Desmond worked, the principle was totally different. You had to give maximum space so that the customer could walk around and choose and best of all be persuaded by something that had not been on the original shopping list. Mr Patel's business was the other end of the market. They came in because they had run out of sugar or they hadn't bought anything for the supper and the shop they intended to go to had been closed. They came for the evening paper and a tin of beans sometimes. Mr Patel said that you'd be surprised how many people must be going home to a lonely evening. He often felt better off standing in his shop talking to whoever came and went.

Desmond's wife Deirdre said she had nothing against Mr Patel personally, he was extremely polite and respectful always, but everything was that little bit dearer there. The place was a mixem gatherem, a bit like those hucksters' shops you didn't go into years ago at home in case things mightn't be quite . . . well, fresh.

And she never knew why Desmond would stop and buy an earlier edition of the paper in the corner shop when he could have got one nearer work and had the pleasure of reading it on the way home.

Desmond found it hard to explain. There was something solid about the little place. It didn't depend on the fluctuations of far-away suppliers and huge multinationals. If Mr Patel noticed a customer asking for something he gave it a lot of thought. Like the time Desmond had asked for red-currant jelly.

'Is it a jam or a condiment?' Mr Patel had asked with interest.

'I think it can be either.' Desmond had been equally interested in the definition. Between them they decided that once it had been bought, it would be placed on a shelf with the mustards, the chutneys and the little green jars of mint sauce.

'Soon I will know exactly the tastes and temperaments of a fine British suburb, I will know enough to write a book, Mr Doyle.'

'I think you know that already, Mr Patel.'

'I am only starting, Mr Doyle, but it is all so interesting. You know the saying they have in your country about all human life is here . . . that's what I feel.'

'All human life is in my job too but I don't welcome it as much as you do.' Desmond smiled ruefully.

'Ah, that's because your job is so much more important than mine.'

Deirdre Doyle would have agreed with him, Mr Patel was right to look with respect at a man like Desmond who though well under fifty was Special Projects Manager at Palazzo. Palazzo was a name like Sainsbury's or Waitrose. Well not quite like them, but in certain areas it was just as well thought of and back home in Ireland where nobody knew any of the others anyway, a Palazzo sounded much grander.

The Patels didn't live in Rosemary Drive, naturally they lived somewhere else, somewhere more suitable for Indian and Pakistani people, Deirdre said, when anyone brought the subject up.

Desmond knew that in fact Suresh Patel, his wife, his two children and his brother lived in the tiny storerooms behind the small shop. Mrs Patel could speak no English and the brother was fat and looked as if he had some illness. He used to sit there and smile perfectly pleasantly but he spoke little and did not seem to be any help in the running of the corner shop.

For some reason that he never totally understood Desmond never mentioned that the Patel family lived there. That their two children, immaculate in school uniform and wearing blazers and spectacles, came out each morning from this tiny place. Desmond felt that somehow it demeaned the Patels to be thought to live in such a small place, and somewhere in his subconscious he felt that Deirdre might think it demeaned the neighbourhood to have Pakistanis actually living there rather than just trading.

The shop was busy in the early morning, people buying papers, bars of chocolate, orange drinks and plastic-wrapped sandwiches. The stuff that kept the commuters more or less alive on their journeys to work. The oil that ran the machinery of British industry.

Not that Desmond felt too cheery about his own part in British industry. He was on his way to work at the big headquarters of Palazzo Foods, the supermarket chain which was now ninth largest in Britain. Desmond had begun to work for it back in 1959 when it was simply called Prince. That was the year he and Frank Quigley had left Mayo and come to London by train, boat and train to make their fortune. They arrived during the heatwave that went on month after month, they thought they had come to paradise.

As Desmond took his regular morning journey down Rosemary Drive into Wood Road and on to the bus stop at the corner he often looked back on those days when things were simpler and when he and Frank worked behind the counters in the two Prince Stores. One day they might be slicing bacon, another day dressing windows. Every day they met the customers and they knew everyone who worked in the shop.

It was Frank who had seen that this was a company where they could rise and rise, it was no stopgap job. Prince Foods were breaking new ground, they were getting bigger, soon they would expand and Frank would be a manager in one branch and Desmond in another if they played their cards right. Frank played his cards magnificently. Desmond had always been slower to see the opportunities. But he saw how everything was changing and saw sadly that the higher he rose, dragged, pulled and cajoled by his friend Frank, the further he got from the people, which was what he had liked about it all in the first place.

Desmond Doyle had been a thin wiry young man then with a thick shock of fair brown hair. His children had often teased him about the old photograph, saying that he looked a proper teddy boy, but their mother wouldn't allow that at all. That was the way all young men of style looked then, she would say firmly. He looked different now, combing his hair in a way where it might look as if it was covering his head, and wearing shirts that had a neck size far wider than he wore that first summer when he had only been able to buy two shirts as his entire wardrobe and there was always one hanging on the back of a chair drying.

He supposed that many people looked back on the old days as good days even though they had been practically penniless days. He certainly did.

He could never understand why people liked the Palazzo Building so much. It was a perfect example of Art Deco, they said, a thirties masterpiece. Desmond always thought it looked like one of those big brutalist buildings you saw in documentaries about Eastern Europe. It was a square menacing-looking place, he thought, it was strange that there was a preservation order on it and articles in magazines talking about its perfect proportions.

Frank had been instrumental in getting that building for Palazzo, it was then the disused headquarters of a motor group that had gone bankrupt. Nobody else had seen its potential, but Frank Quigley who knew everything said that they had to have storage space for stock, they had to have a depot and maintenance centre for their vans and they had to have some kind of central offices. Why not combine them all behind this splendid facade?

A facade is what it was. Wonderful stairways and reception rooms on the ground floor. But upstairs a warren of prefabricated and jerry-built offices and partitions. Accounts had been modernized and gone on line in computers, so that was housed in a modern extension at the back. But there was a strange limbo land on the third floor, a place where there were names on doors and people often bursting in saying, 'Oh, sorry'. There were vague storage areas where panelling that hadn't worked or plastic display units that hadn't fitted were left pending decisions.

There in the heart of this hidden chaos, the unacceptable face of Palazzo, lay Desmond Doyle's workplace. The Special Projects Department. Officially it was the nerve centre of new ideas, plans, concepts and illuminations that would wipe the competition off the map. In reality it was the place where Desmond worked and drew his month's salary and kept his managerial title because he was the boyhood friend of Frank Quigley. Because they went back a long way and because they had set out on the same day over a quarter of a century ago.

Frank Quigley the quiet but powerful Managing Director, the man who had seen the way to jump and jumped with the Italians when it came to takeover time. The man who had married the boss's daughter. It was thanks to Frank that Desmond walked up to the third floor of Palazzo and opened the door of his office with heavy heart.

The Special Projects Department was coming under scrutiny. There had been definite rumours that a big investigation was upcoming. Desmond Doyle felt the familiar knot of sour bile in his stomach and the panic beginning to grip his chest. What did it mean this time? An accusation that the section wasn't pulling its weight, a demand for exact quantifying of how much the last instore presentations had realized, and the projected figures likely from the children's promotional exercises.

The antacid tablets seemed to do no good any more, he was eating them like sweets. He was weary of the confrontations and the need to seem bright. Once that business of looking bright and being on top of things had been the be-all and end-all of his day. Not any more. At an age which the rest of the world persisted in thinking of as young, Desmond Doyle felt an old, old man. Forty-six going on ninety. That's what he would have answered truthfully if anyone had asked him caringly about his age.

His office, blessedly free from the photographs that covered the walls in his home, had a pale print of a Connemara countryside. It looked somehow more mauve, blue and elegant than he remembered it, but Deirdre said it was the very spirit of the West of Ireland and he should hang it there so that it could be a conversation piece. He could talk about it to visitors, tell them this was the place he came from. Those were his roots.

Poor Deirdre, thinking that was the kind of conversation that took place in his box-like cubicle of an office. He was lucky to have walls that were not that rough glass or Perspex, he was lucky to have a desk, a telephone and two filing cabinets. The luxury of chats about roots based on over-pastelized views of County Mayo was not anything he had known. Or would ever know.

He no longer felt that the words stuck with cardboard lettering on his door were important . . . there had been no Special Projects in the old days, it was only a made-up word. There had been real jobs like Stores Development Manager, or Operations Manager. Merchandising Manager. These were what the business was about. Special Projects meant nothing to Desmond Doyle because he knew that in his case it was nothing. In other countries it was a real job, he knew that from reading the retail magazines. In Palazzo Foods it meant only a pat on the back.

Desmond remembered way back reading an advertisement which said 'A title on the door means a Bigelow on the floor'. A Bigelow was some kind of a carpet. It was a lovely innocent advertisement trying to drive young executives mad for status. He had told Deirdre about it once but she had missed the point. Why shouldn't he have a carpet too, she had asked. Perhaps they could get some off-cut of carpet themselves and fit it over the weekend, then it would look important and nobody would have to go to war over it and risk a confrontation they might lose. Wearily at that time he had settled for a small rug, which he kept under his desk so that nobody could see it but assured Deirdre that it gave the place class and superiority.

Desmond wouldn't lose his job in Palazzo even if the whole Special Projects Department was deemed to be useless, a criminal waste of time. It was hardly a department anyway, he had that young pup who was meant to be a trainee and the very occasional services of Marigold, a big Australian girl with a mouthful of teeth and a mane of hair who was on what she called OE, Overseas Experience, and had worked in a funeral parlour, as a dentist's receptionist and in the office of an amusement park, all to get an idea of what the world was like before she went home and married a millionaire from Perth, which was her goal.

She was a handsome friendly girl who would sit on Desmond's desk companionably asking if he had any correspondence or memos to type. She thought typing was the golden key to unlocking the world. 'Tell your girls to learn to type, Dizzy,' Marigold told him often. She never accepted that one of his girls was a BA graduate working in a bookshop and the other was a sort of worker nun. Neither of them would take Marigold's golden key to the world.

If Special Projects was wound up Marigold would be sympathetic, she would tell Dizzy that Quigley was a sod and what's more he always tried to pinch her bum. She'd offer to buy him a beer and tell him he was too good for Palazzo and should look around for something better. The young pup of a trainee would hardly notice, he would go and pick his nose in some other part of the store. The pup's father was an important supplier, he would be kept on no matter what happened.

As would Desmond himself. He had been let go once. Never again. Frank Quigley would see to that. His job or a form of it was his for life. He had almost fourteen years more with Palazzo. The company had a retirement at sixty policy. In fact it was less than fourteen years, it was now only thirteen and a bit. They would find something for him to do in that time.

Desmond Doyle would not find himself explaining his existence and justifying his role to his old friend Frank. No, if there was anything unpleasant like that ahead you could be sure that Frank would have pressing business in the furthest part of the land, or a meeting that was so important it could not be rearranged. Desmond would have to talk to Carlo Palazzo himself. The father-in-law, but in no ways a Godfather figure.

Carlo was a man who thought about his family and his soft leather jackets, he had always wanted to be in the fashion business and now with the profit he was making from Palazzo he could have his showrooms and his life's dream. Carlo Palazzo, a mild-looking Italian whose accent seemed to become more pronounced with every year he spent in North London, made none of the day-to-day decisions about his supermarket empire, he left the running of all that to the bright Mr Quigley who he was sharp enough to spot many years ago as the type of hungry young Irishman who could run it. And who could marry Carlo's daughter too.

There were no children yet and Desmond knew that this was a great sadness, but he kept hoping. Even though it seemed increasingly unlikely with every year that went by, fifteen years of marriage and Renata now well into her thirties.

Carlo was an optimist about his grandchildren. But he was a practical man about his profits and if it were he who would conduct the investigation, Desmond sighed, there would be no emotional confidences today, only harsh facts, and even harsher questions. What has Special Projects added to the sum of Palazzo's profit in the last six months? Just list the achievements please, Desmond. Yes?

Desmond drew his pad nearer to him to get the sorry list together. It wasn't that he had no ideas, he was bursting with ideas, but somehow they got lost in this welter of departments and other pressures and needs.

Like the time he suggested they have a bakery on their own premises. That had been a long time ago and very much ahead of its time. Desmond had not been adventurous enough, he had suggested only that they make brown bread and scones. But his reasoning had been so sound it had been taken over on a larger scale than he had ever dreamed. He had said that the smell of freshly cooked bread was very attractive when a customer came in the door, it was the living guarantee that it was absolutely made that day. The fact they could see it being cooked in hygienic conditions spoke volumes for the general hygiene of the rest of the store as well.

But somehow it had gone from him, it was never the Desmond Doyle idea, or the Special Projects suggestion, it had become part of Merchandising, and then a separate section called Bakery started and there were articles and photographs in all the papers about the baps and the twists and the yeast breads they made. Palazzo breads had become a legend.

Desmond didn't waste too many tears over it, an idea was only an idea, once you gave it to other people then it was no longer yours. In terms of seeing it through it didn't really matter whether you got credit for it or not, it was out of your hands. But if you *had* got credit of course, if you had the reputation of being Mister Ideas in the company then life would have a different colour to it during the working day. There would be a bigger office, a proper name on the door and even one of those carpets. Mr Palazzo would ask him to call him Carlo and invite Desmond and Deirdre to their big summer parties in the large white house that had a swimming pool and a big barbecue. And he would beg Deirdre to try on a soft blue leather jacket that had just come in from Milan and exclaim that it looked so well on her she must have it. As a gift, as a token of the esteem in which they held her husband. The ideas man in Palazzo.

The list was looking scrappy. Marigold came in saying she had a raging hangover which had not been improved in the canteen where she had gone to get some cold orange juice to dilute the miniature of vodka. In the canteen Marigold had heard that Mr Carlo was on the warpath, there had been a less than lovely session with his accountants, and he wasn't going to get enough pocket money to play with those dishcloth rags of leather jackets. So he was about to reorganize everyone. Stupid little wop greaseball, Marigold said, if he was back in Australia he'd be man enough to get the hell out into whatever turned him on like these pathetic frocks and coats rather than pretending he knew how to run a business which everyone knew was run by that gangster Frank Quigley.

Desmond was touched by the partisan nature of Marigold's response.

'Sit down there now and stop exciting yourself, you'll only make your head worse,' he said sympathetically.

Marigold looked at him, her eyes pink and puffy but full of concern.

'Jesus Dizzy, you're too good for this shower,' she said.

'Shush, shush. I'm going past the cold store, will I get you some ice for that? A cure's no good without ice.'

'No wonder you'll never run the bloody place, you're a human being,' said Marigold with her head in her hands.

Marigold had only been with Palazzo six months, she said it was nearly time for her to move on already. She had been thinking of a hotel next, or a job as receptionist in a Knightsbridge hairdressing salon where you might see members of the Royal Family coming in.

Greatly revived by her chilled vodka and orange which she had tried to pursuade Desmond to share without any success, she put her mind to dredging up some details of work done in the section during the period she had worked there.

'Jesus, we must have done *something*, Dizzy!' she said, her face frowning with concentration. 'I mean you were never coming in here every day and looking at that picture of the pale blue outback in Ireland all day, were you?'

'I wasn't, I don't think I was, there always seemed to be things to do but they were other people's things, you see.' Desmond sounded apologetic. 'So they don't count as being from here. It's not going to look very impressive.'

'Where will they send you? If they wind it up?'

'This is one of the smallest offices, they might leave me here, reporting to someone else, you know. Same place, same job, different line of responsibility.'

'They'd never give you the heave-ho?'

He reassured her. 'No, no, Marigold, don't worry about that. No.'

She smiled at him roguishly. 'You mean you know where the bodies are buried?'

'In a way,' he said.

He spoke so softly and sadly Marigold let it go.

'I'll go out and see what I can gather from the letters I typed for you anyway,' she said.

It was more or less as Desmond had thought it would be. Carlo sat in the small office not even remotely impressed by the efforts Marigold made calling him Mr Doyle and talking about people on the telephone and saying he was in conference. Marigold had even been to borrow two china cups and saucers for the coffee rather than use the two scarlet mugs with D and ? on them which were usually brought into play.

Carlo Palazzo spoke about the need to redeploy, to continue to expand, to experiment, never to stand still. He spoke about the competition. He talked about inflation, recession, about industrial unrest and about the difficulty of parking cars. In short, he brought in almost every common topic of gloom to support his reluctant decision that the department *as such* should be fused with other departments and its work, important and useful of course as it was, might best be served by being redeployed.

When he came round to using the word redeployed for the second time Desmond felt that it was like going to the cinema and recognizing the part where you had come in.

He felt a great weariness. A realization that this would happen again and again in the next thirteen and a half years. Until possibly the decision might be that he should work in the car park, that would be the best redeploying.

Desmond's head felt heavy, he wondered how best to explain it to Deirdre that evening. He knew there would be no diminution of salary, he knew there would be no public announcement. Only the title would have gone. He was down to essentials now.

'And do you think I should continue in whatever new deployment is agreed from this room, this office?' he asked.

Carlo Palazzo spread out his big hands. If it were up to him, then of course.

'But it's not, Mr Palazzo?'

It wasn't, it appeared, it was reorganization and taking down some partitions and having an open flow, and a lot more light, and a change in some of the stocktaking.

Desmond waited patiently. He knew that it would be told, and no amount of hurrying tactics would work.

He let his eyes wander to the picture with its unlikely blue skies and its soft grassy slopes. Mayo had never been like that. There had been very big white skies and stony walls and small brown fields. The picture was chocolate-box stuff.

Carlo Palazzo was coming to the point.

The point was definitely upcoming, Desmond thought to himself. he felt the familiar acid taste coming from his stomach to his mouth. Please let there be some kind of office. Something which need never have to be explained. Some part of the building where there would be a person, a person like Marigold who would answer the telephone to Deirdre. Someone who would say 'Hold on and I'll put you through' when his wife rang and asked as she always did to speak to Mr Doyle Special Projects Manager, please. With an upward inflection on the please.

Please let there be some word 'manager' somewhere along the line, and let Deirdre not have to spend the rest of her life phoning a business who would not know who he was, let alone where he was.

'So we thought it best if your work was to be in a roving capacity,' Carlo Palazzo said.

'Not roving, Mr Palazzo,' said Desmond Doyle. 'Please, not roving.'

The Italian looked at him with concern.

'I assure you, Desmond, that the work will be just as important, more important in many ways, and as you know there is no question of changing the salary structure, that will remain with the usual emoluments . . .'

'Any kind of base. Anything at all.' Desmond felt the sweat on his forehead. God Almighty, he was beginning to beg. Why could he not have talked it straight through with Frank Quigley?

He and Frank, who had played on the stony hills of Mayo together, who had never seen a West of Ireland sky like the one in the picture, they knew the same language. Why had the barriers of years meant that he couldn't say to Frank straight out that he must have an office even if it was a doorway leading nowhere? It wasn't much after all these years to give Deirdre, the belief that her husband was of managerial stuff in a large and important retailing organization.

There was a time when he and Frank had been able to talk about anything, anything at all. Like how Frank's father drank away a fortune of compensation in three weeks buying large measures for the whole town. Like how much Desmond wanted to escape from the farm and the silent brothers and sisters who seemed happy to stalk the barren land after the scrawny difficult sheep.

They had told each other of their first conquests with girls when they had come here, two ignorant young paddies in the fifties, they had shared everything from the day they had gone to work for Prince Stores. But then a hunger had taken Frank over, and it must have been about that time that the close friendship died.

And Frank had gone for ever up, for ever and ever, he ran everything now. But the Palazzos had bought out Prince Stores and made it their own. It was known that Carlo Palazzo had never made a decision larger than what sauce he would have on his pasta without consulting Frank Quigley. So it was Frank who was dooming his old pal Desmond to be on a roving basis.

Did Frank not remember Deirdre, did he not know how hard this was going to be for him?

Frank came so rarely to Rosemary Drive these days. But still, every time they met each other it was as if the old days were still the same. They banged each other on the shoulders and laughed, and since Desmond never made anything of being on such a low rung of a ladder they had joined so long ago, Frank equally never made any reference to his own high position. Only at the marriage to Renata Palazzo had the real gulf between them become apparent.

Nobody else from Desmond's level was at the wedding, everyone was many degrees above.

Deirdre had hated that wedding. She had been looking forward to it for months and even believed that she and Renata Palazzo would somehow become great friends. It had always been so unlikely that Desmond had never taken her seriously. Renata was years younger than they were, she was from a different world. Deirdre persisted in thinking of her as an Italian immigrant of her own age who would be shy and needing some kind of sisterly advice.

Desmond would never forget how Deirdre's smile had faded

575

at the wedding when the bright yellow dress and coat made in matching man-made fibre came up against the pure silks and the furs of the other women. She who had left the house so cheerily that morning had been sinking into the background even during the church service when an Italian opera singer was getting through 'Panis Angelicus' for the newlyweds. By the time they had arrived at the marquee and joined the line of guests waiting to be received she was tugging at her dress and his arm.

It had been a black day for her and her hurt had darkened the day for Desmond too.

But none of it had been Frank Quigley's fault. Frank's smile never lessened, not ever in the years since then.

You could always go to Frank. You didn't have to say things in so many words. You could use code.

Where in the name of God was Frank today, this new black day when Carlo Palazzo was telling Desmond Doyle that he would have no office, no door, no telephone on a desk possibly?

Should he ask whether he could shortcut the whole thing for them by putting on one of the beige coats that the men who swept the shops put on, and getting down to work immediately with his bucket and pail and cleaning cloth, wiping the vegetable racks just after the doors closed? Would it perhaps be easier than waiting for half a dozen further slides? But then anger filled him too, he wasn't a stupid man, he wasn't a fool who could be passed over like this. He could feel his face working in a way that was beyond his control. To his horror he saw something like pity in the older man's face.

'Desmond, my friend, please,' Carlo began uncertainly.

'I'm all right.' Desmond stood up behind his small desk. He would have strode across to the window so that the telltale tears in his eyes could subside. But his office wasn't one for striding, he would have had to squeeze past the filing cabinet and possibly knock over the small table or ask Mr Palazzo to move his chair. It was too confined a place for grand gestures. Of course, come next week there would be no place for any gestures at all.

'I know that you are all right. I just don't want you to understand me wrongly. Sometimes even after all these years in this country I can't make myself clear ... you know.'

'No, you make yourself very clear, Mr Palazzo, clearer than I do, and English is meant to be my native tongue.'

'But perhaps I have offended you in something I said. Can I try to say it again? You are so valued here, you have been here so long and your experience is so necessary . . . it is just that circumstances change and there is an ebb and flow . . . everything is being . . . what word will I use . . . ?'

'Redeployed,' said Desmond flatly.

'Redeployed.' Carlo Palazzo seized it and ran with it, not knowing he had already used it twice. His smile was broad. As if this word somehow rescued things.

He saw from Desmond's face that it didn't.

'Tell me, Desmond, what would you like best? No, it's not an insulting remark, not a trick question . . . I ask you what would you like best in work, what way would be the best way for things to work out for you today? Suppose it were possible for you to stay here, would that be your dream, your wish?'

The man was asking seriously, it wasn't a game of going forwards and back. Carlo wanted to know.

'I don't suppose it would be my dream, no. Not to stay in this room as Special Projects Manager.'

'So.' Carlo looked for some silver lining desperately. 'So why then is it so bad to leave it? What other place would have been your dream?'

Desmond leaned on the corner of the filing cabinet. Marigold had decorated the place a little with a few borrowed plants which she must have grabbed from the carpeted offices. Desmond hoped she hadn't actually taken any of Carlo's own greenery. He smiled a little to himself at the thought, and his boss smiled back, looking up eagerly from the chair in front of the desk.

Carlo had a big kind face. He didn't look shifty, he was the kind of Italian who always played the kind uncle or indeed the loving grandfather in a film.

It was Carlo's dream to be a grandfather many times over, to have a lot of little grandsons with half-Irish and half-Italian names running in and out of that huge white house. Children to leave his share of Palazzo to. Did Desmond dream of grand-children too? He didn't know. What a dull man he must be not to know his own dream when he was asked it by this big straightforward man.

'It's so long since I allowed myself to have a dream I suppose I've forgotten what it was,' he said truthfully.

'I never forgot mine, I wanted to go to Milano to work with the fashion,' said Carlo. 'I want to have the finest craftsmen and stitchers and designers all together and to have my own factory with the name Carlo Palazzo.'

'You have your own name over your work,' Desmond said.

'Yes, but it is not what I wanted, not what I had hoped, I only have a little time in what I would have loved. My father he told me I must go into the food business, with my brothers, with my uncles, not playing with clothes like a ladies' dressmaker, he said.'

'Fathers don't understand,' Desmond said simply.

'Your father . . . did he not understand perhaps?'

'No, my father neither understood nor didn't understand, if you know what I mean. He was always an old man. When I was ten, he was old, and it wasn't just that I *thought* it, he looks it in every picture. He only understood sheep and hillsides and silence. But he never stopped me, he said I was right to go.'

'Then how do you mean fathers never understand?'

'I didn't understand. I did all this for my son. I wanted him to have as good an education as possible, I didn't understand when he left.'

'Where did he go?'

It had never been admitted outside Rosemary Drive. Never beyond the walls.

'He ran away, he ran back to the sheep and the stones and the silence.'

'Well, you let him go.' Carlo didn't seem shocked that Desmond's son had run off uneducated to the back of beyond.

'But not with a good grace.' Desmond sighed.

Carlo was still puzzled. 'So did you want a life of high education?'

For some reason the small eager face of Suresh Patel flashed into Desmond's mind, his dark eyes feverish with the wish to heap degrees and diplomas on his family.

'No, not a high education. Just a place, I suppose, a place that was mine.'

Carlo looked around the featureless office, which he probably remembered as being even more featureless over the previous months without its injection of borrowed plants.

'This place? It feels so important?'

Desmond had somehow come to the end of the road.

'To be honest, Mr Palazzo, I don't know. I'm not a man of very strong opinions. I never was. I have ideas, that's why I suppose Frank and you thought I'd be good here. But they are personal ideas, not corporate ones, and I'm inclined to get a bit lost whenever there's redeployment and the like. But I'll manage. I'll manage. I've always managed before.'

He didn't sound frightened now or self-pitying. Just resigned and practical. Carlo Palazzo was relieved that the mood, whatever it had been, had passed.

'It's not going to happen overnight, it will be in two to three weeks, and in many ways it will give you more freedom, more time to think about what you really want.'

'Maybe it will.'

'And there *will* be a title of manager, it hasn't been quite worked out yet but when Frank gets back I'm sure . . .'

'Oh, I'm sure he will,' Desmond agreed readily.

'So . . .' Once more Carlo spread his hands out.

This time he was rewarded with a half smile and Desmond stretched his own hand out as if to shake on something that had been agreed between two men of like mind.

Carlo paused as if something had struck him.

'Your wife? She is well?'

'Oh yes, Deirdre's fine, thank you Mr Palazzo, blooming.'

'Perhaps she might care to come some evening to have . . . to have a meal in our house with us, the family, you know, Frank and Renata and everything . . . You were all such friends in the old days . . . before any of this . . . that's true, yes.'

'That is very kind of you Mr Palazzo.' Desmond Doyle spoke in the voice of a man who knew that no such invitation would be issued.

'That will be good, we will enjoy that.' Carlo Palazzo spoke in exactly the same voice.

Marigold held the door open for the great chief Mr Palazzo. He looked at her with a vague and pleasant smile.

'Thank you, thank you . . . um.'

'I'm Marigold,' she said, trying to iron out her Australian accent. 'I'm lucky enough to work for Mr Doyle. There have been several important calls, Mr Doyle, I told them that you were in conference.'

Desmond nodded gravely, and waited until the footsteps were gone for Marigold to hiss at him, 'Well, what happened?'

'Oh Marigold,' he said wearily.

'Don't "Oh Marigold" me, didn't I make you look good? Didn't you hear me? Bet he thinks a lot more of you now. Saying I was lucky to be working for you.'

'I expect he thinks you're sleeping with me,' Desmond said.

'I wouldn't half mind.'

'You're possibly the nicest girl in the world.'

'What about your wife?' Marigold asked.

'Oh, I don't think she'd like you to sleep with me, not at all.'

'I mean isn't she the nicest girl in the world, or wasn't she once or what?'

'She's very nice, very nice indeed.' He spoke objectively.

'So no chance for me then.' Marigold was trying to jolly him along.

'Palazzo's not the worst. That's a great Irish expression for you, to say a man is not the worst, it's grudging praise.'

'He didn't give you the bum's rush then?' Marigold's face lit up.

'No, he gave me the bum's rush all right.'

'Aw, shit. When? Where?'

'Soon, a week or two when Frank gets back.'

'Frank's not away,' Marigold said furiously.

'No, but you know, we say he's away.'

'And where are they sending you?'

'Here and there, roving apparently.'

'Is there any good in it, any good at all?' Her eyes were tender, her big handsome face concerned, and she bit her lip at the unfairness of it all.

He couldn't bear her sympathy.

'Oh, it's all right, Marigold, there's plenty of good in it. I don't see this as anything we should fight them on the beaches for, do you . . . ?'

He looked around the office and made a theatrical gesture with his arms.

'But roving?' She seemed upset, he had to reassure her.

'It's more interesting than sitting here and seeing nothing at the end of it. I'll roam up and see you from time to time, you'd brighten my day.'

'Did they say why?'

'Redeployment of resources.'

'Redeployment of balls,' Marigold said.

'Maybe, but what's the point?'

'You didn't *do* anything, they shouldn't take your job away.'

'That could be it, perhaps I really *didn't* do anything.'

'No, you know what I mean, you're a manager for God's sake, you've been here years.'

'There's still going to be a manager's title, of whatever sort . . . We don't know yet, we'll know later . . .'

'Later, like when Frank gets back.'

'Shush, shush.'

'I thought you two were meant to be such friends.'

'We were, we are. Now please, Marigold, don't *you* start.'

She saw, sharp and quick, Marigold, and impulsively she said it.

'You mean you're going to have all this with your wife tonight, is that it?'

'In a way, yes.'

'Well, consider me a bit of a dry run.'

'No. Thank you, I know you mean well.'

She saw the tears in his eyes.

'I mean very well, and I'll tell you this: if your wife doesn't understand that you're one of the best . . .'

'She does, she does.'

'Then I'll have to go round to your house and tell her she's got one beaut guy and I'll knock her head off if she doesn't know it.'

'No, Deirdre will understand, I'll have had time to think about it, explain it properly and put it in perspective.'

'If I were you I wouldn't spend any time rehearsing, ring her up, take her out to lunch, go on, find a nice place with tablecloths and buy a bottle of grog, tell her about it straight, there's no perspective.'

'Everyone does things they want to in the end, Marigold,' he said firmly.

'And some people, Dizzy, do nothing at all,' she said.

He looked stricken.

Impulsively she flung her arms around him. He felt her sobbing in his arms.

'I'm such a loudmouth,' she was saying.

'Hush, hush.' Her hair smelled lovely, like apple blossom.

'I was trying to cheer you up, and look at what I ended up saying.'

Her voice was becoming more normal. Gently he released her and held her from him, looking admiringly at the lovely Australian, the same age perhaps as his own Anna or a little older. The daughter of some man out on the other side of the world who had no idea of the kind of jobs this girl was doing and how she entered into them with all her heart. He said nothing, just looked at her until she sniffed herself to some kind of calm.

'Great if the old greaseball had come back and found us in a clinch, would have confirmed everything he suspected.'

'He'd have been jealous,' said Desmond gallantly.

'He would in a pig's eye, Dizzy,' she said.

'I'm going out, I think,' Desmond said.

'I'll tell them you're practising roving if they ask,' she said, almost grinning.

'Don't tell them anything,' he said.

That was what he always said.

He phoned Frank from a call box near one of the entrance gates.

'I'm not sure if Mr Quigley's available, can I say who wants him?'

Long pause. Obviously a consultation.

'No, I'm very sorry Mr Doyle, Mr Quigley's away on business, was this not told to you? I believe Mr Palazzo's secretary was to let you know . . .'

'Sure, I just wondered was he back.' Desmond was mild.

'No, no.' The voice was firm, as if speaking to a toddler who hadn't quite understood.

'If he calls in tell him that . . . tell him.'

'Yes, Mr Doyle?'

'Tell him nothing. Say Desmond Doyle rang to say nothing, like he's been saying all his life.'

'I don't think I quite . . .'

'You heard me. But I'll say it again.' Desmond said the words again and felt some satisfaction at the sound of them. He wondered was he perhaps going mad.

It was the middle of the morning and there was a strange

sense of freedom about walking out through the big Palazzo gates. Like a child being sent home from school with some kind of sickness.

He remembered at the Brothers years ago how he and Frank had mitched off for the day. Nobody knew that word over here, skived is what they called it. They had told the Head Brother that they had inhaled a bag of chemicals in the schoolyard and that their eyes were red and they were choking. They managed to persuade him that the cure would be fresh air.

Desmond could still recall thirty-five years later that freedom, as they ran and skipped over the hills, liberated in every way from the small classroom.

One of the things they had found lacking then was any way of finding people to play with. Everyone else was sitting resentfully in the classroom. They had felt the lack of a gang and had gone home earlier than they would have thought likely.

It was somehow the same today. There was nobody that Desmond could ask to come and play. Nobody to buy a bottle of grog for as Marigold had suggested. Even if he were to take the train in to Baker Street and go to Anna's bookshop she might not be free. And she would be alarmed, it was so out of character. His only son who had been lucky enough to recognize some kind of freedom and run for it was far far away. His other daughter away in her convent would not understand the need that he had to talk, the great urgency to define himself somehow.

It was a poor totting up of twenty-six years in this land that he could think of no other person in the whole of London that he could telephone and ask to meet him. Desmond Doyle had never thought of himself as a jet-setter but he had thought of Deirdre and himself as people with friends, people who had a circle. *Of course* they were. They were going to have a silver wedding anniversary shortly and their problem was not looking for people, it was trying to cut down on numbers.

What did he mean that he had no friends, they had dozens of friends. But that was it. *They* had friends. He and Deirdre had friends and the problem had nothing to do with redeployment or managerial titles, the trouble was a promise made and a promise broken.

He had sworn to her that night so many years ago that he would rise in the business, he would be a name for the O'Hagan family in Ireland to take seriously. He had said that Deirdre would never go out to work. Her mother had never gone out to work, and none of Deirdre's friends who married back in 1960 would have expected to go and look for a job. Ireland had changed since then, had become more like England. Mrs O'Hagan's nose, which seemed to turn up very easily, would not turn today if a young woman went on for further education or took any kind of work to help build a family home.

But those were black days long ago, and the O'Hagan scorn had been hard to bear. And Desmond knew that his promise was given under no duress. He had held Deirdre's small hand and on the night they were about to tell her parents the news, he had begged her to trust him. He remembered his words.

'I always wanted to be in buying and selling, I know it's not the thing to tell your family but even when the tinkers came to town I loved it, there was an excitement about it, about the way they put out their scarves and bright glittering combs on the ground, I knew what it was about.'

Deirdre had smiled at him confidently, knowing he would never bring up anything as alien as tinkers in the O'Hagan household.

'I want *you*,' he had said, 'I want it more than anything in the world and when a man has a dream there's nothing he cannot conquer. I'll conquer the retail business in England. They'll be glad they didn't lose you to a doctor or a lawyer. The day will come when they'll be so glad they settled for a merchant prince.'

And Deirdre had looked at him trustingly as she had always looked ever since.

He supposed that she was still his dream, but why had she not come to his mind when Mr Palazzo had asked him?

Desmond found himself walking the well-trodden path towards home. His feet had taken him on automatic pilot to the bus stop. At this time of day there were no crowds, no queues, how pleasant to be able to travel like this instead of incessant rush hours.

Suppose he *did* ring Deirdre, he knew she was at home, she was working over that infernal silver wedding list again. Surely she would appreciate his honesty and directness?

She loved him in a sort of way, didn't she? Like he loved her. And he did love her. She had changed of course like everyone changed, but it would be ludicrous to expect her to be the fluffy blonde desirable young Deirdre O'Hagan who had filled his thoughts and his heart so urgently. Why wasn't she the dream? She was connected with the dream in a way. The dream was to make good his promise. But he couldn't have told that to Carlo Palazzo in a million years, not even if he had been able to articulate it, which he hadn't. Not until this moment when the bus was approaching.

Desmond hesitated. Should he let the bus go, find a telephone and invite his own wife out to lunch and tell her his own real thoughts? In the hope that they could somehow share them the way they had shared every little heartbeat during that time when they stood strong against the might of the O'Hagans about their marriage.

'Are you getting on or are you not?' the conductor asked him, not unreasonably. Desmond had been standing holding the rail. He remembered Marigold saying to him, 'Some people, Dizzy, do nothing at all.' But he was nearly on the bus.

'I'm getting on,' he said. And his face was so mild and inoffensive that the tired young bus conductor who also wanted a different and a better life abused him no further.

He sorted it out for Deirdre as he walked towards Rosemary Drive, little phrases, little reasoning steps. There would be more scope in a roving managerial position, he would get to know the workings of the company at first hand rather than being tucked away in his own little eyrie. He would explain that Frank had been called away, he would mention that the exact wording was not firmed up but the magic word Manager would be included. He would not mention the Palazzo invitation to supper because he knew it would not materialize.

He felt no bitterness towards Frank for avoiding the confrontation. Nor indeed for initiating the move. Frank was probably right, the functions of Special Projects had indeed been taken over.

Frank at far remove might even be giving him a chance to find a better niche. He wished he could summon up more enthusiasm for this niche, whatever it might be.

It would confuse Deirdre to see him arriving home unexpectedly for lunch. She would fuss and say over and over that he should have warned her. The importance of his news would be lost in a welter of worries about there being nothing at hand.

Desmond decided that he would go into the corner shop, and tell Mr Patel that yet again he had provided a service. They sold pizzas there, not very good ones, wrapped in rather too much plastic and with the wrong ratio of base and topping. Still that might do. Or he might get a tin of soup and some crusty French bread. He didn't remember whether Mr Patel sold chicken pieces, that might be nice.

There were no customers in the shop, but more unusually there was nobody sitting at the till. On the few occasions when Suresh Patel did not sit there himself as if at a throne, still able to advise and direct his tiny empire, there was always another occupant. His silent wife, wordless in English but able to ring up the prices she read on the little labels. Sometimes it was the young owlish son or the pert little daughter. Mr Patel's brother didn't seem capable of manning the family business.

Desmond moved past the central aisle and saw with that lurching feeling of recognition that a raid was in progress.

There was that slow-motion sense of things not being real. Desmond felt as he looked at the two boys in their leather jackets beating the fat brother of Suresh Patel that this was like an action replay when watching a football match.

Desmond felt the old bile, but this time it was a sharper feeling. He thought he was going to choke.

He took two steps backward. He would run out and raise the alarm, he would run around the corner to the street where there would be more people passing by. *And*, if he was honest, where there would be less chance of the two muggers catching him calling for help.

But before he could go any further he heard the voice of Suresh Patel calling to the boys with the bars.

'I beg of you, I beg of you, he is simple in the head, he does not know anything about any safe. There *is* no safe. There is money in the night deposit. Please do not hit my brother again.'

Desmond saw with another shock that he could feel physically in his own stomach that Mr Patel's arm hung at an odd angle. As if it had already been beaten. And already broken.

Even if Marigold had not said to him sadly that there were some people who never did anything at all, he would have done what he did. Desmond Doyle, the man so mild that he had to be moved from an office lest he take root, so meek that he made a young Australian beauty cry over his future, knew suddenly what he had to do.

He lifted the stack of trays which had held the bread delivered that morning and he brought it suddenly down on the neck of the first leather jacket. The boy, who could hardly have been as old as his own son Brendan, fell with a thud to the floor. The other one looked at him wild-eyed. Desmond pushed him, jabbing him with the trays, and manoeuvred him towards the back rooms, the living quarters of the whole family.

'Is your wife in there?' he shouted.

'No, Mr Doyle.' Suresh Patel looked up from the floor like people look up in films when rescuers arrive.

The brother who didn't know where the safe was smiled as if his heart was going to burst.

On and on Desmond pushed and prodded, his strength flooding to him. Behind him he heard voices come into the shop. Real customers.

'Get the police immediately, and an ambulance,' called Desmond Doyle. 'There's been a raid. Go quickly, any private house will let you phone.'

They ran, the two young men delighted to be on the safe end of a heroics job, and Desmond pushed a cabinet up against the door to the room where he had cornered the bewildered boy in the leather jacket.

'Can he get out that way?' he asked.

'No. We have had bars on the window and everything, you know in case something like this . . .'

'Are you all right?' Desmond knelt on the floor.

'Yes. Yes. Did you kill him?' He nodded towards the boy on the floor who was regaining consciousness and starting to groan.

Desmond had taken his iron bar away from him, and stood prepared to deal another blow, but the boy was not able to move.

'No, he's not dead. But he'll go to gaol, by God he'll go to gaol,' said Desmond.

'Perhaps not, but it doesn't matter.' The shopkeeper tried to get himself to his feet. He looked weak and frightened.

'What matters then?' Desmond wanted to know.

'Well, I have to know who will run this shop for me – you

see my brother, how he is, you know how my wife cannot speak, I must not ask the children to desist from school, they will miss their places and their examinations . . .'

Far away Desmond heard a siren, the two heroes were bursting back in saying the Law was on the way.

'Don't worry about that,' Desmond said gently to the man on the floor. 'That will all be organized.'

'But how, how?'

'Have you any relations, cousins, in businesses like this?'

'Yes, but they cannot leave their own places. Each place, it has to make its own way.'

'Yes I know, but when we get you to hospital, will you be able to give me their names? I can get in touch with them.'

'It is no use, Mr Doyle, they will not have the time . . . they must work each in their own.'

His face was troubled and his big dark eyes filled with tears. 'We are finished now. It's very simple to see,' he said.

'No, Mr Patel. I will run the shop for you. You must just tell them that you trust me and that it's not any kind of trick.'

'You cannot do that, Mr Doyle, you have a big position in Palazzo Foods, you only say this to make me feel good.'

'No, it is the truth. I will look after your shop until you come back from hospital. We will have to close it today of course, put up a notice, but by tomorrow lunch time I will have it working again.'

'I cannot thank you . . .' Desmond's eyes also filled with tears. He saw that the man trusted him utterly, Suresh Patel saw Desmond Doyle as a great manager who could do what he willed.

The ambulance men were gentle. They said he had very likely broken a rib as well as an arm.

'It might be some time, Mr Doyle,' said Suresh Patel from the stretcher.

'There's all the time in the world.'

'Let me tell you where the safe is.'

'Not now, later, I'll come to see you in the hospital.'

'But your wife, your family, they will not let you do this.'

'They will understand.'

'And afterwards?'

'Afterwards will be different. Don't think about it.'

The policemen were getting younger, they looked younger

than the villains. One of them was definitely younger than Desmond's son Brendan.

'Who is in charge here?' the young policeman asked with a voice that had not yet gained the confidence it would have in a few short years.

'I am,' said Desmond. 'I'm Desmond Doyle of 26 Rosemary Drive and I'm going to look after these premises until Mr Patel comes back from hospital.'

Father Hurley

Nobody except his sister called Father James Hurley Jimbo, it would have been unthinkable. A man in his sixties with silver hair and a handsome head. He had the bearing of a bishop, and a lot of people thought he looked much more bishop like than many of those who held the office. Tall and straight, he would have worn the robes well, and even better the cardinal's red. But Rome didn't go on appearances, and Father Hurley's name had never been brought to any corridors of power.

It was impossible to find anyone who would speak a word against him. His parishioners in several County Dublin districts had loved him. He was able it seemed to move just fast enough with the changes that came to the Church after the Vatican Council, but not too fast. He could murmur calming things that soothed the most conservative and yet he seemed to go far along the road that allowed the laity to have a say. He wasn't exactly all things to all of his flock but he certainly avoided irritating them.

And in a Dublin where anti-clericalism among the younger liberals was becoming rife, this was no mean feat.

He was not a television priest, he had never been seen on the screen debating any issue. He was not the kind of man who would officiate at the marriage of known atheists having a church wedding just for the show, but neither was he the old-fashioned curate who went to Cheltenham in March with a pocket full of fivers, or cheered on the dogs at a coursing match as they followed the hare. Father Hurley was a travelled educated soft-spoken man. People often said that he looked like an academic. This was high praise. And he was amused that it was sometimes regarded as even higher praise when he was described as looking not like a priest but more like a vicar!

James Hurley seemed to have moved quietly from parish to parish without either an upward or a downward movement. There did not seem to be the sense of advancement that such a well-spoken thoughtful man might have been led to expect, but it was rumoured that he never sought any promotion. You couldn't say he was unworldly, not Father Hurley who liked fine wines and was known to enjoy pheasant and to relish lobster.

But he always seemed totally contented with his lot, even when they had sent him to a working-class parish where he was in charge of fourteen youth clubs and eleven football teams instead of the drawing rooms and the visits to private nursing homes of his previous position.

He had been at school at one of the better Catholic schools in England, not that he ever talked about it. His family had been wealthy people and it was rumoured that he was brought up on a big estate in the country. But none of this ever came from the man himself, he would laugh easily and say that nobody in Ireland should try to shake their family trees for fear of what might fall down. He had a sister who lived in the country with her husband, a country solicitor of substance, and their only son. Father Hurley did speak of this boy, his nephew, with great affection. Gregory was the only part of Father Hurley's private life where he ever volunteered information.

Otherwise he was just a very good and interested listener to other people's stories. Which is why people thought he was such a good conversationalist. He talked only about them.

In the various presbyteries where Father Hurley's life had taken him there were pictures of his mother and father, now dead, in old-fashioned oval frames. There was a family picture taken at Gregory's first Communion, and another one of Gregory's Conferring. A handsome boy with his hand lightly laid on his parchment scroll and his eyes smiling through the camera as if he knew much more than any other graduate who was posing for stiff formal photographs that day but took it all very casually.

For the people who told Father Hurley their own life stories, their worries and their tittle-tattle, Gregory was an ideal conversation piece, they could ask for him, and hear an enthusiastic response, enough to look polite, then they could return to their own tales again. They didn't notice that after a certain date the stories about Gregory never originated with Father Hurley and that his replies were vaguer and less informed than they had been once. He was far too diplomatic to let that be seen. That was

591

another thing people said, he would have been very good at the Department of Foreign Affairs, or a consul or an ambassador even.

When James Hurley was a boy his mother had died and he had always thought of Laura as being a combination of mother, sister and best friend. Laura was five years older than he was, she had been seventeen when left in charge of a big crumbling house, a small crumbling brother and a remote and withdrawn father who didn't give any of himself to his children any more than he had given of himself to his wife or the estate he had inherited.

Father James Hurley knew all that now, but then he had lived in a childlike fear of offending his stern cold father still further. Laura could have gone away to university, he always thought, if it had not been for her little brother. Instead she stayed at home and took a secretarial course in the nearby town.

She worked in the local grocery which was eventually taken over by a bigger firm, then she worked in the local bakery which merged with three nearby bakeries and her secretarial job there was over. She worked as the doctor's receptionist and during her time there he was taken off the medical register for professional misconduct. Laura used to tell her little brother Jimbo that she seemed to have a fairly unlucky effect and a dead hand on those she went to work for. Her little brother Jimbo used to suggest she came to work in his school in the hope that she would close it down.

She encouraged him in his Vocation, she took long walks in the country roads with him, and together they sat on mossy banks and on the stile between the fields and talked about the love of God the way others might have talked about sport or the cinema.

Laura Hurley had knelt with tears in her eyes to receive her brother's first blessing after he had said his First Mass.

Their father had died by this stage, remote and uninvolved to the end. James had become a priest; he might have become a soldier or a jockey, it would have been on the same level of interest for his father.

While away at the seminary James had often worried about Laura. She lived in the gate lodge of what had been their home. The Big House was not really big in terms of the landed estates thereabouts but it had been substantial. But Laura felt no sense of having come down in the world, living in the cottage where once people lived rent free if they opened and closed the gates after the Hurley family. Laura had always said cheerfully that it was much easier to keep a small place than a big one, and since their father had gone first to a nursing home and then to his eternal reward she was alone, so it didn't make sense to run the Big House. When it was sold there were so many debts that had gathered from James being a student, from father being a patient in a private nursing home, that the place had been thoroughly mortgaged. There was little in the bank, there was no dowry for Miss Laura Hurley, faithful sister and dutiful daughter.

Laura never thought like that. She was happy, she walked her two big collie dogs, read her books in the evening by her small fire, and went to work by day for the local solicitors. She said laughingly that she hadn't managed to close them down like she had done to every other business she worked for but she had managed to change them utterly.

Like changing the confirmed bachelor status of young Mr Black. The Mr Black who had once been the most eligible man in the county. At the age of forty he looked at Laura Hurley aged thirty-four and a lot of his iron-hard resolve about staying single, uninvolved and free began to chip away.

Then the letter arrived: 'Dearest Jimbo, you'll never believe it but Alan Black and I are going to get married. We would very much like it if you could perform the ceremony for us. Since we're not in the first flush of youth to put it mildly we won't make an exhibition of ourselves here with everyone coming to stare. We would like to come to Dublin and be married in your parish if that's possible. Dearest Jimbo, I never knew I could feel so happy. And so safe and as if things were meant to turn out like this. I don't deserve it, I really don't.'

Father Hurley always remembered that letter from his sister, he could see it, the words almost tumbling over each other on the small cream writing paper. He remembered the way his eyes had watered with a feeling of pleasure that things really did seem to have some point if this kind woman had found someone generous and good to share her life with her. He couldn't remember Alan Black except that he had been very handsome and rather dashing-looking in the past.

Father James Hurley felt that at twenty-nine he was a man of the world. And in a strange way he felt protective of his older sister as he joined her hand with Alan Black's at the wedding ceremony. He hoped this man with the dark eyes and dark hair just greying at the temples would be good to Laura and understand her generosity and how she had never sought anything for herself.

Several times he found himself looking at them and with a hope that was more than a wish, it was a silent prayer, he willed his sister to have a good relationship with this tall handsome man. Laura's face was open and honest, but even on this her wedding day nobody could call her beautiful, her hair was pulled back and tied with a large cream-coloured ribbon which matched the colour of her suit. The ribbon was large enough to be considered a hat or head covering for church. She had a dusting of face powder and a smile that warmed the small congregation to the heart. But she was not a beautiful woman. Young Father Hurley hoped that the attentions of the handsome solicitor would not wander.

Years later he marvelled at his own callow approach and wondered how he could ever have thought himself any use in advising men and women in their lives on their road to God. In a changing world there never was and never had been anything more strong and constant than the love Alan Black had shown to his bride. From the day that they had come to see him, back suntanned and laughing from their honeymoon in Spain, he should have realized that his own judgements based on appearances and vanity were superficial. Why should Alan Black, a bright intelligent man, not be able to see the great worth, goodness and love in Laura Hurley? After all James Hurley had always seen it himself, why should he think it would pass Mr Black the solicitor by?

And as the years went on he used to go to stay with them. They had done up the little gate lodge and built on extra rooms. There was a new study out at one side of the house filled with books from ceiling to floor, they lit a fire there in the evenings and often the three of them sat in big chairs reading. It was the most peaceful happy place he had ever been.

Sometimes Laura would look up from the chair where she lay curled up and smile at him.

'Isn't this the life, Jimbo?' she'd say.

Other days when he visited she might walk with him through the fields and over the stiles and hedges and ditches they had once owned.

'Did we ever think it would turn out so well, Jimbo?' she said often, ruffling the hair of her young brother who would never be the great Father Hurley to her.

And then they told him they were building a similar long low room at the other side of the house. It was going to be a nursery playroom. They would never call it the nursery, they said, they would call it the child's room whatever his or her name was. Nursery was only a baby name. The name was Gregory, Father James held the baby in his arm for the Baptism. A beautiful child with the long dark eyelashes of his father. Gregory Black.

He was their only child; Laura said they would like to have had a brother or sister for him but it was not to be. They made sure he had plenty of other children to play with. He turned out to be the dream child that every doting uncle hopes for.

He would run from the window seat of his own big low room when he saw the car approaching.

'It's Uncle Jim,' he would shout and the old collie dogs would bark and leap and Laura would rush from the kitchen.

When Alan got back from work the smile was broad and the delight obvious. They loved to see him come for a couple of days mid week. They loved the way he got on so well with their son.

Gregory wanted to be a priest of course, when he was around ten. It was a far better life than working in his father's office, he told them all seriously. As a priest you had to do nothing at all, and people paid you money for saying Masses that you'd be saying anyway, and you could get up on a pulpit and tell them all what to do or else they'd go to hell. Sensing a delighted if half-shocked audience, Gregory went on eagerly. It was the best job in the world. And you could refuse to forgive anyone in Confession if you didn't like them and then they'd go to hell, it would be great.

They came to Dublin to see him too and James Hurley never tired of talking about this warm bright boy. Gregory wanted to know everything, to meet everyone. He could charm crabbed old parish priests and difficult women parishioners who were always quick to fancy slights.

'I think you would be good as a priest actually,' his uncle said to him laughingly one day when Gregory was fifteen. 'An awful lot of it is public relations and getting along with people, you're very good at that.'

'It makes sense,' Gregory said.

Father Hurley looked at him sharply. Yes of course it made sense to present an amiable face towards people rather than a pompous one, of course it was the wise thing to do to take the path that would not bring the wrath of authority around your ears. But fancy knowing that at fifteen. They were growing up a lot faster these days.

When Gregory got his place in UCD he was studying Law, that made sense too, he said. He had to study something and Law was as good a training as anything else, meanwhile it kept his father, grandfather and uncle happy to think another Black was going to come into the business.

'And is that what you are going to do?' Father Hurley was surprised. Gregory seemed to him to be too bright, too lively to settle in the small town. There wouldn't be enough to hold his sharp eyes that moved restlessly from face to face, from scene to scene.

'I haven't really thought it out, Uncle Jim. It's what my mother and father would like certainly, and since I don't know yet it makes sense to let them assume that it's what I'll do.'

Again there was a slight chill in the words. The boy had not said he was lying to his family, he had said that since nothing in this world was definite why cross your bridges before you came to them? Father James Hurley told himself that once or twice when he was saying his Evening Office and when the memory of Gregory's words troubled him. He began to think that he was becoming a foolish fusspot. It was ridiculous to read danger into the practical plans of a modern young man.

Gregory graduated well and was photographed on his own and with his father, mother and uncle.

His father was now white-haired, still a handsome man. He was sixty-three now, forty-two years older than his boy. Alan Black had always said that it didn't matter whether you were eighteen years older than your son or forty-eight years older, you were still a different generation. But that in his case it had been everything and more than he had hoped, the boy had never wanted a motorbike, hadn't taken drugs or brought hordes of undesirables back to the home. He had been a model son.

His mother Laura looked well on the Conferring day. She didn't twitter like other mothers did about having produced a son who could write Bachelor of Civil Law after his name and who would shortly be admitted to the Incorporated Law Society as a solicitor as well. Laura wore a bright pink scarf at the neck of her smart navy suit. She had spent what she considered a great deal of money on a haircut, and her grey hair looked elegant and well shaped. She did not look fifty-six years of age but she did look the picture of happiness. As the crowds milled around the university campus she grasped her brother by the arm.

'I almost feel that I've been too lucky, Jimbo,' she said, her face serious. 'Why should God have given me all this happiness when He doesn't give it to everyone else?'

Father Hurley, who certainly did not look his fifty-one years either, begged her to believe that God's love was there for everyone, it was a matter of how they received it. Laura had always been an angel to everyone, it was just and good that she should be given happiness in this life as well as in the next.

He meant it, every single word. His eye fell on a woman with a tired face and a son in a wheelchair. They had come to watch a daughter be conferred. There was no man with them.

Perhaps she too had been an angel, Father James Hurley thought. But it was too complicated to work out why God hadn't dealt her a better hand in this life. He would not think about it now.

They had lunch in one of the best hotels. People at several tables seemed to know Father Hurley, he introduced his family with pride, the well-dressed sister and brother-in-law. The bright handsome young man.

A Mrs O'Hagan and a Mrs Barry, two ladies treating themselves to a little outing, seemed very pleased to meet the nephew of whom they had heard so much. Father Hurley wished they wouldn't go on about how often and how glowingly he had mentioned the young man. It made him feel somehow that he had no other topic of conversation.

Gregory was able to take it utterly in his stride. As they sat down at their own table he grinned conspiratorially at his uncle.

'Talk about me being good at public relations, you're the genius, just feed them a little bit of harmless family information from time to time and they think they know all about you. You're cute as a fox, Uncle Jim.'

It was rescue from being thought to be the gossipy over-fond uncle, certainly, but it did seem to classify him as something else. Something a bit shallow.

Gregory Black decided that he would practise law in Dublin for a few years in order to get experience. Make all his mistakes on strangers rather than his father's clients, he said. Even his old grandfather now in his late eighties and long retired from the firm thought this was a good idea, and his uncle who had no children of his own. His parents accepted it with a good grace.

'It would be ridiculous to keep him down in a backwater after he's been so long on his own in Dublin,' Laura told her brother. 'And anyway he says he'll come down and see us a lot.'

'Does he just think that or will he really?' Father Hurley asked.

'Oh he will, the only thing that made it difficult for him when he was a student was all the train and bus travel. Now he'll have a car it will be different.'

'A car of his own?'

'Yes, it's Alan's promise. If he got a good degree a car of his own!' She was bursting with pride.

And Gregory's gratitude was enormous. He embraced them all with pleasure. His father, gruff with delight, said that of course in time Gregory would change this model and trade it in for another smarter kind. But for the moment . . . perhaps . . .

Gregory said he would drive it until it was worn out. Father James Hurley felt his heart fill up with relief and pleasure that this dark eager young man should know how much love and need encircled him, and respond to it so well.

His parents went back happily to the country, his uncle went happily back to the presbytery and the boy was free to do what he wanted with his life, with a brand-new car to help him on the way.

And Gregory did indeed visit home, he drove smartly in the entrance of the gate lodge and fondled the ears of the collie dogs, children and even grandchildren of the original collies that his mother had loved so much. He would talk to his father about the law and to his mother about his social life in Dublin.

He seemed to have lots of friends – men and women, Laura told her brother eagerly – they went to each other's houses and they even cooked meals for each other. Sometimes she baked a steak and kidney pie for him to take up to his flat, she always gave him bread and slices of good country ham, and bacon, and pounds of butter. Once or twice James Hurley wondered what did she think they sold in shops around the bedsitterland where his nephew lived, but he didn't ever say anything. His sister loved the feeling that she was still looking after the big handsome son she had produced. Why disturb that good warm feeling? To use his nephew's own words, 'it wouldn't make sense'.

He hardly ever coincided with Gregory back down home because the priest was never free at weekends, Saturdays were busy with Confessions and house calls, Sundays with the parish Masses, the sick calls and the evening Benediction. But when he did get back himself mid week for an overnight now and then he was pleased to see that the pleasure of the visits totally outweighed what might be considered the selfish attitudes of their only son.

Laura talked delightedly of how Gregory had this big red laundry bag she had made him and often he just ran into the kitchen and stuffed all the contents into her washing machine.

She said this proudly as if it had taken some effort. She mentioned not at all that it was she who took them out and hung them up to dry, she who ironed and folded the shirts and had an entire laundry ready packed on the back seat of his car for his return journey.

Alan talked about how Gregory loved coming to have Saturday dinner with them in the golf club, how he appreciated the good wines and nice food that were served there.

Father Hurley wondered why Gregory hadn't on some occasions at least put his mother and father into the car they had bought him and driven them to one of the hotels nearby to treat them to a dinner.

But as usual it made no sense to bring up something so negative. And he remembered with some guilt that he had never thought of treating his sister in the old days. He had a vow of poverty perhaps on his side, but there were things he hadn't thought of then. Maybe it was the same in all young men.

And Gregory was great company. He could talk a lot without saying anything, something that could be a compliment or an insult. In Gregory's case it was something to be admired, praised and enjoyed.

Sometimes Gregory went swimming with his uncle out in Sandycove at the Forty Foot, the men's bathing place. Sometimes he called in to have a drink in the presbytery, where he would raise the nice crystal Waterford glass to the evening light and admire the golden whiskey reflecting in the midst of all the little twinkling shapes of glass.

'Great thing this ascetic life,' Gregory would say, laughing.

You couldn't take offence at him, and it would only be a very churlish person who would notice that he never brought a bottle of whiskey with him to add to the store, ascetic or not.

Father Hurley was totally unprepared for a visit from Gregory in the middle of the night.

'I'm in a bit of trouble, Jim,' he said straight away.

No Uncle, no sorry for getting you out of bed at three a.m.

Father Hurley managed to shoo the elderly parish priest and the equally elderly housekeeper back to their respective quarters. 'It's an emergency, I'll deal with it,' he soothed them. By the time he got into the sitting room he saw that Gregory had helped himself to a large drink. The boy's eyes were too bright, he had sweat on his brow, he looked as if he had already had plenty to drink.

'What happened?'

'A bloody bicycle swerved out at me, no proper light, no reflecting clothes, nothing. Bloody fools, they should be prosecuted, they should have special lanes for them like they do on the continent.'

'What happened?' The priest repeated the words.

'I don't know.' Gregory looked very young.

'Well is he all right, was he hurt?'

'I didn't stop.'

Father Hurley stood up. His legs weren't steady enough to hold him. He sat down again.

'But was he injured, did he fall? Mother of God, Gregory, you never left him there on the side of the road?'

'I had to, Uncle Jim. I was over the limit. Way over the limit.'

'Where is he, where did it happen?'

Gregory told him, a stretch of dark road on the outskirts of Dublin.

'What took you up there?' the priest asked. It was irrelevant but he didn't feel he yet had the strength to stand up and go to the phone to let the guards and the ambulance know there had been an accident.

'I thought it was safer to come back that way, less chance of being stopped. You know, breathalyzed.' Gregory looked up, like the way he had looked up when he had forgotten to take one of the dogs for a walk, or hadn't closed a gate up in a far field.

But this time a cyclist lay on the road in the dark.

'Please tell me, Gregory, tell me what you think happened.'

'I don't know. Jesus, I don't know, I felt the bike.' He stopped. His face was blank.

'And then . . .'

'I don't know, Uncle Jim. I'm frightened.'

'So am I,' said James Hurley.

He picked up the phone.

'Don't, don't!' screamed his nephew. 'For God's sake you'll ruin me.'

James Hurley had dialled the guards.

'Shut up, Gregory,' he said. 'I'm not giving them your name, I'm sending them to the accident, then I'll go myself.'

'You can't . . . you can't . . .'

'Goodnight Sergeant, it's Father Hurley from the presbytery here, I've had a message, a very urgent one, there's been an accident . . .' He gave the road and the area. He thought the time was in the last half hour or so. He looked over at Gregory, the boy nodded miserably.

'Yes, it seems it was a hit and run.'

The words had a disgusting finality about them. This time Gregory didn't even lift his head.

'No, Sergeant, I can't tell you any more. I'm sorry, it was reported to me in the nature of confession. That's all I can say. I'm going out there now to see what happened to the unfortunate . . .

'No, it was just confessed to me, I know nothing about any car or who the person was.'

Father Hurley went for his coat. He caught a sight of his nephew's face and the relief that flooded it.

Gregory looked up at him gratefully.

'I never thought of that, but of course it makes sense, you *can't* really tell because of the seal of Confession.'

'It wasn't Confession, I could tell but I'm not going to.'

'You couldn't break the sacred . . .'

'Shut your face . . .'

This was a different uncle than he had ever seen before.

He took a small bag with him in case he would have to administer the last sacrament to a seriously injured victim on the side of a dark road outside Dublin.

'What will I do?'

'You will walk home. And you will go to bed.'

'And the car?'

'I will deal with the car. Get home and out of my sight.'

The cyclist was a young woman. She was according to the student card in her wallet a Ms Jane Morrissey. She was aged nineteen. She was dead.

The guards said that it was always the same no matter how often they saw it, a dead body on the side of the road when some bastard had not stopped, it was terrible. One of them took off his hat and wiped his forehead, the other lit a cigarette. They exchanged glances over the priest, a pleasant soft-spoken man in his fifties. He prayed over the dead girl and he sobbed as if he were a child.

He did it all for Laura, he told himself afterwards in the sleepless nights, because he couldn't drop off and be in a deep dreamless unconscious state for seven and eight hours a night any more. He had changed it to Confession because if it hadn't been then he would have had to report his sister's only boy as a hit-and-run driver. Even within the sacrament of Confession he should still have urged the boy to confess and admit.

In real life things weren't like an old black and white movie with Montgomery Clift playing the tortured priest in an agony of indecision. Today a priest would insist that if a penitent wanted absolution he must face up to the responsibility of his actions, he must make his restitution.

But James Hurley had thought of Laura.

This was a way to save her. It was a way to tell that weak

son of hers that he was regarding the matter as one between sinner and Confessor. It hadn't a leg to stand on in civil or canon law.

He lied to the Garda Sergeant, he said it had been a hysterical call from someone trying to confess, that he had no idea who the driver was. He lied to the parish priest about the caller in the night, he said it was a man looking for alms.

He lied to his sister when she asked him why he couldn't come down soon and see them again. He said there was a lot on in the parish. The truth was that he couldn't look them in the eyes. He couldn't listen while they told him some new tale of Gregory's excellence.

He had driven Gregory's car to a service station on the other side of Dublin in a place where nobody had known him. He had lied to the garage owner, said that he had driven the parish priest's car and hit a gate. The garage man loved to hear that a priest could do wrong too, he knocked out the dent and he gave it a thorough going over.

'The parish priest will think you kept it in great nick now,' he said, glad to be in on some kind of a game.

'How much do I owe you?'

'Ah, go on Father, there's nothing in it, say a few Masses for me, and my old mother, she's not been well.'

'I don't say Masses in exchange for repairs.' The priest had turned white with fury. 'In God's name man will you tell me how much it cost?'

Frightened, the garage owner stumbled out an amount.

Father Hurley recovered and put his hand on the man's arm, 'Please forgive me, I'm desperately sorry for losing control and shouting at you like that. I've been under a bit of strain but that's no excuse. Can you know how sorry I am?'

Relief flooded the man's face. 'Sure, Father, there's nothing like giving a car a bit of a tip against an old gate for putting the heart across you, and specially in the case of a respectable clergyman like yourself. Think nothing of it, it wasn't even as if there was any harm done.'

Father Hurley remembered the white face of Jane Morrissey aged nineteen, student of Sociology with the side of her head covered in rapidly drying blood. He felt faint for a moment.

He knew his life would never be the same again. He knew he had entered a different kind of world now, a world of lies.

He had placed the keys of the car in an envelope and left them through the letter box of Gregory's flat. He had parked the car in the car port and walked back to the presbytery.

He read in the evening papers about the accident, he listened to the appeal for witnesses on Radio Eireann.

He played a game of draughts with the old parish priest with his mind a million miles away.

'You're a good man, James,' said the old priest. 'You don't let me win like the others do. You're a very good man.'

Father Hurley's eyes filled with tears. 'No I'm not, Canon, I'm a very weak man, a foolish, vain and weak man.'

'Ah, we're all foolish, weak and vain,' said the parish priest. 'But given all that, there's goodness in some of us as well and there certainly is in you.'

But those frightening days were long over now, and still sleep didn't come. He had established an uneasy and formal relationship again with his nephew.

Gregory had phoned at once to thank him for the car.

Father James Hurley had said calmly down the phone, 'I'm afraid he isn't here.'

'But that *is* you speaking, Uncle Jim.' Gregory was puzzled.

'I've told so many lies, Gregory, what's one more?' His voice sounded tired.

'*Please.* Please, Uncle Jim, don't talk like that. Is there anyone there listening to you, you know?'

'I've no idea.'

'Can I come and see you?'

'No.'

'Tomorrow?'

'No. Stay away from me, Gregory. Far far away.'

'But I can't do that, not for ever. I don't want to for one thing, and what about Mother and Father for another thing? It would look . . . well, you know how it would look.'

'I don't think they'd guess in a million years. I think you're safe. They would believe better of you. To them it will be just a small paragraph in the papers, another sad thing that happened in Dublin . . .'

'No I mean about us . . . if we're not going to be speaking.'

'I suppose we'll speak again. Give me time. Give me time.'

Gregory couldn't get through to him, not for weeks. If he turned up at the presbytery his uncle apologized but said he was rushing out on a sick call. If he telephoned it was the same.

Eventually he chose the one place where he knew he could get the undivided attention of the man who was running away from him.

In the Confession box the little partition slid back. Father Hurley's handsome head could be seen leaning on his hand, not looking straight at the penitent, but looking forward and slightly down. In a listening position.

'Yes, my child?' he began comfortingly.

'Bless me Father for I have sinned,' Gregory began the ritual. His voice was too familiar not to be recognized. The priest looked up suddenly in alarm.

'Good God, have you decided to make a mockery of the sacraments as well?' he whispered in a low voice.

'You won't listen to me anywhere else, I have to come here to tell you how sorry I am.'

'It's not me you have to tell.'

'But it is, I've told God already through another priest, I have decided to give a certain amount each month out of my salary to a charity to try and make up, I know it won't. I've given up drink. God, Uncle Jim, what more can I do? Please tell me. I can't bring her back to life, I couldn't have even then.'

'Gregory, Gregory.' There were tears in Father Hurley's eyes.

'But what is the use, Uncle Jim, what good will be served if you don't speak to me, and you don't come back home because you don't want to speak about me? I mean if I had been killed that night too, it would all have been different, you'd have been locked in with my mother and father. So shouldn't we be glad I'm alive anyway even if that poor girl was killed in an accident?'

'By a hit-and-run drunken driver.'

'I know, I've accepted it.'

'But not the punishment for it.'

'But what *good* would it do? Really and truly. It would break Mother's heart and disgrace Father, and humiliate you, and suppose it all came out now, now weeks later, it would look so much worse. We can't relive that whole night. I would if I could . . .'

'Very well.'

'What?'

'Just very well. We will be friends.'

'Ah, I knew you'd find it in your heart.'

'Good, well you were right, I've found it in my heart, now can you allow someone else in to make their peace with God?'

'Thank you, Uncle Jim. And Uncle Jim . . .'

The priest said nothing.

'Will you come and have lunch in my flat some time? Maybe Saturday. No liquor but a couple of my friends. Please?'

'Yes.'

'Thank you again.'

He went to the boy's flat. He met two young men and a girl. They were pleasant easygoing company. They drank wine with their lunch and argued genially about whether the Church still ruled everything in Ireland. Father Hurley was practised in this kind of conversation, most of his friends' children took this line. He was bland and unfailingly courteous, he saw the point of view on this hand, on the other hand and on yet further hands. He had a soothing murmur, an ability to appear to lose a point in order to let the opposition concede a point too.

He watched Gregory carefully. Only mineral water went into his glass. Perhaps the boy was shaken and was trying to start a new life. Perhaps James Hurley really should find it in his heart to try to forgive the boy even if he couldn't forgive himself. He smiled at his nephew and got a warm smile back.

They all helped to clear the table out to the small smart kitchen.

'Hey Greg, what's this bottle of vodka doing, if you've given up the jar?' asked one of his friends.

'Oh, that's from the days before, take it with you.' Gregory spoke easily.

Father Hurley wondered whether his own soul had become somehow poisoned because he had a suspicion that his nephew's eyes were somehow too bright for a boy on plain water, perhaps he had been topping it up with vodka out in the kitchen. The other drink was kept on a sideboard.

But if this was the way he was going to think all the time then there was no point in having any relationship with his nephew at all. He put it firmly from his mind. Into that store of other things he was simply refusing to think about these days.

He went to see Laura and Alan during the week. They were delighted to hear about the presence of the girl at the Saturday lunch party, they thought she might be a current girlfriend.

'She didn't seem to be relating to him specially.' Father Hurley felt like an old lady gossiping at a tea party.

'She's been around for a while,' Laura said happily. 'I think this may be the one all right.'

It had been a strange visit, everything his sister and his brother-in-law said seemed to grate on him.

They told him he was lucky to have certainties. Sometimes in the law there were grey areas.

He smiled grimly as if there were no grey areas in his line of work.

They said how lucky they were with Gregory, the son of a friend of theirs had joined Sinn Fein, first as a legal adviser, then as an active campaigner and then as a fully fledged member of the Provisional IRA.

'At least he had some ideals, however misplaced and mad,' Father Hurley said.

'Jimbo you must be mad, there's no ideals in that lot,' Laura cried.

And as always he smiled self-deprecatingly. There was no way he was going to explain to them that he thought any cause was better than the weak-minded cause of saving your own skin which their son had done. With his connivance.

He looked uneasy and unhappy; Alan Black in his diplomatic way changed the subject.

'Tell us, are you officiating at any nice society weddings these days? We love to feel near the high and mighty of the land through you, Jim.'

No, Father Hurley told them that young people always had some friend of their own to marry them nowadays, they didn't go for old family friends of the parents these days. No, not a posh wedding coming up. A silver wedding though, he said brightly, and in England no less.

They were interested as they always were in everything he did. He explained he had married this couple way back in 1960

– it didn't seem like a quarter of a century ago but that was apparently what it was! The daughters and son of this couple wanted him to attend, they had said it would be meaningless if he didn't have some kind of ceremony for them all.

Laura and Alan thought that it was only right that this couple whoever they were would want Father Hurley again.

'I didn't know them very well,' he said, almost as if talking to himself. 'I know Deirdre's mother Mrs O'Hagan slightly, and I knew Mrs Barry, the mother of the bridesmaid Maureen Barry. But I didn't know the young man at all.'

'You never mentioned them.' Laura was drawing him out.

'Well no, I suppose I marry a lot of people. Some I never see again. I always get a Christmas card from Deirdre mind you, I used not to remember exactly who they were, Desmond and Deirdre Doyle and family . . .' He sighed heavily.

'Did you not like them?' Laura asked. 'It doesn't matter telling us, we don't know them, we won't ever meet them.'

'No, they were perfectly nice, I *did* like them as it happened. I suppose I didn't think they were well suited, that they'd stay together . . .' He gave a little laugh to lighten the mood. 'But there you go, I was wrong. They've been together now for twenty-five years and it don't seem a day too much.'

'They must like each other.' Laura was thoughtful. 'Otherwise they wouldn't want you round and have a big do and everything. Will there be a renewing of vows?'

'I don't know, it was their daughter who wrote to me.'

He relapsed into silence, but silence in the big booklined room of Alan and Laura Black was never anything to worry about.

He thought about that wedding, the year that Gregory was born. He remembered how Deirdre O'Hagan had come into his sacristy saying that she had heard from her mother that he was going on a six-month secondment to London. It was partly a study assignment and partly in case he might want to join the Irish chaplaincy scheme in Britain. There were so few English Vocations, and so many of the Catholic flock were Irish or second-generation Irish who preferred a priest from their own tribe.

Deirdre O'Hagan had seemed distressed and tense. She wanted to know could he organize a marriage for her in the next month or so.

It had all the hallmarks of a shotgun marriage but she would not be drawn into any conversation about the reasons for the speed.

He had asked mildly that she should consider having the ceremony in Dublin but she had been adamant. Her fiancé's people were from the West.

But surely Dublin was nearer to the West of Ireland than London was?

Deirdre O'Hagan whom he had remembered as the pretty giggling university student daughter of Kevin and Eileen O'Hagan who were supportive and well-off parishioners seemed to have developed a will of steel. She was marrying in London, she said it would be a kindness to her family to involve a curate whom they knew and liked, but of course if he wasn't able to she would make other arrangements.

Father Hurley had tried at the time, he thought looking back on it, to involve the girl in some questioning of the suddenness of her decision. He had said that one shouldn't go into matrimony too hastily and for all the wrong reasons.

He had obviously sounded stuffy and inquisitive, for he remembered her voice clear as a bell and cold, very cold.

'Well Father, if one was to take your own attitude to matrimony one would never marry at all and one would suddenly find that the whole human race had died out.'

Despite this poor start the wedding had been perfectly pleasant. The boy's people were simple small farmers from the West, they didn't field a very large contingent. The O'Hagans were there in force. A nice man, Kevin, quiet and thoughtful. He had died some years back but Eileen was still going strong.

The bridesmaid had been that handsome young woman Maureen Barry, who ran the smart dress shops nowadays. He had seen her only the other day when he had said the Requiem Mass for her mother. He wondered would she go across to London for this ceremony. He wondered would he. He sighed again.

'You're not in good form, Jimbo.' Laura was concerned.

'I'd love to be an old settled priest, you know, totally certain about everything, no doubts at all.'

'You'd be unbearable if you were,' she said affectionately.

Alan looked up from his book. 'I know what you mean, it

would be easier if there was just one law and you had to administer it, abide by it. It's all this awful business of trying to judge each case on its merits that confuses things.'

James Hurley looked at his brother-in-law sharply but the solicitor had no hidden meaning, no insight about his son and the trouble he had caused. He was thinking in terms of the district court and a justice being lenient here and strict there according to what he knew of the person before him.

'You'd end up like the Nazis if you couldn't make your own decisions,' Laura consoled him.

'Sometimes they're not right, though.' His face was still troubled.

'You'd never do anything unless you thought it was right at the time.'

'And afterwards? What happens afterwards?'

Laura and Alan exchanged glances. Jim was never like this.

Alan spoke eventually. 'Well at least it's not like a hanging judge in the old days. You didn't actually sentence anyone to death.' It was meant to be reassuring. It didn't really work.

'No. No not to death.'

'Will we take the dogs for a walk?' Laura said.

They walked, the brother and sister, sprightly and strong through the fields that they had walked since they were children.

'If I could help?' she said tentatively.

'No, Laura, I'm a weak man to be letting you see my black side.'

'You're my young brother for all that you're a grand important priest.'

'I'm not grand and important. I never got a parish, I never wanted one. I don't want to take charge.'

'Why should you, then? People don't have to.'

'There are some things they have to take charge of.'

She knew he would talk no more about it, and his brow seemed to clear as they walked home in the fading light.

He knew after that afternoon that if the whole terrible business was to have any value whatsoever he must cease these self-indulgent moods. What was the point of saving them worry on one score only to cause it on another? So, they had been spared from knowing that their son had killed a cyclist while drunk and had failed to stop, that had been peace of mind. Why take that peace away from them again by letting them think that he was cracking up and heading for serious nervous trouble?

In the months that followed he hardened his heart to the doubts and he fought the sense of betrayal when he sat with the only family he ever had or would ever know. He began to laugh easily at his nephew's jokes, and managed not to wince at some of Gregory's more insensitive remarks. The priest told himself over and over that to expect a fallible human being to be perfect was to go against the revealed word of God.

He took pleasure in the simple joy that Gregory Black's parents got from their son. He reminded himself that in all his years of parish work he had never come across a family where there was such peace and genuine accord. Perhaps the price for this might never have to be paid in their lifetime.

He forced his smile not to falter when he saw Gregory helping himself liberally to the gins before dinner, the wines with and the whiskies after. The non-drinking resolution had not lasted very long. Neither had the girlfriend.

'She's too determined, Uncle Jim.' He had laughed as he drove Father Hurley across the country rather too fast for the priest's liking. 'You know everything is an absolute with her. No grey area.'

'It's admirable in its way,' Father Hurley said.

'It's intolerable, nobody can be that sure, that definite.'

'Did you love her do you think?'

'I could have I suppose, but not with all this black and white, honesty or dishonesty, you're either a saint or devil. That's not the way it is in the real world.'

Father Hurley looked at the handsome profile of his sister's son. The boy had forgotten the girl he had killed. The ambiguity and hypocrisy of that night had literally been put out of his mind. He was driving his uncle because Father Hurley's car was out of action, and Gregory had wanted to come down mid week, wanted to talk to his father about a loan. There was something coming up, he had heard a piece of information, the kind of chance that only comes once in a lifetime. Something he really shouldn't know, but if he invested now. Boy!

Father Hurley felt sick that he should be allowed to receive this confidence. But then what was he except another grey-area person? Someone prepared to lie when it made sense. It was a strange visit. Gregory's father seemed apologetic about not being able to raise the money that Gregory needed and a little mystified that he wasn't being told exactly what it was needed for.

Gregory's smile didn't falter but he said he would drive out to be on his own for a while near the lake.

Laura said after he had left that it was very sensible of him to go and work out his annoyance sitting looking at the lake. She said that she wished Alan had just given him the damn money, it would all be his after their time, why couldn't he have it now?

By ten thirty he hadn't come back.

Father Hurley knew he was in the pub, the roadhouse out on the lake drive. He said he'd fancy a walk himself, it was a nice night. It was a three-mile walk. He found his nephew in the bar being refused a drink.

'Come on, I'll drive you home,' he said in what he hoped didn't sound a tone likely to anger his very drunk young nephew.

When they got to the car Gregory pushed him away.

'I'm perfectly able to drive.' His voice was steely.

James Hurley had a choice once the boy was behind the wheel – go with him or let him go on his own.

He opened the passenger door.

The corners were legion and the surfaces were not good.

'I beg you, take it slowly, you don't know what's coming round the corner, there's no way we can see the lights.'

'Don't beg me,' Gregory said, his eyes on the road. 'I hate people who whine and beg.'

'Then I ask you . . .'

They were on top of the donkey and cart before they saw it. The frightened animal ahead reared and was emptying the two old men and their belongings on to the road.

'Jesus Christ.'

Helpless they watched as the donkey, roaring in pain, dragged the cart over the body of one old man and started to slip down the bank towards the lake.

Father Hurley was running towards the cart where two children were screaming.

'You're all right, we're here, we're here,' he called.

Behind him he felt the breath of his nephew.

'You were driving, Uncle Jim, in the name of Christ I beg you.'

The priest didn't stop. He had caught the first little tinker child in his arms and pulled her to safety, then the second, and with all the strength in his body he pulled at the braying donkey too.

'Listen, I beseech you. Think about it, it makes sense. They'll hit me with everything, they can't put a finger on you.'

It was as if Father Hurley hadn't heard him, he had children and cart up to the road where the two dazed old men sat. One was holding his head in his hands and blood was coming through his fingers.

In the moonlight Gregory's face was white with terror.

'They're tinkers, Uncle Jim, they're not meant to be out here without any signs or warning or lights . . . nobody could blame you . . . they heard you saying you were driving me home.'

Father James Hurley knelt beside the old man and forced him to take his hands away so that he could see the wound.

'It's all right my friend, it's all right, when somebody comes we'll get you to the hospital, it'll only be a stitch or two.'

'What are you going to do, Uncle Jim?'

'Oh Gregory.'

The priest looked up with tears in his eyes at the only son of the two people who would realize tonight that perhaps life wasn't meant to be all that good on this earth, and that some people had been too lucky.

Maureen

The one thing Maureen's mother would have insisted on had she been alive was that the funeral be done right. Maureen knew exactly what that meant. It meant that there be sufficient notice in the paper for everyone to attend, that there be a judicious invitation back to the house, not everyone but the right people. Both on the day she was brought to the church and on the following day after the burial itself.

Maureen arranged it meticulously, a last homage to the mother who had given her everything and had made her what she was.

She wore a magnificently cut black coat and asked a hairdresser to come to the house so that she would look immaculately groomed in front of all the people who turned up at the church. Maureen did not consider this vanity, she considered that she was carrying out to the letter her mother's last wishes: that Sophie Barry go to her rest mourned publicly by her exquisite and devoted daughter Maureen, successful businesswoman, person of standing in Dublin.

Her mother would have approved too of the drinks and canapés served in the big drawing room, and the way that Maureen moved among the guests pale but calm, introducing here and thanking there, and always being able to remember if it was a wreath, a mass card or a letter of sympathy that had to be acknowledged.

She had nodded in total agreement to all who told her that her mother was a wonderful woman, because this was only the truth. She nodded that it was better her mother didn't have a long illness, she deplored the fact that sixty-eight was too young to die, she was pleased that so many people told her that her mother had been so proud of her only daughter.

'She never talked about anything else.'

'She had a scrapbook of all your achievements.'

'She said that you were more than a daughter, you were her friend.'

Soothing words, gentle touches, graceful gestures. Just as Mother would have liked it. Nobody got drunk and became boisterous but there was the kind of buzz about the whole proceedings that Mother would have thought the mark of a successful gathering. Several times Maureen had found herself planning to talk to her mother about it afterwards.

But then people often said that this was the case. Particularly when you had been close. And there were few mothers and daughters as close as Sophie Barry and her only child Maureen.

Possibly it was because Sophie was a widow and Maureen had been left fatherless for so many years. Possibly because they looked so alike, people read more into their togetherness than there was. Sophie had only become grey late in her fifties, and when she did it was a steel-dark grey as shiny and glamorous as had been the raven-black hair. She had been a size twelve up to the last day and said that she would die rather than wear one of those tent-like creations that so many women seem to sink into after a certain age.

Sophie's good looks and harsh standards did not always endear her to the more easygoing in her circle. But she had what she wanted from them, their total admiration all of her days.

And Maureen would make sure that it would continue in terms of whatever needed to be done now. The house would not be sold with unseemly haste, the mortuary cards would be simple and black-edged, with some tasteful prayer that could be sent as a memento to Protestant friends too. Not something dripping with indulgence-gaining imprecations, no photograph. Mother would say that's what maids did. Maureen would know better than to insult her memory.

Friends had offered to help her go through her mother's things, it can be upsetting they said, it's often easier if an outsider comes to help. Everything can be divided into categories much less emotionally. But Maureen smiled and thanked them, assuring them that this was something she would like to do herself. She didn't particularly want to go through things alone, but Mother would never have let a stranger look at private papers in a million years.

Father Hurley who had known them for years offered to help.

He said it was often a lonely business and he would be happy even to sit with her as company. He had meant well, and Mother had always liked him, she said he was a credit to the Church, nicely spoken, very cultured, knew everyone who was anyone; high praise from Mother. But still Mother would not have let him become involved in her private papers. A gentle moving sermon yes, exactly the right kind of priest for this parish, but he couldn't be involved in anything personal. That would be for Maureen alone.

Walter would want to help of course. But it was out of the question, Walter had been kept at arm's length during the whole proceedings. Maureen had no intention of marrying him, or of being seen to rely on him. Why then should he be allowed to be present at all the funeral ceremonies as her right-hand man? This would be giving a false impression to all those old biddies, friends of her mother, women who had nothing left to talk about in their own lives and speculated instead about each other's children. Maureen, unmarried at forty-six, must have given them many good years of chat and supposition, she thought with a grim pleasure.

Kind courteous Walter, who was thought to be suitable for her because he too was unmarried, of a good family and had a good practice at the Bar. Maureen knew that if she wanted to she could marry Walter. He didn't love her, and she felt nothing even remotely like love for him. But Walter was the kind of man who wouldn't have expected love at this stage in life. Once when he was a younger man, perhaps an unsuitable dalliance or two, maybe even a real affair that didn't work out.

Walter had his male bonding in the Law Library, he had a busy social life. People always wanted an extra man.

Mother had liked Walter but Mother was far too intelligent to push her towards him. Anyway Mother would have been the last to use the argument about insuring against a lonely old age. Look at her own years as a woman without a man. Her life had been very full.

Once Maureen had made it clear that she had no thoughts about Walter as a life partner her mother had never pushed the notion again. There had been no talk of including Walter in a bridge party, a theatre outing, or in the party made up to go to the Aga Khan Cup at the Horse Show.

Walter was kind, courteous, and could indeed after several glasses of good claret be a little emotional. Sometimes he talked of lonely roads, and sacrificing all else on the altar of one's career. But Maureen would laugh at him affectionately and ask him to consider what on earth she and he had sacrificed. They had lovely apartments, good cars, hosts of friends and freedom to go where they liked. In Maureen's case to London and New York buying clothes, in Walter's to the West of Ireland fishing.

In a Dublin which more and more would have accepted such a state they were not lovers. It had been suggested one evening and rejected, with charm and elegance on each side, and broached once more in case the first refusal had been only a matter of form. But they remained two attractive single people whose eyes often met resignedly over a table, as yet again a hostess had brought them together as an inspired idea for a dinner party.

It was ironic that of all the men who had wandered into Maureen's life the only one that Mother would have considered suitable was the one who came too late, who came along when Maureen knew she didn't want to change her ways. If she had met Walter, a young earnest barrister in his twenties when she had been struggling to establish the shops, she might well have settled for him. So many of her friends had settled for men who they could not possibly have loved in any real sense. These were not great loves, the wedding ceremonies that Maureen had attended all through the 1960s, they were alliances, refuges, compromises, arrangements. Deirdre O'Hagan, who defied everyone and married her first love in that long summer when they had all been in London, that might have been real love. Maureen was never sure. Even though she had been Deirdre's bridesmaid, and they had slept in the same room the night before the wedding, she had not been certain that Deirdre ached for Desmond Doyle and cried out to be with him. As she herself had cried out to be with Frank Quigley.

It was a strange friendship, hers with Deirdre, their mothers wanted them to be friends so desperately that they gave in at the age of fourteen and agreed to go to the same tennis parties, and later the same hops and rugby-club social evenings on Saturday nights.

By the time they got to UCD they were in fact friends of a sort. And they each knew that their salvation lay with the other.

If Maureen said she was going anywhere with Deirdre, then Mother would relax. It was the same in the O'Hagan household, Deirdre could always use Sophie Barry's daughter Maureen as an excuse.

That was why they had been able to go off to London together that summer. The summer they should have been at home working for their degrees. The summer they met Desmond Doyle and Frank Quigley on the boat to Holyhead.

Maureen wondered what Frank Quigley would say if he knew that Mother had died. She didn't know how he talked these days, whether his accent had changed, if he spoke as a lot of Irishmen living twenty-five years in London spoke, with two distinct strands in their voices and telltale words of both cultures coming in at the wrong place.

She had read about him; who hadn't read about Frank Quigley? He was profiled always amongst the Irish who had done well in Britain. Sometimes she saw pictures of him with that sullen-looking young Italian he had married to advance himself still further in the hierarchy of Palazzo.

Frank might be so suave of course nowadays that he would write an elegant note of sympathy on a gilt-edged card. He might be so down to earth and still such a rough diamond that he would say she should have died a quarter of a century earlier.

One thing Maureen knew was that Frank Quigley would not have forgotten her mother, any more than he would have forgotten Maureen.

This was not arrogance on her part, believing that her first love would remember her with the same intensity as she remembered him, when she allowed him into her mind at all. She knew it was true. Still it was irrelevant; he might hear about it from Desmond and Deirdre, but it was hard to say whether they all remained friends still.

Admittedly Desmond still worked in Palazzo, but despite Mrs O'Hagan's great reports of her son-in-law's managerial promotions from time to time, Maureen had the feeling that Desmond had stuck somehow low on a scale, and that all the patronage and friendship from his old friend Frank couldn't pull him any higher.

The day of sorting through Mother's things could not be put off for ever. Maureen decided to go on the Sunday following the funeral. It would not take long if she put her mind to it and did not allow herself to become emotionally upset by everything she touched.

Already she had wept over her mother's glasses in their spectacle case which had been given to her in the hospital. Somehow it seemed sadder than anything else to see the sign of Mother's frail fading eyesight, handed to her in a useless little case. Maureen, usually so decisive, hadn't known what to do with them. They were still there zipped into a side compartment of her handbag. Mother would not have been so soft-hearted. She would have been cool and practical as she had been about everything.

They had only fought once, a long time ago, and it had not been about Frank Quigley nor about any man. Mother hadn't thought that the clothing business looked all right, or sounded respectable enough.

Maureen had blazed her anger, what the hell did it matter how things looked or sounded? It was how they were, what they were about that was important. Mother had smiled a cool infuriating smile. Maureen had stormed out. Up to the North of Ireland first where she got a thorough grounding in retail dress sense from two sisters who ran a smart clothes shop and were pleased and flattered to see the dark handsome young university graduate from Dublin come up to learn all they could teach her. Then she went to London.

It was then that she realized how she had never been really close to Deirdre, they had met rarely while she was there. Deirdre had been tied up with two babies at that stage, and Maureen had been going to trade fairs and exhibitions, and learning what to look for. Maureen told Deirdre nothing of her coldness with her mother for fear that it would go straight back to the O'Hagan household, and presumably Deirdre had secrets, worries and problems that she didn't tell Maureen either.

And anyway the coldness didn't last. It had never been an out-and-out hostility, there were always postcards, and short letters and brief phone calls. So that mother could tell Eileen O'Hagan how well Maureen was doing here, there and everywhere. So that appearances could be kept up. Appearances had been very important to Mother. Maureen determined that she would honour this to the very end, far beyond the grave.

Maureen Barry lived in one of the earlier apartment blocks that had been built in Dublin. She lived ten minutes by foot and two minutes by car from the big house where she was born and where her mother had lived all her life. It had been Mother's home, and Father had married in. For the short married life that they had. He had died abroad when Maureen was six, forty years ago this year.

It would be his anniversary shortly, in three weeks; how strange to think that she would attend the Mass they always had said for the repose of his soul totally on her own. Normally she and Mother went together, for as long as she could remember. Always at eight o'clock in the morning. Mother had said that it was discourteous to involve others in your own personal mourning and memorials. But Mother had always told people afterwards that they had been to the Mass.

The living arrangements were yet one more way in which the relationship between the two women was widely praised. Many another mother would have clung to her daughter and kept her in the family home as long as possible, not noticing or caring about the normal wish of the young to leave the nest. Many a less dutiful daughter might have wanted to go away to another city. To London perhaps or even Paris. Maureen was successful in the fashion world. To have two shops with her own name on them by the time she was forty was no mean achievement. And such smart shops too. She moved from one to another with ease, each had a good manageress who was allowed freedom to run the day-to-day business. It had left Maureen free to buy, to choose, to decide to lunch with the fashionable women whose taste she monitored and even formed. She went to London four times a year and to New York once every spring. She had a standing that her mother would never have believed possible in those bad days, the bad time when they had not seen eye to eye. It hadn't lasted long, and every relationship was allowed to have some valley periods, Maureen told herself. Anyway, she didn't want to think about those days now, not so soon after Mother's death.

It had indeed been so sensible to live apart but near. They saw each other almost every day. Never in all the years since she moved into her apartment did Maureen open her front door and find her mother unannounced on her step. Mother wouldn't dream of calling to a young woman who might be entertaining someone, and wish to do so privately.

It was different about Maureen going back to her old home. No such strictures applied there. Maureen was welcome to call at any time, but Mother managed to let her know that at the end of a bridge party was a particularly suitable time to drop in for a sherry, because everyone could have the chance to admire both the elegant daughter and the evidence of her consideration and devotion to her mother.

On the Sunday she walked to the house where she would never again see her mother walking lightly down the hall to open the door, viewed through the multi-coloured stained glass of the hall-door panels. It felt strange to go to the empty house, because by now there would be no kind friends and relatives staying around as support. Mother's great friend Mrs O'Hagan, Deirdre's mother, had been very pressing and begged Maureen to come and see them, to drop in for supper, to use the O'Hagan house just like she had her old home.

It had been kind, but not the right thing. Maureen wasn't a little girl, she was a middle-aged woman for heaven's sake. It was not appropriate for Mrs O'Hagan to invite her up to the house as she had done thirty years ago when she and Mother had decided that Deirdre and Maureen should be friends.

Mother had always set a lot of store on what Eileen O'Hagan thought about this and that. Eileen and Kevin were her greatest friends. They had always invited Mother to join them at the theatre or the races. They had never to Maureen's recollection tried to find a suitable second husband for her. Or perhaps they had. She would not have known.

As she walked through the sunny streets towards her old home Maureen wondered what life would have been like if Mother had married again. Would a stepfather have encouraged her or fought her when she wanted to take up her career in what she had called the fashion industry and her mother had said was common drapery and glorified salesgirl work?

Would Mother have been coquettish with men years ago? After all Maureen herself did not feel old and past sexual encounters at the age of forty-six, so why should she assume that her mother had? But it was something that never came into their lives.

They talked a lot about Maureen's young men, and how they had all somehow failed to measure up. But they had never talked about any man for Mother.

She let herself into the house and shivered slightly because there was no little fire lit in what Mother had always called the morning room. Maureen plugged in the electric fire and looked around.

Two weeks ago on a Sunday she had come here to find Mother looking white and anxious. She had this pain, possibly indigestion but . . . Maureen had acted quickly, she helped her mother gently to the car and drove calmly to the hospital. No point in disturbing the doctor, calling him away from his Sunday breakfast she had said to Mother, let's go to the outpatients' department, to Casualty. They were there the whole time in a hospital, they would set her mind at rest.

Mother, looking more and more anxious, agreed with her, and even at this stage Maureen had noticed with sinking heart that her mother's careful speech sounded slurred, the words were running together.

They were seen at once, and within an hour Maureen was waiting outside the intensive care to be told the news that her mother was having a massive stroke. One that she might very well not recover from.

Mother recovered, but not her faculties of speech; her eyes, bright and burning, seemed to beg for an end to this indignity.

She could press once for yes and twice for no on Maureen's arm. Maureen had spoken to her alone.

'Are you afraid, Mother?'

No.

'You do believe that you'll get better, don't you?'

No.

'I want you to believe that, you must. No, sorry: of course you can't answer that. I mean, don't you want to get better?'

No.

'But surely for me, Mother, for all your friends, *we* want you to get better. God, how do I say something that you can answer? Do you know that I love you? Very very much?'

Yes, and a lessening of the strain in the eyes.

'And do you know that you are the best mother that anyone could have?'

Yes.

Then she had been tired and not long after that she had slipped into unconsciousness.

They had been right, the friends who had stood in this room, Mother's morning room that got the early light, when they had nodded and said Sophie Barry could not have lived the dependent life of an invalid. It was better that she had been taken quickly away from pain and indignity.

Could it really only have been two weeks since that Sunday morning? It felt like ten years in so many ways.

Maureen unfolded the black plastic sacks. She knew that a great deal of Mother's things could indeed be thrown away, there was no one to gasp and wonder over old mementos of cavalry balls years ago, or programmes of long-forgotten concerts signed with some illegible squiggle. No grandchildren to ooh and aah over worlds gone by. And Maureen in her own busy life would not look at them, a lot of things would go.

She sat at the small writing desk: an antique. She might take it for the hallway of her own flat. It was such an impractical thing dating from a time when ladies only penned little notes or invitation cards. It had nothing to do with today's world. Mrs O'Hagan had been surprised that Maureen was going to remain in her flat. She was sure that Sophie would have wanted her own home to continue in the family. But Maureen was adamant. She lived a life too full to involve cleaning a house with as many nooks and crannies as this. Her own space was custom-made for her, wall-long closets for her clothes, a study with proper filing cabinets as a mini-office, a big room where she could entertain, its kitchen in full view of the dining table so that she could talk to her guests as she served them their dinner.

No, it would be a backwards move to come home to this house. Mother knew that too.

First she went through the finances. She was surprised how fiddly and disorganized Mother had become lately. It was sad to see little notes Mother had written to herself: a reminder here, a query there. It would have been so easy for Maureen to have set up an uncomplicated system like her own, five minutes would have done it, a letter to the bank asking them to pay so much each month to electricity, gas, insurance fund ... It would have cut out all these final demands and letters of bewilderment.

Mother must have appeared much more in control than she was.

Then there was an endless correspondence with a stockbroker. Like everyone of her generation, Mother had believed that wealth was measured in stocks and shares. Only the broker's letters were to be found: Mother had kept no copies of her own side of the correspondence. It was a sorry tale of confusion and disappointment.

Maureen felt weary and sad as she finished the series of responses to what had obviously been querulous demands for information and explanations why shares that everyone knew were excellent seemed to have vanished into nothingness. Briskly Maureen wrote a letter to the broker explaining that her mother had died and asking him to send her details of the nature of the portfolio as it stood now. She wished that she had involved herself more but with Mother there was such a dignity, there was a boundary you didn't cross.

Maureen kept all the letters she had written in her slim briefcase, she would photocopy them later, back at her own apartment. Mr White who had been Mother's solicitor had already congratulated her on her efficiency; he wished that many more young women could be as organized but then of course she hadn't built herself a big business without having a good financial brain and a sense of administration. He had shown her Mother's will, a simple document leaving everything to her beloved daughter Mary Catherine (Maureen) Barry with gratitude for all her years of devoted love and care. The will had been made in 1962. Just after the reconciliation. After Mother had accepted that Maureen was not going to abandon her idea of how she would live her life. Since the day that Sophie Barry had written down her gratitude for the devoted love and care, twenty-three more years of it had been given. Surely she would never have believed that for over two decades Maureen would remain single and remain her close friend.

It was taking more time than she had thought, and she felt a strange sense of loss, different entirely to the grieving at the funeral. It was as if she had lost her idea of Mother as someone almost perfect. This nest of confusion stuffed into the drawers of a lovely writing desk spoke of a peevish old woman, confused and irritable. Not the calm beautiful Sophie Barry who until two weeks ago had sat like a queen in her throne room in this her morning room with its tasteful furnishings. Maureen didn't like discovering this side of her mother.

She had made herself a cup of coffee to give her more energy for the task and reached out resolutely for the next big bulky envelope. She remembered the way Mother used to say, 'Maureen my child, if a thing is worth doing, it's worth doing properly.' That used to apply to anything from cleansing her face twice a day with Mother's special cream and then splashing it with rosewater, to going back and having six more tennis lessons so that she would look that much better at the summer parties. Well if Mother could see her now, something Maureen doubted, she would certainly agree that the devoted daughter was doing the job properly.

She was totally unprepared for the papers she found in the envelope marked Solicitor. She thought it might be some more foostering dealings about shares or pensions, but these were letters from a completely different solicitor, and they were dated forty years ago. There were a series of legal documents, all signed in 1945. And they showed that Maureen's father Bernard James Barry had not died of a virus when he was in Northern Rhodesia just after the war. Sophie Barry's husband had deserted her forty years ago. He had left his wife and child and gone to live with another woman in Bulawayo in what was then Southern Rhodesia.

Maureen realized that for all she knew she might have a father still alive, a man of seventy years, living in Bulawayo, Zimbabwe. That she might even have stepbrothers and sisters, men and women not much younger than herself. The woman described as his 'common law wife' was called Flora Jones and had come from Birmingham in England. Wildly Maureen thought that Mother would have said that Flora was a maid's name.

She wasn't in the habit of pouring herself a stiff drink in the middle of a Sunday morning. Maureen Barry, disciplined in this as in everything else, realized the perils of drinking alone. She had seen too many of her friends lapse into it, at the end of a long hard day with no one to relax with. She had learned this from Mother as she had learned everything. Mother said that widows could slip into tippling if they didn't exercise some control. Widows, what did Mother mean, acting out a lie for forty years?

625

What kind of closeness was it that meant she couldn't tell her only daughter the biggest event of her life? What manner of woman could perpetuate a myth about a man who had to be buried abroad?

With another ripple of shock running through her like the continuous waves after an earthquake, Maureen realized that her mother who had been a sane woman had gone out every May and had a Mass said for the repose of the soul of Bernard James Barry, a man who must have been alive for some if not all of the time that she was doing this.

There was whiskey in a decanter. Maureen smelled it, it reminded her of when she had a toothache years and years ago and Mother would put a whiskey-flavoured piece of cotton wool on the gum to numb the pain. Mother had loved her so much.

Maureen poured out a large measure of neat whiskey, drank it, and burst into tears.

It was a measure of the lonely life she led, she realized, that she had no one to tell. There was no bosom pal to ring up, no house where she could run around and share this staggering news. Like her mother, she had kept aloof from intimacies. There was no man she had let close enough to her thoughts to confide in. Her work colleagues knew nothing of her private life. Her mother's friends . . . oh yes . . . they would be interested. My, my, would she get a hearing at O'Hagans' if she were to turn up with the news.

Flora, Flora Jones. It was like a name from a musical comedy. And now presenting Miss Flora Jones, the Carmen Miranda of our town. There had been letters about divorce, and copies of letters from Mother's solicitor repeating over and over, that not only was there no divorce in Ireland, and that his client was a staunch Roman Catholic, but that this was not the matter at issue, the question at issue apparently had been money. Maureen leafed still unbelieving through the documents . . . kept meticulously in order − this was a younger firmer Mother, more in control forty years ago, wounded and enraged and determined she was going to get the last penny from the man who had betrayed her. A sum had been paid over. A sum which in today's money would have been considered staggering. The solicitor of Bernard James Barry in Bulawayo wrote to the solicitor of Mrs Sophie Barry in Dublin that his client was willing to realize most of his assets in order to provide for his wife and eldest daughter. His client Mr Barry had now, as was already known to Mrs Barry, a second daughter by Miss Flora Jones, a daughter whose birth he was most anxious to legitimize.

Mother's letter of reply to that had been extraordinary, it was written exactly as Mother spoke. Maureen could hear her voice as she read the words. She could literally hear Mother's voice, slow, measured, articulate, a younger stronger voice than of late.

'...while you will understand that there can never be any question of a divorce since it is against the rules of the Church to which we both belong, I cannot legislate for you and your actions in a foreign land. I am writing this letter without the approval of the solicitors but I think you will understand its general drift. I have accepted your settlement for Maureen and myself, I shall pursue you in no court, nor under any jurisdiction. You shall be totally free from me if and only if you never return to Ireland. I shall announce your death. Today is April 15th. If you return this letter to me with your promise that you will never come back to Ireland again, then I will say that you died abroad of a virus on May 15th.

'If this promise is ever broken or if you try to get in touch with Maureen in any way even after she is legally an adult, I can assure you that you will be made to regret it to the end of your days...'

It was the way Mother spoke to a tradesman who had offended her in some way, or to a handyman who had not done a job to her satisfaction.

He had accepted her terms, the man in Bulawayo, the man Maureen had thought was dead for forty years. He had returned the letter, as ordered to do. Attached to it by a small pearl-topped pin was a postcard. A brown sepia picture of mountains and savannah.

The words on the postcard said, 'I died of a virus on May 15th 1945.'

Maureen put her head down on her mother's desk and cried as if her heart would break into little pieces.

She didn't feel the time passing. And when she looked at the clock, the way the hands were placed seemed meaningless. It said a quarter past two or ten past three. It was bright so it must be daytime.

She had come to the house at ten o'clock, she must have been in this semi-trance for over two hours.

She walked around feeling the blood beginning to flow again in her veins. If anyone had looked in the window of the morning room they would have seen a tall dark young woman, looking considerably less than her forty-six years, apparently hugging herself around the waist of her smart navy and pink wool dress.

In fact Maureen was holding in each hand the elbow of the opposite arm, in a physical attempt to hold herself together after this shock.

She felt a rage against her mother, not just because this man had been ordered summarily out of her life, and threatened not to contact his own flesh and blood. But she felt a burning anger that if her mother had kept this secret so successfully for so long, why on earth had she not destroyed the evidence?

If Maureen had never found these papers, she would never have known. She would have been happier, more safe and sure in the world she had built for herself.

Why had her mother been so casual and cruel? She must have known that Maureen would find the evidence some day.

But of course Mother knew that Maureen would not betray her. Maureen would keep up appearances to the end.

Like hell she would. Like bloody hell.

It came to her suddenly that she could do anything she liked about this whole farcical bargain. She had entered into no melodramatic promises about mythical deaths. She had entered into no promise not to contact him for fear of some awful punishment.

By God, she was going to find him, or Flora, or her half-sister.

Please, please may they be alive. Please may she find her father from this welter of documents. The latest being in 1950, confirming a final transfer of assets.

Please God may he still be alive. Seventy wasn't that old.

She began to work with the kind of controlled furious energy that she had not known since the night before her first big high-fashion sale when they were up almost all night in the stockrooms marking clothes down, and recataloguing and estimating the takings of the following day.

This time she approached her mother's belongings with different categories in mind. She found two boxes which she filled with early photographs and memorabilia of herself when a child.

If she did find this man, if he was a man with any heart he would want to know what she looked like at her first Communion, in her hockey outfit, dressed for her first dance.

Items which would have been carefully cut up and destroyed were now filed in boxes and labelled 'keepsakes'.

She sorted and arranged and tidied until she was ready to drop. Then she tied up the bags which were real rubbish, folded the clothes and other items which were to go to the Vincent de Paul, and ordered a taxi to take back the boxes of keepsakes to her own flat.

There wasn't a drawer now that hadn't been emptied and dusted out. Much of the ordinary kitchen equipment would go to Mrs O'Neil who had come to clean for Mother over the years. Jimmy Hayes who did the garden could have the lawnmower and any of the gardening tools he wanted. Maureen also wrote him a letter asking him to take for his own use any plants that he particularly liked, and to have them removed quickly. She had decided now that the house would go on the market as soon as possible.

She laid her hand on the small writing desk. The one she had been going to take for the entrance hall of her own apartment. She patted it and said, 'No'. She didn't want it now. She wanted nothing from here.

The taxi man helped her in with the boxes. Because he was curious she told him that she had been clearing away her mother's effects. He was very sympathetic.

'Isn't it a pity now that you didn't have anyone to help you do a job like that?' he said.

That's what people often said to her in different forms, like wasn't it a wonder that a fine girl like herself had never married and settled down.

'Oh my father would have done everything but he was away, far away,' she said.

She had mentioned her father. She didn't care about the surprised look that the taxi driver gave her, or how odd it was to have a father far away when a mother had died.

She felt that by mentioning him she was making him be alive.

She had a long, long bath and felt better but ravenously hungry. She telephoned Walter.

'I'm being very selfish, and literally using you, so feel free to say no, but are there any nice restaurants open on a Sunday night? I'd love to go out for a meal.'

Walter said nothing could suit him better, he had been doing a particularly tedious kind of Opinion where there seemed to be no solution or a thousand solutions, and one was as hard as the other. He would love to escape from it.

Together they sat and ordered good food and wine by candle-light.

'You look a little feverish,' Walter said with concern.

'I've a lot on my mind.'

'I know, it must have been very distressing today,' he said.

Her eyes seemed to dance at him across the table. She had never looked more beautiful, he thought.

'I know it's not the time, but then there never is any really good time, but perhaps you might think of . . .'

'Yes?'

'Well, should we go on a holiday together, somewhere we would both like, Austria you once said you would like to visit?'

'There's no fishing in Austria, Walter.' She smiled at him.

'There are probably no fashion trade fairs either, but we could manage for two weeks couldn't we?'

'No, Walter, we'd drive each other mad.'

'We could leave each other alone.'

'Can't we do that better living apart?' She gave him a very bright smile.

'There's something on your mind.' He looked hurt and troubled.

'Yes, there is, and I can't tell you now. But please remember tonight and that I wanted to tell you something. I will soon.'

'When?'

'I don't know. Soon.'

'Is it another man? I know that sounds very corny but you have that kind of look about you.'

'No, it's not another man. Not in that sense. I'll tell you, I've never lied to you, and when I do tell, you'll realize.'

'Now I can't wait,' he said.

'I know, neither can I, I wish people worked on Sundays, why does the world close down on Sundays?'

'You and I work on Sundays,' Walter complained.

'Yes, but offices all over the world don't, damn them.'

He knew it wasn't worth asking any more, he would hear nothing. He leaned over and patted her hand.

'I suppose I must love you to let you get away with all of this performance.'

'Oh will you go away to hell, Walter, of course you don't love me, not even in the slightest, but you're a great friend, and I'm sure, though I don't intend to find out, that you're a smashing lay as well.'

The waiter's arrival just at that moment, in time to hear Maureen's extravagant compliment, prevented Walter from saying anything in reply.

She slept a little but not much. She was out of her bed, showered and dressed, by six a.m. The time difference would be three hours. She would start telephoning International Inquiries, and giving the out-of-date numbers, hoping that it would not be too long a haul. She had almost weakened enough to ask Walter if there were international directories of solicitors worldwide that she could study down at the Four Courts, but no, she must give him no details, no hints; later she would tell him. He deserved that. She hadn't decided what she would tell everyone else, when she found her father; if she found him.

It was not as difficult as she had feared. It was probably twenty times as expensive in terms of telephone calls, but she didn't care.

The firm no longer existed in Bulawayo, helpful operators got her listings of other solicitors, finally she found that the original company had moved to South Africa. She found herself talking to people in cities she had never even thought about even if she had acknowledged their names . . . Bloemfontein, Ladysmith, Kimberley, Queenstown.

She found one of the names that had signed one of the letters in Pretoria. Maureen Barry was crisp.

She explained that her mother had died and that it was her last wish that she Maureen should contact her late father: to whom should she now make the inquiries?

It wasn't a file that would have been kept open for forty years, the man told her.

'But you haven't thrown it away. Lawyers don't throw anything away.'

'Can't you inquire at your end?'

'I have, they know nothing, the firm has changed, they say, and it's true that all the documents were handed back to my mother at her request. I have to try at your end.'

He sounded a nice man despite his accent and the way he said *rilly* instead of really and tried to work out what was the best way to go in the *ind* instead of the end.

'I fully realize that this is professional work, to research on my behalf, I am totally prepared to pay a professional fee for your time and expertise,' Maureen said. 'Would you like me to approach you through solicitors here to put it on a more formal basis?'

'No, it seems to me that you are a person who could be dealt with in her own right.'

She could hear him smiling from across the world, a man whom she'd never met in a country she would never visit (nor would any of her friends) on account of its policies. Mother had been heard to say once she felt very sorry for those whites having to give up all their privileges and nice homes. But it hadn't gone down well. Mother hadn't been a fool, she didn't go that route again.

He said he would call her shortly.

'I wonder have you any idea how shortly I hope it's going to be.'

'I think so,' he said in his curious clipped accent. 'If I had just lost one parent and had the hope of finding another I would know that there was a lot of urgency involved.'

She didn't know how she got through the Tuesday and the Wednesday. He phoned her, the man from Pretoria, on Wednesday at 8 a.m. with an address of a solicitor's firm in London.

'Is he dead or alive?' she asked, her hand at her throat waiting for the reply.

'They didn't tell me, truly they didn't tell me.' He sounded regretful.

'But these people will know?' she begged.

'These people will be able to get a message to whoever is concerned.'

'Did they hint?'

'Yes. They hinted.'

'What?'

'That he was alive. That you would be talking to the principal involved.'

'I'll never be able to thank you,' she said.

'You don't know yet whether you have anything to thank me for or not.'

'But I'll tell you. I'll ring you back.'

'Write to me, you've spent enough on telephone calls. Or better come out and see me.'

'I don't think I'll do that, would you be any use to me? What class of an age of a person are you at all?'

'Stop putting on that accent. I am sixty-three, a widower, with a beautiful home in Pretoria.'

'God bless you,' she said.

'I hope he's alive and good to you,' said the stranger from South Africa.

She had to wait an hour and a half before she could talk to the man in the London firm of solicitors.

'I don't know why you're talking to me,' he said in a slightly peeved tone.

'I don't know either,' Maureen confessed. 'But the original agreement was that my father and I should not get in touch during my mother's lifetime. I know it sounds like something from Hans Christian Andersen but this is the way it happened. Can you listen for two minutes, only two? I can explain it quickly, I'm used to business conversations.'

The English solicitor understood. He said he would be in touch.

Maureen began to have far greater faith in the speed of the law than she ever had before. Walter would tell her about delays and adjournments, she knew herself the endless palaver about contracts with suppliers. But suddenly in the middle of the most important event of her whole life she had met two law firms who seemed to understand her urgency. To sense her impatience and respond to it. On Thursday night she checked the answering machine in her flat but there was nothing except a kindly invitation from Mother's friend Mrs O'Hagan to drop in any evening for a sherry just as you did with your own poor mother. And there was a message from Walter who was going to the West of Ireland at the weekend, there would be lots of lovely walks and gorgeous food, he said, as well as fishing. And there needn't even *be* any fishing if Maureen would care to join him.

She smiled. He was a good friend.

There were two clicks where people had hung up without leaving a message. She felt restless, and then annoyed with herself. How could she expect these people to act so swiftly? And suppose her father *was* alive and in England, which was the way it looked now . . . perhaps he didn't want to get in touch, or he did and Flora didn't want him to, or his daughter. She suddenly realized that there might have been other children.

She paced the apartment, walking the length of her long living room, arms hugging each other. She couldn't remember when she had last been like this, unable to settle to anything.

The phone when it rang made her jump and the voice was hesitant.

'Maureen Barry. Is that Maureen Barry?'

'Yes.' She spoke half words, half breath.

'Maureen, it's Bernie,' the voice said. And there was a silence, as if he was waiting desperately to know what she would say.

She was able to say nothing. No words would come out.

'Maureen, they told me you had been trying to get in touch, if that's not so . . .' He was almost ready to ring off.

'Are you my father?' she whispered.

'I'm an old man now, but I was your father,' he said.

'Then you still are.' She forced a lightness into her voice. It had been the right thing to do, she heard him laugh a little.

'I rang before,' he said. 'But it was one of those machines, you sounded so formal I had to ring off without saying anything.'

'I know, people should be hanged for that,' she said. Again it was right, he was relaxing.

'But I rang again just to hear your voice and think: This is Maureen speaking, actually the sound of her voice.'

'And did you like the sound of it?'

'Not as much as now when it's a real conversation. Is it a real conversation?'

'Yes, yes it is.'

There was a silence, but it wasn't a heavy one, it was as if they were both settling into the strange ritual of talking to each other.

'Would you like to meet me?' she asked.

'There's nothing I would like more. But would you be able to come to England to find me? I'm a bit feeble now, I couldn't come to Ireland to see you.'

'That's no problem. I'll come as soon as you like.'

'It won't be the Bernie you used to know.'

She understood he wanted her to call him Bernie, not Father. Mother had always referred to him as poor Bernard.

'I never knew you anyway Bernie, and you only knew me for a short time, it will be no shock to either of us. I'm freewheeling down to fifty, a middle-aged woman.'

'Stop, stop.'

'No, it's true, I'm not actually grey because I have such a regular relationship with a hairdresser . . .' She felt she was burbling on.

'And Sophie . . . she told you . . . before she . . .' He was hesitant.

'She died two weeks ago . . . Bernie . . . it was a stroke, it was quick and she wouldn't have recovered, it was all for the best . . .'

'And you . . . ?'

'I'm fine. But what about seeing you, where will I come, and Flora, and your family?'

'Flora is dead. She died shortly after we left Rhodesia.'

'I'm sorry.'

'Yes, she was a wonderful woman.'

'And children?' Maureen felt this was an extraordinary conversation. It sounded so normal, so run of the mill, yet she was talking to her own father, a man she had thought was forty years dead until four days ago.

'There's just Catherine. She's in the States.'

Maureen was pleased somehow.

'What's she doing there, is she working, is she married?'

'No, she's neither, she's gone with this rock musician, she's been with him eight years now. She sort of goes along wherever he is to make a type of home for him, she says, it's all she ever wanted. She's happy.'

'She's lucky then,' Maureen said almost without thinking.

'Yes she is, isn't she? Because she's not hurting anyone. People say she's a loser but I don't think that, I think she's winning if she has what she wants without hurting anyone else.'

'When can I come and see you, Bernie?' she asked.

'Oh the sooner the better, the soonest the very best,' he said.

'Where are you?'

'Would you believe Ascot?' he said.

'I'll come tomorrow,' she said.

Before she left she went through her post quickly. Hardly anything to do with work came to her apartment, all business mail was addressed to her main shop. There were a couple of bills, circulars and a letter that looked like an invitation. It was from Anna Doyle, the eldest of Deirdre O'Hagan's children, a formal invitation to a silver wedding for their parents and a note saying that she apologized for the ludicrously early notice but she wanted to make sure that the key figures were able to come. Perhaps Maureen could let them know.

Maureen looked at it almost without seeing it. A silver wedding seemed such a small milestone compared to what she was about to embark on herself. She wouldn't think now about whether she would go or not.

It was a very comfortable guest Home, Bernard James Barry had left the colonies in style, Maureen realized. She had hired a car at Heathrow and driven to the address he had given her.

She had taken the precaution of telephoning the Home herself to inquire whether her arrival would not put too much strain on her father, who said he had bad rheumatoid arthritis and was recovering from a mild heart attack.

She had been told that he was in the best of health and was already eager for her to arrive.

He was dressed in a blazer with some colourful crest, he had a carefully tied cravat, he looked the perfect gentleman lightly tanned, a lot of thick grey hair, a cane and a slow walk, but in every way the kind of man her mother would love to have entertained back in Dublin. He had a smile that would break your heart.

'I have the Egon Ronay guide, Maureen,' he said after she had kissed him. 'I thought we should go out and have a proper lunch to celebrate.'

'You're a man after my own heart, Bernie,' she said.

And he was a man after her own heart. There were no apologies, no excuses. In life there were only just so many chances for happiness, he didn't regret his daughter Catherine taking hers, he didn't blame Sophie for seeking happiness through status, it was just that he couldn't stick with it himself.

He had known all about Maureen, he had never lost contact, not until Kevin O'Hagan died. He had written to Kevin at his club and asked him for news of his little girl. He showed Maureen a scrapbook he had made, cuttings from the newspapers about Maureen's shops, photographs cut from society magazines about Maureen at this dance or that reception. Photos too of Maureen with Deirdre O'Hagan, including one showing her in bridesmaid's outfit.

'They're having a silver wedding would you believe this year.' Maureen winced at the picture of the very inelegant 1960 wedding outfits. How could they have known so little then, had she only developed a clothes sense much later?'

Mr O'Hagan had written regularly, it was only when his letter was returned from the club with a note that Maureen's father had heard of his friend's death. He had been instructed to leave no evidence of the correspondence in his house, part of the deal had been that Bernard Barry be mourned as a dead man.

They talked easily, old friends with a lot in common, it seemed.

'Did you have any great love that you didn't follow?' he asked as he sipped his brandy. At seventy he felt entitled to a little luxury like this, he said.

'Not really, not a great love.' She was uncertain.

'But something that could have been a great love.'

'I thought so at the time, but I was wrong, it would never have worked. It would have held us both back, we were too different, it would have been unthinkable in many ways.' Maureen knew that her voice sounded like her mother's as she said this.

She found it easy to tell this man about Frank Quigley, about how she had loved him so much when she was twenty she thought that her whole body and soul would explode. She found it not at all difficult to use such words, although she had never even articulated them before.

She told how she had done everything but sleep with Frank that summer, and the reason she held back was not the usual fear of pregnancy that had held every other girl back, but simply she knew that she must not get more involved than she already was as he would never fit into her life.

'And was this something you believed or was it something Sophie told you?' His voice was gentle, without accusation.

'Oh I believed it, I believed it utterly. I thought there were two types of people, us and them. And Frank was definitely them. So was Desmond Doyle but somehow Deirdre O'Hagan managed to get away with it. I remember at the wedding we were all pretending Desmond's people came from some estate in the West instead of a cabin on the side of a hill.'

'She didn't get away with it entirely,' Maureen's father said.

'You mean Mr O'Hagan wrote to you about that?'

'Yes, a bit. I suppose I was someone he could talk to who wasn't involved, who never would be.'

Maureen told how Frank Quigley had come to Dublin uninvited for her Conferring day. How he had stood at the back of the hall and made whooping sounds and shouted as she went to receive her parchment.

He had called to the house afterwards. It had been terrible.

'Did Sophie order him away?'

'No, you know Mother, well maybe you don't but she wouldn't do that, she killed him with kindness, she was charm itself . . . "Oh and tell me Frank, would my late husband and I have met your people when we were in Westport" . . . you know the kind of thing.'

'I do.' He looked sad.

'And Frank somehow behaved worse and worse, everything she did seemed to make him more bolshie and thick and badly behaved. He took out his comb during supper and combed his hair, you know, looking at himself in that bit of mirror in the sideboard. Oh and he stirred his coffee as if he were going to go through the bottom of the cup. I could have killed him, and I could have killed myself for caring.'

'And what did your mother say?'

'Oh, something like "Have you enough sugar, Frank? Or perhaps you would have preferred tea?" You know, terribly polite, not a hint that anything was out of place unless you knew.'

'And afterwards?'

'Afterwards, she just laughed. She said he was very nice and laughed.'

There was a silence.

'But I went along with it,' Maureen said earnestly. 'I can't say she threw him out, she didn't, she never denied him the house, she even inquired about him from time to time with that little laugh, it was as if somehow by mistake we had invited poor Jimmy Hayes who did the garden in for supper. And I went along with it, because I agreed with her, I went along with her way of thinking.'

'And did you regret it?'

'Not at once, he was so foul-mouthed and called me all the snobby bitches under the sky, he almost proved Mother's point, my point. He said he'd show me, that he would be received in the highest houses in the land, and that one day my crabbed old mother and I would regret that we hadn't welcomed him to our poxy house. That's the way he spoke.'

'Out of hurt.' Her father was sympathetic.

'Yes, yes of course. And of course he *did* become a merchant prince and Deirdre O'Hagan married his equally ignorant and non-acceptable best friend . . . so he was right. His day did come.'

'And is he happy?'

'I don't know, I think not. But maybe he's like a lark in the spring. I don't know.'

'You're lovely, Maureen . . .' her father said suddenly.

'No I'm not, I'm very stupid, was very stupid for too long. It wouldn't have hurt anybody to use your phrase, it wouldn't have hurt anybody at all for me to say to Mother when I was twenty-one that I was off with Frank Quigley, pedigree or no pedigree.'

'Maybe you didn't want to hurt her, after all I had abandoned her, you didn't want it to happen to her twice.'

'Ah, but I didn't know you'd abandoned her, I thought you got an awful virus and died.'

'I'm sorry.' He looked contrite.

'I'm delighted, you old devil,' she said. 'Nothing has given me as much happiness in my whole life.'

'Come on out of that, an old man, ready for a wheel-chair.'

'Will you come and live with me in Dublin?' She asked.

'No, no, my dearest Maureen, I won't.'

'You don't need to be in a home, you're as fit as a fiddle. I can see you well looked after, not in Mother's house, we'll get somewhere together. Some place bigger than my flat.'

'No, I promised Sophie.'

'But she's dead now, you kept your promise while she was alive.'

His eyes were sad.

'No, there is a kind of honour about a thing like this, they'd reassess her, you know, they'd go over everything she said, it would be degrading her afterwards. You know what I mean.'

'I do, but you're being too honourable in a sense, she didn't give you the chance to stay in contact with your own daughter, she didn't give me that chance, she didn't play really fair with us. I thought you were dead until a few days ago.'

'But at least she told you in the end,' said Bernard Barry, his face happy.

'What?'

'Well at least she told you that she wanted you to find me. I heard that from the solicitors. When she knew she was dying she wanted you to have the chance to meet me again.'

Maureen bit her lip. Yes, that was what she had said at the outset, when she was making those early inquiries to Bulawayo.

She looked closely at her father's face.

'I must say I was touched and pleased at that. I thought she was implacable. Kevin O'Hagan told me that there was an anniversary Mass for me every year.'

'I know,' Maureen agreed, 'it's coming up again shortly.'

'So she did something she needn't have done, I owe it to her not to go back and disturb her memory. Anyway, child, I don't know anyone there any more, not since Kevin died, and I'd only be an object of curiosity to them all. No, I'll stay here, I like it, and you'll come and see me from time to time, and your sister Catherine and her young man will come, I'll be in clover.'

Her eyes filled with tears. She would never tell him that Mother hadn't sent her to find him, she would let him think something good as he sat in the sunset thinking he was in clover.

'I'll find lots of excuses to come and see you then, maybe I'll open a shop in Ascot here or in Windsor. I mean it.'

'Of course you do, and won't you be coming over for Kevin's daughter's silver wedding? Won't that be another excuse?'

'I mightn't go to that. Frank Quigley was the best man, you

know, it's meant to be a kind of a reunion of everyone who was there, dredging up all the past memories and everything.'

'Isn't that all the more reason to go?' asked Bernie Barry, the man with the tan and the twinkle in his eye who fell in love on a business trip forty years ago and had the courage to follow his star.

Frank

He never knew why everyone made such a fuss about travelling, Frank loved to get into his car and head off a hundred miles or more along motorways past signposts. He felt free and as if there was a sense of adventure about it all. Even if it was only a catering exhibition that he had been to a dozen times before he enjoyed it. And why wouldn't he? As he often reminded himself, not everyone else on the motorways had a Rover, this year's model, with fitted stereo and radio filling the sleek comfortable world with music. Or whenever he wanted it with *Italian for Businessmen*. Nobody in Palazzo Foods knew that Frank Quigley could understand every single word of Italian spoken in his presence. He never let a flicker of the eye acknowledge that he had understood what might be being said. Even when it was about him. Particularly when it was about him.

Sometimes Frank thought that his father-in-law Carlo Palazzo might have a suspicion, but if he had he kept it to himself. And he would have admired Frank all the more for it. He had let Frank know a long time ago that they had been watching him and grooming him, and that he would never have got to first base with the boss's daughter unless Carlo Palazzo and his brother had wanted it that way.

Frank had known this already, it came as no surprise that a wealthy girl like Renata would be heavily protected by her father and uncles from fortune hunters. He knew that he was suitable because he didn't need to marry the Palazzo Princess to rise in the company. He didn't even need Palazzo, Frank Quigley would have been able to walk into any business in Britain. He had no initials after his name, he had never finished his formal schooling. He didn't need any of it. He had the flair and the ability to work long hard days and nights. They had known all that fifteen years ago when they let him take Renata out to dinner. They knew he would lay no untoward hand on the dark shy heiress to the

Palazzo fortunes until they were wed. And the Palazzos knew that if ever he were to be the teeniest little bit unfaithful to his wife it would be something anonymous and discreet and far from home. There would be no hint of scandal.

Frank sighed about the unwritten rules. He had sailed a little near the wind on one or two occasions but nothing he couldn't handle. Until now. Now the situation was very different, and he needed every moment alone that he could seize in order to work out what to do. If it were business, if it were only business ... ah, then he would know exactly what to do. But Joy East was not business. Not when she was in her yellow tee-shirt and nothing else, walking confidently around her house proud and sure of herself. And sure of him, as he lay there admiringly afternoon after long sunny afternoon smiling at her mane of streaked brown and gold hair, her perfect teeth, her long tanned legs.

Joy East the designer who had got Palazzo into the smart magazines, who had raised their image from the tatty to the stylish, as Frank Quigley had raised their sales and their progress from the mass of small so-called supermarkets to the very front rank. Joy East who had told him the first night they had looked at each other with non-professional eyes that they would be the ideal match. Neither wanted to change their lifestyle, neither was in any position to force the other to do so. Joy wanted her independence and freedom, Frank wanted to remain in his marriage with the boss's daughter. Who better to suit each other than two people with everything to lose by being silly and everything to gain by enjoying each other's company discreetly? She had told him this partly in words, partly by her look and partly by the way she had leaned across the restaurant table and kissed him full on the lips.

'I checked first,' she had said, laughing. 'There's nobody in the place except tourists.'

It had been exciting then, it had continued to be exciting. Frank had rarely met women like Joy. The finer and indeed the main points of the women's movement had passed him by, this new independence seemed to him very exotic. Joy East was proud of her single state, she had almost married, she told him, a very lucky escape when she was twenty-three but she had called it off days before the wedding. Her father had been furious and they still had to pay a huge whack of the wedding reception cost, and the cake, and the limousines. Not to mention all the talk and the fuss. Everyone would have preferred her to get married just to save all the embarrassment. And the man? Oh, lucky escape for him too, Joy thought, laughing and thinking about him not at all.

She lived in a small house on the corner of a road which had been not at all fashionable when she found it but which day by day was seeing the removal vans of ever smarter neighbours. Her white-walled garden was private and had vines on the walls. Her long comfortable living room could fit sixty comfortably at one of her parties. Joy gave wonderful parties and often said that it was terribly easy to flatter and please people by asking them for two hours' drinks and canapés to your house.

And they loved her in Palazzo for doing it. So generous of Miss East, the board always said, above and beyond what Miss East needed to do for them. It bought her further goodwill. Their admiration was unstinting. Joy East could invite clients, press people, foreign contacts and local dignitaries into her house with such ease. She hired caterers and then contract cleaners after-wards. Joy told Frank that it was no trouble, in fact it was positively useful. She had her house cleaned once a month professionally, she had a freezer full of hors d'oeuvres. She always cleared away her ornaments and valuables before any gathering. You never knew if strangers might be light-fingered, much better to leave out forty big blue glass bowls as ashtrays. They had cost £1 each in some warehouse. She had another forty in a cardboard box in the garage. On a high shelf over the small sports car.

Frank Quigley the handsome Managing Director of Palazzo and Joy East the Design Consultant who had been in charge of Palazzo's image from its Art Deco building to its smart carrier bags had been having an affair for three years and they could both say with certainty that nobody knew about it. They were not fooling themselves like so many other lovers in the world who believed that they were invisible. They knew that nobody else had the slightest suspicion. Because they had been very careful and they had lived by a set of rules.

They never telephoned each other except on legitimate busi-ness for the company. And Joy made no telephone calls to the Quigley apartment about anything at all. Once the affair had got under way Renata was never brought to Joy East's house whatever the social occasion. Frank Quigley felt that it would be undignified for his wife to be entertained in a house where he himself had been entertained so many afternoons a week in a very different sense of the word. Frank would not let his wife lay her fur coat across the wide bed where he and Joy had spent so many hours. Even though he swore to himself that Renata would never learn of the relationship, he still felt that he owed it to her not to betray her by pretending to be an equal guest in a house which was in reality so much his home. He didn't think about any other kind of betrayal because Frank had always believed that his strongest quality was an ability to compartmentalize his life. He had always been able to do this. He never thought of his violent drunken father and his weak forgiving mother . . . not once he had left them to live in London. But when he had returned to visit them and his brothers and sisters who had never left the small town in the West of Ireland he brought no tales and even no thoughts of his London life back with him. He had managed to come back if not exactly shabby at least unkempt. None of them would have guessed at his lifestyle in the business world and the social life of retailing. He had bought Renata a shapeless tweed coat for her one-off regulation visit there and had told her they should play down the comfort they enjoyed back in Wembley. Renata had understood very quickly, she had gone almost wordlessly to help in the kitchen with the women while Frank had talked to his brothers, and offered a little investment here and buying into something there . . . all of them polite ways of giving money without being seen to do so. During the four days he had spent in the place where he had grown up, his leather briefcase and hand-made shoes were locked in the boot of the hired car with Renata's silk scarves and jewellery roll.

Frank had said that you diminished everything by trailing one life and one set of memories with you. Better far to live whatever life you were living at the moment to the full with no connecting links.

So a wife could not be brought unawares to the house of a mistress.

Similarly when the Quigleys entertained as they always did at Christmas Miss East would be said to be out of town. They met on common ground all right, like at his father-in-law's, but the conversation was always about work. Frank was literally able to divorce himself from the other side of their life together and talk guiltlessly about plans and projects. He got none of the sense of illicit excitement that he knew others felt about an extra-marital affair. He knew that Joy felt the same. She must have felt the same. After all it was she who had laid down the ground rules.

Joy had been to the forefront in saying they would have no sense of over-responsibility to each other. She was not going to suffer the agonies of the typical Other Woman, she had assured him. There would be no image of poor Joy sitting alone with a sandwich on Christmas Day listening to 'Jingle Bells' on the radio. No, she was thirty when she met him and she had lived ten years more or less alone. She had a hundred places to go for Christmas, and would spend no time feeling abandoned. They would take the time they could have without destroying either their careers or their plans for the future. She was free as the air to go where she pleased without consulting him. If a trip to the States came up she would take it, and he could find other ways of filling those afternoon hours until she returned.

It had been idyllic . . . yes, a real afternoon idyll over three years. In summertime they often sat and drank cold white wine and peeled each other pears and peaches in the warm walled garden. In winter, they sat on the thick rich carpet beside the fire and watched pictures in the flames. At no time did they ever say what a pity that they couldn't get away together for a week, for a holiday or for a lifetime. Renata's name was never mentioned between them. Nor was David, the name of the man in the advertising agency who had great hopes of the lovely Joy East and sent her large bouquets of flowers. Sometimes she went out with him at weekends but so great was the sense of independence between Frank and Joy that Frank never asked whether they slept together or if David's attentions were in any way a threat to his own position. He assumed that David had been kept at arm's length with a convincing story about work and not wishing to get involved.

Frank had listened to the stories of colleagues, men who had as they put it had a little fun, played around a bit, thought they had a good thing going. Always and in every case there had been some disastrous turnabout of events. And it was invariably obvious and predictable to the outsider but never to the man involved. Frank examined his own relationship with Joy as minutely as he would have examined a contract or a proposition put to him in his office. If there were any flaws, then he couldn't see them. Not until the Christmas party at Palazzo last year, which was when the trouble had begun. And even then it had been small and insignificant. At first.

It was all very clearly etched on his mind. Supermarkets found it hard to have Christmas parties like other firms did since they were literally serving the public all hours. But Frank was ever mindful of the importance of some kind of ceremony and group loyalty, particularly at a festive time.

Frank had persuaded Carlo to have the party on the Sunday before Christmas each year, it would be a lunch-time party with Carlo as Santa Claus for the kiddies. Wives and children all came, there were small gifts for everyone and paper hats, and because it was a family day out the usual office party nonsense didn't happen with young secretaries being sick behind the filing cabinets and older managers making fools of themselves doing a striptease.

Renata had always loved it and was very good with the children, organizing games, and paper streamers. Every year for as long as he could remember Frank's father-in-law had looked fondly at his daughter and said that she was so wonderful with the bambinos, wasn't it a pity that there were no bambinos of their own. Every year Frank had shrugged and said that the ways of the Lord were strange.

'It's not for lack of loving,' he would say regularly, and Carlo would nod gravely and suggest that perhaps Frank should eat more steaks, a lot of red meat never did a man any harm. Every year with patience and a smile fixed easily on his face. It was a small price to pay, it was not intended as humiliation, it wasn't received as such. Frank took it as an old man's affectionate and perhaps tactlessly expressed regret. It was one of the few areas where he humoured Carlo Palazzo. In business they spoke as equals, always.

But last Christmas the party had been different. Joy East was usually in charge of decorating the big warehouse where they had the festivities. Not the actual work of pinning crepe up on the walls and laying out the trestles with the sausage rolls and mince pies of course, but with organizing a colour scheme, providing huge paper ornaments, or giant sunflowers as she had done one year. Arranging someone to make mighty bells out of silver paper. Seeing to it that a big green baize-covered table full of gifts be arranged for Santa Claus Carlo and that the photographer from the local and sometimes even national papers be present. Together Frank and Joy had organized a huge Christmas calendar that would have the name of every employee on it. It cost practically nothing to print and yet everyone who worked in Palazzo took it home proudly to keep for the next year. It sometimes changed their mind if they were thinking of leaving. It was hard to leave a place where you were so highly thought of as family that they put your name among the names of board members and senior managers on the calendar.

Last Christmas Joy said she was going to be away in the time before the party. There was this packaging fair she really had to go to. It was important, she needed new ideas.

'But that's on every year at this time and you don't go,' Frank had complained.

'Are you telling me what I can do and can't do?' Her voice had been steely.

'Of course not. It's just that it's become such a tradition . . . your ideas for the Christmas party . . . always. Long before you and I . . . always.'

'And you thought that it would always be so . . . long after you and I?'

'What is this, Joy? If you're trying to say something say it.' He had been brusque to cover his shock.

'Oh I'm never trying to say anything, I assure you. I really assure you of that. Either I say it or I don't say it, there's no question of trying to say anything.'

He had looked at her sharply, her voice had sounded slurred when she was repeating the word 'assure'. It was unthinkable that Joy East had been drinking, drinking in the middle of the day. He put the suspicion out of his mind.

'That's good then,' he had said with false joviality, 'because I'm the same. If I want to say something I say it, we're two of a kind, Joy.'

She had smiled at him oddly, he thought.

When she returned from the packaging fair they met as had been arranged at her house. One of the many things that made it all so safe was that Joy really did work from home with a small bright studio filled with light, and Frank did have legitimate reason to call on her. But even better her house was very near the offices of the firm of accountants they used as tax advisers. Frank had even more legitimate reason to visit them regularly. If his car was ever seen in the area he was well covered.

Joy said she hadn't done much at the packaging fair, it was Mickey Mouse stuff.

'Then why did you go?' Frank had asked, irritated.

He had been responsible for finding other people to take over Joy's work preparing the hall for the party and nobody had anything like her flair.

'For a change, for a rest, for some time off,' she had said, considering her words.

'Jesus, I never think a trade fair is a rest,' he had said.

'It is if you hardly leave your room in the hotel.'

'And what did you do in your room in the hotel that was so important?' His voice was cold.

'I never said it was important. Now did I?'

'No.'

'It wasn't at all important what I did in my room, I read the catalogues, I had room service, I had a lot of nice cold white wine. Oh, and I had a nice Scotsman, head of a stationery firm. But nothing at all important.'

Frank's face had gone white but he was still in control. 'Is this meant to hurt me?' he asked.

'But how could it, we're two of a kind, you've often said it. You have your life with your wife, I have my life with the odd ship that passes in the night. Nothing hurtful there.'

They were lying in her bed. Frank reached out for a cigarette from the slim case on the bedside table.

'I usually prefer you not to smoke here, it does sort of linger in the curtains,' Joy said.

'I usually don't need to smoke here, but the things you're saying sort of linger in my mind and make me anxious,' he said, lighting up.

'Ah, it is all a game, isn't it?' Joy said perfectly amicably. 'I thought about this a long time while I was away. What you and I have is not love, not one of those great passions that make people do foolish things . . . it's just a game. Like tennis, one person serves, the other returns it . . .'

'It's much more than a game . . .' he began.

'Or like chess.' Joy was dreamy now. 'One person makes a

crafty move and then the other responds to it with something even craftier.'

'You know very well what we have, there's no point in finding fancy words for it. We love each other . . . but we have set limits to this love, you and I. And we admire each other and we're happy together.'

'It's a game,' she repeated.

'Well, people who go out to play a game of golf or squash or chess together are friends, Joy, for God's sake, you don't decide to spend a day with someone you don't like. Use this example if it gives you pleasure, keep saying game game game. But it doesn't mean anything. It doesn't change anything. We're just the same. You and I.'

'Oh you *are* playing it well.' She laughed admiringly. 'Trying to diffuse it all, asking no questions about whether there really was a Scotsman or not. I think you'd be a very dangerous adversary in a game.'

He put out his cigarette and reached for her again, he held her close to him and spoke into her long shiny hair with its stripes of gold among the brown and its smell of lemony shampoo.

'Well so would you . . . a terrifying adversary. Isn't it just as well that we're the best of friends and the best of lovers and not enemies at all?'

But he had spoken more cheerfully than he felt, and her body had not been responsive to him. She had a half smile that was disturbing and had nothing at all to do with any pleasure which she might or might not have been feeling.

At the party Joy was dressed in a dazzling navy and white dress. The gleaming white collar was cut low into her cleavage revealing a lot of breast and expensive lace-trimmed brassiere. Her hair seemed to shine out like gold and copper. She looked ten years younger than thirty-three, she looked like a young beautiful girl on the prowl. Frank watched her with alarm as she moved through the crowds of Palazzo employees. This time there was no doubt about it, she had been drinking. And well before she arrived at the party.

Frank felt a cold knot of nervousness in his stomach. Joy sober he could cope with easily, but she was an unknown quantity drunk. His father's terrible and unpredictable rages flashed before him suddenly. He remembered the time that the entire dinner had been thrown into the fire in a fit of temper . . . nearly forty years ago but as clear as yesterday. And what had always stuck in Frank's mind was that his father had not intended to do it, he had wanted to eat his dinner as he told them over and over all night. It had given Frank a fear of drunks, he drank very little himself and he scanned his managers and sales force for signs of the bottle. It was the feeling that you couldn't rely on someone who was so dangerous. They would probably be all right but you couldn't be sure. He looked at the flashing smile and the low neckline of Joy East as she cruised around the room ever refilling her glass at the trestle tables, and he felt not at all sure that the day would end all right.

Her first target was Carlo, struggling offstage into his Santa outfit.

'Wonderful, Mr Palazzo,' she said. 'Wonderful, you go out and knock them dead, tell them what Santa will put in their wage packets if they're good little girls and boys and work like good little ants.'

Carlo looked puzzled. Frank acted quickly to draw her away.

'Joy, where are the tubs for the children? Please?' His voice was urgent.

She came up close to him and he saw her eyes were not focusing properly.

'Where are the tubs?' she asked. 'The tubs are being presided over by your wife. The saintly Renata. Santa Renata.' Her face broke into a big smile. 'That would be a nice song . . . Santa Renata . . .' She sang it to the tune of 'Santa Lucia', and seemed pleased with it so sang it a little louder. Frank moved slightly away. He had to get her out. Soon.

At that very moment Renata appeared to explain that the pink wrapping paper was on the gifts for girls and the blue for boys. One year her father had given the girls horrible monsters and spiders and the boys comb and mirror sets. This time they were taking no chances.

'That's right, Renata, take no chances,' Joy said.

Renata looked at her startled. Never had she seen Joy East looking like this.

'You look . . . very smart . . . very elegant,' Renata said.

'Thank you, Renata, *grazie, grazie mille,*' Joy said, bowing flamboyantly.

'I have not seen you wear clothes like this and look so full of life before . . .' Renata spoke quietly but with a little awe in her voice. She fingered the edge of her expensive but very muted woollen jacket. It had probably cost four times. as much as the striking garment that Joy was wearing but Renata looked like a bird of little plumage, dark hair, sallow skin and designer suit in lilac and pink colours with a braid of lilac-coloured suede at the edge of the jacket, nothing to catch the eye. Nothing at all.

Joy looked at Renata steadily.

'I'll tell you why I look so different, I have a man. A man in my life. That's what makes all the difference.'

Joy smiled around her, delighted with the attention from Nico Palazzo who was Carlo's brother, and from Desmond Doyle and a group of senior management who were all in the circle. Renata smiled too, but uncertainly. She didn't know quite what response she was meant to make and her eyes raked the group as if to find Frank who would know what to say.

Frank stood with the feeling that the ice in his stomach had broken and he was now awash with icy water. There was nothing he could do. It was the sense of powerlessness that made him feel almost faint.

'Was I telling you about this man, Frank?' Joy asked roguishly. 'You see me only as a career woman . . . but there's room for love and passion as well.'

'I'm sure there is.'

Frank spoke as if he were patting down a mad dog. Even if he had no connection with Joy they would have expected him to be like this. Soothing, distant, and eventually making his escape. They must all see now what condition she was in, they must have noticed. Was it only because he knew her so intimately, had traced every feature of her face and body for three years with his hands that he realized she was out of control? Everyone around seemed to be treating it all as normal Christmas high spirits. If he could stop her just now, before she said anything else, then all might not be lost.

Joy was aware she had an audience and was enjoying it. She put on a little-girl voice that he had never heard her use before. She looked very silly, he thought quite dispassionately, in her sober state she would be the first to criticize any other woman with an assumed lisping voice.

'But it's forbidden in this company to love anyone except Palazzo. Isn't that right? We all love Palazzo, we must have no other love.'

They laughed, even Nico laughed, they were taking it as good-natured banter.

'Oh yes, first love the company, then other loves,' Nico said.

'It's infidelity to love anyone else better,' Desmond Doyle said, laughing.

Frank flashed him a grateful look, poor Desmond his old pal from those long-ago days in Ireland was helping him inadvertently, he was taking the heat off. Maybe he could be encouraged to say more.

'Well, you've never been unfaithful, Desmond,' Frank said, loosening his collar. 'You're certainly a long and loyal Palazzo man.' He felt sick in his stomach after he said it, remembering suddenly the time that Desmond had been allowed to go after the rationalization and how he had to fight hard to get him reinstated. But Desmond didn't seem to see the irony. Desmond was about to answer with something cheerful when the voice of Joy East cut in again.

'No one should be married except to the company. When you join Palazzo you must marry the place, marry Palazzo. Very hard to do. Very hard. Except for you, Frank. You managed it all right, didn't you? You really *did* marry a Palazzo!'

Even Nico who was very slow must have realized by now that something was wrong. Frank had to move quickly. But he must not appear to be rattled. He must take it indulgently as anyone would take the public idiocy of a normally exemplary colleague.

'Yes, you're right, and I'm glad you reminded me because my father-in-law will be down on us all like a ton of bricks if we don't get the presents going soon. Renata, should we get the children to line up now ... or does somebody make an announcement. Or what?'

In other years Joy East had arranged everything like clockwork. Renata had a look of relief all over her face. She had thought that there had been an insult, a jibe, but obviously since Frank didn't see one, she had been wrong.

'I think we should tell Papa that the time has come,' she said and moved away towards her father.

'I think we should all tell Papa that the time has come,' Joy said to nobody in particular.

Desmond Doyle and Nico Palazzo exchanged puzzled looks.

'Joy, you must be tired after all that busy time at the packaging conference,' Frank Quigley said loudly. 'If you like I can run you home now before it all gets too exhausting here.'

He saw the relief on a few faces around him, Mr Quigley was always the one to cope with the situation, any situation.

His smile was hard and distant as he looked at Joy. It said in very definite terms that this was her one chance to get out of what she had walked them into. There wouldn't be any other chances. His smile said that he was not afraid.

Joy looked at him for a few seconds.

'All right,' she said, 'let's say I'm tired after the packaging conference, tired and very very emotional, and that I need to be taken home.'

'Let's say that then,' Frank said easily. 'Tell Renata to save me a nice boy present from Santa Claus,' he called out. 'I'll be right back to collect it.'

They looked at him in admiration as he led Miss East who was behaving most oddly out of the big hall and towards the car park.

There was complete silence in the car, not one word spoken between them. At her door she handed him her small handbag and he took out the key. On the low glass table was a bottle of vodka with one third of it gone and some orange juice. A heap of unopened Christmas cards, and a small smart suitcase as if she was going on or had come back from a journey. With a shock he realized that she must not have unpacked her case after her trip to that conference.

'Coffee?' he asked. It was the first word spoken.

'No thanks.'

'Mineral water?'

'If you insist.'

'I don't insist, I couldn't care less what you drink, but I wouldn't give a dog any more alcohol than you've had already.'

His voice was icy cold.

Joy looked up at him from the chair where she had sat down immediately.

'You hate drink because your father was such a drunk,' she said.

'You're telling me what I told you. Have you any further insights or shall I go back to the party?'

'You'd like to hit me but you can't, because you saw your father beating your mother,' she said, a crooked smile on her face.

'Very good, Joy, well done.' His hand was clenched, and he would like to have struck something, a chair, a wall, even to get rid of the tension he felt.

'I said nothing that wasn't true. Nothing at all.'

'No indeed, and you said it beautifully. I'm going now.'

'You are not going, Frank, you are going to sit down and listen to me.'

'Now that's where you're wrong. Since I did have a drunk for a father I am only too used to listening to drunks, it's a useless exercise. They don't remember anything next day. Try telephoning the speaking clock, tell it all to them, they love a good sob story from people with enough drink in them to float a navy.'

'You have to listen, Frank, you have to know.'

'Another time, a time when you can pronounce my name without stumbling over it.'

'About the conference. I wasn't there.'

'So you said, you told me. A Scotsman, well well. Don't tell me it's preying on your mind?'

'I wasn't anywhere near it, I didn't leave London.'

Her voice was odd, she seemed to have sobered up a bit.

'So?' He was still poised to go.

'I went to a nursing home.' She paused. 'To have an abortion.'

He put his car keys in his pocket, and came back into the room.

'I'm sorry,' he said, 'very sorry.'

'You needn't be.' She didn't look at him.

'But why, how . . . ?'

'The pill didn't suit me. I changed the type several times . . . but still . . .'

'You should have told me . . .' He was gentle now. Forgiving.

'No, it was my decision.'

'I know, I know. But still . . .'

'And so I went to this place . . . very nice place actually, it's a real nursing home for other things too, not just terminations as they call them . . .' Her voice shook a little.

He laid his hand over hers, the coldness was forgotten. 'And was it very bad, was it awful?' His eyes were full of concern.

'No.' Her face was bright and she smiled at him, a smile only a little lopsided. 'No it wasn't awful at all. Because when I went in there and went to my room, I sat and thought for a while, and I thought . . . Why am I doing this? Why am I getting rid of a human being? I would *like* another human being around me. I would like a son or a daughter. So I changed my mind. I told them I had decided not to go through with the termination. And I went to a hotel instead, for a couple of days, then I came back here.'

He looked at her, stricken.

'This can't be true.'

'Oh yes, it's true. So now you see why you couldn't just toddle off back to the party. You had to know. It was only fair that you should know. And know everything.'

If he lived to be an old man, something that his doctor said was highly unlikely, Frank Quigley would never forget that moment. The day he learned he was going to be a father, but not the father of Renata's child, not the father who would be congratulated and embraced by the Palazzo tribe. A father who would be ostracized and cut off from the life he had built for himself for a quarter of a century. He would never forget her face as she told him, knowing that for the first time in their very equal relationship she held all the cards. Knowing that drunken and upset and having broken all their rules she was still the one in charge. Because of biology which said that the women bore the children she was winning, and that was the only reason. Frank Quigley would not have been beaten by anything except the human reproductive system.

He had played it just right, of course, at the time. He had telephoned back to base and said that Joy needed a bit of attention. He had sat down and talked to her, but his mind was in overdrive. His words were soothing and supportive, his real thoughts were taking a journey into the future.

He allowed his real reactions only a moment's indulgence while he relished the thought that he had fathered a child. If Carlo knew there would be a lot less of the chat about eating more red meat. If Carlo knew. Carlo must never know. And

Renata would be hurt beyond repair. Not only at the infidelity, the knowledge that an affair had been going on under her very nose for years, but at the fact that this woman had produced a child, the one thing that Renata had failed to do.

As he stroked Joy's fevered forehead and assured her of loyalty and his great pleasure at the news and the way that things had turned out, Frank was working out logically and coldly what he must do next, what avenues were open to him.

As he urged cups of weak tea and thinly sliced bread and butter on the weeping Joy, he listed the possibilities that lay ahead and the disadvantages of each one. When he found the one that had the least dangerous minefield attached to it that was where he would head.

Joy could have the child and he would acknowledge that it was his. He would say that he did not intend to leave his marriage, but felt in fairness that the son or daughter should grow up knowing the care of a father. He considered this for seconds, only to dismiss it.

In a more liberated society this would work. But not with the Palazzos. Not for one minute.

Suppose Joy were to say that she was having the child and that the identity of the father was to remain unknown, undiscussed? Again not something beyond the imaginings in the 1980s for a liberated woman. But again this was the world of Palazzo. It would be frowned upon, it would be speculated about, and worst of all if Joy were ever to hit the bottle again it would all be revealed.

Suppose he were to deny paternity? Literally say that Joy was lying? He wondered why he had even considered this route. Joy was a woman he had intended to spend a great amount of time with, he didn't only love her for the good sex they had, he loved her mind and her reactions to things. Frank asked himself why had this possibility crossed his mind. He had never thought of stabbing Carlo in the back and taking over the company. He had not decided to woo and win Renata only for her money and position. He was not that kind of bastard. So why even entertain the idea of turning his back on the woman who had been his lover for three years, the woman who was going to bear his child? He looked at her, slack-jawed and awkward in the chair. He realized with a shudder how much he feared drink and the effects of it. He knew that whatever happened now, he would never be able to trust Joy, or trust himself to her again.

Suppose he were to persuade her to have the termination, for everyone's sake? There were still two weeks in which it would be safe. Perhaps he could persuade her.

But if he couldn't then he risked a hysterical response. And if she were to go ahead and have the child knowing that he wanted it aborted, then things would be about as bad as they could ever be.

Suppose he were to ask her to go away, to start a new life with a set of glowing references? Joy move away from London? Joy start life afresh with a small baby just to please Frank? It was unthinkable.

Suppose he were to ask her to give the child to him. Suppose that he and Renata were to adopt this baby? The child would inherit the Palazzo millions. Everyone would be pleased. Frank and Renata had done the rounds of the adoption societies, at forty-six he was too old to be an adoptive father. Not a real father as it turned out, but then Nature was never known to be a great supporter of bureaucracy.

But Joy had deliberately decided to have the child because she wanted another human being around her. She would not consider it. Or not now at any rate. Don't dismiss it utterly. She might, later on in the pregnancy. It was unlikely yet not impossible.

And then it would be adopting his own child. That would be very satisfying. In honesty he would have to tell Renata but they need not tell her family . . .

Frank stroked the forehead, administered the cups of tea and thought his own thoughts as he consoled Joy East with murmurs and sounds that would never constitute any kind of promise or contract in the unlikely event of their being recalled.

The weeks had passed somehow. The bad behaviour at the Christmas party was hardly commented upon, Frank was as usual congratulated for having as usual averted any little silliness. Joy was back at work head high in the new year, plans and ideas tripping out of her. There were no recurrences of drinking. Also there were no lazy afternoons by her fireside.

They met for a lunch early in the new year, Frank had said

in front of several of the managers that the place was lacking in anything new. What it needed in these days after Christmas was some pizzazz. He would take Joy East out to lunch and have a brainstorming session, he said. Women always loved a business lunch, and he wouldn't mind one himself. They went to the best restaurant where they were bound to be seen.

She sipped her Slimline Tonic and he drained his tomato juice.

'An expense-account lunch is wasted on us.' Joy smiled at him.

'As you told me that time, I'm a drunk's son, I'm afraid of drink,' he said.

'Did I say that? I don't really remember all the things I said that day. Is that why you don't come to me in the afternoons?'

'No it's not that,' he said.

'Well why not? I mean there's no need for any precautions now, it would be like bolting the stable after the horse had fled . . . we should get value . . .' Her smile was warm and welcoming. Like the old Joy.

'It might be bad for you, they say it's not good at this stage of the pregnancy,' he said.

She smiled, pleased that he was caring. 'But you could come and talk to me anyway, couldn't you?' I've waited a lot of afternoons.'

That was true, she had kept her word about not contacting him. Ever.

'We do have to talk,' he said.

'So, why are we trying to talk in a restaurant where everyone sees us? Those women over there, they're in-laws of Nico Palazzo. They haven't had their eyes off us since we came in.'

'We will be seen in public for the rest of our lives, this is exactly where we must discuss how our lives will continue. If we go to your house we slip into the old ways, we're back in the days when we only had ourselves to consider.' His voice was calm. But she seemed to sense his anxiety.

'You mean you wanted a get-away car and witnesses if I'm going to tell you anything unpalatable. Is that it?'

'Don't be silly, Joy.'

'No I'm not being silly, you're trying to get out of it, aren't you? You're actually scared to death.'

'That's not so, and stop smiling that smile that isn't a real smile. It's a paper-thin smile you put on for customers and contacts. It's not genuine.'

'And what was ever genuine about *your* smile, Frank? Did you not know, your smile never reached your eyes, never. It stopped always around the mouth.'

'Why are we talking like this?' he asked.

'Because you are full of fear, I can smell it,' she said.

'What's turned you against me, did I say anything?' He spread his hand out in wonder.

'You don't need to make those Italian gestures at me, I'm not a Palazzo. What did you say? I'll tell you what you said, you said we should sit down in a public place and make decisions about the rest of our lives. You forget that I know you, Frank, you forget that you and I know when you meet an adversary the first rule is to meet him on common ground, not your territory or his. You're doing that. We both know that if there's a danger of a row the rule is: make sure the meeting is held in a public place. It stops people making scenes.'

'Are you feeling all right, Joy? Seriously?'

'It won't necessarily work, you know, drunk or sober, at home or out I could make a scene if I wanted to.' She looked mulish.

'Of course you could, what *is* this? We're friends you and I, where's the hostility?'

'We are not friends, we are fencing with each other, we are playing games, looking for the advantage . . .'

'Well then, if that's all we are, what on earth are we having a child together for?'

'We're not having a child together,' Joy East said, 'I am having a child.'

There was a look of triumph on her face like he had only seen when she had beaten a rival, won an award or somehow got her way against all the odds.

It was then he knew that she intended him to dangle there, forever watching his step, forever in her power. It was her child, and her decision, but only for as long as it suited her. She was never going to promise him either secrecy or involvement. Her plan was that he should never know. That he would be for ever tied to her.

Frank Quigley had come across schemes like this before, the

supplier who had bought up the market but hadn't told you. He would want you to advertise the produce and then suddenly could raise the price because you were committed. Frank had dealt with that one in his time. Someone had tried it on him, but only once. Frank had smiled and said there was no way he was going to pay more than the agreed price for the product. But wouldn't they look foolish, the man had said, having spent all that money advertising it and then having to admit they didn't have it? No, not at all. Frank had smiled back with easy charm. They would just take another advertisement apologizing that the suppliers had proved unreliable. Everyone would think well of Palazzo for their honesty, the suppliers would be ruined. It had been so simple. But then it had only involved fruit, it hadn't involved a child.

He had brought into play every available ounce of charm that he possessed, and limp as a wet rag at the end of the lunch he congratulated himself that they were at least speaking normally on the surface.

They talked about the company. Twice he made her laugh, real laughter, head thrown back and pealing with mirth. The two women that she had said were Nico's inlaws looked over with interest. But there was nothing for them to take home with them as gossip, this was the most innocent lunch in the history of the world. Otherwise it would not have been here and in full view of everyone.

He had told her about his Christmas and then she told him about hers. She had gone to stay with friends in Sussex. In a big family home where she had been before, full of children, she said.

'Did you tell them?' he asked. He felt the conversation must not be allowed to wander too far from what they were both thinking about lest he be labelled callous.

'Tell them what?' she asked.

'About the baby?'

'Whose baby?'

'Your baby. Our baby if you like but basically, as you said, your baby.'

Joy gave a little purr of satisfaction. It was almost as if she were saying: That's better. That's more like it.

'No,' she said. 'I'm not telling anyone until I've decided what to do.'

And then there was no more. They spoke as they always had

about plans and schemes, and the inadvisability of letting Nico know anything at all that was taking place. The wisdom of Palazzo's buying the new site in that area which was meant to be coming up – Joy was afraid it was coming up too fast. The big houses were changing hands for a lot of money and then even more money needed to be spent on them to make them smart. That kind of people would shop in fancy delicatessens or even go in to Harrod's, she felt, Palazzo's would be wiser to aim for somewhere less ambitious, somewhere where you could get a huge car park. That's the way things were going now.

'We could even try to make a feature out of the car park,' Joy had said excitedly. 'You know how gloomy they look at best, and how they look like places you're going to be murdered in at worst. Perhaps it could all be brightly painted and there could be a covered terrace around it, a type of cloister effect, we could rent space to market stalls, give the place more life . . .'

She had been talking in terms of staying on, Frank had noted.

Joy East, if she were planning anything at all, planned to take three months' maternity leave and return to work once her child was born. Frank was not going to be informed about his role. That was the way she was going to play the game.

He had left that lunch white with fury. Angrier far and determined even more to regain control than he had been before Christmas. He would not be left suspended like this.

If she would not reveal her intentions like any normal person, then he was not going to respond normally.

Two could play a game of cat and mouse.

Long before Joy mentioned her pregnancy to anyone else Frank had made his contingency plan.

Based entirely on Joy's own projections about the need not to go too far upmarket for their customers, Frank Quigley commissioned surveys.

He had explained to the young men and women in the market-research bureau that they wanted confirmation of their belief that they should expand into less well-off areas. The survey was to be done nationwide but on a very small sample. It was the kind of survey which if Frank had seen cold he would have dismissed on the ground that its findings could not possibly be conclusive. But this time he wanted to let the board see from an outside agency that the way forward was to expand, and to leave

North London far behind. To open up on a trial basis in the Midlands, in the North of England even. The key to it would be design and image. Palazzo was to be presented as stylish and desirable. Joy East was the one to create that image.

It would be promotion, it would be a seat on the board for Joy. He would see her once a month at board meetings, true, but he would not see her every day.

And she would not see his father-in-law every day.

And she would not be in danger of meeting his wife.

He had few weapons, he had to outwit her by cunning.

She had to think that the promotion, the move and the change were against his wishes.

The survey which Carlo Palazzo fondly believed he had commissioned himself was complete by March when Joy East broke her news with maximum drama. She announced it under the heading of Any Other Business at the weekly management meeting.

Her eyes had been suspiciously bright. Frank knew what was coming.

'Well I suppose this *is* other business in a way, I bring it up in case you should hear it elsewhere and wonder why I had said nothing of it to my colleagues. I will be seeking three months' maternity leave in July . . . Obviously I'll work around it to make sure that any promotions are well covered but I felt you should know that it was upcoming.' She smiled around sweetly, meeting the eyes of the fifteen men in the room.

Carlo was at a total loss. 'Well heavens, good Lord, I did not even know you were thinking of getting married . . . my congratulations.'

'Oh no, nothing as settled as that I'm afraid.' A tinkly laugh. 'Just a child. We don't want too much of a shock to the system like getting married as well.'

Nico's jaw dropped, the others shuffled their praise and pleasure, but looking sideways at Carlo and Frank to try to gauge the mood of the meeting.

Frank Quigley looked pleasantly surprised and admiringly amused.

'This is very exciting news, Joy,' he said evenly. 'Everyone is delighted for you. I don't know what we'll do without you for three months, but will you be able to come back to us after that?'

The inquiry was warm and courteous, nobody could have seen the way their eyes locked hard across the table.

'Oh yes indeed, I've been busy making arrangements. These things aren't done lightly, you know.'

'No indeed,' he said soothingly.

By this stage Carlo had recovered enough control to be able to murmur a few pleasantries, but he called Frank to his office.

'What are we going to do?' he asked.

'Carlo, it's 1985, it's not the middle ages. She can have thirty children if she wants to. You're not shocked, are you?'

'Yes of course I am. Who is the father, do you think? Is it anybody at Palazzo?'

Frank felt he was acting a part in a play. 'Why should it be? Joy has a full life of her own outside here.'

'But why, why on earth?'

'Perhaps she felt she is in her thirties, she is alone, she might just *want* to.'

'It's a very inconsiderate thing to do,' Carlo grumbled. 'And inconvenient too. Look at the way it will upset our plans for the North.'

Frank spoke very carefully. 'When were you hoping to get that operational, not until the new year? Its planning stages will only be coming on stream in autumn when she comes back to work . . .'

'Yes, but . . .'

'But doesn't it suit you down to the ground, not that you should *say* that to her of course. You were already worried that she might not want the move. Now that she's having a child it might be just what she'd need, new environment, fresh start, more space and room up there, away from London . . .'

'Yes . . .' Carlo was doubtful. 'I think this has thrown a big spanner in the works.'

'Then if that's where you want her, you should make it sound very very attractive for her. Put it to her in a way that it seems just the right step for her to take . . .'

'Perhaps *you* should explain it to her.'

'No, Carlo.' For the second time Frank felt that he was actually acting out a part on stage. 'No, because you see, in a way I don't want to lose her from the London side of things, even though I think in my heart you're right. It's best for the company that she should go up North and get Palazzo into a different league, a national league.'

'That's what I thought,' Carlo said, believing it.

'So I'm the wrong one to persuade her.'

'Suppose she thinks I am banishing her away?'

'She can't think that, Carlo, haven't you all the documentation and surveys and inquiries to prove you were thinking of it ages back?'

Carlo nodded. He had, of course.

Frank let the breath out slowly between his teeth. Nowhere in that whole paperwork did Frank Quigley's name appear, in fact in the files there were several letters dissenting slightly and wondering whether Miss East would be better kept in London. He couldn't be faulted now.

Frank did not have long to wait. Joy burst into his office, eyes blazing and clutching a piece of paper in her hand.

'Is this your doing?' she asked.

'I have no idea what you're talking about.' He was bland, unruffled.

'Like hell you don't, you're sending me away. By God you're not going to get away with this, Frank. I'm not going to be shunted out of your sight when things get too hot to handle.'

'Sit down,' he said.

'Don't tell me what to do.'

He walked past her and called out to his secretary in the next room, 'Diana, can we have a big pot of coffee? Miss East and I are about to have a row and we need fuel.'

'Don't think I'm bowled over by that kind of witticism,' Joy said.

'It wasn't a witticism, it was the plain unvarnished truth. Now what *is* this about? Is this Carlo's plan to put you on the board and give you responsibility for the expansion?'

'Carlo's plan, don't give me Carlo's plan. It's your plan to get rid of me.'

His eyes were cold. 'Don't let's add paranoia to everything else.'

'To what else, what else are you talking about?'

His voice was low and hard. 'I'll tell you what else. You and I loved each other, I still love you. We agreed to make love, you were the one looking after contraception. When it no longer worked for you to look after it, it would have been fair to tell me, and let me be in charge of that side. Yes, Joy, that would have been the fair thing. It was not fair to allow me to conceive a child by accident.'

'I would have thought you'd be glad to prove you were able to,' she snapped.

'No. You would have thought wrong. Then to continue your unfairness you will not let me know what your plans are for the child we conceived. I have agreed that it's your responsibility if that's what you want. You said you would let me know. You have not let me know. You have played some kind of game with me throughout. I don't know any more than I knew at Christmas time.'

She was silent.

'And now you come screaming in here with some cock and bull story that I'm banishing you off to the provinces whereas the truth is that I did everything in my power to get you to stay here. You can believe this or not as you wish but that is the case.'

There was a knock on the door and Diana came in with the coffee. She laid it on the desk between them.

'Is the row over?' she asked.

'No, it's just getting to the peak,' Frank smiled.

'I don't believe you,' Joy said when Diana had left. 'Carlo never had a thought of his own.'

Frank went to a file and showed her a letter. In black and white it said that it might be a waste of Joy East's capabilities to have her tied up away from the nerve centre of the business. He told her that there were more. He could find them if she needed proof.

'Then it's Carlo, he can't bear the shameless unmarried mother bit . . . it's he who's sending me away.'

'Joy, I warned you about the danger of paranoia. If you look through these files that survey was commissioned back in January. Months before you made your announcement.'

'That bloody survey. Who are they anyway? They seem like a Mickey Mouse outfit to me,' she grumbled.

Frank had a moment's regret, she was so sharp no complaint and bright, her thinking was exactly on the same line as his own. What a pity that it had to end in this acrimony and games-playing.

'Well, however they are Carlo believes everything they say,

and they may have a point, you know. You said a lot of it yourself already, long ago, before all this.'

'I know.' She had to admit that this was true.

'So what will you do?'

'I'll make up my own mind without any patronizing pats on the head from you,' she said.

'As you wish, Joy, but may I remind you, this is *my* office and it was *you* who came to see me. It's not unreasonable that I should ask since you seem determined to involve me.'

'When I've decided what I'm going to do, I'll let you know,' she said.

'You said that before.'

'But that was only about *my* child, this is about *your* company. You have a right to know.'

He sat for a long time staring ahead of him after she left, her cup of coffee undrunk. He thought she had looked frightened and a little uncertain. But perhaps he was only imagining it.

She was a clever woman and she knew that she could make him sweat it out not knowing what she was going to say next and where she was going to say it.

He thought about it again that evening in their apartment. Renata sat on one side of their big marble fireplace looking into the flames and he sat on the other. There were often long companionable silences between them. But that night he said nothing at all.

Renata eventually spoke.

'Is it boring sometimes being with me in the evenings?' There was no complaint in her voice. She was asking as she might have asked the time or whether they should turn on the news on television.

'No, it's not boring,' Frank said truthfully, 'It's restful, actually.'

'That is good,' Renata said, pleased. 'You are a very good husband to me, and sometimes I wish I had more fire and light and sparkle.'

'Oh Jesus, I get enough of that at work, it's like a Guy Fawkes bonfire. No, you're fine the way you are.'

And he nodded to himself, as if agreeing with what he had just said. He didn't want to change her for a different model, a brighter shinier brand.

The weeks passed with no further word from Joy, the plans for the expansion continued. Carlo said that Joy East was certainly giving it a lot of attention, whether she intended to go or not was anyone's guess.

'Don't force her,' Frank advised. 'She'll go, but not before she's ready.'

He hoped he had read it right. Because she was succeeding in unsettling him.

He got an ornate invitation to a silver wedding celebration for Desmond and Deirdre Doyle. He looked at it grimly. In ten years possibly he and Renata might be sending out something similar. But he wondered if it were likely.

He wondered also what Desmond had to celebrate, a wedding that everyone had assumed was shotgun even though it turned out not to have been the case. A lifetime of being snubbed by the awful O'Hagan family back in Dublin. A life's work getting nowhere fast in Palazzo. Difficult children. The eldest shacked up with some out-of-work actor, apparently, the boy hightailing it back to Mayo of all places, and Helen. A nun, a very odd, disturbed girl. Frank didn't like to think about Helen Doyle who had appeared twice in his life, both times trailing disaster behind her and around her.

No, the Doyles had little to celebrate, which was probably why they were having this party.

An unlikely outing it was going to be.

But not as unlikely as the outing that Renata told him about when he came home from work.

'Joy East has invited us to dinner, just you and me and her,' she says.'

'Did she say why?'

'I did ask her, and she said she would like to have a talk to us.'

'Is it at her house?'

'No, she said that you always say when something has to be said it should be said on neutral ground.' Renata sounded puzzled.

Frank's stomach churned with fear.

'I don't know what she means by that,' he managed to say.

'Well, she said she's booking a table in this restaurant . . . and that she checked with Diana that you are free, so she telephoned me to see if I were free.'

'Yes. Well.'

'Do you not want to go?' Renata sounded disappointed.

'She's been very odd lately, this pregnancy has unhinged her a bit I think, that and the move . . . not that she's said yes or no to that, by the way. Can we get out of it do you think?'

'Not without being very rude. But I thought you liked her?' Renata looked confused.

'I do, I did, it's not that. She's a bit unbalanced. Leave it with me.'

'She said to ring her tonight.' Renata seemed withdrawn.

'Yeah, I will. I have to go out again anyway. I'll ring her while I'm out.'

He got into his car and drove to Joy's house. He rang the doorbell and knocked, but there was no reply.

He went to a public telephone and called her. She answered immediately.

'Why didn't you let me in?'

'I didn't want to.'

'You *told* me to call.'

'I told you to telephone, it's a different thing.'

'Joy, don't do this, don't have a scene in front of Renata, it's not fair on her, she's done nothing to deserve it, nothing. It's cruel.'

'Are you begging, do I hear you begging?'

'You can hear what you goddamn like, but just think, what harm has she ever done you?'

'Does this mean yes or no to my invitation?' Joy asked in a cool voice.

'Listen to me . . .'

'No, I am not going to listen any more. Yes or no?' There was a threat in the question.

'Yes.'

'I thought so,' said Joy East, and hung up.

It was the same restaurant where they had lunch last January. When Joy's stomach had been flat and when Nico's in-laws had seen them laughing. Now it was different.

Joy, still on mineral water to Frank's enormous relief, was gracious and anxious that they should be well seated and choose wisely from the menu. She did most of the talking, as Frank was edgy and Renata very reserved.

'You know the way in films they say: "You must be wondering why I asked you to come here tonight . . ." ' she tinkled.

'You said you had something to talk about.' Renata was polite.

'I do. I have come to some decisions finally after a lot of thought and I think it's fair that I should tell you about them. Frank because of work . . . and Renata, you because of Frank.'

He felt the floodgates begin to open. God damn her to the pit of hell. It wasn't even a woman scorned, it wasn't that kind of fury. He would have played straight with her. Or straightish anyway.

'Yes?' Renata's voice was anxious. Frank hadn't trusted himself to speak.

'Well, about this baby . . .' She looked from one to the other. And waited. It seemed like an age but it was probably three seconds.

Joy continued: 'I think it is going to change my life much more than I imagined. For a month or two I wondered if I'd done the right thing. Perhaps even at this late stage, I should give the child away, give it to some couple who would have a loving secure home. I might not turn out to be such a great mother figure, all on my own.'

She waited for one of them to deny this politely. Neither of them did.

'But then I thought no. I went into this knowing what it was about, so I must go through with it.' She smiled happily.

'Yes, but what has this to do with us . . . exactly . . . ?' Renata asked. Her face was fearful.

'It has this to do with you. If I were going to give the child to anyone I would most certainly have offered you the chance. You would be such good parents, this I know. But since I'm not, and since you might have harboured some hopes . . .'

'Never . . . I never thought of it,' Renata gasped.

'Hadn't you? I'm sure *you* did, Frank. After all you haven't been able to get any joy out of the adoption societies, Carlo tells me.'

'My father has no right to speak of such things,' Renata said, her face a dark red.

'No, perhaps not. But he does of course. Anyway, it was to make these matters clear that I asked you here, and to tell you that I will be going North, soon, much sooner than anyone expected. I've sold my house here, and bought a really lovely old

Georgian farmhouse in need of repair, but magnificently propor-
tioned, small and beautiful, and a perfect place for a child to
grow up. If he or she is only going to have me around, then the
poor love had better have a pony and somewhere to play as well!'
Her smile was all-embracing.

Renata took a deep breath. 'And will the child's father be
involved at all?'

'Not at all. The father is someone I met casually on a
packaging conference, a ship that passed in the night.'

Renata's hand flew to her mouth in an involuntary gesture.

'Is that so shocking?' Joy asked. 'I wanted to have a child, he
was as good a person as anyone else.'

'I know, I mean it was just that I thought . . .' Her voice
trailed away and she looked at Frank, whose face was stony.

'What did you just think, Renata?' Joy was like honey now.

'I know this is silly.' Renata looked from one to the other. 'I
suppose I was afraid that the child might have been . . . Frank's
child. And that this is why you even contemplated offering it to
us . . . please, I don't know what I am doing talking like this . . .
please.' There were tears in her eyes.

Frank was frozen, he *still* didn't know which way Joy would
jump. He couldn't put out his hand to comfort his wife.

Joy spoke deliberately and slowly: 'Oh, Renata, surely you
couldn't have thought that Frank and I? We're too alike to be a
number, to be the Grand Affair of the century. Oh no. And
anyway. Frank a father, that's not very likely, that wouldn't have
been on the cards, would it?'

'What . . . what do you mean . . . ?'

'Oh, Carlo told me about his problems . . . I'm afraid your
father is very indiscreet sometimes, but only when he knows it
won't go further . . . Please don't say back to him that I ever
mentioned it. But he was always so sad that Frank did not give
him the grandson . . .'

Frank spoke for the first time for a long while. He thought
he had managed to take the shake out of his voice.

'And your child? Shall you tell him it was a one-night stand
in a hotel room?'

'No, no, of course not, something much more romantic and
sad. An untraceable wonderful person, long dead. A poet maybe.
Something sad and beautiful.'

Somehow they finished the meal, somehow they found other things to talk about. The hurt went a little from Renata's eyes, and the lines of tension from Frank's face. And the serenity and bloom of pregnancy settled ever more on Joy East. She paid the bill confidently with her credit card and when Renata went to the Ladies' she sat and looked calmly across the table at Frank.

'Well, you won,' he said.

'No, you won.'

'How did I win, tell me? You frightened me to death and now you're denying me any part in the child's life. How is that winning?'

'You got what you wanted. You got me out.'

'You're not starting that again?'

'I don't need to. I investigated the market-research bureau. They told me you hired them, they even had the date, it was just after we had lunch in this restaurant. As usual it turned out the way you wanted it to. I'm out of your hair. The coast is clear for the next project. I do wonder who she'll be. But I'll never know. Any more than you'll know what it's like to play with a two-year-old, your two-year-old. Because you're not capable of fathering one. That's both your alibi and my excuse for cutting you out.'

'You never told me why. Why all this hate?'

'It's not hate, it's determination. And why? I suppose because you have cold, cold eyes, Frank. I didn't see that until lately.'

Renata was coming back across the room. They stood up, it was time to go.

'You'll be back for the meetings . . . and everything?' Frank said.

'Not all of them, I think if this operation is to be a success, we mustn't let anyone involved think that we keep running to London all the time. Major decisions should be made in the place itself. Otherwise they'll just think they're a little outpost instead of important in their own terms.'

She was right of course, as she had been so often.

He held the door of the taxi open for her. She said she was too big to fit into her little sports car any more.

For a brief moment their eyes met.

'We both won,' she said softly. 'You could put it like that.'

'Or neither of us won,' he said sadly. 'That's another way of putting it.'

And he put his arm around his wife's shoulder as they went to where the Rover was parked.

Nothing would ever be the same between them after tonight. But the world had only cracked a little for them, it hadn't blown apart as it might have. And in a way that was winning.

8

Deirdre

The article said that anyone could be truly beautiful if they would give twenty minutes a day. Deirdre settled herself with a happy little wriggle into her chair and pulled the packet of biscuits towards her. Of course she could give twenty minutes a day. Who couldn't? Lord, weren't we all up and awake for sixteen hours for heaven's sake? Twenty minutes was nothing.

She repeated the words Truly Beautiful. She could hear them being said about her when the day came. Doesn't Deirdre look truly beautiful? Who would think she was married for twenty-five years? Imagine that she's the mother of three grown children.

She sighed with pleasure and began to read. Let's see, what would she have to do? It would be her own little secret, investing this amount of time. The reward would be sensational.

First it said you must assess yourself and list your good points and weak areas. Deirdre took the little silver pen with a tassel on it from her handbag. This was fun, great fun. What a pity she had to do it on her own. Her eldest daughter Anna would say that she was fine as she was, no need to list figure flaws and dry patches in her skin. Her second daughter Helen would say it was ludicrous to be a victim and to think that looks were important, with all the suffering in the world women couldn't afford to take time analysing their blemishes and deciding whether their eyes were deep-set or too close together.

Her son Brendan, far away from her now, living in Ireland on a remote hillside in his father's part of the country . . . What would Brendan say? She found it almost impossible to imagine how Brendan would react any more. She had wept night after night when he had first left home with few explanations and less apologies. Only when he had asked her straight out on the telephone . . . When he had cut across her tears to ask, 'If you had your choice, if you had the power to choose my life what would you have me do that would be so good and so important

674

for us all?' she hadn't been able to answer him. Because to say that she wished things were different was no answer. You couldn't wish a circle to be square or black to be white.

But according to this beauty article there were things you could wish to be different and make them different. Like the shape of your face, a little judicious use of the blusher and the lightener could do wonders. Deirdre looked at the diagrams happily, she *would* learn to do it right. There was nothing worse than people who attempted it and got it wrong, they looked like Coco the Clown.

That was something that she could imagine Maureen Barry saying in the old days. She and Maureen used to have so much fun at one time. Deirdre's mother had been bosom pals with Mrs Barry and so the girls had carte blanche to do anything they liked as long as they were with each other. Deirdre thought back on those holidays in Salthill years ago. She had called the house in Rosemary Drive 'Salthill' as a reminder, but she saw the name on the gate so often that it didn't really suggest the sea and sunshine and total freedom of their teens.

Maureen had been so entertaining those times, there was nothing that they felt they couldn't tell each other. Not until the summer they came to London, the summer that everything changed for both of them.

Deirdre wondered about the girls they had been to university with in Dublin. Did they often wonder what had happened to blonde Deirdre O'Hagan? They would all know of course that she married young, maybe she would even put an announcement of her silver wedding in the *Irish Times*. Rub their noses in it, the uppity ones who had gone on to be barristers or to marry barristers. The types who thought that Dublin was the centre of the universe and had only heard of Harrod's as a place to shop and Chelsea as a place to live. Pinner? They used to say Pinner? as if it was Kiltimagh or somewhere like that. Oh, in *north* London. I see. It was their ignorance that they weren't travelled. But still she would put in an announcement. Or maybe it was something that the children should do . . . a little message wishing them well on the twenty-fifth anniversary. She would check the papers and see how people did things these days.

What a pity there wasn't still that closeness with Maureen Barry. If only the years could be rolled back, she could pick up the phone and ask her. Straight out. And talk to her too about face shaping, and how to shadow the jawline. But she would never ask Maureen anything like that these days. Things had changed completely as the years went by.

There were no friends around here who could share the fun of all this self-improvement. No indeed, her neighbours would think it frivolous and silly. A lot of the women went out to work, they either knew such things anyway or else they hadn't time for it. Anyway Deirdre would never dream of letting them into her business, letting them know that this was a big thing in her life, that it was her one chance to prove that a quarter of a century had added up to something. Deirdre intended to impress her neighbours rather than let them share in the fun. They weren't really important, not like people back in Dublin, but still it was good to let them see that the Doyles were people of importance, of worth.

What would Desmond say if he saw her studying this article so intently? Would he say something flowery like that she was Truly Beautiful already? Or might he just say that's nice in the curious flat way he often said things were nice without engaging in them at all? Or might he sit down and say to her that there was really no need for all this fuss and preparation. Desmond often told her not to fuss. She hated that, she didn't fuss, she just saw to it that things were done right. If somebody hadn't lit a fire under Desmond all these years where would they be now she would like to know?

Deirdre would not share her beauty secrets with her husband. Long long ago in that strange summer when it all began, Desmond would lie on a narrow bed and admire her as she brushed her long fair curls, he would say that he never knew that peaches and cream was anything except a line in a song until he saw Deirdre's lovely face. He would reach over for her and ask if he could help her rub more of that nice cold cream in, maybe down her throat a little, maybe around her neck and arms. Maybe . . . maybe. It was so hard to remember Desmond being like that. But the article in the magazine said that she could recapture all that fresh glow, it was only a matter of proper skin care.

Deirdre would follow every single step, all those upward and circular movements when massaging in the throat cream, all that avoiding the delicate tissue around the eyes. She was going to look right on this day if it killed her. She was going to show them that they had been wrong to pity her twenty-five years ago when she had married Desmond Doyle, a counter hand in a grocery shop, a boy from a poor family in the back of beyond in Mayo. A family that nobody had ever heard of.

This day would be her silvery revenge.

They had all said yes, every single person who had been expected to come. There were some of course who had been asked but knew that they were not meant to come. Like Desmond's odd brother Vincent, the man who never left his mountains and his sheep in that lonely place where Brendan had chosen to spend his life. There had been a message from her son that his uncle very much regretted but it was a bad time to get away. That was the way it should have been done. Deirdre had nodded, pleased at the correct response.

And of course the Palazzos who ran the huge company where Desmond had worked for so long. Unfortunately they couldn't come, a sweet letter from Carlo and Maria, signed personally, wishing them all kinds of happiness and full of regrets that it would coincide with their annual visit to Italy. There would be a gift and flowers. But it was right that they didn't come. They were too high up, they would cramp everyone else's style. And Deirdre's mother who felt able to talk to everyone might discuss with them too closely Desmond's career in the company. She might discover that Desmond had never risen high and had at one stage been let go. This would be at odds with the glowing picture Deirdre always painted.

Frank Quigley and his wife Renata Palazzo said they would love to come. Deirdre thought grimly that Frank, for all his vast success and his unfair advancement up the ladder even before he married the heiress to the Palazzo fortunes, was still a good man to have at a function. He always seemed to know the right thing to say, and said it. She remembered back to their wedding day, Frank had been the best man then, he had been well able to handle anything that had turned up. Including Deirdre's mother and father, with their faces like early Christian martyrs throughout the ceremony and the so-called festivities.

And Father Hurley was coming, he said it would be a marvellous chance to visit a couple whose marriage has worked out so well. Deirdre knew she could rely on kind Father Hurley to say the right thing all evening.

And of course the Irish contingent would arrive. The date had been long fixed in their minds. There had been a possibility that her brother Gerard might not be able to make it but Deirdre had telephoned with such surprise and hurt and bewilderment that somehow his plans had changed. She had told him straight out on the telephone that there was no point in *having* a silver wedding if the family couldn't be there.

'Will Desmond's family be there?' Gerard had asked.

'That's not the point,' Deirdre had said.

Mother was coming of course, and Barbara, they were going to make a long weekend out of it all, come on the Thursday, do a few shows, take in a lot of shopping. Barbara's husband Jack would combine it with a business trip of course. That's what he was always able to do.

And when they arrived they would have drinks on the lawn in Rosemary Drive in the late afternoon. Then they would all go to a special Mass where the priest would refer to blessings of the sacrament of matrimony in general and specific reference to Desmond and Deirdre in particular. Father Hurley would be called on as the priest who married them to say a few words . . . Then after photographs outside the church and everything they would gather back at Rosemary Drive, and champagne would be opened.

There had been no champagne back in 1960 but Deirdre would not let her brow furrow about that. If she were to be truly beautiful she must keep worry lines away from her face.

She told herself that there really was no need to have worry lines. Everything would go perfectly.

And even if . . . no, no, smooth out the temples, don't screw up the eyes.

The beauty plan had suggested you do a Countdown and a Chart. Nothing pleased Deirdre more, she loved making out plans and schedules like this. Anyway she already had her own Countdown to the silver wedding in terms of things to be organized.

Desmond had shaken his head sadly, but men didn't understand the way things were done. Or maybe, Deirdre thought crossly, *some* men did, and those were the ones who got on. Men like Desmond who had never risen in Palazzo, who were leaving and going into partnership in a corner shop. Those men didn't understand.

And because Deirdre was so plugged into her count-down, she knew she had exactly 110 days to go when the telephone rang and it was her mother at the other end of the line.

Mother rang only every second weekend, on Sunday evenings. Deirdre had instituted that practice years ago, they rang each other on alternate Sundays. Sometimes she felt that Mother had little to say, but that couldn't be possible. Mother wasn't good at writing letters so these conversations were Deirdre's lifeline. She remembered everything that was said, and even kept a little spiral notebook by the phone to jot down names of Mother's bridge friends, or of the party that Barbara and Jack had been to, or the concert that Gerard had taken Mother to. Sometimes Mrs O'Hagan would exclaim that Deirdre had the most extraordinary memory for little things. But Deirdre thought it was only natural that you should want to recall matters of moment in your family's life. She was always mildly put out that Mother hardly ever remembered any of her friends, and never inquired about Palazzo or about any of the outings that Deirdre had described.

It was unexpected to hear from Mother in the middle of the week, in the middle of the day.

'Is anything wrong?' Deirdre said at once.

'No, Deirdre, Lord above you sound just like your grandmother.' Kevin's mother always began every greeting by asking was anything wrong.

'I meant it's not your usual time to ring.'

Mother softened: 'No, I know, I know. But I'm in London and I thought I'd try and see could I catch you at home.'

'You're in *London*!' Deirdre cried, her hand flying to her throat. She looked around the living room, untidy and covered with Desmond's papers, plans and projections, notes that he had been discussing with the Patels, the family who ran the shop that he insisted was far more his life's dream than the great Palazzo company. Deirdre herself was dressed in a faded pinny, the place was a mess. She looked out the window fearfully as if her mother were about to come straight in the door.

'Yes, I just got in from the airport. The Underground is marvellous isn't it? Just whizzes you in, door to door almost.'

'What are you doing in London?' Deirdre's voice was almost

a whisper. Had Mother come three months too early for the silver wedding, was there a crisis?

'Oh, just passing through . . . you see the tour leaves from London.'

'The tour? What tour?'

'Deirdre, I told you all about it . . . didn't I? I must have. I've told everyone else.'

'You mentioned no tour to me.' Deirdre was mutinous.

'Oh I must have, maybe I wasn't talking to you.'

'We talk every Sunday night of life, I was talking to you four days ago.'

'Deirdre, is anything wrong dear? You sound so strange. Like as if you're fighting with me or something.'

'I didn't know of any tour, where are you going?'

'Down to Italy first, and then by ship, we pick up the ship in Ancona and head off from there . . .'

'Where do you head off to?'

'Oh a variety of places . . . Corfu, Athens, Rhodes, Cyprus, and some place in Turkey . . .'

'A cruise Mother, you're going on a cruise!'

'I think that's a very grand name for it.'

'It sounds a very grand outing.'

'Yes, well let's hope it won't be too hot out in all those places, I think it's probably not the right time of year to head off . . .'

'Then why are you?'

'Because it came up, anyway enough of this, are we going to meet?'

'Meet? You're going to come here? Now?'

Mother laughed. 'Well thanks a lot, Deirdre, that sounds a great welcome, but actually I hadn't intended on going out to darkest Pinner . . . I thought you might come in and join me for a spot of lunch or coffee or whatever.'

Deirdre hated Anna calling it 'darkest Pinner', it was such an insult, as if the place was off the beaten track. And here was her own mother, who was from Dublin for heaven's sake, who didn't know where anywhere was, and whether it was on or off any track, saying the same thing.

'Where are you staying?' she asked, trying not to let the irritation show.

Mother was in a central hotel, very central she said, it had only taken her two minutes to leave the Piccadilly Line and be in her foyer. Simply remarkable. It would be easy for Deirdre to find too.

'I know how to get there.' Deirdre was white-faced.

'So will we say the bar here at one thirty, will that give you time . . . ?'

Deirdre left a note to Desmond on the table. These days she never knew whether he was going to come back or not during the day. His arrangements with Palazzo seemed to be fluid. Frank Quigley had said there would be proper arrangements made, for a manager like Desmond, setting up on his own, it wasn't a question of severance pay, redundancy, compensation, golden handshakes . . . It was all defined as Proper Arrangements. Deirdre hoped it would be finalized by the time of the silver wedding.

Grimly Deirdre went upstairs and put on her best suit. Her hair was limp and greasy-looking. She had planned to wash it later in the day, now there wasn't time. Her good handbag was being mended, the catch had worked loose. There was a grubby-looking bandage on her wrist where she had burned herself on the oven. She didn't like to open it all up and apply a fresh one, they had told her that it should be done at the hospital.

In low spirits and filled with a vague apprehension Deirdre Doyle set out to meet her mother. She felt drab and unattractive. She looked what she was, she decided, catching a reflection of herself in the window of the train that took her into Baker Street. She looked the middle-aged housewife from the suburbs, married to a not very successful man, no job to exercise her mind, not enough money to dress herself properly. Suffering badly from the empty-nest syndrome. Perhaps more than most: one daughter trying to be accepted in a convent where they wouldn't let her take her vows, another daughter who sometimes didn't come to see her parents more than once in a fortnight, and her son, her beloved son gone, fled to live at the other side of another country.

She was sure that she and Mother would fight. There had been something in the tone of the phone call that she hadn't liked. Mother had been impatient with her, and patting her down as if *she* were the difficult one.

It was extremely irritating but Deirdre would not lose her temper. Years of being reasonable and refusing to raise her voice had meant that there were few arguments in Rosemary Drive.

Deirdre had always prided herself on that. It was something to show for all those years and all that had happened.

Mother was sitting in a corner of the big oak-panelled bar as if she were a regular. She looked very well, she wore a fawn linen jacket and skirt with a cream-coloured blouse beneath, her hair had been freshly done, in fact she must have spent the hour that her daughter used to struggle in to central London sitting peacefully in a hairdressing salon. She looked relaxed and at her ease. She was reading a newspaper and unless she was putting on an elaborate act she seemed to be reading it without the aid of glasses.

A woman of sixty-seven and she looked somehow younger and fresher than her own daughter.

Eileen O'Hagan's eyes looked up just at that moment, and she smiled broadly. Deirdre felt her movements somehow stiffen as she walked across to meet her mother. They kissed and Mother, who was already on friendly terms with the waiter, called him over.

'Just a glass of wine and soda,' Deirdre said.

'Nothing stronger to celebrate your old Mother coming to town?'

'You're never this lady's mother, seesters yes . . .' the waiter said on cue. But it had a ring that was altogether too truthful for Deirdre.

'Just wine and soda,' she snapped.

'Let me look at you . . .' her mother said.

'Don't, Mother, I look badly, I wish you'd told me . . .'

'But if I had then you'd have gone to an immense amount of fuss and worn yourself out . . .' her mother said.

'Then you admit you didn't tell me, that it didn't just slip your mind.'

'It was out of kindness, Deirdre . . . you were always one to go to such efforts, that's why I didn't tell you.'

Deirdre felt the tears sting in her eyes, she fought to keep the hurt tone out of her voice.

'Well all I can say is that it's a pity. Desmond would have loved to have had you to the house, and the girls will be very sorry they've missed their Grannie.'

'Nonsense, Deirdre, Anna's at work. Helen's at prayer . . . Desmond is up to his eyes . . . Why create a great fuss?'

There it was again, that hated word Fuss. Deirdre clenched her fists and saw her mother glance at her whitened knuckles. This was very bad, she had vowed that there would be no argument. She must keep to that.

'Right, well here we are anyway,' Deirdre said in a voice that sounded to her own ears curiously tinny. 'And Mother, you do look remarkably well.'

Her mother brightened up. 'This suit has been a godsend, you know I bought it three years ago in Maureen's shop. Maureen always had great taste, I used to wonder why some of her clothes were so expensive, but her mother always said you paid for the cut and that they never really went out of fashion . . .'

Mother patted the skirt of her outfit with pleasure.

'It should be just the thing for a cruise.' Deirdre tried to sound enthusiastic.

'Well yes, I didn't think there was any point in getting all those floral silks . . . leisurewear, cruisewear they actually call them nowadays. Better to bring something suitable, something familiar, and I have a few cotton dresses for sightseeing.' She looked animated and excited.

'And what possessed you to take off on something like this?' Even as she spoke Deirdre knew that hers sounded like the voice of an older woman remonstrating with a difficult daughter rather than the enthusiasm that there should have been for a self-sufficient parent capable of enjoying herself on her own.

'As I told you, it came up, and I have a friend who was also free at this time, so it seemed only sensible . . .'

'Oh good, someone's going with you.' Deirdre was pleased. Two old ladies on board ship would at least have each other to talk to at the time, and be able to share the memory afterwards. She tried to remember which one of her mother's bridge cronies would have been likely to be accompanying her.

'Yes, and I thought I'd seize the chance of letting you meet each other, not for lunch, we'll have that on our own, but Tony said he'd pop down and say hallo . . . Ah, there he is . . . what timing!'

And as Deirdre felt the base of her stomach fill with lead she realized that her mother was waving at a florid-looking man with a blazer and a red face who was coming across the room rubbing his hands delightedly. Mother was going on a cruise with a man.

'This is nice,' Tony said, crushing Deirdre's hot hand in his own, and telling the waiter that he'd like a large G and T, Cork and Schweppes, ice and slice.

The waiter was puzzled. Mother said affectionately that Irish gin-drinkers were fanatically partisan and only drank the home brew as far as gin was concerned.

'But we're very democratic, we drink the English tonic,' Tony said, beaming around him. 'Well Deirdre, what do you think of all this caper?'

'I've only just heard about it this moment,' she said, hardly able to find the words.

'It should be a great old jaunt altogether,' he said. 'No decisions about whether to go and see places, they come to see you instead. Perfect for the lazy man. And lazy woman.' He actually patted Mother's hand.

'Were you afraid to tell me this too in case I'd fuss?' Deirdre asked, and could have bitten off her tongue.

Tony weighed in before Mother could answer.

'Oh, there you are, Eileen, she's as jealous as the others. Barbara nearly went mad when she heard that her mother was taking me instead of her, and Gerard said that in all decency your mother should take her son instead of a toy boy like myself.' He threw back his head and laughed heartily, and Mother laughed with him.

Deirdre thought, he knows Barbara and Gerard. Why had neither of them said anything about this to her? How dare they keep quiet about something as big as this? And was he serious about Mother taking him, Mother could not possibly be paying for this loud vulgar man. Or was this a joke too?

Mother seemed to read her face. 'Don't worry about a thing, Deirdre my love, it's only his way of going on. Tony's not after the deeds of the house.'

'Fat chance I'd have if I *were* after them,' he boomed. 'Your mother will live for ever, I'll go for the chop one of these days. Hopefully not on the cruise, though a burial at sea would be something to remember, wouldn't it?'

Deirdre felt a genuine sense of nausea. This man who must be almost the same age as her mother, was a serious part of her life. And until this minute nobody had been able to tell her.

She forced the smile back on to her face, and saw her mother's approving glance. She found her mouth dry and bitter as she searched for some suitable words.

But Tony was not a man who would allow silences. He had had her glass refilled, he had commandeered a dish of olives and a bowl of crisps on the ground that one had to have all the trappings. He had assured her that he would take great care of her mother on the cruise, squeezed her hand hard again, and said he would leave the key at reception. The key. The man wasn't even pretending that they had separate rooms. Deirdre felt a sense of unreality wash over her, and she hardly noticed that he had kissed her mother goodbye on the cheek.

Mother had booked a nearby restaurant. It was small and French and expensive. The napkins were thick, the silver was heavy, and the flowers on the table were real and plentiful.

In her twenty-five years living in London Deirdre had never eaten in a place like this and here was her mother, her mother from a small country, a small city compared to this one, ordering as if she were used to it.

She was glad that Mother was making decisions, not only could she not understand the menu but she would not have been able to order, so confused and upset did she feel.

'Why didn't you tell me anything about ... er ... Tony?' she asked eventually.

'Well there wasn't all that much to tell until we decided to go on this cruise together, and then as soon as we set off on that I *did* tell you.' Mother spread out her hands as if it were the simplest thing in the world.

'And Gerard, and Barbara ... do they ... did they ... ?'

'Well they know Tony's a friend of mine, and naturally I told them our holiday plans.'

'And were they ... did they ... ?'

'Gerard drove us to the airport this morning. Tony's right, he's green with envy, he keeps saying it's just what he needs. He works too hard, he *should* take time off, and he can well afford it. Maybe this is the spur.'

'But did he say ... what did he think ... ?'

'He didn't say that he'd take a holiday, and you know Gerard, he probably is thinking about it.'

Could Mother really misunderstand her or was this deliberate? Deirdre was not going to be brushed aside.

'What about Barbara and Jack? What do they think of you going away with a man?'

'Dearest Deirdre, I'm not going away with a man in that sense, I am going away on holiday certainly and I am going with Tony, and yes indeed he is a man. What do you mean, what do they think? They don't think at all, I am perfectly sure.'

'But Jack's family . . .'

As long as Deirdre could remember, Jack's family had been spoken of with some kind of awe. His father was a High Court Judge, his uncle was an Ambassador. Barbara had done what the O'Hagan family had wanted by marrying such style, instead of what she, Deirdre the eldest, had done – marrying a nobody and doing it in a great hurry.

But Mother looked totally bewildered.

'Jack's family?' she repeated as if Deirdre had somehow begun to speak in a foreign language. 'What on earth connection have they with anything?'

'You know . . .'

'I don't think they ever met Tony. No, I'm sure they didn't. Why do you ask?'

Deirdre looked hard at her mother. Mother knew bloody well why she asked. She asked because the high and mighty Jack's family were always mentioned. They had been mentioned since Deirdre's young sister Barbara had started walking out with a son of the well-connected tribe. Deirdre remembered the huge wedding, given for Barbara, with the marquee, the witty speeches, the politicians and the photographers. It had been very different from her own wedding day. And now suddenly Jack's almighty clan didn't seem important any more.

Feeling a flush darken her cheek, she spoke directly to her mother.

'And do you and . . . Tony . . . have any further plans . . . like after the cruise, do you think you might get married or anything?'

'Do try to keep the surprise out of your voice,' her mother said. 'Stranger things have happened, you know. But the answer is no. No plans like that.'

'Oh?'

'And anyway, enough about me and my trip. Tell me about all your doings.' Mother smiled in anticipation.

Deirdre looked dour: 'None of them are anything nearly as interesting as your plans.'

'Come come, Desmond's setting up on his own, *and* you're going to have this whole silver wedding shindig . . .'

It was such a Tony word, shindig. Mother didn't speak like that before.

'Where did you meet him?' Deirdre asked abruptly.

'Desmond?' Now Mother was being playful. 'When you brought him home of course, and told us about the wedding. But you know that.'

'I didn't mean Desmond, and you know that.' Deirdre was cross. 'I meant Tony. How did you become involved with him?'

'We met in the golf club.'

'Tony's a member of the golf club?' The surprise and disbelief were clear in her voice.

'Yes, he plays off twelve,' Mother said proudly.

'But how did he become a member?' Years ago someone flash like Tony could not have been proposed, it would have been as simple as that. Had her Desmond known how to play golf, which he did not, he would not have been acceptable. How could someone like Tony get in?

'I've no idea, I suppose like we all became members.' Mother was vague.

'And do all your other friends know him, did Mrs Barry know him for example?' Deirdre had chosen Maureen Barry's mother, the great social barometer of their Dublin. Surely Tony had not been welcomed in her set?

'Sophie? Yes of course poor Sophie met him from time to time. Sophie Barry didn't play golf, remember, so she wouldn't have known him in that context.'

'Don't tell me Tony plays bridge?'

'No, he's frightfully dismissive of old pussy cats as he calls us, spending hour after cheery hour, day after day dealing cards.'

Mother laughed merrily and suddenly her life seemed much more fun than Deirdre's own. Desperate not to let her mother change the subject again, Deirdre tried once more.

'And Mother please, what does Gerard think? What does he

say? No, not about taking holidays himself, what does he say about you and Tony?'

'I've no idea.'

'You must know.'

'No, I mean how would I know? I only know what he says to me, I've no idea what he says to anyone else. He has a rather nice girlfriend at the moment, he may talk about it with her, but I imagine not.' Mother looked supremely unconcerned.

'But he must . . . surely . . .'

'Listen, Deirdre. Everyone has their own life to lead, Gerard is probably much more worried about his career at the Bar, should he take Silk, should he stop playing the field with these little dolly birds and settle down? He probably worries about his health, he's nearly forty, he may think a lot about cholesterol and polyunsaturated fats. He might wonder whether to sell his flat and buy a house. What time on earth is there for him to spend thinking about his mother? I ask you!'

'But if you're doing something . . . if you're getting into something . . .'

'I'm sure he thinks I'm old enough to look after myself.'

'We all have to look after each other,' Deirdre said a trifle unctuously.

'That's where you are totally wrong, we all have to make very sure we don't interfere in people's lives. That's the great sin.'

The unfairness of it stung Deirdre like the lash of a whip. How *dare* Mother come out with this preachy nonsense about not interfering in people's lives. For a quarter of a century Deirdre had been trying to live up to some kind of image, some expectations for her. She was the daughter for whom there had been such hopes. The eldest of the family, very bright at university, an honours student, she might have taken the Third Sec examination and gone into the Department of External Affairs as it was called then, she might have been on the way to being an ambassador or marrying one. She might have done the Bar as her brother had done. She might have made the brilliant match that her sister Barbara had done.

Instead she had fallen in love one long hot summer, and trapped herself into a strange prison. Where since nothing was good enough for the O'Hagans and their hopes back home then everything must be made to look as if it were.

Deirdre had lived her entire life on this premise, to please the mother who was now sitting opposite her justifying her pitiable relationship with a common flashy man by saying that the main rule of living was not to interfere! It was not possible.

Deirdre spoke very slowly: 'I know what you're saying but I think it's important too not to be entirely self-centred and to take the wishes of others into account as well. I mean, did I or did I not spend all my teenage years hearing about people who were suitable, and people who were not suitable?'

'Not from me you didn't.'

'But you were always wanting to know what people's fathers did, and where they lived?'

'Out of interest.' Mother was airy about it. 'It's always nice to know who people are in case you knew them years ago or something. That's all it was about.'

'No it wasn't, Mother, you and Mrs Barry . . .'

'Oh Deirdre, Sophie Barry had nothing in her whole life except some kind of nonsensical pecking order. Nobody who knew her took a blind bit of notice of it . . .'

'Maureen did.'

'Well more fool Maureen, and anyway I don't think you're right, Maureen lived her own life, made her own way despite all poor Sophie's rubbishing on about being in trade.'

'You mean to tell me that you and Daddy were perfectly happy that I married Desmond? Don't try to tell me that. I won't believe it.'

There were tears in Deirdre's eyes, tears of rage, hurt and confusion. Suddenly the screen was falling away, the mask was being dropped, she knew she was on dangerous ground here. The polite pretence of years was being swept away.

The woman in the fawn linen suit and the cream blouse looked at her with concern. She began to speak and then stopped.

'Now, you can't deny it!' Deirdre was triumphant.

'Child, you're talking about a lifetime ago,' her mother said.

'But what I say is true, you did care, you did care that Desmond wasn't top drawer enough for us.'

'What do you mean for us? We weren't marrying him, you were, he was your choice, the words top drawer weren't even mentioned.'

'Not aloud maybe.'

'Not at all. I assure you, your father and I thought you were too young, of course we did, you hadn't taken your degree, we were afraid you would never get any qualification. In that I suppose we wished you would wait, that was all.'

Deirdre took a deep breath: 'You knew we couldn't wait.'

'I knew you wouldn't wait, that's all I knew. You were very determined. I wasn't going to oppose you.'

'You knew why.'

'I knew you loved him or thought you did, now that you've stayed with him and are dead set on having all this palaver in the autumn then you were probably right, you did love him, and he loved you.'

To Mother it seemed too simple, if you lived together for twenty-five years and were prepared to acknowledge it . . . you loved each other. Deirdre was thoughtful.

'Well isn't that what happened?' Mother was waiting for a yes or a no or an I told you so.

'More or less, but no thanks to anyone at home.' Deirdre was still mulish.

'I don't know what exactly it is you're trying to say, Deirdre. Of all my children I thought you were the most contented. You went for what you wanted, you got it. Nobody forced you to do anything, you had your freedom, you went to university, you could have worked for a living but you never did. Sophie and I used to say that you got everything on a plate, now it seems there's some grievance.'

Mother was interested but not distressed, she was concerned but not unduly curious. She tossed a salad expertly and waited for an explanation.

'Why did you let me marry Desmond if you thought I was too young?'

'I only thought, let's cause the least grief possible in the world. That's what I always think. Your father did think you might be pregnant, but I knew you weren't.'

'How did you know that?' Deirdre's voice was a whisper.

'Because nobody, not even in the far back year of 1960, would have got married to someone just for that reason if she didn't want to. And you weren't. Anna wasn't born until months and months later, quite wiped poor Sophie's eye, I think. I have a feeling she had the same thoughts as your father.'

'Yes.'

'So, Deirdre, what's the federal case as they say? What am I meant to have done? We gave our permission. Was that bad? No. We came to the wedding, that's what you wanted. You said you didn't want a huge showy number and you wanted it in England, we went along with that. We took Barbara and Gerard out of school for the ceremony.

'The house is there for you and Desmond to come over and see us but you never do, you came once and you were so touchy we didn't know what to say to you, everything upset you. We came to see you a few times and we're all heading over to see you again for your silver wedding, something it may be said that isn't at all what we're used to, and somehow still in spite of all this I am the worst in the world, and by implication your father was, and your sister and brother are.'

Eileen O'Hagan mopped up the dressing of her salad with a piece of French bread and looked at her daughter for an explanation.

Deirdre looked at her wordlessly.

The waiter came and took away their plates and discussed at length an apple tart and a burnt cream. Deirdre's mother went into the option with animation, it gave Deirdre a chance to gather her thoughts.

'I ordered one of each, I hate to be directive but I thought it best.'

'That's fine, Mother.'

'And what were we talking about before? Oh I know, Daddy and I were meant to have hated Desmond or something, isn't that it?'

'Not exactly.'

'Well not just not exactly, not at all. We both thought he was very nice, bullied within an inch of his life by you of course but then you'd be bound to be a bossy boots, you get it from me.' Eileen O'Hagan was pleased to have passed on such sterling qualities.

'What did you say about him to each other?' Deirdre's voice was small.

'Daddy and I? Hardly anything. He was providing for you all right, that was what we worried about I suppose in those days, so it was good that this side of it wasn't a problem. I think we were upset that you didn't have a career.'

'I had three children in rapid succession.' Deirdre was defensive.

'Yes, but afterwards. Anyway I suppose we thought that maybe it was a bit hierarchical in that set-up with the Italians, the Palladians . . .'

'The Palazzos, Mother.'

'Yes well, that's about the only negative thought we ever had about Desmond, so you can stop doing your outraged lioness bit about him.'

Mother laughed affectionately.

Deirdre looked at her as if she were someone never seen before.

'And Mrs Barry, was she not questioning you about us?'

'No, sweetheart. To be very honest there wasn't all that much interest at all. Nobody had. You know that yourself about Dublin, out of sight out of people's minds and immediate conversation and interest.'

'But not for you, surely you couldn't have forgotten me, your eldest daughter.' Her lip was trembling.

'Of course I don't forget you, silly thing, but not all the little bitty things that you think were never off our lips, this promotion, that remark that the Palladians passed about Desmond, the time that Anna was at the same reception as Princess Di.'

'It was Princess Michael of Kent.'

'Well you know what I mean, Deirdre, it's not some kind of score card, you know, points for this, minus points for that.'

There was a silence. A long silence.

'I'm not criticizing you, you do know that?'

'Yes, Mother.'

'And even if Kevin and I hadn't liked Desmond, which was not the case, whatever we were allowed to get to know of him we liked very much . . . But suppose we hadn't . . . what would have been the point of saying it or letting it be thought? We weren't going to live your lives for you.'

'I see.'

'When I was married to Kevin my parents were delighted, they crowed and brayed and made me very very uneasy.'

'You should have been pleased.'

'No, I was suspicious. I thought that they wanted me off their hands and I also thought they equated money with some kind of happiness or success. Your father didn't give me much of either.'

'I don't believe you!' Deirdre's mouth was wide open.

'Why shouldn't I tell you this? You and I are middle-aged women, we're talking about life and love. Your father was what they call now a chauvinist pig, in those days we called it a man's man and were meant to be grateful that he wasn't chasing the ladies. He stayed at his clubs every evening until late, you remember that growing up, don't you? I bet Desmond was at home to get to know his children.'

'He wasn't a member of any clubs.' Deirdre sounded wistful.

'And weren't you the better for it? Anyway I always thought I would neither encourage nor discourage any of my children, let them choose for themselves and go along with it.'

'Barbara's wedding . . .' Deirdre began.

'Nearly put us in the workhouse. What a bloody shower, Jack's family. They gave us a wedding list of their guests from their side of the family as long as your arm . . . we decided to do it the way the young couple wanted it. Though Barbara has often said to me she wished they had had less of a send-off, nothing ever lived up to it.'

'Barbara said that?'

'She says it every time she has a glass of sherry, it's hardly breaking a confidence to tell you. She says it in the golf club, and she tried to say it the night she was in the audience at the *Late Late Show* but apparently they didn't get a mike to her.'

For the first time Deirdre laughed a genuine laugh, and the waiter was so pleased he came running with a plate of bon bons and a refill of coffee.

'And I know you think I should be happy with my six grandchildren, your three and Barbara's three. But I never see yours. They grew up without us, and when we did meet them they were like white mice they were so afraid of us. And I was sick to death of Barbara's three when they were at the poisonous stage, we were unpaid unthanked babysitters and now that they're nice and interesting I don't see hide nor hair of them. And I don't think that Gerard is going to give us any news in that direction, but that's his business. I don't want to send him out to mate just so that I can have more people to call me Grannie.'

She looked lively and eager, she did not look like someone

who wanted more people to call her Grannie, let alone someone who had grown-ups who did.

'And suppose you and ... er Tony ... get on well on this cruise, why don't you think there might be a chance of ... well, something more permanent?'

Deirdre somehow felt that if he were accepted by Mother's cronies at home and by her sister and brother he couldn't be quite as common and unsuitable as she had thought at first.

'No, that's not on the cards.'

'As you said earlier, it's not such a barbarous idea.'

'Well, it is really, Deirdre. Or his wife would think so anyway.'

'He's married. Mother, I don't believe it.'

'Oh but you must, I assure you.'

'Does anyone know, is his wife sort of around, are people aware of her?' Deirdre's voice was very concerned.

Her mother was silent for the first time. She looked at Deirdre with a strange expression. It was hard to read her look. It was partly sad and partly as if she had known that things would be like this. There was a little frisson of impatience in the disappointment.

She didn't answer Deirdre's question, she never answered it. She called for the bill, and they walked together back to her hotel.

She said she had a little more shopping to do, and she sent her love to Anna, and to Helen. There was no point in sending love to Brendan, they both knew that he was only rarely in touch. No rapport of weekly phone chats had been established between Deirdre and her son on Sunday nights as there were between Deirdre and her mother.

Eileen O'Hagan said she wished Desmond well, and thought that he was quite right to have left the Palladians or the Palazzos or whatever they were called. A man had to do what a man had to do. And so had a woman.

She said she would send a postcard from somewhere that looked nice and exotic.

She said since Deirdre hadn't offered that she would be sure and give Deirdre's warm wishes to Tony and tell him that Deirdre had said Bon Voyage.

And as she left her daughter who would get the tube back to the station where the Metropolitan line would take her back to Pinner and the table full of preparations for a party 110 days away, Eileen O'Hagan reached out her hand and stroked Deirdre's cheek.

'I'm sorry,' she said.

'What for, Mother? Why are you sorry? You gave me a lovely lunch. It was really good to see you.' And Deirdre meant it.

'No, I'm sorry that I didn't give you more.'

'You gave me everything, I was only being silly, you said yourself that I was the most contented of your children. I never knew that.'

Her mother opened her mouth as if to speak but closed it again, and when Deirdre turned to wave she saw that Eileen O'Hagan's lips were moving. She thought she was just mouthing goodbye.

She was too far away to hear her mother saying, 'I'm sorry that I gave you no notion of happiness. Only how to pretend you are happy and that's no gift at all. It's a burden for your back.'

Deirdre waved again just before she went down the steps to the tube station, and she hoped her mother would stop mouthing at her. After all, here in Piccadilly Circus the whole world could be passing by, and there could be anyone, just anyone, who might see them. Someone from Pinner or someone from Dublin. The world was getting smaller and you should always behave as if you were under some kind of observation, because when it came down to it, that's what we all were most of the time. Under observation.

Silver Wedding

They had set the Teasmaid for seven o'clock.

Desmond had grumbled that it was too early, they would both be worn out by the time the thing began. But Deirdre said it was better far to be ahead of themselves instead of running after themselves all day. Be up and organized before the caterers came.

'They're not coming until three o'clock,' Desmond had said.

'Everything has to be cleared away for them.'

'God Almighty, Deirdre, we're not going to spend eight hours clearing the kitchen worktops. And isn't it all done already anyway?'

She took no notice of him, she poured him out a cup of tea.

For years, since they had moved into separate beds in fact, they had this morning ritual of the electric teamaker on the table between them. It somehow soothed them into the day, took the little edges off the slight sense of morning disappointment that they each seemed to feel.

'Happy anniversary,' he said and reached out for her hand.

'And to you,' she said, smiling. 'Will we give our presents now or later?'

'Whatever you like.'

'Maybe later.' She sipped her tea and ticked off in her mind all the things to be done. She had an appointment at the hairdresser, and a manicure as a special treat. Her new outfit was hanging on the wardrobe under its cellophane wrapping. She hoped it was a good choice, the woman in the shop had been very pushy, kept calling her Madam and speaking to her as if she wasn't there. Madam would look very well in pale colours, Madam doesn't want to grow old before her time. Madam could do with a little detail on the shoulder if Madam really insists that she won't wear shoulder pads.

Deirdre would like to have worn pads, almost everyone did nowadays like the women in *Dynasty* and *Dallas*, but she remem-

bered that time years ago when she had bought a very uphol-
stered-looking jacket and Maureen Barry had laughed at it and
called it Deirdre's Marshal Bulganin outfit. She daren't risk that
again. Or risk even the memory of it.

She knew that whatever Maureen wore today it would be
stunning, it would take all the attention away from her, away
from Deirdre whose party it was. The woman in the shop said
she couldn't believe that Madam was really celebrating a silver
wedding, but that was in the shop. The woman was anxious to
flatter her and make a sale.

The woman hadn't seen Maureen.

She would take the limelight today as she had taken it
twenty-five years ago. When the bride had looked pink and
frightened and flustered, and the bridesmaid had looked dark and
cool and elegant in a plain pink linen dress and a big pink flower
in her hair. And Frank Quigley had never taken his eyes off her.
From one end of the day to the other.

Would it be the same today? Would the great Frank Quigley
remember his passion for Maureen Barry with regret as the one
thing he didn't win in his life? Knowing Frank he would probably
have turned it into a success rather than a failure. Look at the
bigger and better prize he had won. Married to the entire Palazzo
fortune. He wouldn't have had that if Maureen had accepted him
all those years ago.

But she wouldn't think destructive thoughts. Not today, today
was her day more than her wedding day had ever been. She had
worked hard for it, put in long hours, long years. Deirdre Doyle
would have today.

Desmond looked at his face in the bathroom mirror. It looked
back at him, younger he thought than it had done a while ago.
Or maybe he just imagined that, because he felt better. He didn't
have that constant pain in the base of his stomach that he used
to have going in to Palazzo. He enjoyed leaving the house now.
Mornings were so much easier.

He had suggested that he and Suresh Patel start a newspaper
delivery service in the area. People would like to have a paper to
read in their homes if it arrived before seven. And it was a great
success. It was run by the owlish boy who kept the accounts
meticulously and also delivered the papers before heading off to
school. He dropped the *Daily Mail* into Rosemary Drive for

Desmond too, and it meant that he could read it and leave it for Deirdre.

He was annoyed with her that she had not wanted Suresh Patel and his wife to come to the silver wedding.

'It's only for people who were at the ceremony,' she had complained.

'John and Jean West weren't there,' he had countered.

'Don't be silly, Desmond, they're our next-door neighbours.'

'Well Suresh is my partner isn't he?'

'Only very recently, and anyway he won't know anyone.'

'Half of them won't know anyone.'

'Be reasonable, can't you, his wife doesn't even speak English. What am I to say to people, this is Mrs Patel, Desmond's partner's wife who can only nod and smile?'

He had left it. But it rankled. He felt sure that if Suresh Patel was having some ceremony in his house, the Doyles would have been invited. But it wasn't worth a major row, if he had won then he would have had to look after the Patels all evening. And there were so many other things to concentrate on. Like his son was coming back ... of his own free will to be there for the celebrations. Perhaps now that he too had been able to escape from a world that had frightened him they might have more in common. Perhaps the old prickliness would have softened if not gone altogether.

And he would be glad to see Father Hurley again, he was a kind man. Even in those bad far-off days when priests were meant to be disapproving of sin and anticipating the sacrament of matrimony and everything. There had been no condemnation when he had gone and asked Father Hurley if he could arrange to marry them as quickly as possible. Even quicker.

'Are you sure?' Father Hurley had asked.

'Oh yes, the tests were positive,' Desmond had said, fighting the panic.

'No, I meant are you both sure this is what you want to do? It's for life.'

It had been an odd question at that time. Desmond had paid little heed to it. The only important thing had been could the priest get them married in three weeks, so that their child would not be impossibly premature. The child that was never born. The child that miscarried on Christmas Eve.

He wondered had Father Hurley ever thought about it, whether the priest who had after all baptized Anna realized that she was born a full fourteen months after the shotgun wedding. And that a sister or brother had been lost before that.

Desmond sighed. Father Hurley probably had enough to think about in an Ireland which was rapidly catching up with the rest of the world in terms of godlessness. He would be unlikely to spend time speculating about what had happened in marriages made a quarter of a century ago.

Anna woke around seven in her flat in Shepherds Bush, she went straight to the window to see what kind of day it was. Good, a bright crisp autumn day. London was lovely in autumn. The parks were at their best. She had been walking last night with her friend Judy, and they had seen possibly a dozen different shades of gold and orange on the trees. Judy said that in America up in New England they had special tours and holidays for Leaf Peekers, for people who came to peek at the leaves changing colour. You could organize that in London too.

Anna was going to work for the morning. She would only be in the way in Rosemary Drive, things would be up to high doh there, the less people there were about the better. She would go there around three, the same time as the caterers, just to keep Mother out of their hair and from driving them up the walls. She had begged Helen not to turn up until five, the official time that the celebrations began. The thought of letting her sister Helen loose on any house where professional caterers were preparing a meal was enough to frighten anyone.

Helen was in very poor form at the moment, there had been some problem yet again in the convent. Apparently the rest of the Community didn't want Helen to take her vows and be a permanent member of the house. This was what Anna was reading between the lines, Helen of course was reading nothing of the sort, seeing only a series of petty irritations, confusions and obstacles.

Anna sighed. If she was in a religious community, which was possibly the last place on earth she would want to end up, then the very very last person on earth she would like with her was Helen, there was something very unsettling about Helen's very presence. On the few occasions she had come to see Anna in the bookshop it had been a matter of trying to hold on to big piles of books in displays – no other customer knocked them over but Helen would. Like she had actually swept the credit-card machine off the cash desk, breaking the glass on a display cabinet. Like her coat always caught somebody's cup of coffee. Not a restful presence anywhere. She hoped that Helen wouldn't say the wrong thing too often this evening.

What could she say that would be terrible? Well, something about Brendan, along the lines of wasn't it great we forced him to come back ... Which wasn't the case, but Father would think it was. Or about Father having left Palazzo and working with a terribly nice Paki. Helen was the only person Anna knew who actually used words like Paki and Eyetie. Yes, she could refer to Renata Quigley as an Eyetie.

Anna padded off in bare feet to make herself a cup of instant coffee. Another pleasure and advantage of not living any more with Joe Ashe. It had to be real, the coffee, it had to be freshly ground in a machine that would split your head apart. She would not like to live for ever on her own, but she was daily finding more and more positive things about not living with Joe Ashe.

He had left as good-naturedly and easily as he had arrived. He had kissed her on the cheek and said that she was being very heavy over nothing. He had said he'd miss her, and he had taken quite a few of her records, and a very expensive rug she had bought for their bed. She had watched him fold it, and had said nothing.

'You did give me this as a present, I think?' He had smiled lightly.

'Sure, Joe,' she had said. She would not be heavy over a bedspread. Only about another woman in her bed.

Judy had been very good over the break-up.

'I'm always here, ring me if you feel a bit bleak. I'll listen. Don't ring him out of loneliness, only ring him if you could take him back.'

Friends were great, Anna thought, real pure gold. Friends understood when you got infatuated with people, and didn't mind you going mad for a while, they were still there when the infatuation was over. As it nearly was. Very very nearly.

And she wasn't going to embark on anything again for a long while. Ken Green understood that, he had said that he wanted the smell of Joe Ashe's rather sickly aftershave well gone from the place before he came round in earnest. Ken was very droll. He got on very well with her father too, which was odd, and persuaded Dad and Mr Patel to take a small selection of his paperbacks to display with the magazines, just in case there was a market, he had said . . . and of course there had been. Father and Mr Patel were going to expand. There was an opening for a bookshop in the area. Ken had even suggested that Anna might think of opening one herself, in conjunction with them.

'Too near home,' she had said.

'Maybe you're right.' Ken was agreeable but not in the way Joe Ashe agreed with people. Joe agreed for an easy life, Ken because he had thought it out. She half wished she had asked him to the silver wedding do, but it was far too public a commitment, Mother's friends would whisper, and Grandmother O'Hagan would be bound to want to know everything even though there was nothing to know. Brendan had arrived in London early, off the boat train in Euston. It coincided with the morning rush hour. He stood watching for a quarter of an hour while the commuter population of that part of London buzzed and scuttled and darted up ramps and down stairs, down to taxi queues, in to grab a quick breakfast standing at a counter, leaping on to escalators. They looked so self-important, he thought, as if whatever petty job they were racing to was important, as if they were people of substance. And this is what his father and mother would like him to be doing, racing down from Rosemary Drive to catch a train to Baker Street, and another tube to somewhere like here. It was a preposterous way to live, and all to be able to *say* to someone that this was success.

Brendan knew he must not spoil his gesture in coming to the celebration by voicing these thoughts.

And he also remembered that Vincent had warned him to buy some proper clothes to wear for the occasion.

'You'll always be able to use a good suit, lad,' his uncle had said.

'Aw no, Vincent, not a suit, I'd never wear a suit for God's sake.'

'Well that's what we wore in my day. But then a jacket and trousers.'

'An anorak maybe?' Brendan had brightened.

'Not an anorak, you gobdaw, not for a big party in their house, a smart dark jacket, navy maybe and light blue trousers. Sure you'll have them hanging out of you at the next dance you go to here.'

His uncle had given him folding money. It was a sacred trust to buy something smart to wear. He had written to Anna, telling her how much he had to spend. He had hoped she wouldn't make fun of him, but he had wronged her even to suspect she might do such a thing.

Her letter was enthusiastic and grateful, she told him that Marks or C and A or any High Street store would have a bewildering selection, and that she was touched and pleased that he was going to so much trouble. She wrote that she herself was going to wear a dress and jacket in navy and white with awful bits of lace trimming on both, because she thought it would please Mother, it looked what Mother called dressy and Anna called yucky but it was Mother's day. Anna wrote how she had told Helen that since Vatican Two nobody expected nuns to arrive in places dressed in sackcloth and ashes, but of course Helen would suit herself, as always.

Maureen Barry came out of Selfridge's and thought she saw Desmond's and Deirdre's son Brendan walking down Oxford Street with a huge Marks and Spencer's bag as if he had bought half the shop.

But she decided that this was ridiculous. There were twelve million people in London, why should she see a member of the family she was thinking about?

And for all she knew the boy might still be in the West of Ireland, there had been some kind of coldness. Her mother had told her that not long before she died. She said that Eileen O'Hagan had said that there had been some great cover-up but the facts were that the son of Deirdre and Desmond had run away, and run of all places back to the very townland his father managed to escape from. The same place that Frank had run from. Maureen told herself to be reasonable. Even if the boy was in London, he would surely be out in Pinner helping to set up tables for the function. She must stop being fanciful and thinking she had this town down to size as she did Dublin. Only that morning at the hotel she had thought she saw Deirdre's mother, in the distance across the dining room, in fact it had been so like her she was nearly going across to say hallo but the woman had been joined by a flashy-looking man wearing a blazer with a big crest of some sort. Perhaps it was the sign that she needed glasses. She smiled, remembering how they had all told each other years ago when coming to work in London that they should get false teeth and spectacles on the National Health, it had seemed a scream to need either.

It was good to be back in London again, Maureen thought, she had a spring in her step and three credit cards in her wallet. She was merely going on a reccy as the film people called it, a little prowl examining the style in other people's boutiques and in the big fashion stores. And if she wanted to she could stop and buy herself any treat she wanted. She walked in a cloud of the expensive perfume she had just bought in Selfridge's, she had bought her father a jaunty cravat there too. He would look well in that, and he would like the fact that she had thought him a cravat man.

Helen Doyle sat in the kitchen of St Martin's with both her hands round the mug of coffee as if to get some warmth from it. It was not a cold morning but not even the bright shafts of sunlight coming in the window seemed to warm her. Across the table sat Sister Brigid, the others had gone. They must have known that the confrontation was coming, they had either gone back to their rooms or gone about their business.

A yellow cat with a broken paw looked trustingly up at Helen. She had found it and made a sort of splint which helped it to walk. The others said she should take it to the cats' home, but this would be curtains for the yellow cat, Helen said. It wouldn't eat much, they could mind it surely.

It was just one more sign of Helen around the house, and another chore. It would be impossible to expect Helen to feed or clean after the cat *all* the time. The cat began a very loud purring and arched its back to be stroked. Tenderly Sister Brigid lifted it up and carried it out to the garden. She came back and sat beside Helen. She looked straight into the troubled eyes and spoke.

'You have so much love and goodness to give,' she began. 'But this is not the place.'

She saw the lip, the lower lip that Helen had been biting nervously, begin to tremble. And the big eyes fill with tears.

'You're sending me away,' Helen began.

'We could sit here all morning, Helen, you could call it one thing, I could call it another. I could say that you must find yourself and what you are looking for in some other surroundings, you will say that I am throwing you out, turning you away from St Martin's.'

'What did I do this time?' Helen looked piteous. 'Was it the cat?'

'Of course it wasn't the cat, Helen, there's no one thing, one incident. Please know that . . . could you *try* to understand that it's not a punishment, not an exam where you pass or fail? It's a choice and this house is our life, we chose it and we have to choose how it will be shared.'

'You don't want me, you've all decided at a meeting, is that it?'

'No it's not it, there was no court passing sentence on you. When you came here in the first place it was on the understanding that . . .'

Helen interrupted hotly. 'In the old days nuns couldn't pick and choose who they had with them, if you didn't like another member of the community that was hard luck, you had to offer it up, it was part of the sacrifice . . .'

'Nobody dislikes you . . .' Sister Brigid began.

'But even if they did, in the old days it wouldn't have been a matter of a popularity contest like it is now.'

'If there were a popularity contest there are many ways you'd come out on top. And anyway looking back on the old days they were bad old days, in the very old days girls could be thrown into convents literally if they were wild or disappointed in love or something. That was a fine way to build a community.' Brigid was firm.

'That didn't happen to me, nobody forced me, in fact they tried to keep me back with them.'

'That's why I'm speaking to you today.' Brigid was gentle. 'Today no false optimism about when you will take your vows. Because you won't, Helen, not here with us. It would be unfair for me as head of this house to let you go to a family celebration in the belief that you were well on the way towards being a nun in our Order. One day you will thank me from the bottom of your heart. Today I wanted you to look at your family with different eyes, look at the other options . . .'

'You mean I'm out today. I can't come back here tonight!' Helen was stricken.

'Don't be so dramatic . . .'

'But when? If you're giving me notice, when do you want my room?' Helen was hurt and bitter.

'I thought that if you could think for a while, don't do any more work, just think, take stock of yourself, and what you might want to do . . .'

'When?' Helen repeated.

'Christmas seems a good time.' Brigid was firm. 'Say two or three months. You should know by Christmas.'

Frank and Renata Quigley planned the day ahead.

'Will I dress up or down?' Renata asked.

'Up as high as you can go,' he smiled.

'But that wouldn't be considered . . . I don't know . . . showing off a bit?' Renata was doubtful.

'Oh, you couldn't please Desmond's wife, if you're too casual you didn't make the effort, if you do make the effort you're overdressed . . .'

'So?'

'So let her have something she'll be glad to have in the photographs. The woman's a monster for snapping this and that. Every time someone farts it's recorded in that place.'

'Frank, really!'

'No, you don't know what they're like. Seriously though, their place is coming down with framed photographs. I remember a wall full of them at least.'

'That's nice in a way.'

'Yes, it would be if there was anything to remember. Anything to celebrate.'

'But you were friends, why do you talk like this?'

'I was friends with Desmond, never with Deirdre, anyway she resented me being free, she was afraid – rightly, I think – that poor old Desmond would feel tied down by comparison. Still we'll dress ourselves up to the nines and dazzle their eyes out.'

She smiled back at him. Frank was so cheerful these days,

705

since they had come to so many decisions. There was the expansion of the business. It was going ahead up North, and it did not mean as Renata had feared that Frank would be away a lot. No, he hardly ever travelled there, her father and uncle did, and of course Mrs East had been very much part of it. Even with the baby boy, she seemed to thrive on work. Some women were able to do everything, Renata thought sadly.

Still, things were good nowadays, and this morning she was going to get injections and vaccinations, shots needed for the journey. Frank would go to work as he did almost every Saturday, he said it was so quiet in the big Palazzo building that he could dictate peacefully and get more done in an hour than he normally did in a week of ordinary days. She reminded him to get a haircut. He was looking a bit shaggy around the neck.

Frank didn't need to be reminded, he would go to Larry and have hot towels as well as a trim. He would wear his best suit, and the new shirt. If Maureen Barry was going to look at him she would admire what she saw. That was why he had asked his wife to dress up too. When Renata had the full works she looked very well. Maureen Barry would not be able to say that the man she rejected had to marry a colourless mouse with money.

Father Hurley had a great place to stay when he came to London, he always described it as a cross between a luxury hotel and a gentlemen's club. It was in fact a religious house, a simple place now where they rented most of their high-ceilinged rooms as office space. Once these had been parlours with polished tables holding copies of *Missionary Annals*. It was an oasis to come back to after a day in such a big noisy city. Father Hurley found the morning a little overtiring, it was good to know that he could come back to this house and have a rest.

His friend Daniel Hayes was Principal, a soft-spoken man who seemed to understand a great deal without having to have things explained in words. He had known last night when he asked after Father Hurley's nephew that this was not an avenue to travel any further. Diplomatically and with the polished ease of years Father Hayes slipped to another topic. Father Hayes also seemed to know that his old friend James Hurley was somehow uneasy about the silver wedding he was going to attend.

'I can tell you, Daniel, you don't know them from a hole in

the ground, a nice young pair, she a real product of Dublin Four
. . . though we didn't know the phrase then. He was a bit of a
rough diamond from the West of Ireland without a penny to bless
himself. Anyway the usual story, and she was well and truly
pregnant, and I knew the family, *her* family that is, and could I
marry them in a flash.'

'And you did?' Father Hayes prompted.

'Well I did of course, what else did we do in those days?
Cover the shame, hide the sin, get the thing regularized as soon
as possible . . .'

'And did it not work out . . . they are still together?'

'I know, Daniel, it's just that there's something odd there.
Firstly they didn't have a child.'

'What?'

'Oh, they did later, three of them. But not at the time. They
sort of played at being married, pretended it . . . as if they were
taking parts in a play . . . Right, Desmond will play the Husband
and Deirdre will play the Wife.'

'I expect a lot of people do that.'

'Yes, I expect they do, and there's ways in which we're playing
at being priests. But do you know what I mean? As if the whole
thing didn't ring true. Like Deirdre sending me a picture of them
all on a picnic or somewhere, blinking into the light, as if she
had to prove it to people.'

'Prove what?'

'Lord, I don't know, that they were a normal family or
something.'

'They might be just very unhappy,' Daniel Hayes said. 'A lot
of people are, seriously. They go into these marriages with such
ridiculous expectations. I never thought that all the celibacy bit
seemed too much of a hardship to me . . .'

'Me neither,' Father Hurley agreed. His face was sad.

'Of course when it does work, it must be the greatest thing
in the world, a friendship so real and true you'd trust the other
with your life . . . We never had that, James.'

'No indeed.' Father Hurley still seemed down.

'But your sister had it, didn't she? I remember your telling
me that you thought she had a totally good relationship, that they
seemed to know each what the other was about to say, and then
smiled when they said it.'

'True, but their life hasn't been easy...'

Father Hayes interrupted him. 'Of course not, but it's only that kind of relationship we're talking about... It would surely buoy them up when things were bleak. You don't see anything like that in this wedding you're going to in Pinner.'

Father Hurley had been successfully diverted. 'No, it's going to be a lot of empty phrases, like it was a quarter of a century ago.'

'Ah, that's what we're here for, James,' laughed his friend. 'If the priests can't put a bit of conviction into meaningless comforting phrases... then I ask you... who can?'

The caterers arrived at three o'clock. It had all been arranged weeks ago. But Philippa of Philippa's Catering knew a fusser when she saw one, and Mrs Doyle had all the characteristics of someone who could raise a Class-A fuss. There were to be canapés and drinks for an hour or so then the party would proceed to a Roman Catholic church where there would be a Mass, and the Doyles would say aloud that they renewed their marriage vows. Then pink and triumphant they would return to Rosemary Drive, it would now be heading on for seven, there would be more drinks and the guests would be asked to help themselves to a cold buffet – salmon, and cold chicken in a curry mayonnaise. There would be warm herb bread with it. Philippa, having seen the size of the house and the smallness of the oven, had advised against hot food, she had convinced Mrs Doyle that people would most certainly think it was a *real* meal even if it was cold and there were no potatoes.

As Philippa unloaded crates from her van and set up her centre of operations in the Doyles' small kitchen she hoped that someone might have been detailed to distract this woman with the freshly done hair and the obviously new manicure who held her hands awkwardly as if the varnish would chip.

Mercifully a daughter arrived, a sensible-looking girl, dark and intelligent. She was carrying her own outfit on a hanger. Through the kitchen window Philippa had seen her thanking a man who had driven her. The girl had leaned back into the car and kissed him. Philippa liked to see something like that, it made a change in the highly tense homes she often found herself working in.

Still if it weren't for the weddings, the bar-mitzvahs, the silver weddings, the retirement parties, where would her business be? She thought that Mrs Doyle and her husband must both be barking mad to go back into a church and say publicly that they were still married. As if it weren't obvious. As if anyone else would have either of them! However, question it not, just keep unpacking, get the table decoration started, and maybe send in a tray of tea to the bedroom so that the mother and daughter could be kept up there.

'You look absolutely beautiful, Mother,' Anna said. 'You haven't a line on your face, did you know that? You're like a young girl.'

Deirdre was pleased. 'Oh stop it now, you're going too far.'

'I mean it. And isn't your hair great! Very elegant in all those swoops.'

Deirdre looked at her daughter's short dark shiny head of hair.

'Of course if *you* went to the hairdresser a bit . . . just now and then for a nice set . . . you'd look very much better. I know it's smart nowadays to wash your hair every day in the shower . . .' Deirdre was trying to be helpful.

I know, Mother . . . Oh look, isn't this marvellous, a pot of tea . . . brought to us on a tray! *This* is the life, isn't it?'

Deirdre frowned. 'I wish your father was back, he's going to be running late. I don't know what he had to go down to Patel's for . . .'

'It's not Patel's, it's the Rosemary Central Stores, Mother, *and* Dad is the joint owner, *and* Saturday is very busy, so obviously he's going to help Suresh *and* he'll be back in plenty of time. You know Dad.'

'What time's Brendan coming?'

'He should be here anytime. He was looking round a bit, he said he didn't want to come too early and be in the way.'

'Lord, wouldn't you think he'd come . . .'

'And of course he'll be here tomorrow and the next day and the next.'

'And why he couldn't stay in his own home . . .'

'Mother, Brendan's back now, isn't that what we all hoped? He's staying with me because it's easier, handier. He's going to be here every day seeing you.'

'His father could easily have moved all those boxes and files from his room.'

'It's not *his* room any more, no more than *my* room is mine, it'd be pointless having them waiting for us, much better letting them be offices and for filing and everything.'

'Helen's room is still there, and she's off in a convent.'

'It's always wise to give Helen somewhere to lay her head, you never know when she'll need it.' Anna sounded resigned.

'Will I change now, do you think?'

'Why don't you wait a little bit longer, Mother, we'll get hot and sweaty if we get into our finery too soon.'

'I hope it's going to be all right.'

'It's going to be magnificent. Everyone you want is coming to it ... we don't have to raise a finger ... they'll all be as impressed as hell.'

'Not that we're trying to impress anyone,' Deirdre said firmly to her daughter.

'No indeed, what would be the point?' Anna asked, wondering could her mother be serious. What was this about if it wasn't to wipe eyes around the place, show Grandmother O'Hagan what style they lived in, let Maureen Barry know that life in Pinner was full of sociability, point out to Frank Quigley that though Desmond hadn't married the boss's daughter he had still done well for himself. Show Father Hurley what a good strong Catholic way of life went on in what he probably thought of as Heathen England. Let the neighbours see what a team they could field, thirty people, and caterers, and speeches and a good non-vintage champagne for the toasts. What was all that if it wasn't intended to impress?

When they heard the commotion downstairs of someone beating on the side door and voices being raised they knew Helen had arrived. She didn't want to come in the front door to inconvenience people so she had been trying to push open the side door, and because boxes of wine were against it she had been having difficulties. She was handed a cup of tea very briskly by Philippa of Philippa's Caterers and pointed upstairs.

Helen came into the room, they knew by the droop of her shoulders that something was wrong. Anna hoped that they might get away without discussing it.

'Doesn't Mother look terrific, Helen?' she cried.

'Great,' Helen said dutifully and absently.

'And Brendan's going to be here any moment.'

'Is he staying here?' Helen asked.

'No, we ... er ... thought it would be ... more suitable if he stayed at my place. He's there now changing, I left the key for him under a plant pot. More suitable, more central, closer to things.'

'What things?' asked Helen.

'Any things.' Anna gritted her teeth.

'So he's not sleeping here tonight?'

'No, he wouldn't even consider ...' Deirdre was beginning.

'Anyway his room is an office for Dad now, so ...'

'Is my room an office for Dad?' Helen asked.

'No of course not. Why do you ask?'

'I thought I might sleep here tonight,' Helen said. 'If it's no trouble, that is.'

Anna held her breath. She didn't trust herself to speak. So Helen had decided to leave her convent. And she chose now to tell everyone. *Now*, one hour before Mother's and Father's silver wedding party. Anna fixed her eyes on the two dressing gowns that hung on the back of the door. Father's had a long cord. Perhaps Anna could take this and strangle Helen, or would that in the long run mean further disruption? It was hard to know.

She was saved from having to work it out because Brendan had arrived. He ran lightly up the stairs and his mother and sisters ran to meet him. He looked tanned and well, they thought, and handsome too, in a smart navy jacket, a sparklingly white shirt and a tie with a discreet design on it.

'I got silver colours in the tie, I thought it would be suitable,' he said.

Deirdre Doyle looked at her only son with pride. There would be no need to apologize for Brendan today nor explain him away. Whatever kind of life he was leading in that backwoods, at least he had dressed up today when it mattered. And he was going to be pleasant to people, not hanging back and muttering. She would not have dared to hope for this much.

Desmond came back in plenty of time to wash and change, and at five minutes before the official starting time Philippa was able to pronounce that they all looked magnificent, and that everything was under control.

More and more in her business she felt it was a matter of calming down the hostess and family just as much as preparing a good menu and serving it well.

They stood in their sitting room. The doors to the garden were open, they were ready. With as little comment as possible Anna had found an outfit to suit Helen among their mother's clothes. It was a simple green skirt and a long cream-coloured over-blouse. It was simple enough to have been the nunnish kind of clothes she wore ... if she wanted it to be. But also it was perfectly adequate as lay clothes too, if that was the route she chose.

Any moment now the guests would arrive. The Doyles had refused a drink from Philippa, saying that they would need to keep their heads clear.

Philippa noticed that there were no private moments between them. They didn't squeeze each other's hands and say: Fancy, a silver wedding! They didn't seem excited in themselves over the event, only that it was being marked.

The first to arrive was Grandmother O'Hagan. Deirdre's eyes raked the taxi to see if she would be followed by Tony. But mercifully Mother had decided to come unaccompanied. And just as she was being ushered in Frank's and Renata's car pulled up. The florist's van arrived with a huge floral arrangement from Carlo and Maria with many many regrets, and warmest wishes on a wonderful family occasion. It had been arranged the previous day by Frank Quigley's secretary who had also left a message with Carlo Palazzo's office noting that it had been done.

And when the Wests next door had peered out and seen the place filling up, they arrived, and they were followed by Father Hurley who had been driven there by his friend Father Hayes.

'Won't Father Hayes come in too and have a drink?' Deirdre Doyle had said. You couldn't have too many priests at something like this.

Father Hayes was tempted just to a sherry, he said it was wonderful in this world where so many people took marriage so lightly to find a couple whose love had survived for so long.

'Well yes.' Deirdre had been pleased by the compliment if somewhat startled by the way it was expressed.

At that moment Maureen Barry arrived.

She must have left her taxi at the corner of Rosemary Drive, she walked easily through the gate and up the little path to the door. The guests were both in and outside the house, it was one of those warm autumn evenings that made it not totally ridiculous to be in the open air.

Maureen seemed to expect all eyes to be on her, yet there was nothing vain or coquettish about the way she came in.

She wore a lemon-coloured silk suit, with a lemon and black scarf. She was slim and tall and her black hair shone as if it were an advertisement for shampoo. Her smile was bright and confident, as she turned with excitement from one to another.

She said all the right things and few of the things that were in mind. Yes, that was Brendan she had seen this morning struggling with a big green Marks and Spencer's bag. Obviously the outfit he was wearing now. Perfectly adequate, but think what a big handsome boy could look like if he had been dressed by a tailor.

Yes, amazingly it *had* been Deirdre's mother that she had seen that morning at breakfast with the rather over-obvious-looking man. Was it possible that the great and esteemed Eileen O'Hagan was having a relationship? How her father would enjoy hearing of that, when she went to Ascot to see him tomorrow.

She kissed her friend Deirdre and exclaimed with pleasure over the wonderful dress. In her heart she wondered how Deirdre could have fallen for the obvious-looking lilac, the matronly garment with the self-colour embroidery at the shoulder. It was a pastel Mother of the Bride outfit. Deirdre deserved better, she could have looked so well. *And* the dress had probably cost a fortune as well.

The Doyle girls didn't look smart either. Helen seemed to be wearing a blouse and skirt, perhaps that was the nearest that the Order could come to letting her wear home clothes. Anna, who was quite striking if she had just left herself alone, was wearing a very tarty-looking navy and white outfit: everywhere there could be a white frill there was one, at the neck, on the hem, at the wrists. It was like a child's party frock.

And Frank.

'How well you look, Frank, it must be years and years,' she said.

'But it's impossible that for you time has stood still,' he said, mocking her tones by imitating her, very slightly.

Her eyes hardened.

'Renata, this is Maureen Barry, she and I played bridesmaid and best man at the great occasion twenty-five years ago. Maureen, this is Renata, my wife.'

'I'm delighted to meet you.'

The two women took in each other's clothes at a glance.

Maureen saw a girl with a nondescript face and well-cut designer garments, carefully made up and wearing discreet jewellery. If that gold chain was what she thought it was Renata Quigley was wearing the price of several houses in Rosemary Drive around her neck.

'Frank tells me you are a very successful businesswoman, and you have high fashion shops.' Renata spoke as if she had learned a little speech. Her accent was attractive.

'He's building me up a bit too much, Renata, two small outlets, but I am thinking of opening up over here. Not in London, more out Berkshire way.'

'I was sorry to hear that your mother died,' Frank said. He lowered his voice suitably.

'Yes, it was sad, she was very lively and opinionated always, she could have had many more years. Like Mrs O'Hagan over there.' Maureen nodded in the direction of Deirdre's mother who was holding forth in a corner.

Renata had moved slightly away to talk to Desmond and Father Hurley.

'Of course she hated me,' Frank said, not letting his eyes leave Maureen's.

'Who? I beg your pardon?'

'Your mother. She hated me. You know that, Maureen.' His eyes were hard now. Like hers had been.

'No, I think you're quite wrong, she never hated you. She spoke very well of you always, she said you were very nice, that one time she met you. I remember her standing in the morning room at home and saying, "He's a very nice boy, Maureen." ' As Maureen spoke she re-created her mother's little laugh, the unkind dismissal, the sense of amused wonder.

It was the most cruel thing she could have done.

But he was asking for it, arrogant, handsome and powerful, playing with people's lives, and planning what they would buy and where they would buy it.

'You didn't marry?' he asked. 'There wasn't anyone you could marry?'

'Not anyone I did marry, no.'

'But you were tempted, perhaps a little here and there . . .' His eyes still held hers. They hadn't faltered under her sarcasm, her reproducing her mother's deadly voice.

'Oh Frank, of course I've been tempted here and there, like all business people are. That has nothing to do with being married. I'm quite sure you have found the same in your life. I'd be *very* surprised if you didn't. But to marry and settle down, there has to be a reason for that.'

'Love maybe, or attraction even?'

'Not enough, I think. Something more prosaic like . . .' She looked round and her glance fell on Deirdre. 'Like being pregnant maybe, or else . . .' She looked round the room again and stopped when she was looking at Renata.

But she wasn't quick enough, Frank said it first.

'Like money?' he said blandly.

'Exactly,' she said.

'Not very good reasons, either of them.'

'Well, certainly not the pregnancy one. Even more specially when it turns out not to have been a real one.'

'Did you ever find out what happened?' Frank asked.

Maureen shrugged. 'Lord, I wasn't even told that there was any question of it in the first place, so I wouldn't be told that the danger had passed or whatever.'

'I think she had a miscarriage,' Frank said.

'Did Desmond tell you that?' She was surprised.

'Not a bit of it, but it was their first Christmas in London, and I was in a bit of a bad way, a bit let down and feeling very lost. I asked could I spend Christmas with them, the excuse was Deirdre wasn't well. She looked badly too. I think that's what it was.'

He sounded much more human, her eyes had softened and she felt his had too.

'What bad luck to tie themselves into all this, for nothing, over a false alarm,' she said.

'They may like it, the children could be some consolation,' Frank argued.

They were talking like friends now, old friends who hadn't seen each other for a while.

Philippa was relieved when the party began to decamp towards the church. She had no idea and didn't even want to imagine what went on there, but she knew it was some kind of important landmark for them. Not just to serve food and drink but go back to the same kind of a church where the whole thing had begun. She shrugged cheerfully as she organized the collection of glasses, the airing of the room. At least this bizarre kind of two-tier arrangement gave them a chance to clear up the hors d'œuvres part of things and let them lay out the salads without interruption.

The church was at a nice easy walking distance, that was why it had been thought a feasible plan. If they had all to get lifts and taxis and sort out who went with whom it would have taken for ever.

They all knelt in a little group, the thirty people who formed the silver wedding party.

It was a perfectly normal Mass, many of them congratulated themselves that they didn't need to go tomorrow since a Saturday-evening attendance was sufficient in these liberated days.

Some like Anna who didn't go anyway did not see the great incidental advantage.

Brendan always found Mass a social event back home with Vincent. He didn't think his uncle believed in any kind of God, but he went to Mass on a Sunday as regularly as he would go to get petrol, or to the marts to buy sheep. It was part of the life they lived.

Helen prayed hard at the Mass so that God would tell her what was right. If Sister Brigid said that she was running away, what was it from and which was the right direction if the convent was the wrong one? If she could have some kind of sign. It wasn't much to ask.

Father Hurley asked himself why did he feel that this was all some kind of charade, almost a television version of renewal of vows? Any moment now someone would say 'Cut. Can we take that again from the top?' He didn't feel this about any other aspect of his ministry. There was just something he didn't like about a public reiteration of something that was said and meant a long time ago. Yet the faithful were always being asked to renew their baptismal vows, so why did he feel uneasy in this instance?

Frank looked at Maureen in the church and thought what a

fine-looking woman she was, full of spirit, so like Joy East in many ways. He thought briefly of Joy and of his son who was called Alexander. The son he would never get to know.

It had been thought inappropriate to take pictures at the church. It wasn't as if it were a real wedding, they would look a little ancient to be photographed, Deirdre tittered, hoping that someone would disagree with her.

Maureen did, strongly.

'Come on now, Deirdre, I still have to take the plunge and when I do I'll want banks of photographers outside,' she said.

'And after all people get married at *any* age, any age at all,' Deirdre's mother said, which caused Deirdre's heart to lurch a little.

'And with the way the church is going, maybe even the clergy will get married, Mother, and Father Hurley will be coming down the aisle in a morning suit,' Helen said.

They laughed at that, particularly Father Hurley, who was rueful and said that even if he was forty years younger he wouldn't be able to take on such an undertaking.

And soon they were back in Salthill, 26 Rosemary Drive. The neighbours who had not been invited waved and called out greetings, the lights were on and soon the supper was under way.

'There's a lot of conversation, like at a real party,' Deirdre said to Desmond almost in disbelief.

Her face was flushed and anxious, her hair had fallen from its hard lacquered layers and seemed softer somehow. There were beads of perspiration on her forehead and upper lip.

He felt strangely touched by her anxiety.

'Well it *is* a real party,' he said, and he touched her face gently with his hand.

It was an unfamiliar gesture but she didn't draw back, she smiled at him.

'I suppose it is,' she agreed.

'And your mother is getting on well with everyone,' he said encouragingly.

'Yes, yes she is.'

'Brendan's looking in fine shape, isn't he? He said he'd be very interested in coming down to the Rosemary Central Stores tomorrow morning to see how it operates.'

She was surprised. 'He's going to come the whole way across from Shepherd's Bush early in the morning when he could have stayed here in his own room?' She was still peeved that he wouldn't stay.

'It's not his own room, Deirdre, it's the office.'

'There'd have been room for him,' she said.

'Yes, and he will stay some time. But as a visitor.'

'As part of the family,' she corrected him.

'As a visiting part of the family,' he corrected her back.

It was gentle. But the Desmond Doyle of a few months back would not have done it. He would have been too anxious, too willing to play the parlour game of lies, backing up whatever story Deirdre told her mother and Maureen Barry about his mythical prowess at Palazzo, trying all the while to engineer these conversations out of the hearing of Frank or Renata who would know them to be untrue.

How restful it was at last for Desmond Doyle to have his own position, his own place. To be for the first time his own person, not Palazzo's person. It gave him by a grim irony the kind of confidence that his wife had always wanted to see in him, but which would have for ever escaped him in Palazzo land.

'Mother is actually talking normally to Dad,' Brendan whispered to Anna at the other side of the room. 'Does this happen often?'

'Never saw it happen before,' she said. 'I don't want to take away from your sense of wellbeing, but I do think that you have captured a very rare sighting, make the most of it.'

And indeed as they looked the little tableau broke up. One of the caterers was speaking to Mother, there was a slight problem in the kitchen.

'It's bound to be Helen,' Anna said sadly. And it was.

Helen was all for putting candles on the gateau, she had bought twenty-five of them and had rooted through the bottom of the dresser to find old cake tins holding the plastic candle holders. She could only find fourteen. She could not think why.

'Probably because that would be the age at which normal people wouldn't really want any more,' Anna said crisply. 'All right, Mother, go back to the guests. I'll cope with it.'

'It's not a question of coping with it.' Helen was hurt and angry now. 'I was just making a little gesture so that we could be festive.'

Philippa of Philippa's Caterers said that the written agreement had been a gateau with toasted almonds to be applied at the last moment to the cream topping, the toasted almonds to read: Desmond and Deirdre October 1960.

'I think it *is* better like that, Helen, don't you?' Anna spoke as she might have spoken to a dog that was foaming at the mouth or a four-year old who was severely retarded. Ken Green said he spent a lot of his life speaking to people like this, it got you a reputation for being very patient, slightly thick, and a person who could be relied on in any crisis. Anna remembered that Ken always said that the more enraged he was the more slowly he spoke.

'Don't you think we should leave the caterers to it, Helen?' Anna said, enunciating every word very clearly and slowly.

'Oh piss off, Anna, you're a pain in the arse,' Helen said.

Anna decided that they were definitely coming to the end of Helen's term of life in a religious order.

Helen had flounced out into the garden.

'Shall I go after her?' asked Philippa the caterer.

'No, she's probably safer out there, there's no one she can insult beyond reprieve, and not too much she can break.' Anna thought that Ken would be proud of her and wondered why she was thinking of him so much anyway.

Helen sat and hugged her knees in the garden where she had sat, misunderstood and thinking herself unloved, all the years of her childhood. She heard footsteps behind her. Anna no doubt asking her to come in and not to make a scene, Mother telling her not to sit on damp stone, Grandmother O'Hagan about to ask when was she ever going to be professed. She looked up. It was Frank Quigley.

A terror seized her throat and she felt a momentary light-headedness. It was of course impossible that he was going to touch her, molest her in her parents' home.

But he looked so menacing in the dark.

'I heard from your father that you're thinking of leaving St Martin's,' he said.

'Yes. They want me to go, they threw me out.'

'I'm sure that's not true.'

'Sister Brigid says the others don't want me.' She realized as she spoke that she sounded like a child of five years of age with her thumb in her mouth.

'Sister Brigid is far too fond of you to think that, let alone say it.'

'How do you know? You only saw her that night, that awful night.' Helen's eyes had become as big as dinner plates. The memory of the time she had tried to steal a baby for Frank and Renata Quigley, the night that had turned out so badly, and when the real descent had begun in St Martin's.

'No, Helen, I've met Sister Brigid many times since then,' Frank said. 'We didn't speak of you much, we had other things to talk about . . . She was giving me advice. She gave me very good helpful advice, I have you to thank for that.'

'I meant well that night, I really thought it would have suited everyone.'

'It might have, you know, but we couldn't do it that way, always running, always hiding, always pretending. That's not the way to live.'

'That's the way I've always lived.' Helen sounded rebellious and defensive.

'No, no, it isn't.'

'In this house we always pretended, we still are tonight.'

'Shush,' he said soothingly.

'How did you learn to be so upright and not to have to act like the rest of us?'

'I'm not upright. You of all people should know that.' Frank spoke seriously. 'I have done things I am ashamed of, one of them with you. I am very, very ashamed of that.'

For the first time since that day in his apartment Helen Doyle looked Frank Quigley in the eyes. For the first time for many years in any encounter she said absolutely nothing.

'I was always hoping that you would meet somebody nice and somebody young and tender, someone who would put that strange sad day into some kind of perspective for you. Show you that while it was important in one way in many others it was not important at all.'

Still Helen said nothing.

'So I supposed I was sorry when you went into St Martin's, because I always thought then that what happened might appear magnified.'

'I never thought about it again,' Helen said. She looked at him as she told him the lie, her eyes confident and her head held high.

He knew she was lying but it was important that she didn't realize.

'That is so much the right way to be, and it certainly puts me in my place.'

He smiled at her. Ruefully, admiringly. He got it just right. And he could see she was beginning to feel better.

'So what will you do when you do leave, if you're going to?'

'I'll leave. I don't know yet. Maybe I need time to think.'

'Is this the place to do your thinking?' He looked uncertainly up at Salthill, 26 Rosemary Drive.

'Maybe not.'

'Maybe you should go away, right away from London. You're good with children, Brigid tells me, very good.'

'Yes, I like them. Certainly. They don't get as upset as adults.'

'Could you mind one? For a year or two while you're thinking?'

'Do you know one?'

They seemed to talk as equals, her fear of him fell away.

'I do, his name is Alexander. I don't know him but I know his mother. However she and I had a fight and she doesn't like me, if I suggested you she would say no. If she were to advertise, and say if you were to apply . . .'

'Wouldn't it be too much of a coincidence?'

'No, we can do it through Carlo: she asks Carlo about a nanny. Carlo says the daughter of one of his ex-managers, she knew your father.'

'Is it Miss East?'

'Yes.'

'What did you fight about?'

'This and that.'

'Is Alexander nice?'

'I don't know, Helen.'

'But you'd like to know?' She seemed to have grown up in minutes.

'I'd love to know.'

'Fine,' said Helen Doyle. 'I have to do my thinking somewhere, it might as well be with Alexander East.'

The cake was produced and cut. And when everybody had a slice of rich gateau on a plate, Desmond tapped on a glass and said that Frank Quigley who had done the honours so well a quarter of a century ago was going to say a few words.

Frank stood forward, he said that it was a great happiness and a great honour to be asked to speak. He made it seem both.

Those who listened felt for a moment that he was lucky to have been invited.

He said that he remembered the day when Deirdre, looking roughly the same as she did tonight, had made this commitment; she was young and beautiful, she had her life ahead of her, there were many decisions to make, many paths to choose. She had chosen Desmond Doyle. Smoothly he brought them from the marriage through the early days of Palazzo, to the joys of children, to their luck in each and all of these children, a daughter rising high in the book trade – Palazzo had tried to poach her, but with no success. Another daughter giving her entire life to looking after people, and a son with a love of the land. These were three rich rewards for Deirdre and Desmond to look at and see their hopes realized.

He himself had not been so fortunate in the early days, he hadn't met anyone he loved until later on in life. His gaze passed gently over Maureen standing cool and admiring in her lemon silk dress. But then he too had known the happiness of married life, though unfortunately unlike Desmond he had not been given the joy of fathering three fine children. But his heart was happy tonight and in no sense tinged with the envy that it might have held over the years. At the weekend he and Renata were going to Brazil, where a legal adoption had been arranged, and where they were going to take home with them and give a home to a girl called Paulette. She was eight months old. Nuns had arranged the papers. She would be very much younger than his friend Desmond's children but he hoped that the friendship would be there always, as his had been. A lifelong friendship, he said. Some things never change.

It had been masterly, there were a few tears brushed away, and the champagne glasses were raised.

Everyone was touched by Frank. Every person in the room. Even Maureen Barry.

'My God, you are one performer,' she said to him admiringly.

'Thank you, Maureen.' He was gallant and suave.

'No, I mean it. You always were. You didn't have to try so hard, just to prove my mother wrong, to prove me wrong.'

'But your mother loved me, she said I was a very nice young man.' He put on her mother's voice. It was a good imitation.

'I'm glad about the child,' she said.

'Yes, so are we.'

'And will I see you all when I open my shop in England?'

'It will be a time before Paulette will be old enough for your clothes.'

'Oddly enough I'm having a children's boutique too.'

'Well then.' His smile was warm. But not warm enough.

Maureen thought she would discuss it with her father. The old rascal was full of advice. She wasn't going to let drop a prize like this again.

Father Hurley said he wanted to use the phone, but there appeared to be a queue. Anna was speaking to someone.

'Sure, come round,' she was saying. 'Listen to me, Ken Green, this is 1985, we are all free to make our own choices. My choice is that if you choose to be here that would be great.' There was a pause.

'And I love you too,' she said, hanging up, surprised with herself.

Deidre's mother was on the phone next.

'Yes Tony, perfectly satisfactory, no opportunity. No, no, not reneging on anything, but you know the whole art of life is knowing the right time to say things. Yes, yes. Nothing changed. Absolutely. Me too. Lots.'

Father Hurley picked up the telephone to tell Father Hayes that he was getting a mini-cab back, he would be sharing it with several others, a large car had been ordered.

Yes, he said, it had been delightful, he just felt he mustn't take up the phone, other people might be telephoning people to say they loved them.

No, he said testily to Father Hayes. He wasn't even remotely drunk, he had just been sitting listening to a woman and her granddaughter talking on the telephone. That was all.

The move to go was general now. But there was a sense of something not quite completed.

Deirdre found the camera. She had a new film in it all ready for the occasion, she ran into the kitchen where Philippa's team were busy putting polythene on the leftovers and storing them in the fridge. There would even be things for the freezer.

Deirdre explained how the camera worked and Philippa listened patiently. It was a characteristic of this kind of woman that they thought their cameras were complicated.

They gathered around the couple in a semicircle. They smiled. The camera flashed and flashed again.

Amongst the pictures in the roll of twenty-four there would be one which was bound to look good when enlarged, would look just right. There would be the picture of The Silver Wedding on the wall, for everyone to see. Everyone who came to Rosemary Drive from now on.

THERMOANALYTICAL
METHODS OF
INVESTIGATION

THERMOANALYTICAL METHODS OF INVESTIGATION

By Paul D. Garn

DEPARTMENT OF CHEMISTRY
THE UNIVERSITY OF AKRON
AKRON, OHIO

1965

ACADEMIC PRESS   New York · London

68863/
4·10·66

ACADEMIC PRESS INC.
111 Fifth Avenue, New York, New York 10003

United Kingdom Edition published by
ACADEMIC PRESS INC. (LONDON) LTD.
Berkeley Square House, London W.1

Library of Congress Catalog Card Number: 65-18426

PRINTED IN THE UNITED STATES OF AMERICA

D
543.086
GAR

Preface

Although the art of differential thermal analysis has reached a maturity that warrants a detailed and critical examination of the experimental methods used, the current literature still reveals a lack of knowledge of such basic considerations as heat transfer and atmospheric effects.

This monograph provides extensive discussions of the important parameters used in differential thermal analysis, thermogravimetric analysis, and related fields. It is designed principally for the research worker who finds, or has reason to believe, that one or more of the thermoanalytical techniques may prove useful to him. Furthermore, it will be of great aid to those who have to purchase an instrument and are not familiar with its many advantages and disadvantages. Finally, for the specialist in the techniques of thermal analysis, it provides a comprehensive discussion of design features which will enable him to construct an instrument suitable for his purposes.

The many variables affecting the course of a change in state, and hence the appearance of the thermogram, are considered. Examples from the literature are cited to demonstrate the merits or demerits of particular methods. These range from the rather prosaic effects of dilution or heating rate to the disordering effects of radioactive decay. A few examples are cited only to illustrate the range of applicability of the techniques.

Most of the parameters are discussed stressing particularly the relation to differential thermal analysis, but nearly all of them will affect thermogravimetric analysis, electrical resistance, dilatometric, or other measurements since they affect the course of the thermally induced process.

The general topic of thermoanalytical investigations is truly interdisciplinary, being useful in the earth sciences of geology, mineralogy, and oceanography; the natural sciences, notably metallurgy, chemistry, and ceramics; biological sciences such as botany and agronomy; and in chemical and food processing, and medical and forensic technology.

This work is concerned with the behavior of the sample material and the effects of the treatment to which it is subjected. The type of apparatus used will influence the behavior of the sample because of its direct effect on the treatment of the sample, thus discussions of types of apparatus are necessary. Since the commercial apparatus of today may not be available even a year from now, an aggregation of photographs of apparatuses is not offered; in fact, specific descriptions are avoided. If, for example, one of the features claimed for an apparatus is the small sample needed, the advantages and disadvantages of small samples can easily be reviewed. Hence the discussion is pertinent to the particular advantage claimed for the apparatus.

This monograph was written almost entirely while I was employed at the Bell Telephone Laboratories, Murray Hill, New Jersey. The concentration on techniques rather than on data of immediate and commercial interest would not have been possible at many industrial laboratories. The library, drafting shop, and stenographic services provided so liberally by the Bell Telephone Laboratories brought the preparation of this monograph within the realm of possibility to a working chemist.

For the background training and experience which made this work possible, I am indebted to the late Dr. William M. MacNevin, my preceptor at The Ohio State University, and to Dr. Wilfred E. Campbell, formerly of Bell Telephone Laboratories. For their helpful discussions and reviews of substantial parts of the manuscript I am grateful to Drs. Ralph Hansen and Patrick Gallagher, both of Bell Telephone Laboratories, and to Mr. Emlyn Rowland, then of Leeds and Northrup Co. For his major contribution in criticizing the entire manuscript, I am especially thankful to Dr. Robert Bohon of 3M Company. Because of his careful examination of this book, many passages that were clear to me are now also clear to the reader; he also caught errors of omission and transcription. I should also like to thank, for their helpful discussions, Drs. John Lundberg and John McChesney of Bell Telephone Laboratories and Dr. H. James Harwood of The University of Akron.

To Polly, my beloved wife, and to our children, Michael and David, I am grateful for their patience with my almost continual absence, evenings and weekends, for a couple of years.

Akron, Ohio   PAUL D. GARN
October, 1965

Contents

Chapter I

Changes in State on Heating

Chapter II

Differential Thermal Analysis

Chapter III

Operational Parameters

Chapter IV

Apparatus for Differential Thermal Analysis

Chapter V

Evaluation of Differential Thermal Analysis Curves

Chapter VI

Kinetics

Chapter VII

Atmosphere Control

Chapter VIII

Special Techniques

Chapter IX

Thermogravimetric Analysis

Chapter X

Thermogravimetric Apparatus

Chapter XI

Simultaneous Measurements

Chapter XII

Other Techniques

Chapter XIII

Miscellaneous Topics

Chapter XIV

Analysis of Gaseous Decomposition Products

Chapter XV

Recording, Control, and Power Equipment

Chapter XVI

Miscellaneous Apparatus and Information

Chapter XVII

Apparatus Design

Appendix I

Appendix II

Calibration Data

Appendix III

Acknowledgments

The author is deeply grateful to Bell Telephone Laboratories, Incorporated for releasing the previously unpublished data contained herein and for providing him with drafting, stenographic, and library services during the preparation of most of this book.

The author acknowledges with thanks the use of published data from a number of journals and other publications. He is grateful to the following publishers and commercial or scientific organizations for permission to use the listed figures:

American Ceramic Society (*Journal* and *Bulletin*)—II-6, 7, 9, 16; III-3, 11, 17, 18; IV-11; V-4, 5, 7, 8; VI-4, 5, 6, 7, 8, 9; VII-4, 18; VIII-11, 12, 13, 29; X-6; XI-10; XII-4, 10, 11, 12, 17;
American Journal of Science—III-4, 5, 6; IV-8.
American Mineralogist—I-9; II-14, 15, 19, 20, 21, 22; III-25, 27; IV-5, 6, 7, 18; V-9, 12, 15; VII-3, 9; XIII-5, 8.
Analytica Chimica Acta—I-7; VI-15.
Analytical Chemistry—II-23; III-7, 10, 15, 19, 20, 21; IV-2, 10, 12, 13, 21, 22, 23, 24, 28, 29, 30, 31; V-19, 20, 21, 22; VI-10, 11, 12, 13; VII-1, 2, 5, 13, 16, 28; VIII-17, 18, 19, 25, 26, 30, 31, 32; IX-1, 2, 4, 8, 9, 10, 11, 14; X-2, 3, 5, 7, 12, 13, 14, 15; XI-1, 11, 12, 13, 14, 15, 16; XII-7, 8; XIII-3, 4, 16, 17, 19; XIV-2, 3, 4, 5, 11, 12, 13, 14, 15, 18, 19, 20, 21, 22, 23, 24; XVI-3; XVII-4.
Berichte der Deutschen Keramischen Gesellschaft—VIII-23, 24.
Brennstoff-Chemie—XI-9.
Bulletin Societé Chimie de France—VII-8, 9, 10.
Bulletin Societé Française Ceramique—X-19, 20.
Bulletin Societé Minéralogie et Cristallographie Française—XI-5, 6, 7.
Canadian Journal of Chemistry—X-9, 10, 16, 17; XIII-12, 18.
Clay Mineralogy—V-3.
Economic Geology—XV-6.
Fuel—VIII-14, 16.
Geologie e Mijnbouw—IV-19; V-16, 17.
Journal of Applied Chemistry—III-30.
Journal of Applied Polymer Science—II-18; V-23, 24; XII-5, 6; XV-7.
Journal of Chemical Education—X-11.

Journal of Inorganic and Nuclear Chemistry—XI-2.
Journal of Less-Common Metals—IV-33.
Journal of Pharmaceutical Science—I-11; XII-13.
Journal of Polymer Science—XIII-2, 13.
Journal of Scientific Instruments—X-8; XII-2; XVI-5.
Journal of the American Chemical Society—VI-1, 2; XIII-6, 7.
Leeds and Northrup Co.—XVI-1.
Materials Research Standard—VII-25, 26.
Microchemical Journal—VIII-1.
Mineralogical Society (London)—II-24.
Nature—IX-5, 6; XIII-14, 15.
Physics and Chemistry of Glasses—II-25, 26; III-26.
Reviews of Scientific Instruments—VII-20; X-4; XII-14, 15, 16; XVII-6, 7.
Schaevitz Engineering Co.—XVI-7, 8.
Talanta—IX-3; XIV-6, 7, 8, 9, 10.
Textile Research Journal—XIII-1.
Transactions of the British Ceramic Society—IV-20, VI-3.
Transactions of the Metals Society, AIME—I-8.
Wiley (Interscience)—VIII-2, 3, 4, 5, 6, 7.

CHAPTER I

Changes in State on Heating

1.1. Introduction

An appropriate beginning for a monograph of this nature is an explanation of the need for it—a justification of its existence. The work deals mainly with differential thermal analysis and thermogravimetric analysis, since these are the most popular techniques. These are the best known and the most used and yet they have developed almost independently and certainly unsystematically. There have been reportorial works in differential thermal analysis and an array of data from thermogravimetric analysis. The need for this book stems from the inability of users of orthodox techniques in either field to obtain data that can be generally related unequivocally to the data obtained with the same material but using a different apparatus, or to obtain data by differential thermal analysis which can be generally related unequivocally to thermogravimetric data obtained even by the same person on the same material.

In 1952, MacKenzie and Farquharson (M6) reported some results of differential thermal analysis studies of standard mineral specimens by a number of observers—with no attempt to control the type of apparatus used by each. The results are disturbing. Curves obtained by MacKenzie on the standard minerals are shown in Fig. I-1. Since clay mineralogists

1

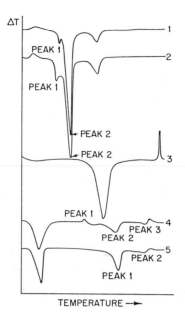

FIG. I-1. Thermograms for the *standard* minerals reported by MacKenzie and Farquharson (M6). The minerals are: 1, bauxite; 2, bayerite; 3, kaolinite; 4, Mississippi bentonite; and 5, Wyoming bentonite.

Specimens of each material were sent to each participant in the study.

generally use peak temperatures as comparison points MacKenzie and Farquharson showed the results in this manner. They found that for the same peak various observers reported temperatures varying by as much as 100°C!

FIG. I-2. Distribution of peak temperatures as reported by MacKenzie and Farquharson (M6). The classes of apparatus having sufficient members to warrant grouping are:

	A	B	C	D	E	F
Type of Specimen Holder:	Metal	Metal	Metal	Ceramic	Ceramic	Metal
Position of Temperature Thermocouple:	Inert	Specimen Holder	Inert	Inert	Various	Various
Sample weight (gm)	<1.0	<0.5	0.5–15	<1.0	—	—
Heating rate (°C/minute)	9–10	11–14	14–16	9–11	—	—

The range of data is related to the type of apparatus by the shading.

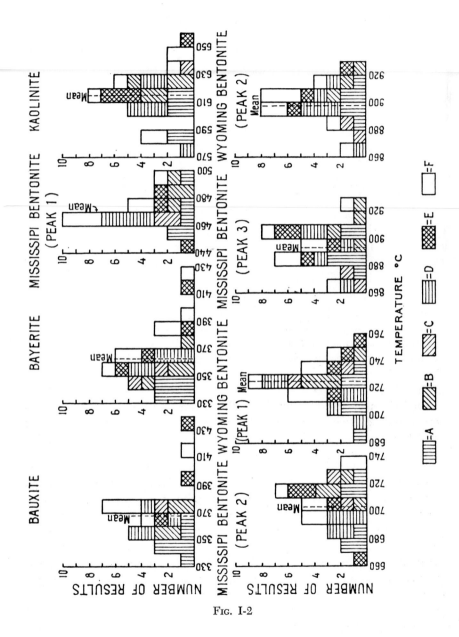

Fig. I-2

The uncorrected peak temperatures are shown for some common classes of apparatus in Fig. I-2. Bauxite (peak 2) not only yielded a 100°C range for all types of apparatus but even for the same general type yielded differences of 30–50°C not occasionally but routinely. This latter statement ignores the wider variations in the catch-all classes E and F. Even when (Fig. I-3) the data were corrected to yield the temperature of the sample rather than the block or inert material, the scatter was still serious indeed.

These results are not unusual. Kissinger (K29) examined the effect of heating rate—and, to a lesser degree, sample dimensions—on peak temperature and found variations of the same (100°C) magnitude. Webb and Heystek (W11) assembled a considerable array of thermal data on carbonates and offer a number of curves for chalybite (naturally occurring ferrous carbonate) as shown in Fig. I-4. Data of this kind will lead naturally and invariably to controversy among the various workers—each of whom can get, for a single mineral on his own apparatus, very reproducible curves which bear little resemblance to the equally reproducible curves obtained by someone else on *his* apparatus.

There must necessarily be an explanation for the divergent results which find their ways into the literature. Specimens do not customarily behave according to whim. Under the same thermodynamic conditions specimens of the same material can be expected to do the same things at the same temperature whether the measured variable is temperature, time, weight, length, electrical conductivity, thermal conductivity, or even color.

Deviations in any measured variable from time to time or from observer to observer or disagreement among the various measured variables must then be a result of the measuring technique. A principal objective of this book is to explore the reasons for the lack of agreement that does exist and provide some clarification. Another objective is to provide basic instruction in the principal tools common to thermal analysis and in the techniques of the principal methods of thermal analysis.

The literature appearing in the various scientific journals has been consulted and is cited freely to show the development of the art. Some technical literature is not reasonably accessible to the author and some available reports may have been overlooked. In addition, the author has deliberately omitted mere compilations of curves without interpretation and those reports which are obviously of no significance. The technical literature contains a liberal portion of data which may now be evaluated or reinterpreted in light of current knowledge. Since the errors were most frequently the result of inadequate knowledge of the atmosphere effect, a clear understanding of Chapter VII is essential.

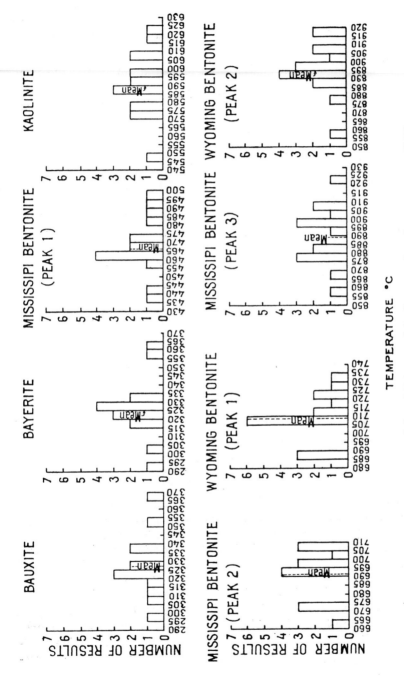

FIG. I-3. Distribution of data (5°C intervals) of corrected peak temperatures (M6).
If the several apparatus were equivalent the deviations would approach the error in temperature measurement, ca. 2–5°C.

1.2. Scope

The field of thermal analysis may be considered to comprise the following fields, as described:

(1) Differential thermal analysis—the measured variable is the temperature difference between the sample and a contiguous reference material, generally, as they are heated or cooled. Any change in state which takes place fairly rapidly can be detected. It is closely related to calorimetry.

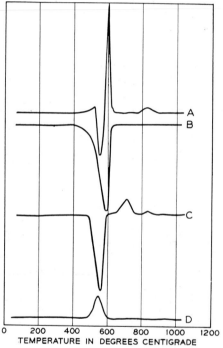

Fɪɢ. I-4. Thermograms of chalybite: A, in open sample holder; B, in nitrogen atmosphere; C, in sample holder with loosely fitting cover; D, fine-grained chalybite, loosely packed without cover. From Webb and Heystek (W11).

The same mineral will show grossly different thermograms depending on its surroundings.

(2) Thermogravimetric analysis—the measured variable is the change in weight of the sample as it is heated, cooled, or programmed through some temperature interval. Oxidation, reduction, dehydration, decomposition, volatilization, drying, reaction with the atmosphere, reaction yielding a volatile product, and similar occurrences are amenable to observation.

(3) Dilatometry—the measured variable is the size of the specimen, frequently as measured along a chosen axis but sometimes as measured by volume change. Generally, the information desired is gained directly, but the results also disclose phase changes.

(4) Microscopy—the observed variable may be the color, shape, optical rotation, or index of refraction of the sample. Changes occur from the same phenomena that may be detected by differential thermal analysis.

(5) X-ray diffraction—the measured variable is the intensity of a reflection. The quantity determined from the angles of the diffraction peaks is the crystal lattice spacing. Disappearance of the peak implies disappearance of the associated crystal structure.

(6) Calorimetry—the quantity measured may be the temperature of the sample or temperature change of its surroundings. The same effects as in differential thermal analysis are observable. Heats of reaction, heat capacities, and heats of transition can be measured with greater accuracy than in differential thermal analysis.

(7) Conductivity—the measured variable is the electrical resistance or some function of the resistance. The data yield a measure of the order of the sample, e.g., the degree of perfection of crystalline materials. The imperfections may be due to impurities as well as crystal defects.

(8) Effluence analysis—the measured variable may be the thermal conductivity, density, or volume of the gas given off while the sample is heated. Qualitative analysis of the decomposition products is an aid in interpreting or identifying the reaction taking place.

(9) Differential calorimetry—the measured variable is the temperature difference between the sample and the furnace. Occurrences detectable by differential thermal analysis can be detected by differential calorimetry.

The list could be continued by additions such as dielectric properties, in which the measured quantity will itself be of interest, or thermoelectric emf or magnetic properties, in which the data might be used principally for detection of a change.

The first two subjects will be covered in considerable detail; the remaining topics will be treated quite briefly as they relate to nonequilibrium thermal analysis, even though some are extensive fields in their own right. Note that these properties or occurrences are characteristic of the state of combination, i.e., the compound, rather than the elemental species comprising the compound.

1.3. Phenomena Detectable by Thermal Analysis

The several types of changes of state commonly observed by differential and other kinds of thermal analysis necessarily involve heat, whether or not this heat provides the means of detection and/or measurement of the change. Consider first the nondestructive changes in state.

Any material has a free energy content $F = H - TS$ where H is the heat content, T is the absolute temperature, and S is the entropy. Any system will tend to reach whichever of the possible states has the least free energy at the temperature of the system; hence, if a material is in a given crystalline structure and it is taken to a temperature at which another structure has a lower free energy, it will tend to change to the more stable structure. This transformation may be very slow (e.g., aragonite $\rightarrow$ calcite) but the tendency to transform is real. Consider a material heated from room temperature up to T_f as indicated in Fig. I-5.

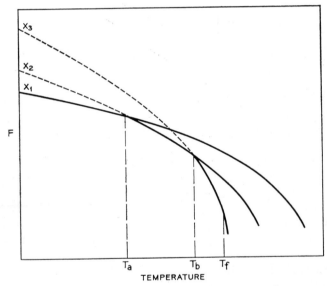

Fig. I-5. Representation of the free energies of three states of a material as functions of the temperature.

The thermodynamically stable state is that with the least free energy. Any other state will tend to change to the stable form.

The free energy of the stable state at room temperature changes with temperature indefinitely along the curve X_1. Let us consider, though, that there is another possible arrangement of the atoms of our sample and that the free energy of this arrangement follows the curve X_2. At T_a the two structures have the same free energy and can coexist but at higher temperatures the second structure has a lower free energy and is consequently more stable and the first structure will tend to disappear as the atoms or ions rearrange to form the second. This appearance of a more stable crystal structure may occur several times as the sample is heated, as at T_b, or the more stable state need not be another crystalline phase. The more stable state may be the liquid or vapor in which cases the material will tend to melt, boil, or sublime.

Generally, these reactions are rapid and a given state will not exist in detectable amounts outside the temperature limits prescribed. (Exceptions will be treated later.) The temperatures of coexistence of phases are variously transition, melting, boiling, or sublimation points.

These points of equal free energy are decidedly not without heat effects. The equality of F_{X_1} and F_{X_2} does not imply equality of H_{X_1} and H_{X_2} or S_{X_1} and S_{X_2}. These quantities normally change by measurable amounts. The change in H is of principal concern. This ΔH, $H_{X_2} - H_{X_1}$, is the measured or detected quantity in several techniques in thermal analysis.

Figure I-6 shows a reasonably typical variation of H with tempera-

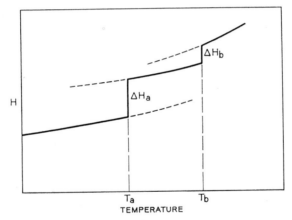

Fɪɢ. I-6. Representation of heat content vs temperature for a material undergoing two changes of state.

The heat content of any single form of a material increases continuously with temperature. At T_a or T_b additional heat must be supplied to change the material to the other form.

ture. This might be, for example, chemical reaction at a and melting at b; except for the relative values of ΔH_a and ΔH_b it might be a crystalline phase transformation and melting; it might be a simple melting and boiling. No matter, each involves a quantity of heat being added to the system at (ideally) a constant temperature and the occurrence can be detected and generally measured. Heats of solution and second-order phase transformations can also be measured and detected.

A change in weight may result from boiling, sublimation, dehydration, decomposition, combustion, oxidation, absorption, desorption, and perhaps a few other occurrences. Let us ignore the first two ordinary volatilizations as trivial cases. The latter two are special problems beyond the normal scope of thermal analysis; they are generally measured isothermally. Some of the apparatus and techniques are applicable.

The observations of weight changes immediately distinguish changes in (condensed) state from the occurrence listed above but this is a collateral use. The principal value of weight measurements is in the relative accuracy of the numbers obtained. It is not a good means of independent determination of the temperature of those occurrences, but is of immense value in determining what is occurring. Weight gain or loss (Fig. I-7) is directly related to the quantity of material reacting.

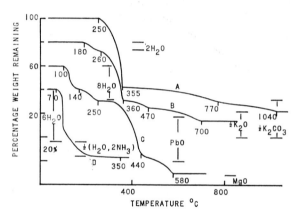

Fig. I-7. Thermal decomposition curves of metal diliturates and of magnesium ammonium phosphate hexahydrate: A, Potassium diliturate, 373.8 mg heated at 300°C/hour; B, Magnesium diliturate octahydrate, 109.5 mg heated at 65°C/hour; C, Lead diliturate dihydrate, 37.6 mg heated at 150°C/hour; D, Magnesium ammonium phosphate hexahydrate, 106.8 mg heated at 65°C/hour. From Berlin and Robinson (B47).

The several weight losses can be measured and these quantities related to the specific occurrences.

The measuring of dimensional changes on heating is of considerable significance in metallurgy, ceramics, physics, and glass-making. In those fields, the information desired is that which is determined, namely, how much does a given material expand (or contract) in a given direction when heated to a given temperature. A complete treatment of the subject is obviously beyond the scope of this book. The technique is treated herein as a means of gathering the information obtainable from anomalies or discontinuities in thermal expansion, e.g., detection of phase changes or sintering or determination of the state of oxidation or densification.

In the normal course of heating a solid crystalline material, the increasing thermal energy brings about lattice vibrations of increasing amplitude. In an isotropic crystal or in random assemblies of crystals the material expands. In single crystals of low symmetry the increasing amplitude of vibrations may be so directed that while the whole crystal grows in size it may actually contract along one axis. In any case, the expansion along the various axes of an anisotropic crystal can (like other properties) vary according to the direction of observation. Along with the ordinary expansion discontinuous changes in dimensions occur at phase transitions (see above). These discontinuous changes may be used to detect changes of state (Fig. I-8).

The changes in dimensions may be detected or determined by means other than direct measurement of the length or breadth of a specimen. Electron, or more commonly, X-ray diffraction techniques determine the geometric relationship of the nuclei within the crystal; hence, variation

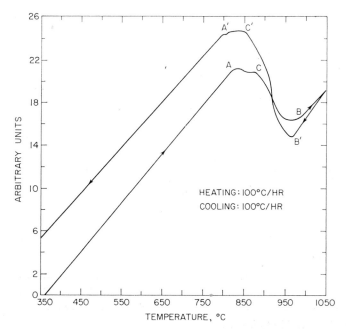

Fig. I-8. Thermal expansion of zirconium. From Intrater (I3).
The change in state ca. 850°C brings about a change in dimensions.

of the interplanar spacing may be used to measure the expansion along a given axis. Obviously, the disappearance or appearance of a reflection may be used to detect a discontinuous change in state, i.e., phase change, decomposition, etc. (Fig. I-9).

Most nonmetallic crystalline materials are poor conductors of electricity—their valence bands are filled and there is only an occasional electron in a conduction band. During a phase transformation, the transitory disorder in the crystal leads to nondiscrete energy levels and

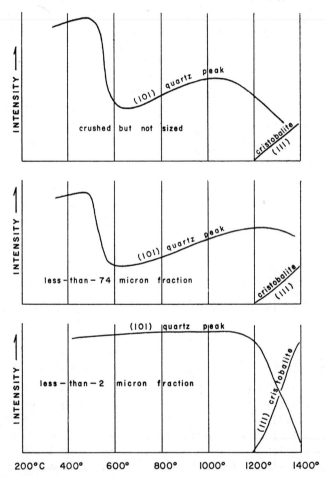

Fig. I-9. Intensity of quartz (101) X-ray diffraction peak as a function of temperature. From Wahl *et al.* (W2).

The change in arrangement of the nuclei changes the intensity of a given reflection, hence detecting the appearance or disappearance of a phase.

a diminished energy gap between valence bands and the lowest-lying conduction levels. While this disorder exists, the electrical conductivity of the specimen may be several orders of magnitude higher than for either of the ordered states (Fig. I-10).

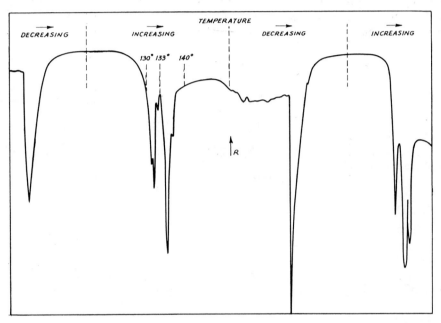

Fɪɢ. I-10. Electrical resistance variation with temperature in silver iodide. From Garn and Flaschen (G10).

As the specimen undergoes a transformation the electrical resistance decreases sharply.

Optical properties are easily observed at low temperatures. If the material is well-ordered and large enough so that single particles may be observed directly or microscopically, any discontinuous change may be observed quite without regard to the energy involved (Fig. I-11). Organic materials are especially good subjects since fair-sized molecules may find several ways to crystallize at various temperatures and a phase transformation may be little more than an unkinking of a carbon chain.

Analysis of the gaseous products of a reaction or decomposition will yield rather specific information concerning the nature of the reaction. The specific reaction can often be deduced from the temperature and the presence—or absence—of a particular product. Quantitative data may be obtained (see Chapter XIV).

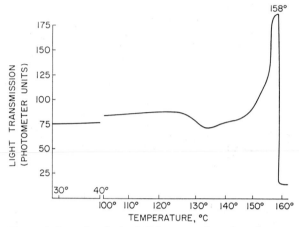

Fig. I-11. Transmission of polarized light as a function of temperature. From Reese *et al.* (R11).

A change in state will change the degree of rotation of the polarized light.

1.4. Dielectric Constant

The dielectric properties will vary as a result of decomposition or phase changes (Fig. I-12). Changes in symmetry due to a crystallographic transformation, possibly but not necessarily induced by a decomposition, may bring about a change in the rotational freedom of the molecule or ion so as to change the dielectric constant.

1.5. Thermoelectric Emf

The discontinuities in thermoelectric potentials with temperature may be used for the study of metals or alloys.

1.6. Magnetic Properties

Magnetic susceptibilities will change discontinuously for some materials for some changes of state and hence may be used to detect these changes.

1.7. Summary

Nearly any property of a material may be used to detect a change in state, but some are better than others. Several types of measurement will yield information of direct interest, e.g., dilatometry. If the purpose of the experiment is only to detect changes rather than to measure properties, any type of measurement suitable for the material can be used. Differential thermal analysis is most used because it is experimentally convenient and the occurrence of changes of state are quite apparent from the record. The interpretation is quite another matter.

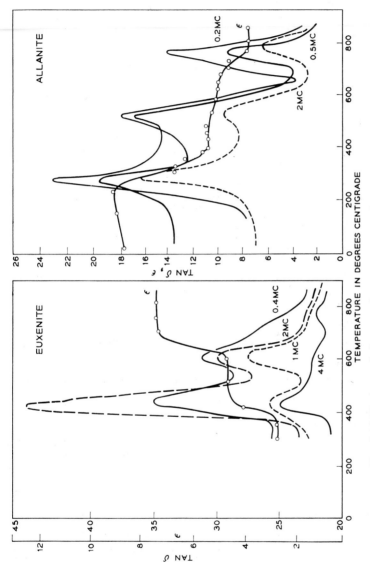

FIG. I-12. Dielectric behaviors of metamict minerals. From Ukai (U2).
The change in structure is reflected in a change of dielectric constant, ϵ, and in dissipation factor, tan δ.

CHAPTER II

Differential
Thermal Analysis

2.1. Description

Differential thermal analysis is a technique by which thermal effects are measured, usually as the sample is heated or cooled. It is of use or assistance in quantitative and semiquantitative analysis. The basic technique is simple and straightforward; it is related, of course, to calorimetry.

Consider first an adiabatic calorimeter to which heat is being added at an essentially constant rate (Fig. II-1). The temperature of the calorimeter will increase also at an essentially constant rate. Now let us insert in the calorimeter a sample which undergoes a reaction requiring the absorption of heat. This time, as the calorimeter is heated, the temperature varies in a slightly different manner because of the heat capacity of the specimen; nevertheless the temperature increases in an approximately linear manner until the temperature of the reaction is reached (Fig. II-2). Since the sample is at a temperature at which it *can* undergo reaction, it *will* undergo reaction and a portion of the heat that otherwise would have raised the temperature of the calorimeter is instead absorbed by the sample without change of temperature. When the necessary heat, dictated by the nature of the material and the size of the sample, has been supplied, the additional heat again raises the temperature of the calorimeter. This additional quantity of heat that must be added without changing the temperature of the samples is specifically the heat of reaction and may be, of course, the heat of fusion, decomposition, or transition depending upon the nature of the reaction taking place.

The temperatures measured in calorimetry are often high and the quantities of interest are frequently the differences between large numbers. This type of measurement is inherently subject to error, since the uncertainties in the two separate temperature readings may approach the

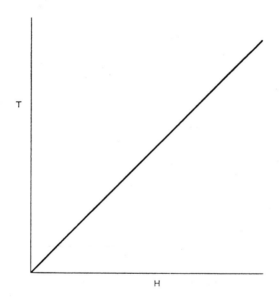

Fɪɢ. II-1. Temperature as a function of heat input for a calorimeter without a specimen.

As heat is added to the isolated system the temperature of the system rises approximately linearly.

same magnitude as the desired difference. This temperature that is measured, however, is basically a difference itself. It is most generally the difference between the furnace or calorimeter temperature and an ice bath temperature as measured with a thermocouple junction in the furnace opposing a reference junction immersed in an ice bath. Let us now take the reference junction out of the ice bath and put it in a second (empty) calorimeter and heat the two of them simultaneously. We have now a nearly zero signal since the temperature difference is small. Under ideal conditions the displacement is due only to the heat capacity of the sample. Now as the sample reaches the reaction temperature the sample begins to lag behind the reference material because a portion of the heat supply is required to carry out the reaction (Fig. II-3). When the reaction is complete a new, nearly constant signal is obtained. (This is the essence of differential calorimetry.) Subsequent reactions may be detected in a similar manner. Now, however, the magnitude of the signal imposes a possible limitation on the sensitivity of the method. So let us move the reference junction into the same calorimeter or furnace and

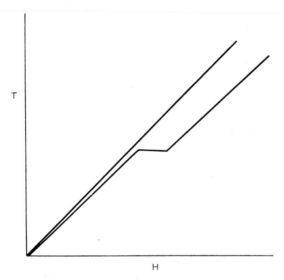

T

H

FIG. II-2. Temperature as a function of heat input for a calorimeter with a specimen.

The calorimeter temperature rises a bit more slowly because the specimen must be heated too. When the transformation temperature is reached an additional quantity of heat must be added to change the specimen to the new form.

permit heat to flow between the sample and reference thermocouples, but not too freely. In this case (Fig. II-4) as the sample is heated there is a very slight deviation of the signal from zero until the reaction temperature is reached. The reaction goes on as before and a temperature signal is obtained, but now, with the possibility of exchange of heat with the reference region, heat flows from the reference region to the sample region and the temperature of the sample again approaches that of the reference region. The subsequent reaction is detected in essentially the same manner. Now we are in position to use highly sensitive measurements since the temperature difference will return to near zero after the

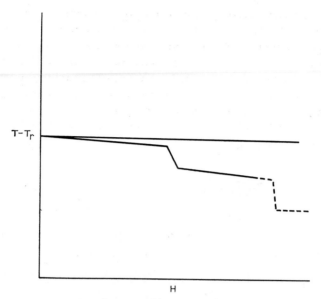

FIG. II-3. Temperature as a function of heat input for a calorimeter with a moving reference temperature.

Relatively small temperature differences need to be measured.

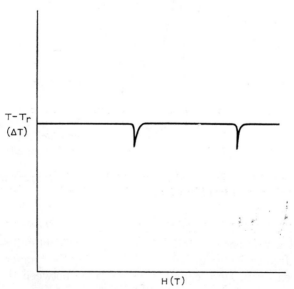

FIG. II-4. Differential thermal analysis.

By permitting a temperature difference to decay the system is ready to detect a subsequent thermal effect with a high degree of sensitivity.

completion of each reaction, so that detection of a subsequent reaction is not inhibited or prevented.

If, now, we call $T_r - T$, ΔT, and plot this function against the temperature rather than heat input, and if we put the sample thermocouple into the specimen and the reference thermocouple in a rather similar specimen of inert material, we have the essential ingredients of differential thermal analysis. We can, in fact, put the sample and the reference materials in a single block as in Fig. II-5 so that exchange of heat can be quite rapid. Chapter IV shows a variety of methods of containing the sample.

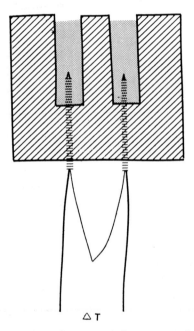

Fig. II-5. Typical sample block showing placement and connection of thermocouples.

The thermocouples are connected in opposition, i.e., the temperature difference, ΔT, is measured between two like wires.

Differential thermal analysis, then, is generally performed by heating a sample and a reference material in rather close contiguity—permitting moderately free exchange of heat—and measuring the temperature difference between them. Here ends the resemblance between the apparatus used by the various observers.

Evaluation or use of data reported by other workers is difficult because of the many effects which can influence the peak height, temperature, or shape. Identification of a material by comparing temperatures derived from an experimental curve with temperatures cited in the literature would be foolhardy. MacKenzie (M4) and co-workers have compiled a punched-card index of differential thermal analysis data in which the two principal peaks of materials are listed as reported by each worker. The forty-four reports cited for kaolinite cover a range of 540–660°C for the dehydroxylation and 995–1060°C for the exotherm. Still another report (K31) gives 665°C as the peak temperature—at a heating rate of 20°C/minute. Similarly, the thirty-one reports (M4) on dolomite have a 740–820°C range for the dolomite decomposition and 830–1010°C for the subsequent calcite decomposition. It is quite apparent that, in the present state of the art, any use of data obtained by another observer must be done with considerable caution.

Before discussing the several operational parameters, an understanding of some rather basic topics is needed. The apparent simplicity of the technique leads the uninformed to assume that satisfactory data may be obtained, for example, by sticking a pair of thermocouples into a specimen and a reference and lighting a fire under them. The inevitable result of such work will be data which are not interpretable or relatable to other data, hence a subjective consequence—conviction by the user and others who see the data that the technique has no value.

First of all, we must be aware of the occurrences in a specimen being heated. This requires a nodding acquaintance with the heat-flow equation

$$\nabla^2 T = \frac{\rho c}{k} \frac{\partial T}{\partial t}$$

where the operator ∇ refers to the derivative with respect to the coordinate system chosen. In the case of unidirectional flow, the equation is simply

$$\frac{\partial^2 T}{\partial x^2} = \frac{\rho c}{k} \frac{\partial T}{\partial t}$$

where x is the distance from the reference point, ρ is the density, c is the heat capacity, k is the thermal conductivity, and $\partial T/\partial t$ is the rate of heating. The terms ρ, c, and k are often combined in a single term, a, the thermal diffusivity:

$$a = \frac{k}{\rho c}.$$

The various forms of the heat-flow equation apply to a homogeneous system; at a boundary of any sort there is a discontinuity beyond which another expression must be applied—with the appropriate new values of ρ c, or k. Boundaries will exist, for example, between the heater and furnace tube, between furnace tube and block, between block and specimen, and even between the parts of the specimen that have and have not undergone the thermal reaction being studied.

2.2. Sample Size and Geometry

Most users of differential thermal analysis agree that a proper shape for a sample is a cylinder heated, as symmetrically as possible, from the outside. The uniform approach of heat to the center permits the highest convenient symmetry and hence little disturbance of the peak shape due to irregularities of heat flow. Other shapes have been used (see Chapter III); many occasions will arise on which the cylinder may be impractical (see Chapter VIII).

There is a natural tendency among users of differential thermal analysis to attempt to work with smaller and smaller samples. This urge is obviously laudable (but see below); not only is the utility of the technique extended but also the errors inherent in the use of large samples are avoided or diminished.

The major problem in the use of large sample holders is the finite time required for an advancing temperature front to permeate the sample. Recall now that as a small particle is heated to a temperature at which it will undergo a phase transformation the increase in temperature will be continuous until the transition temperature is reached. The sample remains at that temperature while absorbing sufficient heat to undergo the transformation and then, and only then, it will pass heat onward to a particle further from the heat source. We may picture then a cross section of a cylinder containing a sample undergoing a phase transformation. A thermocouple is placed at the center of the cylinder. Hence at the time that the material at the edge of the sample begins its transformation, flow of heat to the center diminishes sharply. Since the reference thermocouple is continuing its increase in temperature a difference signal is immediately obtained. The rate of advance of the transition temperature front is governed by the rate of supply of heat to the sample and by the thermal diffusivity of the new phase. In any case a finite time is required A thin cylinder will require a shorter time for the reaction (Fig. III-16) to go to completion and, hence, the thermal deflection will occupy a shorter interval of temperature and consequently will be less likely to interfere with the detection of subsequent transformations or reactions. More than enough compensation for the diminished initial signal can be gained by electronic amplification.

The use of small specimens must be undertaken judiciously; however, the question immediately arises: is the sample representative of the whole? The present author has described techniques for the use of milligram quantities of samples, but he has also encountered irreproducibility (see Chapter VIII) for the reason cited. The use of small samples just for the sake of using small samples is nonsense; each problem ought to be considered separately and the technique chosen according to the needs of the problem.

2.3. The Behavior of a Specimen Undergoing a Transformation

Any specimen whose temperature is being raised by application of heat to the outside cannot possibly be at a uniform temperature; this should be obvious. Less obvious is the manner in which the temperature changes within the specimen as it undergoes a transition. Smyth's (S36) treatment, although a few simplifying assumptions were required, is the best treatment of which the present author is aware. The major criticism is the assumption that the density, specific heat, and thermal conductivity all remained constant.

Smyth chose to consider a pair of infinite slabs with the sample between. The distance from side to center could be subdivided mathematically into a number of slabs such that if the boundary conditions were known the temperature of each slab could be easily calculated. The progress of the reaction inward could then be followed.

Let us now restrict our discussion to the simplest system and later expand it to include some description of decompositions and such. We will concern ourselves with a reversible crystallographic phase transformation which is reasonably rapid, i.e., any typical transition. For such a system, the temperature uniquely describes the phase present except at precisely the transition temperature. Any particle at a temperature lower than this transition temperature will necessarily have the lower-temperature structure, while any above will equally certainly be in the high-temperature form. Let us now heat a specimen—along with a reference material—from below to above the transition temperature and let us form the materials in slabs heated from both sides so that we can use Smyth's figures. The reference material will assume some temperature gradient which will vary slowly with changes in thermal diffusivity so that the temperature of the center lags behind that of the wall (Fig. II-6a) by a nearly constant amount.

The specimen under observation must behave differently in the region of the transition or we would see no differential temperature. As the wall exceeds—slightly—the transition temperature the sample in contact with the wall transforms and then is able to continue to pass on heat to succeeding layers (Fig. II-6b). The high-temperature form will set up a

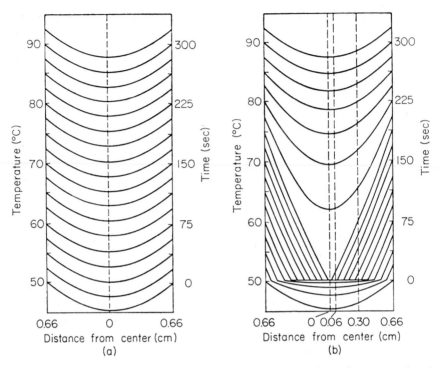

FIG. II-6a. Temperature distributions in the reference material at intervals of 18.75 sec. (S36).

The gradient at any point in the reference will assume a nearly constant value depending on the heating rate, the geometry, and the thermal diffusivity of the material.

FIG. II-6b. Temperature distributions in the test material at intervals of 18.75 sec. *There is a discontinuity in thermal gradient at the reaction front.*

(Note that the temperature gradient is not constant. For any short temperature range during steady temperature rise

$$\frac{\partial^2 T}{\partial x^2} = \text{constant}.$$

This is apparent from the obvious need for each segment to pass inward enough heat to supply *all* segments between it and the center. The amount of heat passed on is proportional to the temperature difference so a linearly varying temperature difference will give, under the conditions stated, a uniform change of temperature for each segment, i.e., a steady state.)

rather different gradient than that in the low-temperature form both because of a change in diffusivity and—more important—because of the
need to transport an additional quantity of heat. Assuming uniform conditions over the slab, a more-or-less discrete interface will move inward
from the surface toward the center. The transforming material acts as a
heat sink during the moment of transformation, but this sink is—in effect
—of infinite thinness so that the infinite heat capacity at the transition
temperature is reflected as a discontinuity in the temperature gradient
(Fig. II-7). The discontinuity is, of course, at the transition temperature.
The gradient in the high temperature form must obviously be higher than
in the low; it is the change in this latter gradient that is of particular
interest.

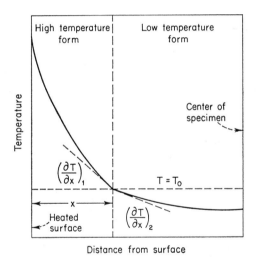

FIG. II-7. Temperature gradients close to boundary between low- and high-
temperature forms. From Smyth (S36).
*The reaction front appears as a moving boundary between the low- and high-
temperature forms.*

In effect, the center of the slab has seen, at a distance, a constantly
rising temperature which has caused a similar but delayed rise in its own
temperature.

At the start of the transition the center no longer sees the rising temperature but a constant temperature front advancing toward it from the
wall (Fig. II-8). The events outside this front influence the center only
by their influence on the movement of the front.

The temperature difference between the center and the front becomes smaller as time passes and because the movement of the front is slowed by its need to carry out the transformation the gradient inside the front can become very small. Eventually, the reaction front reaches the center, i.e., the center reaches the transition temperature, and this center is suddenly exposed to the relatively high temperature gradient. Since this temperature gradient is higher than that in the reference, the center be-

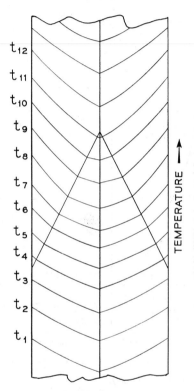

FIG. II-8. Temperature distribution at successive times.

The actual form of advance of the front at transition temperature, T, will probably not be linear. The relative diffusivities of the two forms will determine the shape.

gins to gain in temperature more rapidly than the center of the reference, decreasing the temperature lag. This event is, of course, the peak in the differential temperature. The return to a new steady state will be governed by the thermal diffusivity of the high-temperature form.

Now let us consider—qualitatively—the effect of geometry, the specific question being to what degree the discussion above pertains to the more common cylindrical sample cavity. The same general arguments hold, of course; the specimen will still experience a movement of a reaction front inward—this time from all directions perpendicular to the front.

The form of the operator is different, the expression now being

$$\frac{\partial^2 T}{\partial r^2} + \frac{1}{r}\,\frac{\partial T}{\partial r} = \text{constant}$$

with the same assumptions as before. Qualitatively, this means that near the center the heat is supplied noticeably faster than in the case of the slab, but this is rather obvious from inspection anyway. The result is a sharper peak; the general form will vary somewhat depending on the thermal diffusivities of the two forms.

The behavior of a material undergoing decomposition will be complicated by the transitory presence of reaction products; this will be discussed at greater length in Chapter VII.

The flow of a gas through the specimen will affect the appearance of the peak because it supplies a second heat transfer mechanism acting perpendicular to the conductive flow of heat. The influence of the gas flow will be highly dependent on (1) the sample material because of its thermal conductivity, heat capacity, density, and surface characteristics; (2) the particle size because of the area of contact between particles and the surface area available for heat exchange with the gas; (3) the flow rate because of the greater or lesser heat that the gas may bring or carry away; (4) the temperature because of the changing importance of conduction and radiation with temperature; and (5) the nature of the gas because of differences in heat capacity and thermal conductivity.

For many samples, the total effect is going to be small and will decrease with increasing temperature, but the user of dynamic atmospheres must be aware of the possibility of a significant error in unfavorable cases.

2.4. The Shape of the Differential Temperature Peak

Smyth's (S36) calculations also permitted description of the shape of the differential peak and the effect of the manner of plotting. [The reader must bear in mind that assumptions have been made (p. 23) to permit these computations.] For his slab specimens he obtains the plots of Fig. II-9a, b and c. Considering now the effect of the cylindrical heat flow the form can be modified somewhat. In essence, the first two plots are ΔT vs time and the third is ΔT vs temperature, so the first two are the same curve with a displacement equal to the temperature drop in the reference.

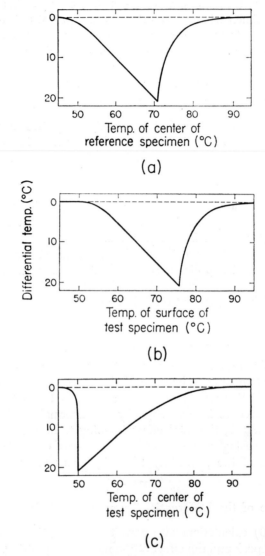

Fig. II-9. Calculated plots for a slab heated from both sides. (a) Differential temperature plotted against the temperature at the center of the reference material. (b) Differential temperature plotted against the surface temperature of the test or the reference sample. (c) Differential temperature plotted against the temperature at the center of the test specimen. From Smyth (S36).

These plots are based on assumed equalities of k, ρ, *and* c *for both low- and high-temperature forms.*

Note that there is no reason to expect a differential thermal analysis peak to be symmetrical; the conditions after the peak temperature is reached are quite different from the initial conditions. The latter part of the curve is a period of temperature equalization; its shape will depend on the thermal diffusivity of the high-temperature form of the material.

The curves are somewhat exaggerated. The difference signal is shown as increasing linearly with time (Fig. II-9a and b) during most of the approach to the peak. This is definitely not the general case in cylindrical cavities. He shows also a rapid approach by the center of the specimen (Fig. II-9c and Fig. II-6b) to the transition temperature and, apparently, a constant temperature for a couple of minutes while the transition goes to completion. This is unrealistic; the heat required to bring the center to the transition temperature must flow under the influence of a temperature gradient, implying that the temperature must be changing continually. While some part of the specimen is in the low-temperature form, the center can reach the transition temperature only asymptotically.

Experimentally, the peaks look like those of Figs. II-10 and II-11. The specimen was cycled automatically for several hours, giving the multiple

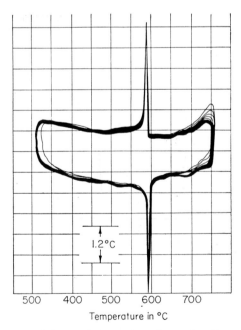

1.2°C

500 400 500 600 700

Temperature in °C

Fig. II-10. Repetitive differential thermal analysis of potassium sulfate in Type 310 stainless steel block; heating rate, 8°C/minute.

Both the peaks and the programming are highly reproducible.

trace shown in Fig. II-10. A time-based record was obtained simultaneously; the peaks in Fig. II-11 are a pair of these. Note in Fig. II-11 that
there is no straight-line portion of the curve as the transition progresses;
there is curvature at all points. The nearly straight portion has been used
from time to time in empirical estimations of transition temperature, but
no basis on which to expect a straight-line portion exists. After the peak
the return to a base line is rapid because it is now limited only by the
thermal diffusivity of the high-temperature form.

Figure II-10 contains ten cycles. The peak heights were determined
from the time-based record of which Fig. II-11 is a portion. The base was

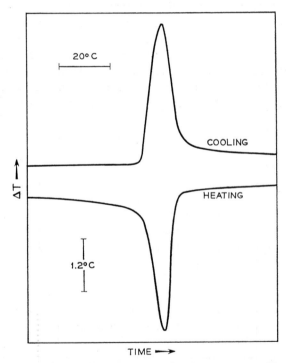

Fig. II-11. Differential thermal analysis curve for the potassium sulfate transition.
The differential temperature is plotted against time.

chosen arbitrarily as the point of rapid departure from (on cooling) and
approach to (on heating) the steady state. The peak height and the average and median deviations on heating were 2.70 inches, 0.022 inch, and
0.025 inch, respectively. Similarly, the cooling peak height and average
and median deviations were 2.67 inches, 0.014 inch, and 0.015 inch, re-

spectively. The root mean square deviations were, on heating, 0.030 and, on cooling, 0.022 inch, respectively. The root mean square deviations then are 1.1% on heating and 0.8% on cooling.

Exact matching of the heating and cooling peaks even on ideally reversible phase transformations would be rare. The differences in thermal properties between the high- and low-temperature forms are ordinarily great enough to cause noticeable differences. Consider the case in which there is a sizable increase in thermal diffusivity in the high-temperature form. On heating, the movement of the reaction front is aided by the existence of the high-diffusivity material between the front and the surface and the return to the base line is quick. On cooling the specimen, as the reaction front moves inward, it leaves behind it an increased barrier to flow of heat, so that the heat of transformation serves to delay the cooling of the inner regions. The return to the base line is also slowed because the heat must be lost by and through this lower-diffusivity material.

The plot in Fig. II-10 shows not only the reproducibility possible with good control equipment but also the significant points of measurement. Note that the peaks on heating and on cooling are at essentially the same temperature. Allowing for a small amount of supercooling, this is the proper result. The center is the hottest point during cooling, so its temperature depends on the rate at which heat is lost from the sample to the block and from the block to its environment.

The steady state that is set up is interrupted when the edge of the specimen reaches the transition temperature. As the transition front moves inward, the cooling of the center is slowed because the heat of transition must be carried away to permit the front to move. The slow approach of the center to the transition temperature results in a relatively steep indication on a ΔT vs T_{sample} plot. Actually, the peak temperature is the temperature at which the transition front has reached the center and is hence the transition temperature. The fact that the heating and cooling peaks do not agree may be attributed to the tendency of many materials to superheat or supercool. Potassium perchlorate appears to superheat rather more than most materials (Fig. II-12). The sharp departure from the base line on heating and the large displacement of the cooling—relative to the heating—curve indicate this. Heat conduction along the thermocouple may lead to a displacement, but this should be about the same on heating or cooling.

The reader must remember that the description thus far has been limited to phase transformations. The complicating features of decompositions will modify the appearance of the thermogram somewhat for reasons which will be pointed out after discussion of the atmosphere effect (Chapter VII).

2.5. Exothermal Reactions

Reversible phase changes are always endothermal; this must follow from the Mass Action Law, for if a reaction tended to give off heat as the material was heated, it would tend to raise the temperature of the substance and accelerate the reaction, and similarly the material on cooling would—at the start of the transformation—take up heat and again accelerate the change. The two phases could not coexist. It follows from this consideration that any phase change which gives off heat as the specimen is heated must be irreversible. There are several conditions which permit these exothermal effects.

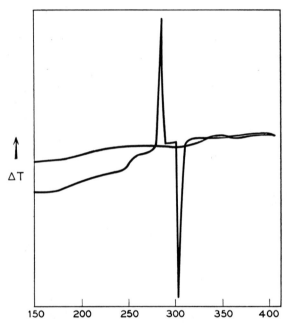

Fig. II-12. Differential thermal analysis curves for the potassium perchlorate transition. The differential temperature is plotted against the specimen temperature.
The lack of overlapping superheating and/or supercooling.

Chemical reaction is an obvious source of heat. Oxidations will ordinarily yield an exothermal peak; the special case of combustion invariably will.

Crystalline rearrangements are a common cause of exothermal effects; the prerequisite for such an event is the formation, by some means, of an unstable phase. The origin of the unstable phase will influence the thermal behavior so the ordinary causes must be examined; the thermal behavior will depend most on whether the unstable phase occurred by an act upon the specimen by an outside agency or by the customary behavior of the material.

In the former classification will fall quenching or distorting of the specimen; these two quite different acts have the same general effect. If a specimen is heated to such a temperature that a new phase is formed—one which is not stable at ordinary temperatures—and the specimen is chilled quickly, e.g., by dropping it in liquid nitrogen, it may not transform completely to the low-temperature form because the transformation proceeds slowly enough that the mobility of the ions drops essentially to zero before they can move to their proper location. The high-temperature form is "frozen-in"; it may persist indefinitely at room temperature.

Consider now the heat content plots in Fig. II-13 and bear in mind that (Fig. I-5) the free energy of this frozen-in phase is higher than that of the low-temperature form so the tendency to transform is always present. If the specimen is now heated, the probability of reversion to the lower state becomes greater because of the added vibrational energy. When the temperature becomes high enough, the ions are sufficiently mobile to regain the low-temperature form. As they drop into their

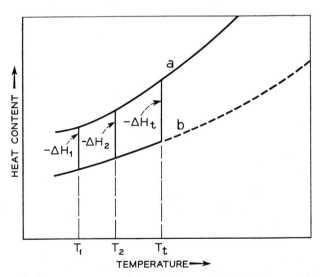

Fig. II-13. Heat content vs temperature for a material having a crystallographic phase transition.

If the material in the high-temperature form a is cooled rapidly far below the transition temperature, T_t, it may retain the a structure. If it is now heated it may give up its surplus energy below T_t and revert to the stable form b. The energy released will vary with the temperature at which the event occurs.

proper places, the excess energy must be given up in the form of heat; the amount of this heat will depend on the temperature at which the reversion takes place. Reversion at T_1 of Fig. II-13 would yield a heat effect of ΔH_1 while if the specimen remained in the high-temperature form until T_2 the heat effect would increase to ΔH_2. (In the general case, the heat capacities of the higher-temperature species are greater so $d\Delta H/dT$ is positive.) If, by some chance, the material did nothing prior to the transformation temperature, there would be no heat effect because the transformation would no longer be needed.

Note that a very thoroughly quenched specimen ought to persist in the high-temperature form to greater temperatures than a less well-quenched specimen because it has a regular structure; imperfections (see below) would tend to cause earlier reversion. Variations in quenching will cause variations in both temperature and magnitude of the thermal effect.

Any treatment of the specimen which distorts the lattice markedly may also produce exothermal effects (see Chapter III). The resulting structure will not have the long-range regularity of a well-quenched specimen; in fact, a fairly continuous variation from the ordered interior to the greatly distorted or even amorphous surface ought to occur. This high-energy condition, like the quenched state, can persist until the vibrational movement is enough to permit reversion to the ordered lattice. Since the reversion will tend to heat the specimen locally, the commencement of reversion may heat the next most disordered neighbors enough so that they in turn drop back, giving up their energy to the next, etc. The reversion could in this case appear as a well-defined exotherm. One may also postulate, however, a condition in which small region after small region gives up energy without inducing any reversion by neighbors. The observed effect in this latter case would be an apparent decrease in the heat capacity of the entire specimen. An example is brannerite.

Brannerite is a multiple oxide of titanium and uranium of rather variable composition. Apparently, during the time since its formation, the internal bombardment due to its own radioactive decay has rendered it amorphous—at least to the limits of detection by X-ray diffraction. A result of this occurrence is that various specimens of the mineral show different thermal effects and the thermal effects of most interest are exothermal (Fig. II-14); the additional energy taken up during the destruction of the original lattice is released as the various ions again fall into an ordered arrangement. Variations of these exothermal effects have been related by Kulp, Volchok, and Holland (K47) to the age of the mineral.

Adler and Puig (A1) showed that if specimens of brannerite from Cordoba, Spain, were heated at 550°C for varying periods the first exothermic reaction diminishes (Fig. II-15) while the second peak increases.

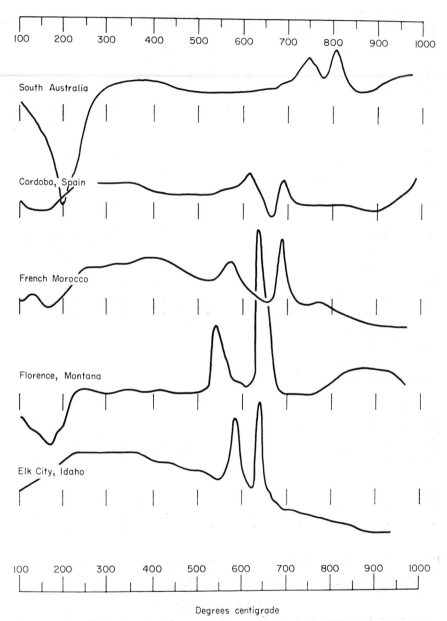

FIG. II-14. Thermal curves of brannerite. From Adler and Puig (A1).
*The variable appearance of thermograms of the mineral is due partly to its varia-
ble composition but partly also to its history.*

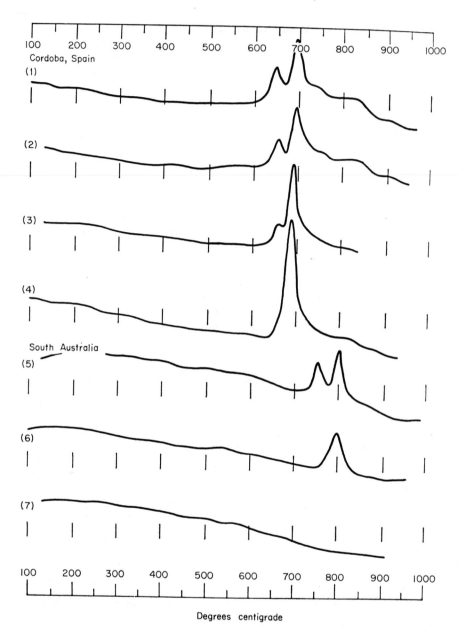

FIG. II-15. Progressive heating of brannerites: (1) 3 hours at 550°C; (2) 5 hours at 550°C; (3) 7 hours at 550°C; (4) 9 hours at 550°C; (5) 1 hour at 685°C; (6) 3 hours at 705°C; (7) 6 hours at 770°C. From Adler and Puig (A1).
The annealing permits reordering of the lattice.

After 9 hours heating at 550°C, the first peak appears only as a barely discernible shoulder on the second peak. Adler and Puig pointed out that the area under this last peak was greater than the combined area under the two peaks for the untreated material. They attributed this increased area after the heat treatment to absorption of thermal energy from the furnace. This is, of course, a rather improbable event; the heating would tend to enable movement toward a *more* rather than a *less* stable state. A more likely explanation can be found by observing the shifting base line.

In the run on the unheated specimen there is a continual exothermic tendency. This may be only ordinary base line drift but it may also be principally—or at least substantially—reversion to a stable crystal structure. The appearance of peaks at reproducible temperatures implies the existence of metastable states. The two metastable states in the brannerite from Cordoba are clearly, even though not greatly, separated. The rather deep "valley" between them, ca 660°C, implies only that there are not many highly energetic particles or regions in the second (more stable) of the two metastable states. The heating at 550°C permits movement enough to allow the higher-energy state regions to drop to the lower-energy state as shown not only by the enhancement of the second peak at the expense of the first but also by the gradual shifting of the first peak to higher temperatures as the material gains in stability. The increase in area of the single peak over the sum of the two peaks is due not to any absorption of energy from the furnace but to the consolidation of the high-energy states into a fairly narrow energy band. The base line shift because of the annealing process not only increases the population of this band but also shifts the reference line giving a further increase in area.

Similarly, the heating at progressively higher temperatures (curves 5, 6, and 7 of Fig. II-15) moves the first peak to a somewhat higher temperature, then destroys it—with some gain by the second peak. Heating for several hours on a temperature (770°C) corresponding to a point on the return slope of the first peak in an unheated specimen completely removes the second peak because the ions can move around enough to revert to the ordered arrangement.

Quenching and distortion will have one important common characteristic: irreproducibility. Stable states are obviously more easily produced and repeated than unstable states; the apparently exact reproduction of a given state of quenching should be difficult and in most cases fortuitous. (Quenching of very sluggish systems, e.g., polymer melts, is very probably an exception to this last statement.)

The last major group of exothermal reactions comprises those reversions which occur as a part of the ordinary behavior of the specimen. In a number of cases, a reaction occurs such that it leaves a metastable product which sooner or later reverts to a stable form. Two well-known examples are the kaolin minerals and basic magnesium carbonate.

The kaolin minerals undergo two reactions in particular which distinguish them and which are used for identification: a dehydroxylation in the 500–700°C range and an exothermal rearrangement ca. 1000°C. The dehydroxylation of kaolinite yields a product generally referred to as *meta*-kaolinite; the structure and nature of it have been the subject of considerable discussion. Whatever the nature of this intermediate, it rearranges ca. 1000°C to mullite or γ-alumina plus cristobalite—possibly depending on the specimen, possibly on the experimental conditions during and after the dehydroxylation.

Similarly, the dehydroxylation-dehydration of basic magnesium carbonate apparently leaves the material with the original lattice even after several of the constituent particles have gone out of it. This is unstable, of course, so it soon collapses to the magnesium carbonate–magnesium oxide structure. In carbon dioxide atmospheres the collapse is a multistep process.

The outstanding feature of exothermal reactions of this last type is the reproducibility of the effect. Under ordinary experimentation, the initial reaction produces a repeatable intermediate state, so this intermediate state collapses or reacts at a repeatable temperature. These exothermal reactions can properly be used as part of an identification.

2.6. Second-Order Transitions

Second-order transitions involve a discontinuous change in heat capacity. Occurrence of such a transition during a differential thermal analysis run will result in a change in direction which, with small samples, will be discernibly angular.

The over-all shape of the thermal effect will depend on the type of material. Second-order transitions in inorganic materials such as Curie points involve an increase in heat capacity (or specific heat) followed by a sudden decrease (Fig. II-16). This bears a moderate resemblance to ordinary first-order transitions and the peaks will vary in appearance from being just small (because of no true heat of transition) peaks (Fig. II-17) down to mere discontinuities in the base line.

In contrast, polymeric materials will ordinarily show an increase (Fig. II-18) in specific heat at the glass transition temperature as motion of chain segments becomes possible.

Since there is no mechanism for additional absorption up to the time of the transition temperature, the appearance of the thermogram will be quite different from that of an inorganic specimen. If the angle is not

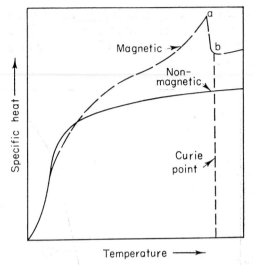

Fig. II-16. Specific heat for a magnetic and a nonmagnetic material. From Blum *et al.* (B57).

The heat capacity increases just prior to the Curie point but since no phase change occurs there is no ΔH of transition. The heat capacity simply drops off suddenly.

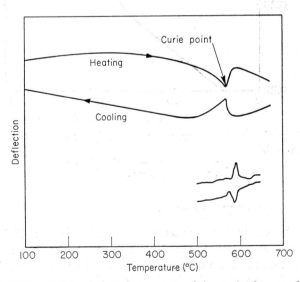

Fig. II-17. Differential thermal analysis curves of (upper) Blum *et al.* (B57) and (lower) Garn (G6).

The present author obtained the lower peaks using the sample holder of Fig. IV-15b.

well-defined and if the heating rate is high enough to obtain a sizable deflection the thermal effect observed will appear almost sigmoidal, but tending to return toward some value of ΔT lower than the peak (see Chapter V, Sec. 5.6).

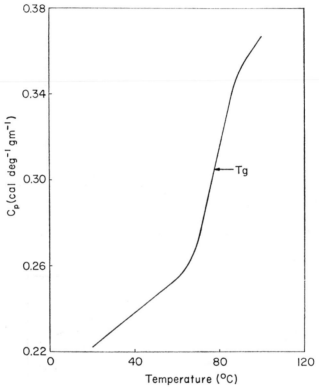

FIG. II-18. Specific heat vs temperature for a polymer about the glass transition. From Strella (S65).

For polymers, the specific heat increases at the glass transition because another mode of absorption of energy becomes possible.

2.7. Measurement of Temperature

At present, temperature measurement can be done sufficiently accurately by thermocouples and recording potentiometers. The accuracy will be dependent on the type of measuring system as described in Chapter XVII. Linearity—or approximate linearity—of recorder response to temperature requires considerable effort. The quantity usually recorded is the thermal emf, the nonlinearity of which varies considerably from one combination to another (see Fig. XVI-1). Thermocouples become contaminated and most other systems use comparison measurements so occasional calibration is worthwhile.

If the experimenter is not measuring the sample temperature directly —or indirectly by measuring the reference temperature—the system should be calibrated. The calibration will provide a measure of the temperature lag in the system or, more specifically, a measure of the temperature difference between the sample and the point of measurement. This calibration will be necessary for unusual experimental techniques which the investigator may concoct for use in special problems.

More sensitive determinations can be made by use of thermistors, but for most purposes at present such a high degree of sensitivity is not needed.

The ingenious work of Barshad (B9) is principally of historical importance now but the technique of temperature calibration will be of occasional interest and we shall have reason to examine some of his conclusions. Barshad contrived a temperature scale by using small quantities of known materials in the sample or reference wells to give a number of thermal effects (Fig. II-19) which then served as temperature indices. This procedure eliminated need for temperature-measuring apparatus, resulting in a comparatively economical apparatus. (The technique of differential thermal analysis has been developed to a level such that one would now use Barshad's procedure only for instruction or as a shift.)

The inclusion of these several materials is not necessarily a very serious handicap considering that only a few milligrams are used while his sample can hold well over ½ gm. of alumina. By including two or three of these salts (Fig. II-20), Barshad suggests, the operator may obtain a temperature scale if he has any justification for assuming that the heating rate is essentially linear. If the variation in the rate of heating is small, a few more points would help establish the scale.

In addition, Barshad devised a way to check the sensitivity of his differential thermocouple, galvanometer, and optical system at the temperature range of any reaction. He added a portion of a temperature indicator to some of the sample and placed this around the thermocouple (with undiluted sample above and below it). In the reference well he placed small quantities of other temperature indicators to bracket the peak as closely as possible. Since the first temperature indicator was chosen to give a thermal effect as near as possible to the maximum deflection of the sample peak, a rather large deflection already existed when this indicator showed its effect (Fig. II-20). By interpolation, the operator could determine the reference temperature at the time the indicator in the sample went through its change and, knowing the temperature at which the change took place for that indicator, he could ascertain the temperature

difference, relate this to the magnitude of the deflection, and calculate
the sensitivity. This was particularly necessary for any quantitative work
because galvanometers are current-drawing instruments. For potentiometer recorders, this procedure would be less important. A major objection
to the general technique is that it yields curves as given in Fig. II-20,
where most of the effects are from the added materials. We can assume
that Barshad also ran specimens with few or no indicators.

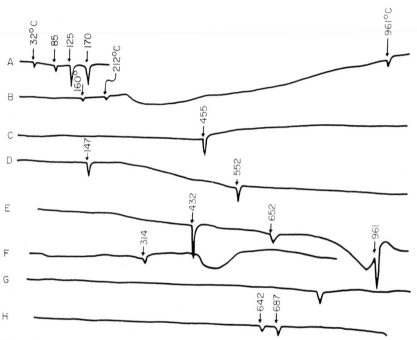

Fig. II-19. Differential thermal analyses curves of salts useful for temperature
calibration. From Barshad (B9). The salts are: A, 10 mg NH_4NO_3; B, 3 mg $AgNO_3$;
C, 2 mg AgCl; D, 15 mg AgI; E, 20 mg Ag_2SO_4; F, 2 mg $NaNO_3$; G, 2 mg NaCl;
H, 3 mg Na_2MoO_4.

*The salts were dispersed in 10 mg of Al_2O_3 and centered around the thermocouple.
As many salts as the operator felt were needed could be incorporated into the
reference.*

Barshad's work showing the effect of distance from the thermocouple
on the area of the peak has greater significance than has been noted. The
rapid decrease (Table II-1) of the measured thermal effect of kaolin and
the striking variation in the curves for ammonium nitrate (Fig. II-21)
show that only the material near the thermocouple has a worthwhile effect on the thermocouple. The rest is of no value and need not exist.

Ergo, huge samples are of no merit; smaller samples will produce nearly the same effect. Note that 2–15 mg of temperature indicator is generally enough to give a sizable thermal effect. Let us confine the conclusion, however, to the phase transformations; other factors enter into decomposition reactions.

Note that the exothermic reaction shows a quite different peak height vs position relation from that of the phase changes. The rush of hot gases

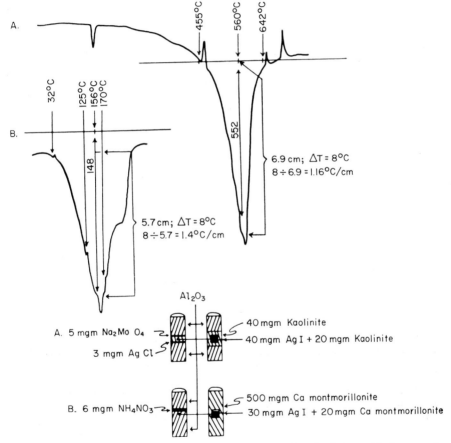

Fig. II-20. DTA curves of a Ca-montmorillonite and a kaolinite with impressed temperature reference points suitable for measuring the sensitivity of the DTA apparatus. The silver iodide peaks at 552°C in A and 148°C in B occur at reference temperatures of 560° and 156°C, respectively. The 8°C lag in each case gives a measure of the sensitivity of the recording system at that temperature. From Barshad (B9).

The variation is due to nonlinearity of thermal emf.

from the bottom past the thermocouple can be expected to show a noticeable thermal effect while a similar reaction at the top will push the hot gases into the surrounding atmosphere. Note further that the phase changes, unlike the decomposition, show a somewhat greater effect at the top. This is due to lack of symmetry; the material at the bottom is in contact with the metal block and can gain heat quickly while the material at the top has a corresponding exposure to the atmosphere. Since it cannot gain heat quickly the temperature will lag more and the deflection will be greater. Let us confine the conclusion, again, to the phase transformations.

TABLE II-1

PEAK AREA OF THE ENDOTHERMIC BREAK IN THE
DIFFERENTIAL THERMAL ANALYSIS CURVES OF
50 MG OF KAOLINITE DISPERSED IN AN INCREAS-
ING VOLUME AND CENTERED AROUND THE
THERMOCOUPLE

Volume of sample (cm³)	Peak area (cm²)
0.040	4.06
0.130	3.02
0.220	2.55
0.310	2.23
0.400	1.94
0.490	1.62

2.8. Effect of Dilution with an Inert Material

Specimens are often diluted with aluminum oxide or other inert material. In some cases, this dilution is to avoid such a high-temperature difference signal that it cannot be kept on the scale of the recording system; another reason is to try to match heat-transfer characteristics of specimen and reference, a third reason is to obtain a series of specimens of varying concentrations to enable quantitative estimation of the active material in another specimen. So long as the effect examined is a change in state rather than a decomposition the effect of dilution should be only the diminution of the peak area and height. The temperature of the change should be unaffected by dilution.

One hazard that can be avoided by dilution is sintering. Some powdered materials will shrink on heating to such a degree that the specimen must pull away from the sample holder. The heat-transfer changes and the base line will ordinarily shift.

If the purpose is to match heat-transfer characteristics substantial dilutions are required. If the material used as reference is used to dilute the sample, the effect of small additions is a diminution of both heat effect and base line signals so there is no gain. As the effect of dilution is nonlinear, the sample eventually assumes very nearly the same heat-transfer characteristics as the reference; since the signal from the heat effect is attenuated linearly, a gain in signal-to-noise ratio is achieved. Electronic amplification can restore the differential temperature peak to a readable level and with a lesser base line displacement.

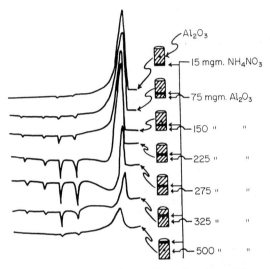

Fig. II-21. DTA curves of 15 mg of NH₄NO₃ placed at different positions with respect to the thermocouples. From Barshad (B9).
The maximum response is obtained when the thermocouple is in contact with the active material.

Dilution—as a technique for smoothing base lines—must be used with considerable caution, otherwise the experimenter will have difficulty reconciling his data to others. Again it is matter of diffusion of atmospheres in and out during decompositions, oxidations, and such. Compare the several curves of Fig. II-22 and compare these to Fig. I-4. At the low concentrations, the over-all reaction

$$2FeCO_3 + \tfrac{1}{2}O_2 \rightarrow Fe_2O_3 + 2CO_2$$

can proceed almost without hindrance because the diluting particles create additional diffusion paths for gases without a corresponding need for said gases. The oxygen can diffuse in rapidly enough to sustain the highly energetic oxidation. As the siderite concentration is increased the nitrogen and freshly released carbon dioxide fill the open regions enough to slow the oxidation briefly (curve H). At one-third siderite (curve G), the carbonate decomposition, needing no gas supply, is proceeding rapidly enough to balance the heat effect of the oxidation. As the concentration of siderite is increased, the ratio of inert-to-active material decreases so the effect of diffusion is quite pronounced.

The over-all effect, then, is a change in shape of the curve so great that there is no discernible relation between the more dilute and the undiluted specimens.

We may conclude from this that samples which decompose may show —upon dilution—a marked change of shape of their differential thermal analysis peaks under static atmosphere conditions. Dynamic atmos-

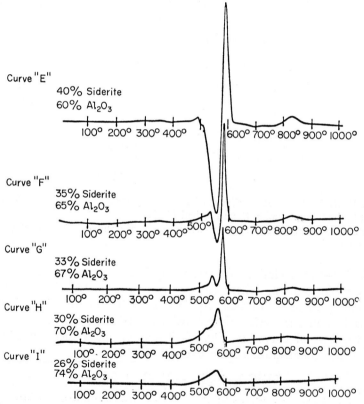

FIG. II-22. Differential thermal analyses of diluted specimens of siderite. From Rowland and Jonas (R33).

The shape of the "peak" changes markedly because of the changing access of oxygen.

pheres will maintain an essentially fixed concentration of each component about each particle so dilution should present no untoward results.

Barrall and Rogers (B7) show (Fig. II-23) that liquid diluents can be useful with solid specimens. In essence, the liquid surrounding the particles represses dehydration because the gaseous layer on the surface approaches the equivalent of an atmosphere of water vapor (see Chapter VII). When the water vapor pressure exceeds atmospheric, the decomposition proceeds. On Carborundum, the escape of water vapor permits a less sharp decomposition. Barrall and Rogers (B7) also pointed out that solubility of the specimen in the liquid diluent would depress the melting point, but this is to be expected.

The reason that dilution is effective in matching heat-transfer characteristics is that the surface properties, rather than bulk properties, present the greater resistance to flow of heat. Consider an aggregation of

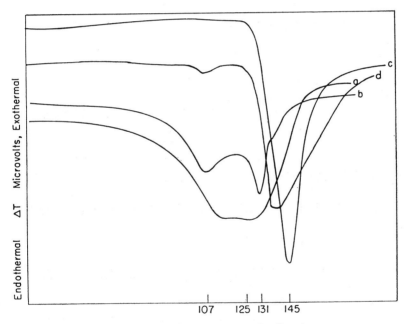

Fig. II-23. Differential thermograms of copper acetate and copper sulfate at a heating rate of 15°C per minute and a ΔT sensitivity of 200 μv per 3 inches. (a) Copper sulfate diluted to 6.5% with Carborundum; (b) Copper sulfate diluted to 20% with Nujol; (c) Copper acetate diluted to 20% with Nujol; (d) Copper acetate diluted to 6.9% with Carborundum. From Barrall and Rogers (B8).

The Nujol traps and retains the water until the vapor pressure approaches the ambient pressure.

particles of sample material, *s*, and of diluent, *D*, with the understanding that the diluent is the same material as the reference. The addition of a small portion of *D* to a specimen comprised previously only of *s* has little effect on the heat-transfer characteristics of the specimen because the great majority of contacts are still between particles of *s*.

As greater numbers of *D* replace *s*, the *s–s* contacts diminish, being replaced by *s–D*, contacts. In the region of predominance of *s–D* contacts the conduction of heat will be limited to something approximating the conductance of particles of the poorer conductor. At either end of the range, i.e., high *s–s* or *D–D* contacts, the conduction would approach that of particles of the pure material. The diluents generally used are not good conductors (in aggregations of particles); for this reason they are effective in the middle range. It is only necessary to diminish the *s–s* contacts to a relatively small fraction to approach fairly close to the heat conductance of the pure diluent and hence the reference.

2.9. Pretreatment of Specimens

Like most other questions in thermal analysis the preparation of a specimen for differential thermal analysis must be considered separately for each specimen or group of specimens. Some authors have found it expedient to premelt specimens to erase any effects of thermal history; others are interested specifically in this same thermal history. The experimentor may wish to compare a number of specimens "as received" and possibly again in some standard initial state.

In general, the decision will depend on the use to which the data will be put. If the study is of the intrinsic properties of pure material, pretreatment to eliminate effects of impurities and history would be proper; if the study is of the effect of some condition or act or if processing decisions depend on some details of the raw material, pretreatment is, in diagnostic jargon, contraindicated.

Some pretreatment to eliminate a material or to bring the specimen to the chosen standard initial state may be useful. The most frequently used pretreatments for eliminating interferences are acid-leaching to remove carbonates and hydrogen peroxide treatment to remove organic matter. The present author has used the acid-leaching (G12) but has no experience with the latter. Beech and Holdridge (B22), however, show an example (Fig. II-24) of the effect of such a treatment. Several clays have substantial amounts of organic matter because of the conditions of formation; ball clays are among them. Oxidation of the organic matter during differential thermal analysis in air or even degradation in nitrogen will throw considerable doubt on any data inferred from thermal effects below ca. 700°C so the pretreatment is imperative. The peroxidetrated clay shows thermal effects easily identified as typical of kandites.

Other kinds of clays are subject to variation of the loosely held water according to source and recent history. The variations cause substantial differences in the low-temperature portion of the thermogram; this in turn gives rise to doubt of identity of specimens. MacKenzie and Farquharson (M6) recommended a standard treatment for clays to bring them to a reproducible state of hydration. The clays are equilibrated over a saturated solution of magnesium nitrate.

The importance of knowing the starting material in solid-state reactions is shown rather clearly by some data of Wilburn and Thomasson

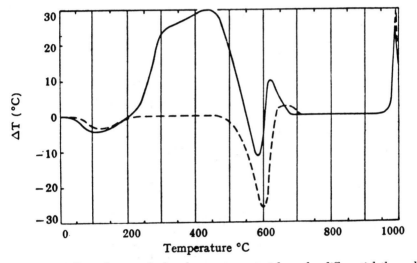

Fig. II-24. Effect of removal of carbonaceous material on the differential thermal curve of a black ball clay: ———, original clay; - - - -, clay after removal of carbonaceous matter. From Beech and Holdridge (B22).

The oxidation of the organic matter could easily obscure a reaction. Note that the peak ca. 600°C is shifted downward in the original clay due to dilution of the atmosphere.

(W34) shown in Figs. II-25 and II-26. These authors were studying reactions of glass-making materials. The silica types used, both better than 99% pure, were Loch Aline sand for the coarser grain sizes and Welsh silica flour for the finer. They found that these reacted quite differently with calcium carbonate (Fig. II-25).

The possibility that particle size difference was the reason for the differences in reactions—particularly C as compared to A or B in Fig. II-25—was checked by Wilburn and Thomasson by reacting calcium carbonate with similar grain size ranges of each type of silica. They ground some Loch Aline sand to pass 200 and 300 BSS and compared the reactions of 200–300 BSS and 300–350 BSS Loch Aline sand with those of Welsh silica flour of the same size ranges (Fig. II-26). While there are minor differences between the two fractions of either silica, the two silicas react quite differently from each other; in fact, the Loch Aline sand tends to form more calcium orthosilicate while the Welsh silica flour favors the formation of calcium metasilicate.

The use and description of specially prepared materials is commendable. From time to time research workers in thermal analysis, as well as in other fields, have taken elaborate precautions to assure themselves of

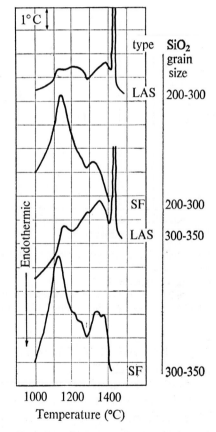

Fig. II-25. Differential thermal analyses of $3SiO_2$–$2CaCO_3$ mixtures with different types of silica and various grain sizes. $CaCO_3$ to pass 300 BSS. From Wilburn and Thomasson (W34).

The possibility existed that the particle size influenced the mode of reaction.

nearly perfect samples or sample materials. A question arises: "How can a procedure be checked by another observer without a similar preparation of sample materials?" Kissinger, McMurdie, and Simpson (K31) are to be commended for their approach:

"Reagent grade $MnCO_3$ and $FeCO_3$ were used in this study. Each of these compounds was also made in this laboratory by hydrothermal methods, care being taken to insure purity of the product. Since the materials prepared in this way did not differ significantly from the reagent grade material, the more readily available reagent grade was used."

The experimentor reporting extensive or elaborate preparative procedures should, like Kissinger *et al.*, also verify the need for them.

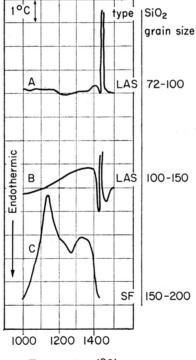

Fig. II-26. Differential thermal analyses of $3SiO_2$–$2CaCO_3$ mixtures with different types of silica and various grain sizes. $CaCO_3$ to pass 300 BSS. From Wilburn and Thomasson (W34).

The behavior is dependent on the history rather than the particle size of the specimen.

2.10. Summary

Differential thermal analysis comprises the heating and/or cooling of a specimen and reference and measuring the difference in temperature between them. Sample sizes can range over several orders of magnitude and should be chosen to suit the problem. Cylindrical specimens are most often used but other shapes can be used. The shape of the peak will depend on sample size and shape.

Exothermal reactions may occur either because of sample treatment or because of the nature of the sample itself.

Temperature calibration should be done occasionally on all systems and always on new experimental apparatus.

Dilution or pretreatment can have drastic effects on the shape of the peak.

CHAPTER III

Operational Parameters

3.1. Introduction

The major work of P. L. Arens, *A Study on the Differential Thermal Analysis of Clays and Clay Minerals* (A12), comprises an exceedingly thorough examination of differential thermal analysis empirically and to a limited degree theoretically. Because of the significance of this work, his conclusions are reviewed and the points he raised are examined in the following sections. (The relative unavailability of the work led to extensive repetition in the following paragraphs.)

Arens suggests a number of experimental factors affecting the shape of differential thermal analysis curves:

(*a*) rate of temperature rise of the furnace;
(*b*) nature of the sample holder;
(*c*) depth and radius of the sample holes in the holder;
(*d*) the measurement sites of both furnace and differential temperatures;
(*e*) nature and proportions of the thermocouples;
(*f*) the nature of the inert substance;
(*g*) the tightness of packing of the clay and inert substance in the holes;
(*h*) the effect of covering the sample holes; and
(*i*) the composition of the furnace atmosphere.

Since Arens is principally interested in clay minerals, he looks for additional factors:

(*j*) the particle size of the clay minerals present;
(*k*) the degree of crystallization;
(*l*) the cations absorbed; and
(*m*) the presence of admixtures in the clay.

He further points out that the recorded results are determined primarily by items *a, c, d, g, h, i, j,* and *k*.

He concludes regarding the effect of rate of temperature rise:

(1) There exists a systematic difference between the reactions accompanied by a loss in weight and those not accompanied by it.
(2) Types of reaction accompanied by a loss of weight are strongly influenced by the heating rate; with increasing heating rate the peak temperatures increase, as do also the peak height and peak area. But the peak range, measured as the time of reaction, decreases.
(3) If the furnace temperature is measured in the clay sample, those types of reactions in which there is no loss in weight are not affected as regards peak temperature, but are affected as regards peak height, range and area.
(4) From the results of experiments with varying heating rate, all other factors being kept constant, it is possible to compute empirically the reaction temperatures for zero rates of heating (static dehydration, etc.). These "asymptotic" reaction temperatures are of importance for correlating DTA with dehydration studies.

From his experiment with varying types of sample holders he concludes:

(1) Nickel blocks yield DTA curves with relatively flat endothermal and sharp exothermal reactions.
(2) Ceramic blocks yield curves with sharp endothermal and relatively flat exothermal reactions.
(3) All types of reactions undergo influences of the sample holder, irrespective of whether the reactions are accompanied by loss of material or not.
(4) No noticeable peak shifting is observed.

From a number of runs Arens concludes:

(1) The depth and radius of sample holes greatly affected the appearance of thermal reactions accompanied by changes in weight, as regards peak temperature, peak height, and total duration of reaction.

(2) Reactions not accompanied by changes in weight are not affected as regards peak temperature, and only slightly as regards peak height.

(3) It is possible to mask or to enhance reactions, by varying the depth and radius of the sample holes.

From his other experiments and without special examination of the effect of placement of the differential thermocouple junctions, he offers these conclusions:

(1) Deep placement of the differential thermocouple junctions in the samples yield DTA curves with relatively strong endothermic reactions in the low-temperature range and flat endothermic reactions in the high ranges.

(2) Exothermic reactions (in the high-temperature range) are recorded the best with deep placement of the differential thermocouple.

(3) For most reactions the thermocouple should be inserted in the samples without protective cover.

(4) Thermocouples fixed in the sample holders are a great advantage as regards reproducibility of data.

He summarizes the effect of the inert substance as follows:

(1) The inert material should have thermal characteristics (specific heat, heat conductivity, thermal diffusivity) as closely equal as possible to those of the clay. This requirement is never fully realizable, because the thermal characteristics of clay undergo rather sudden changes accompanying the reactions.

(2) If the furnace temperature is measured in the inert substance, an apparent peak shift is observed, the amount of which is increased with increasing radius of sample holder and increasing heating rates. This holds for all types of reactions.

(3) It is recommended that furnace temperature be measured in the clay sample.

(4) The use of calcined clay, of the same sample as is to be investigated, as inert material has no fundamental advantages over the use of calcined alumina, provided particle size distribution of the latter is not different from the clay.

Similarly, he concludes:

(1) Differences in density of packing are the most common causes of deviations from straight zero lines in temperature ranges where no reactions occur.

(2) Hard packing, considered the easiest to reproduce, is recommended for most cases, to obtain recordings with pronounced reactions and with straight zero lines.

(3) Loose packing gives rise to faint reactions, the effect lying in the same direction for all types of reaction, except probably the oxidation reaction.

Since the covering or not of the sample hole and the influence of the composition of the furnace atmosphere are so closely related, his conclusions on these two points are offered as a single unit:

(1) Covering the sample holes exerts considerable influence upon the appearance of reactions when there is a change in weight of the reactant (Fig. III-1).

(2) Reactions accompanied by loss in weight (dehydration, loss of CO_2) may be enhanced by covering while a peak shifting upwards occurs.

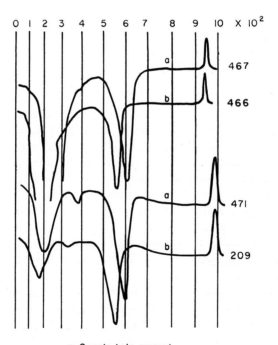

a. Sample hole covered
b. Sample hole uncovered

FIG. III-1. Thermograms of halloysite (466, 467) and of indianaite (209, 471) with covered and uncovered sample holes. From Arens (A12).

The restriction of decomposition product gases affects the temperature of decomposition.

(3) Reactions accompanied by gain in weight (oxidation) may be fully inhibited by the covering or may not be well-defined.

(4) Though covering may aid in certain cases to obtain straight zero lines, it should be avoided for general prospecting purposes.

(5) The composition of the atmosphere affects considerably the initiation and course of reactions accompanied by changes in weight.

(6) The initiation and course of dehydration reactions are influenced by the partial vapor pressure of water. The decomposition reactions of carbonates are influenced by the partial vapor pressure of CO_2 and the oxidation reactions are influenced by the partial vapor pressure of O_2 in the furnace atmosphere.

3.2. Rate of Temperature Rise

Whether or not the rate of temperature rise has a significant effect on the peak temperature depends not only on the nature of the sample but also on the manner of containing the specimen. If the sample undergoes only a change in state, the nature of the sample holder is immaterial, except for heat-transfer problems. The effect of a change of heating rate will be small in such cases and any effect will be related principally to heat-transfer considerations. Arens (A12) used heating rates of 6, 12, 18, and 21°C per minute on quartz and found no noticeable shift of transition temperature. Even the exothermic effect in kaolin was little affected.

The reactions involving loss in weight show a quite different behavior. Peak shifts of 75° are reported for kaolinite and all the weight loss reactions behave in the same manner [Kissinger (K29) found even greater shifting; see Chapter VII].

These peak shifts with temperature are quite normal and easily explained (see Chapter VII); the gases that are given off tend to inhibit further decompositions. These gases will diffuse out of the sample chamber, but this need for effusion means that the concentration of the gas will be time-dependent.

The higher the heating rate, the less gas will diffuse out before the reaction becomes very rapid. The fact that the initially released gas does not have time to diffuse out means that the concentration of gas can increase to some particular level with less total decomposition.

Assume—purely arbitrarily—that at the peak temperature at some heating rate the average partial pressure of water vapor in the vicinity of the last particles of a hydrate to decompose is one-third of an atmosphere. This heating rate is slow enough to permit fairly good interchange of gases between sample holder and furnace. If we hurry the reaction along on a run at a higher heating rate, this one-third of an atmosphere partial pressure will be reached with less than complete decomposition for two reasons. The time interval between the start of decomposition and the achievement of this partial pressure has not allowed the same amount of effusion, and the presence of the water vapor in higher concentration has repressed the decomposition. Yet at this same pressure of water vapor our sample should be at the peak temperature of the first experiment. Since we still have undecomposed material, the peak temperature in this second run must obviously be higher than that in the first.

A greater problem than mere peak shifting is the possibility of different degrees of peak shifting; i.e., differential thermal analysis peaks of a single specimen may be shifted unequally in such a manner that one of them is obscured. A prime example is the series of thermograms of gypsum (Fig. III-2) obtained by Dilaktorskii and Arkhangel 'skaja

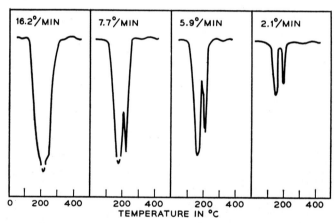

Fig. III-2. Effect of heating rate on the dehydration of gypsum. From Dilaktorskii and Arkhangel 'skaja (D11a).

Very high heating rates may completely mask a thermal effect.

(D11a). At very high heating rates the second peak is nearly covered by the first. We may reasonably assume that the rapid heating produces water vapor so rapidly that it cannot diffuse away from the specimen nearly so fast as it is supplied (see Chapter VII). By the time the center of the specimen has reached the first decomposition temperature under the extant atmosphere conditions—ca. one atmosphere of water vapor—the outside of the specimen, in contact with the wall, is already warm enough to start the second decomposition. This decomposition will go quite rapidly since no atmosphere change will impede it; the first and second reaction peaks are consequently very close together.

As the heating rate is lowered the temperature difference across the sample becomes lower, not only because thermal diffusion can transfer heat and hence can keep the specimen nearer thermal equilibrium but also because diffusion of water vapor out of the specimen diminishes the temperature required for this decomposition. At a quite low heating rate the first reaction is essentially complete before the second begins.

Not merely the separation of reactions but the general appearance of thermal effects can be affected by the heating rate. During the heating of ferrous carbonate (Fig. III-3), for example, the higher rate of heating causes evolution of carbon dioxide rapidly enough to slow the diffusion of oxygen back into the specimen holder. This causes a broadening and flattening of the oxidation exotherm so that the oxidation is not complete until the specimen is more than 50°C hotter than at the slower rate. Atmosphere effects are discussed in Chapter VII.

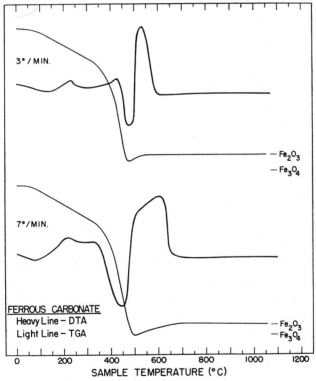

Fɪɢ. III-3. Differential thermal analysis-thermogravimetric analysis patterns of FeCO₃ at 3° and 7°C per minute. From Kissinger *et al.* (K31).

Different rates of heating may cause substantial alteration of the appearance of the thermogram.

As early as 1923, Houldsworth and Cobb (H25) reported the influence of the rate of temperature rise on the reaction ranges of kaolinite; i.e., at high-temperature-rise velocities the dehydration reaction is delayed over 100°C above the "equilibrium" temperature. There are several factors involved in the shift in temperature and in the increase in area of the peak that accompanies the increase in temperature. At low heating rates the decomposition product of kaolinite, that is, water vapor, can diffuse out into the atmosphere readily and the partial pressure of water is never high. The entire decomposition may then be carried out without the partial pressure even approaching one atmosphere.

Accounting for the peak area is rather more difficult. The difficulty arises principally from the need to offer a mechanism or hypothesis that will explain the increased area with increasing rate of temperature rise for kaolinite as well as for the inversion of quartz [cf. Arens (A12)]. While there is no shift in temperature for the quartz inversion the rate of change of peak area with heating rate is approximately the same as for the decomposition of kaolinite. Consequently, the change of heat of reaction with the temperature cannot be cited to explain this change in area.

The probable cause of the increasing area with the higher heating rates is again the problem of heat transfer. A differential signal exists because the heat is being used for a process other than increasing the temperature, but this other process cannot continue indefinitely because the quantity of sample is limited. This differential signal is dependent on—among other things—the amount of material reacting at any given time; this in turn depends on the rate at which heat is supplied. The given amount of material will require a given number of extra calories to carry out the process so the rate of supply of extra heat integrated over the time this extra heat is supplied ought to be directly proportional to the quantity of material. The error lies in failure to detect the heat and the failure is due to the technique. The ease of heat transfer which makes differential thermal analysis useful in detecting reactions imposes a hardship in measuring the amount of heat.

In essence, the low rates of heating allow heat to diffuse in or out of the specimen in a manner only slightly affected by the reaction. With differential temperatures of a few tenths of a degree the flow in both specimen and reference are still nearly the same. Now let the heating rate be increased, say, three times. A steeper gradient within the specimen and reference will be set up and a steady state ensues in which the differential temperature is again zero or nearly so.

As the transition temperature front with its additional heat requirement moves inward, the wall continues to rise steadily in temperature, but as the center approaches the transition, its heating rate tends to decrease because it sees, essentially, a constant temperature front moving inward from the wall and shielding the center from the higher gradient between this front and the wall. There is, consequentially, a volume— substantial at first but constantly diminishing—which is influenced only secondarily by the temperature of the wall. This is the reason not only for the larger differential temperature but also, because the transport of heat is dependent on time as well as temperature, for the greater $\int \Delta T \, dt$. The hot wall simply cannot supply heat at the rate required by the heat capacity of the specimen until it has also supplied that necessary to carry out the transition.

An optimum heating rate cannot often be determined immediately or *a priori* so a generally useful heating rate is used routinely or for initial examination. Most apparatus are designed to permit several rates. The most common heating rate is 10°C/minute. It is the rate used most often by the present author (see Chapter XVII) and is the one recommended to the International Geological Congress (M6). For quantitative work a constant heating rate is recommended (see Chapter V).

Discussion of the effects of rate of heating must include the work of Keith and Tuttle (K14) who used rates on the order of 0.5°C per minute in their study of quartz. For lack of temperature-recording techniques that are really suitable for the purpose, they selected a pair of materials having crystallographic phase changes closely above and below the quartz inversion and obtained the inversion temperatures by interpolation as shown in Fig. III-4. Note that it is only necessary for their needs that the cooling—or heating—be nondiscontinuous through the range between the cryolite and potassium sulfate inversions; it can be nonlinear so long as it is always reproducibly nonlinear.

With this slow heating rate Keith and Tuttle were able to study variations in quartz. Not only were they able to recognize variations within a single quartz deposit as in Fig. III-5, but even differences within a crystal as in Fig. III-6. We may reasonably conclude that low heating rates are usable and necessary for detecting differences in close-lying inversion temperatures.

3.3. Influence of the Sample Holder

The means of supporting the sample and providing for temperature measurement has been the subject of abundant controversy. Let us recall the description of differential thermal analysis in Chapter II and consider specifically the step from differential calorimetry to differential thermal analysis. We permitted heat to flow between the sample and the reference materials in order that the difference signal might return to zero, thus enabling detection of a number of successive reactions. The passage of heat between the sample and the reference specimens necessarily reduces the temperature difference and, therefore, the signal available for detection and measurement. The use of differential thermal analysis is a sacrifice of total sensitivity to gain another kind of sensitivity —sensitivity to any thermal effect almost independent of previous occurrences. We must examine, then, the consequences of the extreme cases of well-separated specimens as in differential calorimetry and of rather intimately connected specimens as in a high-conductivity differential thermal analysis sample block.

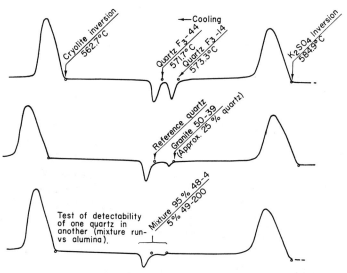

Fig. III-4. Chart records illustrating thermal curves for inversion on cooling (rising-temperature records are similar). From Keith and Tuttle (K14).

The inversion break temperature is taken as the beginning of the heat effect, defined as the intersection of a line drawn through the first straight portion of the thermal curve with the base line.

Considerable evidence has been presented to show that sample holders in the form of isolated cups have greater sensitivity than blocks. The present author (G12) has done his part in continuing the discussion, concluding that isolated cups will provide a gain in sensitivity but that the sample vessel must be thick enough to provide temperature homogeneity around the sample.

The author has since concluded that to rely on one type of sample holder for all types of samples would be to risk failure in studying half or more of the samples that have needed examination; the author has,

ply of a little extra heat, but this will not normally be of any consequence unless one is attempting to describe the curve mathematically
(see Chapter V).

3.6. Influence of the Nature and Proportions of the Thermocouples

The present author reports, in another chapter, work in which metal
shields over the thermocouples were used routinely. In other works, thermocouple wires as small as 0.003 inch and as large as 0.030 inch have
been used. There is no significant qualitative effect. A systematic evaluation of quantitative effects was not made, except to note that there is a
considerable loss of sensitivity with shielded thermocouples and particularly a sluggish response with shielded thermocouples with ungrounded
junctions.

Vassallo and Harden (V3) report (Fig. III-20) that change from 40- to
28-gage thermocouple wire resulted in a 15% diminution in peak height,

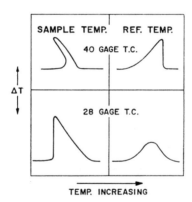

FIG. III-20. Character of boiling endotherms using sample and reference temperature measurement. From Vassallo and Harden (V3).
The curve at the upper left is typical for specimens that superheat.

but this is a change from 0.08 mm to 0.32 mm diameter wire in tubes
that are only 1.5 to 2.0 mm in diameter. The larger thermocouple wires
occupy a significant cross section of the sample tube.

Since the thermocouple must be heated (or cooled) to deliver the
proper indication there must be some deleterious effects with unduly
large thermocouples because of the heat capacity and thermal conductivities of the wires. Some authors (see Chapter V) have found it necessary to take the thermal properties of the thermocouple wires into
account, but this will generally be unnecessary.

in fact, had to develop nearly a dozen ways to hold particular specimens. Let us examine the effect of the sample holder on a simple phase transformation (Fig. III-7). The thermal effect is quite sharply defined in the block, A, and in the thicker-walled cups, B and C. The return to the base line is rapid in A because the specimen diameter is small and the total magnitude of the specimen does not matter greatly. B and C are more spread out because the system is approaching more closely differential calorimetry; in these cases, and in D and E, the entire specimen has to be warmed up so the transfer of heat to and throughout the sample will take a greater time. The ratios of the total heights to the half-widths of the deflections are about 25, 23, 39, 11, and 14 for

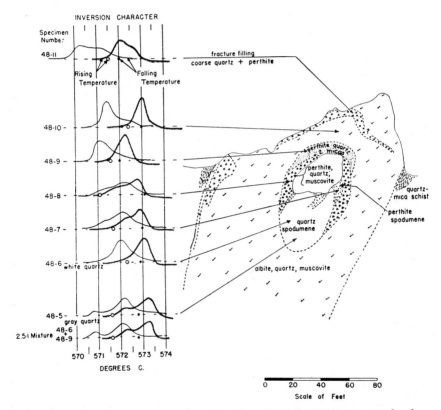

Fig. III-5. Quartz inversion results of Keith and Tuttle (K14) on samples from the Helen Beryl Mine pegmatite, Custer County, South Dakota, shown in relation to a vertical section after M. H. Staatz and J. J. Norton of the U. S. Geological Survey.

At least four different types of quartz can be recognized and each sample shows evidence of containing more than one type of quartz.

A, B, C, D, and E, respectively. The apparent reason for the relatively
low peak heights for D and E is the relatively poor conduction around
the sample holder itself; this would result in a nonuniform temperature
at the edge of the specimen and hence a nonsymmetrical thermal gradient. This nonsymmetrical thermal gradient would mean, in turn, that
some portion of the material in the immediate vicinity of the thermocouple would, during steady heating, be at some higher temperature
than another corresponding portion. When this warmer region begins to
transform—before the other—the usual heat flux from that direction is
diminished and the center of the sample begins to lag in temperature;
i.e., the endotherm begins. The endothermic reaction will progress at
different rates in different directions and hence will occur over a greater
time interval and the center will not be the last region to reach the
transition temperature (Fig. III-8). This will appear also as a greater

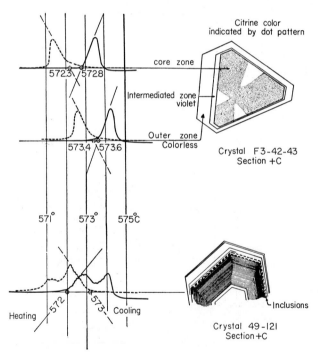

FIG. III-6. Character of the heat effect obtained on two zoned single crystals.
Crystal F3–42–43 was separated into two fractions as illustrated and the inversion
of each fraction is shown (solid lines = thermal effect on heating, dashed lines =
thermal effect on cooling). From Keith and Tuttle (K14).

The very low heating rate permits clear distinction of materials transforming at
temperatures only a degree apart.

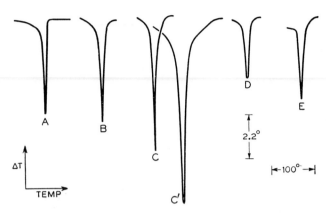

FIG. III-7. Thermograms of 170 mg of potassium sulfate in various specimen holders. The sample size was determined by the capacity of the block. A, Platinum block cavities 5 × 10 mm. B, Platinum cups, 0.6-mm wall, 6–8 mm ID × 10 mm. Aluminum oxide, ca. 110 mg, mixed in with 170 mg specimen to fill cup. Cups supported in firebrick block. C, Same specimen as B, but cups supported on wire loops. D, Quartz cups, 1-mm wall, ca. 6 mm ID × 10 mm. Aluminum oxide, ca. 20 mg, mixed with specimen to fill cup. Cups supported on wire loops. E, Platinum cups fabricated from 0.06-mm sheet, same specimen as B and C. Cups supported on wire loops.

The relative broadness of D and E suggests the need for good thermal conductivity around the specimen.

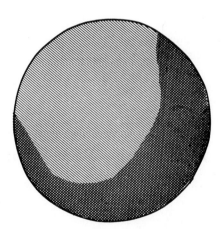

FIG. III-8. Representation of an unsymmetrically heated specimen. The progress of the high-temperature form (crosshatched area) will leave material untransformed (diagonal lines) when the center reaches the transition temperature.

Transfer of heat around the specimen should be more rapid than transfer of heat into the specimen.

temperature interval so the endotherm is spread out to a greater degree than in the case of the thicker specimen holders (see Chapter II).

The transfer of heat from the edge of the sample container into the sample has been treated by Speil (S40), Vold (V10), Arens (A12), Vold and Vold (V11), Sewell and Honeybourne (S19a), Smythe (S36), and Allison (A4). There is, however, an almost equally significant problem of transferring the heat from the furnace winding to the sample surface. In considering this problem let us assume only at this time that the sample and reference material are in symmetric locations within a cylindrical vertical furnace. Now let us consider a common case of a ceramic tube with the heater winding on the outside heating a sample block inside the tube. There is customarily no direct mechanical contact between the furnace tube and the sample block.

The question now arises concerning the choice of materials for the sample block. The question of block vs cup will be considered separately. Even the casual observer will realize immediately that a metallic block provides greater temperature homogeneity within the block than does a ceramic or other nonmetallic block. The relative mass of metallic and ceramic blocks will be discussed later. The immediate question of the relative efficiency of moving the heat to the sample entails consideration of thermal conductivity, heat capacity, and thermal emissivity. At lower temperatures the heat-transfer coefficients of the two types of block and furnace wall to air must be considered as well as the thermal conductivity of air or other vapor. At the temperatures at which radiation is the principal method by which heat is conveyed, the relative emissivity of the two materials is of major importance. Polished metallic strips have emissivities ranging from less than 0.1 near room temperature to the order of 0.23 at 1000°C. From the equation for rate of interchange of heat between bodies A and B

$$Q_{ab} = \frac{\sigma(t_a^4 - t_b^4)}{(1/\epsilon_a) + (1/\epsilon_b) - 1}$$

where Q_{ab} is the rate of heat flow from A to B, σ is the Stefan-Boltzman constant, t_a and t_b are the temperatures of surfaces of A and B, respectively, and ϵ_a and ϵ_b are the thermal emissivities of these surfaces. If one takes the emissivity of the ceramic furnace tube as being essentially one, the equation is then readily converted to

$$Q_{ab} = \sigma \epsilon'_b (t_a^4 - t_b^4)$$

and the heat exchange is essentially a function of the emissivity of the block material. Obviously thermal energy can be transported from heater winding to block much more rapidly if the block is a ceramic rather than a polished metal. Since the total heat capacities of, say, nickel, platinum, and alumina are never the same for a sample block of a given size, the relative merits of these types of sample blocks must be considered with special regard to the heat-transfer characteristic, bearing in mind at all times that completely free flow of heat is not necessarily desirable.

Arens (A12), from a rather limited number of runs, concluded that ceramic blocks gave sharp endothermic reactions while nickel block gave sharp exothermic reactions (Fig. III-9). His evidence is too scanty to draw conclusions of this type. An equally valid conclusion from the evidence at hand is that ceramic blocks are more sensitive in the lower-temperature regions than nickel blocks but that nickel blocks are more sensitive at higher temperatures. Below red heat, the relatively low heat

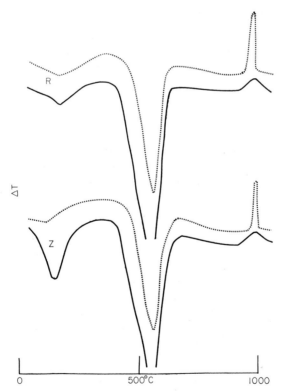

Fig. III-9. Thermograms of kaolinite from, R, Renau, and Z, Zettlitz, in nickel (• • • • •) and in ceramic (———) blocks. From Arens (A12).
The relative sensitivities of the blocks vary with temperature.

conductivity of alumina results in a comparative thermal isolation of the sample and reference, all other conditions being equal. As the temperature is increased and radiation takes a greater part in the transfer of heat, the relatively high emissivity of alumina compared to nickel permits transfer of heat quite readily from the blocks to the sample. At such temperatures nickel tends to play the same part as did the alumina at the lower temperatures; that is, the poor transfer of heat from sample to sample block or vice versa permits a sharper indication of a reaction. This explanation should apply to low thermal conductivity ceramics. The present state of ceramic art permits use of high-density formulations of some fairly conductive ceramics.

The thermal conductivity of high-density alumina is roughly the same as many of the high-temperature alloys but still only about one-quarter that of commercially pure nickel or ca. one-tenth that of aluminum. Competing with the effect of the thermal conductivity is the effect of the thermal emissivity. A third property influences the transfer of heat: the interfacial or surface characteristics of the block.

The emissivity determines, to a very great extent, how much heat is transferred from one body to another. Bear in mind that high emissivity also implies ready absorption of energy. If a ceramic and a nickel surface were each exposed to a hot surface under identical conditions the surface of the ceramic would heat faster. If a nickel and a ceramic *body* were similarly exposed the interior temperature of each body would depend on the thermal conductivity as well as the emissivity. While the outside of the ceramic body may be heating up quite rapidly the relatively high diffusivity of the nickel might well permit the center of the latter body to heat more rapidly at first.

The effect of interfacial layer characteristics is often severe. These layers take two forms—solid oxide or corrosion layers and the static gas which adheres to any surface. The oxide layer can—and often will—be the major resistance to the flow of heat; a metal block whose heat must traverse an oxide layer may—under steady-state heating—have a negligible temperature gradient. The static gas layer is of somewhat less importance because it is present on all materials and partly because it influences only the heat transfer by conduction (including convection).

To evaluate the relative heat-transfer characteristics, the present author heated a pair of geometrically identical sample holders (Fig. III-10), one of nickel and the other of high-density alumina, and measured the temperature difference between their centers. The sample holders were set on $\frac{1}{4}''$ (nominal) alumina two-hole rods and calcined alumina powder was put in each and pressed tight. A vertical furnace was put in place and power supplied from a motor-driven autotransformer. The immediate response (Fig. III-11) was a more rapid heating of the alumina holder. The thermocouple at its center showed a continually increasing lead until the Curie temperature of nickel was reached. The sharp change in thermal conductivity (Fig. III-12) permits the nickel-enclosed sample to heat more rapidly until the differential temperature approaches (and slightly exceeds) zero ca. 900°C.

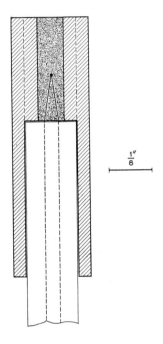

$\frac{1''}{8}$

Fig. III-10. Cross sectional view of trial sample holders of nickel and alumina. From Garn (G9).

The alumina sample holder comprised a (nominal) ¼ OD tube cemented into a longer ¼ ID tube; the nickel holder was machined to the same dimensions.

The sample holders were interchanged in a second run to avoid any errors due to accidental misalignment. There was no difference in shape and the difference in magnitude was negligible.

The thermal conductivity of the nickel is, through the whole temperature range, substantially larger than that of alumina, yet the alumina transmits heat to the specimen faster at the lower temperatures. It is frequently as easy to test the myths and misconceptions as it is to try to justify them.

3.4. Design of the Sample Block

The depth and radius of the sample wells are quite naturally a part of the total design of the sample block. The designs are extremely varied; sample cavities and blocks are not necessarily round. The design is partly dependent on the means of support. In the horizontal furnace supports can be devised for a wide range of shapes with equal ease because the specimens are not symmetric about the furnace axis anyway. In the vertical furnace a cylindrical block is virtually the only shape used. Arens (A12) used several shapes in his studies (Fig. III-13) and other authors have contributed other structures.

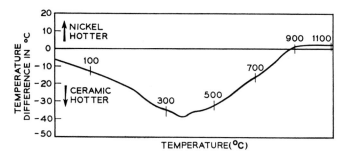

Fig. III-11. Temperature differential between alumina- and nickel-enclosed samples vs temperature of one of the samples. From Garn (G9).
The alumina transmits heat more readily than the nickel over most of the range. The nonlinearity of heating rate is typical of motor-driven autotransformers.

The thin-walled arrangements pose a special problem, particularly when the individual chambers are in contact. One assumption generally made in the use of a block is that the temperature gradient within the block is virtually zero. This is an essential prerequisite for symmetric heating of the specimens. A narrow wall between sample and reference specimens can hardly be at the same temperature as the portions more directly exposed to the hot furnace wall, but if the sample wells are reasonably spaced the metal cross section will be sufficient to maintain a fair approximation to uniformity. If the wells are separated to such a degree that they are near the edge of the block a rather similar problem exists but this time the narrow portion of the metal is a source (relative to the specimens) of heat. The degree of asymmetry of heating will be heavily dependent now on the rate of transfer of heat to the block—as well as on the conductivity within the block. Both of these quantities change with temperature. A reasonable guide is to maintain a thickness of metal at least equal to the well diameter all around each cavity.

The block will be supported, generally, by an insulating material, not to keep heat from it but to avoid what would amount to a distortion of the temperature distribution in the block. For vertical furnaces, such as the present author generally uses, the block may be supported on the ceramic tubes that carry the thermocouple wires, in the manner of Fold-vari-Vogl and Kliburszky (F11) (Fig. III-14). The present author uses stepped holes rather than stepped ceramic tubes to position the block. In

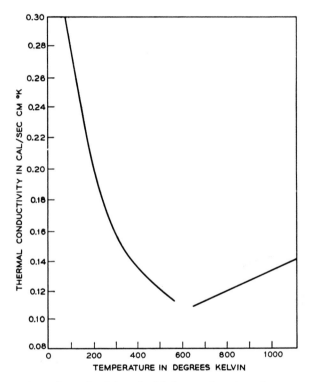

Fig. III-12. Thermal conductivity of nickel as a function of temperature. From Goldsmith *et al.* (G27).
The change at the Curie temperature is quite pronounced.

horizontal furnaces the present author has used both alumina and fire-brick to support blocks such as that in Fig. III-15. Stone (S51) supported his sample block directly on the metal gas-flow tubes.

Assuming some given heating rate, a large cavity will have a large temperature drop from side to center. This implies that by the time the center reaches a given temperature the side is at a substantially higher temperature. Since a temperature effect will have its beginning at the

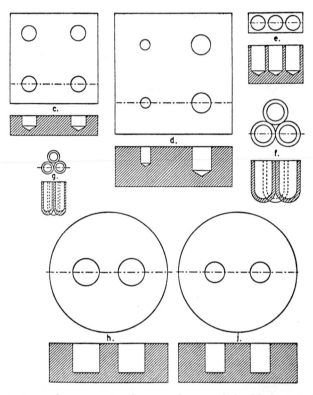

FIG. III-13. Top and cross sectional views of some of the blocks tested by Arens (A12).

The variety of blocks gives a wide range of ease of transfer of heat.

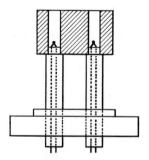

FIG. III-14. Sample block supported by thermocouple tubes (F11).

By minor changes in design a dynamic atmosphere can also flow through the supporting tubes.

time the wall reaches the reaction temperature and its ending when the *center* reaches the reaction temperature, the effect will be spread out in time.

We may also conclude (Fig. III-16) that a smaller-diameter specimen will have a lower drop and the peak will be over a narrower time range. The relative smallness of the peak need not be a great disadvantage since electrical amplification can be used; on the contrary, the small differences from the block temperature will mean a low drift of the base line because the temperature drop from block to center of sample or reference cannot be large and hence their difference cannot be large.

Data by de Jong (J9) tend to show, from sets 2, 5, and 6 of Fig. III-17, that depth of placement of the thermocouple has only a minor effect on

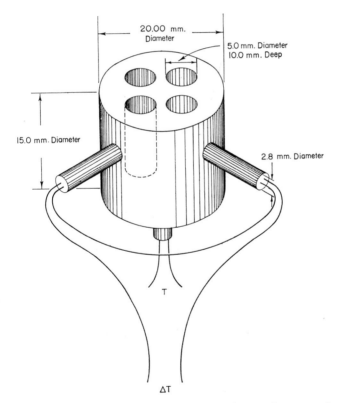

Fig. III-15. Sample block showing method of introducing thermocouples for furnace temperature, T, and differential temperature, ΔT. From Garn and Flaschen (G12).

The four holes permit interpolation of temperatures in the manner of Keith and Tuttle (K14).

peak area in full, covered sample cavities. The conclusion is not firmly based on these data because the thermocouple bead is relatively close to the bottom in each case; Barshad's work cited in Chapter II showed the end effect quite clearly.

The various widths of set A show an increasing thermal isolation of the thermocouple because of the relatively low thermal diffusivity of the specimen. This larger area is not necessarily a desirable attribute (see Chapter II). The fourth set in Fig. III-17 shows the diminution of the peak area due to a lesser quantity of specimen in the immediate vicinity of the thermocouple.

The general case may be stated quite simply: the longer and narrower the sample cavity the greater will be the effect of the atmosphere gen-

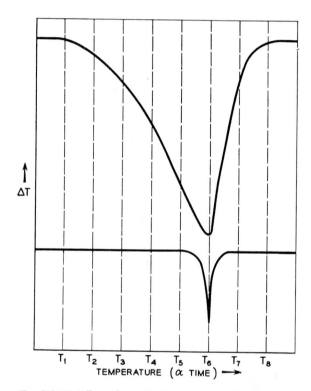

Fig. III-16. Effect of sample diameter on width of peaks.

A material which reacts at a temperature T_6 will appear to begin reacting at a much lower temperature (when ΔT is plotted against the temperature at the center) because the outside of the specimen is already at T_6. The lower edge-to-center temperature difference in the smaller specimen yields peaks of lesser magnitude but better definition.

erated by the sample itself and the less the effect of the composition of the ambient gas. The data in Fig. III-17 show that the effect reaches a virtual limit.

There should be no magic number expressing the length-to-depth ratio; in fact there will be occasions for most observers to use shallow as well as deep sample cavities (see Chapter VII). The actual dimensions should be selected, then, on the basis of experimental convenience and conformity with other parts of the apparatus. Bear in mind that in a dynamic atmosphere (see Chapter VII) or in a vacuum the length of the cavity is immaterial so long as it is the sample temperature rather

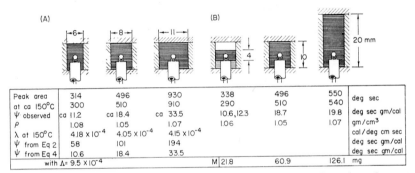

	(A)			(B)			
Peak area	314	496	930	338	496	550	deg sec
at ca 150°C	300	510	910	290	510	540	
ψ observed	ca 11.2	ca 18.4	ca 33.5	10.6,12.3	18.7	19.8	deg sec gm/cal
ρ	1.08	1.05	1.07	1.06	1.05	1.07	gm/cm³
λ at 150°C	4.18×10^{-4}	4.05×10^{-4}	4.15×10^{-4}				cal/deg cm sec
ψ from Eq 2	58	101	194				deg sec gm/cal
ψ from Eq 4	10.6	18.4	33.5				deg sec gm/cal
with $\Lambda = 9.5 \times 10^{-4}$				M 21.8	60.9	126.1	mg

Fig. III-17. Test results for $CuSO_4 \cdot 5H_2O$ diluted with α-Al_2O_3 (weight ratio, 1:7). (A) Samples of different diameter and equal height and (B) samples of different height and equal diameter. From de Jong (J9).

The considerable change in depth of thermocouples in the last two examples yields only a slight change in the peak area, but this is partly because the thermocouple bead is the same distance from the bottom in each case.

than that of the flowing or evolved gas that is measured. In other words, one cannot pass a gas through a thin layer of specimen and hope to have a good measure of the specimen temperature. The dynamic gas should pass through a sufficient thickness of specimen that thermal equilibrium is approached quite closely.

In a nondynamic atmosphere and with samples of rather substantial size, i.e., more than a few millimeters in diameter, the user may wish a cavity with a length-to-width ratio of two or more so that the heat supply comes principally from the sides. This is not particularly important for detection but those who wish to make calculations from data obtained using a block have enough other troubles. (See Chapter V.)

3.5. Placement of Thermocouples

The manner of recording T and ΔT and controlling (programming) T will depend greatly on the apparatus available, but a few simple considerations must be borne in mind; variations can be made successfully, but the consequences must be understood.

Since knowledge of the behavior of the specimen as its temperature is changed is the object of the study, the best temperature to measure and record is that of said specimen. If the thermocouple junction is placed in the center of a cylindrical specimen and an endothermic reaction is observed the thermocouple is at the place where the reaction last occurs. When the center finally reacts, the lag behind the reference is at its greatest and hence the peak of the endotherm is the reaction temperature. When practical, then, the temperature of any sizable specimen should be recorded from the center of the sample.

The maximum sensitivity and sharpness of reactions will certainly be obtained by maximum thermal and atmospheric isolation of the detecting thermocouple junction so that the surrounding material—whether sample or inert—will exert the maximum effect on the temperature of the thermocouple bead. No implication that this is necessary nor the best arrangement is implied. The present author has repeatedly—and successfully—used thermocouples with protective cover (Fig. VIII-5) at the edge of a sample. Under these conditions, however, very small samples were used. Arens' conclusions on the effect of placement of thermocouples were apparently based on curves in which the atmosphere effect overshadowed the geometric.

If the experimenter needs to control from the recording thermocouple, as did the present author for some years, two quite usable locations were available: the block, if one is used, or the reference specimen. In the latter case, the transition or decomposition temperature may be found easily by adding or subtracting the difference temperature; the control thermocouple is rather isolated from the heater, causing thermal lag, so especially good control apparatus is required.

Recording and controlling the block temperature would permit better control but at the price of some uncertainty in the actual specimen temperature. We can assume—with some reservations—that we know the temperature of the interface between block and specimen but the drop to the interior of the specimen is not known; there is also no convenient and continuous method for determining the drop. Said temperature drop will vary from specimen to specimen and from temperature to temperature and the variation will be discontinuous at thermal effects. For simple phase transitions no great problem exists; the beginning of the deflection is the reaction temperature. For decompositions the temperature of the center of the specimen will be of greater interest and a two-step measurement will be of use.

If the temperature drop in the reference material is known as a function of temperature for the heating rate used, this value and the differential temperature may be added to the block temperature to obtain the specimen temperature. This temperature drop will vary with both material and heating rate. In small-diameter cavities the errors become less and possibly negligible. The differential signal is diminishing too, but the discontinuities at reaction temperatures can still be detected easily even at small thicknesses of specimen material.

> Note that control of the specimen temperature is decidedly impractical for ordinary differential thermal analysis. The temperature-control device would lose control at the very time when smoothness of control was most needed. At the start of, for example, a simple endothermic phase change the control device will receive a sudden call for more heat. Assuming a typical separation of heat source from a sample a few intermediate layers must be heated more rapidly before the effect is felt by the specimen. In the meantime, the specimen temperature is lagging still further behind the programmed temperature, so the demand for heat continues to increase. By the time the reaction is complete, the surroundings are overheated and the temperature will rise at a rate greater than the programmed rate. The sensing thermocouple will cease to call for heat and the furnace input will be cut back sharply. When the programmed temperature again catches up there will be another demand because the specimen temperature is rising only slowly or may even by falling. How soon the control system can return to the program will depend very much on the type of control system and the care used in its adjustment, but in any case the apparatus will be off control for some time after the start of the reaction. During this time, it is incapable of dependable and reproducible detection of additional thermal effects and thereby has lost a significant part of the usefulness of differential thermal analysis.

The detection of this one thermal effect would not be inhibited but the shape of the deflection would likely be more than usually dependent on particle size, packing, etc.

The general problem of placement of the control thermocouple is discussed in Chapter XV.

Improper positioning of sample and reference thermocouples within the specimens will result in a diminution or deformation of the differential signal. Ordinarily this will be quite undesirable, although there are conceivable uses for deliberately nonsymmetric arrangements. In general, the aim is to obtain the maximum and best-defined signal available under the experimental conditions. This position will—in most systems—be at the center of symmetry or at the point corresponding as nearly as possible to it.

> Understand, however, that the goal here is the maximum information. The application of the general principles to specific problems will sometimes be experimentally unfeasible. Good, usable data can be obtained with other arrangements. See also Cole and Rowland's (C20) observations on the effect of placement of the thermocouple wires.

In the usual cylinder the best thermocouple location is along the axis as would be expected; in Smyth's (S36) slab arrangement a central plane is the most isolated position. Smyth's calculations of the effect of thermocouple position provide a convenient starting point, and we can extend his conclusions qualitatively to the cylindrical cavity. Fig. III-18a and b show time-based plots, but these can be related easily to a temperature-based curve; let us first examine the events against a time base.

Let us note that the temperature differences generally encountered in differential thermal analysis are often quite small. A phase change involving a temperature differential of 2°C can be detected quite routinely. Yet on a range of 1000°C, this 2°C corresponds approximately to the dead zone of a good controller (L3a). This means that small deflec-

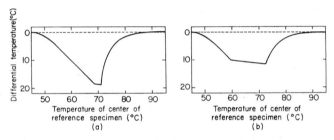

Fig. III-18. Effect of having the thermocouple displaced (a) 0.06 cm and (b) 0.30 cm from the center of the test specimen. From Smyth (S36).

The discontinuity occurs as the reaction front passes the thermocouple (see also Fig. III-8).

tions will have only a slight influence on the control system. This magnitude of signal is obtained with small samples undergoing crystallographic phase transitions; meltings, decompositions, and phase transitions in large samples will often produce a signal in excess of this. These larger signals will invariably influence the programming of the temperature because of the transitory lag (or lead) of the temperature compared to the programmed rate.

In short, if the thermal effects are small in magnitude the program control signal can be taken from a point in or near the sample—without serious upset of the program. Unless the differential signal is already known to be small the wiser course is to program from some other point. The user of this technique *must* use small samples.

As the transition proceeds, the temperature of a point not at the center will lag further and further behind the reference temperature as previously discussed. As the transition front reaches this point, the temperature at the point is no longer affected directly by the high "heat capacity" at the front. The temperature is now dependent on the new thermal diffusivity and the temperature difference between the wall and the now-receding front. A discontinuity is the natural result. The temperature rises more swiftly so that the differential temperature does not increase at the same rate as before. Whether or not the differential temperature will increase or decrease slightly will depend on the relative diffusivities of the two forms. The point will not, however, begin a rapid climb to a zero differential temperature because the unreacted material still behaves as a heat sink. The differential temperature may decrease somewhat, but only when the transformation is complete does the final return to the base line begin. The time that the point spends in the high-temperature form before the transition is complete is directly related to the displacement from the center and hence the flattened region in Fig. III-18 is greater with the larger displacement.

The general form of the plot is applicable to the cylindrical sample holder but the two-dimensional flow of heat (instead of unidirectional) will tend generally to smooth any changes. The converging flow of heat tends to diminish the difference in temperature so that the curve features will be somewhat less sharply defined. Thermocouple assymmetry, then, like assymmetric heating (Fig. III-8), will yield a less sharp peak; the degree of rounding will vary with the amount of assymmetry.

Barrall and Rogers (B7) examined the relation of heating rate and thermocouple location to the measured peak temperature. Their furnace arrangement is shown in Fig. IV-10. Note that heat transfer to the specimens is deliberately very poor. Under such conditions, a rapid heating rate will cause an apparent upward shift (Fig. III-19) of the peak temperature. The material does not actually remain in the solid state to higher temperatures as suggested by Fig. III-19 but rather the lag between block and thermocouple has increased substantially as the heating rate increased. Locating the measuring thermocouple in the specimen provides a reproducible peak temperature for the simple reason that the measurement is made where the measured event is occurring. So long as the thermocouple is at the center and the process is rapid the maximum signal occurs when the material around the thermocouple bead reaches the reaction temperature.

The use of a second thermocouple within the sample or reference for measuring the total temperature is fairly common. Since this not only disturbs the symmetry of heating but provides another path for heat leakage, compensation is applied in the form of a dummy thermocouple in the reference or sample. When the recording circuit is a potentiometric device requiring no current at balance, no further problems are encountered (see Chapter XV). With most multirange recorders—and particularly X-Y recorders—a new problem arises.

Most general purpose adjustable-range recorders use a voltage divider in their input circuit. This requires a current flow even when no change is being recorded. This in turn requires that work be drawn from the furnace. If the temperature is being recorded from the sample or reference, an unbalance is created. The unbalance arises because the work

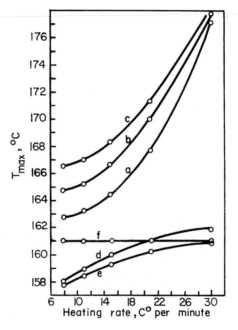

Fig. III-19. Peak temperature of (diluted) salicylic acid melting as measured in the block (a,b,c), the reference (d,e), and the sample (f). Curves a, d, and f refer to the same sample weight. From Barrall and Rogers (B7).

Variations in thermal lag at the several locations will be dependent on heating rate; the actual melting point will not.

drawn as electrical energy must be supplied as thermal energy, decreasing the temperature of the thermocouple itself and its immediate surroundings. This unbalance will be accentuated if the temperature is being recorded from one junction of the differential thermocouple. The solution in either is to draw an equal amount of work from the other thermocouple. This is done by putting a resistive load across the other thermocouple to match the recorder input. This maneuver requires sup-

3.7. Choice of Inert Substance

Under steady heating conditions with no reaction, the observed temperature difference depends both on the ease of heat transfer within the reference or inert material (thermal conductivity) and on the amount of heat necessary to raise the temperature of the material (heat capacity). The quantities of interest are the density, specific heat, thermal conductivity, and particle size. The first three of these are related in a term called the thermal diffusivity, a, which is defined by

$$a = \frac{\lambda}{\rho c}$$

where λ is the thermal conductivity, ρ is the density, and c is the specific heat.

Arens derives an expression for the steady-state temperature difference,

$$\triangle T = \frac{1}{4}\frac{dT}{dt}\,r^2\,(\frac{1}{a'} - \frac{1}{a})$$

where dT/dt is the heating rate, r is the radius of the cavity, and a' and a are the thermal diffusivities of the sample and reference, respectively.

But while the density and thermal conductivity are generally known for solids in large sizes, the effective density and the effective thermal conductivity will depend on particle size and packing. Smith (S34) relates the thermal conductivity of a powder to the volume fractions of air and solid. He gives

$$\lambda = \lambda_a P_a + \lambda_s P_s$$

where P_a and P_s are the volume fractions of air and the powdered substance. For ordinary purposes the contribution of air can be neglected but even the packing must be carefully controlled as part of any effort to obtain a zero base line.

The underlying problem in achieving a low ΔT and hence a nearly zero base line is that of matching the thermal diffusivity of the reference (or inert) material to that of the specimen. The problem in achieving also a zero base line drift is that of matching the thermal diffusivity of the inert material to that of the specimen at *all* temperatures in the range studied. Note, from the expression (see above) for the steady-state temperature difference, that the difference is a direct function of the heating rate; i.e., at higher heating rates the drift will be larger. With a single reference material, this matching is obviously not possible for more than a few fortuitously chosen specimens. Some base line deviation and indeed some drift is to be expected unless the observer has made a special effort to match the reference to the specimen. In the absence of such precautions, a base line of nearly zero and which does not drift is prima-facie evidence of a low-sensitivity apparatus.

It is for this same reason that one need not be perturbed when a base line is not the same before and after a reaction. Even in crystalline rearrangements but especially in decompositions the thermal conductivity and the specific heat of the product will differ from that of its initial form; in decompositions, too, the density must change. Attaining the same thermal diffusivity after the reaction as before the reaction would be strange indeed. This is one of the effects which frustrate attempts to derive exact expressions for quantitative differential thermal analysis.

The dilution of materials may also result in apparent changes because of sorption of the material and/or decomposition products. Barrall and Rogers (B7) have shown (Fig. III-21) the sorption of water and alcohols

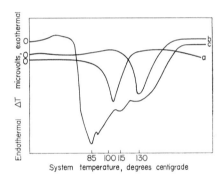

FIG. III-21. Differential thermograms of vapors sorbed on glass beads and alumina at a heating rate of 7.9°C per minute and a ΔT sensitivity of 200 μv per 3 inches. a, Water sorbed on 0.029-mm glass beads. b, Water sorbed on calcined alumina. c, Methanol, ethanol, and water sorbed on calcined alumina. From Barrall and Rogers (B7).

Affinity of the "inert" material for vapors may lead to data that is difficult to interpret.

on their calcined alumina diluent. If a sample material contained some adsorbed water, an undiluted specimen might well lose this water in the 60–100°C range without any very noticeable effect. In a specimen diluted with calcined alumina, evolved water would be immediately absorbed by the alumina and not lost again until the specimen was substantially over 100°C as in Fig. III-21. The comparatively rapid release then might provide a spurious peak which could impel the observer to seek the material in the specimen which gives a peak at, e.g.,

127°C. On the other hand, if water initially adsorbed on the sample material could be reliably adsorbed by the diluent and later desorbed over a narrow temperature range to give a well-defined peak, a useful and convenient method for detection of—specifically—adsorbed water might result.

The present author generally uses calcined alumina as diluent or inert material but has used other materials for special problems. Magnesium oxide, powdered fused quartz, manganese magnesium ferrite, and even powdered silicon have been useful, as well as organic materials for organic problems. The author has no particular procedure to recommend in selecting an inert material except to try substances as like the sample as possible. When a special problem requires a special reference material, it is selected quite empirically. Fortunately, the problem does not arise often. A drifting base line does not discompose the author unless there is some chance that an effect might be missed, but this would require a very rapid drift. Of course, if one were trying to measure the peak area anything more than a very small drift could not be tolerated; the operator must choose his reference material to suit the particular problem. Of prime importance, the base line drift—or shift—must be reproducible. So long as the deviation is reproducible it will be, or at least can be, compensated for in calibration. The resulting error will be relatively small.

Careful matching of the inert material to the sample material, in those cases in which it might be successful, is seldom profitable except in those cases in which a larger number of samples are to be run and compared with one another.

3.8. Effect of Packing

The tightness of packing affects the thermogram in two ways: in all cases it affects the transfer of heat from the wall of the sample cavity to the thermocouple junction, but in decompositions it also affects the diffusion of gases in or out. Let us consider the effects in that order.

In the absence of any forced passage of gas or a need to modify diffusion, forced passage of tight packing is generally preferable; not only does it decrease the thermal gradient by increasing the thermal conductivity (see above discussion on choice of inert material) but it is more reproducible. Kissinger (K29), on the other hand, was able to get reproducible packing by treating the specimens uniformly—tapping the side of the sample vessel to compact the specimen. To a limited degree, packing differences may be used to alter the diffusivity and thereby help to match reference to sample, but this can only be recommended as a shift. Arens (A12) found rather severe differences (Fig. III-22) on thermograms of quartz and kaolinite. Unduly loose packing of the specimen yields the effect of a long-drawn-out endotherm because the lower thermal conductivity produces a larger temperature lag.

The effect of packing on decompositions will depend on the conditions of atmosphere accessibility (see Chapter VII). If one is using a closed-chamber sample holder the packing should be tight simply to delay any appreciable reaction as long as possible.

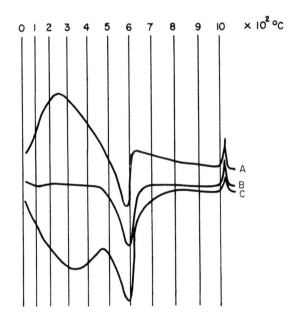

FIG. III-22. The influence of tightness of packing on differential thermal analysis records: A, tightly packed kaolinite, loosely packed reference; B, kaolinite and reference tightly packed; and C, loosely packed kaolinite and tightly packed reference. From Arens (A12).

The tighter packing provides better heat conduction and leads to base line displacement if the packing is poorly matched.

In a static atmosphere with a comparatively thin specimen (see Chapter VII) the sample needs to be compacted only slightly. This is necessarily a compromise between the very loose packing which would inhibit diffusion less and the tighter packing which facilitates heat transfer.

A dynamic atmosphere has its own special problem. Since "diffusion" occurs under the influence of a gaseous pressure gradient, the packing may be relatively tight; the flow will be controlled, in part, by the pressure drop across the specimen. A very firmly packed specimen might possibly have a sufficient pressure difference across it to affect the reaction temperature but this is rather unlikely. The firm packing does permit better heat exchange between solid and gas as well as between particles. A dynamic atmosphere differential thermal analysis sample, then, should be packed firmly unless there is reason to believe that there is a deleterious effect on the particular system under study. In short, the degree of packing is a matter of convenience. The present author is generally concerned with the nature of the reaction rather than the magnitude of the heat effect, so only moderate reproducibility of packing is sufficient; the specimen is usually pressed down with a rod (or drill bit) held fairly firmly between thumb and two fingers.

If the peak height or area is to be measured and compared to another, somewhat more attention to reproducibility is needed. Whether Kissinger's (K29) technique is sufficient or whether the material must be compacted with considerable force will probably depend on the material involved. The present author is not prepared to offer a generally applicable opinion; the experimenter is constrained to assure himself that he can obtain reproducible curves.

Note, however, that reproducible packing is not necessarily good packing; the reproducible packing should still be firm enough to permit reasonable heat flow. While Kissinger's technique is, from the present author's experience, generally suitable for clays and many inorganic powders, it would not be suitable, for example, for some of the hydrated carbonates of magnesium. These might be compacted only 20% by tapping but an additional 50% by pressing. The data are experimental but only approximate.

3.9. The Effect of Covering Sample Holes

Covering the sample holes has an effect ascribed by some to the elimination of direct radiation from the furnace wall into the specimen. While this radiation or lack thereof may have some small effect, the change in results is principally an atmosphere effect (see Chapter VII). The cover inhibits, to some degree, the diffusion and escape of gaseous reaction products or ingress of reacting gases. Arens (A12) reported specifically on the effect of covering the sample holes on thermograms of two clay minerals (Fig. III-1). Note that there is no shift of the exothermic reactions.

The present author has found that simply loosely covering the sample holder is not adequate. It will cause a shift of temperatures, of course, in reversible or oxidation reactions, but the peak shifting is not so great as in a closed-chamber sample holder because the vapor pressure of the reaction product gas does not reach the ambient pressure. This shows *per se* that there is diffusion both ways and the ambient atmosphere can enter the sample hole. This raises the possibility—or indeed the probability—that the atmosphere within will not be reproducible temperature by temperature from run to run and hence the peak temperatures will similarly be less reproducible than they ought to be. Differences in particle size might cause sufficient difference in reaction rates that the exchange of gases has a significant effect. Bear in mind that the equilibrium vapor pressure expression says nothing about rate of decomposition.

Consider two specimens of clay, identical except for particle size. Since we can assume that under a given set of temperature and partial pressure conditions the rate of diffusion of the gaseous decomposition product within the particle affects the rate of decomposition, we can also assume, for convenience, that our smaller particles are of such a small size that diffusion within the entire solid particle occurs instantly. We shall further assume for the purpose of this discussion that the larger particles are of such size that diffusion within the particle takes a measurable time. Now let us heat these two specimens in lightly covered sample holes allowing a small exchange of gases and also in a closed-chamber sample holder allowing—in effect—gases to escape but not enter.

As the specimens are heated, the finer particles will tend to decompose first in either sample holder but the increase of the partial pressure prevents complete decomposition immediately. Since we have both a rising temperature and a tendency to dilute by ingress of the ambient atmosphere the reaction in the lightly covered sample hole continues at an ever-increasing rate until the material is exhausted. The increase in rate of decomposition is partially vitiated by the increase in gaseous diffusion rate with temperature. Under the same conditions, the larger particles will begin to decompose in much the same manner, but as soon as the decomposition has progressed a few layers deep, it can no longer maintain equilibrium as could the smaller particles. The progress of the decomposition now depends more and more on the increase of the reaction rate with temperature, but it is obviously not at equilibrium with the atmosphere within the sample hole. Since the reaction rate increases exponentially with temperature there will finally be a rapid decomposition of the remainder of the specimen; in order to achieve such a rate, the temperature has probably reached the point corresponding to an equilibrium vapor pressure equal to the ambient atmosphere. Compare this set of events with those in the closed-chamber sample holder.

As stated above, the smaller particles will tend to react first simply because it is the nature of small particles to react more readily than large (surface imperfections, i.e., unsatisfied valences such as at corners, occur more frequently on small particles than on large, other parameters being equal), but the surface of the larger particles does not lag far behind. Since only enough of either specimen to satisfy the equilibrium vapor pressure requirement will decompose, not much really happens. Very little of the material needs to decompose to keep the partial pressure increasing properly, so the problems arising from slow diffusion in the solid particles will probably not be of any concern. The temperature meanwhile is increasing to that corresponding to equilibrium at the ambient pressure. As the temperature increases, the reaction rate increases and so does the diffusion rate within the particles, even though the net reaction is inconsequential. By the time the partial pressure within the chamber exceeds the ambient pressure and gas begins to leave rapidly, the total rate of decomposition of the large particles is fairly rapid and the decomposition will be complete not much later than that of the finer particles. Depending on the identity of the material and the particle sizes, the peak shift may be so small as to be imperceptible. It will almost certainly be negligible.

The relative ease of diffusion into the covered hole raises the possibility of reaction with the atmosphere but at a rate that may be so low as to leave some doubt (from the thermogram alone) that a reaction even occurred. An oxidation, for example, may well begin at the usual temperature, but the limited supply of oxygen limits the rate so that it is spread out over a wider temperature range than in an uncovered hole. Note, however, that if the ambient atmosphere were pure oxygen rather than air the consumption of oxygen would draw in an equal volume of oxygen and the reaction would go on because a steady (actually an increasing) supply is available. In air, on the other hand, as a volume of oxygen is used less than one-fifth of this volume is brought in as direct replacement. Any further supply must be supplied by diffusion (see also Chapter VII).

The present author uses a long thin cylindrical diffusion path instead of a cover as a barrier, but even a 3-inch path no more than 0.003 inch thick and $\frac{1}{4}$ inch in diameter does not completely prevent oxidation. The edges of the hemispherical sample (Fig. III-23) sometimes show signs of oxidation with appropriate samples; nevertheless there may be striking differences in the nature of the reactions.

3.10. The Influence of the Composition of the Furnace Atmosphere

The advantages of using a known atmosphere are covered extensively in other parts of this book. The discussion here will be limited to the effects of ambient air. Even in static heating dehydration experiments Nutting (N16) found "In the lower range of temperature, weight curves vary with the humidity, an effect which vanishes above about 160°C." Since a material will have no tendency to lose weight until its vapor pressure exceeds the ambient partial pressure (Chapter VII), a crystalline hydrate that may be stable up to a given temperature on a very damp day will decompose at a lower temperature on a dry day. Arens (A12) gives a range of 30–40°C for kaolinite.

Similarly, the decomposition temperatures of carbonates—as measured in ambient air—may well vary from laboratory to laboratory, being generally higher for laboratories in cities or associated with manufacturing plants, ranging from 300 to 600 ppm (C11a). The magnitude of the temperature shift will depend on the extant relative concentrations of carbon dioxide and, of course, the heat and temperature of decomposition of the particular carbonate.

3.11. The Particle Size of Clay Minerals

Arens (p. 55) also discusses the particle size of the clay, reporting the work of Kelly and co-workers, Perkins, Speil, and Kulp and Kerr. These workers all report that the grinding of clays results in a decreased intensity of reaction (see Chapter II). This decreased intensity of reaction is

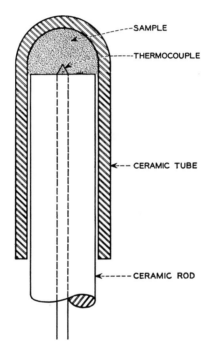

FIG. III-23. Closed-chamber sample holder for differential thermal analysis. *The long diffusion path inhibits but does not completely prevent exchange of gases.*

related to the crystallinity effect also discussed by Arens. The effect of the grinding is to raise the surface energy of the clay or other material such that a portion of the material will react at a considerably lower temperature. The surface energies of the various particles should follow some statistical relation and a continuous breakdown of particles would occur from this lower temperature of initiation up to the original temperature of reaction.

3.12. The Nature of the Clay Minerals Present

The fact that the thermogram depends for its appearance on the nature of the material present is naturally of basic importance in differential thermal analysis; we are concerned here with the effect of one material on the thermogram of another. Arens (A12, p. 52) refers to the work of Agafonoff (A2), Orcel (O6), and Caillère and Hénin (C2), showing peak shifting as a consequence of mixing. Caillère and Hénin compared the effect to the lowering of melting points of mixed systems. Arens disagrees, pointing out, "the reaction temperatures are not systematically lowered in DTA, but sometimes increase by the presence of admixtures. There exists consequently a fundamental difference between the two phenomena." The present author agrees. This effect generally should be traceable to the evolution of dissimilar gases in the case of lowering the reaction temperatures or similar gases in the case of raising the reaction temperature. In the case of the dissimilar gases, the formation and movement of either gas is necessarily going to sweep out the other gas, thereby lowering the partial pressure of the second gas. If the reactions occur simultaneously, each gas acts strongly to reduce the partial pressure of the other, and in turn its own partial pressure is being held to a lower value than would otherwise occur. The raising of a reaction temperature can occur in those cases in which a reaction has already occurred such that the interstices are at least partially filled with the product gas. This rather substantial increase in the partial pressure of this gas raises the reaction temperature for the subsequent decomposition (see Chapter VII).

An example of the effect of an earlier reaction is in the work of Webb and Heystek (W11) who show that (Fig. III-24) dehydration of magnesium hydroxide delays the decomposition peak of calcium hydroxide ca. $50°C$ higher than in the absence of magnesium hydroxide even though the first dehydration is essentially over by the time the calcium hydroxide peak would otherwise begin. The cause is simply the high concentration of water vapor left behind among the particles. The calcium hydroxide is diluted to 10% in each case but the alumina dilution has air rather than water vapor to displace so the reaction occurs at a relatively low temperature. The peak temperature is lower than in pure calcium hydroxide (ca. $585°C$) because of the dilution effect; i.e., the ease of diffusion is about ten times greater per unit of water vapor or hydrate so the vapor pressure is less likely to approach ambient pressure and the hydrate can decompose at a lower temperature than with a pure sample.

Diffusion of water vapor out of the sample matrix is as important in the magnesium hydroxide dilution as raising the temperature; the de-

hydration peak is still lower than that of pure calcium hydroxide, showing that even with the high initial concentration the water partial
pressure does not maintain the value reached during decomposition of
pure calcium hydroxide.

3.13. Comparison of Records Obtained with Different Equipment

Arens obtained a "general equation" for the comparison of reaction
temperatures in curves obtained with different DTA equipment:

$$\hat{T} = T_{observed} - \tfrac{1}{4} r^2 C \,(1/fa - 1/f'a') - Q \log T/4.571 \, b(b - \log p),$$

in which $\hat{T}'$ is the asymptotic reaction temperature in degrees Centigrade or Kelvin; $T_{observed}$ is the experimentally obtained initial or
peak reaction temperature; r is the sample cavity radius in centimeters;
C is the heating rate in degrees Centigrade per second; f and f' are
dimensionless constants; a and a' are the thermal diffusivities of the
sample and reference materials, respectively, in square centimeters per
second; Q is the heat of reaction in calories per mole; p is the appropri-

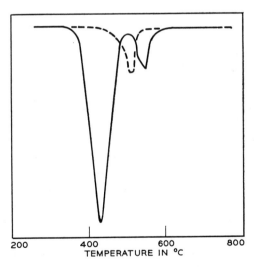

Fɪɢ. III-24. Thermograms of calcium hydroxide diluted with: ———, magnesium
hydroxide; - - -, alumina. From Webb and Heystek (W11).

*The prior decomposition of the magnesium hydroxide leaves behind an atmos-
phere greatly enriched with water vapor; this vapor raises the decomposition temperature of the calcium hydroxide. A rather abrupt beginning of the record decomposition should be expected.*

ate pressure in millimeters of mercury; and b represents the variation in the heat of reaction with temperature.

In his comparisons, Arens used the ambient partial pressure of the appropriate gas when using the initial observed temperature and assumes $p = 760$ mm of mercury when using the peak observed temperature. The first assumption is reasonable only in those cases in which no reaction has occurred prior to the one under examination; for if a reaction has occurred which involves evolution of a gas, the composition of the vapors within the sample has been modified. Diffusion of gases into and out of the sample is a reasonably rapid process; nevertheless, a substantial modification of the atmosphere composition may remain for many minutes and consequently 100 or more degrees. The second assumption is clearly incorrect. In conventional sample holders, i.e., sample blocks or cups with top openings of the same order of magnitude as the depth, the partial pressure of the product gas does not reach one atmosphere. If the pressure did equal one atmosphere at the peak, the reaction would show no effect of covering the sample holes and yet Arens shows from his own work the effect of covering sample holes for two clays, halloysite and indianaite. His plots show clearly a difference on the order of 50°C in the peak temperature for the 600°C peak.

Arens proves the applicability of this equation by a substitution of some data obtained from runs using kaolinite from Zettlitz, and obtains the numerical values $\hat{T} = 480 - 9 - 57 = 414°C$. He cites an expected value of $\hat{T}$ of $420 \pm 10°C$. (The above data were for the initial temperatures of the deflection.) He then inserted the appropriate data for the peak observed temperature leading to the equation $\hat{T} = 590 - 9 - 162 = 419°C$. This appears to be a good agreement until one realizes that the temperature of initiation is suspect. Arens' data from Zettlitz kaolinite shows clearly that there is a reaction between 100 and 200°C and, since this reaction probably is a dehydration, $\log p$ is almost certainly too low and consequently the largest correction value is likewise too low; hence the apparent agreement is unrealistic.

Arens also relates this general equation to qualitative analysis by showing that when an asymptotic reaction temperature could be calculated the material causing the deflection could be determined. He cites a clay as an example, finding a $\hat{T}$ of 598°C and in Table 10, p. 86, he cites the $\hat{T}$ for calcite as 610°C. It is appropriate to examine the definition of T' on p. 78: "We define T' as the absolute temperature at which the reaction starts and finishes in a time approaching infinite, under a heating rate $C = 0$ and under a vapor pressure of the volatile component approaching 0." This temperature is necessarily one at which the vapor pressure cannot be measured. Hence, if a vapor pressure can be measured this asymptotic reaction temperature value is incorrect. Let us look first at calcite and its cited asymptotic reaction temperature of 610°C. Smyth and Adams (S35) found a dissociation pressure of ca 2 mm Hg in this temperature range. Similarly for kaolinite and its suggested asymptotic reaction temperature of 420°, there is present a sizable concentration of water vapor contributed partly by the ambient atmosphere and partly by the reaction. [Nutting (N16) reports an initiation temperature in the order of 380°C.]

The values cited by the comparison of data by different observers show only a moderate agreement and hence could fit other expressions for the asymptotic reaction temperature equally well. Because of the considerable uncertainty in the values which must be used, there is sufficient error in this expression and its use so that its validity is questionable. On the other hand, its invalidity is also not proved. The lack of any really suitable method for comparison of results from apparatus to apparatus points up the necessity for obtaining differential thermal analysis curves under known thermodynamic conditions.

Nonetheless, if Arens' work had been more generally known—and used —by others active in the field, the art of differential thermal analysis would have advanced more rapidly than it has. It would still remain an art, however, for while Arens observed well and reached generally well-founded conclusions of a qualitative nature, his approach to a quantitative treatment of differential thermal analysis was not soundly based.

Arens (A12) assumed that if two substances or objects, not necessarily alike, are heated in the same furnace at the same rate, each will be supplied with the same number of calories. This means that at a constant heating rate $dT/dt = $ constant; so also is $dQ/dt = $ constant. MacKenzie and Farmer (M5) pointed out two such cases, the first in Arens opening assumptions on theoretical considerations (cf. Chapter IV of ref. A12). Arens, ignoring for the moment the thermal conductivity, set down the expressions, for the inert sample,

$$c_1 = \frac{Q}{m_1(T_2 - T_1)}$$

and for the clay sample,

$$c_2 = \frac{Q}{m_2(T_2' - T_1)}$$

where c_1 and c_2 are the heat capacities and m_1 and m_2 the masses. He then stated "Q is equal for both samples in one and the same furnace." With this assumption he concludes that one can obtain a straight base (or zero) line when $c_1 m_1 = c_2 m_2$, which conclusion has been quoted and acted upon by later workers. Obviously, since (T_2-T_1) must equal (T'_2-T_1), the equality must be

$$\frac{Q_1}{m_1 c_1} = \frac{Q_2}{m_2 c_2}$$

and therefore the condition necessary for a straight zero line is simply that, if one sample has a higher $m \times c$ than the other, more heat must be supplied to it, but see Chapter II.

Similarly, MacKenzie and Farmer call attention to the time-of-reaction equation

$$t = \frac{qm}{(c_1 m_1 + c_2 m_2 + \ldots)} \cdot \frac{1}{C}$$

where q is the number of calories needed to raise the temperature from the initial temperature, T_i, to the final temperature, T_f, at heating rate C. This equation is not valid; MacKenzie and Farmer attribute its non-applicability to the assumption that the quantity T_f-T_i is independent of heating rate; the present author suspects that it is a recurrence of the uniform addition of heat assumption. In his discussion of nickel and ceramic sample blocks Arens states "the heat supplied per unit of time (dQ/dT) is the same in one furnace for all types of blocks. . ." (see Sec. 3.3).

MacKenzie and Farmer also disagreed with Arens' derivation of an expression for the area under an endothermic peak, part of which is the heat flow into the sample. Arens describes this as

$$\int_0^t \Delta T_2 \, dt \text{ (heat supply)} = \frac{Q m_1}{c_1 m_1 + c_2 m_2 + \ldots} \int_0^t \frac{1}{2} \, dt$$

which is the integration of a straight line; i.e., the flow of heat into the sample is constant during the course of the reaction.

MacKenzie and Farmer raised objections to Arens "asymptotic reaction temperature" which he calculates from

$$T_{\text{observed}} - \hat{T} = \frac{Q}{4.571(b - \log p)} - \frac{Q}{4.571 \, b}$$

where $b = \Sigma v \cdot 1.75 \log T + \Sigma v\epsilon + \log 760$,
      Q = heat of reaction,
      p = partial pressure of gaseous product in mm Hg,
      $\hat{T}$ = the asymptotic reaction temperature,
      v = number of moles of gas formed, and
      ϵ = conventional chemical constant.

The term "log 760" arises from Arens' assuming that (1) the maximum rate of reaction occurs at the peak temperature and (2) the partial pressure of the reaction product is then equal to the ambient pressure. Mac-Kenzie and Farmer take exception to the first and the present author to both of these statements. The assumption of most rapid reaction at the peak temperature is at variance with practically all other observers. The peak temperature occurs—in an endothermal reaction—at the *time* when the point of measurement lags in temperature most behind the reference or furnace temperature. This is obviously true from the manner of measurement. In a cylindrical sample reacting uniformly about the axis, this ought to be at the time the material at the axis reacts, but since the reaction front or surface is shrinking it is hardly likely that the maximum rate of reaction is reached at that time. The present author believes that the temperature of maximum rate of reaction cannot be identified from a differential thermal analysis peak. It should depend not only on the geometry of the sample but also on the relative thermal diffusivities before and after the reaction, the heat of reaction, the ease of diffusion of the gas evolved and the ambient gas, and very decidedly on the heating rate (see Chapter V for other opinions).

The second assumption is only a poor approximation. One of the major reasons for variation of peak temperature with heating rate is the variation of the atmosphere within the sample. A slow heating rate permits interchange of product with ambient gas rapidly enough to avoid a really great enrichment; an extremely high heating rate will enable the product gas to sweep out nearly all the ambient gas; intermediate heating rates will yield an intermediate condition. This peak temperature will even vary with depth of placement of the thermocouple, because the ambient atmosphere partial pressure will be quite pronounced near the top of the sample well.

3.14. Effect of Particle Size and Grinding

A naturally formed surface of a mineral particle can be presumed to be fairly stable, otherwise it would have reverted to a stable state before reaching the thermal analysis laboratory. Recently formed surfaces are quite a different problem. The added surface activity of ground or milled samples is demonstrated strikingly by the Schaller and Vlisidis' (S8) report that powdered siderite had spontaneously oxidized at ambient temperatures. The ferrous iron content, reported as FeO, decreased from 59.42 to 6.23% in 29 years and to 0.74% in 43 years. Chunks of siderite do not oxidize in a similar time. Similarly, freshly formed surfaces can be expected to react at lower temperatures or more vigorously in thermal analysis studies, as (Fig. III-25) do the asbestos specimens described by Martinez (M19).

Even among naturally formed particles one may reasonably expect to find differences in reactivity depending especially on particle size. Let us consider the effect of subdivision of a cube, but let us first recall that a particle is unlikely to be equally reactive all over its surface. Corners or other discontinuities will tend to react before a smooth surface. Even different crystal faces will differ in reactivity.

Assume for the moment that we have a cube of some material and that it is a perfect single crystal of unit length. It has, of course, eight cor-

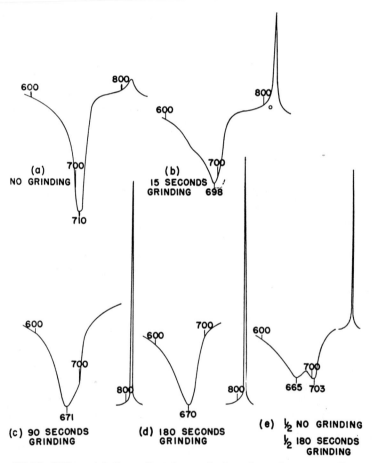

Fig. III-25. Differential thermal analyses of chrysolite asbestos samples ground in Wig-L-Bug for varying lengths of time. From Martinez (M19).
The short-term grinding has produced a substantial change in the thermal effects.

ners, twelve edges with a total length of twelve units, and six faces with a total area of six square units. Let us now subdivide this crystal into perfect single crystals one-tenth unit on the side. These thousand crystals have eight thousand corners, twelve thousand edges with a total length of twelve hundred units, and six thousand faces with a total area of sixty square units. The less reactive portions of the surface increase slowly compared to the much more reactive corners and edges. Continue the subdivision and again the more reactive portions multiply rapidly so that a gram or a cubic centimeter of a material may have a wide range of "active regions," depending on the particle size. The reactivity can then be expected to vary inversely with the particle size.

These differences in reactivity are unimportant for most materials at room temperature. (If the reactivity were substantial, some process would have occurred to relieve this driving force.) If the particles are heated, though, this hitherto negligible difference in reactivity can become important. As the sample approaches a temperature at which even a plane surface will react the discontinuities, whether corners, edges, or cracks, will naturally tend to react first—hence finer particles tend to react to a greater extent at a given temperature.

It is not necessary to postulate cubes; any geometry leads to the same general conclusion: assuming that natural materials are the same in reactive behavior except for particle size, the smaller particles will be more reactive (Fig. III-26) because as the surface area is increased so are the unsaturated valences, especially at discontinuities whether they are corners, edges, cracks, lattice defects, or just plane surface.

The artificial diminution of particle size by grinding yields more striking results than does separation of naturally occurring particles. The naturally occurring particles have had time for degeneration of the surface irregularities which lead to increased reactivity. Corners and edges are rounded, cracks become cleavages, and the new edges become curves. Even impurities may disappear from the surface perhaps by leaching; the particle may be covered by materials adsorbed on the surface. Contrast this condition with freshly formed surfaces.

A newly formed surface has a degree of disorder greatly dependent on the method of formation of the surface: precipitation cannot be expected to form the same type of surfaces as grinding, so even specimens of a small particle size range may show considerably different thermal effects. The newly formed surfaces from either grinding or precipitation will not have had much opportunity to react in any way to destroy the active regions, so there should be a marked difference between these and well-aged surfaces. Let us examine some data showing these various effects.

Kulp, Kent, and Kerr (K42) crushed a sample of Santa Fe calcite and sieved the powder to separate various size fractions. Their data (Fig. III-27) show only a slight reduction in reaction temperature in four size fractions down to 200 mesh. They extended the range of study to smaller particles by grinding some of the finest fraction to pass the 200-mesh screen. Now an effect appears more clearly, the reaction begins at a distinctly lower temperature, and at 900°C the deflection is greater than for the next larger size, yet the temperature range of the reaction is well above that of either the deep sea sedimentary calcite or the freshly precipitated calcium carbonate.

We can safely assume that crushing a sample—as Kulp, Kent, and Kerr did—will cause cleavage along reasonably well-defined crystal directions so that, while new faces are formed, reactivity of the particle is not increased very much. Grinding of 120–200 mesh particles to pass 200

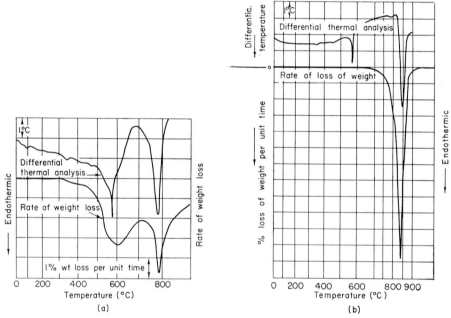

Fɪɢ. III-26. Differential thermal analysis and rate of loss of weight against temperature for 85 mole parts SiO_2–15 mole parts Na_2CO_3 mixture: (a) both grain sizes below 300 BSS; and (b) both materials between 72 and 100 BSS. From Thomasson and Wilburn (T7a).

The higher reactivity of the smaller particles is reflected in the substantial reaction below 700°C in (a). The lowered final reaction temperature in (a) is due to the formation of a eutectic between the sodium carbonate and the silicate formed by the early reaction.

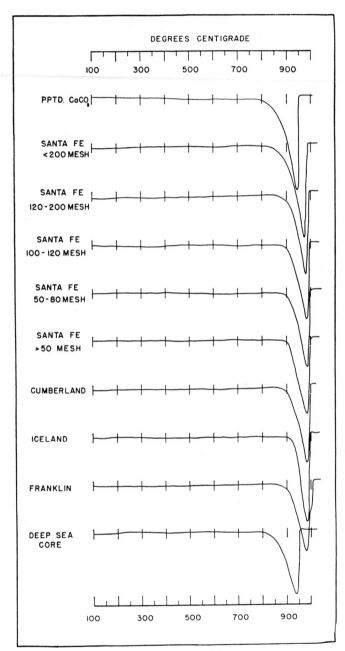

FIG. III-27. DTA curves of various specimens of calcite and of various particle sizes for the Santa Fe–Iceland spar. From Kulp *et al.* (K42).

The precipitated calcium carbonate and that from the deep sea core have relatively high reactivity.

mesh does not constitute a major operation but the initiation and completion of the decomposition both occur at lower temperatures; this is due partially to decrease of particle size and partly to distortion of the lattice which we shall consider further below. The passage of a particle through a 200-mesh sieve implies only that two perpendicular directions can be defined such that at no point in the particle does the width along either of these exceed 74 μ. The third dimension is unspecified; acicular particles have some reasonably substantial probability of getting through. We know from this that the particles which get through the sieve can still have an average cross section of 74 μ or more. We can surely assume that the average size is at least 50 μ. Newly precipitated crystals can be expected to have imperfectly formed faces and edges and usually a small particle size. Sedimentary carbonate ought to be small (sedimentary clays are in the order of 5 μ) but the surfaces should be uniform. Whether the effect is due to particle size alone or surface imperfections as well as particle size, the decomposition temperature range of these calcium carbonates is lower than that of a lightly ground specimen.

When particles are subjected to more vigorous treatment more striking results than a mere shift in temperature may be obtained. Dry grinding, usually done by ball milling, is a repeated abrasion of the particle under the impact of the falling balls. Strains are built up in the surface layers so that they will tend to undergo reaction more readily because of the high-energy state.

McLaughlin (M28) showed the change in reaction temperatures for dickite, a clay mineral related to kaolin. The curves are shown in Fig. III-28. He started with the 2–20 μ fraction (nearly all the material was in this range) and ground it in a mechanical mortar and pestle. The dry-ground samples show an immediate drop in reaction temperature of a portion of the material (curve 2), with some remaining apparently unchanged. After 6 hr no trace of the original material remains and the total 500–700°C dehydration peak has lost much of its magnitude.

The simultaneous appearance of an endothermic peak in the 100–300°C range indicates prior water adsorption but, more important, the great spread of this water loss is evidence that the water is held by a range of bonding strength. These forces arise from the high energy of the distorted surface; the localized heating and the shearing forces resulting from each impact leave their mark in the form of a greatly disturbed surface layer. McLaughlin reports that X-ray diffraction lines began to disappear after 2 hours dry grinding and noticeable changes in the lattice dimensions occurred, particularly an increase along the Z axis. Other spacing showed both increases and decreases. The high surface energy is most strikingly demonstrated by the enhanced exothermic reaction shown by the dry-ground specimens ca. 980°C. Now that a temperature is reached at which another form is more stable the individual ions can move around and rearrange to the new crystal structure. The additional energy from the lattice distortion on the surface is now readily lost and appears as increased heat of reaction.

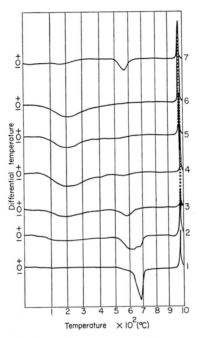

Fig. III-28. Differential thermal curves for dickites: 1, unground material; 2, ground 2 hours; 3, ground 6 hours; 4, ground 15 hours; 5, ground 24 hours; 6, ground 140 hours; 7, ground wet 60 hours. From McLaughlin (M28).
The wet grinding (curve 7) has relatively little disruptive effect on the crystallinity.

In contrast to all this, the specimen ground wet for 60 hours shows a slight broad low-temperature endotherm, a broadening and lowering (by ca. 120°C) of the normal dehydration, and a quite normal exotherm at 980°C. The lowering of the temperature appears to be the ordinary particle size effect; the broadening is probably due to a great increase in particle size range. McLaughlin points out that "the material ground wet 60 hours lies intermediate in size between 2 hours and 6 hours dry grinding" and concludes that "very long periods of wet grinding would be needed to reach the equilibrium which is apparently obtained after

15 hours dry grinding." The present author disagrees. The effect of 60 hours wet grinding can probably not be achieved by 2–6 hours of dry grinding nor will the effect of 15 hours of dry grinding be duplicated by a couple of months of wet grinding.

Wet grinding in moderation brings about some changes in reactivity but frequently, at least, these changes are in the direction of enhanced peaks. Caillère and Hénin (C2a) have shown (Fig. III-29) that chlorite minerals show better definition of peaks after wet grinding and a general simplification of the thermogram. The lowering of temperatures by grinding is probably due simply to the relative ease of escape of the water from the smaller particles. In a controlled-atmosphere experiment (using water vapor), the peaks would presumably begin at the same temperature in both samples, but the peaks for the ground sample would be extremely sharp compared to those of the unground material.

A large portion of the distortion of the surface of the dry-ground par-

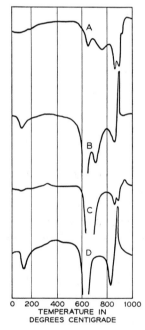

TEMPERATURE IN
DEGREES CENTIGRADE

Fig. III-29. Differential thermal curves for: A, leuchten bergite, Beramy, Madagascar, -60 mesh; B, same mineral particles $<2\ \mu$ esd.; C, clinochlore, Besafotra, Madagascar, -60 mesh; D, same mineral, particles $<2\ \mu$ esd. From Caillère and Hénin (C2a).

The exothermic peaks in B and D have shifted enough to obscure any evidence for the second part of the double endothermic peaks in A and C.

ticles is due to the local heating resulting from the impact and shearing. The wet-ground specimen does not show distortion to nearly the same degree simply because each impact, each scrape, and each abrasion is fluid-cooled. Any significant tendency to heat a portion of a surface would bring about vaporization of a little of the grinding fluid in contact with the surface so that the areas that reached temperatures much above the boiling point would be rare indeed.

The effect of particle size, then, is related to the method of producing the particle size. Wet grinding—not necessarily wet with water—should produce much less of a surface distortion than dry grinding. The effect of dry grinding is to produce a high-energy surface—probably quite useful in preparing materials for reaction—which cannot be depended on to show thermal effects closely like those of the original material. Dempster and Ritchie (D10), for example, dry-ground quartz enough to form a surface layer (M3) thick enough, apparently, to insulate the interior and prevent detection of the low-energy a-β transition at 573°C. The coating formed was probably similar to fused quartz, i.e., amorphous and with little tendency to crystallize. Since the a-β transition represents little movement as well as little energy, even repeated passage through the transition would not likely crystallize much of the amorphous layer. The added layer through which heat must pass and the irregularity of that layer could easily cause diffuseness of the peak sufficient to render its existence uncertain.

Whether or not the means of dry grinding has a great influence on the nature of the surfaces produced has not—to the present author's knowledge—been established. Some inferences may be drawn by comparing the McLaughlin work discussed above with that reported by Gregg *et al.* (G42). These latter authors studied kaolinite rather than dickite but these minerals are very similar—at least from a nonmineralogist's viewpoint. Gregg, Parker, and Stephens milled a china clay (95% kaolinite with some mica, tourmaline, feldspar, and quartz) in a pebble mill at 25 rpm for 1000 hours, taking samples at intervals for measurement of specific surface, apparent density in carbon tetrachloride, bulk density *in vacuo,* particle size distribution, and base exchange capacity. In addition specimens were studied by X-ray diffraction, dissolution in hydrochloric acid, and thermogravimetry.

In general, the particles decreased in size but eventually began to agglomerate so that the specific surface and the base exchange capacity passed through a maximum about midway through the grinding period. Of special interest are the weight-loss curves. Figure III-30 shows the rate of weight loss as a function of temperature, Δ_W/Δ_T vs T. Compare the curves for 576 hours to that for 2 hours in Fig. III-26.

The inference from the limited data would be that ball (or pebble) milling—like wet grinding—is much slower than mortar-and-pestle grinding. This may be true, but there is at least a high probability that the results differ in kind as well as in degree. Recall that McLaughlin found changes in spacing but still a recognizable X-ray diffraction pattern in specimens ground dry for 140 hours. On the other hand, Gregg *et al.* report that the X-ray diffraction lines "become progressively broader and weaker against a darkening background until, at 1000 hours, no pattern

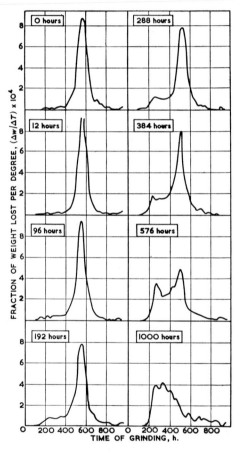

Fɪɢ. III-30. Grinding of kaolin. The thermogravimetric analysis of the ground samples. In each graph the fractional loss of weight per degree is plotted against the temperature of the furnace. The time of grinding is marked on each sample. From Gregg *et al.* (G42).

Only after ca. 20 days milling does the kaolin peak at 600°C diminish greatly.

could be identified." Even mild-acid treatment restored the pattern of kaolinite only up to the 576-hour sample.

Just how different the two treatments ought to be is rather hard to judge. The falling of a ball or pebble results in a fairly reproducible impact but how this impact is distributed among the particles on which the ball falls will probably vary along with the particle size and shape. We may easily infer, nevertheless, that a given impact will cause a range of effect from a high tendency to fracture the particles directly in line with the impact to a greater tendency to shear the particles to the side of the line of impact, but of course the force diminishes with the cosine of the angle. A mechanically driven mortar and pestle will have principally a shearing action. Note here that a manually operated mortar and pestle will have a range of behavior from crushing to shearing depending on the operator and the sample. This effect would likely be highly irreproducible if it were measurable. Fortunately the reduction of particle size to the 100-mesh range will not often produce noticeable surface effects. Few experimenters will go to finer size ranges manually.

The conclusion to be reached is that, if the particle size of a specimen must be reduced, even the method used must be chosen with consideration of possible effects. This applies especially to the very fine sizes. As we reduce the particle size of a material by some given method, at some point the effects of surface irregularities will become noticeable against the behavior of the bulk material. As the size reduction continues this surface layer becomes a greater portion of the whole particle and will determine the behavior of the particle to a greater and greater extent. The sample sizes at which the surface effect appears or predominates can be expected to vary not only with the manner of particle size reduction but also from material to material.

3.15. Summary

The values of the several parameters must be chosen to suit the problem. A high rate of heating will offer more sensitivity for detection at a risk of loss of resolution. Depending on the type of apparatus, peak shifting may or may not occur with a change in heating rate.

The material chosen for the sample block will depend on the temperature range. Ceramic materials are available with thermal conductivities as good as commonly used high-temperature alloys and with superior surface heat-transfer properties.

For changes in condensed states, the design of the sample block can introduce small aberrations due to assymmetry of heating of the sample. For decompositions or reactions producing or using a gas pronounced changes will appear with different designs arising from differences in accessibility to the atmosphere. The nature of the change will depend on the atmosphere and the material.

Thermocouples are generally placed as near as possible to the center of symmetry to obtain the maximum signal. Other arrangements are usable but the form of the differential signal will be different. The size of the thermocouple will have a relatively small effect unless the wire— or shield—is large enough to conduct appreciable heat to or from the sample.

The inert substance ought to be chosen to match the total heat-transfer characteristics of the material being studied, but these characteristics often change drastically upon occurrence of some thermal event. An empirically chosen reference material (such as calcined aluminum oxide) is often used. The sample may also be diluted to a point at which the thermal properties of the diluent obscure those of the sample; the diluent is used also as the reference material.

The particle size and often the means of obtaining the particle size will influence the peak shapes. On very fine particles the surface characteristics obtained by grinding may predominate.

CHAPTER IV

Apparatus for Differential Thermal Analysis

4.1. Introduction

For many reasons, most workers in the field of differential thermal analysis have constructed their own apparatus. The principal reason has been the usually well-founded conviction that no apparatus with which he was familiar would give him the particular information he needed. We may assume that the new features introduced in a particular apparatus were usually of some benefit in the type of study for which it was designed. To extrapolate this assumption to conclude that any particular innovation is of general utility would be rash. The discussion of apparatus following relates to specific types and includes in many cases the present author's evaluation.

Some discussion of principles pertaining especially to differential thermal analysis is included. More general topics are explained or described in Chapters XIV–XVI. Special types of sample holders are described in this chapter even though some properties or characteristics of sample holders in general are discussed in Chapters II, III, and V.

Except to illustrate a particular feature, the extant commercially available apparatus are not discussed in detail. A description would become obsolete almost during the printing time for a book not only because of additions but also because of changes. We will be concerned herein with principles by which to judge the suitability of an apparatus. A list of suppliers is offered in Appendix I.

4.2. Furnace Orientation

Whether a horizontal or a vertical furnace should be used will depend mostly on individual preferences; both have advantages. Horizontal furnaces can generally be constructed for greater ease of manipulation; a track allowing rather accurate positioning can be easily supported on a bench top, making the sample support easily accessible to the operator. Vertical furnaces of some contemporary designs will have the sample position at or above eye level when set on a standard bench. If the heating element with insulation is heavy and/or bulky it matters little for a horizontal furnace but the support mechanism becomes a rather important consideration in vertical furnaces. The heater support mechanism must move to expose or enclose the sample support without change in orientation except along the straight-line extension of the furnace tube axis and without appreciable vibration or other disturbance such as flexing of the support. The ordinary relay rack is not strong enough. The lighter and smaller furnaces currently available alleviate most of the support problem so the relative merits of the two systems can be examined with somewhat less regard for mechanical considerations.

A horizontal tube furnace generally comprises a resistance wire or ribbon wound on the exterior of a ceramic tube and with insulation outside of this winding (Fig. IV-1). The horizontal furnace [patterned after that of W. Coffeen (C18)] used by the author for several years is shown in Fig. IV-2. It moved on a ball slide fastened to a steel mounting plate; this steel plate was set on a benchtop. Since all parts are fixed in relation to the mounting plate and the mounting plate was under no strain, devising a sample support could be done easily with the assurance that clearances would be maintained when the furnace was moved into operating position—subject, of course, to heating effects.

The horizontal furnace will have, if wound uniformly, a temperature gradient along the axis or any line parallel to the axis whose magnitude will depend greatly on the length/width ratio. After the high gradient at the ends, the temperature (under steady-state heating) will increase toward the center not because the heater winding is any hotter or the insulation is any better but because the center cannot radiate heat to appreciably cooler surfaces. It is obvious from this consideration that a long, narrow tube-and-winding will have a low gradient in the middle region. Since long tubes are often impractical, ways of conserving heat or otherwise decreasing the gradient are used. One practical solution is the supplying of additional heat to the ends of the windings (see Chapter XVII). In addition, the ends of the tube are insulated inside as well as practicable. In Fig. IV-2, the detail 19 is a firebrick plug extending approximately 2 inches into the heated region. Like most users of horizontal furnaces the author then assumed that the central portion of the

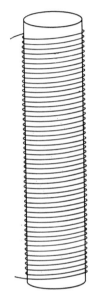

Fig. IV-1. Helical winding on insulating tube.
The winding is cemented into place with a material having high thermal conductivity to equalize the temperature.

furnace was, for all practical purposes, uniform. One may question rather seriously whether the uniformity of temperature is maintained under high heating rates. The need to heat the end plugs introduces the problem of convection currents because these plugs are insulators and not easily heated. Likely as not the principal source of heat for warming the plug surface (at least below 600–700°C) is convection. In the absence of such precautions a very favorable condition for the occurrence of a sizable convection current is set up: a vertical wall substantially cooler than the gas inside and a heat source at the bottom. If the inside of the tube is comparatively empty a current will probably become established. The presence of the heat source around the sides of the tube ought to result in turbulence but will probably not stop the flow.

The construction of a vertical tube furnace poses somewhat different problems from those associated with horizontal furnaces. Most problems are connected with the greater opportunity for convection because there will generally be a greater height of open volume heated along the edges. Note, too, that a vertical cylinder with heated walls can permit a continuous smooth flow of gas up the walls and down the center while the flow in the same cylinder in a horizontal position will become turbulent before an appreciable velocity is reached. A uniform temperature zone is much easier to achieve, then, in a horizontal than in a vertical furnace; it is essential therefore that the advantages of the vertical arrangement be examined carefully and critically.

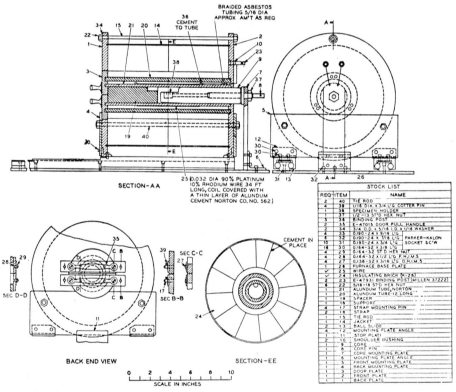

Fig. IV-2. Conventional furnace for differential thermal analysis. From Garn and Flaschen (G12).

The horizontal furnace is moved into place around the sample block. Double-wound ends provided a low-temperature gradient in the center of the furnace (see Chapter XVII).

A vertical furnace has the significant advantage that specimens, liquid or solid, may be placed symmetrically about the axis; this permits uniform exposure to heating at all temperatures. A vertical thermal gradient is necessarily going to exist and this gradient is almost certain to be larger than that in a horizontal furnace. This is no real cause for alarm, however, because under the same heating conditions the temperature variation at any point should be reproducible (but see below). So long as the sample is at a reproducible height and the temperature is being measured either at the sample or at the same height no significant errors should occur.

The use of a vertical furnace requires some caution. An open-end tube or one in which a cold region exists above the hot zone can lead to rather striking convection currents. The author discovered with some dismay that the earlier vertical furnaces wound for him were subject to a temperature oscillation that might persist for 100–300°C. The oscillation was not a "hunting" of the control apparatus since—once started—it continued even if the furnace power was turned off for a short time. The author eventually deduced that surges of gas were set up because of the unfavorable temperature gradient (see Fig. IV-3).

This unfavorable temperature gradient occurred for two reasons, insufficient insulation at the top and termination of the windings ½ inch from the top of the tube. The top of the furnace chamber may be 50°C or more cooler than the region within the windings. Since the author began winding his furnaces himself the temperature gradient in the top 2½ inches is generally on the order of 20°C; no evidence of surges of air have been seen. This was accomplished by extending the winding of the furnace to the top of the tube. Note that the temperature-inversion problem did not occur in the furnace shown in Fig. IV-2 even when it was mounted vertically; this is presumably because the plug (detail 19) which was above the sample was inserted well within the windings and consequently was quite well heated. Further, there was only a small open region between the sample and this plug.

These surges of gas are probably of little importance when the thermocouple is hidden deep in a block with a nondynamic atmosphere; the cool gas has to encounter many hot surfaces before reaching the thermocouple bead. However, in dynamic-atmosphere operation in the Lodding-Hammell (L10) manner one must examine the origin and possible effects of these surges. The author can only speculate on this extension of the surge phenomenon because the short-term cooling one might expect is highly irreproducible. Consider, though, a furnace in which windings are terminated noticeably short of the end of the tube (Fig. IV-4b). At very high flow rates of gas there is probably sufficient turbulence in the top of the chamber to force a reasonable mixing. At some poorly defined flow rate—probably heavily dependent on temperature and composition—the turbulence is insufficient to prevent significant cooling at the very top of the chamber. At still lower flow rates the gas rising beside the block from the lower part of the chamber can flow across the upper surface of the block and through the sample and reference

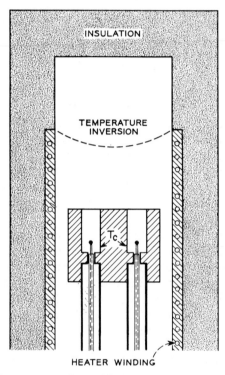

FIG. IV-3. Cross section of top end of early model of vertical furnace.
The cold end caused oscillation of temperature as the inversion broke down and re-established itself.

without appreciable disturbance of the temperature distribution in the upper chamber; this is the potentially most troublesome situation. We have now a condition in which a general flow of gas produces no stirring so the gas in the top of the furnace may cool. The gas in the region of the winding is heated but, with no driving force to assure continual mixing, a temperature inversion is established—a sort of micro Los Angeles. This unstable condition is unlikely to persist for a considerable time so after a little while the cooler gas drops down the middle of the tube as far as the block, warm gas replaces the cooler gas, the cool gas—mixed somewhat with warm gas—flows down through sample and reference and hence is disposed of, and now the temperature-inversion cycle may begin again.

The time of the breakdown of the temperature inversion concerns us here. The cool gas entering the sample or reference cavity will tend to cool rather than heat the specimen and will cause a spurious signal of short duration. The problem is compounded if one is controlling (programming) from either the sample or reference thermocouple for

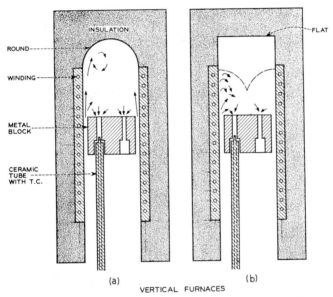

Fɪɢ. IV-4. Cross sections of furnaces showing dynamic gas flow.
Round ends and higher windings prevent establishment of significant temperature inversions.

the cooling—or cessation of heating—will bring about an increase of power input (see Chapter XVI). Proof or disproof of these speculations is not easily acquired; the curves obtained by the author show deviations in accord with the events described. When one is working with a high-sensitivity system in which the total heat capacity is small the gas surges are large enough to ruin the experiment. The surges do not occur with a properly wound furnace.

The fact that thermal gradients will exist must be accepted; the problem becomes a dual one of decreasing the gradient so far as practical and then decreasing the effect of that which remains by careful arrangement of the parts. The most important source of trouble is the top end of the furnace hot zone. In uncontrolled atmosphere furnaces and in some controlled atmosphere furnaces there is no serious problem; one simply inserts a firebrick plug into the heated zone far enough so that it is well-heated. In closed-end tubes—such as the present author generally uses—no such easy way out exists.

Small vertical temperature gradients are of little importance except insofar as they affect gas flow. A pair of specimens at the same level and symmetrically placed with respect to the axis of the furnace tube will still reach the same temperature; the gradient should be small to compensate for errors in locating. The author has repeatedly put < 10-mg samples in small tubes placed over the ends of shielded thermocouples and obtained good thermograms with a low base line drift.

Further, a block will equalize the temperature within itself quite well even if the top and bottom edges are adjacent to furnace wall sections several degrees different in temperature. Conduction within the block—except at quite high temperatures—transfers heat more rapidly than from furnace wall to block.

In horizontal furnaces a common technique used to provide a uniform temperature zone is to wind the ends closer than the center (Fig. XVI-1). This technique is worthless in vertical furnaces because of the existence of the thermal gradients. Consider especially the closer winding at the top. Gases flowing up the wall become very hot just below a cool surface. The temperature inversion discussed earlier can become serious indeed. Table IV-1 shows data for just such a furnace, with the winding of 1 inch of 16 turns/inch, 3 inches of 10 turns/inch, and 1 inch of 16 turns/inch ending about ⅝ inch from the top of the tube. A variable autotransformer was set successively at a series of convenient points and the furnace allowed to reach a steady state as indicated by the

TABLE IV-1

TEMPERATURE INVERSION IN TOP OF CLOSED-END TUBES
AT SOME ARBITRARILY CHOSEN TEMPERATURE

	Single-wound End		Double-wound End	
	Top	1.0 inch below top	Top	1.0 inch below top
T_1	1125	1138	1100	1202
T_2	902	915	795	915
T_3	668	670	628	722
T_4	450	450	495	560
T_5	356	351	301	314

thermocouples. The data are compared to similar data obtained using a furnace having a uniform winding extending above the end of the furnace tube. The cementing and insulating of the two furnaces were the same.

The closer winding which is of real value in horizontal furnaces neither avoids the temperature inversion nor provides a uniform temperature zone in the central region. The nearest to uniformity provided by such a winding is in the close-wound region, but that is also a hot zone just below a cold zone; such a zone would be treacherous indeed.

In such furnaces, the top must be heated in some manner. The most convenient way is to extend the winding beyond the closed end of the tube.

4.3. Amplification

The differential signal from any of the less energetic reactions will require amplification for most recorders. To a limited degree, amplification can be obtained in the sample holder itself by use of a thermopile (Fig. IV-5) in which the junctions are alternately in the sample and reference

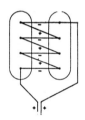

FIG. IV-5. Schematic diagram of a multiple differential thermocouple. From Lodding and Sturm (L12).
The signals are additive so the emf would be four times that of the conventional technique.

specimens; Lodding and Sturm's (L12) arrangement is shown in Fig. IV-6. The sample-holder design must permit locating a number of thermocouple junctions at equivalent positions, in this case the center line of a rectangular parallelopiped.

This technique for amplification has one very distinct advantage—the effects due to size and positioning of thermocouple beads are averaged over the set so that any base line drift *due to these causes* is diminished even while the differential signal is increased. Note, however, that drift due to the differing properties of the specimens is amplified, too. Lodding and Sturm show (Fig. IV-7) thermograms of quartz to illustrate

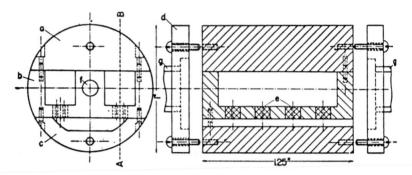

Fig. IV-6. Specimen holder for a four-unit multiple differential thermocouple. The line A-B refers to the cross section shown on the right. From Lodding and Sturm (L12).
The rectangular cross section permits easiest positioning of thermocouple beads.

the technique. The base line signal is low in magnitude so a peak of fairly low magnitude could be detected.

Another nonelectronic means of amplifying the differential signal can be used easily with optical detectors. The signal is fed into a mirror galvanometer and the movement detected by photocells some distance away. The displacement of the beam is obviously proportional to the distance. The signal may be attenuated by shunting to obtain less sensitive operation. Keith and Tuttle (K14) arranged a split photocell on a recorder pen carriage (Fig. IV-8) so that the photocell and hence the pen followed the beam deflection.

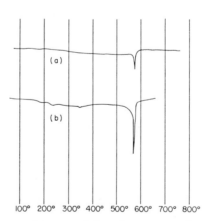

100° 200° 300° 400° 500° 600° 700° 800°

Fig. IV-7. Thermograms of quartz: (a) with conventional unit, (b) with multiple differential thermocouple. From Lodding and Sturm (L12).
The small inflections ca. 250° and 350°C may be due to impurities.

Generally, electronic amplification will be used. Stabilized electronic amplifiers with high signal-to-noise ratio and low drifts are available. The total amplification of the amplifier-recorder combination should be adjustable, but only in fixed steps. A continuously variable range will almost certainly be less reproducible than a fixed range and has little to offer in compensating advantages while a fixed-step adjustment ought to be accurately reproducible from day to day.

Similarly, a stepwise zero adjustment has a substantial advantage over a continuous adjustment. This zero adjustment ought to be on the slide-wire shunt on the recorder. The reason for having a stepwise adjustment is that the zero can be known at all times, permitting change in amplification with knowledge of the effect. (With continuous adjustments on amplification and zero, by the time the operator has made a couple of changes during a run he has probably lost track of zero and possibly of amplification factor so that he no longer knows the magnitude of his signal.) The reason for putting the zero shift on the shunt is that a compensating signal is avoided. The compensating signal technique introduces more components and more noise. The present author has used both techniques; in the differential thermal analysis apparatus described in Chapter XVII a compensating signal is used because operation in the slidewire circuit is impractical. When the thermogravimetric control and recording apparatus (Chapter XVI) is used—as it is occasionally—for a differential thermal analysis experiment, the author shunts the slidewire to shift the zero.

If an external compensating signal is to be used, a calibrated potentiometer should be used if the zero is to be shifted more than one or two scale ranges away from center. For zero shifts on scale or not far off scale the shifting signal can be applied between amplifier and recorder. At this higher signal level contact noise and such is rarely troublesome. Nearly any amplifier will give a linear output at twice its rated output, particularly under these conditions; the electrical load is, in effect, diminished.

4.4. Placement of Control Thermocouples

In most types of furnaces, any location chosen for a control (programming) thermocouple is a compromise between smoothness of control and precise linearity of temperature rise. For maintaining a steady temperature in the interior of a furnace, assuming no change in demand, keeping the temperature of the heating element nearly constant is quite obviously the best way, for a steady-state heat flow will be established that will be unchanging with time. If the temperature of the furnace winding is controlled, however, the system is insensitive to

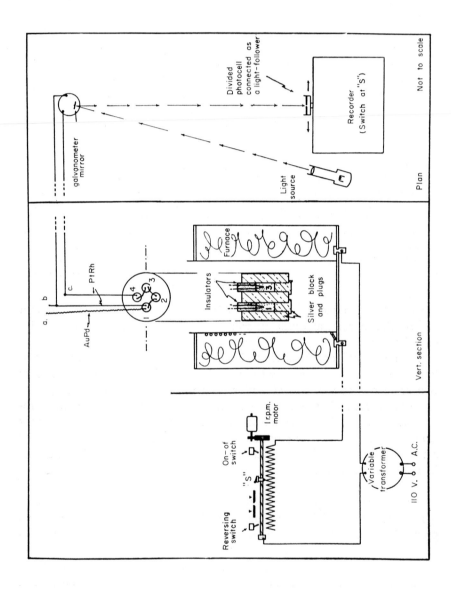

changes in demand; that lack of sensitivity made necessary the earlier assumption (see above) of constant demand. Let us move to the other extreme in control points, i.e., within the material being heated, and consider the behavior of the control system.

If the system happens to be at a steady state and any control functions are in a nonvarying condition, the temperature may possibly remain constant. (Note that in the absence of any proportioning action the steady state is highly improbable.) Any unbalance that does occur is likely to initiate oscillations about the control temperature simply because the heater must gain or lose in temperature to compensate for the unbalance, but this gain or loss is not received immediately at the control point.

> A cooling of the control point, for example, brings about an increase in the heater temperature but all intervening materials must also be heated before the control point is brought back to the set temperature. Since these intervening materials are now warmer than they would be in a steady state the control point is also made warmer than the set temperature so that the heater needs to cool. The intervening materials likewise cool to below their steady-state temperature and the process repeats. The magnitude and frequency of this "hunting" oscillation depends on the nature and quantity of material between the heater and the control point and the type of control system (which determines the relation between any unbalance and the resulting temperature of the windings).

Some types of control systems permit some oscillation as a matter of course; this oscillation would be characteristic of ON-OFF, HIGH-LOW, or adjustable autotransformer control. For many applications it is not troublesome but for accurate smooth control better systems are needed. Even with good control systems the problem of location of the control point is not solved completely. With a control point at the windings the material being heated is at a lower temperature and this lower temperature depends on the demand, i.e., the amount of heat the winding must supply to its surroundings to keep itself (and the control point) at the set temperature. On the other hand, if the control point is in the material being heated a change in temperature will incur exaggerated changes in the temperature of the winding which may induce hunting.

Let us now impose a new condition—a moving set point or temperature. This is the condition of real interest to us, a regular increase or decrease in temperature with time—so we need to consider what point in

Fig. IV-8. Mirror galvanometer with beam follower. Samples in silver block: (1) unknown quartz; (2) cryolite; (3) reference quartz; (4) K_2SO_4. From Keith and Tuttle (K14).

Up to the limit imposed by mechanical vibration the galvanometer movement can be amplified by further separating the beam follower from the galvanometer.

our system is to rise in temperature at a constant rate. Let us first return the control point to near the furnace winding and note the effect on the region in which a differential thermal analysis specimen might be placed.

As shown above, the interior of the furnace will not be at the control temperature; further, this difference will change with temperature and heating rate. This difference is not generally severe; the initial lag due to low conductivity at room temperature diminishes gradually until a dynamic "steady state" is achieved.

Now put the control thermocouple in the specimen. As heating begins the lag shown in Fig. IV-9 will require the heating winding to supply

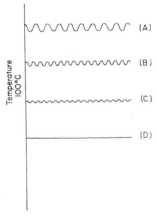

FIG. IV-9. Temperature variation in specimen with control thermocouple located in: (A) isolated cup; (B) metal alloy block; (C) furnace cement ⅛ inch outside of heater winding; and (D) against inside wall of furnace tube.
The control thermocouple should be near the heater for smooth control.

heat rapidly. Since the heater winding is able to heat its environment to some limit far above room temperature, it may warm the furnace tube 100°C or more too high before the control thermocouple is brought to the control point. But now the heater shuts down and the overheated tube keeps up with the moving control point for a while. Since the heater is actually cooling there must soon come a time when the control thermocouple temperature begins to lag behind the control point and a new surge must begin. This effect diminishes at higher temperatures because heat transfer becomes more rapid. The behavior shown in A can be alleviated by proper adjustment of proportional band reset and rate action to approach that shown in D. Note that the controlled temperature is now at the location where the control is wanted; on the other hand, the adjustment of the process control variables, i.e., proportional band, etc., may need to be different for each type of experimental arrangement. This can be a minor nuisance in determining the settings, but once these are found the operator needs only to remember to make the changes when required.

The author's control apparatus was designed to operate from the recorded temperature which means that the control point must be in the sample, the reference, the block, or at some reasonably equivalent point. Generally the block temperature was recorded (and controlled). The later use of more sensitive arrangements required careful readjustment for each system.

4.5. Sample Holders

The use of a sample block is common perhaps to the extent of being prevalent; nevertheless, a considerable number of workers use other types of specimen holders. These may range from a moderate increase in isolation of specimens by inserting a poor conductor between block and specimen to a complete (within the hot zone) isolation of the specimen supports. The present author uses the entire range.

For slight isolation a poorly conducting sleeve may be set in the specimen cavities. Providing the length of the specimen is significantly greater than the diameter this will provide some isolation with the comforting knowledge that the outside of that sleeve is at a uniform temperature.

Somewhat greater isolation is provided by inserting nonmetallic cups into blocks (Fig. IV-10); much greater isolation can be obtained by supporting the specimen only (Fig. IV-11) by the thermocouple wires. The latter degree of isolation is approximated also by support by the thermocouple insulator. Many varying intermediate degrees of isolation have been reported, e.g., Figs. IV-12, IV-13, IV-15, and VI-34.

The effect of the increasing separation is a matter of degree; the approach toward differential calorimetry carries with it the risk of failure to separate—or possibly even to recognize—close-lying thermal effects.

Bohon (B59) enclosed samples of explosives in small cups which were set on the ends of shielded thermocouples. The samples were enclosed by threaded caps either (Fig. IV-12) to seal in the sample and products or to retain the sample but allow interchange of gases between the sample and the furnace atmosphere. (The present author has used similar cups but *sans* cover to allow free access of atmosphere to the sample.)

The apparatus used by Bohon is shown in Fig. IV-21. Note that the Inconel thermocouple sheaths and the baffle plates form a heat conduction path between sample and reference. The interchange of heat is significant (B61) and, in fact, the degree of thermal isolation—and hence sensitivity—can be varied somewhat by adding, subtracting, or repositioning these baffle plates.

A somewhat unusual sample arrangement has been reported by Sabatier (S2), by West (W24), and by Rey and Kostomaroff (R18). Three rather isolated cylinders (Fig. IV-13) hold the sample, reference, and a second reference in which to measure the temperature. The temperature reference cylinder may sometimes contain sample rather than an inert material. The fact that there are three sample vessels instead of two

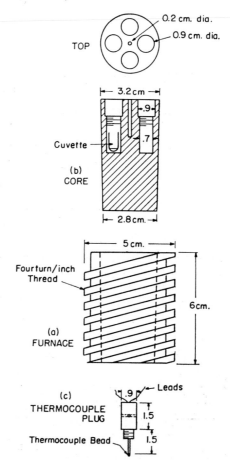

Fig. IV-10. Differential thermal analyses block. (a) Furnace block, Alcoa aluminum rod stock; (b) cuvette carriage core; (c) thermocouple and mounting. From Barrall and Rogers (B7).

The very coarse winding is of no importance because the block equalizes the temperature. The cuvette provides some thermal isolation of the specimens.

means that they must necessarily be spread out more than two need be and, hence, a portion of each is very near the hot wall. Garn and Flaschen (G12) have pointed out the potential danger of nonuniformity of temperature around the specimen. The wall of the cylinder must be thick enough to transmit heat rapidly, otherwise the reaction front does not move symmetrically from the entire circumference and the peak is spread over a wider range of time and (indicated) temperature. The effect will diminish with increasing temperature.

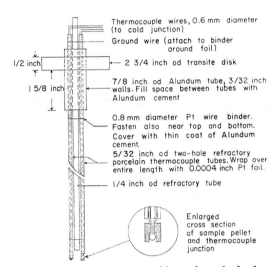

Thermocouple wires, 0.6 mm diameter (to cold junction)

Ground wire (attach to binder around foil)

1/2 inch

2 3/4 inch od transite disk

1 5/8 inch

7/8 inch od Alundum tube, 3/32 inch walls. Fill space between tubes with Alundum cement

0.8 mm diameter Pt wire binder. Fasten also near top and bottom. Cover with thin coat of Alundum cement.

5/32 inch od two-hole refractory porcelain thermocouple tubes. Wrap over entire length with 0.0004 inch Pt foil.

1/4 inch od refractory tube

Enlarged cross section of sample pellet and thermocouple junction

FIG. IV-11. Details of thermocouple assembly and method of supporting sample pellet. From Newkirk (N7).

If the specimen melts the liquid can cling to the thermocouple bead. No thermal contact exists between sample and reference except by radiation (see Chapter VIII.

The nature of the surface of the sample block is as important as the properties of the bulk material. A nickel block may conduct heat more readily within itself than a ceramic block but its emissivity is far lower. This can result in better heat transfer in the ceramic because the temperature drop between wall and block is accentuated. Figure IV-14 is a purely arbitrary representation of this condition. While the metal block has a nearly zero gradient in it, it heats the sample less because it cannot absorb radiation so well as the ceramic.

The isolated sample sleeves in the preceding figure might better be ceramic than platinum.

The author has used a great variety of specimen holders for various studies. The use of a vertical furnace with easily interchanged support pieces makes possible many changes in geometry. Support rods with one, two, four, or even more holes of various sizes enable use of shielded or wire thermocouples in a multitude of arrangements. Two specimen holders in which both sample and reference thermocouples were led through a single ¼ inch ceramic tube (centered in the furnace) are shown in Fig. IV-15. The open-cup holder shown in Fig. IV-15a is used to provide good accessibility of (or to) the furnace atmosphere (see Chapter VII).

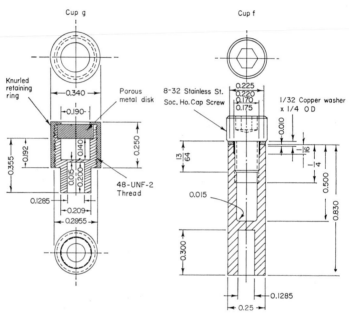

FIG. IV-12. Typical sample cups used by Bohon (B59). *Left:* Isobaric cup g. Porous metal cup permits passage of gases but retains solid sample. *Right:* Isochloric cup f. Dead soft copper gasket provides pressure seal.

The isochloric cup permits pressures of several thousand pounds per square inch.

The reference thermocouple may be placed in a similar cup (and the two symmetrically placed) if the slight base line drift is a problem but for most purposes a thermocouple not quite touching the cup is adequate.

The holder shown in Fig. IV-15b was used with some relatively small samples for which finding reference materials would have been a tedious problem. This resembles a thermal conductivity measurement and the displacement of the base line does indeed depend on the thermal diffusivity but discontinuities are easily detected.

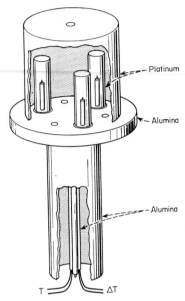

Fɪɢ. IV-13. Sample-holder arrangement using a third cavity in which to measure the furnace temperature.

Platinum sleeves are set into the alumina support plate so that the thermocouple bead is centered and along the axis.

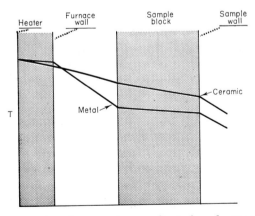

Fɪɢ. IV-14. Representation of temperature gradients from heater to sample well.

The temperature drop between furnace wall and sample block is high because of the low emissivity (and absorptivity) of metals.

Figure IV-16 shows a block used for samples which melt and for which a dynamic atmosphere is not needed. The block is set on the support rods used with the standard blocks and the thermocouple led through to re-enter the sample cavity from the top.

4.6. Programming

The general problem and techniques of programming are discussed in Chapter XV. Let us note here the need for programming by observation of the effect of a linearly varying voltage input. See Table IV-2.

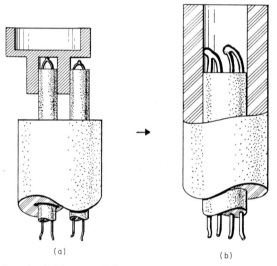

(a)   (b)

Fɪɢ. IV-15. Sample holders used by the author for (a) controlled-atmosphere accessibility and (b) changes in state of certain powdered specimens.

The wall separating the thermocouple and sample in (a) is thin enough to permit sensitive detection of effects. The measurement in (b) is the temperature drop from edge to center. The size of the thermocouple wire is exaggerated.

As part of a study of the kaolinite decomposition in water vapor at various pressures, the present author wished to heat the specimens to ca 700°C and cool without appreciable overshoot in temperature. The only apparatus in the author's custody which would permit controlled heating followed by complete shutdown at a preset temperature was that designed originally for thermogravimetric work. The "control" comprised a motor-driven autotransformer and a limit switch on the recorder. In practice, the voltage input was increased steadily until the thermocouple in the center of the specimen reached 720°C at which time the furnace power was shut off. The heating rate was not constant, but was fairly reproducible (10%) as the decomposition region was approached.

4.7. Recording of Data

The recording of data from a differential thermal analysis requires the simultaneous measurement of the temperature, T, and the temperature difference, ΔT. These may be recorded together or separately in a number of ways. The general problem of recording data is discussed in Chapter XVII; we are concerned here with a comparison of techniques.

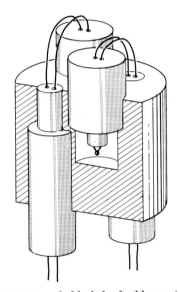

Fig. IV-16. Sample block for fusible specimens.
The holder was designed in this form to permit easy interchange with the dynamic atmosphere blocks.

The two major recording methods of interest here are (1) T and ΔT vs t, i.e., plotting of both functions on a time-based recorder, and (2) ΔT vs T, i.e., plotting of ΔT on a temperature-based recorder. The accuracy of recording is not the question; with good equipment there would be no difference. The comparison must be on the usefulness of the records. The author is firmly convinced that a time-based—whether or not on the same chart as ΔT—record of temperature is needed, since the operation of control devices cannot be taken on faith. [The need for monitoring is especially great if a range of types of operations is planned, while if the apparatus is to be used, run after run, on a single type of sample (control laboratory type of operation) any failure might possibly be recognized quickly without monitoring.]

The temperature-based record has certain elements of convenience: the records are all the same size and can be stored easily; two or three runs can be recorded side by side for easy comparison; for a fixed range and the proper graph paper, the temperature at any point may be read directly from the chart. The major deficiency is that it does not provide a time-dependent record of events that are themselves time-dependent.

TABLE IV-2

TEMPERATURE OF A KAOLINITE SPECIMEN, CA. 0.20 GM, DURING HEATING WITH LINEARLY INCREASING VOLTAGE SUPPLY TO BASE METAL WOUND FURNACE (FINAL VOLTAGE, 78 VOLTS)

Time (minutes)	Temperature (°C)	Heating rate, average over two intervals of time (°C/minute)
0	20	—
5	22	0.8
10	28	1.6
15	38	2.6
20	54	3.6
25	74	5.0
30	104	7.4
35	148	9.4
40	198	10.2
45	250	11.4
50	312	13.0
55	380	14.2
60	454	15.4
65	534	15.6
70	610[a]	16.0
75	700	—

[a]Reaction temperature range.

The time-based record has somewhat different advantages: the record can be expanded or shortened by changing chart drive speed without effect on the recording ranges; any irregularities in heating or other performance failures can be seen readily; and it provides in interpretable record of events even while the sample temperature is changing very slowly. The major deficiency is that an active experimenter encounters storage problems.

Let us now consider the relative effects of time- and temperature-based recording. First consider a phase transformation as shown in Figs. II-10 and II-11. The peaks of Fig. II-10 are quite sharp, far more so than those of Fig. II-11. The latter figure could be made to approach the former by slowing the chart speed, but that would put a much greater slope on the temperature indication and make more difficult the task of reading the temperature. On the other hand, if a measurement of area were desired, the ΔT vs T would be useless (See Chapter V) since the advance of the chart is not constant.

The major hazard in the use of temperature-based recorders is the possibility of overlooking close-lying effects in phase studies (this might apply to polymer work). Figure IV-17 shows a portion of a cooling cycle of a BaF–LiF mixture in which there are three close-lying thermal effects. The entire range of the peak is only 12°C, so the chart of the

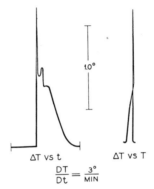

ΔT vs t   ΔT vs T

$$\frac{DT}{Dt} = \frac{3°}{MIN}$$

Fɪɢ. IV-17. Simultaneously recorded temperature-based and time-based thermograms of a BaF–LiF mixture.
The close-lying effect would not have been detected on a temperature-based recording.

X vs Y recorder (0–1500°C span) moves only slightly—not even the width of the tracing line—between the start of the deflection and the third peak. There is, in fact, a slight elevation in temperature during this period because of supercooling prior to the start of the solidification. Each of the three effects is clearly seen in the time-based plot.

It is true enough that expansion of the T scale to, say, 50°C or less full scale would permit detection of these changes. Use of this scale expansion (with the required zero offset circuitry) would require the willingness to rerun a portion of samples just to examine peaks. Reruns might also be required with time-based recording but the need to make the rerun would be clear. The equivalent of scale expansion is accomplished by the present author by setting limit switches on the temperature pen so that the chart drives only when the temperature is within the selected limits. Only a small amount of chart paper is run off even though the entire run might be quite long in time.

The present author uses both a time- and a temperature-based recorder, often simultaneously (see Chapter XVI). If only one recorder were to be used this author would unhesitatingly choose a time-base, recording T and ΔT on a single chart using a two-pen recorder.

4.8. Multiple Sample Holders

There are advantages in simultaneous differential analysis of a number of samples. It makes possible direct comparison of thermograms of two or more samples, the same sample in a series of dilutions, or comparison specimens for qualitative identification. The major problem of identity of temperature programming from run to run, while still highly desirable, can be avoided for work *specifically limited* to comparisons. In more general work in which the features of each thermogram are expected to have some meaning the usual requirements of nondiscontinuous and reproducible heating rates still apply and the heating rate is preferably linearly programmed.

The question of arrangement of sample cavities in a multiple block is reasonably simple. If the block is fairly conductive one may safely assume that the temperature is the same at the perimeter of each cavity so that, as in Fig. IV-18, the sample and reference may not even need

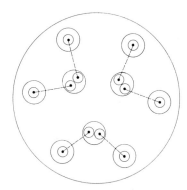

Fɪɢ. IV-18. Multiple differential thermal analysis in a single block (K43). The (numbered) sample holes are symmetrically placed but their accompanying reference functions are unsymmetrically placed in holes not symmetric with the sample holes.

The noncentered reference thermocouples appear to be quite satisfactory. The small base line drift that would probably occur with most samples would be of little consequence in this phase diagram work since it would appear in all thermograms and hence not indicate differences in specimens.

to be symmetrically placed. For many inorganic systems this would be a satisfactory arrangement. Kulp and Kerr (K43) were obtaining phase diagram data. It was convenient to obtain data from a set of six compositions simultaneously. Note that while sample and reference are not symmetrically placed, each sample well is symmetric with the others so even if a radial temperature gradient should exist, the only effect would be a base line displacement of each plot; the samples would still be exposed to the same temperature at their perimeters.

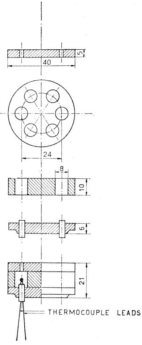

Fig. IV-19. Sample block for multiple DTA; dimensions in millimeters. From de Bruijn and van der Marel (B85).

The three-part block can be cleaned easily.

Another type of multiple differential thermal analysis sample block is that of de Bruijn and van der Marel (B85) shown in Fig. IV-19. This one has radial symmetry and, of course, accommodates three sample-and-reference pairs. It can be disassembled for easy cleaning. One of the interesting features, probably inadvertent, is that with an assembly like this the user could diminish end effects by choosing poorly conducting interfaces and have an uncommonly good approach to symmetric heating.

4.9. Controlled-Atmosphere Furnaces

The physical chemical basis for controlled atmospheres is elucidated in Chapter VII; our purpose here is to show only some of the equipment used. The effect of neutral atmospheres or atmospheres of gases which take part in a reaction is a comparatively recent development; the common practice was, of course, to establish a procedure for running a differential thermal analysis and to relate unknown samples to known specimens. This was reasonably satisfactory for mineralogical use in the days when the technique was used only to establish identity. As equipment was improved the users in all fields attempted to learn more about the reactions themselves.

A natural consequence of this shift in emphasis was a more careful evaluation of sample holders. Disputes such as that centered around the mineral ferrous carbonate, siderite, drew attention to the problem of atmosphere control (see Chapter XIII).

From this increased emphasis on atmosphere effects came the use of controlled-atmosphere furnaces. These evolved quite reasonably; the earliest were simple adaptations of existing apparatus followed by those designed specifically for controlled-atmosphere work. Whitehead and Breger (W30), for example, enclosed a more-or-less standard differential thermal analysis furnace is a vacuum chamber principally to avoid oxidation of organic materials in their samples.

Saunders and Giedroyc (S6) recognized the need for inert (nitrogen) as well as oxidizing (air) atmospheres in differential thermal analysis. They arranged their crucible assembly inside a quartz tube (Fig. IV-20) which they could evacuate and flush several times before adjusting their gas flow through the tube. Their sample cavity was also provided with a cover so that even the controlled atmosphere could be kept free from contact with the sample.

The use of supra-atmospheric pressures is also a consequence of controlled atmospheres; if a furnace must be sealed so that it can be pumped out or so there is no interchange of gas there is nothing to prevent the operator from adding more gas—up to the mechanical limits of the equipment. The general reasons for use of sub- or supra-atmospheric pressures will be discussed in Chapters VI and VII.

A more special use is in the study of explosives; here there is a distinct effect of pressure other than the usual atmosphere effect. The burning, ignition, or detonation behavior of explosives and propellants is dependent frequently on the *total* gas pressure rather than the pressure of some particular gas having some part in the reaction. Bohon (B59) constructed a furnace (Fig. IV-21) having a Monel tube surrounding the specimens and pressure-sealed to the base. Several hundred pounds of pressure can be applied to a sample by pressurizing the entire furnace chamber.

Application of a controlled pressure to a reasonably large chamber gives an approximately constant composition of gas—subject to short-term variations in the vicinity of the sample—and a constant pressure be-

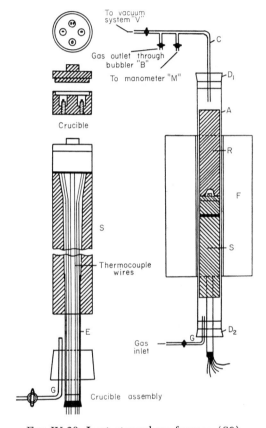

FIG. IV-20. Inert atmosphere furnace (S6).
The atmosphere sweeping up the sides of the tube can remove decomposition products or prevent oxidation.

fore, during, and after the reaction. Another technique found necessary by Bohon was the use of closed containers (Fig. IV-12) which could be pressurized before closing (Fig. IV-22) to provide a quite high initial pressure within only the sample container; the furnace chamber can be operated at atmospheric pressure. This technique permits higher pressures with relatively inexpensive equipment but it requires confinement of product gases with a consequent change in composition *and* increase in pressure as the decomposition reactions proceed.

Whether or not this is a disadvantage depends on the particular experiment; a general answer cannot be given. Berg and Rassonskaya (B40) used supra-atmospheric pressures on more nearly reversible reactions (see Chapter VII, Sec. 7.12).

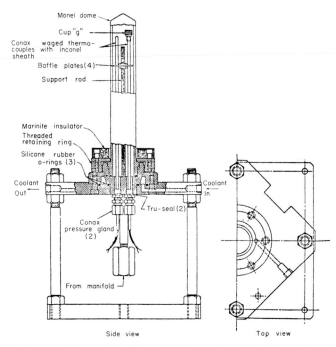

FIG. IV-21. Pressure furnace for differential thermal analysis. From Bohon (B59).
The lower O-ring seals retain the coolant, the upper seal provides the pressure seal. Baffle plates serve as radiation shields as well as adjustable thermal bridges between sample and reference.

4.10. Subambient Temperatures

The state of a specimen of nonliving material is prescribed by—among other things—the temperature. Each material behaves in a manner dictated by its own characteristics as its heat content is changed. It follows that the common temperatures 273.18°K, 298.18°K, or 373.18°K are of no general importance to such matter. There are thermal events which take place below room temperature quite like those associated with higher temperatures. The only difference in the study of these effects is that we must remove heat from the furnace and sample; this requires different apparatus from that customarily used. The difference, however, is intrinsically quite small.

Accurate control of temperature by exerting control only on a cooling process is not common; on the other hand, very extensive experience in control of heating processes can be drawn upon. The natural result is that an apparatus designed for subambient temperatures will comprise an uncontrolled or not closely controlled means of lowering the temperature and a means of controlled electric heating. The controlled heating

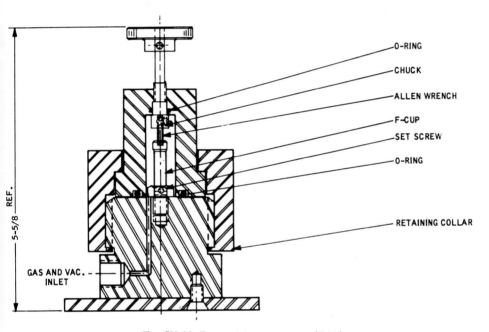

FIG. IV-22. Pressurizing apparatus (B60).
A high pressure of a known gas can be applied to the specimen. The composition may change drastically in the course of the reaction.

can then supply the compensating energy with quite ordinary equipment.

The actual apparatus design will depend on the nature of the problem. Two examples will be cited—one providing high thermal homogeneity within the system, the other providing a high degree of isolation.

Vassallo and Harden (V3) supplied cooled nitrogen to the outside of a metal block by use of a helical winding of tubing around the block (Fig. IV-23). Some cooling control can be obtained by varying the flow of the nitrogen. The presence of the heater at the center of the block raises the possibility of a substantial temperature gradient in the block so that noticeable differences in temperature at the inner and the outer edges of the sample might occur; careful programming and control would be needed (see Sec. 4.11).

Reisman (R12) used a Dewar flask which could be filled with liquid nitrogen for cooling (Fig. IV-24). While he uses isolated containers instead of a block, there is no reason why the same general plan could not be used with a block. The existence of a substantial surface area implies that some degree of control of cooling can be applied by varying the pressure over the liquid nitrogen. This control would be difficult to program accurately but the smooth variations would make the heating

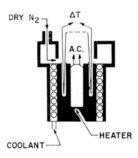

FIG. IV-23. Cross section of heater-cooler differential thermal analysis block. From Vassallo and Harden (V3).

In addition to the cooling gas, dry nitrogen is swept across the top of the block to avoid water condensation or oxidation.

control easy. Note that the heater is between the cooling system and the sample. This arrangement assures that the sample assembly will be affected by a single heat source—or sink; the temperature of this heat source, the wall surface, will presumably be changing smoothly so that no extreme or rapidly changing gradients will occur.

This latter arrangement, with the heat supply interposed between the cooled region and the specimen, is the more common design. In effect, one simply puts a fairly ordinary furnace in a cold environment. The direct contact of heat source and heat sink with the block can be made to work but extra effort is almost certainly required.

4.11. Internally Heated Blocks

Differential thermal analysis blocks are generally heated from external sources for good reason: homogeneity of temperature throughout the block can be approached more closely. Although many designs do not provide real symmetry—for example, a horizontal tube furnace enclosing a cylindrical block whose axis is in a vertical position—they do generally provide a fairly uniform environment. Heat can reach the block from the furnace wall in a pattern which at least approaches symmetry. But symmetry is only a part of the problem. Let us first examine the relative quantities of heat which must be transferred to or from the block and their effects on homogeneity or the temperature changes.

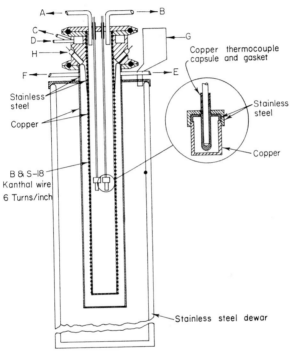

Fɪɢ. IV-24. Differential thermal analysis cryostat, 190 to 400°C. A and F, Vacuum valves; B and E, Bleeder valves; C, water inlet; D, water outlet; G, Funnel—liquid N_2 (supply to outer stainless steel Dewar); H, Stupakoff seals (2). From Reisman (R12).

The heater helps provide the precise control of the temperature "seen" by the specimens.

Consider the blocks of Fig. IV-25 in which axially symmetric blocks are heated internally and externally. The externally heated blocks must receive from the furnace wall enough heat to raise the temperature of the block, the sample and reference, and the support and measuring accessories. This implies a furnace wall hotter than the block but only sufficiently hotter to maintain the heat flow. The actual amount of heat transferred will change only slightly over a few hundred degrees and the change will be smooth.

Note that the flow of heat is converging; the relatively large source of heat to the block, i.e., the outer edge, provides heat to an effective cross section which diminishes with distance. This means that even the curvature of the temperature distribution will be less steep in most of the block.

Contrast this with an internally heated block. The small circumference in contact with the heater must convey approximately the same heat to the block assembly as before but through a considerably diminished area. The temperature gradient near the heater is necessarily considerably greater.

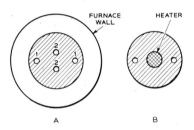

Fɪɢ. IV-25. Representation of blocks heated from A, a furnace wall and B, an interior heater.

Because of the difference in paths, the thermal gradient will be different in the two cases and the outer sample well (1) of block A will see a larger gradient than the inner (2) well.

Let us demonstrate the effect by a simple exercise which is descriptive enough to give some relative numbers but which lacks any vitiating assumptions. That we are dealing with a portion of a long cylinder, i.e., ignoring end effects, is the only controversial assumption. This assumption will change some numbers but will not affect the conclusion.

The equation for steady-state radial flow of heat in a cylinder is

$$q = \frac{2\pi kl(T_2 - T_1)}{\ln (R_1/R_2)}$$

where q is the quantity of heat crossing a radius, k is the thermal conductivity, l is the length, and T_2 and T_1 are the temperatures at radii of R_2 and R_1, respectively. This does not, however, take into account the consumption of heat in simply raising the temperature. Treatments of unsteady-state problems of this nature are—to the best of the author's knowledge—lacking in the literature, so we will use an ingenuous approach which yields answers in the form we are seeking.

Let us put some imaginary boundaries in the blocks of Fig. IV-25. First assume that the internal heater has a radius one-fourth that of the block and that the contact between them is perfect and hence radially symmetric. Now assume a constant heat capacity over a small range of temperature so that we may say that introduction of Q calories per unit time will raise the temperature at the programmed rate and, for the purposes of the immediate discussion, no heat is lost.

For any imaginary radius we can now calculate the area within and without the radius and also the quantity of heat which must cross that boundary. To avoid assigning specific values we will deal in fractions of R, A, and Q. The heat passing a boundary inward is proportional to the area within the boundary and the length of the boundary is proportional to the radius so

$$\frac{Q_{in}}{c} = \frac{Q}{2\pi r} \times \frac{a_{in}}{A}$$

where c is the circumference at r. This yields a measure of the heat flux, the quantity of heat passing unit length of boundary, and hence a measure of the temperature gradient which must exist at that boundary. Since we are dealing with fractional quantities and treating A as unity we can simplify to

$$\frac{Q_{in}}{c} = \frac{Q}{2\pi} \times r.$$

For the internal heating, the quantity of heat passing a boundary is proportional to the area outside the boundary so

$$\frac{Q_{out}}{c} = \frac{Q}{2\pi r} A(1 - a_{out}).$$

The values shown in Table I are calculated for several radii from these formulas. The plot in Fig. IV-26 relates the temperature gradients to the radius for the internally and externally heated blocks under the conditions assumed. Only at $0.7R$ do the gradients compare. The outer pair of specimen walls of block A of Fig. IV-25 would be in regions of temperature gradients approximating those of block B although the variation in gradient from inner to outer edge is considerably less. The inner pair are in regions of temperature gradient much smaller than around the outer holes.

The discussion so far as assumed no heat transfer out of the block. In case A of Fig. IV-25 this is a reasonable approximation, the heating of support structures and thermocouple leads can be neglected. When the block is hotter than its surroundings, it becomes the apparent heat source and flow of heat can no longer be neglected. But note that this heat loss will be affected by the temperature difference between the block and its surroundings (and also by the actual magnitude of the temperature), the geometry, and the atmosphere. Unfortunately, this loss will vary during a run in a manner which will itself differ with, particularly, change of atmosphere. We can, however, note the general effect by plotting some losses in terms of assumed fractions of Q; i.e., the heat crossing a boundary outward must be that previously calculated plus a given quantity so that

$$\frac{Q_{out}}{c} = \frac{QA}{2\pi r}\left(1 - \frac{a}{A}\right) + \frac{Q^*}{2\pi r}.$$

Figure IV-27 shows the effect of heat losses only up to a value equal to the useful heat, Q, although it can easily exceed Q.

The data show that a changing Q^* brings about a change in the thermal environment at the sample well. Since a change in Q^* is inevitable, so is its consequence.

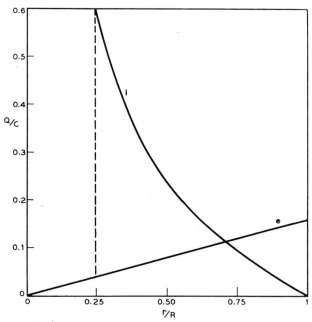

Fig. IV-26. Relative temperature gradients as functions of r/R for internal (i) and external (e) heating. The data of Table IV-3 are plotted using Q_{out}/c at the boundary of the internal heater as the reference value ($= 1.00$).

The temperature difference between inside and outside wall of a sample cavity will be greater for the internally heated block except very near the edge.

4.12. Thermistors as Detecting and Measuring Transducers

The development of differential thermal analysis techniques and apparatus has been an unsteady advance. The entry of a new device or technique may not be generally noted because the reports failed to demonstrate clearly the advantages or new possibilities inherent in the development. For example, controlled atmospheres—even static—have real value, but not until Stone wrote a series of articles demonstrating the use of controlled dynamic atmospheres (see Chapter VII) did many workers do more than speculate about the effect of ambient atmospheres.

TABLE IV-3

EFFECT OF DIRECTION OF HEAT FLOW ON TEMPERATURE
GRADIENT DISTRIBUTION IN CYLINDRICAL BLOCK ASSUMING
NO RADIATION OR CONVECTION LOSSES AND AN INTERNAL
HEATER RADIUS OF $0.250R$

$\dfrac{r}{R}$	$\dfrac{a_{in}}{A}$	$\dfrac{a_{out}}{A}$	$\dfrac{Q_{in}}{c}$	$\dfrac{Q_{out}}{c}$
0.125	0.016	0.984	0.020	—
0.250	0.062	0.938	0.040	0.596
0.375	0.137	0.863	0.060	0.366
0.500	0.250	0.750	0.080	0.239
0.625	0.390	0.610	0.100	0.156
0.750	0.562	0.438	0.119	0.093
0.875	0.765	0.235	0.139	0.043
1.000	1.000	0.0	0.159	0.000

r = radius of boundary under consideration,
R = outside radius,
a_{in} = area inside r,
a_{out} = area outside r,
A = area enclosed by R,
Q_{in} = quantity of heat per unit time moving inward past r,
Q_{out} = quantity of heat per unit time moving outward past r,
c = circumference at r.

The lack of impact is frequently the author's own fault. The introduction of even a minor improvement must be reported with a considered evaluation of its probable use. This ought to take the form of demonstrations of solutions of difficult problems or a clear comparison of techniques.

An example from recent literature of an opportunity lost is the work of Pakulak and Leonard (P4) who reported on the use of thermistors in differential thermal analysis (Fig. IV-28). Obviously thermistors can be used within their temperature limitations and, since they are small and have a low heat capacity but a high temperature coefficient of resistance, a worthwhile extension of technique ought to be obtainable. Very tiny samples in contact with the thermistors ought to yield rather large signals in a properly designed bridge. Further, the low-energy transitions of many organic materials could be detected. Comparison of thermal data with microscopic observation using a hot stage not only could have excited interest but also might have stimulated other workers.

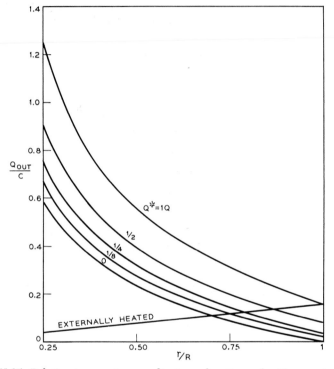

Fig. IV-27. Relative temperature gradients as functions of r/R assuming various relative heat losses, Q^*.

Since Q^* will change with temperature as well as several other parameters the relative environment of a sample cavity in an internally heated block will not remain constant.

In the actual report, Pakulak and Leonard noted that "Because this curve [Fig. IV-29] has a logarithmic nature, using the thermistors directly in a measuring circuit would result in an extremely poor temperature scale. Readings at one end of the scale would show a very small resistance differential for a given temperature differential; those at the opposite end would have very large resistance differentials." So they sacrificed the principal advantage of the thermistor by shunting it by at least an order of magnitude at low temperatures (Fig. IV-30). Having discarded most of the sensitivity and finding there was still more than they could use with ordinary high-heats-of-reaction samples, they diluted the sample twenty to sixty times to obtain readable thermograms (Fig. IV-31) and used a relatively slow (2°C/minute) rate of heating. They even measured the temperature using a thermistor; the temperature lag in their sensing assembly may account for their temperatures of 104, 117,

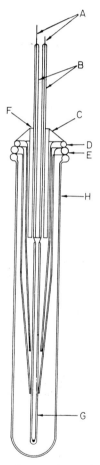

FIG. IV-28. Thermistor sensing element for differential thermal analysis: A, output leads; B, Teflon sleeve; C, electric resistor cement; D, 1 mm centrifuge tube; E, 1.5 mm centrifuge tube; F, two-hole ceramic tube; G, thermistor; H, test tube (P4).

A matched pair of thermistors replaces the differential thermocouple.

and 131°C for the copper sulfate pentahydrate peaks. The first peak is the loss of two waters, the second is the vaporization of these waters.

Rotation of their bridge through 90° would have permitted elimination of the shunts (Fig. IV-32). With thermistors at R_1 and R_2 and ignoring the balancing resistor, R_B, since

$$\frac{\Delta E}{E} = \frac{R_1}{R_2} - \frac{R_3}{R_4} = \frac{R_1}{R_2} - C$$

a fractional change in R_1, e.g., $R_1 + 0.04\,R_1$, will have the same effect at any value of R_1, since R_2 is changing at essentially the same rate. The

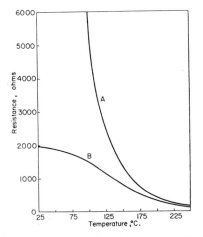

Fig. IV-29. Relationship of resistance of a thermistor and of a thermistor and its shunt to temperature: A, resistance of a thermistor vs temperature; B, combined parallel resistance of a thermistor and its shunt vs temperature (P4).

At the lower temperatures most of the sensitivity of the thermistors is lost by shunting.

zeroing or balancing potentiometer could be put between R_3 and R_4. Some adjustment of resistance might be necessary for impedance matching (see Chapter XV). This matching could be done by using an amplifier or a cathode follower. In spite of the handicap imposed on the system the thermograms obtained by Pakulak and Leonard (Fig. IV-31) show rather good sensitivity.

Some observers might be tempted to use thermistors for all four legs of the bridge, and put, perhaps, an indexing or comparison specimen on one or more of the others or a similar specimen on the opposite leg to double the effect. This may indeed be feasible. Some makers discourage use of thermistors for all four legs of a bridge but the present author has done just that in a chromatograph in which two detectors read into a single recording channel.

The temperature limits are the major problem. The present author has not, to date of writing, found thermistors made for general use above 500°C. Some interesting low-energy transitions occur at lower temperatures so thermistors can have great utility. The best solution to the resistance change problem will no doubt be the use of more than one pair of thermistors. The user might need to have a choice of perhaps five or six sets, each set having a different optimum temperature range.

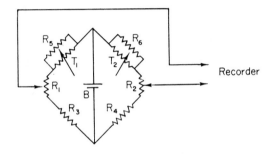

R₁,R₂ = 100Ω   Potentiometer
R₃,R₄ = 1000Ω ±1%
R₅,R₆ = 2000Ω ±1%
T₁,T₂ = Thermistors – 100,000Ω at 25 °C
B   = 1 1/2 volt dry cell

Fig. IV-30. Direct current bridge for differential thermal analysis (P4).
The recorder is "looking into" about 1400 ohms near room temperature and only about 100 ohms near 250°C. Maximum sensitivity occurs when the effective resistance of the shunted thermistor is 1000 ohms at around 250°C.

4.13. Insulation

Operation of an uninsulated furnace can be both uneconomical and uncomfortable. Well-insulated furnaces can be maintained above 1000°C with 200–300 watts. We are generally concerned in thermal analysis with heating and cooling so (1) the furnace heater must have sufficient power to raise the temperature at the desired rate and (2) the furnace must lose heat rapidly enough to cool reasonably quickly. These arguments lead generally to low-mass, lightly insulated furnaces or to furnaces with built-in cooling arrangements. The cooling arrangements are generally those used also in subambient temperature work (Sec. 4.10).

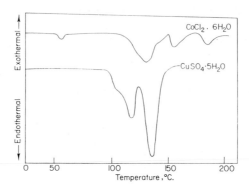

FIG. IV-31. Thermograms of copper sulfate pentahydrate and cobalt chloride hexahydrate (P4).

The thermograms show reasonable sensitivity but slow response; the response behavior is probably due to the isolation of the sensing element.

The present author frequently uses lightly insulated furnaces, confining the heat by the protective cement and outer tube at lower temperatures and by a radiation shield at higher temperatures.

The radiation shield functions by reflection back to the furnace of a substantial portion of the heat radiated. The shield itself, since it can radiate heat outward, does not reach nearly the same temperature as the furnace surface. It functions best in vacuum systems such as that of Martin and Edwards (M15) shown in Fig. IV-33 but it can be used also in air. The slow corrosion of the inside shield in air diminishes the effectiveness after a while but this can be replaced easily.

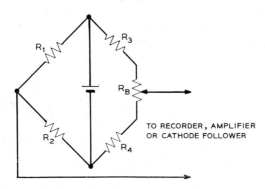

FIG. IV-32. Suggested circuit for thermistor. R_1 and R_2 are matched thermistors; R_3 and R_4 are fixed resistors.

Since a thermistor shows a fractional change in resistance with temperature the sensitivity of this arrangement would change only slowly with temperature.

The radiation shield surrounding a hot furnace in air will be cooled by convection; a very unsteady-state heat-transfer situation arises in which the heat loss can easily vary somewhat from minute to minute. In differential thermal analysis, the heating and cooling of the furnace present a changing demand on the power supply which is far greater than any demand changes from changes in cooling effects. For slowly varying temperature for differential thermal or thermogravimetric analysis the present author cannot recommend the use of radiation shields. A well-insulated furnace will provide greater temperature stability, longer life for the winding, lower power requirement, and a cooler laboratory. If the well-insulated furnace has provision for cooling, the same furnace

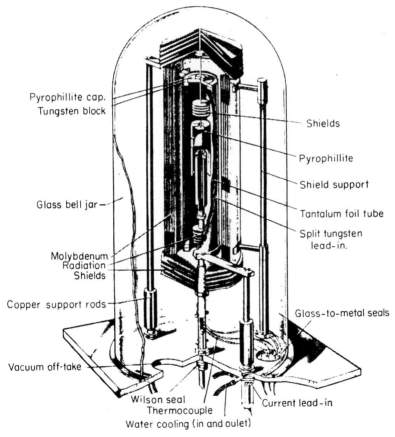

Fɪɢ. IV-33. Thermal analysis furnace using radiation shielding. From Martin and Moore (M16).

The shielding restricts heat by reflection and performs effectively as insulation.

could have all the advantages cited at the disadvantages of significantly greater cost and size.

The ordinary commercial insulating materials are well-known: firebrick, magnesium oxide, etc. For not extremely high temperatures, a relatively new material, potassium titanate, can be used. The thermal conductivity is much less than that of magnesium oxide.

4.14. Summary

There is no one superior instrument for differential thermal analysis. The basic apparatus will need to be selected or constructed for the problem on which it will be used.

Horizontal furnaces can be constructed with very low-temperature gradients; vertical furnaces will have noticeable gradients but provide more nearly symmetric heating.

The type of sample holder is chosen principally on the basis of the desired degree of isolation and atmosphere accessibility. Multiple sample holders are useful for comparison runs.

Quantitative measurements other than peak height will ordinarily require a time-based record. An X vs Y recorder plotting ΔT vs T does not show as much; the X vs Y records are more convenient to store.

Controlled-atmosphere furnaces are useful for studying decomposition or oxidation reactions. Pressure effects can also be studied.

CHAPTER V

Evaluation of Differential Thermal Analysis Curves

5.1. Introduction

Before making any detailed study of quantitative measurements or mathematical treatments some concept of the magnitudes involved will be of help. Several clearly different types of reactions could be chosen ranging from decompositions or combustions to crystallographic phase transformations on to second-order transitions. Because of the oft-encountered assumptions of temperature homogeneity and of unchanging or nonaffecting atmosphere the best starting point is a chemical decomposition.

Let us examine the decomposition of calcium carbonate in some detail. We shall mount the specimen in a usual manner—a long cylinder of which we will take a right section. We will consider the outside of the cylinder to be heating at a regular rate. We shall assume, for our immediate purposes, that the decomposition is extremely rapid although this is not essential to the discussion.

As the specimen is heated a temperature gradient is set up from the edge to the center which reaches a nearly steady state. An exactly

149

steady state would require a heat capacity, thermal conductivity, emissivity (if the experiment goes above, say, 400°C), heat-transfer coefficient from container to sample, and heat-transfer coefficient from particle, all constant with temperature, or a fortuitous combination of circumstances. But since we have a quasi-steady state, we can find relations describing the gradient within the specimen merely assuming that certain quantities are constants over any small temperature interval.

Recall the heat flow equation for cylinders. A form of the temperature distribution which satisfies the differential equation is

$$T = \beta \left(t - \frac{R^2 - r^2}{4a} \right)$$

where β is the heating rate, T is the time, R is the outside radius, r is the radius of the point under consideration, and a is the thermal diffusivity.

Now
$$\frac{\partial^2 T}{\partial r^2} + \frac{1}{r}\frac{\partial T}{\partial r} = \text{constant},$$

so substituting our previous expression for T we obtain

$$\frac{\beta^2 T}{2a} + \frac{1}{r}\cdot\frac{\beta r}{2a} = \frac{\beta}{a}$$

obeying the general heat flow equation $\nabla^2 T = \dfrac{\beta}{a}$.

Using the temperature equation given, we can calculate the temperature difference, $T_w - T_c$, from wall to center during the steady temperature rise:

$$T_w - T_c = \frac{\beta R^2}{4a} = \frac{\beta \rho c R^2}{4k}.$$

We can then insert known or estimated values for the heat capacity, c, the density, ρ, the thermal conductivity, k, and the radius, obtaining a numerical value for this temperature difference. Assume, for the purposes of illustration, the values shown in the accompanying tabulation for the calcium carbonate decomposition.

	$CaCO_3$	CaO
k	0.0070	0.017 cal/sec cm/deg
c	0.27	0.24 cal/gm/deg
ρ	2.7	1.3 gm/cm^3
β	$= 6.0°C/min = 0.10°C/sec$	
R	$= 0.30$ cm	

(The density we have taken is for a well-packed specimen, nearly 90% crystal density for calcite, assuming no shrinkage or loss of weight.)

From the preceding equation we can readily calculate the temperature drops from wall to center as 0.20°C and 0.10°C for calcium carbonate and calcium oxide, respectively. (This produces a base line shift of 0.10° or 4 μv using chromel-alumel thermocouples.) Let us next consider the energy involved in the decomposition, i.e., 44 kcal/mole or 440 cal/gm of calcium carbonate.

Imagine first the instantaneous addition of the necessary quantity of heat (for decomposition) simultaneously to our sample and to an extremely stable reference material. The temperature rise of the inert specimen would be ca. 1800°C. Quantities of heat of this magnitude require a tremendous temperature gradient for transport. Since this addition of heat is clearly unrealistic, imagine that we are carrying out a decomposition in our sample holder in such a manner that the last 1% of the sample decomposes in 1 second. We can calculate that 1 cm length of specimen will require 300 calories so we must supply 3 calories to the center. Since we are only concerned with the order of magnitude, we use the steady-state equation

$$\Delta T = \frac{q}{2\,k\pi} \ln \frac{R}{r},$$

the real case being much worse. We are dealing now with a layer of calcium oxide but neglecting the uncertain correction for change in mass,

$$\Delta T = \frac{3.0 \times 2.3}{2 \times 0.017} \approx 64°.$$

This means that to carry out the decomposition so that the last bit occurs at 1% per second we must heat the sample enough to provide at least a temperature drop of 64°C from the wall to the reaction front. The limiting factor in a decomposition of this kind is not the rate of reaction but the supply of heat to the decomposing material. Obviously the heat supply problem is accentuated in thermogravimetry wherein the sample is customarily isolated from the heat source.

Note that each of the quantities involved in the idealized heat transport is changing discontinuously at the time of decomposition and that other quantities are varying continuously with temperature. Deeg (D9) points out that sixteen variables have to be considered even after omitting emissivity; Dilaktorskii and Arkhangel'skaja (D11a) list twenty-five.

The thermal effects during a phase or second-order transition will be less marked but note that the lesser magnitudes call for more careful avoidance of background signal. The residual signal due to actual changes in thermal properties of the sample and reference is relatively large compared to the discontinuous event being studied. The temperature gradients in a polymer undergoing a glass transition, for example, are ordinarily much smaller than in a decomposition but by no means negligible; gradients are—in fact—to be expected because of the low thermal conductivities of such materials.

5.2. General Remarks

There are three important reasons for mathematical treatments of differential thermal analysis curves; of basic interest are the attempts to describe the curves in terms related to the events occurring with the aim —simply—of understanding the process. Another use for measurements is the quantitative determination of materials, or, if the material is known, the determination of energy changes; the third is to estimate the rates of reaction of the material from the slope or from the instantaneous magnitudes of the differential temperature.

So far, the mathematical treatments have been inadequate. Vitiating flaws exist in the treatments offering a precise description. The purely empirical procedure of obtaining a calibration curve is in general use. Nevertheless, the events occurring during a differential thermal analysis are reproducible physical phenomena and are subject to known physical laws and relationships; the problems are that: (1) several processes must be treated simultaneously; (2) the nature of some processes may be changing during the run or vary with the environment; (3) the applicability of a treatment of a particular segment of the process may depend on the history and condition of the specimen; and (4) the several types of reactions render the use of any single description unworkable.

Under (1) we must consider the problems of heat transfer and temperature control and these are already severe (mathematically) in the simple case of a rapid and reversible phase change. If the furnace wall, for example, is programmed to raise in temperature at a constant rate the change in heat-transfer coefficients from wall to block and from block to specimen means that the actual heating rate of the specimen is varying slowly. Programming the rise of the block temperature eliminates only the first but accentuates the problem of control. Within the sample the heat transfer in unreacted and reacted materials will differ and will vary with temperature. During the reaction the temperature distribution within the block will vary because of the change in demand by the sample.

Under (2) we must consider not only the effect of atmosphere and changing atmosphere (Chapter VII) but also the possibility that the over-all reaction being studied is actually a stepwise process whose individual reactions may—and probably do—have heats of reaction and/or of activation which vary greatly and differently with temperature.

Under (3) we must consider effects of particle size and history on heat transfer and surface energy as well as effects of packing on uniformity of heating within the specimen.

Under (4) we must consider the obvious existence of processes that are decidedly rate-controlled, others that are diffusion-controlled, and still others that are instantaneous.

For all these reasons assumptions and approximations are made concerning various parts of the several processes; in many cases the assumptions are clearly not related to the physical event, in others the relation is tenuous at best. The inability to describe the curve satisfactorily leads immediately to inability to integrate mathematically and calculate the amount of material or the heat of reaction from the area and already known parameters such as heat capacity and thence to the need to calibrate the apparatus to determine the effective magnitude of all the parameters under the conditions of the experiment.

This lack—to date—of a really satisfactory treatment should not excuse the active practitioner of thermal analysis from study of the extant treatments. These can still lead to some better understanding of the processes involved and perhaps to some new and superior approach. This chapter necessarily treats both empirical and mathematical approaches to analytical, thermodynamic, and kinetic problems in thermal analysis.

The endothermic peak appearing in differential thermal analysis results from the deviation of the temperature of the material in contact with the thermocouple or other measuring device from the programmed (directly or indirectly) temperature. The cause of the deviation is a change in the thermal characteristics of the sample material. The manner in which the change in properties will affect the heating in the vicinity of the thermocouple depends on the nature and magnitude of the change and, to a limited degree, on some mechanical considerations.

If the change in properties comes as a result of a change in state other than volatilization the change will occur along a moving boundary as described in Chapter II and the movement will be determined by the sharpness of the discontinuity (related to the heat of transition) and the thermal properties of both the high-temperature and the low-temperature forms. The endothermic peak is essentially a record of the movement of this boundary so that it, in turn, reflects the changes in thermal properties. In the case of chemical reaction or decomposition the movement of the boundary can be modified by atmosphere effects, or, in some cases, by a rate-controlling step.

Chemical reactions, including decompositions, will generally be sufficiently rapid that we can assume a clear boundary between unreacted and reacted materials; some, however, are very decidedly rate-controlled* so that each particle reacts or decomposes over a finite time.

*The term *rate-controlled* is used to describe reactions, including decompositions, in which the chemical reaction rate is slow enough so that it determines the over-all rate of reaction. In this sense such reactions may be differentiated from those in which the over-all rate is determined by the supply of heat or by diffusion of gases.

In the latter case the moving boundary would be spread out to a skewed curve. The several effects cited will each affect the magnitude of the differential temperature and, if any quantity is to be calculated from the differential temperature, the several others will need to be considered.

5.3. Peak Shape

The detailed shape of the differential thermal analysis peak has been the subject of considerable empirical treatment as well as some mathematical description. The empirical treatments quite naturally preceded the mathematical as the users of differential thermal analysis sought ways of relating sets of data to each other and to the composition of the materials. The manner of description normally included the magnitude of the peak and some temperature selected to represent the reaction. The mode of selection of the temperature can be surmised: it would be the temperature which remained most nearly constant with changes of quantity of active material, nature of other materials present, heating rate, and any other variables coming to the mind of the experimenter. The fact that the temperatures chosen were frequently heavily dependent on apparatus and procedure was not recognized.

Although the quantitative measure generally chosen was the area of the peak, the difficulty of circumscribing this area properly (Section 5.4) has led to other methods of measurement. Similarly, the shape of the peak has been used to deduce information needed for kinetic studies.

In general, endothermic deflections will look somewhat like one of those in Fig. V-1. A typical phase transformation will comprise (Fig. V-1, A) a continually increasing rise until very near the peak, a slightly rounded peak, and a rapid return to the base line [which may be displaced from the original base line (see Chapter II)]. If the process is seriously rate- or diffusion-controlled the deflection will be relatively broad and the peak (Fig. V-1, C) decidedly rounded. Deflections hav-

ing some characteristics of each type may occur in lesser degrees of rate
or diffusion control or in cases of inadvertent limitation of decomposition
products. The oft-mentioned straight-line portion (Fig. V-1, B) may occur in quite large specimens or with a fortuitous combination of thermal
properties. There is no reason to expect such a region to be characteristic
of all deflections.

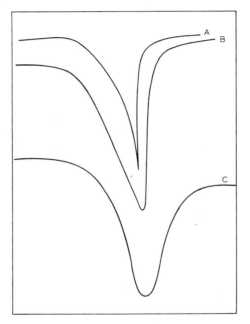

Fig. V-1. Typical thermograms for: A, a rapid phase transition; B, a phase transition deflection with a straight-line section; and C, a rate-controlled reaction.
Simple treatments are impracticable because the shape depends on the nature
of the thermal effect.

The shape of the peak is dependent not only on the nature of the
material but also on its manner of containment. The presence or absence
of a heat sink close to the specimen can and will modify the reaction and
hence modify the thermogram. Figure V-2 shows a repetitive thermogram of potassium sulfate; compare this with Fig. II-10. In Fig. V-2,
the sample holder was an alumina sleeve which fitted over the supporting tube and extended above it, forming a sample well quite isolated
from a similar reference well. Not only is interchange of heat avoided
but also each specimen is in contact only with a thin ceramic wall of
fairly low heat capacity (not counting the supporting tube). The heat
supplied to or taken from the sample must therefore have just come

from or be immediately supplied to the furnace wall. (The sample cavity in the block was also ¼ inch nominal ID.) Differences in appearance are quite apparent in both the time-based and the temperature-based (Figs. V-3 and II-11) thermograms. In Fig. II-11 the presence of the heat sink enables a rapid return to the base line on heating through the transformation and a very noticeable shift in the base line. The reverse effect, i.e., a sharp break *away* from the base line, is seen on cooling. The change in thermal properties of the material exercise a de-

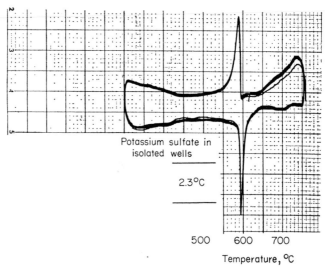

Potassium sulfate in
isolated wells

2.3°C

500　　600　　700

Temperature, °C

FIG. V-2. Repetitive (seven-cycle) thermogram of potassium sulfate in isolated alumina wells.

Compare with Fig. II-10.

cided effect. In Figs. V-2 and V-3, on the other hand, the sharper deviations from the base line are, in each case, the initial deviations from the base line. The return to the steady state is essentially asymptotic. This is quite reasonable since the isolated specimens comprise, in effect, a differential calorimetry arrangement. The gain in sensitivity, roughly a factor of 2, (note difference in scale) carries the penalty of a lack of sensitivity for close-lying reactions. For seven cycles in Fig. V-2 the peak heights and root mean square deviation were 2.16 ± 0.016 and 1.97 ± 0.01 inches for heating and cooling, respectively. The root mean square deviations are 0.7 and 1.0%, respectively.

The several temperatures that have been used to characterize a deflection include the temperature of onset of transition or decomposition, the intersection of the extensions of the base line and of the "straight-line portion" of the deflection, a similar intersection using an extension of the slope at the inflection point, the temperature at the inflection point, the intersection of extensions of the "straight-line portions" of the rising and falling sides of the deflection, the peak temperature, the temperature of "maximum rate of reaction," and temperature of completion of reaction. These methods are empirical. The peak temperature is the temperature

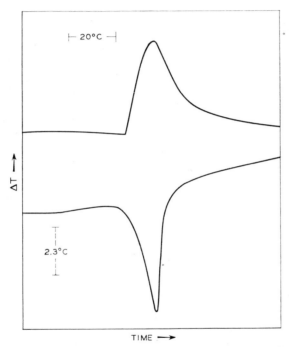

⊢ 20°C ⊣

2.3°C

TIME ⟶

Fig. V-3. Thermogram of potassium sulfate in isolated wells.
The inflection is larger but the return to the base is slower than shown in Fig. II-10.

of interest when the measuring thermocouple is at the center of the specimen. If the measured temperature is that of the edge of the sample. e.g., the block temperature, the temperature of the beginning of the reaction is the important datum. Other points of measurement on or from the peak have no simple significance.

Guiochon (G53) has registered an objection to the use of the term "temperature of onset of decomposition," pointing out that the Arrhenius law, $\kappa = Ae^{-E/RT}$, describing the temperature dependence of reaction rates indicates only that the rate of any reaction will generally decrease along with the temperature. He states further that "there is absolutely no reason why this rate suddenly becomes zero, although it may be that no apparatus can detect it below a certain value of the temperature, characteristic of the apparatus, not of the reaction." This is a quite valid criticism, yet temperatures such as that of "onset of decomposition" are still measured and reported. This is because a more-or-less reproducible temperature is observed under a given set of conditions. The reason must be that the initial (ambient) atmosphere already contains some of the gaseous decomposition product; the presence of a partial pressure of the gas will delay a noticeable decomposition and ultimately permit what appears to be an almost immediate finite rate (see Chapters III and VII).

The temperature at which this finite rate appears will be dependent on the geometry as well as on the heating rate of the sample, but only to a small degree on the rate of flow of a gas over the specimen. (The flow of gas will have a much greater effect after the appearance of the weight change, when the concentration of gas over the sample might limit the diffusion outward.) The vapor remaining within the specimen can affect subsequent decompositions (Fig. III-22).

The general pattern of action in deriving expressions describing the differential thermal analysis peak is to set up a mathematical model, make a number of simplifying assumptions, state the established laws and/or relations for heat conduction or temperature variation, substitute in these laws the quantities applicable to the particular problem, and finally manipulate the expressions until a usable form is obtained. The approach is perfectly straightforward. It is notably unsuccessful because the assumptions necessary to permit convenient mathematical description are not ordinarily physically valid. (This criticism is especially applicable to decomposition reactions, yet these same reactions are cited commonly in evaluating quantitative techniques.)

As Sewell and Honeyborne (S19a) point out, these assumptions are commonly that none of the several quantities needed in the mathematical expressions change during the thermal effect (see Chapter II). These quantities include the thermal conductivity, heat capacity, density and hence the thermal diffusivity, and heat of reaction. (Sewell and Honeyborne carefully restrict their own treatment to reversible phase changes and thermodynamically irreversible decompositions obeying a first-order law with the comment that the type of reactions such as the decomposition of calcite "appears too complex for a general treatment to be useful.")

The quantities assumed as constant all change with temperature but even if we ignore the continuous change of each of these we can scarcely ignore the sudden change in thermal conductivity, for example, when a sample melts. Even crystallographic phase changes differ considerably. The a-β transition in quartz involves two hexagonal structures and a rather small heat of transition. One might expect the listed quantities to be rather similar at temperatures above and below the transition. In contrast, barium titanate undergoes a rhombic-cubic transformation ca. 120°C. This transition also marks the disappearance of ferromagnetic properties (Curie point). To expect the listed quantities to remain nearly the same above and below this transformation would be exceedingly optimistic.

This nonconstancy of important quantities means, essentially, that a simple relation between heat of reaction and temperature difference or peak area does not exist for differential thermal analysis. This does not mean that reasonably accurate quantitative techniques cannot be found. The simplest—and probably the best available—procedure will be the use of differential calorimetry.

Differential calorimetry has its own quota of disadvantages and hence is certainly not a cure-all. If a reaction can be isolated—in point of time— from any other and there is no easy flow of heat between sample and reference a rather good measure of the heat of reaction should be obtainable.

5.4. Precision Analysis

With the increasing use of differential thermal analysis, there is inevitably a compulsion to improve the numerical precision so that accurate heats of transition or decomposition may be obtained or, conversely, by determining the heat effect of the reaction in the sample and in the pure material, an accurate quantitative analysis may be performed.

Various degrees of success have been claimed but success has generally been accompanied by penalties. In several cases, the term "differential thermal analysis" has been used quite loosely; the authors have reported on a technique which can be more reasonably classed as differential calorimetry.

In general, the attempts to describe a differential thermal analysis peak are characterized by unwarranted assumptions based on mathematical convenience; these assumptions were intended to render the differential temperature describable by an expression requiring no great manipulation. These assumptions are recognized as approximations and the final expressions were intended as no more than good representation.

If a certain term, expression, or relation—whether known or unknown

—describes a physical being or process, an approximation must be a simpler term, expression, or relation describing the same phenomenon but not so well as the proper term. Substitution of one process for another is out of bounds. To ignore the physical realities is to vitiate the final result which, one may presume, the author had hoped to use for some real events. In evaluating an expression which purportedly describes a differential thermal analysis curve due to some specific type of thermal effect, one may often save time by examining the assumptions made. If some part of the assumed behavior of the system is unrealistic the final expression may be, in effect, nothing more than an exercise in mathematical manipulation.

Differential thermal analysis was defined previously (Chapter I) as a technique in which heat is allowed to flow from the sample to the reference or vice versa. The function of this heat flow is to permit equalization of the temperature and enable detection of any subsequent reaction. Obviously one may inhibit this heat flow by thermal isolation of the sample, but this tends to cause deflections to persist unduly long times, nullifying the advantages of differential thermal analysis. Admittedly this is a matter of degree; there is no clear separation between differential calorimetry and differential thermal analysis.

The major criterion in the several mathematical representations of the differential thermal analysis curves is whether or not the devisor of the expression was able to ignore the thermal conductivity of the specimen. If this quantity is found to have no effect on the results, the technique used is differential calorimetry and the reader will find that the writer has his sample vessels supported by rods—generally ceramic—or set on a ceramic plate or otherwise isolated from the reference material.

Differential calorimetry is certainly a worthy technique, but the prospective user must be aware of its shortcomings. Differential calorimetry will permit determination of heats of reaction or transition at the cost of loss of ability to measure or perhaps even detect reactions occurring soon after the first. The interval in which interference would occur varies with heating rate and heat of reaction. The calculations are simple and calibration is not even needed in favorable designs. Comparison with a known specimen is sufficient.

Vold (V10) got rather good agreement with literature values for the heats of fusion of stearic and benzoic acids. She recognized that her apparatus was a differential calorimeter and—even more laudably—recognized that confinement of vapors was necessary. On this latter point, she differed from the general run of workers reporting quantitative techniques even though these would consistently use decomposition reactions for calibration.

Quantitative measurements on reversible transformation ought not to be difficult; Grimshaw (G46), for example, found $\beta \rightarrow \alpha$ quartz inversion reproducible to less than 2% diluted in diluted (with alumina) natural specimens. This is quite understandable; the transition temperature is not affected seriously by the rate of heating or cooling and the porosity of the mass is unimportant because no gases have to find their ways in or out. Note, however, that Arens (A12) (see Chapter III) reports that the area of the quartz peak increases with heating rate. The present author believes this to be a heat-transport problem, but in any case the rate of heating should be controlled and reproducible.

Boersma (B58) chooses to go back to differential calorimetry. He points out quite justly several shortcomings of differential thermal analysis and offers a solution. "These shortcomings can be overcome by a new measuring technique (new sample holder) [Fig. V-4] and a new method of diagram interpretation (curve synthesis) [Fig. V-5]."

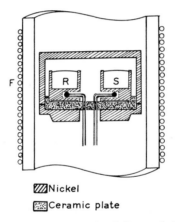

///Nickel

Ceramic plate

Fig. V-4. Boersma's (B58) sample holder for differential thermal analysis: S, sample; R, reference material; F, furnace.

The isolation of the specimen and reference holders prolong the temperature effects. Better quantitative data may be obtained for completely separable effects but these completely separable effects are less likely to be found.

Boersma's formulas were derived for nickel blocks, in which the thermal conductivity of the block was considered to be so much greater than that of the specimen that its effect could be ignored, and for ceramic blocks, in which the thermal conductivity of the block was taken into account. The equations are given below, together with that for the proposed sample holder.

A. Nickel Blocks
    (1) Cylindrical cavity:

$$\int_{t_1}^{t_2} \theta_0 dt = \text{peak area} = \frac{qa^2}{4\lambda}$$

where θ_0 = differential temperature,
        q = heat of transformation per unit volume,
        a = radius of cavity, and
        λ = thermal conductivity of sample material.

    (2) Spherical cavity:

$$\int_{t_1}^{t_2} \theta_0 dt = \frac{qa^2}{6\lambda}.$$

    (3) Flat plate:

$$\int_{t_1}^{t_2} \theta_0 dt = \frac{qa^2}{2\lambda}.$$

B. Ceramic Block
    A solution exists only for the spherical case:

$$\text{peak area} = \frac{qa^2}{6} \left(\frac{2}{\lambda_c} + \frac{1}{\lambda} \right)$$

where λ_c is the thermal conductivity of the ceramic block.

C. Proposed Sample Holder (Differential Calorimeter)

$$\int_{t_1}^{t_2} \theta \, dt = \frac{mq}{G}$$

where m = mass of sample and G = heat-transfer coefficient between small nickel container and surrounding nickel.

The sample holder is perfectly suitable for differential calorimetry since, as Boersma points out, the volume or thermal conductivity of the sample does not affect the peak area. They do, however, affect seriously the time interval over which the peak must be observed and therefore can seriously decrease the sensitivity. With samples of any moderate size the peak may easily become so spread out that it overlaps another and Boersma's calculation can be applied to neither. For this eventuality he proposes the use of "curve synthesis."

Curve synthesis is a technique by which curves for known pure minerals might be added electrically to match the curve obtained from a specimen containing these minerals. Templates are made of curves of the pure minerals and of the specimen. These are examined by a light beam–photocell arrangement and the responses from the several known materials individually attenuated until their sum—as observed on an oscilloscope—reproduces the curve of the unknown. The amount of each material is proportional to the attenuator setting. (The circuit as shown would tend to *average* rather than *sum* the several inputs. In order to add the various input signals should appear across resistors in *series* rather than *parallel.*)

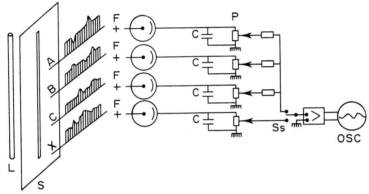

Fig. V-5. Curve synthesis for differential thermal analysis: L, lamp; S, slit; A, B, C, and X, moving templates; F, photocells; C, integrating condensers; P, calibrated potentiometers; Ss, selector switch; and OSC, cathode ray oscillograph. From Boersma (B58).
By optically adding fractions of components Boersma attempted to match the thermogram of the unknown mineral.

The method takes no account of curve shifting by other components (see Chapter VII) and it assumes that the operator is comparing curves of *all* the components; further, comparison of the curves directly will lead the operator to match—or try to match—peak heights rather than areas. The present author does not agree with Boersma's closing statements on the advisability or ease of manipulating an integral curve rather than the raw data. Further, the present author has not heard of any successful use of the curve synthesis procedure. If the data were obtained using a properly chosen dynamic atmosphere, the procedure might well be successful. The present author does not imply that matching peak heights rather than area is an error (see Chapter II). The peak height must be shown to be a linear function of concentration or some empirical correction would need to be applied. This correction might be dependent on the other materials present. A further complication is the quite common shift in peak temperature with concentration as shown in Fig. V-6.

Boersma also formulated the expressions below for the deviation of the peak because of the presence of the thermocouple (Fig. V-7), accounting both for the altered geometry and for heat leakage along the thermocouple wires.

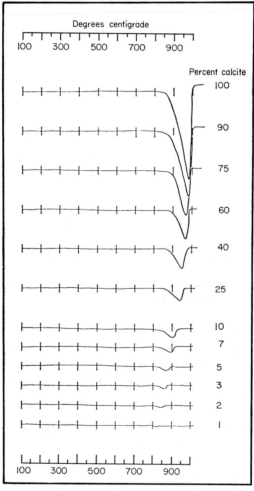

Fig. V-6. DTA curves of calcite-alundum mixtures. The calcite is Iceland spar ground to 120–200 mesh. From Kulp *et al.* (K42).
Decompositions will customarily show a shift in temperature with dilution.

Correction Added for Thermocouple Interference
(1) Spherical cavity:

$$\int_{t_1}^{t_2} \theta_0 dt = \frac{qa^2}{6\lambda} \cdot \frac{\alpha}{1 + \Lambda/\lambda}$$

where a (correction for altered geometry) equals $1 - r_0^2/a^2 \, [3 - 2r_0/a]$ and Λ (heat leakage correction) equals

$$\lambda_p \frac{r_0}{l} \frac{A}{4\pi r_0^2} \left[1 - \frac{r_0}{a} \right]$$

where r_0 = radius of thermocouple bead,
  λ_p = thermal conductivity of thermocouple wire, and
  A = cross section of leads.

(2) Cylindrical cavity

$$\int_{t_1}^{t_2} \theta_0 dt = \frac{qa^2}{4\lambda} \frac{1 - \dfrac{r_0^2}{a^2} (1 + 2 \ln a/r_0)}{1 + \dfrac{A}{l} \cdot \dfrac{\lambda_p}{\lambda_s} \cdot \dfrac{\ln a/r_0}{2\pi n}}$$

where l = length of leads.

Two years later, de Josselin de Jong (J9) reported his evaluation of the Boersma (B58) equations. He found, like Speil (S40) but unlike Arens (A12), peak areas essentially independent of heating rate. Several equations for areas or temperature differences predict this independence. The question must necessarily be resolved. If one side or the other has not committed a gross error then the experiments must differ in some important way.

In his determination of the calibration factor for heats of reaction de Jong (J9) finds that a given sample (and thermocouple) height but a varying diameter will yield calibration factors, Ψ, which agree with

$$\Psi = \frac{\text{peak area}}{\omega} = \frac{\rho \alpha^2}{4\lambda} \left\{ \left[1 - \frac{r_0^2}{a^2} \left(1 + \ln \frac{a}{r_0} \right) \right] \left[1 + \frac{\Lambda}{\lambda} \ln \frac{a}{r_0} \right] \right\}$$

values calculated from where ω = quantity of sample, obtained from Boersma (B58). But when the height of the sample is varied, the calibration factor cannot be predicted. Figure III-15 shows that the height of the thermocouple neither maintained (*a*) a symmetric position in the sample nor (*b*) a fixed position with respect to either end. His data have undoubtedly met with objections on the first point but his conclusion answers such: "samples 10 and 20 mm high show practically the same area which indicates that it is not the total amount of the reacting material that counts but only the amount present in a disc of unit height." True! so far as it goes, but only because his point of

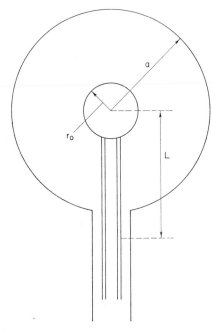

Fig. V-7. Heat leakage through thermocouple wires of lengths *l*. From Boersma (B58).

The presence of sizable metal leads coming from the point of measurement can have a serious effect on sensitivity.

measurement has become deep enough to decrease (almost to vanishing) the effect of exchange with the outside atmosphere. This is strictly analogous to Arens (A12) observation that "deep placement of the differential thermocouple junctions in the samples yield DTA curves with relatively strong endothermic reactions . . . in which the omission of the latter part of the quotation is deliberate (see Chap. III). The peak temperatures should be increasing asymptotically like the area. These temperatures are not shown.

Note: There is a deplorable compulsion to calibrate or evaluate for quantitative work using reactions involving a weight loss; yet only a few authors give *any* sign of recognition that the atmosphere has any importance. The heat of decomposition of copper sulfate pentahydrate is *not* the same when expanding against one atmosphere of water vapor as when expanding against the few millimeters of vapor pressure in the ambient atmosphere. This is because the reactions occur at different temperatures. In the usual sample holder the vapor pressure is at some undeterminate place between those limits. At best, the partial pressure of water approaches one atmosphere during the latter part of the decomposition. The 220 cal per gram determined by de Bruijn and van der Marel (B85) applies to the apparatus and conditions including the relative humidity of the ambient atmosphere. For any other apparatus or conditions the figure is an approximate value. It can be used (with reasonable care) to demonstrate similarity of condition. It may NOT be treated as a fixed, known value. It *must* not be used for calibrating an instrument.

The total heat of the change

$$CuSO_4 \cdot 5H_2O_{(25°C)} \rightarrow CuSO_4 \cdot H_2O_{(200°C)} + 4H_2O_{(0.01\ atm,\ 200°C)}$$

could be determined and would be a fixed quantity by whatever path the change took place. The differential thermal analysis apparatus measures the heat effect only within the sample—more specifically, only in the vicinity of the thermocouple. The heat required to drive off the water will be detected but the temperature dependence of the calibration factor will not.

Boersma's equations, according to de Josselin de Jong, predict (Fig. V-8) that $\Psi/\rho a^2\lambda$ (a function of the heat loss through the thermocouple wires) reaches a maximum for r_0/a of 0.2; i.e., the greatest peak area or

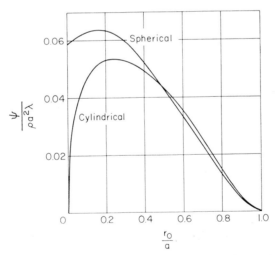

Fig. V-8. Graph of calibration factor ψ according to Boersma's eqs. (4) and (5) for $\Lambda/\lambda = 2$ and for different ratios of thermocouple junction, r_0, vs sample diameter. From de Jong (J9).

The conclusion apparent from the plot would be that one uses different size thermocouple beads for different size sample cavities and that there is a drop in sensitivity with an excessively fine couple (or with a small couple in a large specimen).

the least fractional loss through the thermocouple wires occurs when the thermocouple radius is ca. one-fifth of the sample radius. Further, if one decreases this thermocouple radius toward zero, the function for a spherical sample holder drops off only slightly but for a cylindrical sample holder the value drops rapidly toward zero! One may, then, decrease sensitivity greatly if one uses a small junction in a cylindrical sample but not in a spherical sample—if the relation is valid.

5.5. Area Measurement and the Parameters Influencing It

Examine now the quantity used as a measure of heat of reaction or amount of material, i.e., the peak area. This area is the summation—over the time of the deflection—of the temperature difference,

$$A = \int_{t_1}^{t_2} \Delta T \, dt.$$

The ΔT is the difference in temperature between the sample and reference but the universal assumption in deriving expressions is that the heat of reaction heats or cools the sample and its crucible. A sample block cannot be treated in the same manner because not only will the reaction in the sample heat or cool the block but it will also heat or cool the reference, in either case diminishing the ΔT signal. This effect on the reference is time-dependent and will have a greater effect with the slower heating rates. A high heating rate will carry the reaction to completion before the effect is felt or at least before it reaches the same magnitude. A more rapidly heated specimen may then show a higher apparent heat of reaction than a less rapidly heated specimen. The effect is not seen with isolated cups (differential calorimetry) since there is no rapid transfer of heat from sample to reference.

The discussion above may lead the reader to plan immediately to use the isolated specimen holder so a review of the advantages and disadvantages is in order. The isolated sample and references offer the greater sensitivity to *a* reaction because the heat of reaction needs to affect only the sample and the container; a given quantity of heat can bring about a greater temperature change than if the sample were in a block and, from this, a greater temperature difference than if there is a "low-impedance" path for heat between the sample and the reference. On the other hand, the dissipation of excess heat or recovery of a deficit of heat by an isolated sample is slow for the very same reason. The lack of reasonably free exchange of heat between sample and reference means that thermal effects will be spread over a large temperature range.

The block, with its relatively free exchange of heat, suffers a diminution of peak height and area but permits approach of temperature equilibrium very quickly after completion of one reaction so that a subsequent reaction may be observed as a separate reaction. This is the prime advantage of differential thermal analysis.

The author does not imply that either technique is superior per se to the other. The author uses both and modifications of both. The author does hope to convince the reader that the choice of sample holders must be made on the basis of the problem at hand. Dependence on either one alone prevents thorough exploitation of thermal analysis.

Eriksson (E5) points out that the peak area in differential thermal analysis is always a linear function of the heat of reaction *if* the heat is being produced or consumed at the *same rate at every point in the sample*. For most differential thermal analysis work this is per se a trivial solution since finite times and decidedly finite temperature lags are involved. In conventional apparatus reactions may take 10 or more minutes, the reaction finally ending at a temperature 100°C higher than at its inception. Obviously Eriksson's argument does not apply to such a case, but consider now a small sample one in which essentially every particle is in contact with a common heat sink of low heat capacity. The function of this sink is more to equalize temperature than to supply or remove heat. Under these conditions Eriksson's condition is met or closely approximated and we may conclude that for small specimens not compacted into a sphere or cylinder his relation might hold. The problem of measuring temperature change becomes quite difficult in such an experiment.

Under the conditions generally used in differential thermal analysis the heat of reaction is not being generated or consumed equally in all parts of the sample because thermal gradients do exist. Barshad (B9) showed (Fig. V-9) that the measured heat effect was, in effect, proportional to the amount of heat consumed per unit volume, i.e., the concentration of the active material.

Another source of concern in quantitative differential thermal analysis is the variation of atmosphere which occurs principally in decomposition reactions. It is accompanied, therefore, by peak shifting with changing heating rate. This is reasonable. The peak area is a measure of the heat of reaction, ΔH. The reaction temperature is dependent on the partial pressure of any gaseous product in contact with the specimen, i.e., within the bulk of the specimen. At high heating rates the gas does not diffuse out rapidly enough to maintain any resemblance of equilibrium. The reaction temperature is increased according to the van't Hoff relation, $d(\ln p)/dT = \Delta H/RT^2$, but ΔH is not a constant. Some further effects must be considered.

From Kirchoffs law $(d\Delta H/dT)_p = C_p$; thus

$$\Delta H = \Delta H_0 + \int_0^T \Delta C_p dT \tag{1}$$

and

$$\frac{d \ln K_p}{dT} = \frac{d \ln P}{dT} = \frac{\Delta H_0}{RT^2} + \frac{1}{RT^2}\int_0^T \Delta C_p dT.$$

Ignoring variation with T in ΔC_p,

$$\ln \frac{P_2}{P_1} = -\frac{\Delta H_0}{R}\left(\frac{1}{T_2} - \frac{1}{T_1}\right) + \frac{\Delta C_p}{R}\ln\frac{T_2}{T_1}. \tag{2}$$

This ΔC_p term can, and often will, be greater than the ΔH_0 term so that the observed ΔH increases quite rapidly with increasing partial pressure.

Let us examine the problem graphically (Fig. V-10). At low heating rates the product gas, e.g., water from kaolinite, can diffuse away rapidly enough so that only a small fraction of an atmosphere is present at any time. The material decomposes at T_1 to form dehydrated kaolinite and water absorbing a quantity of heat ΔH_1. These necessarily have some given heat content, H_1, at T_1 and this heat content increases with temperature in a manner dependent on the heat capacities of the prod-

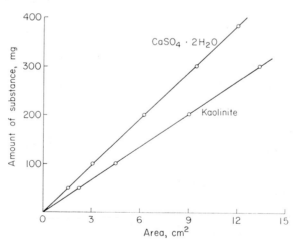

FIG. V-9. Peak areas of the endothermic breaks in DTA curves of various amounts of kaolinite and $CaSO_4 \cdot 2H_2O$. From Barshad (B9).

The materials were dispersed in sufficient quantities of alumina to yield the same volumes.

ucts. At T_2 the heat content is H_2. Now consider a second specimen heated at a higher rate, thereby decomposing at a higher temperature, T_2, because of the increased partial pressure of water vapor, P_2. Since the products must have a heat content of H_2, the heat of reaction at temperature T_2 is ΔH_2 which is obviously greater than ΔH_1.

Now let us insert some values in Eq. (2) and evaluate the significance of the source of error, using the data of Arens (A12) for the specific heats of kaolinite and calcined kaolinite, 0.201 and 0.428 cal/gm/°C, respectively. The molar heat capacities are 51.1 and 75.0 cal/mole/°C, respectively, but we have yet to consider the 2 moles of water. These add another 18.0 cal/mole°C. The change in heat capacity, ΔC_p, is then 62 cal/mole°C. Now, using Arens' peak shift values, i.e., peak temperatures of 545 and 620°C for heating rates of 6 and 10°C/minute, respectively, and using the value of 200 cal/gm as the heat of decomposition, Eq. (2) can be partially evaluated,

$$\log \frac{P_2}{P_1} = -\frac{200 \text{ cal/qm} \times 260 \text{ qm/mole}}{2.3 \times 2.0 \text{ cal/mole deg}}\left(\frac{1}{893°C} - \frac{1}{820°C}\right)$$

$$+ \frac{62 \text{ cal/mole deg}}{2.3 \times 2.0 \text{ cal/mole deg}} \log \frac{893}{820}$$

$$= 1.1 + 0.5 = 1.6$$

and the partial pressure of water vapor within the specimen chamber at the peak temperature is about forty times as high for the rapid

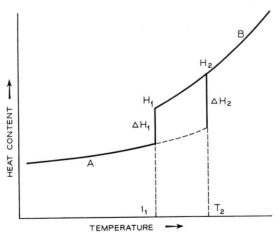

Fig. V-10. Heat content as a function of temperature: A, initial material; B, products.

Since the difference between the total heat contents varies with temperature, so must the heat of reaction or decomposition.

heating rate as for the slow. This value is very likely an exaggeration but there is, nevertheless, a marked effect.

The peak areas can hence be expected to be different at different rates, because at the higher heating rate a higher fraction of the kaolin stays in the unreacted state to any given temperature in the reaction range. This is in addition to the variation in area with equal increments of heat.

That even a given amount of heat does not cause the same magnitude of thermal effect at all temperatures has been shown by Sabatier (S2) and by Foldvari-Vogl and Kliburszky (F12). Sabatier selected materials whose heats of decomposition are well-known from the literature and which decompose at various temperatures, and related the peak area to the heat. His data are shown in Table V-1; they show a progressive

TABLE V-1

Substance	Temperature of dissociation (°C)	Heat of dissociation (Q) (cal/gm)	Area (S) (mv sec/gm)	Q/S
Gypsum	160	153	1720	0.089
$ZnCO_3$	425	114	965	0.118
$MgCO_3$	565	302	2160	0.140
$CaCO_3$	875	404	2120	0.190

diminution in response of the differential signal to a given quantity of heat as the temperature increased.

Even more convincing are the data of Foldvari-Vogl and Kliburszky (F12). They didn't rely on other measurements of heats of decomposition, but measured the effect of known quantities of heat applied electrically. They inserted a resistance heater in the form of a 5.6-ohm spiral filament in one of the sample crucibles and passed a current of 0.68 ampere through it for a period of 3 minutes (1100 cal) each 100°C as the sample was heated to ca. 1000°C. The areas (Fig. V-11) show a progressive decrease with temperature which shows the same general form as reported by Sabatier for actual reactions.

The conclusion to be reached is clearly that one cannot calibrate an apparatus for quantitative measurements at a temperature significantly removed from the temperature at which it will be used. A more positive thought, however, is that one might routinely compare peaks to an electrical standard rather than to the heat from another run; for example, after completion of the heating the furnace could be cooled to the approximate reaction temperature and a quantity of heat approximating the reaction heat added electrically. This would enable convenient comparison with a precisely known amount of heat at essentially the reaction temperature. Exact return to an arbitrarily defined reaction temperature would be pointless; bear in mind that the calibration factor varies by about 10% in an interval of 100°C in Foldvari-Vogl and Kliburszky's apparatus.

This electrical calibration would require a special apparatus. For general or infrequent use calibration with known amounts of known materials would suffice; Ellis and Mortland (E1) suggest those shown in Fig. V-12.

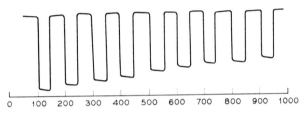

FIG. V-11. Differential temperature and area produced by adding identical quantities of heat at intervals of temperature rise. From Foldvari-Vogl and Kliburszky (F12).

The area per calorie decreases with increasing temperature.

The problem of integrating the area of a differential thermal analysis peak to measure the quantity of heat taken up or evolved has led to a variety of empirical solutions. We are not concerned here with the form of the peak nor with the significance of any part of the deflection; our immediate concern is the evaluation of the integral of $\Delta T\ dt$ from the moment the reaction begins to the moment ΔT returns to the base line. The method of integration can be selected from any of a number of techniques, e.g., measurement by planimeter, square-counting, weighing of the peak area, summation by trapezoidal rule. The major problem is selection of a reference line, that is, the line delineating the boundary at the open end of the recorded peak.

As a general rule materials undergoing reaction or transformation will show a quite marked change in thermal diffusivity and, hence, the steady-state temperature difference, i.e., baseline, will change. This effect may be diminished by dilution or by separation of sample and thermocouple but the peak is also attenuated, although not to the same degree. Further, the question of homogeneity of the dispersed sample will arise. Let us consider, for the time being, only specimens consisting wholly of a sample material whether or not it is already impure.

Figure V-13 shows Berg's (B26) thermogram for potassium nitrate illustrating his techniques for choosing the limits of simple curves. Transitions or reactions in which there is no substantial change in base line offer no difficulty; the base line is extrapolated from one side to the other and the area is clearly established. When there is a substantial change in the base line as the second transition, a slightly more involved procedure is required. Berg, like Deeg (D9), treated such reactions as occurring on a front moving inward from the edge of a circle so that, at

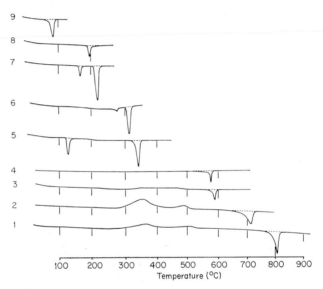

Fɪɢ. V-12. Differential thermal analyses curves of materials used for heat of reaction calibration: (1) NaCl, 8.3%, 0.226 gm; (2) RbCl, 22.7%, 0.232 gm; (3) K_2SO_4, 52.8%, 0.280 gm; (4) quartz, 100%, 0.283 gm; (5) KNO_3, 41.2%, 0.215 gm; (6) $NaNO_3$, 21.7%, 0.230 gm; (7) $AgNO_3$, 53.0%, 0.273 gm; (8) NH_4Cl, 17.2%, 0.208 gm; (9) *m*-/dinitrobenzene, 32.7%, 0.185 gm. The specimens were diluted with alumina. From Ellis and Mortland (E1).

Several calibration materials are needed because of the variation of heat indication with temperature.

the time the centrally located thermocouple reached the peak deflection, the transition was complete. The latter part of the curve, then, is simply a return of the center of the sample to a temperature approximating that of its surroundings. This asymptotic return depends only on the magnitude of the deflection and on the thermal characteristics of the specimen and not on the actual heat of reaction generated in or taken up by the sample material. This does not avoid counting the area but it does provide a basis for choice of the reference line. On the basis of the considerations set forth above, in those cases where the thermal characteristics of the sample change enough so that the sample becomes warmer than the reference after the transition, Berg drops a perpendicular from the peak of the deflection to the zero line and joins this intersection to the initial and final portions of the curve. More involved peaks or combinations of peaks require more elaborate treatment as Berg needed to use in his quantitative evaluation of dolomite-bearing minerals. Figure V-14 shows the somewhat overlapping peaks of dolomite mixed

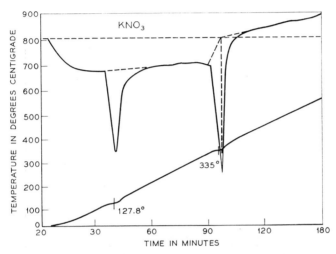

Fig. V-13. Thermogram of potassium nitrate showing ways of selecting the base line. From Berg (326).

The area is selected on the premise that the thermal effect after the peak is due only to a return to the base line.

with calcite and Berg's method of separating the two peaks. The method is intrinsically arbitrary.

Other possible ways of delineating the peak area to be measured include a slanted line joining an empirically selected beginning of the peak to an empirically selected end of the peak, extension of the lower-temperature base line to meet the high-temperature side of the peak, or, if these would not meet, the extension of the higher-temperature base line to meet the initial side of the peak. Both base lines might be extended also to join a perpendicular at the peak temperature. All of these are arbitrary and may be selected on the basis of the shape of the peak; any error will likely be within the experimental error due to other causes so long as peaks of the same shape (preferably of the same type of sample) are being compared.

If the instrument is being calibrated with one material for subsequent use with another, considerable risk of inaccuracy is incurred because the area that may or may not be included in the count can be a significant fraction of the total area. Note that simple experimental error is not involved here; either curve might be reproducible and repeatable. The question is whether to ignore a section—on one or the other of the curves—which could reasonably be included. Unfortunately, the derived expressions offer no help. The before and after base lines are *assumed* to be the same.

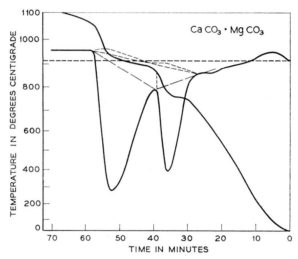

Fɪɢ. V-14. Thermogram of dolomite showing the separation of areas of overlapping curves. From Berg (B26).
The separation is arbitrary but the error will be a small part of the total area.

An essential feature in measuring the peak area is reproducibility of the total curve. For decompositions the atmosphere effect requires special care by the operator, particularly in packing the sample. A quite sensitive measure of the reproducibility of packing will be the reproducibility of the peak temperature. Despite the considerable body of evidence (i.e., reports) that reproducibility of curves can only be achieved by firm packing of the samples, Kissinger (K29) found that peak temperatures were better reproduced "by loading the sample into the holder, with no packing other than gentle rapping around the outside of the holder. The standard deviation of an individual measurement was found to be 2.6°C, calculated from 25 pairs of duplicate determinations." This attention to reproducibility is convincing.

The reason for this reproducibility lies only partly in the mode of packing; it rests as much or more on the sample geometry. Kissinger used, principally, a tube ³⁄₈ inch by 1¼ inch long. The sensing thermocouple is well-buried. Its atmospheric environment is not pure air certainly, but neither is it pure water vapor. At this distance from the surface, the reaction product (water vapor) cannot escape readily so the partial pressure of water is substantial. With the lesser barrier to diffusion than in a tightly packed sample, this partial pressure will reach some maximum value, probably before the peak temperature, determined principally by this case of diffusion and the heating rate. The observed peak temperature is properly the peak temperature at that particular water vapor pressure. Because of variations in sample holder design, variations in peak temperature will occur and variations in the calculated activation energies must result.

Kissinger's data (Table V-2) shows the peak temperature as a function of heating rate for the ³⁄₈ inch and for some ⅛ inch by ½ inch long sample holders. The differences in peak temperature are in the order of 80°C for the same material, the same heating rate, but a different sample holder.

A further advantage of the thinner samples is the lesser error in establishing transition or "decomposition" temperatures. The huge samples popular in early differential thermal analysis work led to a number

TABLE V-2

DIFFERENTIAL THERMAL ANALYSIS MEASUREMENTS (K 29)

Heating rate[a] (°C/minute)	Peak temperature (°C)				
	A	B	C	H–12	H–13
(a) ³⁄₈ inch holders					
12.5	640	642	635	629	629
10	625	632	615	616	614
6	611	614	611	603	597
4.5	598	599	592	588	583
3	588	584	574	582	568
(b) ⅛ inch holders					
12.5	557	563	544	553	553
10	549	553	530	547	542
6	537	538	520	530	533
4.5	525	528	511	519	517
3	514	523	499	512	508

[a] Heating rates given are nominal values. The actual rates were measured individually for each pattern and varied slightly from pattern to pattern.

of rather arbitrary geometric devices for obtaining a temperature to be designated as the characteristic temperature for that event. When simple phase transformations are spread out graphically over 50°C and de-hydrations extend over a spread of more than 100°C, these empirical single temperatures are rather unconvincing.

There is, of course, no question that areas can be measured and, if the analyses are made under properly chosen conditions, related quite well to the quantity of material present. Barshad (B9) showed that the con-centration was more closely related to area than total quantity. Some limitations must be observed, but these are generally restricted to de-composition reactions.

Wittels (W35) demonstrated, nevertheless, that a high heating rate (30°/minute) could be used for measurement of high heats of reaction (calcium carbonate, 40 kcal/mole) on small undiluted samples. He re-ports good linearity of peak area with sample mass from 0.30 to 3.00 mg (Fig. V-15), the smaller quantity giving a heat of reaction of 0.12 cal. In a later work (W36) he shows that the area to mass relation is non-linear for samples greater than 60 mg in the case of tremolite, a calcium magnesium silicate hydrate.

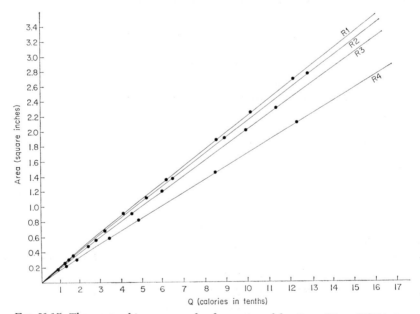

Fɪɢ. V-15. Thermographic response for four rates of heating: R1 = 30°C/minute; R2 = 22.5°C/minute; R3 = 15°C/minute; R4 = 10°C/minute. From Wittels (W35). *The area per calorie varies somewhat with rate of heating but not with the amount of heat.*

Wittels pointed out that "samples of large mass are to be avoided when measuring small heat changes by differential thermal analysis" partly on the basis of the data noted above. The present author agrees enthusiastically—especially with the principal clause. The present author does not extend this agreement to the derivation by Wittels of an expression for the heat of reaction. The treatment was empirical; the approach was chosen on the basis of similarity of Wittels' area vs quantity plot to a plot of the function e^x. No theoretical justification is offered.

Wittel's success can be attributed easily to the fact that in this sample size range he finds the area dependence to be linear because he is generating carbon dioxide rapidly enough to form a reproducible atmosphere, i.e., nearly all CO_2. The heat of decomposition will be the same for a range of sample sizes. The higher limit (Fig. V-15) is set by the decreasing response to material at some distance away. Its closeness to the container walls becomes increasingly significant. For smaller samples the limit would be dictated to some degree by a similar reason; i.e., in the same container a relatively greater portion is in good thermal contact with the wall rather than the thermocouple. A very important contribution, however, is the probability that a large and variable fraction of the *ambient* atmosphere permeates the sample. This would be true in the upper part of the specimen and as the sample becomes smaller a centered thermocouple necessarily approaches the top.

In diluted samples some range of near constancy of atmosphere can be obtained with the result that both upper and lower limits could be pushed further. The lower limit would again be the failure to generate an atmosphere at a rate sufficient to keep the heat of reaction nearly constant. The upper limit would be set by the influence of the thermal characteristics of the material on those of the diluted specimen.

With the aid of the data of de Bruijn and van der Marel (B85) we can gain some better picture of the effects. Figure V-16 shows a calibration curve in which the heat in calories is plotted against the area of the peak. The samples were, for convenience, mixed with the required weight of alumina to make up 400 mg; note that we are dealing with *weight per cent* and not concentration. The plot actually has a very straight-line region up to about 20 calories. Near this point corresponding to one-quarter or more of the less-energetic materials a noticeable curvature begins and the data are less well-related from compound to compound. The thermal characteristics of the individual materials will generally begin to exert an influence (on the thermal conductivity for example) on the thermal behavior of the entire specimen. In spite of the curve having been extended unduly far with some of the materials it does show that the heat measured can be related quite well to the amount of material reacting or decomposing. As Barshad (B9) showed (Fig. V-9) the material ought to be dispersed in a constant volume and dispersed to such an extent that the thermal characteristics of the diluent determine those of the whole specimen. In de Bruijn and van der Marel's work the drop in heat effect with large concentration is shown in Fig. V-17. The small deviation by the barium chloride dihydrate is probably due to the lesser volume of a given weight.

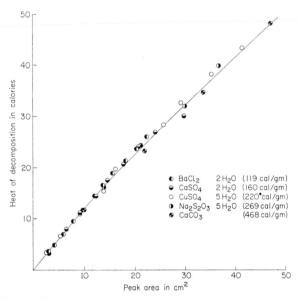

◑ BaCl$_2$	2 H$_2$O	(119 cal/gm)
◕ CaSO$_4$	2 H$_2$O	(160 cal/gm)
○ CuSO$_4$	5 H$_2$O	(220*cal/gm)
◐ Na$_2$S$_2$O$_3$	5 H$_2$O	(269 cal/gm)
✶ CaCO$_3$		(468 cal/gm)

Fig. V-16. Calibration of differential thermal analysis apparatus. Heats of decomposition of some pure substances diluted with inert α-Al$_2$O$_3$, the total in the sample holder being 400 mg. *Peak area and heat of decomposition for loss of H$_2$O from CuSO$_4$·5H$_2$O to CuSO$_4$·H$_2$O. From de Bruijn and van der Marel (B85).

The well-diluted specimens show a linear relation because the thermal characteristics of the sample material do not contribute greatly to those of the entire specimen.

5.6. Evaluation of Heats of Reaction

The differential thermal analysis technique can be used to determine heats of reaction or of decomposition. Several methods of calculating these quantities have been offered by the difficulties arising from the changing characteristics render these methods inexact. Nevertheless they must be examined and the inaccuracies pointed out so that the pitfalls may be avoided without discarding the entire work.

The question of the exact significance of the differential thermal analysis peak of a decomposition reaction was taken up by Foldvari-Vogl and Kliburszky (F12), who analyzed the steps in the heating and cooling, resolving the heat effects into six quantities. The quantities are given below, with some clarification by the present author.

(1) A quantity of heat, q_1, is needed to heat the specimen from ambient temperature, T_0, to the initial temperature of the thermal effect, T_i, so

$$q_1 = m_1 \int_{T_0}^{T_i} c_1 \, dT + H_1$$

where m is the mass, c is the heat capacity, and H_1 comprises any heat effects at temperatures lower than the reaction under investigation.

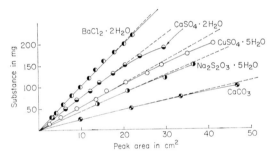

FIG. V-17. Calibration of differential thermal analysis apparatus. Peak areas for endothermal reactions of some substances diluted with inert α–Al_2O_3, the total in the sample holder being 400 mg. From de Bruijn and van der Marel (B85).
The relationship is linear for well-diluted materials.

(2) Some further heat, q_2, is required to change the lattice energy, the decomposition product from the specimen, and, in the case of water, vaporize it, as well as raise the temperature of the residue to the final temperature of the experiment, T_f. (Foldvari-Vogl and Kliburszky used the example of a mineral containing an OH radical so they could later show that for some minerals most of the heat effect detected by differential thermal analysis was heat of vaporization of water rather than the heat required to break chemical bonds.)

If the final temperature coincides with the return to a base line of a differential thermal analysis plot, the area under the curve is a measure of q_2. The changing heat capacity during the course of the reaction ought (except in rate-controlled processes) to be a rather small correction since at their very rapid heating most of the reaction will take place under one atmosphere of water vapor or other product gas and hence over a small temperature range.

Then on cooling:

(3) The decomposition residue is cooled to the ambient temperature, releasing a quantity of heat, q_3, which is not identical with q_1 because both mass and heat capacity are different, so

$$q_3 = m_3 \int_{T_f}^{T_0} c_3 \, dT + H_3$$

where the quantities are defined as previously, except referring now to step (3).

(4) Cooling the product gas (assume it to be water vapor) to 100°C liberates a quantity of heat, q_4.

(5) Condensing the water vapor at 100°C liberates a quantity of heat, q_5.

(6) Cooling the liquid water to ambient temperature liberates a quantity of heat, q_6.

Note that if the product gas were a permanent gas, step (5) would be dropped and steps (4) and (6) would be a single entry.

Now if the decomposition process is carried out in a calorimeter (Foldvari-Vogl and Klibursky's is described in Chapter XII), the quantity of heat supplied, Q, can be measured by the time and magnitude of an electric heating current. The quantity of heat recovered by heating of the calorimeter can be determined from the temperature rise and the total heat capacity. The difference, ΔQ, is an algebraic sum of all six steps, i.e.,

$$\Delta Q = -q_1 - q_2 + q_3 + q_4 + q_5 + q_6.$$

All of these quantities can be determined experimentally except q_2, so that, from known values plus whatever further measurement is needed, q_2 may be calculated.

The value of q_2 determined in this manner is not time-dependent. The change in base line which is common in differential thermal analysis has no bearing, since if the specimen is heated beyond completion of the reaction the difference in heat capacity between unreacted material and residue does not appear in the final determination. The heat required to raise the temperature of the residue appears again as a part of q_3 *so long as no other reaction occurs.*

In essence, Foldvari-Vogl and Kliburszky determine the heat of reaction at room temperature and relate it to differential thermal analysis measuring or calculating the necessary quantities to evaluate the heat of reaction at the temperature of the reaction. The appropriate relationship is

$$\frac{\partial \Delta H}{\partial T} = \Delta C_p$$

so

$$\Delta H_T = \Delta H_{T_d} + \int_{T_0}^{T} \Delta C_p \, dT.$$

The integral on the right comprises the terms described by Foldvari-Vogl and Klibursky as q_1, q_3, q_6.

Their technique ought to be useful not only for evaluation of heats of reaction but even as a quantitative tool. If another reaction occurred prior to the one under investigation, the effect could be calculated if the data are available or the material might be given a preheating to eliminate the interference.

Note that, unlike differential thermal analysis, calorimetric technique does not register heat of vaporization of water as part of the heat of reaction; the heat used in the vaporization is recovered on cooling. This is a major source of error in some dehydrations, those in which the reaction may reasonably be interpreted as $A \cdot xH_2O \rightarrow A + xH_2O(l)$ followed by $xH_2O(l) \rightarrow xH_2O(g)$. Dehydrations or dehydroxylations above the critical temperature of water ($374°C$) would have no vaporization step but the heat of condensation is still recovered.

The figures obtained by Foldvari-Vogl and Kliburszky (F12) will differ from data obtained by differential thermal analysis, as pointed out above, by $\int \Delta C_p \, dt$; in most cases involving hydrates the heat of vaporization will appear as a major portion of this heat, so the values by these authors will be lower than differential thermal analysis (or high-temperature calorimetry) values by this heat of vaporization. In the case of gypsum, they found, by differential thermal analysis, 170 cal/gm and, by their calorimeter, 34 cal/gm. From this latter datum they calculate q_2, the heat of dehydration, as 151 cal/gm.

Sewell and Honeyborne (S19a) treat a differential thermal analysis block and sample arrangement as a multitude of points each obeying a temperature function which is specifically a function of position and time. Each of these points continues its course of temperature rise without regard for the behavior of adjacent particles or points except for certain regions during the temperature interval of the thermal effect. The temperature difference, ΔT, can be treated as the difference between the function $T(P_1,t) - T(P_2,t)$. P_1 is specifically the location of the thermocouple in the sample and P_2 the location of the thermocouple in the reference specimen. The block containing the sample and reference material is assumed to be close to but not touching a furnace wall whose temperature is programmed at a constant rate so that $T = \beta t$. Heat conduction from the furnace wall to the block is assumed to be a function only of the temperature difference between the wall and the surface of the block. All of the quantities with the exception of temperature and time are assumed to be constant before and after the reaction has taken place as well as during the course of the reaction. The treatment is further limited to reversible phase changes and to thermodynamically irreversible decompositions obeying a first-order law.

All points except within the sample and all points in the sample except during the reaction or phase change obey the ordinary heat flow equation $\kappa_i \nabla^2 T = \partial(T)/\partial t$ where the subscript i may refer to any point within the system. During the reaction, the equation for points within the test specimen has an additive term

$$\kappa_s \nabla^2 T = \frac{\partial T}{\partial t} + \frac{L}{C_s} \frac{\partial \alpha}{\partial t}$$

where L is the heat of reaction and α is the fraction of material at P that has reacted at time t. The use of this fraction term demands a continuity of state which is not generally accepted; it implies that in any small region there is a mixture of reacted and unreacted material whose relative amounts are temperature- and time-dependent. The use of the term may be warranted in time-dependent decompositions but probably not in any reversible phase transition.

The customary heat flux continuity equations must also be obeyed; in essence what goes in one side of a boundary must come out the other.

$$\lambda_s(\partial T/\partial n)_s + \lambda_b(\partial T/\partial n)_b = 0$$

and

$$\lambda_r(\partial T/\partial n)_r + \lambda_b(\partial T/\partial n)_b = 0$$

where $\partial T/\partial n$ is the temperature gradient perpendicular to the surface at the point under consideration. On the surface of the block, this continuity equation takes a different form; while the heat transfer into the block is, as above, the thermal conductivity multiplied by the temperature gradient, any heat transfer from the furnace wall to the block depends upon the temperature difference at that point. Assuming the furnace wall at that point to have a temperature equal to βt, the temperature function for the point on the surface of the block is $T(P)$ and the difference between these two terms is multiplied by the heat-transfer coefficient $H(P)$,

$$-\lambda_b(\partial T/\partial n) = H(P)[T(P) - \beta T]$$

where β is the heating rate. Since this H is the sum of two terms, H_R and H_C, heat-transfer coefficients for radiation and for conduction, respectively, and since neither of these is independent of temperature, the assumption that the total heat-transfer coefficient is independent of temperature introduces a serious source of error.

During ordinary operation of the differential thermal analysis run, a steady state will occur or ensue in which the temperature at any point lags behind the programmed wall temperature by some function of its position so that, in general, $T = \beta t - f(P)$, where $f(P)$ depends on the heat-transfer characteristics both of the materials between the point under consideration and the wall and also on the heat-transfer and heat-absorption characteristics of the material further from the wall and to which it must transmit heat. With all the assumptions of temperature independence previously set down the temperature at any point will reach a fixed lag behind the programmed temperature and then heat smoothly at the programmed heating rate of β; hence, the temperature difference between point one and point two, the sample and reference, will reach some magnitude and, until a reaction occurs, have zero slope.

In order to use this $f(P)$ it must be shown that it has the same form as $T(P)$ to the extent of obeying the rules set down so far. Substitution in the general heat-flow equation yields identical results because—on the left hand side—βt is not a function of the coordinate so its derivative with respect to position drops out; $f(P)$ is not a function of time so it drops out, leaving β, which is the heating rate.

In the interface relation, the derivative of βt with respect to position again drops out, leaving the same equation but in f instead of T.

Similarly, on the block surface, the substitution allows the βtr to be subtracted. The same thing happens in the differential temperature at the steady state.

Having established a model for the behavior during the steady temperature rise, Sewell and Honeyborne turn their attention to the events during the phase change. They introduce the peak area function, an integral between two times, one before and one after the reaction, at both of which the temperature differential has returned to a base line which is time- and temperature-independent.

$$W(P) = \int_{t_0}^{t_2} [\beta t - f(P) - T(P,t)]dt$$

where t_2 is a time after completion of the reaction; thus

$$\text{area} = \int_{t_0}^{t_2} [(\Delta T)_0 - (\Delta T)]dt = W(P_1) - W(P_2).$$

In essence, this peak area function is the integral of the difference between the actual temperature and the temperature which is prescribed by the previous considerations. It is, then, the integral of a peak one might observe if the temperature at a point were plotted against the symmetrically located point, the symmetry being with respect to a plane between a sample and the reference specimens. Since this peak area function, $W(P)$, is a function of $T(P)$, we can substitute W into the several equations which T and f must obey and ascertain whether or not the results have any meaning; we shall, in effect, evaluate one side of the equation.

One can easily dispose of the parts that take no direct part—whose roles are as counterpoise, containment, and measuring accessories. This is done by expanding $\kappa\Delta^2 W$ by simply inserting the definition of W on the right-hand side and since $\kappa\Delta^2 f$ is equal to $=\beta$ and $\kappa\Delta^2 T$ equal to $\partial(T)/\partial t$ we get an expression which we recognize as $f(P)$ evaluated between t_0 and t_2, but since $f(P)$ is not a function of time the evaluation is zero.

Similarly, insert W in the equation of continuity at interfaces and expand W by definition, noting that βT is not a function of position, and rearrange terms. Two expressions, one involving F and one involving T, are obtained but each of these expressions goes to 0 at an interface as does, then, the expression involving W. In essence, this establishes that W is continuous across any interface. Again, on the surface of the block, W behaves in the same manner as T or F.

The behavior in the specimen is of greatest importance. Again, expanding W and substituting, the first two terms in the brackets drop out leaving the term involving the several thermal properties times a evaluated between t_0 and t_2. But a goes from 0 before the reaction to 1 after the reaction leaving

$$\nabla^2 W = \frac{-L\rho_s}{\lambda_s}.$$

Thus, from the several results and with the assumptions previously stated, Sewell and Honeyborne conclude that the peak area is proportional to the heat of reaction per unit volume of test sample and is independent of the heating rate so long as it is linear, the rate at which the reaction takes place, or the specific heat of the test sample. It does, however, depend on the conductivities of the several materials of the furnace as well as the heat transfer between the surface of the block and the furnace wall.

Sewell and Honeyborne recognized the several limitations of the treatment just described, but treatments which do take into account, for example, that thermal conductivities, specific heats, diffusivites, and conductances are functions of temperature become at least unwieldy or even intractable.

Complete and exact analysis of the differential thermal analysis peak will require methods of at least this degree of complexity. If we now add in the fact that $f(P)$ is not a function *only* of P but has a temperature dependence it becomes apparent that solution would be impractical. (The temperature dependence of f arises from the variations in heat capacities and thermal conductivities with temperature.) Further, it is apparent that within the sample $f(P)$ [or $f(P, T)$] would have a discontinuity during and because of the thermal event. The discontinuity arises from the change in identity of the material.

The treatment by Deeg (D9), on the other hand, takes into account the changing thermal properties in a nonexplicit manner, but he finds it necessary to point out that, in most cases, it will be impossible to provide a self-contained analytical form of the solution; hence, in the evaluation of basic equations, reliance will have to be placed mainly on numerical and graphical processes.

In addition to Deeg's refusal to make assumptions purely to simplify the mathematics, he treats the reaction temperature range differently. He uses the "advancing reaction front" approach, stating, in effect, that except for a very brief period of time the material at a given point is either in one form or the other—no fractions.

In his treatment, he uses Dirac's δ function (C13)

$$W_B = \lim_{\epsilon \to 0} W \cdot \int_{T_r - \epsilon}^{T_r + \epsilon} \delta(T/T_r) dT$$

which is a step function.

The two approaches to the transition temperature region are compared in Fig. V-18. A segment of time bracketing the transition is taken and the fraction reacting at some given point is plotted. Sewell and Honeyborne's treatment dictates a skewed curve—skewed because of the temperature dependence of the rate of transformation. Deeg's treatment dictates an immediate rise to some high rate followed by a fall to zero when the material at that point has been exhausted. The summations are equally predictable, a nonsymmetric sigmoid curve compared to a rapid rise.

Sewell and Honeyborne's acceptance of coexisting reacted and unreacted material implies a finite and substantial time of reaction of a particle; this implies in turn a rate-determining step. Deeg implies that when the sample reaches a transformation temperature it simply transforms. Deeg's treatment is more descriptive of phase changes but is quite unsuitable for those decompositions which do have a rate-

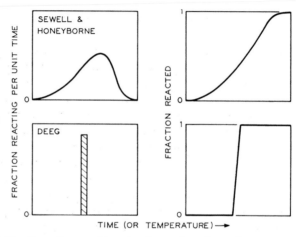

Fig. V-18. Fraction of any arbitrarily chosen bit of sample reacting or reacted as a function of time (or temperature) as the specimen is heated steadily.

Sewell and Honeyborne's (S19a) treatment assumes coexistence—in a limited region and for a finite time—of reacted and unreacted material; Deeg's (D9) treatment assumes instantaneous or very rapid conversion. For the entire sample, Sewell and Honeyborne's calculations yield a relatively broad peak compared to Deeg's.

determining step. The former treatment shows the effects of studies on clay minerals. Many of their reactions have rate-determining steps and Sewell and Honeyborne's use of the a term takes this into account even though they carefully restrict the applicability of their treatment to reversible phase changes or decompositions obeying a first-order law.

Whether or not a particular thermal effect is rate-controlled can be established fairly easily by two kinds of experiments by changing the heating rate under identical thermodynamic conditions or by changing the size of sample.

The identity of the thermodynamic conditions is crucial; if the reaction is a gas-forming decomposition, the atmosphere surrounding the material should be the pure gaseous product at the same pressure in each experiment or a dynamic atmosphere comprising the product gas. Significant change in temperature of reaction, e.g., peak temperature, with change in heating rate implies a rate-determining step.

Changing the sample diameter, on the other hand, will affect the shape but the peak temperature—measured along the axis of a cylindrical sample—should remain the same if the process is fast i.e., not rate-controlled. The peak will become sharper with the smaller samples. In a rate-controlled process, on the other hand, the shape of the curve ought to remain very nearly the same.

The sharper peaks available with the smaller specimens are not an argument for general use of very small samples. The injudicious use of milligram amounts can lead to sampling errors that often render the data almost meaningless.

Vold (V10) prepared a formula by which heats of reaction could be calculated from differential thermal analysis curves. For a close approach to validity, her final equation must be used with data obtained with a block-type specimen holder, yet she carefully used a pair of

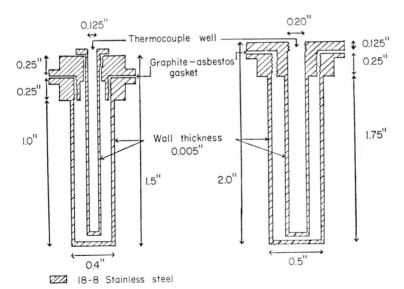

FIG. V-19. Differential calorimeter cells. From Vold (V10).
These cells are suspended in air within a cylindrical furnace. Any vapor was either confined within the cell or allowed to diffuse out through a small orifice.

isolated cells (Fig. V-19). Vold first sets down equations describing the heat flow into the specimen and into the reference:

$$\frac{dq_s}{dt} = K_s(T_w - T_s) + \sigma(T_r - T_s) + \alpha_s(T_0 - T_s) \tag{3A}$$

$$\frac{dq_r}{dt} = K_r(T_w - T_r) + \sigma(T_s - T_r) + \alpha_r(T_0 - T_r). \tag{3B}$$

dq/dt is the rate at which heat is received by the sample or reference, K_s and K_r are the heat-transfer coefficients between the furnace wall and sample or reference, and σ and α are heat-transfer coefficients between the specimens and from specimen to the outside environment at T_0.

The "furnace wall" must necessarily be a surface which presents a uniform appearance to sample and reference specimens *and* from which these specimens may take heat directly; if this is not the case, we must add some more terms. In Vold's apparatus, these would include a term describing the temperature of the outer wall of the cell, a pair of terms describing the transfer of heat to and from the air in the furnace, and, of course, a term describing the transfer of heat through the air. The terms would be nearly identical most of the time so the differences would be small most of the time. Unfortunately, the differences would assume a significant value at a most inopportune time, i.e., during the thermal effect. The heat-transfer coefficients will all be dependent on the nature of the interface between the sample and its container. One can easily deduce what types of specimens will cause severe changes: samples which melt, samples which shrink away from the walls, samples whose decomposition residue has a greatly diminished density, etc. The possibility of significant change would be present quite generally. The isolated sample cell wall will lag in temperature behind the reference cell wall so we have an increased rate of supply of heat to the sample cell, but we have neither a T_w that applies to both cells nor equal rates of heating.

Vold next points out the identity

$$\frac{dq}{dt} = \frac{dH}{dt} = \frac{dH}{dt}\frac{dT}{dt} \tag{4}$$

and segregates the heat content arising from the heat of reaction,

$$\frac{dq_s}{dt} = C_s\frac{dT_s}{dt} + \Delta H\frac{df}{dt} \tag{5}$$

where df/dt is the fractional rate of transformation, and, by substitution, subtraction, and simplification obtains

$$\frac{\Delta H}{C_s}\frac{df}{dt} = \frac{dy}{dt} + A(y - y_s) \tag{6}$$

where $y = \Delta T$, $A = (K_r + a_r + 2\sigma)/C_s$, and

$$y_s = \frac{\left[(C_s - C_r)\dfrac{dT_r}{dt} + \delta K(T_w - T_s) - \delta a(T_s - T_0)\right]}{K_r + \alpha_r + 2},$$

where δK and δa take account of asymmetry in heat transfer. The term y_s is assumed to be a steady-state function of y, essentially a constant for a given experiment or set of conditions. $(C_s - C_r)$, however, is most unlikely to remain constant. In phase transformations, this is often a fair approximation, but in a decomposition such an event would be purely fortuitous; a sizable change in C_s is the rule rather than the exception.

Vold finds the transformation complete when $dy/dt = -A(y - y_s)$, since df/dt is again zero. This point is found by plotting $\log (y - y_s)$ vs t (Fig. V-20); this time of deviation from linearity moving down-

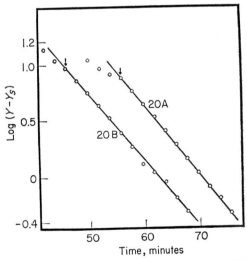

FIG. V-20. Plot for determining constant A. From Vold (V10).

A governs rate at which a thermal steady state is re-established after a transformation occurs. Arrows mark time at which transformation is finished; subsequent points lie on straight lines.

ward in time) marks the time of completion of the reaction. This time corresponds to a point some time after the maximum deflection as in Fig. V-21 (see Section 5.3). Figure V-22 shows the relation between the total and differential heating curves. The reader should keep in mind also that all these "constants" are temperature-dependent.

Note that Vold took no account of the heat transfer within the specimen. There is no objection to this in differential calorimetry, in which entire area is used in computation, but it would be a serious matter in other cases where σ has a significant value. It enters into Vold's work because she was measuring temperatures at the center of specimen and reference and calculating point-by-point values. The rather tardy completion of reaction is probably due to thermal inhomogeneity resulting from loss of heat upward along the sample cells.

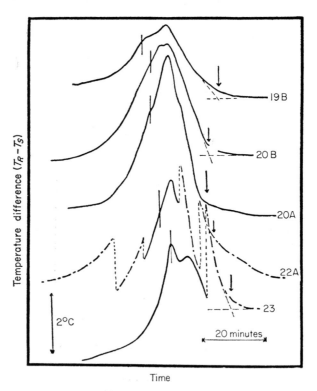

FIG. V-21. Differential heating curves of stearic and benzoic acids. From Vold (V10).

From the points designated by arrows, since reaction is "complete," ΔT returns asymptotically to a new steady-state value.

5.7. Second-Order Transitions

The effect of a discontinuous change of some property on the thermal behavior has been treated by Deeg (D9) with emphasis on its application to differential thermal analysis. The sudden change in a property —whether C_p, ρ, k, or other, will influence the transfer of heat and consequently cause a thermal effect in differential thermal analysis (see Chapter II, Sec. 2.6). The special case of polymers has been examined by Strella (S65).

Strella assumed a cylindrical model in which he lets the surface temperature of the unreacted material hold constant at the glass transition temperature as the interface between the two forms moves in toward the center and, meanwhile, the higher temperature form is treated as a cylinder whose inside diameter is decreasing.

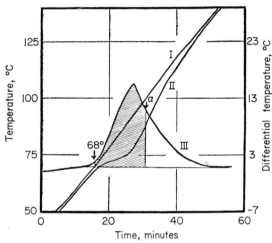

Fig. V-22. Total and differential heating curves for stearic acid and Nujol: I, heating curve for Nujol cell; II, heating curve for stearic acid cell; III, differential heating curve.

At 68°C melting begins. a is time at which calculation shows that melting is completed. Shaded area is that taken into account in calculating ΔH.

From the decay of the temperature distribution in the initial form and the corresponding growth of the resulting form he obtains an expression for the temperature differential between surface and center,

$$\Delta T = \frac{\beta a^2}{4k_2}(1 - e^{-k_2\alpha,t}) + \frac{\beta a^2}{4k_1}e^{-k,\alpha,t}$$

where β is the heating rate, a the radius, k and k_2 the thermal diffusivities, a the first root of the (Bessel) equation $J_0(\alpha a) = 0$, and t the time from the initiation of the transition.

The equation implies a sigmoidal form for ΔT vs T and Strella further deduces that, considering the exponential nature of the equation for ΔT, a plot of log T_{gi} vs heating rate should be linear and extrapolation to zero rate should yield the correct glass transition temperature. Taking the T_{gi} as the inflection points of a number of curves obtained at different heating rates (Fig. V-23) he constructed the plot of Fig. V-24. From Fig. V-24 he obtained a value of 110°C for the correct glass transi-

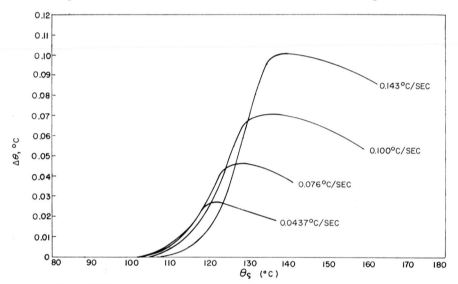

Fɪɢ. V-23. Differential temperature vs surface temperature for a polymethyl-methacrylate heated at several rates. From Strella (S65).

The change occurs over a substantial time at these not very low heating rates (2.6 to 8.6°C/minute).

tion temperature of polymethylmethacrylate, which "compares quite favorably with Rogers and Mandelkern's value of 105°C (R28). Thus the prediction that the extrapolation of T_{gi} to zero rate would yield the value of the glass transition temperature is considered correct."

As his equation stands, the high-temperature form is not growing at the same rate as that at which the low-temperature form is disappearing; i.e., the decay terms, $e^{-k_n a^2 t}$, should be the same if we are to accept the concept as it stands. The influence of the increased heat capacity may establish the rate at which the interface moves.

The method of extrapolating the data apparently doesn't matter much. The intercept is about the same whether the temperature is in °C as in Fig. V-24 (the mantissa only) or in °K as Strella used for atactic polypropylene. For that matter, a linear plot, i.e., T_{gi} vs heating rate, of Strella's data yielded 109°C as the "correct glass transition temperature." Further, the initiation of the glass transition should designate the transition temperature when ΔT is plotted against surface temperature. From Fig. V-23, this occurs in the 102–106°C range.

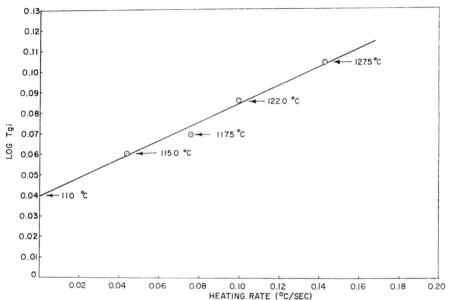

Fɪɢ. V-24. Logarithm of the indicated glass transition temperature vs heating rate for polymethylmethacrylate. From Strella (S65).

Extrapolation to zero heating rate is used to estimate the correct glass transition temperature.

5.8. Summary

Quantitative treatment of differential thermal analysis curves by other than empirical methods is impractical at present. Detailed calculations of simultaneous processes would require computers and a set of equations and data not presently available.

The changing of thermal properties as a material is being heated implies that return to the same base line as before the reaction is unlikely. Empirical methods are used to delineate the peak. So long as there are no overlapping peaks a high degree of isolation (as in differential calorimetry) favors accurate quantitative determinations.

Approximate mathematical descriptions of differential thermal analysis curves have been devised, but in order to render the expressions tractable assumptions not in agreement with physical reality are needed. Some inferences may be drawn from the models assumed.

CHAPTER VI

Kinetics

6.1. Introduction

While most crystallographic phase transformations and some decomposition reactions proceed so rapidly that the observed rate of reaction is due to some other limiting feature, some reactions including decompositions proceed at a measurable rate even when atmosphere and temperature conditions are favorable. (Note here that the *observed* rate of change will depend on the *slowest* of the processes involved.) This rate will ordinarily depend on the quantity of unreacted material present and the temperature of the sample. The nature and pressure of the surrounding atmosphere may or may not have a significant effect other than influencing heat transfer. A review of chemical kinetics is outside the scope of this book; any elementary physical chemistry text will provide sufficient background.

One major problem in the study of the kinetics of a reaction by thermoanalytical methods has been the failure to take account of all the factors which might influence the rate. An important question in evaluating kinetic data is whether or not the data are independent of geometry of the specimen. If a reaction can truly be described as first order, then the weight loss should occur in the same manner in a crucible as in a closed chamber or on a flat plate. If, on the other hand, the reaction depends on the nature of the atmosphere surrounding the particles or on the ease of heat transfer—in the case of a changing temperature—the shadow of doubt may reach the proportion of a heavy cloud.

6.2. Homogeneous Reactions

One of the more frequently quoted expressions for rates of reaction is that of Borchardt and Daniels (B67). The expression was derived very specifically for a system in which the (liquid) sample and reference are stirred (Fig. VI-1) so that the temperature of the sample or reference may reasonably be considered to be uniform. Intrepid followers have applied the expression to solid-state reactions without satisfying this homogeneity condition. There are twelve assumptions involved in Bor-

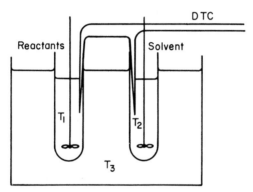

Fig. VI-1. Differential thermal analysis apparatus of Borchardt and Daniels (B67) for obtaining kinetic data for reaction occurring in solution.
The stirring assures temperature homogeneity.

chardt and Daniels' derivation. We will consider only six of them, including (1) the uniform temperature condition above.

We have already (Chapter II) seen how a reaction front proceeds from the wall of the sample holder inward in solids so the extension of the expression to solids is automatically void because the uniform temperature assumption is out of the question. Three of the assumptions are —at best—approximations; these are (2) the heat-transfer coefficients of reactants and products are equal, (3) the heat capacities of reactants and products are equal, and (4) these quantities, plus the heat of reaction, do not change over the temperature range of reaction. Note that these three (see below) are the only ones which would require the temperature difference to return to zero after the reaction and, further, Borchardt and Daniels' plot (Fig. VI-2) does *not* show a return to zero even with stirred liquid specimens.

Assumption (2) will depend greatly on the nature of the materials and the container surface. Just as heat transfer in solids is governed greatly by the nature of interfaces, so can we hypothesize that adsorption of solute on the container surface will influence the heat-transfer coefficient. The relative polar characteristics of solute (both unreacted and reacted) and solvent must be considered.

Assumption (3) will probably be reasonable in dilute solutions of such a nature that the heat of solvation is low. A substantial fraction of the heat-capacity difference could be due to desolvation. Dilution of the specimen will diminish the signal so a compromise must be made. Bor-

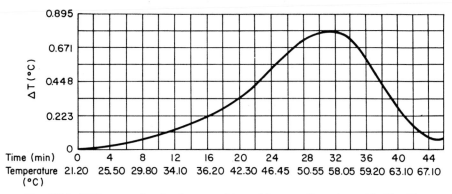

Fɪɢ. VI-2. DTA curve for the decomposition of benzenediazonium chloride. Temperature difference between the reactant solution and inert liquid is plotted as a function of temperature and time. From Borchardt and Daniels (B67).

Even under especially good experimental conditions the differential signal cannot be expected always to return to zero.

chardt and Daniels used a 0.4 M solution, which is not very dilute; a heat-capacity difference can reasonably be expected. At this level of concentration, the change in heat capacity before and after the reaction can well be significant.

Note, too, that formation of a second phase would affect the heat capacity of the solution. If a reaction product were an immiscible fluid or insoluble the likelihood of unchanging thermal characteristics would indeed be remote.

Assumption (4) is related to this last effect since $d\Delta H/dT = \Delta C_p$ and, of course, desolvation and desorption from the surface would both be temperature-sensitive.

These three assumptions, then, are only approximations when applied to stirred liquid samples; applied to powdered solid specimens they are untenable.

The assumption (5) that the heat effect—as measured by the differential temperature—is proportional to the number of molecules reacting in unit time can be applied only to thermally homogeneous systems. It is satisfactory for the stirred samples but not for solids. That the heat effect detected by a thermocouple is influenced by the distance of the reacting materials from the thermocouple has already been shown (Chapter II). The reaction of a given quantity of sample at the edge of the specimen will not produce the same effect as reaction of the same quantity adjacent to a centrally located thermocouple. The reaction of a cylindrical sample is not proceeding most rapidly at the peak of the differential temperature; in many cases it is complete.

The assumption (6) that the kinetics of a reaction can be described by a single rate constant is acceptable for systems that might be studied by Borchardt and Daniels' method but its applicability to solid reactants must be approached with caution and vertified for the system under investigation.

6.3. Heterogeneous Decompositions

A considerable weakness of such extensions—or original derivations, for that matter—is that in the systems of most interest, i.e., decompositions, these various "constants" undergo rather drastic change. Decompositions such as that of kaolin cannot be expected, in the usual nondynamic atmosphere experiment, to follow a single rate expression; nor can decompositions be expected to follow a single rate expression if the concentration of reaction products is allowed to vary.

Freeman and Carroll (E14) by appropriate differentiation, integration, and division, proceed from $k = Z \exp - (E^*/RT)$ where k is the specific rate constant, Z is the frequency factor, E^* is the activation energy, and R is the gas constant, and

$$ -\frac{dX}{dt} = kX^x $$

where X is the concentration, mole fraction, or amount of reactant and x is the order of reaction, to find

$$ \frac{-(E^*/R)\Delta(1/T)}{\Delta \ln X} = \frac{\Delta \ln(-dX/dt)}{\Delta \ln X} - x. $$

That conclude, of course, that a plot of

$$ \frac{\Delta\left(\frac{1}{T}\right)}{\Delta \log X} \quad \text{vs} \quad \frac{\Delta \log(-dX/dt)}{\Delta \log X} $$

should result in a straight line with a slope of $\pm E^*/2.3R$ and an intercept of $-X$. Freeman and Carroll proposed to take the necessary data from a single thermogravimetric experiment in which several tenths of a gram of sample were heated at a rate of 10°C/minute.

Implicit in their derivation were the assumptions that (1) the order of reaction is the same throughout the reaction, (2) the atmosphere had no effect, and (3) the temperature was the same throughout the specimen. The first of these assumptions is not necessarily correct; the other two are clearly untenable (see Chapter II). In their experiment using calcium oxalate monohydrate, not only will the presence of air, rather than water vapor, permit variations in the vapor pressure of water within and about the sample and hence affect the rate of dehydration, but also the air affects the nature of the second reaction. In air, the carbon monoxide moiety of the oxalate ion oxidizes readily to carbon dioxide. The reaction is rapid and sharply exothermic. In Freeman and Carroll's experiment, this reaction took five minutes as compared to the few seconds it would take in a smaller sample. The reason for this is discussed in greater detail elsewhere (Chapter VII), but in essence the rate is dependent on the entry of oxygen; however, diffusion of the oxygen inward is inhibited by the nitrogen which diffuses in too but is not consumed and by the carbon dioxide which is being evolved. The third reaction, decomposition of calcium carbonate, is a rapid and reversible reaction. It will proceed at a rate far more dependent on the diffusion outward of the carbon dioxide than on a reaction rate constant. Furthermore, the size of specimen used by Freeman and Carroll is in the range frequently used in older differential thermal analysis apparatuses; at 10°C/minute, temperature differences of 20°C or more are easily obtained.

On the other hand, Murray and White (M45) measured the rate of weight loss of kaolin under constant (furnace) temperature and concluded that the dehydroxylation in the 500–600°C range is a first-order reaction. They eliminated the extracrystalline water by heating to constant weight at 430°C; they then raised the furnace temperature rapidly to the desired temperature and observed the weight loss as a function of time. They plotted their data with the appropriate coordinates and concluded that over the bulk of the decomposition range the decomposition followed a first-order law.

Murray and White wrote the first-order law in the form

$$\frac{dl}{dt} = k(l_\infty - l)$$

where l_∞ is the total (see below) loss of combined moisture and l is the actual loss at time t. This yields the integrated form

$$\log\left(\frac{l_\infty - l}{l_\infty}\right) = -kt.$$

This equation has the interesting property that "l_∞ cannot be assumed as known but is got by plotting the logarithm of the amount decomposed in a constant time interval Δt against t, the time at the beginning of the interval"; in other words, l_∞ is *not* the amount of water which is lost all together but is simply an integration constant. If this expression is to have any physical significance the magnitude of l_∞ must be quite close to the actual total weight loss; otherwise we must look for another effect. Actually, the magnitude of l_∞ is sufficiently different to cast some doubt.

One other effect is the rate at which the material reaches the decomposition temperature. Obviously, if a sample held in, say, a crucible is exposed to a hot surface the temperature will not rise instanteously to the new temperature; heat must be transmitted from the surface to all parts of the interior. Since heat will flow only from a warmer to a cooler body a temperature gradient must necessarily exist. (Any treatment demanding an assumption of equal temperatures throughout a specimen during heating is automatically suspect.) Let us examine the possible effect of geometry by use of some simplifying heat-transfer assumptions that have at least some resemblance to physical reality. In addition, let us assume that under the extant conditions of water vapor pressure, particle size, and previous history there is some one temperature at which each particle will decompose.

> The assumption of a reaction temperature is used here only as a tool to show some relative effects. There is no reason to doubt that the dehydroxylation of kaolin and similar decompositions of a number of other minerals are rate-controlled. For our purposes, however, we can raise the temperature high enough to cause a conveniently high rate of reaction. The real fact of the rate control will only bring about a diffuseness of boundaries between reacted and unreacted material.

Now recall the conditions of the Murray and White experiments, i.e., the rapid heating of a furnace to a temperature above the decomposition temperature and measurement of weight loss vs time of a crucible suspended therein. Let us consider a full crucible with length $>>$ diameter. Concede that the crucible wall will reach the decomposition temperature instantaneously and the material in contact with the wall will decompose. The wall continues heating to the furnace temperature and transmits heat to the specimen. The outer material of the specimen receives heat from the direction of the wall, warms up to the decomposition temperature, decomposes, and subsequently passes heat onward to the material farther in—which performs in the same manner. Consequently, there is a decomposition temperature front advancing toward the center uniformly from the vertical wall (neglecting small effects at the bottom) ahead of which front is unreacted material and behind which is reacted material. As this front advances its diameter and hence its area decrease. If we assume that this front advances at a uniform rate,* $dr/dt =$ constant, where r is the radius of the front, and the area must be proportional to r. This implies that the quantity reacting is proportional to r.

The volume of the unreacted material is proportional to r^2, i.e.,

$$V = \pi r^2 h$$

so that

$$\frac{dV}{dr} = 2\pi h \cdot r$$

but $dr/dt =$ constant, hence

$$\frac{dV}{dr} \cdot \frac{dr}{dt} = \frac{dV}{dt} = 2\pi h \cdot r\kappa \text{ constant} = \kappa r = \frac{\kappa(V)^{1/2}}{\pi h}.$$

The cylindrical crucible may be simple to treat since if the length is sufficiently greater thas the diameter the effects of atmosphere will disappear; this ease of mathematical treatment does not bring about any closer resemblance to physical reality. Let us now consider the common practice; this practice would lead to use of an ordinary crucible, length 1.3–2 times the diameter, partly filled with the specimen. This approximates the condition discussed in Chapter VII. But the events described therein lead to the establishment of a reaction front which as a simplification could be treated as spherical.

Let us make the same assumption of constant advance (dr/dt is constant) but now the volume must be expressed differently, i.e.,

$$V = \frac{4}{3}\pi r^3$$

or

$$\frac{dV}{dr} = 4\pi r^2$$

so

$$\frac{dV}{dr} \cdot \frac{dr}{dt} = \frac{dV}{dt} = 4\pi\kappa r^2 = V^{2/3}.$$

Under these conditions the disappearance of unreacted material will follow a one-half order rate law in a cylinder and a two-thirds order law in a sphere.

---

*This is no more real than Murray and White's assumption of uniform temperature. The intent here is to show the probable effect of geometry on the rate of reaction.

With different assumed geometries, then, different conclusions may be reached with these—and presumably with any—assumptions. (Note that if the material were laid on a flat surface and this surface were kept at a steady, uniform temperature the reaction would appear to be zero order.) The conditions stated above do not coincide with physical reality. There are complicating effects—principally thermal diffusivity change and heat of reaction—which would affect the advance of the reaction front. Nevertheless, the appearance of a first-order decomposition can be approximated by nonfirst-order reactions for reasons of geometry and atmosphere. In the poorly defined geometry represented by a partly full crucible in an uncontrolled atmosphere an extensive treatment would be a waste of time.

This discussion obviously does not establish the actual order of the kaolin decomposition. It is intended only to show that there is considerable reason to question the conclusion of Murray and White. A first-order reaction would depend only on the quantity of unreacted material and the temperature; yet Stone (S60) and the present author have shown an atmosphere dependence and Murray and White "have had certain indications that sample size, type of container, and other environmental factors may have an appreciable effect on the rate of decomposition observed."

Murray and White (M46) extended their consideration of the kinetics of kaolin decomposition to calculate the shape of differential thermal analysis curves. In particular, they calculate a peak temperature which they also describe as the temperature at which the reaction is proceeding most rapidly. This is consistent with their assumption of temperature homogeneity but not with physical reality. The effect might be achieved, however, by thoughtful or fortuitous placement of thermocouples. Note from Fig. VII-9 that under the heating conditions specified the last portion of material to decompose is not at the center, but below the center. A thermocouple at the center of the specimen would show probably a maximum or possibly a sharp change in slope as the reaction front passed it. (The nature of the change would depend on the relative thermal diffusivities before and after the reaction as well as on the heat of decomposition. The situation is probably not analogous to Smyth's (S36) exercise showing the effect of noncentered placement of thermocouples.) Regardless of the shape of the curve one may safely say that the reaction is not yet complete at the time or temperature of the differential thermal analysis peak in a process whose rate is determined (limited) by chemical kinetics.

We can eliminate the heating from the bottom by the simple expedient of specifying a depth much greater than the diameter. We have not eliminated the top; i.e., diffusion of gases will still occur, although the effect will be attenuated in the lower regions. This means that the reaction front will advance only slightly inward before the atmosphere enrichment will require the major movement of the front to be from the top down. A thermocouple at the center (with half the specimen beneath it) will now show a maximum while a very substantial portion of the specimen has not yet reacted. Note that if the thermocouple is sufficiently deep in the sample hole the effects of the ambient atmosphere can perhaps be neglected for most work: the partial pressure of the product gas will be high enough by the time the reaction front reaches the thermocouple location that small deviations may be unnoticeable. The thermocouple would have to be placed deep enough so that no dilution effect could be seen.

Murray and White's decomposition curves calculated from the rate constants obtained from the thermogravimetry data are shown in Fig. VI-3. They bear a rather good resemblance to differential thermal

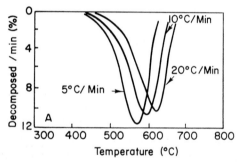

Fig. VI-3. Percentage decomposition per minute against temperature during heating of Supreme kaolin at constant heating rates of 5, 10, and 20°C/minute. From Murray and White (M46).

Calculated decomposition curves assuming first-order reaction kinetics with rate constants determined by static methods. At low heating rates the decomposition proceeds more rapidly than at higher rates!

analysis curves until the effect of heating rate is studied with a little care. These curves show the effect of heating rate on peak temperature in the proper direction, but the relative magnitudes of the peaks are decidedly not in agreement with experiment. The specimen heated at 5°C/minute reaches a greater rate of decomposition than that heated at 20°C/minute! Yet, the former spends about 20 minutes at rates greater than 4%/minute while the latter spends only about 5 minutes at such rates. According to Murray and White's calculations, the depletion of unreacted material becomes the major effect when the decomposition is about 70% complete causing the dehydroxylation to slow down; this figure corresponds to the peak temperature or "turning point"; it is also a figure accepted both frequently and uncritically as the degree of reaction to be expected at the peak temperature—for any reaction. Note that Murray and White cited evidence found and advanced a hypothesis. They recognized the probability of effects of water vapor, for example, and they were aware of the lowering of "dehydration temperatures" at subatmospheric pressures. These latter points would naturally not be known by later workers whose only contact with Murray and White's work is through reading of abstracts.

Sewell (S19) extended Murray and White's work to take account of thermal gradients in the specimen. *With the assumption that Murray and White were correct in their basic conclusion* Sewell pointed out that the turning point, i.e., the temperature at which the reaction proceeds most rapidly, could be expressed by

$$\exp{(E/RT_M)} = ART_M{}^2/\beta E$$

where T_M is the turning point temperature, β is the heating rate, E is the activation energy, and A is a constant (from the Arrhenius rate equation). Sewell derived relationships between T_M and the peak actually observed in differential thermal analysis. Unfortunately, the expression for the temperature of the center of the specimen predicts that the peak temperature for dilute samples should be higher than for undiluted samples. This is obviously not in accord with physical evidence (see Chapter III, so Sewell concludes that the equation describing a first-order reaction "cannot be regarded as more than a first approximation to the laws describing the dehydration of kaolinite" and suggests the possibility of an atmosphere effect.

Let us remember now that a first-order reaction is one in which the reaction proceeds (at a given temperature) solely as a function of the quantity of the—or one of the—reactants. For the kaolinite dehydroxylation this would obviously be the unreacted material. The intervention of any physical condition or property other than quantity and temperature requires some other classification.

Brindley and Nakahira (B79) have concluded that if the effect of water vapor can be eliminated the dehydroxylation is indeed first order. They measured the rates of decomposition of a number of discs of kaolinite of various thicknesses, plotted log w/w_0 vs t (Fig. VI-4), extrapolated the values for various thicknesses to zero thickness (infinitely thin disc), and found a straight-line relationship which corresponds, of course, to a first-order reaction. (The w/w_0 is the fraction of total weight loss.) The times taken to reach a given fractional weight loss, w/w_0, vary in quite good agreement with a linear relationship $tw/w_0 = c + kh$, where h is the thickness and hence c is the time at zero thickness; the agreement appears to be good not only in the initial (straight-line) portion but also in the curved part of the plot.

Brindley and Nakahira use the rate constants determined from the initial portions of the curve to establish the inherent behavior of kaolinite; they were able to show (Fig. VI-5) that the rate constant at each of several temperatures varied linearly with thickness. They established further that an Arrhenius plot is linear *only* for infinitely thin discs (Fig. VI-6). The same general behavior was demonstrated by halloysite, another kandite.

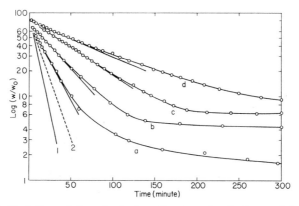

Fig. VI-4. Variation of log (w/w_0) with time for kaolinite disks heated at 497°C; (w/w_0) is expressed as a percentage of the total weight loss by dehydroxylation. Curves a, b, c, and d correspond to disks of thickness 0.38, 0.83, 1.55, and 2.68 mm, respectively. Curve 1 is the extrapolated curve for an infinitely thin disk and curve 2 corresponds to a very thin layer of uncompacted powder. From Brindley and Nakahira (B79).

The weight loss is decidedly dependent on the geometry of the specimen.

These experiments do indeed indicate that the kaolin dehydroxylation is kinetically a first-order reaction, but the reader must bear in mind that these experiments are quite different from those of Murray and White. The stated warning by Brindley and Nakahira, also implicit in the curvature of the weight loss data of Fig. VI-4, that at temperatures in the 450–520°C range kaolinite tends to react only to some given degree, must be also remembered. Murray and White had also noted that there was no clear line of demarcation between the loosely held water and water of constitution.

Neither of these pairs of authors has really eliminated the effect of water vapor. The concentration of water in ambient air is far from negligible, yet the variation might be small enough to escape notice. According to handbook (L1a) values, at 25°C a change from 84% to 42% relative humidity means a drop in absolute humidity from 20 to 10 mm of mercury. As a sample is heated, the water diffuses out of the particles of the specimen as long as the temperature is high enough to vaporize said water in the face of this extant partial pressure. Even assuming that the water vapor can escape from the furnace into the surrounding

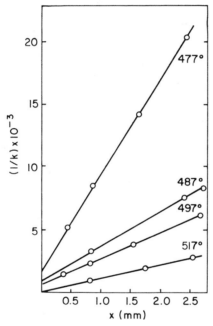

Fig. VI-5. Variation of reciprocal rate constant, $1/k$, vs disk thickness for kaolinite disks at various temperatures. From Brindley and Nakahira (B79).
The distance through which vapor must diffuse has a very clear effect on the rate.

atmosphere, the partial pressure in the furnace can only drop toward that of its surroundings; it cannot drop below. This would explain the tendency toward incomplete dehydroxylation in Brindley and Nakahira's work if a real equilibrium vapor pressure exists.

In recent work, Holt, Cutler, and Wadsworth (H22) have studied kaolinite under rather different conditions. They, too, point out the need for experimentation which avoids the effect of water vapor and proceed to heat their specimens in vacuum. The specimen was applied to a platinum screen as a paste or slurry, then dried at 130°C in preparation for the dehydroxylation.

The data, obtained by heating at pressures less than 1 μ of Hg, indicate that the rate of dehydroxylation is inversely proportional to the thickness of the dehydrated layer, i.e.,

$$\frac{dx}{dt} = \frac{k}{x}$$

where x is the thickness of the dehydrated (or dehydroxylated) layer. This means, of course, that

$$x^2 = 2kt$$

or, since the fraction reacted, R, is proportional to x for this constant-area arrangement, $R^2 = 2kt$

This is the parabolic rate expression and indicates that the decompo-

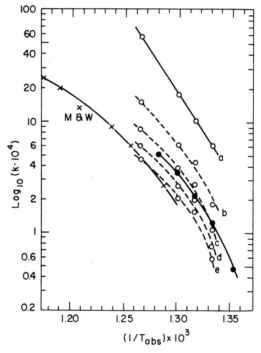

Fig. VI-6. Arrhenius plots for log k vs $1/T$ (absolute for kaolinite). Curves a, through e correspond to disks of thickness 0, 0.5, 1.0, 1.5, and 2.0 mm, respectively. Curve (M&W) shows data by Murray and White. Solid circles show experimental data for sample held in a small platinum crucible. The Arrhenius plot is linear only for curve a corresponding to the infinitely thin disk. From Brindley and Nakahira (B79).

In an infinitely thin specimen the decomposition should follow a first-order law.

sition process is diffusion-controlled, slowing down not from scarcity of material but from the increasing difficulty of eliminating products. Holt *et al.* report that the linear relationships (Fig. VI-7) between R^2 and t hold to 50% decomposition "after which it starts to change" in a direction not specified. They attribute the nonlinearity to a "decrease in surface area brought about by the fact that the smaller particles are completely dehydrated before the large particles." In essence, this means that the rate of reaction is governed by diffusion within the individual particle rather than through the pores in the bulk of the specimen.

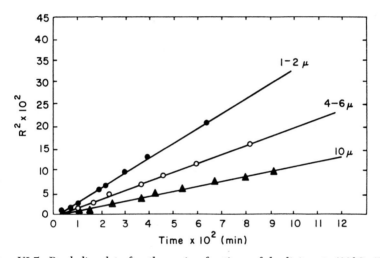

FIG. VI-7. Parabolic plots for three size fractions of kaolinite at 400°C. From Holt *et al.* (H22).
Up to 50% decomposition the rate is inversely proportional to the amount reacted.

The intrinsic similarity of decompositions of the various particle sizes of Fig. VI-7 is demonstrated in Fig. VI-8, in which Holt, Cutler, and Wadsworth arbitrarily selected fractional decomposition, $R = 0.30$, and obtained an expression for $2k$ and substituted so that

$$R^2 = R_{0.30}^2 \, \tau/\tau_{0.30}$$
$$= 0.090 \, \tau/\tau_{0.30}$$

where $\tau_{0.30}$ is the time during any run at which $R = 0.30$. Now the data from the three particle size fractions can be plotted together as in Fig. VI-8. The behavior of each of the three fractions is quite similar to that of the others.

Holt *et al.* also showed at low pressures of water vapor the parabolic relationship held; increasing water vapor decreased the rate (Fig. VI-9) of decomposition in a linear manner at these lower pressures. They report that at moderate pressures, e.g., 4.5 mm of Hg at 420°C, the process undergoes some change that renders the kinetics of the decomposition first order, in agreement with the several studies in air. The major conclusion which one might reach is that, while knowledge of the kinetics of dehydroxylation of kaolin under a number of sets of experimental conditions has been obtained, the intrinsic behavior may not yet be known. The pressed discs of Brindly and Nakahira (B79) are quite different from the dried slurry of Holt, Cutler, and Wadsworth as were the

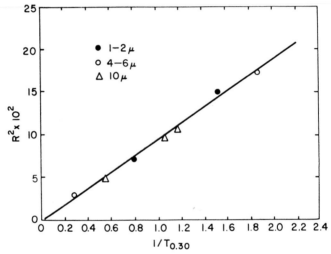

FIG. VI-8. Plot of R^2 vs $1/T_{0.30}$ at 400°C using three size fractions. From Holt et al. (H22).

The agreement indicates that the actual differences in rates are due only to differences in area.

environments used. Neither set of authors could measure initial behavior satisfactorily because (even disregarding the fact that the control temperature is not reached quickly by the sample) the basic measurement constitutes a small change in a large quantity. This is a procedural error common to nearly all these experiments. While the present author has no desire to minimize the utility of thermoanalytical techniques in general, he also advocates selection of the best tool for the job at hand. The proper measurement—certainly for the initial behavior and probably for the whole experiment—is the rate at which water is released. Weight loss is only an indirect measure of it.

The fact that a thermocouple junction measures the temperature of its immediate surroundings cannot be used to infer that more distant materials do not affect the temperature at all. The magnitude of any effect will depend on the geometric relation; material between the specimen and the heat source, for example, must inevitably influence the heating of the specimen. This effect was neglected by Kissinger (K30) in his evaluation of shapes of peaks and the relation of these shapes to

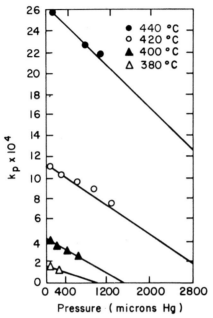

FIG. VI-9. Parabolic rate constant vs water vapor pressure at four temperatures. From Holt *et al.* (H22).

At low pressures the rate constant varies inversely with the pressure of water vapor.

the order of the decomposition kinetics. He set up expressions for the quasi-steady-state heating: at the center of the reference,

$$T_r = T_0 + \phi t - \frac{\phi \rho c a^2}{4k}$$

and at the center of the sample

$$T_s = T_0 + \phi t - f\left(\frac{dq}{dt}\right)$$

where ϕ is the heating rate, a is the radius of the cylindrical specimens, $f(dq/dt)$ is a function of the reaction rate, dq/dt being the rate of heat absorption per unit volume, and the other terms have their usual significance.

The differential temperature,

$$\theta = T_s - T_r = f\!\left(\frac{dq}{dt}\right) - \theta\,\frac{\rho c a^2}{4k}$$

and

$$\frac{d\theta}{dt} = f'\!\left(\frac{dq}{dt}\right)\frac{d^2q}{dt^2}.$$

From this last equation he concluded that when d^2q/dt^2 was zero $d\theta/dt$ must necessarily be zero. Since $d^2q/dt^2 = 0$ implied maximum rate of reaction and $d\theta/dt = 0$ a maximum temperature difference, the peak in the differential thermal analysis deflection must occur at the moment of the maximum rate of reaction. In the utopian case, i.e., reaction occurring equally in all parts of the specimen and unchanging thermal characteristics, this would be a reasonable conclusion.

The conclusion still represents—approximately—the behavior of the material in the immediate vicinity of the thermocouple, but only so far as the small region can be considered to react homogeneously. The temperature of this region has already, during the quasi-steady-state heating, lagged behind the outside of the specimen by several degrees. The material at the edges will continually be at a higher temperature than that at the point of measurement and the progress of the reaction takes up heat that would otherwise serve to warm the central region, accentuating the difference in rate. The material at the periphery will be significantly further reacted than that at the center at any time after the reaction starts until that at the edge is approaching complete reaction. As the reaction at the edge subsides it can pass on in greater amounts the energy necessary to carry out the reaction in the central regions. Note that a cylinder with some arbitrary thin wall, say 1/1000 inch, occupies a much greater volume of space with the same radius as the sample holder (i.e., at the edge of the sample) than with a radius of, say 10/1000 inch, enough to surround the thermocouple. Much more of the sample is at the higher temperature. We can easily infer that the maximum rate of reaction occurs well onto the low-temperature side of the peak; when the center of the sample reaches the maximum temperature lag in most cases the reaction is nearly complete.

(All this takes no account of the atmosphere effect which will cause a reaction rate variation from top to bottom of the specimen holder. All the materials cited by Kissinger show such effects.)

We have seen that Kissinger's method is an approximation because the basic assumption is invalid. Since no rigorous treatment exists approximation must be used; it is advisable, hence, to examine the closeness of the approximation to physical reality. Kissinger ascertains an expression for the temperature of maximum rate of reaction in terms of the order and extent of reaction by differentiating the rate expression

$$\frac{dx}{dt} = A(1 - x)^n e - (E/RT)$$

with respect to t and setting the expression equal to zero, obtaining

$$\frac{E\phi_2}{RT_m} = An(1 - x)_m^{n-1} e - (E/RT_m)$$

where the subscript m refers to conditions at the peak temperature. [Compare with Sewell's (S19) equation assuming first-order kinetics.]

By integrations and substitutions Kissinger arrives at $n(1 - x)^{n-1}_m = 1 + (n-1) (ZRT_m/E)$ which says that as n becomes smaller so also does the quantity of material not yet decomposed at T_m. This agrees in principle with the implied observation that in a reversible phase transformation (zero order) the reaction is complete when the peak temperature is reached. From the variation in the quantity decomposed at T_m with order of reaction Kissinger proposed the use of a "shape index" to estimate the order of reaction. Figure VI-10 shows his calculated plots for several orders of reaction.

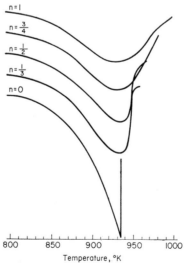

FIG. VI-10. Effect of order of reaction on plots of reaction rate vs temperature for constant heating rate, frequency factor, and activation energy. $E/R = 20,000$; ln $A = 16.00$. From Kissinger (K30).

The activation energy and frequency factors are arbitrarily selected but their influence on the relative shapes is small.

From these curves, or from curves in general, the slopes at the inflection points are taken (Fig. VI-11) and the ratio of these slopes is used as a measure of the assymmetry of the peak. At these inflection points d^3x/dt^3, the rate of change of reaction rate, i.e., $d^2/dt^2 \, (dx/dt)$, is zero, so Kissinger does the differentiations and with some substitutions is able to calculate the relation between shape index and order of reaction as shown in Fig. VI-12.

The straight line of the lower plot is described by

$$n = 1.26S^{1/2}.$$

Some curves showing the experimentally determined S and n are shown in Fig. VI-13.

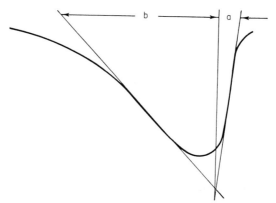

Fɪɢ. VI-11. Method for measuring amount of asymmetry in an endothermic differential thermal analysis peak. Shape index = $S = a/b$. From Kissinger (K30).

Actual determination of an inflection temperature is not required. The probable error in determining the slope is less when the inflection point is difficult to establish.

These apparent orders of reaction are obviously influenced by experimental conditions since agreement among authors is not very good. Particle size and geometry of the specimen will have a considerable influence, especially since the atmosphere is not that of the gas being evolved.

With the understanding that some invalid assumptions have been made and approximations are introduced, Kissinger's method can be used as a rough guide to the apparent order of the rate law followed by various decompositions *under the experimental conditions used;* the shapes of the curves vary in the proper manner.

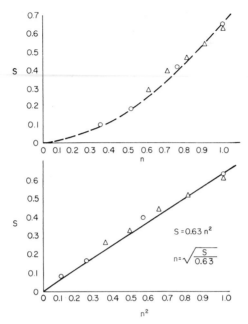

FIG. VI-12. Values of shape index S plotted as functions of n and n^2. KEY: $\triangle$, calculated; $\bigcirc$, measured on curves of Fig. VI-10.

The relatively good agreement between calculated and measured slope ratios shows only the consistency of the mathematics.

6.4. Reversible Decompositions

Calcium carbonate is frequently cited as an example of a reversibly decomposing salt. The temperature at which it begins to decompose is determined by the pressure of carbon dioxide in contact with the surface of the particle. Janz and Lorenz (J4) have reported that when the prescribed temperature is passed, either heating or cooling, the material begins to decompose or recompose very quickly; this says nothing about the rate but shows that even the occurrence or nonoccurrence is dependent on the carbon dioxide pressure. Cremer and Nitsch (C26) studied the decomposition by volumetric measurements (avoiding the very marked heat-transfer problem found in thermogravimetry) at various pressures (Fig. VI-14) of carbon dioxide. They deduced that overlapping processes of nucleation and crystal growth would explain the data and, further, that at a given pressure the reaction is of the two-thirds order. This is in agreement with crystal growth dependence.

The many treatments of reaction rates by thermal analysis appear to

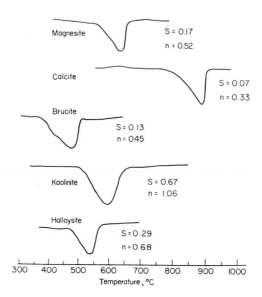

Fig. VI-13. Typical differential thermal analysis peaks for materials used in present study. From Kissinger (K30).

The calcite decomposition—which is probably not rate-controlled—approaches $n = 0$.

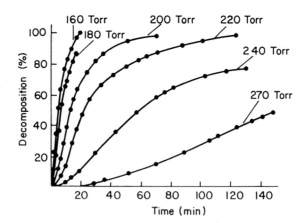

Fig. VI-14. Decomposition of calcium carbonate at 850°C. From Cremer and Nitsch (C26).

The rate of decomposition varies greatly with the pressure of carbon dioxide.

show a common disbelief in equilibrium or reversible processes. The idea of a simple reversible dehydration or similar process obeying a first-order rate law is patent nonsense; the probability of its following first-order kinetics is vanishingly small. Chapter VII treats the atmosphere effect in detail; we shall see herein sufficient evidence to impress on the reader the need to study Chapter VII.

Berlin and Robinson (B48) used thermogravimetry in their study of reaction rates. They had derived a relation for the reciprocal of the absolute temperature,

$$\frac{1}{T} = -\frac{R}{E_2}\Big[\ln\Big(\frac{d\alpha}{dT}\Big) - \ln(1-\alpha)^Z - \ln A_0\Big(\frac{\Gamma M}{W_0 N} S_2 \nu \bar{N}\Big)\Big]$$
$$+ \frac{R}{E_2}\ln\Big(\frac{dt}{dT}\Big)_c$$

wherein a is the fraction decomposed, Z is the exponent describing the change in area, A, at the interface between reacted and unreacted species such that $A = A_0(1-a)^Z$, and

$$\Gamma = \Big(1 - \frac{\nu_B M_B}{\nu_A M_A}\Big)^{-1}.$$

They suggest the use of a T_2, the temperature at which the reaction is virtually complete, as a means of relating data obtained by different authors in different laboratories on different types of equipment. (Their T_2 is found by estimating from the plot or data the temperature of the last detectable change in weight.) By measuring T_2 at several heating rates and plotting $1/T_2$ vs $\ln (dt/dT)_c$, they anticipated a straight line with a slope R/E_2 and an intercept of

$$\frac{R}{E_2}\ln A_0\Big(\frac{\Gamma M}{W_0 N} S_2 W N\Big).$$

Now let us examine the assumptions. There is, of course, the implied assumption of temperature homogeneity but in addition they recognize that da/dT and $(1-a)^Z$ are dependent on the thermobalance, assuming, however, that they remain constant for a given balance. Since the exponent Z is, in essence, the order of the reaction kinetics followed, said order varies from thermobalance to thermobalance.

The plot yields an activation energy from the slope and it is with this that we are concerned. Using the data of Richer and Vallet (R19), they obtain plots A and B of Fig. VI-15. The plots yield activation energy values of 44 kcal per mole for the decomposition of calcium carbonate in nitrogen and 210 kcal per mole in carbon dioxide. Since the determination of activation energies is a popular pastime, let us examine now their physical significance.

The activation energy is a quantity which takes into account the fact that thermodynamically favorable reactions do not proceed spontaneously and speedily. It may be pictured as an energy barrier separating the stable species such that a quantity of energy must be added to either species to produce an activated species which may or may not become the other species as it gives up its energy. In a reversible reaction a sufficient number of particles are being supplied with this activation energy so that there is a recognizable tendency for interchange and consequently equilibrium. Equilibrium implies that in a given time the

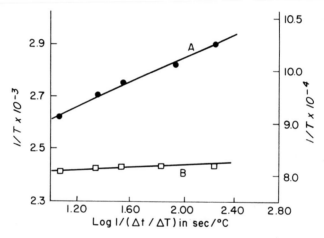

FIG. VI-15. Relation between temperature of completion of the decomposition and the heating rate. $1/T$ x 10^{-4} scale: (A) $CaCO_3$ powder in dry N_2; (B) $CaCO_3$ powder in CO_2. From Berlin and Robinson (B48).
The slope is R/E_2 where E_2 is the activation energy. For calcium carbonate the value varies greatly with composition of the atmosphere.

number of particles leaving any state is equal to that entering the state; i.e., for a single one-step reaction the forward and reverse rates are equal. In the case under consideration, the nature of the activated species can be deduced easily; it must be an energized calcium carbonate,

$$CaCO_3 \rightleftharpoons CaCO_3{}^* \rightleftharpoons CaO + CO_2.$$

Figure VI-16 shows a two-dimensional representation of a one-step process such as we are considering. A particle ($CaCO_3{}^*$) that can pass over the barrier can fall into either stable phase A ($CaCO_3$) or B + C ($CaO + CO_2$) without regard for the state from which it came; thus the rate equation in either direction must include a term expressing the probability that the particle will pass over the barrier rather than dropping back.

The forward reaction rate constant, using rather simplified kinetics, may be expressed by

$$k_f = A_f \theta_f(P) \exp - (E_f/RT).$$

where A_f is a constant lumping together all the terms we do not presently wish to compare and $\phi_f(P)$ is some function of the pressure of carbon dioxide.

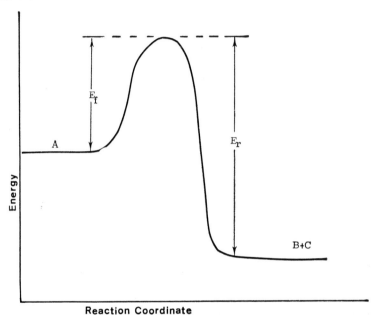

Reaction Coordinate

Fig. VI-16. Two dimensional representation of energy relation of reaction $A \rightarrow B + C(g)$.

The activated state formed by adding energy E_f to E_a can go to either stable state. The activated state for the reverse reaction requires not only energy Er but joining of B and C. It, too, can fall to either stable state.

This atmosphere dependence of the forward reaction ought to be a very secondary effect, probably related to diffusion of gas out of a particle. This much is in qualitative agreement with the data of Cremer and Nitsch (C26). However, the direct effect of this limiting step may be to permit a transitory equilibrium pressure of carbon dioxide within the particle. In this (quite probable) case, the true rate of reaction is likely zero order, but appearing to decrease with decreasing concentration of unreacted because of the increasing diffusion path as the surface and subsurface layers react. This diffusion step would vary with total pressure as well as with carbon dioxide pressure because the outward migration of carbon dioxide would be repressed somewhat by a high concentration of gases (i.e., a shorter mean free path). Even should the measured forward rate have an apparent dependence on the pressure of carbon dioxide this may well be due to other causes than to $\phi_f(P)$ in the rate expression having real significance. Measurements of the rate of decomposition as a function of particle size and total pressure as well as carbon dioxide pressure would be needed to resolve the question. Cremer and Nitsch (C26), working with pure carbon dioxide atmospheres and a single type of calcite, deduced that the rate of decomposition is determined by a nucleation velocity and the growth rate of the CaO crystallites—and that these two processes are dependent on the pressure of carbon dioxide.

Returning to the question of the activation energy, this quantity is evaluated by calculating the rate of the reaction at each of several temperatures and plotting an appropriate function of temperature (e.g., log k vs $1/T$ for first-order reactions). The activation energy is calculated from the slope of the plot. The calculation assumes that the chemical reaction is the rate-controlling step in the process and that the observed rate of reaction is a true description; i.e., the entire specimen is undergoing reaction at that rate at the moment under consideration. If this is not the case, some qualifications must be made.

Wendlandt (W18), for example, calculated the activation energy for the dehydration of calcium oxalate monohydrate (Fig. VI-17) as 27 kcal/mole, using the method of Borchardt (B66). Comparing this value to Freeman and Carroll's (F14) 22 kcal/mole, Wendlandt points out "the slight difference between results may be attributed to the effect of particle size, heating rate, furnace atmosphere conditions, and so on." Which curve of Fig. VI-17 he used was not specified.

This activation energy is a physical quantity whose value should not vary significantly with experimental conditions. If there is a severe variation the experimental procedure is at fault. The technique for reconciliation of thermogravimetric data from one apparatus to another takes no account of atmosphere effects and neglects entirely the fact that the rate of recombination of carbon dioxide and calcium oxide is increasing with the pressure of carbon dioxide (in the immediate vicinity of the particles) as well as with temperature.

6.5. Critique

Attempts to apply methods using a progressively changing temperature to determine a highly temperature-dependent quantity (the rate of reaction) have generally lost touch with the straightforward approach of making the easiest measurement. In the case of kaolinite, for example, the measurements of the rate of reaction involved problems in heat transport, in temperature homogeneity, and in atmosphere effects. These arose from the thermal isolation and the shape and method of support of the sample. Further, the initial stages of the decomposition are of special interest, but at that stage thermogravimetric methods have their smallest validity. (The entire sample and support are being weighed to establish—by difference—the loss of a very small part of the entire weight.)

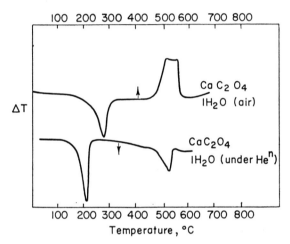

FIG. VI-17. Differential thermal analysis curves of calcium oxalate monohydrate. From Wendlandt (W18).
The peak (200–300°C) for the dehydration was used to calculate the activation energy by the method of Borchardt (B66).

Let us instead support this sample on a thermostatted heat sink in such a manner that it can take up heat rapidly from the sink and let the sample be in a thin layer so that the temperature gradient is indeed negligible. Now let us pass across the sample a stream of gas so that the gaseous decomposition products are carried from the sample into a detector such as is used in gas chromatography.

Since these detectors can measure in the microgram range the measurement of the initial decomposition can be performed with more sensitivity than with a thermobalance and yet the sensitivity can be adjusted easily to measure higher concentrations with the same relative accuracy. Under these conditions the sample temperature is known and is known to be very close to uniform. The only problem remaining is that of the changing atmosphere.

The effect of the changing atmosphere can at least be diminished considerably by good contact between gas and sample. If the incoming gas stream contains none of the product gas, the partial pressure will not be known but will be small. A better arrangement would be to supply a gas stream having a known concentration of the product gas (water in the case of kaolinite). With such a stream the concentration of water vapor is at least some minimum value; whether or not it rises substantially will depend on design and flow. A differential detector can still measure the small increase due to decomposition.

From this point on, the design of the system will be determined by the nature of the information sought. A partial pressure carbon dioxide can be supplied for carbonate decompositions or even a mixture including both carbon dioxide and water vapor if both may be given off. For irreversible reactions any ordinary carrier gas could be used. If analysis of products is required, repetitive gas chromatography would be useful (see Chapter XIV).

6.6. Summary

Like quantitative descriptions of differential thermal analysis curves, attempts to establish the kinetics of a reaction from thermogravimetric or differential thermal analysis data require untenable assumptions. The mathematics required for a rigorous treatment does not lend itself to a practicable solution. Several additional data, e.g., changes in heat capacity and thermal conductivity, would be needed.

The atmosphere effect must be taken into account. Reversible decompositions will be affected by accumulation of products. Irreversible reactions may be affected by accessibility of reactant.

Use of other experimental techniques is indicated.

CHAPTER VII

Atmosphere Control

7.1. Introduction

Many of the reactions studied by differential thermal analysis involve weight loss and this weight loss is often the result of a more-or-less reversible decomposition. The effect of the surrounding atmosphere is therefore of extreme interest. It is the author's experience that a simple description of the effect of atmosphere is not convincing; examples of misleading data are necessary. This chapter will contain a more extensive review than was considered appropriate for other topics.

Let us note first a range of effects on a single material, ammonium perchlorate, without an attempt to reach any conclusion except that the conditions of the experiment have a decided effect and hence the experimental conditions must be controlled—or at least known. Figure VII-1 shows Stone's (S58) data using dynamic atmospheres. The reaction in the 400°C region is a decomposition whose products vary from author to author.

The influence of the atmosphere on the behavior of the specimen can be varied by design. To some degree it will depend, in nondynamic systems, on the sample geometry. For a given sample geometry the effect will depend on whether the atmosphere is static, flowing, or dynamic. For our purposes a flowing atmosphere is defined as one in which the gas is passed through the furnace and around or over the sample holder and a dynamic atmosphere is one in which the gas passes through the sample cavity or chamber. A static atmosphere is one in which there is no forced flow of gas. The most important influence is, of course, the nature of the gas in relation to the reaction under investigation.

Bohon's (B59) curves on the decomposition of ammonium perchlorate

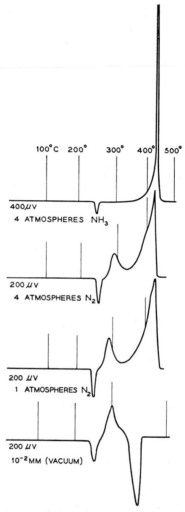

Fɪɢ. VII-1. Effect of pressure and gas composition on decomposition of NH_4ClO_4 diluted 1:1 with alumina. From Stone (S58).

The purely exothermal reaction in ammonia changes with atmosphere composition and pressure to an endothermal reaction under vacuum. In the absence of ammonia a lower-temperature exothermal reaction appears.

(Fig. VII-2) under some rather special conditions appear prima facie to disagree with Stone's (Fig. VII-1) data; qualitatively they can be related. The curves are shown here for easy comparison; the explanation is postponed to Section 7 of this chapter.

7.2. History and Critique

Rowland and Lewis (R34) were among the early users of controlled, static atmospheres. While a part of their work was concerned with use of a neutral atmosphere to avoid combustion or other oxidation, the more interesting curves are those obtained using carbon dioxide (Fig. VII-3).

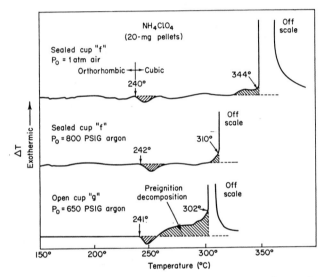

FIG. VII-2. Effect of pressure and product escape on pyrolysis of ammonium perchlorate (20 mg pellets). From Bohon (B59).
The mass action law requires that the presence of a product gas should inhibit a decomposition.

Siderite is cited elsewhere (Chapter II) in pointing out the evils of orthodox sample holders. In oxygen the lesser heat effect of the carbonate decomposition is completely hidden. Rowland and Lewis state: "between 450°C and 530°C the endothermic effect of the dissociation of CO_2 is accompanied by oxidation of FeO, so that the first part of the curve is a compromise. When a temperature of 530°C is attained, sufficient CO_2 is liberated to prevent the oxidation of the FeO, and a modified endothermic loop is registered. At about 570°C the evolution of CO_2 decreases enough so that the FeO can oxidize, and an exothermic loop is recorded. The small exothermic mound between 750°C and 850°C is registered when the iron oxide becomes hematite. In a CO_2 atmosphere the iron is not oxidized and a larger, uninterrupted endothermic loop is obtained."

The magnesite and calcite curves show clearly the effect of an atmosphere of the product gas. The deflections break away from the base

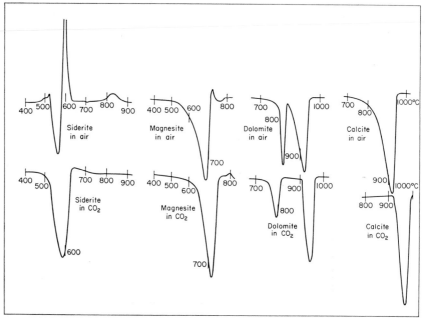

Fig. VII-3. Carbonates heated in air and in carbon dioxide. From Rowland and Lewis (R34).

Temperatures of reactions vary and in some cases the nature of the reaction is different.

line more sharply and at higher temperatures than in air. This behavior is to be expected since the temperature must become high enough to cause an equilibrium vapor pressure of one atmosphere instead of the 2×10^{-4} atmospheres common in ambient air.

The effect of pressure change in controlled atmospheres is rather strikingly demonstrated by Stone's (S54) data shown in Fig. VII-4. The peak for magnesite is shifted only slightly while that for a calcite impurity is shifted by ca. 200°C. This might lead one to conclude from the van't Hoff relation that the heat of decomposition of magnesite is much greater than that of calcite. While this is apparently true, reaching such a conclusion from only the evidence here would be reasoning in circles since heats of decomposition are often determined from just this sort of shift of decomposition temperature. A very necessary step is to establish the reversibility of the decomposition.

An interesting approach to the question of atmosphere was taken by Hill and Murphy (H13). They heated a sample block from below with a heat lamp. This block was encased in three pieces of firebrick. The top piece had a piece of aluminum foil in the hollowed cover section. They report that the second peak in Fig. VII-5, "although much lower than the reported boiling point of 220.3°C, corresponds to the volati-

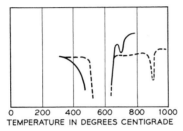

O   200   400   600   800   1000
TEMPERATURE IN DEGREES CENTIGRADE

Fig. VII-4. Differential thermal analysis of magnesite in carbon dioxide: _____ 16.5 mm of Hg; - - - - - - - 750 mm of Hg. From Stone (S54).
The calcite peak is shifted much more than the magnesite.

lization of 1,4-dibromobenzene from the sample holder. The position of the lamp ensures the existence of a thermal gradient in the system, which provides a driving force for the sublimation [sic] of 1,4-dibromo-benzene. . . . Thus, nonequilibrium conditions exist providing for continuous removal of the gaseous phase and replenishment from the liquid. Because of this, liquid-gas transitions would be expected to give broader peaks, at temperatures below recorded boiling points." The authors report this as a perfectly reasonable phenomenon to be accepted and endured! They fail to point out what possible use one might have for volatilization temperatures under uncertain conditions. The arrangement would have no use whatsoever for mixtures since the composition would be continuously changing in the volatilization temperature range; yet as a separation technique it must obviously rank as somewhat less than trivial.

The solution is confinement of the vapor so that it must reach a vapor pressure essentially equal to the ambient pressure before it could escape from the immediate vicinity of the sample. The answer was available in the literature. Vold (V10) had reported 10 years earlier—an experiment in which water vapor was made to escape through a hole drilled in the side of the sample cell. This confinement made certain that the water vaporized under a partial pressure essentially equal to the ambient pressure.

Kissinger *et al.* (K31) had a much better knowledge or understanding of the atmosphere effect. They believed "the decomposition of the

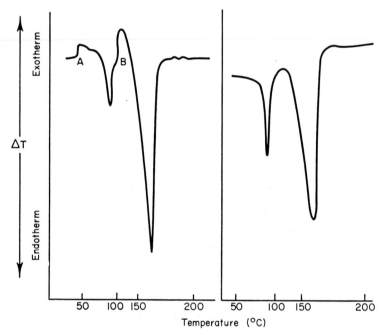

Fɪɢ. VII-5. Differential thermal analysis of 1,4-dibromobenzene. *Left:* 50% in Al₂O₃; manual control. *Right:* 20% in Al₂O₃; programmed voltage. From Hill and Murphy (H13).

When no design precautions are taken a process involving vaporization will yield good results only by chance.

type solid → solid plus gas takes place essentially at a pressure of one atmosphere of the gas evolved when studied by the DTA-TGA under conditions . . . described." They did overestimate the difficulty of diffusion of gas into the sample from the ambient atmosphere. The ⅜-inch opening at the top of the sample holder presents a tremendous area for exchange of gas with the atmosphere above; further, the ⅜-inch total cross section of the sample also permits diffusion from the surface down into the bulk of the sample. At temperatures in the region of 400°C carbon dioxide and oxygen molecules are traveling at a velocity of 20,000 sample holder lengths per second; even considering the tremendous number of collisions, the rate of diffusion within the sample will be high. The only reasonable barrier to interchange of gases is a long narrow path.

7.3. Effect of Interchange of Gases

Consider Fig. VII-6, in which a vessel containing a sample is decomposing reversibly, giving off vapor X into an atmosphere of N. The sur-

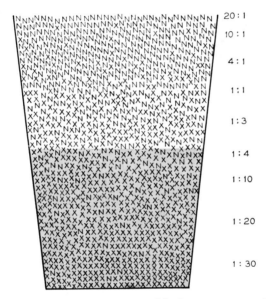

Fig. VII-6. Crucible containing reversibly decomposing specimen.
As decomposition product X is formed it tends to diffuse out into the ambient atmosphere. Since the diffusion is slow amongst the particles of sample the relative amounts of the neutral atmosphere, N, and X will vary with depth in the container. The N : X ratios shown were selected arbitrarily.

rounding gas being initially pure N the concentration of N will vary at some given instant with depth in the vessel, both above and within the specimen. The diminution in N with depth is obviously the result of the evolution of X, but even while this gas is being evolved some N will remain in—or reach—all parts of the vessel simply because gases diffuse rapidly. Of greater importance, the proportion of N and X is not the same in various parts of the vessel. Let us consider the consequence of this rather obvious fact.

As the vessel is heated the walls will reach a "decomposition temperature" first and the reaction will begin. Product X will displace some N initiating a concentration gradient essentially perpendicular to the walls. The center is not yet hot enough to decompose and the concentration of X is a further bar to decomposition so the material toward the center is unaffected as yet.

While the concentration of X is increasing in the bulk another effect— the interchange with the ambient atmosphere—begins to exert an influence. The material near the top of the sample has a lesser concentration of X because of diffusion interchange with N from the environment, i.e., the X diffuses out and N diffuses in. Therefore, this material will react fairly soon after that which is in contact with the wall even though material nearer the wall but deep within the specimen is at a higher temperature. This latter material must reach a still higher temperature because of the concentration of X amongst the particles.

The concentration gradient of X (Fig. VII-7 and VII-9) at the sides is steep in the immediate vicinity of the reaction surface because this is the source of product X, but a more-or-less steady change should go on toward the center with a nearly steady-state vertical gradient set up when diffusion and decomposition are balanced.

The temperature, on the other hand, advances steadily from the sides.

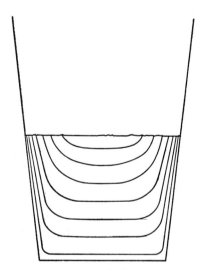

Fɪɢ. VII-7. An arbitrary representation of the concentration gradient of product gas during the early stages of a decomposition.

The concentration is initially high along the sides because that is where the reaction is preferentially occurring and diffusion is slow.

If the temperature lag due to absorption of the heat of reaction is neglected, the temperature distribution in a large thin-walled vessel can
be described by Fig. VII-8.

The atmosphere in the immediate vicinity of a given small particle
dictates the temperature at which that particle will decompose. Each of
the product gas isobars establishes an area which must reach a unique
temperature. These isobars are in continual motion; obviously the product
X concentration around any particle will tend to diminish after that
particle has decomposed.

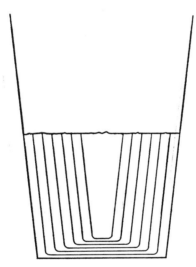

Fig. VII-8. An arbitrary representation of the temperature gradient during a
decomposition.
The heat is supplied mostly through the sides of the vessel.

All of this means that a large and bulky sample decomposing in contact with an atmosphere other than the product gas is constrained by
known physical laws to have a sizable temperature range of decomposition. It further means that the actual conditions under which various
parts of the sample decompose are thermodynamically different (Fig.
VII-9), and in at least a few cases the observer risks the occurrence
of different reactions in different parts of the vessel. This effect accounts
in turn for the nonstoichiometric weight losses obtained more than
occasionally.

The deplorable consequences described above may be avoided, even
with large samples. Obviously if a single product gas is involved decomposition in an atmosphere of that gas will avoid different reactions re-

gardless of sample geometry. If another atmosphere is used it may be kept in dynamic contact with the sample in the manner of Stone (S50) or Lodding and Hammell (L11), or if it is administered as a static or quasi-dynamic atmosphere in the manner of Rowland and Lewis (R34) or Saunders and Giedroyc (S6), respectively, the sample must be in a thin layer in the manner devised by the present author (G17) or Paulik, Paulik, and Erdey (P11) to permit rapid interchange with whatever atmosphere is supplied and hence to maintain an atmosphere within the sample approximately like that above. A third solution is to avoid diffusion from the atmosphere into the sample (G16). Let us examine, with the aid of thermodynamics, the origin of the troubles and the reasons why the solutions are available.

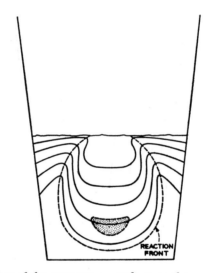

Fɪɢ. VII-9. The effect of the temperature gradient on the concentration gradient. *The reaction temperature is prescribed by the concentration so that the reaction front moves in more rapidly at the top. The front moves downward rather fast, too, so that the last material to react is usually a pellet close to, but not at, the bottom.*

7.4. Reversible Decompositions

Take the case of a reversible decomposition of a carbonate,

$$MCO_3 \rightleftharpoons MO + CO_2.$$

This reaction is governed by both rate and equilibrium constants but let us assume that at the temperatures of interest both the decomposition and recomposition proceed very rapidly; we can then ignore rate constants and concern ourselves with the more important problem of equilibrium.

The equilibrium constant for such a reaction is expressed as

$$K = \frac{[MO]\,[CO_2]}{[MCO_3]},$$

but since the oxide and carbonate are both solids their activities (or concentrations) are generally taken arbitrarily as unity so that

$$K = [CO_2]$$

or

$$K = P_{CO_2};$$

that is, the possibility that the oxide and carbonate will coexist at some given temperature depends only on the pressure of carbon dioxide over the system. If the pressure actually existing is not the equilibrium pressure the reaction will proceed in the direction which will tend to bring about this condition.

From this we can see that at some reasonably high temperature if a carbonate is put under a vacuum it will decompose completely, while if an atmosphere of carbon dioxide were supplied to it it would stay as the carbonate. The only condition permitting coexistence of both solid species is maintenance of the equilibrium pressure, but this is a difficult condition to impose on a system by external control. Deviation in either direction will permit disappearance of one species or the other.

Let us examine the actual physical occurrences in a system comprising a specimen of our metal carbonate, MCO_3 and, over it, an infinite volume at a fixed total pressure of carbon dioxide. Since one of the initial conditions is existence of the carbonate, the temperature of the system is below that for which the fixed pressure is the equilibrium pressure, so let us heat the specimen. When the carbonate reaches and exceeds the appropriate temperature, it will begin to decompose and will continue to do so until it is gone. Now let the specimen cool. When the temperature drops below the equilibrium temperature for this fixed pressure of carbon dioxide the oxide will begin to take up carbon dioxide and convert back to the carbonate. Again the process will go to completion without much regard for the amount of temperature drop. Let us contrast these occurrences with those in a slightly different system.

Consider the same system, a quantity of metal carbonate in an infinite volume with the same pressure of carbon dioxide, but now this carbon dioxide pressure is not the total pressure. Let us add some other gas so that this carbon dioxide pressure is only a few per cent of the total pressure. Again let us heat the specimen. Again the specimen will reach and exceed the same equilibrium temperature but now the evolution of carbon dioxide from the carbonate causes an enrichment of the gas in the immediate vicinity of the specimen so that the decomposition will be retarded. Given sufficient time, however, the carbon dioxide can diffuse away into the infinite volume bringing the partial pressure in the immediate vicinity back toward the initial partial pressure remitting additional carbonate decomposition. Note that the end result is the same: the carbonate will decompose completely. Now let this specimen cool. When the temperature drops below the equilibrium temperature the specimen begins to convert back to the carbonate, depleting the carbon dioxide supply in the immediate vicinity. Since an infinite volume is available, more carbon dioxide diffuses in, allowing further reconstitution of the carbonate. Again the end result is the same; there is, however, a quite different speed of reaction because of the effect of diffusion.

7.5. Pressure-Temperature Relation

We have seen from the above discussion that at a given pressure of carbon dioxide there is some definite temperature at which the metal carbonate will decompose. We can infer that there is a definite relationship governing the equilibrium pressure at various temperatures. The relationship may be found with the aid of a few statements from rather elementary thermodynamics. Remember that for such reactions

$$K = P_{CO_2}$$

but

$$\Delta F = RT \ln K, \qquad \text{so } \Delta F = RT \ln P_{CO_2}$$

or

$$\frac{\Delta F}{T} = R \ln P.$$

The variation of the change of free energy with temperature is given by

$$\frac{d(\Delta F/T)}{dT} = \frac{-\Delta H}{T^2}$$

so

$$\frac{d(R \ln P)}{dT} = \frac{-\Delta H}{T^2} \text{ or } \frac{d \ln P}{dT} = \frac{-\Delta H}{RT^2}.$$

This is the familiar van't Hoff expression. Several important considerations may be deduced easily from examination of a typical plot of this expression, as in Fig. VII-10.

Consider again the vessel shown in Figs. VII-6 to VII-9 and assume that the material in it has an equilibrium pressure of P_a at ambient temperature T_A, but that the ambient partial pressure of carbon dioxide is P'_A. The material is obviously stable. Let us heat the specimen. Upon reaching T'_A the material may start to decompose but any decomposition raises the partial pressure of carbon dioxide in the immediate vicinity in turn slowing the decomposition. The carbon dioxide, however, can and will diffuse away so if heating was stopped just above T'_A the material would decompose as rapidly as the product gas could diffuse away. We are concerned, generally, with dynamic systems so let us

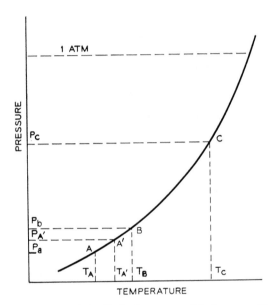

Fig. VII-10. Van't Hoff plot for a reversible decomposition.
At any temperature to the right of that corresponding to the actual local partial pressure the material will tend to decompose, to the left, recompose.

continue the heating. The decomposition of the carbonate will enrich the gas in the immediate vicinity so that as a material reacts the material near it sees a change in environment; as the partial pressure is increased to P_b the material in that environment cannot decompose until T_B is reached. If diffusion is slow because of geometry and sample size the partial pressure of carbon dioxide may reach P_c so that the decomposition is not completed until T_C is reached. This reaction which will occur at any static temperature above T'_A is now, because of somewhat inhibited diffusion, spread out over the temperature range from T'_A to T_C.

Let us consider some effects of various sample and atmosphere arrangements to avoid this spread-out temperature range problem. Conside first the behavior we might expect in a dynamic atmosphere with a partial or total pressure equal to P_b. A dynamic atmosphere is specifically a stream of gas passing through the sample; each particle may be assumed to be surrounded by an atmosphere identical with that entering the sample vessel.

As soon as the temperature exceeds T_B the sample will begin to decompose. This condition is essentially the same as a sample decomposing in an infinite volume of carbon dioxide at a total pressure of P_b so the sample will decompose completely at any temperature above T_B. Note that diffusion is unimportant because an atmosphere with a carbon dioxide pressure of P_b is continually supplied to each particle. The time required for the reaction will be generally dependent on the rate at which heat can be supplied to the specimen.

Reactions taking place in a dynamic atmosphere of the gas produced during the reaction will, in general, take place in a very narrow temperature range. The start of the reaction should be clearly manifest.

Take now a quite open sample vessel and put in it a thin layer of the specimen. Expose this now to a *static* atmosphere with a *partial* pressure of carbon dioxide of P_b. (In an atmosphere comprising only carbon dioxide this reaction would occur quickly as described earlier but it is important to consider a more general case.) When the temperature T_B is reached and exceeded the decomposition begins, as usual, but with the thin, spread-out sample diffusion of carbon dioxide out of the sample is rapid and the sample decomposes rapidly over a short temperature range. Under the same heating conditions the decomposition in this mixed atmosphere will occur over a somewhat longer temperature range than would the decomposition in pure gas (because of the need for diffusion), but this range will be considerably smaller than for the same reaction at the same heating rate in a crucible or block because the diffusion is so much more rapid.

7.6. Inhibited Diffusion

Let us now consider the opposite extreme in atmosphere accessibility. This time we will put the sample in a cavity opening to the atmosphere only through a long narrow tube (Fig. VII-11). The cavity is packed with the powdered sample so that the only air remaining in it is the small amount between particles. From Fig. VII-12 we can deduce the behavior of the specimen. Assuming for this case that the ambient partial pressure does not exceed P_A, as the temperature exceeds T_A, the equilibrium vapor pressure exceeds P_A and decomposition begins. The first hint of decomposition brings about a substantial increase in the amount of gas present so that an equal volume of gas must be forced out of the cavity. The gas forced out will be mostly air, so that the partial pressure of the product gas is increased from P_A to P_1. Considering that the volume expansion from the solid to the gas is likely to be on the order of 1000 and that the open space among the particles is likely to be only a few per cent, one may conclude that the amount of material which needs to be decomposed to increase the partial pressure significantly is quite small. This increase, however, is but the first of a series of infinitesimal steps. When the temperature exceeds T_1 a further quantity must be decomposed raising the partial pressure to P_2 raising the decomposition temperature to T_2 raising the pressure to P_3 raising the decomposition temperature to T_3, etc.

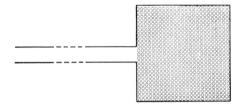

Fig. VII-11. Closed or inhibited diffusion vessel.
Gas can escape easily under a pressure gradient but exchange of gases is slow in the absence of a pressure differential.

This series of infinitesimal steps will continue until P_i is equal to P_{atm}, still with the decomposition of only a small part of the sample. The atmospheric pressure is of course the limit since a diffusion path does exist through the long narrow tube. Since this diffusion path does exist the sample can decompose rapidly and over a small temperature range. Thus, by preliminary decomposition of a very small portion of the sample material, the bulk of it is decomposed, at one atmosphere pressure, over a small temperature range.

The general effect is a narrowing of the reaction temperature range, consequently permitting better discrimination for close-following reactions and probably a more reproducible peak area. (This latter should follow because the effect of packing on diffusion into and out of the sample will disappear.) In practice the long diffusion path need not be tubular. The author uses cylinder-and-piston sample holders for thermogravimetry (Fig. VII-13) and for differential thermal analysis (Fig. III-23). The clearance is about 0.05 mm in either device.

Note that the decomposition occurs at the ambient total pressure rather than at specifically one atmosphere. Hence one may bring about the decomposition of a material at any experimentally convenient pressure. The gas surrounding the vessel need not bear any resemblance to the product gas yet because the movement of gas occurs in just one direction; the decomposition will take place under the applied pressure of the product gas. This consideration is of some importance in studying samples whose products might be difficult to handle in a pure state or in substantial amounts.

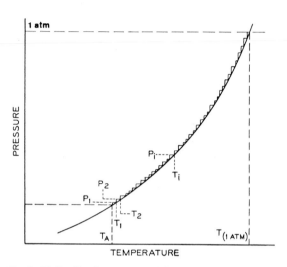

Fig. VII-12. Van't Hoff plot for a reversible decomposition with inhibited diffusion.

As the material decomposes the newly formed gas displaces the ambient air in a series of infinitesimal steps, each in turn raising the temperature required for continued decomposition. Most of the material decomposes only when the ambient temperature is reached.

7.7. Some Results

Essentially concurrent with the author's work (G16, G17) on sample holders for thermogravimetry, Paulik and co-workers (P11) were discovering the merits of a shallow sample holder. Since their concern was, in part, for more effective use of their particular apparatus (P10), they attached a thermocouple to the underside of their platinum pan (Fig. VII-14) and rested the pan on three points on the support tube. Their comparison of curves used different materials from the present authors—but the results are in agreement in principle. Figure VII-15 shows their results for calcium oxalate dihydrate, one of a number of excellent test specimens. The center group of curves is the sort of data Paulik *et al.*

obtain directly by derivative thermogravimetric analysis (see Chapter X). The thin layer of specimen does not permit build-up of water vapor, so the dehydration occurs more readily. The oxalate decomposition is exothermic in air

$$CaC_2O_4 + \tfrac{1}{2}O_2 \rightarrow CaCO_3 + CO_2$$

but endothermic in carbon dioxide (curves 3)

$$CaC_2O_4 \rightarrow CaCO_3 + CO.$$

Note that the differential thermal analysis in the crucible (curve 2) shows what might be interpreted as a pair of exotherms. This sort of

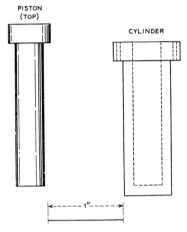

Fig. VII-13. Sample holder for thermogravimetry in self-generated atmospheres. From Garn and Kessler (G16).
Closed-chamber specimen holder. The piston provides a greatly restricted opening and hence highly inhibited diffusion of gases (see also Fig. III-23).

trouble often occurs with crucibles or other massive samples. It becomes clear on careful deliberation that the air within the sample and that diffusing in could oxidize the first carbon monoxide formed, but the carbon monoxide and dioxide tended to keep oxygen out of the crucible so the decomposition required heat until it slowed down enough so that oxygen could diffuse in again to react with the remaining carbon monoxide. The total decomposition reaction, then, comprises a single exothermic and a single endothermic reaction. The exothermic reaction involves a greater quantity of heat (compare curves 1 and 3), and under reasonably well-defined thermodynamic conditions one or the other reaction will be seen while under the unsteady, uncertain, and uncontrollable conditions in a crucible both reactions may or may not be observed. The exact nature of the curve will depend both on the geometry and the heating rate. Note too that the carbonate decomposition in the crucible begins at a temperature, ca. 630°C, at which the shallow pan-in-air decomposition is proceeding rapidly but the reaction is not complete until about the same temperature (>900°C) as in the carbon dioxide atmosphere. See also Figure VI-17.

Calcium oxalate monohydrate does not always show an exotherm when heated in air. Freeman and Edelman, in their examination of electrical derivative techniques (F15), obtained a thermogram (Fig. VII-16) much like the one Paulik *et al.* obtained in carbon dioxide (up

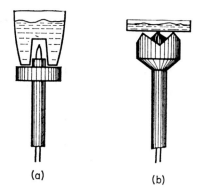

(a)   (b)

Fig. VII-14. The sample holders of Paulik *et al.* (P11).
The thin layer of specimen in (b) does not permit a high concentration of product gas to accumulate.

to about 700°C), but this was because the initial dehydration of the quite large and deep sample drove the air out. Loss of carbon monoxide presumably occurred in an atmosphere initially of water vapor. It is quite apparent that air did not diffuse to the region of the thermocouple until the decomposition was complete.

Pyrite (Fig. VII-17) is much less simple. In the shallow pan in air two oxidations can occur but one (iron) effects a weight gain while decomposition of the disulfide—to what appears to be an oxysulfide and sulfur (which oxidizes)—effects a weight loss. The differential thermogravimetric (DTG) analysis plot looks rather like the differential thermal analysis of calcium oxalate hydrate in a crucible in air (Fig. VII-15). Here, though, it appears to be a question of initiation temperatures and rates. Oxidation of ferrous iron obviously begins before decomposition of the disulfide. Just as obviously the disulfide decomposition is more rapid than the iron oxidation, since the thermogravimetric as well as the "DTG" curve shows a continuation of iron oxidation at the end of the first reaction. The final weight loss—to the oxide—is apparently endothermic.

Curves obtained in the crucible in air are uninterpretable except for gross features. The iron oxidation begins followed quickly by a general but erratic disulfide decomposition. One might guess that the ingress of oxygen from the air is not a uniform process—that there is reasonable

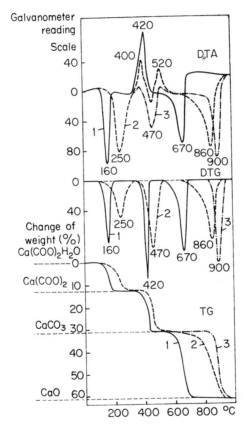

FIG. VII-15. The decomposition of calcium oxalate hydrate: Curves 1 in air in the free-diffusion sample holder of Fig. VII-14b; curves 2 in air in the crucible of Fig. VII-14a; and curves 3 in carbon dioxide in the crucible. From Paulik *et al.* (P11).

Note that curves 2 and 3 coincide in the first step in each case because the carbon dioxide is not evolved. The nature of the atmosphere is immaterial except to the extent that water vapor may be present.

evidence that surges occur. Accounting for each of the peaks in the "DTG" curve would require, first of all, a vivid imagination. This paragraph is, admittedly, opinion; one might make a case for some intermediate sulfides, citing the curves obtained in nitrogen. From there it is a simple step to postulate, in turn, corresponding oxysulfides.

Figures VII-1 and VII-2 or ammonium perchlorate may now be related and the apparent inconsistencies elucidated. Note that the specimen

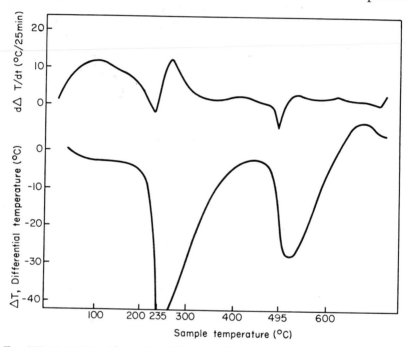

Fɪɢ. VII-16. DDTA (derivative differential thermal analysis) and DTA curves of calcium oxalate monohydrate. From Freeman and Edelman (F15).

Ten-gram samples in glass test tubes were used so the calcium carbonate decomposition was not reached.

sealed in air not only must retain its decomposition products in the immediate vicinity but must decompose in the presence of a very substantial pressure of one of them (oxygen). The total pressure is not of great interest; the partial pressure of any product gas is. Compare first with Stone's curve in ammonia; in each case the supression is considerable. Now compare the first curve of Fig. VII-2 with the second; no product gas is initially present so the decomposition occurs at a lower temperature. Since the gases are restricted, the temperature of the rapid decomposition is still set back more than in the third case.

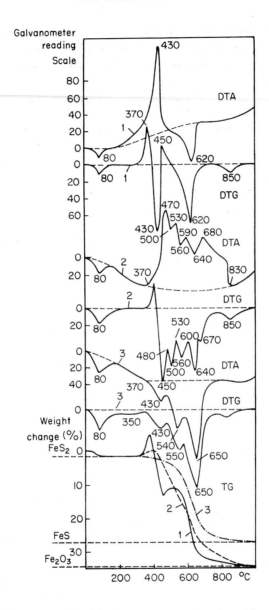

Fɪɢ. VII-17. Thermal analysis of pyrite. Curves 1 in air in the shallow sample holder; curves 2 in air in the crucible; and curves 3 in nitrogen in the crucible. From Paulik *et al.* (P11).

The rapid surges in curves 2 might be the result of several quite similar steps; the oxidation of some of the sulfur not only depletes the atmosphere but also fills the crucible with a heavy gas which slows down the entrance of oxygen for a time.

In the open cup experiment the initially formed products can diffuse away readily and their effect is only slightly felt. This would correspond to the dynamic nitrogen atmospheres used by Stone but modified by the slowness of diffusion.

> The reader may question the applicability of the mass action law to an exothermic reaction. The discussion in Chapter II pointed out only that crystallographic phase changes were unquestionably irreversible if exothermic. While we may conclude prima facie that the decomposition of a perchlorate is irreversible and that equilibrium states are hence nonexistent, we might admit that a particular reaction is possibly reversible but that the thermodynamic equilibrium highly favors the decomposition. But this concession may not be required here since we can suggest an alternative. From Stone's curve obtained in vacuum, we might very easily postulate an endothermic (and probably reversible) step preceding—and prerequisite to—the exothermic decomposition such that the exothermic decomposition does not occur until a sufficient concentration of products (probably within the particles) has been built up.

7.8. Effect of Presence of Gas Other than Product or Reactant

Before introducing the concept of dynamic atmosphere it is appropriate that we make an overwhelming case against improper control of atmosphere. We will examine a few experiments in which the present author has concluded that interpretation or technique was faulty because of atmosphere effects. These are selected only as examples; there are many, many thermograms, including some of the present author's, that could be more informative if redone with proper atmosphere control.

The work by Crandall and West (C25) on oxidation of cobalt-alumina mixtures shows the problems encountered when the experiment is not planned specifically to obtain the information needed. Their use of the standard differential thermal analysis technique (G41) led to some rather doubtful conclusions (Fig. VII-18). Crandall and West apparently took the thermocouple temperature as the temperature of the entire specimen. The present author's interpretation of their differential thermal analysis data—assuming that the thermocouple bead is at or very near the center of the specimen—is that the indicated peak temperature occurs in the higher temperature runs at the time the reaction front reaches the bead. The present author also takes issue with their conclusions on rate-controlling factors. At the lower temperatures, oxygen reaches all particles very soon and the oxidation proceeds inward at each particle. The rate-controlling factor cannot be the diffusion of oxygen but has to be the oxidation rate of the cobalt. At higher temperatures, e.g., 700°C, the oxidation is so rapid that it depletes the oxygen. As oxygen diffuses into the nitrogen atmosphere in the sample vessel, it is taken avidly by the first unoxidized cobalt it encounters; at this temperature, then, the rate-controlling factor must necessarily be the diffusion of oxygen. The reaction front moves into the sample vessel at a progressively slower rate because of the progressively longer diffusion path, accounting for the tailing-off after the maximum.

The studies could have been more lucid had oxygen been used in place of air. The depletion of the oxygen at the reaction front draws in—purely as a volume change effect—only about an 18% replacement.

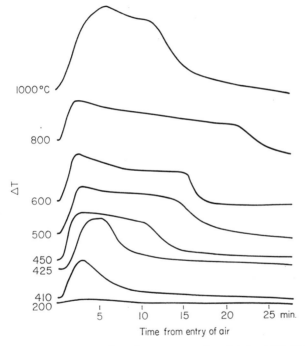

Fig. VII-18. Differential thermal oxidation curves for 50% Co—50% Al$_2$O$_3$ mixtures at high temperatures. From Crandall and West (C25).

The present author suggests that the rate-determining step at the higher temperatures is the diffusion of oxygen into the sample cavity.

In effect, oxygen is diffusing from an 18% level at the top of the sample vessel to the reaction front at a 0% level. Suppose, though, that oxygen had been used. The oxygen would sweep in as a replacement for that used up. While the reaction would be very rapid at the higher temperatures, the rate-controlling step ought to be the oxidation of the metal. A dynamic atmosphere like that suggested by Stone (S58) would be most helpful in this study. A stream carrying definite partial pressures of oxygen at a high flow rate would give a nearly uniform environment to the entire sample.

Kissinger and co-workers (K31) made an attempt to interpret the decompositions of manganous and ferrous carbonates by simultaneous differential thermal analysis and thermogravimetric analysis and by X-ray and electron diffraction. The X-ray and electron diffraction techniques are, of course, static-heating experiments but conclusions may still be drawn with caution. The differential thermal and thermogravimetric analysis experiments provide good correlation of data between the two techniques since the data were obtained simultaneously with essentially identical specimen holders. Identical specimen holders provide for similar inhibitions of diffusion of product or reactive gases. Such determinations provide relatable information which does not necessarily have any thermodynamic significance. Their data on all carbonates are subject to reinterpretation.

A cylindrical sample holder $\frac{3}{8}$ inch in diameter and $1\frac{1}{4}$ inch in depth can provide a rather extensive range of environments during a decomposition. Their assumption that ferrous carbonate necessarily decomposes first to ferrous oxide and carbon dioxide, the ferrous oxide then oxidizing to ferric oxide, is not well-supported by the data which they show. The more probable interpretation, under equilibrium conditions at least, is that the first reaction to occur is the oxidation of a part of the ferrous iron to the ferric iron on and near the surface. This gives rise to the slight exothermic effect shown in their 3°C per minute heating rate (Fig. III-3). This oxidation cannot take place in the mass of the specimen because of the ensuing decomposition with evolution of carbon dioxide. The oxidation does continue wherever oxygen can get into the sample from the surface. The process of oxidation and the process of decomposition are quite separate phenomena except when evolution of carbon dioxide prevents the oxidation of ferrous to ferric iron.

Borchardt (B65), in his apparatus for instructional purposes, used a block with holes 2 inches deep, thereby achieving, inadvertently, atmosphere confinement to a greater degree than is customary. Since his thermocouple junction was only slightly raised from the bottom the conditions set forth for a closed-chamber sample holder were approached. for this reason he was able to show the two-step dehydration of $BaCl_2 \cdot 2H_2O$. His text and thermogram also suggest that part of the time the first decomposition of $CuSO_4 \cdot 5H_2O$ and the vaporization of the resulting liquid water could be detected as separate steps. A high degree of reproducibility and ease of interpretation could be gained by adding sample to a depth of about $\frac{1}{4}$ inch, then inserting a close-fitting rod to create a long narrow diffusion path.

The attempt by Walton (W3) to achieve greater sensitivity by forming the sample into a pellet has been mentioned previously (Chapter VI). Examine the 600°C dehydroxylation shown in Fig. VIII-12. The deflection starts at a significantly lower temperature in the isolated sample and continues to essentially the same temperature as in the block. The attentive reader will conclude that the reaction begins at a low temperature because of the exposure to the atmosphere. To this extent it resembles the free-diffusion sample holders. This is simple enough. Let us next consider the sample block and the sample dimensions. Within the $\frac{3}{8}$-inch-diameter sample cavity there is no less than $\frac{1}{2}$ inch of greatly compacted sample between the thermocouple and the atmosphere. This is enough distance to prevent rapid diffusion and the last parts of the sample decompose, in effect, under nearly one atmosphere of water vapor.

Actually with such a heavily compacted body the $\frac{1}{2}$-inch separation between thermocouple and atmosphere is more than enough. The $\frac{3}{16}$-inch lateral separation appears to be enough. In other words, the latter part of Walton's isolated-sample dehydration curve shows that the center of the specimen is decomposing under ca. one atmosphere of water vapor.

The resemblance of the exposed pellet curves to a melange of "free-diffusion" and "closed-chamber" effects is due to the sample size, yet this problem can only be vitiated—not eliminated—by decreasing the size, so long as the pellet technique is used at all. Brindley and Nakahira (B80) reported that even with thin and loosely compacted samples the isothermal dehydroxylation of kaolin proceeded as a first-order reaction ($-dx/dt = kx$, where x is the quantity of unreacted material) at first, then slowed down. With pressed-disc samples, the reaction was slowest both initially and finally for the thickest samples. Relating this information back to the case of the pellets, the material on the surface is not influenced by the amount of material beneath it. The dehydroxylation will begin at a low temperature. The water vapor that forms inside cannot diffuse out readily and hence inhibits the decomposition until either the water vapor diffuses out or the temperature is raised, permitting a higher vapor pressure of water. The question of the order of reaction is discussed in Chapter VI.

Even the choice of "inert" atmospheres can affect the behavior of the sample and hence the appearance of the thermogram. The use of helium, for example, will cause severe deviations because of its special properties of very high diffusivity and thermal conductivity. As a dynamic gas it will provide another—and important—means of heat transfer, tending to diminish differential signals by serving as an infinitely large heat sink. This behavior contributed to the diminished signal found by the present author (Chapter XIV) in one of his early experiments in effluent gas analysis.

Wendlandt's (W18) curves for calcium oxalate monohydrate in air and in helium provide a striking example. The endothermic peaks in the 200–300°C range are the same process in each case, the dehydration of the monohydrate, yet if these peaks were separately presented, even an experienced observer might well fail to recognize them as the same process occurring in the same material. The reasons for the difference in the peaks are the two cited properties of helium. See Figure VI-17.

The major effect is the rapidity with which helium interchanges with other gases. The entry of helium in among the particles lowers the partial pressure of water vapor, enabling decomposition at a lower temperature. A secondary effect is the improved transfer of heat by this interparticulate helium. The more uniform temperature within the sample permits decomposition over a narrower range of temperatures.

The conclusion to be reached is necessarily that decompositions require precise control of the atmosphere. The mere supply of a particular gas over the sample holder is not enough; indeed, from Section 7.6 control of the gas *over* the sample holder may not be necessary.

7.9. Dynamic Atmosphere Differential Thermal Analysis

One of the most significant steps in thermal analysis since the introduction of the differential thermocouple was the development of apparatus permitting the passage through the sample of selected and controlled dynamic atmospheres. This was mainly the work of Stone (S50–S55, S58, S60), with an improved (in some ways) approach later by Lodding and Hammell (L10, L11). Some work had been reported (R34, S6) in which the sample—enclosed in a cavity or cup—was heated in an atmosphere of a selected neutral, reducing, oxidizing, or product gas. Product gas is used here and elsewhere in this book to mean a gas resulting from a decomposition.) Even with the usual rather massive samples, static atmosphere heating is a perfectly sound technique so long as the object is to avoid a decomposition, for example, the use of nitrogen or argon to avoid an oxidation, or if a single decomposition occurs and the atmosphere is the product gas.

Consider first a case in which a hydrated carbonate is heated in a static atmosphere of carbon dioxide and let us arbitrarily select this hydrated carbonate such that the water and carbon dioxide are given off at widely separated temperatures. (This latter condition is only a convenience). As the sample is heated to the decomposition range of the hydrate the dehydration will begin and will proceed at a rate tending to set up an equilibrium pressure of water vapor. Since the original atmosphere was not water vapor its real identity is almost immaterial. (Diffusion rates of water vapor in various gases will have a small effect.) The hydrate will tend to decompose over a wide range of temperatures just as though the atmosphere had been air.

The dehydration completed, the sample approaches in temperature the decomposition range of the carbonate. Since a large temperature interval was specified most of the water vapor will have diffused out of the sample holder. The decomposition begins, then, in an atmosphere of carbon dioxide with a small amount of water vapor. The onset of decomposition, at a temperature determined by the relative amounts of water and carbon dioxide deep in the sample holder, expels the water vapor as the decomposition proceeds. Most of the decomposition occurs in the atmosphere of the product gas and hence over a small temperature range.

Now let these same reactions occur with a lesser temperature interval between the decompositions. The hydrate decomposition will tend to remain the same but the onset of the carbonate decomposition will occur at a lower temperature because the water vapor has not had time to diffuse out. Still the effect may not be great since a small amount of carbon dioxide will expel the water vapor; but consider the logical extension, i.e., the case in which the equilibrium vapor pressure of carbon dioxide over the carbonate has a measurable value within the decomposition range of the hydrate. Now as the hydrate decomposes, and the water vapor partial pressure increases, the partial pressure of carbon dioxide necessarily decreases. At some temperature the hydrate decomposition is occurring rapidly enough to diminish the partial pressure of carbon dioxide below the equilibrium vapor pressure of carbon dioxide and the carbonate will begin to decompose. A mixture of water vapor and carbon dioxide will be given off from the sample because the presence of either of the gases will diminish the partial pressure of the other and accelerate the reaction producing that other. Eventually, the lower-temperature hydrate decomposition will run its course, the temperature difference signal will approach—but not reach—the base line, and the remainder of the carbonate will decompose. Note that even the dehydration will be complete at a lower temperature than if the carbonate decomposition did not occur so soon. [This is the lowering of the decomposition temperatures of mixtures noted by Arens (A12) and by Webb and Heystek (W11).]

Now examine the effect of a dynamic atmosphere of carbon dioxide on the same systems. The effect is quite straightforward. The water vapor is swept out rapidly and never achieves any substantial partial pressure. The dehydration occurs at a significantly lower temperature and has no effect on the carbonate decomposition. The dehydration peak is not particularly well-defined. The carbonate decomposition takes place sharply over a small temperature range determined by the actual pressure of the carbon dioxide. To complete the picture, however, we must consider a static atmosphere of water vapor and dynamic atmospheres of water vapor and of a mixture of water vapor and carbon dioxide.

In static water vapor the hydrate will remain unchanged until the equilibrium vapor pressure reaches the furnace pressure. If the hydrated carbonate has no appreciable equilibrium pressure of carbon dioxide we have no serious complications; at the appropriate temperature the hydrate will begin to decompose. Since the hydrated specimen is at a higher temperature than it could reach in the carbon dioxide atmosphere, let us assume that at this temperature we have a few millimeters vapor pressure of carbon dioxide from the carbonate. The dehydrated carbonate will tend to decompose to maintain the pressure but the dilution in the water vapor keeps the pressure low—and not only due to diffusion. The movement of the freshly released water vapor from the bulk of the sample into the surrounding atmosphere sweeps the particles with a pro tempore dynamic atmosphere of water vapor. Initially, then, the carbonate decomposes rapidly—as long as the dehydration continues. When there is no hydrate to decompose the carbonate decomposition will slow to a rate only sufficient to keep each particle surrounded by the equilibrium vapor pressure of carbon dioxide as long as possible. The reaction will proceed as described in Section 3 of this chapter.

In a dynamic atmosphere of water vapor (pure or diluted) the hydrated carbonate will again be stable until the equilibrium vapor pressure reaches the pressure (or partial pressure) of water vapor in the steam. At this point it will start to decompose and if the carbonate has an appreciable vapor pressure (as we postulated before) it will also begin to decompose. In this case, however, the dilution of the carbon dioxide continues so that the carbonate decomposition peak follows close behind the dehydration peak and is not well-separated from it.

Lastly, consider a dynamic atmosphere of a mixture of carbon dioxide and water vapor. The proportions are not very important as long as there is a substantial fraction of each; let us arbitrarily use, for example, carbon dioxide saturated with water vapor at 25°C before it enters the furnace. The hydrate will begin to decompose when the equilibrium vapor pressure exceeds the partial pressure of water in the gas stream. Assuming a flow rate sufficient that the carbon dioxide partial pressure is not changed substantially, the hydrate will decompose completely—over a short temperature interval—without effect on the carbonate. At the appropriate temperature the carbonate will in turn decompose, also over a short temperature interval. The two reactions are now, however, clearly separated in temperature and in time. The degree of separation in temperature would depend, for a given material, on the actual partial pressures of the two gases. The separation can hence be varied by changing said pressures.

Note that the arguments above can describe, just as well, a mixture of a carbonate and a hydrate. The only difference would be that the equilibrium vapor pressures would now be independent of each other; i.e., the discontinuity of carbon dioxide pressure as the hydrate decomposed would not occur. Similarly, the arguments are by no means limited to carbon dioxide and water. Figure VII-1 shows the effect of ammonia in repressing a reaction in which one of the product gases is ammonia.

7.10. Apparatus for Dynamic Atmosphere Differential Thermal Analysis

Two varieties of dynamic atmosphere differential thermal analysis furnaces are in common use, that (Fig. VII-19) described by Stone (S58) and that (Fig. VII-20) described by Lodding and Hammell (L10); they differ basically in the direction of flow of the gas. Stone introduces the gas into a manifold below the furnace chamber from whence it is admitted to the sample and the reference through a pair of capillaries. After passing upward through the specimens it mixes with the chamber gas which may or may not be the same gas.

> The present author very strongly suggests the use of the same gas unless there is good reason to use another. Back-diffusion of the chamber gas can occur even at moderately high rates of flow of gas.

In the Lodding–Hammell apparatus the dynamic gas is sent first into the furnace chamber from which it flows downward through the sample and reference and out through the tubes which also support the block and lead the thermocouple wires.

Each technique basically has its own advantages which render it better —for some purposes—than the other. Each can be modified, however, to obtain some of the attributes of the other; there is, for example, no chemical reason why the operation of either cannot be inverted to resemble the other. The barriers are physical and mechanical.

With the understanding that modifications are possible in either case we will consider and compare the basic design of each.

The Stone apparatus uses a sample block heated by a furnace element quite separate from the gas enclosure. The block is secured to the gasflow tubes. Since the furnace element is positioned on the base by water and electrical connections and the block is also carefully positioned, the heater and the block are positioned quite reproducibly with respect to one another. The Lodding–Hammell apparatus uses ceramic cups (which are, in essence, sleeves set part way over the support rods) heated by a furnace winding applied over the furnace chamber tube. Since the support rods and the furnace chamber tube are secured at some distance from the hot zone, the cups and the furnace are less

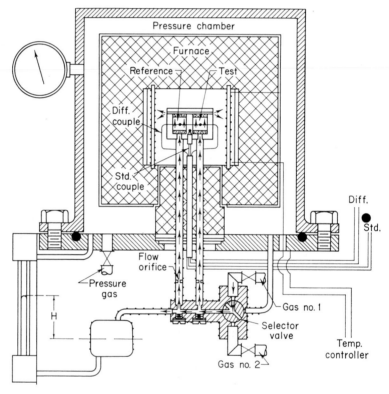

Fig. VII-19. Dynamic atmosphere differential thermal analysis furnace. (Courtesy of Robert L. Stone Co.)

The dynamic gas flows upward from manifold through orifices and specimens and escapes into the pressure chamber.

likely (in the absence of special techniques) to be reproducibly and symmetrically positioned. If a block is substituted for the cups, a substantial misalignment may permit the block to touch the furnace wall and be heated very unsymmetrically. The use of varying pressure on the O-ring seal to position the furnace with respect to the specimen is of little use because it would need to be done not only at each run but even during each run, using the differential signal as a guide. This might compensate for gross differences in the thermal properties of sample and reference materials when this sort of compensation is not particularly desirable. Further, balancing the heating in this manner is a unidirectional adjustment. The information gained is only that sample and reference specimens are symmetric with respect to a plane perpendicular to and at the midpoint of a line joining the sample and reference thermocouple junctions. The specimens may still be much closer to the furnace

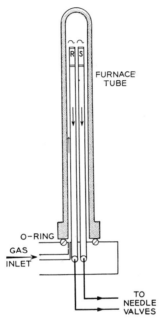

Fig. VII-20. Dynamic atmosphere furnace of Lodding and Hammell (L10).
The dynamic gas passes from the furnace chamber through the specimens out of the furnace and thence through flow measuring and control equipment.

wall on one side than the other; such positioning will tend to smear out the thermal effect. This type of positioning error would be quite irreproducible.

The present author uses a modification of the Lodding–Hammell furnace because of its other advantages but eliminates the positioning error. The furnace flange (Fig. VII-21) determines the positioning of the furnace chamber accurately; the O-ring is used properly only as a sealant. The support rods are positioned so that the top ends of the rods are directly above the support tube positioning holes in the base. When assembled, then, the sample and reference, whether in block or cup, are symmetrically positioned with respect to the furnace.

Letting the gas flow downward through the specimens then out of the furnace permits (*a*) collection of product gases for continual repetitive

or subsequent analysis (see Chapter XIV) with minimum dilution and
(*b*) separate and nearly independent control of flow through the two
specimens. The flow of gas can be monitored to assure not only actual
rate but also volume. Variations due to differing impedance to flow or to
possible clogging can not only be detected but also corrected.

Water vapor cannot be used as a dynamic gas in the Lodding–Hammel
method except at pressures or partial pressures less than the ambient
temperature vapor pressure, at least with practices current at the time
of writing. The Stone method permits the preheating and superheating

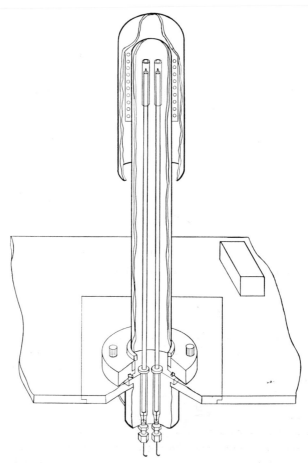

Fɪɢ. VII-21. Dynamic atmosphere differential thermal analysis furnace. (Courtesy
of Apparatus Manufacturers, Inc.)

*The author's design provides for reproducible positioning as well as for micro-
samples and the several types of atmosphere control.*

of the water vapor so that dry steam can be introduced to the sample cavity.

Preheating of gases is not only possible but also necessary with the Stone method. The entry of gas at ambient temperature into a sample at—say—400°C could bring about a rather severe temperature gradient at a right angle to the ordinary gradient. The Lodding–Hammell method uses gas from the furnace chamber which can be assumed—in the absence of a nearby cold surface (see Chapter III)—to be very near block or cup temperature at any heating rate. Preheating without a separate controller would produce an effect which varied with heating rate and possibly with temperature.

A properly constructed furnace of the Lodding–Hammell type can be used easily with isolated samples because the temperature gradients in the hot zone are low. This likewise permits a flexibility of sample support —for example, microsamples as described in Chapter VIII, Sec. 8.2—which is impracticable in a zone heated only from the sides and with a very sizable cool surface above it.

Techniques requiring a change of dynamic gases are generally easier with the Stone technique. The hold-up volume of the manifold is low and the transition from the initial to near the final composition is swift (Fig. VII-2). In the Lodding–Hammell arrangement the furnace chamber must also be cleansed of the initial gas so that the complete change might well take several minutes.

Handling of fusible samples is similar in the two methods. The sample may be mixed with enough diluent to hold it when molten or small cups may be put in the sample chamber. The latter is easier with the Lodding–Hammell arrangement because the cup can rest against the thermocouple bead.

7.11. Experimental Results

The utility of controlled and/or dynamic atmospheres is seldom exploited to near its capabilities. Indiscriminate use will lead to a lack of appreciation of the merits of control. Comparisons of the effects of dynamic gases that have no significantly different action on the specimen (e.g., nitrogen and helium or, usually, oxygen and air) are uninformative and hence useless.

In planning an experiment the degree of confinement and the nature of the possible reactions must be considered. The use of a controlled atmosphere—except to prevent a reaction such as oxidation or if the atmosphere is a product of the reaction being studied—when the specimen is not in good contact with the atmosphere is quite without merit. Likewise, if the nature of the reaction is known and a single gas is

involved a dynamic flow is not ordinarily beneficial. Since the temperature or even the nature of the reactions can vary with atmosphere,
definitely known conditions must be used; the use of these definitely
known conditions is rewarded by more informative thermograms.

Fig. VII-23 shows thermograms obtained from a coprecipitated magnesium manganese iron oxalate hydrate. (The desired heating product is
magnesium manganese ferrite.) Each curve is different from the others
not from lack of control of heating conditions but because the environ-

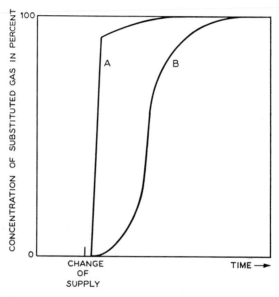

FIG. VII-22. Representation of the time dependence of gas proportions during
change of gases in the (A) Stone and (B) Lodding–Hammell furnaces.

*The change will not be completely sharp in the Stone furnace because the gas
in the differential manometer will exchange very slowly. The entire furnace chamber
volume of the Lodding–Hammell furnace damps the change. The change should be
effectively complete in the latter in a small number of minutes.*

ment of the specimen was established for each thermogram. The curve
obtained in the closed chamber shows a quite sharp dehydration ca.
200°C and a less well-defined oxalate breakdown peaking ca. 460°C.
This latter is—for most oxalates when heated separately—an evolution of
carbon monoxide to form the appropriate metal carbonate; some, however, lose carbon dioxide to yield the metal unless oxygen is available
(see Figs. VIII-6 and XI-15). In either case this a highly irreversible
decomposition so a carbon dioxide atmosphere could not be expected

to have a substantial effect. In dynamic carbon dioxide, therefore, this peak is rather similar to that obtained in the closed chamber. The slight downward shifting suggests that the temperatures ought to be sensitive to carbon *monoxide* pressure since the major effect here is dilution of the carbon monoxide.

The dehydration peak is shifted to ca. 170°C in dynamic carbon dioxide because the water vapor is swept out rapidly and can achieve only a low vapor pressure. Roughly the same effect is observed in dy-

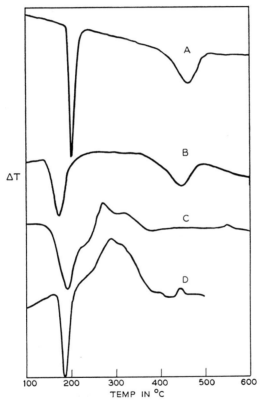

FIG. VII-23. Thermograms of coprecipitated magnesium manganese iron oxalite hydrate in A, closed-chamber sample holder; B, dynamic CO_2; C, dynamic O_2; and D, shallow pan sample holder in air. No attempt was made to obtain equal peak heights in the various runs. Thermogram D was terminated at 500°C because the sample holder was aluminum.

Since materials may show greatly different thermograms under different atmosphere conditions, well-selected atmosphere conditions can be used to derive information about a sample.

namic oxygen but the shift is not so great because the bottled oxygen has a higher water content than the "bone dry" carbon dioxide.

The exothermic peaks ($250-350°C$) in the dynamic oxygen are–as one might expect–due to the oxidation of the various oxalate species (see Fig. VIII-3).

The presence of oxygen permits oxidation of the carbon monoxide moiety of each species more or less separately. While it is reasonable to assume that a mechanical mixture of the oxalates would show a greater definition of oxidation peaks, the coprecipitated material will have intermediate energy states at boundaries of crystallites or at metal ion substitutions. The later oxidation ca. $550°C$ is probably manganese going to the $+3$ state.

In static air the behavior of the material is much as in dynamic oxygen except for the oxidation ca. $450°C$. Note that the principal oxidation peaks are not quite the same shape as in dynamic oxygen. This is understandable; in dynamic oxygen the partial pressure of other gases cannot become very high and each particle is surrounded by a continually refreshed atmosphere of oxygen while in static air the oxygen in the vicinity of the specimen becomes depleted not only because of use but because of the formation of the carbon dioxide. Four volumes of carbon dioxide are formed for each volume of oxygen reacting and, since a volume of oxygen diffusing in from an air atmosphere also brings along more than four volumes of nitrogen, it is clearly possible to blanket the specimen and prevent–briefly–an oxidation that would otherwise have occurred during the general oxidation.

We can see from this last curve the possible hazard of a static atmosphere. Such anomalies will be particularly apparent when the specimen reacts with the–or part of the–atmosphere to form another gas. If the product were a solid (oxide, for example) the only effect of reaction with a part of the atmosphere would be dilution as in the case of Crandall and West (C25) (see Fig. VII-18).

The important feature in dynamic atmosphere work is that reactions may be selectively affected. The sweeping through of carbon dioxide during a dehydration has the same effect as nitrogen, argon, or cyclobutane; i.e., the concentration of water vapor is kept extremely low and the dehydration takes place at a lower temperature than in even a static atmosphere. If a subsequent (reversible) decomposition of the sample produces carbon dioxide the peak will be very clearly defined compared to the corresponding peak in other gases. Even for rather similar reactions separations of peaks can be accomplished. The van't Hoff relation describes the manner of change independently for each reaction. If a pair of dehydrations are describable by the two curves of Fig. VII-24 and the intersection occurs very near the ambient partial pressure of water the peaks will not be separable by ordinary techniques but can be by proper atmosphere control.

Consider the case of gypsum, calcium sulfate dihydrate. Fig. VII-25 shows thermograms of the dihydrate and the two hemihydrates. Note that the hemihydrates are already beginning to decompose before the dihydrate is completely gone. This would quite obviously present diffi- culties if one were to attempt to detect or measure a small quantity of

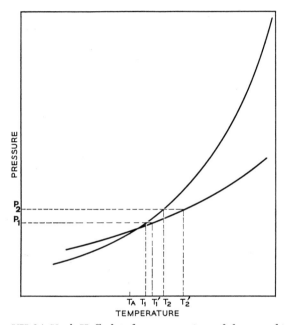

Fɪɢ. VII-24. Van't Hoff plots for two reactions of the same kind.
Even though the two reactions may occur together at some particular pressure a change in pressure will separate them on the temperature scale. The separation, $T_i'-T_i$, will vary regularly with pressure.

dihydrate in either hemihydrate unless, of course, one controls the atmosphere properly. Kuntze (K48) showed (Fig. VII-26) that such control was easily achieved for this particular case.

In Fig. VII-26a, even 1% of the dihydrate is barely discernable in a dry atmosphere; this would be true at the slower heating rate, too. The reason is that at the low water vapor pressure the hemihydrate begins to decompose at about the same temperature as the dihydrate in water vapor, however, the hemihydrate decomposition is set back enough (Fig. VII-26b) so that $\frac{1}{10}\%$ dihydrate is readily detected and measured.

7.12. Pressure Effects

The variation of the temperature or even nature of thermal effects with atmosphere has now been demonstrated, along with the concept of variations with pressure (Fig. VII-1, VII-2, and VII-4; see also Fig. V-29). Not only can the use of pressure changes be informative in studying an already known effect but also the use of pressure effects can lead to discovery of, for example, new states of matter (G8).

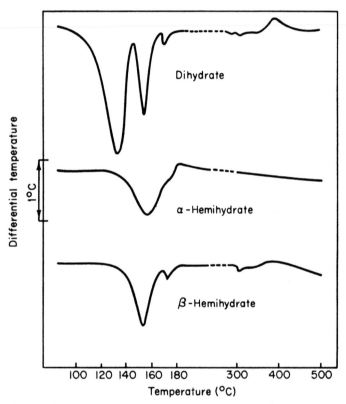

FIG. VII-25. Differential thermograms of synthetic hydrates of calcium sulfate. From Kuntze (K48).

The dihydrate goes to the β-hemihydrate at atmospheric pressure.

The apparently simple dehydration of barium chloride dihydrate becomes rather complex at pressures above atmospheric. At one atmosphere the weight loss occurs in two steps, the first near 100°C so that the water can vaporize immediately and the second well above the boiling point. If we increase the pressure on the system we change the boiling point of water in a well-documented manner (L1a); further, we change the temperatures of the weight losses in a manner depending on the heat of dehydration so we can calculate this quantity if we wish. But of even more interest, we may reach a pressure at which some new crystal structure or composition is stable.

Figure VII-27 shows this author's data at several pressures. The data were obtained using the closed-chamber sample holder of Fig. III-14 in a furnace like that of Fig. VII-21. Supra-atmospheric pressures were

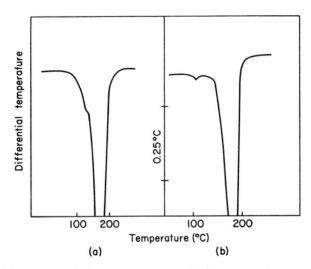

FIG. VII-26. Differential thermograms of hemihydrates containing small amounts of dihydrate. (a) Dry atmosphere, 1% dihydrate, rate of heating 10 cal per min. (b) Atmosphere saturated with water vapor, 0.1% dihydrate rate of heating 6 cal per min. From Kuntze (K48).

The differing heats of dissociation of the hydrates permit separation of peaks by changing the pressure.

obtained by applying a gas pressure to the furnace chamber from a cylinder. The identity of the pressurizing gas is essentially immaterial; whatever is used, the decomposing hydrate must supply an equal pressure before the decomposition can become rapid.

At pressures above one atmosphere the initial loss of water simply leaves a wet sample; the water does not vaporize until a higher temperature, the second peak, is reached. In addition, another thermal effect is indicated by the small peak separating from the second dehydration. At four atmospheres this new effect is well-separated, but at eight atmospheres still another effect appears. Whether or not these two additional effects are both weight losses is not clear at the time of writing. It is probable that many hydrates have several forms with lesser hydration at elevated pressures. Modification of furnace design to permit higher pressures will allow greater latitude in studying these.

Other possible and inadvertent effects of use of pressure must be recognized. Consider a particle of a clay at a temperature in the dehydroxylation range. The water must diffuse out of the particle as part of the total process. If the atmosphere is something other than water, diffusion outward is more rapid if the pressure is low than if it is high since there are less of the other molecules bouncing about at the low pressure.

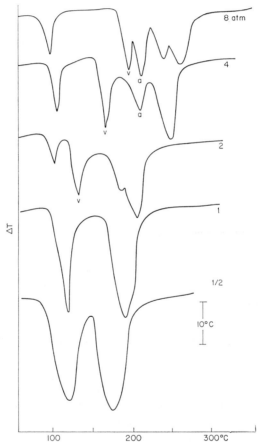

Fig. VII-27. Thermograms of barium chloride dihydrate in self-generated atmospheres at various pressures. From Garn (G8a).
At the higher pressures new phases appear.

Stone's (S58) data on Ca-montmorillonite (Fig. VII-28) show the effect. Even a dynamic atmosphere, keeping the water vapor at the surface near zero, causes a considerable shift of dehydration or dehydroxylation temperatures.

Note that this shift will be seriously time-dependent because the nitrogen and water are continually interchanging. The appearance of the thermogram would be significantly dependent on heating rate. In a water

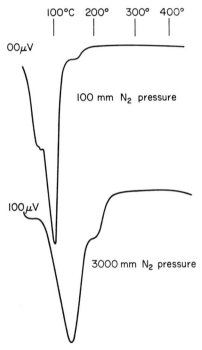

FIG. VII-28. Removal of low-temperature water of a Ca-montmorillonite. From Stone (S58).

At the higher pressure the diffusion outward is repressed so the thermal effects occur at higher temperatures.

atmosphere, whether dynamic or self-generated, the diffusion takes place by reason of a pressure differential created by the decomposition. Any change in appearance of the thermogram would be solely due to the rate of dehydroxylation, not diffusion.

Berg and Rassonskaya (B40) observed pressure effects with the assembly shown in Fig. VII-29. They set a crucible containing the sample into the pressure chamber and also had no provisions for highly inhibited interchange with the pressurizing gas; consequently their data were not so well-defined as can be obtained by the present author's technique.

7.13. Summary

Most of the reported examples of use of dynamic atmospheres are designed to extract specific information rather than to show the benefits thereof. For the present purpose, the offering of an extensive series of comparisons would become tedious. The purpose of this chapter was to

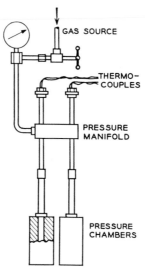

Fɪɢ. VII-29. Pressure system for thermal analysis at elevated pressures. From Berg and Rassonskaya (B40).

No matter what the pressurizing gas—unless it reacts with the sample—the atmosphere during a decomposition becomes principally the product gas at the applied pressure.

demonstrate the need for atmosphere control of some sort so that the experimenter could choose the optimum conditions for the particular experiment. Some general examples of applications are given in Chapter XIII.

In brief, the static controlled atmosphere combined with easy interchange of gases provides a control over reversible (and some irreversible) reactions in which the atmosphere is a reactant or product, without effect on other reactions. If another reaction should evolve another gas, there is obfuscation to some degree reaching as a limit the equivalent of no atmosphere control. It is best used for study of specific reactions and by using the gas undiluted.

A dynamic atmosphere provides a control over reactions in which the dynamic gas is a reactant or product similar to the static atmosphere but with a different influence on reactions yielding other gases as products; i.e., these other gases are kept at very low levels of concentration so that the decompositions occur at lower temperatures while those involving the dynamic gas as a product occur at higher temperatures. The technique has the advantages that the type of reaction may be easily identified by changing the identity or pressure of the dynamic gas and that gaseous decomposition products may be easily swept out for identification or determination (see Chapter XIV).

The self-generated atmosphere provides better-defined peaks for decompositions without the need for specific control of atmosphere. It is used as the principal exploratory technique and on those occasions when supplying an atmosphere of the decomposition product gas is impracticable.

CHAPTER VIII

Special Techniques

8.1. Introduction

Differential thermal analysis is by no means a perfected art. The apparatus commonly used in differential thermal analysis has evolved by reason of its applicability to a reasonably wide range of problems. The great utility of the technique, however, leads to its use in cases wherein the usual methods are of marginal or submarginal value. The enterprising observer will thereupon devise a modification more suited to his needs.

The user of differential thermal analysis as a research tool must be willing to evaluate his own particular needs and change his approach accordingly. This will be more successful than just dropping a sample into whatever apparatus is around and hoping the curve will be helpful.

8.2. Small Samples

Over the period of development of differential thermal analysis, the size or weight of sample generally used has naturally decreased. The use of 10 gm or so of sample brings about uncertainty because at moderate heating rates the temperature drop from edge to center will be a score or more degrees. This raises the possiblity of a second reaction already beginning at the edge influencing the flow of heat inward and hence affecting the shape of the observed peak.

266

There are very understandable investigations of smaller samples. The present author, when there is reason, uses samples down to the tenths of a milligram range instead of the 20–200 mg which generally yield more reliable data. These small samples must be used with caution lest they become an experiment in instrumentation rather than a source of information about the sample.

Thermal analysis of extremely small (1 mg) samples imposes special problems because of the need for concurrent temperature homogeneity between sample and reference and low heat capacity and conductivity of the sample holder. The thermal isolation of the sample is necessary to provide a reasonable lag or lead in temperature to permit detection of the thermal event; this isolation causes unusual difficulties in providing a reference thermocouple at an almost exactly equivalent point. The almost exactly equivalent point is a point which undergoes temperature changes very similar to the sample point under all ordinary heating and cooling cycles. Such a point is required because of the ultimate need or desire for higher amplifications. Presently available techniques and commonly available detecting and recording apparatus are quite easily able to detect the low energies of decompositions or even phase transformations in samples no larger than a few micrograms. The real gains in sensitivity must come from design of the sample environment. Generally, microsamples will be examined by differential calorimetry, i.e., comparatively isolated sample holders, because of the greater sensitivity. This isolation should be modified only so much as may be necessary to (1) reduce drift to reasonable limits and (2) permit separation of close-lying reactions (see Chapter III).

Rogers (R26) uses micro differential thermal analysis for a quite understandable reason. His samples are principally explosives. Since the decomposition is exothermic and atmosphere-independent, the atmosphere accessibility is of no importance. The principal function of his sample holder (Fig. VIII-1) is to provide a compact sample in good thermal contact with the reference material. The reference material

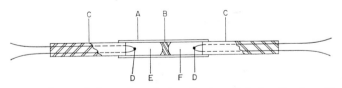

Fig. VIII-1. Differential thermal analysis cell: A, cell body; B, plug; C, thermocouple insulation; D, thermocouples; E, sample compartment; and, F, reference compartment. From Rogers (R26).

Sample and reference are in good thermal contact, leading to low drift.

could probably have been omitted and the thermocouple pushed against the barrier. Any small base line drift would be trivial compared to the effects in which he was interested.

The present author's work with small samples (G5) was done with full cognizance of the importance of atmosphere accessibility and hence took a route somewhat different from those of other workers. Attempts to provide good temperature agreement while retaining some thermodynamic significance led to development of sample holders which comprise a means of measuring the temperature of a thin layer of material. There is obviously no merit in having an extensive area covered by this sample; hence the small area and the thin layer result in a small sample, 0.1 to 2 mg. This free-diffusion technique then becomes necessarily a microtechnique. The advantages of essentially reproducible and nearly constant atmosphere conditions are obtained only with rather small samples in any reasonable size furnace. The advantages of the other extreme in atmosphere accessibility, i.e., the inhibited-diffusion sample holder, are described in Chapter VII. Design to accommodate smaller samples was simple.

The free-diffusion sample holders comprise, in general, a thin sheet of metal to which one or more fine dissimilar wires has been welded. One form comprises a heavy wire (0.020 inch) platinum vs platinum–10% rhodium thermocouple to which a 0.005-inch sheet of gold is welded (Fig. VIII-2). A 0.005-inch platinum–10% rhodium wire is welded to the bottom of a slight depression in the sheet. The fine wire must be of the same composition as one of the thermocouple wires so that the gold may function as the joining member of a differential thermocouple.

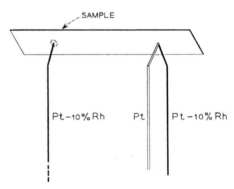

SAMPLE

Pt–10% Rh   Pt   Pt –10% Rh

FIG. VIII-2. Micro free-diffusion sample holder. From Garn (G5).
The gold sheet acts as the joining wire of the differential thermocouple. The sample is placed directly over the junction with the fine wire.

The relatively heavy wire of the thermocouple provides at least a small heat sink so that thermal effects in the sample are not transmitted along the foil sufficiently to affect the temperature signal. The fine wire and thin foil are used to afford as high a degree of thermal isolation as practicable. The need for a thin layer of specimen with a reasonably homogeneous temperature not only permits the use of small samples but also implies that a reference material—to give more or less compensating temperature effects—is not needed.

The sample holder (Fig. VIII-2) is supported on a ceramic tube inside a vertical furnace. The leads are connected to an amplifier and an *x-y* recorder such that the temperature is measured across the thermocouple leads directly while the potential difference between the two platinum–10% rhodium wires (ΔT) is amplified before being fed into the recorder.

The thermogram of cobalt oxalate hydrate (Fig. VIII-3) shows good

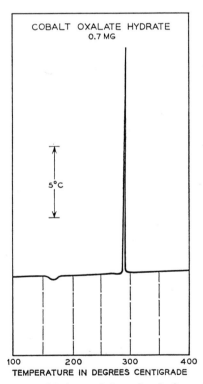

FIG. VIII-3. Thermogram of 0.7 mg cobalt oxalate hydrate. From Garn (G5).
The ease of entry of oxygen permits rapid enough oxidation to cause a 15°C exothermic deflection.

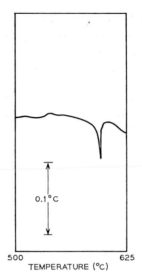

TEMPERATURE (°C)

Fɪɢ. VIII-4. Thermogram of potassium sulfate (0.1 mg). From Garn (G5). *The local cooling permits ready detection of phase transformations.*

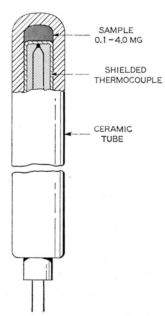

Fɪɢ. VIII-5. Inhibited-diffusion sample holder for small samples. From Garn (G5).

Even with shielded thermocouples very small effects can be detected.

agreement with the weight loss ·curve of Chapter XI. Any remaining error is most likely in the temperature measurement in thermogrametry. Thermograms of phase transitions are not affected by the nature of the sample container. Figure VIII-4 shows the α-β transition in a 0.1-mg sample of potassium sulfate.

The inhibited-diffusion sample holder (Fig. VIII-5) comprises, in its simplest form, a glass or ceramic sleeve fitting snugly over a commercial shielded thermocouple, $\frac{1}{16}$ OD. Reaction products which escape freely

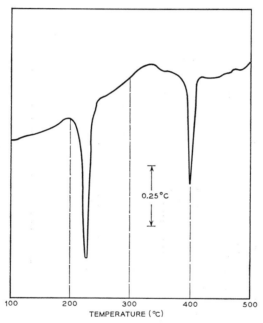

0.25°C

100   200   300   400   500
TEMPERATURE (°C)

Fig. VII-6. Thermogram of 0.3 mg cobalt oxalate hydrate. From Garn (G5).
The inhibited diffusion eliminates exterior atmosphere effect for small samples as well as large. Compare with Figs. VIII-3 and XI-15.

from the free-diffusion sample holder are retained because of the long, narrow escape path. The major portion of the decomposition takes place in one atmosphere of the product gas, and consequently the reactions occur at some higher but more reproducible temperature than with other sample arrangements. Reactions with atmosphere oxygen do not take place.

Figure VIII-6 shows a thermogram of cobalt oxalate hydrate and Fig. VIII-7 shows one of copper sulfate pentahydrate. Even with the small 0.3- and 2.0-mg samples the deflections are well-defined. The base line drifts significantly because of the difficulty of matching but the drift is not enough to inhibit measurement.

The work of Mazières (M21) with specimens in the tens of micrograms range shows both a particular use and a limitation of small samples. The use is in the study of effects of lattice strain or imperfection, in this case induced by irradiation; the limitation is the possibility that a particular sample of the material under investigation might show deviations in behavior of no interest in the particular study. The furnace is shown in Fig. VIII-8.

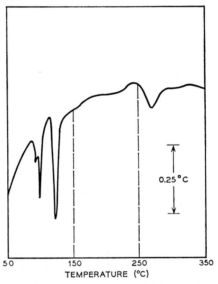

Fɪɢ. VIII-7. Thermogram of copper sulfate pentahydrate. From Garn (G5).
The effect of the first dehydration and subsequent vaporization of water ca 100°C can be seen clearly.

The three microsample holders are used in the manner described in Chapter IV, Sec. 4.5. There is, of course, no sample block of the usual type. The heat effect need only be large enough to affect the temperature of the very small cup. This is surrounded by a chamber which is—hopefully—very symmetrically heated. The great sensitivity is shown in Fig. VIII-9, where the droplet of mercury has enough heat of fusion $(2.8 \times 10^{-5}$ cal) to produce a melting endotherm of more than half a degree. (A furnace designed to permit subzero operation was used.)

The study of effects of radiation, strain, etc., might very advantageously be carried out by microtechniques. Figure VIII-10 shows data on irradiated lithium fluoride. Note the variation in curves a, e, f, and g;

the conclusion is clearly that the history of the particle has a very important effect on the thermogram.

A more general conclusion is that, if one obtains thermograms of single particles or small assemblages of particles, the thermal and physical history of the individual particles will show effects superimposed on the thermal effects characteristic of the material. In larger quantities the variations among the individual particles would be diluted and only the characteristics common to all would persist. It follows that if one plans to study the intrinsic properties of a material one must use a specimen in which nonintrinsic properties can be destroyed or at least diluted. The thought of running enough differential thermal analyses for a statistical treatment is appalling.

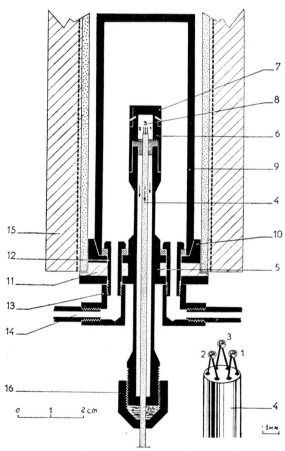

Fig. VIII-8. Furnace and sample holder for differential thermal analysis of very small samples. From Mazières (M21).

Samples down to a few micrograms can show very easily detectable thermal effects.

In summary, very small samples can be used effectively if used intelligently. Atmosphere control is just as important as with larger samples and must be used with more care. The characteristics peculiar to a given particle may have sufficient effect on the thermogram to lead the user to ascribe these characteristics to the whole sample (see also Chapter XI, Sec. 11.1).

8.3. Pelleted Samples

Walton (W3) attempted to obtain better sensitivity (Fig. VIII-11) by pressing the specimens into pellets and supporting these pellets on the

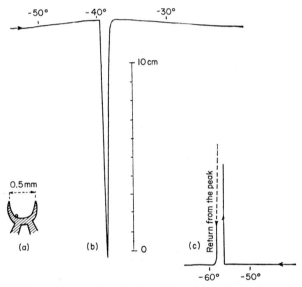

Fig. VIII-9. Thermogram of a droplet of mercury, showing heating and cooling peaks. From Mazières (M21).

The melting of 10 µg Hg gives a signal of ca. 0.8°C.

thermocouple insulators but otherwise isolated from the furnace wall. He compared these pellets with similar ones heated in a block and reported "a much greater sensitivity . . . in the low-temperature range than with . . . the Inconel block." This means that in the dehydration of kaolin a greater pen deflection was obtained with the isolated sample than with an identical pellet in the block. This is no guarantee that the curve is more useful.

The inflection (curve C, Fig. VIII-12) for the isolated sample is about 20% greater in peak height than for the pellet in the block (curve B); unfortunately, it is also about 60% broader. This means that any other reaction overlapping this nearly 200°C interval will interfere and be interfered with. Sensitivity, however, must be judged on the ability of the technique under examination to detect a material in small quantities, to detect it as a separate entity in a mixture, or to separate reactions within a single material. Obtaining a greater deflection is not in itself a suitable goal. The curves offered by Walton would lead the present author to choose the block technique. The reasons for the appearance

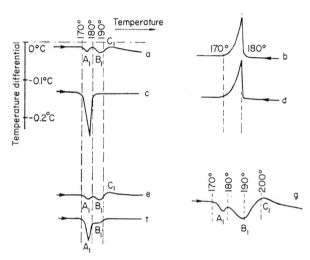

FIG. VIII-10. Thermograms of irradiated fragments of lithium fluoride: a, first heating, b, first cooling, c, second heating, and d, second cooling of a single fragment; e, part of another fragment; f, the other part of this fragment after preheating at < 160°C; and g, rapid (30°C/minute) heating of another fragment of the same crystal. From Mazières M21).

On very small samples, localized effects can appear to have significant influence in the characteristics of the material.

of the thermograms of the isolated samples are discussed in Chapter VII. The broad low-temperature deflection in curve C is probably due to differences in heat transfer. The emissivity of the calcined reference can be expected to be higher than that of the sample (see Chapter III).

Pellet techniques can be useful, however; they, like other techniques, must be used with discretion—selecting the best method to obtain the most instructive data. Newkirk (N7), for example, uses a pellet technique for phase equilibria studies. Since no decompositions are involved, the exposed surface is not in itself advantageous; the advantage lies in the elimination of any sample holder at all. The work reported is in the 1300–1500°C range so heat transfer occurs principally by radiation. A sample holder serves no function except—when necessary—to hold the sample.

Newkirk presses his samples in a mold and sinters them at a temperature ca. 50°C below the first liquidus formation. A hole is drilled in the specimen, it is slid over the thermocouple wires, and the thermocouple

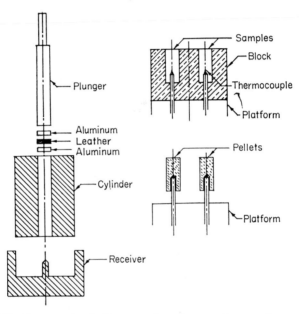

Fɪɢ. VIII-11. Cross sectional diagram of equipment for pressing and mounting pellets. From Walton (W3).

The pellets are supported by the thermocouples and are exposed directly to the wall of the furnace.

wires are joined in a rather large bead (0.025-inch wire, 0.070-inch bead). The bead then supports the sample (Fig. IV-11). Another simplification is possible here, the elimination of a reference body. To the thermocouple, the sample appears at a shield, shading it in part from direct radiation from the furnace wall, i.e., intercepting much of the radiation and reradiating at a lower temperature. This condition can be easily simulated by drawing the reference couple up so that it is partially recessed in the protection tube. Quite satisfactory curves (Fig. VIII-13) were obtained.

8.4. Fluidized-Bed Differential Thermal Analysis

A case in which improper use of a new approach vitiated the results was the fluidized-bed differential thermal analysis reported by Basden (B14, B15). His arrangement, shown in Fig. VIII-14, provides for fluidizing both the external heat-transfer medium and the pair of specimens.

A fluidized bed is an arrangement in which a bed of particles levitate by reason of an upward gas stream through the bed. Figure VIII-15 shows the nature of the velocity-of-flow effect of the gas stream. At low flows, the gas must penetrate the bed by diffusing through the tedious paths between the particles; as the flow is increased, the pressure drop across the bed increases. At some point dependent on the nature (particle size, density, etc.) of the bed the upward push exceeds the downward pull of gravity and the particles will be lifted. Lifting of the

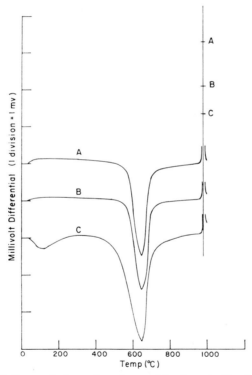

Fig. VIII-12. Differential thermal analyses of kaolin: A, Hand-packed specimen heated in Inconel block; B, pressed, dried sample heated in Inconel block; and C, pressed, dried sample heated in air. From Walton (W3).

The exposed pellet technique shows a greater deflection (C) but its broadness shows an even greater increase; this leads to a greater possibility of overlapping reactions.

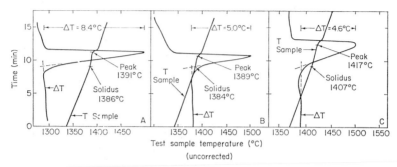

Fɪɢ. VIII-13. Typical differential thermal analysis curves obtained by pellet method for some compositions in the system CaO–2CaO•Fe$_2$O$_3$–12CaO•7Al$_2$O$_3$. From New-kirk (N7).

The absence of any sort of heat sink permits a quite large ΔT signal.

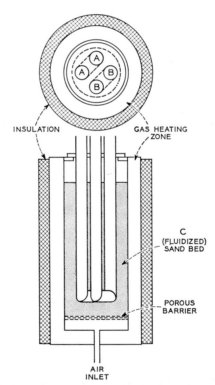

Fɪɢ. VIII-14. Fluidized-bed differential thermal analysis apparatus. From Bas-den (B14).

Fluidized-bed heat transfer is used not only for the gross heating of sample and reference but also to achieve thermal homogeneity within each of the two speci-mens.

particles expands the openings so the pressure gradient across the bed drops rather sharply. This would tend to permit the particles to drop back into a bed except that the consequent formation of narrow paths would increase the (local) upward force and the particles would again levitate. The result is a rapid, more-or-less turbulent movement of the particles both vertically and laterally. This rapid movement and the consequent frequent collisions provide rapid transfer of heat and hence very good temperature homogeneity within the bed.

If Basden had fluidized either the heat-transfer bed or the pair of specimens, some advantage should accrue for reasons explained below; fluidizing both gave the plots shown in Fig. VIII-16 and in which the

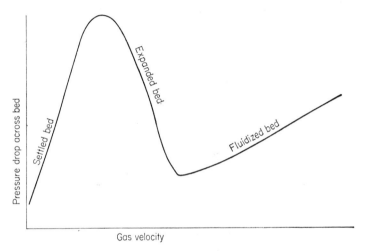

Fig. VIII-15. Fluidization of finely-divided solids. From Zenz and Othmer (Z1).
When the gas velocity becomes high enough, the particles lift with little motion, allowing a decrease in the pressure drop. Continued increase in gas velocity lifts the particles so that they are individually supported and free to move.

principal distinguishing features are (besides the peaks due to introduction of steam) the sudden shifts (ca. 40°C) due to agglomeration of the Liddell and Greta specimens. The general trend of oxidation shown in the bottom set of curves illustrates the over-all problem.

The benefits of fluidized-bed systems are derived from the rapid motion, but this rapid motion brings about the loss of identity of any single particle and hence the inability to measure the properties (especially the temperature) of any except the whole group. Consider a relatively cool fluidized bed in contact with a suddenly heated wall. While the mass of the bed is still cool, the particles impinging on the wall are heated to a temperature far greater than their counterparts away from the wall. The hot particles circulate into the cooler regions, losing heat to the cooler particles they encounter but leaving many particles pro tempore untouched and still cool. The apparent temperature of the bed rises nonetheless because any measuring device we would care to use treats the particles on a statistical basis. We have, then, in such a system a distribution of particle temperatures over a range from the initial

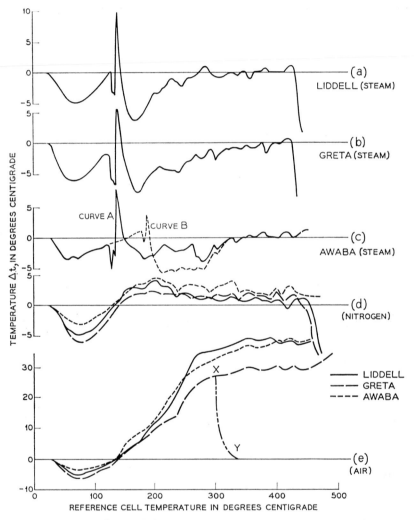

Fɪɢ. VIII-16. Differential thermal analysis of coals by the fluidized-bed technique. From Basden (B15).

Other than the effect of steam injection the only sharply defined feature is the agglomeration of two of the coals.

(for a short time) temperature to something approaching the wall temperature.

Now examine the technique used by Basden. The sample and reference cells are set into a hot fluidized bed thus reproducing the conditions just described. Some of the coal particles are heated substantially above the measured temperature; others are not. When—in the presence of oxygen—the particle can oxidize, it will oxidize, contributing to an exothermal indication at a relatively low temperature. The general exothermic trend in Fig. VIII-16 is due, then, to a steady increase in the rate at which the particles reach the reaction temperature. A number of reasons can be advanced for the leveling off. One of these is the combination of the decrease in unreacted particles and the increase in ease of reaction. (Since the particle is already approaching temperature, the likelihood of a collision raising it to the reaction temperature is increasing.) Another condition contributing to the trend is the probability of successive reactions. In fluidized-bed specimens, these will necessarily be smeared together for the reasons given above. Still another factor contributing to the poor resolution in Basden's studies is the probable interruption of exothermic reactions by cooling. Recall that in a non-fluidized bed of particles heated from a wall a temperature gradient from the wall inward (Chapter II) will be set up. For endothermic changes, a reaction front moves from the wall inward as the temperature of reaction is reached and passed. An exothermic reaction, on the other hand, can supply not only heat to continue its own temperature rise but also heat to warm the neighboring—inward—particles so that they, too, reach the reaction temperature. The process (unless a second phase such as oxygen is needed but is in short supply) is self-sustaining and is consequently rapid. Now contrast this to Basden's fluidized-bed thermal analysis.

Assume only that each particle will react chemically with oxygen (other than by ordinary combustion) as long as the particle is at or exceeds some temperature T_r and as long as the particle is not completely reacted. Let a fluidized bed of these particles be exposed to a suddenly heated ($<T_r$) wall. The first multitudes of collisions will probably not raise a significant portion of the entire specimen to T_r but eventually this must happen. As previously described, the hot particle—in the normal course of circulation—will collide with many cooler particles and give up heat to them, warming them—but to temperatures less than T_r. The net effect is a partially reacted particle and a number of particles warmer than they would have been in the ordinary course of heating; the over-all effect is an exothermal trend. As the general temperature level is raised, the partial oxidations will occur more and more fre-

quently, and the general effect shown to the observer—by the recording equipment—will be an increasing exothermic effect while the measured temperature is still below T_r. The increase must stop eventually because of the formation of completely reacted particles, but since these are ready for further oxidation in this stepwise process the shape of the curve would be difficult to predict. The curves given by Basden are, at least, not in contradiction to this discussion.

The fluidized-bed technique for maintaining a nearly uniform temperature in the specimen, we may conclude, will lead to uninterpretable results if a wide range of particle temperatures is permitted. It would be necessary to control the rate of rise of the wall temperature. The use of fluidized beds for both specimens and heat transfer in differential thermal analysis is subject to uncertainty because the huge (apparent) thermal conductivities leave little to measure. Use of a fluidized bed for heat transfer to an orthodox specimen could be quite useful because of the temperature homogeneity.

Fluidized-bed specimens may lead to some interesting results. Eriksson (E5), for example, showed that the peak area was proportional to the heats of reaction if the reaction were occurring at the same rate throughout the specimen. Borchardt and Daniels (B67) derived expressions for determining the kinetics of reactions assuming temperature homogeneity; they necessarily confined their use to stirred liquids. Fluidized beds may permit better use of Eriksson's work and a *valid* extension of Borchardt and Daniels' work to reactions of solids. The experiment would best be done in rather isolated specimen holders.

8.5. Furnaces Providing Visual Observation of Specimens

There is occasionally a need—and frequently a desire—to keep the specimen under visual observation during the heating cycle. There is no question that the observation may be useful. Hogan and Gordon (H20) attacked the problem by heating their test tube specimen holders from below with a laboratory electric "burner" (Fig. VIII-17). They pointed out that thermomicroscopy was not well-adapted for measuring thermal effects because of the space needed for the sample and measuring elements. Programming and recording were both inhibited greatly by heat-transfer problems after the appearance of a liquid phase (Fig. VIII-18); part of their difficulty in programming was due to the relatively small heat reservoir and part to the location of the control point for their controller. A control point should not be located at any point where it might be affected by short-term variations in the specimen, i.e., heat effect, unless one is deliberately permitting the disturbance (see Chapter IV). A better approach ought to be the use of an ordinary quartz tube furnace with some apertures in the winding to permit the visual observation.

The most important consideration is the avoidance of any direct path for loss of heat, i.e., there must be a heated surface or a space containing heated gas between the specimen and the observer. This is because the observer does not see the part of the specimen the thermocouple "sees"

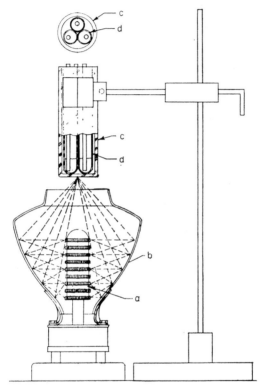

Fig. VIII-17. Schematic diagram of electric Bunsen burner and sample tubes: a, Heating element; b, aluminum reflector; c, quartz tube; d, borosilicate glass sample tubes. From Hogan and Gordon (H20).

The sample can be observed from the side as well as the top.

and hence is looking at a part of the specimen which is almost certainly at a measurably different—and likely at a severely different—temperature from that indicated by the recording system. In Hogan and Gordon's apparatus the temperature of the observed material is no doubt hotter than that near the thermocouple; on the other hand, if a sample block is heated directly and one attempts to look at the surface of a specimen, the observed point is no doubt cooler than the indicated temperature. A transparent dome above a directly heated block will require deep immersion of the specimen so that observation would be impractical. The high convection currents would cause the outer portion of the block to lag too greatly behind the inner regions. A filled sample cavity would experience a considerable gradient at elevated temperatures.

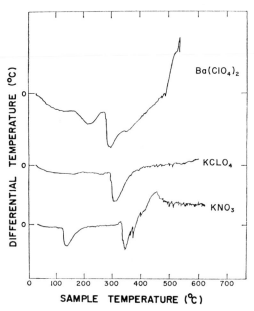

FIG. VIII-18. Representative DTA curves obtained by using electric Bunsen burner. From Hogan and Gordon (H20).

The exothermic displacement of the signal after appearance of the liquid phase is due to the greater transparency of the liquid to the radiated heat. The "noise" may be due to sample movement resulting from bubbling.

The disparity in the case of the block will increase with temperature for the quite obvious reason that loss or gain of heat by radiation becomes more important. If the block is heated from an exterior wall by radiation and/or convection, the problem will be serious only if a large portion of the exposed spherical angle projects toward cool surfaces.

8.6. Change of Atmosphere

Differential thermal analysis need not be done only by changing the temperature regularly. Thermal effects are in some cases detectable upon changing the total pressure or the partial pressure of a gas. Stone (S58, S59) uses both techniques. In studying catalysts he raises the temperature in an inert atmosphere then injects the desired atmosphere and observes the transient change in temperature resulting from the absorption or, more particularly, the chemisorption of this gas on the active catalyst. The heat generated is taken as a measure of catalytic activity.

Crandall and West (C25) used a rather similar technique in studying the oxidation of cobalt. The sample was brought to the selected temperature in flowing nitrogen and a flow of air substituted for the nitrogen. Oxidation of the cobalt is observed as an exothermic reaction. The reaction was not instantaneous; measurements continued for ca. 30 minutes. The reasons for the slowness of reaction are discussed in Chapter VIII.

Stone (S58) also diminished the pressure as a function of time to determine the moisture content of samples. Within a porous somewhat moist specimen an equilibrium will be set up between the moisture on the particles and in the air in the interstices. This condition can persist because the exchange of air between the sample and its surroundings is slow. Now let us decrease the pressure at a steady rate. The adsorbed water will tend to evaporate to maintain the partial pressure corresponding to the vapor pressure at the room temperature, but eventually the total pressure will be diminished below the vapor pressure (see Chapter VII) and evaporation will be accelerated, giving a measurable thermal effect. Stone provides the example shown in Fig. VIII-19. The evaporation will cool the sample, tending toward a steady state in which the new temperature will correspond to a water vapor pressure equal to the instantaneous total pressure. Since the total pressure is decreasing constantly, the evaporation cannot cool the sample to a steady state, but the over-all effect of the accelerated evaporation is a rather sharp thermal effect which can be related to the total moisture.

Stone uses the peak height as a measure of the moisture content. Essentially the peak height—rather than the area—would be a measure of the mass of water available for evaporation at the time the vapor is suddenly pulled away. At room temperature heat transfer will not be very rapid so that the peak height should depend directly on the amount of water (hence indirectly on the total amount of water) and inversely on the heat capacity, with only one condition: the evaporation must be rapid; the entire peak should be obtained in a few seconds. If, because of surface conditions, the evaporation becomes slow, some more elaborate calibrations may be needed.

8.7. Pyrosynthesis

Dunne and Kerr (D17) measured thermal effects during pyrosynthesis by differential thermal analysis while investigating a series of solid solutions of lead sulfide (galena) and lead selenide (clausthalite) using the technique previously reported by Bollin *et al.* (B62). They sealed the weighed constituents into a Pyrex tube having a thermocouple recess (Fig. VIII-20). A similar tube was used as reference. The reaction temperature increased as the sulfur was increased (Fig. VIII-21 and VIII-22). Differential thermal analysis curves (in air) of the synthesized materials are interpreted by the authors as evidence for a con-

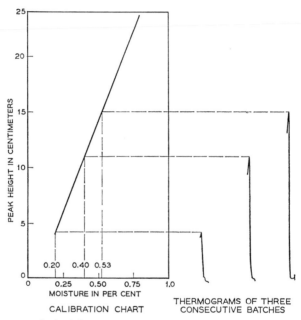

Fɪɢ. VIII-19. Method of determining moisture content of dry powders by evacuation. Sample, undiluted; thermogram, room temperature; instrument range, 20 μv. From Stone (S58).

The sudden vaporization as the furnace pressure is brought below the vapor pressure of water provides a measure of the amount of water.

tinuous series of solid solutions, even though some of these curves show two distinct oxidation peaks (D17). These two minerals have nearly the same lattice parameters so one might readily suspect a complete series of solid solutions. The present author is not ready to dispute the conclusion but he is ready to point out that the thermal data offered are not adequate proof. An alternative interpretation of Figs. VIII-21 and VIII-22 can be supplied.

Consider the curves shown in Fig. VIII-21. They are characterized by a huge exothermic peak due to reaction of lead with sulfur, selenium, or both. Selenium reacts ca. 160°C and sulfur ca. 210°C, 50°C difference. The exotherms go off scale in each case indicating—from examination of the description of Bollin *et al.* (B62)—a temperature difference substantially greater than 12°C. This large difference is indicated on a thermocouple separated from the reacting specimen by a layer of Pyrex so it is easily conceivable that the temperature within the sample reached 210°C and initiated the lead-sulfur reaction. Since this is exo-

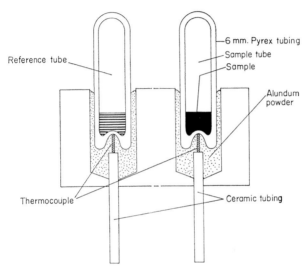

FIG. VIII-20. Sealed-tube specimen holders for relatively low-temperature thermal analysis. From Bollin *et al.* (B62).
The recess in the tube ensures that a large spherical angle around the thermocouple is directed toward the sample.

thermic there would be no recognizable indication with the experimental method used. (The present author has found sudden temperature increases of more than 100°C in some reactions.) The variation of initiation temperature with quantity of the lower temperature–reacting species is almost certainly no more than a concentration effect. The sharp increase of initiation temperature at the high-sulfur end is a consequence of the lack of enough selenium to raise the temperature locally to the lead-sulfur reaction temperature.

In this sort of experiment it is essential that the *sample* temperature be recorded rather than the furnace or reference temperature (see Chapter IV).

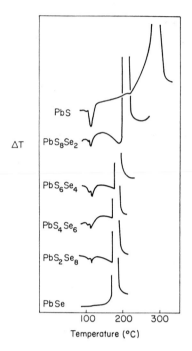

FIG. VIII-21. Differential thermal pyrosynthesis (DTP) curves. The samples comprise a 20 mole % synthetic PbS-PbSe series. From Dunne and Kerr (D17). *Endothermic deflections are to the right.*

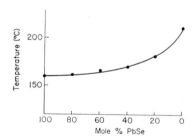

FIG. VIII-22. Pyrosynthesis reaction (formation) temperature vs molar composition. The samples listed are those whose DTP curves are given in Fig. VIII-21. From Dunne and Kerr (D17).

The reaction temperature is increased only slightly until the sulfur content is very high.

8.8. Differential Calorimetry

In Chapter I differential calorimetry and differential thermal analysis were compared on the basis of sensitivity and the reasons and precautions set forth. We are now in a position to examine a particular type of differential calorimetry, i.e., that in which the temperatures of the sample and reference containers provide the differential signal.

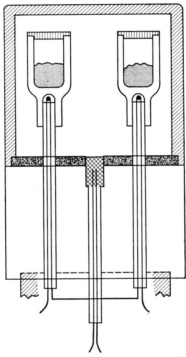

Fig. VIII-23. Sample holder for dynamic differential calorimetry. From Schweite and Ziegler (S15).
    For isolated reactions, heat changes can be measured with good precision.

Schweite and Ziegler (S15) used sample holders of the type shown in Fig. VIII-23 to obtain quantitative data on some decompositions. Note that these differ from Boersma (B58) sample holders in that Boersma measured the temperature in the major heat-transfer path while Schweite and Ziegler provided no special heat path but simply compared the temperatures of the bottom portions of the holders. The temperature distribution within the specimen is of no concern since the measurement is made over the entire thermal effect. Reproducible data on isolated heat effects can be and have been obtained in this manner.

The measurement of temperature of the sample holder yields a thermogram with a smoothed-over indication of the thermal event, the actual
heat absorption or evolution having to cause a change in temperature of
the sample holder as well as that of the sample itself. Further, the temperature of the sample itself is not known particularly well, the possible
error being very greatly dependent on the sample holder size and design.

Note that a relatively large specimen will have a major influence on
the measured temperature with a reasonably thin sample container but
the temperature gradients within the sample are also large and the center of the sample may be at a temperature quite different from that
measured. Similarly, if the sample is small in relation to the holder the
temperature effect becomes dependent on possible variations in heat
transfer to the specimens; even though these variations are relatively

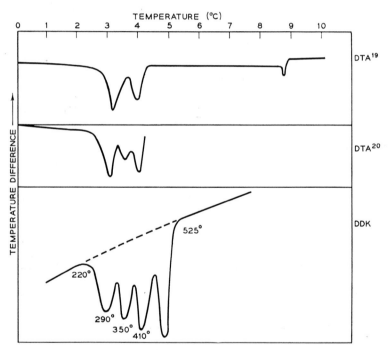

Fig. VIII-24. Dynamic differential calorimetry and differential thermal analysis of
lead carbonate. From Schweite and Ziegler (S15).

*The temperature gradient in the sample and the lack of heat transfer between
sample and reference inhibit approach of the signal to any base line between peaks
because (1) both reactions are occurring at the same time in different parts of
sample and (2) the "decay" time of the temperature difference is too great.*

minor in a large sample because of averaging, a change in the heat transfer for any reason would cause a more serious change in temperature lag than in a large sample. Figure VIII-24 shows Schwiete and Ziegler's thermogram of lead carbonate. The additional peak is not explained.

The present author uses specimen holders rather similar to those of Schwiete and Ziegler (Fig. IV-15), but only when the information sought calls for that particular technique.

8.9. Heats of Explosion

The violently exothermic reaction of an explosion provides an essentially instantaneous quantity of heat which—even with special apparatus —would be impracticable to measure continuously. The customary method of determining heats of explosion is by calorimetry, but since this normally requires a substantial sample there is a need for a method better adaptable to small samples. Bohon (B60) used a form of differential calorimetry, the apparatus for which is described in Chapter IV. In essence, Bohon measures the decay curve as the sample cell returns to the furnace temperature to calibrate the apparatus. The heat generated during the explosion is then calculated from the area under the peak in the conventional manner (see also Vold V10).

Providing that the heat is generated over a brief interval of time as in Fig. VIII-25 and assuming near constancy of heat capacity, emissivity,

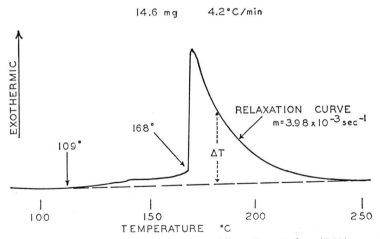

FIG. VIII-25. Thermogram of JPN propellant. From Bohon (B60).

The change in temperature with time after the explosion is used to measure the heat of explosion. JPN is a homogeneous solid propellant comprising principally nitroglycerin and nitrocellulose.

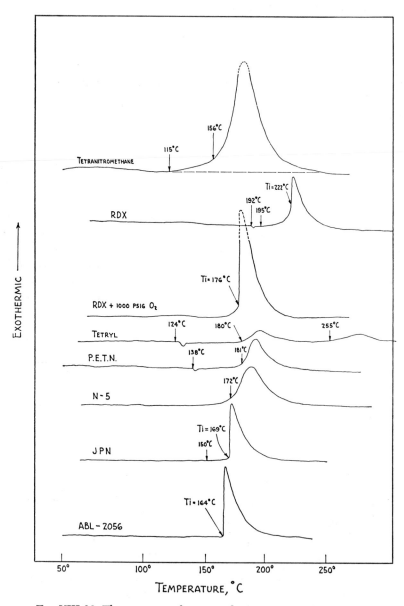

FIG. VIII-26. Thermograms of some explosives. From Bohon (B60).
The reaction in some cases is very rapid, indicated by a steep rise from the base line.

and such, the return follows the decay law,

$$\frac{d\Delta T}{dt} = -m\Delta T.$$

Experimentally the return to the base line follows the decay law only approximately so actual measurement of the area under curve is more suitable. The area measurement would have to be used in those cases (Fig. VIII-26) where the reaction was slower.

8.10. Freezing Range Measurements in Clays

The melting point of a pure bulk material can be reasonably expected to be reproducible; when the material is deformed its melting behavior may change very appreciably. From a thermodynamic point of view a layer of water absorbed on a clay is deformed relative to bulk water. It follows that determination of the temperature range through which the water on a wet clay melts might be related to the amount of water actually absorbed. Rosenthal (R31) used the arrangement shown in Fig. VIII-27 to measure "freezing ranges" of clay-water mixtures, relating data such as those of Fig. VIII-28 to the plasticity of the clay, a high

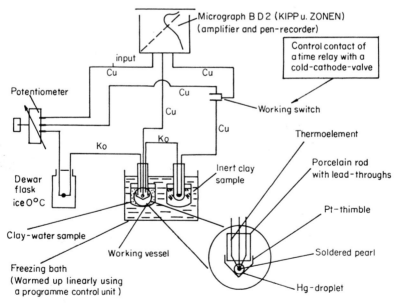

Fig. VIII-27. An apparatus for the freezing analysis of clay-water systems. From Rosenthal (R31).

Any supercooling effects are eliminated by cooling at least to −55°C.

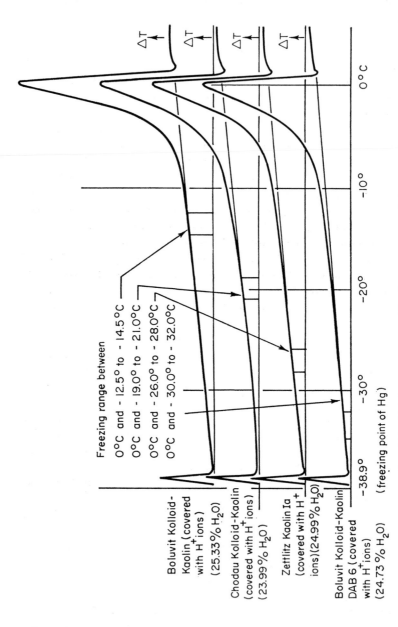

Freezing range between

0°C and -12.5° to -14.5°C
0°C and -19.0° to -21.0°C
0°C and -26.0° to -28.0°C
0°C and -30.0° to -32.0°C

Boluvit Kolloid-Kaolin (covered with H⁺ ions) (25.33% H_2O)

Chodau Kolloid-Kaolin (covered with H⁺ ions) (23.99% H_2O)

Zettlitz Kaolin Ia (covered with H⁺ ions)(24.99% H_2O)

Boluvit Kolloid-Kaolin DAB 6 (covered with H⁺ ions) (24.73% H_2O)

-38.9°   -30°   -20°   -10°   0°C

(freezing point of Hg)

Fig. VIII-28. Freezing curves of kaolin. From Rosenthal (R31).
The lower the temperature of the "freezing range" the greater the plasticity.

degree of water adsorption—indicated by a wide freezing range—corresponding to a high plasticity.

8.11. Derivative and Differential Techniques

In differential thermal analysis we have already departed from use of the primary signal, i.e., the temperature of the sample. We have done so in order to gain sensitivity in detecting changes. An important question is whether or not there is any advantage in continuing further. The procedures can (prima facie) be very simple and for crystallographic phase changes the interpretation should in fact be simple. Let us first consider the differential techniques and subsequently the derivative.

Double differential thermal analysis is a technique in which a reactive specimen is compared with a reactive reference. The present author has attempted—on a few occasions—to detect shifts in reaction temperature of superficially identical specimens by treating one as sample and the other as reference. This is done in the hope that equal reactions at identical temperatures will cancel each other's thermoelectric effect and supply a straight-line plot. Another method of use is to attempt to subtract the thermal effect of one (or more) materials so as to permit better observation and measurement of the thermal effect of another component. One example of the author's use of this technique was an attempt to measure the Curie point shift in isotopes of nickel (S9). Samples of Ni^{60} and Ni^{62} were compared with Ni^{58}. Readable variations were obtained although no conclusion could be reached because impurities, especially copper, could have affected the Curie point to a greater degree than the additional mass.

A prospective user of the method must necessarily demonstrate that his sample containers are heated very uniformly. If either leads the other in temperature, its contents will begin to react first and show a portion of the thermal effect. This will soon be cancelled or diminished by the thermal effect in the other container. Since the reaction in the first container is concluded while reactive material is still present in the other, the total thermal effect will finish with a more or less symmetric (to the first) deflection.

The major proponent of the technique is McLaughlin (M29). His optimism is not entirely justified but with proper care the technique should be of use in special problems. McLaughlin's illite: kaolinite mixtures are, in general, attempts to observe and measure illite in the presence of kaolinite. He concedes that "the quantitative analysis of kaolinite and illite mixtures are . . . fraught with difficulties. . . ." One of these difficulties was his inability to subtract out the kaolinite reactions by placing an equal amount (diluted with alumina) in the "reference" cavity. One source must—in this case—be unsymmetric heating.

McLaughlin also points out the effect of wet and dry mixing on the high-temperature reactions: ". . . in wet mixes the exothermic peak (ca. 950°C) due to kaolinite is considerably lower in temperature . . ." and "a tendency also for the 850°C endothermic reactions due to illite to sharpen. . . ." Although McLaughlin specifies only "mechanical mixing" a reasonable assumption is that a ball mill was used. Ball milling for extended periods has been shown to be deleterious to differential thermal analysis peaks (M28). Shaking in water may in time cause as many fractures of crystals but water is immediately available for adsorption on any active regions as well as to prevent local heating.

Let us now compare the effects of the grinding with the wet mixing. The additional surface energy gained during the dry grinding lowers and broadens the differential thermal analysis endotherm because it produces surface regions with a wide range of energies. The first reactions must consequently be rather diffuse in the dry mix compared to a thoroughly hydrated wet mix. But this only applies to the first reaction in which a recrystallization takes place. From this point on the reactivity will depend on the other attributes of the mixing methods, i.e., differences in particle size, crystallinity, and intimacy of mixing. The "sharpening" of the 850°C illite endotherm is probably the result of comparing a fully hydrated with an incompletely hydrated system. The lowering of the kaolinite exotherm is attributed by McLaughlin to catalysis by the breakdown products of the illite, but Stone and Rowland (S60) and the present author (G9) have found that decomposition of kaolinite in water vapor tends to lower the temperature of and broaden the exotherm (Fig. VIII-29).

In the use of this technique, the experimenter must satisfy himself that symmetry of heating exists. A reasonable test is the use of identical specimens in each cup in a separate run. These specimens must have (in ordinary differential thermal analysis) an endotherm or exotherm with at least as great a slope and maximum deflection as the specimens under investigation. A double differential thermal analysis of these specimens will establish limits of significance for the sample of interest; that is, a deflection must be greater than the maximum deflection in the test run before any confidence may be placed in its reality. The same criterion must be established for the subtraction of thermal effects.

Almost inevitably, any worker determined to perform double differential thermal analysis must sacrifice uniformity of heating of the individual specimens, i.e., cylindrical chambers, in favor of symmetric heating of the two specimens. For this purpose, some type of gradient heating arrangement may be best. An example, conceived but not tested by the author, would comprise a three-leaved bar with cubic sample cavities cut into the center leaf. The loaded sample holder would be inserted partly into a vertical furnace and allowed to heat from the top down. The atmosphere effect would be essentially that of a closed chamber.

A technique using two identical samples but having asymmetry of heating *and* of thermocouples was proposed by Freeman and Edelman (F15). Two 18-mm-diameter test tubes were set in an eccentrically located Nichrome block; the test tube nearer to the wall had a thermocouple junction 5 mm from the bottom of the tube while the junction in

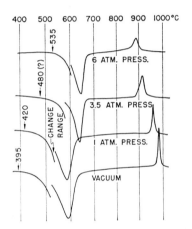

Fig. VIII-29. Thermograms of kaolinite under different pressures. From Stone and Rowland (S60).

The fact that the water vapor pressure must reach different levels in the several runs leads to a change in environment during dehydroxylation sufficient to affect the exothermic reaction substantially.

the other tube was 8 mm from the bottom. The sample nearer the furnace is somewhat warmer as the furnace heats up and consequently reaches the temperature of any thermal event more quickly. In the case of a phase transition, such as in Fig. VIII-30, the temperature differential drops toward zero as the transition front moves inward. (Note that this is an experimental ΔT rather than $d\Delta T/dt$; the scale shown by Freeman and Edelman is calculated.) It drops very near to zero because the ordinary heating of the "reference" brings its temperature at the thermocouple close to the transition temperature as the material near the "sample" thermocouple undergoes transition. The assymmetry of the latter portion of the upper plot is due to the geometric asymmetry. Both samples are returning toward steady-state heating but are not at identical points (in time) of the return nor is the temperature differential taken between corresponding points.

The appearance of such a plot will be sensitive to spacing and to heating rate. This could be alleviated somewhat by putting the differential thermocouple in a single sample (see Fig. IV-15b).

The general purpose derivative techniques suggested by Campbell *et al.* (C4) use electromechanical amplification to obtain a signal large enough to differentiate and record without further electronic amplification. The slidewire shaft of the recorder measuring the primary function

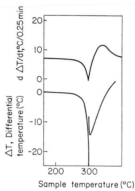

FIG. VIII-30. Derivative differential (upper) and differential (lower) thermal analyses of potassium perchlorate. From Freeman and Edelman (F15).

The upper curve measures the differential temperature between eccentrically located samples. Symmetry cannot be expected.

(Δt, Δw, etc.) is fitted with a "retransmitting" slidewire. Movement of this slidewire as the recorder pen moves changes the voltage (Fig. VIII-31) read off the slidewire at the contact. This voltage is supplied to a differentiating capacitor; since direct current cannot flow through a capacitor the charge on the capacitor will follow the position of the slidewire. If this charge should change due to movement of the slidewire, a current must flow through the resistor on the right-hand side to charge—or discharge—the differentiating capacitor to the new level. This flow of current creates a potential drop which can be measured by the second recorder (see Chapter XV).

Generally, in constructing such a circuit one would choose capacitors and resistors so that the time constant, RC, was less than the pen speed (time required for full-scale travel) of the recorder and the resistance was not greater than the input impedance of the recorder. Too large a time constant will mean that the recorder can follow a charging current and produce a record showing a false rounding or slow approach to a steady value, much like an overdamped balance or galvanometer. Too large a resistance will result in loss of sensitivity. Campbell *et al.* were faced with an additional problem, a "noisy" recorder. Their solution was a smoothing capacitor across the recorder input. Since this capacitor has to be charged and discharged, it becomes the major contributor to the time constants of 4 seconds for the upper and 40 seconds for the lower circuit. They offer the curves shown in Fig. VIII-32.

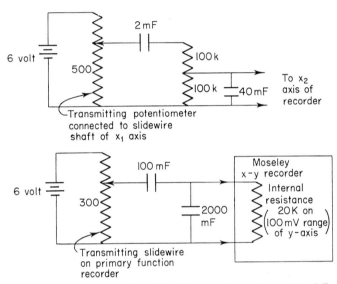

Fig. VIII-31. Circuit diagram for *R-C* differentiation. Top: *R-C* differentiating circuit for use with potentiometric recorders. Bottom: *R-C* differentiating circuit for use with Moseley *x-y* recorder. From Campbell (C4).

The movement of the recorder pen shaft changes the voltage on the differentiating capacitor causing a current to flow during and shortly after the movement. The heavy filtering by the 40- and 2000-mfd capacitors is required to avoid signals due to the "jitter" of the recorder shaft on which the transmitting slidewire is mounted.

Their major error was in their choice of the signal to differentiate. The jitter that is common on a number of kinds of recorders does not—or should not—affect the input signal appreciably. This input signal can be differentiated by a similar circuit (Fig. XVI-9) and amplified electronically if necessary to produce a rapidly responding system. The same type of circuit may be inserted between amplifier and recorder. The present author has done this merely as an exercise and obtained good, readable curves (Fig. VIII-33). Since the present author has not yet seen any real gain in the use of a derivative signal in differential thermal analysis, the resistor and capacitor were soon put back in the electrical-parts drawer. (Thermogravimetry is quite another question; see Chapter X.)

8.12. Sealed Tube Sample Holders

A frequently occurring problem involves samples which decompose before melting or at least before the thermal effect of interest. If the product gas is easily handled and if the equilibrium pressure is not very high, ordinary controlled atmosphere techniques may be used. If, however, the pressure is unduly high or if the gas is not easily handled, sealed sample holder techniques may be needed (see also Sections 8.7 and 8.9).

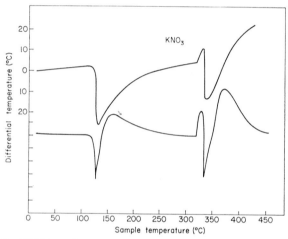

FIG. VIII-32. DDTA and DTA curves of potassium nitrate. From Campbell *et al.* (C4).

The asymmetry in the lower plot is attributable not only to the sample but also to mechanical and electrical characteristics.

Many fluorides, for example, have quite substantial fluorine vapor pressures below their melting points. The pressure at the melting point of the salt may be several atmospheres. Fluorine is, of course, quite difficult to handle at these pressures and temperatures near 1000°C. In the author's laboratory the customary solution is the use of sealed tubes (see Fig. VIII-34). These sealed-tube sample holders are constructed from 20 mil platinum–20% rhodium commercially available tubes. The tubes are ¼ inch in diameter. In use, a 1- to 2-inch section of tubing is cut off with an ordinary tubing cutter, and one end is crimped with a cable cutter fitted with rounded jaws to permit crimping without breaking the metal. The crimped end is then welded securely using a carbon arc.

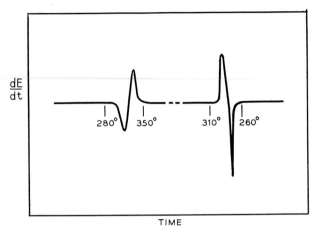

Fɪɢ. VIII-33. Derivative differential thermal analysis curves for potassium per-chlorate using the differentiating circuit of Fig. XVI-9 at the output of the amplifier. *The asymmetry is almost entirely attributable to the sample (see Fig. II-11).*

The sample is now loaded into the open end to the extent of one-eighth to one-third the total depth of the tube, and the open end is crimped and welded in the same manner as the other end. The welding takes only a few seconds and the tube is held in a vise which serves as a heat sink. No evidence of decomposition of sample was encountered. At this point, or, if the operator is confident, after the thermocouple wires are attached, the tube is safety-tested. This is customarily done

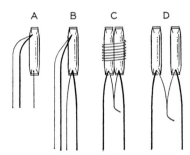

Fɪɢ. VIII-34. Ways of connecting sealed-tube sample holders: A, Single thermo-couple and single wire; the thermocouple may be at top or bottom. B, Two thermo-couples; fairly smooth furnace control is possible using the upper thermocouple while the sample temperature is read from the lower. C, Sample and reference tubes, joined; the tubes are held together by a wrapping of wire. D, Sample and reference tubes, separated.

The separated tubes offer best ultimate sensitivity while the joined tubes offer superior resolution of close-lying effects. The ΔT signal was taken from the platinum wires in each case.

by placing the tube in a muffle at a temperature at least approximating the maximum temperature to be reached during the thermal analysis. In the absence of any audible or visual evidence of failure, the sample tube may be used. The thermocouple system may comprise a platinum vs platinum 10% rhodium thermocouple and a platinum wire. The platinum–platinum rhodium is spot-welded to the tube near one end and the platinum wire is spot-welded to the tube near the other.

Now with the tube properly supported in the furnace the thermo-couple wires may be connected to the recorder treating the two platinum wires as the outside legs of a differential thermocouple, the platinum-rhodium tube being the joining member. If the temperature measured is that of the top of the tube, the temperature difference between the top and the bottom is measured by the differential thermocouple; thus any inflections detected can be associated quite accurately with the tempera-ture of the sample itself. Thermal effects can reach the thermocouple at the top, resulting in a less neat thermogram without in any way affecting the validity of the data. This arrangement was used during a portion of the work because the measuring thermocouple was part of the control system. A temperature gradient is built up along the tube with the type of furnace the author was using at that time but the thermal effects (Fig. VIII-35) are still clearly defined. The gradient quite naturally in-

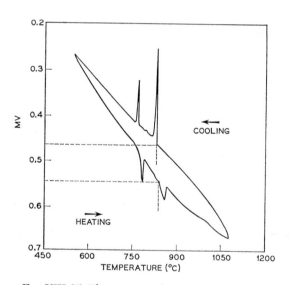

Fig. VIII-35. Thermogram of a BaF_2–LiF mixture.
The phase changes are sharply defined and reproducible even though a substan-tial temperature difference is set up.

creases with temperature and is somewhat different on the cooling from on the heating cycle.

Somewhat more elaborate systems were also used with a reference sealed tube. These were connected as shown in Fig. VIII-34 for various needs, i.e., varying degrees of isolation and, hence, sensitivity (see Fig. VIII-36).

Sealed tubes are not necessarily a good general technique. In phase diagram work, for example, there is the everpresent possibility of segregation and *de facto* variation in composition. Repetitive heating could lead to very well-defined segregation which might remain relatively

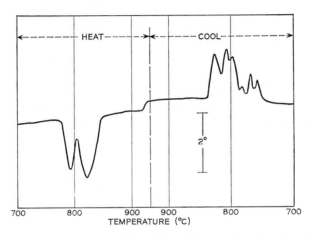

FIG. VIII-36. Thermograms of a chromyl fluoride–potassium fluoride mixture using the twin-tube arrangement of Fig. VIII-34c.

The ease of heat transfer approaches that of a block so that good separation of effects is possible.

steady from cycle to cycle. The small holders will not prevent segregation but the high sensitivity will make detection easier. The symptom is a changing temperature of one or more thermal effects from cycle to cycle. Segregation is inevitable in phase diagram work. The freezing-out of one phase separates it from the melt so that the two phases cannot generally reunite at any significant rate on heating. For this reason the heating cycle of a specimen undergoing a number of changes is likely to show a very few effects while the cooling cycle shows, as in Fig. VIII-36, each effect. The segregation becomes serious only if it persists while the sample is supposed to be molten.

An additional possibility which might vitiate the results is decomposition of the specimen. In small sealed tubes any reversible decomposition will not go far unless the vapor pressure at the melting point is very high. Whether or not an irreversible decomposition has occurred must be determined by examination of the specimen after the thermal study is complete.

8.13. Summary

There are many variations on the general method of differential thermal analysis, each having some advantages. The user of the technique is well-advised to prepare to take advantage of more than one approach.

Very small samples can be used quite easily, even with control of atmosphere effects. The lower size limit will be set by the applicability of the data to the whole specimen.

Pelleted samples present a large surface for interchange of gases with the atmosphere. If this is taken into account, the technique is useful. It presents the ultimate in practicable sample isolation.

Fluidized-bed heating may be usable for heat transfer to samples or within the sample itself but not both. If the use within the sample is successful, some valid kinetic data may be obtainable.

Visual observation of specimens during heating will require special design to avoid strong convection currents.

Changing of atmosphere or pressure can yield useful information. The furnace should permit dynamic-atmosphere or free-diffusion operation.

Several types of reactions may be studied. If the atmosphere needs to be excluded or the products contained, sealed sample holders of various types may be used.

Derivative or differential techniques could be usable if careful preparation were made.

CHAPTER IX

Thermogravimetric Analysis

9.1. Introduction

For the purpose of this discussion, consider thermogravimetry to comprise continuous or frequently repeated measurement of the weight or change in weight of a specimen as it is subjected to a temperature program. Generally, it will include automatic and continuous recording of weight or change of weight as the sample is heated. The temperature programming and/or control is usually of the same general nature as for differential thermal analysis and is described in another chapter. The concern here is over the means of weighing, the conditions affecting the specimen, and the significance of results.

The measurement of weight and temperature as the specimen is being heated is not simple. Before considering the mechanical and electrical systems needed let us first consider some of the special problems. These problems comprise principally heat transfer and the consequent temperature lag, changes in buoyancy, and movement of gases by convection or by design.

9.2. Heat-Transfer Effects

The fact that the specimen is being weighed requires that mechanical contact with the specimen be extremely slight; otherwise the sensitivity and possibly the accuracy of the measurement will be impaired. This condition then requires that heat be transferred from, generally, a nearby hot wall to the specimen holder. In turn, a temperature difference between wall and specimen is implied, and we can deduce easily that a temperature measurement anywhere but in the specimen will be in error. This error must be evaluated to determine whether or not trying to place the thermocouple in the specimen is worthwhile. If a satisfactory measurement can be made from a thermocouple supported very near the specimen, the additional mechanical linkage involved in leading thermocouple wires to the specimen is another and unnecessary source of error.

Newkirk (N5) made a quite thorough study of sources of error in Chevenard thermobalance; from the present author's experience the data cited herein are applicable to thermobalances generally. (A Chevenard thermobalance comprises a torsion balance, a counterweighted assembly to support the specimen above the level of the beam, and a furnace surrounding the specimen holder.) Newkirk programmed the temperature rise of his furnace and measured at several temperatures the difference in temperature between his control thermocouple in the furnace and another thermocouple in the crucible. The results in Fig. IX-1 show the extent of the lag. His data agree qualitatively with those the present author obtained with a bottom-loaded balance (Chapter XVII).

The error could be expected to be small at lower heating rates; fortunately these are the heating rates more commonly used in thermogravimetry. But now consider the effect of the specimen. In the Chevenard balance, like many others, a very light specimen holder

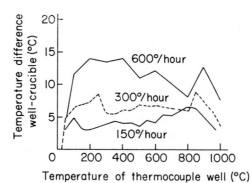

Fig. IX-1. Effect of heating rate on temperature lag of the specimen holder. From Newkirk (N5).

The difference does not continue to increase with temperature because heat-transfer processes become more effective at higher temperatures.

is used and consequently the specimen contributes much or most of the heat capacity. It is not surprising, then, that the presence of a specimen alters the temperature lag noticeably. Newkirk made a set of measurements corresponding to those shown in Fig. IX-1, but with quantities of calcium oxalate hydrate in the crucible. The data in Fig. IX-2 show the increased lag for the dehydration ($CaC_2O_4 \cdot H_2O \rightarrow CaC_2O_4 + H_2O$) and for the subsequent decomposition of calcium

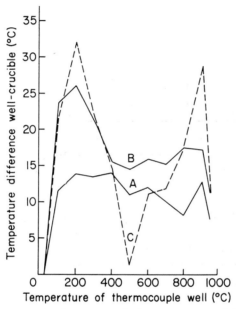

FIG. IX-2. Temperature lag due to sample. Decomposition of $CaC_2O_4 \cdot H_2O$. Heating rate 600°C/hour: A, crucible only; B, crucible + 0.2 gm $CaC_2O_4 \cdot H_2O$; C, crucible + 0.6 gm $CaC_2O_4 \cdot H_2O$. From Newkirk (N5).
The temperature lag varies the most at the temperatures of greatest interest.

carbonate ($CaCO_3 \rightarrow CaO + CO_2$); in between, however, the larger specimen gives off enough heat during the oxalate decomposition ($CaC_2O_4 + \frac{1}{2}O_2 \rightarrow CaCO_3 + CO_2$) to bring the crucible very near the furnace temperature. The important feature is that the reaction changes the temperature lag in the reaction region, so special effort or precautions would be necessary to get reliable temperatures of reaction from thermogravimetry.

It must be recognized that thermogravimetry will only rarely approach equilibrium. The transfer of sufficient heat to warm the sample may take place quite readily but decomposition of a few hundred milligrams of sample will require such a quantity of heat that the temperature will lag severely (see Chapter V, Sec. 5.1). Figure IX-3 shows the curves of Belcher *et al.* (B23a) on potassium acid phthalate in which a heating rate as low as 0.5°C/minute gives an effect much closer to a heating rate ten times as fast than to a zero heating rate. The results obtained by thermogravimetry may well appear to be significant because repeatable numbers can be stated. Nevertheless, the data must be interpreted with some understanding of the physical or chemical processes.

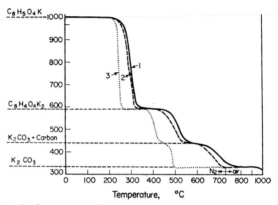

Fig. IX-3. Weight loss curves for potassium acid phthalate at (1) 5°C/minute, (2) 0.5°C/minute, and (3) isothermal heating at successively higher temperatures. From Belcher *et al.* (B23a).

Isothermal heating will bring about reaction at far lower temperatures than is customary in thermogravimetry. Thermogravimetric data must be used with great caution in estimating thermal stabilities.

9.3. Buoyancy and Gas Flow

When a specimen is heated in ambient air or any gas of comparable density, the apparent weight changes with temperature due to the change in weight of the displaced gas; the specimen appears to gain weight as it is heated. Simons, Newkirk, and Aliferis (S26) have examined the effect; their curve is shown in Fig. IX-4. The weight change is more rapid at lower temperatures. The simple solution is to decrease the volume of the sample holder but there are advantages to larger sample vessels. The effect must be recognized; from there on a choice of procedures is available. The principal choices are (1) calibration and correction and (2) use of twin furnaces. The former procedure is easier; the latter is generally better.

An apparent buoyancy effect can result from application of power to the heater windings as a step function. The sudden application of a

higher voltage heats the furnace wall quickly but because—at low temperatures—heat is transferred to the sample holder mainly by convection,
the flow velocity increases markedly. The rapid rising of gas along
the wall displaces the cooler gas down the center so that it impinges on
the sample holder, creating thereby an apparent weight gain. Lukaszewski (L17) has given (Fig. IX-5) rather dramatic evidence of the effect.
The effect is transitory because it depends for its existence on a rather
drastic temperature difference between wall and specimen holder. It
will be aggravated by a cold top (see Chapter IV); even though

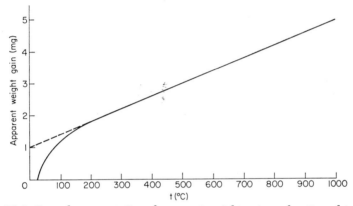

Fɪɢ. IX-4. General representation of apparent weight gain as function of temperature. From Simons *et al.* (S26).
*The gain in weight is the diminution of weight of the gas displaced by the
specimen holder plus the specimen.*

Lukaszewski had inserted a plug well into the heated zone (Fig. IX-6)
the plug surface is slow to heat because of the poor thermal contact and
will remain relatively cool because it can conduct heat to the top of the
furnace. Alumina is not a very good thermal insulator; magnesia would
have been better.

Controlled atmospheres are used in thermogravimetry for various purposes (see Chapter VII). One important use is the shifting of decomposition temperatures as illustrated in Fig. IX-7. The separation of reactions should be observable and controllable in thermogravimetry just as
in differential thermal analysis.

As thermogravimetry is usually practiced, very often the choice is simply between an oxidizing and a nonoxidizing atmosphere. In the latter
case, there is reason to have a flowing rather than a static atmosphere.
A flowing atmosphere is, by definition, an atmosphere which moves past,
around, and/or over a specimen but not through it. The fact that there

is a flow in the vicinity of a specimen being weighed creates some rather severe problems. A general movement of gas past a body exerts a force on it. Movement of gas may arise inadvertently, for example by convection, as well as by intention. Newkirk (N5) has made some useful measurements on the Chevenard balance. The present author believes them to be generally applicable.

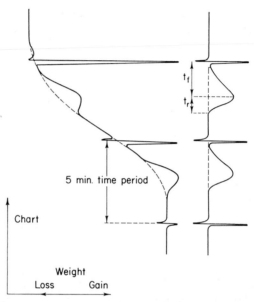

FIG. IX-5. A thermogravimetric record (diagrammatic), showing the effect of thermal pulsing in the furnace: t_r, rise time; t_f, fall time. From Lukaszewski (L17). *The sharp pulses are time marks.*

The usual technique for atmosphere control with Chevenard balances is to bring the gas in at the top of the furnace tube and let it escape through the opening at the bottom through which the sample support rod passes. The downward movement of the gas pushes down slightly on the sample holder, as shown in Fig. IX-8; this effect varies, naturally, with rate of flow of gas.

Duval (D18a) has suggested that proper venting of the furnace at the top could permit flow of air from bottom to top (convection) so as to avoid the apparent weight gain. Newkirk examined the effect of venting (Fig. IX-9) and found rather wide variations. The top opening of 0 mm has already been discussed. The buoyancy effect, however, is mitigated by an upward sweep of air if a small opening is provided. If the top is completely open, the sweep of air becomes a rush, and the

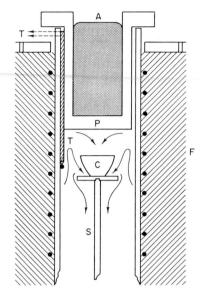

FIG. IX-6. The hot zone of a standard thermobalance furnace: A, alumina powder; P, refractory ceramic plug; T, thermocouple; F, furnace wall; C, crucible; S, support assembly. From Lukaszewski (L17).
   A cool surface above a heated zone will accentuate convection.

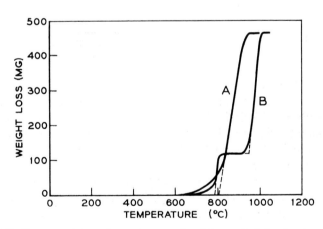

FIG. IX-7. Decomposition of a mixture of calcite and dolomite in streams of (A) air and (B) carbon dioxide. From Gibaud and Gelosa (G24).
   The decomposition temperature of calcite is heavily dependent on the pressure of carbon dioxide.

sample appears to lose weight rapidly. An 8-mm opening yields a quite small effect but Newkirk points out that this is dependent to some degree on heating rate.

For the type of work Duval does—i.e., examination of analytical precipitates to determine whether or not they are suitable for a rapid thermogravimetric analysis—the solution is easily deduced: establish, by trial and error, the conditions which will yield an apparent weight gain of near zero for a crucible of given mass and geometry and a precipitate

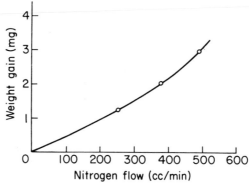

Fɪɢ. IX-8. Effect of gas velocity on apparent weight gain of one porcelain crucible at room temperature. From Newkirk (N5).

This error should increase somewhat with temperature because both volume and velocity of the gas will increase.

of a given volume. This sort of answer is hardly suitable for general purpose thermogravimetry, so under ordinary conditions users of thermobalances will need to evaluate the flowing atmosphere and buoyancy effects for each type of specimen holder and sample volume.

One technique for avoiding convection streaming when a flowing gas is used by heating the gas and passing it from top to bottom of the furnace in the manner of Vassallo (V3). He filled the upper portion of his furnace tube with glass wool (Fig. IX-10) and because the glass wool was partly in the heated zone the incoming nitrogen had plenty of warm surface to encounter before it entered the open part of the chamber. Not only is the gas hot but it would tend to emerge from the glass wool at a fairly uniform rate; this uniformity of flow should also lead to more uniform temperature distribution.

9.4. Twin-Furnace Operation

The soundest way to avoid errors from gas flow and convection is by balancing the effects both figuratively and literally. If one suspends or supports a holder with an appropriate amount of nondecomposing material in an identical furnace and any gas and voltage supplies are fed equally to each, all the physical effects on the sample should be felt equally by this reference; no movement or force should register except change in weight by the sample. Note that both hot-zone volumes and cold-zone volumes should be balanced.

Obviously, this type of operation calls rather specifically for an equal-arm beam balance, but there are a number of reasons for using such a

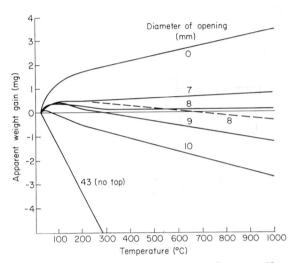

FIG. IX-9. Effect of top opening on apparent weight gain. Chevenard thermobalance, heating rate 300°C/hour: —, one porcelain crucible, Coors 230-000 (about 4 gm); - - -, two crucibles. From Newkirk (N5).
The apparent weight loss with two crucibles is probably because the moving stream of air has an additional edge to push on.

balance anyway (see Chapter X). The advantages to be gained are several: the calibrations and corrections are avoided; one may use specimen holders of considerable variety; one may use the differential technique of deKeyser (K22).

The present author uses twin-furnace operation. The Ainsworth thermobalance (G13) (Chapter XVII) had been equipped with two furnaces from the beginning; conversion to top-loading simply meant that shorter, lighter furnaces were mounted above instead of below the beam. No new problems were encountered and some were avoided (see Chapter IV).

A major—but often unrecognized—problem in systems using a gas flow is the possibility of contamination due to the upstream diffusion of oxygen, for example. Consider a Chevenard balance operated in a reasonably customary manner with a gas—perhaps nitrogen—entering at the top and exiting through the support-rod hole. There is, true enough, an outward flow that will tend to decrease the entry of oxygen but note that an operator will use as small a flow as he deems safe to avoid disturbing the measuring process. Even at room temperature oxygen is bouncing around at about ½ km per second so the idea of a noticeable percentage being able to ricochet against the general flow presents no strain on one's credulity.

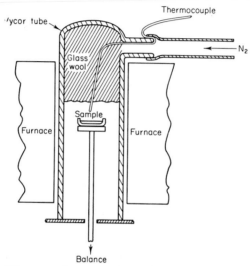

Fɪɢ. IX-10. Modifications of Stanton thermobalance. From Vassallo and Harden (V3).

A more nearly uniform temperature is achieved and mechanical disturbance avoided by bringing preheated gas in at the top.

The present author has encountered the problem a few times—enough to make him wary. In general, whenever a system is designed so that two nonidentical gases meet and mixing ahead of the designed meeting point is undesirable special care in design or use will be required. Early models of a commercial gas-density detector permitted diffusion from the sample stream back to the detectors; gases evolved by samples in the Lodding–Hammill type of furnace will diffuse upstream to the furnace chamber unless a small orifice or a high-velocity flow is provided; the Stone type of furnace can permit chamber gas to diffuse back to the sample, so the operator is well-advised to use the same chamber gas as dynamic gas unless there is good reason not to.

This diffusion upstream can be avoided by causing at some point a very high velocity flow or by introduction of a long, narrow flow path. In many applications the high velocity would be undesirable so the long path must be used.

Soulen and Mockrin (S39b) put a long exit path for the flowing gas in their Chevenard balance (Fig. IX-11) but for a different reason. They wished to prevent condensation of decomposition products on the cold support rod. The present author suggests that a major part of the improvement was due to the more effective inhibition of oxidation.

9.5. Top-Loading vs Bottom-Loading

The analytical balance is designed so that the material being weighted-is suspended from the beam. If one plans to make a series of weight

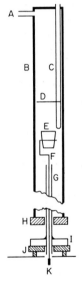

Fig. IX-11. Section through nickel muffle with nickel sleeve in place around crucible support: A, gas entry tube, $\frac{1}{4}$-in. nickel tube, to Teflon coupling and inlet hose; B, nickel muffle, $1\frac{5}{8}$ in o.d. $\times$ $\frac{1}{8}$ in. wall, $16\frac{1}{8}$ in. long; C, nickel thermowell, $\frac{1}{4}$ in. o.d. $\times$ $\frac{1}{32}$ in. wall, bottom $9\frac{3}{4}$ in. from bottom of muffle; D, baffle welded to thermowell to divert incoming gas stream, $11\frac{1}{16}$ in. from bottom of muffle; E, crucible; F, crucible support; G, nickel sleeve, $\frac{1}{4}$ in. o.d. $\times$ $\frac{1}{32}$-in. wall, $8\frac{15}{16}$ in. over-all length, passes through and is silver-soldered to its base, I; H, threaded cap for muffle; I, nickel base soldered to sleeve G, 2 inches diameter $\times$ $\frac{3}{8}$ in. thick, bottom $\frac{7}{16}$ in. from bottom of sleeve; J, ceramic platform; K, bottom of crucible support. From Soulen and Mockrin (S38b).

The downward flow of nitrogen through the tube enclosing the crucible support effectually prevents upward diffusion of oxygen.

measurements on a hot sample, one puts a balance above a furnace and inserts some heat shields. It is natural that many thermobalances have been designed from that point of view. The present author has constructed three of that type. For most purposes their operation is satisfactory. In controlled atmosphere work (in closed systems) there are some disadvantages.

Consider a balance with one or two furnaces beneath it and equipped with some shields through which the support wire passed. [The non-controlled atmosphere thermobalances (G3) constructed by the present author had three significant barriers to the passage of hot air from furnace to balance: a split disc directly on top of the furnace tube; the metal table on which the balance sat; and the metal base which supported the balancing mechanism. Each of these, and the bottom of the balance case, had a ¼-inch hole for passage of the support wire. Rising heat was spread quite effectively.] So long as hot gases are kept out of, and from the bottom of, the balance case, no trouble from heat should occur. In an open system, the heat can be led away easily. Now let us attach the furnace to the balance by some air-tight contrivance so that we may use a vacuum or pressure and so that we may use a controlled static atmosphere. This mechanical connection greatly diminishes our ability to spread or otherwise dispose of heat. Let us consider the consequences.

Heat is transferred to the balance by conduction and convection. Conduction along the walls of the furnace tube ought to be a fairly trivial problem; in a moderately long tube there is plenty of opportunity to lose heat to the surroundings. One might even encourage this with a fan or cooling coil. The problem inside is not so simple. Convection implies the presence of a gas so let us note first that, if the thermobalance is being operated in a vacuum, there should be no trouble; the amount of heat that can be transported up a support wire can be neglected easily.

When a substantial amount of gas is present, the possibility of conveying heat to the balance chamber increases enormously and provisions must be made to avoid this transfer. We face, however, the condition of having a cold zone above a hot zone. The measures taken to avoid transfer of heat may induce erratic behavior; see Chapter IV on the effect of a temperature inversion in differential thermal analysis. We cannot, for example, interpose a cold surface with no other precautions; this would set up a rather forceful stream of gas and induce a temperature-dependent error. The present author used a series of discs, each with a hole in the center but otherwise nearly filling the tube, to stop radiation and convection. This was partly successful; the balance could be used quite satisfactorily under diminished pressures but much less well at atmospheric. More precisely, at atmospheric pressure it did not operate satisfactorily at high temperatures. Some combination of interposing a barrier and cooling should work satisfactorily, but the mechanical problems led the present author to look with favor on top-loading.

Top-loading results in an array of hot and cold zones in their proper order; this immediately eliminates convection and diminishes conduction. The problems that arise are mechanical; they require some special effort but nothing very difficult. One mechanical problem is that of furnace handling. Bringing a tube furnace upward to enclose a sample holder is not difficult even by hand, i.e., without mechanical guides. It is less easy to bring a furnace down to enclose a sample holder without touching it so a mechanical contrivance will be helpful to lower and lift the furnace or furnaces.

The ordinary beam balance supports the load from hooks which are in turn supported by knife edges. This flexible suspension requires that the center of mass of the load on each end of the beam be below the hook so a top-loading sample holder must be counterweighted, as in Fig. IX-12, for the sample assembly to keep it in a reproducible position in the furnace. (Since the weight of the assembly is—in effect—at the knife edge, any tilt may permit unequal heating, but the measurement of the weight will not be affected.) The weight of the counterbalance and sample holder assembly should not exceed the rated maximum loading for the balance; the change in sensitivity of the balance should then be of no concern. Most important, the counterbalance should be designed so that it is not the weight-limiting feature. The counterweight should be short and have a substantial cross section; if a significant part of the mass is near the fulcrum it is of little use. The material near the fulcrum should be only of sufficient mass to provide rigidity.

The lever arm relation is a summation, i.e., for the top portion

$$W_T D_T = \sum_{d=0}^{d=l} w_n d_n$$

where w and d refer to weight and distance from the fulcrum and l is the total length; a similar summation of the top portion holds for the bottom. But to keep the sample support in a vertical position

$$W_B D_B > W_T D_T$$

in any position of the support arm. Since the total weight is limited, the length may need to be extended. An arrangement using relatively little weight to good advantage, then, would comprise an appropriate mass at the end of a rod or tube. In the present author's design the sample-supporting tube is 12 inches, but the counterweight rod is 20 inches long. The counterweight need not be equal in weight to the sample and sample holder, but was made sufficiently heavy to keep the support tube vertical. The actual length of the counterweight tube will generally be limited by the space available.

9.6. Connections to Balance Beam

Mechanical connection to the beam or suspension system of balances is to be avoided wherever practicable; even thermocouple leads must be tolerated only as a necessary evil. If the measurement system requires connection between the moving and stationary parts there are ways of making any damping, drag, or tension effects rather small. The manner of attaching electrical connections depends on their use. Thermocouple connections may be made through fine copper or thermocouple wires (see Chapter XVI). For displacement-measuring systems a connection

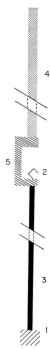

Fig. IX-12. Counterweight for top-loaded beam balance.

The counterweight (1) should be as far from the fulcrum (suspension hook) (2) as is experimentally convenient. The counterweight support (3) should be a thin-walled plugged tube. This and the upper tube (4) are cemented into the bracket (5). The sample holder is set on top of the rod. Thermocouple wires may be led through the rod.

permitting limited movement with as little drag or tension as possible is required; Reisman (R12) and the present author use single large loops of fine wire. For null balance the present author prefers a helix which can be easily bent or stretched so that at null the wire has no influence on the beam position (Fig. IX-13).

For current-carrying wires the connection should be made where the inevitable drag or tension will have the least effect, i.e., near the center knife edge on a beam suspension balance; Waters (W8), for example, passes the coulometer current through a helix attached to the beam near the central support.

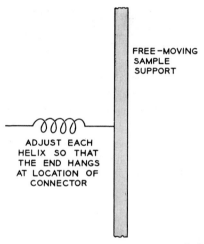

FREE–MOVING
SAMPLE
SUPPORT

ADJUST EACH
HELIX SO THAT
THE END HANGS
AT LOCATION OF
CONNECTOR

Fig. IX-13. Thermocouple connection to balance.
The helix can be bent until the end rests without force on its stationary terminal. When secured, there will be no appreciable effect on the balance.

In general, the deleterious effects of mechanical connections may be diminished most in a null or force-restored null balance because the same force—if at all measurable—is operative at all times since the beam remains in the same position. [Papailhau (P5a)—see Chapter X—even connects gas-carrying tubes to his sample support.] Any significant force will manifest itself only by an increase in the unbalance required to initiate restoring action. Whether or not the effect will be significant in a pseudo-null balance will depend on the magnitude of the force.

The arguments advanced above are not limited to beam balances. They apply to as well to spring, torsion element, or any other support system. The essential distinctions here are only between the devices that do or do not operate at or near a null position.

An exception might be granted in a case in which the mechanical connection is made through a sensing element; for example, Bartlett and Williams (B12) used a strain gage on the beam end opposite the sample suspension. The vertical strain from balance table to beam was measured to follow the weight change.

Intermittent mechanical contact between a moving and a stationary support system is not necessarily deleterious; as long as the beam or other moving part can move to its proper position after each disturbance the balance operation need not be impaired. Note that the intermittent rebalancing action used by Ewald (E8) should not have any effect on a beam already at null because the position-indicating arm is first locked in position by a movement parallel to the knife edge, the rebalancing movement—if any—takes place, and the indicating arm is finally released. No torque is exerted about the knife edge except by the specimen or the chain.

Now consider the position-sensing device (Fig. IX-14) used by Simons *et al.* (S26) with a Chevenard balance. The contact plate is driven downward by the recording mechanism until contact is made whereupon the recorder mechanism reverses the drive, withdrawing the contact plate until the connection is broken; the contact plate and hence the recorder sense the extent position of the beam, but in so doing a small force is exerted briefly.

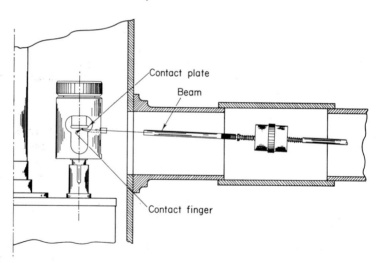

Contact plate

Beam

Contact finger

Fig. IX-14. Position-sensing mechanism for pen-recording Chevenard thermobalance. From Simons *et al.* (S26).

The slight intermittent force from the contact plate will tend to keep the beam free-moving.

This small force, even though it is present about half the time, may actually improve the sensitivity by providing an additional cyclic movement which will particularly aid in eliminating surface tension effects in oil dampers, etc. In heavier systems such as one may use on an equal-arm beam balance the cyclic movement will help to overcome inertia. The very noticeable solenoid action of linear variable differential transformers may perform a quite similar function.

Whether or not this movement is a real help will depend very heavily on the particular design. The important conclusion from this discussion is that it is not per se an adverse condition.

9.7. Precautions

Balance mechanisms, whether beam, spring, or other, are generally designed for sensitivity rather than sturdiness and general invulnerability.

Vibration is a common and well-known hazard so that it need not be discussed in great detail, with one exception. There is a moderately widespread belief that analytical-type balances are unsuitable for long-term operation as thermobalances because of wear of the knife edges. Modern laboratory buildings will not often be subject to enough vibration to cause any short-term error at analytical accuracy. (If the vibration is sufficient, other balances will need vibration-free mounts.) The author's three thermobalances showed no signs of deterioration in sensitivity during his use of them even though some runs lasted for over 2 days.

Whether or not such wear does occur, the best policy is to choose the instrument that will perform best in the intended use. If the choice, on this criterion, is an analytical balance type of thermobalance, the sensitivity can be checked every few months for signs of loss of sensitivity from wear. A good test for many systems is observation of the electrical displacement or restoring signal on a galvanometer to see whether or not the signal changes smoothly as the weight changes. Evaporation of a drop of isopropanol should be sufficient. The signal should be taken as near as possible (electrically) to the transducer.

Vacuum balances will, of course, degas as the system is pumped down. As little paraphernalia as possible should be within the evacuated volume. Metal, glass, and many other smooth surfaces well-exposed present no great problems. Confined spaces will slow the pump-down (as well as changes of atmospheres).

In addition, for high-vacuum operation, the out-gassing of components must be taken into account, along with possible changes in frictional coefficients of moving components.

Corrosive gases must be kept out of the balance mechanism region. (The term "corrosive gas" may require different definitions for different apparatus.) If a corrosive gas is being used or formed some counterflow of a "safe" gas can be used to keep the corrosive gas away from the balance mechanism. The opening connecting the balance chamber to the weighing chamber must be a reasonably long and narrow path to avoid back-diffusion (see Chapter VII).

Some materials will creep badly; for example, oxides that form glasses readily may creep over the wall of a crucible and up or down the support. If there is a large temperature gradient, part of the sample may be very significantly hotter or colder than the remainder.

Magnetic effects must be carefully avoided. The first thermobalance constructed by the author (G3) was put to use by another group in a study of polymer additives. The balance oscillated through nearly its full 100 mg range. The low-temperature furnace used in place of the platinum wound furnace had many turns and their stainless steel sample holder responded nicely to a magnet. The holder had been pulled against the side of the tube and the friction caused a dead zone of ca. 80 mg.

9.8. Summary

The need to isolate the sample mechanically from its immediate surroundings accentuates the heat-transfer effects seen in differential thermal analysis. Further, the new problem of mechanical forces arising from buoyancy and intended or unintended gas flow must be taken into account.

The generally poor heat transfer leads to low heating rates.

Buoyancy can be corrected for by calibration or automatically compensated by twin-furnace operation.

Convection is avoided by proper furnace design, most easily by use of top-loaded balances.

Connections to the sample support must afford extremely small torques or, in the case of null balance instruments, small or very highly reproducible torque.

CHAPTER X

Thermogravimetric
Apparatus

10.1. Introduction

The devices used to perform continuous weighings while heating a sample have been quite varied. A remarkable degree of ingenuity has been thrown into the outwardly simple problem of providing a minute-by-minute record of the weight of a sample as it rests in a furnace. The devices must be classed first in the two broad categories, beam-balances and other weighing devices.

The beam balance is to the weighing device much as differential thermal analysis is to calorimetry; that is, by hanging an essentially equal weight on the other end of the beam small changes in weight may be detected. Both high accuracy and high sensitivity are possible. Weighing devices in general provide a measure of the total weight. The taring or reference point is commonly electrical and is essentially independent of the actual weighing mechanism. Because of this arrangement the weighing device must attempt to detect small differences in a large quantity and relate these differences to a reference whose constancy depends in large part on the stability of the electrical and electronic systems. The user of any such weighing machine is constrained to use as light a sample support as possible so that the sample is a substantial fraction of the total weight. He must then sacrifice the advantages of massive or closed-chamber sample holders. The user of a balance of ordinary analytical characteristics, on the other hand, can load a 120-gm sample holder with 80 gm of his specimen and measure a 90-mg loss with an accuracy approaching that of an analytical balance or certainly to ca. 0.2 mg—a change of 1 in 4×10^5 in sample weight. The present author has a strong bias in favor of equal-arm-beam null balances; in some special cases it may well be expedient to use some other weighing device but this author knows of no case in which such devices are demonstrably superior under comparable conditions.

10.2. Beam Balances

The analytical balance is frequently used in construction of automatic recording balances. It is designed to operate at null; i.e., the weight suspended from one end of the beam is counterbalanced by adjusting the *weight* suspended from the other end of the beam so that the beam, when free to move, will remain in a horizontal position and the pointer is at the center of the scale. The definition of null balance is necessary because it has been misused. The analytical balance may be put to use as an automatic recording balance in four ways: null balance, force-restored null balance, pseudo-null balance, and displacement measurement (Fig. X-1).

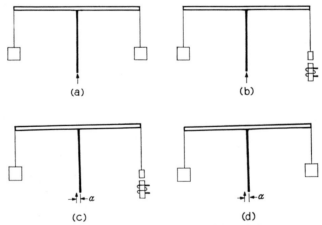

FIG. X-1. Various ways of using an equal-arm beam balance as an automatic and/or recording balance. (a) Null balance; the weight is adjusted to keep the beam balanced. (b) Force-restored null balance; a force, e.g., magnetic, is applied to compensate for changes in weight. (c) Pseudo-null balance; a force which varies with displacement keeps the balance near null. (d) Displacement measurement; for small angles the displacement is very nearly proportional to the weight change.

10.3. Null Balance

The null balance system is not only esthetically pleasing, especially to the physical or analytical chemist, but also inherently more stable. Basically, the balance does not require frequent calibration or checking. The only question that should arise is: "Does the balancing system function?" The question of linear response does not appear. The primary need is a system for adding or removing weight in response to an unbalance signal such that the unbalance signal is caused to disappear when the weight is rebalanced.

The present author has built two null balance instruments (G3) (Fig. X-2). In each case, a linear variable differential transformer was used as an unbalance detector. The unbalance signal supplied a servoamplifier-motor arrangement with directional as well as go-no-go information. The motor moved the balancing chain to restore balance. These were true null balance instruments since the differential transformer and core were adjusted so that at balance there was no force exerted on the balance beam and the motor was not driving. The beam was first balanced with all power off and the chain position noted. With the power on but

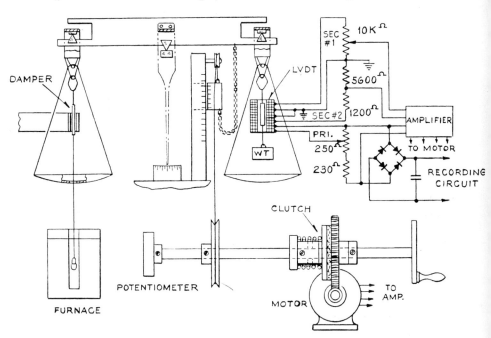

Fig. X-2. Outline drawing of automatic recording balance. From Garn (G3).
The magnetic and electrical nulls are adjusted to coincide with the mechanical null. The balance is always at null except during a weight change.

the motor disconnected from the chain, the transformer core was adjusted along the threaded support rod until the balance stayed at null. [This step is necessary because of the solenoid action of the transformer on the core except when the core is centered (see Chapter XVI).] With the balance now truly at null, the electrical system was adjusted so that the motor did not drive. With the gear train reconnected, the sensitivity was adjusted to a minimum "dead zone" and stable nonhunting operation. That the balance was operating at null could be checked at any time by shutting off the electrical power. In the absence of maladjustment the beam remained stationary.

In the first of these two thermobalances (this instrument is presently in use by another group at Bell Laboratories), a commercial servo-amplifier of the type often used in strip chart recorders was used. There is obviously no need to convert the transformer output to direct current when it must be converted back within the amplifier. A better solution is to bypass the chopper and feed the signal directly to the first amplifier stage. To avoid misconnection resulting in phase reversal, the transformer was supplied directly from the amplifier. Both of these worthy purposes could be accomplished easily by removing the converter (chopper) from its socket and substituting a plug wired to the transformer input and output circuits. The second thermobalance, still in use by the author at the time of writing, makes use of a commercial transformer-amplifier-motor combination.

A rather similar apparatus was constructed by Hyatt *et al.* (H30) using a dual photocell detector to operate the chain-drive motor. The operation of this sort of balance with any reasonable drive speeds brings about a situation in which unbalance produces a constant restoring velocity for all except very small displacements. For these small displacements the restoring velocity is proportional to displacement. The chain motion continues until balance is reached, but the beam moves beyond null because of its momentum, and the chain must move again to correct this false unbalance. For these small displacements the chain velocity decays exponentially as the beam swings toward null; that is, since

$$\frac{dv}{dt} = -kx,$$

$$v = e^{-kt},$$

but the chain has already been driven past the proper balance position and hunting normally ensues.

Three corrective measures are available. One is to slow the movement of the chain so that the beam and load can follow closely enough to enter the detector dead zone before the chain has moved enough to move the rest point beyond the dead zone. This is the solution adopted by Hyatt *et al.* who drive the chain at 0.1 mg/second over a 100-mg range. [The present author (G3) uses a drive speed of about 0.5 mg/second over a 100-mg range. This faster range is suitable for nearly all samples. A few exothermic decompositions cannot be followed accurately.] The second solution is velocity damping using the magnetic damping apparatus normally supplied with analytical balances and perhaps augmented with fluid or additional magnetic damping. The third is the addition of electronically controlled magnetic damping.

An ingenious combination recording and balancing system was devised by Ewald (E8). He supplied the unbalance signal from photoelectric cells to an electromechanical strip chart recorder (Fig. X-3). The pen shaft of this recorder also raised—or lowered—a balancing chain so that a direct record of the amount of chain was obtained.

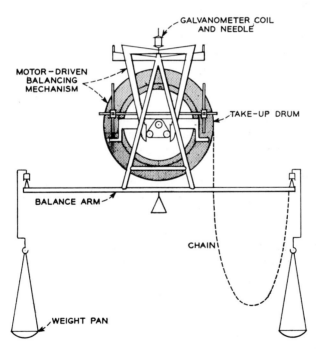

Fig. X-3. Null-type recording balance constructed from mechanical galvanometric recording potentiometer. From Ewald (E8).

At a moderate sacrifice of sensitivity the recording system becomes the balancing system as well. The period and/or damping of the balance must be adjusted so that the balance is not on a back swing at the time of the next balancing action.

In general, null balance instruments suffer from a limited range. The chain-adjusting types described above are limited to the range prescribed by the chain. This limitation is not severe because (1) sample size can usually be adjusted, (2) chains of different weights can be used, (3) more than one point of suspension on the beam can be provided, or (4) weights may be added or subtracted automatically when the chain reaches the limit of travel. The major barrier to substantial downward change of range by either (2) or (3) above is the inherent sensitivity of the balance. The author, once having a prescribed sample size and a need—or at least desire—for greater sensitivity, soldered a pointed wire on the opposite (center) end of the adjusting screw supporting the chain. With the chain end supported at this new point, a range of ca. 29 mg, instead of the usual 100 mg, was obtained. The weight-loss record was quite satisfactory.

10.4. Force-Restored Null Balance

The force-restored null balance instrument differs from the true null balance instrument only in the method by which the balance is maintained at the null position. This is generally, of course, by the action of a solenoid pushing—or pulling—on a core suspended from one end of a beam. In an automatic balance (not a thermobalance) the author helped design, a differential transformer-amplifier-motor combination like that described in the previous section was geared to a helical potentiometer which supplied the solenoid. The voltage across a precision resistor was read. The voltage across the helical potentiometer could be changed to obtain different sensitivities, e.g., ranges of a few milligrams up to several grams.

Among the force-restored null balance apparatuses is the automatic recording vacuum microbalance of Cochran (C17), who used a servo-system to adjust the current through a solenoid to bring the beam back to its original position much as described above. The detector (Fig. X-4) is a variable permeance inductor. The two portions of the winding of the inductor form two legs of an alternating current bridge so that a change in the relative inductive reactances introduces an unbalance. The unbalance supplies a potential to a servoamplifier which moves a balancing potentiometer, steadily changing the restoring force until the unbalance signal disappears.

The balancing circuit is customarily adjusted so that the electrical null coincides with the mechanical null which implies that at balance the transducer should have no effect on the balance system, although Cochran says "the transducer exerts forces of several hundred to zero micrograms on the probe, depending on position, frequency and voltage." Ob-

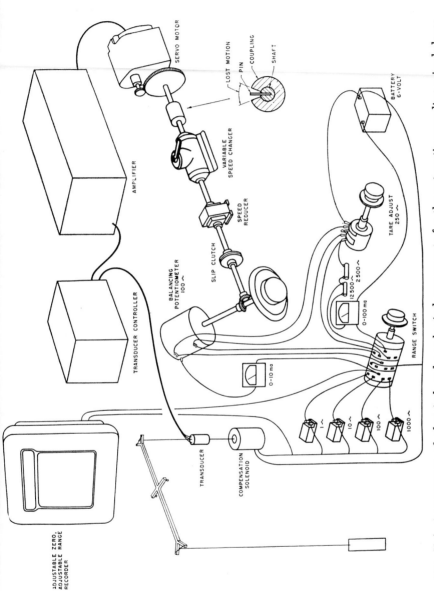

FIG. X-4. Arrangement of electrical and mechanical components for the automatic recording microbalance. From Cochran (C17). *The built-in "lost motion" permits recording of slowly varying weight changes without providing damping.*

viously, when an unbalance occurs, the change in inductive reactance must appear as a magnetic pull, but this should disappear when balance is restored.

No electrical or mechanical damping was used by Cochran. He avoided the problem neatly by building in a "dead time" as opposed to a "dead zone." His mechanical coupling deliberately employs a "lost motion" angle so that a reversal of signal must exist for some time before it results in a change of restoring force. Under these conditions, as the balance is driven back to—and beyond (see below)—null position the resulting reversal of signal would tend to cause oscillation, but even though the beam may move beyond null for a few seconds the lost motion is not used up before the beam has swung back to null and on to the side of the original displacement. The driving motor then starts back in the first direction without ever having transmitted any movement to the balancing potentiometer. The oscillation will die out mechanically without any effect if the balance is at null. Note, however, that there is no real loss of sensitivity because if the balance is not at null the oscillations will not be centered about null and eventually the greater portion of time spent on one side of null will cause the motor to nudge the potentiometer one to several times until the oscillation is centered. This "lost motion" type of operation requires that the dead time be not less than one-half the period of the balance. There is consequently a sacrifice of response speed.

The need for this dead time substitute for damping is partly the result of design. It appears to the present author that the servoamplifier is almost constantly overloaded with signal. Cochran reports that "the servomotor runs at nearly constant speed." One must infer from this that any appreciable displacement will bring forth a full-speed approach from the balancing system. Since the signal cannot reverse until the null point is passed, the beam position will change at an essentially constant rate toward null. Because of inertia, it must necessarily lag somewhat so that, by the time the beam position is at null, the restoring force is already too great—or too little—to maintain the null, so from this and from its momentum the beam will overshoot. In the ordinary course of events position-correcting action will not begin until about one and one-half periods have elapsed. The correction ought to be completed in a few periods.

The behavior just described should have no important effect on the type of study Cochran reports (oxidation of aluminum). A continually changing weight will give a record appearing to waver back and forth about a line which should be a satisfactory index. For systems in which discrete weight losses or gains are to be measured the arrangement is probably unsatisfactory, but then one hardly ever tries to study these systems on microbalances because the question whether or not the small sample was representative would arise.

10.5. Pseudo-Null Balance

The pseudo-null balance instrument uses, in general, a restoring force to keep the balance beam near null, but the magnitude of this restoring force is governed by an unbalance signal. Since a displacement signal is required to maintain the restoring force, that force cannot act to return the balance to null without destroying the displacement signal that must exist to initiate the restoring force, etc.

Consider a general case in which a displacement signal controls the current through a solenoid. The measured quantity is the voltage drop across a resistor in the solenoid circuit and, hence, the current through the solenoid. The one controlling requirement is that throughout the range of the balance

$$i = k\Delta w$$

where i is the current through the solenoid, Δw is the change in weight, and k is a proportionality constant.

In order to generate this current, a displacement from null, x, must exist. Without specifying the nature of the detector, let us assume that the current generated is directly proportional to the displacement, i.e.,

$$x = k'i.$$

Now let there be a change in weight, Δw_1, and let a steady state ensue, so that

$$i_1 = k\Delta w_1$$

and

$$x_1 = k'i_1 = k'k\Delta w_1$$

except that a portion of the weight is represented by the displacement, x_1. This is not an obvious problem since if the change in weight is doubled, i.e., $\Delta w_2 = 2\Delta w_1$,

$$x_2 = 2k'k\Delta w_1,$$

twice as much weight is represented by the displacement itself. In the absence of any change except in weight, the system is capable of supplying a proper measure of a change in weight, as long as the balance beam is held close to the null position, that is, in the limited region where displacement may be considered proportional to changes in weight.

In most pseudo-null balances the displacement is kept small; hence, nonlinearity of the current-displacement relation is not a significant problem because the measured quantity is the restoring force and the error will be the additional (or lesser) voltage required to bring the beam from the proper (linear) control point to the actual control point. (For the purpose of this limited discussion the control point is the position of rest at which the displacement signal generates restoring force necessary to maintain the displacement.) The pseudo-null instrument generally has a high signal/displacement relation so that the displacement error is small. This high response to position change brings about two requirements: dynamic damping and good voltage stabilization.

Consider a beam at balance with a zero restoring force and let a change in weight occur. The beam tends to move to the position which provides the appropriate restoring force. The momentum of the beam and load carries the beam beyond the "control point" as defined above whereupon a strong restoring force stops and reverses the motion and carries the beam beyond the control point in the other direction, etc. Since the restoring force is proportional to the displacement, i.e.,

$$\frac{d^2x}{dt^2} = -kx,$$

we have a classical harmonic oscillator. This oscillator will tend to hunt unless damped. This damping will generally need to be acceleration damping as practiced by Brown *et al.* (B83) or Mauer (M20) rather than the velocity damping provided by the usual magnetic dampers.

The high signal/displacement relation alone is enough to require good voltage stabilization. Consider a system at rest at some reasonable displacement and vary the power supply voltage. Since the detecting system is off null, it will immediately see a change in signal strength almost irrespective of the nature of the detector. This will require a change in position of the beam to restore (nearly) the original restoring force. A recurring variation in the supply voltage will cause recurring momentary deviations with small persistent deviations. This is in an ideal system in which the same supply variation did not affect the damping circuitry. In a nonideal (real) system, the damping circuit will sense the variation in supply voltage as a change in displacement signal and supply an opposing force where none is needed. This causes a real displacement, and the balance oscillates, at least briefly. For the reasons given, a pseudo-null balance instrument must be provided with a good voltage-stabilized power supply.

The linearly increasing displacement signal is simply the easiest to use for illustration; it is common with electrical displacement detection systems but not with optical systems; long-term stability is essential. A circular spot of light activating one of two photocells would be reasonably typical. Brown *et al.* (B83) used such a spot arranged so that there was a small dead zone between the two photocells. (This dead zone does not seem to serve any useful purpose since a displacement is required to do any measuring.) When the spot falls on a photo-cell the area increases rapidly and nonlinearly as the spot moves onto the photocell. They very naturally fitted this detector with a highly effective damping system. Without it a small overshoot due to mechanical momentum could supply a restoring force large enough to start the balance back toward null and possibly into the dead zone. If the momentum carries the beam beyond null and the light spot encounters the other photocell, a sharp surge of current in the solenoid would arrest the beam and start it back in the original direction where it would again encounter a surge, leading to anharmonic oscillation. Their damping system provided a current opposing any change so that the beam would move at a low velocity as long as the restoring force was not equal to the gravitational force at that displacement. The damping current kept the movement slow enough so that the signal could die out and the beam could stop without overshoot.

10.6. Displacement Measurement

The displacement-measuring instrument depends on the nearly linear variation of displacement angle with change in weight. The assumption of linearity is satisfactory for small angles since $\sin a \approx a$. Only the ordinary magnetic damping is required, but because a signal proportional to displacement must be generated this system, too, must have a voltage-stabilized power supply. In this case, the voltage stabilization need be only as good as the accuracy required, since no parts will tend to initiate hunting.

Figure X-5 shows a simple displacement-measuring system. The

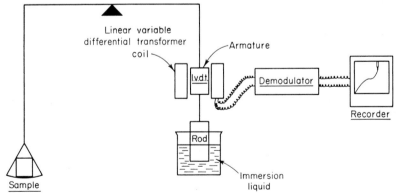

Fig. X-5. Schematic diagram of converted analytical balance for automatic recording. From Gordon and Campbell (G35).

For small angular displacements the signal is proportional to the weight change.

linear variable differential transformer (Chapter XVI) gives an output quite reproducibly dependent on position. The limit of use will be dictated by the balance at both extremes. The sensitivity will depend on the minimum weight difference needed to cause the balance to move and the usable range will be limited by the curvature of E vs w plot. Calibration will be required.

10.7. Miscellaneous Beam Balance Systems

Several variations in detecting or balancing systems have been tried. Whether or not a particular system becomes popular is not solely dependent on its capabilities; there are important human factors in play, too. The unique feature of the system may be beyond a potential buyer's or builder's experience; for example, not many—in the author's opinion —would venture to build a sensitive weight-measuring system using strain gages as sensing elements, yet they have been used. Very few of those who might need recording balances are familiar with strain gages. Similarly, the unique feature of the measuring system might be relatively inconvenient to use and would be rejected summarily on this account. This is not an entirely unreasonable attitude; in many cases, the user will be interested only in the data—not in the means of obtaining them. A third human factor is predilection or prepossession. The present author, for example, is quite unlikely to consider use of a spring for a weighing device under ordinary conditions of experimentation; on the other hand, some workers look with dismay at the use of knife edges for the protracted periods common in thermogravimetry.

Some variations used in connection with beam balances are reviewed below with comments where appropriate. The reader may pick and choose if he plans to build or be better prepared if he plans to buy.

Capacitance null indication was used by Crandall and West (C25) in their thermobalance (Fig. X-6). The detector itself is not at a null condition, but the oscillator circuit may be tuned so that the balancing motor reverses at the mechanical null. The actual detecting elements in a system of this kind would be a pair of plates—one stationary, one attached to the beam—forming a capacitance in the grid circuit of the oscillator. This circuit is then tuned so that an output-stage relay will operate or fall back when the balance is at null. A motor connected to the relay then drives the chain in the appropriate direction.

The fact that the chain is always moving is only a minor disadvantage. The moving parts will wear out faster, but since the balance is always swinging the sensitivity is somewhat better than in the case where a deflection of some minimum value is needed to operate the balancing mechanism. The mechanical backlash—even if very small—can avoid the appearance of a wavy record. This mechanical backlash ought to be the limiting feature on the sensitivity of recording. The amplitude of this backlash will depend on the speed of the motor and the period of the balance. The actual period of oscillation will not be that of the free-swinging balance; the balance will perform as a driven oscillator, but the frequency of this driven oscillator will depend on the variables cited above. If the motor drive is slow, the period of the driven oscillation

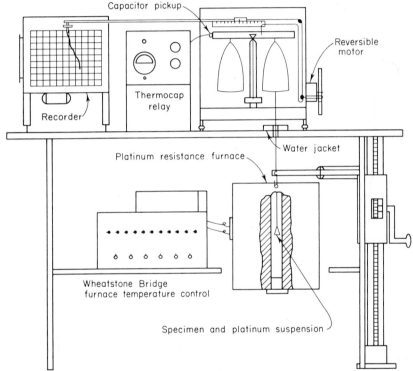

Fɪɢ. X-6. Automatic recording balance with furnace. From Crandall and West C25).

The recording pen is coupled mechanically to the chain-drive mechanism.

will approach that of the balance and the amplitude will be low. Let the speed be increased and the amplitude, too, will increase; from the time of the swing of the balance past null to the time of its passing in the other direction the motor will be driving at full speed in a single direction. The actual speed must be a compromise between that needed to follow a weight change properly and that which gives a decently small wiggle.

The long-term (few-hour) drift of the oscillator would probably not be serious. The null detector can be reset very conveniently at the start of a run, but, on the other hand, this resetting is almost certainly necessary.

A magnetic repulsion system has been used to maintain a balance beam at an apparent null (Fig. X-7). The detecting beam oscillates with small amplitude about a null position. When the balance beam tends to move because of a change of weight the increased or decreased repulsion makes the upper beam tend to follow. The upper beam is returned to null

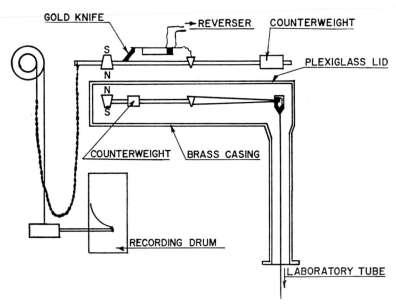

FIG. X-7. Testut null-type vacuum thermobalance with servo-operated chain for restoring force and electromechanical null detector. From Gordon and Campbell (G35).

Essentially all control and measuring equipment is outside the chamber.

so that the lower beam is constrained to return to nearly null. The nearness of approach to null will depend on the strength of the magnetic field. In general, the behavior is similar to the pseudo-null balances described earlier.

Another technique for adding or subtracting weight is by electroplating a metal onto or stripping it from an electrode hanging from the beam. Waters (W8) used a photoelectric detector to drive an amplifier which pushed an electric current through an electrolytic cell in the proper direction so that the weight of the hanging electrode assembly equalled that of the sample assembly (Fig. X-8). This is intrinsically a null system—as long as a displacement exists a restoring action continues. The measured quantity is the current flowing through the cell so the primary record is essentially a derivative, the rate of change of weight with time. Integration of the current presents the user with the total weight change as a function of time. The balancing and recording systems should be very dependable; if this arrangement were to be used in a controlled atmosphere or vacuum system the electrode support ought to pass through a small orifice and the electrolyte covered with a layer of vacuum pump oil.

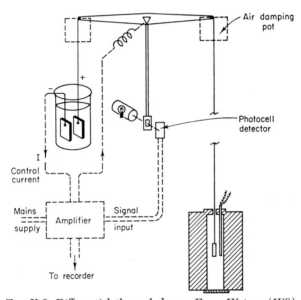

FIG. X-8. Differential thermobalance. From Waters (W8).
The beam is kept at null by electrochemical addition or subtraction of weight. The current required to maintain balance is recorded; this current is initiated and controlled by means of the photocell detector.

10.8. Nonbeam Systems

Some thermobalances use direct suspension of the sample. Magnetic suspensions have been used in other applications (B19) and a thermobalance using a magnetic suspension is reportedly being prepared for commerical sale.

Spring suspensions are often used. Some springs, including quartz-fiber springs, have been used for sensitive measurements of weight (or apparent weight) in closed systems many times. Hooley (H23) used

such a spring in a thermobalance (Fig. X-9), measuring the displacement with a linear variable differential transformer whose core was
part of the suspension system and whose coils were outside the enclosure.
The sample then hangs down into a furnace chamber. The entire volume
may be evacuated or a gas may be made to flow through the chamber to
supply a constantly replenished known atmosphere.

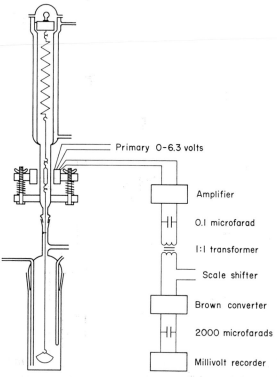

Primary 0–6.3 volts

Amplifier

0.1 microfarad

1:1 transformer

Scale shifter

Brown converter

2000 microfarads

Millivolt recorder

FIG. X-9. Balance and the recording circuit. From Hooley (H23).
The spring enclosure is water-cooled to provide uniform response along the spring.

Hooley showed (Fig. X-10) that there is a linear region for the spring
he used. Within this region the output of the differential transformer is a
reasonably accurate measure of the weight. The total load for linear
response is about 0.7 gm for the spring he used. The situation of a cold
zone above a hot zone (see Chapter IX) is unavoidable with this type
of suspension.

Wendlandt (W19) devised a strain gage support from which he sus-
⌐ his specimens (Fig. X-11). The system should be relatively
      ⌐le; Wendlandt cites a tolerance of a 1-lb overload without

damage for ±0.15-ounce gage, a fiftyfold overload. On the other hand the capacity is low and very frequent calibration is likely to be needed.

Other systems may permit top-loading. The cantilever support used by Kertzmann (K18) shown in Fig. X-12 allows quite rigidly prescribed positioning of the specimen but at the sacrifice of considerable sensitivity since the support arms must resist torque in any direction but the vertical.

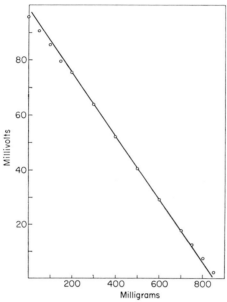

Fig. X-10. The linear region for spring D^1. From Hooley (H23).
This particular spring can be used from about 250 to 700 mg with a two-point calibration.

10.9. Pressure Thermobalances

Rabatin and Card (R1) constructed a high-pressure (600 psi) thermo-balance (Fig. X-13) using a torsion balance and an optical displacement-measuring system. The furnace is mounted above the balance to avoid convection heating of the balance itself. The top contains not only the furnace but also (Fig. X-14) a thermocouple placed so that it is within the sample crucible when the top is let down into place. At 7°C/minute they obtained the curves shown in Fig. X-15. At high pressures the reactions are not necessarily the same as at ambient pressure. Operation at a series of pressures may supply useful thermodynamic data.

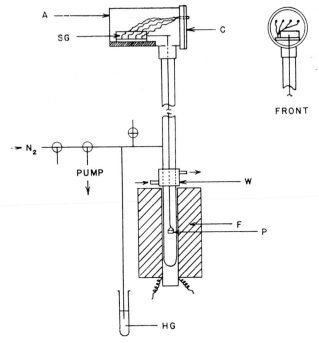

FIG. X-11. Schematic drawing of strain gage thermobalance. From Wendlandt (W19). A, aluminum cylinder housing; SG, strain gage transducer; C, plastic disc; W, water-cooled standard taper joint; F, furnace; and P, sample pan.

The position of the sample supporting arm is sensed by the relative changes in resistance of the gage arms.

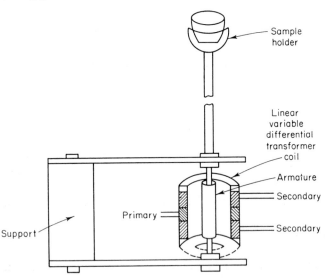

FIG. X-12. Cantilever deflection-type load cell with differential transformer as transducer for measuring. From Kertzmann (K18), as given by Gordon and Campbell (G35).

A somewhat different approach to high pressures was taken by Biermann and Heinrichs (B50a). They enclosed a horizontally positioned
spring in a side arm on their chamber and supported their specimen and
holder in the furnace above (Fig. X-16). The detecting and damping
system provided the counterweight. Since their displacement-measur-

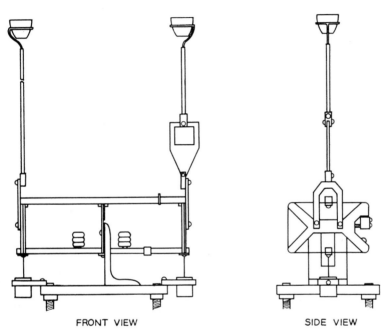

FRONT VIEW   SIDE VIEW

Fig. X-13. Torsion thermobalance assembly for pressure operation. From Rabatin
and Card (R1).

*The right-hand arm was used for counterweighting and supporting the displace-
ment-indicating flag. This single-furnace thermobalance compensates for buoyancy
changes due to pressure but not for temperature.*

ing transducer, a single-ended linear variable differential transformer
(see Chapter XVI), was inside they needed to provide adjusting devices
to "zero" the support mechanically. This is no great problem; a number
of sealing devices which allow movement of shafts are commerically
available.

The single-ended transformer (see Chapter XVI) permits simpler circuitry than would a null type; the phase angle is always the same so
directional discrimination is not needed. The useful sensitivity will depend on the reproducibility of the bending of the torsion arm. Their
curve for Mohr's salt (ferrous ammonium sulfate hexahydrate) is given
in Fig. X-17.

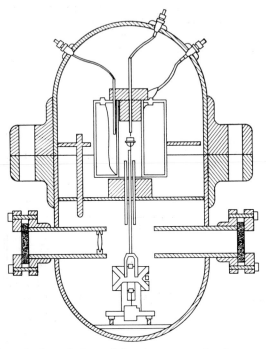

Fɪɢ. X-14. Cross section of thermobalance pressure chamber. From Rabatin and Card (R1).

A thermocouple is positioned so that when the top is put in place the junction is within the sample crucible. The rounding of the right-angle corners in the pressure vessel contributes greatly to safety by diminishing stress fatigue.

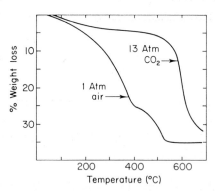

Fɪɢ. X-15. Thermograms for decomposition of manganous carbonate in air and in 13 atm carbon dioxide. From Rabatin and Card (R1).

The presence of carbon dioxide represses the decomposition of the carbonate and the absence of oxygen prevents oxidation of MnO to Mn_2O_3 until rather high temperatures are reached.

Note that both of these high-pressure thermobalances have the furnace *above* the weighing mechanism. The present author has found top-loading to be better (in closed systems) even at somewhat subatmospheric pressures. At elevated pressures the gas would inevitably heat the balance chamber in a suspended-sample arrangement. Interposition of a cooling barrier would set up severe currents at only a few hundred degrees.

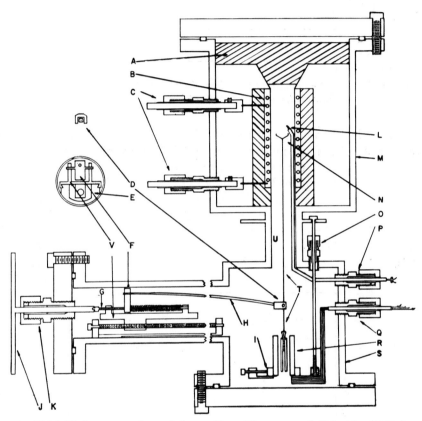

FIG. X-16. High-pressure thermobalance. From Biermann and Heinrichs (B50a). *The position-sensing transducer is also the counterbalance.*

10.10. Differential Thermogravimetry

Just as differential thermal analysis makes use of transient differences in temperature as a means of detection—and sometimes of measurement—of a reaction, so one may also use transient differences in weight. Consider the reasonably typical weight-loss curve in Fig. X-18, curve A.

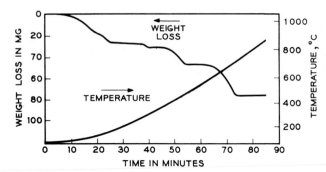

Fig. X-17. Thermogram obtained on heating Mohr's salt. From Biermann and Heinrichs (B50a).

The weight changes are attributed to loss of water, water, ammonia plus hydrogen, ammonia plus sulfuric acid, and, finally, sulfur trioxide.

Since we have no generally successful way to permit mass to enter or leave a specimen we must regain equilibrium by allowing our reference to change in the same manner. Figure X-18, B, shows a pair of curves slightly displaced in temperature and the difference between them. This difference is approximately the derivative of the original curve and such a signal may be obtained by plotting the derivative curve. That technique is discussed elsewhere (Chapter VIII); we are here concerned with the differential curve; how to get it and how useful it is.

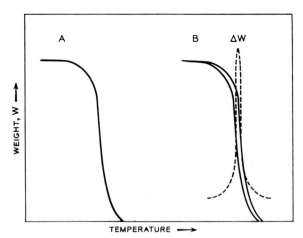

Fig. X-18. Differential thermogravimetry by the twin-furnace technique.

If two weight losses as in curve A occur closely spaced in time so that they overlap as in B, a difference signal ΔW gives an indication of the rate of weight loss.

The technique of de Keyser (K22) is perfectly straightforward. He heats two identical samples in a twin-furnace balance as shown in Fig. X-19. One of the furnaces being slightly hotter than the other, de Keyser obtains the difference between the two separate plots as illustrated in Fig. X-18, B. His comparison of differential thermal and differential thermogravimetric analyses of magnesium carbonate (apparently a basic magnesium carbonate) is shown in Fig. X-20.

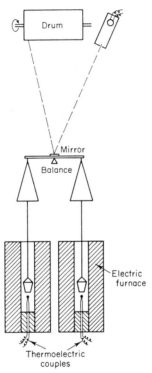

Fɪɢ. X-19. Twin-furnace differential thermogravimetry apparatus. From de Keyser (K22).

Identical samples in two furnaces—one lagging slightly in temperature—give transient indication of weight changes.

The general similarity of the curves in Fig. X-20 could be predicted; differential thermogravimetry has the same general advantages over thermogravimetry that differential thermal analysis has over calorimetry (Chapter II). It has a distinct advantage over differential thermal analysis in that the base line must necessarily return to zero in the absence of a reaction. Obviously it use is limited to study of those reactions involving a reasonably rapid weight change. Kaolin, for example, will show the drying and dehydration but not the exothermic reaction ca. 1000°C (see Chapter VIII). This is not necessarily a disadvantage.

The present author has strong doubts that satisfactory quantitative data may be derived from the technique even though de Keyser suggests that if one determines the total weight loss the weight loss of any

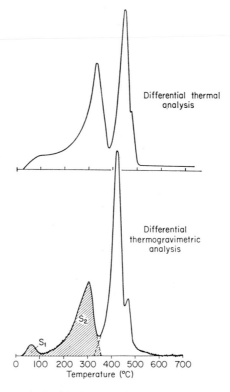

Differential thermal analysis

Differential thermogravimetric analysis

S_2

S_1

0   100 200 300 400 500 600 700
Temperature (°C)

FIG. X-20. Differential thermogravimetric and thermal analyses of "magnesium carbonate." From de Keyser (K22).

one reaction may be calculated from its relative area. The major problem is the nonconstancy of the $\Delta W/\Delta T$ that one is trying to measure; a second is the nonequal rates of reaction and nonequal temperature dependence of rates of reaction when two or more weight losses are involved.

The nonconstancy of ΔT is an apparatus problem and is not easily solved; de Keyser used a resistor in series with one of the furnace windings and apparently fed both from the same power supply. This in effect means that a set and almost constant fraction of the total voltage is dissipated in the resistor and furnace no. 2 of Fig. X-19 will have a voltage input of, say, 95% that of furnace no. 1. At higher and higher temperatures and hence voltage input the relative power total dissipation, $P = E^2/R$, remains the same but in the lagging furnace circuit we encounter a greater and greater lag because not all of the lesser power in the furnace no. 2 circuit is dissipated in the furnace. If, for example, the furnaces have 10 ohms resistance and the lagging resistor is ½ ohm, the actual relative power dissipation in the lagging furnace is 0.91. This naturally brings about a greater and greater temperature difference between the furnaces and hence between the specimens. Under the best conditions otherwise equivalent reactions would give quite different areas. All this does not gainsay the utility of the technique for detecting and studying reactions.

Before considering ways of obtaining a more nearly constant ΔT for the differential let us examine more carefully the nature of the measurement, i.e., the quantity we are attempting to measure, and evaluate the utility of the data. We are bringing about two separate reactions which proceed independently and we are measuring as a function of *time* the difference in completeness of the two reactions. (Whether we plot this difference against time or temperature has not the slightest effect on the reaction.) The rate of reaction is a function of both temperature and time so that the actual measurement is

$$\int_0^t \int_{T_r}^{T+\Delta T} f(T,t) \, dt \, dT - \int_0^t \int_{T_r}^{T} f(T,t) \, dt \, dT.$$

The fact that the rate of reaction changes with temperature means an unsymmetric peak must be expected because a unit of area does not have the same quantitative significance at various times during the course of the reaction. If a unit of area cannot be expected to maintain the same value (in milligrams per second) during one reaction, one cannot hope that a unit of area during some later reaction would have meaning even close to that in the previous reaction. Even assuming a constant ΔT, not only would the second peak be asymmetric within itself but the different rate constant and activation energy will cause a different response.

It can be argued justly that asymmetry in a reaction peak does not affect its utility for quantitative measurements. The objection is raised only for those cases in which (1) area is assigned a definite value and summation of the area under a deflection is considered to be evidence that some precisely stated quantity of material reacted or (2) two or more reactions occur and, from knowledge of the total weight loss, changes in weight are attributed to the various reactions in proportion to the areas of their peaks, i.e.,

$$\frac{\Delta W_1}{A_1} = \frac{\Delta W_2}{A_2} = \frac{\sum_i \Delta W_i}{\sum_i A_i}.$$

Quantitative measurements will require calibration using known quantities of the reacting species under well-controlled conditions.

Since the technique ought to be useful in qualitative work, it is worth while to consider possible improvements. The use of a resistor for lagging one furnace has already been shown to have serious disadvantages, yet the entire value of the system is concerned with this temperature difference. The use of two separate control systems is likely to permit fairly wide and rapid variations in a small ΔT; this would probably have no advantage. One furnace must be programmed and the other made to follow at some definite separation.

Since the system is now being considered principally for qualitative studies, we are not concerned with a very precise interval of temperature. It is enough that one can maintain an approximate ΔT and that this ΔT does not change rapidly or discontinuously. The appropriate control technique is to maintain a constant potential difference between thermocouples in the two furnaces (Fig. X-21). The variation with temperature of thermocouple response should be of no significance here.

Note also that this technique provides a convenient means of controlling sensitivity of selectivity of a process. By adding a way to vary the voltage added across the resistor (Fig. 21b) one may order a small ΔT for high selectivity or a large ΔT to avoid overlooking slow reactions. Too large a ΔT may permit reactions to go to completion in one furnace at a time. This is potentially a limit to the sensitivity.

The related technique of derivative thermogravimetry as described by Paulik *et al.* (P10) (see Chapter XI) depends on the rate of mechanical movement of the sample and support. Since it is not an absolute measurement, it would tend to be insensitive at low rates of weight loss. The derivative technique of Waters (W8) would be usable since it is a null balance technique.

The reader must bear in mind, while evaluating the technique, that it is—or should be—capable of detecting loss of a milligram or so in a 100-gm sample without interferring with detection of another reaction. Similarly, loss of even a number of grams will not interfere with the subsequent detection of milligram quantities.

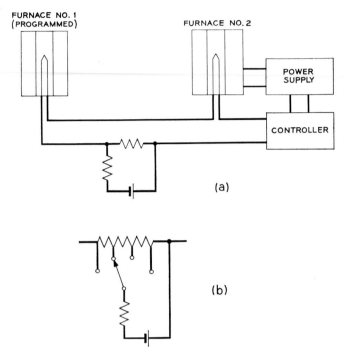

Fɪɢ. X-21. Suggested control system for differential thermogravimetry.
With the left-hand furnace controlled by the programming equipment the right-hand furnace can be made to lag or lead by a (a) fixed or (b) an adjustable amount. An added signal of zero in (b) would permit simple twin-furnace operation.

10.11. Summary

Beam balances may be operated at null by true mechanical balance or by use of a restoring force. They may be held near null by application of a restoring force or the displacement of the beam can be measured.

Nonbeam balances usually comprise some spring device. The displacement is usually measured but null operation is practicable.

While nonbeam balances can be made very sensitive to absolute weight change, the beam balances can measure (with good accuracy) a much smaller percentage weight change.

Differential and derivative thermogravimetry are often useful or convenient. Differential thermogravimetry has better potentialities but its use requires considerable care.

CHAPTER XI

Simultaneous Measurements

11.1. Introduction

In the separate practice of the arts of differential thermal and thermogravimetric analysis it will occur to many workers that, since both techniques involve observation of a sample during heating, the two measurements could be done simultaneously and poor correlation of data eliminated *ipso facto*. The advantages accruing from getting more than one set of data from the same sample at the same time are reasonably clear. A comparison of the two sets may be made with assurance that a reaction or other phenomenon apparent from one set of data can be related to an event apparent from the other set at the same temperature (or time); further, there is a *prima facie* saving on equipment and time. The first argument as it stands is true enough, but serious question of the need or advisability of correlating data in this way can be raised; the second is potentially a snare and a delusion.

The present author has from time to time concluded that two or more techniques could be used simultaneously and proceeded to carry out the experiments. While these experiments have been reasonably successful (e.g., G18 and G7), the general utility of the combination may not be worth the expenditure of time, equipment, and energy. In the second paper cited (G7) the benefits to be derived from a frequent qualitative analysis of the gaseous decomposition products of a thermal analysis were obvious. The nature of the reaction could be determined rather easily and the products of successive reactions could be separately identified. Mixtures of two gases could be separated into their components. An apparatus was assembled which could perform a differential thermal analysis and a continuous thermal conductivity measurement on the effluence, and, more important, at fixed intervals of time the effluence was sampled by a gas chromatograph (see Chapter XIV).

The concept was quite satisfactory; each analysis could be carried out; the method was discontinued anyway. The occurrence of trouble in one of the techniques was frequent enough to discourage use of the combination. In more recent experiments a sample is heated and the gases repetitively sampled for gas chromatography but, aside from measuring the temperature, nothing else is attempted. A separate sample is taken for differential thermal analysis. Since equipment is available a continuous gas analysis can be run as a possible aid in correlating data, but this is an added benefit only occasionally used. The important set of information is generally the differential thermal analysis.

In advocating simultaneous differential thermal analysis and thermogravimetric analysis or any such combination, the argument may have sometimes been raised that, unless the measurements are made simultaneously, they have no significance; they were not made on the same few hundred granules and another portion might behave quite differently. We may presume that a chemist with analytical training would not advance such a claim, for an important part of such training is in intelligent sampling.

If the sample is not representative of the whole, conclusions based on the behavior of the sample may not be extended to the whole. If the sample is properly taken to be representative of the whole, another portion properly taken should also be representative of the whole, and the behavior of one portion can be related to the behavior of the other, and the properties determined on these portions can be attributed to the whole.

The present author has encountered several types of opportunities for improper sampling. A common case is that in which a reaction—usually thermal—has not proceeded in the same manner or to the same degree in one part of the vessel as in another (see Chapter V). Another case is that in which a surface exposed to the air oxidizes or takes up water to a different degree than the interior. A third case is that in which each particle has characteristics somewhat different from others. An example of this third case is a polymer the present author studied rather briefly. The material was in coarse granules, so a few—or even one—could be used as a specimen. The results were highly irreproducible because the polymer had been strained deliberately and each granule could be expected to differ from any other. The selection of two pieces having essentially identical thermal properties would have been fortuitous. In each of these cases there are real differences, and the operator must either sample properly or refrain from making sweeping conclusions from a little bit of dust.

The possibility of irreproducible sampling is also the most probable lower limit to the size of a differential thermal analysis specimen (see Chapter VIII). The smallest practicable specimen, in the opinion of the author, will be that below which any quantity fails to show the thermal effects observable in a larger quantity. Extremely small specimens, such as those used by Mazieres (M21), will presumably be used only for studies of reversible phenomena or with the understanding that the properties of the specimen are not necessarily representative of any larger quantity.

Let us return now to the first reason for simultaneous determinations. The importance of designing an experiment to obtain unambiguously the information needed cannot be overemphasized. It is not enough to point with pride at some curves and relate a bump on one to a cant on another in serene confidence that the same event caused both. This is hardly thermal analysis. Ideal conditions for each of the techniques discussed in this monograph differ and, indeed, they differ even within a single general technique such as differential thermal analysis. The apparatuses for simultaneous determinations are perforce restrictive; the need to make one measurement must necessarily influence or limit the manner in which the second measurement must—or may—be made. If a compromise is made which sacrifices any advantage of either technique, the gain is probably not worthwhile; there is—in fact—a real possibility that the data are entirely meaningless.

The author does not by any means imply that simultaneous measurements should not be made—only that they must be made properly. Several of the techniques mentioned in Chapters I or XII could be done in combinations without detriment to any.

11.2. Differential Thermal plus Thermogravimetric Analysis

A case in which data may be vitiated with particular ease is that of simultaneous thermogravimetric and differential thermal analysis. Generally one may obtain data having relatability by simultaneous use of well-known techniques (Fig. XI-1). In the former case, orthodox techniques call for a moderately large sample and slow heating rates but in the latter case smaller samples and faster rates are the rule. The use of thermogravimetry implies a weight change and probably more than one.

If a leg of a differential thermocouple is stuck into the relatively large thermogravimetry sample and a slow heating rate is used the thermal effects—being time-dependent—will be small in magnitude and quite spread-out (in time). Recording ΔW or ΔT vs T (X-Y recorder) will eliminate time effects but see Chapter IV. If the heating rate is increased substantially, the weight loss reaction may be finished at the edges before the effect is even noticeable at the center. This temperature difference might be enough that a subsequent reaction would begin before the material at the center had undergone its first reaction.

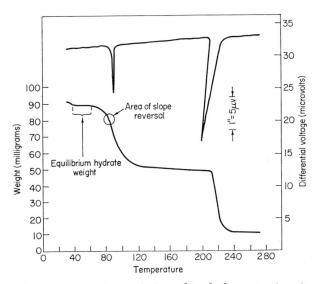

FIG. XI-1. Simultaneous differential thermal and thermogravimetric analysis of cesium carbonate hydrate at an average heating rate of 0.33°C/minute. From Reisman (R12).

A high-sensitivity amplifier and ΔT vs T recording shows temperature effects clearly but note that the lower-temperature thermal effect appears to occur over only part of the weight change.

In differential thermal analysis, one deliberately and with aforethought induces a temperature difference at the moment of reaction in apparatus designed to enhance this temperature difference as much as possible without preventing detection of subsequent reactions. In thermogravimetric analysis, one would like the specimen to lose instantaneously whatever weight it ought to lose under the experimental conditions. In the former technique, a temperature gradient within the sample is necessary and desirable; in the latter, a gradient must be avoided as far as possible and a minimum endured only reluctantly. In the former, dependence of magnitude of signal is naturally a function of heating rate; in the latter, any shift in reaction temperature with heating rate is to be deplored. The two techniques are not compatible. A combination must inevitably compromise the utility or sensitivity of one or the other technique, at least with the techniques common at the time of writing.

If one chooses to employ a high rate of heating, and thus get sensitive differential thermal analysis, temperature gradients within the sample will consequently spread out the weight loss. This will be the extent of the impairment if one is using an atmosphere of the product gas or a closed chamber (Chapter VII); in other cases atmosphere effects will displace the reaction temperature. If, on the other hand, one heats the material slowly, one loses a considerable part of the sensitivity of the differential thermal technique.

Agreement of thermogravimetric and differential thermal analysis data may be obtained in a number of ways. The author has a strong bias in favor of sets of data each obtained under the same known and reproducible thermodynamic conditions whether or not the data were obtained on the same sample at the same time; other attempts to obtain agreement are possibly meaningless. It is quite true that decomposition curves may be obtained which show thermal effects and weight changes in the same temperature ranges. Three popular ways are by simultaneous measurements of weight and temperature on the same specimen, simultaneous measurements on separate but contiguous specimens, and measurements of the two effects in separate experiments but in the same (type of) sample holder.

The good agreement in temperature of the thermal and the mass effects can lead to—or be used to support—some quite unwarranted interpretations or oversimplifications. An example of the latter is Borchardt's measurement of initial reaction rates from differential thermal analysis data (B66). Borchardt derives an equation for the rate of reaction, i.e., the fraction converted per unit time:

$$\frac{-dn/n_0}{dt} = \frac{2\Delta T}{\tau \Delta T_{max}}$$

where he assumed (*a*) that the differential thermal analysis peak can be approximated by a triangle of base τ and height ΔT_{max} and (*b*) that the rate of reaction so calculated applies to the temperature at which the height of the peak is ΔT. By using only low values of $\Delta T/\Delta T_{max}$ he found "initial reaction rates" for magnesium, carbonate, calcium carbonate, and kaolinite. For verification he obtained thermogravimetric curves using a sample holder of the same internal geometry. These sample holders were cavities—open at the top—$\frac{1}{4}$ inch in diameter and $\frac{3}{8}$ inch deep. The furnace atmosphere was static air and the heating rate 12°C/minute.

Borchardt selected a $\Delta T / T_{max}$ value of $\frac{1}{10}$, determined the corresponding temperatures from the differential thermal analysis plots (Fig. XI-2), and calculated the reaction rates shown in Table XI-1. From the thermogravimetric data, he measured the rate of weight loss ("observed

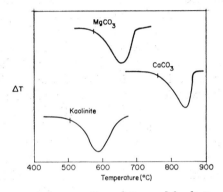

Fig. XI-2. DTA patterns of magnesite, calcite, and kaolinite. The marker on the curve indicates the point where $\Delta T = 0.1 \, \Delta T_{max}$. From Borchardt (B66).
The weight loss ratios at the 0.1 ΔT_{max} were calculated from the first-order reaction law and compared with the experimental values.

rate" of Table XI-1) at nearly the same temperatures and found reasonable agreement. The agreement is reasonable but the assumption that these numbers then describe the rates of reaction for these materials at the given temperatures is not. Each number applies only to the *particular* sample geometry with the *particular* packing at the *particular* heating rate because the decomposition is not occurring at the same rate in all parts of the vessel.

TABLE XI-1

"INITIAL REACTION RATES" DETERMINED BY BORCHARDT (B66)

Material	DTA temperature (°C)	Calculated rate (%/minute)	Observed rate (%/minute)
MgCO₃	579	1.67	1.90 at 580°C
CaCO₃	762	2.11	2.78 at 759°C
Kaolinite	506	1.29	1.28 at 506°C

The very earliest decomposition takes place, of course, in air, but there is a fairly rapid increase in carbon dioxide (or water) concentration. Even with the loose packing of the calcium carbonate, 8.27% of theoretical density, particle size, 6.3 μ, by the time 1% of the material had reacted enough carbon dioxide had been liberated to fill the intergranular voids a couple of times. Nevertheless, these voids are not filled with product gas because of interchange with the ambient atmosphere. The rapidity of interchange will depend not only on the geometry of the sample holder but also on the ease of diffusion within the voids. With this loose packing the interchange could indeed be rapid. Because of this loss of carbon dioxide to the ambient atmosphere, most of the reaction is occurring either near the surface where the carbon dioxide concentration has been attenuated by diffusion or at the wall where the material is hotter than in the interior of the specimen holder (see Chapter VII). The reaction rate is consequently an average rate applicable only to the conditions of that particular experiment. The data would be essentially reproducible and would have significance if they were obtained in an atmosphere of the product gas. Note, however, that two of these materials used as examples are quite different in nature, the simple decomposition of a carbonate as compared to dehydroxylation of a layered mineral (see Chapter VI). A quite different heating rate dependence can be expected.

By a variation on standard techniques, a reasonable approximation to simultaneous differential thermal and thermogravimetric analysis might be performed without serious impairment of either technique. Consider again the requirements: (1) the decomposition or other reaction must cause a measurable deviation from steady-state heating; (2) the temperature must be virtually the same throughout the sample.

The latter requirement is met easily by the thin-layer technique previously discussed, except that the sample holder is no longer massive. Since we can measure the temperature of the sample we no longer need to assure ourselves that the sample temperature is increasing steadily. We may, then, use a low–heat capacity but high–thermal conductivity component in contact with the sample and follow its temperature. This arrangement might take the form of a thin metallic disc—isolated thermally from the furnace walls—on which the sample rests. Its temperature could be compared with that of a point near—but not in contact with—it. This device could be readily adapted to either the free-diffusion or the closed-chamber sample holder (Fig. XI-3 and XI-4) (see Chapter VII). The signal from a measuring thermocouple in contact with the metal disc is compared with the signal from a thermocouple slightly below it.

The result is not strictly differential thermal analysis but the same sort of data can be obtained: a small signal with some drift and the thermal effects imposed on it. The usual amplification and recording apparatus would be needed. (The author is merely suggesting, not advocating.)

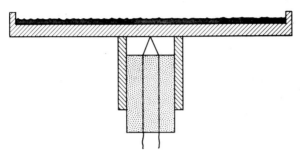

FIG. XI-3. Free-diffusion sample holder for top-loading balance.
The holder is set down on the support rod which also carries the thermocouple.

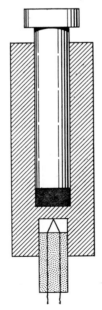

FIG. XI-4. Closed-chamber sample holder for top-loading balance.
The thickness of the barrier between the sample and thermocouple should be inversely dependent on the skill of the fabricator. The mass of the holder may prevent its use on any but beam balances.

11.3. Apparatus for Simultaneous Differential Thermal and Thermogravimetric Analysis

One important attempt at simultaneous differential thermal and thermogravimetric analysis was that of Papailhau (P5a), who constructed a weighing apparatus (in which he could do differential thermal analysis at the same time and on the same sample) which remained at a stationary balance point by reason of a variable fluid displacement action on a cylinder fastened to the sample support (Fig. XI-5). A weight loss causes the breaking of an electrical circuit. The breaking of the circuit causes a motor to lift a second cylinder from the fluid to decrease the displacement by the first by changing the level of the fluid. An index coupled with the motor movement follows the position of the control

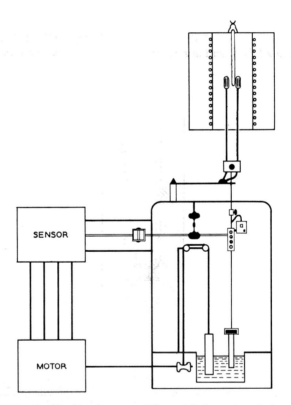

Fig. XI-5. Apparatus for simultaneous differential thermal and thermogravimetric analysis. From Papailhau (P5a).

The temperature effects and weight loss of a single specimen are measured. The fluid level is changed to maintain null.

cylinder, either recording its position on a strip of paper or registering it
on a millivoltmeter.

Papailhau (Fig. XI-6) adds another feature—a dynamic atmosphere.
A dynamic atmosphere (see Chapter VII) is potentially extremely useful because it permits determinations by both techniques under thermodynamically known and reproducible conditions, so some of the
objections to simultaneous determinations are not applicable (Fig. XI-7).
The major problems are mechanical. Note (Fig. XI-6) that Papailhau
uses a straight length of tubing. Any significant curvature would bring
about a noticeable change in torque with any change in gas flow because an increase in flow—and hence in pressure—would tend to

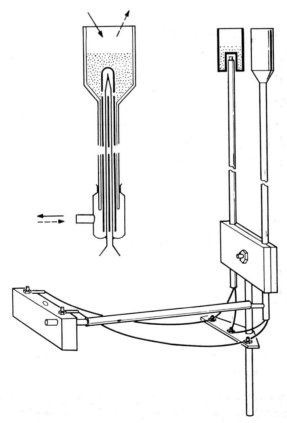

Fig. XI-6. Arrangement for passing a controlled atmosphere through a sample and
measuring both temperature and weight changes. From Papailhau (P5a).

*The mechanical connections have relatively little effect since the balance operates
at null.*

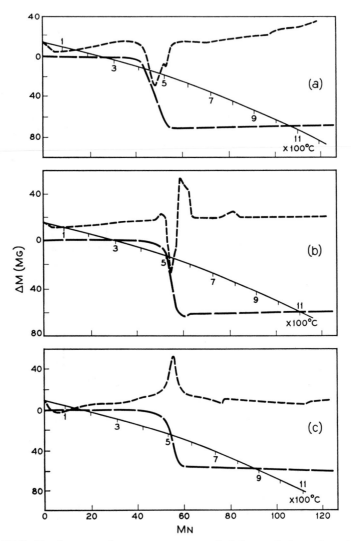

F_{IG}. XI-7. Simultaneous thermogravimetric and differential thermal analysis of siderite in dynamic flow of (a) nitrogen, (b) air, and (c) oxygen. From Papailhau (P5a).

The known thermodynamic conditions in (a) and (c) permit accurate interpretation. The attenuated oxygen supply in (b) leads to incomplete reaction (see Chapter VII).

straighten the tube. If Papailhau were measuring displacement instead of maintaining a null position his calibration curve would be just that —a curve.

The matter of inserting a thermocouple into the sample has been faced—and solved—a number of times. The present author uses a helix of fine wire bent so that the stationary end hangs naturally to the point at which it is fastened (see Chapter IX). Papailhau uses a direct lead with only a slight loop. This is effective in his apparatus because it is a null instrument. Since there is no appreciable change in position any force which might be exerted between the fixed and movable parts will at least be constant.

The same constant-force argument can be applied to the tubing joining the fixed and movable parts. While the coupling might have some effect on the sensitivity, no other error is involved as long as the flow of gas is constant.

Papailhau used samples ranging from 165 to 300 mg in a geometry approximating a crucible. The thermal effects agree, of course, with the weight changes but these weight changes are quite drawn-out affairs. Any sizable reaction extends over at least 100°C. Part of the reason for the wide temperature range is the heating rate, part is the size of the sample. Papailhau heated his samples at the common differential thermal analysis rate of 10°C/minute. This is far too fast to obtain reasonable transfer of heat to a sample (see Chapter III), and especially is it difficult to heat a mass of 0.3 gm at such a rate and expect to have anything approaching uniformity. Even the dynamic atmosphere does not help for, like Stone (S50), he brings the gas to and through the sample and into the furnace chamber but, unlike Stone, he does not preheat the gas.

Paulik and co-workers (P10) used a sort of mechanical derivative with electrical pickup to do simultaneous differential thermogravimetry and, on the same specimen, thermogravimetry and differential thermal analysis. The sample and a reference material are heated in the same furnace (Fig. XI-8) and ΔT, ΔW, and dw/dt are all plotted as functions of time. The dw/dt signal arises from movement of a coil within a permanent magnet; this response should be accurately linear as long as the beam is very nearly at null and the magnet and coil are so designed that electrical response is linear with movement.

The useful weight loss range of a balance of this type is dictated by (1) the mechanical range of linear electrical response and (2) the mechanical range of constant displacement response $d\theta/dw$. Another limit is imposed on the differential thermal analysis. Movement of the sample with relation to the reference should tend to displace the base line because of the temperature gradient within the furnace.

Weltner (W13) reports curves as shown in Fig. XI-9 using the apparatus of Paulik *et al.* (P10), where the thermogravimetric curve is also shown to demonstrate how much more informative is derivative thermogravimetric analysis as compared to simple thermogravimetric analysis. The present author believes that the thermogravimetric curve could be made decidedly more informative by proper attention to sample holders (see Chapter VII). Paulik *et al.* (P11) later improved the sample holder (Fig. VII-14).

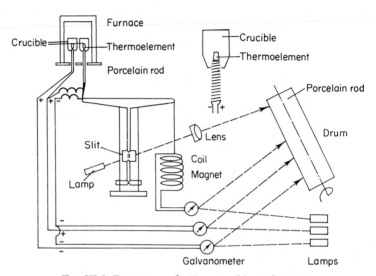

Fig. XI-8. Derivatograph. From Paulik *et al.* (P10).
The balance position is recorded directly by use of a slit on the point arm and T, ΔT, and dw/dt by use of appropriately connected galvanometers.

The technique is obviously usable to detect reactions and has the advantage over the deKeyser (K22) technique in that the area of a deflection is relatable directly to the loss in weight—as long as the limitations given above are heeded.

The technique should not be extended to very low-mass weighing devices because of the possibility of regenerative feedback between galvanometer and detecting coil. A very light balance could possibly have an oscillation period somewhere nearly equal to the period of the galvanometer. Displacement of the galvanometer during the change of position of the magnet induces an opposing voltage during the deflection —i.e., work is done on the galvanometer—but, as the movement drops to zero and reverses, the return of the galvanometer to its rest or zero position induces a voltage opposing the drop-off of detecting coil voltage and hence aiding the movement of the magnet—i.e., work is done by the galvanometer. This work would tend to carry the magnet beyond its new rest point so that it would need to return, thereby starting a galvanometer motion in the other direction, etc. Fortunately, the amount of work that could be done by the galvanometer would not be sufficient to sustain oscillation. The extra deflection would be a nuisance and could at times hinder interpretation of the curve.

This oscillation has an analog occasionally encountered by the unwary. If one attempts to supply a potential to a fairly high-speed, low-range, recording potentiometer from a potentiometer having a short period galvanometer as a null indicator, oscillation may occur if the galvanometer is neither locked nor shorted. Unless

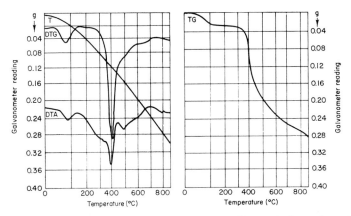

Fig. XI-9. Simultaneous thermogravimetric and differential thermal analysis of coal. From Weltner (W13).

The DTG and DTA curves show good agreement; the TG plot shows little detail.

the recording potentiometer slide-wire contact is already at the proper potential the unbalance will cause motion of both the meter movement and the recorder slide-wire. The slide-wire movement will tend to stop at the set potential but the meter is probably deflected full scale. Its movement back to null induces a voltage which sends the recorder slide-wire further in the direction of initial movement, causing the meter to deflect the other way, causing the recorder to overshoot again. The major difference between this case and the galvanometer-magnet coil case is that this former is a driven oscillator. The work supplied to the slide-wire permits continuous oscillation.

An example of the problems encountered in simultaneous determinations is offered by Kissinger *et al.* (K31) in their studies on manga-

nese(II) carbonate (Fig. XI-10). The differential thermal analyses in
the 400–600°C region show striking effects at the highest heating rate
compared to the lower heating rates—yet at this highest heating rate,
the detail of the weight loss curve is lost, leaving very little to which to
relate these effects. The weight loss curve at 10°C/minute, for example,
loses the shoulder ca 450°C seen at the lower heating rates but shows
no new detail which might be related to the very sizable thermal effects.
These authors were careful to use the same geometry for both speci-

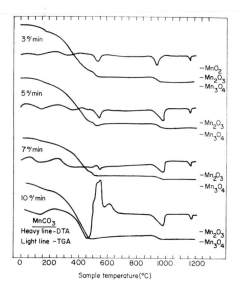

FIG. XI-10. Differential thermal analysis and thermogravimetric analysis patterns
of reagent-grade manganese carbonate, MnCO₃, at various heating rates. From
Kissinger *et al.* (K31).

*The differential thermal analysis shows the most detail at heating rates at which
thermogravimetric analysis shows the least.*

men holders; the loss of detail is due to incompleteness of one reaction
before the start of the next, partly because of the high heating rate and
partly because of the atmosphere effect (see Chapter VII).

The atmosphere can be taken into account rather easily. The thin-
layer technique—affording free interchange of gas between sample and
atmosphere—has been used by McAdie (M24) for simultaneous differential thermal and thermogravimetric analysis. He uses two pans suspended on the same rod (Fig. XI-11) and measures the temperature of
each by use of a thermocouple pressed into a hole in the disc. By control

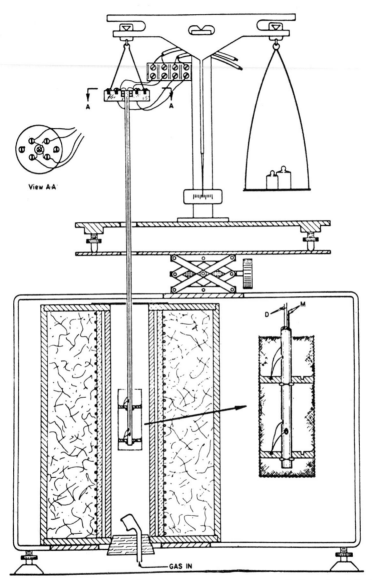

Fɪɢ. XI-11. Simultaneous thermogravimetric and differential thermal analysis apparatus using free-diffusion sample holders. From McAdie (M24).

Since known thermodynamic conditions can be obtained, the data are meaningful.

of the flowing atmosphere, decomposition steps can be separated as shown in Fig. XI-2 and XI-3.

The simultaneous determinations by Reisman (R12) were done under a considerable range of heating rates with the intention of keeping the specimen near equilibrium at all times. His specimens were contained in

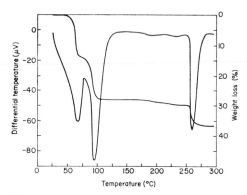

Fig. XI-12. Simultaneous thermogravimetric and differential thermal analysis of copper sulfate pentahydrate in air. From McAdie (M24).

The constant partial pressure of water vapor permits clear separation of the first two steps of the dehydration. Compare with Fig. XI-14.

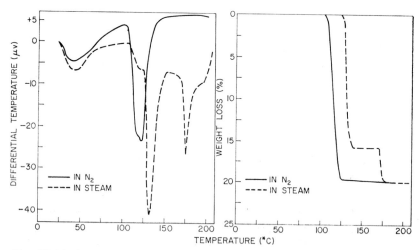

Fig. XI-13. Simultaneous thermogravimetric and differential thermal analysis of calcium sulfate dihydrate in nitrogen and in steam. From McAdie (M24).

The clear separation of the first reaction permits a better quantitative measurement of the dihydrate than by differential thermal analysis.

split crucibles mounted at the end of a counterpoised rod, both thermal effects and weight change being measured on the same sample. The work is in large part vitiated, unfortunately, by his choice of sample holders. His inability to obtain more than a minor slope anomaly for $CuSO_4 \cdot 3H_2O$ (Fig. XI-14) at a heating rate of 0.56°C/minute must be compared to McAdie's well-developed plateau (Fig. XI-12) at about twice the heating rate or to the present author's very clear break (G4) at 2°C/minute. The partial pressure of water vapor is by no

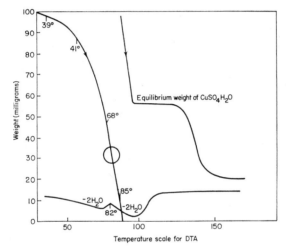

Fig. XI-14. Partial simultaneous differential thermal and thermogravimetric analysis of copper sulfate pentahydrate at ca. 0.56°C/minute. From Reisman (R12).

The lack of a clear inflection is due to nonhomogeneity of the sample during the dehydration. Some material has gone to the monohydrate before all the pentahydrate has gone to the trihydrate.

means equal throughout the crucible, and consequently the material is not all in the same state nor is the relative composition constant from top to bottom.

Similarly, the thermal and mass effects in rubidium carbonate hydrate are very probably well-described by his heating of a sample in an oil bath except that the solid crust is almost certainly the anhydrous carbonate. The crust forms quickly over the melt, showing further loss until the water vapor pressure can break through—rather than diffuse through —when the temperature is raised sufficiently.

An interesting method of detection of changes of state makes use of the adsorption of diffusing gas at interfaces between crystalline regions.

Bussiere *et al.* (B91) devised a simultaneous differential thermal analysis, thermogravimetric analysis and effluence detection using this principle. The applicability of the method would be rather uncommon but this does not imply that it may not be of great value in some particular case.

Thorium, on radioactive decay, gives off the short-lived rare gas, thoron. The gas diffuses out of the crystal of a thorium salt in the normal course of events, some escaping before further decay, but some part of the gas will tend to remain in interstices, along grain boundaries, and at other high-energy sites. During reactions or simple phase transformations, the grain boundaries are disturbed and the gas can escape more easily. If a stream of gas is passed over—or preferably through—the specimen and it is monitored by a radiation detector somewhere downstream, the additional radioactivity during a disruption can be detected. A simultaneous recording of thermal effects, change of weight, and radioactivity is shown in Fig. XIV-17.

Note that the second weight loss, the conversion of the dihydrate to the monohydrate, is reflected only by a gradual increase in radioactivity of the gas stream. This is because even a reversible event would show a time-dependent response to the "emanation analysis"; the gas must have an opportunity to return to a stable level. If the heating were stopped at 100°C and at a later time the sample were rerun, it is possible that the dehydration in the 150–200°C range would also be shown by increased "emanation." In this case, however, another behavior might be encountered. The first dehydration has very probably already caused a change in crystal structure; this one need not. Water might well be driven off without severe disturbance of the lattice and without this disturbance no disruption of grain boundaries is likely to occur. The decrease in emanation ca 300°C is very probably a dilution effect during the decomposition of the oxalate ion.

In any case in which simultaneous determinations are contemplated, the experimenter must consider whether any of the measured phenomena are time-dependent or history-dependent. If any are, special care in planning the experiment is required. Note that even in the common practice of simultaneous differential thermal and thermogravimetric analysis the differential signal is time-dependent while the weight of the specimen may be time-dependent, but for a reversible decomposition in a controlled atmosphere it is much more temperature-dependent.

In most cases the advantage lies with execution of separate experiments, each planned to extract information in the best possible manner. The present author does thermogravimetric and differential thermal analysis on separate apparatuses and at different times (Chapter XVII) yet has no trouble obtaining relatable data. The important consideration is the agreement of thermodynamic conditions, in particular the atmosphere and its degree of confinement (see Chapter VII). Figures XI-15 and XI-16 show thermogravimetric and differential thermal analysis data for cobalt oxalate hydrate and lead carbonate in which there is no difficulty relating the effects.

Nearly the ultimate in simultaneous operations was attempted by Blazek (B55) who constructed a thermobalance with provision for recording a differential thermal analysis and a gaseous decomposition

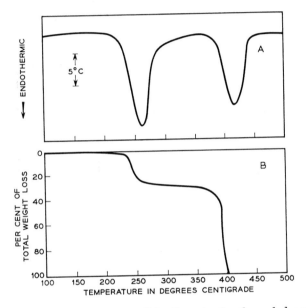

Fig. XI-15. Thermal (a) and mass (b) effects in the thermal decomposition of cobalt oxalate dihydrate in a closed-chamber sample holder (Figs. III-23 and VII-13). From Garn (G4).

The dehydration and the loss of carbon dioxide show clear agreement. The cobalt oxalate is degraded to the metal.

product analysis simultaneously with the thermogravimetric analysis. Like Kissinger *et al.* (K31) or McAdie (M24) he used separate specimens but unlike these other authors he did not use the same geometry. The furnace (Fig. XI-17) had two chambers, one for the thermogravimetric analysis and the other for the gas and differential thermal analysis. The latter chamber (Fig. XI-18) has separate holders for the differential thermal analysis and for the gas analysis samples. Fortunately Blazek used only inert gases passing through the furnaces so that, while each specimen might react somewhat differently as a function of time, the disagreement would be relatively small. The need to place three different sample holders so that each is heated equally is already rather difficult when they are the same shape; vertical furnaces can be expected to have temperature gradients. When at least one of the samples (differential thermal analysis) is necessarily going to be heated unsymmetrically because of its shape, really good agreement is out of the question. The one simultaneous differential thermal and thermogravimetric analysis reported (Fig. XI-19) shows poor agreement. While the differ-

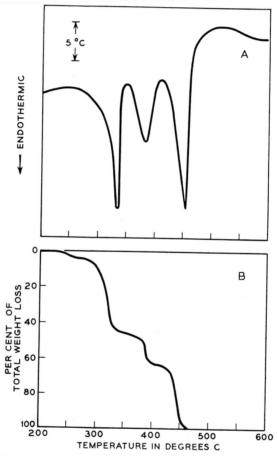

FIG. XI-16. Thermal (a) and mass (b) effects in the thermal decomposition of lead carbonate in a closed-chamber sample holder. From Garn (G4).

Each loss of carbon dioxide is clearly separated because the decomposition—in each experiment—occurs in an atmosphere of carbon dioxide.

ential thermal analysis peak coincides with the completion of the weight loss at the lower-temperature weight loss ca. 300°C, it occurs ca. 100°C after the weight loss at the higher-temperature decomposition.

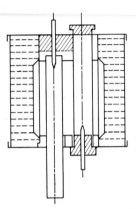

FIG. XI-17. Section of furnace. From Blazek (B55).
The thermogravimetric sample is in a crucible–supported from the balance beneath–in the left-hand chamber.

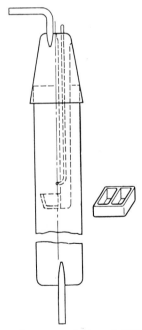

FIG. XI-18. Quartz casing for gas analysis and DTA. From Blazek (B55).
The several containers are not all positioned for equal heating.

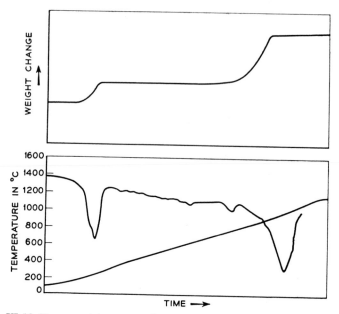

Fig. XI-19. Decomposition curve of manganous sulfate. From Blazek (B55).
The thermogravimetric sample is probably located higher in its chamber than is the differential thermal analysis sample in its chamber. Not only is the temperature higher but also the heat transfer would be better.

11.4. Summary

The conditions of sample size, geometry, heating rate, etc., which are best for one type of measurement may be quite incompatible with the conditions best for another. Properly chosen experiments can yield better data by separate experiments. Differential thermal analysis combined with thermogravimetry will often lead to poor results.

Nevertheless, if compatible techniques (see also Chapter XII) are chosen and experimental conditions set up so that any needs incident to the taking of one masurement have no influence on any other, a number of parameters can be measured simultaneously and the data will have meaning.

CHAPTER XII

Other
Techniques

12.1. Introduction

From time to time problems appear in which differential thermal or thermogravimetric analysis is unsuccessful. Assuming that a thermal technique for dynamic analysis is needed, one of several special techniques may be appropriate. The techniques discussed in this chapter are generally less useful than differential thermal or thermogravimetric analysis and for this reason are unlikely to be widely used; nevertheless any of them might be useful in some specific case. The techniques may be used as detection methods or, in some cases, as primary measurements providing specifically the desired information.

No exhaustive examination of the literature in these fields has been undertaken; rather specific examples have been selected. This chapter is intended in large part to acquaint the experimenter with these other modes of attack on a problem. A secondary purpose is to offer sufficient instruction to enable the experimenter to avoid some of the possible troubles.

12.2. Dilatometry

The measurement of dimensions or volume as the material is heated or cooled is principally useful when these specific data comprise the in-

formation sought. As a means of detecting changes in state it is advantageous in only a few cases. Nevertheless it can be used and the reader
should have some acquaintance with the techniques and limitations.
Note that the relative nonutility for *detecting* changes does not imply
nonutility for *studying* the changes.

Several techniques for measuring linear expansion are useful. Dial
gages, micrometers, telescopes, linear variable differential transformers,
interferometers, and X-ray diffraction patterns have all been reported.

All of these except the last measure the linear expansion of the specimen as it is set in the apparatus. For nonisotropic materials the expansion
will presumably differ and additional experiments with differently oriented samples may be needed. X-ray diffraction measurements yield
expansion data for all directions if the lines have been properly cata-
logued.

During the preparation of this monograph an experimental dilatometer
for both sub- and supra-ambient temperatures was constructed at Bell
Telephone Laboratories by H. A. Sauer (S7). The measuring and programming systems were the same for both ranges but since the heat
conducting and insulating problems are different in the two ranges different test chambers were used. In either case the test chamber (Fig.
XII-1) is heated or cooled by a circulating gas whose temperature is
controlled by the programmer. Measurements may be recorded, then,

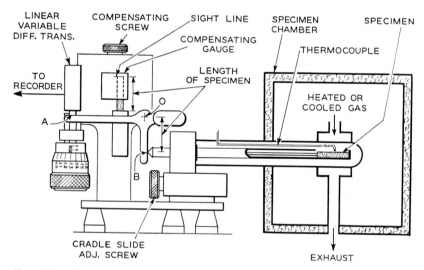

FIG. XII-1. Programmed dilatometer providing sub- and supra-ambient temperatures. From Sauer (S7).

Linear expansion of a rod is recorded directly as a fractional change.

as the specimen is heated, as it is cooled, or at constant temperature.

The sensing element is a linear variable differential transformer whose rectified output is recorded directly. The mechanical linkage to the transformer is through an adjustable mechanical amplifier (the pivot arm). Adjustment of the compensating screw of Fig. XII-1 to bring the top of the specimen to the sight line moves the pivot arm so that the contact point from the bearing rod is precisely one sample length from the fulcrum. In effect, the linear variable differential transformer sees a fixed length of specimen, in this case 100 mm long, and the change recorded is the change in 100 mm of specimen. The transformer may be moved by the micrometer screw for calibration and for zeroing.

Volume expansion is of special value for organic materials and particularly those which are not highly oriented. (Mechanical measurements of linear expansion generally require some firm mechanical contact which could cause deformation of soft specimens.) Fluid displacement is, of course, the simplest method of observing volume changes.

The usefulness of the technique for organic materials is a consequence of the low thermal conductivity of these materials and the occurrence of glass transitions in polymeric materials. The low heating rates ordinarily needed to obtain a reasonably small temperature gradient render the base line discontinuity difficult to detect. Higher rates of heating that cause a significant time lag between the initiation of the change at the edge and completion at the center quite naturally cause a rounding of the discontinuity. While these transitions can usually be detected by differential thermal analysis, static methods such as dilatometry are at least not out of place and are sometimes necessary.

The system of Loasby (L9) illustrates the use of volume expansion. The changing displacement of the sample in Fig. XII-2 is converted to linear motion by the bellows. The large sample and relatively small volume of oil permits rather good sensitivity. The maximum sensitivity is obtained by (1) designing the sample so that it just barely fails to touch the sides at maximum temperature and (2) adding just enough oil to the bellows to bring it out of contact with the sample. Some mechanical amplification can easily be obtained by enclosing the specimen in a rigid container attached to a narrower bellows or, of course, by measuring the volume expanding into a narrow tube. The former would usually be unnecessary because adequately sensitive measurements for most purposes can be made without the mechanical amplification. The second would simply require a different method of measurement. The volume expansion dilatometer can be constructed over a considerable range of sensitivities depending on the particular needs of the user. For temperatures more than just slightly different from ambient the sample chamber of Fig. XII-2 would be enclosed in a thermostatted bath. Note that the specimen need not be a single massive piece. While this massive specimen would provide better sensitivity, small chunks of material can be used. These latter could be expected to reach thermal equilibrium more quickly.

The dilatometers using position-sensing transducers to obtain an electrical signal to record will generally need to be calibrated. The calibration may, in fact, be required before and/or after each run; the linear

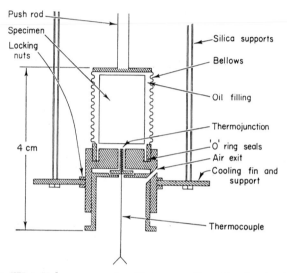

FIG. XII-2. Volume expansion dilatometer. From Loasby (L9).
Expansion or contraction in all directions is converted to unidirectional movement.

variable transformer often used gives a good, sensitive measure of changes of position but an essential part of the experiment will be the simulation of the run by an accurately known change. Lieberman and Crandall (L7) devised a self-calibrating dilatometer (Fig. XII-3) which recorded change in fractions of a fixed unit. They attached an optical grating to the end of their support rod so that it moved as the specimen expanded or contracted and passed a light beam through this and another grating. The measured intensity of the light falling on a photocell is recorded but only an uncalibrated measurement is needed. If the output is simply adjusted so that the recorded maximum and minimum intensities do not go off scale, a plot such as that in Fig. XII-4 will be obtained as the sample expands or contracts. For a 500 lines per inch grating, a full deflection is obtained then for each 0.00100 inch of movement and the sensitivity will likely be limited by the perfection of the grating, i.e., the accuracy of reading of the maxima and minima. The accuracy will only be compromised in that particular cycle; the integral traverses of grating lines will be unaffected. An absolute accuracy of, say, ½% of scale, rather than a relative accuracy, is obtained.

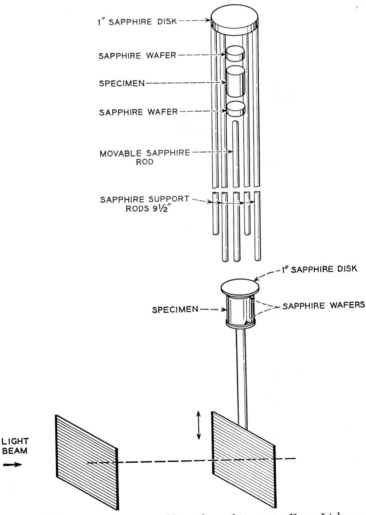

FIG. XII-3. Dilatometer stage assembly and sapphire parts. From Lieberman and Crandall (L7).

The resolution within a half cycle will depend on the collimation of the light and the alignment and quality of the gratings because of their effect on the sharpness of the maxima and minima.

The slight possibility of misinterpretation of the data due to reversal of direction of travel when the intensity happens to be at a maximum or minimum can be avoided; the present author would use a grating with one end shielded so that successive intensity maxima became greater or less as the specimen expanded or contracted. By the time another maximum has passed the actual direction of travel would be unequivocally known.

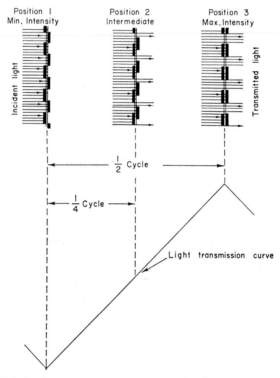

Fig. XII-4. Relation between grating position and light transmission. From Lieberman and Crandall (L7).

Within a half cycle the effect of grating defects is small because the total intensity from a large number of apertures is measured.

Thermal expansion data may also be obtained by X-ray diffraction, but this is ordinarily a static technique (see, for example, Campbell's array of data on magnesium oxide (C5).

Another type of optical recording was used by Dannis (D2). He rested one leg of a tripod carrying a mirror on the specimen and recorded the position of the light beam (Fig. XII-5) in a manner similar to that of Keith and Tuttle (K14). The use of photoresistors is probably more covenient experimentally than the phototube used by Keith and Tuttle. Dannis obtained the curve of Fig. XII-6 using the apparatus. The temperature was recorded from a 38-gauge thermocouple to avoid any extraneous movement due to springiness or differences in thermal expansion of the thermocouple wires (D1).

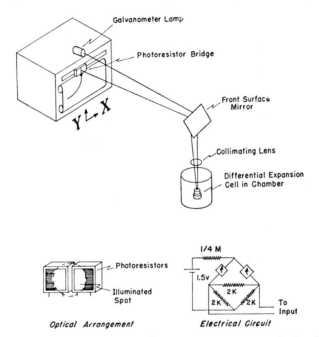

FIG. XII-5. Schematic arrangement of expansion apparatus with details of photo-resistor arrangement. From Dannis (D2).

The expansion or contraction of the specimen displaces the mirror. The pen carriage moves to keep the photoresistor cells in the reflected beam.

12.3. Electrical Measurements

The electrical properties of a solid material can be of use in detecting changes of state. Consider, for example, a well-crystallized ordinary salt or oxide which can undergo a crystallographic phase transformation. In either form the energy levels are well-defined and are properly filled, leaving a very few electrons in the high-energy conduction levels. During a phase transformation, however, an unrest appears. The movement of ions from the one configuration to the other quite necessarily disturbs the order of the system as the valence electrons settle into their new energy states. During this transitory disorder electrons are relatively free to move and, under the influence of an electric field, conduct current.

If we measure the resistance of a pure material as it is heated, then we may expect a decrease in resistance during the time of transition followed by an increase to some not necessarily equal level. The extent of the decrease and the temperature or time interval over which it occurs should be dependent not only on the nature of the material but also—to a lesser degree—on its history.

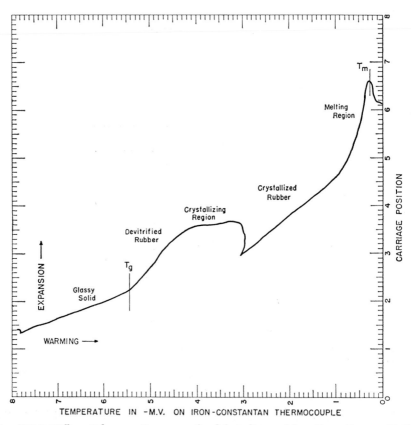

FIG. XII-6. Differential expansion curve of polybutadiene rubber. From Dannis (D2). *Changes in state can be detected by changes in rate of expansion.*

The ease of detection of polymorphic phase changes will depend on the experimental apparatus and technique. Reisman *et al.* (R16) measured the voltage drop across a specimen in series with a known resistance, thereby obtaining actual resistance values. The present author, with Flaschen (G11), preferred to use a resistance bridge and obtain only an indication of change. Neither set of authors used the alternate technique so a critical comparison is not available.

The latter authors (G11) were only able to detect very easily not only the effect due to a drastic phase change (Fig. XII-7a) in a pure material and to the corresponding transition in a solid solution with an isomorphic material (Fig. XII-7b) but even the effect due to the relatively small shift (Fig. XII-7c) during the a-β quartz transition. Melting points (Fig. XII-7d) would present no difficulty even with very simple equipment.

An important virtue of the technique is that highly accurate temperature programming is not needed. The time or temperature range of the deflection should be unaffected by relatively small—but even abrupt —changes in heating rate. The magnitude of the deflection should be affected by the heating rate because at higher heating rates a greater portion of the sample could be expected to be changing at a given time (Fig. XII-8).

The example shown in Fig. XII-8 is unusual in that the resistance increases during the transition. Barium titanate has a positive temperature coefficient of resistance whose range and magnitude depend on the nature and quality of impurities.

The polarizability of a material varies only slowly with temperature in the absence of any change in state. The mobility during a change permits relatively great movement during the time that the ion is in a disordered state so that the dielectric constant increases and subsequently decreases, yielding plots with temperature similar to that of I-13.

12.4. X-Ray Diffraction

A technique only recently approaching its real potentialities in thermal analysis is X-ray diffraction. The analysis of samples at room temperature after heating to some temperature at which the observer believes a given—but no other—reaction has taken place is simple X-ray analysis and need not be treated here. Of substantially greater interest are studies performed on heated samples.

Several authors have reported results using X-ray diffraction on samples held at an elevated constant temperature. These constant-temperature studies are perfectly straightforward for crystal structure measurements, including the detection of crystallographic phase transformations. Ordinary changes in crystal structure can be located on the temperature scale with an accuracy limited by the accuracies of control and measurement of the temperature of the sample. A few diffraction patterns taken at temperature intervals in the vicinity of the suspected transition will narrow the range; a few more will bracket it more closely and the

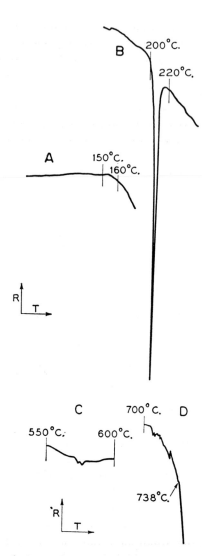

Fɪɢ. XII-7. Change of electrical resistance during phase changes for: (a) single crystal of potassium niobate; (b) ceramic of potassium niobate-tantalate (0.90:0.10); (c) single crystal of quartz; and (d) powdered sodium bromide. From Garn and Flaschen (G11).

The indications may be a brief period of disorder (a), *a well-defined change in temperature coefficient* (b), *or sharp discontinuity* (d) *in resistance. In* (d) *the recorder pen went off scale during the deflection starting at 738°C. The earlier minor change is due to premelting.*

transition temperature may then be determined with a preciseness dependent on the accuracy of the apparatus and the diligence of the operator. Similarly, the cell dimensions may be determined at each of a number of temperatures to determine the thermal expansion coefficient.

For those samples which decompose, especially reversibly, to give off a gaseous product the arguments previously advanced concerning the agreement between differential thermal analysis and thermogravimetric analysis apply. More accurately, the arguments apply with special force because of the geometry of the specimen. In differential thermal analy-

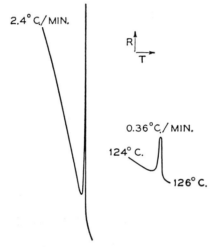

Fɪɢ. XII-8. Change of electrical resistance with temperature for barium titanate single crystal. From Garn and Flaschen (G11).

The transient positive temperature coefficient of resistance occurs over a considerable temperature range in ceramic compositions.

sis without a dynamic atmosphere the orthodox sample geometry is a cylinder exposed to the atmosphere only at one end. The temperatures of interest are found at some high heating rates. The X-ray sample, on the other hand, is a tiny cylinder exposed over the whole surface except for the support end, a small wedge also with most of the surface exposed, or a rather thin layer with one side (nearly half of the total surface area of the bulk sample) exposed. This sample is then heated at one temperature for about the same length of time as that during which the differential thermal analysis sample was heated through its whole range. If there is another decomposition (reversible) within the next hundred degrees it is almost certain to take place during these 2 or more hours. Control of the atmosphere might prevent the unwanted reaction. Solid-state reactions could not be prevented by these controlled atmospheres.

Weiss and Rowland (W12) devised a technique for oscillating the goniometer across a selected X-ray diffraction maximum. This scanning permits repetitive automatic examination of a single diffraction as the sample is heated. Since the limits of travel of the goniometer are known, any excursions of the maximum intensity due to lattice expansion may be measured. The principal objective, however, is the detection of the appearance, disappearance, or sudden shift of position of a diffraction due to a change in state.

The shift in position can be observed readily because the scanning limits are within the background region and have already a moderate

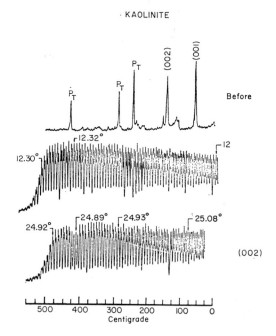

Fɪɢ. XII-9. Heating-oscillating patterns of the first and second order of the basal spacing of kaolinite. From Weiss and Rowland (W12).

As the temperature increases, the peak shifts to a higher 2θ due to lattice expansion. This is shown by the increase in intensity at the low-angle limit. In the 475–525°C region, the peak disappears because of the decomposition of the kaolinite. Note that the decomposition of this rather thin film is well under way at 500°C (see Chapters V and VII).

intensity. Since the limits are in regions of fairly high $(dI/d2\theta)$ slope and this slope has opposite signs at either end, a slight shift of the diffraction will cause an increase in the background at one end and a decrease at the other. An example of the data of Weiss and Rowland is shown in Fig. XII-9, with some explanatory additions by the (present) author.

After the room temperature diffraction record is obtained (Fig. XII-9), the goniometer is set to scan as small a range as is practicable. These limits take into account the background slopes and any expected shift in the maximum and obviously depend to a fair degree on the previous experience or knowledge of the operator concerning the specimen. The background intensity limits are preferably equal and of moderate intensity at the beginning. The furnace program is started and the scanning continued automatically. At Weiss and Rowland's 5°C/minute heating rate, the specimen's diffraction peak was scanned at 3°C intervals.

Rowland *et al.* (R35) have reported on a small sample mount, Fig. XII-10, and a program control, Fig. XII-11, designed to drive the sample holder temperature to 1000°C. The tiny heating element is in good contact with the sample so the temperature indication and response to programming should be very satisfactory.

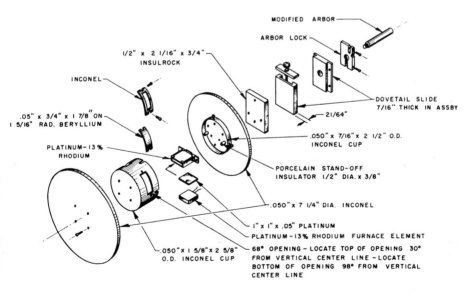

Fig. XII-10. Cutaway drawing of components of specimen holder for oscillating-heating X-ray diffraction studies. From Rowland *et al.* (R35).
The sample is heated from below by the furnace element.

The control system is not well-designed for the heater described, since the control variables are not permitted to operate over their full range. From their description, the furnace element has a hot resistance of 8 ohms and their controller needs to supply no more than 80 watts. Since $E^2/R = P = 80$ watts $= E^2/8$ ohms, E is in the order of 25 volts at maximum power input. With line voltage input, the system should always be operating at 75%, or more, turndown. The control current from the amplifier must necessarily perform with three quarters of its range inaccessible. With this type of furnace, Rowland, Weiss, and Lewis no doubt were able to control well even without proportional band, etc., corrections. The control thermocouple is so close to the heater that response is immediate.

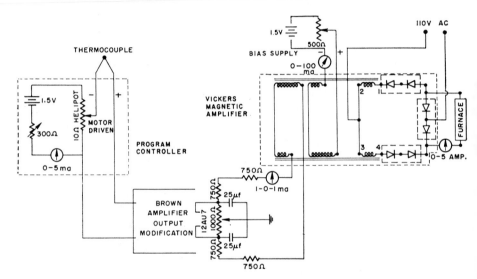

Fɪɢ. XII-11. Schematic diagram of program controller. From Rowland *et al.* (R35). *The linear thermocouple output programming provides a somewhat nonlinear temperature program but this is less serious than in differential thermal analysis.*

Examine Rowland, Weiss, and Lewis' data for the decomposition of a sodium montmorillonite-glycol complex (Fig. XII-12). Bear in mind that (1) the descriptive numbers are taken from the goniometer setting and, in accordance with X-ray diffraction practice, are twice the angle that the reflecting plane makes with the beam; (2) since $n\lambda = 2d \sin \theta$, the angle θ and the lattice spacing are inversely related, hence an increasing 2θ implies a diminishing spacing; (3) complexes of this nature formed at room temperature are not necessarily in their most stable state and diminution in size on heating is to be expected; and (4) increase in relative stability is indicated by increased intensity of the peak since the peak intensity is a measure of the order of the system. Rowland *et al.* point out: "Sodium montmorillonite also forms a two-layer glycol complex with a spacing at 5.17° 2θ (17.2 a.u.). As the temperature is increased this complex stabilizes and reaches maximum stability between 50° and 70°C. at a spacing of 5.20° 2θ (17 a.u.). Above 70°C. the intensity begins to decrease and by 80°C. there are remnants of the two-layer complex mixed with a separate one-layer complex. At about 90°C. the one-layer complex begins to stabilize at 6.53° 2θ (13.6 a.u.)

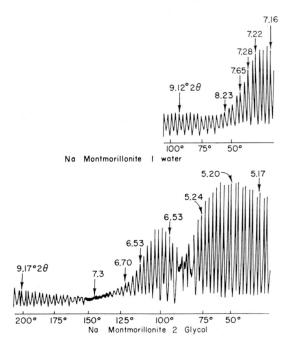

Fɪɢ. XII-12. Oscillating-heating diagrams of sodium montmorillonite with water and with glycol layers. From Rowland *et al.* (R35).
The increasing order of a newly formed species can be observed.

and reaches maximum stability between 100° and 110°C. Thereafter, the intensity begins to decrease and by 120°C. the one-layer complex has collapsed to a spacing of 6.70° 2θ (13.2 a.u.). The remaining glycol is driven off and at 160°C. the spacing is 9.10° 2θ (9.7 a.u.), which represents the collapsed lattice without glycol."

Now let us consider the details of construction of the furnace arrangement used as an example, but with the clear understanding that, since the design elements to be discussed are quite generally used, the criticisms expounded apply equally generally. We will note only briefly the atmosphere effect since that is covered elsewhere. The changing atmosphere will influence decomposition patterns and, since the ease of diffusion in and out of the furnace will vary from one design to another, the temperatures of decomposition will be more or less unique to the apparatus.

An equally serious flaw exists in the heating arrangement. The specimen is in good thermal contact with the heater on one side; the other side is exposed to unheated surfaces. At low temperatures the gradient across the specimen will be relatively small (except during a reaction) but at high temperatures the increasing radiation of heat from particle to particle of the specimen is quite unlikely to compensate for the radiation from the face of the sample which is also increasing.

A high-temperature X-ray specimen could be heated more satisfactorily by radiation from a source not in mechanical contact. (Remember that the X-ray beam only penetrates a few layers.) A thin specimen on an insulating material could be used satisfactorily.

12.5. Thermomicroscopy

Observation of phase changes of bulk samples is perfectly feasible—within narrow limits. Temperature gradients can lead to sizable errors. These same gradients will cause even rapid changes to occur over a large time interval. Polarized light cannot be generally used. For these reasons optical thermal analysis is normally done microscopically and the specimen is heated on a specially designed hot stage. Since microscopists have in effect pre-empted the field, the term thermomicroscopy came into use rather than optical thermal analysis. That convention is followed herein.

We may best consider thermomicroscopy in two parts depending on the temperature range. The lower range comprises all temperatures—above and below room temperature—at which the specimen is not very thermally luminous; the higher range comprises the temperatures at which the sample is thermally luminous. Naturally there is some overlapping since the observations possible at room temperature are not rendered impossible discontinuously as the sample becomes faintly luminous. Let us consider only the more generally applicable lower-temperature thermomicroscopy and further confine our attention to the range from room temperature to a few hundred degrees centigrade. Cold stages are available commercially but the same effects are observed as may be seen in different specimens at more convenient temperatures. The problems involved are roughly the same.

Thermomicroscopy in this range is of rather moderate use in inorganic studies but is an important tool for most organic work. The size and complexity of nearly any organic molecule renders optical isotropy impossible. Polarized light may be used to detect very sharply the growth, disappearance, or rearrangement of crystals. (A major hazard is that such observation is likely to become an avocation.) Since the detailed techniques of thermomicroscopy can properly constitute a separate volume, only basic instruction will be offered herein. The reader may find a more extensive treatment in McCrone's (M25) book, from which the present author has learned much.

The observation of thermal effects is generally done on specimens placed on an ordinary microscope slide, covered with a cover glass, and set on a heating stage. The temperature of the hot-stage block is measured by use of a thermometer inserted in the block. Two problems immediately arise: thermal homogeneity and measuring error.

The thermal homogeneity of the slide is not even assumed ordinarily; instead, an empirically chosen set of conditions is used so that the small area under observation is nearly isothermal. The principal condition is a fairly rigorously controlled slow heating rate. The observed temperature of thermal effect depends strongly on the heating rate.

The measuring error is closely related to the thermal inhomogeneity. Consider a heating stage being heated at some customary rate such as 2°C/minute and assume that the heating has been proceeding for several minutes and a nearly steady-state transfer of heat to the sample prevails. The sample is in a part of the slide not in contact with the block—since we shall want to pass light through the sample; further, the thin cover glass over the specimen is in close proximity to the microscope objective—a fairly large heat sink that does not much exceed room temperature. A significant difference in temperature must therefore exist between the sample and the thermometer.

The first of these sources of error is dependent on heating rate, the second on temperature. The use of prescribed conditions of heating and observation will permit reproducibility—generally—even though there is a real error.

The existence of these difficulties should not cause the reader to shun the technique. One may look with dismay at the temperature measurement without losing sight of the extensive qualitative information which may be derived therefrom.

Thermomicroscopy is generally carried out by visual observation but there is no reason why this observation cannot be mechanized. Reese *et al.* (R11) set up an arrangement (Fig. XII-13) which permits detection of polymorphic phase transformations by measurement (recording) of light intensity. The light is polarized and analyzed by crossed polarizing filters; this has the advantage that melting is detected rather specifically by the drop in intensity of transmitted light. This condition exists because the occurrence of an isotropic organic solid is rare among the materials likely to be studied. The light intensity is adjusted at the start of the run; any change thereafter—excluding ordinary drift—should be relatable to some change in state of the specimen. Figure I-11 shows their results for amobarbital.

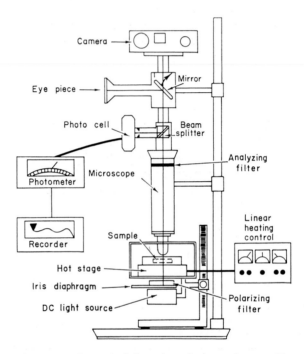

Fɪɢ. XII-13. Apparatus for optical detection of phase changes. From Reese *et al.* (R11).

The change in intensity of the polarized light may be detected instrumentally or visually and a photograph taken.

12.6. Thermal Conductivity

Any property which shows a discontinuous change may be used to detect and determine the temperature at which the change occurs, including thermal conductivity, the bête noir of the many derivers of equations for differential thermal analysis. Claussen (C16), who refers to his technique as differential thermal conductivity analysis, studied the shift of the α-γ iron transformation at pressures up to one hundred thousand atmospheres using a nickel reference for the iron piece under study (Fig. XII-14). The furnace arrangement is rather ingenious. The entire

assembly is within the pressure device and the heating elements surround the specimens. Claussen provides his temperature gradient by
stacking discs of lava against the nickel equalizing disc at one end and
alumina discs against the equalizing disc at the other. Since the lava has
a higher thermal conductivity than the alumina the disc at that end
will be hotter and a gradient will be set up.

Claussen assumes that in the absence of a phase change the temperature at the center of the nickel reference strip ought to be the same as
the temperature at the center of the iron specimen because of the

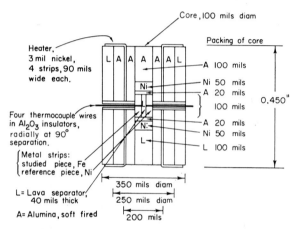

Fɪɢ. XII-14. Complete differential thermal conductivity analysis cell design. From
Claussen (C16).

*A temperature gradient exists between the ends of the strips because of the dif-
ference in thermal conductivity between the lava and alumina discs in the ends.*

equalizing blocks at the ends. He is then forced to offer a very questionable explanation for the base line drift of the typical curves 2, 3, and 4
of Fig. XII-15. This explanation involves a possible high heat flux between the heater strips and the test strips (across the alumina bushing).
He observed also that "more perfect maxima ΔT curves were obtained
with cells containing nickel heaters than with Nichrome heaters." He
attributes this to heater characteristics: "Nickel would tend to produce a
hot spot. Nichrome would produce more even heat."

A more probable reason for the base line drift is the continual change
in the temperature gradient. The difference in thermal conductivity of
the reference and test specimens (nickel is about twice as good a conductor as iron in the transformation temperature region) would be of no

importance if the temperature difference between the equalizer blocks were constant. The central points would be at the same temperature in steady-state heating while no discontinuous change was occuring anywhere in the specimen. On the other hand, if the temperature difference between the equalizer blocks varies, the temperature gradients within the metal specimens will vary over their lengths and the midpoint of neither will necessarily have a temperature halfway between the temperatures of its ends. Further, the two midpoints will not change to the same degree because of the difference in thermal conductivity and its influence on the heat transfer to the specimens. Therefore, if the temperature difference between the equalizer blocks is increasing—or decreasing, for that matter—the ΔT signal will become larger. The drift of curves 2, 3, and 4 is to be expected in this system.

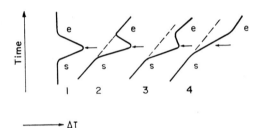

Fɪɢ. XII-15. Typical ΔT curves on recorder charts: s = start of transformation; e = end of transformation; → = transformation half-completed. From Claussen (C16).
  The marked base line drift could prevent detection of transitions; any more severe drift would render curve 4 quite doubtful.

Claussen shows (Fig. XII-16) a variation in transformation temperature rather different from Strong's (S68) data. Neither cites the purity of the test specimen. Differences in impurities might account for the apparent discrepancy. The differences in results with different heater materials are much more likely due to a change in construction whether planned or inadvertent.

The technique could be improved by providing a reference specimen more nearly like the sample. The material most like the sample would be another specimen of the same material. If two such pieces were used and spacers added to the high-temperature end of one and to the low-temperature end of the other, the gradient within the pieces would be nearly the same but with a geometric and temporal displacement. Now if thermocouples are attached to appropriate points a small differential signal with small drift could be obtained. This near equality of temperature ought to be very significantly disturbed during the traverse of the phase change in the specimens. While there would be small changes in heat flow across the boundary, this initial perturbation as the hotter end of one and then the other specimen began the transformation should be small in comparison to the effects seen as the transition passed one and then the other of the thermocouple locations.

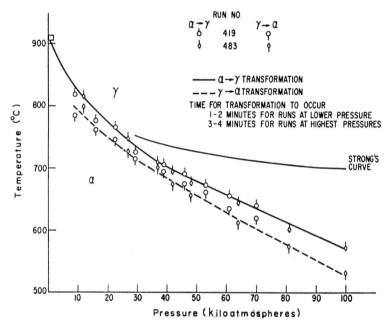

FIG. XII-16. Effect of pressure on α-γ transformation in iron. Pressure calibration is based on the transitions for Bi and Ba, which were assumed to occur at 24,800 and 77,400 atmospheres, respectively. From Claussen (C16).

The difference in temperature of transition on heating and cooling ranges from ca 15 to 04 C.

The more prosaic thermal conductivity measurements, in which the data wanted are actually the values directly obtained, can be done in a multitude of ways. As in most of the techniques described in this monograph no one manner is of general applicability. Kingery (K28) discusses a number of methods including spherical and cylindrical configurations for the sample. His cylindrical test assembly (K27) is shown in Fig. XII-17. Note that the thermocouple junctions are centered along the axis and that the axis is relatively long. A major problem is the avoidance of axial heat flow. This axial heat flow will be least, of course, where the axial temperature distribution is most nearly uniform.

End effects and such are eliminated by use of spherical sample holders but the problems of uniform heating and obtaining precisely concentric sample, containers, and central heater are severe. Beck (B20) has, in effect, inverted the technique; he devised a spherical sample container

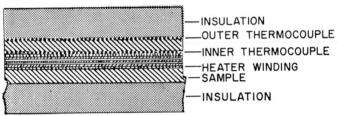

—INSULATION
—OUTER THERMOCOUPLE
—INNER THERMOCOUPLE
—HEATER WINDING
—SAMPLE
—INSULATION

FIG. XII-17. Cross section of cylindrical assembly for measuring thermal conductivity. From Kingery (K27).

The heat dissipated by the electrical resistor must be conducted outward. The temperature difference and dimensions of the sample and the amount of heat dissipated are used to calculate the thermal conductivity.

with only a thermocouple at the center (Fig. XII-18). The containing block was heated and the temperature difference between block and sample measured. The uniformity of packing is questionable indeed, but since Berg was concerned with detection of effects (Fig. XII-19) rather than precise measurement of effects the relative inaccuracy is not important. Note, however, that even a close approach to a real measurement of thermal conductivity is obtained only between thermal effects.

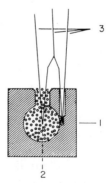

FIG. XII-18. Spherical sample holder for thermal analysis. From Berg and Sidorova (B41).

Although thermal conductivity in nonsteady-state heating could be measured the device is useful for detecting phase changes.

12.7. Calorimetry

The change in temperature of a specimen or system including specimen as heat is added can be related to the heat of reaction. Several
approaches are used depending on the information sought. The heating
may be stepwise, continuous, a single pulse, or supplied by the sample.

If the heat capacity is of principal interest the calorimetry will generally be done stepwise on moderately large specimens. In such a case a
calorimeter of the type shown in Fig. XII-20 may be used. The addition
of a known quantity of heat to the central assembly by supplying a

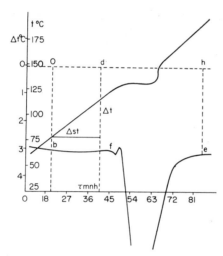

Fig. XII-19. Thermogram obtained with the sample holder of Fig. XII-18. From
Berg and Sidorova (B41).

In essence, the plot yields a differential thermogram with a nonzero base line.

known electric power for a measured time is followed by the diffusion
of this heat throughout the specimen. The ensuing steady temperature,
when reached, is measured and another quantity of heat added. The
empty calorimeter must be calibrated because of the rather substantial
mass of the heater and sample holder assembly.

Since at temperatures substantially different from ambient the loss of
heat to the surroundings could become a source of significant error, the
common practice is to surround the sample holder with a jacket whose
temperature is controlled to match the surface of the sample holder
(ΔT of Fig. XII-20 is maintained at zero) by the outer heater. This becomes, then, an adiabatic calorimeter. Insulation from the outside condition simplifies control. The temperature of the sample need not be

measured at the edge as shown in Fig. XII-20 since the equilibrium temperature is measured, it can be done anywhere.

Heats of reaction can be measured in this type of calorimeter, but if the heat of reaction data are to be referred to room temperature an isothermal calorimeter would more often be used. In this type of apparatus the outside is maintained at some chosen temperature (for relatively imprecise measurements on short-term reactions, moderate insulation from ambient temperature is enough) and the rise or fall of the calorimeter temperature is measured. This rise or fall is deliberately made to

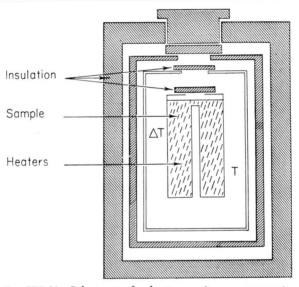

Insulation

Sample

Heaters

ΔT

T

FIG. XII-20. Calorimeter for heat capacity measurements.
From this general plan the more complex design for minimizing mechanical contacts and other sources of heat loss can be evolved.

be of low magnitude so that the actual change in temperature has little influence on the values obtained. A water jacket or other heat sink is generally used.

Much high-temperature calorimetry has been done by the "drop" method, in which a sample is brought to thermal equilibrium at the temperature of interest, a release mechanism is operated, and the sample falls into a calorimeter in which the sample's total heat content difference between the initial and final temperatures is measured. This heat content refers, obviously, to the specimen in whatever form it was at the time it was dropped. Heats of decomposition are not determinable in this manner; some kind of adiabatic system with controlled atmosphere or isothermal system with special provisions would be needed. Foldvari-Vogl and Kliburszky (F12) have constructed an apparatus especially for determining heats of reaction for events occurring at elevated temperatures and have eliminated the possible error involving the heat content of the released gas. Under reasonably favorable conditions, it should be very useful.

Their calorimeter comprises an externally insulated copper vessel containing 200 ml of water, a calorimetric bomb, and a small furnace inside the bomb. This small furnace has an inside winding; the filament is in direct contact with the sample. A thermocouple is centered in the furnace. The bomb has connected to it a capillary tube 50 cm long through which gaseous products escape. This capillary tube is immersed nearly all its length in the water of the calorimeter so that any gas leaving the hot zone gives up its heat before escaping.

In use, the sample is placed in the small furnace and the bomb closed. The system is allowed to come to thermal equilibrium, then a measured current is passed through the heating coils until the indicated temperature of the specimen rises to some point at which the reaction is known to be complete. The furnace is turned off, and the bomb is allowed to cool; the heat is given up to the surrounding water. The temperature rise of the water is measured in the usual manner. By comparison of the heat added electrically and the heat recovered thermally the heat of reaction at ambient temperature may be determined. By substituting appropriate values for the heat capacities of all species involved, the heat of reaction at the elevated temperature may be calculated (see Chapter V).

The rapid heating is a probable source of trouble. The rapid heating insures a temperature lag within the sample that may reach 100°C or more during the 2- or 3-minute heating. If another reaction occurs at a temperature very close to that of the reaction being studied, the user might have to settle for a longer heating time to avoid drastic overshoot. The material in contact with the heater can become very substantially hotter than the inside even when no reaction occurs; this condition is aggravated during any change of state (see Chapter III).

12.8. Summary

Measurement of any of a number of properties can be useful in interpreting the events that occur as a substance is heated. Some of these may be performed simultaneously or in combination with differential thermal or thermogravimetric analysis. These latter techniques are the most used because the returns in information (compared to the effort and expense) are greater.

CHAPTER XIII

Miscellaneous Topics

13.1. Introduction

The description of techniques necessarily included some illustrations of use but these were chosen for their applicability to the discussion, not for their subjective interest. This chapter contains some discussion of applications of thermoanalytical methods of investigation to particular materials or problems. Examples are offered, frequently only reportorially, to show the range of utility of the methods. On the other hand, further discourses on a few topics are presented.

13.2. Polymers

Since the seeming relegation of an important field of science to only a section may arouse the ire of dedicated polymer chemists, let it be clearly understood that much of the book is about polymers—just as much as any other class of materials. Other materials, however, undergo reactions more quickly or otherwise show more clearly the effects associated with the parameters under discussion.

The major differences between polymeric and other materials are

(a) the thermal effects are relatively slow and (b) thermal effects occur at less well-defined temperatures because the material is not really homogeneous. Coupled with these annoyances are those found with organic materials in general, i.e., low heats of transition or fusion and poor thermal conductivity.

Smaller organic molecules or ions have shapes that are complex relative to most inorganic molecules and ions; further, polyfunctionality is common and this may include not only different kinds of functional groups but similar groups with somewhat different reactivities resulting from differences in their structural environment. For these reasons, many organic materials can enter into a multiplicity of crystal structures. Organic materials in general are hence suitable materials for study by thermoanalytical methods and, conversely, thermoanalytical methods will supply considerable information about said organic materials. Now consider the special problems of polymeric materials.

Long-chain molecules moving around in a solution or melt cannot be expected to achieve—on precipitation, evaporation, or cooling—the same degree of order found in smaller organic and in inorganic materials. Polymethylene chains, for example, tend to look about the same all down their lengths. A molecule, finding itself in need of an energetically acceptable resting place on solidification, would have little tendency to seek out an end to end or any other specific relation with its neighbor. Neither would a part of the molecule, entering into the solid phase after another part had already situated itself, check down its own length to ascertain that methylene segments match one for one along the length.

Consider now that the nearest neighbor of some given part of a long-chain molecule is quite likely to be another portion of the same molecule. If these parts are not greatly separated the stability of the solid can be increased (due to interactions) compared to the stability of a pairing with a distant part or with a part of another molecule. Given enough time, the molecule will tend to form a single crystal by folding back on itself so that chain segments lie alongside each other (B51). The length of the typical chain segment may be kinetically or thermodynamically controlled but the actual length of a given segment may be different because of branching. That is, random imperfections will tend to move (with the attached carbon) to the fold, leaving, if necessary, somewhat longer or shorter chain segments in the immediate vicinity.

We have at this point an assembly of chain segments all interconnected. Even assuming that this is truly a single crystal, i.e., having no chains held jointly with another crystal, we have a range of energy states. If we heat this crystal to the onset of rotation it is quite apparent that the chain segments at the edge have a lesser barrier to rotation than the more central segments, hemmed in as they are by their neighbors. Consider also the melting: segments at the edges will gain some freedom at lower energies (and temperatures) than those surrounded by their fellows and the end of the chain, if exposed, will tend also to move freely. In either case these are local differences from strains caused by imperfections and variations in segment length.

Because of all these complications, polymeric materials cannot be expected to show transition points as sharp, as well-defined, as insensitive

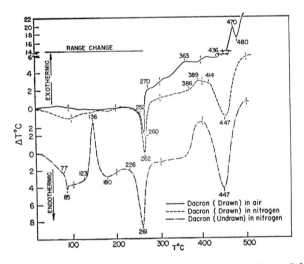

Fig. XIII-1. Differential thermal analysis curves of Dacron. From Schwenker and Beck (S16).

The undrawn fiber shows a second-order transition at 77°C and crystallization at 136°C.

to heating rate and other parameters as can be found in simpler organic materials, let alone inorganics. Nevertheless, differential thermal analysis is a highly useful tool in the study of polymers. This is not because of any particular ease of use but because other methods of investigation also fail to yield clear-cut and reliable answers without considerable effort.

As an identification technique differential thermal analysis is useful as a comparison tool. Some assemblages of curves have been published but these will be of little value unless the thermogram of the material to be identified is obtained on the same type of apparatus. For this reason they are not reviewed. Even assemblages of curves or data on inorganic materials are not likely to show much agreement when different types of apparatus are used (see Chapter II, Sec. 2.1). To expect to sort out the relatively poorly formed peaks of polymeric materials would be unrealistic and to use a particular experimental procedure only in the hope of getting a curve that looks like someone else's is a waste of time. If comparison with the published literature is to be attempted, the proper procedure is to interpret the curves so far as is possible, then to compare the data: temperatures of peaks or second-order transitions, relative peak heights or areas, etc.

In the case of polymers it is especially unwise to plan to make all sorts of important discoveries by dropping a sample into a commercial instrument and pushing a switch (see Chapters III, IV, and VIII). The sample holder must be designed for the experiment. Hay (H8), for example, melts his samples *in situ* and quenches or anneals them. His principal interest is in the intrinsic properties of the polymer. His apparatus would not be suitable for study of drawn or extruded fibers or resin-forming reactions nor does it pretend to be.

Schwenker and Beck (S16), on the other hand, need to use the sample with a minimum of pretreatment since they are concerned with, for example, the effects due to mechanical history (Fig. XIII-1). These effects very likely present one of the most fruitful uses of differential thermal analysis in the study of polymers.

13.3. Mechanical Effects in Polymers

The crystalline form obtained by careful annealing of a polymer is of substantial interest because it is a characteristic of that material and study of the crystal can lead to knowledge of the material. Polymers are not often made just to permit study of their properties. They are formed into usable articles by extrusion, spinning, molding, and similar processes so it is essential that we study their behavior under all this pulling and pushing.

The purpose here is only to point out that the orientations and disorientations due to mechanical treatment—or mechanical strain due to thermal treatment—will necessarily have a heat effect associated with them. This may be reflected in a slow evolution or absorption of heat and hence manifested only by a change in heat capacity. More likely, however, is the occurrence of similar events of the same energy in many parts of the specimen, which regions then evince themselves over a narrow temperature range. This range may be narrow enough so that a well-formed peak is obtained.

An example of the effect of stretching is given in Fig. XIII-1. Ke (K11a) provides an example of the effect of quenching (Fig. XIII-2), showing the thermal effects resulting when the high-temperature form— or something approximating it—is retained by rapid cooling to low temperatures (see Chapter II).

13.4. The "Integral Procedural Decomposition Temperature"

The comparison of polymers on the basis of thermal stability is quite difficult because of the wide variety of possible behaviors. Even disregarding any atmosphere effects such as oxidation, the start of decomposition may be the degradation of a side group while the chain remains

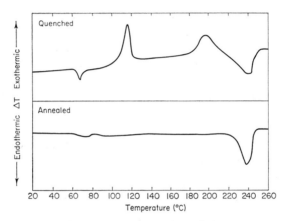

FIG. XIII-2. Thermograms of polyethylene/diethylene terephthalate. From Ke (K11).
The quenched specimen shows crystallization effects well below the melting point.

intact. At some higher temperature further decomposition occurs, eventually affecting the entire material. On the other hand, under identical heating conditions, another substance might degrade completely in a single step and a third decompose in some other manner but leave a residue at the upper limit of heating. Doyle (D14, D15) puts these various behaviors on a common numerical basis by use of an arbitrarily defined "integral procedural decomposition temperature."

This integral procedural decomposition temperature, or *ipdt,* is derived from the weight loss vs temperature plot under rigidly controlled experimental conditions. The weight loss is assigned to a single temperature, the *ipdt,* at which the area under the curve (Fig. XIII-3) could be represented as a rectangle bounded by the residual weight fractions 1.00 and 0.00, 0°C, and T_A. Thus, "in T_A, it is *pretended* that all materials volatilize completely in TGA to 900°C and do so at a single temperature."

This does not really take into account the refractoriness of some materials. Some polymers contain inorganic fragments which may remain at the arbitrary termination of heating. To take account of this, Doyle introduces a correction K^*/K to this area which essentially moves up the base of the rectangle from a residual weight fraction of zero to the actual fraction remaining at 900°C. Without this correction, a material degrading at a low temperature but leaving a substantial residue would have an *ipdt* indicating good stability. As a comparison, Doyle shows the *ipdt*'s (Fig. XIII-4) of a series of polymers, some containing inorganic portions, and relates them to the temperatures of half weight loss.

A set of data such as that obtained by Doyle can be quite useful for comparing polymers as long as the data are obtained in the same manner and probably by the same equipment. Taking a datum from the set for use in another comparison or even taking an *ipdt* as having some physical significance would indeed be risky.

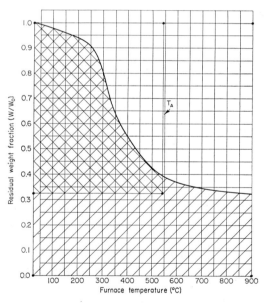

FIG. XIII-3. The thermogravimetric analysis curve areas A^*, ////, and K^*, cross-hatching. From Doyle (D15).

By use of both corrections, account is taken of the residual weight.

13.5. Dolomite and Siderite Decompositions

The decomposition of dolomite has attracted considerable attention because of the quite different nature of the two endothermic peaks. The first peak is quite well-established as being the decomposition of the dolomite structure rather than the decomposition of a magnesium carbonate moiety of a mixed crystal. The decomposition temperature is not significantly affected by the usual change: dilution, subatmospheric

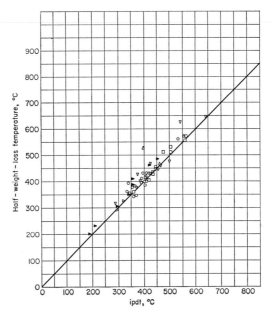

Fig. XIII-4. Half weight loss temperature vs *ipdt* for fifty-four polymers containing: ●–C, H, N, O; △–F; □–SI: ▲–B, P; ▼–Cu, Fn, Be. From Doyle (D15).
The corrected temperature agrees well with the temperature at which half the weight loss has occurred.

pressure, etc. Strangely enough, an atmosphere of carbon dioxide seems to lower rather than raise the decomposition temperature. Berg (B25a) showed that the presence of alkali-metal compounds could also lower the decomposition temperature but simply washing the sample eliminated the effect. Ivanova and Tatarskii (17) have shown that dilution of dolomite with up to 85% kaolin causes "no substantial and consistent lowering of the decomposition temperature."

The lowering of the dolomite peak temperature in the presence of carbon dioxide is interesting not only because this behavior is contrary to ordinary experience but also because there is an accompanying change in the shape of the peak (Fig. XIII-5). If one considers only the atmosphere effect the van't Hoff relation would be obeyed only in the event of a negative heat of decomposition; admittedly a negative heat of reaction could be obscured by the positive heat of reaction (decomposition) of the magnesium carbonate formed by decomposition of the

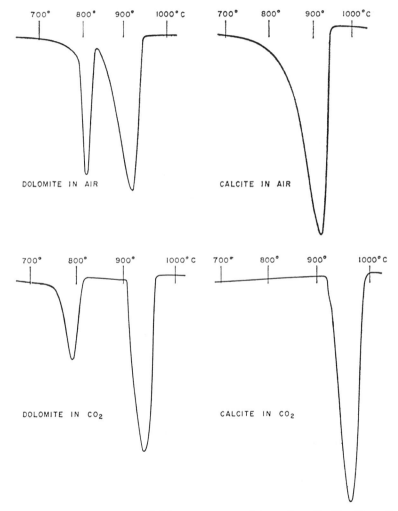

Fig. XIII-5. Decomposition of dolomite in air and in carbon dioxide. From Rowland and Lewis (R34).

The presence of carbon dioxide lowers the decomposition temperature of the dolomite but raises the decomposition temperature of the residual calcium carbonate.

dolomite. The exact behavior would depend on the heat capacities of the various substances as well as on the heats of reaction since $d(\Delta H)/dT = \Delta C_p$.

Take note of the several effects which lower the decomposition temperature: the presence of carbon dioxide, the presence of certain salts. The latter tends to distort the surface of the crystal but another effect must be postulated for the former.

Consider now that dolomite is presumably unstable at temperatures near the decomposition temperature, lacking only the necessary activation energy for decomposition. The soluble salts provide the energy by distortion of the lattice. The carbon dioxide, on the other hand, lowers the activation energy requirement by providing another reaction mechanism—one requiring a lower activation energy. Haul and associates (H7) have demonstrated the exchange of carbon dioxide between calcite and carbon dioxide atmosphere.

The advent of another mechanism could be expected to change even the shape of the curve. In effect, the over-all decomposition changes from a principally temperature effect whose reaction rate is determined by the transport of heat to a kinetic effect whose reaction rate is determined substantially by the interchange with the atmosphere.

The decomposition of siderite or chalybite (natural ferrous carbonate) presents an interesting problem in competing reactions. The ferrous carbonate (Fig. 1-4) will decompose to magnetite and oxides of carbon in a nonoxidizing atmosphere in the vicinity of 500°C; in an oxidizing atmosphere, on the other hand, the ferrous ion moiety will tend to oxidize to ferric in the same region. In air the exothermic response is far greater than the endothermic response if there is a reasonable opportunity for oxidation. From this, it has been concluded that the evolution of carbon dioxide from ferrous carbonate requires little energy compared to that given off by the oxidation of ferrous to ferric oxide.

Careful examination of siderite curves in air or oxygen will disclose a tendency for oxidation to begin before the carbonate decomposition. Examination will also disclose that there is a correspondence between the magnitude of the carbon dioxide evolution endotherm in air and the later oxidation peak ca 840°C.

Let us hypothesize that two quite separate reaction paths exist and that the path taken by any small segment of the specimen is determined only by the presence or absence of oxygen at the instant of change. In the absence of oxygen, the reaction is endothermic, the products being carbon dioxide, carbon monoxide, magnetite, Fe_3O_4, and—apparently under some conditions—ferrous oxide. If oxygen is available, we may hypothesize the oxidation as the first step, but this would yield ferric carbonate—an unstable structure. This unstable material would decompose exothermally to yield ferric and/or ferrosoferric oxide. The major point here is that the carbon dioxide from the oxidation path is not driven off endothermally. Hence, the curve showing both reactions cannot be interpreted by simply considering that the endothermic carbonate decomposition must be going on but the heat of oxidation is so great that the endotherm may be masked. The carbon dioxide evolution that does not take up heat gives off heat instead. The endothermic portion of the curve is only a measure of the amount of lower oxides formed; this is subsequently indicated also by the oxidation peak ca 840°C. Handbook (L1a) values for heats of formation indicate that the endothermic decomposition would show a heat effect not much less than that of the oxidation.

In static oxidizing atmospheres, whether air or oxygen, the oxidation process is self-limiting because the carbon dioxide produced will tend to prevent oxidation of more material but diffusion interchange of gases would enable some continuation except for the other reaction. The material that has no oxygen available when it would otherwise be ready to react will react (possibly several degrees later) by decomposition, also producing carbon dioxide and thus sustaining the condition. Whether or not the thermogram will show any further oxidation will depend on the geometry—including location of the thermocouple—and state of dilution (see Chapter II) of the specimen.

13.6. Study of Metathetical Reactions at Elevated Temperatures

Differential thermal analysis is a useful tool in the observation or study of reactions between solids at elevated temperatures. The extension to include the effect of some materials on the decomposition of others is but a short step.

One interesting application of metathetical reactions in recent years has been the re-examination of the Hedvall effect by Borchardt and Thompson (B70). The Hedvall effect refers to the enhanced reactivity of solid materials during a crystallographic transition.

Borchardt and Thompson repeated the experiment of Hedvall and Heuberger, obtaining the curves of Fig. XIII-6, in which the endothermic peaks in (a) and (c) are good evidence for the formation of barium and strontium carbonates. These were samples that had been exposed to air. On the other hand, if the same starting materials, protected from the atmosphere and well-mixed as before, were heated to substantially above the reaction temperature indicated by the exotherm, the materials retained their identity. Further, both barium and strontium oxides showed endothermic peaks which suggested the possibility of melting of a eutectic oxide-hydroxide system to provide a liquid phase. [Balarew (B3) had suggested that the Hedvall effect appeared because of the formation of a liquid phase which could then provide a low-energy reaction path for the metathesis.]

Borchardt and Thompson (B70) made direct observations on silver nitrate mixtures with the alkaline earth oxides and found that reaction occurred at the appearance of a liquid phase, i.e., melting of silver nitrate (Fig. XIII-7), not at the phase transition about 50°C lower in temperature. These and other data led Borchardt and Thompson to ques-

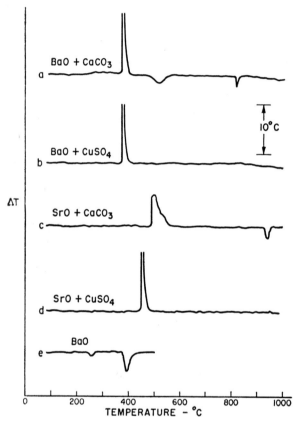

Fig. XIII-6. Differential thermal analyses of barium oxide and mixtures of barium and strontium oxides with calcium carbonate and with copper sulfate. From Borchardt and Thompson (B68).

The exothermic peaks indicate reaction at fairly low temperatures. The high-temperature endothermic peaks confirm the formation of barium and strontium carbonates.

tion the actual existence of a Hedvall effect, at least in the original narrow sense of an increased reactivity *while* the transformation is taking place.

The effect of impurities in changing the reactivities or even reactions of materials is demonstrated well by Martin's (M17) data on clay-carbonate mixtures, from which Martin concludes that measurement of carbonates in natural soils could possibly miss nearly half of the carbonate present. Lowering of the decomposition temperature of dolomite by

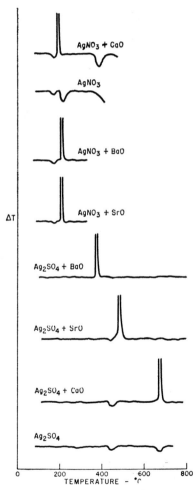

FIG. XIII-7. Differential thermal analysis of binary mixtures with silver nitrate and with silver sulfate. From Borchardt and Thompson (B70).

A liquid phase has apparently facilitated the metathetical reaction.

addition of soluble salts had been demonstrated by Berg (B25a) and Graf (G38), but dolomite is a rather special case; calcite is relatively unaffected by such impurities. Nevertheless, the natural soil containing calcite, curve E of Fig. XIII-8, shows little sign of calcium carbonate although if the soil is washed (curve G) there appears a very pronounced

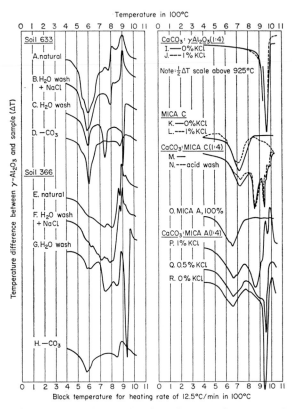

Fig. XIII-8. Thermograms of natural soils and prepared mixtures showing anomalous carbonate peaks. From Martin (M17).

The presence of soluble salts permits interactions which alter the thermogram quite substantially.

calcite peak ca 900°C. Now if sodium chloride is added to a suspension of this water-washed clay and the material is dried, this sample yields a thermogram (curve F) nearly identical to the original material.

Note, apropos of the Borchardt and Thompson work, that sodium chloride melts at 800°C and that thermograms E and F begin an exothermic deflection in this region. This existence of even a relatively small quantity of liquid phase could bring about the destruction of calcium carbonate by, in effect, precipitation of calcium silicate. The presence of this liquid phase could render the metathesis sufficiently rapid to compete with the decomposition.

13.7. Clay Minerals as a Continuous Series

Keeling (K12) has compared several measurements on clay minerals and suggested that they may be considered to be a continuous series describable in terms of the ratio of combined water to the specific sur-

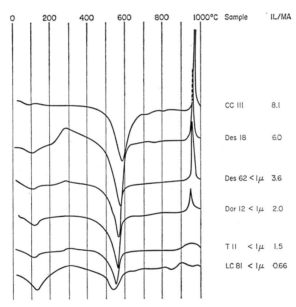

Fig. XIII-9. Differential thermal analyses of clays. From Keeling (K12). *The figures on the right are a measure of the water/area ratio.*

face. Infrared absorption and X-ray diffraction data as well as differential thermal analysis (Fig. XIII-9) show, with a decreasing water/surface ratio, "progressive increase in size and peak temperature of the adsorbed moisture endotherm, a decrease in size and peak temperature of the breakdown [dehydroxylation] endotherm at 500–600°C, and a decrease in definition and peak temperature of the 900–1000°C exotherm." He relates these structural properties to the plasticity and green strength which are important in the ceramic art, but relation to more precisely measurable parameters may sometime be instructive.

13.8. Biological Studies

This section will be limited to the presentation of a few examples of biological samples. The potential range of application is great. Here in particular effluence analysis would be useful.

The thermograms of ankle bone and of hemoglobin, Fig. XIII-10 and XIII-11, show possible use in medical studies while the thermograms of

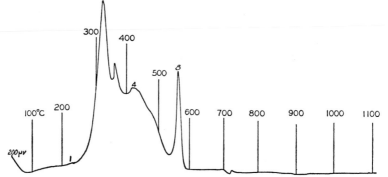

Fɪɢ. XIII-10. Thermogram of ankle bone leached in chloroform for 24 hours. (Courtesy of Robert L. Stone Co.)

The residue from the chloroform leaching may be of aid in studying bone composition.

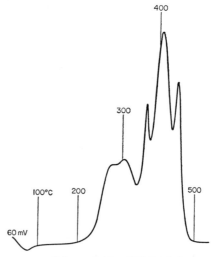

Fɪɢ. XIII-11. Thermogram of hemoglobin—70% fetal from cord blood; 1 atm, O_2 (1 wt. H + 7 wt. Al_2O_3). (Courtesy of Robert L. Stone Co.)

Some oxidations occur prior to the combustion. The peaks might provide a quick test for the sources of the blood.

wood and its extracts, Fig. XIII-12, and of plant gums and acids, Fig. XIII-13, suggest possible botanical applications.

13.9. Fractional Thermogravimetric Analysis

The technique devised by Waters (W7) in which some components leaving a sample during decomposition are trapped within the weighed assembly may be very useful in studies in which more than one reaction may be going on simultaneously. Waters constructed his sample holders

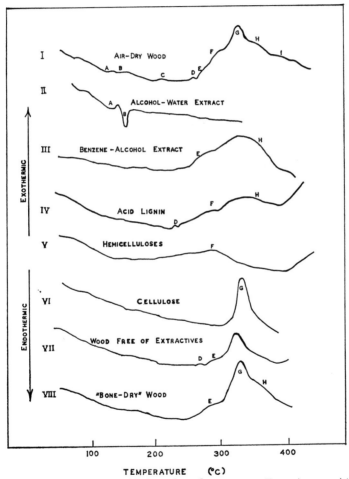

Fig. XIII-12. Thermograms of balsam fir and its extracts. From Arsenan (A14).
The multiplicity of components renders the thermogram of the original material uninterpretable; separation of components by extraction or distillation would be an essential step.

(Fig. XIII-14) such that gases from the sample had to pass through adsorbents to escape.

The study will require a number of runs to learn the manner in which each component is driven off from the sample. Waters used the technique in the study of coals (Fig. XIII-15) in which there are a number

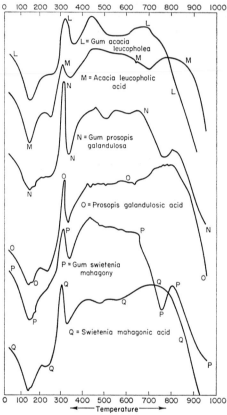

FIG. XIII-13. Thermograms of plant gums and gum acids. From Kulshrestha (K47a). *Effluence analysis would be very helpful in further characterization.*

of each of several types of materials coming off. A more specific effluence analysis (Chapter XIV) would be extremely tedious and very possibly pointless.

13.10. Detection of Formation of Compounds

The present author showed (G14), several years ago, that the product obtained by alkaline hydrolysis of maleate esters was not the same as that obtained by a similar hydrolysis of maleic anhydride. One piece of evidence cited (G12) was a comparison of differential thermal analysis curves of the two materials (Fig. XIII-16). From several pieces of evidence we (G14, G19) advanced the hypothesis that dimerization occurred during hydrolysis of the esters and that the potassium salt of the dimeric acid crystallized as a hemialcoholate. The thermogram of the potassium maleate appears to be that of a well-crystallized material with some very sharply defined reactions. The hemialcoholate, after losing the alcohol, shows a general similarity to the potassium maleate without the good definition of the oxidation of the various parts of the molecule.

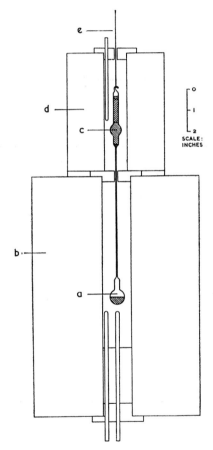

Fɪɢ. XIII-14. Apparatus for fractional thermogravimetric analysis: a, sample bulb; b, furnace; c, absorption tubes; d, subsidiary furnace; e, suspension wire to balance. From Waters (W7).

The absorption tube, c. may be packed with several adsorbents or chemisorbents. allowing only selected materials to escape.

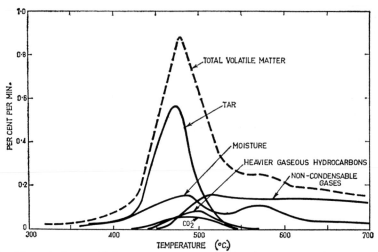

FIG. XIII-15. Fractional thermogravimetric analysis of a coking coal. From Waters (W7).

A quantitative analysis as well as the temperature dependence is obtained.

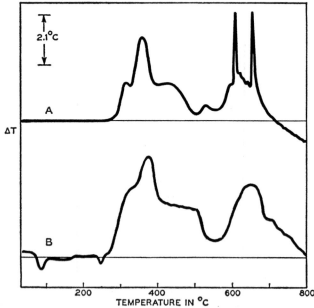

FIG. XIII-16. Thermograms of saponication products from (A) maleic anhydride and (B) diethyl maleate. From Garn and Flaschen (G12).

The general similarity of the exothermic reaction indicates a general similarity of the two potassium salts. The potassium maleate in (A) is more crystalline and would be expected to yield sharper peaks. The initial endotherm in (B) is due to decomposition of an alcoholate.

(Similar curves were published by Rey and Kostomaroff (R18). Since no reference is made to the present author's work, said present author is uncertain whether or not Rey and Kostomaroff have confirmed the observation.)

The subsequent experience of the present author would dictate a rather different approach, permitting a quite conclusive resolution of the problem by techniques within the scope of this monograph. There is, for example, no reason why an atmosphere of ethyl alcohol cannot be used in either differential thermal analysis or thermogravimetric analysis. The expected shift of temperature of the initial decomposition in Fig. XIII-16 would confirm the nature of the alcoholate. Alternatively, effluence analysis could be used to identify the decomposition product. The methods appropriate to structure analysis would still be needed to establish or refute the dimerization.

13.11. Qualitative Identifications

The usual organic identification procedures of mixed melting points or determining the melting points of derivatives can be carried out readily by differential thermal analysis. Chiu (C11) demonstrated the utility of a simple process of derivative formation by heating a mixture of triethyl-amine and picric acid (Fig. XIII-17) and showing the formation of the

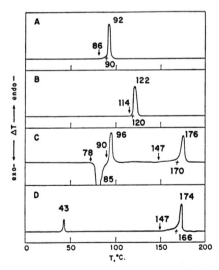

Fɪɢ. XIII-17. Thermogram showing formation of triethylamine picrate. From Chiu (C11). (A) triethylamine; (B) picric acid; (C) reaction mixture of triethylamine and picric acid; (D) rerun of residue from C.

The melting point of the derivative is obtained very quickly. A rerun of the residue would be advisable.

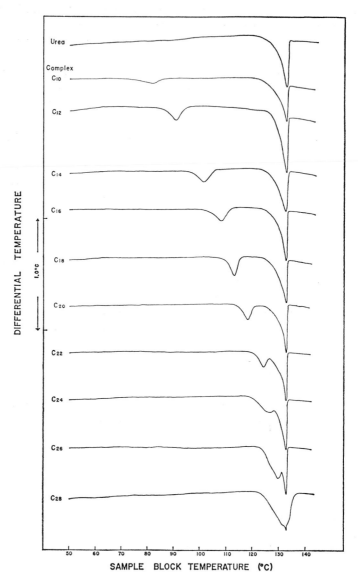

Fɪɢ. XIII-18. Differential thermograms of urea and a series of urea–*n*-paraffin complexes. From McAdie (M23).

The dissociation temperature increases with carbon number up to the melting point of urea.

picrate derivative. The rerun, as shown in Fig. XIII-17d, should be carried out routinely. Thermal effects occurring in the product but below the reaction temperature may be helpful. With nonstoichiometric mixtures some of one reactant may interfere.

Molecular complexes, such as the inclusion complexes of methylnaphthalenes (M33a) or urea (K33a), not only are interesting chemically but also can be useful. The urea complexes of n-paraffins were studied by McAdie, who reported the variation (Fig. XIII-18) of decomposition temperature of the complex with the chain length of the adduct.

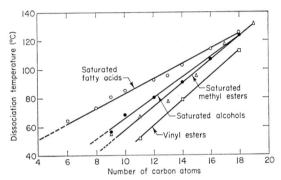

Fig. XIII-19. Dissociation temperatures of urea complexes as functions of number of carbon atoms in the adduct. From Knight *et al.* (K33a).
Several classes of materials vary in similar manners.

Knight *et al.* had found similar variations in other classes of compounds (Fig. XIII-19). The value found should be of help in identifications and differential thermal analysis should be an expeditious manner of finding that value.

13.12. Summary

The uses of thermoanalytical techniques are many and varied. Anomalies may be disclosed and investigation of these will sometimes lead to new knowledge.

CHAPTER XIV

Analysis of Gaseous Decomposition Products

14.1. Introduction

As used herein, effluence analysis is defined as the qualitative and/or quantitative analysis of gaseous products given off during the heating of a specimen. We can study these gases most easily by the types of detectors generally used in gas chromatography. Many analyses of such products have appeared in the literature in contexts not directly related to thermal analysis but since a reader may plan to use similar methods the author feels justified in extending his remarks and evaluations beyond the general scope of this book.

14.2. Heating of Specimens

The solid material being studied has been or can be heated in several manners and for multiple purpose studies as well as specifically for the analysis of the decomposition products. The most common of the multiple determinations would be simultaneous differential thermal analysis and effluence analysis; the effluence from a thermogravimetric analysis could also be analyzed, but this will invariably be accompanied by considerable dilution. In any event, in such simultaneous determinations the heating program and heating conditions are fairly rigidly prescribed

420

by the requirements of the other technique. In those cases in which the sample is heated specifically for analysis of gaseous decomposition products, a fairly wide range of heating conditions can be and have been used. Examples could include slow heating of a rather massive sample to some fixed temperature or, at the other extreme, flash heating by use of a high-intensity source of visible and infrared radiation. A common technique, intermediate between these, is the practice of placing the sample on a heater (wire) or in a heater specially formed, then applying a predetermined voltage to the heater so that the specimen heats in an uncontrolled but approximately reproducible manner. In contrast to this latter, the specimen can be heated in some programmed manner as would be typical in the simultaneous determinations.

14.3. Simultaneous Determinations

Let us use as a starting point the present author's work with some simultaneous determinations; this work has been, of late, generally concerned with problems such that simultaneous differential thermal analysis and effluence analysis would have obvious benefits. In previously reported work, the author (G18) has connected a dynamic-atmosphere differential thermal analysis to various devices for detecting gaseous products and/or establishing the nature of the products.

One arrangement used is shown in Fig. XIV-1. In this arrangement a gas is supplied to the furnace chamber under sufficient pressure to cause a reasonable flow—this flow varies with the type of experiment—downward through the sample and through the reference materials. The gas passing through the reference is used as the reference gas in the thermal conductivity detector and the gas passing through the sample is compared with it. Any gaseous decomposition product whose thermal conductivity, k, is different from that of the "chamber gas" will then produce in the thermal conductivity detector a different cooling effect than the pure chamber gas during the time that the product gas is passing through the detector. The magnitude of the differential signal from such a detector is, at low concentrations, proportional to the quantity of the product gas passing through at the moment, so that integration of the area under a total deflection is a measure of the quantity of the gas evolved, provided the gas is known.

In the arrangement of Fig. XIV-1, the gas which passed through the sample then goes into the gas density detector. This detector has the advantage (over the thermal conductivity detector) that it is not only a quantitative measuring device but also to some extent qualitative. It has a further advantage that the sensitivity of the detection can be adjusted by judicious selection of carrier gas since the density or "apparent molecular weight" is the only property of importance in the measurement. One potential advantage is that some effluent species may be completely blanked out by use of a mixed carrier gas of the same density. A small quantity of some other gas could be detected in the presence of a large mass of the first.

The gas density detector depends for its operation on the effect of minor changes of flow in the vertical column on the total flow in tubes connected to the top and bottom of a vertical column. Let us assume that

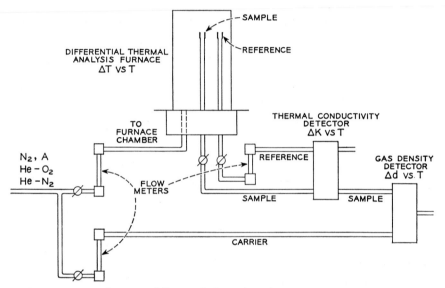

Fɪɢ. XIV-1. Combination differential thermal analysis and double effluence analysis.

The transient changes in the sample stream are detected in chromatographic-type analyzers.

in the device shown in Fig. XIV-2 a steady-state flow into the ports both on the right and in the center has been established so that we have a steady-state cooling of the detector elements. Now at some point upstream we inject a small quantity of a product gas, as we might in the normal course of a decomposition in differential thermal analysis. If this product gas is heavier than the carrier gas, the change in density, of course, will be an increase and, hence, the sample plus carrier gas will tend to flow downward to a greater extent than upward. This downward flow will decrease slightly the flow in the lower supply tube (coming from the right) and increase slightly the flow in the upper supply tube; this change in flow in the supply tubes produces a change in the cooling effect on the detector elements, an increase on the upper and a decrease on the lower.

The differential flow at any moment is proportional to the change in density of the sample plus carrier gas from that of the carrier gas alone, permitting, of course, a quantitative measurement of the material passing through—assuming that it is a single gas. Note, however, that the density of the sample plus carrier gas is dependent not only on the quantity of sample but also on the nature of the sample; that is, a gas which, pure, is only slightly heavier than the carrier gas will at a given level of concentration produce some fixed differential flow while a gas

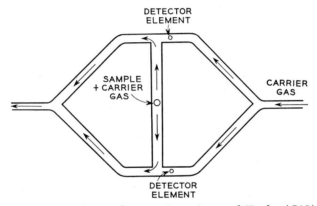

Fig. XIV-2. Gas density detector. From Garn and Kessler (G18).
A change in density of the sample gas produces a greater flow upward or downward. This in turn changes the flow of the reference gas.

substantially heavier than the carrier gas will at the same concentration produce a significantly greater differential flow. Because of this, qualitative as well as quantitative information can be obtained. If the sample gas is unknown, a second experiment with a carrier gas of different density will provide data for calculation of the real or apparent molecular weight of the sample. (If the sample is a mixture of gases, the apparent density will be dependent on their relative proportions and their relative densities in the pure state). If the number of possibilities is quite limited, a simpler identification is possible by bracketing the density of the suspected gas in two runs; for example, if there is reason to believe that the specimen gives off oxygen when heated in an inert atmosphere, an experiment using nitrogen as the carrier gas will show that the sample is more dense while a second experiment using argon will show that the sample gas is less dense, and if necessary direct comparison of the areas will show whether or not the apparent molecular weight of the gas is 32.

The present author has used this type of identification in several cases. Two are cited below. In some studies of cobalt oxalate hydrate the nature of the second step was not known with certainty. Most oxalates decompose in a nonoxidizing atmosphere by loss of carbon monoxide producing the corresponding carbonate. A cobalt oxalate resulting from the heating of the dihydrate decomposed ca. 400 C to yield what appeared to be a finely divided metal. In closed-chamber differential thermal analysis experiments with air as the furnace atmosphere, this metal powder had, around the opening along the support tube, evidence of oxide formation. The question was resolved by effluence analysis with density detection using nitrogen as the carrier gas. Figure XIV-3 shows a temperature-based, simultaneous differential thermal analysis and effluence analysis of cobalt oxalate dihydrate. A curve similar to the lower curve of Fig. XIV-3—but recorded on a time base—was obtained and the areas below and above the two peaks were measured. If a mole of cobalt oxalate dihydrate decomposes directly to the metal, 2 moles of carbon dioxide are released, and since 2 moles of water are also released the areas should be in direct relation to the density difference. The density difference between water and nitrogen, assuming ideal gas, etc., is 28—18 or 10 gm per mole while the difference between carbon dioxide and nitrogen would be 44—28 or 16 gm per mole. The ratio of areas then should be 1.6 if the decomposition is directly to the metal. Within a few per cent, attributable to experimental error, this is the result obtained; thus the gas must be carbon dioxide. Note that in this experiment carbon monoxide, having a molecular weight of 28, would not have shown its presence at all because its density is the same as that of nitrogen.

A case in which nitrogen and argon were used to establish the evolution of oxygen concerned the decomposition of lanthanum oxalate hydrate. Some plots are shown in Fig. XIV-4. We are concerned here with the reaction just above 700°C in which a material heavier than nitrogen but lighter than argon is evolved. From the nature of the system this is obviously oxygen. Note, too, that in the region of 400°C in nitrogen there is a substantial increase in density while in argon there is an increase followed by a sharp but transient decrease. The increase is attributable to the volution of carbon dioxide and the decrease to carbon monoxide, which is also evolved and whose presence would pass unnoticed in the nitrogen experiment.

Figure XIV-5 shows the decomposition of lanthanum oxalate hydrate in oxygen using the arrangement shown in Fig. XIV-1. In the low-temperature region the water loss is shown as a series of endothermic reactions, as a series of increases of the thermal conductivity and decreases in density. In this experiment no carbon monoxide is given off; instead, the carbon monoxide is oxidized to carbon dioxide, accounting both for the sharp increase in density around 350°C and the sharp exotherm in the differential thermal analysis plot. The thermal conductivity decreases. In the 750°C region we again see a decomposition yielding carbon dioxide since the density becomes heavier; the thermal conductivity decreases but the differential temperature first shows evi-

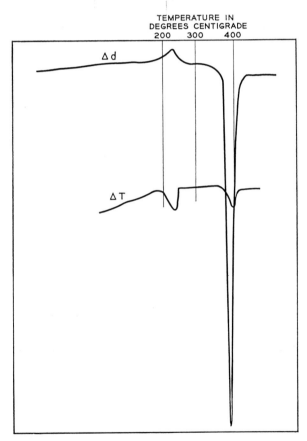

Fig. XIV-3. Differential thermal and effluence density analysis of cobalt oxalate dihydrate: $\Delta d = d$ carrier gas $- d$ effluent gas. From Garn and Kessler (G18).

The areas of the differential density deflection can be related to the mass and concentration of the decomposition product.

dence of an endothermic reaction followed by an exothermic rearrangement of some sort.

While these particular sets of curves were obtained during single runs
with all measurements being made simultaneously, this is not by any
means a necessary procedure. Separate experiments would be just as
instructive and possibly experimentally more convenient as long as they
were planned properly.

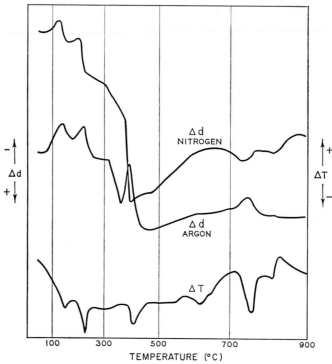

Fɪɢ. XIV-4. Identification of gaseous products by use of gas density detector.
From Garn and Kessler (G18).

*Use of nitrogen and argon discloses evolution of carbon monoxide ca 370°C and
oxygen ca 750°C.*

14.4. Gas Chromatography

In many cases a more specific identification than described above may
be needed because at some stages in the decomposition more than one
product may be given off. For such cases the addition of gas chromatography is useful. Gas chromatography as ordinarily practiced would be
relatively ineffective; it would measure all the decomposition products

up to the time of sampling. Specific identification of the product of a particular reaction requires that the sampling be made for that reaction alone; that is, any reaction products from previous decompositions are already removed from the site of sampling. This can be done readily by an arrangement such as that shown in Fig. XIV-6. In this system a furnace such as that shown in Fig. XIV-1 or Fig. VII-21, is used to carry

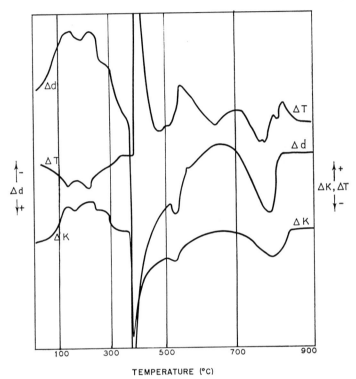

TEMPERATURE (°C)

Fig. XIV-5. Simultaneous measurement of differential temperature (ΔT), density (Δd), and thermal conductivity (Δk) of the effluent gas. From Garn and Kessler (G18).

Fairly precise interpretation of the effects can be made by use of the several curves.

out the thermal decomposition. The carrier gas which passes through the sample may, if desired, be passed through a thermal conductivity cell for a continuous and general survey of decomposition products, but more important, it passes through a pair of sampling valves with, in some cases, an interposed water trap. These sampling valves operate at programmed intervals to withdraw samples of gas from the stream and pass them through chromatographic columns and detectors. The programming is done by trial and error. For the Fluoropak column, and separately for the split column, flow conditions were determined which gave adequate separation. An adjustable cam timer was then connected to the sampling valves so that during each revolution one sampling valve would open for 5 seconds, then close, and after the selected interval of

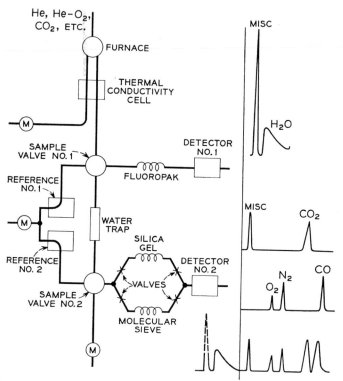

Fig. XIV-6. Gas train and switching for repetitive dual sampling chromatography. From Garn (G7).

Sample valve No. 1 transfers a 3-ml sample and No. 2 a 5-ml sample. Sampling interruptions have been deleted in copying (see Fig. XIV-7).

time the other valve would open and close. The oven temperature, the flow rates, and the sampling times were chosen for each type of experiment specifically to permit rapid sampling. In effect, each sampling occurs soon after the last expected peak from the previous sampling.

The Fluoropak column, when used, permits all nonpolar and slightly polar materials to run through rapidly but holds up the water long enough to give separation and permit measurement.

The second sampling valve in turn withdraws a specimen from the stream and directs it through a split column and to a second detector. This split column has silica gel in the one side and a molecular sieve in the other, the silica gel holding up the carbon dioxide but passing the other permanent gases through rapidly while the molecular sieve separates the permanent gases. Proper adjustment of the relative flows permits appearance of the carbon dioxide conveniently in the interval of time between the appearance of nitrogen and of carbon monoxide from the molecular sieve. The chromatogram resulting from the presence of all the gases but water is shown at the right for each column and at the bottom for a complete cycle. Figure XIV-7 shows a chart section with a

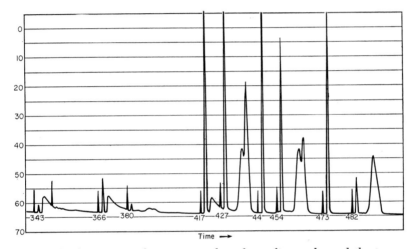

Fig. XIV-7. Chart section showing a number of sampling cycles and the temperature at which the sample was taken. From Garn (G7).

The temperature at the moment of sampling is measured and the reaction occurring at that temperature thus described (see Fig. XIV-6). Alternate samplings, e.g., 417° and 446°C, are into the Flouropak column; the others go through the split-column.

number of cycles, the appearance and disappearance of peaks reflecting the beginning and subsidence of reactions as the specimen material is heated.

Examination of several cycles of the chromatographic analysis permits the following of a single reaction, or, more important, a series of reactions, by the relative heights or areas of peaks. Figure XIV-8 shows such a series. The left-hand set of analyses are solely for water, those to their immediate right are the associated samplings for the permanent gases, and those at the far right a subsequent series of analyses for the perman-

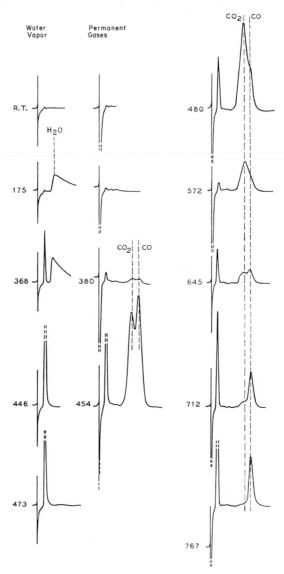

FIG. XIV-8. Reproduction of several chromatographic analyses from the chart of which Fig. XIV-7 showed a part. The temperatures of sampling are indicated. From Garn (G7).

The appearance and disappearance of specific products can be followed easily (see Fig. XIV-6).

ent gases. No water appeared in the later analyses so they are not shown. Note that even in the water analysis an indication of the increasing concentration of other gases was apparent from the growth of the peak just prior to the rather broad water peak. Similarly, even though the carbon dioxide and carbon monoxide peaks run together at high concentrations, the sharp peak shortly after the sampling, due to the permanent gases other than carbon dioxide passing rapidly through the silica gel column, gives an indication of the concentration of carbon monoxide even when the peak is almost obscured by the carbon dioxide. At the higher temperatures carbon dioxide evolution ceases and carbon monoxide is the only product detected.

The data from one run are tabulated in Fig. XIV-9 along with the differential thermal analysis and differential conductivity curves. The water is given off over a rather wide range and the peaks are poorly defined in this dynamic atmosphere of helium; then the decomposition of oxalate occurs very sharply and the interrupted peak on the thermal conductivity curve can be related to the more or less continual evolution of carbon dioxide coupled with the quickly terminated evolution of carbon monoxide. The new appearance of carbon monoxide at higher temperatures is also apparent. The high drift in the differential thermal analysis signal is a result of sintering of the specimen and consequent change in the heat transfer from the side to the center of the specimen. One might conclude from these particular curves that Δk is a more sensitive measurement than ΔT and in some cases this could be justified. Consider, however, that this particular experiment used a helium atmosphere and the thermal conductivity change is at a maximum [a dynamic atmosphere of helium would seldom be picked for differential thermal analysis (see below)]. Further, differential thermal analysis detects changes of state which the thermal conductivity of the gas stream obviously cannot reflect.

Some of the earlier exploratory work with the combination of chromatography with differential thermal analysis shows the hazard of vitiating data from one of the techniques. Figure XIV-10 shows some differential thermal analysis curves for an ocean sediment specimen obtained with air and with helium as dynamic atmospheres. While the analysis in helium was being performed, a technician took chromatographic samples by manual operation of a sampling valve at regular intervals (G15). There is no difficulty following the appearance of carbon monoxide and the appearance and virtual disappearance of carbon dioxide in the decomposition products, but there is significant difficulty in finding related. One may not conclude that combinations of techniques will be any thermal effects in the helium run to which the gas evolution may be necessarily useful. Simultaneous determinations are of benefit only under those conditions in which neither technique is greatly compromised. The planning of separate experiments for each technique will often be more fruitful.

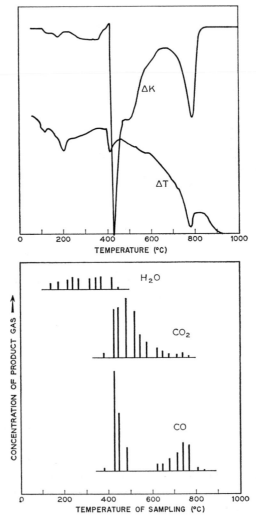

Fig. XIV-9. Tabulated chromatographic peak heights related to the simultaneously obtained differential thermal analysis and thermal conductivity analysis of the effluent stream. From Garn (G7).

The sudden appearance of carbon monoxide and dioxide is indicated also by the plots. The curves, however, give no hint of the relative amounts of CO_2 and CO.

14.5. Critique

With all the experimental problems of simultaneous analysis and the distinct probability that separate experiments could be better controlled or more instructive, nevertheless the simultaneous-determinations technique is generally superior to point-by-point sampling for the same types of analyses. Let us consider the technique devised by Murphy *et al.* (M42) in which a differential thermal analysis was performed of poly(vinyl chloride) in an evacuated vessel which had connections also (Fig. XIV-11) to some previously evacuated sampling tubes for mass spectrometry. The object is, of course, to determine the identity of

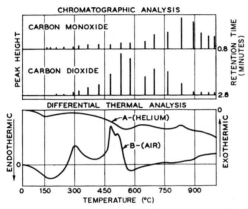

Fɪɢ. XIV-10. Differential thermal analyses of an ocean sediment related to the effluence analysis. From Garn (G7).

The appearance and disappearance of the gases can be related to the peaks of curve A but curve B bears no appreciable resemblance because the reactions are quite different.

the gaseous products coming off at various stages of the heating, but consider the required procedure. One must first make a trial run in order to establish the temperatures which may be of interest. After selecting the sampling temperatures a rerun must be made with operator monitoring in order that the selected samples may be taken at the proper time, and finally the gaseous samples taken must be conveyed to the other instrument, in this case a mass spectrometer, and analyzed individually. All of this is perfectly possible and may be justified on the basis of the need for information about a particular sample, but there immediately arises the problem of the need for an operator to make a judgment on probably inadequate data. That is, on a specimen with which the operator is not familiar, a single thermogram is seldom sufficient to establish the identity of a given reaction.

In this technique the choice of sampling points is obviously extremely important, yet the example shown by Murphy *et al.* (M42) in Fig. XIV-12 involves what is apparently an error in choice. They sampled at 300 and 400°C, the lower temperature being at the peak of an endothermic reaction and the higher temperature at what they describe as a flat exotherm. They found, as they expected, hydrogen chloride evolved at 300°C, and we may infer that they had expected similar evolution at 400°C for they reported that no hydrogen chloride was evolved without specifying the presence or absence of any other material. The absence of any material evolved in the 400°C region should not be a surprise; that

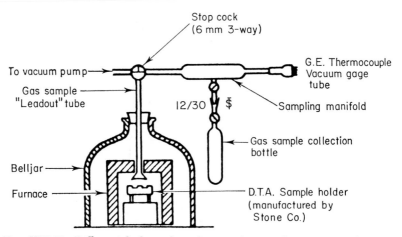

Fig. XIV-11. Differential thermal analysis with point-by-point sampling. From Murphy *et al.* (M42).

Since the gas samples are analyzed separately a small number would be taken at temperatures selected by the operator.

region is almost certainly not an exotherm or due to any reaction at all. It is far more likely a simple change in base line due to the change in thermal properties of the specimen. The important point here is not that they made an error and their information needs reinterpretation but that such an error is easily possible with point-by-point sampling techniques.

Let us now consider an arrangement in which the gas given off by a heated specimen is swept by a carrier gas into a thermal conductivity detector. In the arrangement described by Ayres and Bens (A19), the sample cells are test tubes set in a metal block as shown in Fig. XIV-13. A differential thermal analysis is performed on the specimen and the plot from the thermal conductivity cell is related to the differential thermal analysis plot. The carrier gas passes through a preheater and then flows over the sample and reference specimens and thence into the detector cell; note that the gas does not pass *through* the specimen, so the atmosphere surrounding the particles will vary depending on the nature of the product gas and the depth of the particle within the total specimen. The upper layers are continually exposed to an atmosphere of essentially pure helium, but during a decomposition the helium will be displaced by the product gas and, especially near the bottom, the particle will experience an enrichment of the product gas concentration.

The effect of the enrichment within the bulk of the specimen will vary depending on the nature of the sample. Reactions having any appreci-

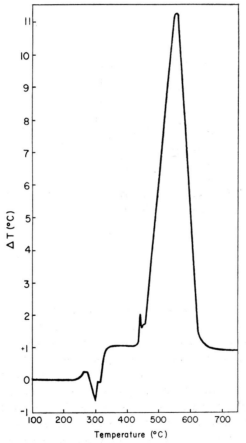

Fig. XIV-12. Differential thermal analysis of poly(vinyl chloride) showing sampling temperatures. From Murphy *et al.* (M42).

The necessity for operator judgment based on limited information is more subject to error than programmed sampling.

able semblance of reversibility will be spread over a range of temperatures because of the atmosphere effect, yet not to the same extent as
would be the case in the absence of a moving atmosphere because we
can consider any product gas to be diffusing outward into a zero-level
concentration above the specimen (cf. Chapter VII). For a reversible
reaction, then, this technique will yield differential thermal analysis
curves intermediate between those obtained in static atmospheres or in
dynamic atmospheres as cited previously. The effluent gas analysis will

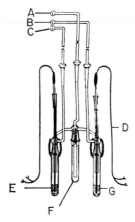

Fɪɢ. XIV-13. Differential thermal analysis apparatus providing detection of
evolved gases: (A) sweeping gas inlet; (B) gas train to detector, sample; (C) gas
train to detector, reference: (D) thermocouple probe leads; (E) reference cell with
glass beads; (F) sweeping gas preheater, with glass wool; (G) sample cell, with
sample and glass beads. From Ayres and Bens (A19).

*The carrier gas sweeps over the sample, carrying toward the detector gases that
diffuse out of the sample.*

closely parallel the differential thermal analysis curve. Irreversible decompositions, such as the perchloric decomposition and many organic
decompositions, will be virtually unaffected by any movement of the
atmosphere because these reactions proceed rapidly when the decomposition temperature is reached regardless of the ambient atmosphere.
The detection of the effluent gas can be expected to agree less well
than in the case of the reversible reactions because a tailing off is essentially certain to follow a rapid exothermic reaction; in addition to the
burst of gaseous products spewed into the carrier stream, these products
displace the carrier gas from the nooks and crannies within the specimen
and some reasonable interval of time will be required for this material
to diffuse out of the specimen and into the gas stream. In reversible

reactions, under this type of conditions, there is very probably a diminution in the rate of formation of the product gases. Their concentration increases and, toward the bottom of the sample vessel, unreacted material may yet exist after the peak temperature difference has passed. The return to the base line will be slow because of this continuing reaction and during the same period these last portions of product gases will be diffusing out of the specimen and into the gas stream in ever-decreasing quantities; the effect in the gas detector is, then, rather similar to the differential thermal analysis peak.

Let us examine the data obtained by Ayres and Bens using ammonium perchlorate; but first we can well review the reactions of ammonium perchlorate under a small variety of conditions. Differential thermal analysis curves in various atmospheres were obtained by Stone (S58); his data are shown in Fig. VII-1 (see also Fig. VII-2). In an ammonia atmosphere the entire decomposition occurs at one temperature because the presence of the ammonia represses the initial decomposition. In any other gas a preliminary decomposition occurs which is only slightly pressure-dependent. The final decomposition temperature remains the same. Note that this initial decomposition is not a *necessary* prelude to the exothermic decomposition. The evidence so far suggests that in the absence of ammonia this initial decomposition comprises the loss of all or part of the ammonia. We might hypothesize either a double salt remaining at this stage or, if all the ammonia is lost, that the perchloric acid vapor pressure has not yet reached one atmosphere.

In vacuum the final decomposition is not exothermic at all. We may infer that the ammonium perchlorate decomposition products from the initial reaction volatilize and the material is swept out before decomposition.

In any case, the curve obtained by Ayres and Bens in helium (Fig. XIV-14) would correspond to the third of Stone's curves, i.e., the one obtained in nitrogen at one atmosphere. The difference in the nature of the flowing or dynamic gas between the two experiments is of no consequence as long as the gas does not enter into any sort of reaction with the specimen. The drawn-out initial decomposition and the tailing off of the gas evolution after the final decomposition can be attributed to the manner of passing the gas across the sample as explained above.

Less volatile products will cause a rather different trouble, but the problem is apparently purely physical and could be corrected by redesign of the apparatus. Ayres and Bens also show decomposition curves for nitroglycerin and a propellant (Fig. XIV-15). Note that at the upper extremes in temperature an evolution of gas appears to take place with no evidence of a thermal effect. This is more likely due to the condensation of a decomposition residue in a cooler part of the glassware and subsequent vaporization of the residue as the heating continues and that part of the glassware reaches a sufficiently high temperature.

Ayres and Bens called attention to the possible troubles due to condensation; the present author's contribution is the delineation of events within the sample.

Another use of simultaneous differential thermal analysis and a form of effluence analysis was of a very special kind; Bussiere and co-workers (B91) constructed an apparatus. (Fig. XIV-16) in which they could si-

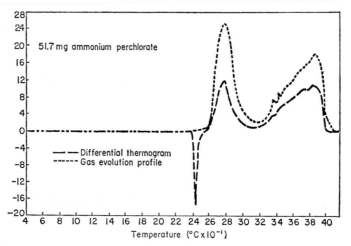

FIG. XIV-14. Decomposition of ammonium perchlorate in a flowing atmosphere of helium. From Ayres and Bens (A19).

The evolved gases do not enter the stream instantaneously so tailing-off can be expected.

multaneously perform differential thermal analysis, thermogravimetric analysis, and a measure of the emanation from thoron. Their work is based on the absorption of thoron along the interfaces between crystallites. The sample used was thorium oxalate hydrate. The radioactive decay of thorium produces (also radioactive) thoron, part of which escapes and part of which is trapped in the interfaces or interstices and, at best, moves slowly to the particle surface. When, however, the material undergoes a change of state, the disruption of the crystals permits more ready escape of the thoron from among the crystallites.

Bussiere *et al.* (B91) passed a gas stream across their specimen and into a detector in which the radioactivity of this gas stream (due to the thoron) was measured. The data of Fig. XIV-17 are not easily interpreted at first sight. The first dehydration is unambiguous; each of the measurements demonstrates an effect which we can accept as decomposition to the dehydrate as stated by Bussiere and associates. The second weight loss and accompanying endotherm are clear enough, but there is no corresponding event in the emanation measurement. Further,

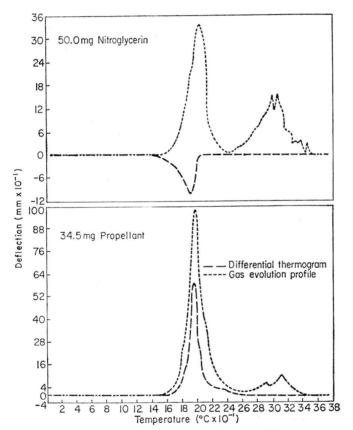

Fig. XIV-15. Decomposition of nitroglycerin and a propellant. From Ayres and Bens (A19).
The comparatively nonvolatile residues apparently condense and are driven slowly toward the detector.

in the final decomposition, not only does the thermogravimetric curve indicate a single, smooth weight loss while the differential thermal analysis curve shows a pair of reactions, but the emanation curve even shows a decrease rather than the predicted increase.

The two-step final endotherm shown by the differential thermal anal-

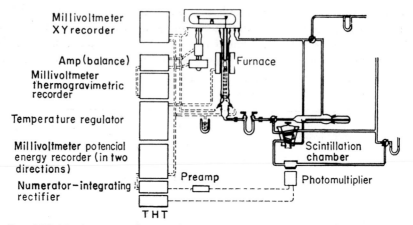

Millivoltmeter
XY recorder

Amp (balance)
Millivoltmeter
thermogravimetric
recorder

Temperature regulator

Millivoltmeter potencial
energy recorder (in two
directions)
Numerator–integrating
rectifier

Furnace

Scintillation
chamber

Preamp   Photomultiplier

T H T

Fɪɢ. XIV-16. Apparatus for simultaneous differential thermal analysis, thermo-gravimetric analysis, and radioactive emanation detection. From Bussiere *et al.* (B91).

The radioactive gas is a decay product of thorium. Dilution and delay could be important problems.

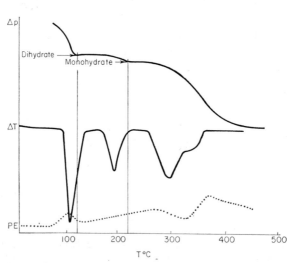

Fɪɢ. XIV-17. Simultaneous measurement of weight loss, thermal effects, and emanation of thorium oxalate hydrate. From Bussiere *et al.* (B91).

The weight loss curve does not show the double thermal effect ca 300°C nor can the emanation curve be related prima facie *to either.*

ysis could be the decomposition of the oxalate first to the carbonate and subsequently to the oxide. On moderately large specimens and with no useful atmosphere control, these two decompositions will or at least can overlap enough to give a single thermogravimetric weight loss. The present author will not attempt to explain the slow rise in the emanation between about 120 and 250°C. The decrease in the region of 300°C may possibly be due to dilution; the evolution of the other gases may become such a significant part of the total gas flow that the flow through the counter is increased and the quantity of thoron present in the counter at any moment consequently decreased. As the rapid evolution diminishes the increased concentration is again apparent. The method is interesting and may be particularly useful in special cases. As a general technique, it suffers from the disadvantages that it does not provide a complete and unambiguous response to events in the specimen and, further, that it requires the presence of thorium or some other radioactive material producing a radioactive gas with a short half-life.

14.6. Determination of Gaseous Products Only

Let us now consider some experiments in which the gathering of information was confined to study of the gaseous products of decompositions. These range from systems in which only the event is of interest to systems in which the products are measured quite specifically both qualitatively and quantitatively. One of the former type is that of Rogers and associates (R27) in which (Fig. XIV-18) the specimen was pyrolyzed in a stream of helium. The organic vapors from the pyrolysis chamber are oxidized to water and carbon dioxide in the combustion tube to avoid condensation as well as to enhance sensitivity. (The conversion of a molecule of some fairly complex organic material to many molecules of

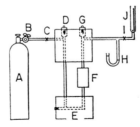

Fɪɢ. XIV-18. Schematic drawing of pyrolysis apparatus: A, carrier gas supply; B, pressure regulator; C, flow-control needle valve; D, reference thermal conductivity; E, pyrolysis chamber F, combustion tube; G, active cell; H, monometer; I, pressure-control needle valve; J, rotameter.

The oxidation of the products in the combustion tube avoids the condensation encountered by Ayres and Bens (A19).

carbon dioxide and water will quite naturally enhance the signal obtained in passing through the thermal conductivity cell.) [Bohon (B60) has used this type of pyrolysis chamber without the combustion tube; in this way he was able to collect the combustion products.] The pyrolysis block (Fig. XIV-19) is heated by commerical cartridge heaters through a temperature program. The data gained from the thermal conductivity measurements are simple indications of decompositions without identification (Fig. XIV-20) except, in some cases, by the temperature at which

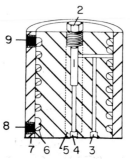

Fig. XIV-19. Pyrolysis block: 1, pyrolysis chamber; 2, nickel plug; 3, carrier gas inlet; 4, carrier gas outlet; 5, cartridge heater wells (two); 6, helical threads cut in inner body of block; 7, outer shell of block; 8, cooling jacket inlet; 9, cooling jacket outlet.

Because of the high temperatures, the inlet and outlet are sealed by use of model airplane spark plug gaskets or dead-soft copper washers.

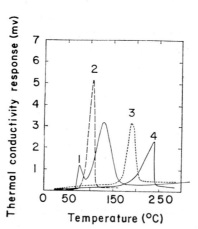

Fig. XIV-20. Pyrolysis curves: 1, 10 mg NaHCO$_2$ contaminated with Na$_2$CO$_3$•H$_2$O; 2, 10 mg CaSO$_4$•2H$_2$O; 3, 10 mg tetryl; 4, 10 mg hexanitrosobenzene.

The decomposition reaction must be inferred since no specific identification is obtained.

the decomposition occurs. This apparatus has the advantage over the Ayres and Bens apparatus that the conversion to carbon dioxide and water rids the system of easily condensable materials which might later vaporize and give a false signal.

These simple indications of decompositions are useful principally in establishing temperatures of decomposition, but with known products the technique can also be used as a quantitative measure with the same confidence as gas chromatography since the same type of detector is used. The user must know the product gases very specifically, or at least know that the same material containing the same proportions of carbon and hydrogen will come off from each sample tested. If this knowledge is not available with certainty, more detailed analyses may be in order. It is necessary only to substitute a technique for analysis instead of, or as well as, detection of the gaseous products. There is no reason why programming of the temperature is not still possible. The most generally useful technique for analysis of these effluent gases is gas chromatography; in the reported work seen by the present author, these sample materials have been vaporized into the carrier gas stream and carried immediately into the chromatographic column.

14.7. Qualitative Identification of Decomposition Products

In general, the direct injection of the decomposition product gases into the chromatograph is done by rapidly heating the material in the gas stream, the means of heating being usually the sample container as well. Experimenters principally interested in the chromatographic analysis can very easily overlook the importance of the manner of heating, and, indeed, this is a common occurrence. The specimens are heated rapidly so that the product gases appear in the chromatograph as a single pulse of gases; identification of the gases given off at intermediate temperatures is not attempted.

The transfer of heat from the heater wire to the sample material is a source of variation and error with specimens of appreciable thickness. Jennings and Dimick (J5) avoided the heat-transfer problem by evaportating the specimen on the heater wire using aqueous phosphoric acid to supply hydrogen and oxygen for the decomposition reaction. Their sampling apparatus is shown in Fig. XIV-21. They examined the effect of temperatures from 550 to 1100°C, finding that for thymine there was no appreciable difference in the pyrolysis pattern, that is, the identities and relative quantities of products. An example of their work is shown in Fig. XIV-22 where the lower plot gives by integration a measure of the volatile components. The first composite peak is likely to be permanent gases. These data show their reproducibility on repetition of the experiment as indicated in Table XIV-1. This is not the sort of reproducibility one would expect from an ordinary chromatographic analysis so the deviation or irreproducibility must be related to the pyrolysis technique. The nonlinearity in Jennings and Dimick's calibration data may still possibly be a heat-transfer problem; the thin specimens with good exposure to the atmosphere may partly volatilize without decomposition while the thicker specimens being heated from the inside may be subject only to the same absolute quantity of vaporization and hence a smaller percentage effect. The probability that the thicker specimens

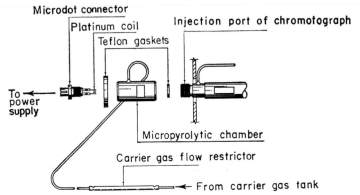

Fɪɢ. XIV-21. Exploded view of pyrolytic accessory. From Jennings and Dimick (J5).

Evaporation of a thin layer of sample onto the heater wire leads to good thermal contact and comparatively uniform heating.

reach higher temperatures locally may also lead to some variation in the relative quantities of the several products even though the identities of the products remain the same. Jennings and Dimick were also able to distinguish quite clearly between positional isomers; cytosine and isocytosine showed quite different proportions of products under similar pyrolysis conditions.

Quite different heating conditions were used by Strassburger *et al.* (S62); these authors used a much lower-temperature pyrolysis in their studies of methyl methacrylate copolymers. They heated their pyrolysis coil, shown in Fig. XIV-23, to about 450°C with 10 to 15 mg of specimen contained therein. At that temperature and in the absence of oxygen and hydrogen a relatively nonvolatile residue is formed. The reactions causing the formation of the residue also introduce distinct nonlinearities into the calibration for quantitative measurements so that, for example, the sample weight-to-peak area ratio varies by a factor of 2 in the methyl methacrylate–ethylene dimethacrylate copolymer.

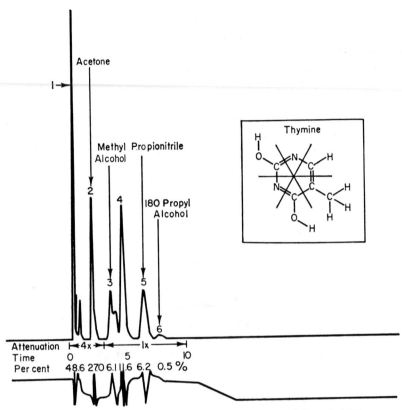

Fig. XIV-22. Pyrolysis of thymine. From Jennings and Dimick (J5).
The relative quantities of products are determined by the manner of splitting of the molecule and recombinations of the fragments.

TABLE XIV-1

COMPOSITION OF THYMINE PYROLYSIS PRODUCTS (J5)

Peak No.	RRT[a]	Per cent	Standard deviation
1	b	45.8	3.6
2	0.28	31.7	4.4
3	0.49	5.6	1.1
4	0.64	10.5	1.7
5	0.88	3.8	2.5
6	1.04	1.1	0.7

[a]RRT refers to relative retention time to benzene (7.2 minutes) on Hallcomid M-18 at 62°C.

[b]Represents a group of peaks.

14.8. Dependence of Products on Conditions of Their Formation

While some of the authors cited indicate that the pyrolysis products are the same over a wide range of pyrolysis conditions, to assume this happy circumstance for any given material to be studied would be exceedingly optimistic. A thin layer of material in contact with a heating element or other form of hot surface at a temperature approximating the ultimate decomposition temperature of the material may transmit heat rapidly enough to permit the entire film to decompose at essentially the same time and more or less at the same temperature. The material in contact with the heated surface does not necessarily rise in temperature greatly above the surface of the film. If this heated surface were several hundred degrees, say, above the ultimate decomposition temperature, rapid decomposition of the inner portion of the film could

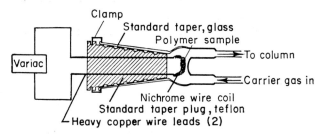

Fig. XIV-23. Sample introduction system. From Strassburger *et al.* (S62). *Solid pieces of material were placed in the heater coil.*

change the conditions of heat transfer substantially. With very thin specimens the problem will arise only in the extreme cases because the heating of the surface is not instantaneous; the heat capacity of the wire itself will cause some delay in reaching the final temperature, permitting a similar smooth rise by the specimen material.

If a thick sample is placed in contact with a heating element and the heating element is supplied with a sudden application of an electric current, the relatively low thermal conductivity of the typical organic specimen will permit the establishment of a high (and not necessarily continuous) temperature gradient through the specimen. The over-all effect will depend on the nature of the sample holding system. If the material has been deposited on a wire or other surface by evaporation of a solvent so that there is a continuous layer on the heating surface, the material next to the heating surface may well be heated slowly enough so that low-temperature decomposition products might form, but these decomposition products cannot escape and will consequently be subject to further decomposition. If particles are merely laid upon the heating surface the portion of the surface initially in contact may be heated slowly enough to undergo a low-temperature decomposition, but the new layers of material subsequently touching the heated surface are being subjected to a progressively hotter surface bringing about the possibility of a different decomposition mechanism.

The change in products obtained with change of pyrolysis conditions has been demonstrated by Martin and Ramstad (M18) who used flash pyrolysis to decompose cellulose in the sample chamber of a two-stage column. They separated the permanent gases on a gas-solid absorption column using polypropylene glycol. The specimen was heated by flash photolysis; that is, intense radiation from a flash tube or arc source was directed on the specimen for a short length of time, the temperature reached depending both on the intensity and the time of exposure. They induced momentary temperatures in the sample in excess of 600°C with intense radiation of a millisecond duration and compared the results with a slower pyrolysis in the 250 to 350°C range induced by less intense radiation lasting for several seconds. The plots are shown in Fig. XIV-24.

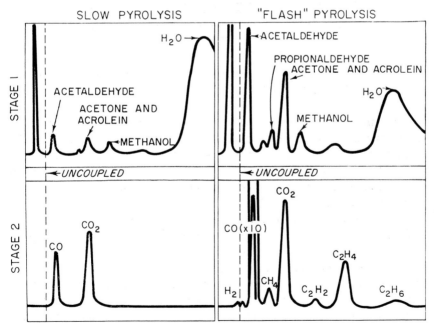

FIG. XIV-24. Chromatograms of cellulose pyrolysis products. From Martin and Ramstad (M18).

The manner of splitting and recombination is decidedly temperature-dependent.

The decomposition products are carried into the polypropylene glycol column where the permanent gases are impeded only slightly. These are led from the glycol column into the activated charcoal column where the gases are separated, the columns being uncoupled immediately after passage of the permanent gases from stage 1 into stage 2. The slow pyrolysis produces only carbon monoxide and carbon dioxide among the permanent gases while the flash pyrolysis produces significant quantities of the lighter hydrocarbons. The principal feature of the partition column curves is the greatly diminished water relative to the other components in the flash pyrolysis. While it is the major component, two of the other peaks at least surpass it in height. Note, too, that the magnitude of the carbon monoxide peak in the flash pyrolysis is more than ten times that of the carbon dioxide peak while in the slow pyrolysis it is somewhat smaller. Explanation of these variations would require further knowledge of the system, but a safe general conclusion can be stated: variations in the rate of heating of an organic specimen may cause different products or different relative quantities of products.

14.9. Other Possibilities

Now let us consider some of the extensions of effluence analysis; first of all, changes in the carrier gas used with the intention of encouraging or inhibiting some particular reaction. The use of helium-oxygen and helium-nitrogen mixtures has already been discussed in relation to determining the steps of an inorganic reaction. In this case, the helium-oxygen mixture permitted the oxidation of carbon monoxide while the absence of the oxygen brought about decomposition without oxidation. Similarly, small quantities of oxygen in the carrier gas stream would permit oxidation or partial oxidation of the specimen or the presence of hydrogen might permit saturation of organic carbon chains. This is not being recommended as a general technique but as a modification of procedure which might yield useful information. Repetitive sampling into the column in the manner practiced by the present author (see above) would yield successive lots of decomposition products as the temperature was increased.

Repetitive sampling for chromatography need not be an intermittent withdrawal of a portion of a gas stream. An alternative procedure, having some substantial advantages, is repetitive instanteous heating to successively higher temperatures. This may be done by extending Martin and Ramstad's (R18) technique to a *programmed* flash pyrolysis.

In this procedure the sample is within the gas stream at all times. At selected time intervals—depending on the nature of the columns and products—and flow conditions, light flashes of progressively higher intensity are directed at the sample. The heat generated within the sample due to optical absorption raises the temperature to a degree determined by the heat capacity and nature and quantity of the specimen. Some measure of the thermal effects may be obtained by relaxation time measurements as discussed later. The temperature can sooner or later be raised to a temperature at which some decomposition will occur. The millisecond—or less—pulse brings about a sudden expulsion of gas into the chromatographic gas stream. This sudden sampling inserts a very small "slug" of the gaseous products which means, in turn, comparatively narrow peaks as the components pass through the detector.

The major problem is the usual one of temperature inhomogeneity. The possibility of momentary temperature differences of hundreds of degrees across the sample forces the use of thin samples—essentially a monolayer of particles. Even so, the illuminated side of a particle may be completely decomposed while portions of the dark side are yet in the original state.

The enforced use of a very small sample is not such a handicap as it might appear *prima facie*. Since the sampling consists of heating the entire sample briefly to each of the successively higher temperatures the entire effluence is injected into the chromatographic column—rather than a comparatively small fraction as in repetitive sampling from a gas stream. This represents a gain of 30 to 100 to compensate for the diminution in sample size.

Measurement of the temperature could be done with a high-speed, probably oscillographic, recorder. Relaxation time studies of the variation of temperature after each flash are potentially of considerable use in investigation of thermal properties and behavior of freshly formed and freshly disrupted surfaces and crystals. Conversely, programmed flashing could be used to induce reaction of a solid—or liquid—specimen with the atmosphere. A reaction which is not strongly exothermic could be carried out using a multitude of low-energy and/or short pulses and some information on relative activities of surface regions gained.

Decompositions of specimens can be carried out directly in the sampling locations of other analytical instruments as well as chromatographs or chromatographic type of detectors, and similarly the decompositions can be programmed either stepwise or continuously. Two types of analyzers are of particular promise, optical and mass spectrometers. Decomposition into say, an infrared absorption spectrometer sample tube would be of particular interest if a particular compound or functional group were being monitored. Fairly high resolution would be required to obtain unambiguous reults. There is the advantage, however, that the appearance of the product could be followed during the entire decomposition, and if the decomposition is programmed some measure of the temperatures of appearance of various products may be obtained.

Of the mass spectrometers, the time-of-flight spectrometer would be of special interest because of the high frequency of repetitive sampling possible. Decomposition in a chamber connected to the spectrometer by an appropriate orifice would make possible the gathering of kinetic data on decompositions.

Relating the events recorded by these various techniques needs to be done with great care. Bussiere *et al.* (B91) compared curves obtained by their simultaneous determinations (see above) with those obtained on other (apparently single purpose) apparatus. An example is the pair of differential thermal analysis plots of Fig. XIV-25. Bussiere *et al.* conclude that it is preferable to make all the measurements simultaneously to obtain agreement in the interpretation of a given reaction. This is a fairly

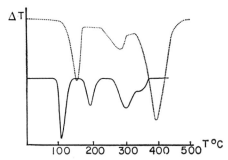

Fig. XIV-25. Comparison of differential thermal analyses of $Th(C_2O_4)_2 \cdot 6H_2O$: _____, simultaneous with thermogravimetric and emanation analyses; ......, in a separate apparatus. From Bussiere *et al.* (B91).

Differences in both the temperatures and the manners of the decompositions are apparent.

common attitude. The present author has contended (G4)—and still contends—that, unless the data from each technique have some real significance, attempts to relate them are seldom gainful even when apparently successful. The agreement that is almost unavoidable in simultaneous determinations can give the observer an entirely unwarranted confidence in whatever he chooses the curves to mean.

14.10. Summary

When a gas is given off during a thermal decomposition it is no longer necessary to speculate on its identity to describe the reaction. Gases can be identified quite easily, directly or indirectly. The specificity of the analysis should be chosen to fit the problem at hand.

Simultaneous meaasurements may be very helpful but proper care in design of the experiment is important.

When a sample is degraded thermally with the intent of only analyzing the gases, the problems incident to heating of the sample have not lost their importance. Pyrolysis products from even mildly complex organic molecules can be different under different heating conditions.

Programmed pyrolyses should provide more significant data.

CHAPTER XV

Recording, Control, and Power Equipment

15.1. General

Since nearly all recording of differential thermal analysis data will be done by the use of strip chart recording potentiometers, a reasonably complete description of their operation is appropriate. A nonhistorical survey of other techniques will be found later in the chapter.

Strip chart recording potentiometers may be X vs t or X vs. Y. In the latter case the Y signal either moves the chart back and forth under the X pen support or moves the carriage supporting the X pen back and forth as needed. In either case, the position of the pen with respect to the chart indicates the value of the Y signal.

15.2. Recording Potentiometers

Recording potentiometers are of special value in differential thermal analysis because of their null balance characteristic; i.e., no current is drawn from the measuring elements except when their potential is changing, and even during a process of change the currents drawn are negligibly small. In essence, the potential from the thermocouple or amplifier is compared with the potential of a moving contact on a slide-

452

wire (Fig. XV-1). The comparison circuit includes an amplifier and motor arranged so that if an unbalance in potential does exist this unbalance is amplified and supplied to the motor. The motor moves the contact on the slide-wire to a position at which the unbalance signal is returned to zero. A recording pen is connected mechanically to the slide-wire contact shaft, so that movement of the contact resulting from a changing input potential leaves a record on the moving chart paper.

The signal from the thermocouple or differential thermocouple is, of course, a direct current potential. In order to amplify the unbalance potential to a sufficient voltage to drive a motor, the signal must be converted to a nonsteady, e.g., pulsating, potential. In standard commercial recorders, the usual procedure is to convert the direct potential to a non-

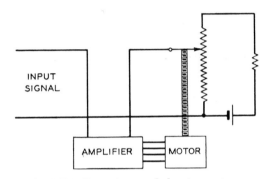

Fɪɢ. XV-1. Potentiometer balancing system.
The amplifier detects any difference between the slide-wire contact and the input potential and causes the motor to drive the slide-wire to eliminate the difference.

sinusoidal alternating potential by means of a "chopper." This chopper applies the potential to a pair of primary transformer windings alternately by mechanical switching. These windings are so connected that the secondary winding has induced in it a series of pulses, each opposed to the last (Fig. XV-2). The result is a potential which is alternating at a frequency determined by the rapidity of the mechanical switching. The wave is sufficiently pure that it can be amplified and used to drive the balancing motor with a moderate amount of filtering of harmonics.

The mechanical switching is commonly synchronous with the supply frequency so that the amplified frequency on a 60-cps supply voltage is also 60 cps. This condition will normally cause an inquiry by the neophyte because of the obvious possibility of electrical pickup from dozens of nearby sources; the choice of frequency must be justified in some manner. The principal reason for the choice is the customary one—saving of money.

The amplified voltage fed into the grid of the output stage of the amplifier being an alternating current of known frequency, the plates of a push-pull output stage can be fed with an alternating voltage of the same frequency (Fig. XV-3) rather than with a direct current supply. This permits the elimination of a fair-sized rectifier and filter for the plate

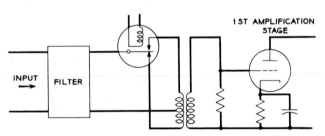

FIG. XV-2. Amplifier input.

The amplifier dc input is "chopped" by the vibrating contacts to send the current alternately through each of the two halves of the transformer primary winding.

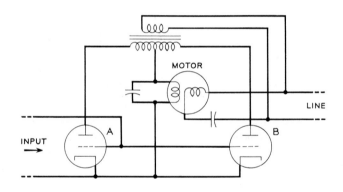

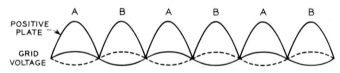

FIG. XV-3. Push-pull output to motor.

The grids of tubes A and B follow the driver signal together but only one plate at a time is positive. In the diagram at the bottom the plate in tube A is positive while the grids are positive (solid line) so the tube conducts. When the plate of tube B is positive the grids have gone negative and the tube does not conduct. If the input signal were reversed, the grid voltage would follow the dotted line and tube B would conduct.

supply. Interference from electrical pickup is avoided by filtering the input.

In circuits like that of Fig. XV-3, the electron tubes are acting essentially as switches. A positive signal on the grid while the plate is positive allows a current to flow. The phase of the grid signal is in phase—or 180° out of phase—with the plate potential so that the presence of a grid signal means that either tube A or tube B will conduct. The motor will move rapidly toward the rebalancing position. Zero signal on the grids will permit some current to flow each half cycle, causing a tendency for the motor to rotate in each direction in turn and hence a noticeable "jitter." A capacitor across the motor leads provides some damping by smoothing the pulsations somewhat, introducing thereby a dc component.

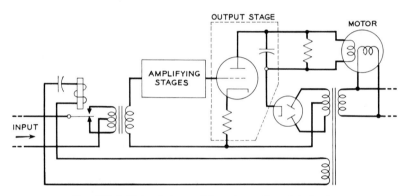

FIG. XV-4. Output stage with motor as the plate load.
The phase shift in the amplifier plus that caused by the capacitor in the chopper-drive circuit equals 90°.

With an amplifier output of the supply frequency a relatively small alternating current motor may be used to obtain bidirectional drive since one field can be supplied directly from the line. Any frequency other than line frequency would require a power supply large enough to drive the entire measuring system.

More elegant systems supply the output plate with a direct (but not heavily filtered) current (Fig. XV-4). The motor winding is the plate load. A moderate direct current flows all the time applying some continuous damping on the motor movement. Zero signal on the grid allows a direct current flow to damp motor movement completely. The phase shift (90°) necessary to provide direction of control is supplied principally by operating the converter (chopper) out of phase, taking into account the small phase shift through the amplifier.

15.3. Phase Shift

The phase shift in either case performs the same general function as the capacitor in an ordinary split-phase motor. This type of motor has no electrical connection between rotor and stator; it depends on an induced field arising from sets of adjacent coils; these coils obviously cannot be supplied with currents all in phase with each other or there would be no net effect. The phase shift need not be 90° for unidirectional drive but it must be quite specifically 90° for most reversible motor applications; any sizable deviation will cause a difference in power in the two directions—an obviously pointless condition.

Whether this phase shift causes a "lag" or "lead" of the control-winding current in relation to the line-winding current depends on the polarity of the input voltage to the amplifier. Since the direction of the motor rotation depends on whether it sees a "lag" or "lead," it, too, reflects the polarity of the input signal and is thus able to move in the proper direction to drive the error signal back to zero.

15.4. Input Impedance

Since the chopper amplifier does have a transformer input stage, a real—though small—electric current must flow when an off-balance condition exists. Design and construction for high input signal strength is obviously simpler than for low signal strength. For this reason recording potentiometers are most readily available for signal strength of 400–1000 ohms input impedance. Thermocouples are well below this level (0–15 ohms) so that a base-metal thermocouple can be connected directly to a fairly sensitive (−0.5 to +0.5 mv) recording potentiometer and reasonably good thermograms obtained. This span represents ca. ± 11°C for a Chromel-Alumel thermocouple.

Some thermistors and strain gauges may exceed the upper limits of input impedance. In this case the recording potentiometer must be selected partly on the basis of its input impedance. Commercial recorders are available with input impedance greater than one megohm.

15.5. Recording Potentiometer as a Signal Follower

The normal function of a strip chart recording potentiometer is to measure and record a potential, but the possibility of otherwise using its circuitry should not be overlooked. The author, for example, has used a second slide-wire, mounted on the same shaft as the ordinary slide-wire contact, to follow the movements of the chain of an automatic balance (G3). Before the days of Zener diodes, one had a choice of manual, semiautomatic, or automatic standardization of measuring slide-wires.

Essentially this required a very stable battery or cell in the recorder or else the appearance—at regular intervals—of standardization resets. In addition, if a movement was to be followed by converting that movement into an electrical signal, that circuit likewise had to be especially stable.

Consider now a circuit in which the same voltage supply is fed to two slide-wires adjusted to match electrically (Fig. XV-5). If the moving contacts are in such a position that no voltage difference exists between them, a change in the voltage at the source will change the voltage of either moving contact with respect to any reference except the other moving contact. This voltage difference remains zero. If this potential between the two moving contacts is amplified and used to drive one of the contacts back to the balance point, the result is a servo system which is insensitive to changes in supply voltage.

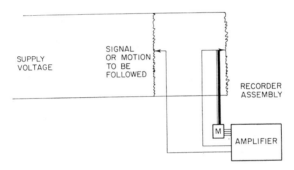

Fɪɢ. XV-5. Recorder amplifier used to follow rather than measure a signal.
Since the two slide-wires are fed from the same voltage, the system is insensitive to ordinary voltage changes.

In the application cited, a potentiometer was mounted on the shaft from which the balance chain was driven. This potentiometer was fed from the same electrical source as the second slide-wire on the recorder shaft. The intrinsic slide-wire was disconnected from the recorder amplifier. The difference signal from the moving contacts was fed into this amplifier. When a difference existed, the recorder shaft was moved by the motor to return the difference signal to zero. Since the pen is driven by the same shaft, the pen provided a continuous indication of the position of the potentiometer and hence the chain. Since the chain was itself actuated by an independent circuit which kept the balance continuously at null, a weight change record could be obtained overnight or over other intervals too long for reliable voltage supplies.

15.6. Recording Potentiometer as Position Follower

Another use of a recorder as a position indicator was more direct (Fig. IV-8). Keith and Tuttle (K14) mounted a split photocell on the pen carriage of a recording potentiometer. The recorder amplifier was fed from the photocell circuit so that the pen carriage moved in the direction of more intense illumination. When the light flow on the two sides of the photocell was equal, the carriage remained at rest.

Keith and Tuttle connected their (DTA) differential thermocouple to a mirror galvanometer so that the light beam fell on the path of the photocell. The pen then followed the galvanometer light beam to give the ΔT plot. A reasonably long light path and a sensitive galvanometer will yield a quite satisfactory optical amplification. The "noise" in this case would be mechanical in origin. See also Dannis (D2).

15.7. Recording Potentiometer as Position Adjuster

The servo features in strip chart recorders have been used to provide direct balancing in thermogravimetry. Ewald (E8) used the recorder shaft to pay out or take up chain. The pen position indicated the amount of chain paid out.

Ordinary single-pen recording potentiometers are available in ranges suitable for temperature measurement as well as for much of the differential temperature measurement. The multitude of available types permits a great latitude of choice of input signals for thermogravimetric analysis.

15.8. Special Types of Recorders

For thermal analysis studies, in which some other quantity must be related to the temperature, comparison of T from one strip chart with $f(T)$ from another is inconvenient and unnecessary. Reference marking or "pipping" indicators will be described later. Modern design generally calls for simultaneous recording on a single chart. The principal types of recorders for this purpose are X vs Y, multipen, multipoint, and multichannel.

An X-Y recorder is frequently used to obtain a direct plot of $f(T)$ vs T. Plotting of weight loss vs time in thermogravimetry is a reasonably satisfactory technique because variations in the rate of heating are relatively insignificant compared to differential thermal analysis.

For differential thermal analysis, however, the maintenance of an essentially constant rate of heating is essential. To use an X-Y recorder with no monitoring apparatus is to place complete faith in an unsupervised control system. A failure or defect in the programming will appear as a spurious thermal effect which may not be recognized. X-Y recorders are often used in differential thermal analysis with motor-driven auto-transformer power supplies. The nonlinear temperature increase is concealed by the ΔT vs T plot. An X-Y recorder is useful but the temperature should be separately monitored. A relatively inexpensive galvanometer recorder with an independent thermocouple is sufficient.

Multipen recorders provide independent measuring circuits, each operating over the entire range of the chart. There is necessarily a displacement of one record with respect to the other since the pens must be able to pass one another. The author makes use of several two-pen recorders including one whose chart movement depends on temperature rather than time, that is, an X_1, X_2 vs Y recorder.

A multipoint recorder is one in which a simple measuring circuit scans, repetitively and in sequence, a number of input signals; the number may be as high as a few dozen. These recorders have quite limited use in thermal analysis because of their noncontinuous plotting; their principal use would be in multiple differential thermal analysis. In general, one would be constrained to do studies involving gross samples so that a reading every 4 to 24 seconds is adequate. The more serious limitation is the fact that all circuits to be measured must have the same range. Putting a number of ΔT signals on one chart is really no great problem, nor is putting a number of temperature signals, but to try to put a temperature signal and a difference signal on the same multipoint recorder means that one signal has to be given one or two extra treatments. Specifically one needs to amplify or attenuate one signal so that it agrees in span magnitude with the other and, in addition, a bias must be inserted to shift the zero. By this time, enough equipment and effort are used up so that a multipen recorder would have been cheaper. Nevertheless, it can be done.

Kauffman and Dilling (K8), in the early days of electronic recording, converted a 0–10 mv multipoint potentiometric recorder to a 0–0.4 mv instrument so that temperature differences could be measured directly, then they fed the temperature signal (from the reference couple) into a voltage divider, R10 and R11 of Fig. XV-6. Since they were recording three thermograms they added a different bias to each of the three differential signals, accomplishing the double purpose of separating the traces and establishing the zero line at a more convenient place than at the recorder zero at the right-hand edge of the chart.

Both temperature and differential temperature were recorded by a single pen in the arrangement used by Keavney and Eberlin (K11b). At a preset interval the input was switched from ΔT by a timing switch long enough to allow a suitable measurement of T. The peaks for T in

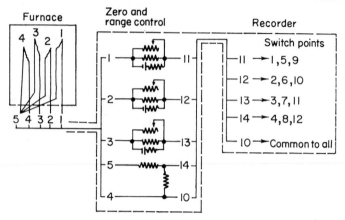

FIG. XV-6. Multipoint potentiometer to record both T and ΔT. From Kauffman and Dilling (K8).

The recording circuit is switched successively to each of twelve sets of contacts, in this case paralleled in four sets of three each. The fourth set records a fraction of the thermocouple electromotive force.

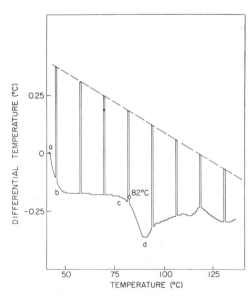

FIG. XV-7. Temperature and differential temperature of the glass transition in polystyrene. From Keavney and Eberlin (K11b).

The recording technique is economical but a large recorder dead zone results.

Fig. XV-7 can be interpolated easily to give the value at any point. Quite good data were obtained but note that Keavney and Eberlin had to set their recorder sensitivity to a low value to avoid a very messy record (because of the sudden large pen movements). The low sensitivity causes the stepping in the record. This particular nuisance could be avoided by addition of a damping resistor on the motor drive and a time-delay relay so that the movement would be damped heavily as the pen changes but the damping resistor is shorted during normal operation.

A multichannel recorder provides (generally two) side-by-side measuring systems each with limited chart travel. While they lack the readability of multipen recorders, there is a more or less compensating gain in that the two signals may be related more accurately by reading across —with reference to the printed chart lines—than by measuring the pen displacement.

15.9. Galvanometer Recorders

In addition to the recording potentiometer, a number of types of galvanometer recorders are available. These are meter movements generally equipped with some low-friction means of marking the position on the moving chart paper. Alternatively, the meter arm may be periodically arrested and pressed against the chart. The low-friction marking may be properly extended to the zero-friction devices using optical or thermal methods.

In general, these galvanometric measuring devices are less expensive than recording potentiometers and require less maintenance. Operationally, they are somewhat inferior to recording potentiometers because they draw current and hence the heat source must do some work on the thermocouple. The withdrawal of this energy changes the temperature distribution in the region of the thermocouple. Also, the current drawn from the thermocouple produces a voltage drop across the resistance of the thermocouple leads. This voltage subtracts from the voltage produced by the thermocouple, and its magnitude changes with change in resistance of the leads due to aging and ambient temperature variations. The change in thermal gradient is of little importance when the thermocouple and meter are being used for measurement or control near the furnace windings or in a heavy sample block but in work needing high sensitivity a recording potentiometer must be used.

15.10. Miscellaneous Notes on Recording

Here we must differentiate between recording potentiometers and recorders with a potentiometric circuit. A recording potentiometer compares the full magnitude of an incoming signal directly with a signal from a slide-wire or equivalent; a recorder with a potentiometric measuring circuit has instead a tapped resistance in which the *voltage drop* across a portion of the resistance is measured—with a potentiometric circuit. The requirement that there be a voltage drop to measure implies a current flow, which is precisely what a recording potentiometer avoids. These recorders with potentiometric circuits are characterized in general by a multitude of ranges.

For most purposes, including more general temperature measurements, this type of recording is satisfactory. Even for differential thermal analysis they present no disadvantage if the furnace or block temperature is being measured or if sample sizes are large. The moment one attempts to measure directly the temperature of small specimens, sample or reference, from or near the differential thermocouple, the work drawn from the specimen to maintain the required current flow will upset the temperature distribution and cause a smoothly increasing (with temperature) base line (see Chapters III and IV). The differential signal, however, can be fed into such a recorder after amplification because this small current drawn from the output of the amplifier will not affect the input circuit and because the work drawn would be very, very small. Remember that measurements of T are with reference to ambient temperature or a fixed reference temperature while ΔT is measured with reference to a junction at nearly the same temperature.

The function of the amplifier-motor combination was performed on some early recorders by a galvanometer and a mechanical linkage from the chart drive motor. The unbalance between the slide-wire and input signal was supplied to the galvanometer. Periodically (ca every 2 seconds) the galvanometer movement would be arrested and the deflection of the pointer arm would determine the action of a clutch. The clutch could drive the slide-wire either way with a limit of nearly an inch per operation. This sort of movement is satisfactory for monitoring differential thermal analysis furnace temperatures but not for programming or for recording the differential temperature itself. It would be suitable for use in programming a low-speed thermogravimetry furnace.

A rather different approach to the comparison-signal problem involves the use of strain gauges as a replacement for the slide-wire. The strain gauge is a device whose electrical resistance is changed by mechanical strain.

The input signal is treated in the same manner as in a slide-wire potentiometer. The motor drive responds to a difference signal to increase and decrease strain to restore the unbalance to zero. The advantages are the infinite resolution and the lack of moving electrical contacts. The first is of only moderate interest since the resolution of a slide-wire, i.e., the voltage increment per turn, is one of the lesser problems. The instruments having accuracies of ¼% of full scale have three or more turns within their error tolerance; the existence of ten times this number would be of little benefit. The moving-contact avoidance is of real value. The range of movement of the strain gauges is so small that nonlinearity constitutes no problem.

15.11. Power Supplies

The means of controlling the temperature of a furnace—even before one attempts to program it—are so varied that a complete separation of topics is not practicable. In general we shall consider first the power supplies—ranging from switches through thyratrons—as the physical method of limiting at the will of the operator the power input to the furnace. We shall then consider control systems—to the extent that they are separable—as the means by which the operator indicates his wishes to the power supply. We shall subsequently examine programming techniques by which the user—prior to the beginning of an operation—gives the control system all instructions required to carry out said operation.

During the discussion it will be expedient to refer to combinations of power supplies, controllers, and even programming in a manner intended for over-all clarity. The author has been unable to consign each type of unit to a separate paragraph or two and still offer a hope for a general understanding of the whole exposition, but, as far as is practicable, the various devices will be described separately.

15.12. Variable Autotransformer

A simple and popular power supply device is the variable autotransformer. (In this day and age, the use of a variable resistance is almost inconceivable.) An autotransformer comprises a single winding with a number of connections for input and output voltages (Fig. XV-8). As a step-down transformer, it is the inductance analog to a resistance-type voltage divider. Alternating currents may be stepped up as well as down. A variable autotransformer, then, is a device with provision for changing the output in a large number of small steps. In commercial practice, this variable autotransformer normally takes the form of a toroidal winding of several dozen to a few hundred turns arranged so that a wiping contact may sweep around to make electrical connection with any turn. Actually two or three turns are touching the wiping arm at the same time; this multiple contact avoids momentary open circuits and arcing. The number of turns and the size of the wire is dependent on the voltage supply and the current rating. The flux density within the core is determined by the current input and the number of turns. An autotransformer may be used for lower than rated input voltage but not for higher. This rated input voltage should not be exceeded significantly since the core would become overloaded, i.e., magnetically saturated. The autotransformer may also be operated in reverse, but, since the output voltage is then something approximating an ordinary supply voltage, the advantages of this arrangement are generally trivial.

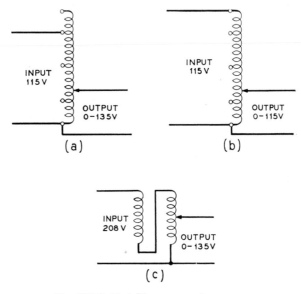

FIG. XV-8. Variable autotransformers.

When power is supplied to less than the full winding but may be taken from the full winding (a), a voltage step-up can be obtained. Applying power to the entire winding (b) permits variation only up to supply voltage. If power can be taken from less turns than it is applied to (c), there is a voltage step-down.

The variable—or adjustable—autotransformer can increase or decrease the furnace power to bring the temperature back to the set point. It has two advantages over the saturable-core rector (see below): it may be selected to match the largest load, yet will perform in the same manner for smaller loads (except see below) and it has a zero turndown. On the other hand, the adjustment action is by no means stepless. Unless the control system is adjusted so that it is on the verge of "hunting," adjusting action may change the input voltage several volts. A few seconds later, a reverse change nearly as great may take place. On very rapid-response heating systems, the time constant of the motor-driven transformer may approach that of the system resulting in an unstable control which will continually oscillate. On a very rapid-response differential thermal analysis or differential calorimetry furnace, the result may be a scalloped base line. For other systems, nothing is lost by having a slower-response furnace. The reader may argue that a control system should ordinarily be adjusted so that it is on the verge of "hunting"; this is correct—ordinarily. Operation of a rapid-response furnace in this manner is quite satisfactory as long as nothing is changed. Let a sample block be used in place of cups or a ceramic block in place of nickel and the control system may go into oscillation. This is normally a problem only on very rapid-response furnaces.

15.13. Saturable-Core Reactor

A saturable-core reactor comprises a laminated iron transformer core with a power and a control winding (Fig. XV-9). To understand its operation, it is necessary to review the role of the iron core in transformers and chokes.

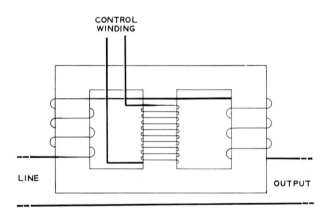

Fɪɢ. XV-9. Saturable-core reactor.
Supply of part of the flux density from the control coil decreases the impedance to alternating current.

As the voltage in a coil increases, the magnetic field in the coil increases. In the absence of a material of high permeability, the region within the coil is quickly saturated, i.e., reaches its maximum flux density, and little impedance is offered at power frequencies. If an iron core is now inserted into the coil, the possible flux density is much greater. The work necessary to build up a field is consequently much larger and a sizable impedance to alternating current is offered.

The impedance offered by the winding depends, then, on the flux density which the current through the winding must generate. Movement of an iron core in and out of the coil is a possible but not practical means of control. An easier way to limit the flux density in the core is to provide some portion of the possible density in some other way. This may be done readily from another (control) winding on the same core. If this second coil should now supply 80% of the saturation flux density, the first (power) coil would now supply only the other 20% and the winding would offer only one-fifth of the maximum inductive impedance to the flow of alternating current. The control coil uses a low direct current, e.g., 0–5 ma, but a relatively very large number of turns makes it able to supply a saturation flux density.

The current through the control winding can be varied readily, rapidly, and continuously so that the saturable-core reactor has an advantage over the position-adjusting system, i.e., continuous variation within its range as well as nearly instantaneous response. There are also some disadvantages: nonzero turndown and the necessity of designing or selecting for the particular load.

The nonzero turndown is simply the result of having a continuous circuit at all times. Even at maximum impedance, some current will flow. A characteristic value of this current is 3% of full load. The selection requirement is, in part, related to the nonzero turndown. If, for example, a 0.5-kw load were connected to a 2.0-kw reactor, not only would the turndown current tend to be about four times too high, but also the higher resistance load would become a more significant portion of the voltage drop and the voltage on the furnace might be 15% or more of the supply voltage. Obviously, control at low temperatures would be out of the question with an oversized reactor.

The other reason that a saturable-core reactor must be matched to its load is simply the dc resistance of the winding. At full saturation by the control winding, the reactor appears only as a resistive load. Its resistance must be low enough and the windings large enough to permit dissipation of the rated power in the load.

As in the ON-OFF control, the furnace input is varied to keep the temperature at or near the set point—with an immense difference. Since the voltage drop across the reactor can be varied in an infinite number of steps, the power dissipated in the furnace can likewise be varied in an infinite number of steps. If one supplies a control signal which can be varied similarly, one may control without anything resembling the discrete increases and decreases found with ON-OFF controllers; instead, as the temperature drops below the set point, the power input increases in a stepless manner to bring the furnace back up in temperature. As the temperature rises, the power input is cut back.

This and other current—or voltage—adjusting controllers benefit greatly from proportional band, rate time, and reset action. These devices are outlined in a later section.

15.14. Controlled Rectifier

The ordinary form of the controlled rectifier at the power levels of interest here is the thyratron. This may be an electron tube or, more recently, a solid-state device—in essence, a king-size transistor.

The electron tube thyratron is a gas-filled tube with a heater and three, or more, working electrodes. As in ordinary electron tubes connected as amplifiers, electrons are emitted from the heated cathode (Fig. XV-10) but their flow toward the positively charged anode is inhibited

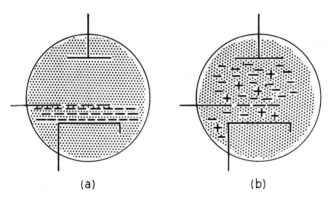

(a)   (b)

FIG. XV-10. Electron tube thyratron.
While the bridge is kept sufficiently negative (a) the tube does not conduct; if the grid permits flow (b) the movement of electrons toward the plate will ionize the gas and the positive ions will prevent the grid from regaining control until the conduction is stopped externally.

or prevented by the negatively charged grid. Like an amplifier, for a given grid voltage some anode potential will be sufficient to draw some electrons past the grid and toward the anode. Unlike the amplifier, once the flow has started the grid no longer can control it. The current through the tube either is zero or is limited by the load and the anode dissipation. This lack of control is the result of ionization of the gas within the tube. An electron accelerated toward the anode collides with gas atoms with sufficient energy to ionize a few before reaching the anode. This supplies not only more electrons but also positive ions. These latter are attracted not only to the cathode but also to the more negatively charged grid. Since current flow in the grid circuit is limited by a resistor to a small value, these positive ions tend simply to depolarize the grid. [If the current were not limited, the grid would supply electrons to the positive ions, thereby acting as a second (cold) cathode and losing control anyway.]

The thyratron discharge ends only when the anode voltage is not sufficient to sustain the flow, i.e., when an electron is not accelerated rapidly enough to ionize gas particles. When this occurs, no positive ions are formed to depolarize the grid and the grid discharges the ions near it, becomes negative, and rather abruptly shuts off the flow of electrons to the anode.

For most applications, the thyratron is supplied with an alternating potential so that the anode voltage drops to zero each cycle. During the following half cycle, the anode is less positive than the grid so that the tube could not conduct anyway. Typical operation characteristic of a thyratron is shown in Fig. XV-11.

The current flow through a thyratron is controlled by varying the grid voltage and thus limiting the fraction of the half cycle during which the tube conducts. The control signal may be an alternating potential whose phase angle (with respect to the anode supply) is shifted so that it is more negative than the control characteristic (Fig. XV-11) until the proper time of firing. A controlled-rectifier system for furnace program control would more generally make use of a direct current control supply, which adjusts the phase angle of the alternating current grid potential as a function of its magnitude. The same control signal used in saturable-core reactor systems can be used in some controlled-rectifier systems.

A solid-state thyratron has similar over-all performance even though it functions rather differently.

15.15 Ignitron

The ignitron is a controlled rectifier used to supply greater amounts of power than are common in thermal analysis. Its operation is generally similar to that of a thyratron.

15.16. Control System

Furnaces with constant rates of heating with either constant or linearly increasing voltage input have not yet been constructed. Further, reproducibility of response from one furnace to another is poor. The need or desire for a reasonably constant heating rate over the full temperature range or from one furnace to another leads directly to temperature control.

Consider first static control, i.e., setting of a control point to a given temperature or condition representing a given temperature, comparing

this set point to the actual temperature, and from the difference determining the voltage input to the furnace. A simple case is an ON-OFF
regulator of the bimetallic strip type. There are a multitude of ways of
adjusting the voltage input, a number of ways in which the off-balance
signal is detected, and a few corrections which may be added to more
sophisticated systems. These may well be discussed before approaching
the problem of moving the set point.

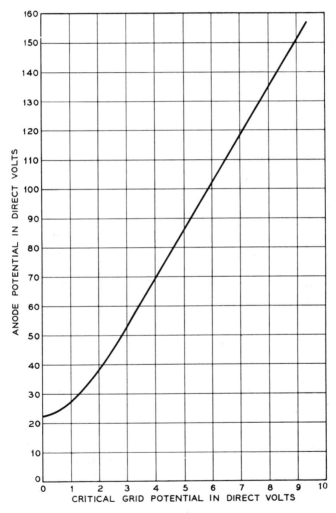

FIG. XV-11. An example of control characteristics of a thyratron.
The instantaneous anode cathode voltage must exceed that shown at the instanta-
neous grid cathode (negative) potential. Both values may be continuously changing.

15.17. ON-OFF Control

The increase in temperature to above the set point opens a switch or de-energizes a relay and removes power from the furnace. Voltage input is, then, either zero or a set voltage. This set voltage may be the line voltage or may be the output from an autotransformer. With an autotransformer an additional safety feature is available; i.e., the supply voltage may be that which will just barely bring the furnace to the maximum temperature at the desired heating rate. It cannot then go far above that temperature even with a constant supply voltage.

15.18. HIGH-LOW Control

The ON-OFF control may be changed easily to a HIGH-LOW control such that when the sensing point in the furnace reaches or exceeds the control temperature the electric power is not switched OFF but to a lower voltage—a voltage known to be too low to maintain the control temperature. This may be done in several ways; for example a load in series with the furnace might be short-circuited when the furnace is below the control point, the control switch opening up the short circuit as the control point is reached so that a portion of the voltage drop is dissipated in this load. By close adjustment of the HIGH-LOW inputs not only can the temperature fluctuations be made small but the cycle time can be made long. The essential condition is that under all operating conditions the higher voltage is sufficient to keep the furnace at or above the control point and the lower voltage is under no conditions sufficient to maintain the furnace at the control point.

An autotransformer can be switched to perform nearly the same function. The switching arrangement will depend partly on the power requirements. If the voltage output needed is somewhere close to the maximum, switching of the output is feasible (Fig. XV-12a) if there is no objection to having the furnace winding ca 20 volts above ground potential at the lowest point. This switching will add or subtract 17 or 20 volts depending on the input connection. If the output voltage requirement is low, say in the order of 30 volts average, switching between 20 and 40 volts is a considerable change. For such cases input switching (Fig. XV-12b) is better. Now, regardless of position of the moving contact, the output voltage will increase by about 17% when the control operates, and in the example cited the switching can be between $27\frac{1}{2}$ and $32\frac{1}{2}$ volts, giving both longer cycle time and lower variation than the arrangement in Fig. XV-12a. With the generally low-current requirements (< 20 amp) of modern thermal analysis apparatus switching on the primary is quite satisfactory. For very high currents the surge that occurs if the switching occurs at the peak of the voltage cycle might cause mechanical damage.

Any HIGH-LOW switching must be based on certain knowledge that the furnace requirements will always lie between the two positions; otherwise the system can go out of control.

The ON-OFF or HIGH-LOW control may also be used with the other power supplies in which case their only advantage is in avoiding switching the relatively high furnace current. With either the saturable-core reactor or the controlled rectifier, a HIGH-LOW control system could be set up easily with a dc supply and a few resistors.

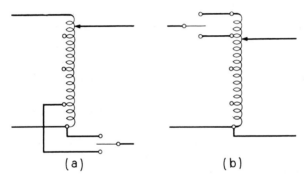

(a)   (b)

Fɪɢ. XV-12. Autotransformer connections for HIGH-LOW control. *Switching the output (a) adds or subtracts a fixed voltage while switching the input (b) changes the output by a fixed percentage.*

An even more nearly constant temperature can be obtained by attaching a reversible drive motor to an adjustable autotransformer and connecting the sensing element so that the autotransformer output is slowly increased while the furnace temperature is below the control point and slowly decreased while the furnace temperature is above the control point. Now the controller and power supply combination has a complete range of inputs. In event of a sudden increase in load the autotransformer will move until the control point is again reached. (The slow drive is to avoid serious overheating in just such a case.) For steady-state heating the autotransformer will necessarily cycle up and down through a small voltage range because of the constant driving one way or the other.

This system has a wider range of control than the HIGH-LOW and a smoother control with less tendency to overheat than the ON-OFF. The drive speed is necessarily a compromise between the high speed the operator might wish to use for rapid adjustment for large changes and the low speed required to avoid serious overshoot or large-amplitude cycling.

Again, such a control system could use a saturable-core reactor or a controlled rectifier by driving a potentiometer to vary the control signal. Under almost steady-state conditions the control will be quite superior to the ON-OFF or HIGH-LOW, but there is, nevertheless, a built-in cycling that can be objectionable and almost certainly will be objectionable in low-lag furnaces. (The reader must bear in mind that each step in improvement must be made at some cost in dollars or the equivalent.) The next step is the introduction of proportioning control.

15.19. Proportioning Control

The comparison of the temperature of the furnace with the desired temperature and adjustment of the voltage or current input according to the magnitude of the deviation is proportioning control. It differs from the reversible-drive autotransformer and related systems in that the change or rate of change in furnace input is principally a function of displacement or deviation rather than of time. The simplest form of proportioning control would comprise a device which independently interrupts the furnace input to a greater and greater degree as the furnace temperature increases in the region of the control point. This can be done on optical systems by moving a shutter back and forth such that it does not interrupt the light beam when it is far below the control point (large galvanometer deflection) but because of its sinusoidal motion interrupts for longer and longer periods as the temperature increases. The temperature reaches a steady-state position at which the electric power is supplied to the furnace at the right proportion of the time to maintain that temperature. The actual control temperature will deviate from the set point by an amount which varies slightly and regularly over the range of the instrument.

Electric meter (millivoltmeter) indicator-controllers can be equipped with a similar function. When the indicating pointer moves below the control point an electric impulse is supplied that drives the meter movement upscale so that if the temperature is only slightly below the control point the indicator will pass it and the power will be shut off. Since the impulse to the movement is also discontinued the pointer will drift back toward the control point. The impulse is rather small so the power will remain on except when the furnace temperature is within a few degrees of the control point and will be shut off an increasing percentage of the time until the temperature exceeds the control point.

Electronic controllers not making use of mechanical inertia have other means of modifying response in order to avoid cycling. Electronic circuits, fortunately, are not limited by the need to move parts, so, while their action must often be tempered to cope with a slow reacting system, these moderating influences can be adjusted to suit the individual needs. These are dynamic corrections based on the actual deviation or the rate of change of deviation. Their function is to bring about a very rapid return to the control point without serious overshooting. The corrections are: proportional band, rate of approach or reset, and rate time. The first two can be used with proportioning control systems; since the last is closely related the description of all is postponed until after the introduction of feedback control.

15.20. Feedback Control

Up to this point, we have considered systems whose power input to the process was related in a simple manner to the deviation of the temperature signal from a set point. The controller (Fig. XV-13a) compares the temperature signal with the temperature signal it has been instructed (set) to maintain and adjusts its signal to the power supply in such a manner as to correct or reduce the error. This action occurs and continues without regard for recent history or for possible future events. A controller without feedback must have capabilities suited specifically to its function; otherwise there is a risk of loss of control and possible damage to the process or apparatus. As an example, an autotransformer

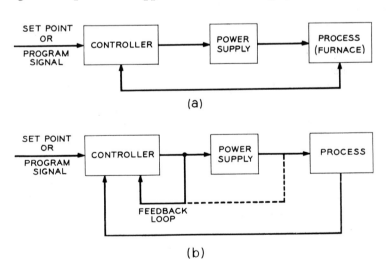

FIG. XV-13. Control systems without and with feedback.

A simple control system as in (a) recognizes and acts on the instantaneous condition of the process; introduction of a feedback loop (b) permits modification of the action according to amount and rate of change of error.

driven in one direction or another by a HIGH-LOW switching controller might be set to driving upward due to some temporary cooling (furnace door opened) and at the cessation of the demand be in a position that could bring the temperature far above the control point, yet it would still drive upward until the furnace did reach the set temperature because the controller had no information about the position of the auto-transformer. Providing such information will permit a more flexible control system; i.e., it can adjust the process input to correct for a greater degree and a greater variety of processes unbalances. This arrangement by which the controller is supplied with information describing the input to the process so that it may adjust this input not only from temperature signal set point comparison but also from present input and rate of change of input is feedback control.

Figure XV-13b shows the full control loop with the added feedback loop. Whether the information comes from the input to or the output from the power supply depends generally on the nature of the power supply. If an adjustable autotransformer is used, the feedback information must be the output or position; if a saturable-core reactor or a controlled rectifier is used, the input signal can be used just as easily.

Now we have a control device supplied with three signals: the control or set point signal, the furnace temperature signal, and the furnace input signal. The controller can not only relate the temperature to the set point but also make use of the furnace input signal to monitor and modify its action. With electronic rather than mechanical information, greater flexibility is possible because modifying actions may be obtained very readily. These actions may be made to operate over wide ranges and at adjustable speeds, so that a single control unit can—with changes in instructions by resetting of dial knobs—control a small laboratory furnace or a room-size furnace, perhaps even with the same power unit. Rate time and reset are secondary modifying actions; the primary action is *proportional band.*

15.21. Proportional Band

Adjustment of the proportional band expands or contracts the portion of the full range over which proportioning of any kind occurs. If the deviation is beyond this range the controller should turn the power supply full ON or full OFF. For very slow response systems proportioning action may be required over 50% of full range; i.e., if the control unit range is 1000°C, a 500°C interval about the control point is within the proportioning zone (Fig. XV-14). With a control point of 600°C and a cold furnace full power would be applied until the sensing point reached ca 350°C at which time turndown or time proportioning would begin. If this furnace should "line out" at 600°C and then be reset down to 200°C the control unit would turn down or off until the furnace temperature dropped to ca 450°C and would then apply larger and larger quantities of power until the furnace "lined out" at the new temperature.

Rapidly responding systems could be operated with a proportional band of a few per cent so that with the same range (1000°C) the furnace would heat or cool at full rate until the temperature was within 20–40°C of the control point.

While the proportioning control helps in quickly regaining the control point region, it operates over the entire proportional band region without discrimination; i.e., the furnace will reach some temperature within the proportioning region such that the power input—under the influence of proportional band operation—is just sufficient to maintain that tempera-

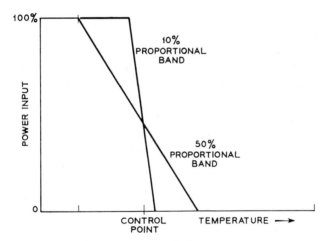

Fig. XV-14. Variation of power input with deviation (of temperature) from control point.

A smaller proportional band accentuates the response to small deviations.

ture. This temperature has no fixed relation to the control point because proportional band operation alone has no way to recognize the control point. For control point recognition *reset action* is added.

15.22. Reset Action

Consider that due to a process unbalance of some sort the temperature is displaced from the control point. Reset action modifies the proportional band action at a rate proportional to this displacement and the length of time away from control point. This modification is in effect an electrical shifting of the proportional band region up- or downscale to increase or decrease the power input. The rate of this shift can be modified so that the proportional band is shifted downscale or upscale from several per cent per minute to several minutes per per cent.

This reset action is the only part of the circuit which knows when to stop, but the nature of its action dictates that it cannot stop without overshoot unless its action is very slow.

Let us assume a large (because we need a door) electric muffle on control. Let us open the door for half a minute to put in a specimen. During this half minute the furnace cools somewhat and the recorder pen moves downscale. Reset action moves slowly to aid by shifting the proportional band position—thus accentuating the effect—and the temperature moves back toward the control point. During all this time reset action has been pushing the proportional band region further upscale. When the temperature reaches the control point the proportional band has been shifted enough to maintain a furnace temperature higher than the control point, so the temperature must necessarily overshoot. During the overshoot the proportional band is shifted downscale again so that with proper adjustment for that sort of demand change the furnace will be on control after a cycle or two. The possibility of serious overshoot after a large demand change leads to the need for *rate action.*

15.23. Rate Action

Rate action acts in a manner similar to reset action in that it, too, shifts the proportional band range; the difference is in the source of the control signal. While reset action is proportional to displacement of the recorder pen from the control point, rate action is proportional to the rate of change of displacement, i.e., the speed, irrespective of position, at which the pen is moving. Rate time thereby tends to slow down the pen motion by shifting the proportional band in the proper direction. In the case of the opened door the first action is the upscale shift of proportional band partly because of reset but mostly because of rate action. When the temperature has dropped as low as it will the rate action stops, but immediately begins to bring the proportional band region downscale again as the temperature starts to climb. Now it competes with reset action, but, for the furnaces common in thermal analysis, rate action should have the greater influence here. As the temperature approaches the control point it slows down its rate of approach and reaches the control point with no overshoot (in a carefully adjusted system).

15.24. Moving Control Point

The description of the various features of feedback control referred to a set control point, applicable to steady-state heating. The same elements will behave in essentially the same manner with a driven set point (Fig. XV-15). Consider the usual case—a linear (with time) heating rate. The control point is being driven upscale at a constant rate. The proportional band region is following at a rate modified by the other actions. Since we are trying to heat at a linear rate the recorder pen is moving at a nearly constant rate so the proportional band is shifted upscale by a nearly constant amount. Variations in the rate action are a small part of the total rate action in fairly rapid heating (several degrees per minute), so the over-all effect of properly adjusted rate action is to move the proportional band region upscale an amount dependent on the heating rate so that reset action can maintain close control. Reset action should now be able to move the proportional band up and down to maintain even the moving control temperature.

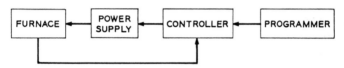

Fig. XV-15. Programmed control system.

The introduction of a program unit permits the operator to give time-based instructions to the control unit.

The author's experience is that settings derived from static heating are satisfactory for linear heating and cycling at linear rates. The author's power programming and control system comprise—at the time of writing —an L & N Series 60 Current Adjusting Type controller, a retransmitting slide-wire on the temperature pen of an X_1, X_2 vs t recorder, a cam-driven slide-wire programmer, and a silicon controlled rectifier. Since the temperature range is 0–1500°C or 0–1200°C, the initial position of the cam calls for a temperature below ambient; thus at the start of a program there is a brief time with no action, but the temperature pen eventually starts upscale forming an angle with the room-temperature portion of the trace rather than a curve. Similarly when the preset limit is reached, the furnace temperature begins dropping within a few seconds. When the programmer is set for cycling between preset limits, the temperature trace plots from one limit to the other at a uniform rate, cutting sharply back toward the other limit yet repeating these limits within ca 3°C over as many as eight cycles.

15.25. Programming

The imposition of the desired time-temperature cycle on the furnace and/or sample is called programming. Programming may range from the trivial but sometimes useful case of application of a constant—for example, line—voltage on a furnace designed to reach a particular temperature in a particular time to a multiple-step raising of the temperature with adjustable hold times and separately adjustable heating rates. The choice will be dictated by requirements and available funds.

The programming device comprises the parts and/or units necessary to retain and carry out the instructions of the operator. The degrees of complexity will depend on the flexibility desired for the program and the control accuracy needed.

The common devices are motor-driven adjustable autotransformers and cam-driven or screw-driven set point controllers. The first is simplest. Each of the others has features contributing to greater flexibility as well as some limitations. The performance of a programming unit is obviously tied quite closely to the controller and/or power supply.

15.26 Motor-Driven Adjustable Autotransformer

The adjustable autotransformer is the most widely used technique for controlling and varying the voltage input to furnaces. The simplest technique offering fair control, linear voltage programming, comprises the variable autotransformer driven at a selected but constant rate by an electric motor. The nearness to linearity of the temperature rise will depend on the furnace winding and construction. An approach to linearity over a portion of the range is all that a linear increase of voltage input can afford (Fig. XV-16).

The power input to a furnace with a purely resistive load is determined by $W = E^2/R$.

The heat losses from a furnace are by a variety of mechanisms, none of them proportional to the square of the voltage input. Radiation losses are a function of the fourth power of the absolute temperature while thermal conduction is proportional to the difference in temperature between the hot and the heating body. We may expect, then, a slow initial rise in temperature following, more or less, the E^2 relation because heat loss is not yet very rapid. As the temperature increases so does the heat loss, but because of the T^4 dependence of the radiative loss the heating rate not only stops increasing but will decrease. The only region approaching a linear rate of heating is that in which the conductive and convective heat losses and the radiative heat loss are changing in a manner approximating the changing power input so that net power input is fairly steady for an extensive period of time.

The heating of the base metal-wound furnace (Fig. XV-16) demonstrates the problem. At the slow driving rate the heating rate increases, maintains an almost steady state, and eventually begins to decrease. The heating rate ca 900°C is 50% greater than at 200°C. If we choose arbitrary criteria of performance we can conclude that a heating rate range with no more than 20% variation extends from ca 350 to 1100 C, but if we wish no more than 10% variation the most extensive range is from ca 400 to ca 850 C.

At the faster driving the rate has not yet started to decrease at 1100°C. A nearly constant range extends from ca 600 to 1100°C. The rate in the

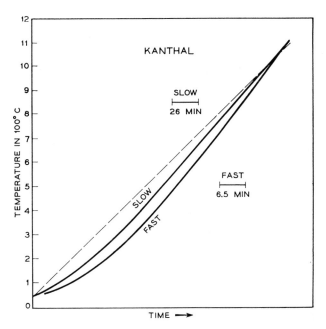

Fɪɢ. XV-16. Temperature vs time for a linear increase of voltage input to a base metal-wound furnace.

A very slow rise at first results from relatively poor thermal conductivity at low temperatures. The rapid increase in power $(W = E^2/R)$ *causes an increasing heating rate.*

900–1100°C range, however, is twice that at 150°C. If we apply the same criteria as before, the 20% variation range is from ca 400 to 1100°C and the 10% variation range from ca 600 to 1100°C. Other base metal windings would perform similarly.

The variation of heating rate is not so pronounced for platinum-wound furnaces because the resistance increases with temperature. The power input consequently is a function of a nonintegral $(1 < n < 2)$ power of E and therefore of time. At the slower heating rate, the slowdown of heating (Fig. XV-17) due to radiation losses is quite apparent. Never-

theless, the 20% variation range extends from ca 200 to at least 1400°C.
The longest 10% variation range is from ca 200 to 850°C.

In the faster heating, the slowing is less than 10%, so the 20% variation range extends from ca 350 to over 1400°C and the longest 10%
range from ca 625 to over 1400°C.

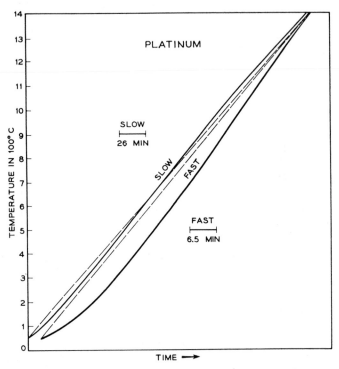

Fig. XV-17. Temperature vs time for a linear increase of voltage input to a
platinum-wound furnace.
*The increasing (with temperature) resistance of the winding tends to diminish the
power input so that a nearly linear heating rate is maintained for a substantial range.*

In these experiments the heating was stopped (automatically) well
below the operational limits of the two furnaces because of the high
heating rates. The temperature measured was, of course, the interior
temperature. The windings would be substantially hotter—and possibly
approaching their melting points—at the high heating rates. A furnace
offering a nearly linear temperature increase when driven by a linearly
increasing voltage is little more than fortuitous. Nevertheless, a variable
autotransformer driven by a constant-speed motor through a set of gears
will provide a fairly reproducible heating program rather economically,

provided conditions are essentially the same each run.

The sameness of conditions will very definitely include the initial temperature. In well-insulated furnaces the ambient temperature is not very important (within the ordinary laboratory ranges) but lightly insulated furnaces may heat at somewhat different rates from day to day depending on the temperature and humidity. To even hope for reproducibility, the operator must permit the furnace to cool to the ambient temperature before reuse.

15.27. Motor-Driven Set Point: ON-OFF Controllers

In general, the use of ON-OFF controllers for differential thermal analysis work must be approached with considerable caution. The imposition or sudden removal of a substantial voltage will, with most furnace arrangements, show a definite pickup in the thermocouple circuit. In addition, the very real cycling of temperature in the furnace may be observed. Here, especially, one must pay careful attention to the relative positions of heater control point and sample. An ON-OFF control will obviously introduce cycling at the control point. This control point, equally obviously, must be at a point close to the heater, and preferably between the heater and the sample. The geometry should be such that the path for conduction of the heat is shorter from heater to control point than from control point on to the sample. In this manner, the sharp cycling unavoidable with ON-OFF controllers will be, or may be, damped sufficiently that the oscillation has no apparent effect on the time-temperature relation at the sample point.

The ON-OFF switching might be used to operate an autotransformer drive so that when the temperature is below the control point a motor drives the autotransformer but when the temperature overtakes the control point the autotransformer remains stationary. This technique would avoid nearly all the undesirable consequences of use of ON-OFF programming.

The most probable consequence of this technique is a saw-toothed heating curve if the autotransformer drive is very much faster than the programming needs; in this use the drive should be on most of the time. This would require different drive speeds for significantly different heating rates.

In general, the motor-driven set point controllers comprise arrangements by which a control point is moved across the face of an indicating meter or recorder, and the unbalance or difference between the control point and the indicated actual temperature actuates electrical circuitry to produce some more involved type of control than simple ON-OFF switching.

15.28. Cam-Driven Set Point

A cam programmer comprises a motor-driven cam (Fig. XV-18a) which changes the position of a set point as a function of time. The cam may be cut for linear rise (Fig. XV-18a) as well as for linear rise and

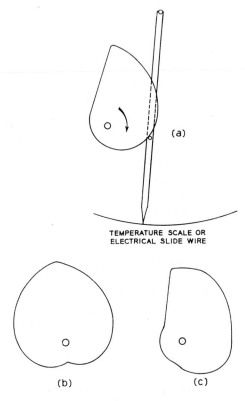

TEMPERATURE SCALE OR
ELECTRICAL SLIDE WIRE

Fig. XV-18. Cam programmer
The rotation of the cam moves a contact or set point according to a fixed pattern.

fall (Fig. XV-18b) or nonlinear rise (Fig. XV-18c) of temperature. It may contain one hold time or several, depending on the needs of the system. The rates of heating or cooling may vary from step to step in a complex program.

On the other hand, the program time is limited to one revolution of the cam. The existence, then, of a long hold time might mean that a heating step would be such a small part of the total rotation that accurate cutting of the cam would be difficult. While the total rotation time might be extended by the use of percentage timers (Chapter XVI), the problem is unchanged because the relative—rather than actual—times are the controlling factors.

The turning of the cam displaces the riding arm a greater or lesser distance or angle from the axis. The arm is mechanically coupled to a slide-wire or other device which permits a comparison of positions of the set point and the actual temperature indicator. The error signal is sent along to the control unit for appropriate action.

By the cam method the temperature rise may be made very nearly linear with time if special precautions are taken. These precautions comprise ways of compensating for the nonlinearity of thermocouple electromotive force (emf) with temperature. One technique is the "linearized" slide-wire for the temperature measurement. The "linearization" may be accomplished by tapping (electrically) the slide-wire at several points and shunting these several sections with resistors selected to keep the rate of angular displacement, $d\theta/dT$, of the new shaft (Chapter XVI) very nearly constant over the recorder span. The set point drive may then be linear with time. The nearness of approach to linearity is obviously dependent on the number of taps. The greater the number of taps, properly placed and shunted, the less the deviation from linearity. Since the slide-wire must first be tapped and then the shunting resistances calculated and installed, construction of a linearized slide-wire with very small deviation (less than 0.5%) becomes expensive. This increasing cost might—if only very minute deviations can be tolerated—justify a tapered slide-wire. The tapered slide-wire is nonuniformly wound and by the variation in windings compensates for the nonlinearity of the thermal emf. (Where dE/dT is high, the turns are close together; i.e., $dE/d\theta$ is high, so that $d\theta/dT$ is constant.)

Cam-driven set points may use compensated cams for the same purpose. The cam is cut so that the set point variation is similar to the emf variation. In this case, the temperature slide-wire may be uniform, i.e., $dE/d\theta$ constant; the chart paper should be compensated. The corresponding arrangement on the motor-driven set point (across the recorder scale) is a nonlinear drive. The worm in which the set point rides may have a nonuniform cut so that the set point travels faster in the region where dE/dt is larger.

An approximation to a linearly increasing temperature is often obtained by use of a linear drive over a millivolt, i.e., nonlinearized, temperature scale. This is less expensive than the other techniques and hence will often be used in conjunction with galvanometer indication or recording. The error in temperature will be as high a 3% in a 0-1000°C range using Chromel-Alumel thermocouples. The heating rate based on this system would vary by over 15%.

15.29. Screw-Driven Set Point

Screw-driven set points comprise a recorder or indicator, a set point which may be moved across the scale, a drive system, and an error-detecting system. This system has a distinct advantage in programming in that times—including relative times—are not rigidly circumscribed. If, for example, one wished to observe cooling curves after driving the sample up in temperature at some given rate and then holding at a constant temperature for varying times, the only limit on the "soak" time would be the range of the timer available. The heating and cooling rates would be practically independent.

A number of adjustable switches can be provided on some programmers. These permit the user to modify the program when the indicator reaches the preset temperature. He might, for example, heat a furnace very rapidly to some given temperature, then introduce a percentage timer or the drive to cut the drive speed to the desired rate for the continued heating.

The screw-driven set point can be as reproducible in heating rate as the cam-driven set point assuming full time (no percentage timers) in each case. The temperature limits will not be so reproducible on the screw-driven set point, nor will multiple heating rates, because of the difficulty of resetting the switch or timer positions precisely.

The linearity or nonlinearity of heating rate will depend on the recording or indicating system. A nonlinearized system will have the errors described in the previous section. One could supply a nonuniform cut on the driving worm but the expense would be difficult to justify. The best arrangement currently available would use a linearized slide-wire.

15.30. Eccentrically Driven Potentiometer

Another approach to the problem of approximating a linear temperature rise was taken by Satava and Trousil. They positioned their comparison potentiometer off-center (Fig. XV-19) so that the steady driving of the potentiometer would produce a reference potential (for their furnace control thermocouple) which would rise at a rate corresponding closely to that of the Pt vs Pt-Rh thermocouple. The agreement (Fig. XV-20) can be quite good, certainly a far better approximation than the straight-line variation pretended in simple programming devices.

15.31. Summary

Null balance potentiometers perform best for recording thermoanalytical data. The recording potentiometer may be used as part of a servo loop as well as an ordinary measuring device.

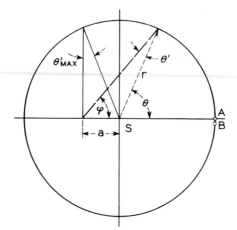

FIG. XV-19. Eccentric positioning of the programming potentiometer to obtain nonlinear time dependence of potential (S5).

The fact that different arcs are swept out by a given angle at different positions provides a curved E vs t dependence.

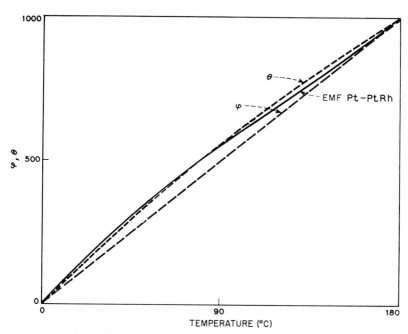

FIG. XV-20. Comparison of the angular position of the potentiometer, the potential at the contact, and the potential of a Pt vs Pt-Rh thermocouple (S5).

The shift in the axis produces good approximation of the thermoelectric potential curve with a simple cam modification.

For complete and unchanging systems the saturable-core reactor permits good stepless control, but where different types of experiments will be done the controlled rectifier is superior because it can control a wide range of loads.

The control unit should provide a continuous, stepless signal to the power supply and this signal should be modified by proportional band, rate, and reset action.

The choice between cam- and screw-driven (or otherwise driven) set points depends on the general nature of the work planned. Cam programmers give high reproducibility at the price of relative inflexibility of operation.

CHAPTER XVI

Miscellaneous
Apparatus
and Information

16.1. Thermocouples

The usual method of measuring temperature and change of temperature in thermal analysis is by use of thermocouples; these are junctions of dissimilar metals or alloys welded, soldered, swaged, or otherwise held in contact. The relative electronic energy levels give rise to a potential between the two. If the two materials are connected electrically at some other point so that a complete circuit is made, a similar potential will be established at that junction. If both junctions are at the same temperature the potentials are equal but, since these potentials are temperature-dependent, if the two junctions are at different temperatures the potentials will be different in the two and electric current can flow. This is the Seebeck effect. If one of the two materials is now opened (electrically speaking) the potential difference between the two ends can be measured and used to determine the temperature difference between the junctions. (The flow of current can also be made to do useful work but this is not within our immediate interest.) Unfortunately this potential is not a linear function of temperature difference; on the other hand, some combinations of metals have a variation with temperature which is close enough to being linear to permit use of linear measuring circuits with fair accuracy.

From this point on the discussion will assume the materials to be in the form of wires, for the simple reason that a wire form is the one most commonly used; the reader should understand that a wire of one material secured to a surface of another metal or alloy can be used to measure the temperature at the point of contact.

The thermoelectric effect obeys certain laws:

(1) No thermoelectric potential is established in a homogeneous electrical conductor regardless of temperature gradient along the wire.

> This statement implies that wires may be led from hot furnaces to measuring apparatus at room temperature without loss of accuracy.

(2) If one of the dissimilar wires is cut and each end joined to a wire of a third material and both of these latter junctions are at the same temperature, the thermoelectric potential is not affected.

> This statement follows from the first by applying the earlier stated law to the third material. It implies that connection may be made to other kinds of wires and hence to measuring apparatus without any effect. It is only necessary to keep these junctions at the same—but not necessarily steady—temperature.

(3) The observed thermoelectric potential is the sum of the potentials characteristic of each junction at its temperature.

> This statement implies that one may keep all junctions save one at some uniform temperature and, knowing this temperature, determine the temperature of the other junction. Similarly, if two junctions are at temperatures different from the rest, the thermoelectric potential will be the sum of or the difference between (depending on how they are connected) the individual potentials with respect to the potential at the temperature of the remaining junctions. A multiple-junction array can be assembled into a thermopile. A given difference in potential, in turn, represents a given difference in temperature from that reference temperature. The nonlinearity (Fig. XVI-1) of the thermoelectric potential with temperature precludes any other inference except as an approximation.

While any combination of dissimilar metals and alloys could be used to obtain a thermoelectric potential, only a few are in practical use; the principal considerations are the magnitude of the thermoelectric potentials, the reproducibility of potential from one thermocouple to another, and the stability of the combination in use. Table XVI-1 shows the commonly used thermocouples, their useful ranges, and the potential difference for an arbitrarily selected interval. Tables of thermoelectric potentials are given in Appendix II.

The maximum temperatures shown are not absolute limits; they are the temperatures at which extrapolated values reach an arbitrarily selected uncertainty. Calibrations are obtainable for somewhat higher temperatures but the user should realize that the possible error is becoming substantial.

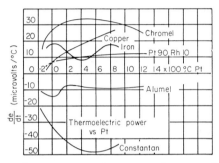

Fig. XVI-1. Thermoelectric powers of common thermocouple elements against Pt. From Finch (F7).

None of the combinations have a linear or even linearly changing response to temperature.

TABLE XVI-1

THERMOCOUPLES IN COMMON USE WITH THEIR USUAL AND MAXIMUM SERVICE TEMPERATURES AND A MEASURE OF THEIR SENSITIVITIES.

	Temperature range (°C)		
Thermocouple pair	Usual	Maximum	$E_{300°C} - E_{200°C}$
Platinum vs platinum-10% rhodium	0 to +1450	1700	0.880
Chromel vs Alumel	−190 to +1100	1350	4.08
Iron vs constantan	−190 to + 760	1000	5.55
Copper vs constantan	−190 to + 300	600	5.58

There are several techniques for joining thermocouple wires; the important criterion is whether or not a joint is small enough that it will itself contain no temperature gradients under the conditions used. From there on, sturdiness, sensitivity, ease of handling, and external circuitry must be considered.

Sturdiness calls for large sizes, sensitivity for small, while ease of handling calls for moderation in size. Since the present author customarily reads temperatures by true (recording) potentiometers, wire sizes from 0.0015 to 0.030 inches in diameter have presented no problems in measurement (see Chapter XV).

Thermocouple wires can be jointed by electric arc, flame heating, soldering, or pressure. When a butt-welded junction is needed it is generally formed by use of a dc carbon arc.

Parallel-wire or twisted-wire junctions can be made by forming the junction, moistening with a flux, and arc-welding, flame-welding, or soldering. The arc-welding can be done by carbon or mercury arc simply and easily. The process requires a melting together of the two wires. This is done by connecting one lead from a power source to one or both thermocouple wires and the other to an electrode and touching the junction to the electrode. The author presently uses a mercury arc apparatus comprising a pool of mercury covered with a layer of tricresyl phosphate. The tricresyl phosphate serves as a flux (D3) so that no preparation of the wires other than skinning and twisting is required. The mercury pool cannot be used with copper so connection to the mercury pool in the author's apparatus is by a carbon rod. Copper-constantan junctions are made by touching the junction to the carbon rod under the surface of the tricresyl phosphate.

Arc-welding by electrical discharge is often useful. By this technique a bank of capacitors is charged to some chosen voltage and this charge is subsequently dissipated to form the thermocouple by use of a carbon rod to produce a carbon arc by direct welding of the wires or by welding a wire to an object of the other thermocouple material (see Fig. VIII-2). This technique has the advantage that completed thermocouples can also be joined to surfaces, e.g., sample cups or crucibles as well as the tubes of Fig. VIII-34.

Soldering is frequently used for low-temperature work. The thermocouple wires are twisted or simply held against each other and silver solder applied using a torch (and flux) or soft solder may be applied with an iron. Only a short length should be soldered so that temperature homogeneity will not be in doubt.

16.2. Recording of Temperature—Millivolt Recorder

Since thermocouple wires will show a thermal emf with the copper conductors ordinarily used in measuring apparatus it is necessary to make the connections properly to avoid or compensate for the effect. Whether to avoid or compensate depends on the measuring system; some recorders have built-in compensation, but let us consider first measurement of temperature with a millivolt recorder, a potentiometer, or a galvanometer. If a thermocouple is connected directly to the terminals of any of these devices with no precaution whatever, the potential measured depends on the difference between the thermojunction temperature and that of the terminals of the measuring device. This is clearly an unsuitable condition for continuously measuring temperatures; room temperatures change and recorders warm up. A convenient solution for short times is the insertion of the junctions to copper in an ice bath. An ice bath has the advantages of being easily prepared and being already a temperature reference (0.0 . . .°C). Now the potential measured is dependent on the difference between the thermojunction temperature and 0°C, obviously quite a convenient arrangement. Since only a little care is needed in preparation of an ice bath it is a very popular system for providing a cold junction.

Unfortunately, the ice bath depends for its constancy of temperature on melting of the ice so these baths—even in Dewar flasks—require occasional attention. The ice must be replenished and firmly packed and water must be drawn off, so for protracted measurements other reference points may be more convenient. The other major reference temperature is the boiling point of water, achieved readily and steadily by immersion of the reference junction in a refluxing water bath. With a good condensing system the loss of water vapor is inappreciable so measurements extending over several days can be made. The only trouble with a boiling water bath as a reference junction thermostat is that setting it up is a nuisance.

16.3. Recording of Temperature—Compensated Recorders

To enable the customer to avoid the need for preparing a reference junction of any sort, makers of recording potentiometers supply built-in compensation for temperature ranges. This compensation comprises a temperature-sensitive resistance which shifts the scale slightly (Fig. XVI-2) but, because of the circuit arrangement, changes the zero-potential position markedly.

Assume a 0–1000°C scale and the entire system initially at a room temperature of 25C°. We then wish the recorder pen to indicate 25°C even though no thermal emf exists so the slide-wire zero must be $25/1000$ upscale. This is a simple matter: resistors R_1 and R_2 establish the reference point by their relative magnitudes. (The actual resistance is of no great concern in this discussion.) Now let the thermojunction be at some elevated temperature, T; the potential difference measured by the recorder is $T - 25°C$ but since the zero potential is shifted upscale the temperature shown is $T°C$.

Note in Fig. XVI-2 that the thermocouple leads join the copper recorder leads in the vicinity of R_1; in some recorders the connections are actually enclosed by the resistor, in others they are merely close by. Since the resistance of R_1 is temperature-sensitive, if the temperature should change the potential drop across R_1 would change; the potential at point P therefore changes and the zero-potential point on the slide-wire shifts from point O toward A if the temperature rises and toward B if it falls. The actual temperature error due to use of a compensator instead of a thermostatted reference junction is small.

Whether a reference junction or a compensator is used the thermo-couple materials or properly chosen equivalent must lead from the thermojunction to the reference junction or the recorder terminals. For the base metal thermocouples the common practice is to use thermo-couple wire even if the run is fairly long but for noble metal thermo-couples special extension wires are often used for reasons of economy. These extension wires are alloys chosen or made to give very low ther-moelectric potentials with the thermocouple wires. This nonsensitivity to temperature must apply for a range from the reference temperature to the actual temperature of the junction between extension and ther-mocouple wires.

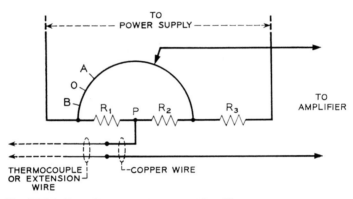

Fɪɢ. XVI-2. Recording potentiometer with cold junction compensation.
Temperature-sensitive resistance changes zero point toward A if the temperature rises and toward B if it falls.

Note that connection of sets of dissimilar wires may take place through another conductor without effect as long as the temperatures at the actual points of connection are the same. This permits the use of connector blocks whether or not the wires are held in actual contact with each other. Note, too, that a differential thermocouple need not be connected through any sort of reference junction. Assuming that two like wires are connected together and no other connection is made to them, the other two like wires—from which the differential signal is measured—may be connected directly to copper at any convenient point.

The present author generally—but by no means always—uses lead wire alloy plugs for interconnections. For millivolt recorders, an arrangement such as that used by Vassallo and Harden (V3) is perfectly satisfactory (Fig. XVI-3). The only precaution necessary in changing to copper leads is that, within each set of terminals, the temperature must be uniform; this is not difficult within usually acceptable limits of error. The apparatus more recently assembled uses spring clip terminals to hold wires together. These terminals are enclosed by a metal block which serves to keep the temperature *uniform; constant* temperature is unnecessary.

Recording potentiometers provided with temperature ranges will normally be equipped with the appropriate extension or thermocouple wire from the terminals to the cold junction. These recorders may be

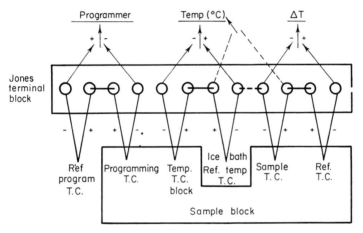

Fig. XVI-3. Thermocouple junctions for temperature programming, temperature, and differential temperature measurements. From Vassallo and Harden (V3).

A connector block (at a uniform temperature) permits convenient change or replacement of individual thermocouples.

ordinary millivolt recorders, they may be ordinary millivolt recorders designed for nonlinear scales and chart paper, or they may have a "linearized" slide-wire. The choice of scales depends on the need, with appropriate attention to cost.

If one is only recording temperature the second choice is the best. The cost is only slightly more than the ordinary millivolt recorder. If a two-pen recorder is used and the other variable is not temperature one of the other choices is more appropriate. Presumably the other variable can be measured best on linear paper, as, for example, weight change or differential temperature. An ordinary millivolt recorder will require correction for the less than linear E vs T relation; for a few hundred dollars more this correction can be made negligible by use of a linearized slide-wire.

Recall that in a recording potentiometer the range is determined (Fig. XVI-4) by the relation between R_A and the resistance, R_{eq}, equivalent to the slide-wire R_S and its parallel resistors R_B and R_C, i.e.,

$$\text{measuring range} = E_x \; \frac{R_{eq}}{R_A + R_{eq}}.$$

The zero is established by the relative magnitudes of R_B and R_C and the slide-wire contact position can supply a linearly varying portion of the potential drop across $R_B + R_C$. This slide-wire can be made to supply an approximation to a thermocouple output by tapping it at a number of points and shunting it with several resistors instead of two (Fig. XVI-4b). Now the slide-wire can supply a varying portion of the potential drop across $R_B + R_D + R_E + R_J$, but this potential will

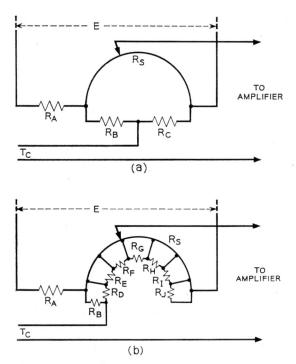

(a)

(b)

Fig. XVI-4. Recording potentiometer circuits giving (a) a linear measure of thermal emf and (b) a nearly linear measurement of temperature. R_B is the temperature-compensation resistor.

R_C *is replaced in* (b) *by shunt resistors whose number and values are selected according to the type of thermocouple. Another possible arrangement would comprise a complete set of linearizing resistors shunted by* R_B *and* R_C.

vary in a series of linear segments designed to give a good approximation to the actual thermocouple output. With the linearized slide-wire the temperature may be recorded on the same linear chart as another variable without much error in reading the temperature.

In any case, if a highly accurate temperature reading is needed a potentiometer may be used to reproduce the pen position and the correct temperature determined from the potentiometer reading.

16.4. Photocells

A common method of obtaining a signal related to the degree of unbalance in thermogravimetry is by use of a photocell so arranged that movement of the balance beam permits more or less light on the sensitive region. This method is useful for general purpose displacement measuring of moderate sensitivity and for sensing in pseudonull balance systems. The photocell comprises one or two light-sensitive elements whose resistance varies inversely with the amount of light impinging upon them. This change in voltage drop due to the change in resistance can be amplified and measured or used to control a power input or a balancing device.

16.5. Capacitance Detection

The electrical capacitance of a pair of neighboring plates or other conductors is governed, among other things, by their separation. If one is free to move with respect to the other, the capacitance will change. By suitable equipment, this capacity change can be measured or used to initiate some operation. The displacement detector used in the pseudo-null balance of van der Breggen and Wouterlood (B74), shown in Fig. XIV-5, detects the increase of one capacitance and consequent decrease of the other as the center plate, attached to a balance beam, moves. The circuit ought to be more sensitive if the resistors and diode rectifiers

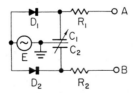

Fig. XVI-5. Differential capacitance detector. From van der Breggen and Wouterlood (B74).

Change in position of the central plate changes the voltage of A *relative to* B. *(D_1, D_2 = OA72; R_1, R_2 = 470 kohm, 0.5 watt, high stability.) This signal controls the restoring force of a magnet.*

were interchanged; the continuous flow of the alternating current and reading-off of the resulting voltage drops would provide a better response than reading the current flow between the plates.

A capacitance measurement of this type will be approximately linear over only a narrow range. Since the capacitance varies inversely with the square of the distance, only in the center will an increment of displacement in one direction have an effect equal (in absolute magnitude) to a similar displacement in the other. The rapidly increasing increments of signal at greater displacements might make the detector useful in a true or force-restored null balance.

16.6. Strain Gauges

The stretching of a wire brings about a small change in its electrical resistance simply because of dimensional changes. Some metal alloys have special characteristics so that the resistance of a wire under strain provides a stable and reproducible measure of the elongation. Wires of such alloys are assembled into conveniently used units so that the user may attach them to material under strain.

The gauges may be connected in any standard resistance measuring circuit but the customary arrangement is a bridge. This bridge may have two gauges as in Fig. XVI-6, in which the second gauge is unstrained

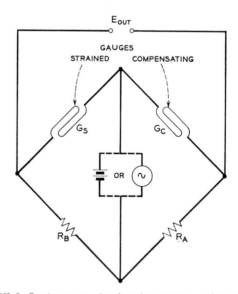

Fɪɢ. XVI-6. Strain gauge circuit using compensating gauge.
R_A and R_B could be replaced by another G_S and G_C, respectively, to double the sensitivity.

and merely compensates for temperature variations. Note that if the strained and compensating gauges (G_s and G_c, respectively) both change in resistance by the same fraction the potentials at points s and c change by very nearly the same amount and the output voltage E_{out} is virtually unaffected.

A strain gauge can be applied to a strip of spring steel or to a drill rod or to any material which is elastically deformed. (A primary requirement is, of course, that the material on which the gauge is mounted will respond reproducibly to strain.) A sample can then be supported in a manner such that a change in weight (or length) can be detected and measured.

16.7. Variable Differential Transformers

A variable differential transformer comprises three windings and a movable core; an example is given in Fig. XVI-7. This is specifically a

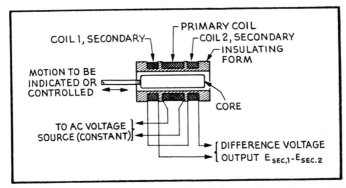

Fig. XVI-7. Operation of the linear variable differential transformer (LVDT). *Movement of the core changes the relative inductive couplings of the two secondaries with the primary.*

linear variable differential transformer because the motion detected is along the axis of the transformer. (Rotary variable differential transformers may be used to measure angular displacement, but the linear variety is of more interest here.) As long as the core is symmetrically located with respect to the two secondaries, the outputs are equal and, if properly connected, opposite in phase. There is essentially no net voltage; a quite small residual voltage is still present because of the phase angle shift in the transformer but for most applications this is not important.

Let us move the core toward the left, toward point A in Fig. XVI-8, and let us measure the instantaneous output from the secondaries at some constant point on the alternating current wave. When the core is at point A, a voltage will appear which will diminish as the core is moved toward the center because the inductive coupling between the primary and the left-hand secondary is decreasing while that between the primary and the right-hand secondary is increasing. As the core moves past the center O and toward B, the output from the right-hand secondary becomes greater than that from the left-hand secondary and the instantaneous voltage changes sign.

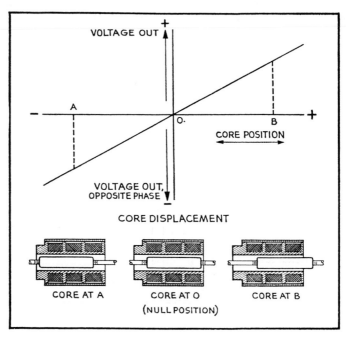

Fɪɢ. XVI-8. LVDT output voltage and phase as function of core position, linear graph.

Both magnitude and direction of displacement can be measured.

The important features are: (1) as the core passes the center (null) position, there is a phase shift of 180°; and (2) the output voltage varies linearly with displacement. The first feature makes possible null-seeking systems, and the second permits measurement of displacement or servo systems to follow displacement. Some linear variable differential transformers are single-ended, i.e., designed to measure only displacement.

Since a current is passing through the primary, it follows that there will be some tendency for the transformer to act as a solenoid, pulling on the core to bring it to the center or null position. The force varies with displacement and inversely with excitation frequency. This force must be taken into account in displacement-measuring balances, but in null-seeking devices the effect can be eliminated by adjustment so that the magnetic null coincides with the mechanical null of the balance (see Chapter X).

16.8. Electrical Differentiation

A measure of the rate of change of a direct electric current can be obtained easily by the circuit shown in Fig. XVI-9. Under steady-state conditions the potential across capacitor C is equal to the potential drop across R, i.e., $E_C = i_1 R_1 = E$. If the potential drop should increase, electrons would flow through R_2 until $E_C = E$, resulting in a

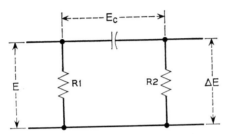

Fig. XVI-9. Differentiating circuit.

When a change in E occurs, the capacitor must charge or discharge to return E_C to zero. The voltage drop across R_2 gives a measure of the rate of change of E.

transient potential drop, $i_2 R_2$, across R_2. This potential drop is proportional to the difference between E and E_C, i.e., the effective charging voltage; the capacitance of C and the resistance R.

A high capacitance will obviously need a large quantity of electricity to charge it; therefore, at some given current i_2 the time needed to change a capacitor will vary with the capacitance. Similarly, a given capacitor can be charged (or discharged) more rapidly at a high current (low resistance) than at a low; the time required for a capacitor to charge or discharge will vary with the resistance in series with it.

For some instantaneous change in E, E_C will approach E at a rate determined by the magnitude of the change and by R and C. Specifically, the approach follows a first-order reaction (radioactive decay) relation, i.e.,

$$\frac{dx}{dt} = -kx,$$

for this particular case,

$$\frac{d\Delta E}{dt} = \frac{-\Delta E}{RC}.$$

Instead of the half-life of the reaction, the commonly used measure of such a circuit is the time constant, $R \cdot C$, which gives the time required for the voltage to decay to 1/2.3 of its original value.

Now it is apparent that if a circuit is constructed with a long time constant and the potential is changed by some increment, the approach of E_C to its new value will be slow. A measurable ΔE will persist for a considerable time. Such a condition has limited utility; the measurement of ΔE will fail to show much more than the grosser features of successive changes of E. If, on the other hand, a very small time constant circuit is used the capacitor will approach its new potential so rapidly that the ΔE signal cannot be measured conveniently. With a small time constant the value of E_C is never far different from E except in the case of instantaneous changes; the measured ΔE will more closely approach the true value of dE/dt than with a large time constant circuit. The selection of a differentiating circuit is based principally on the rapidity of variation of the signal and on the speed of response of the measuring apparatus.

Consider two quite different cases, (I) a thermogravimetric apparatus which supplies a signal proportional to the sample weight and (II) a differential thermal analysis apparatus operating under rather ordinary conditions. In case I the signal will be slow to change compared to case II. If the same derivative circuit were used the time constant suitable for differential thermal analysis would be too small for thermogravimetric analysis and as a result the ΔE signal would be unnecessarily and inconveniently small. On the other hand, a large time constant giving acceptable results for following thermogravimetric measurements would obscure any rapid variations in differential thermal analysis signals.

The choice of circuitry must be a compromise between high signal strength and reasonably accurate following of the dE/dt signal. If one is recording the signal, there is no real need or value to have a time constant smaller than the balancing time of the recording system. From this minimum time constant one makes whatever increase he finds necessary to obtain a useful (both measurable and meaningful) ΔE vs t plot. Since the voltage across R_2 is the quantity usually measured, the value of this resistor should be equal to the maximum permissible input impedance of the measuring apparatus; this will permit use of only as much capacitance as may be needed and will enable the closest practicable following of dE/dt.

If the differentiating circuit is supplying other electric or electronic circuitry, the time constants are generally much smaller simply because the absence of mechanical motion removes the greatest obstacle to close following of the potential E.

16.9. Electrical Filtering

The occasional need for conversion of an alternating or pulsating current to a direct current raises immediately the problem of filtering. The charging and discharging of a capacitor through a resistor was described briefly in the previous section. The possibility of spreading out the change of potential over a substantial period of time was pointed out there as something to avoid; under different circumstances it is highly desirable. In each case, one must consider how much filtering needs to be supplied; too much will slow any response to change as well as being extra trouble to supply while too little may give erratic response and irreproducible and inaccurate results. The amount of this filtering is not highly critical; a factor of two or three has little effect, but only a little thoughtlessness is needed to throw in one hundred-fold too much filtering.

The R part of the time constant is often beyond the direct control of the user. The load to be supplied makes certain requirements which have to be met. Power supply filtering is just a special case in which a very appreciable current needs to be smoothed.

Let us consider a case in which a 60-cps differential transformer output is to be measured on a direct current recording potentiometer. If the transformer output is supplied to a full-wave rectifier (Fig. XVI-10a) a pulsating current of 120 cps is obtained. Let us assume that our recording potentiometer has an input impedance maximum of 400 ohms and that the signal we need to measure will drive the recorder approximately full-scale (no voltage divider is needed). Let us put in a capacitor with a capacitance of 25 μf. The time constant is 400 ohms $\times 25 \times 10^{-6}$ farads or 0.01 second. From the decay relation this means that the capacitor will discharge more than half of its stored energy before it is charged by the next pulse.

If the time constant were increased by about two orders of magnitude the capacitor would discharge less than 1% of its stored energy before being charged by the next pulse. This is a rather convenient rate. (Note that if the input signal drops suddenly the capacitor will follow at this less than 1% per cycle rate because the input potential would have no effect until the capacitor potential dropped below it; on the other hand, an increase in potential will be followed at a rate determined by the time constant of the rectifier-capacitor system.)

We can make this one hundred-fold increase in the time constant most easily by increasing the total resistance (Fig. XVI-10b) but this means that if the proper input resistance is maintained the signal drops proportionately. The alternative would be to increase the capacitance, but

2500 μf consumes both space and funds. (The apparently simple expedient of using electrolytic capacitors is unwise because these devices often develop spurious voltages.)

In the event that the entire signal is needed a stage of amplification may be the best solution; a high-impedance recorder is another possibility. Whatever solution is used the circuit will be a compromise between the speed of response that accompanies the low time constant and the higher signal level that goes with a higher time constant. Whatever the

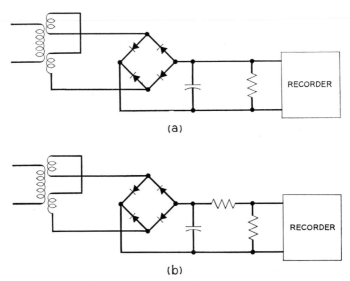

(a)

(b)

Fig. XVI-10. Transformer rectifier circuit with filter.

The signal appearing at the recorder in (a) will reach slightly less than the peak voltage and will vary sinusoidally by a magnitude determined by R·C. Attenuation by inserting the additional resistor in (b) will decrease the magnitude of the signal but will decrease the sinusoidal variation additionally by increasing the time constant.

frequency, the time ought to fall in the 5–20 cycle range as a first approximation. For higher frequencies this might be extended to, say, 0.05–0.2 second. For special cases, further extensions in either direction may be desirable.

Filtering of a signal which is part of a servo loop is a special case in which a fairly long time constant is desirable. Consider the same type of signal as before except that now it will be fed into an amplifier which operates a motor which in turn brings the signal back to zero. We cannot use a full-wave rectifier because we could then drive in only one direction; instead, we oppose two half-wave rectifiers (Fig. XVI-11). (We are assuming here that there is good reason to use a dc input amplifier as part of the servo system.) Even though both signals may be—and usually are—rather high, the servo amplifier sees only the difference. Since the capacitors will be charged up to nearly peak voltage at each cycle, each must maintain its voltage essentially undiminished during the next half cycle while the other is being charged. Too rapid a discharge would cause the servomotor to tend to drive in opposite directions each half cycle so that it would sit and hum. Worse, it would impose a condition by which the amplifier would see enough of a signal to actually get the motor turning only when a substantial difference existed; the sensitivity would be lowered. An extremely high time constant might possibly cause hunting because of the persistence of the signal.

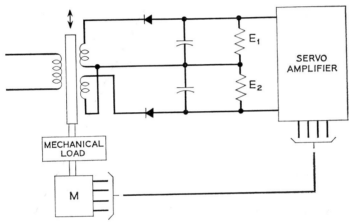

Fig. XVI-11. Servo systems using rectification and filtering.
The servo amplifier drives in the direction indicated by the sign of $E_1 - E_2$.

16.10. Phase Relations

Filtering in the servo system described above is a necessary companion to expediency. If the signal could be applied to the amplifier with the proper phase relation no filtering at all would be needed.

The author has done this sort of thing but instead of supplying the unbalance signal to the normal input he supplied it directly to the input transformer (see Chapter X). The only provision for phasing was to make certain that the motor drove in the proper direction. Correct phasing would have been fortuitous; the amplifier is probably quite heavily overloaded.

Proper phasing could be obtained by proper selection of a series capacitor but an easier solution is to smooth the output. Bear in mind that the only function of the ΔE is, essentially, to destroy itself. We are not interested in its magnitude but we are interested in following changes rapidly. A substantial time constant means overshoot and hunting but an inadequate filtering might permit the potential to drop off while the amplifier needs the maximum signal. A time constant of only a couple of cycles would maintain a readable signal without serious impairment of the response time.

16.11. Impedance Matching

One may find, in appropriate texts, evidence that maximum power can be transferred electrically when the output impedance of the supply circuit is equal to the input impedance of the receiving circuit. A complete discussion is outside the scope of this book, but a few selected applications may be described.

In furnace power circuits one may generally feed a high-impedance load from a low-impedance source; e.g., a furnace drawing a maximum of 8 amp may be fed from a 20- or 50-amp autotransformer without trouble. The major exception is due to loss of control sensitivity as with a saturable-core reactor rated for low load impedance feeding a high-resistance load. The opposite is not practical. Supplying a low-impedance load from a high-impedance source will have results ranging from non-functioning of the apparatus to damage to the source.

In electronic gear the same general considerations hold, including the possibility of damage to the source if moderate powers can be drawn. In these cases, the impedance matching must be considered simply for protection of apparatus. At still lower power levels, i.e., where the actual amount of power is insignificant, the penalty for mismatch of impedance is loss of sensitivity, failure of the receiving circuit to respond.

The impedance (resistance) of a thermocouple will range from less than 1 ohm to 70 or 100 ohms. This is a low resistance and a thermocouple can thence supply essentially any ordinary electronic circuit, amplifier, recorder, etc. (The higher-resistance thermocouples may not be able to supply galvanometer recorders or indicators.) We do encounter the problem of amplifying thermistor bridge or other high-resistance bridge circuit signals.

In essence, stable amplification of a direct current signal requires that a small current flows. Similarly, a recording potentiometer will require current flow during any unbalance. (In a true recording potentiometer there is no drain on the measured circuit except after a change and until balance is restored.) In the case of the dc amplifier the current flow across the input grid resistor must be enough to establish the proper grid bias voltage. If the output impedance from the source is excessive, the current flow will set up a sizable voltage drop in the source circuit, detracting thereby from the input voltage in the amplifier. The amplified signal will not reflect accurately the voltage it is ostensibly measuring.

The recording potentiometer will show a different effect. In this case, some minimum voltage drop must appear across the input stage grid resistor before the output stage can supply enough energy to start the motor. A reasonably common set of values might be 1000 ohms nominal input impedance with 1 μv sensitivity. This means that a source of no more than 1000 ohms and having a net unbalance of 1 μv will supply enough voltage drop to start the balancing motor. Higher source impedances may require several microvolts, open circuit, to be able to supply 1 μv, closed circuit. This results in a range of voltages on each side of the balance voltage within which not enough power can be supplied to the recorder amplifier to cause it to operate; this is a "dead zone." The symptom of a large dead zone on the record is a "stepping" of the recorded signal.

One can operate outside the rated impedance limits of recorders or amplifiers when it is expedient. The penalties are severe only if they are unrecognized, the principal effect being slower speed or response. Habitual operation beyond the limits recommended by the maker is unwise. The author indulges in the practice only when testing of a hypothesis would otherwise have to await acquisition of a suitable instrument. If there is need for continued use of the new system, proper instrumentation is bought or otherwise acquired.

16.12. Noninductive Furnaces

The ordinary helical winding on a furnace tube sets up an electric field. The effect of this field on differential thermal analysis apparatus is not really well-known. (In thermogravimetric analysis it requires use of a nonmagnetic sample holder.) The present author used noninductively wound furnaces for a short time. These were wound by bending the wire around a pin at one end of the zone and applying two windings (i.e., from the midpoint of the piece of resistance wire out toward both ends) side by side. This resulted in the entire input voltage being applied across an insulation-filled gap not much more than a millimeter wide. When the furnace became hot the insulation broke down and the platinum-rhodium furnace winding followed suit.

Noninductive windings can be applied as two separate coils. The essential features are that they have very nearly the same number of turns, pass very nearly the same amount of current, and are quite close to each other. One winding can be of a good conductor and serve only as a compensator.

The author subsequently eliminated noise by inserting a grounded platinum shield inside the furnace tube. In recent work shielding has ordinarily been needed only for temperatures above 1000°C, when using base thermocouple wires. The author is not absolutely convinced that noninductive furnaces are useful but he is performing some experiments on a hopefully better way of applying a noninductive winding on a ceramic tube furnace.

16.13. Induced Currents and Noise

Recall that when a steady direct current is flowing through a conductor a magnetic field exists around that conductor. If that current should increase or decrease, so would the field. Similarly, if a magnetic field encompasses a conductor and the magnetic field changes in strength, an emf is induced in the conductor.

If an alternating current is flowing, the field is constantly increasing, decreasing, reversing, etc. This smooth change may be a source of interference, i.e., hum spurious steady signals, etc., but filtering and simple shielding are usually sufficient protection for any single major component. To avoid the effects of induced emf's of different levels in different parts, the chassis or frames of the several components are grounded. This is often done by grounding each frame or chassis separately to a metal cabinet but is better done by connecting all the frames together by a ground lead. Each component with very much metal, i.e., recorder, furnace base, program unit, etc., should be grounded to a common point with separate wires.

In severe cases, stray currents may be induced in metal cabinets. Two components grounded to each other as well as each to the cabinet will constitute a "ground loop" such that current may flow. (This situation is analogous to the grounding of a circuit at two points which are not supposed to be at the same potential.) The author avoids the problem by mounting the several components in a wooden cabinet and grounding them individually to a common point.

When a discontinuous change of current occurs in a conductor the field increases or decreases sharply and seldom smoothly. The making or breaking of a switch, for example, sets up a field quite irregularly so that a multitude of frequencies will be induced in nearby conductors. Loose contacts will often have the same effects. These spurious signals in the very low-level differential temperature signal may cause pips, jitter, and other forms of noise in the thermogram.

Thermoelectric noise in the furnace winding may cause a high-level "hash" at temperatures in the vicinity of 800°C. Symmetry of conductors appears to be of great help here. The author had considerable noise in an early horizontal furnace (G12). It was eliminated by use of a grounded platinum cylinder inside the furnace tube. The vertical furnaces the author presently uses do not appear to be subject to this type of noise. If such noise should appear, the proper procedure is to (1) check connections very carefully, (2) ground any component that can be grounded, and (3) shield any suspected source.

In some cases a component exposed to induce noise cannot be grounded; this is often the case with thermocouples which feed amplifiers which are already grounded. Assuming a dc signal, as in a thermocouple, ac noise can be bypassed to ground by use of large nonelectrolytic capacitors. In severe cases a choke input to the amplifier may be needed along with the capacitors.

16.14. Summary

Thermoelectric potentials result when dissimilar metals are in contact. Connection of other wires to thermocouple wires must be at a known, constant, or compensated temperature for a measuring thermocouple; for differential temperatures, the connections must only be at the same, though perhaps not steady, temperature. Variations in photoelectric effects, capacitance, resistance, and magnetic effects are often used in thermogravimetric and other apparatus.

Electrical techniques and problems are described.

CHAPTER XVII

Apparatus
Design

17.1. General

The design of an apparatus can be a reasonably simple affair, provided one has (1) the performance requirements for the final assembly clearly in mind, (2) a reasonably thorough knowledge of available components and their characteristics, and (3) several years of experience. For the rest of us, periods of indecision and uncertainty, occasional compromise, and frequent revision must be expected and considered routine. One gains experience only by doing and to a lesser degree one can establish performance requirements only from experience. The other aid in design, knowledge of components, is part of one's collateral education gained sometimes by experience but more often by diligent study at the time of need.

The material presented in the accompanying sections is intended to diminish the uncertainty and indecision. The need for compromise may be alleviated by a clearer understanding of performance requirements. The need for revision may possibly be lessened for the same reason, but new techniques, new components, new problems, plus the awareness of ways to meet the new requirements might bring about fairly frequent revision even for an experienced user. Cognition of the possibility of modifying or adapting a commercially available apparatus may tip the balance in favor of purchase rather than construction, particularly for the neophyte. The final sections describe, purely as examples, assemblies designed by the author.

The experimenter must keep in mind at all times that the means of handling the sample is of prime importance. Once an experimental procedure has been selected the design problem becomes quite general. For example, when the type of sample holder and furnace for a differential thermal study has been chosen, the programming and recording system will likely be very like some other assembly. This is all to the good; if a different type of problem arises, another furnace and/or sample holder can be substituted.

17.2. To Design or Not to Design

A person experienced in thermal analysis and who needs new apparatus will probably design it; he is convinced that commercially available equipment does not fill his needs; to a considerable degree he is right.

Apparatus manufactured for general sale is constrained to nonspecificity; in order that it may serve the needs of many reasonably well the maker must shun the features which improve it for only limited purposes and which limit its utility for other purposes or increase its cost unnecessarily. One experienced in the art can immediately see disadvantages in any given commercial apparatus. Whether the new requirements of the user can be met better by purchase and modifications or by construction according to the user's own design is a question not always answered objectively.

The neophyte has a quite different problem; he does not even know to what degree the commercial apparatus will satisfy his needs; he must evaluate the conflicting advice of various authorities; he can foresee obstacles to obtaining funds for design of an apparatus at any short interval after purchase of a complete apparatus. Only the most enlightened management is likely to understand that even good scientists are not always able to invade new fields without error. Perhaps the course of action can best be decided by evaluation of one's own attitude. He who wants a tool to get an answer and who cares not how it happens must settle for the available apparatus. He who is ready and willing to study the technique and apparatus critically can well undertake the problem of modifying or designing to suit his special needs.

The author places himself squarely with the norm in his response to an apparatus problem. A few years ago an apparently expensive packaged apparatus was put on the market. The author was investigating such apparatus for his own use. He rejected the commercial ready-to-use apparatus in favor of design and construction around a commercially available principal component. The final apparatus was significantly more expensive than the commercial unit but had the quality of filling —after several further modifications—the special needs of the author; yet the author has recommended the commercial unit for those who had not had the experience essential for such design or who had no needs beyond its capabilities.

Unfortunately one may expect little aid, comfort, or encouragement from manufacturers of materials. If the designer of a furnace should follow strictly the conditions recommended by these manufacturers and was still able to construct the furnace, it would certainly have a life expectancy of 30 years, far more than the useful life of the rest of the apparatus. A maker of platinum wire, for example, points out that platinum windings should not be cycled up and down in temperature; crystallization of the wire would shorten the life of the winding. The author has cycled such a furnace several hundred times with no evidence that it was near failure. The furnace was taken out of service because of obsolescence, a much greater hazard in this work.

17.3. To Design

The previous question having been settled, consideration of the real problem may begin. Assume now that a differential thermal analysis apparatus of an orthodox type is to be constructed for use to 1500°C at a heating rate not less than 10°C/minute and that only the furnace and programming apparatus are under consideration. The first problem is obviously the size and nature of the furnace. The temperature range will narrow the choice of windings to platinum or an alloy for the ordinary tube furnace.

Design of the windings, i.e., size and quantity of wire, will depend on the size and construction of the furnace and the voltage supply. All of the furnace parameters are interrelated. This requires an attempt at simultaneous consideration of ease and quality of control, degree of insulation, size of heated chamber, rate of heating, etc.

A furnace with plenty of insulating material around it does not necessarily require less power to heat it than a similar furnace with less insulation. The insulating material must be heated, too. The heavily insulated furnace is less subject to minor fluctuations in temperature. Because of its mass, changes in input voltage are less immediately apparent as changes in temperature. This means that rather simple programming apparatus will give a smooth nondiscontinuous heating curve. The reader should not infer a linear or even a highly reproducible heating rate. These both may require good control equipment. (A heavily lagged furnace driven by a voltage increasing at a fixed rate should have a fairly reproducible heating rate; if this voltage input is programmed the heating rate can be reasonably close to linear. Both statements assume that the furnace is essentially at room temperature at the start of the program.) One quality is certain. The furnace will take a long time to cool. Another run can be made the following day.

A lightly insulated furnace will be more affected by changes in supply voltage; it will require sensitive and quick-acting control apparatus to maintain a programmed temperature rise; good apparatus can program the furnace with good precision because of the rapid response; the furnace will cool quickly.

Returning now to the problem of heating to 1500°C, one may select a power input on the basis of experience when possible. Otherwise a reasonably safe estimate is 1500 watts. This is a beginning.

Consider next the type of voltage or current control. Assuming the supply voltage is 115 volts ac, one has available 115 volts with an ON-OFF controller (included only for information; an ON-OFF program would not be used with a platinum winding; see Chapter XIV), 115 or 135 volts with an adjustable or driven autotransformer, about 105 volts with a properly loaded saturable-core reactor, and about 110 volts with a solid-state controlled rectifier. This maximum voltage is needed to calculate the furnace resistance (see the following section). Choose, for the purpose of this discussion, an autotransformer. (The other cases are even simpler.) If the transformer is connected to give 0–135 volts, the relation is $P = E^2/R = 1500$ watts $= (135 \text{ volts})^2/R = 1.7 \times 10^4/R$ and $R = 11^+$ ohms. If the autotransformer is connected to deliver 0–115 volts, $R = 9^-$ ohms. The windings then must have a resistance of 9^- or 11^+ ohms at a temperature somewhat above 1500°C. This last is important since platinum has a relatively high-temperature coefficient or resistance.

Choosing the 11^+ ohms for this problem and assuming the winding may reach 1600°C the electrical resistance must be about 4.5 ohms at room temperature. (Platinum and platinum alloys have high positive temperature coefficients of resistance which must be taken into account. The high-temperature resistance is used in calculating the amount of wire.) This 4.5 ohms must obviously be a long length of fairly thick wire rather than a short length of fine wire, but since the cost of the winding for a given power dissipation varies as the fourth power of the diameter, i.e., $\$ = kd^4$, a compromise must be made. The author has generally used 0.032-inch wire in this power range. The oldest furnace was in use for about 7 years before removal from service. It has not shown any signs of deterioration.

There must be enough turns on a tube furnace (probably no less than six turns per inch) so that no noticeable image of the winding shows through the tube to the heated chamber. The total number will now depend partly on the use of the furnace. A horizontal furnace will need a sizable constant-temperature zone so the winding will occupy 6 to 8 inches for a differential thermal analysis furnace. In a vertical furnace the same wire can be distributed along 4 to 5 inches since gradients are going to exist anyway. In vertical furnaces, we rely on symmetry. At the same distance from the axis at any given height the temperature should be the same. If a high-conductivity block is used to contain the sample, temperature differences at symmetric points will be very small.

Horizontal furnaces are subject to "end effects," i.e., greater heat loss at the end of the wound portion simply because the adjacent region in the one direction is not heated. The furnace designer will generally compensate for this by doubling the number of turns in the last inch on either end (Fig. XVII-1). This is an arbitrary choice. Very close compen-

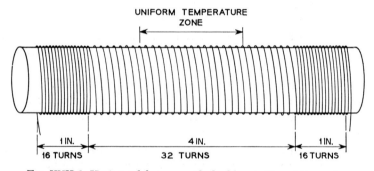

UNIFORM TEMPERATURE ZONE

1 IN.   4 IN.   1 IN.

16 TURNS   32 TURNS   16 TURNS

Fɪɢ. XVII-1. Horizontal furnace with double winding at the ends.
The additional heat at the ends will provide a nearly uniform temperature zone in the center section because heat loss to the ends is avoided.

sation over any sizable temperature range is neither likely nor often expected. The object of this and winding is to present to the uniformly wound center section an adjoining region at nearly the same temperature so that finally the center region of the center section has a temperature gradient within it sufficiently low that it can be considered as a uniform temperature region.

17.4. Power Supply

The selection of a power supply for differential thermal analysis depends on the funds available and the demands to be placed on it. A simple ON-OFF supply is out of the question for any but very heavily lagged furnaces; even on these the induced emf'ts may introduce serious noise. For lighter, quick-response furnaces an ON-OFF control will show clearly in the record of any but the most precisely balanced sample and thermocouple assemblies; this objection would not apply to thermogravimetric furnaces. The application of line voltage to a cold winding is generally without serious consequences to the winding, but the sudden heating of this winding may very well cause other troubles. A winding directly on a ceramic tube, for example, may crack the tube after repeated use of an ON-OFF controller. Once the furnace is hot this problem ceases to exist. When the tube is already hot the sudden heating of an area a couple of hundred degrees is not serious, but the sudden heating of a small area to a thousand degrees higher than the neighboring area causes severe strains in any material.

A platinum or platinum alloy furnace winding would also rule out a simple ON-OFF control because of the high-temperature coefficient of resistance. A winding designed to dissipate 1000 watts at 1500°C will dissipate roughly 2500 watts at room temperature. One may safely assume that somewhere along the winding there will be a point at which the rapidly heating wire cannot dissipate heat to its surroundings rapidly enough to keep the wire temperature below its melting point. In a matter of a few seconds the winding burns out.

Another result which will arise in differential thermal analysis but not in thermogravimetric analysis from the use of an ON-OFF controller is electrical interference. Switching of currents in the 5–20 amp range in the general vicinity of a system measuring a few tens of microvolts is an invitation to trouble on two counts. If the power supply and the recording system are fed from the same supply line there is likely to be a very decidedly noticeable change in line voltage. This will affect recorders which are not strictly null balance potentiometers or moving-coil galvanometers. Specifically it can and generally will affect recorders which measure voltage drop across a resistor. The other source of electrical interference is electromagnetic radiation; i.e., the making and breaking of the contacts with the incident sparking transmits a damped wave which has fairly high intensity close by. [The author has had interference from a percentage timer on a cam-drive motor (½ amp) in spite of shielded thermocouples, a null balance recording potentiometer, and a regulated and isolated power supply.] This radio-frequency wave can be picked up as a very high-level noise signal within the recorder-amplifier circuit where the input filter has no effect.

To summarize, ON-OFF controllers are generally not suitable for thermal analysis. They should certainly not be used in any system in which low-level electrical signals are to be measured. They should not be used with a furnace having a helical winding directly on a ceramic tube. Since they are inexpensive and will for this reason be considered in design of apparatus, a positive set of limitations is in order. ON-OFF controllers may be used in a slow-response system where the temperature fluctuations of the winding are not felt appreciably at the sample. They may be used when the measurement does not make use of a low-level electrical signal or when this signal is measured on a galvanometer or similar instrument; hence they may be used for thermogravimetry with most recording systems, or high-temperature X-ray diffraction or the like, or even for differential thermal analysis if one is using samples gross enough to permit direct recording from base metal differential thermocouples.

If the designer of an apparatus decides that an ON-OFF supply cannot be used he still has several possible systems of varying the furnace power. The next simplest is an adjustable autotransformer. The adjustable autotransformer is nearly as versatile as the ON-OFF controller; i.e., it needs to fit the largest demand but will supply smaller currents equally well. It can be used very satisfactorily on much more rapidly responding systems than the ON-OFF controller since the voltage output will change no more than a few volts at a time. It is far less likely to cause electrical interference because the moving of the contact from one turn to the next only exchanges a shorted turn for a lesser but significant load, or vice versa. The only disadvantage of the adjustable autotransformer is the discrete increments of voltage and this disadvantage manifests itself only on rapid-response systems. The effect on rapid-response systems will be to cause a wavy base line when a low-level signal is being measured and if there is some thermal asymmetry in the sample block. In summary, the adjustable autotransformer is a good general purpose power supply which may be used with any but very rapid-response systems.

> We will use the adjustable autotransformer as the general example in this chapter partly because it is a useful device and partly because the planning of cam drives for other power supplies is rather similar.

The adjustable autotransformer must be compared with two continuously adjustable systems, the thyratron and the saturable-core reactor. These three systems have a wide enough range of applicability that for many applications any one of the three is quite satisfactory.

The thyratron may be turned down to zero output like the adjustable autotransformer but it cannot step up the voltage as the autotransformer can; in fact there is a loss of a few volts at maximum power and this must be taken into account when designing the furnace. The voltage variation is continuous rather than in discrete steps. It may be selected on the basis of maximum demand without sacrifice of performance at lower powers. The author's experience is that a silicon controlled rectifier (solid-state thyratron) power supply is an excellent power supply.

The saturable-core reactor is similar to the thyratron in that the voltage variation is continuous and there is a small voltage drop at maximum power. It has two interrelated disadvantages, the nonzero turndown and its need to be matched to the load to provide suitable control. This means that if one uses a significantly different furnace than the reactor was designed to supply one must replace the reactor or make other adaptations. This adaptation would usually take the form of a dummy load, just a resistor dissipating the difference between the actual and the rated load. If the new furnace requires a greater power input than the reactor can control, a new reactor is obviously required; a reactor wound to control a 500-watt load and having a 10-volt internal drop would have a drop nearly three times as large if a 1500-watt load were substituted. The dissipation within the reactor would be about eight times as large and the reactor windings would likely burn out the first time the control system called for full power.

In summary, the saturable-core reactor is a perfectly good control system for apparatus in which the heating requirements are not likely to be changed greatly and in which the nonzero turndown is of no consequence. For research instrumentation, in which different sized loads may be used, its use is ill-advised.

For most purposes the designer of an apparatus should by now have a reasonably firm concept of the right controller for his particular system. If special problems do not lead to special ways of heating (Chapter VIII) one of the systems discussed above should perform quite satisfactorily. For a general purpose research apparatus the author favors the solid-state thyratron. The author is well-aware that in the assembly of an apparatus it is sometimes expedient to compromise for reasons of price, delivery, and availability of packaged subassemblies. Such a compromise may now be made with some fairly accurate knowledge of the consequences.

17.5. Program Controllers

Several general modes of control are used: linear (with time) voltage increase, programmed voltage increase, programmed temperature increase, linear (with time) temperature increase, and variations approximating the last.

The first-named program control is generally a motor and gear train attached to an adjustable autotransformer. The gears are selected and arranged to drive the autotransformer at a speed calculated to reach maximum voltage (end of travel) not long after the temperature limit is reached. These are interdependent quantities and must be guessed ahead of time with some provision for closer approximation after the system is tested. Since the designer can only estimate his power requirements for any reasonably fast heating rate, he has presumably left a margin of safety and expects to reach his maximum planned temperature at the desired heating rate when the voltage output is 120–125 volts out of the possible 135 volts. He must now plan his autotransformer drive to reach 120–125 volts at the time his furnace is supposed to reach the temperature limit, with some provision for adjustment after trial. This adjustment will be a gear change for precise and reproducible changes but may be a proportional timer for approximations. The rate of heating may be varied in the same ways—reproducible changes by gear changes, approximation with a percentage timer.

A programmed voltage increase would generally take the form of a nonuniformly driven autotransformer, i.e., $d\theta/dT \neq$ constant. The variable rate of adjustment of the shaft angle, θ, may be the deliberate imposition of grossly nonuniform heating or it may be an attempt to obtain a constant temperature rise with a simple program and control system.

Since the dissipated power, W, is equal to E^2/R, a uniform rate of voltage increase will give a nonuniform power increase. On the other hand the conduction losses are roughly proportional to the temperature, so this effect modifies the nonlinearity of temperature rise which the first effect causes. With furnaces having hot outside walls the radiation loss (proportional to T^4) will have a further modifying effect at high temperature. Obviously, a furnace and a uniformly ($d\theta/dT =$ constant) driven autotransformer which yield a linearly (with time) increasing temperature within the furnace is a purely fortuitous combination. For this reason the rate of drive of the autotransformer may need to be modified to compensate for those effects.

Any modification of the drive speed must be established for a given type of furnace. Any given modification is likely to be impractical if two or more types of furnaces must be driven from the same program controller. The deliberate gross modification, such as a discontinuous change in heating rate, is quite practical.

The programmed or linearly driven autotransformer supplies power to a furnace at a rate not directly related to the temperature within that furnace. There must necessarily be a means of cutting off power unless the furnace can operate indefinitely at the maximum supply voltage. Two limiting devices may immediately be suggested: an adjustable limit on the travel of the autotransformer or, preferably, an adjustable limit switch on the temperature recorder.

In summary, both kinds of voltage drive have the serious disadvantage that their action is not related to the quantity (temperature) being changed. They can provide a nondiscontinuous rise in temperature with smooth changes in heating rate, except for very low-lag furnaces. A simple motor-driven autotransformer is the least expensive system by which a reasonable and somewhat nearly reproducible heating rate may be obtained. It is extremely sensitive to line voltage fluctuations, as can be seen from the derivative, $dW/dE = 2E/R$.

An infrequently occurring source of error with these controls is long-term supply voltage fluctuation. Commercial power systems should be quite stable; a few institutional systems with large daily variations may remain. [One university had a system so heavily overloaded that a graduate student is reported to have had to make measurements only in the early Sunday morning hours (before 6 o'clock) because this was the only time the voltage was reasonably nearly constant.]

Programmed temperature increase and linear (with time) temperature increase are generally accomplished with driven set points or variations on the latter. A common form of the driven set point is the temperature indicator or strip chart recorder with an additional index pen. This index pen is driven across the scale according to a schedule and its position is constantly compared with that of the temperature pen. Their relative positions determine the signal sent to the controller and hence the signal to the power supply.

Consider a case in which the designer of the apparatus expects to need 1100°C maximum and a heating rate of 10°C/minute. Assume that he knows that the voltage input to his furnace must be 120 volts at the time the sample reaches 1100°C at an average rate of 10°C/minute. Since this is slightly higher than ordinary line voltage, the usual 115 volt input, 0–135 volt output connections will be used. The transformer must travel eight-ninths of its span in 110 minutes but its span is about 320° or eight-ninths of a full circle. The autotransformer must then turn

$$\frac{8 \text{ revolutions}}{9} \times \frac{120 \text{ volts}}{135 \text{ volts}} \times \frac{1}{110 \text{ minutes}},$$

1 revolution/140 minutes.

Low-speed motors are large and expensive; gears are easily selected and used. The designer selects a set of gears to reduce the, say, 1800 revolutions/minute to 140 minutes/revolution. This 250,000 : 1 reduction is done in several steps, possibly including a commercial gear box or starting with a motor already geared down. This is the simplest arrangement. From this point, the designer begins to add features intended for protection of apparatus, for increased versatility, or for convenience in operation.

17.6. Auxiliary Components or Functions

These added features may include a number of the following as well as some others the author has not thought of.

SLIP CLUTCH

The slip clutch is a standard feature. It permits manual adjustment or reset of the variable autotransformer or any driven component.

POWER RELAY

The power relay is a useful device for enabling shutdown of power from a number of points and thus permits more flexible circuitry. A small current flow in the relay winding controls a much larger current through the contacts.

LIMIT SWITCH

The limit switch is one device used for terminating or changing the cycle. It may operate to stop the autotransformer drive, reverse the drive (see below), shut off all power, change the drive speed, or start a timer.

REVERSIBLE MOTOR

The reversible motor is useful generally in differential thermal analysis but has only occasional value in thermogravimetry. The programmed decrease in temperature would be instituted on operation of the limit switch (see above). A pair of limit switches could be arranged to cause the reversible motor to drive repeatedly up and down, providing a cycling between the preset limits.

PILOT OR INDICATOR LIGHTS

Indicator lights in various colors can serve a multitude of useful purposes. Essentially, they tell the operator—at a glance—what parts of the apparatus are or should be functioning. For example, in a simple system, lights on (1) the main switch, (2) the motor circuit, and (3) the furnace power circuit would immediately indicate (1) whether or not anything should be happening, (2) whether or not the programmer has reached its limit, and (3) whether or not there should be power supplied to the furnace.

Whether or not any of this information is trivial or superfluous depends on the circuit.

TEMPERATURE LIMIT SWITCH

Temperature-actuated adjustable switches may be obtained on many recorders. These may be used to shut off the furnace as a protection feature or used in place of the limit switches on the autotransformer drive.

INTERNAL TIMER

The timer may be used in place of the limit switch where protection is not an important requirement. The timer may also be used to shut down the apparatus when it is to be left unattended for long periods.

FUNCTION SWITCHES

A few switches wired to modify operation rather than only to turn it on or off can be very useful. A switch permitting the furnace either to remain hot or to cool when the program limit is reached, and one short-circuiting timer contacts or manually reversing the drive motor can add considerably to the utility of the apparatus.

PERCENTAGE TIMER

The percentage timer comprises a clock motor and a cam-operated switch designed so that the "closed time" of the switch is adjustable from a few per cent to 100% of the time. It is used generally to adjust heating rates or chart speeds, by opening and closing the motor circuit (Fig. XVII-3). It should not be used to control directly current flows more than a few tenths of an ampere in the vicinity of low-level signals such as in differential thermal analysis.

GEAR CHANGE

If the same program controller is used for several purposes, a gear change arrangement is essential. The operation of a percentage timer to slow down a driver motor is reasonably good, but for any high degree of reproducibility of a lower drive speed a known gear change is far superior and avoids an important source of noise.

METERS

A voltmeter to show that the controller is supplying a voltage and an ammeter to show that the furnace is using it will generally be enough.

With some control systems, the control signal may be shown instead. Saturable-core reactor and solid-state thyratron systems generally show only the control current.

RELAYS

Large furnace currents may require large switches. These switches may be so large that their presence on a control panel is inconvenient. The furnace power is better switched by use of a relay which in turn may be operated by use of a small switch. Use of a relay permits all sorts of switching devices to turn on or off the furnace power under specified conditions. Relay control of the operating power likewise permits a high degree of automatic control and, hence, untended operation.

For special circumstances, slow-acting or slow-releasing relays might be applicable. A more useful special type would be the time-delay relay which closes or opens a circuit after preset periods of time, less than 1 second on up.

THERMOCOUPLE BREAK PROTECTION

Occasionally thermocouples will fail and occasionally operators will fail to make proper connections. If the thermocouple involved is a control thermocouple, the system will call for heat with no indication when the control point is reached or exceeded. The usual result is a burned-out furnace.

To protect the equipment from such a mishap, a thermocouple break protection circuit is used. In essence, this circuit provides a false signal when a break occurs tending to drive the temperature indication upscale so that the control system will shut down the power. The break protection circuit (Fig. XVII–2) comprises, in its simplest form, a dry cell and a limiting resistor. The limiting resistor is so chosen that (a) the voltage drop across the indicating galvanometer will exceed the range of the meter or (b) the voltage drop across the amplifier input is sufficient to cause the motor to drive the slide-wire.

A galvanometer-type control unit will suffer a slight offset in its ordinary operation because the circuit must be capable of supplying, e.g., 10 to 50 mv to the meter. Through the comparatively low-resistance thermocouple, however, the drop is considerably smaller, so that the offset will generally be only a few degrees. Since the protection circuit only needs to supply a few microvolts to a potentiometric circuit, the presence of the circuit is unnoticeable. Note that any low-impedance connection across the thermocouple terminals renders the protection circuit inoperative. This means, first, that a short-circuited thermocouple or extension will still permit furnace burnout and, second, that connection of another measuring device to the same thermocouple will inactivate the protection.

The present author has found it expedient to add this protection circuit to his control equipment.

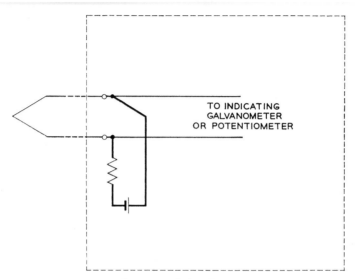

TO INDICATING
GALVANOMETER
OR POTENTIOMETER

Fɪɢ. XVII-2. Thermocouple break protection circuit.
In event of an open circuit outside the controller the low current from the battery circuit is sufficient to drive the temperature indication upscale to the limit. No protection against short-circuited thermocouples is provided.

17.7. Complete Assemblies

The various apparatus designed completely or partly by the author are described herein, not in a spirit of advocacy but as a reference or point of departure for a would-be designer. The reasons for the components will be offered so that the reader may pick and choose as fits his need or fancy. With the exception of the first thermobalance, each apparatus has been packaged in a metal (or, most recently, wood) cabinet designed specifically for that apparatus. The reader may suggest that this operation decreases the versatility of the several parts of the assembly. The author does not admit this to be a handicap. The "versatility" phase of the author's career ended when some interesting differential thermal analyses had to be postponed while some rather long thermogravimetric analyses were completed, the thermogravimetric and differential thermal analysis apparatus sharing the program controller and recorder at that time.

The design of an apparatus to do a multitude of operations is an eternal and personal challenge. Success would probably bring deep satisfaction. The result of such an attempt may be little more than a monument to the designer's conceit; it is per se an admission that there is not a potential significant need for any one of the several manifestations of the creation. The author prefers to assemble an apparatus to perform a particular function; if some additions can be made without interfering with its principal function and the additions extend its utility, well and good—as long as there is no compromise on its performance of its principal task. If the special characteristics of an apparatus are such that some portion can be used to great advantage in another type of apparatus, the author would choose an opportune time and convert the one apparatus to the other—to the extent of dismantling the first if necessary. If the second apparatus is successful, the question of reconverting or replacing components in the first can be argued on tenable grounds. The author is at the time of writing awaiting such a strategic moment to metamorphose an apparatus currently in his custody.

17.8. Thermobalance

The second thermobalance constructed by the author was, like the first (G3), a null balance driven chain instrument. The heater power is supplied through a motor-driven adjustable autotransformer. The control circuitry is shown in Fig. XVII-3. Since platinum-wound furnaces are used most of the time, the possibility of inadvertently supplying line voltage to the furnace must be avoided. This is done by use of a microswitch operated by a cam on the autotransformer shaft. The cam is positioned so that the microswitch is operated only while the output voltage is no more than about 4 volts. This switch closes the furnace relay circuit and, since a hold circuit is incorporated therein, the autotransformer may be turned up. The function of this arrangement is to require the operator to turn back the autotransformer manually before a supply voltage is available to the furnace. From then on the operator may adjust the voltage manually—the autotransformer being fitted with a slip clutch and the drive motor with a switch—or it may be increased at any of four standard speeds by use of two sets of gears. Any of these speeds may be further decreased, in a less reproducible manner, by setting of the percentage timer in the motor circuit.

In the absence of operator intervention the autotransformer is driven to higher voltage output until the adjustable limit on the temperature pen shaft is reached. The motor will stop driving or the entire furnace circuit will shut down at this point, depending on the position of the HEAT ONLY–HEAT AND HOLD switch. (Since this limit switch is the only device which automatically stops the autotransformer, the recorder is wired so that it is on at any time the furnace is on. It may also be turned on separately.)

On very extended runs, at heating rates, for example, of less than

1°C per minute, the strip chart record may be inconveniently long, so the chart drive is equipped with a percentage time to slow it down. For runs in which no record is necessary or in which there is an extended heating period with no weight loss the chart drive can be shut off completely.

The balance may be operated independently of the recorder since the recording circuit has no bearing on the balance operation. Since the recorder amplifier would tend to drive the weight-change pen off scale if no signal were applied, the recording circuit is supplied from the recorder rather than from the balance. The weight-change pen always reproduces the chain position whether or not the balance is operating.

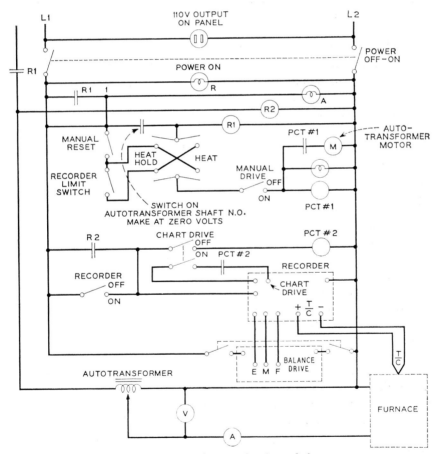

Fɪɢ. XVII-3. Control circuit for thermobalance.
A reasonably extensive choice of operations is available by the addition of a few components.

The chain-drive motor may also be shut off for occasional checking of the balance. A dummy load is substituted to avoid damage to the servo amplifier.

The entire unit is packaged in a metal cabinet fabricated for it. It comprises a box 36 inches high including the casters and resembles the cabinet of Fig. XVII-5. Of the 4-foot length slightly more than half is clear working space for the balance; the remainder is occupied by a permanently mounted box which contains the recorder, the switching, the electrical connections to the balance, and a drawer for storage of gears, sample holders, etc. Beneath this box are the autotransformer and its drive, the balance amplifier and adjusting potentiometer, the adjusting potentiometers for the recording circuit, and two percentage timers (autotransformer and chart). The speed change gear shafts for the autotransformer extend out the front of the cabinet. A hinged cover encloses the gears. This section of the cabinet is thermally insulated internally from the other side. The section under the balance contains the furnaces and their supports. These are small, well-insulated tube furnaces which hang from supports positioned beneath the balance pan hooks. The support wires for the sample holders pass through ¼-inch holes in the balance pans, the floor of the balance case, the base on which the balancing mechanism is mounted, and the top of the cabinet.

Access to the furnace compartment is by a door, latched at the top and hinged on rollers at the bottom, which may be swung down and pushed back to recess below the furnace compartment. Access to the other compartment and to the control and recording compartment above is by lift-out panels at the side and rear, respectively.

17.9. Differential Thermal Analysis Apparatus

The present differential thermal analysis equipment is an example of evolution of an apparatus. It began its existence in 1953 (G12) as a reasonably advanced design. The control and programming system (Fig. XVII-4) performed very well with the furnace used. For some time, the programming and recording equipment served a dual purpose since conversion of thermogravimetric use required physical addition only of an auxiliary slide-wire on the 5–0–5 millivolt pen shaft.

To use the apparatus for thermogravimetry the operator needed to: (a) plug in the thermogravimetric furnace in place of the differential thermal analysis furnace; (b) change gears to program at a lower rate; and (c) remove the amplifier input plug and substitute two single-lead plugs.

Similarly, when electrical resistance monitoring (G11) was more useful than thermal measurements, a resistance ratio bridge with supply voltage and adjustable resistances was packaged in a small box and attached to one side of the control panel. This could be put to use by (a) changing furnace leads and (b) replacing the differential thermocouple lead (at the amplifier input) with the output from the bridge. A zero-adjusting circuit was added at the comparatively high signal level between the amplifier and recorder. (This is feasible because the linear range of the amplifier extends well beyond its working range and this type of monitoring could use even the nonlinear range still further out.) (See Chapter IV, Sec. 4.3.)

At one point a copper-constantan range was added on the temperature pen to permit measurements below room temperature. This has sub-

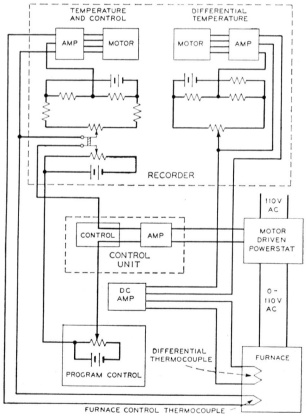

Fig. XVII-4. Block diagrams of control and recording apparatus for differential thermal analysis (G12).

The furnace control signal is also the recorded temperature signal.

sequently been changed to a Chromel-Alumel range so that the recorder now has a 0–1500°C Pt vs Pt-10% Rh range and a 0–1200°C Chromel vs Alumel range (selected by a switch) on one pen and a 5–0–5 millivolt range on the other pen. The reason for having two ranges so close together is not so much to gain accuracy in temperature measurement as to permit measurement from one of the differential thermojunctions whether base metal or Pt vs Pt-Rh couples were being used.

The apparatus was repackaged in a metal cabinet at about this point. An *X–Y* recorder was added for some special work. The cabinet provided a reasonably centralized control system with at least as convenient access to the various components as before. It also provided a work area directly associated with the furnaces. This was concurrent with the change to the Lodding–Hammell (L10) type of furnace so that a relatively small table-top area was sufficient.

The advent of effluence analysis—made practicable by the Lodding–Hammell technique—brought new needs and, hence, new instrumentation. It is clearly inconvenient and a source of error to measure two dependent variables on two separate recorders and subsequently relate both records to temperature; further, repetitive gas chromatography of the effluence was planned, and this has distinctly different chart speed requirements. To permit simultaneous recording from differential thermocouples and a gas density detector, a Leeds and Northrup two-pen *X–Y* recorder was added in place of the single-pen *X–Y* recorder. This X_1, X_2 vs Y recorder plots, when needed, both the differential temperature and the differential gas density against temperature. The temperature drive has a fixed 0–1500°C Pt vs Pt–10% Rh range and a second range governed by a range-change card similar to that used by Leeds and Northrup in their Speedomax Model H. The two X ranges are 1 and 10 mv with live end point, both slide-wires being equipped with switches to center the zero point or move it to the left margin.

To make room for this recorder, the amplifier disappeared into the cabinet (Fig. XVII-5) where it is set on its side in such a position that the range switch may be operated conveniently by use of a jointed rod connecting the knob on the front with the switch on the chassis. The range-change switch operates at low signal levels and should be left encased in the amplifier chassis. The output switch could be removed easily from its panel position so it is mounted directly on the cabinet. The *X–Y* recorder was completely removed from service with this differential thermal analysis apparatus.

The removal of these two units provided space not only for the new recorder but also for a drawer. This drawer is a very worthwhile addition to the apparatus. It is used to store change gears for recorder or

Fig. XVII-5. Differential thermal analysis apparatus.
The lower recorder can record ΔT and another function vs T. The upper recorder plots ΔT and T against time.

programmer, pen cleaners, sample holders, sample blocks, thermocouples, thermocouple extension leads, a pencil, spare nuts and O-rings, as well as miscellaneous items. Another useful addition was an electrical outlet for using soldering irons or an electronic voltohmmeter.

A connector panel was added more recently—after changing to frequent use of commercial shielded thermocouples. This is wired to permit connection of the differential thermocouples to the control and recording circuits when desired. The plugs in the center row are connected to the sample and reference plugs below so that patch cords can be plugged into center and top rows, thus connecting reference and sample thermocouples with control and recording circuits. This is by no means a necessary condition, since most of the furnaces have or can be fitted with thermocouples in special wells near the winding and several of the furnace bases have a third thermocouple. (The term "most of the furnaces" can be taken literally. Obviously, when one is experienced in the art, furnaces can be designed and wound cheaply. Experimenting with furnace design is therefore not only possible but practical. On the other hand, acquiring this degree of experience can be expensive.) The several furnace bases represent two adapted from the Lodding–Hammell concept and various experimental special purpose types. The one shown in Fig. XVII-6 is used for closed-chamber differential thermal analysis of small samples (Fig. VIII-5). These special purpose bases are essentially devices for holding one or more ceramic tubes so that one or two sample holders can be positioned in the hot zone. In the example given, two stainless steel–shielded thermocouples with exposed #36 Chromel-Alumel junctions are led through a two-hole, $\frac{1}{4}$ inches OD, $\frac{3}{32}$ inches ID, alumina tube. This tube is held by the base so that the samples are held at the selected level in the furnace. The sample and reference materials are placed in tubes (closed at one end) which fit rather snugly over the thermocouple shield. These are slid over the thermocouples— lifting the base from its stand and tilting the assembly to avoid spilling— so that the thermocouple bead is buried in the sample or reference material (see Chapter VIII). For some work, a block—resembling an inverted sample block—is set on top to equalize temperatures as much as possible.

The control connection on the thermocouple panel goes to the senior recorder for a very good reason: the temperature pen shaft of that recorder is equipped with a slide-wire which is a basic part of the control system (see above). The author considers a time-based temperature recorder to be a necessary part of any differential thermal analysis apparatus (see Chapters V & XVI). The second pen of this recorder may be used with the chromatograph so that, when repetitive chromatography is being done on the effluent gas from a furnace, the qualitiative data may be referred to the temperature at the time of sampling, thus permitting better identification of the reaction products with the thermal effect (see Chapter XV).

The most recent important change in the apparatus has been in the control system. The adoption of rapid-response furnaces led to a troublesome cycling effect on the temperature difference signal when some special techniques—and high amplification—were used. This is a natural occurrence for control systems using adjustable autotransformers since the voltage changes are necessarily discrete. A new control unit and a solid-state thyratron power supply were substituted for the old unit and the adjustable autotransformer. The program unit and the recorder were unchanged. Since all the furnaces had been designed for 0–135 volt operation, some would not heat satisfactorily at 0–115 volts. The 115-volt supply had to be led into an autotransformer and the stepped-up voltage (135 volts) fed into the power supply. This power supply is far more rapid in response and, with the present furnaces, gives a much more nearly linear heating rate than the adjustable autotransformer.

Since the photograph was made an adjustable-zero circuit has been added, along with switching to permit recording the amplifier output on the X,X vs Y, the X,X vs t, or both recorders while shorting the input of either recorder not in use. This arrangement permits recording of the differential signal as a function of temperature, time, or both. Also, a thermoelectric device which gives a small direct current indication of an alternating current or voltage was connected to the output of the power supply. This provides a convenient method of recording power input to the furnace.

17.10. Controlled Atmosphere Thermobalance

Because of the frequent need for controlled atmosphere thermogravimetry another thermobalance was constructed. Basically it was a commercial automatic recording balance (Ainsworth RV-AU2) fitted with a pair of furnaces (Fig. XVII-6). The balance was purchased as a semimicrobalance but the behavior was initially so erratic—apparently due to convection—in any appreciable atmospheres that it was converted to ordinary analytical range operation. The problem of significant convection currents was diminished by introduction of a series of plates between the hot zone and the balance chamber. These served both as barriers to passage of streams of hot or cold gases (convection) and as radiation shields in vacuum operation. The support wire passed through a $\frac{1}{4}$-inch hole in the center of each.

The arrangement was suitable for rather limited work but for general

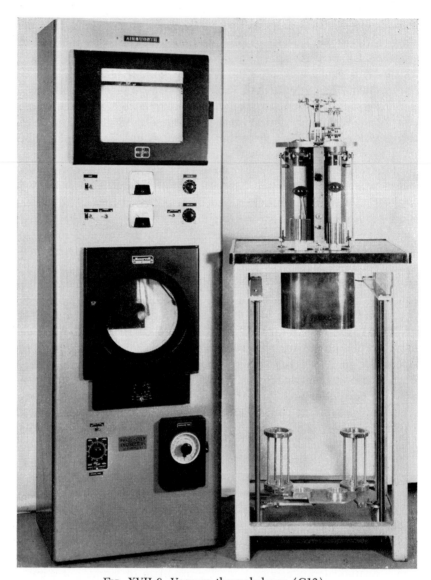

FIG. XVII-6. Vacuum thermobalance (G13).

The furnace support arrangement permitted easy operation of the balance even with the long furnace tubes. The apparatus was subsequently converted to a top-loading arrangement.

high-temperature work at near-atmospheric pressure its operation was "noisy" so the assembly has subsequently been converted very successfully to top-loading (see Chapter IX). A metal dome was formed and fitted to receive furnaces rather similar to the differential thermal analysis furnaces. A 12-inch metal ring was grooved to take an O-ring on each side and so provide a vacuum seal between the dome and the base. Two counterweighted support tubes were hung from the beam; the lower ends hanging in brass tubes were connected to the furnace openings in the base. The upper ends were ceramic tubes; thermocouple wires were led through one of the tubes and joined at the top and so that the sample holder sat directly on the bead. Connection is made to these thermocouple wires in the manner used by Reisman (R12) (see Chapter X). The sample temperature is recorded and occasionally programmed (see Chapter XV); generally the furnace is programmed.

The control power is supplied through the contacts of relay No.1 (Fig. XVII-7). This relay winding is wired through another set of contacts to provide a "hold" circuit. Any momentary break in the relay circuit will permit the relay to "drop out" and remain in the nonoperated condition until the operator again pushes the Main Power ON button. This momentary contact button is in parallel with the hold contacts and so completes the relay winding circuit. The circuit may be interrupted and the power shut off by the Main Power OFF button or by opening all four parallel sets of contacts in the "lockup" mechanism in such a manner that they are all open at the same time. This is discussed later. (A limit switch was later added on the temperature pen shaft.)

With the main power on, the balance and furnace may be turned on. The interval and percentage timer motors and the cam driver in the program unit are now supplied with power. The program and control units are left on simply because electronic equipment will normally function better if left on. This is not done with all equipment because of the problem of attacking components internally to separate the functions which must be shut off from those which may remain on.

The furnace relay switches on the moving contact of the variable autotransformer rather than on the primary supply to avoid the surges of power that occur when line voltage is suddenly connected to a transformer which has a sizable load on its secondary. The voltmeter and ammeter monitor only one of the two furnaces with the expectation that the other similarly wound furnace will differ only negligibly. The principal function of the second furnace is to permit buoyancy compensation so the temperature need only be approximately the same. If differential thermogravimetry were to be attempted, a second controller would be used (see Chapter X).

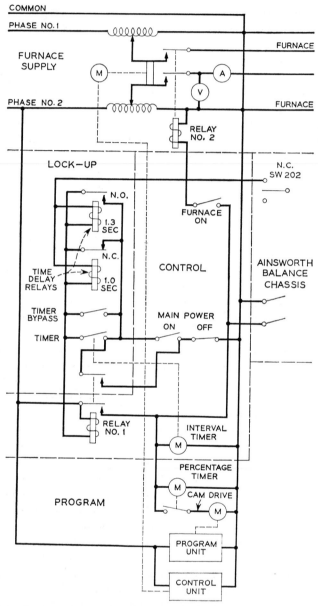

FIG. XVII-7. Circuit diagram for control system. From Garn *et al.* (G13). *The lockup circuit permits extensive unattended operation. The program could be terminated by a temperature limit switch as well as by the timer.*

The automatic lockup mechanism of the balance operates to lift the beam from the knife edges and reset it, compensating for any displacement due to building vibration. The present author devised a way to use this mechanism to assist in timed automatic shutdown.

The lockup, in addition to the parts of the manual lockup and the timing mechanism, comprises a motor geared to a wheel fitted with an eccentric pin which slides a shaft which, in turn, operates the manual lockup. The beam is lifted about 0.8 second after the start of the cycle and is released again about 1.8 seconds after the start of the cycle. The electrical impulse which initiates the lockup cycle remains on for about 15 seconds. These conditions require that shutdown occur during—and only during—this 1-second interval. This is done with a pair of electronic time-delay relays and a hold circuit on the power relay. The relay may be released from the main power switch or the shutdown circuit.

When the shutdown circuit is not in use the time-delay relays are bypassed by the timer bypass switch. When the timer circuit is in use the time-delay relays are bypassed by the timer contacts until the expiration of the preset time. When the timer contacts open the relay hold current passes through the time-delay relay contacts so that when they are next activated the thermobalance is shut down with the balance beam locked up.

The time-delay relay circuit opens the hold circuit 1.0 second and closes it 1.3 seconds after the lockup cycle is initiated. The circuit closure is necessary to avoid shutdown while the initiating signal is still on (15 seconds) but the beam has been restored to its operating position. Runs of a couple of days duration have been terminated—generally on a weekend—without operator attention.

17.11. Another Differential Thermal Analysis Apparatus

The apparatus in use by the author at the time of publication is similar in many ways to the previous design. It has a cam-programmed silicon controlled rectifier power supply, but the Leeds and Northrup Series 60 control unit has with it a Speedomax H recorder, so the control system is independent of the recording system. As first choice, a two-pen X_1, X_2 vs T recorder was used.

If long-duration experiments are needed, an X–Y recorder will be installed. The use of a ΔT vs T plot is now feasible since the temperature program is being monitored independently. The programming thermocouple would be moved nearer the sample and the *proportional band* and the *rate* and *reset* actions of the controller readjusted; the change of thermocouple position would provide a better measure of the sample temperature and the readjustment would be necessary because the furnace temperature—at the point of measurement—would not be responding as quickly as before.

The temperature pen shaft of the recorder is equipped with a switch by which the chart only moves when the pen is *on-scale*. This permits the substitution of a small millivolt range and biasing the temperature signal *off-scale*. This, in turn, allows measurement of a small part of a long run, conserving paper and space, without sacrificing the advantages of time-based recording. One use planned for this arrangement involves the study of an inorganic reaction in the 900°C range. A 5.0-mv range card would provide a span of about 125°C full scale. Biasing the measuring circuit with 37 mv would permit recording from just below 900°C to slightly above 1000°C. With a moderately fast chart speed, good peak area measurements can be obtained.

The amplifier is connected directly to the line and left on. This minimizes drift which would be most marked during warm-up.

A rectifier and voltage-dividing potentiometer are wired to an independent manual input control for the power supply. This permits the setting of a repeatable voltage input to the furnace quite separate from the normal control functions.

Two pressure gauges and a regulator are mounted on the panel and some flowmeters will be added. These are interconnected with polyethylene and /or nylon tubing with fittings which allow easy interchange of connections. The interchange of connecting tubing is not quite as easy as manipulating a number of valves but this approach consumes less space and design time and presents a lesser number of places which may leak.

The controlling recorder has two switches operated by the pen shaft. One is used as a limit switch. It is wired into the *hold* circuit of the main relay so that if the switch opens the whole apparatus quietly ceases to operate. This switch is normally set at the furnace limit but may be set at some lower value to prevent—for example—the melting of certain kinds of samples. The second switch is used as a function switch and may be set to stop the program drive and hold the temperature, to reverse the drive to allow the furnace to cool, to shut off the furnace while leaving the recorder on, or to shut down the whole apparatus.

The electrical and plumbing gear are all mounted in a plywood cabinet (stained to match the laboratory furniture) and the furnace assembly is fastened to the side. The several connections are brought out at positions which allow easy connection to whatever furnace assembly is in use. The wooden box not only presents an electrical advantage but also makes possible very easy modification. New components can be added without the aid of a machinist. The whole apparatus is mounted on casters.

A gas density detector is being added for effluence detection and analysis (Chapter XIV). If repetitive chromatographic analyses are undertaken, most of that equipment will be housed separately.

17.12. Summary

The design of an experimental apparatus requires a background of experience and knowledge gained principally firsthand (as by the author) or vicariously (as by the reader). Once the small nucleus has been chosen with the help of the first fourteen chapters, these last three will aid in design of the portion greater in bulk and cost.

Two thermobalances and two differential thermal analysis assemblies are described, along with miscellaneous parts or functions that may be of use.

References

(A1) Adler, H. H., and Puig, J. A., Thermal behavior of brannerite. *Am. Mineralogist* **46**, 1086–1096 (1961).

(A2) Agafonoff, V., Mineralogical study of soil. *Trans. 3rd Intern. Congr. Soil Sci., Oxford* pp. 74–78 (1935).

(A3) Aliev, B. D., and Aliev, G. M., Effect of the addition of cadmium on the thermal and electrical conductivity of selenium. *Izv. Akad. Nauk Azerb. SSR, Ser. Fiz.-Mat. i Tekhn. Nauk* **5**, 85–90 (1960).

(A4) Allison, E. B., Quantitative thermal analysis of clay minerals. *Clay Minerals Bull.* **2**, 242–254 (1955).

(A5) Anderson, A. C., Salinger, G. L., and Steyert, W. A., Specific heat and thermal boundary resistance of liquid helium-3. *Phys. Rev. Letters* **6**, 331–334 (1961).

(A6) Anderson, D. A., and Freeman, E. S., Characterization of saturated polyesters by differential thermal analysis. *Anal. Chem.* **31**, 1697–1700 (1959).

(A7) Anderson, D. A., and Freeman, E. S., Differential thermal analysis of potassium per chlorate. *Nature* **195**, No. 4848; **196**, No. 4849, p. 1297 (1962).

(A8) Anderson, H. C., Differential thermal analysis of epoxide reactions. *Anal. Chem.* **32**, 1592–1595 (1960).

(A9) Anderson, H. C., Differential thermogravimetry versus differential thermometry in studying the pyrolysis of polymers. *Nature* **191**, 1088–1089 (1961).

(A10) Andrianov, K. A., and Manucharova, I. F., Study of polyorgano siloxanes and polyorgano elemento siloxanes thermostability using the method of differential thermal analysis. *Izv. Akad. Nauk SSSR, Otd. Khim. Nauk* No. 3, pp. 420–424 (1962).

(A11) Anikin, A. G., and Dugacheva, G. M., Determination of small heat effects by a thermographic method at temperatures below 0-deg. *Dokl. Akad. Nauk SSSR* **135**, 634–637 (1960).

(A12) Arens, P. L., "A Study of the Differential Thermal Analysis of Clays and Clay Minerals." Excelsiors Foto-Offsets, 1951.

(A13) Ariesan, V., Ionescu, C., Tilinca, A., Cojocaru, Z., and Pitea, M., Application of the micro thermal method in the study of certain binary barbiturate-alkaloid systems. *Farmacia (Bucharest)* **9**, 65–73 (1961).

536

(A14) Arsenan, D. F., The differential thermal analysis of wood. *Can. J. Chem.* **39**, 1915–1919 (1961).

(A15) Arutiunova, L. B., and Ravich, G. B., Combined micro thermal and spectroscopic investigation of polymorphism among higher fatty acids. *Dokl. Akad. Nauk SSSR* **135**, 837–839 (1960).

(A16) Asaba, T., and Hikita, T., Thermal decomposition of lithium perchlorate. *Kogyo Kagaku Zasshi* **63**, 1890–1893 (1960).

(A17) Ashby, G. E., and Kellagher, R. C., An apparatus for the study of thermoluminescence from minerals. *Am. Mineralogist* **43**, 695–706 (1958).

(A18) Austin, J. B., Thermal expansion of nonmetallic crystals. *J. Am. Ceram. Soc.* **35**, 243–253 (1952).

(A19) Ayres, W. M., and Bens, E. M., Differential thermal studies with simultaneous gas evolution profiles. *Anal. Chem.* **33**, 568–572 (1961).

(B1) Bachelet, M., and Christen, M., Effect of renewing the atmosphere on the thermal decomposition of calcium carbonate. *Compt. Rend.* **251**, 2961–2963 (1960).

(B2) Balandin, A. A., Tolstopyatova, A. A., and Kokenko, I. R., Catalytic conversion of iso propyl alcohol and hydrocarbons on titanium di oxide (anatase) using differential thermocouple. *Izv. Akad. Nauk SSSR, Otd. Khim. Nauk* pp. 2096–2102 (1960).

(B3) Balarew, D., Z. *Anorg. Chem.* **160**, 92 (1927).

(B4) Balygin, I. E., Transformation of amorphous quartz into crystalline during thermal diffusion of silver. *Kristallografiya* **6**, 727–732 (1961).

(B5) Barney, J. E., Remote operation of single-pan balance for weighing in inert atmospheres. *Anal. Chem.* **33**, 1294–1295 (1961).

(B6) Barnier, Y., Pauthenet, R., and Rimet, G., Thermal variation of the anisotropy constants and the spontaneous magnetization of cobalt in the hexagonal phase. *Compt. Rend.* **252**, 2839–2841 (1961).

(B7) Barrall, E. M., and Rogers, L. B., Differential thermal analysis of organic samples. Effects of geometry and operating variables. *Anal. Chem.* **34**, No. 9, 1101–1105 (1962).

(B8) Barrall, E. M., and Rogers, L. B., Differential thermal analysis of organic compounds. Effects of diluting agents. *Anal. Chem.* **34**, No. 9, 1106–1110 (1962).

(B9) Barshad, I., Temperature and heat of reaction calibration of the differential thermal analysis apparatus. *Am. Mineralogist* **37**, 667–694 (1952).

(B10) Bartenev, G. M., and Kongarov, G. S., Dilatometric determination of polymer compatibility. *Vysokomolekul. Soedin.* **2**, 1692–1697 (1960).

(B11) Barthomeuf, D., Perrin, M., and Trambouze, Y., Study of the exothermal phenomenon detected in silica-alumina gels during their thermal evolution. Test of the generalization. *Compt. Rend.* **252**, 4154–4156 (1961).

(B12) Bartlett, E. S., and Williams, D. N., Continuous recording laboratory thermobalance. *Rev. Sci. Instr.* **28**, 919–921 (1957).

(B13) Barton, C. J., Friedman, H. A., Grimes, W. R., Insley, H., Moore, R. E., and Thoma, R. E., Phase equilibriums in the alkali fluoride-uranium tetrafluoride fused salt systems. I. The systems $LiF–UF_4$ and $NaF–UF_4$. *J. Am. Ceram. Soc.* **41**, 63–69 (1958).

(B14) Basden, K. S., Fluidized bed differential thermal analysis. *Fuel* **39**, 270–272 (1960).

(B15) Basden, K. S., Low temperature reactions in fluidized-bed coal pyrolysis. *Fuel* **39**, 359–360 (1960.)

(B16) Bates, L. F., and Barnard, R. D., Electrical resistivities and magnetic susceptibilities of some stable and metastable uranium-molybdenum alloys. *Proc. Phys. Soc. (London)* **77**, 691–699 (1961).

(B17) Baumann, E. W., Thermal decomposition of amberlite IRA-400. *J. Chem. Eng. Data* **5**, 376–382 (1960).

(B18) Bayliss, P., and Warne, S. S. J., Effects of the controllable variables on differential thermal analysis. *Am. Mineralogist* **47**, 775–778 (1962).

(B19) Beams, J. W., Hulburt, C. W., Lotz, W. E., Jr., and Montague, R. M., Jr., Magnetic suspension balance. *Rev. Sci. Instr.* **26**, 1181 (1955).

(B20) Beck, C. W., Differential thermal analysis curves of carbonate minerals. *Am. Mineralogist* **35**, 985–1013 (1950).

(B21) Beckett, R., and Winfield, M. E., The thermal decomposition of thorium oxalate. *Australian J. Sci. Res.* **A4**, 644–650 (1951).

(B22) Beech, D. G., and Holdridge, D. A., Testing clays for the pottery industry. *Trans. Brit. Ceram. Soc.* **53**, 103–133 (1954).

(B23) Behl, W. K., and Gaur, H. C., Differential thermal analysis of magnesium chloride hydrates. *Proc. Natl. Inst. Sci. India* **27A**, 33–37 (1961).

(B23a) Belcher, R., Erdey, L., Paulik, F., and Liptay, G., A derivatographic study of potassium hydrogen phthalate. *Talanta* **5**, 53–57 (1960).

(B24) Belov, K. P., and Nikitin, S. A., Low-temperature transformation in the crystal of manganese ferrite. *Kristallografiya* **5**, 726–731 (1960).

(B25) Beretka, J., Differential thermal analysis of yttrium iron garnet. *Phys. Chem. Solids* **24**, 169–170 (1963).

(B25a) Berg, L. G., Influence of salt admixtures upon dissociation of dolomite. *Compt. Rend. Acad. Sci. URSS* **38**, 24–27 (1943).

(B26) Berg, L. G., On area measurements in thermogram for quantitative estimation and the determination of heats of reaction. *Compt. Rend. Acad. Sci. URSS* **49**, 648–51 (1945).

(B27) Berg, L. G., New method of physicochemical investigation of phases in mixtures. *Izv. Sek. Fiz.-Khim. Anal., Inst. Obshch. i Neorg. Khim. Akad. Nauk SSSR* **19**, 249–255 (1949).

(B28) Berg, L. G., Thermographic determination of the heat of phase transitions. *Tr. Pervogo Sov. Termogr. Kazan* pp. 59–66 (1953).

(B29) Berg, L. G., The thermographic investigation of some dehydration processes. *Izv. Kazan Filiala Akad. Nauk SSSR, Ser. Khim. Nauk* No. 4, 133–139 (1957); see *Chem. Abstr.* **54**, 6282 (1960).

(B30) Berg, L. G., and Burmistrova, N. P., Thermographic analysis of salts with simultaneous determination of temperature effects and electrical conductivity. *Zh. Neorg. Khim.* **5**, 676–683 (1960); see *Chem. Abstr.* **55**, 3261 (1961).

(B31) Berg, L. G., and Ganelina, S. G., Calcination of dolomite. *Izv. Kazan Filiala Akad. Nauk SSR, Ser. Khim. Nauk*, pp. 83–89 (1955); see *Chem. Abstr.* **51**, 18499 (1957).

(B32) Berg, L. G., Ganelina, S. G., Rassonskaya, I. S., and Teitel'baum, B. Ya., Improvements of methods of thermographic investigation. *Tr. Pervogo Sov. Termogr. Kazan* pp. 42–47 (1953).

(B33) Berg, L. G., Gromakov, S. D., and Zoroatskaya, I. V., An accelerated method of study of diagrams of state by means of thermography., *Dok. Akad. Nauk SSSR* **125**, 78–79 (1959).

(B34) Berg, L. G., Leperhkov, I. N., and Rassonskaya, I. S., Thermographic analysis of salts. *Tr. Pervogo Sov. Termogr. Kazan* pp. 171–181 (1953).

(B35) Berg, L. G., Mochalov, K. N., Kurenkova, P. A., and Amoshina, N. P., Thermogravimetric study of bromoplatnic acid. *Izv. Kazan Filial Akad. Nauk SSSR, Ser. Khim. Nauk* No. 4, 127–132 (1957); see *Chem. Abstr.* **54,** 5312 (1960).

(B36) Berg, L. G., and Rassonskaya, I. S., Rapid thermal analysis. *Dokl. Akad. Nauk SSSR* **73,** 113–115 (1950).

(B37) Berg, L. G., and Rassonskaya, I. S., Thermographic method of determination of dissociation pressure. *Izv. Sekt. Fiz.-Khim. Anal., Inst. Obshch. i Neorg. Khim. Akad. Nauk SSSR* **22,** 140–154 (1953); see *Chem. Abstr.* **52,** 3497 (1958).

(B38) Berg, L. G., Rassonskaya, I. S., and Buris, E. V., The thermographic dissociation pressure of some salts. *Izv. Sekt. Fiz.-Khim. Anal., Inst. Obshch. i Neorg. Khim. Akad. Nauk SSSR* **27,** 239–250 (1956); see *Chem. Abstr.* **50,** 15195 (1956).

(B39) Berg, L. G., and Yagfarov, M. Sh., The effect of some factors on the character of thermographic recording. *Tr. Pervogo Sov. Termogr. Kazan* pp. 53–58 (1953).

(B40) Berg, L. G., and Rassonskaya, I. S., Thermographic analysis at high pressures. *Dokl. Akad. Nauk SSSR* **81,** 855–858 (1951).

(B41) Berg, L. G., and Sidorova, E. E., Temperature conductivity determination by using the method of the differential thermal analysis with applications. *Bul. Inst. Politehn. Iasi* **5,** No. 9, 95–102 (1959).

(B42) Berg, P. W., Influence of the fine and coarse fractions of a clay on the results of differential thermal analysis. *Ber. Deut. Keram. Ges.* **30,** 231–235 (1953); see *Ceram. Abstr.* p. 133 (1954).

(B43) Berg, P. W., The influence of the size of the particles of clay on the results of the differential thermal analysis. *Kemisk* **34,** 49–54 (1953).

(B44) Bergeron, C. G., Russell, C. K., and Friedberg, A. L., Thermal analysis of lead borate glasses during crystallization. *J. Am. Ceram. Soc.* **46,** 246–247 (1963).

(B45) Bergstein, A., and Vintera, J., Thermal decomposition of manganese (II) carbonate. *Chem. Listy* **50,** 1530–1539 (1956).

(B46) Berkelhamer, L. H., An apparatus for differential thermal analysis. *U. S. Bur. Mines, Tech. Paper* **664,** 38–55; *U. S. Bur. Mines, Rept. Invest.* **3762** (1944).

(B47) Berlin, A., and Robinson, R. J., Thermo gravimetric determination of magnesium, potassium and lead by precipitation with dilituric acid. *Anal. Chim. Acta* **24,** 224–234 (1961).

(B48) Berlin, A., and Robinson, R. J., Thermo gravimetric determination of ethylene DI amine and quinine with dilituric acid solubilities of some poly methylene DI amine diliturates. *Anal. Chim. Acta* **24,** 319–328 (1961).

(B49) Berlin, A., and Robinson, R. J., Thermogravimetric analysis. Temperature limits and rate of heating. *Anal. Chim. Acta* **27,** 50–57 (1962).

(B50) Bernstein, L., and Beals, R. J., Thermal expansion and related bonding problems of some (III-V) compound semiconductors. *J. Appl. Phys.* **32,** 122–123 (1961).

(B50a) Biermann, W. J., and Heinrichs, M., A simple thermobalance for studies over a pressure range of 0 to 60 atmospheres. *Can. J. Chem.* **40,** 1361–1367 (1962).

(B51) Billmeyer, F. W., Jr., "Textbook of Polymer Science." Wiley (Interscience), New York, 1962.

(B52) Binnington, D. S., and Geddes, W. F., An automatic recording balance. *Ind. Eng. Chem., Anal. Ed.* **8**, 76–79 (1936).

(B53) Bishui, B. M., and Dhar, R. N., Indian mica. Effect of dry grinding on differential thermal analysis. *Central Glass Ceram. Res. Inst. (India) Bull.* **8**, 15–22 (1961).

(B54) Blau, M., and Carlin, J. R., Industrial applications of radioactivity. *Electronics* **21**, 78–82 (1948).

(B55) Blazek, A., *Silikaty* **1**, 158–163 (1957).

(B56) Blazek, A., Electronic thermobalance with simultaneous registration of differential thermal analysis curves and of curves of decomposition gas product analysis. *Hutnicke Listy* **12**, 1096–1102 (1957).

(B57) Blum, S. L., Paladino, A. E., and Rubin, L. G., Differential thermal analysis technique for determining Curie points. *Am. Ceram. Soc. Bull.* **36**, 175–177 (1957).

(B58) Boersma, S. L., A theory of differential thermal analysis and new methods of measurement and interpretation. *J. Am. Ceram. Soc.* **38**, 281–284 (1955).

(B59) Bohon, R. L., Differential thermal analysis of explosives and propellants under controlled atmospheres. *Anal. Chem.* **33**, 1451–1453 (1961).

(B60) Bohon, R. L., Approximate heats of explosion using differential thermal analysis. *Anal. Chem.* **35**, 1845–1852 (1963).

(B61) Bohon, R. L., Private communication (1964).

(B62) Bollin, E. M., Dunne, J. A., and Kerr, P. F., Differential thermal study of pyrosynthesis. *Science* **131** 661–662 (1960).

(B63) Bollmann, W., Phase transformation of cobalt., *Acta Met.* **9**, 972–974 (1961).

(B64) Bondarenko, A. V., Kiselev, V. F., and Krasil'nikov, K. G., Thermal dehydration of silica and certain properties of its surface. *Dokl. Akad. Nauk SSSR* **136**, 1133–1136 (1961).

(B65) Borchardt, H. J., Differential thermal analysis. An experiment for the physical chemistry laboratory. *J. Chem. Educ.* **33**, 103–107 (1956).

(B66) Borchardt, H. J., Initial reaction rates from differential thermal analysis. *J. Inorg. Nucl. Chem.* **12**, 252–254 (1960).

(B67) Borchardt, H. J., and Daniels, F., Application of differential thermal analysis to the study of reaction kinetics. *J. Am. Chem. Soc.* **79**, 41–46 (1957).

(B68) Borchardt, H. J., and Thompson, B. A., Reactions of solid alkaline earth oxides. I. BaO and SrO. *J. Am. Chem. Soc.* **81**, 4182 (1959).

(B69) Borchardt, H. J., and Thompson, B. A., Reactions of solid alkaline earth oxides. II. CaO and MgO. *J. Am. Chem. Soc.* **82**, 355–357 (1960).

(B70) Borchardt, H. J., and Thompson, B. A., Reactions of alkaline earth oxides. III. A re-examination of the Hedvall effect. *J. Am. Chem. Soc.* **82**, 5630–5632 (1960).

(B71) Bowen, C. H., Data for interpretation of differential thermal curves. *Eng. Expt. Sta. Ohio State Univ., Circ.* **56** (1954).

(B72) Bradley, W. F., Burst, J. F., and Graf, D. L., Crystal chemistry and differential thermal effects of dolomite. *Am. Mineralogist* **38**, 207–217 (1953).

(B73) Bragg, W. L., "Atomic Structure of Minerals." Cornell Univ. Press, Ithaca, New York, 1937.

(B74) van der Breggen, J. C., and Wouterlood, H. J., Novel displacement detector and its application in a recording thermobalance. *J. Sci. Instr.* **37**, 297 (1960).

(B75) Bretsznajder, S., Leyko, J., and Blum, A., Rate of nuclei formation of a new solid phase in the course of thermal dissociation of magnesium carbonate. *Bull. Acad. Polon. Sci., Ser. Sci. Chim.* **8**, 605–608 (1960).

(B76) Brewer, L., and Greene, F. T., Differential thermal analysis of the Si–SiO$_2$ system. *Phys. Chem. Solids* **2, 2868** (1957).

(B77) Brewer, L., and Savitsamos, P., A study of the Ge–GeO$_2$ system by an inductively heated DTA apparatus. *Phys. Chem. Solids* **2**, 284–285 (1957).

(B78) Brindley, G. W., "The Kaolin Minerals: X-ray Identification and Crystal Structures of Clay Minerals," pp. 32–75. Mineral. Soc., London, 1951.

(B79) Brindley, G. W., and Nakahira, M., The kaolinite-mullite reaction series: III, the high-temperature phases. *J. Am. Ceram. Soc.* **42**, 319–324 (1959).

(B80) Brindley, G. W., and Nakahira, M., X-ray diffraction and gravimetric study of the dehydration reactions of gibbsite. *Z. Krist.* **112**, 136 (1959).

(B81) Brockdorff, U. V., and Kirsch, K., *Electrotech. Z.* **71**, 611 (1950).

(B82) Brokaw, R. S., Thermal conductivity and chemical kinetics. *J. Chem. Phys.* **35**, 1569–1580 (1961).

(B83) Brown, F. E., Loomis, T. C., Peabody, R. C., and Woods, J. D., The design construction and some uses of an automatic recording balance. *Proc. Iowa Acad. Sci.* **59**, 159–169 (1952).

(B84) Brown, F. H., Jr., and Duwez, P., The systems zirconia-lanthana and zirconia-neodymia. *J. Am. Ceram. Soc.* **38**, 95–101 (1955).

(B85) deBruijn, C. M. A., and van der Marel, H. W., Mineralogical analysis of soil clays: I. Introduction and differential thermal analysis; II. Example of mineral analysis by X-ray diffraction and differential thermal analysis. *Geol. Mijnbouw* [N.S.] **16**, 69–83 and 407–428 (1954).

(B86) Bulgakova, T. I., and Zaitsev, O. S., Thermogravimetric investigation of the reaction of formation of a nickel-magnesium ferrite. *Vestn. Moskov. Univ., Ser. II: Khim.* **16**, No. 4, 33–35 (1961).

(B87) Bundy, F. P., Effect of pressure on EMF of thermocouples. *J. Appl. Phys.* **32**, 483–488 (1961).

(B88) Burriel-Marti, F., and Garcia-Clavel, M. E., Reactions between solids. Application of thermogravimetric analysis to the study of reactions between alkaline earth hydroxides and sulfates. *Anales Real. Soc. Espan. Fis. Quim.* (*Madrid*) **B57**, 99–104 (1961).

(B89) Burriel-Marti, F., and Garcia-Clavel, M. E., Application of the thermogravimetric method to dehydration problems. Hydrates of strontium and barium hydroxides. *Anales Real. Soc. Espan. Fis. Quim.* (*Madrid*) **B57,** 111–116 (1961).

(B90) Burriel-Marti, F., and Garcia-Clavel, M. E., New technique for the determination of the percentage of the reaction between two substances in the solid state. *Anales Real. Soc. Espan. Fis. Quim.* (*Madrid*) **B57**, 105–110 (1961).

(B91) Bussiere, P., Claudel, B., Renouf, J. P., Trambouze, Y., and Prettre, M., Study of solid phases by simultaneous use of thermogravimetry, differential thermal analysis, and the emanation method. *J. Chem. Phys.* **58**, 668–674 (1961).

(C1) Cabane, J., and Bernard, J., Role of diffusion in the thermal decomposition of alkali per chlorates. *Bull. Soc. Chim. France* pp. 36–40 (1961).

(C2) Caillère, S., and Hénin, S., Thermal analysis and its interpretation. *Trans. Intern. Ceram. Congr.*, **1948** pp. 137–150 (1948).

(C2a) Caillère, S., and Hénin, S., *in* "The Differential Thermal Investigation of Clays" (R. C. Mackenzie, ed.), pp. 207–230. Mineral. Soc., London, 1957.

(C3) Calvert, E., A new compensated differential microcalorimeter. *Compt. Rend.* **226**, 1702–1704 (1948).

(C4) Campbell, C., Gordon, S., and Smith, C. L., Derivative thermoanalytical techniques. *Anal. Chem.* **31**, 1188–1191 (1959).

(C5) Campbell, W. J., Thermal expansion of magnesium oxide—An interlaboratory study. *U. S. Bur. Mines, Rept. Invest.* **6115** (1962).

(C6) Caro, P., and Loriers, J., Thermolysis curves of some oxalates of rare earths. *J. Recherches Centre Natl. Recherche Sci. Lab. Bellevue (Paris)* **39**, 107–118 (1957).

(C7) Carpeni, G., Hamann, Y., Haladjian, J., and Perinet, G., Isohydric point. Isohydric polygermanate containing two potassium, five germanium, and eleven oxygens. Irreversible transformation of the solid phase in aqueous solutions. Electrometry, thermogravimetry, and X-rays. *Bull. Soc. Chim. France* pp. 1093–1908 (1960).

(C8) Cecil, O. B., and Koerner, W. E., Gas and heat evolution from thermally unstable materials. *Ind. Eng. Chem.* **53**, 475–478 (1961).

(C9) Chaly, V. P., and Shor, O. G., Thermographic investigation of the hydroxides of certain metals. Binary systems of hydroxides. *Ukr. Khim. Zh.* **27**, 7–11 (1961).

(C10) Chaly, V. P., Shor, O. G., and Rozhenko, S. P., Thermographic investigation of the hydroxides of certain metals. Binary systems of hydroxides. *Ukr. Khim. Zh.* **27**, 3–6 (1961).

(C10a) Chanh, Nguyen-BA, Thermal diagram of the solid state of the ternary system constituted of sodium, potassium, chloride, and bromide. *J. Chim. Phys.* **58**, 500–505 (1961).

(C10b) Chiu, J. Identification of organic compounds by differential thermal dynamic analysis. *Anal. Chem.* **34**, 1841–1843 (1962).

(C11) Chiu, J., Visual observation in differential thermal analysis. *Anal. Chem.* **35**, 933 (1963).

(C11a) Cholak, J., The nature of atmospheric pollution in a number of industrial communities. *Proc. 2d Natl. Air Pollution Symp.*, 6–15 Stanford Res. Inst., Los Angeles, 1952.

(C12) Chughtai, A. R., and Badaruddin, Thermal decomposition of alkaline earth sulphates. *Pakistan J. Sci. Ind. Res.* **3**, 52–56 (1960).

(C13) Churchill, R. V., "Operational Mathematics." McGraw-Hill, New York, 1958.

(C14) Cimino, A., and Parry, G. S., Interdomain symmetry in the reversible phase transformation of potassium cyanide. *Nuovo Cimento* [10] **19**, 971–980 (1961).

(C15) Claudel, B., Perrin, M., and Trambouze, Y., Nature of reactions observed by differential thermal analysis. *Compt. Rend.* **252**, 107–109 (1961).

(C16) Claussen, W. F., Detection of the $\alpha - \gamma$ iron phase transition by differential thermal conductivity analysis. *Rev. Sci. Instr.* **31**, 878–881 (1960).

(C17) Cochran, C. N., Automatic recording vacuum microbalance. *Rev. Sci. Instr.* **29**, 1135–8 (1958).

(C18) Coffeen, W., Private communication (1952).

(C19) Cola, M., and Castellani-Bisi, C., Thermal decomposition of metallic sulfites. *Gazz. Chim. Ital.* **91**, 173–186 (1961).

(C20) Cole, W. F., and Rowland, N. M., Abnormal effect in differential thermal analysis of clay minerals. *Am. Mineralogist* **46**, 304–312 (1961).

(C21) Collins, G. A., and Swan, A. G., Differential thermal analysis of minerals. *Can. Mining Met. Bull.* **508**, 533–538 (1954).

(C22) Comeforo, J. E., Fischer, R. B., and Bradley, W. F., Mullitization of kaolinite. *J. Am. Ceram. Soc.* **31**, 254–259 (1948).

(C23) Costa, D., and Costa, G., Thermal differential analysis. I. Decomposition of amides of cellulose. *Chim. e Ind.* (*Milan*) **33**, 71–76 (1951).

(C24) Costa, D., and Costa, G., Application of differential thermal analysis to the determination of characteristic temperature. II. Thermal decomposition of several sugars. *Chim. e Ind.* (*Milan*) **33**, 708–711 (1951).

(C25) Crandall, W. B., and West, R. R., An oxidation study of cobalt-alumina mixtures. *Am. Ceram. Soc. Bull.* **35**, 66–70 (1956).

(C26) Cremer, E., and Nitsch, W., The kinetics of the thermal decomposition of calcium carbonate. *In* "Science of Ceramics," Proc. 1961 conf. (G. H. Stewart, ed.), pp. 295–303. Academic Press, New York, 1962.

(C27) Crouthamel, C. E., and Johnson, C. E., Thermogravimetric decomposition of thorium 8-hydroxy quinolate. *Talanta* **8**, 377–380 (1961).

(C28) Cuthbert, F. L., and Rowland, R. A., Differential thermal analysis of some carbonate minerals. *Am. Mineralogist* **32**, 111–116 (1947).

(C29) Cuthbert, F. L., and Rowland, R. A., *Am. Mineralogist* **32**, 591 (1947).

(D1) Dannis, M. L., Thermal expansion measurements and transition temperatures. *J. Appl. Polymer Sci.* **1**, 121 (1959).

(D2) Dannis, M. L., Thermal expansion measurements and transition temperatures. II. An automatic recording system. *J. Appl. Polymer Sci.* **4**, 249–250 (1960).

(D3) Dannis, M. L., Private communication (1964).

(D4) Danusso, F., and Polizzotti, G., Application of differential thermal analysis to isotactic polymers of substituted styrenes. *Makromol. Chem.* **61**, No. 1, 157–163 (1963).

(D5) Das, I. S. S., Differential thermal analysis in ceramic research and industry. *Indian Ceram.* **1**, 167–176 (1954).

(D6) Das, I. S. S., Differential thermal analysis in ceramic research and industry. *Indian Ceram.* **1**, 207–215 (1954).

(D7) Das, I. S. S., Differential thermal analysis in ceramic research and industry. *Indian Ceram.* **1**, 289 (1954).

(D8) Dean, L. A., Differential thermal analysis of Hawaiian soils. *Soil Sci.* **63**, 95–105 (1947).

(D9) Deeg, E., Basis for theoretical treatment of differential thermal analysis. Conclusions for practice. *Ber. Deut. Keram. Ges.* **33**, 321–329 (1956).

(D10) Dempster, P. B., and Ritchie, P. D., Surface of finely ground silica. *Nature* **169**, 538–539 (1952).

(D11) Deshpande, V. T., and Sirdeshmukh, D. B., Thermal expansion of tetragonal tin. *Acta Cryst.* **14**, 355–356 (1961).

(D11a) Dilaktorskii, N. L., and Arkhangel'skaja, L. S., The thermal analysis method. *Proc. 5th Conf. Exptl. Mineral. and Petrogr., Moscow, 1956* pp. 88–96. Acad. Sci. USSR, Moscow, 1958.

(D12) Dollimore, D., Griffiths, D. L., and Nicholson, D., Thermal decomposition of oxalates. Thermo gravimetric analysis of various oxalates in air and in nitrogen. *J. Chem. Soc.* pp. 2617–2622 (1963).

(D13) Dollimore, D., and Nicholson, D., Thermo-gravimetric analysis of some complex oxalates. *J. Inorg. Nucl. Chem.* **25,** 738–740 (1963).

(D14) Doyle, C. D., Evaluation of experimental polymers. *WADD Tech. Rept.* No. 60–283 (1960).

(D15) Doyle, C. D., Estimating thermal stability of experimental polymers by empirical thermo gravimetric analysis. *Anal. Chem.* **33,** 77–78 (1961).

(D16) Doyle, C. D., Kinetic analysis of thermogravimetric data. *J. Appl. Polymer Sci.* **5,** 285–292 (1961).

(D17) Dunne, J. A., and Kerr, P. F., Differential thermal analysis of galena and clausthalite. *Am. Mineralogist* **46,** 1–11 (1961).

(D18) Duval, C., "Inorganic Thermogravimetric Analysis." Elsevier, Amsterdam, 1953.

(D18a) Duval, C., Remarks to article by W. W. Wendlandt: Thermolysis of ammonium 12-molybdophosphate. *Anal. Chim. Acta* **20,** 270 (1959).

(D19) Duval, C. Use of thermogravimetry and of infrared spectrophotometry for following solid-state reactions. *Acta Chim. Acad. Sci. Hung.* **32,** 281–293 (1962).

(D20) Duval, C., History of the development of thermogravimetry. *Chim. Anal. (Paris)* **44,** No. 5, 191–194 (1962).

(D21) Duwez, P., and Martens, H., Dilatometric study of sintering of metal powders compacts. *Trans. AIME* **185,** 571–577 (1949).

(E1) Ellis, B. G., and Mortland, M. M., Comparison of two methods of determining heats of reaction by differential thermal analysis. *Am. Mineralogist* **47,** 371–378 (1962).

(E2) Erdey, L., and Paulik, F., Thermal study of precipitates. I. Metal oxalate precipitates. *Magy. Tud. Akad. Kem. Tud. Oszt. Kozlemen.* **5,** 461–476 (1955).

(E3) Erdey, L., and Paulik, F., Thermal study of precipitates. II. Aluminum hydroxide precipitates. *Magy. Tud. Akad. Kem. Tud. Oszt. Kozlemen.* **5,** 477–487 (1955).

(E4) Erdey, L., Paulik, F., and Paulik, J., Differential thermogravimetry. Nature 174, 885–886 (1954).

(E5) Eriksson, E., Problems of heat flow in differential thermal analysis. *Kgl. Lantbruks-Hogskol. Ann.* **20,** 117–123 (1953) (in English).

(E6) Ern, V., Differential thermal analysis of a cubic modification of barium titanate. *J. Am. Ceram. Soc.* **46,** 295–296 (1963).

(E7) Escoffier, P., and Gauthier, J., Thermo-magnetic study of some inorganic neutral and basic salts of copper. *Compt. Rend.* **252,** 271–272 (1961).

(E8) Ewald, P., Recording automatic balance. *Ind. Eng. Chem., Anal. Ed.* **14,** 66–67 (1942).

(E9) Eyraud, I., Automatic absorption balance. *J. Chim. Phys.* **47,** 106 (1950).

(E10) Eyraud, C., and Goton, R., Theoretical and experimental considerations in differential heat analysis. *Compt. Rend.* **240,** 423–425 (1955).

(E11) Eyraud, C., Goton, R., and Prettre, M., A study of the dehydration of gibbsite by the simultaneous use of thermogravimetry under reduced pressure and differential thermal analysis. *Compt. Rend.* **240,** 1082–1084 (1955).

(E12) Eyraud, C., Goton, R., Trambouze, Y., The, T. H., and Prettre, M., The decomposition of alumina hydrates by differential enthalpy analysis. *Compt. Rend.* **240,** 862–864 (1955).

(F1) Faust, G. T., Differentiation of aragonite from calcite by differential thermal analysis. *Science* **110**, 402–403 (1949).

(F2) Faust, G. T., Thermal analysis studies on carbonates: I. Aragonite and calcite. *Am. Mineralogist* **35**, 207–224 (1950).

(F3) Fedulov, S. A., Venevtsev, U. N., Zhdanov, G. S., and Smazhevskaya, E. G., high temperature X-ray and thermographic studies of bismuth ferrite. *Kristallografiya* **6**, 795–796 (1961).

(F4) Felix, W. D., McDowall, M. A., and Eyring, H., Differential thermal analysis of natural and modified wool and mohair. *Textile Res. J.* **33**, 465–470 (1963).

(F5) Feurer, I., Radioactive electronic detector. *Anal. Chem.* **20**, 1231–1237 (1948).

(F6) Fialkov, A. S., and Davidovich, Y. G., Linear thermal expansion of materials consisting of graphite and other coal products. *Zh. Prikl. Khim.* **34**, 300–306 (1961).

(F7) Finch, D. I., "General Principles of Thermoelectric Thermometry," Tech. Publ. ENS2(1). Leeds & Northrup Co., Philadelphia, Pennsylvania, 1962.

(F8) Fischer, W., and Abendroth, H. J., Thermal analysis by the plotting of the piston-sink curve. Melting diagram of the sodium chloride–sodium oxide system. *Z. Anorg. Allgem. Chem.* **308**, 98–104 (1961).

(F9) Flanagan, T. B., Effect of the conditions of dehydration upon the subsequent thermal decomposition of lead styphnate. *Trans. Faraday Soc.* **57**, 797–808 (1961).

(F9a) Fleck, W. E. P., Jones, M. H., Kuntae, R. H., and McAdie, H. G., The differential thermal analysis of natural and synthetic hydrates of calcium sulfate. *Can. J. Chem.* **38**, 936–943 (1960).

(F10) Flom, D. G., Dynamic mechanical spectrometry by means of rolling friction measurements. *Anal. Chem.* **32**, 1550–1554 (1960).

(F11) Foldvari-Vogl, M., and Kliburszky, B., New viewpoints on the theory and practice of differential thermal analysis. *Acta Geol. Acad. Sci. Hung.* **2**, 215–229 (1954) (in German).

(F12) Foldvari-Vogl, M., and Kliburszky, B., On the determination of heats of dissociation of minerals. *Acta Geol. (Budapest)* **5**, 187–195 (1958).

(F13) Frederickson, A. F., Derived differential thermal curves. *Am. Mineralogist* **38**, 1023–1025 (1954).

(F14) Freeman, E. S., and Carroll, B., The application of thermoanalytical techniques to reaction kinetics. The thermogravimetric evaluation of the kinetics of the decomposition of calcium oxalate monohydrate. *J. Phys. Chem.* **62**, 394–397 (1958).

(F15) Freeman, E. S., and Edelman, D., Simple method for derivative differential thermal analysis. *Anal. Chem.* **31**, 624–625 (1959).

(F16) Freeman, E. S., and Gordon, S., The application of the absolute rate theory to the ignition of propagatively reacting systems. The thermal ignition of the systems lithium nitrate-magnesium, sodium nitrate-magnesium. *J. Phys. Chem.* **60**, 867–871 (1956).

(G1) Gadzhiev, S. N., and Sharifov, K. A., Use of thermistors in calorimetry. *Zh. Fiz. Khim.* **35**, 1147–1149 (1961).

(G2) Gafner, G., Thermal aspects of the growth of thin films by vacuum sublimation. *Phil. Mag.* [8] **5**, 1041–1048 (1960).

(G3) Garn, P. D., Automatic recording balance. *Anal. Chem.* **29**, 839–841 (1957).

(G4) Garn, P. D., Thermal analysis—A critique. *Anal. Chem.* **33**, 1247–1251 (1961).

(G5) Garn, P. D., Thermal analysis of small samples. *Proc. Intern. Symp. Micro-chem. Techniques, State College, Pennsylvania, 1961* (N. D. Cheronis, ed.), pp. 1105–1109. Wiley (Interscience), New York, 1962.

(G6) Garn, P. D., Thermal detection of Curie temperatures. Presented at *140th Meeting Am. Chem. Soc.* (*Div. Anal. Chem.*), Washington, D. C. (1962).

(G7) Garn, P. D., Some problems in the analysis of gaseous decomposition products. *Talanta* 11, 1417–1432 (1964).

(G8) Garn, P. D., Differential thermal analysis using self-generated atmospheres at sub- and supra-atmospheric pressures. *Anal. Chem.* 37, 77–78 (1965).

(G9) Garn, P. D., Comparison of sample holder materials for differential thermal analysis. *J. Am. Ceram. Soc.* in press (1964).

(G10) Garn, P. D., and Flaschen, S. S., Unpublished measurements (1956).

(G11) Garn, P. D., and Flaschen, S. S., Detection of polymorphic phase transformations by continuous measurement of electrical resistance. *Anal. Chem.* 29, 268–271 (1957).

(G12) Garn, P. D., and Flaschen, S. S., Analytical applications of a differential thermal analysis apparatus. *Anal. Chem.* 29, 271–275 (1957).

(G13) Garn, P. D., Geith, C. R., and DeBala, S., Furnace mounting and control system for Ainsworth vacuum automatic recording balance. *Rev. Sci. Instr.* 33, 293–297 (1962).

(G14) Garn, P. D., and Gilroy, H. M., Determination of maleic anhydride in polyesters. *Anal. Chem.* 30, 1663–1665 (1958).

(G15) Garn, P. D., and Kessler, J. E., Unpublished measurements (1960).

(G16) Garn, P. D., and Kessler, J. E., Thermogravimetry in self-generated atmospheres. *Anal. Chem.* 32, 1563–1565 (1960).

(G17) Garn, P. D., and Kessler, J. E., Free diffusion sample holder. *Anal. Chem.* 32, 1900 (1960).

(G18) Garn, P. D., and Kessler, J. E., Effluence analysis as an aid to thermal analysis. *Anal. Chem.* 33, 952–954 (1961).

(G19) Garn, P. D., Vincent, S. M., and Gilroy, H. M., Unpublished measurements (1956).

(G20) Geller, R. F., and Yavorsky, P. J., Effects of some oxide additions on thermal length changes of zirconia. *J. Res. Natl. Bur. Std.* 35, 87–110 (1945).

(G21) Gerard-Hirne, J., and Lamy, C., Identification of clays by differential thermal analysis. *Bull. Soc. Franc. Ceram.* pp. 26–40 (1951); see *Ceram. Abstr.* p. 93 (1952).

(G22) Gerdanian, P., and Dode, M., Use of a Eyraud-Ugine thermobalance. *Bull. Soc. Chim. France* pp. 1348–1351 (1961).

(G23) Gheith, M. A., Differential thermal analysis of certain iron oxides and oxide hydrates. *Am. J. Sci.* 250, 677–685 (1952).

(G24) Gibaud, M., and Gelosa, M. M., Application of the thermobalance to the determination of mixtures of chalk, magnesium calcium carbonate and dolomite. *Chim. Anal.* (*Paris*) 36, 153 (1954).

(G25) Glasner, A., and Steinberg, M., Thermal decomposition of lanthanum oxalate. *J. Inorg. Nucl. Chem.* 16, 279–289 (1961).

(G26) Glass, H. D., High-temperature phases from kaolinite and halloysite. *Am. Mineralogist* 39, 193–207 (1954).

(G27) Goldsmith, A., Waterman, T. E., and Hirschhorn, H. V., "Handbook of Thermophysical Properties of Solid Materials." Macmillan, New York, 1961.

(G28) Golubenko, A. N., and Rezukhina, T. N., Application of the method of hydrostatic weighing to the study of heterogeneous equilibria. *Zh. Neorg. Khim.* **6**, 674–678 (1961).

(G29) Goodkin, J., Solomons, C., and Janz, G. J. Calorimeter for heats of fusion of inorganic compounds. *Rev. Sci. Instr.* **29** 105 (1958).

(G30) Gordon, B. E., and Denisov, A. M., Thermal decomposition of crystal hydrates obtained by crystallization of metastable and of labile supersaturated solutions. *Ukr. Khim. Zh.* **19**, 368–371 (1953).

(G31) Gordon, M., Recent advances in the theory of thermal degradation of heterodisperse polymers. *Soc. Chem. Ind. (London) Monograph* **13**, 163–83 (1961).

(G32) Gordon, S., and Campbell, C., Differential thermal analysis of inorganic oxidants: Nitrates. *U. S. Govt. Res. Rept.* No. PB-116622 (1954).

(G33) Gordon, S., and Campbell, C., Synchronizing and reference marking of photoelectric and potentiometric recorder curves. *Am. Ceram. Soc. Bull.* **34**, 372–374 (1954); see *Ceram. Abstr.* p. 25 (1956).

(G34) Gordon, S., and Campbell, C., Differential thermal analysis of inorganic compounds. Nitrates and perchlorates of the alkali and alkaline earth groups and their subgroups. *Anal. Chem.* **27**, 1102–1109 (1955).

(G35) Gordon, S., and Campbell, C., Automatic and recording balances (Review). *Anal. Chem.* **32**, 271–289R 1960).

(G36) Goubeau, J., and Walter, K., Thermal decomposition and the infrared spectra of beryllium dimethyl. *Z. Anorg. Allgem. Chem.* **322**, 58–70 (1963).

(G37) Govorov, A. A., and Granovskii, I. G., Apparatus for the complex thermal analysis. *Zavodskaya Lab.* **27**, 115–116 (1961).

(G38) Graf, D. L., Variations in differential thermal curves of low-iron dolomites. *Am. Mineralogist* **37**, 1–27 (1952).

(G39) Grant, D. H., and Grassie, N., Thermal decomposition of poly (*t*-Butyl methacrylate). *Polymer* **1**, 445–455 (1960).

(G40) Grauerman, L. A., Karantsevich, L. G., Ul'yanova, T. S., Use of differential dilatometric curves for the investigation of fats and fat mixtures. *Maslob.-Zhir. Prom.* **26**, No. 11, 13–18 (1960).

(G41) Gray, T. V., Detwiler, D. P., Rase, D. E., Lawrence, W. G., West, R. R., and Vennings, T. C., "The Defect Solid State." Wiley (Interscience), New York, 1957.

(G42) Gregg, S. V., Parker, T. W., and Stephens, M. J., The grinding of kaolinite. II. A more detailed study. *J. Appl. Chem.* **4**, 666–674 (1957).

(G43) Griffith, E. J., Thermogravimetric analysis of complex mixtures of hydrates. *Anal. Chem.* **29**, 198–202 (1957).

(G44) Grim, R. E., Differential thermal analysis of prepared mixture of clay minerals. *Am. Mineralogist* **32**, 493–501 (1947).

(G45) Greenwood, C. T., Knox, J. H., and Milne, E., Analysis of thermal decomposition products of carbohydrates by gas chromatography. *Chem. & Ind. (London)* pp. 1878–1879 (1961).

(G46) Grimshaw, R. W., The quantitative estimation of silica minerals. *Clay Minerals Bull.* **2**, 2–7 (1950).

(G47) Groot, C., and Troutner, V. H., Automatic recording thermobalance. *Anal. Chem.* **29**, 835–839 (1957).

(G48) Gruver, R. M., Differential thermal analysis studies of ceramic materials: I. Characteristic heat effects of some carbonates. *J. Am. Ceram. Soc.* **33**, 96–101 (1950).

(G49) Gruver, R. M., Differential thermal analysis studies of ceramic materials: II. Transition of aragonite to calcite. *J. Am. Ceram. Soc.* **33**, 171–174 (1950).

(G50) Gubergrits, M., Influence of heating conditions on the distribution of oil shale thermal decomposition products. *Izv. Akad. Nauk Eston. SSR, Ser. Fiz.-Mat. i Tekhn. Nauk* **9**, 343–357 (1960).

(G51) Guichard, M. M., Continuous study of dehydration by means of a hydrostatic compensation balance. *Bull. Soc. Chim. France* **37**, 251–253 (1925).

(G52) Guichard, M. M., A hydrostatic compensation balance. *Bull. Soc. Chim. France* **39**, 1113–1115 (1926).

(G53) Guiochon, G., Thermogravimetric measurements. *Anal. Chem.* **33**, 1124–1125 (1961).

(H1) Haase, R., Hoch, K., and Schoenert, H., Thermo-elements. Evaluation of measurements. *Z. Physik. Chem. (Frankfurt)* [N.S.] **27**, 421–438 (1961).

(H2) Harmelin, M., Study of chromium sulfate by thermogravimetry and infrared absorption spectroscopy. *Compt. Rend.* **252**, 4142–4144 (1961).

(H3) Hasegawa, H., Precipitated calcium carbonates with thermal balance. *Yakugaku Zasshi* **80**, 1739–1742 (1960).

(H4) Hashimoto, H., Thermal decomposition of calcium carbonate—annealing process and electric conductivity. *Kogyo Kagaku Zasshi* **64**, 250–255 (1961).

(H5) Hashimoto, H., and Itoo, M., Recording microthermobalance. *Kogyo Kagaku Zasshi* **64**, 1515–1517 (1961).

(H6) Haul, R. A. W., and Heystek, H., Differential thermal analysis of the dolomite decomposition. *Am. Mineralogist* **37**, 166–179 (1952).

(H7) Haul, R. A. W., Stein, L. H., and Louro, J. D., Exchange of carbon-13 dioxide between solid carbonates and gaseous carbon dioxide. *Nature* **167**, 241–242 (1951).

(H8) Hay, A. W., Private communication (1963).

(H9) Hedvall, J. A., Einführung in die Festkörper Chemie. Vieweg, Braunschweig, 1952.

(H10) Hedvall, J A., Thermal decomposition of dolomite. *Z. Anorg. Allgem. Chem.* **272**, 22–24 (1953).

(H11) Hegedus, A. J., Sasvari, K., and Neugebauer, J., Thermal and X-ray analytical investigation of the reaction of tunsten trioxide and carbon monoxide. *Acta Chim. Acad. Sci. Hung.* **26**, 113–128 (1961).

(H12) Hermodi (Morovky), A., and Salmon, A., Thermal decomposition of ammonium per chlorate in the presence of magnesium oxide. *Bull. Res. Council Israel* **9A**, 206–207 (1960).

(H13) Hill, J. A., and Murphy, C. B., Infrared heating applied to differential thermal analysis. *Anal. Chem.* **31**, 1443–1444 (1959).

(H14) Hill J. A., Murphy, C. B., and Schacher G. P., Thermal decompositions of copper (II) acetate monohydrate. *Anal. Chim. Acta* **24**, 496–497 (1961).

(H15) Hirone, T., Maeda, S., and Tsuza, N., *Rev. Sci. Instr.* **25**, 516–517 (1954).

(H16) Hirota, M., Kitakaze, H., and Seki, K., Automatic recording apparatus for the compound thermal analysis. *Yogyo Kyokai Shi* **69**, 97–102 (1961).

(H17) Hock, C. W., and Arbogast, V. F., Measuring melting points and rates of crystallization of polymers by recording changes in birefringence. *Anal. Chem.* **33**, 462–465 (1961).

(H18) Hogan, V. D., and Gordon, S., A thermoanalytical study of the binary oxidant system potassium perchborate-barium nitrate. *J. Phys. Chem.* **62**, 1433 (1958).

(H19) Hogan, V. D., and Gordon, S., Thermoanalytical study of the reciprocal system $2KNO_3 + BACL_2 \rightarrow 2KCL + BA(NO_3)_2$. *J. Phys. Chem.* **64**, 172–173 (1960.

(H20) Hogan, V. D., and Gordon, S., Apparatus for observing physical changes at elevated temperatures. *Anal. Chem.* **32**, 573–574 (1960).

(H21) Hogan, V. D., Gordon, S., and Campbell, C., Differential thermal analysis and thermogravimetry applied to potassium perchlorate-aluminum-barium nitrate mixtures. *Anal. Chem.* **29**, 306–310 (1957).

(H22) Holt, J., Cutler, I. B., and Wadsworth, M. E., Rate of thermal dehydration of kaolinite in vacuum. *J. Am. Ceram. Soc.* **45**, 133–136 (1962).

(H23) Hooley, J. G., Recording vacuum thermobalance. *Can. J. Chem.* **35**, 374 (1957).

(H24) Horton, G. K., Thermal expansion of metals at low temperatures. *Can. J. Phys.* **39**, 263–271 (1961).

(H25) Houldsworth, H. S., and Cobb, J. W., The behavior of fireclays, bauxites, etc., on heating. *Trans. Brit. Ceram. Soc.* **22**, 111–137 and 344–348 (1923).

(H26) Howard, W. H., The glass temperatures of polyacrylonitrite and acrylonitrite-vinyl acetate copolymers. *J. Appl. Polymer Sci.* **5**, 303–307 (1961).

(H27) Hummel, F. A., Properties of some substances isostructural with silica. *J. Am. Ceram. Soc.* **32**, 320–326 (1949).

(H28) Hummel, F. A., Significant aspects of certain binary compounds and solid solutions. *J. Am. Ceram. Soc.* **35**, 64–66 (1952).

(H29) Huzan, E., Abbiss, C. P., and Jones, G. O., Thermal expansion of aluminum at low temperatures. *Phil. Mag.* [8] **6**, 277–285 (1961).

(H30) Hyatt, E. P., Cutler, I. B., and Wadsworth, M. E., Apparatus for thermogravimetric analysis. *Bull. Am. Ceram. Soc.* **35**, 180–181 (1956).

(H31) Hyatt, E. P., Cutler, I. B., and Wadsworth, M. E., Calcium carbonate decomposition in carbon dioxide atmosphere. *J. Am. Ceram. Soc.* **41**, 70–74 (1958).

(I1) Iida, Y., Sintering of high purity nickel. Dilatometry. *J. Am. Ceram. Soc.* **41**, 397–409 (1958).

(I2) Inoue, M., and Saito, T., Application of differential thermal analysis. Application to polymorphism. *Yakugaku Zasshi* **81**, 615 (1961).

(I3) Intrater, J., Dilatometric investigation of vacuum-melted zircaloy-2. *Trans. Met. Soc. AIME* **221**, 567–572 (1961).

(I4) Ivanov, O. S., The use of N. S. Kurnakov's pyrometer for differential thermal analysis and calorimetric studies of microsamples. *Izv. Sekt. Fiz.-Khim. Anal. Inst. Obshch. i Neorg. Khim. Akad. Nauk SSSR* **25**, 26–40 (1954).

(I5) Ivanov, V. E., Shapoval, B. I., and Amonenko, V. M., Inner friction method for the study of phase transformation in zirconium and beryllium. *Fiz. Metal. i Metalloved.* **11**, No. 1, 52–58 (1961).

(I6) Ivanova, L. I., Relation between the heat capacity of solids and the phase transition temperature. *Zh. Fiz. Khim.* **35**, 2120 (1961).

(I7) Ivanova, V. P., and Tatarskii, V. B., Thermograms of mixtures of dolomite and kaolin. *Dokl. Akad. Nauk SSSR* **73**, 341–343 (1950).

(J1) Jacobs, P. W. M., and Kureishy, A. R. T., Thermal decomposition of nickel oxalate dihydrate. *Trans. Faraday Soc.* **58**, Pt. 3, 551–560 (1962).

(J2) Jacque, L., Guiochon, G., and Gendrel, P., Applications of kinetics to thermogravimetry. *Bull. Soc. Chim. France* pp. 1061–1069 (1961).

(J3) Jaffray, J., and Viloteau, J., The thermal and dilatometric analysis of chromic oxide. *Compt. Rend.* **226**, 1701–1702 (1948).

(J4) Janz, G. J., and Lorenz, M. R., A dynamic method for the dissociation pressures of carbonates. *Rensselaer Polytech. Inst. Project* No. 441.35, *Tech. Rept.* No. 6 (1960).

(J5) Jennings, E. C., Jr., and Dimick, K. P., Gas chromatography of pyrolytic products of purines and pyrimidines. *Anal. Chem.* 34, 1543–1547 (1962).

(J6) Johns, I. B., Mcelhill, E. A., and Smith, J. O., Thermal stability of organic compounds *Ind. Eng. Chem., Prod. Res. & Develop.* 1, No. 1, 2–6 (1962).

(J7) Johnson, G. B., Hess, P. H., and Miron, R. R., Relative degree of cure in unsaturated polyester—styrene copolymer as determined by differential thermal analysis. *J. Appl. Polymer Sci.* 6, 195–205 (1962).

(J8) Johnson, N. M., and Daniels, F., Luminescence during annealing and phase change in crystals. *J. Chem. Phys.* 34, 1434–1439 (1961).

(J9) de Jong, G., Verification of use of peak area for quantitative differential thermal analysis. *J. Am. Ceram. Soc.* 40, 42–49 (1957).

(J10) Joyner, T. B., and Verhoek, F. H., Products of the thermal decomposition of some cobalt ammine azides. *J. Am. Chem. Soc.* 83, 1069–1072 (1961).

(K1) Kadlets, O., and Dubinin, M. M., Kinetics of thermal decomposition of solid substances. Thermal decomposition of silver carbonate. *Izv. Akad. Nauk SSSR, Otd. Khim. Nauk* pp. 390–396 (1961).

(K2) Kalinina, A. M., Conversion of silica during high-temperature reactions of synthetic kaolinite. *Zh. Neorg. Khim.* 6, 2109–2119 (1961).

(K3) Kalinkina, B. A., Kozlova, N. I., Nikolaev, I. N., and Stepanchikov, A. A., Thermal decomposition of coals and their mixtures. *Izv. Akad. Nauk SSSR, Otd. Tekhn. Nauk, Met. i Toplivo* No. 6, 156–160 (1960).

(K4) Kamecki, J., and Trau, J., Thermal and thermogravimetric analysis of hydrated cupric chloride. *Bull. Acad. Polon. Sci., Cl. III* 3, No. 2, 111–115 (1955) (in English).

(K5) Karan, C., Barium titanate-potassium fluoride phase diagram. *J. Chem. Phys.* 22, 957 (1954).

(K6) Karan, C., and Skinner, B. J., $BaTiO_3$-KF phase diagram. *J. Chem. Phys.* 21, 2225 (1953).

(K7) Kasner, B., and Hartwig, K. Differential thermogravimetric analysis. *Tonind.-Ztg. Keram. Rundschau* 84, 471–475 (1960).

(K8) Kauffman, A. V., Jr., and Dilling, E. D., Differential thermal curves of certain hydrous and anhydrous minerals, with a description of the apparatus used. *Econ. Geol.* 45, 222–224 (1950).

(K9) Kaurkovskii, V. I., Automatic thermoregulation with a thermocontrol element. *J. Appl. Chem. USSR (English Transl.)* 25, 743–747 (1952).

(K10) Ke, B., Differential thermal analysis of high polymers. Poly amides. *J. Polymer Sci.* 50, 87–98 (1961).

(K11) Ke, B., Differential thermal analysis of high polymers. Some low-temperature transitions. *J. Polymer Sci.*, Part B, Vol. 1, 167–170 (1963).

(K11a) Ke, B., Differential thermal analysis of high polymers. IV. Saturated linear polyesters. *J. Appl. Polymer Sci.* 6, 624–628 (1962).

(K11b) Keavney, J. J., and Eberlin, E. C., The determination of glass transition temperatures by differential thermal analysis. *J. Appl. Polymer Sci.* 3, 47–53 (1960).

(K12) Keeling, P. S., The common clay minerals as a continuous series. *In* "Science of Ceramics," Proc. 1961 Conf. (G. H. Stewart, ed.), Vol. 1. Academic Press, New York, 1962.

(K13) Keena, A. G., Differential thermal analysis of the thermal decomposition of ammonium nitrate. *J. Am. Chem. Soc.* **77**, 1379–1380 (1955).

(K14) Keith, M. L., and Tuttle, O. F., Significance of variation in the high-low inversion of quartz. *Am. J. Sci.*, Bowen Vol., Pt. 1, 203–252 (1952).

(K15) Kelly, H. J., and Harris, H. M., An automatically recording thermal-expansion apparatus. *J. Am. Ceram. Soc.* **39**, 344–348 (1956).

(K16) Kelly, W. C., Application of differential thermal analysis to identification of the natural hydrous ferric oxides. *Am. Mineralogist* **41**, 353–355 (1956).

(K17) Kerr, P. F., and Kulp, J. L., Differential thermal analysis of siderite. *Am. Mineralogist* **32**, 678–680 (1947).

(K18) Kertzmann, J., Presented at *130th Meeting Am. Chem. Soc. (Div. Anal. Chem.), Atlantic City, N. J.* (1956).

(K19) Kessler, M. F., and Romovackova, H., Experiences with differential thermal analysis of coal and coke. *Fuel* **40**, 161–170 (1961).

(K20) Ketov, A. N., Pechkovskii, V. V., Varskoi, B. N., and Starkov, N. P., Thermal decomposition of copper sulfate. *Zh. Prikl. Khim.* **34**, 517–521 (1961).

(K21) de Keyser, W. L., A study of kaolin and some Belgian clays. III. Discussion of results. *Ann. Mines Belg.* **40**, 357–429 and 711–806 (1939).

(K22) de Keyser, W. L., Differential thermobalance—new tool of research., *Bull. Soc. Franc. Ceram.* pp. 2–5 (1953).

(K23) de Keyser, W. L., The thermal behavior of kaolin and of clay minerals. *Silicates Ind.* **24**, 117–123 and 190–196 (1959).

(K24) Khu, C. T., and Novoselova, A. V., Thermal analysis of the potassium fluoride–lanthanum fluoride–potassium fluoberyllate system. *Zh. Neorg. Khim.* **6**, 2148–2157 (1961).

(K25) Khutsaidze, A. L., Apparatus for thermal analysis with a programmed regime. *Soobshch. Akad. Nauk Gruz. SSR* **26**, 681–686 (1961).

(K26) Kirillova, E. I., Matveeva, E. N., Potapenko, T. G., Rachinskii, F. Y., and Slovachevskaya, N. M., Effect of organic compounds on thermal decomposition of poly vinyl butyral. *Plasticheskie Massy* No. 5, 15–19 (1961).

(K27) Kingery, W. D., Thermal conductivity. VI. Determination of conductivity of aluminum oxide by spherical envelope and cylinder methods. *J. Am. Ceram. Soc.* **37**, 88 (1954).

(K28) Kingery, W. D., "Property Measurements at High Temperatures." Wiley, New York, 1959.

(K29) Kissinger, H. E., Variation of peak temperature with heating rate in differential thermal analysis. *J. Res. Natl. Bur. Std.* **57**, 217–221 (1956) (Res. Paper No. 2712).

(K30) Kissinger, H. E., Reaction kinetics in differential thermal analysis. *Anal. Chem.* **29**, 1702–1706 (1957).

(K31) Kissinger, H. E., McMurdie, H. F., and Simpson, B. S., Thermal decomposition of manganous and ferrous carbonates. *J. Am. Ceram. Soc.* **39**, 168–172 (1956).

(K32) Kitamura, N., Kashiwase, Y., Harada, J., and Honjo, G., Electron diffraction study of the phase transition of hydrogen sulfide at −170-Deg.-C. *Acta Cryst.* **14**, 687–688 (1961).

(K33) Kleber, W., and Noack, H., Dielectric measurements on powdered minerals with comparative differential thermal analysis determinations. *Chem. Erde* **21**, 5–23 (1961).

(K33a) Knight, H. B.; Witnauer, L. P.; Coleman, J. E.; Noble, W. R., Jr.; Swern, D. Dissociation temperatures of urea complexes of long-chain fatty acids, esters and alcohols. *Anal. Chem.*, **24**, 1331–4 (1952).

(K34) Kobayashi, I., Thermal decomposition and air-oxidation of some uranium compounds. *Rika Gaku Kenkyushu Hokoku* **36**, 710–713 (1960).

(K35) Kofler, A., Microthermal analysis of the system NaNO₃–KNO₃. *Monatsh.* **86**, 643–652 (1955).

(K36) Kopp, O. C., and Kerr, P. F., Differential thermal analysis of pyrite and marcasite. *Am. Mineralogist* **43**, 679–697 (1958).

(K37) Kopp, O. C., and Kerr, P. F., Differential thermal analysis of sphalerite. *Am. Mineralogists* **43**, 732–748 (1958).

(K38) Kornienko, V. P., Kinetics and chemical mechanism of thermal decomposition of formates and oxalates. *Sb. Nauch. Rabot Akad. Nauk Beloruss. SSR, Inst. Khim.* No. 5, 92–99 (1956); see *Chem. Abstr.* **52**, 6906 (1958).

(K39) Kornienko, V. P., Effect of the nature of the cation on the thermal decomposition of oxalates. *Ukrain. Khim. Zh.* **23**, 159–167 (1957); see *Chem. Abstr.* **51**, 12617 (1957).

(K40) Krogmann, K., Thermal decomposition of nickel formate. *Z. Anorg. Allgem. Chem.* **308**, 226–241 (1961).

(K41) Krueger, J. E., and Bryden, J. G., Apparatus for combined thermogravimetric and differential thermal analysis. *J. Sci. Instr.* **40**, 178–182 (1963).

(K42) Kulp, J. L., Kent, P., and Kerr, P. F., Thermal study of the Ca–Mg–Fe carbonate minerals. *Am. Mineralogist* **36**, 643–670 (1951).

(K43) Kulp, J. L., and Kerr, P. F., Multiple thermal analysis. *Science* **105**, 413 (1947).

(K44) Kulp, J. L., and Kerr, P. F., Improved differential thermal apparatus. *Am. Mineralogist* **34**, 839–845 (1949).

(K45) Kulp, J. L., and Trites, A. F., Differential thermal analysis of natural hydrous ferric oxides. *Am. Mineralogist* **36**, 23–44 (1951).

(K46) Kulp, J. L., Wright, H. D., and Holmes, R. J., Thermal study of rhodochrosite. *Am. Mineralogist* **34**, 195–219 and 285 (1949).

(K47) Kulp, J. L., Volchok, H. L., and Holland, H. S., Age from metamict minerals., *Am. Mineralogist* **37**, 709–718 (1952).

(K47a) Kulshrestha, V. K., Differential thermal studies on plant gums. *J. Polymer Sci.* **58**, 791–808 (1962).

(K48) Kuntze, R. A., Determination of small amounts of gypsum in calcium sulfate hemi hydrate by differential thermal analysis. *Mater. Res. Std.* **2**, 640–642 (1962).

(L1) Lambert, A., A recording electronic balance for the study of sedimentation or thermogravimetry. *Bull. Soc. Franc. Ceram.* **45**, 19 (1959).

(L1a) Lange, N. A., "Handbook of Chemistry" Handbook Publishers, Sandusky, Ohio, 1956.

(L2) Larson, H. V., Myers, I. T., and LeBlanc, W. H., Method of linearizing thermistor thermometer data in calorimetry. *J. Sci. Instr.* **38**, 400–401 (1961).

(L3) Laval, J., Thermal expansion of crystalline media. *J. Phys. Radium* **22**, 451–458 (1961).

(L3a) *Leeds & Northrup (Phila.) Bull.* ND46–33(107) (1962).

(L4) Le Floch, G., Le Montagner, S., and Rousselot, M. M., Apparatus for differential thermal analysis. *J. Phys. Radium* **23**, 959–960 (1962).

(L5) Leicester, J., and Redman, M. J., Thermal decomposition of the nickel and cobalt salts of aliphatic acids. *J. Appl. Chem.* (*London*) **12**, 357–365 (1962).

(L6) Li, Y. S., Thermal and tensimetric analysis of the aluminum chloride-ammonium chloride system. *Zh. Neorg. Khim.* **5**, 2804–2807 (1960).

References

(L7) Lieberman, A., and Crandall, W. B., Design and construction of a self-calibrating dialatometer for high-temperature use. *J. Am. Ceram. Soc.* **35**, 304–308 (1952).

(L8) Lloyd, S. V., and Murray, J. R., A simple, automatic high-temperature thermal analysis apparatus. *J. Sci. Instr.* **35**, 252–254 (1958).

(L9) Loasby, R. G., A simple volumenometer. *J. Sci. Instr.* **38**, 306 (1961).

(L10) Lodding, W., and Hammell, L., High temperature pressure-vacuum furnace. *Rev. Sci. Instr.* **30**, 885–886 (1959).

(L11) Lodding, W., and Hammell, L., Differential thermal analysis of hydroxides in reducing atmospheres. *Anal. Chem.* **32**, 657–662 (1960).

(L12) Lodding, W., and Sturm, E., A new method of differential thermal analysis employing multiple thermocouples. *Am. Mineralogist* **42**, 78–82 (1957).

(L13) Lohmann, I. W., An electronic recording analytical balance. *J. Sci. Instr.* **21**, 999–1002 (1950).

(L14) Longuet-Escar, Mme. V., Reactions in the solid state at low temperatures in the presence of water. *Bull. Soc. Chim. France* p. 153 (1949).

(L15) Longwell, P. A., and Sage, B. H., Thermal decomposition of N-hexane at high pressures. *J. Chem. Eng. Data* **5**, 322–330 (1960).

(L16) Lowell, T. L., Thermal expansion of alpha-uranium single crystals. *J. Nucl. Mater.* **3**, 67–71 (1961).

(L17) Lukaszewski, G. M., Accuracy in thermogravimetric analysis. *Nature* **194**, 959–961 (1962).

(M1) Macarovici, C. G., and Macarovici, D., Thermogravimetric study and X-ray study of the dehydration and thermal decomposition of a basic carbonate of magnesium. *Acad Rep. Populare Romine, Filiala Cluj, Studii Cercetari Chem.* **11**, 281–288 (1960).

(M2) Mackenzie, R. C., Differential thermal analysis apparatus. *Anales Edafol. Fisiol. Vegetal (Madrid)* **11**, 159–184 (1952).

(M3) Mackenzie, R. C., "The Differential Thermal Investigation of Clays." Mineral. Soc., London, 1957.

(M4) Mackenzie, R. C., "Scifax Differential Thermal Analysis Data Index." Cleaver-Hume Press, London, 1962.

(M5) Mackenzie, R. C., and Farmer, V. C., Notes on Arens' theory of differential thermal analysis. *Clay Minerals Bull.* **1**, 262–266 (1952).

(M6) Mackenzie, R. C., and Farquharson, K. R., Standardization of differential thermal analysis technique. *Proc. 19th Session Intern. Geol. Congr., Algiers, 1952* pp. 183–200 (1953).

(M7) Majumdar, A. J., and Roy R., System $CaO-Al_2O_3-H_2O$. *J. Am. Ceram. Soc.* **39**, 434–442 (1956).

(M8) Makarov, S. Z., Arnold, T. I., Stasevich, N. N., and Shorina, E. V., Systems having concentrated hydrogen per oxide. Thermal analysis of copper per oxide compounds *Izv. Akad. Nauk SSSR, Otd. Khim. Nauk* pp. 2090–2095 (1960).

(M9) Malard, C., Thermal decomposition of simple and double selenates of cobalt and of potassium, rubidium, and cesium. *Compt. Rend.* **252**, 2238–2240 (1961).

(M10) Mallya, R. M., and Murthy, A. R. V., Hydrated basic nickel carbonates. Potentiometric study of precipitation. Preparation of basic nickel carbonates and their differential thermal analysis. *J. Indian Inst. Sci.* **43**, 65–96 (1961).

(M11) Mallya, R. M., and Murthy, A. R. V., Basic carbonates of nickel. Thermo-gravimetric behavior of basic nickel carbonates. Thermal decomposition of basic nickel carbonates in vacuum and the nature of the surfaces. Formation and configurations of basic nickel carbonates. *J. Indian Inst. Sci.* **43**, 131–157 (1961).

(M12) van der Marel, H. W., Quantitative differential thermal analysis of clay and other minerals. *Am. Mineralogist* **41**, 222–244 (1956).

(M13) Markin, T. L., Thermal decomposition of americium (III) oxalate. *J. Inorg. Nucl. Chem.* **7**, 290–291 (1958).

(M14) Markov, P. J., and Peschew, P. D., Study of the kinetics of the reaction between N-butyl iodide and magnesium by differential thermal analysis. *Compt. Rend. Acad. Bulgare Sci.* **14**, 175–178 (1961).

(M15) Martin, A. J., and Edwards, K. L., Linear voltage temperature furnace for thermal analysis. *J. Sci. Instr.* **36**, 170–172 (1959).

(M16) Martin, A. J., and Moore, A., The structure of beryllium, with particular reference to temperatures above 1200°C. *J. Less-Common Metals* **1**, 85–93 (1959).

(M17) Martin, R. T., Clay-carbonate-soluble salt interaction during differential thermal analysis. *Am. Mineralogist* **43**, 649–655 (1958).

(M18) Martin, S. B., and Ramstad, R. W., Compact two-stage gas chromatograph for flash pyrolysis studies. *Anal. Chem.* **33**, 982–985 (1961).

(M19) Martinez, E., The effect of particle size on the thermal properties of serpentine minerals. *Am. Mineralogist* **46**, 901–912 (1961).

(M20) Mauer, F. A., Analytical balance for recording rapid change in weight. *Rev. Sci. Instr.* **25**, 598–602 (1954).

(M21) Mazières, C., Differential thermal microanalysis, physical-chemical applications. *Bull. Soc. Chim. France* pp. 1695–701 (1961).

(M22) Mazières, C., Microsamples, thermal phenomena that are connected with structural transformations. *Ann. Chim. (Paris)* **6**, 575–622 (1961).

(M23) McAdie, H. G., Thermal decomposition of molecular complexes. 1. Urea–n-paraffin inclusion compounds. *Can. J. Chem.* **40**, 2195–2203 (1962).

(M24) McAdie, H. G., Simultaneous thermal analysis using the open pan type of sample holder. *Anal. Chem.* **35**, 1840–1844 (1963).

(M25) McCrone, W. C., "Fusion Methods in Chemical Microscopy." Wiley (Interscience), New York, 1957.

(M26) McKeand, I. J., and Hursh, R. K., A tungsten coil furnace for high-temperature X-ray diffraction investigations. *J. Am. Ceram. Soc.* **38**, 63–65 (1955).

(M27) McLaughlin, R. J. W., Quantitative differential thermal analysis. *Am. J. Sci.* **252**, 555–566 (1954).

(M28) McLaughlin, R. J. W., Effects of grinding on dickite. *Clay Minerals Bull.* **2**, 309–317 (1955).

(M29) McLaughlin, R. J. W., Differential thermal analysis of kaolinite-illite mixtures. *Trans. Brit. Ceram. Soc.* **59**, 178–187 (1960).

(M30) McLaughlin, R. J. W., Effect of dilution on the shape of differential thermal curves of kaolinite. *Trans. Brit. Ceram. Soc.* **60**, 177–189 (1961).

(M31) McLaughlin, R. J. W., Geochemistry of some kaolinitic clays. *Geochim. et Cosmochim. Acta* **17**, 11–16 (1959).

(M32) Medlin, W. L., The preparation of synthetic dolomite. *Am. Mineralogist* **44**, 979–986 (1959).

(M33) Middlehurst, J., Mercury switch for establishing the true electrical zero in precise thermocouple measurements. *J. Sci. Instr.* **38**, 165 (1961).

(M33a) Milgrom, J., Inclusion complexes of methylnaphthalenes *J. Phys. Chem.* **63**, 1843–1848 (1959).

(M34) Misra, M. L., Gipta, M. M., and Upadhyaya, V. G., Assam and Rewa sillimanite-dehydration, DTA, and thermal expansion study. *Refractories J.* **31**, 399–401 (1955).

(M35) Mitchell, B. D., and Mackenzie, R. C., An apparatus for differential thermal analysis under controlled atmosphere conditions. *Clay Minerals Bull.* **4**, No. 21, 31 (1959).

(M36) Morita, H., and Rice, H., Characterization of organic substances by differential thermal analysis. *Anal. Chem.* **27**, 336–339 (1955).

(M37) Morrison, R. D., and Lachenmayer, R. R., Thin film thermocouples for substrate temperature measurement. *Rev. Sci. Instr.* **34**, 106–107 (1963).

(M38) Muan, A., and Somiya, S., Phase equilibrium studies in the system CaO–FeO–Fe_2O_3–SiO_2. *J. Am. Ceram. Soc.* **42**, 603–613 (1959).

(M39) Muller, R. H., Instrumentation. *Anal. Chem.* **32**, No. 13, 107A (1960).

(M40) Muller, R. H., and Garman, R. L., Electronic recording analytical balance. *Ind. Eng. Chem., Anal. Ed.* **10**, 436–440 (1938).

(M41) Muller, N. W., and Peck, R. E., Simple automatic and recording balance. *Ind. Eng. Chem., Anal. Ed.* **15**, 46–48 (1943).

(M42) Murphy, C. B., Hill, J. A., and Schacher, G. P., Differential thermal analysis and simultaneous gas analysis. *Anal. Chem.* **32**, 1374–1375 (1960).

(M43) Murray, J. A., Fischer, H. C., and Shade, R. W., M.I.T. Fellowship Report. *Proc. Natl. Lime Assoc.* (*Wash., D. C.*) **49**, 95–116 (1951).

(M44) Murray, P., and Allison, E. B., The monoclinic to tetragonal phase transformation in zirconia. *Trans. Brit. Ceram. Soc.* **53**, 335–361 (1954).

(M45) Murray, P., and White, J., The kinetics of clay decomposition. *Trans. Brit. Ceram. Soc.* **48**, 187–206 (1949).

(M46) Murray, P., and White, J., Kinetics of the thermal dehydration of clays. IV. Interpretation of the differential thermal analysis of the clay minerals. *Trans. Brit. Ceram. Soc.* **54**, 204–238 (1955).

(N1) Nakai, Y., Powdered preparations. Theoretical consideration of tablet disintegration process by thermal analysis. *Chem. Pharm. Bull.* (*Tokyo*) **9**, 796–800 (1961).

(N2) Nakamura, Y., Differential thermal analysis of phenol- form aldehyde resin. *Kogyo Kagaku Zasshi* **64**, 392–395 (1961).

(N3) Narsimhan, G., Thermal decomposition of calcium carbonate. *Chem. Eng. Sci.* **16**, 21–30 (1961).

(N4) Nechitailo, N. A., Tolchinskii, N. M., and Sanin, P. I., Thermal analysis in the study of polymer destruction. *Plasticheskie Massy* No. 11, 54–57 (1960).

(N5) Newkirk, A. E., Thermogravimetric measurements. *Anal. Chem.* **32**, 1559–1563 (1960).

(N6) Newkirk, A. E., and Laware, R., Thermogravimetric analysis of potassium hydrogen phthalate *Talanta* **9**, 169–173 (1962).

(N7) Newkirk, T. F., Differential thermal analysis above 1200°. *J. Am. Ceram. Soc.* **41**, 409–414 (1958).

(N8) Newman, P. C., Phase changes in In_2Se_3. *Z. anorg. allgem. Chem.* **299**, 158–159 (1959) (in English).

(N9) Nikitina, E. A., and Buris, E. V., Thermographic investigation of important saturated heteropolyacids. *J. Gen. Chem. USSR* (*English transl.*) **26**, 717–720 (1956).

(N10) Nikolaev, A. V., and Shubina, S. M., Differential thermal microanalysis. *Vopr. Petrog. i Mineral. Akad. Nauk SSSR* **2**, 427–432 (1953).

(N11) Nishiyama, Z., Shimizu, K., and Sugino, K., Martensite transformation in thin foils. *Acta Met.* **9**, 620–622 (1961).

(N12) Norin, R., The decomposition products of kaolinite. *Geol. Foren. Stockholm Forh.* **66**, 15–8 (1944).

(N13) Norton, F. H., Hydrothermal formation of clay minerals in the laboratory. *Am. Mineralogist* **24**, 1–17 (1939).

(N14) Notz, K. J., and Jaffe, H. H., Correlation of TGA and DTA temperatures in decomposition reactions. *J. Am. Ceram. Soc.* **43**, 53–54 (1960).

(N15) Nozaki, F., and Morikawa, K., Surface composition and chemical properties of the supported nickel catalysts X-ray analysis, infrared spectrum analysis and differential thermal analysis. *Kogyo Kagaku Zasshi* **64**, 1568–1573 (1961).

(N16) Nutting, P. G., Some standard thermal dehydration curves. *U. S. Geol. Surv. Profess. Papers* **197E**, 197–217 (1943).

(O1) O'Connor, J. R., Use of thermo electric effects during crystal growth. *J. Electrochem. Soc.* **108**, 713–715 (1961).

(O2) Oetting, F. L., and Gregory, N. W., Heat capacity of and a transition in iron(II) iodide above room temperature., *J. Phys. Chem.* **65**, 173–175 (1961).

(O3) Ogimachi, N. N., Corcoran, J. M., and Kruse, H. W., Thermal analysis of systems of hydrazine with propyl alcohol, isopropyl alcohol, and allyl alcohol. *J. Chem. Eng. Data* **6**, 238–239 (1961).

(O4) Okada, Y, and Ameniya, A., Effect of atmosphere on radiation-induced cross-linking of polyethylene. *J. Polymer Sci.* **50**, S22–S24 (1961).

(O5) Okuda, H., Kato, S., and Iga, T., Formation of mullite from kaolin minerals at the temperatures lower than 900. *Yogyo Kyokai Shi* **69**, 149–160 (1961).

(O6) Orcel, J., and Caillère, S., Differential thermal analysis of clays and montmorillonites *Compt. Rend.* **197**, 774 (1933).

(O7) Oriani, R. A., and Murphy, W. K., Differential calorimeter for heats of formation of alloys. *J. Phys. Chem.* **62**, 303 (1958).

(O8) O'Shaughnessy, M. T., Fundamental ideas of polymer chemistry. (Contract AF-04(695)-69) Report No. TDR-69(2240–54)TN-1, DCAS-TDR-62-118.

(O9) Osipov, A. I., Infringement of Boltzmann's distribution in the process of thermal dissociation of molecules. *Dokl. Akad. Nauk SSSR* **137**, 833–835 (1961).

(O10) Otsubo, Y., and Yamaguchi, K., Thermochemical properties and reaction processes of alkali carbonate–iron(III) oxide systems as investigated by means of differential thermal method. Lithium carbonate–iron(III) oxide system. Sodium carbonate–iron(III) oxide system. *Nippon Kagaku Zasshi* **82**, 557–562 (1961).

(P1) Paciorek, K. L., Lajiness, W. G., and Lenk, C. T. Differential thermal analysis of fluoro-elastomer systems. *J. Polymer Sci.* **60**, 141–148 (1962).

(P2) Paciorek, K. L., Lajiness, W. G., Spain, R. G., and Lenk, C. T., Differential thermal analysis of fluorinated polymers. *J. Polymer Sci.* **61**, 415–435 (1962).

(P3) Padmanabhan, V. M., Saraiya, S. C., and Sundaram, A. K., Thermal decomposition of oxalates, *J. Inorg. Nucl. Chem.* **12**, 356–359 (1960).

(P4) Pakulak, J. M., Jr., and Leonard, G. W., Thermistorized apparatus for differential thermal analysis. *Anal. Chem.* 31, 1037–1039 (1959).

(P5) Palei, P. N., Sentyurin, I. G., and Skylreiko, I. S., Application of thermogravimetry in analytical chemistry. *Zh. Anal. Khim.* 12, 318 (1957).

(P5a) Papailhau, J., Apparatus for simultaneous thermogravimetric and differential thermal analysis. *Bull. Soc. Franc. Mineral. Crist.* 82, 367–373 (1959).

(P6) Parker, C. J., Hathaway, J. C., and Blackmon, P. D., Some curves from a portable differential thermal analysis unit. *U. S. Geol. Surv. Bull.* 1021G, (1956).

(P7) Partridge, E. P., Hicks, V., and Smith, G. W., A thermal, microscopic, and X-ray study of the system $NaPO_3-Na_4P_2O_7$. *J. Am. Chem. Soc.* 63, 454–466 (1941).

(P8) Pask, J. A., and Warner, M. F., Fundamental studies of talc. I. Constitution of talcs. *J. Am. Ceram. Soc.* 37, 118–128 (1954).

(P9) Pask, J. A., and Warner, M. F., Differential thermal analysis methods and techniques. *Am. Ceram. Soc. Bull.* 33, 168–175 (1954).

(P10) Paulik, F., Paulik, J., and Erdey, L., Derivatograph. *Z. Anal. Chem.* 160, 241–252 (1958).

(P11) Paulik, F., Paulik, J., and Erdey, L., Effect of the atmosphere which is formed within the sample on the case of derivatographic investigations. *Acta. Chim. Acad. Sci. Hung.* 26, 143–148 (1961).

(P12) Pavel, L., and Fojtik, L., New method of thermal analysis of clay minerals— rapid derivative thermal analysis. *Sb. Cesk. Akad. Zemedel. Ved, Rostlinna Vyroba* 4, 863 (1958).

(P13) Pearce, J. H., and Mardon, P. G., Apparatus for combined thermal analysis and dilatometry. *J. Sci. Instr.* 36, 457 (1959).

(P14) Peco, G., Differential thermal analysis of clays. *Ceramica (Milan)* [N.S.] 7, 48–52 (1952).

(P15) Pedregal, J. D., and Aparicio-Arroyo, E., Fluoride-based ceramics. *In* "Science of Ceramics," Proc. 1961 Conf. (G. H. Stewart, ed.), Vol. 1. Academic Press, New York, 1962.

(P16) Pegolotti, J. A., and Young, W. G., Allylic rearrangements. Reactions of A- and gamma-trifluoromethyl allyl alcohols with thionyl chloride and thermal decomposition of the chlorosulfinate intermediates. Displacement reactions in trifluoromethyl allyl systems. *J. Am. Chem. Soc.* 83, 3251–3261 (1961).

(P17) Penther, C. J., Abrams, S. T., and Stross, E. H., Semiautomatic thermal analysis apparatus. *Anal. Chem.* 23, 1459–1466 (1951).

(P18) Perlin, S. M., Gilman, T. P., and Leites, A. Z., Degree of consolidation of unsaturated polyester resins by the dilatometric method. *Plasticheskie Massy* No 10, 64–68 (1960).

(P19) Peters, H., and Wiedemann, H. G., Thermalbalance of high accuracy and wide application. *Z. Anorg. Allgem. Chem.* 298, 202–211 (1959).

(P20) Peters, H., and Wiedemann, H. G., Thermal decomposition of calcium oxalate and calcium carbonate on a thermobalance of high accuracy. *Z. Anorg. Allgem. Chem.* 300, 142–51 (1959).

(P21) Peterson, A. H., Analytical balance + differential transformer + recording potentiometer = recording microbalance. *Instr. Automation* 28, 1104–1106 (1955).

(P22) Phillips, B., and Muan, A., Stability relationship of calcium ferrites: Phase equilibria in the system 2 $CaO-Fe_2O_3-FeO\cdot Fe_2O_3-Fe_2O_3$ above 1135°C. *Trans. Met. Soc. AIME* 218, 1112–1118 (1960).

(P23) Phillips, N. D., and Wagoner, C. L., Use of differential thermal analysis in exploring minimum temperature limits of oil-ash corrosion. *Corrosion* **17**, 396T–400T (1961).

(P24) Pietri, A., Haladjian, J., Perinet, G., and Carpeni, G., Isohydric Point. Hydrated germanium dioxide, preparation, thermogravimetry, and X-rays. *Bull. Soc. Chim. France* pp. 1909–1913 (1960).

(P25) Pirisi, R., and Mattu, F., Differential thermal analysis of sodium and ammonium oxalates. *Chimica (Milan)* **8**, 283–287 (1953).

(P26) Polizzotti, G., X-ray and differential thermal analyses on a Sicilian montmorillonitic clay. *Chim. Ind. (Milan)* **43**, 154–158 (1961).

(P27) Primak, W., Fuchs, L. H., and Day, P., Effects of nuclear reactor exposure on same properties of vitreous silica and quartz. *J. Am. Ceram. Soc.* **38**, 135–139 (1955).

(P28) Proks, I., and Siske, V., Study of $CaCO_3 \rightleftharpoons CaO + CO_2$ reaction by differential thermal analysis. *Chem. Zvesti* **12**, 275–283 (1958).

(P29) Proks, I., and Siske, V., Apparatus for the performance of differential thermal analysis at low temperatures. *Chem. Zvesti* **15**, 309–314 (1961).

(R1) Rabatin, J. G., and Card, C. S., Simple recording thermobalance for vacuum and pressure studies. *Anal. Chem.* **31**, 1689–1692 (1959).

(R2) Radchenko, O. A., and Koperina, V. V., Thermal analysis applied to the study of dispersed organic matter of rocks. *Dokl. Akad. Nauk SSSR* **135**, 713–716 (1960).

(R3) Radzikovskaya, S. V., and Samsonov, G. V., Vacuum thermal method of preparation of cerium and lanthanum mono sulfides. *Zh. Prikl. Khim.* **34**, 671–672 (1961).

(R4) Ralls, J. W., and Elliger, C. A., Thermal transformations of O-alkyl-lactims. *Chem. & Ind. (London)* p. 20 (1961).

(R5) Rao, C. N. R., Yoganarasimhan, S. R., and Faeth, P. A., Brookite-rutile transformation. *Trans. Faraday Soc.* **57**, 504–510 (1961).

(R6) Rao, K. V., Dielectric loss and thermal bleaching of calcite irradiated by X-rays. *Phys. Chem. Solids* **20**, 193–196 (1961).

(R7) Rase, D. E., and Roy, R., Phase equilibria in the system $BaO–TiO_2$. *J. Am. Ceram. Soc.* **38**, 102–113 (1955).

(R8) Raudsepp, I. Y., Instrument for differential recording of electro conductivity changes in polythermal analysis. *Zh. Fiz. Khim.* **35**, 665–668 (1961).

(R9) Ravich, G. B., and Burtsev, U. N., Effect of polymorphism on thermal conductivity. *Dokl. Akad. Nauk SSSR* **137**, 1155–1157 (1961).

(R10) Razuvaev, G. A., Terman, L. M., and Petukhov, G. G., Mechanism underlying the thermal decomposition of percarbonates in solution. *Dokl. Akad. Nauk SSSR* **136**, 628–630 (1961).

(R11) Reese, D. R., Nordberg, P. N., Eriksen, S. P., and Swintosky, J. V., Technique for studying thermally induced phase transitions. *J. Pharm. Sci.* **50**, 177–178 (1961).

(R12) Reisman, A., Isobaric dissociation studies of alkali-metal carbonatehydrate using simultaneous differential thermal analysis–thermogravimetric analysis. *Anal. Chem.* **32**, 1566–1574 (1960).

(R13) Reisman, A., and Holtzberg, F., Phase equilibria in the system potassium carbonate-niobium pentoxide by the method of differential thermal analysis. *J. Am. Chem. Soc.* **77**, 2115–2119 (1955).

(R14) Reisman, A., Holtzberg, F., Berkenblit, M., and Berry, M., Reactions of the group VB pentoxides with alkali oxides and carbonates. III. Thermal and X-ray phase diagrams of the system K_2O and K_2CO_3 with Ta_2O_5. *J. Chem. Soc.* **78**, 4514–4520 (1956).

(R15) Reisman, A., and Karlak, J., Observations on the differential thermal analysis of copper sulfate pentahydrate. *J. Am. Chem. Soc.* **80**, 6500 (1958).

(R16) Reisman, A., Triebwasser, S., and Holtzberg, F., Phase diagram of the system potassium niobate–potassium tantalate by the methods of differential-thermal and resistance analysis. *J. Am. Chem. Soc.* **77**, 4228–4230 (1955).

(R17) Remizova, A. A., and Tamarin, A. A., Effect of admixtures on the anomaly of thermal expansion near the melting points. *Izv. Vysshikh Uchebn. Zavedenii, Fiz.* No. 6, 152–156 (1960).

(R18) Rey, M., and Kostomaroff, V., Physico-chemical interpretation of differential thermal analysis. *Silicates Ind.* **24**, 603 (1959).

(R19) Richer, A., and Vallet, P., On the method of study of chemical systems by variation of the mass during linearly increasing temperature, its application to the pyrolysis of calcium carbonate in netrogen and carbon dioxide and to the study of gravimetric methods. *Bull. Soc. Chim. France* pp. 148–151 (1953).

(R20) Richmond, J. C., and Stewart, J. E., Spectral emittance of ceramic-coated and uncoated specimens of incaved and stainless steel. *J. Am. Ceram. Soc.* **42**, 633–640 (1959).

(R21) Ringwood, A. E., Aspects of the thermal evolution of the earth. *Geochim. Cosmochim. Acta* **20**, 241–259 (1960).

(R22) Roberts, A. L., and Brindley, G. W., A review of clay mineral research in the University of Leeds. *Clay Minerals Bull* **1**, No. 1, 15–17 (1952).

(R23) Roberts, A. L., and Grimshaw, R. W., The quantitative determination of minerals by thermal analysis. *Trans. 2nd Intern. Ceram. Congr., 1950* p. 71 (1950).

(R24) Robertson, R. H. S., Thermal decomposition of dolomite. *Nature* **172**, 998–1001 (1953).

(R25) Rodot, M., Thermomagnetic ambielectronic effects and mechanism of the electronic relaxation in semiconductors of groups III and V. *Compt. Rend.* **252**, 2526–2528 (1961).

(R26) Rogers, R. N., Simple microscale differential thermal analysis of explosives. *Microchem. J.* **5**, 91–99 (1961).

(R27) Rogers, R. N., Yasuda, S. K., and Zinn, V., Pyrolysis as an analytical tool. *Anal. Chem.* **32**, 672–678 (1960).

(R28) Rogers, S. S., and Mandelkern, L., *J. Phys. Chem.* **61**, 985 (1957).

(R29) Romo, P. C., and Lynch, T. W., U. S. Patent 2,705,418 (1955). Differential thermal analysis of minerals.

(R30) Ropp, R. C., and Aia, M. A., Thermal analysis of phosphor raw materials. *Anal. Chem.* **34**, 1288–1291 (1962).

(R31) Rosenthal, G., A study of the plasticity of mono-ionic clays. "Science of Ceramics," Proc. 1961 Conf. (G. H. Stewart, ed.), Vol. 1. Academic Press, New York, 1962.

(R32) Rowland, R. A., and Beck, C. W., Determination of small quantities of dolomite by differential thermal analysis. *Am. Mineralogist* **37**, 76–82 (1952).

(R33) Rowland, R. A., and Jonas, E. C., Variations in differential thermal analysis curves of siderite. *Am. Mineralogist* **34**, 550–558 (1949).

(R34) Rowland, R. A., and Lewis, D. R., Furnace-atmosphere control in differential thermal analysis. *Am. Mineralogist* **36**, 80–91 (1951).

(R35) Rowland, R. A., Weiss, E. V., and Lewis, D. R., Apparatus for the oscillating-heating method of X-ray powder diffraction. *J. Am. Ceram. Soc.* **42**, 133–138 (1959).

(R36) Rubin, T., Johnston, H. L., and Altman, H. W., Thermal expansion of rock salt. *J. Phys. Chem.* **65**, 65–67 (1961).

(R37) Rudin, A., Schreiber, H. P., and Waldman, M. H., Measurement of polyethylene oxidation by differential thermal analysis. *Ind. Eng. Chem.* **55**, 137–140 (1961).

(S1) Sabatier, G., Effect of the dimensions of chlorite crystals on their thermal differential analysis curves. *Bull. Soc. Franc. Mineral.* **73**, 43–48 (1950).

(S2) Sabatier, G., Determination of heats of transformation by differential thermal analysis. *Bull. Soc. Franc. Mineral.* **77**, 953–968 and 1077–1083 (1954).

(S3) Saibova, M. T., and Berg, L. G., Thermographic phase analysis of certain salt mixtures. *Uzbeksk. Khim. Zh.* No. 1, 15–22 (1961).

(S4) Sastry, B. S. R., and Hummel, F. A., Studies in lithium oxide systems. V. $Li_2O-Li_2O \cdot B_2O_3$. *J. Am. Ceram. Soc.* **42**, 216–218 (1959).

(S5) Satava, V., and Trousil, Z., Simple construction of an apparatus for automatic DTA. *Silikaty* **4**, 272–277 (1960).

(S6) Saunders, H. L., and Giedroyc, V., Differential thermal analysis in controlled atmosphere. *Trans. Brit. Ceram. Soc.* **49**, 365–374 (1950).

(S7) Sauer, H. A., "An Experimental Dilatometer." To be published, 1964.

(S8) Schaller, W. T., and Vlisidis, A. C., Spontaneous oxidation of a sample of powdered siderite. *Am. Mineralogist* **44**, 433–435 (1959).

(S9) Schawlow, A. L., and Garn, P. D., Unpublished measurements (1958).

(S10) Schnitzer, M., and Hoffman, I., Thermogravimetry of the organic matter of a podzol soil. *Chem. & Ind.* (*London*) pp. 1397–1398 (1961).

(S11) Schnitzer, M., Wright, J. R., and Hoffman, I., High temperature thermogravimetry of chlorides and sulphates. A study of the application to soils. *Anal. Chim. Acta* **26**, 371–377 (1962).

(S12) Schnitzer, M., Wright, V. X., and Hoffman, I., Use of the thermobalance in the analysis of soils and clays., *Anal. Chem.* **31**, 440–444 (1959).

(S13) Schroeder, J., and Stanik, T., Automatic apparatus for differential thermoanalysis. General description and results of check measurements. *Chem. Stosowana* **4**, 397–406 (1960).

(S14) Schuele, W. J., Preparation of fine particles from bimetal oxalates. *J. Phys. Chem.* **63**, 83–86 (1959).

(S15) Schweite, H. E., and Ziegler, G., Principles and applications of the method of dynamic differential calorimetry. *Ber. Deut. Keram Ges.* **35**, 193–204 (1952).

(S16) Schwenker, R. F., Jr., and Beck, L. R., Jr. The differential thermal analysis of textile and other high polymeric materials. *Textile Res. J.* **30**, 624–626 (1960).

(S17) Sekine, Y., Mechanism of thermal decomposition of urea–formaldehyde resin. *Kogyo Kagaku Zasshi* **63**, 1657–1659 (1960).

(S18) Seto, J., Study on amino acids by using a thermobalance. *Bunseki Kagaku* **9**, 939–945 (1960).

(S19) Sewell, E. C., The consequences for differential thermal analysis of assuming a reaction to be first order. *Clay Minerals Bull.* **2**, 233–241 (1955).

(S19a) Sewell, E. C., and Honeyborne, D. B., in "The Differential Thermal Investigation of Clays" (R. C. Mackenzie, ed.), pp. 65–97. Mineral. Soc., London, 1957.

(S20) Shiba, S., Differential thermal analysis of the systems aluminum soap–hydrocarbon. Bull. Chem. Soc. Japan 34, 809–816 (1961).

(S21) Shiba, S., Differential thermal analysis of aluminum soaps. Bull. Chem. Soc. Japan 34, 804–808 (1961).

(S22) Shiloss, J. C., Thermal analysis of the $CrCb_2$–NaCl system. J. Phys. Chem. 64, 1566–1567 (1960).

(S23) Sidorovich, A. V., and Juyshinskii, E. V., Specific features of the thermal expansion of polyethylene terephthalate crystallized after preliminary stretching. Vysokomolekul. Soedin. 3, 161–163 (1961).

(S24) Simchen, A. E., Application of the kinetics of phase transformation to the thermal decomposition of potassium chlorate and potassium per maganate. J. Chim. Phys. 58, 596–601 (1961).

(S25) Simchen, A. E., Fusion point and the thermal decomposition of potassium perchlorate. J. Phys. Chem. 65, 1093–1095 (1961).

(S26) Simons, E. L., Newkirk, A. E., and Aliferis, I., Performance of a pen recording chevenard thermobalance. Anal. Chem. 29, 48–54 (1957).

(S27) Simons, J. H., Scheirer, C. L., Jr., and Ritter, H. L., Magnetic weighing and gas density balances. Rev. Sci. Instr. 24, 36–42 (1953).

(S28) Siske, V., and Proks, I., New arrangement for differential thermal analysis. Chem. Zvesti 12, 185 (1958).

(S29) Siske, V., and Proks, I., Differential thermal analysis of carbonates in carbon dioxide current. Chem. Zvesti 12, 201–208 (1958).

(S30) Sklyarenko, I. S., and Chubukova, T. M., Analytical applications of thermo gravimetry. Thermogravimetric study of plutonium compounds. Zhur. Anal. Khim. 15, 706–710 (1960).

(S31) Sklyarenko, U. S., Sklyarenko, I. S., and Chubukova, T. M., Thermogravimetry in analytical chemistry. Thermogravimetric study of lanthanum carbonate. Zhur. Anal. Khim. 16, 417–421 (1961).

(S32) Skorik, A. I., and Boldyrev, V. V., Arrangement for investigating the kinetics of thermal degradation of solids during irradiation. Zh. Fiz. Khim. 35, 1370–1371 (1961).

(S33) Smith, C. S., A simple method of thermal analysis permitting quantitative measurements of specific and latent heats. Am. Inst. Mining Met. Engrs., Inst. Metals Div., Tech. Publ. 1100, 9 pp. (1939).

(S34) Smith, W., The thermal conductivity of dry soils. Soil Sci. 53, 453–460 (1942).

(S35) Smyth, F. H., and Adams, L. H., The system calcium oxide–carbon dioxide. J. Am. Chem. Soc. 45, 1167 (1923).

(S36) Smyth, H. T., Temperature distribution during mineral inversion and its significance in differential thermal analysis. J. Am. Ceram. Soc. 34, 221–224 (1951).

(S37) Somiya, T., and Hirano, S., Thermal decomposition of oxalates and of nitrates of lanthanum, cerium, praseodymium, neodymium and samarium in the atmosphere of carbon dioxide. J. Soc. Chem. Ind. Japan 34, 495–613 (1931).

(S38) Sosman, R. B., "Properties of Silica," Am. Chem. Soc. Monogr. No. 37. Chem. Catalog Co., New York, 1927.

(S38a) Soulen, J. R., Calculation of thermogravimetric data by electronic digital computer. *Anal. Chem.* **34**, 136–137 (1962).

(S38b) Soulen, J. R., and Mockrin, I., Improved methods of using the thermobalance to determine thermal stabilities. *Anal. Chem.* **33**, 1909–1912 (1961).

(S39) Spatz, S. M., Thermal decarboxylation of diaryl fumarates to stilbenes. *J. Org. Chem.* **26**, 4158–4160 (1961).

(S40) Speil, S., Berkelhamer, L. H., Pask, J. A., and Davies, B., Differential thermal analysis. Its application to clays and other aluminous materials. *U.S. Bur. Mines, Tech. Paper* **664** (1945).

(S41) Speros, D. M., and Woodhouse, R. L., Quantitative differential thermal analysis. Heats and rates of solid-liquid transitions. *Nature* **197**, 1261–1262 (1963).

(S42) Spinedi, P., and Franciosi, O., Thermodifferential precision analysis. *Ricerca Sci.* 22, 2323–39 (1952).

(S43) Splitek, R., Automatically operated apparatus for differential and gravimetric thermoanalysis. *Hutnicke Listy* 13, 697 (1958).

(S44) Sriraman, S., and Shanmugasundaram, V., Thermomagnetic study of mercury and dilute amalgams of sodium and potassium. *Bull. Chem. Soc. Japan* **34**, 1288–1290 (1961).

(S45) Srivastava, O. K., and Murthy, A. R. V., Thermal decomposition of cerous oxalate in vacuum. *J. Sci. Ind. Res. (India)* **208**, 96–101 (1961).

(S46) Srivastava, O. K., and Vasudevamurthy, A. R., Thermo gravimetric behavior of lanthanum, thorium and cerium oxalates in an atmosphere of carbon dioxide. *Current Sci. (India)* **29**, 470 (1960).

(S47) Stegmüller, L., Differential thermalanalysis apparatus. *Sprechsaal Keram.* **86**, 1–8 (1953).

(S48) Stephenson, J. L., Smith, G. W., and Trantham, H. V., Automatic recording of weight and temperature for vacuum-sublimation studies. *Rev. Sci. Instr.* **28**, 381–382 (1957).

(S49) Stepko, I. I., Romanova, G. P., and Chmel, N. G., Effect of thermal treatment on gas evolution from a germanium surface. *Ukr. Fiz. Zh.* **5**, 705–707 (1960).

(S50) Stone, R. L., Differential thermal analysis of clay materials under controlled thermodynamic conditions. *Ohio State Univ. Stud. Eng. Expt. Sta. Bull.* **146** (1951).

(S51) Stone, R. L., Apparatus for differential thermal analysis under controlled partial pressures of water, carbon dioxide, other gases. *J. Am. Ceram. Soc.* **35**, 76–82 (1952).

(S52) Stone, R. L., Differential thermal analysis of kaolin-group minerals under controlled partial pressures of water. *J. Am. Ceram. Soc.* **35**, 90–99 (1952).

(S53) Stone, R. L., Preliminary study of the effects of water vapor pressure on thermograms of kaolinitic soils. *Proc. 2nd Natl. Conf. Clays and Clay Minerals, 1953* pp. 315–323. Natl. Acad. Sci.–Natl. Res. Council (Publ. No. 327), Washington, D. C., 1954.

(S54) Stone, R. L., Thermal analysis of magnesite at carbon dioxide pressures up to six atmospheres. *J. Am. Ceram. Soc.* **37**, 46–47 (1954).

(S55) Stone, R. L., Effect of water vapor pressure on thermograms of kaolinitic soils. *Proc. 2nd Natl. Conf. Clays and Clay Minerals, 1953* pp. 315–323. Natl. Acad. Sci.–Natl. Res. Council (Publ. No. 327) Washington, D. C., 1954.

(S56) Stone, R. L., Determinative tests of aid in the design of driers and kilns. *Am. Ceram. Soc. Bull.* **36**, 1–5 (1957).

(S57) Stone, R. L., Laboratory tests on the oxidation characteristics of a Texas shale. *Am. Ceram. Soc. Bull.* **36**, 172–173 (1957).

(S58) Stone, R. L., Differential thermal analysis by the dynamic gas technique. *Anal. Chem.* **32**, 1582–1588 (1960).

(S58a) Stone, R. L., Private communication (1962).

(S59) Stone, R. L., and Rase, H. F., Differential thermal analysis. New techniques for testing silica-alumina catalysts. *Anal. Chem.* **29**, 1273–1277 (1957).

(S60) Stone, R. L., and Rowland, R. A., DTA of kaolinite and montmorillonite under water-vapor pressures up to six atmospheres. *Proc. 3rd Natl. Conf. Clays and Clay Minerals, 1954* pp. 103–117. Natl. Acad. Sci.–Natl. Res. Council (Publ. No. 395), Washington, D. C., 1955.

(S61) Stone, R. L., and Weiss, E. J., Examination of four coarsely crystalline chlorites by X-ray and high-pressure differential thermal analysis techniques. *Clay Minerals Bull.* **2**, 214–222 (1955).

(S62) Strassburger, J., Brauer, G. M., Tryon, M., and Forziati, A. F., Analysis of methyl methacrylate copolymers by gas chromatography. *Anal. Chem.* **32**, 454–457 (1960).

(S63) Straus, S., and Madorsky, S. L., Thermal stability of poly di vinyl benzene and of copolymers of styrene with di vinyl benzene and with trivinyl benzene. *J. Res. Natl. Bur. Std.* **65A**, 243–248 (1961).

(S64) Strekalovskii, V. N., Bessonov, A. V., Vlasov, V. G., and Sidorenko, F. A., Phase transformation during reduction and oxidation of uranium oxides. *Fiz. Metal. i Metalloved.* **11**, 400–403.

(S65) Strella, S., Differential thermal analysis of polymers. 1. The glass transition. *J. Appl. Polymer Sci.* **7**, 569–579 (1963).

(S66) Strella, S., Differential thermal analysis of polymers. II. Melting. *J. Appl. Polymer Sci.* **7**, 1281–1289 (1963).

(S67) Strizhkov, B. V., Lapitskii, A. V., and Vlasov, L. G., Preparation and thermographic study of barium, lead, and strontium titanyl oxalates. *Zh. Prikl. Khim.* **34**, 673–674 (1961).

(S68) Strong H. M., The experimental fusion curve of iron to 96,000 atmospheres. *J. Geophys. Res.* **64**, 653 (1959).

(S69) Stross, E. H., and Abrams, S. T., The phase behavior of the system sodium stearate-cethane. *J. Am. Chem. Soc.* **72**, 3309–3310 (1950).

(S70) Sturm, E., Quantitative differential thermal analysis by controlled heating rates. *J. Phys. Chem.* **65**, 1935–1936.

(S71) Suga, H., Chihara, H., and Seki, S., Crystallochemical study by the differential thermal analysis. Device of automatic recording and program control for the differential thermal analysis. *Nippon Kagaku Zasshi* **82**, 24–29 (1961).

(S72) Suga, H., Nakatusuka, K., Shinoda, T., and Seki, S., Crystallochemical study by the differential thermal analysis. Detection of phase transition. *Nippon Kagaku Zasshi* **82**, 29–32 (1961).

(S73) Suleimanov, A. S., The nature of exothermic effect in magnesium carbonates. *Tr. Pervogo Sov. Termagr. Kazan* pp. 200–204 (1953).

(S74) Sun, M. S., Differential thermal analysis of shattuckite. *Am. Mineralogist* **46**, 67–77 (1961).

(S75) Sundquist, B. E., and Mondolfo, L. F., Heterogeneous nucleation in the liquid-to-solid transformation in alloys. *Trans. Met. Soc. AIME* **215**, 157–164 (1961).

564 References

(T1) Taft, R. W., Evidence for phenyl cation with an odd number of pi electrons from the aqueous thermal decomposition of the diazonium ion. *J. Am. Chem. Soc.* **83**, 3350 (1961).

(T2) Takakura, E., and Yasoshima, Y., Thermal decomposition of potassium titanyl sulfate. *Kogyo Kagaku Zasshi* **63**, 1569–1570 (1960).

(T3) Teitel 'baum, B. Ya., and Berg, L. G., Thermal analysis of registration of the volume of evolved gases. *Zh. Anal. Khim.* **8**, 152–157 (1953).

(T4) Teitel 'baum, B. Ya., and Dianov, M. P., Method of recording thermomechanical curves of polymers. *Vysokomolekul. Soedin.* **3**, 594–601 (1961).

(T5) Teitel 'baum, B. Ya., Iagfarova, T. A., Dianov, M. P., and Gubanov, E. F., Thermal transformations of certain rubbers as investigated by the method of thermomechanical curves. *Dokl. Akad. Nauk SSSR* **140**, 1132–1135 (1961).

(T6) Templeton, L. K., and Pask, J. A., Formation of $BaTiO_3$ from $BaCO_3$ and TiO_2 in air and CO_2. *J. Am. Ceram. Soc.* **42**, 212 (1959).

(T7) Thall, E., An automatic recording balance. *Can. Mining Met. Bull.* No. 145, 663–670 (1946).

(T7a) Thomasson, C. V., and Wilburn, F. W., The application of differential thermal analysis and thermogravimetric analysis to the study of reactions between glass-making materials. Part 2. The sodium carbonate-silica system with minor batch additions. *Phys. Chem. Glasses* **1**, 52–69 (1960).

(T8) Torkar, K., and Bertsch, L., Aluminum oxide and aluminum hydroxide. Effect of sodium ions on the formation and the thermal decomposition of bayerite. Effect of small amounts of sodium on the thermal decomposition of boehmite. *Monatsh.* **92**, 525–33 and 746–755 (1961).

(T9) Torkar, K., and Egghart, H., Aluminum oxide and aluminum hydroxide. Effect of hydrolysis conditions on the formation of aluminum hydroxide from aluminum ethylate. *Monatsh.* **92**, 755–768 (1961).

(T10) Torkar, K., Egghart, H., Krischner, H., and Worel, H., Aluminum oxide and aluminum hydroxide. Thermal decomposition of very pure aluminum hydroxide. *Monatsh.* **92**, 512–525 (1961).

(T11) Treloar, F. E., Measurement of polymerization kinetics by dilatometry. *Polymer* **1**, 513–514 (1960).

(T12) Tryhorn, F. G., and Wyatt, W. F., A recording hydrostatic balance of simple design. *Trans. Faraday Soc.* **23**, 238–242 (1927).

(T13) Tsurinov, G. G., "Pyrometer of N. S. Kurnakov." Acad. Sci. USSR, Moscow, 1953.

(T14) Turner, R. C., Hoffman, I., and Chen, D., Thermogravimetry of the dehydration of magnesium hydroxide. *Can. J. Chem.* **41**, 243–251 (1963).

(U1) Ugai, Ya. A., Thermographic investigation of the decomposition of bivalent metal oxalates. *Zh. Obshch. Khim.* **24**, 1315–1321 (1954).

(U2) Ukai, Y., Thermal investigation of mineral by means of dielectric behavior. *Mem. Coll. Sci. Univ. Kyoto, Ser. B* **22**, 185–198 (1955) (in English).

(U3) Ukai, Y., Korekawa, M., and Mochida, Y., The dielectric behavior and the X-ray investigation on some metamict minerals. *Kobutsugaku Zasshi* **2**, 252–262 (1955).

(U3a) U. S. Weather Bur., Private communication (1964).

(U4) Urbanski, T., Semenczuk, A., and Gorski, W., Thermal analysis of the system 1-chloro-2,4-dinitrobenzene–picryl chloride. *Bull. Acad. Polon. Sci., Ser. Sci. Chim.* **8**, 487–488 (1960) (in English).

References 565

(V1) Vainstein, E. E., and Kotlar, B. I., Fine structure of the X-ray telluride within the range of antiferromagnetic transformation temperatures. *Dokl. Akad. Nauk SSSR* **136**, 133–135 (1961).

(V2) Vand-Der-Lugt, W., and Poulis, N. J., Magnetic phase transitions of cobalt chloride. *Physica* **26**, 917–921 (1960).

(V3) Vassallo, D. A., and Harden, J. C., Precise phase transition measurements of organic materials by differential thermal analysis. *Anal. Chem.* **34**, 132–135 (1961).

(V4) Venkateswarlu, K., and Sriraman, S., Diamagnetic susceptibility of oxalate, tartrate, and citrate ions. *Trans. Faraday Soc.* **53**, 438–441 (1957).

(V5) Vickery, R. C., and Muir, H. M., Anomalous thermo-electric properties of gadolinium selenide. *Nature* **190**, 336–337 (1961).

(V6) Vieweg, R., and Gast, T., Recording microbalance for the measurements of diffusion through plastic membranes. *Kunstostoffe* **34**, 117–119 (1944).

(V7) Vinogradova, E. N., Vasil'eva, L. N., Use of differential thermocouple during ebullioscopic determination of molecular weight of oil products. *Khim. i Tekhnol. Topliv i Masel* **6**, No. 1, 57–61 (1961).

(V8) Vlasov, A. Y., and Antonov, I. V., Thermal magnetic hysteresis and thermal hysteresis of the magnetostriction of nickel-copper alloys. *Izv. Sibirsk. Otd. Akad. Nauk SSSR* No. 8, 121–124 (1961).

(V9) Vlasov, L. G., Lapitskii, A. V., and Strizhkov, B. V., Thermographic and thermogravimetric study of oxalato niobates. *Vestn. Mosk. Univ., Ser. II, Khim.* **16**, No. 1, 57–58 (1961).

(V10) Vold, M. J., Differential thermal analysis. *Anal. Chem.* **21**, 683–688 (1949).

(V11) Vold, M. J., and Vold, R. D., The phase behavior of lithium stearate in cetane and in decahydronaphthalene. *J. Colloid Sci.* **5**, 1–19 (1950).

(V12) Vold, R. D., Grandine, J. D., and Vold, M. J., *Polymorphic transformations* of calcium stearate and calcium stearate monohydrate. *J. Colloid Sci.* **3**, 339–361 (1948).

(V13) Vratny, F., Kern, S., and Guliotta, F., Thermal decomposition of cerium(III) nitrate hydrate. *J. Inorg. Nucl. Chem.* **17**, 281–285 (1961).

(V14) Vyrodov, I. P., Differential thermal analysis of the ternary system. Magnesium oxide-magnesium chloride-water. *Zh. Prikl. Khim.* **34**, 1208–1218 (1961).

(W1) Wada, G., Rapid evaluation of the activation energy of chemical reactions in solutions by differential thermal analysis. *Nippon Kagaku Zasshi* **81**, 1656–1661 (1960).

(W2) Wahl, F. M., Grim, R. E., and Graf, R. B., Phase transformations in silica as examined by continuous X-ray diffraction. *Am. Mineralogist* **46**, 196–208 (1961).

(W3) Walton, J. D., Jr., New method of preparing clay samples for differential thermal analysis. *J. Am. Ceram. Soc.* **38**, 438–443 (1955).

(W4) Warne, S. S. J., Differential thermal analysis of siderite. *Bull. Soc. Franc. Mineral. Crist.* **84**, 234–237 (1961).

(W5) Warne, S. S. J., and Bayliss, P., Differential thermal analysis of cerussite. *Am. Mineralogist* **47**, 1011–1023 (1962).

(W6) Waterbury, G. R., Douglass, R. M., and Metz, C. F., Thermogravimetric behavior of plutonium metal, nitrate, sulfate, and oxalate. *Anal. Chem.* **33**, 1018–1023 (1961).

(W7) Waters, P. L., Recording differential thermogravimetric balances. *Nature* **178**, 324–326 (1956).

(W8) Waters, P. L., New types of recording differential thermobalances. *J. Sci. Instr.* **35**, 41–46 (1958).

(W9) Waters, P. L., Fractional thermogravimetric analysis. *Anal. Chem.* **32**, 852–858 (1960).

(W10) Webb, T. L., Comparative performance of nickel and porous alumina sample holders for differential thermal analysis. *Nature* **174**, 686–688 (1954).

(W11) Webb, T. L., and Heystek, H., *in* "The Differential Thermal Analysis of Clays" (R. C. Mackenzie, ed.), pp. 329–363. Mineral. Soc., London, 1957.

(W12) Weiss, E. J., and Rowland, R. A., Oscillating reacting X-ray diffractometer studies of clay mineral dehydroxylation. *Am. Mineralogist* **41**, 117–126 (1956).

(W13) Weltner, M., Derivatographic analysis of the thermal decomposition of coal. *Brennstoff-Chem.* **42**, 40–46 (1961).

(W14) Wendlandt, W. W., Inexpensive automatic-recording thermobalance. *Anal. Chem.* **30**, 56–58 (1958).

(W15) Wendlandt, J. J., Thermal decomposition of scandium, yttrium and rare earth metal oxalates. *Anal. Chem.* **30**, 58–61 (1958).

(W16) Wendlandt, W. W., Thermal decomposition of the rare earth metal oxalates. *Anal. Chem.* **31**, 408–410 (1959).

(W17) Wendlandt, W. W., An inexpensive differential-thermal-analysis apparatus. *J. Chem. Educ.* **37**, 94–96 (1960).

(W18) Wendlandt, W. W., Reaction kinetics by differential thermal analysis. *J. Chem. Educ.* **38**, 571–573 (1961).

(W19) Wendlandt, W. W., A controlled atmosphere thermobalance. *J. Chem. Educ.* **38**, 556–558 (1961).

(W20) Wendlandt, W. W., A new apparatus for simultaneous differential thermal analysis and gas evolution analysis. *Anal. Chim. Acta* **27**, 309–314 (1962).

(W21) Wendlandt, W. W., Automatic digital recording thermobalance. *Anal. Chem.* **34**, 1726–1727 (1962).

(W22) Wendlandt, W. W., George, T. D., and Horton, G. R., Thermal decomposition of thorium(IV), uranium(IV), and the rare-earth metal(III) oxalate hydrates. Differential hermal analysis and weight-loss studies. *J. Inorg. Nucl. Chem.* **17**, 273–280 (1961).

(W23) Werner, P. E., Kierkegaard, P., and Magneli, A., Note on the thermal expansion of the tungsten bronzes of potassium, rubidium and cesium. *Acta Chem. Scand.* **15**, 427–428 (1961).

(W24) West, R. R., High-temperature reactions in kaolin-type clays. *Am. Ceram. Soc. Bull.* **36**, 55–58 (1957); see *Ceram. Abstr.* p. 96 (1957).

(W25) West, S. F., and Audrieth, L. F., Differential thermal analysis of some heteropoly acids of molybdenum and tungsten. *J. Phys. Chem.* **59**, 1069–1072 (1955).

(W26) Westman, S., Phase transition in vanadium(IV) oxide. *Acta Chem. Scand.* **15**, 217 (1961).

(W27) White, G. K., Anomalous thermal expansion of chromium. *Australian J. Phys.* **14**, 359–367 (1961).

(W28) White, T. R., Melting behavior of crystalline polymer fibers. *Nature* **175**, 895–896 (1955).

(W29) Whitehead, W. L., The vacuum differential thermal analysis of coals. *Conf. Origin and Constitution of Coal, Crystal Cliffs, Canada, 1950* pp. 100–105. Nova Scotia Dept. Mines, Nova Scotia Res. Found., 1950.

(W30) Whitehead, W. L., and Breger, I. A., Vacuum differential thermal analysis. *Science* 111, 279–281 (1950).

(W31) Whittemore, O. V., Jr., and Ault, N. N., Thermal expansion of various ceramic materials to 1500°C. *J. Am. Ceram. Soc.* 39, 443–444 (1956).

(W32) Wijk, H. F. Van, Impurity determination by thermal analysis. Melting curve of a quickly frozen sample. *Anal. Chim. Acta* 24, 41–45 (1960).

(W33) Wijk, H. F. Van, and Smit, W. M., Impurity determination by thermal analysis. Melting curve of a gradually frozen sample. *Anal. Chim. Acta* 23, 545–551 (1960).

(W34) Wilburn, F. W., and Thomasson, C. V., Application of differential thermal analysis and thermogravimetric analysis to the study of reactions between glass-making materials. Calcium carbonate-silica system. *Phys. Chem. Glasses* 2, 126–131 (1961).

(W35) Wittels, M., The differential thermal analyzer as a microcalorimeter. *Am. Mineralogist* 36, 615–621 (1951).

(W36) Wittels, M., Some aspects of mineral calorimetry. *Am. Mineralogist* 36, 760–767 (1951).

(W37) Woerner, P. F., and Wakefield, G. F., High temperature thermobalance. *Rev. Sci. Instr.* 33, 1456–1457 (1962).

(W38) Wolk, B., Relationship between thermal decomposition and microstructure of alkaline earth carbonates. *J. Electrochem. Soc.* 105, 89 (1958).

(W39) Wolski, W., Formation of ferrites at low temperatures. *Roczniki Chem.* 34, 1815–1818 (1960).

(W40) Wood, E. A., The question of a phase transition in silicon. *J. Phys. Chem.* 60, 508–509 (1956).

(Y1) Yagfarov, M. Sh., New method of quantitative thermography. *Zh. Neorg. Khim.* 6, 2440–2443 (1961).

(Y2) Yamaguchi, S., Thermo magnetic analysis of cobalt with an electron beam. *Z. Metallk.* 52, 284–285 (1961).

(Y3) Yamaguchi, T., Amagasa, M., and Uchiyama, S., Studies on thermal degradation of polyvinyl alcohol with thermobalance. *Kobunshi Kagaku* 18, 406–410 (1961).

(Y4) Yankwich, P. E., and Copeland, J. L., Pyrolysis of lead oxalate; isotope effects and product composition. *J. Am. Chem. Soc.* 79, 2081–2086 (1957).

(Y5) Yasuda, Toshio, and Araki, Y., Effect of pressure on the room-temperature transition of poly(tetrafluoroethylene) and its heat of transition. *J. Appl. Polymer Sci.* 5, 331–336 (1961).

(Z1) Zenz, F. A., and Othmer, D. F., "Fluidization and Fluid Particle Systems." Reinhold, New York, 1960.

(Z2) Zinov'ev, A. A., and Babaeva, V. P., Thermal decomposition of perchloric acid. *Zh. Neorg. Khim.* 6, 271–282 (1961).

(Z3) Zarnoretschki, O. S., and Peschew, P. D., Differential thermal analysis of the raw materials for preparing hard magnetic oxide materials. *Compt. Rend. Acad. Bulgare Sci.* 13, 559–562 (1960).

General References

"A Study of the Differential Thermal Analysis of Clays and Clay Minerals," by P. Laurent Arens. Excelsiors Foto-Offset, Gravenhage, 1951.

"Inorganic Thermogravimetric Analysis," by C. Duval. Elsevier, Amsterdam, 1953.

"The Differential Thermal Investigation of Clays," edited by Robert C. Mackenzie. Mineral. Soc., London, 1957.

"Differential Thermal Analysis: Theory and Practice," by W. J. Smothers and Y. Chiang. Chem. Publ. Co., New York, 1958.

"Automatic Recording Balances" (Review), by S. Gordon and C. Campbell. *Anal. Chem.* **32**, 271–289R (1960).

"Analytical Chemistry of Polymers," edited by Gordon M. Kline: chapter by H. E. Kissinger and S. B. Newman in Part II. Wiley (Interscience), New York, 1962.

"Differential Thermal Analysis" (Review), by C. B. Murphy, *Anal. Chem.* **34**, 298–301R (1962).

"Thermal Analysis" (Review), by C. B. Murphy, *Anal. Chem.* **36**, 347–354R (1964).

"Thermal Analysis Review" (Series), edited by J. P. Redfern. Stanton Instruments, Ltd., London. (A continuing series started in 1962.)

APPENDIX I

The listed firms supply thermoanalytical apparatus in the U.S.A. In each case the method is indicated by "DTA" for differential thermal analysis, "Dil" for dilatometry, or "TGA" for thermogravimetry. Equipment for simultaneous measurements is simply indicated by both classes. Accessory equipment or component apparatus (such as furnaces or balances) are not listed unless the item is specifically for one or more of the fields covered, for example, shielded thermocouples are made for other purposes as are amplifiers and programmers. A borderline case would be the Ainsworth Vacuum Recording Balance, around which the author has built thermobalance assemblies. Differential calorimeters are classed with differential thermal analysis apparatus.

Since new firms frequently enter the field, the prospective purchaser should also look in recent "Buyers Guides" or similar listings. The author does not guarantee completeness.

American Instrument Co. 8030 Georgia Ave. Silver Spring, Md.	DTA TGA	Wm. J. Hacker and Co. P. O. Box 646 West Caldwell, New Jersey	DTA TGA Dil
Apparatus Manufacturers, Inc. P. O. Box 184 Kent, Ohio	DTA TGA	Harrop Precision Furnace Co. 3470 E. Fifth Ave. Columbus 19, Ohio	DTA TGA Dil
C. W. Brabender Instruments, Inc. 50 E. Wesley St. So. Hackensack, New Jersey	TGA	Metrimpex Nader–U 21 Budapest, V., Hungary	DTA TGA
Brinkmann Instruments, Inc. Cantiague Rd. Westbury, L. I., New York	Dil	Mettler Instrument Corp. 20 Nassau St. Princeton, New Jersey	DTA TGA
Burrell Corporation 2223 Fifth Avenue Pittsburgh 19, Penna.	DTA TGA	The Perkin-Elmer Corp. 750 Main Ave. Norwalk, Conn.	DTA
Cahn Instrument Co. 15505 Minnesota Ave. Paramount, California	TGA	Schuco Scientific 250 W. 18th St. New York 11, New York	DTA TGA
E. I. duPont de Nemours and Co., Inc. Instrument Products Div. Wilmington 98, Delaware	DTA TGA	Robert L. Stone Co. 3316 Westhill Dr. Austin 4, Texas	DTA TGA
Eberbach Corp. P. O. Box 1024 Ann Arbor, Michigan	DTA	Technical Equipment Co. 917 Acoma St. Denver 4, Colorado	DTA TGA

Calibration Data

A. Thermocouple e.m.f.'s

The values tabulated on the following pages are taken from National Bureau of Standards Circular 561 by way of Leeds and Northrup Company Bulletin 077989, Issue 2.

A.1. CHROMEL VS ALUMEL

Thermal e.m.f. in millivolts compared to a reference junction at 0.0°C.

°C	0	1	2	3	4	5	6	7	8	9
0	0.00	0.04	0.08	0.12	0.16	0.20	0.24	0.28	0.32	0.36
10	0.40	0.44	0.48	0.52	0.56	0.60	0.64	0.68	0.72	0.76
20	0.80	0.84	0.88	0.92	0.96	1.00	1.04	1.08	1.12	1.16
30	1.20	1.24	1.28	1.32	1.36	1.40	1.44	1.49	1.53	1.57
40	1.61	1.65	1.69	1.73	1.77	1.81	1.85	1.90	1.94	1.98
50	2.02	2.06	2.10	2.14	2.18	2.23	2.27	2.31	2.35	2.39
60	2.43	2.47	2.51	2.56	2.60	2.64	2.68	2.72	2.76	2.80
70	2.85	2.89	2.93	2.97	3.01	3.05	3.10	3.14	3.18	3.22
80	3.26	3.30	3.35	3.39	3.43	3.47	3.51	3.56	3.60	3.64
90	3.68	3.72	3.76	3.81	3.85	3.89	3.93	3.97	4.01	4.06
100	4.10	4.14	4.18	4.22	4.26	4.31	4.35	4.39	4.43	4.47
110	4.51	4 55	4.60	4.64	4.68	4.72	4.76	4.80	4.84	4.88
120	4.92	4.96	5.01	5.05	5.09	5.13	5.17	5.21	5.25	5.29
130	5.33	5.37	5.41	5.45	5.49	5.53	5.57	5.61	5.65	5.69
140	5.73	5.77	5.81	5.85	5.89	5.93	5.97	6.01	6.05	6.09
150	6.13	6.17	6.21	6.25	6.29	6.33	6.37	6.41	6.45	6.49
160	6.53	6.57	6.61	6.65	6.69	6.73	6.77	6.81	6.85	6.89
170	6.93	6.97	7.01	7.05	7.09	7.13	7.17	7.21	7.25	7.29
180	7.33	7.37	7.41	7.45	7.49	7.53	7.57	7.61	7.65	7.69
190	7.73	7.77	7.81	7.85	7.89	7.93	7.97	8.01	8.05	8.09
200	8.13	8.17	8.21	8.25	8.29	8.33	8.37	8.41	8.46	8.50
210	8.54	8.58	8.62	8.66	8.70	8.74	8.78	8.82	8.86	8.90
220	8.94	8.98	9.02	9.06	9.10	9.14	9.18	9.22	9.26	9.30
230	9.34	9.38	9.42	9.46	9.50	9.54	9.59	9.63	9.67	9.71
240	9.75	9.79	9.83	9.87	9.91	9.95	9.99	10.03	10.07	10.11
250	10.16	10.20	10.24	10.28	10.32	10.36	10.40	10.44	10.48	10.52
260	10.57	10.61	10.65	10.69	10.73	10.77	10.81	10.85	10.89	10.93
270	10.98	11.02	11.06	11.10	11.14	11.18	11.22	11.26	11.30	11.34
280	11.39	11.43	11.47	11.51	11.55	11.59	11.63	11.67	11.72	11.76
290	11.80	11.84	11.88	11.92	11.96	12.01	12.05	12.09	12.13	12.17
300	12.21	12.25	12.29	12.34	12.38	12.42	12.46	12.50	12.54	12.58
310	12.63	12.67	12.71	12.75	12.79	12.83	12.88	12.92	12.96	13.00
320	13.04	13.08	13.12	13.17	13.21	13.25	13.29	13.33	13.37	13.42
330	13.46	13.50	13.54	13.58	13.62	13.67	13.71	13.75	13.79	13.83
340	13.88	13.92	13.96	14.00	14.04	14.09	14.13	14.17	14.21	14.25
350	14.29	14.34	14.38	14.42	14.46	14.50	14.55	14.59	14.63	14.67
360	14.71	14.76	14.84	14.84	14.88	14.92	14.97	15.01	15.05	15.09
370	15.13	15.18	15.22	15.26	15.30	15.34	15.39	15.43	15.47	15.51
380	15.55	15.60	15.64	15.68	15.72	15.76	15.81	15.85	15.89	15.93
390	15.98	16.02	16.06	16.10	16.14	16.19	16.23	16.27	16.31	16.36
400	16.40	16.44	16.48	16.52	16.57	16.61	16.65	16.69	16.74	16.78
410	16.82	16.86	16.91	16.95	16.99	17.03	17.07	17.12	17.16	17.20
420	17.24	17.29	17.33	17.37	17.41	17.46	17.50	17.54	17.58	17.62
430	17.67	17.71	17.75	17.79	17.84	17.88	17.92	17.96	18.01	18.05
440	18.09	18.13	18.17	18.22	18.26	18.30	18.34	18.39	18.43	18.47
450	18.51	18.56	18.60	18.64	18.68	18.73	18.77	18.81	18.85	18.90
460	18.94	18.98	19.02	19.07	19.11	19.15	19.19	19.24	19.28	19.32
470	19.36	19.41	19.45	19.49	19.54	19.58	19.62	19.66	19.71	19.75
480	19.79	19.84	19.88	19.92	19.96	20.01	20.05	20.09	20.13	20.18
490	20.22	20.26	20.31	20.35	20.39	20.43	20.48	20.52	20.56	20.60
500	20.65	20.69	20.73	20.77	20.82	20.86	20.90	20.94	20.99	21.03
510	21.07	21.11	21.16	21.20	21.24	21.28	21.32	21.37	21.41	21.45
520	21.50	21.54	21.58	21.63	21.67	21.71	21.75	21.80	21.84	21.88
530	21.92	21.97	22.01	22.05	22.09	22.14	22.18	22.22	22.26	22.31
540	22.35	22.39	22.43	22.48	22.52	22.56	22.61	22.65	22.69	22.73
550	22.78	22.82	22.86	22.90	22.95	22.99	23.03	23.07	23.12	23.16
560	23.20	23.25	23.29	23.33	23.38	23.42	23.46	23.50	23.54	23.59
570	23.63	23.67	23.72	23.76	23.80	23.84	23.89	23.93	23.97	24.01
580	24.06	24.10	24.14	24.18	24.23	24.27	24.31	24.36	24.40	24.44
590	24.49	24.53	24.57	24.61	24.65	24.70	24.74	24.78	24.83	24.87

A.1. CHROMEL vs ALUMEL (*Cont.*)

°C	0	1	2	3	4	5	6	7	8	9
600	24.91	24.95	25.00	25.04	25.08	25.12	25.17	25.21	25.25	25.29
610	25.34	25.38	25.42	25.47	25.51	25.55	25.59	25.64	25.68	25.72
620	25.76	25.81	25.85	25.89	25.93	25.98	26.02	26.06	26.10	26.15
630	26.19	26.23	26.27	26.32	26.36	26.40	26.44	26.48	26.53	26.57
640	26.61	26.65	26.70	26.74	26.78	26.82	26.86	26.91	26.95	26.99
650	27.03	27.07	27.12	27.16	27.20	27.24	27.28	27.33	27.37	27.41
660	27.45	27.49	27.54	27.58	27.62	27.66	27.71	27.75	27.79	27.83
670	27.87	27.92	27.96	28.00	28.04	28.08	28.13	28.17	28.21	28.25
680	28.29	28.34	28.38	28.42	28.46	28.50	28.55	28.59	28.63	28.67
690	28.72	28.76	28.80	28.84	28.88	28.93	28.97	29.01	29.05	29.10
700	29.14	29.18	29.22	29.26	29.30	29.35	29.39	29.43	29.47	29.52
710	29.56	29.60	29.64	29.68	29.72	29.77	29.81	29.85	29.89	29.93
720	29.97	30.02	30.06	30.10	30.14	30.18	30.23	30.27	30.31	30.35
730	30.39	30.44	30.48	30.52	30.56	30.60	30.65	30.69	30.73	30.77
740	30.81	30.85	30.90	30.94	30.98	31.02	31.06	31.10	31.15	31.19
750	31.23	31.27	31.31	31.35	31.40	31.44	31.48	31.52	31.56	31.60
760	31.65	31.69	31.73	31.77	31.81	31.85	31.90	31.94	31.98	32.02
770	32.06	32.10	32.15	32.19	32.23	32.27	32.31	32.35	32.39	32.43
780	32.48	32.52	32.56	32.60	32.64	32.68	32.72	32.76	32.81	32.85
790	32.89	32.93	32.97	33.01	33.05	33.09	33.13	33.18	33.22	33.26
800	33.30	33.34	33.38	33.42	33.46	33.50	33.54	33.59	33.63	33.67
810	33.71	33.75	33.79	33.83	33.87	33.91	33.95	33.99	34.04	34.08
820	34.12	34.16	34.20	34.24	34.28	34.32	34.36	34.40	34.44	34.48
830	34.53	34.57	34.61	34.65	34.69	34.73	34.77	34.81	34.85	34.89
840	34.93	34.97	35.02	35.06	35.10	35.14	35.18	35.22	35.26	35.30
850	35.34	35.38	35.42	35.46	35.50	35.54	35.58	35.63	35.67	35.71
860	35.75	35.79	35.83	35.87	35.91	35.95	35.99	36.03	36.07	36.11
870	36.15	36.19	36.23	36.27	36.31	36.35	36.39	36.43	36.47	36.51
880	36.55	36.59	36.63	36.67	36.72	36.76	36.80	36.84	36.88	36.92
890	36.96	37.00	37.04	37.08	37.12	37.16	37.20	37.24	37.28	37.32
900	37.36	37.40	37.44	37.48	37.52	37.56	37.60	37.64	37.68	37.72
910	37.76	37.80	37.84	37.88	37.92	37.96	38.00	38.04	38.08	38.12
920	38.16	38.20	38.24	38.28	38.32	38.36	38.40	38.44	38.48	38.52
930	38.56	38.60	38.64	38.68	38.72	38.76	38.80	38.84	38.88	38.92
940	38.95	38.99	39.03	39.07	39.11	39.15	39.19	39.23	39.27	39.31
950	39.35	39.39	39.43	39.47	39.51	39.55	39.59	39.63	39.67	39.71
960	39.75	39.79	39.83	39.86	39.90	39.94	39.98	40.02	40.06	40.10
970	40.14	40.18	40.22	40.26	40.30	40.34	40.38	40.41	40.45	40.49
980	40.53	40.57	40.61	40.65	40.69	40.73	40.77	40.81	40.85	40.89
990	40.92	40.96	41.00	41.04	41.08	41.12	41.16	41.20	41.24	41.28
1000	41.31	41.35	41.39	41.43	41.47	41.51	41.55	41.59	41.63	41.67
1010	41.70	41.74	41.78	41.82	41.86	41.90	41.94	41.98	42.02	42.05
1020	42.09	42.13	42.17	42.21	42.25	42.29	42.33	42.36	42.40	42.44
1030	42.48	42.52	42.56	42.60	42.63	42.67	42.71	42.75	42.79	42.83
1040	42.87	42.90	42.94	42.98	43.02	43.06	43.10	43.14	43.17	43.21
1050	43.25	43.29	43.33	43.37	43.41	43.44	43.48	43.52	43.56	43.60
1060	43.63	43.67	43.71	43.75	43.79	43.83	43.87	43.90	43.94	43.98
1070	44.02	44.06	44.10	44.13	44.17	44.21	44.25	44.29	44.33	44.36
1080	44.40	44.44	44.48	44.52	44.55	44.59	44.63	44.67	44.71	44.74
1090	44.78	44.82	44.86	44.90	44.93	44.97	45.01	45.05	45.09	45.12
1100	45.16	45.20	45.24	45.27	45.31	45.35	45.39	45.43	45.46	45.50
1110	45.54	45.58	45.62	45.65	45.69	45.73	45.77	45.80	45.84	45.88
1120	45.92	45.96	45.99	46.03	46.07	46.11	46.14	46.18	46.22	46.26
1130	46.29	46.33	46.37	46.41	46.44	46.48	46.52	46.56	46.59	46.63
1140	46.67	46.70	46.74	46.78	46.82	46.85	46.89	46.93	46.97	47.00
1150	47.04	47.08	47.12	47.15	47.19	47.23	47.26	47.30	47.34	47.38
1160	47.41	47.45	47.49	47.52	47.56	47.60	47.63	47.67	47.71	47.75
1170	47.78	47.82	47.86	47.89	47.93	47.97	48.00	48.04	48.08	48.12
1180	48.15	48.19	48.23	48.26	48.30	48.34	48.37	48.41	48.45	48.48
1190	48.52	48.56	48.59	48.63	48.67	48.70	48.74	48.78	48.81	48.85

A.1. CHROMEL VS ALUMEL (*Cont.*)

°C	0	1	2	3	4	5	6	7	8	9
1200	48.89	48.92	48.96	49.00	49.03	49.07	49.11	49.14	49.18	49.22
1210	49.25	49.29	49.32	49.36	49.40	49.43	49.47	49.51	49.54	49.58
1220	49.62	49.65	49.69	49.72	49.76	49.80	49.83	49.87	49.90	49.94
1230	49.98	50.01	50.05	50.08	50.12	50.16	50.19	50.23	50.26	50.30
1240	50.34	50.37	50.41	50.44	50.48	50.52	50.55	50.59	50.62	50.66
1250	50.69	50.73	50.77	50.80	50.84	50.87	50.91	50.94	50.98	51.02
1260	51.05	51.09	51.12	51:16	51.19	51.23	51.27	51.30	51.34	51.37
1270	51.41	51.44	51.48	51.51	51.55	51.58	51.62	51.66	51.69	51.73
1280	51.76	51.80	51.83	51.87	51.90	51.94	51.97	52.01	52.04	52.08
1290	52.11	52.15	52.18	52.22	52.25	52.29	52.32	52.36	52.39	52.43
1300	52.46	52.50	52.53	52.57	52.60	52.64	52.67	52.71	52.74	52.78
1310	52.81	52.85	52.88	52.92	52.95	52.99	53.02	53.06	53.09	53.13
1320	53.16	53.20	53.23	53.27	53.30	53.34	53.37	53.41	53.44	53.47
1330	53.51	53.54	53.58	53.61	53.65	53.68	53.72	53.75	53.79	53.82
1340	53.85	53.89	53.92	53.96	53.99	54.03	54.06	54.10	54.13	54.16
1350	54.20	54.23	54.27	54.30	54.34	54.37	54.40	54.44	54.47	54.51
1360	54.54	54.57	54.61	54.64	54.68	54.71	54.74	54.78	54.81	54.85
1370	54.88	54.91								

Appendix II

A.2. IRON VS CONSTANTAN

Thermal e.m.f. in millivolts compared to a reference junction at 0.0°C.

°C	0	1	2	3	4	5	6	7	8	9
-190	-7.66	-7.69	-7.71	-7.73	-7.76	-7.78				
-180	-7.40	-7.43	-7.46	-7.49	-7.51	-7.54	-7.56	-7.59	-7.61	-7.64
-170	-7.12	-7.15	-7.18	-7.21	-7.24	-7.27	-7.30	-7.32	-7.35	-7.38
-160	-6.82	-6.85	-6.88	-6.91	-6.94	-6.97	-7.00	-7.03	-7.06	-7.09
-150	-6.50	-6.53	-6.56	-6.60	-6.63	-6.66	-6.69	-6.72	-6.76	-6.79
-140	-6.16	-6.19	-6.22	-6.26	-6.29	-6.33	-6.36	-6.40	-6.43	-6.46
-130	-5.80	-5.84	-5.87	-5.91	-5.94	-5.98	-6.01	-6.05	-6.08	-6.12
-120	-5.42	-5.46	-5.50	-5.54	-5.58	-5.61	-5.65	-5.69	-5.72	-5.76
-110	-5.03	-5.07	-5.11	-5.15	-5.19	-5.23	-5.27	-5.31	-5.35	-5.38
-100	-4.63	-4.67	-4.71	-4.75	-4.79	-4.83	-4.87	-4.91	-4.95	-4.99
-90	-4.21	-4.25	-4.30	-4.34	-4.38	-4.42	-4.46	-4.50	-4.55	-4.59
-80	-3.78	-3.82	-3.87	-3.91	-3.96	-4.00	-4.04	-4.08	-4.13	-4.17
-70	-3.34	-3.38	-3.43	-3.47	-3.52	-3.56	-3.60	-3.65	-3.69	-3.74
-60	-2.89	-2.94	-2.98	-3.03	-3.07	-3.12	-3.16	-3.21	-3.25	-3.30
-50	-2.43	-2.48	-2.52	-2.57	-2.62	-2.66	-2.71	-2.75	-2.80	-2.84
-40	-1.96	-2.01	-2.06	-2.10	-2.15	-2.20	-2.24	-2.29	-2.34	-2.38
-30	-1.48	-1.53	-1.58	-1.63	-1.67	-1.72	-1.77	-1.82	-1.87	-1.91
-20	-1.00	-1.04	-1.09	-1.14	-1.19	-1.24	-1.29	-1.34	-1.39	-1.43
-10	-0.50	-0.55	-0.60	-0.65	-0.70	-0.75	-0.80	-0.85	-0.90	-0.95
(-)0	0.00	-0.05	-0.10	-0.15	-0.20	-0.25	-0.30	-0.35	-0.40	-0.45
(+)0	0.00	0.05	0.10	0.15	0.20	0.25	0.30	0.35	0.40	0.45
10	0.50	0.56	0.61	0.66	0.71	0.76	0.81	0.86	0.91	0.97
20	1.02	1.07	1.12	1.17	1.22	1.28	1.33	1.38	1.43	1.48
30	1.54	1.59	1.64	1.69	1.74	1.80	1.85	1.90	1.95	2.00
40	2.06	2.11	2.16	2.22	2.27	2.32	2.37	2.42	2.48	2.53
50	2.58	2.64	2.69	2.74	2.80	2.85	2.90	2.96	3.01	3.06
60	3.11	3.17	3.22	3.27	3.33	3.38	3.43	3.49	3.54	3.60
70	3.65	3.70	3.76	3.81	3.86	3.92	3.97	4.02	4.08	4.13
80	4.19	4.24	4.29	4.35	4.40	4.46	4.51	4.56	4.62	4.67
90	4.73	4.78	4.83	4.89	4.94	5.00	5.05	5.10	5.16	5.21
100	5.27	5.32	5.38	5.43	5.48	5.54	5.59	5.65	5.70	5.76
110	5.81	5.86	5.92	5.97	6.03	6.08	6.14	6.19	6.25	6.30
120	6.36	6.41	6.47	6.52	6.58	6.63	6.68	6.74	6.79	6.85
130	6.90	6.96	7.01	7.07	7.12	7.18	7.23	7.29	7.34	7.40
140	7.45	7.51	7.56	7.62	7.67	7.73	7.78	7.84	7.89	7.95
150	8.00	8.06	8.12	8.17	8.23	8.28	8.34	8.39	8.45	8.50
160	8.56	8.61	8.67	8.72	8.78	8.84	8.89	8.95	9.00	9.06
170	9.11	9.17	9.22	9.28	9.33	9.39	9.44	9.50	9.56	9.61
180	9.67	9.72	9.78	9.83	9.89	9.95	10.00	10.06	10.11	10.17
190	10.22	10.28	10.34	10.39	10.45	10.50	10.56	10.61	10.67	10.72
200	10.78	10.84	10.89	10.95	11.00	11.06	11.12	11.17	11.23	11.28
210	11.34	11.39	11.45	11.50	11.56	11.62	11.67	11.73	11.78	11.84
220	11.89	11.95	12.00	12.06	12.12	12.17	12.23	12.28	12.34	12.39
230	12.45	12.50	12.56	12.62	12.67	12.73	12.78	12.84	12.89	12.95
240	13.01	13.06	13.12	13.17	13.23	13.28	13.34	13.40	13.45	13.51
250	13.56	13.62	13.67	13.73	13.78	13.84	13.89	13.95	14.00	14.06
260	14.12	14.17	14.23	14.28	14.34	14.39	14.45	14.50	14.56	14.61
270	14.67	14.72	14.78	14.83	14.89	14.94	15.00	15.06	15.11	15.17
280	15.22	15.28	15.33	15.39	15.44	15.50	15.55	15.61	15.66	15.72
290	15.77	15.83	15.88	15.94	16.00	16.05	16.11	16.16	16.22	16.27
300	16.33	16.38	16.44	16.49	16.55	16.60	16.66	16.71	16.77	16.82
310	16.88	16.93	16.99	17.04	17.10	17.15	17.21	17.26	17.32	17.37
320	17.43	17.48	17.54	17.60	17.65	17.71	17.76	17.82	17.87	17.93
330	17.98	18.04	18.09	18.15	18.20	18.26	18.32	18.37	18.43	18.48
340	18.54	18.59	18.65	18.70	18.76	18.81	18.87	18.92	18.98	19.03
350	19.09	19.14	19.20	19.26	19.31	19.37	19.42	19.48	19.53	19.59
360	19.64	19.70	19.75	19.81	19.86	19.92	19.97	20.03	20.08	20.14
370	20.20	20.25	20.31	20.36	20.42	20.47	20.53	20.58	20.64	20.69
380	20.75	20.80	20.86	20.91	20.97	21.02	21.08	21.13	21.19	21.24
390	21.30	21.35	21.41	21.46	21.52	21.57	21.63	21.68	21.74	21.79

A.2. IRON VS CONSTANTAN (*Cont.*)

°C	0	1	2	3	4	5	6	7	8	9
400	21.85	21.90	21.96	22.02	22.07	22.13	22.18	22.24	22.29	22.35
410	22.40	22.46	22.51	22.57	22.62	22.68	22.73	22.79	22.84	22.90
420	22.95	23.01	23.06	23.12	23.17	23.23	23.28	23.34	23.39	23.45
430	23.50	23.56	23.61	23.67	23.72	23.78	23.83	23.89	23.94	24.00
440	24.06	24.11	24.17	24.22	24.28	24.33	24.39	24.44	24.50	24.55
450	24.61	24.66	24.72	24.77	24.83	24.88	24.94	25.00	25.05	25.11
460	25.16	25.22	25.27	25.33	25.38	25.44	25.49	25.55	25.60	25.66
470	25.72	25.77	25.83	25.88	25.94	25.99	26.05	26.10	26.16	26.22
480	26.27	26.33	26.38	26.44	26.49	26.55	26.61	26.66	26.72	26.77
490	26.83	26.89	26.94	27.00	27.05	27.11	27.17	27.22	27.28	27.33
500	27.39	27.45	27.50	27.56	27.61	27.67	27.73	27.78	27.84	27.90
510	27.95	28.01	28.07	28.12	28.18	28.23	28.29	28.35	28.40	28.46
520	28.52	28.57	28.63	28.69	28.74	28.80	28.86	28.91	28.97	29.02
530	29.08	29.14	29.20	29.25	29.31	29.37	29.42	29.48	29.54	29.59
540	29.65	29.71	29.76	29.82	29.88	29.94	29.99	30.05	30.11	30.16
550	30.22	30.28	30.34	30.39	30.45	30.51	30.57	30.62	30.68	30.74
560	30.80	30.85	30.91	30.97	31.02	31.08	31.14	31.20	31.26	31.31
570	31.37	31.43	31.49	31.54	31.60	31.66	31.72	31.78	31.83	31.89
580	31.95	32.01	32.06	32.12	32.18	32.24	32.30	32.36	32.41	32.47
590	32.53	32.59	32.65	32.71	32.76	32.82	32.88	32.94	33.00	33.06
600	33.11	33.17	33.23	33.29	33.35	33.41	33.46	33.52	33.58	33.64
610	33.70	33.76	33.82	33.88	33.94	33.99	34.05	34.11	34.17	34.23
620	34.29	34.35	34.41	34.47	34.53	34.58	34.64	34.70	34.76	34.82
630	34.88	34.94	35.00	35.06	35.12	35.18	35.24	35.30	35.36	35.42
640	35.48	35.54	35.60	35.66	35.72	35.78	35.84	35.90	35.96	36.02
650	36.08	36.14	36.20	36.26	36.32	36.38	36.44	36.50	36.56	36.62
660	36.69	36.75	36.81	36.87	36.93	36.99	37.05	37.11	37.18	37.24
670	37.30	37.36	37.42	37.48	37.54	37.60	37.66	37.73	37.79	37.85
680	37.91	37.97	38.04	38.10	38.16	38.22	38.28	38.34	38.41	38.47
690	38.53	38.59	38.66	38.72	38.78	38.84	38.90	38.97	39.03	39.09
700	39.15	39.22	39.28	39.34	39.40	39.47	39.53	39.59	39.65	39.72
710	39.78	39.84	39.91	39.97	40.03	40.10	40.16	40.22	40.28	40.35
720	40.41	40.48	40.54	40.60	40.66	40.73	40.79	40.86	40.92	40.98
730	41.05	41.11	41.17	41.24	41.30	41.36	41.43	41.49	41.56	41.62
740	41.68	41.75	41.81	41.87	41.94	42.00	42.07	42.13	42.19	42.26
750	42.32	42.38	42.45	42.51	42.58	42.64	42.70	42.77	42.83	42.90
760	42.96	43.02	43.09	43.15	43.22	43.28	43.35	43.41	43.48	43.54
770	43.60	43.67	43.73	43.80	43.86	43.92	43.99	44.05	44.12	44.18
780	44.25	44.31	44.38	44.44	44.50	44.57	44.63	44.70	44.76	44.82
790	44.89	44.95	45.02	45.08	45.15	45.21	45.28	45.34	45.40	45.47
800	45.53	45.60	45.66	45.72	45.79	45.85	45.92	45.98	46.05	46.11
810	46.18	46.24	46.30	46.37	46.43	46.50	46.56	46.62	46.69	46.75
820	46.82	46.88	46.94	47.01	47.07	47.14	47.20	47.27	47.33	47.39
830	47.46	47.52	47.58	47.65	47.71	47.78	47.84	47.90	47.97	48.03
840	48.09	48.16	48.22	48.28	48.35	48.41	48.48	48.54	48.60	48.66
850	48.73	48.79	48.85	48.92	48.98	49.04	49.10	49.17	49.23	49.29
860	49.36	49.42	49.48	49.54	49.61	49.67	49.73	49.79	49.86	49.92
870	49.98	50.04								

Appendix II

A.3. PLATINUM VS PLATINUM–10% RHODIUM

Thermal e.m.f. in millivolts compared to a reference junction at 0.0°C.

°C	0	1	2	3	4	5	6	7	8	9
0	0.000	0.005	0.011	0.016	0.022	0.028	0.033	0.039	0.044	0.050
10	.056	.061	.067	.073	.078	.084	.090	.096	.102	.107
20	.113	.119	.125	.131	.137	.143	.149	.155	.161	.167
30	.173	.179	.185	.191	.198	.204	.210	.216	.222	.229
40	.235	.241	.247	.254	.260	.266	.273	.279	.286	.292
50	.299	.305	.312	.318	.325	.331	.338	.344	.351	.357
60	.364	.371	.377	.384	.391	.397	.404	.411	.418	.425
70	.431	.438	.445	.452	.459	.466	.473	.479	.486	.493
80	.500	.507	.514	.521	.528	.535	.543	.550	.557	.564
90	.571	.578	.585	.593	.600	.607	.614	.621	.629	.636
100	.643	.651	.658	.665	.673	680	.687	.694	.702	.709
110	.717	.724	.732	.739	.747	.754	.762	.769	.777	.784
120	.792	.800	.807	.815	.823	.830	.838	.845	.853	.861
130	.869	.876	.884	.892	.900	.907	.915	.923	.931	.939
140	.946	.954	.962	.970	.978	.986	.994	1.002	1.009	1.017
150	1.025	1.033	1.041	1.049	1.057	1.065	1.073	1.081	1.089	1.097
160	1.106	1.114	1.122	1.130	1.138	1.146	1.154	1.162	1.170	1.179
170	1.187	1.195	1.203	1.211	1.220	1.228	1.236	1.244	1.253	1.261
180	1.269	1.277	1.286	1.294	1.302	1.311	1.319	1.327	1.336	1.344
190	1.352	1.361	1.369	1.377	1.386	1.394	1.403	1.411	1.419	1.428
200	1.436	1.445	1.453	1.462	1.470	1.479	1.487	1.496	1.504	1.513
210	1.521	1.530	1.538	1.547	1.555	1.564	1.573	1.581	1.590	1.598
220	1.607	1.615	1.624	1.633	1.641	1.650	1.659	1.667	1.676	1.685
230	1.693	1.702	1.710	1.719	1.728	1.736	1.745	1.754	1.763	1.771
240	1.780	1.789	1.798	1.806	1.815	1.824	1.833	1.841	1.850	1.859
250	1.868	1.877	1.885	1.894	1.903	1.912	1.921	1.930	1.938	1.947
260	1.956	1.965	1.974	1.983	1.992	2.001	2.009	2.018	2.027	2.036
270	2.045	2.054	2.063	2.072	2.081	2.090	2.099	2.108	2.117	2.126
280	2.135	2.144	2.153	2.162	2.171	2.180	2.189	2.198	2.207	2.216
290	2.225	2.234	2.243	2.252	2.261	2.271	2.280	2.289	2.298	2.307
300	2.316	2.325	2.334	2.343	2.353	2.362	2.371	2.380	2.389	2.398
310	2.408	2.417	2.426	2.435	2.444	2.453	2.463	2.472	2.481	2.490
320	2.499	2.509	2.518	2.527	2.536	2.546	2.555	2.564	2.573	2.583
330	2.592	2.601	2.610	2.620	2.629	2.638	2.648	2.657	2.666	2.676
340	2.685	2.694	2.704	2.713	2.722	2.731	2.741	2.750	2.760	2.769
350	2.778	2.788	2.797	2.806	2.816	2.825	2.834	2.844	2.853	2.863
360	2.872	2.881	2.891	2.900	2.910	2.919	2.929	2.938	2.947	2.957
370	2.966	2.976	2.985	2.995	3.004	3.014	3.023	3.032	3.042	3.051
380	3.061	3.070	3.080	3.089	3.099	3.108	3.118	3.127	3.137	3.146
390	3.156	3.165	3.175	3.184	3.194	3.203	3.213	3.222	3.232	3.241
400	3.251	3.261	3.270	3.280	3.289	3.299	3.308	3.318	3.327	3.337
410	3.347	3.356	3.366	3.375	3.385	3.394	3.404	3.414	3.423	3.433
420	3.442	3.452	3.462	3.471	3.481	3.490	3.500	3.510	3.519	3.529
430	3.539	3.548	3.558	3.567	3.577	3.587	3.596	3.606	3.616	3.625
440	3.635	3.645	3.654	3.664	3.674	3.683	3.693	3.703	3.712	3.722
450	3.732	3.741	3.751	3.761	3.771	3.780	3.790	3.800	3.809	3.819
460	3.829	3.839	3.848	3.858	3.868	3.878	3.887	3.897	3.907	3.917
470	3.926	3.936	3.946	3.956	3.965	3.975	3.985	3.995	4.004	4.014
480	4.024	4.034	4.044	4.053	4.063	4.073	4.083	4.093	4.103	4.112
490	4.122	4.132	4.142	4.152	4.162	4.171	4.181	4.191	4.201	4.211
500	4.221	4.230	4.240	4.250	4.260	4.270	4.280	4.290	4.300	4.310
510	4.319	4.329	4.339	4.349	4.359	4.369	4.379	4.389	4.399	4.409
520	4.419	4.428	4.438	4.448	4.458	4.468	4.478	4.488	4.498	4.508
530	4.518	4.528	4.538	4.548	4.558	4.568	4.578	4.588	4.598	4.608
540	4.618	4.628	4.638	4.649	4.658	4.668	4.678	4.688	4.698	4.708
550	4.718	4.728	4.738	4.748	4.758	4.768	4.778	4.788	4.798	4.808
560	4.818	4.828	4.839	4.849	4.859	4.869	4.879	4.889	4.899	4.909
570	4.919	4.929	4.939	4.950	4.960	4.970	4.980	4.990	5.000	5.010
580	5.020	5.031	5.041	5.051	5.061	5.071	5.081	5.091	5.102	5.112
590	5.122	5.132	5.142	5.152	5.163	5.173	5.183	5.193	5.203	5.214

A.3. Platinum vs Platinum—10% Rhodium (*Cont.*)

°C	0	1	2	3	4	5	6	7	8	9
600	5.224	5.234	5.244	5.254	5.265	5.275	5.285	5.295	5.306	5.316
610	5.326	5.336	5.346	5.357	5.367	5.377	5.388	5.398	5.408	5.418
620	5.429	5.439	5.449	5.459	5.470	5.480	5.490	5.501	5.511	5.521
630	5.532	5.542	5.552	5.563	5.573	5.583	5.593	5.604	5.614	5.624
640	5.635	5.645	5.655	5.666	5.676	5.686	5.697	5.707	5.717	5.728
650	5.738	5.748	5.759	5.769	5.779	5.790	5.800	5.811	5.821	5.831
660	5.842	5.852	5.862	5.873	5.883	5.894	5.904	5.914	5.925	5.935
670	5.946	5.956	5.967	5.977	5.987	5.998	6.008	6.019	6.029	6.040
680	6.050	6.060	6.071	6.081	6.092	6.102	6.113	6.123	6.134	6.144
690	6.155	6.165	6.176	6.186	6.197	6.207	6.218	6.228	6.239	6.249
700	6.260	6.270	6.281	6.291	6.302	6.312	6.323	6.333	6.344	6.355
710	6.365	6.376	6.386	6.397	6.407	6.418	6.429	6.439	6.450	6.460
720	6.471	6.481	6.492	6.503	6.513	6.524	6.534	6.545	6.556	6.566
730	6.577	6.588	6.598	6.609	6.619	6.630	6.641	6.651	6.662	6.673
740	6.683	6.694	6.705	6.715	6.726	6.737	6.747	6.758	6.769	6.779
750	6.790	6.801	6.811	6.822	6.833	6.844	6.854	6.865	6.876	6.886
760	6.897	6.908	6.919	6.929	6.940	6.951	6.962	6.972	6.983	6.994
770	7.005	7.015	7.026	7.037	7.047	7.058	7.069	7.080	7.091	7.102
780	7.112	7.123	7.134	7.145	7.156	7.166	7.177	7.188	7.199	7.210
790	7.220	7.231	7.242	7.253	7.264	7.275	7.286	7.296	7.307	7.318
800	7.329	7.340	7.351	7.362	7.372	7.383	7.394	7.405	7.416	7.427
810	7.438	7.449	7.460	7.470	7.481	7.492	7.503	7.514	7.525	7.536
820	7.547	7.558	7.569	7.580	7.591	7.602	7.613	7.623	7.634	7.645
830	7.656	7.667	7.678	7.689	7.700	7.711	7.722	7.733	7.744	7.755
840	7.766	7.777	7.788	7.799	7.810	7.821	7.832	7.843	7.854	7.865
850	7.876	7.887	7.898	7.910	7.921	7.932	7.943	7.954	7.965	7.976
860	7.987	7.998	8.009	8.020	8.031	8.042	8.053	8.064	8.076	8.087
870	8.098	8.109	8.120	8.131	8.142	8.153	8.164	8.176	8.187	8.198
880	8.209	8.220	8.231	8.242	8.254	8.265	8.276	8.287	8.298	8.309
890	8.320	8.332	8.343	8.354	8.365	8.376	8.388	8.399	8.410	8.421
900	8.432	8.444	8.455	8.466	8.477	8.488	8.500	8.511	8.522	8.533
910	8.545	8.556	8.567	8.578	8.590	8.601	8.612	8.623	8.635	8.646
920	8.657	8.668	8.680	8.691	8.702	8.714	8.725	8.736	8.747	8.759
930	8.770	8.781	8.793	8.804	8.815	8.827	8.838	8.849	8.861	8.872
940	8.883	8.895	8.906	8.917	8.929	8.940	8.951	8.963	8.974	8.986
950	8.997	9.008	9.020	9.031	9.042	9.054	9.065	9.077	9.088	9.099
960	9.111	9.122	9.134	9.145	9.157	9.168	9.179	9.191	9.202	9.214
970	9.225	9.236	9.248	9.260	9.271	9.282	9.294	9.305	9.317	9.328
980	9.340	9.351	9.363	9.374	9.386	9.397	9.409	9.420	9.432	9.443
990	9.455	9.466	9.478	9.489	9.501	9.512	9.524	9.535	9.547	9.559
1000	9.570	9.582	9.593	9.605	9.616	9.628	9.639	9.651	9.663	9.674
1010	9.686	9.697	9.709	9.720	9.732	9.744	9.755	9.767	9.779	9.790
1020	9.802	9.813	9.825	9.837	9.848	9.860	9.871	9.883	9.895	9.906
1030	9.918	9.930	9.941	9.953	9.965	9.976	9.988	10.000	10.011	10.023
1040	10.035	10.046	10.058	10.070	10.082	10.093	10.105	10.117	10.128.	10.140
1050	10.152	10.163	10.175	10.187	10.199	10.210	10.222	10.234	10.246	10.257
1060	10.269	10.281	10.293	10.304	10.316	10.328	10.340	10.351	10.363	10.375
1070	10.387	10.399	10.410	10.422	10.434	10.446	10.458	10.469	10.481	10.493
1080	10.505	10.517	10.528	10.540	10.552	10.564	10.576	10.587	10.599	10.611
1090	10.623	10.635	10.647	10.658	10.670	10.682	10.694	10.706	10.718	10.729
1100	10.741	10.753	10.765	10.777	10.789	10.801	10.812	10.824	10.836	10.848
1110	10.860	10.872	10.884	10.896	10.907	10.919	10.931	10.943	10.955	10.967
1120	10.979	10.991	11.003	11.014	11.026	11.038	11.050	11.062	11.074	11.086
1130	11.098	11.110	11.122	11.133	11.145	11.157	11.169	11.181	11.193	11.205
1140	11.217	11.229	11.241	11.253	11.265	11.277	11.289	11.300	11.312	11.324
1150	11.336	11.348	11.360	11.372	11.384	11.396	11.408	11.420	11.432	11.444
1160	11.456	11.468	11.480	11.492	11.504	11.516	11.528	11.540	11.552	11.564
1170	11.575	11.587	11.599	11.611	11.623	11.635	11.647	11.659	11.671	11.683
1180	11.695	11.707	11.719	11.731	11.743	11.755	11.767	11.779	11.791	11.803
1190	11.815	11.827	11.839	11.851	11.863	11.875	11.887	11.899	11.911	11.923

A.3. Platinum vs Platinum—10% Rhodium (*Cont.*)

°C	0	1	2	3	4	5	6	7	8	9
1200	11.935	11.947	11.959	11.971	11.983	11.995	12.007	12.019	12.031	12.043
1210	12.055	12.067	12.079	12.091	12.103	12.115	12.127	12.139	12.151	12.163
1220	12.175	12.187	12.200	12.212	12.224	12.236	12.248	12.260	12.272	12.284
1230	12.296	12.308	12.320	12.332	12.344	12.356	12.368	12.380	12.392	12.404
1240	12.416	12.428	12.440	12.452	12.464	12.476	12.488	12.500	12.512	12.524
1250	12.536	12.548	12.560	12.573	12.585	12.597	12.609	12.621	12.633	12.645
1260	12.657	12.669	12.681	12.693	12.705	12.717	12.729	12.741	12.753	12.765
1270	12.777	12.789	12.801	12.813	12.825	12.837	12.849	12.861	12.873	12.885
1280	12.897	12.909	12.921	12.933	12.945	12.957	12.969	12.981	12.993	13.005
1290	13.018	13.030	13.042	13.054	13.066	13.078	13.090	13.102	13.114	13.126
1300	13.138	13.150	13.162	13.174	13.186	13.198	13.210	13.222	13.234	13.246
1310	13.258	13.270	13.282	13.294	13.306	13.318	13.330	13.342	13.354	13.366
1320	13.378	13.390	13.402	13.414	13.426	13.438	13.450	13.462	13.474	13.486
1330	13.498	13.510	13.522	13.534	13.546	13.558	13.570	13.582	13.594	13.606
1340	13.618	13.630	13.642	13.654	13.666	13.678	13.690	13.702	13.714	13.726
1350	13.738	13.750	13.762	13.774	13.786	13.798	13.810	13.822	13.834	13.846
1360	13.858	13.870	13.882	13.894	13.906	13.918	13.930	13.942	13.954	13.966
1370	13.978	13.990	14.002	14.014	14.026	14.038	14.050	14.062	14.074	14.086
1380	14.098	14.110	14.122	14.133	14.145	14.157	14.169	14.181	14.193	14.205
1390	14.217	14.229	14.241	14.253	14.265	14.277	14.289	14.301	14.313	14.325
1400	14.337	14.349	14.361	14.373	14.385	14.397	14.409	14.421	14.433	14.445
1410	14.457	14.469	14.481	14.493	14.504	14.516	14.528	14.540	14.552	14.564
1420	14.576	14.588	14.600	14.612	14.624	14.636	14.648	14.660	14.672	14.684
1430	14.696	14.708	14.720	14.732	14.744	14.755	14.767	14.779	14.791	14.803
1440	14.815	14.827	14.839	14.851	14.863	14.875	14.887	14.899	14.911	14.923
1450	14.935	14.946	14.958	14.970	14.982	14.994	15.006	15.018	15.030	15.042
1460	15.054	15.066	15.078	15.090	15.102	15.113	15.125	15.137	15.149	15.161
1470	15.173	15.185	15.197	15.209	15.221	15.233	15.245	15.256	15.268	15.280
1480	15.292	15.304	15.316	15.328	15.340	15.352	15.364	15.376	15.387	15.399
1490	15.411	15.423	15.435	15.447	15.459	15.471	15.483	15.495	15.507	15.518
1500	15.530	15.542	15.554	15.566	15.578	15.590	15.602	15.614	15.625	15.637
1510	15.649	15.661	15.673	15.685	15.697	15.709	15.721	15.732	15.744	15.756
1520	15.768	15.780	15.792	15.804	15.816	15.827	15.839	15.851	15.863	15.875
1530	15.887	15.899	15.911	15.922	15.934	15.946	15.958	15.970	15.982	15.994
1540	16.006	16.017	16.029	16.041	16.053	16.065	16.077	16.089	16.100	16.112
1550	16.124	16.136	16.148	16.160	16.171	16.183	16.195	16.207	16.219	16.231
1560	16.243	16.254	16.266	16.278	16.290	16.302	16.314	16.325	16.337	16.349
1570	16.361	16.373	16.385	16.396	16.408	16.420	16.432	16.444	16.456	16.467
1580	16.479	16.491	16.503	16.515	16.527	16.538	16.550	16.562	16.574	16.586
1590	16.597	16.609	16.621	16.633	16.645	16.657	16.668	16.680	16.692	16.704
1600	16.716	16.727	16.739	16.751	16.763	16.775	16.786	16.798	16.810	16.822
1610	16.834	16.845	16.857	16.869	16.881	16.893	16.904	16.916	16.928	16.940
1620	16.952	16.963	16.975	16.987	16.999	17.010	17.022	17.034	17.046	17.058
1630	17.069	17.081	17.093	17.105	17.116	17.128	17.140	17.152	17.163	17.175
1640	17.187	17.199	17.211	17.222	17.234	17.246	17.258	17.269	17.281	17.293
1650	17.305	17.316	17.328	17.340	17.352	17.363	17.375	17.387	17.398	17.410
1660	17.422	17.434	17.446	17.457	17.469	17.481	17.492	17.504	17.516	17.528
1670	17.539	17.551	17.563	17.575	17.586	17.598	17.610	17.621	17.633	17.645
1680	17.657	17.668	17.680	17.692	17.704	17.715	17.727	17.739	17.750	17.762
1690	17.774	17.785	17.797	17.809	17.821	17.832	17.844	17.856	17.867	17.879
1700	17.891	17.902	17.914	17.926	17.938	17.949	17.961	17.973	17.984	17.996
1710	18.008	18.019	18.031	18.043	18.054	18.066	18.078	18.089	18.101	18.113
1720	18.124	18.136	18.148	18.159	18.171	18.183	18.194	18.206	18.218	18.229
1730	18.241	18.253	18.264	18.276	18.288	18.299	18.311	18.323	18.334	18.346
1740	18.358	18.369	18.381	18.393	18.404	18.416	18.427	18.439	18.451	18.462
1750	18.474	18.486	18.497	18.509	18.520	18.532	18.544	18.555	18.567	18.579
1760	18.590	18.602	18.613	18.625	18.637	18.648	18.660	18.672	18.683	18.695

A.4. COPPER VS CONSTANTAN

Thermal e.m.f. in millivolts compared to a reference junction at 0.0°C.

°C	0	1	2	3	4	5	6	7	8	9
-190	-5.379	-5.395	-5.411	....	....	....	....	....	....	....
-180	-5.205	-5.223	-5.241	-5.258	-5.276	-5.294	-5.311	-5.328	-5.345	-5.362
-170	-5.018	-5.037	-5.056	-5.075	-5.094	-5.113	-5.132	-5.150	-5.169	-5.187
-160	-4.817	-4.838	-4.858	-4.878	-4.899	-4.919	-4.939	-4.959	-4.978	-4.998
-150	-4.603	-4.625	-4.647	-4.669	-4.690	-4.712	-4.733	-4.754	-4.775	-4.796
-140	-4.377	-4.400	-4.423	-4.446	-4.469	-4.492	-4.514	-4.537	-4.559	-4.581
-130	-4.138	-4.162	-4.187	-4.211	-4.235	-4.259	-4.283	-4.307	-4.330	-4.354
-120	-3.887	-3.912	-3.938	-3.964	-3.989	-4.014	-4.039	-4.064	-4.089	-4.114
-110	-3.624	-3.651	-3.678	-3.704	-3.730	-3.757	-3.783	-3.809	-3.835	-3.861
-100	-3.349	-3.377	-3.405	-3.432	-3.460	-3.488	-3.515	-3.542	-3.570	-3.597
-90	-3.062	-3.091	-3.120	-3.149	-3.178	-3.207	-3.235	-3.264	-3.292	-3.320
-80	-2.764	-2.794	-2.824	-2.854	-2.884	-2.914	-2.944	-2.974	-3.003	-3.033
-70	-2.455	-2.486	-2.518	-2.549	-2.580	-2.611	-2.642	-2.672	-2.703	-2.733
-60	-2.135	-2.167	-2.200	-2.232	-2.264	-2.296	-2.328	-2.360	-2.392	-2.423
-50	-1.804	-1.838	-1.871	-1.905	-1.938	-1.971	-2.004	-2.037	-2.070	-2.103
-40	-1.463	-1.498	-1.532	-1.567	-1.601	-1.635	-1.669	-1.703	-1.737	-1.771
-30	-1.112	-1.148	-1.183	-1.218	-1.254	-1.289	-1.324	-1.359	-1.394	-1.429
-20	-0.751	-0.788	-0.824	-0.860	-0.897	-0.933	-0.969	-1.005	-1.041	-1.076
-10	-0.380	-0.417	-0.455	-0.492	-0.530	-0.567	-0.604	-0.641	-0.678	-0.714
(-)0	0.000	-0.038	-0.077	-0.115	-0.153	-0.191	-0.229	-0.267	-0.305	-0.343
(+)0	0.000	0.038	0.077	0.116	0.154	0.193	0.232	0.271	0.311	0.350
10	0.389	0.429	0.468	0.508	0.547	0.587	0.627	0.667	0.707	0.747
20	0.787	0.827	0.868	0.908	0.949	0.990	1.030	1.071	1.112	1.153
30	1.194	1.235	1.277	1.318	1.360	1.401	1.443	1.485	1.526	1.568
40	1.610	1.652	1.694	1.737	1.779	1.821	1.864	1.907	1.949	1.992
50	2.035	2.078	2.121	2.164	2.207	2.250	2.293	2.336	2.380	2.423
60	2.467	2.511	2.555	2.599	2.643	2.687	2.731	2.775	2.820	2.864
70	2.908	2.953	2.997	3.042	3.087	3.132	3.177	3.222	3.267	3.312
80	3.357	3.402	3.448	3.493	3.539	3.584	3.630	3.676	3.722	3.767
90	3.813	3.859	3.906	3.952	3.998	4.044	4.091	4.138	4.184	4.230
100	4.277	4.324	4.371	4.418	4.465	4.512	4.559	4.606	4.654	4.701
110	4.749	4.796	4.843	4.891	4.939	4.987	5.035	5.083	5.131	5.179
120	5.227	5.275	5.323	5.372	5.420	5.469	5.518	5.566	5.615	5.663
130	5.712	5.761	5.810	5.859	5.908	5.957	6.007	6.056	6.105	6.155
140	6.204	6.254	6.303	6.353	6.403	6.453	6.503	6.553	6.603	6.653
150	6.703	6.753	6.803	6.853	6.904	6.954	7.004	7.055	7.106	7.157
160	7.208	7.258	7.309	7.360	7.411	7.462	7.513	7.565	7.616	7.667
170	7.719	7.770	7.822	7.874	7.926	7.978	8.029	8.080	8.132	8.184
180	8.236	8.288	8.340	8.392	8.445	8.497	8.549	8.601	8.654	8.707
190	8.759	8.812	8.864	8.917	8.970	9.023	9.076	9.129	9.182	9.235
200	9.288	9.341	9.394	9.448	9.501	9.555	9.608	9.662	9.715	9.769
210	9.823	9.877	9.931	9.985	10.039	10.093	10.147	10.201	10.255	10.309
220	10.363	10.417	10.471	10.526	10.580	10.635	10.689	10.744	10.799	10.854
230	10.909	10.963	11.018	11.073	11.128	11.183	11.238	11.293	11.348	11.403
240	11.459	11.514	11.569	11.624	11.680	11.735	11.791	11.847	11.903	11.959
250	12.015	12.071	12.126	12.182	12.238	12.294	12.350	12.406	12.462	12.518
260	12.575	12.631	12.688	12.744	12.800	12.857	12.913	12.970	13.027	13.083
270	13.140	13.197	13.254	13.311	13.368	13.425	13.482	13.539	13.596	13.653
280	13.710	13.768	13.825	13.882	13.939	13.997	14.055	14.112	14.170	14.227
290	14.285	14.343	14.400	14.458	14.515	14.573	14.631	14.689	14.747	14.805
300	14.864	14.922	14.980	15.038	15.096	15.155	15.213	15.271	15.330	15.388
310	15.447	15.506	15.564	15.623	15.681	15.740	15.799	15.858	15.917	15.976
320	16.035	16.094	16.153	16.212	16.271	16.330	16.389	16.449	16.508	16.567
330	16.626	16.685	16.745	16.804	16.864	16.924	16.983	17.043	17.102	17.162
340	17.222	17.281	17.341	17.401	17.461	17.521	17.581	17.641	17.701	17.761
350	17.821	17.881	17.941	18.002	18.062	18.123	18.183	18.243	18.304	18.364
360	18.425	18.485	18.546	18.607	18.667	18.727	18.788	18.849	18.910	18.971
370	19.032	19.093	19.154	19.215	19.276	19.337	19.398	19.459	19.520	19.581
380	19.642	19.704	19.765	19.827	19.888	19.949	20.011	20.072	20.134	20.195
390	20.257	20.318	20.380	20.442	20.504	20.565	20.627	20.688	20.750	20.812

B. Heat Effects

As an aid in calibration, the materials listed may be used. The enthalpy values used were selected from Rossini (R31a), Kelley (K14a), handbook (L1a) and a tabulation already prepared by Bohon (B61). No decompositions have been included because the heat of reaction will be significantly dependent on the conditions of the experiment. Values at intervals along the temperature scale have been included because the observed thermal effect from a given quantity of heat varies with temperature. Some materials with large heat effects and some with small have been included.

Temperature	Material	Melting or inversion	Enthalpy change (cal./gm.)
64	Stearic acid	m	47.6
32.1	Ammonium nitrate	i	4.75
125.2	Ammonium nitrate	i	12.6
169.6	Ammonium nitrate	m	16.2
121.8	Benzoic acid	m	33.9
239	Potassium bifluoride	m	20.2
254	Lithium nitrate	m	88.4
273	Sodium nitrate	i	9.5
306.0	Sodium nitrate	m	41.1
327.4	Lead	m	5.89
412	Silver sulfate	i	6.1
440	Sodium molybdate	i	70.9
455	Silver chloride	m	22.0
583	Potassium sulfate	i	12.3
650	Manganous chloride	m	71.3
800	Sodium chloride	m	117
961	Silver	m	25.0
1069	Potassium sulfate	m	52.6

APPENDIX III

To assist the purchaser of an apparatus or accessories for thermogravimetric or differential thermal analysis the questions below are provided.
While there are no "book answers," the answers may still be found in the
book, i.e., for many questions there will be no general answer but the
discussion herein may suggest the best answer for the particular problem.
It is likely that no apparatus will answer the needs perfectly. At this point
a decision must be made as to whether to accept the closest approach or
to assemble an apparatus. This will probably be resolved by just one or
two of the questions that are of particular importance for the particular
problem.

The purchaser of thermogravimetric apparatus should also take note
of many of the questions suggested for differential thermal analysis, particularly if he is giving any thought to relating the data.

Differential Thermal Analysis

(a) Furnace Assembly
 1. What range of sample sizes can be used?
 2. Can dynamic atmospheres be used and effluent gases detected?
 3. Can static controlled atmospheres be used?
 4. What pressure ranges can be used?
 5. Can dynamic water vapor be used?
 6. Can sample holders be interchanged to accommodate different
    types of samples?
 7. Is low-temperature operation possible?
 8. Do phase transitions and melting of inorganic materials occur
    at the same temperatures at different heating rates?

9. Is the recorded temperature that of the sample, reference, block or other point? Can the point be chosen?

(b) Programming System

1. Is there a temperature vs. time record, either with ΔT or as part of the programmer?
2. Can the programmer reproduce the same curve on a reversible phase change for several cycles?
3. Can the programmer be made to reverse and repeat (cycle)?
4. Will the programmer and power supply drive furnaces of different wattages without extensive readjustment?

(c) Recording System

1. Can the recorder and amplifier produce (as a minimum requirement) a deflection to the edge of the chart with a ΔT of not more than 2°C without appreciable noise?
2. Can the recorder produce a record of ΔT of convenient length for examination over the chosen temperature range?
3. Can the recorder, without major adjustment, record ΔT vs. time to permit quantitative measurements?

Thermogravimetric Apparatus

1. Is the sample supported above or below the measuring system?
2. What provisions exist to prevent heating of the measuring system?
3. If the measuring system is a beam balance, would any inadvertent heating be symmetric?
4. Is there a way to compensate for buoyancy changes?
5. Can controlled atmospheres be used?
6. Can subambient and supraambient pressures be used?
7. Can corrosive atmospheres be used without damage to the measuring system?
8. Where is the temperature measured?
9. Will the furnace and sample holder design permit nearly uniform heating of the sample?

Author Index

Numbers in parentheses are reference citations and mean that an author's work is referred to although his name is not cited in the text. Numbers in italic show the page on which the complete reference is listed.

A

Abbiss, C. P., *549*
Abendroth, H. J., *545*
Abrams, S. T., *557, 563*
Adams, L. H., 93, *561*
Adler, H. H., 34, 35, 36, *536*
Agafonoff, V., 90, *536*
Aia, M. A., *559*
Alier, B. D., *536*
Aliev, G. M., *536*
Aliferis, I., 308, 309(S26), 320(S26), *561*
Allison, E. B., 66, *536, 555*
Altman, H. W., *560*
Amagasa, M., *567*
Ameniya, A., *556*
Amonenko, V. M., *549*
Amoshina, N. P., *539*
Anderson, A. C., *536*
Anderson, D. A., *536*
Anderson, H. C., *536*
Andrianov, K. A., *536*
Anikin, A. G., *536*
Antonov, I. V., *565*
Aparicio-Arroyo, E., *557*
Arbogast, V. F., *548*

Arens, P. L., 53, 56, 57, 60, 66, 67, 70, 72, 84, 85, 86, 88, 90, 93(A12), 161, 165, 166, 171, 249, *536*
Ariesan, V., *536*
Arkhangel'skaja, L. S., 58, 151, *543*
Arnold, T. I., *553*
Arsenan, D. F., 413, *537*
Arutiunova, L. B., *537*
Asaba, T., *537*
Ashby, G. E., *537*
Audrieth, L. F., *566*
Ault, N. N., *567*
Austin, J. B., *537*
Ayres, W. M., 434, 436, 438, 439, 441, *537*

B

Babaeva, V. P., *567*
Bachelet, M., *537*
Badaruddin, *542*
Balandin, A. A., *537*
Balarew, D. Z., 408, *537*
Balygin, I. E., *537*
Barnard, R. D., *538*
Barney, J. E., *537*
Barnier, Y., *537*
Barrall, E. M., 47, 79, 80, 83, 122, *537*

583

Subject Index

A

ABL-2056, 292
Absorption spectrometer, 449
Activation energy, 199, 205, 217
  by distortion of the lattice, 406
  calculated from rate of the reaction, 220
  lowered by providing another reaction mechanism, 406
Activation energies, physical significance, 217–220
Adjustable limit switch, 516
Agreement of data, 354
Alkaline earth oxides, 408–409
Alumina, thermal conductivity, 68
γ-alumina, 38
Ammeter, 519
Ammonium chloride, 174
Ammonium nitrate, 42, 43, 45
Ammonium perchlorate, 223–225, 242–244, 437, 438
Amplification, 115–7
Amplification, adjustable, fixed steps, 117
  electronic, 117
  optical, 116, 118
  thermopile, 115
Amplifiers, stabilized electronic, 117

Ankle bone, thermogram, 412
Apparatus design, 508–521
Apparatus for simultaneous determinations, 352
Apparent weight gain, 312
Array of hot and cold zones, 317
Arrhenius law, 157
Asymptotic reaction temperature, 91, 94
Atactic polypropylene, 194
Atmosphere, dynamic, 46
  influence of, 223
  nonaffecting, 149
  variation of, 169
Automatic balance, 456
Automatic recording vacuum microbalance, 329
Autotransformer, adjustable, 478–481, 511, 514
  motor-driven, 126

B

Balance, automatic lockup, 532, 533
  automatic recording, 324
  beam, 323
  corrosive gases, 322
  degassing, 321
  displacement measurement, 324, 333–4

595